钱迎倩论文集

《钱迎倩论文集》编辑委员会　主编

科　学　出　版　社

北　京

内 容 简 介

本书汇集了已故植物学家钱迎倩先生及其与同事或学生合作发表的学术论文和科普文章等86篇。其中生物技术与生物工程研究方面的论文29篇，生物安全与分子生态学研究方面的论文24篇，生物多样性保护研究方面的论文12篇，科学普及与考察见闻方面的文章21篇。本书比较全面地反映了钱迎倩先生的学术成就，特别是对中国植物科学发展的贡献。本书还收录了钱先生不同时期工作和生活的珍贵照片。附录的5篇文章较全面地总结了钱迎倩先生的科学人生。

本书可供从事植物科学和生物多样性保护方面的研究人员和相关专业的师生参考。

图书在版编目(CIP)数据

钱迎倩论文集/《钱迎倩论文集》编辑委员会主编. —北京：科学出版社，2011
ISBN 978-7-03-030973-0

I. ①钱… II. ①钱… III. ①生物学–文集 IV. ①Q-53

中国版本图书馆 CIP 数据核字(2011)第 080854 号

责任编辑：王 静 马 俊/责任校对：张凤琴
责任印制：钱玉芬/封面设计：北京美光制版有限公司

科学出版社 出版
北京东黄城根北街16号
邮政编码：100717
http://www.sciencep.com

北京佳信达欣艺术印刷有限公司 印刷
科学出版社编务公司排版制作
科学出版社发行 各地新华书店经销
*
2011年5月第 一 版 开本：787×1092 1/16
2011年5月第一次印刷 印张：41 1/2 插页：8
印数：1—800 字数：972 000

定价：168.00 元
（如有印装质量问题，我社负责调换）

序　　言

钱迎倩先生 1954 年毕业于复旦大学，后又到南京大学读研究生，1957 年毕业。自 1959 年起在中国科学院植物研究所工作，1987 年起到中国科学院生物科学与生物技术局工作，1993 年起调到广西壮族自治区科学院工作，1994 年底又回到植物研究所工作直至 1999 年退休。从研究生毕业到退休的 42 年间，钱迎倩先生在科学研究和科技领导工作中都作出了出色的贡献。

他在原生质体培养和细胞融合研究领域做出了不少开创性的工作。他不仅成功地对大豆和烟草原生质体进行了分离和纯化，而且将这两种不同科植物的原生质体进行了融合，得到了异科原生质体融合后的异核体。他所带领的研究组率先在国际上成功地获得了攻关多年未能突破的玉米原生质体再生植株，成为当年该学科领域的重大新闻，受到了国内外同行的好评。在后来的水稻原生质体的游离和培养、美味猕猴桃原生质体再生植株和无性系变异以及多种植物原生质体的超低温保存上都获得不少重要的研究成果。

在科技领导方面，他历任植物研究所植物细胞学研究室副主任、主任，植物研究所副所长、所长。1987 年 2 月任中国科学院生物科学与生物技术局局长，1993 年 2 月至 1994 年 12 月任广西壮族自治区科学院院长。在任所长期间，他充分发挥老一辈科学家在学科建设方面的作用，鼓励研究人员开展国际前沿和与国民经济密切相关的研究课题；落实党和国家的知识分子政策，采取多种措施调动职工积极性；为适应研究所领导体制改革的要求，积极探索所长负责制条件下的研究所运行机制改革；恢复和健全学位工作制度，选送青年研究人员出国深造，以加强研究所的队伍建设。在任局长期间，他十分关注前沿学科领域动向，积极推动中国科学院生物多样性、全球变化、细胞分子进化以及系统生物学等领域的研究。同时，在当时科研经费困难的情况下，关心和支持分类区系研究、“三志”编研、标本馆和植物园建设等基础性工作。他还积极支持华西亚高山植物园和神农架生物多样性定位研究站的建立和发展。钱迎倩先生是个有强烈社会责任感的人，退休以后以极大的热情投入到科学普及工作中，2000 年 9 月至 2008 年 5 月期间，作为中国科学院科学家演讲团成员，他走遍了全国 10 个省、2 个直辖市，演讲 320 场，听众达 8 万多人，他的演讲受到各地听众的广泛好评。他所在的老科学家科普演讲团获得由中宣部、教育部、科技部等部委颁发的“第二届中国青少年社会教育银杏奖”。从上可见，钱先生无论在研究上、管理上，还是社会事业上，都为我们树立了良好的榜样。

印象中，我第一次认识钱迎倩先生是在“文革”结束后不久，上海植生所成立细胞生理研究室，罗士韦先生带我和几位同事到植物所访问吴素萱先生和细胞室。随后，1978 年夏，我俩一起参加由胡含先生带队的中国科学院代表团参加在加拿大卡尔加里召开的国际植物组织培养会议。以后，由于我们在同一研究领域工作，后他又调院里工作，接触颇多。他去广西参加组建广西科学院的工作并担任首任院长时，我已到院里担任副院长，期间到广西去看过他，也为他的开拓精神所感动。钱迎倩先生在做人方面给我留下了极其深刻的印象，可以简单地概括为正直、谦和、大度、关爱、担当。这是我三十多年来与他相处的切身体会。

钱迎倩先生离开我们一年了，他的音容笑貌不时浮现在我的脑海中。他的一生几乎全部奉献给了中国科学院的生命科学事业，不仅为我们留下了具有标志性的研究成果和科学事业发展的成就，更为我们，特别是年青一代，留下了宝贵的精神财富。他将永远活在我们的心里。值此《钱迎倩论文集》即将出版之际，谨以此文寄托对钱先生的敬佩和怀念之情。最后，感谢编辑小组同仁们的善意和辛苦。

是为序。

许智宏

2011年4月20日

一 生 经 历

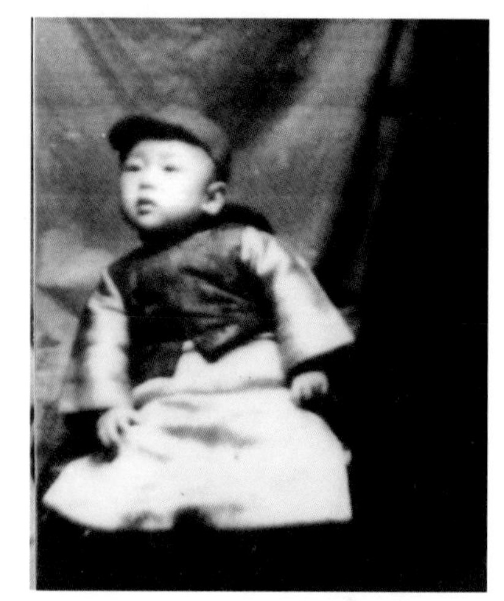

幼儿钱迎倩

1947年，省立上海中学初三16班毕业照(后二排右一)

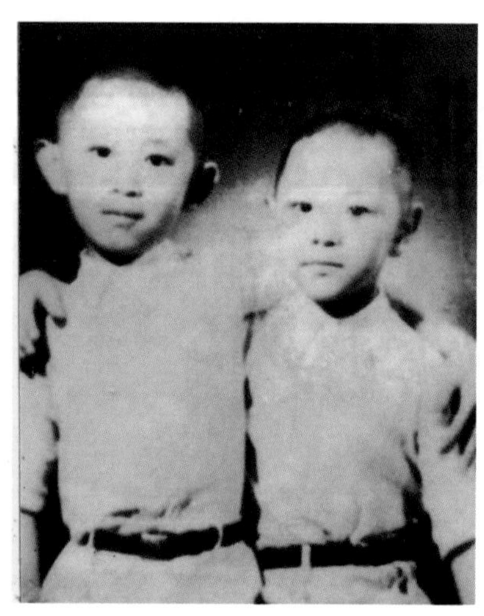

儿童钱迎倩(右一)与哥哥钱岳倩

1953年，复旦大学大学实习

1954年，复旦大学生物系低等植物专业组同学合影

大学时代钱迎倩

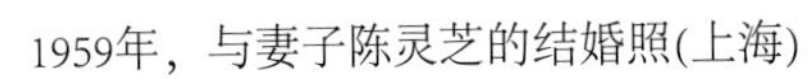

1959年，与妻子陈灵芝的结婚照(上海)

1960年，与妻子陈灵芝的婚后合影(北京)

1982年，与加拿大植物生物技术研究所国际同行合影

1978年，与吴素萱教授，同事周云罗、蔡起贵(从左至右)在实验室

1983年，参加全国植物细胞融合工作会议(二排右四)

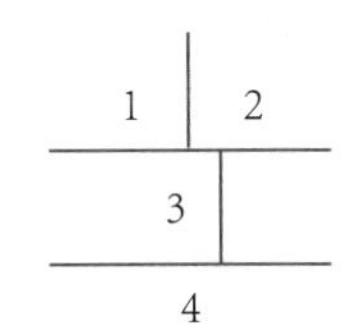

1. 1991年，参加第二届猕猴桃国际研讨会(新西兰)
2. 1992年，参加濒危动植物种国际贸易公约缔约方大会(CITES，日本京都)
3. 1995年，参加印度-马来半岛生物多样性保护会议(泰国)
4. 2005年，参加生物安全国际研讨会(中国南京，一排右三)

1983年，为汤佩松先生80寿辰祝寿

1983年，春节看望研究所老领导杨森同志

1983年，接待来访外宾

1985年，参加植物学会秘书长会议
(重庆，照片为钱迎倩先生笔迹)

1984年，接待国家领导人陈慕华视察中科院植物所植物园

1989年，参加昆明动物所建所30周年纪念活动

1990年，参加昆明动物所细胞与分子进化开放实验室论证会

1990年，在西双版纳植物园调研（中间为时任副院长李振声，左一为时任院办公厅主任栾中新）

1994年，与中科院生物局王贵海(左一)、孟广震(右一)副局长合影

1990年，参加中国科学院生物学部常委会(后排右四)

1993年，考察广西山口红树林保护区

1990年，参加中国动物志第三届编委会

1994年，与妻子和中科院生物局同事合影

1996年，考察广西科学院植物所

2005年，为小学生讲科普知识

2007年，科普演讲

2007年，山东诸城与学生合影

1987年，与妻子、同事和博士研究生合影

1995年，与博士研究生恽锐(左一)和魏伟(右一)于昆明

1991年，与妻子、同事和研究生共渡元旦新年

2005年，复旦大学百年校庆期间看望谈家桢教授

1990年，与妈妈、妹妹合影

1992年，与妻子陈灵芝、女儿钱云杉、儿子钱雪松合影

1992年，60寿辰纪念

2009年，钱迎倩夫妇金婚纪念日合影

2002年，70寿辰纪念

2008年，与哥哥钱岳倩合影

2008年春节，与全家和哥哥家人的全家福

目　　录

生物技术与生物工程研究

生物安全与分子生态学研究

生物多样性保护研究

科学普及与考察见闻

附　录

生物技术与生物工程研究

本文原载：中国植物学会三十周年年会论文摘要汇编. 1963. 中国植物学会编. 北京：中国科学技术情报研究所，182-183

玉米花粉的人工萌发

钱迎倩　吴素萱

(中国科学院植物研究所)

为了解决植物杂交育种、遗传学、生理学及细胞学上的问题，很多学者对花粉进行了研究。人工萌发对研究花粉的问题提供有利的条件，但是不同植物的花粉要求在适宜的环境条件下才能正常萌发和生长。禾本科植物的花粉一般在人工萌发条件下得到的结果都是不够理想的。对玉米花粉的人工萌发，则不易掌握其要求的湿度，一般培养基的湿度较高，花粉容易破裂，较低则不易萌发。除 Kubo(1958)的工作报导外，玉米正常萌发的萌发率都在 30%以下。据 Kubo 的报导，在十月份玉米萌发率可达到 100%。但在我国北方十月份已不是玉米正常的生长季节。我们在 7 月份，亦即玉米盛花期进行了玉米人工萌发的实验。

实验材料是玉米品种华$_{53}$自交系。所用的培养基是 2%琼脂、10%~20%明胶、15%~20%蔗糖的混合胶体，其中尤以 2%琼脂、15%明胶、15%蔗糖的浓度为佳。取混合胶体一滴(约 0.1ml)用玻璃棒均匀地涂在载玻片上(约占面积 24mm × 24mm)。在室温(28°~29℃)下播种花粉，然后将载玻片放在直径为 12cm 并具有湿润滤纸的培养皿内。每培养皿内以 1.3ml 的水润湿滤纸。

玉米花粉萌发率的高低及花粉管生长的长度除决定于适宜的培养基外，还决定于载玻片上所涂培养基的厚度以及花粉采得后插入培养基的时间及密度。Gotch(1931)在播入培养基前将花粉曝露在空气中一个半小时。Conger(1953)认为鸭跖草花粉在播种前必须不能潮湿。他将收集的花粉保存在干燥器内。我们对放在干燥器内及曝露在空气中的花粉作了对比实验。早晨 9 时采集花粉，在一般情况下不管曝露在空气中或放在干燥器中 1~2h 后播种，都可得到满意的结果。其中尤以放在干燥器中的结果较佳。播种的密度过低一般花粉不能萌发，甚至破裂了。即使花粉能够萌发，花粉管亦生长不良。密度过高花粉亦不易萌发，花粉管生长不正常。一般在 × 10 × 10 的视野内均匀地播入 150~180 粒花粉则可得到良好的结果。

本实验按上述条件进行人工萌发，萌发率最高可达到 91.5%。花粉管长度在四个半小时内最长为 1600μm，平均长度为 1352μm。在其中能观察到动态的精子，这一点可说明花粉管的萌发是正常的。

本文原载：实验生物学报. 1980. 13(4): 456

小黑麦叶片细胞全能性的探讨

钱迎倩　周云罗　马诚　蔡起贵

(中国科学院植物研究所)

由于对禾谷类叶片细胞及原生质体培养的失败，有人怀疑禾谷类叶片细胞是否具有全能性。我们用小黑麦幼叶作材料，对此课题进行了探讨。取 4cm 左右的第一片无菌幼叶，从基部 3mm 以上开始，每隔 3mm 切断，叶段顺序在附加有 2mg/L 2，4-D，500mg/L 水解乳蛋白及 1000mg/L 酵母提取物的 MS 基本培养(简称 MS-a)上进行暗培养，4、5d 后，开始有愈伤组织出现，基部 3mm 往上到 12mm 的各切段可诱导出大量愈伤组织，频率分别为 96%、79%及 45%。个别情况下 15~18mm 的切段也有愈伤组织，培养 12d 后逐步分化出大量的根。出现愈伤组织 10d 后的材料，当转移到 1200Lux 光照下培养，50 天左右在原培养基(MS-a)上分化了苗。已获 8 棵形态正常的小植株，并已种入土壤中。在幼叶上用墨水作标记实验，证明即使 3~6mm 的叶段在今后分化了叶鞘的成熟叶子上，这部位还是处于叶片的位置。用第一片幼叶在各种不同培养基，不同光照及萌发条件下作了诱导愈伤组织及分化的实验。结果说明小黑麦幼叶愈伤组织的诱导对培养基及外界条件的要求并不苛刻。但愈伤组织的质地及分化机能有异，在 PRL-4 培养基上，色白、质松，在原有培养基上不易分化，而在 MS-a 及 MS-P 培养基上，色淡黄、质致密，易分化大量根，光照对愈伤组织的诱导稍有抑制作用，用不同组合的生长素和细胞分裂素作了分化苗的实验，在具 0.04mg/L NAA，0.5mg/L GA_3 及 2mg/L 6BA 的 MS 分化培养基上得一棵绿苗，在 0.2mg/L 玉米素，0.2mg/L 2，4-D，0.5mg/L GA_3 及 3.5mg/L IAA 培养基上得多棵形态不正常的白苗。用第二片幼叶做实验，说明只在叶子基部 3mm 向上到 12mm 处可诱导出愈伤组织及分化根。并对幼叶分上(18mm 以上的幼叶，不能诱导出愈伤组织)、中(12~15mm，能诱导愈伤组织，但量少，不易长大)，下(3~12mm 叶段，可大量诱导出愈伤组织)，三部分用聚丙烯酰胺凝胶电泳进行可溶性蛋白的分析表明。上部只有 2、4、7 三条带明显，6 带隐约可见，中部比下部少 1、5 两条带，下部共有 12 条带，量比中部带要多。实验证明：小黑麦幼叶下部细胞具全能性。

本文原载：科学通报. 1980. (22): 1045-1048

小黑麦幼叶外植体的植株再生

钱迎倩 周云罗 蔡起贵

(中国科学院植物研究所)

通过细胞诱变及细胞杂交等遗传操作的途径，改良谷物的性状是国际上普遍关注的一个重要研究课题，其中从原生质体起源的细胞能够再生植株又是高等植物遗传操作的先决条件。但是禾谷类作物的原生质体培养当前存在很多困难，培养成植株的例子还很少。主要原因是叶肉原生质体再生细胞后未能进行有规则的连续分裂，因此，曾有人提出过禾谷类叶细胞是否有全能性的问题[1,2]。

这几年已有少量从禾谷类幼叶诱导得愈伤组织及再生植株的报道[3-5]。可是对禾谷类叶片细胞全能性的基础研究还是比较缺乏。为此，我们以小黑麦叶片为材料着手开展这方面研究。本文仅报道以小黑麦幼叶诱导出愈伤组织及其植株的再生。

材料与方法

八倍体小黑麦种子由中国农业科学院供给。种子在 0.1%硫酸十二烷基钠(SLS)溶液中洗涤 10min，用清水冲洗后在无菌条件下浸入 70%的酒精 15s，再转到 0.1%$HgCl_2$溶液中灭菌 10~15min，最后用无菌水冲洗 3 次。灭菌的种子放在无菌培养皿中的湿润滤纸上，25℃黑暗条件下萌发。取长 1~4cm 的幼叶作为实验材料。剥去胚芽鞘，取出第一片幼叶。从叶子基部开始顺序每隔 3mm 切下一叶段。由于最基部的 3mm 长的叶段里面包有生长锥及第二片叶的叶原基，所以弃去不用。而取 3mm 以上的 5 个叶段顺序地往下列培养基中 25℃黑暗下或光照条件下诱导愈伤组织。培养基的组成是 MS[6]基本培养基，并附加水解乳蛋白 500mg/L，酵母提取物 1000mg/L，2，4-D 2mg/L 及蔗糖 40g/L。

此外，还在幼叶上做了标记实验。采用不同苗龄正常条件下生长的幼苗，分别剥去胚芽鞘。在叶子基部向上 3~6mm 的位置上用碳素墨水作标记，并让其在土壤中继续生长。待第一片叶分化出叶鞘和叶舌后，即可查明所接种的叶段在叶子上所处的位置。

结果与讨论

1. 愈伤组织的诱导

在上述培养条件(见材料与方法)下 3d 左右，有的叶段开始膨大，培养 4~5d 后，就开始有肉眼可见的愈伤组织出现。愈伤组织多数发生在切段向叶基部的一端(图 1a)。但有的愈伤组织也可能在切段向叶尖的一端或在切段的中部产生(图 1b)。

不同的叶段愈伤组织发生的情况是很不一样的。对 24 个幼叶的 120 个叶段进行统计的结果说明从幼叶基部开始到 12~15mm 的切段，在一定的培养条件下都可以诱导出愈伤组织。其中尤以 3~6、6~9、9~12mm 的三种切段为多。诱导频率分别为 96%、79%及 45%。在个别的情况下，培养 15d 左右后，在 15~18mm 的切段上也可以见到有愈伤组织的发生(表 1)。此外，当用 1cm 左右的幼叶作材料时，甚至在叶尖部切段的切口处也诱导出愈伤组织(图 1c)，有关愈伤组织的生长势，3~12mm 的切段都是比较旺盛的，其中尤以 6~12mm 的切段为最旺。

表 1　幼叶不同叶段愈伤组织的诱导致*

培养时间/d 愈伤组织数 叶段/mm	6	9	12	15
3~6	19	23	23	23
6~9	16	17	18	19
9~12	8	11	11	11
12~15	1	5	5	5
15~18	0	0	0	1

* 24 片幼叶各叶段的统计数。叶段是从幼叶基部向上计算。

2. 愈伤组织器官的建成

在小黑麦幼叶愈伤组织上形成根是很容易的。将叶段接种在上述的培养基上，即可产生愈伤组织，随着愈伤组织的长大，12d 左右开始有根的发生(图 1d)。

在不同叶段的愈伤组织上根的分化与愈伤组织的发生和生长势有密切的联系。表 2 说明在 3~12mm 叶段的愈伤组织上都可有大量根的发生，而在 12~15mm 叶段上的愈伤组织偶尔也有根的分化。

在原来的培养基上，我们还得到了苗的分化。有一组实验是先把叶段置于黑暗条件下培养，当愈伤组织出现 10d 左右后，再把培养物转放到白天为 28℃，1200 勒克司 10h 光照条件，晚上为 25℃黑暗条件下培养。愈伤组织上不断地形成大量的根。40d 后将长有大量根的愈伤组织分成若干块，再移回原来培养基上并在上述光照条件下继续培养。10d 左右出现了苗的分化(图 1e)。目前已得到 8 棵小植株，这些小植株在形态上基本上是正常的。另外，愈伤组织上还出现不少具有绿色的小点和小块，但这些绿色点或绿色块在很长时间内一直还保持原状，没有见到有苗的分化。在一系列有生长素和细胞分裂素不同组合的分化培养基上我们也试验了苗的分化，结果将另文报道。

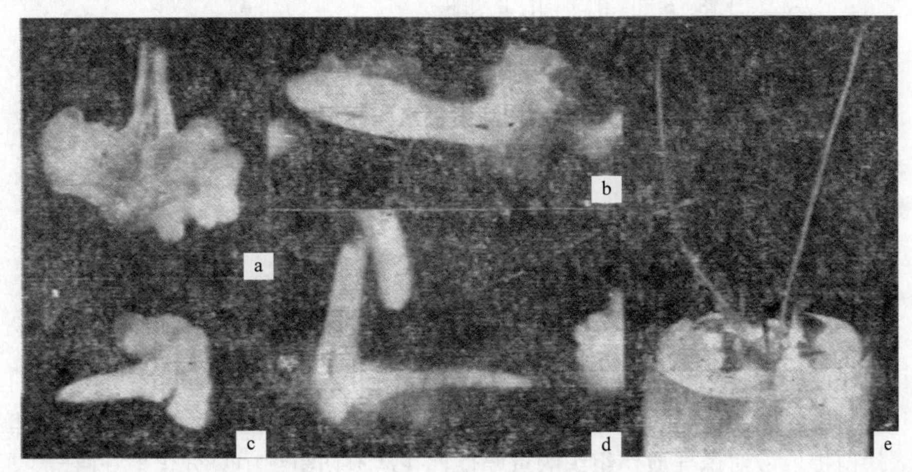

图 1

a. 愈伤组织多数发生在小黑麦幼叶切段的下端切割面上；b. 在叶段的中部也可以有愈伤组织的发生；c. 用 1cm 长的幼叶作材料，由叶尖切段起源的愈伤组织；d. 叶段培养 12d 左右就开始有根的发生；e. 小黑麦幼叶再生的小植株

表 2 不同叶段愈伤组织上根的分化*

分化根的愈伤组织数 / 叶段/mm / 培养时间/d	3~6	6~9	9~12	12~15
12	5	8	2	0
15	5	8	5	1

* 24 片幼叶上各叶段的统计数。

3. 幼叶上的标记实验

8 片不同长度的幼叶(图 2，I-VIII)，用炭素墨水在基部向上 3~6mm 位置上作标记，来鉴定在今后分化出叶鞘的叶子中标记所处的位置，其中 5 个幼叶长 1~2cm，另外 3 个幼叶都已分别伸出胚芽鞘 2~4.5cm。最长的一个幼苗作标记时全长已达 7.5cm 左右。作标记后的植株在土壤中自然生长。5d 后，所有 8 片叶子都已分化出叶鞘和叶舌，并且第二片叶子已经抽出。图 2 说明当叶子继续长大后，所有 8 个幼叶上标记的黑点全部位于叶片的部分，而不在叶鞘上。至于黑点所处的位置，则随当时作标记时的苗龄而异。作标记时的叶子越小，今后黑点在叶片上的部位越高，反之越低。这就证实了在诱导愈伤组织实验时所用的最低的一个叶段，即 3~6mm 叶段，已确实是处于叶片部位。实验所得的一切愈伤组织是由叶片来源而不是叶鞘诱导而得。这就是说，小黑麦幼叶基部 15mm 甚至 18mm 长叶段的细胞确实是具有全能性的。

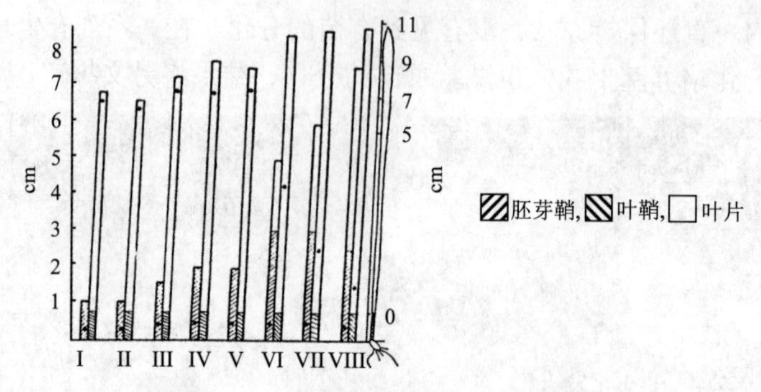

图2　小黑麦幼叶标记实验示意图

I-VIII 共 8 个植株，左边表示开始作标记时植株的长度，右边表示分化叶鞘、叶舌后叶片的长度。黑点表示标记在叶片上的位置

目前还没有看到从禾谷类成熟叶片诱导出愈伤组织的报道。Koblitz 等[3]报道了从大麦叶片的“生长区”分离的细胞能产生愈伤组织并再生绿色植株。他们强调了在培养基中加入幼苗提取液对诱导愈伤组织的重要性，并从愈伤组织中只分化得一棵苗[4]。最近 Dale 等[7]从大麦叶鞘的基部居间分生组织区得到叶片愈合组织，但这些愈伤组织未能进一步分化，而随着叶鞘的死亡而死亡。我们的研究结果与小麦[5]的相似，在不加入幼苗提取液的培养基上可以得到大量愈伤组织，虽然植株可以再生，但频率较低。如何进一步提高植株的再生率，值得进行深入研究。

参考文献

[1] Potrykus, I., Harms, C. T. & Hörz, H. *Cell Genetcis in Higher Plants* (Dudits, D. et al. Eds.), Publishing House of the Hungarian Academy of Sciences, Budapest, 1976, 129~140

[2] Bhojwani, S. S., Evans, P. K. & Cocking, E. C., *Euphytica,* 25 (1977), 343~360

[3] Koblitz, H., Scheunert, E. U. & Saalbach, G. *Abstr. 4th Intern. Congr. Plant Tissue & Cell Culture,* Calgary, 1978, No. 124

[4] Saalbach, G., Koblitz, H., *Plant Sci. Lett.,* 13 (1978), 165~169

[5] 陈惠民, 滕世云, 于家驹. 植物学报, 22(1980), 112~110

[6] Murashige, T., Skoog, F., *Physiol. Plant.,* 15(1962), 473~497

[7] Dale, P. J. & Deambrogio, E., *Z. Pflanzenphysiol.,* 94(1979), 65~77

本文原载：Theor. Appl. Genet. 1982. 62: 301-304

Chromosomal and Isozyme Studies of *Nicotiana tabacum-Glycine max* Hybrid Cell Lines*

Y. C. Chien[1] K. N. Kao[2] L. R. Wetter[2]

(1 Institute of Botany, Academia Sinica, Peking of China; 2 Prairie Regional Laboratory, National Research Council of Canada)

Summary The chromosomal stability of a number of somatic hybrids derived from soybean [*Glycine max* (L.) Merr.] and *Nicotiana tabacum* var. 'Xanthi' were investigated. Several of the hybrid cell lines retained more than half the complement of *N. tabacum* chromosomes after 7 months of culturing. A number of chromosomal abnormalities were observed. The hybrids were positively identified by employing isozyme analysis of several dehydrogenases and aspartate aminotransferase.

Key words Isozymes; Somatic hybrids; Chromosomes

Introduction

Somatic hybridization has become an useful tool for studying the parasexual modification of plant cells and hopefully an experimental system for producing novel plants. Plants have been produced from somatic hybrid calli derived from different genera, e.g. *Solanum tuberosum-Lycopersicon esculentum* (Melchers et al. 1978), *Datura innoxia-Atropa belladonna* Krumbiegel and Schieder 1979), *Arabidopsis thalliana-Brassica napus* (Gleba and Hoffmann 1978, 1979) and *Daucus carota-Aegopodium podagraria* (Dudits et al. 1979).

Chromosome elimination is a common phenomenon in intergeneric fusion products (Binding and Nehls 1978; Gleba and Hoffmann 1978; Kao 1977; Power et al. 1975; Wetter and Kao 1980). Kao (1977) reported that in the somatic hybrids of soybean-*Nicotiana glauca* all of the soybean chromosomes and only a few *N. glauca* chromosomes were retained after 6 months of culturing. Still fewer *N. glauca* chromosomes were evident after 36 months (Wetter and Kao 1980). This paper reports on the hybrids resulting from the somatic fusion of soybean and *Nicotiana tabacum* protoplasts. The result indicates that greater chromosomal stability has been achieved as identified by chromosome and isozyme analyses of hybrid cell lines.

---

* NRCC No. 20130; Communicated by G. Melcher.

Materials and Methods

Protoplasts of soybean [*Glycine max* (L.) Merr.] from a suspension culture were used as one of the fusion partners. The average number of chromosomes in the cells of these cultures was 60. Protoplasts from fragments of young leaves of *Nicotiana tabacum* var. 'Xanthi' were used as the other fusion partner, the chromosome number of which was 48.

The methods for isolation of protoplasts, fusion and culture of single heterokaryocytes in Cuprak dishes have been described elsewhere (Kao 1977). When the hybrids grew to a 100 to 200 cell cluster, they were transferred into the wells of Cooke Histo-plates (Dynatech Laboratories, Inc. 900 Slaters Lane, Alexandria, Virginia, USA 22 314). The plates were sealed with Parafilm. The reason for the transfer is that the wells of Histo-plates are larger than the Cuprak dishes and allow for the utilization of more medium for vigorous growth. One month after fusion the hybrid calli were visible to the naked eye and they were then transferred to Falcon plastic dishes (60mm×15mm) where they grew to colonies 2 to 3mm in diameter. Cell samples taken at different stages were fixed with acetic acid-ethanol, stained with modified carbol fuchsin and examined under a Zeiss research microscope (Kao 1975).

The isozymes studied were performed with the hybrid calli described above. The preparation and protein estimation was carried out as described previously (Wetter 1977). The electrophoretic investigations were done, except for some modifications, as described in a previous report (Wetter 1977). The experiments were performed on a 5% gel rather than a 7% gel. The isozyme patterns for alcohol, 6-phosphogluconate and shikimate dehydrogenase were stained as described by Wetter and Kao (1976). The aspartate aminotransferase was visualized by employing the method of Wetter (1977).

Results

Chromosomes

Fixation and staining of cells, regenerated from protoplasts, 48h after PEG treatment revealed that 14.8% of them were heterokaryocytes. The majority of them had one soybean and one *N. tabacum* nucleus, however multinuclear heterokaryocytes were also observed. *N. tabacum* chromosomes (Fig. 1) were easily distinguished from soybean chromosomes (Fig. 2), the former are thicker and longer than the latter. No premitotic nuclear fusion was observed in the heterokaryocytes.

Heterokaryocytes underwent their first division within 2 to 3days as compared to soybean protoplasts which start to divide within 24h and *N. tabacum* within 2 to 4days. Within 4days after fusion one could easily distinguish the hybrid clusters from the parental clusters by observing the arrangement of the green chloroplasts within the cells. Chloroplasts in dividing *N. tabacum* were evenly distributed while they tended to form clusters in the hybrid cells. Hybrid clusters could be recognized 20days after fusion by the external morphology and trace of green coloration.

Considerable variation was noted in the chromosomal distribution in the heterokaryocytes. Complete sets of soybean and *N. tabacum* were retained in the hybrid cells during the first division. Rearrangement in *N. tabacum* chromosomes was detected beginning with the second division. At this stage, loss of *N. tabacum* chromosomes were evident. The variation in number and morphology of *N. tabacum* chromosomes was dramatic as shown in Figure 3. The daughter cell "a" had a larger number of *N. tabacum* chromosomes, while the daughter cell "b" had only a few *N. tabacum* chromosomes. In both cells most of the *N. tabacum* chromosomes were abnormal in appearance.

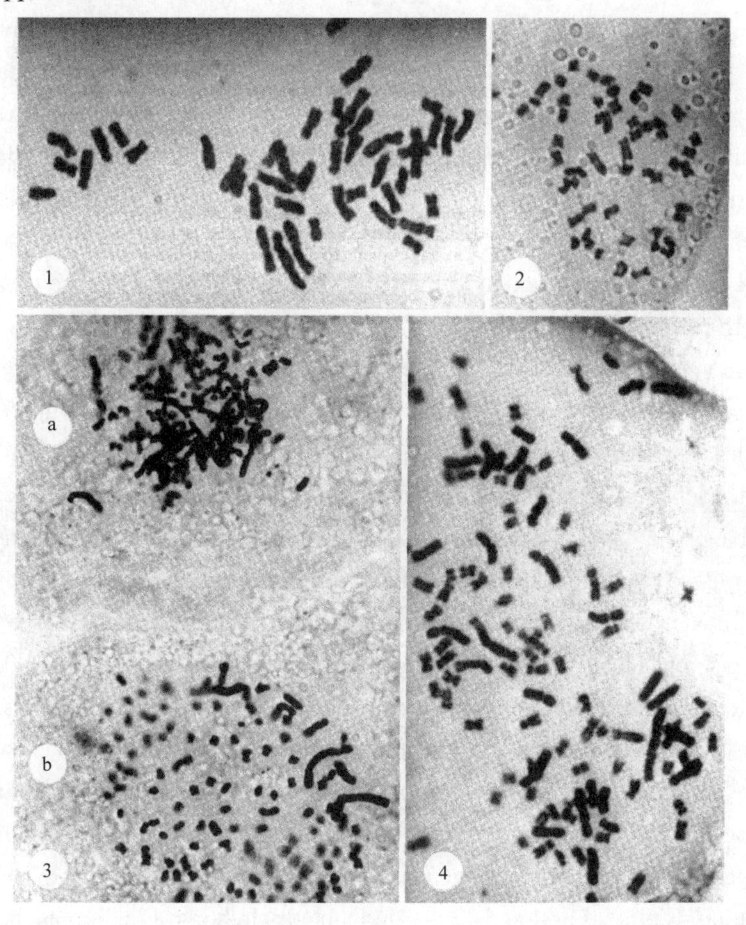

Figs. 1-4

1 Chromosomes in a *Nicotiana tabacum* cell; 2 Chromosomes in a cultured soybean cell; 3 a and b Unequal distribution of *Nicotiana tabacurn* chromosomes in two daughter cells of a *N. tabacum* - soybean hybrid. The hybrid was at the two cell stage; 4 Chromosomes in a cell of a nine month old *N. tabacurn*-soybean hybrid cell line (Figs. 1, 2 and 4 are enlarged to the same magnification)

A total of 21 hybrid cell lines were isolated. After 3 months of culturing, approximately two-thirds of the *N. tabacum* chromosomes were retained in some hybrid lines, many of these however contained abnormal chromosomes. After 6 to 7 months of culturing two very distinct classes could be distinguished in the hybrid cell lines. One class (hybrid lines No.3, 4, 7, 9 and 12) had retained more than half the *N. tabacum* chromosomes in the majority of the cells (Fig. 4). In many of the cells there was still evidence of abnormal chromosomes, e.g. long chromosomes as well as chromosomal bridges. The second class (hybrid lines No.5, 6, 10, 11, 13 and 14) had lost nearly all the *N. tabacum* chromosomes except for a very low number of cells which still retained a number of *N. tabacum* chromosomes. The remaining hybrid lines were intermediate in nature. None of the hybrid cell lines indicated any obvious changes in number and structure of the soybean chromosomes.

Isozymes

Several different isozyme systems, in addition to those found in Fig. 5, were investigated, e.g. lactate, formate and glucose-6-phosphate dehydrogenase, as well as esterase, acid phosphatase and superoxide dismutase. They were not utilized because pattern differences between parents were not great enough to be useful in identifying the hybrid lines. Twenty-one hybrid lines were assayed but only 6 representative lines are shown in Fig. 5. The study was carried out over a 7 month period.

The 4 enzyme systems chosen for the investigation, all show clear evidence of having achieved successful hybridization. The alcohol dehydrogenase zymogram (Fig. 5 a) shows that the hybrid lines have a 2-banded pattern (see hybrids 3, 4 and 12), the top band is derived from *N. tabacum*, the lower band from soybean. The majority of the hybrid cell lines expressed only the soybean band. The band derived from soybean is much more intense in the hybrids than in the parent while the opposite is true for the band derived from *N. tabacum*.

The shikimate dehydrogenase zymograms clearly illustrate that the same cell lines are hybrids (No.3, 4 and 12 in Fig. 5 b). The doublet seen with an R_f of 0.56 and 0.60 is derived from *N. tabacum* while the broad zone over a R_f of 0.32 to 0.45 is an expression in part of soybean. This broad zone could also indicate the presence of genes from *N. tabacum* that are expressed by the 2 band seen at R_f 0.42 and 0.44. It is not possible to ascertain whether the 3 cell lines (No.5, 10 and 11) are true hybrids or contain only soybean information.

The 6-phosphogluconate dehydrogenase is one of the more interesting systems studied in this investigation. Cell lines 3, 4 and 12 are undoubtedly hybrids (Fig. 5 c) as they have bands which are derived from both soybean and *N. tabacum*. However there is considerable variation, cell line 3 contains all the bands from the parents while cell line 12 does not express all the *N. tabacum* bands in the R_f 0.38 to 0.42 region. Further more only cell line 3 expresses the doublet at R_f 0.56, while 4, 5 and 12 exhibit a single band in this region. The remaining cell lines 10 and 11 as well as those not shown here indicate that they are also hybrids as they exhibit bands from soybean and *N. tabacum* in the R_f 0.40 to 0.48 area.

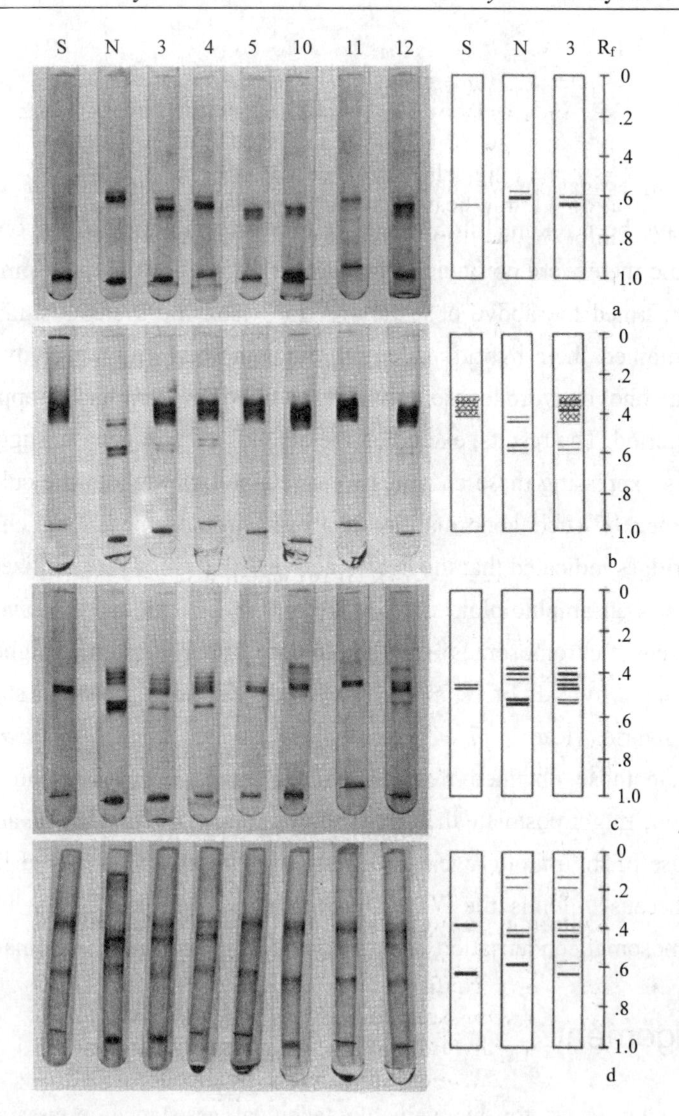

Fig.5a-d

a Electrophoretic patterns of alcohol dehydrogenase, b shikimate dehydrogenase, c 6- phosphogluconate dehydrogenase, d aspartate aminotransferase obtained for *N. tabacum* (N), soybean (S) and various hybrids. The schematic diagram on the right depicts patterns for the parents and one of the hybrids (3)

Three cell lines 3, 4 and 12 very definitely were hybrids when the enzyme, aspartate aminotransferase (Fig. 5 d), was employed. The 2 bands (R_f0.40 and 0.65) present in soybean were always observed in the above cell lines, in addition the *N. tabacum* band with R_f of 0.46 was also present. It is interesting to note that the *N. tabacum* band at R_f0.61 was only faintly evident in line 3 while absent in the other lines. The 3 hybrids exhibited a hybrid band at R_f 0.43. *N. tabacum* had a slow moving doublet (R_f 0.19) which was very faint in cell lines 3 and 4. The other cell lines including those not shown in Fig. 5 could not be distinguished from soybean.

Discussion

In the present investigation we have shown that more than half of the *N. tabacum* chromosomes have been retained in 5 hybrid cell lines for a period of 7 months of culturing, during which time there were no obvious changes in the soybean chromosomes. The isozyme studies have confirmed the above observations, in 3 isozyme systems studied the 5 hybrid lines have maintained their hybrid pattern throughout the 7 month study. The exception appeared to be alcohol dehydrogenase in which the hybrid pattern had disappeared at the end of the 7 month period. The results, excluding the alcohol dehydrogenase, suggested that genes on chromosomes expressing these enzymes were retained throughout the culture period. The continued presence of such abnormalities as ring chromosomes, long chromosomes and chromosomal bridges indicated that the hybrid cell lines have not yet stabilized.

N. tabacum is an amphidiploid derived from *N. sylvestris* and *N. tomentosiformis* and therefore has 4 sets of chromosomes. The double dose of chromosomes might account for the fact that the somatic hybrids of *N. tabacum*-soybean appear to be more stable than the *N. glauca*-soybean hybrids (Kao 1977). The protoplasts isolated from *N. tabacum* leaves divided more readily than those obtained from *N. glauca* leaves. Since soybean protoplasts also divided readily one might postulate that perhaps more nuclei of *N. tabacum* and soybean were in the same phase of the mitotic cycle and thus led to more stable hybrid lines. One might speculate that because of this the *N. tabacum* chromosomes were less likely to undergo premature chromosomal condensation, then fragmentation and finally elimination.

Acknowledgement

We thank Mr. John Dyck for his valuable technical assistance in assaying the various isozymes.

References

Binding, H.; Nehls, R. (1978): Somatic cell hybridization of *Vicia faba* +*Petunia hybrida*. Mol. Gen. Genet. 164, 137~143

Dudits, D.; Hadlaczky, B.Y.; Bajszar, G.Y.; Koncz, C.S.; Lazar, G.; Horvath, G. (1979) Plant regeneration from intergeneric cell hybrids. Plant Sci. Lett. 15, 101~112

Gleba, Y.Y.; Hoffmann, F. (1978): Hybrid cell lines *Arabidop-sis thaliana* +*Brassica campestris*: No evidence for specific chromosome elimination. Mol. Gen. Genet. 165, 257~264

Gleba, Y.Y.; Hoffmann, F. (1979): Arabidobrassica: Plantgenome engineering by protoplast fusion. Naturwissenschaften 66, 547~554

Kao, K.N. (1975): A chromosomal staining method for cultured cells. In: Plant Tissue Culture Methods (eds. Gamborg, O.L.; Wetter, L.R.), pp.63-64. Saskatoon, Canada: Prairie Regional Laboratory, Nat. Res. Counc.

Kao, K.N. (1977): Chromosomal behaviour in somatic hybrids of soybean - *Nicotiana glauca*. Mol. Gen. Genet. 150, 225~230

Krumbiegel, G.; Schieder, O. (1979): Selection of somatic hybrids after fusion of protoplasts from *Datura innoxia* Mill. and *Atropa belladonna* L. Planta 145, 371~375

Melchers, G.; Sacristan, M.D.; Holder, A. (1978): Somatic hybrid plants of potato and tomato regenerated from fused protoplasts. Carlsberg Res. Commun. 43, 203~218

Power, J.B.; Frearson, E.M.; Hayward, C.; Cocking, E.C. (1975): Some consequences of the fusion and selective culture of petunia and *Parthenocissus* protoplasts. Plant Sci. Lett. 5, 197~207

Wetter, L.R. (1977): Isoenzyme patterns in soybean-*Nicotiana* somatic hybrid cell lines. Mol. Gen. Genet. 150,231~235

Wetter, L.R.; Kao, K.N. (1976): The use of isozymes in distinguishing the sexual and somatic hybrids in callus cultures derived from *Nicotiana*. Z. Pflanzenphysiol. 80, 455~462

Wetter, L.R.; Kao, K.N. (1980): Chromosome and isoenzyme studies on cells derived from protoplast fusion of *Nicotiana glauca* with *Glycine max -Nicotiana glauca* cell hybrids. Theor. Appl. Genet. 57, 273~276

本文原载：Can. J. Bot. 1983. 61: 639-641

Effects of osmolality, cytokinin, and organic acids on pollen callus formation in *Triticale* anthers

Y. C. Chien*, K. N. Kao

(Prairie Regional Laboratory, National Research Council of Canada)

Triticale anthers with pollen at middle to late uninuclcatcd stages were cultured individually in Falcon micro test II tissue culture plates. The results indicate that when the anthers were cultured in the same growing conditions the differences in pollen callus formation among anthers from the first and second florets in the same spikelet were not statistically significant. whereas the differences in callus formation among anthers from different spikes (or plants) were statistically significant. These results suggest that comparisons of treatment effects should be made between samples consisting of anthers from the same spikelet only. Benzyl adenine (BA) and higher osmolality enhanced pollen callus induction, while a higher concentracion of organic acids suppressed it. Under optimal conditions 31% of anthers formed callus, while the number of pollen calli per 100 seeded anthers was as high as 130. The pollen calli were able to develop into plants; however, the frequency was relatively low.

Introduction

Induction of pollen plants in anther culture of *Triticale* has been reported (Ono and Larter 1976; Orlikowska 1977; Sun et al. 1973; Sun et al. 1980). However, the frequency was very low. One of the problems in studying nutritional requirements in anther culture is that it is difficult to obtain a meaningful result when random samples are used, because there are great variations among samples (spikes or spikelets). Such problems can be overcome if comparisons of treatments are made by using anthers from the same floret or spikelet as suggested by Kao (1981).

Here, we are reporting the results of the effects of sugars, organic acids, and plant growth substances on *Triticale* pollen callus formation by a single anther culture method.

---

* Visiting scientist. Present address: Institute of Botany, Academia Sinica, Peking, China.

Material and methods

An octoploid *Triticale* variety 96 was used as experimental material. After vernalization the seeds were planted in the greenhouse in February and were transplanted, or planted directly, in the field in early April. Anthers were removed aseptically from *Triticale* plants from May 15 to July 15, 1981. A single anther was placed in 200 μL of a liquid medium in the well of a Falcon micro test II tissue culture plate. Anthers containing pollens at middle to a late uninucleate stage were used. Three basic media used were (*i*) K1 medium (Kao 1981); (*ii*) medium A (pH 5.5) supplemented with 20 mL of coconut water (Kao and Michayluk 1981), and (*iii*) N6 medium (Chu et al. 1975). The pH values of all the media were adjusted to 5.5. The amounts of plant growth substances, sugars, and organic acids used in each of the experiments are stated in the Results and discussion.

A sample consisted of 16 anthers, each of them was obtained from a single spikelet from the same spike. Since the first and second florets in a spikelet are usually in a similar stage of development, six identical samples could be made by distributing the six anthers from each of the 16 spikelets into each of the samples.

Comparison of treatment effects were always made among identical samples. Usually 7-14 spikes were used as replica tions in each experiment. Statistical analyses were made following the model:

$$X_{ij} = \mu + \alpha_i + \beta_i + e_{ij}$$

where α_i = treatment effects, β_i = replication (spike) effects, e_{ij} = sampling variation (see Snedecor 1962, p. 296).

Anthers were incubated in near darkness at 25℃. When the calli grew to a size of 1-2mm in diameter (ca. 30-40days), they were placed on K1, medium A, and N6 agar media with 0.5mg/L 2,4-D and 1mg/L zeatin riboside or without any plant growth substances at 25℃ and under constant illumination (ca. 1000 lx, cool-white fluorescent).

Table 1 Effects of osmolality and kinetin on pollen callus formation in *Triticale* anther culture

Osmolality of The medium (estimated), mOs	Sucrose, g/L	Glucose, g/L	Kinetin, mg/L	% of anthers with pollen calli*	
				Expr. 1 (Kl medium)	Expt. 2 (medium A)
240	60	0	0	1.0 (7)	1.1 (2)
350	35	25	0	6.6 (17)	4.3 (24)
350	35	25	0.5	12.6 (78)	15.9 (80)

* The values given in parentheses represent the number of pollen calli per 100 seeded anthers.

Results and discussion

Based on the experiments the following observations were made.

A certain osmotic pressure level has to be maintained in a culture medium to induce young pollen grain in the anthers to divide as well as inhibit the growth of anther walls (Sun et al. 1980; Keller et al. 1975; Kao 1981). Osmolality had a profound effect on pollen callus formation in *Triticale*. A medium containing 100 g/L sucrose (which contributes ca. 290mOs) or a combination of 35 g/L glucose and 25 g/L sucrose (which contribute ca. 270mOs) induced more pollen calli than a medium containing only 60 g/L sucrose (which contributes ca. 180 mOs) (Tables 1 and 2). The differences were statistically significant.

Two different types of calli were found in *Triticale* anther culture: the dense and creamy-color type which originated from pollen grains and the whitish loose calli which originated from the broken end of filaments. Cytokinin not only increased the frequency of pollen callus fromation but also inhibited the growth of filament calli. The inhibition of callus formation from filaments by cytokinin was also observed by Sun et al. (1980). About 13% of the anthers (or 78 pollen calli per 100 anthers plated) produced pollen calli in a medium containing 0.1mg/L zeatin riboside and 0.5mg/L kinetin, whereas only 7% of the anthers produced pollen calli (or 24 pollen calli per 100 anthers plated) in the same medium containing 0.1mg/L zeatin riboside only (Table 1). On an equimolar basis, BA was most effective in inducing pollen callus formation.Thirteen percent of anthers produced pollen calli (or 29 calli per 100 anthers plated) in a medium containing 2.58μM (or 0.58mg/L) BA, 7% in the medium with 2.58 μM (0.55mg/L) kinetin, and only 2% in the medium with 2.58μM (0.916mg/L) zeatin riboside (Table 3). The 2,4-D level in all the above media was at 4mg/L.

Table 2 Effects of various amounts of sucrose and organic acids on pollen callus induction in *Triticale*

Organic acids* (mg/L)	% of anthers with pollen calli†	
	100g/L sucrose	60g/L sucrose
35	14.4 (52)	4.2 (8)
70	11.1 (37)	3.2 (11)
140	7.9 (19)	3.2 (10)

* A mixture of sodium pyruvate, malic acid, fumaric acid, and citric acid at a ratio of 1 ∶ 2 ∶ 2 ∶ 2. N6 medium with 1mg/L 2,4-D and 0.5mg/L kinetin.

†The values given in parentheses represent the number of pollen calli per 100 seeded anthers.

Table 3 Effects of different cytokinins on pollen callus formation in *Triticale* anther culture

Cytokinins*	% of anthers with callit†
Zeatin riboside (0.916mg/L or 2.58 μM)	2.1 (3)
Kinetin (0.55mg/L or 2.58 μM)	7.2 (14)
6-Benzyladinine (0.58mg/L or 2.58 μM)	12.8 (28)

* In medium A with 4mg/L 2,4-D.

† The values given in parentheses represent the number of pollen calli per 100 seeded anthers.

Table 4 Variation in frequencies of pollen callus formation in anthers from the first and second florets in the same spikelets

Sample No.*	% of anthers with pollen calli†
1	16.2 (45)
2	15.1 (68)
3	17.8 (59)
4	18.1 (70)
5	22.1 (70)
6	17.1 (73)

*The anthers were cultured in N6 with 2mg/L2, 4-D, 0.5mg/L kinetin, and 35mg/L organic acids. The samples were replicated seven times (spikes = replications).

†The values given in parentheses represent the number of pollen calli per 100 seeded anthers.

Table 5 Variation in frequencies of pollen callus formation in anthers from different spikes

Spike No.*	% of anthers with pollen calli †
1	6 (34)
2	5 (5)
3	31 (129)
4	2 (2)
5	29(101)
6	18 (60)
7	26(91)

*Six replications (anthers within spikelets). medium as in Table 4.

†The values given in parentheses represent the number of pollen calli per 100 seeded anthers.

Adding organic acids to the culture medium was found to have a beneficial effect for culturing plant cells at a very low population density (Kao and Michayluk 1975). The results here indicate that a higher concentration of organic acids (140mg/L) was harmful to the induction of pollen callus. We have yet to determine whether a lower concentration (35mg/L) has any beneficial effect to pollen callus induction in *Triticale* (Table 2).

No statistical differences were found in frequencies of callus formation among samples when the anthers were placed on the same medium (Table 4). The frequencies of callus formation in anthers from different spikes varied from 2 to 31 % and the number of pollen calli per 100 anthers varied from 2 to 129 when they were cultured in the same medium (Table 5). The differences were statistically significant. The differences among spikes were likely derived from genetic variation (Sun et al. 1980; Foroughi-Wehr et al. 1976), environmental conditions (Keller et al. 1975), and (or) different ages of flowers (Nitsch and Nitsch 1969). These results clearly indicate that in *Triticale*, spikes as sampling units should not be used since variations among spikes could be much greater than variation among treatments. Treatment effects could only be revealed when samples are made of anthers from the same florets or spikelets as mentioned in the method.

Plant formation was observed on all the agar media tested. Among 1297 pollen calli placed on the agar media, 52 green planllets and 82 albino plantlets were obtained. Part of the reason for this low frequency of plant regeneration might be due to the fact that many calli were aborted before they were placed on the agar because too many calli were competing for a limited amount of medium in the well of the plate. It was not uncommon to find over 10 calli in a well.

References

Chu, C. C., C. C. Wang, and C. S. Sun. 1975. Establishment of an efficient medium for anther culture of ricc through comparative experiments on the nitrogen sources. Sci. Sin. 28: 659~668.

Foroughi-Wehr, B., G. Mix, H. Gaul, and H. M. Wilson. 1976. Plant production from cultured anthers of *Hordeum vulgare* L. Z. Pflanzenzuecht. 77: 198~204.

Kao, K. N. 1981. Plant fonnation from barley anther cultures with Ficoll media. Z. Pflanzenphysiol. 103: 437~443.

Kao, K. N., and M. R. Michayluk. 1975. Nutritional requirements for growth of *Vicia hajastana* cells and protoplasts at a very low population density in liquid media. Planta, 126: 105~110.

——1981. Embryoid formation in alfalfa cell suspension cultures from different plants. In Vitro, 17: 645~648.

Keller, W. A., T. Rajhathy, and J. Lacopra. 1975. In vitro production of plants from pollen in *Brassica compestris*. Can. J. Genet. Cytol. 17: 655~666.

Nitsch, J. P., and C. Nitsch. 1969. Haploid plants from pollen grains. Science (Washington, D.C.), 163: 85~87.

Ono, H., and E. N. Larter. 1976. Anther culture of *Triticale*. Crop Sci. 16: 120~122.

Orlikowska, T. 1977. Induction of androgenesis *in vitro* in *Secaie cereale* and *Triticale*. Genet. Pol. 18: 51~59.

Snedecor, G. 1962. Statistical methods. The lowa University Press, Ames.

Sun, C. S., C. C. Wang, and Z. C. Chu. 1973. Cytological studies on the androgenesis of *Triticale*. Acta Bot. Sin. 15: 163~173.

Sun,J. S., Z. Q. Zhu, J. J. Wang, and P.M. A. Tigerstedt. 1980. Studies on the anther culture of *Triticale*. Acta Bot Sin. 22: 27~31.

本文原载：植物学通报. 1984. 2(1): 1-7

植物原生质体的应用

钱迎倩

(中国科学院植物研究所)

一、前言

植物原生质体已越来越引起人们的兴趣。在细胞生物学、遗传学、植物生理学甚至分子生物学的基础研究方面，原生质体作为理想的实验体系已为更多的人所了解。在植物育种及作物改良方面，也正引起植物育种工作者的重视。

植物原生质体是被脱掉了细胞壁、仅有质膜包围、裸露而生活的植物细胞。质膜在生命活动中的作用极为重要，例如信息传递、能量转换、物质运输等生命现象都与质膜有密切的关系。原生质体作为一个裸露的细胞，为植物质膜的结构与功能的研究提供了有利的条件。过去在整体水平上进行的细胞壁生物合成的研究，所获得的资料是有限的。而原生质体再生细胞壁的过程，是研究壁生物合成最好的机会。此外，人们利用原生质体裸露而具生活力的特性，已在细胞水平上揭示了一系列生命过程的本质。

近十几年来的研究进展已充分说明原生质体可以摄取外源物质，经过各种方法诱导的异源原生质体可以互相融合，融合体可能再生成杂种植株。在马铃薯叶肉原生质体培养方面所得到的结果，说明有一些作物品种在通过培养而不作任何处理的情况下，有可能从中筛选出具有实用价值的新品系。这就进一步展示了原生质体在应用上的潜在可能性。

原生质体研究的进展是非常快的。科学家们已做了大量的工作，本文根据已经获得的结果作一简要介绍。

二、细胞壁再生和质膜的研究

1. 细胞壁再生

由于原生质体能再生新的细胞壁，通过透射电镜、扫描电镜、冰冻蚀刻，免疫荧光以及多糖染色等手段，对于在壁形成过程中质膜、细胞器以及微管(质膜内表面上一种细胞骨架)的作用方面已积累了一定的资料。

在分生组织、快速生长的悬浮培养细胞与特化了的细胞的原生质体之间，细胞壁开始形成的速度是很不一致的。用来源于蚕豆属(*Vicia*)的悬浮培养物的原生质体作实验证明，分离后 10~20 分钟内原生质体就开始有初生壁的合成，并在 24h 内微纤丝可沉积成网状[52]；而来源于烟草叶片的原生质体则要经过 3~24h 后才开始有初生壁的合成[6]。来源于成熟叶片与幼嫩叶片的原生质体，其细胞壁形成的开始时间也是不相同的，前者较后者要晚一点。如在培养基中加入适量的香豆素(coumarin)则可抑制细胞壁的形成或大大延缓细胞壁形成的时间[5]。这些资料对于进行原生质体融合和病毒侵染机理等实验研究是很有参考价值的。

新细胞壁开始是由松散而有组织的微纤丝网组成[52]。当微纤丝过于稀疏时，大多数的基质多糖流失在周围的培养基中[47]。到微纤丝沉积至足够数量后，基质就被保留下来，两者结合并逐步形成致密的细胞壁。由纤维素组成的做纤丝的沉积是在质膜上发生的[36]。在壁形成过程中，质膜内表面的微管在决定微纤丝沉积的方向上起着很重要的作用[36]。也就是说，微管控制着微纤丝形成的方向。而在初生壁生长期间，基质成分的合成和沉积与高尔基体是密切相关的[36]。此外，壁形成过程中内质网明显增加，它们与质膜平行地成片出现，这就间接提供了内质网与壁形成有关的证据[35]。

2. 质膜的研究

由于原生质体的质膜充分暴露，对它进行研究就有很大的方便。例如用特殊的钨磷酸-铬酸(PTA-CrO_3)染色后，染料强烈地与植物质膜结合，从而证实了质膜中存在糖类[37]。质膜也可以与改良的高碘酸-锡夫(PAS)起反应而着色，又一次说明质膜中有糖类的成分。至于糖类在质膜中是属于质膜本身的一部分还是细胞壁的一种残余或先驱物，目前尚不清楚。此外，植物原生质体的表面可与一种外源凝集素——伴刀豆球蛋白 A (ConA)相结合而引起原生质体聚集[15]。ConA 具与原生质体相结合的能力，人们可把它作为一种探针去测试原生质体的表面。用胡萝卜原生质体作材料，还发现 ConA 是通过糖类基团与质膜中的特异位点相结合而发生作用的[16]。这对于了解质膜的结构与功能是有帮助的。

实验证明原生质体表面带有负电荷。Ca^{++}和 Mg^{++}等两价阳离子能消除膜电位，聚乙二醇、高 Ca^{++}、高 pH 以及 $NaNO_3$ 等融合诱导剂也是从改变原生质体表面的电荷而引起聚集，从而起融合作用的[21]。此外，应用免疫荧光及负染技术对转板藻 (*Mougeotia*) 和高等植物原生质体质膜内表面上皮层微管的大小、结构和分布进行研究后，进一步提供了微管控制微纤丝沉积方向的证据[24，48]。

三、在细胞水平上研究抗逆性和其他生理现象

植物对低温、脱水以及有毒环境等逆境的抵抗反应是在细胞水平上进行的。过去在整体水平上进行研究受到了各种干扰，而用原生质体作材料则可排除干扰，大大有助于这方面的研究，对于阐明植物抗逆性的生化过程及在细胞水平上所发生的一些现象是非常有利的。

原生质体可以作为测定植物抗寒力的一种工具。简令成等[1]用三种不同抗寒力小麦品种的原生质体作了耐冻性的测定。结果说明小麦原生质体经冰冻处理后的存活率和品

种的抗寒力成正相关。关于脱水的问题，原生质体形成的本身就是细胞放在高渗溶液中经质壁分离的一个脱水的过程。对于细胞在高渗溶液中脱水的代谢状况的了解还是很不够的。有人认为脱水会产生不可逆的代谢变化。但也有人认为原生质体在生理上是正常的，因为经培养后可以恢复并再生成完整的植株。这个问题还需作进一步的研究。至于病原菌引起的毒害问题，已经证明病原微生物甘蔗长蠕孢菌产生的毒素——长蠕孢醇苷和玉米长蠕孢菌产生的蠕孢菌毒素，均与寄生植物质膜上的特定部位结合。抗毒素的玉米品系分离的原生质体对毒素具高度的抗性。分离得的膜蛋白也不与毒素相结合，因此可以通过原生质体体系来阐明毒素的作用机理。

用植物原生质体作为工具来研究植物细胞的生理现象也是非常有用的。例如植物细胞对一些化合物的反应，过去是用整体植株、组织或单个细胞来进行研究的，由于植物有维管系统和细胞壁，它们具有各种各样的酶足以使某些化合物改变性质或只能有限的进入植物体；而利用原生质体有摄取外界化合物的特性，或材料用脂质体包起来后再作引入，这就有利于在细胞水平上进行细胞对各种化合物反应的研究。

原生质体也可以用来研究光合作用或光呼吸等一些基本的生理过程。Nishimura 等[29]测定了菠菜叶片原生质体的 1，5-二磷酸核酮糖羧化酶的生物合成，发现其活性与菠菜叶片组织是一样的。实验也证明分离的菠菜原生质体的光呼吸过程与叶片组织中的也是一致的。过去用叶片组织来测定这些生理过程时，要从叶片中把具活性的叶绿体分离出来并纯化。用原生质体来测定时就不必进行叶绿体的分离，这在保持细胞器之间的相互关系方面要比分离的叶绿体好得多。这一点是重要的，例如过氧化物酶体在光呼吸过程中是很重要的细胞器，在研究光呼吸过程时，应该把它与叶绿体同时存在的情况下来进行，这样能得到更正确的结果[20]。

Zeiger 等[54]的研究指出：原生质体可用来研究分化了的或高度特化的细胞的生理过程。他们从洋葱和烟草表皮的成熟保卫细胞中分离得原生质体，这些原生质体在蓝光下与正常保卫细胞一样地膨大。所以，进一步对保卫细胞原生质体进行研究，将有助于搞清楚保卫细胞开闭的机理。

四、植物和病毒相互关系的研究

老的方法是用叶片组织来作病毒侵染机理的研究。如烟草花叶病毒是在用金刚砂把叶片表皮磨破后接种的，一次接种只能有 10^6~10^{10} 个病毒颗粒进入。而用烟草叶片原生质体则效率大大提高。对于悬浮培养物原生质体来说，在 10 分钟之内其中的 80%~100% 原生质体每个都可接种上 10^3 的烟草花叶病毒[42]。自从 Takebe 1969 年第一次用烟草叶肉原生质体作为寄主系统以来[44]，许多病毒也可在其他许多植物种内侵染。目前，有关病毒的繁殖过程、病毒核酸和蛋白质的合成、病毒对植物细胞的毒害以及植物对侵染的抵抗等方面都已积累了不少资料[43]。

1980 年以前，作病毒侵染多数用叶片原生质体，但用叶片组织有病毒扩散得慢、不可能同步侵染以及复制等缺点。虽然也可用体外培养的细胞作为实验体系，可是由于接种困难，成功的很少。给人以脱分化的快速生长的悬浮细胞培养物对病毒的繁殖是不利的错觉，但近年来的研究已改变了这个观点。实验说明比起叶肉原生质体来，悬浮培养物更为有利，特点是可得到大量的无菌材料以及可以避免一些麻烦。例如叶肉原生质体由于有叶绿体和大的中央液胞使在分析时必须把病毒大分子分离出来[45]。

五、不同类型细胞和细胞器的分离

1. 不同类型细胞的分离

叶片是由不同类型的各种细胞组成的，这些细胞从解剖学的角度和生理功能上看是不一样的。通过匀浆的方法所得到的是各种类型细胞的混合物。由于难以把不同类型的细胞分离开，得到的结果就不免产生误差。而植物原生质体则提供了解决这问题的方法。例如叶片放在酶溶液中处理后，根据不同组织的细胞所需酶解时间的不同，可以顺序地分别收集不同类型的细胞。Ku 等的实验[23]已能将草本植物叶片中一般叶肉薄壁细胞和维管束鞘薄壁细胞分开。然后分别测定不同类型细胞中酶的含量。经测定，C_4禾谷类植物叶片中叶肉原生质体中有较高的磷酸烯醇丙酮酸(PEP)羧化酶活性，而 1，5-二磷酸核酮糖(RuDP)酶的活性只在维管束鞘薄壁细胞中发现。从而表明 C_4 途径的羧化阶段是在叶肉原生质体中进行，而脱羧作用及随后的 Calvin-Benson 途径的羧化过程是在维管束鞘细胞中进行的。也就是说，C_4碳固定的酶是存在于叶肉原生质体中，而维管束鞘细胞中的酶是把 C_4 途径最初固定的产物转化成 C_3 和 C_6 化合物。

花瓣中具花青素的细胞处于亚表皮细胞层内。根据具色素的原生质体比不具色素原生质体比重为高的原理，通过差速离心可把花瓣经酶解后所得混合原生质体中的两者分离开[49]。从花瓣原生质体还可取得完整的液胞制备品。例如来源于郁金香花瓣原生质体的液胞，经分析说明其中 95%是具色素的液胞，而 5%是不具色素的液胞。

2. 细胞器的分离

过去对细胞器的分离是采用机械破碎、研磨或超声等方法。这些方法的缺点是细胞器很娇嫩受不了强力而大量破坏。原生质体作为分离细胞器的材料是非常理想的，用改变渗透压或如 TritonX-100 这类洗涤剂来处理，在温和的条件下把质膜破碎，释放出的细胞器就非常完整。然后再通过离心可分别收集到质膜、液胞、细胞核、叶绿体、线粒体和过氧物体。这种方法得到的细胞器对于研究单个细胞器的功能、结构与功能的关系或者作细胞器对原生质体的引入都是非常有用的。

例如，从玉米[18]、小麦[49]、菠菜[30]等植物的叶片先分离得原生质体，然后在温和条件下破碎得到叶绿体，纯化后以作光合作用、光呼吸以及核酸和蛋白质合成研究之用。研究发现，纯化方法不同可导致不同的结果。用蔗糖密度梯度纯化，制备品干净，但 CO_2 固定能力低[30]；用差速离心法得到的叶绿体 CO_2 固定效率高[34]，但缺点是有其他细胞器污染而纯度差[33]。利用原生质体也可以分离到大量的细胞核。经合成 RNA 和蛋白质能力的测定，说明分离到的核具完整的功能。但在结构上可能由于在分离过程中使用了去污剂而丧失了核的外膜[19]。

过去关于高等植物液胞的资料不多，原因是缺乏能大量分离和纯化有生理活性的完整液胞的方法。液胞在成熟细胞中占有90%以上的体积，它在调节渗透压、贮藏及消化方面的功能虽已积累了一定的知识，可以预料在大规模分离到液胞后可更多的了解到有关液胞的内含物、结构和液胞膜的运输特性。已有证据说明液胞具溶酶体的功能[25]，里面含有各种水解酶和蛋白质水解酶[31,32]。

六、遗传操作

利用原生质体是裸露的植物细胞的特性，可作外源遗传物质引入、融合以及转化的研究。原生质体是遗传操作研究的理想的材料系统。

外源遗传物质或细胞器的引入

原生质体可以摄取叶绿体、细胞核、病毒、噬菌体、核酸甚至塑料小球等物质。植物原生质体的摄取有两种可能的途径，即胞饮作用和融合[12]，这是两种很不相同的过程。

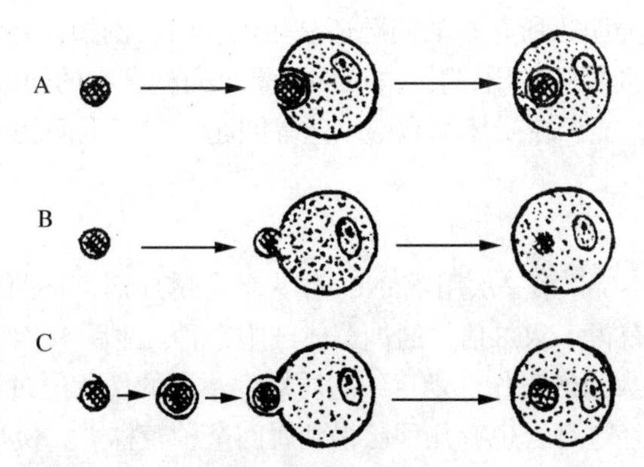

图1 胞饮作用示意图

A. 质膜内折的胞饮作用；B. 膜的融合；C. 材料被脂质体包裹，通过脂质体与膜融合后摄入

图1说明了胞饮作用(A)是包括有质膜内折的过程，使最后进入原生质体中的物质包有一层质膜；而融合的过程(B)意味着外源物质的膜与原生质体进行了融合，因此最后进入原生质体中去的物质是丧失了其外膜的。摄入是通过那一条途径往往需要用电子显微镜的观察来加以肯定。Fowke[12]强调了要考虑到这一点的重要性。至今在引入研究方面虽已作了不少工作，但得到理想结果的不多。原因之一是可能在引入前供体(例如细胞器)本身由于受各种条件的影响，已经不是完整的，或者由于是通过融合过程而摄入的，造成摄入的细胞器已失去了外膜。

原生质体摄取塑料小球的实验，帮助了人们对胞饮机理的了解[41]。塑料小球首先是粘着在质膜上，然后通过质膜的内折摄入，粘着的过程显然是由于静电力的作用，而小球进入原生质体是需借助于能量并发生得非常迅速的过程。关于叶绿体摄入研究，瑞典科学家早在1974年就开展了[4]，他们通过聚乙二醇的诱导把藻类叶绿体摄入到胡萝卜原生质体中去。以后 Davey[9]的工作说明由于分离的叶绿体趋于很快的解体以及融合后叶绿体膜与质膜融合，造成摄入到原生质体的细胞质中的实际上仅仅是叶绿体的内含物。这就造成了摄入叶绿体研究的困难。至今还没有令人信服的完整叶绿体被原生质体摄入的报道。如在技术上作改进后，这条途径对于细胞器的发育、遗传和核质的关系方面的研究都是非常有利的。

至今有关摄入的机理或核在受体原生质体中的命运是不清楚的。近年来有人建议用微原生质体(miniprotoplast)的方法[50]，也就是把原生质体放在细胞松弛素 B 中处理后，通过高速离心，可以得到在细胞核外包有少量细胞质的微原生质体。然后将这种微原生质体通过融合摄入到异源原生质体中去。由于还包有薄层的细胞质，因此还不能认为是纯粹的核移植。在微生物摄入方面，人们希望通过把具功能的固氮酶转移到非豆科植物中去，固氮细菌和蓝藻引入到高等植物原生质体中并不困难。但据报道引入后，原生质体未存活下来，内共生也未建立起来[10, 27]。

为了使细胞器或微生物被摄入后保持它们的完整性，近年来发展了脂质体(一种脂类小泡)作摄入研究[13, 26]细胞器等可先用脂质体包起来，使脂质体与原生质体膜融合，这样可使进入原生质体内的是完整的细胞器(图 1C)。这方面的研究在动物上做得多，在植物上也陆续有所开展。

关于外源遗传物质引入所存在的问题还是相当多的。例如，外源 DNA 的引入，由于遇到细胞质中一系列酶的作用，引入的 DNA 是否完整存在的问题，外源 DNA 能否整合到受体 DNA 中去，能否在受体细胞中表达等问题。对以上问题的争议还是很多的。

1. 体细胞杂交

70 年代初期 Carlson[7]第一次用 $NaNO_3$ 作为融合诱导剂，把两种不同烟草的原生质体进行融合，成功地获得了双二倍体的烟草体细胞杂种。此后 10 年来，种间杂种特别是烟草的种间杂种已有大量的工作。烟草细胞质雄性不育的性状通过细胞融合带给了胞质杂种。属间原生质体经过融合也有几种已得到属间杂种植株[38]。例如，土豆-西红柿、曼陀罗-颠茄、拟南芥菜-芸苔、胡萝卜-羊角芹以及颠茄-烟草[14]等。遗憾的是至今这些属间杂种还都是不育的。科间一般都只获得杂种细胞系，还未见到能分化成植株的报道。这些科间杂种细胞系经过一段时间培养后，往往是某一亲本的染色体大量被排除直到全套染色体被排除，但也有保留一半以上的报道[8]。

最近，有的科学新闻还报道了已能把牛细胞和西红柿原生质体融合并已获得体细胞杂种[3]。但未见到正文。

2. 转化研究

转化一词起源于细菌的研究，现借用在高等植物上。例如，引起双子叶植物形成冠瘿是与根癌土壤杆菌菌体内的 Ti 质粒有关。当细菌进入植物细胞中后，可把质粒释放到寄主细胞内，而 Ti 质粒上的 T-DNA 片段又可整合到寄主细胞核的 DNA 上，从而引起转化。

植物原生质体可作为转化研究的理想的受体系统。原生质体是无壁的单个细胞，这就便于把转化了的细胞分离出来进行纯系增殖。从而克服过去用根癌菌在整株植物上进行感染而可能得到中间混杂有正常细胞的嵌合体。这种嵌合体给分析带来可能的误差。这方面研究已有成功的例子，如 Davey 等用根癌菌 Ach5 处理烟草原生质体再生细胞已得到了转化肿瘤组织[11]。此外，还可用分离的 Ti 质粒或 T-DNA 直接作原生质体转化的研究，如 Davey 实验室还用分离的 Ti 质粒处理矮牵牛原生质体。这些由原生质体来源的转化了的细胞能在无外源激素培养基上生长 24 个月，并具 LPDH(一种控制合成或降解 opine 的脱氢酶，opine 的存在与否是转化成败的证明)的活性。以后用烟草作材料也得到了成功[22]。

此外，把溶菌酶处理过的根癌菌原生质球和长春花原生质体用聚乙二醇诱导融合，也能出现转化[17]。还可以用肿瘤组织的原生质体与正常细胞的原生质体通过融合进行转化。这方面在烟草-烟草及烟草-矮牵牛上都已有了报道[2, 53]。

七、无性系的筛选

从亲本的体细胞(而不是从特化的性细胞)无性繁殖所产生的生物有机体称为无性系。通过无性系进行繁殖称作无性繁殖。无性系的基因组像有性繁殖机体的基因组一样，在某些方面可能产生变异。这些变异可为育种工作者在改良植物品种时找到可选择的源泉。原生质体无性繁殖再生的植株会产生可能有用的各类表型变异，因此可以设想原生质体无性繁殖系在作物改良中有可能起到作用。

1973 年，Shepard 等发现，从烟草叶肉原生质体再生的无性系群体中，在未作任何诱变处理的情况下，大约每 250 个再生植株中有一株叶片上可出现杂色斑点。这特征并能通过有性杂交传到子代[39]。他们从此联想到，如果把原生质体技术应用到经常发生体细胞突变的作物上，也许可能产生更多有用的遗传变异。因此他们研究了品种为 *Russet burbank* 的马铃薯原生质体。发现由原生质体产生的大多数马铃薯植株不仅与亲本不同，它们彼此之间也很不相同。在这些无性系中有许多变异，变异大致可分为两类：一类是野生型的畸形体，染色体数已有改变；另一类是表型变异体，它们个体间的差异是微细的，染色体数不变或仅有细微的差别。变异也表现在改变了对致病有机体的敏感性上，如某些变异体对马铃薯早疫病的致病菌不如亲本那样敏感。又如有约 2%原生质体无性系对马铃薯晚疫病的抗性高于亲本。其后代也还保持着它们的抗性水平。

他们从 *Russet burbank* 品系的原生质体无性系中选出 65 个进行了检定。被测定的复杂性状几乎全部都存在着表型的变异，没有一个彼此相似或是亲本的复制品。园艺性状方面，连遗传上最复杂的特性如块茎产量也发生变异。他们还对另外三个马铃薯品系的原生质体进行了研究，同样观察到了相似的变异性[40]。

可是根据 Wenzel 报道[51]，在他们研究的二倍体马铃薯品系方面，表型变异在原生质体无性系群体中并不是经常出现的一种特征。分析 Shepard 和 Wenzel 两人所得结果的差别，可能是由于研究材料基因型的不同或者是培养方法不一样而影响到变异的频率和类型。

八、其他

此外，还可以通过叶肉原生质体培养得到无病菌的植株。如 Mori[28]用荧光抗体染色检查证明烟草叶片暗绿色区域只有少量或没有病毒。取这区域的叶片分离得原生质体，从中可获得再生的无病毒植株。

原生质体不仅对冻害的基础研究是一个合适的材料，并且作为基因库的种质贮存也是一种理想的材料。Takeuchi[46]做了地钱、胡萝卜的培养细胞以及大豆愈伤组织和大麦、小麦叶肉细胞来源的原生质体冰冻贮存。他们把原生质体用 5%二甲亚砜和 10%葡萄糖混合物保护后作预冻，然后直接放到−196℃的液氮中。经过长期贮存后，大麦、大豆、地钱、小麦和胡萝卜的生活原生质体的量分别为 68、60、40、33 及 30%。地钱的原生质体的细胞壁再生率可达到 80%。两天后就开始分裂，最后形成小细胞团并再生成正常的原叶体。胡萝卜也能再生小植株，其他有的也可有愈伤组织的再生。

综上所述，我们可以看到原生质体在基础和应用研究方面不仅已取得了成绩，并存在着巨大的潜势，值得国内各有关科学工作者的重视。

参考文献

[1] 简令成等，1980，植物学报，22: 17~21

[2] 李向辉等，1982，中国科学，B 辑，3: 223~228

[3] Anomymous, 1983, *New Scientist,* 97 (1351): 888

[4] Bonnett. H. T. and Eriksson T., 1974, *Planta.* 120: 71~79

[5] Burgess, J. and Linstead. P. J., 1977, *Planta.* 133: 267~273

[6] Burgess, J. and P. J. Linstead, 1979, *Planta.* 146: 203~210

[7] Carlson, P. S., 1972: *Proc. Natl. Acad. Sci., U. S. A.,* 69: 2292~2294

[8] Chien, Y. C. (钱迎倩), Kao, K. N. and Wetter. L. R., 1982, *Theor. App. Genet.,* 62: 301~304

[9] Davey, M. R., Frearson E. M. and Power J. B., 1976, *Plant Sci. Lett.,* 7: 7~16

[10] Davey, M. R., 1977, Applied and Fundamental Aspects of Plant Cell Tissue and Organ Culture, Springer-Verlag, Berlin and New York. pp. 551~662

[11] Davey, M. R., Cocking, E. C., Freeman, J., Pearce N. and Tudor. I., 1980, *Plant Sci Lett.,* 18: 307~313

[12] Fowke, L. C. and Gamborg, O. L., 1980, *Intl. Rev. Cytology.* 69: 9~51

[13] Clles, K. L., 1978, Proc. Intl. Congr. Plant Tissue Cell Cult., 4th Calgary, Alberta.pp. 67~74

[14] Gleba, Y. Y., Momot. Y. P., Cherep. N. N. and Skarzynskaya, M. V., 1882, *Theor. App. Genet.,* 62: 75~80

[15] Climelius, K., Wallin A. and Eriksson. T., 1974, *Physiol. Plunt.* 31: 225~230

[16] Climelius, K., Wallin A. and Eriksson. T., 1978, *Protoplasma,* 97: 291~300

[17] Hasezawa, S., Nagata, T. and Syono, K., 1981, *Mol. Gen. Genet.,* 182: 206~210

[18] Hortath, C., Droppa M., Mastardy. L. A., 1978, *Planta,* 141: 230~244

[19] Hughes, B. C., Hess, W. M. and Smith, M. A., 1977, *Protoplasma,* 93: 267~274

[20] Inoué. K., Nishimura, M. and Akazawa, T., 1978, *Plant Ceil Physiol.,* 19: 317~325

[21] Kao, K. N., 1980, Plant Cell Culture: Results and Perspectives. pp. 195~205. Elsovier/North Holland Biomedical Press

[22] Krens. F. A., Molendijk, L. and Schilperoort, R. A., 1982, *Nature.* 296: 72~74

[23] Ku. S. B ., Edwards. C. E. and Kanai R., 1978. *Plant Cell Physiol*., 17: 615~620

[24] Marchant. H. J. and, Hines. E. R. 1979, *Planta.* 146: 41~48

[25] Matile, P., 1978, *Ann. Rev. Plant Physiol.*, 29: 193~213
[26] Mattews. B., Dray S., Widholm, J. and Ostro M., 1979. *Planta*, 145: 37~44
[27] Meeks J. C., Malmberg R. L. and Wolk C. P., 1978: *Planta*. 139: 55~60
[28] Mori. K., Hasokawa D. and Yamashita. T., 1982, Proc. 5th Intl. Congr. Plant Tissue and Cell Culture, Plant Tissue Culture. 803~804
[29] Nishimura. M. and, Akazawa, T., 1975: *Plant*: Physiol., 55: 712~716
[30] Nishimura, M. and Graham. D. and Akazawa T. 1976. *Plant Physiol.*, 58: 309~314
[31] Nishimura. M. and, Beevers. H., 1978, *Plant Physiol.*, 62: 44~48
[32] Nishimura. M. and Beevers. H., 1979. *Nature* 277: 412~413
[33] Quail. P. H., 1978. *Ann. Rev. Plant Physiol.*, 30: 425~484
[34] Rathnam. C. K. M. and Edwards, G. E., 1976, *Plant Cell Physiol.*, 17: 177~186
[35] Robenek, H. and Peveling. E., 1977, *Planta*, 136: 135~145
[36] Robiason. G. 1977, Advances in Botanical Research, Acade and Press, New York, V. 5, pp. 89~151
[37] Roland. J. C., 1978, Electron Microscopy and Cytochemistry of Plant Cell. Elsevier. Amsterdam, pp. 1~32
[38] Schieder. O. and Vasil. L. K., 1980. *Intl. Rev.. Cytology. Suppl.*, 11B: 21~46
[39] Shepard. J. F. and R. E. Totten, 1977. *Plant Physiol.*, 60: 313~316
[40] Shepard. J. F., Bidney. D. and Shahin. E. A., 1980, *Science*. 208: 17~24 (中译文，科学，1982, 9, 75)
[41] Suzuke. M., Takebe I., Kajita S., Honda Y. and Matsui C., 1977, *ExP. Cell Res.*, 105: 127~135
[42] Takebe, I., 1975. *Ann. Rev. Phytopathol .*, 13: 105~125
[43] Takebe. I., 1977. Comprehensive Virology. V. II. pp. 237~283. Plenum Publ. Corp., New York
[44] Takebe. I., Otsuki. Y. and Aoki S., 1969. *Plant and Cell Physiol.*, 9: 115~124
[45] Takebe. I., Kikkawa, H. and Nagata T., 1982, Prod. 5th Intl. Congr. Plant Tissue and Cell Culture. Plant Tissue Culture. pp. 655~658
[46] Takeuchi. M., Matsushima, H. and Sugawara Y., 1982. Proc. 5th Intl, Congr. Plant Tissue and Cell Culture, Plant Tissue Culture. 797~798
[47] Takeuchi. Y. and A. Komanine. 1976. *Planta*, 140: 227~232
[48] Valk. P. V. D., Rennie P.J., Connolly, J. A. and .Fowke L. C., 1980. *Protoplasma*, 105: 27~43
[49] Wagner, G. J. and Siegelman. H. W., 1975. *Science*, 190: 1298~1299
[50] Wallin, A., Glimelius, K. and Eriksson T, 1978, *Z. Planzenphysiol.*, 87: 333~340
[51] Wenzel, G., Schieder,O., Przewozny T., Sopory S. K., Melchers G., 1979, *Theor. Appl. Genet.*, 55: 49~55
[52] Williamson, F. A., Fowke, L. C., Weber G., Constabel F. and Gamborg O. L., 1977, *Protoplasma*, 91: 213~219
[53] Wullems, G. J., Molendijk, L. and Schilperoort R. A., 1980, *Theor. Appl. Genet.*, 56: 203~208
[54] Zeiger, E. and P. K. Hepler, 1976: *Plant Physiol.*, 58: 492~498

本文原载：Acta Hort. 1991. 297: 51-55

Advances in Actinidia Research in China

Qian Ying-qian[1] Yu Dong-ping[2]

(1 Dept. of Biosciences and Biotechnology, Academia Sinica, Beijing;
2 Development and Service Centre for High Quality Agri-Products Ministry of Agriculture, Beijing)

Abstract China has the most abundant wild *Actinidia* resources in the world. Exploration of these resources, selection and breeding, tissue and cell culture, and postharvest physiology and storage studies carried out during the last 10 years, are summarised in this paper. Commercial development and utilization are also discussed.

Additional Index Words selection, breeding, tissue culture, postharvest physiology, storage

1 Introduction

China has the most abundant and diverse *Actinidia* resources and wild germplasm in the world. It was the first country to reognise and describe *Actinidia.* The biological characteristics, growing environment and uses of *Actinidia* have been recorded in many ancient Chinese books such as “Er Ya” and “Compendium of Material Medicine” (Bencao gangmu). In the latter it was described as follows; “It looks like a pear, its colour is as good as a peach and the rhesus monkey likes to eat it”. A fossil leaf of *Actinidia* was discovered in Gucha County, Guixi Province by scientists of Nanjing Institute of Geology and Paleobiology, Chinese Academy of Sciences, in 1977. It dates from the Miocene epoch and is 26~20 million years old. This discovery provides important data for studying the evolution of *Actinidia.*

Actinidia was introduced into New Zealand, Europe and other countries at the beginning of this century. The famous cultivar ‘Hayward’ was selected in New Zealand and kiwifruit industries are now being developed with tremendous speed all over the world. However, as noted by Ferguson *et al.* (1990), ‘Hayward’ was selected from a very small population of the species *Actinidia deliciosa.* This means that only a very small part of the gene pool has been exploited. More research is needed to further develop kiwifruit industries.

2 Exploration of Actinidia resources

The taxonomy and geographical distribution of *Actinidia* species were described by Liang Chou-Fen (1984). Although there is a long history of exploration of *Actinidia* resources, large-scale exploration was from 1978 to 1989. Seventeen-hundred

Acta Horticulturae 297, 1991
Kiwifruit II

specimens and 299 different fruits were collected from 15 provinces including Yunnan, Guangxi, Hunan and Sichuan. Fifty-seven species (including 18 endangered species and 33 endemic species), 39 varieties and 5 forms were identified by taxonomists and agronomists. Some other specimens are still being identified. Most of the new taxa were discovered in Yunnan Province. Table 1 shows that Yunnan and Guangxi had the most taxa. No taxa have yet been discovered in Qinghai, Ningxia, Xinjiang and Neimong provinces. The ecological environment and horizontal and vertical distribution of *Actinidia* taxa were also studied. This provided the scientific basis for further development and conservation of resources of *Actinidia.* The "Monograph of *Actinidia*" is now in preparation.

Table 1 Taxonomic unit of *Actinidia* in provinces of China

Provinces	Species	Varieties	Form
Yunnan	11	22	4
Guangxi	7	22	4
Hunan	9	18	1
Sichuan	9	12	3
Guizhou	6	14	1
Jiangxi	4	15	2
Zhejiang	2	17	1
Guangdon	5	15	—
Hubei	4	15	—
Fujian	5	13	—
Shanxi	3	9	1
Anhui	2	9	—

Continued

Provinces	Species	Varieties	Form
Henan	2	8	—
Gansu	1	6	—
Taiwan	4	5	—
Jiangsu	—	4	—
Liaonig	2	2	—
Xiangton	1	2	—
Xiangsi	—	2	—
Hebei	1	1	—
Jilin	2	—	—
Heilongjian	1	1	—
Tianjin	1	—	—
Beijing	2	—	—

3　Selection and Breeding

3.1　Selection

Cultivation of *Actinidia* on a small scale began 300 years ago in Huang Yan County, Zhejiang Provinee and 29 years ago a small garden was established in Bejjing Botanical Garden, Institute of Botany, Academia Sinica. However, the progress of kiwifruit research was slow.

Fourteen-hundred promising strains were selected from wild *A. chinensis, A. deliciosa* and *A. arguta,* and 6 germplasm nurseries were established in China. Eighteen selections are undergoing further evaluation. Selections of *A. chinensis* include 'Hua-guang' No. 2 and No. 4 from Henan Province, '79~1' and '79~2' from Jiangxi Province, 'Lu-bian-qing' from Beijing Botanical Garden, 'LQ-8' and 'LQ-25' from Zhejiang Province and 'Ya-xia No.20' from Fujian Province. Selections of *A. deliciosa* include 'Qing-mei' and "Chang-an" from Shanxi Province, 'Qing-cheng No.10' and 'Chuan-mi No.4' from Sichuan Province. The fruits of these selections are large, uniform and beautiful. The vitamin C contents range from 250~300mg/100g fresh weight among the *A. chinensis* selections and from 200~370mg/100g fresh weight among the *A. deliciosa* selections. The three species with the highest vitamin C contents were *A. eriantha* (up to

1014mg/100g fresh weight), *A. latifolia* (up to 880mg/100g fresh weight) and *A. farinosa,* a recently discovered species from Yunnan Province (1350~1637mg/100g fresh weight). Some selections are cold tolerant, drought tolerant or show wide climatic adaptability. *A.arguta* ang *A.kolomikta* have been planted in Heilongjian Province. These species can tolerate temperatures below −40℃ and grow and develop fairly well. Fruit of some selections of *A. chinensis* and *A.deliciosa* have a rich, fine flavour. The flesh can be red, yellow or jade green. About 100 plants of a red-fleshed selection have been planted and the yield of these was more than 1000kg. Some selections of *A. chinensis* have a maximum soluble solids concentration of 20%. One dwarf strain has been selected. It is 1m tall and has a 0.8 × 1m canopy. It has short internodes and is stress tolerant. The fruits are nearly round in shape and moderate in sugar and acid content. Their size is in keeping with commercial requirements.

3.2 Interspecific hybridisation and embryo rescue

This work was mainly undertaken by scientists of the Institute of Botany in Beijing and the Wuhan Institute of Botany, Academia Sinica. Between 1982 and 1989, 80~100 interspecific crosses were made. Most were compatible and many hybrid progenies have been obtained. Some combinations, however, did not succeed or produced only a few normal embryos because of high rates of embryo abortion. Embryo culture of young embryos has been carried out and abortive embryos of the following combinations have been rescued;

1. *A. deliciosa* var. *deliciosa* × *A. arguta*
2. *A. deliciosa* var. *deliciosa* × *A. eriantha*
3. *A. deliciosa* var. *deliciosa* × *A. chinensia* var. *chinensis*
4. *A. chinensis* × *A.kolomikta*
5. *A. chinensis* var. *chinensis* × *A. melanandra*
6. *A. arguta* × *A. melanandra*
7. *A. arguta* var. *arguta* × *A. chinensis* var. *chinensis*
8. *A. arguta* × *A.deliciosa*
9. *A. melanandra* × *A. chinensis*

The hybridisation of three combinations (5, 6 and 8) was achieved by cooperation between Chinese and New Zealand scientists. Hybrids from crossed 1 and 4 have now reached the fruiting stage. The shape of fruits and the leaves of hybrids of *A. deliciosa* × *A.arguta* resemble those of the *A. deliciosa* parent. The hybrid vines and fruits are otherwise similar to those of the *A. arguta* parent. The fruits are green, hairless, 30~50g in weight, early maturing with jade green flesh and a vitamin C conten of 120~150mg/100g fresh weight. *A. deliciosa* × *A. eriantha* hybrids are near tetraploid in chromosome number and are expected to flower next season. *A. chinensis* has been pollinated with *A. deliciosa* pollen supplied by DSIR, New Zealand, in an attempt to breed good flavoured fruit with good storage life. More than 10crosses between *A. chinensis* and *A. eriantha* have been performed by scientists of the Wuhan Institute of Botany from 1985 to 1989. The progenies were diploid and showed many intermediate characteristics compared with the parental species. Some pistillate and staminate plants were highly sterile. They produced double flowers in a range of colours. Some flowered 4~5 times each year compared with 2~3 times for the paternal parent and only once for the maternal parent. The average vitamin C content was higher in the hybrids than in the parental species (1181mg/100g fresh weight compared with 150~250mg/100g fresh weight for the maternal parent species and 800~1300mg/100g fresh weight for the paternal parent species. Pollen germination and fertilisation studies have been carried out.

4 Tissue and cell culture of *A ctinidia*

The culture of stem segments of *A. deliciosa, A. chinensis* and *A. eriantha* has been reported by Gui (1979). Regenerated plants grew vigorously. Endosperm culture of *A. chinensis* and *A. deliciosa* was carried out by Gui *et al.* (1982) and regenerated plants were obtained. Endosperms from three interspecific hybrids were also cultured by Mu et al. (1990). Many regenerated plantlets, pistillate and staminate, have been transferred into gardens in China. Obvious variation has been observed in staminate flower morphology, fruit size, vitamin C content and soluble solids concentration. Protoplast culture of *A.chinensis* was studied by Tsai (1988) and regenerated plants grew vigorously in Wuhan and Beijing and should bear fruit next season. Cryopreservation of stem fragments was carried out at the Institute of Botany, Beijing and regenerated plants were obtained.

5 Post-harvest physiology and storage

The optimum maturity for harvesting, ethylene production, the role of polygalacturonase, activity of superoxide dismutase and effects of low oxygen on storage have been studied at Academia Sinica institutes in recent years. A new compound extracted from a wild plant species was found by scientists of the Wuhan Institute of Botany to delay the decomposition of kiwifruit.

6 Development and utilization

Although the qualities of kiwifruit were largely unrecognised in China for a long time, in the last 10 years kiwifruit has been named "King of Fruits" and "Crown of Vitamin C". Commercial production bases have now been established. In 1990, the yield was 5,000 tonnes from 4,000 ha. Various processed products including juice, gum, candy, wine and canned kiwifruit were produced. Studies of medicinal uses of kiwifruit have also been made in China. The use of kiwifruit in cancer prevention (Song and Xu 1988) an d treatment of cardiovascular disease has been reported.

Research and development of kiwifruit is still in the initial stages in China. Conservation of resources, cultivar breeding, processing, storage and management, and so on, have to be improved.

7 Acknowledgements

The authors would like to express their gratitude to Professors Zhang Jie, Mu Xi-jin, An He-xiang, Tsai Da-rong, Li Yu, Liu Shi-ye and Xiong Zhi-ting for their kind permission to incorporate their data in this paper and for providing original data. We would also like to thank Fu Yan-feng and Meng Xiao-xiong who kindly typed and read the manuscript.

References

Ferguson, A. R., Seal, A. G., and Davison, R. M., 1990. Cultivar improvement, genetics and breeding of kiwifruit. Acta Hort. 282: 335~247

Gui, Y-L., 1979. Induction callus and regeneration of plantlets in stem segment culture of Chinese gooseberry. Acta Bot. Sin. 21: 339~344

Gui, Y-L., Mu S-K., and Xu T-Y., 1982, Studies on morphological differentiation of endosperm plantlets of Chinese gooseberry *in vitro*. Acta Bot. Sin. 24: 216~221

Liang C-F., 1984. *Actinidia*. In: Feng K-M. (ed.), Flora Reipublicae Popularis Sinicae, Vol. 49/2 Science Press (Beijing), pp. 196~268: 309~324

Mu S-K., Fraser L. G., and Harvey C. F., 1990. Initiation of callus and differentiation of plantlets from endosperm of *Actinidia* interspecific hybrids. Scientia. Hort. 44: 97~106

Song P-J., ans Xu Y-I., 1988. The effects of *Actinidia chinensis* Planch in the prevention of cancer. V. Inhibitory effects on the formation of N-nitrosoproline in vitro in rats and men. Acta Nutri. Sin. 10: 50~55

Tsai C-K. (Cai Q-G.), 1988. Plant regeneration from leaf callus protoplasts of *Actinidia chinensis* Planch. var. *chinensis*. Plant Sci. 54: 231~235

本文原载：生物工程进展. 1990. 10(1): 1-17(34)

植物细胞工程进展

钱迎倩　邹吉涛　张士波　王铁邦

(中国科学院植物研究所)

生物工程在农业、轻工、医药卫生等等国民经济各主要领域上显示出其越来越重要的作用。世界上不管是发达国家或发展中国家都投入了大量的人力、物力来进行广泛的研究。不少研究成果已在应用上发挥了强大的威力。但是，应该说生物工程目前尚处于发展的初级阶段，随着人们对生命现象认识的不断深化，以及生命科学基础研究的发展，生物工程将会给人类带来更大的福音。

细胞工程是生物工程的一个组成部分。包括分支领域的面也很广，本文仅从植物原生质体培养，植物体细胞杂交，染色体工程以及植物遗传转化研究的进展作一介绍：

高等植物原生质体的研究进展

近年来，高等植物原生质体的研究，取得了很大突破。一直难于培养的禾本科主要农作物比如水稻、玉米、小麦、甘蔗；以及豆科的大豆等，都相继成功地从原生质体再生植株。并且在这些再生系统的基础上，水稻、玉米两种主要农作物外源基因的转化植株，以及水稻融合杂种都已获得成功。

原生质体培养技术的进展,令人最感兴趣的是单个原生质体的培养和遗传操作技术。

原生质体也是细胞生物学、生理学、病理学等基础研究的理想材料。至今利用原生质体进行研究较多的是细胞壁的形成以及细胞膜的结构、功能、微管、微丝及其他细胞骨架系统的研究。

总之，高等植物原生质体各方面的研究，已取得了令人鼓舞的成绩。下面将分别阐述各方面近年内所取得的结果。

一、高等植物原生体质培养的新进展

(一) 原生质体的培养技术

高等植物原生质体培养最常规的是液体浅层培养和琼脂糖固体平板培养。近年来，培养技术有了很大改进，特别是单个原生质体的培养技术。其次是饲喂层培养和琼脂糖念珠状小块培养法。

(a) 单个原生质体的培养

Koop 等(1983)在烟草和蔓陀罗的细胞培养中发展起来一种微培养技术[1]，经过改进以后，成功地用来进行单个植物细胞的选择，以及再利用一系列的自动装置将它们转入微滴进行培养[2]。这整个微培养技术首次成功地将芸苔的单个原生质体进行培养并再生了植株[3]。同时，利用这套技术可以在单细胞水平上研究不同类型原生质体的生理特性，相互之间的作用以及单个原生质体的遗传操作等，特别是有利于两个种单个原生质体的融合，原生质体合并亚原生质体，甚至于原生质体与质粒 DNA 的融合[4]。至于这套技术的详细操作过程和设备可参看 Schweiger 等(1987)的一篇综述[2]。

(b) 饲喂层培养法和琼脂糖念珠状小块培养法

饲喂层培养法，即将原生质体培养在饲喂层细胞的上面。利用它们促进原生质体的分裂和生长。这种培养方法在玉米的原生质体培养[5, 6]以及其他植物的培养中能大幅度地提高分裂频率。

琼脂糖念珠状小块培养法，即将包埋原生质体的琼脂糖作成念珠状小块放在液体浅层中培养。这种培养方法在小麦[7]和水稻[8]，以及鸭茅[9]的原生质体培养中都能提高分裂频率。

(二) 重要高等植物原生质体的植株再生

重要高等植物，如禾本科的主要农作物，以及豆科的栽培大豆等等的原生质体培养，一直是十分困难的。但近五年内，禾谷类的水稻、小麦、玉米、甘蔗和最近成功的小米，高粱等以及豆科的大豆、赤豆都已相继突破。

木本植物，主要是指果树和乔木树种，近年来成功的报道也越来越多。

下面分别对上述的重要高等植物的原生质体培养及药用植物的培养结果作一介绍。

(1) 禾本科作物

禾本科作物包括了最重要的几种粮食作物：如小麦、水稻、玉米，以及重要的经济作物甘蔗。八十年代以前，它们的原生质体培养一直很困难，因为借用模式种以及双子叶植物的培养方法，例如利用器官或组织直接游离原生质体进行培养都未能成功地再生植株，仅得愈伤组织。但 1980 年，Vasil 等，利用珍珠谷的胚性悬浮细胞游离得到原生质体，并成功地通过胚胎发生、再生得到小植株[10]。这是首次禾本科植物的成功报道，特别是提出了一条不同于双子叶植物的崭新途径，标志着禾谷类植物原生质体的重大进展。利用这一途径，在其他禾本科的草本，比如羊草和紫狼尾草都相继获得成功[11, 12]。

近年来，利用胚性的愈伤组织或胚性的细胞悬浮系来游离原生质体这一方法，分别在水稻[13,14,15,16,17,18,19]玉米[5,20,21,22,23]小麦[24,25]甘蔗[26]上成功地获得植株再生。小偃麦[27]高粱[28]和小米[29]最近也已得到成功。并且水稻[18]玉米[5,21,22,23]甘蔗[26]均获得可育成熟植株。大麦[30]和黑麦草[31]仅得到白化苗。

从禾本科植物已成功的报道中可以看出，没有一个普遍适用的培养方法或培养基，因此，今后对不同的种，甚至同种不同基因型还是应该摸索不同的培养基和培养条件。例如水稻的籼稻和粳稻的培养条件就有差别。

禾本科植物原生质体培养成功的关键大体上在于以下三个方面：基因型，游离原生质体的材料，培养基及培养方法。

(a) 基因型：基因型的重要与否主要决定于诱导胚性愈伤组织的成功与否。有人认为基因型是十分关键的；但也有人认为基因型与再生能力的关系是很复杂的、间接的。分化能力主要受到生理和环境因素的影响。因它们影响了植物生长调节剂的合成、运输以及可利用性[32]，原生质体的胚胎发生可以是间接地即通过愈伤组织阶段，也可以是直接来自原生质体。人工合成的2，4-D，可在许多禾本科植物上广泛用来作生长素，诱导和长期保持胚性能力。成熟了的或已经有所分化的细胞能够抑制胚性的表达，供体植株以及组织的生理状况，原生质体游离的步骤、培养条件都可能影响形态发生的途径。从这些方面推测，外植体的生理及发育状况对胚胎发生的控制可能比基因型更为重要。但真正对原生质体再生植株的过程还了解的太少。只是在细胞培养的胚胎发生中发现了一些生化标记[33]。这为原生质体再生植株的机理研究提供了进一步研究的线索。

从重要农作物的成功报道中，基因型还是有限的，如玉米仅几个细胞系：(A188，B73—1，杂种 4 号，sh2sh2 等)获得成功；相对来说水稻基因型比较广泛，至今不仅粳稻、籼稻也有许多成功的[19,34,35]。这种局限性的根本，在于胚性愈伤组织诱导的局限。随着诱导和保持胚性愈伤组织的进一步完善，基因型将会不断地扩大。

(b) 游离原生质体的材料一般均为胚性愈伤组织或悬浮细胞系，从已成功的报道中未见到利用非胚性的能再生植株。因此现在普遍承认原生质体具有用来游离的材料同样的分化能力。一般利用胚性的悬浮细胞系比较容易成功，比如玉米[5,21,22]，小麦[24,25]均利用胚性悬浮细胞系；但也有直接利用固体培养的胚性愈伤组织，如水稻[18]成功地获得植株再生。

(c) 培养方法和培养条件：这两方面在禾本科与双子叶植物之间没有明显的差别。培养方法一般为液体浅层培养[20]，饲喂层培养[5,21,22]，琼脂糖固体培养或琼脂糖念珠状小块培养[36]。培养基也是常用的 N_6[37]，MS[38]，Kmsp[39]，但也有不少根据不同的材料配制特殊的培养基，如蔡起贵等(1987)利用水稻原生质体培养基(Ⅰ)来培养玉米[20]；Harris等(1988)的小麦工作是利用专门配制的培养基，其中附加多种氨基酸以及增加 V_{B1} 的量[24]；水稻上利用特殊的 RY-2 培养基(去掉无机氮源，增加氨基酸的量)成功地获得植物再生[16]。一般对原生质体不作任何特殊的预处理。但 Abdullch 等(1986)报道若对水稻原生质体进行 45℃预热处理能提高原生质体的分裂频率[40]。

总而言之，禾本科植物成功地从原生质体再生植株。首先必须具备能游离大量成活的原生质体的胚性愈伤组织或悬浮细胞系，这是成功的关键；其次是选择合适的培养基、培养方法、培养条件。一般来说常规的方法和培养基都是适用的。

(2) 豆科植物

豆科植物是仅次于禾谷类植物的一类重要经济作物，特别是食用豆类，包括大豆、花生以及其他豆类。豆科的其他草本植物：例如苜蓿、三叶草，也是重要的牧草。近年来，它们的原生质体培养有不少成功的报道，特别是栽培大豆的成功[41]。

(a) 食用豆类作物：虽然利用大豆成熟胚[42]以及各种外植体[43]都能再生植株，但利用它们游离的原生质体仅得到愈伤组织[44,45,46,47]直至卫志明等(1988)利用未成熟子叶游离得到原生质体，在 Km8p 基本培养基上培养，最后在四个栽培种上都成功地获得植株再生[41]。

野生大豆是一类重要的基因资源，因此它们的原生质体能再生植株对各种研究工作也是十分有用的。至今，已有两种野生大豆 *Glyline canescens*[48] *G. soja*[49]和 *G. clandestina*[42]成功地植株再生。

(b) 牧草类豆科植物原生质体的培养：虽然籽苗是一个很好的游离原生质体的材料，但野生苜蓿类主要集中在对子叶原生质体的培养。Gilmour 等(1987)利用三种培养方法进行比较，结果认为，利用苜蓿白化苗的原生质体与野生种原生质体混合培养，能使 5 个野种原生质体的植板率高达 60%以上。三种野苜蓿能经胚胎发生途径再生植株；但这三种以及 *Medicago varia* 和 *M. difalcaia* 最合适的再生途径是经愈伤组织的器官发生[50]。

条件培养基饲喂层培养和微孔膜培养室培养都有利于原生质体的培养[50]。例如野苜蓿和苜蓿利用条件培养基，在密度为 10^3~10^2/ml 的条件下原生质体都能生长；苜蓿、驴食草和 *Trifolium arvense* 利用微孔膜培养(即下面是一层琼脂糖层，上面是一层含有饲喂原生质体的液体培养基，中间是微孔膜培养室；所要培养的目的原生质体就在其中)，能使 50/ml 原生质体或更少均能诱导形成愈伤组织。培养室内的原生质体分裂频率与外面饲喂原生质体的分裂频率相近。所利用的微孔膜的最适孔径为 5~12μm。

三叶草植物相对比较困难些。至今已有三种三叶草植物 *Trifolium rubens*[51]，*T. hybridum*[52]，和 *T. repens*[53,54]，成功地从原生质体获得植株再生。对有的种，虽然利用选择的基因型能提高无根苗的再生频率，但还是不能克服诱导根的困难。在分析 *T. hybridum* 和 *T. repens* 的再生具根植株时初步发现一些细胞学和形态学上的异常现象。*T. repens* 再生植株的染色体倍性取决于游离原生质体的材料。若利用叶片的原生质体只能再生二倍体植株，若利用悬浮细胞则能产生四倍体。

(3) 木本植物的原生质体培养

木本植物的原生质体培养进展一直很慢。这是由于木本植物具有明显的幼年与成年生长之分，从而难于掌握制备有用的原生质体。但近几年来，随着草本植物原生质体培养的飞速发展，木本植物的进展也异常迅速。大概已有 10 余种木本植物能成功地从原生质体再生植株，特别是两个针叶树种火炬松[55]与白云杉[56]，已成功地再生胚状体。

木本植物用来游离原生质体的材料。一般用无菌苗的叶片，例如杨树[57]、洋梨；也有用愈伤组织，比如中华猕猴桃[58]、榆树。但游离最好的还是利用悬浮细胞系。特别对于难于得到原生质体的针叶树来说，例如火炬松与白云杉，成功地再生胚状体的关键在于利用了悬浮系。美国鹅掌楸[56]利用悬浮系成功地从原生质体再生植株。这一结果与禾本科植物的培养有相同之处。所以说木本植物成功地借用了禾本科植物的培养经验。

木本植物原生质体的培养一般都利用常规的方法，比如液体浅层法，琼脂糖固体培养法。但 Kirby(1979)在对花旗松原生质体培养时，提出了用铺垫聚酯纤维的培养方法[59]。此法有利于气体交换并使有害物迅速从生活细胞周围扩散，因此促进原生质体的生长。Russell(1988)在杨树的原生质体培养中，设计了一种能漂浮在液体培养基上的多聚酯筛孔片[57]。这种片子上有许多小孔，孔径为 150μm。游离后的原生质体转移到平皿内的筛板上，使原生质体漂游或吸附在筛网纤维上。这种方法可以使有活力的原生质体与细胞碎片及无生活力的原生质体分开，前者浮游在筛板上。后者则沉入底部，“净化”了原生质体的培养环境，有利于原生质体的生长，成功地从三个杨树无性系的原生质体再生植株。

木本植物原生质体培养的培养基一般利用 MS，Km 以及 B_5[60]；但也有利用特殊配制的例如中华猕猴桃的 TCCW[58]，美国鹅掌楸的特别培养基，针叶树的 LP[56]培养基。培养的原生质体密度一般 1×10^5/ml 左右均可。培养条件一般为暗培养温度 25°~28℃.

(4) 药用植物

药用植物也是一类重要的经济植物。关于药用植物原生质体培养的研究，虽不像禾本科植物那么多，但至今也有不少成功的报道。例如曼陀罗[61]、石龙芮[62]龙葵[63]、地黄[64]、希腊毛地黄[65]、川芎[66]、石防风[67]、三叶半夏[68]等都已成功地再生植株；愈伤组织再生的有枸杞[69]、龙胆[70]等。

游离原生质体的材料，一般都用叶片[62,63,64,65,68]，但也有用胚轴[66]或叶片诱导的愈伤组织[69]。所利用的酶与其他的双子叶植物类似，即常用的纤维素酶 (EA_3-867 或 OnozukaR-10)与离析酶(Macerozyme R-10)，有时附加一些崩溃酶[69]或蜗牛酶[67,68]，并且实践结果表明蜗牛酶对伞形科植物原生质体游离是十分重要的。

原生质体的培养方法一般是常规的液体浅层培养法，但某些药用植物在方法上的改良能大大提高原生质体的植板率。例如用组份浓度差液体——固体双层培养法能大大促进三叶半夏原生质体的分裂与生长[68]。所利用的培养基一般是常用的 MS 或修改的 MS 作为基本培养基，也有用 NT[59]或 Km8p[64]或特异的 D_2[65]。附加的激素一般也为常用的 2,4-D，6-B_A，玉米素等，同时附加一些椰乳、水解酪蛋白等有机复合物均有一定的促进作用；肌醇在龙葵中有促进作用，但在地黄中无作用，因此不同的植物需不同的营养条件，因为内部的代谢是不同的。同样，氨基酸复合物(谷酰胺、精氨酸、甘氨酸、天冬氨酸)能促进地黄原生质体的持续分裂与细胞团的形成。再生愈伤组织的分化，也包括器官发生与胚胎发生两条途径[68]。

药用植物的主要用途是它内含的药用化合物。因此，改良的主要目的是如何提高内含物的含量。它的合成有的在整株植物中，有的仅在叶片、果实等器官中，也有的在愈伤组织阶段同样能合成。因此对药用植物的改良，例如通过无性系变异的方法来筛选可在愈伤组织阶段上来进行[71]。但利用原生质体技术作药用植物的改良，必须注意之点是一定要在保持药用植物原有功效的基础上提高含量，而且没有附加对人体的有害化学试剂。因此改良的药用植物在推广之前，必须经医疗部门的详细检验方为有效。

二、植物原生质体融合研究进展

植物原生质体的融合，即将不同来源的原生质体融为一体以创造新的体细胞杂种。这不仅克服了常规杂交育种的远缘不亲和性，还为体细胞遗传学的研究提供了新机会，也为植物的遗传操作提供了新的方法。

在获得，以至评价体细胞杂种之前，首先必须克服许多技术上的问题。

(1) 原生质体的融合与异核体的形成

目前，原生质体的融合方法常用的是两种：化学方法与电融合方法。化学方法用得最多的是聚乙二醇(PEG)加高 Ca^{++}高 pH 的处理[72]。人们还使用了诸如葡聚糖硫酸酯，聚乙烯醇和盐类混合物等不同化合物。电融合方法包括两个步骤：第一步，将原生质体植板在低导电率的培养基中的两个电极之间，在电极间加入高频交流电场(0.5~1.5MHz)。通过一种称之为双向电泳的过程，原生质体的表面电荷发生极化，此时的原生质体具有偶极子的性质，并沿电场线方向朝较高电场强度的区域迁移。在原生质体迁移时会与其他原生质体接触，形成与电场线平行的原生质体链。电融合的第二步是施用一次或多次足够强的短时(10~100μs)直流电脉冲(1~3kv/cm)，以引起可逆性膜破裂(形成“小孔”)。在原生质体开始融合时，应短时重复施加交流电场以保持原生质体间的紧密结合状态，然后使电场强度降至零。这种方法初始报道时仅局限于少量原生质体的融合[73,74]。但近来发展很快，现在在一次实验内大量原生质体能同时融合[75,76]。

原生质体融合与原生质体培养一样，没有一个在任何条件下，都行之有效的操作方法。大多数情况下，只能适当控制细胞的死亡数与融合体形成数之间的比例。一般来说，悬浮细胞的原生质体，对抵抗化学方法的损害能力要比叶片的原生质体强得多。至于电融合与化学融合相比，是否优越，需要进一步的研究和分析；但目前的一些结果表明，似乎电融合存在一定的优越性[76]。

(2) 异核体的筛选

融合体的筛选方法，主要归两类：1)基因组互补选择法，2)融合体的机械分离法。前者就是利用融合杂体的缺陷互补，使得融合体在特殊附加物条件下能正常生长，而双亲的原生质体不能生长。例如：Hamill 等(1983，1984)利用烟草的 SRI 突变体的抗链霉素质粒与烟草的 nia-30 突变体的硝酸还原酶核缺失体融合，成功地获得双突变体的杂种[77,78]。后者在正常情况下，是用微吸管来分离异核体[79,80]，然后培养在饲喂细胞中，从中可以将异核体选择出来。例如，矮牵牛的白化饲喂细胞用来培养黄化烟草与烟草的融合杂种[78]。

异核体也可用双亲之间肉眼可见的差别来检测，例如：一方是含有叶绿体的叶肉原生质体，另一方是悬浮细胞的原生质体。若双亲之间没有明显可见的差别，那可以人为地用荧光染料标上颜色，在紫外光条件下，鉴测融合杂种。

人工分离异核体是一项既要有技术又比较花时间的方法。最近利用荧光活化细胞分离法(FACS)能大大改进这一方法[81]。

(3) 融合的结果

原生质体融合的目的是企图克服常规远缘杂交的不亲和性。确实，早期的一些实验结果也表明了远缘种之间的原生质体是能够融合的[82]。利用这种技术企图获得亲缘关系上相距十分远的融合杂种是非常困难的[83]，主要是由于遗传上的不稳定性。此外实验表明线粒体与叶绿体基因组，在融合杂种中，与核基因组是相互独立的，这一现象十分有价值。一般来说，叶绿体基因组在融合杂种中重组现象偶尔出现在融合体中[84]。

线粒体基因组，与叶绿体基因组相反，在大量的融合体中出现重组现象[85,86]。

(4) 体细胞杂种在农业上的应用

(a) 核杂种

亲缘关系太远的融合杂种，由于遗传上的不稳定性，目前来看在育种上的意义还不是很大。大多数育种目的，并不是需要不同属之间的杂交，只要将近缘种的有用特性引入栽培品种就足够了。为了达到这个目的，融合杂种必须具有育性。这方面近来已引起了人们的注意。

Pental 和 Cocking(1985)曾指出，三倍体的合成，对野生种的有用基因导入栽培品种是有价值的[87]。这种方法的一个很好的实例，就是 *Nicotiana glutinosa* 的单倍配子体原生质体与烟草的双倍叶片原生质体融合，获得高度可育的三倍体杂种[88]。

融合杂种内，不同种间染色体的同源性，可能引起减数分裂过程中的染色体不分开，进而导致后代育性的降低和非整倍体的产生。除此之外，融合体的染色体倍性也影响融合杂种的育性。例如，Ehlenfeldt 和 Helgeson(1987)发现六倍体比四倍体植物具有更强的育性[89]。

(b) 细胞器的转移

利用原生质体融合，重新组合细胞器或其中的部分基因在农业上是十分有价值的。例如：利用 γ 射线照射的芸苔的抗 triazine(由叶绿体基因控制)原生质体与线粒体标记的雄性不育变异体融合，获得既具有 triazinein 的抗性，又具有雄性不育特性的融合杂种[90]，这是常规育种所不能达到的。其他类似的例子还很多[91,92]。

综上所述，植物原生质体融合作为整个育种程序的一部分是十分有用的。当然它作为基因转移技术，今后将会面对两个方面的挑战：①新的有性杂交方法，例如胚与子房的培养[93,94]；②根癌农杆菌的基因转移[95,96]。尽管如此体细胞融合在植物生物技术中仍然是很重要的，也是十分有用的。

三、染色体工程研究进展

现代生物技术已完全克服了种间生殖隔离的限制，使种间、属间甚至亲缘关系较远的分类群之间的基因转移成为可能。目前这种基因转移主要包括染色体水平的基因重组和分子水平的 DNA 重组，有时二者之间没有明显区别。前者主要在亲缘关系较近的分类群之间转移基因组；染色体或染色体片段，其结果产生双二倍体、部分双二倍体、异附加系、异代换系和易位系。其中双二倍体、部分双二倍体和易位系比较稳定、染色体工程法创制的生产品种主要是易位系，其次是双二倍体，其他类型主要作为育种的中间素材为人们所利用。在小麦育种中，非整倍体系统是选育异代换系和易位系的理想受体系统[97]；异附加系则是外源基因转至受体的有效桥梁种[98]，染色体片段的转移主要通过诱导部分同源染色体配对而实现[99]。

在高等植物进化及品种栽培过程中多倍体起了重要的作用。目前已有黑麦属(*Secale*)、冰草属(*Agropyron*)、偃麦草属(*Elytrigia*)、山羊草属(*Aegilops*)、大麦属(*Hordeum*)，簇毛麦属(*Haynaldia*)、披碱草属(*Elymus*)、和滨麦属(*Leymus*)等八个属和小麦属(*Triticum*)的属间杂交成功的合成了双二倍体[100]。无疑这将为小麦染色体工程育种利用这些近缘属的基因奠定了基础，这些双二倍体的可利用的基因资源主要有抗盐性[101]，抗白粉病[102,103]，抗锈病[104]，抗小麦黄花叶病[103]，蛋白含量高[105]等。远缘杂交结合幼胚培养是获得杂种植株的关键。

小麦和玉米[106]，小麦和高粱[107]这样的超远缘杂交也能受精形成合子，但合子在进行有丝分裂时玉米、高粱染色体丢失。这说明禾本科植物的受精机制差别不是很大。充分利用有性过程转移某些基因还大有潜力。染色体排斥现象在小黑麦早期育种中也普遍存在，但最终还是进入了粮食作物的行列。

二倍体种出现非整倍体往往是致死的，而多倍体种天然就存在非整倍体，应用最普遍的是小麦的非整倍体系统，如单体、缺体和端体等。这种非整倍体系统是染色体工程法改良小麦的理想受体系统。除早已广泛应用的“京华”1 号小麦单体系统外，近年来我国又选育成了普通小麦品种“Abbondanza”[108]、“杨麦 1 号”[109]、“京红 1 号”、“中7902”、和“丰抗 13 号”[110]等单体系统。这些单体系统在植物育种中起了重要作用。但由于配子形成过程中单价体迁移、自交后代中单体频率低，而且其后代中，二体、缺体和单体共存。每一代都要做大量的细胞学工作以检出单体，这给单体育种带来了极大的不便。李振声等对兰粒小麦的选育克服了一般单体的不足[111]，该单体为普通小麦 × 长穗偃麦草(*Elytrigia elongatum*，$2n = 70$)后代中选出的单体代换系，细胞学分析表明来自长穗偃麦草的 4Ael 染色体代换了普通小麦 4D 染色体，在 4Ael 染色体上有使种子胚乳的糊粉层呈兰色的兰色基因，糊粉层的颜色受胚乳的基因组控制，因此，兰单体的自交后代种子有四种颜色，即深兰、中兰、浅兰和白色。深兰为两体代换系，中兰和浅兰为单体，白色种子是缺体，在二体的胚乳中有三份兰色基因，中兰的胚乳中有二份兰色基因，来自于雌配子，而浅兰的胚乳中只有一份兰色基因。由雄配子传递而来，缺体的胚乳不含兰粒基因而为白色。这种缺体自交可育，是用缺体回交法创制异代换系的好材料，到目前为止，已将 4Ael 染色体上的兰色基因转移至小麦其他染色体上培育成 4D、5A、3A、3D、2D、4A 和 6A 七种兰单体(全套为 21 个)。如果能够育成全套兰单体小麦，将对小麦染色体工程育种起很大的促进作用。

缺体因生长势弱、结实率差、并且有转变成三体的倾向，因此染色体工程育种中缺体的作用一直不太明显。最近育成了减数分裂稳定结实、正常的小麦缺体 4D[111]，在此基础上又选育成了小麦“Abbondanza”，自交可育的缺体 12 个，分别是 1B、2A、2D、3B、3D、4D、5A、6A、6B、6D、7A 和 7B，向缺体转移所缺染色体的部分同源染色体很容易形成异代换系(112)。

除小麦外，黑麦(*Secale cereal*)(113),甜菜等(114)的非整倍体也有报道。

染色体工程在植物改良中的应用

1. 小黑麦

目前生产应用的小黑麦大多数是次级 6*x* 小黑麦，其来自黑麦的 R 组染色体已被修饰，一般都丧失了黑麦染色体的端粒。往往是小麦的 A、B 组染色体齐全，并由小麦的 D 组染色体和黑麦的 R 组染色体重组构成其第三个染色体组。最近有人发现在 8*x* 小黑麦和 6*x* 小黑麦杂交后代中选择表型类似于 8*x* 小黑麦的类型,这些类型大多数为 $2n = 42$。许多是 D 组染色体和 A、B 组染色体的代换类型，其中 6A/6D 的代换频率极高(115)。

利用 4*x* 小黑麦改良 6*x* 小黑麦的工作这几年非常引人注目，其大致程序为，创制染色体重组类型的 4*x* 小黑麦，再由这种 4*x* 小黑麦和小麦的二倍体种杂交合成全新的 6*x* 小黑麦，4*x* 小黑麦减数分裂稳定、育性正常，它具有完整的黑麦 R 组染色体，另一组染色体可以是来自普通小麦的 A、B 或 D 组染色体。也可以是来自偃麦草属的 E 组或山羊草属的其他组染色体，另一个方面，4*x* 小黑麦的第二组染色体可以由分别来自以上各组的数目不等的染色体重组而成。但其染色体基数仍然是 $x = 7$。而且没有部分同源染色体的重叠。如由来自小麦 A 组的几条和 B 组的 $7-n$ 条染色体构成(AB)组染色体，也可以由分别来自 A 组的 *m* 条，B 组的 *n* 条和 D 组的 $7-m-n$ 条染色体组成新染色体组(ABD)往往将这样的 4*x* 小黑麦组型写成(AB)(AB)RR，(ABD)(ABD)RR 等，由此可见在 4*x* 水平，各组染色体可以自由重组，形成丰富多样的小黑麦，如利用以下的程序已选育成了全新的 6*x* 小黑麦(116,117,118)。

(AB)(AB)RRRR($2n = 42$) × AABBDD

(AB)(AB)RR($2n = 28$) × AABBDDRR =F_1(AB)ABDRR

↓自交或和 AABBRR 杂交

$$\left.\begin{array}{l}\mathrm{AA(BD)(BD)RR}\\ \mathrm{BB(AD)(AD)RR}\\ \mathrm{(AD)(AD)(BD)(BD)RR}\end{array}\right\} 2n = 42$$

理论上讲，小黑麦 ABRR 可产生 128 种类型的配子，除纯 A、B 组染色体外，其余 126 种均为 A 和 B 组染色体重组构成的重组型配子。从 A_6B_1 到 A_1B_6，事实上，在波兰的 4*x* 小黑麦(AB)(AB)RR 中，重组的染色体组以 BABAAAA(A_5B_2)、AABBAAB(A_4B_5)、BABAABA(A_4B_3)三种组合形成的染色体组频率最高。此外，用 1 粒小麦(*Triticum monococum* A^mA^m)(118)、节节麦(*Aegilop squarrosa* $D^{4a}D^{4a}$)(118)(119)等和黑麦杂交育成了新的 4*x* 小黑麦，这样几乎整个小麦亚族(Triticineae)所有种的基因都可为小黑麦和小麦所利用。

染色体鉴定本是一件很繁琐的工作,尽管黑麦R组染色体有特殊的N-带和C-带模式,小麦的A、B、D组染色体显N-带,但实际工作中分带的重复性很差,而且往往不稳定,因而用染色体分带法鉴定的结果不得不用小麦双端体系统作最后确证。最近有人用对小麦D组染色体专一性很强的P^{ASI}、DNA克隆作探针成功地检测了小黑麦中D组的染色体或染色体片段,并发现小麦D组的染色体可以以任意组合形式代换6*x*小黑麦中A组、B组及(AB)组的部分同源染色体(120),但这种方法还不能确认是具体哪条染色体。

在重组类型的小黑麦中,基因竞争特别突出,如在4*x*小黑麦(AB)(AB)RR中,当随体染色体1B、6B和1R同时存在时,只有1B染色体的核仁组织区有活性,在没有1B和6B时,1R染色体的核仁组织区才有活性,另外,在4*x*小黑麦$D^{sq}D^{sq}RR$中只有D^{sq}组的随体染色体表现核仁活性,而黑麦1R的核仁组织区受到抑制。在这种情况下,显然被抑制的基因是多余的(121)。

2. 小偃麦

小麦-偃麦草杂交已到了出品种的阶段,利用前几年合成的八倍体小偃麦和普通小麦杂交育成了整套小偃麦异附加系(122)。有些株系表现对锈病免疫,白粉病和根瘤病也很轻,蛋白质和赖氨酸含量较高,小偃麦异附加系主要通过8*x*小偃麦和普通小麦杂交F_1自交,后代选择二体附加系,或杂种F_1与普通小麦回交选择单体附加系,然后由单体附加系自交选择二体附加系($2n = 44$),异附加系是染色体工程育种的重要素材(123)。

"缺体回交法"选育异代换系是行之有效的。如普通小麦缺体4D($2n = 40$)和8*x*小偃麦杂交,F_1用缺4D普通小麦回交两次,得到$2n = 42$类型就是异代换系,结果表明偃麦草染色体4E代替了4D形成4E/4D代换系,如果用普通小麦缺4D和小偃麦4E异附加系杂交则人工选育这种异代换系就更容易了。如图所示:

普通小麦缺4D(20W″)×小偃麦4E附加条(21W″ + 4)

↓

20W″+ 4D′+ 4E′

↓ ⊗ 选择

20W″+ 4E″

代换系是比较稳定的,有时代换系直接成为优良品种,另一方面各代换系间相互杂交可形成偃麦草染色体的重组。并导致重组染色体出现,因一条染色体上的基因有利有弊,把各染色体上的有利基因结合在一条染色体上很有必要(124)。

3. 小簇麦

在普通小麦、硬粒小麦和簇毛麦杂交的基础上,用硬粒小麦—簇毛麦双二倍体(AABBVV),和硬粒小麦回交已选育出硬粒小麦—簇毛麦单体附加系6个,普通小麦和簇毛麦杂种F_1再与普通小麦回交的后代中利用标记性状、核型分析、染色体组型分析技术和N-带分析技术已选育成普通小麦—簇毛麦二体异附加系5个,分别是V_2、V_3、V_4、V_6、V_7,异代换系一个(V_2)同时还鉴定出易位系4个,异代换系V_2抗白粉病,并利用这些抗性基因已育成了一些小麦优良株系(125)。

此外，象小麦和大麦这样难以杂交的属间杂交育种亦取得了一定成绩，如在苏联球茎大麦(*Hordeum bulbosum*，$2n = 28$)和普通小麦杂交，F_1再和普通小麦5B单体回交，选育成6个小大麦(Wheat-*Hordeum*)二体异附加系。有些附加系抗小麦黄花叶病，表明大麦染色体上的基因能够在小麦遗传背景上表达[126]。

植物育种与改良的前景

染色体工程转移基因带有很大的盲目性，即便有目的、有针对性的转移外源基因或染色体片段也只限于部分同源染色体的部分同源片段，在一组染色体中只允许一种部分同源片段存在而排斥第二种；另外，由于基因间的紧密连锁，染色体工程法只能将连锁群一起转移而无法区分其利弊只将有利基因转移至受体种，所以细胞遗传学家单方面的能力很有限，他们有必要和分子生物学家合作进行基因的鉴定、定位、分离并转移至象小麦等受体种，这无疑将加速植物改良的进程。

四、植物遗传转化研究进展

植物遗传转化较之于植物生物技术的其他领域更具有工程化的意义。从某种意义来讲人们可以根据具体目标按照既定的意图进行品质改良。而在染色体工程及狭义的细胞工程水平上，由于基因的紧密联锁，难以在不改变其他性状的基础上达到改良品种的目的。

遗传转化的首要问题是分离到适当的目的基因。人们从不同的改良品种的目的出发。报道大量可用于植物遗传转化的外源基因。其中包括：用于改良蛋白质含量的贮藏蛋白基因[127][128]，用于抗病毒的多种植物病毒卫星RNA[129,130]及外壳蛋白*c*DNA[131,132]克隆，用于抗虫的苏云金杆菌毒蛋白基因[133,134]，抗除草剂基因[135,136]等。同时可用于转化研究中筛选及鉴定的报告基因也有大量报导。(表1)。

表1 Selectable and Scorable markers

Neomycine posphotransferase	Bevan et al 1983 Nature 304: 184
Hygromycin posphotransferase	Lloyd et al 1986 Science 234: 464
Bacterial dihydrofolate reductase	De Block et al 1984 EMBO J. 3: 1681
mammalian dihydrofolate reductase	Eichholt et al 1987 Som. Cell & Mol. Gent 13: 67
streptomycin phosphotransferase	Jones et al 1987 M. G. G. 210: 86
EPSP synthase	Shah et al 1986 Science 233: 478
acetolactate synthase	Haughn et al 1988 M. G. G. 211: 266
bromoxynil nitrilase	Stalker et al 1988 Science 242: 419
phosphinothricin acetyltransferase	De Blook et al 1988 EMBO J 3: 1681
2,4-D monooxygenase	wiilmizer 1988

续表

nopline synthase	Depicker et al 1982 J Mol. Appl. Genet. 1: 561
octopine synthase	De Greve et al 1983 J Mol. Appl. Genet. 1: 499
beta galactosidase	Hemer et al 1984 Bio/Techno. 2: 520
chloramphenical acetyltransferase	De Block et al 1984 EMBO J3: 1681
firefly laciferase	Ow et al 1986 Science 234: 856
bate glucuronidase	Jefferson et al 1988 EMBO J 6: 3901

此外，分离了一些在植物中调节基因来表达的启动子及其他有用的元件，其中包括高效表达的CaMV35S启动子。光调节的rbcS启动子，一些器官、胚胎、块茎等专一性的启动子。

就目前而言，转化植物细胞的方法主要分两大类。一种是广泛用于双子叶植物的根癌农杆菌(Agrobacterium)(137)介导的转化，另外一种是DNA直接引入法，包括PEG(138,139)电击穿(140)基因枪(141)等方法。前者适用于部分对农杆菌敏感的植物品种，而对大多数单子叶植物则无能为力。DNA直接导入法适宜于所有种类的植物，但要以原生质体或体外培养细胞为受体材料。一方面原生质体培养不是在所有的植物中都能再生植株，同时体外培养的植物细胞极易发生体细胞变异(142)，这对于遗传操作都是不利的因素。

1. 农杆菌介导的遗传转化

从八十年代初期，农杆菌转化植物细胞系统完善以后，植物遗传转化研究发生了突飞猛进的进展，这种格兰氏阴性菌含有一个大质粒—Ti 质粒(诱瘤质粒)，该质粒中有一个DNA区段，即T-DNA，可以整合到植物基因组上去。而且T-DNA上插入外源DNA片段并不影响整合，所以为转化植物细胞提供了一个方便的桥梁(141)。

野生型Ti质粒可大到200kb，限制性酶切图谱比较复杂，一种限制酶就往往有十多个酶切位点，在进行基因操作上很不方便，因此要加以改造，除了致瘤的一些范围成为缺失的所谓disarmed质粒，人们又发展了一种称之为中间载体(intermediated vector)的质粒。它既可在大肠杆菌中复制，又可以在农杆菌复制，将目的基因插入中间载体，再使这一载体质粒从大肠杆菌进入根瘤农杆菌后再用于转化。目前广泛应用的双元载体就是利用农杆菌介导而转化植物的良好载体(143)。

抗病毒植物基因工程是近几年来利用根瘤菌转化的最突出的结果。从植物抗病毒交叉保护得到的启发，Powell等(144)于1986年首先作了这方面研究。他们克隆了烟草花叶病毒(TMV)外壳蛋白的cDNA构建了CaMV35S启动子，用外壳层的cDNA，嵌合基因转化烟草叶片(disc transformation)(145)，以卡那霉素为选择条件，筛选出了转化植株。转基因植物自交后代能够显著的延长病毒侵染病灶的出现。

抗病毒遗传工程得到的转基因植物可被期望即将应用于实际生产中。在烟草[146]及番茄中业已证明：烟草花叶病，苜蓿花叶病毒以及番茄花叶病毒和黄瓜花叶病毒[147]外壳蛋白在转基因植物中表达，能够以交叉保护的方式抵抗病毒的侵染。

近年通过类似方法获得的抗土豆病毒(potato virus x)[148]的两种栽培土豆品种的转基因植物也已报道。其中颇为有趣的现象是 potato virus x 的外壳蛋白基因在转化的试管苗中表达非常低弱，而移栽至土壤三天后，就有较高水平的表达。在这类研究中还有一个优点是用了转化再生(transformation/regeration)系统，避免了因愈伤组织的继代培养而产生的体细胞无性系变异。

这方面工作的生产效益是显著的，以番茄为例，由于病毒的侵染，对照产量减少26%~35%而工程植株几乎不受任何影响[146]。

我国在抗病毒植物遗传工程研究中也已取得很大进展。中国科学院微生物所的研究者们用自己合成的黄瓜花叶病毒卫星 RNA 的 cDNA 通过农杆菌转化烟草叶片，得到了烟草抗病毒工程植株。另外还将烟草花叶病毒外壳蛋白的 cDNA 通过农杆菌整合到烟草染色体组内，获得了当代转基因抗病毒植株。云南昆明植物研究所也培育出能抗病毒的工程植株，得到了能延迟病症 4~25 天的结果。

抗除草剂植物遗传工程[136]的大量报道集中在抗草甘膦(glyphosate)植物品种的培育上。草甘膦在细胞内的作用对象是 EPSP 合成酶，草甘膦抑制了 EPSP 合成酶活性，使细胞内莽草酸代谢途径受阻，导致芳香族氨基酸缺少，莽草酸积累，引起植物死亡[149]。

草甘膦抗性可由两种途径进行遗传改良，一种是引入过量表达 *EPSP* 酶基因[150]，从而拮抗草甘膦的抑制作用。有报道从抗草甘膦的矮牵牛突变种中分离合成到 EPSP 合成酶 cDNA 联接于 CaMV35S 启动子，转移到对草甘膦敏感的矮牵牛植物中，由于 EPSP 合成酶的过量表达，转基因植株对草甘膦具有明显的抗性。另一种途径是用对草甘膦不敏感酶基因(芳香族氨基酸合成酶基因，*aro*A gene)转化植物。在烟草中，通过转化 *Salmonella typhimurium* 的芳香族氨基酸合成酶的变异基因(*aro*A)，获得了对草甘膦有抗性的工程植株[151]。

中国科学院遗传研究所等单位的科研人员继美国之后，利用龙葵抗阿特拉津 *PsbA* 基因转化育成了抗阿特拉津大豆植株。他们通过子房微注射的方法将 PsbA 基因导入大豆叶绿体基因组中，其抗性可通过世代遗传。

现在已培育出了数种抗除草剂的转基因植物，许多大的化学农药公司都在为自己特有的除草剂培养抗性作物品种。

植物抗虫基因工程所基于的主要基础是目前已克隆到的多个苏云金芽孢杆菌 δ-内毒素基因[152–155]该蛋白编码于苏云金芽孢杆菌的大质粒上。对害虫(50 多种)有广泛的毒杀作用。

不同苏云金杆菌来源的毒蛋白对不同的昆虫的毒害作用不同。除广泛应用的对鳞翅目及双翅目昆虫专一性毒蛋白外，现已克隆到针对鞘翅目昆虫的毒蛋白基因[134]。

番茄及烟草的抗虫工程植株都已得到，害虫侵食毒蛋白基因表达了的转基因植物后，产生厌食等症状而导致死亡。尽管害虫以番茄的转基因植物为食能生存 4 天，但其生长却大大受到影响而植株因为减少了虫害其生长受到了很小的影响[156]。由于目前的研究中还没有应用到器官专一性表达的启动子,大多的工作中用的是非特异性表达的CaMV35S启动子，因而在番茄果实中也能检测到该基因的表达。由于δ-内毒素对人体是否有毒尚不清楚，再者非特异性表达对植物体内能源消耗也是个不利因素，因而有些实验室正在致力于分离损伤性诱导基因表达的启动子。

据悉中国农科院生物技术研究中心的研究人员们已将杀虫毒素基因转移到水稻原生质体中，并再生出幼苗。而且在油菜原生质体中也得到了瞬时表达，使工程化植物走向实用化目标迈出了一大步。

作物不仅在蛋白质含量，而且在蛋白质必需氨基酸的组成上都有可改良的余地。禾本科植物种子蛋白赖氨酸含量很少，而双子叶植物(包括某些豆科植物品种)蛋白则缺少含硫氨基酸。必需氨基酸的最佳平衡是为营养值而进行种质改良的目标之一。目前大量的种子贮藏蛋白基因已被克隆，转化及表达了的工程植株也有大量报道。较为突出的是富硫氨基酸蛋白基因的克隆。这种富硫蛋白基因转移到牧草中，对畜牧业的发展将会起到很大的促进作用。另外，现在已克隆到一种甜蛋白基因 *thaumatin* gene(157)，其甜度可为糖的上万倍，这种基因如被应用到水果类植物研究中，能从营养及味道两个角度上达到改良的目的。此外利用反义 RNA 控制果实成熟的过程，控制花青素代谢中的关键酶的基因表达，以增加花卉色彩的多样性等均已取得良好进展。

这类工作遇到的最大问题同样是如何控制其器官专一性高效表达。即能够使外源基因在植物发育的特定时期及特异器官中表达，这样才能使植物体内营养成分达到最佳利用的效果。目前菜豆种子贮藏蛋白基因，其特异性表达启动子已被克隆，并被应用到转化中，得到了在种子中专一性表达。单子叶植物胚乳专一性表达的启动子也已被克隆，估计不久也会被应用于单子叶植物品质改良的研究中。

近几年来利用农杆菌进行遗传操作的一个新的趋向是开发利用发根农杆菌(Agrobacterium rhizogenesis)(158)发根农杆菌中含有能够诱导毛根(hairy root)的 Ri-质粒,其转化机理类似于根癌农杆菌。Ri-质粒中的 T-DNA 整合到植物细胞基因中，能够诱发大量毛根的分化。这些毛根可以在无外源激素的培养条件下进行大量的扩增。有报道可以利用这些快速扩增的毛根生产次生代谢物质，如色素及生物碱等。目前为止，由毛根产生的东莨菪碱、阿托品、尼古丁和甜菜碱都有报道。这些体外扩增毛根中的次生代谢物质含量与植物体根的含量差异不大，而且随着继代培养也没有减少的明显趋势。(158)(159)这种方法可为药用植物特别是从根部提取药用成分的植物，进行次生代谢物质工厂化生产提供一个简便易行的途径。

2. 电击穿法及基因枪法直接导入 DNA

大多数单子叶植物，特别是一些重要的禾谷类农作物对农杆菌并不敏感，因此要采用其他化学的及物理的直接导入法。报道中较多的两个方法是电击穿法(138)及基因枪法(139)。

电击穿法导入外源基因的基本原理是瞬时连续的高压电脉冲，在质膜上击穿了许多小孔，复原的过程中外源 DNA 被吞噬到细胞内。该方法所用的植物受体材料大多为原生质体，亦可以用小的细胞团。以 CAT 基因(氯霉素乙酰转移酶基因)转化甜菜为例(160)最适的原生质体密度为 2×10^5/ml 以 750v/cm 的电压，脉冲时间为 99.9μs，连续三个脉冲,脉冲间隔为9.9秒一般转化缓冲液中所用的质粒DNA为50ng/ml,浓度大于100ng/ml并不能增加转化频率。

对于悬浮培养细胞，在2~10个细胞左右的细胞团，用500v/cm的电压连续多个电脉冲，也能检测到CAT基因的瞬时表达，但其转化频率却大大低于以原生质体为材料。

为了摆脱原生质体再生的困难，有人只用果胶酶处理细胞团，产生5~15个细胞的细胞团,这些细胞经过与原生质体同样刺激后,其转化频率大约为原生质体的40%~50%。

细胞来源及生理条件是影响转化频率的一个不可忽视的条件。一般来讲，各种来源的原生质体都可用电击穿法转化，但叶片原生质体忍受电刺激的幅度比悬浮细胞来源的原生质体要窄得多。而且其最适密度也低得多(1/4)。另外处于分裂中期的细胞最适于转化。

另一种基因直接导入法是基因枪法。[139]这种方法最突出的特点是可以用植物组织直接作为转化的受体材料，不仅可以用体外培养的愈伤组织，而且可以直接用胚。[161]这种方法不仅可以把外源基因带到核基因组中，也可以带到线粒体及叶绿体中。研究中利用包有质粒DNA的直径约为1.2μm的铅弹(也有用金的)射击放在一个滤膜支持物上的植物材料，子弹的速度、密度及子弹表面用以吸附的Carrier DNA及$CaCl_2$浓度都会影响到转化频率。用基因枪法转移DNA的报道大多集中在以玉米为材料的研究上。

在我国，随着国民经济的发展，人们不仅对粮食作物的产量，而且对其品质会提出越来越高的要求，由于自然环境的恶化，对抗逆性作物品种培育的要求也越来越显得紧迫。植物遗传转化近几年的突出成果，使活跃于植物生物技术领域的科研工作者充满了信心，植物生物技术将是解决这些重要课题的主要途径。

参考文献

[1] Koop, H. U. etal, (1985) J. Plant Physiol, 121: 245~247
[2] Schweiger, H. G., etal, (1987) Theor. Appl Genet. 73: 769~783
[3] Spanqenberg, G, etal, (1986) Physiol Plant, 66: 1~8
[4] Spanqenberg, G., (1987) Proc of 7th Int Protoplast Sym., Wageningen, the Netherlands, 1978, 151~157
[5] Rhodes, C. A., etal, (1988) Biotechnology, 6: 56~61
[6] Ludwig, S. R., etal, (1985) Theor. Appl. Genet., 71: 344~350
[7] Maddock, S. E., (1987) Plant cell Reports, 6: 23~26
[8] Thompson, J. A., (1986) Plant Sci, 47: 123~133
[9] Horn, M. E., (1988) Plant Cell Reports, 7: 371~374
[10] Vasil, V. etal, (1981) Ann Bot, 47: 669~678
[11] Lu, C. Y., etal., (1981) Z. Pflanzenphysiol, 104: 311~318
[12] Vasil, V. etal., (1983) Z. Pflanzenphysiol, 111: 233~239
[13] Fujimura, J. etal, (1985）Plant Tiss Cult. Letf, 2: 74~75
[14] Toriyama, k. etal, (1985) Plant Sci, 41: 179~183
[15] 王光远等(1986)植物生理学通讯，6: 49
[16] Yamada, Y. etal, (1986) Plant Cell Reports, 5: 85~88
[17] 雷鸣等(1987)科学通报 32: 1428~1430
[18] 王光远等(1987)实验生物学报 20: 253~257
[19] 孙宝林等(1989)科学通报 15: 1177~1179

[20] 蔡起贵等(1987)植物学报 29: 453~458
[21] Shillito, R. D. etal, (1989) Bio/ technology 7: 581~587
[22] Prioli, L. M. etal, (1989) Bio/ technology 7: 589~584
[23] Sun, C. S. (孙敬三) etal, (1989) Plant Cell Reports, 8: 313~316
[24] Harris, R. etal, (1988) Plant Cell Reports, 7: 337~340
[25] 王海波等(1989) 中国科学，B 辑 8: 828~834
[26] Srinivasan, C., etal, (1986) Plant Physiol, 126: 41~48
[27] 王铁邦等(1989)(已完成稿)
[28] Wei zhi-ming (卫志明) etal, (1989) Plant Cell Reports, (submitted)
[29] 董晋江等(1989)植物生理学通讯 2: 56~57
[30] Luhrs, R. etal, (1988) Planta, 175: 71~81
[31] Dalton, S. J, (1988) J. Plant Physiol, 132: 170~175
[32] Vasil, I. K. (1987) J. Plant Physiol, 128: 193~218
[33] Stuart, D. etal, (1985) Biotechnology in Plant Seience, Academic Press, 35~47
[34] Kyozuka, J. etal, (1988) Theor Appl Genet, 76: 887~890
[35] Lee, L., etal, (1989) Planta, 178: 325~333
[36] Kyozuka, J. etal, (1987) Mol Gen Genet, 206: 408~413
[37] Chu, C. C. (朱至清) etal, (1975) Sci Sinica, 18: 659~668
[38] Murashige, T. etal, (1962) Physiol Plant, 15: 473~497
[39] Kao, K. N. etal, (1975) Planta, 126: 105~110
[40] Abdullah, R. etal, (1986) Bio/technology, 4: 1087~1090
[41] Wei, Z. M. (卫志明) ctal, (1988) Plant Cell Reports, 7: 348~351
[42] Hammatt, N. etal, (1987) J. Plant Physiol., 128: 219~226
[43] Wright, M. S. etal, (1987) Plant Cell Reports, 6: 83~89
[44] Kao, K. N. (1970) Mol Gen Genet, 150: 225~230
[45] Xu, Z. H. (许智宏) etal, (1985) Sci Sinca, Ser. B, 28: 386~392
[46] Kao, K. N etal, (1981) In Vitro, 17: 645~648
[47] Lu, D. Y. etal, (1983) Z. Pflanzenphysiol, 111: 389~394
[48] Newell, C. A. etal, (1985) Plant Cell Tiss Organ Cult, 4: 145~149
[49] Wei, Z. M (卫志明) etal, (1989) Plant Sci, (submitted)
[50] Gilmour, D. M. etal, (1987) Plant Sci, 48: 107~112
[51] Grosser, J. W. etal, (1984) Plant Sci lett, 37: 165~170
[52] Webb, K. J. (1984) Planta, 162: 1~7
[53] Bhojwani, S. S. etal, (1982), Plant Sci lett, 26: 265~271
[54] Ahuja. P. S. etal, (1983) Plant Cell Reports, 2: 269~272
[55] Gupta, P. K. etal, (1987) Bio/technology, 5: 710~712
[56] Attree, S. M, etal, (1987) Plant Cell Reports, 6: 480~483
[57] Russell, J. A. etal, (1988) Plant Cell Reports, 7: 59~62
[58] Tsai, C. K. (蔡起贵) (1988) Plant Sci, 54: 231~235
[59] Kirby, E. C. etal, (1979) Plant Sci lett, 14: 145~154
[60] Gamborg, O. L. etal, (1968) Exp Cell Res, 50: 151~158
[61] Purner, I. J. etal, (1978) Plant Sci lett, 11: 169~176
[62] Dorion, N. etal, (1975) Plant Sci lett, 5: 325~331
[63] 王光远等(1983)植物学报 25: 111~113
[64] Xu, Z. H. (许智宏)etal, (1983) Plant Cell Reports, 2: 55~57
[65] Li, X. H., (李向辉)(1981) Theor. Appl. Genet., 60: 345~347
[66] 李忠谊等(1986) 植物学报，28: 50~54
[67] 李忠谊等(1987) 植物学报，29: 354~356
[68] 吴伯骥等(1986) 中国科学，B 辑, 29: 267~271
[69] 孙勇如等(1982) 植物学报，24: 477~479

[70] 周云罗等(1985) 植物学报，27: 148~150
[71] Kirsi-Marja etal, (1986) Planta Med, 52: 6~12
[72] Kao, K. N. etal, (1974) Planta, 115: 355~367
[73] Zimmermann, U. etal, (1981) Planta, 151: 26~32
[74] Vienken, J. etal, (1974) Physiol Plant, 53: 64~70
[75] Watts, J. W. etal, (1984) Biosci Rep, 4: 335~342
[76] Negrutiu, I. etal, (1986) Theor Appl Genet, 72: 279~286
[77] Hamill, J. D. etal, (1983) Heredity, 50: 197~200
[78] Hamill, J. D. etal, (1984) J. Plant Physiol, 115: 253~261
[79] Patnaik, G. etal, (1982) Plant Sic lett, 24: 105~110
[80] Hein, T. etal, (1983) Theor. Appl. Genet., 64: 119~122
[81] Afonso, C. L. etal, (1985) Bio/Technology, 3: 811~816
[82] Dudits, D. etal, (1976) Can. J. Genet Cytol. 18: 263~269
[83] Chien, Y. C. (钱迎倩) etal, (1982) Theor Appl Genet, 62: 301~304
[84] Medgesy, P. etal, (1985) Proc Natl Acad Sci USA, 82: 6960~6964
[85] Galun, E. et al, (1982) Mol. Gen. Genet, 186: 50~56
[86] Pelletier, G. etal, (1983) Mol Gen. Genet, 191: 244~250
[87] Pental, D. etal, (1985) Hereditas Suppl, 3: 83~92
[88] Pirrie, A. etal, (1986) Theor Appl Genet, 72: 48~52
[89] Ehlenfeldt, M. K. etal, (1987) Theor Appl Genet, 73: 395~402
[90] Yarrow, S. A. etal, (1986) Plant Cell Reports, 5: 415~418
[91] Menczel, L. etal, (1986) Mol Gen. Genet, 205: 201~205
[92] Kumashiro, T. etal, (1986) Jap J. Breed, 36: 39~48
[93] Iwai, S. etal, (1986) Plant Cell Reports, 5: 403~404
[94] Belivanis, T. etal, (1986) Plant Cell Reports, 5: 329~331
[95] Bevan, M. (1984) Nuc Acid Res, 12: 8711~8721
[96] Paszkouski, J. etal (1984) EMBO J., 3: 2717~2722
[97] Sears, E. R. (1954) Missouri Ag. Exp Sta, Res Bull 572: 1~59
[98] O'Mara, J. G, (1940) Genetics, 24: 509~523
[99] Riley, R. etal, (1958) Nature, 182: 713~715
[100] Cauderon, Y. (1986) Genetic Manipulation in Plant Breeding, Walter de Gruyter & Co, Berlin New York, 83~104
[101] Forster, B. P. etal, (1987) Z. Pflanzenzuchtg, 98: 1~8
[102] 刘大钧等(1986) 作物学报, 12: 155~162
[103] 成均康等(1989) 遗传, 11: 1~4
[104] Chen Dawei, etal, (1986) Proc I Inter Sym Chromosome Engi in Plants, Xian, China, 30
[105] Gills, R. S. etal, (1988) Theor Appl Genet, 75: 912~916
[106] Laurie, D. A. etal, (1986) Can. J. Genet Cytol, 28: 313~316
[107] Laurie, D. A. etal, (1988) Z. Pflanzenzuchtg, 100: 73~82
[108] 薛秀庄等(1988) 作物学报，14: 82~85
[109] 童一中等(1987) 作物学报，13: 261~262
[110] Zhang Yu-lan etal, (1986) Proc I Inter Sym Chromsome Eagi in Plants, Xian, China, 21~22
[111] Li Zhen-sheng (李振声)etal, (1986) Cereal Res Commu, 14: 133~137
[112] Xue xiu-zhuang etal, (1986) Proc I Inter Sym Chromosome Engi in Plants, Xian, China, 22~24
[113] Zeller, F. J. etal, (1987) Genome, 29: 58~62
[114] Jung, C. etal, (1987) Z. Pflanznzeuchtg. 98: 205~214
[115] Gustufson, J. P. etal, (1989) Z. Pflanzenzuchtg. 102: 109~112
[116] Lukaszewski etal, (1987) Genome, 29: 554~569
[117] Baum. M. etal, (1988) Z. Pflanzenzuchtg. 100: 260~267
[118] Krolow, K. D. etal, (1986) Genetic Manipulation in Plant Breeding, Walter de Gruyter & Co, Berlin New York, 105~118

[119] Bernard, S. (1987) Theor Appl Genet, 74: 55~59
[120] Lukaszewski, A. J. (1987) Genome, 29: 425~430
[121] Cermeno, M. C. etal, (1983) Genetic Manipulation in Plant Breeding, Walter de Gruyter & Co, Berlin New York, 137~139
[122] He Meng-Yuan etal, (1986) Proc I Inter Sym Chromosome Engi. In Plants, Xian, China, 28~29
[123] 钟冠昌等(1987) 作物学报, 13: 187~192
[124] 张学勇(1987) 西北植物所硕士学位论文
[125] Liu Da-jun etal, (1988) proc 7th Int. Wheat Genet., Sym. Cambridge, England. 355~361
[126] 汪丽泉等(1988) 遗传学报, 15: 1~8
[127] Sun, S. M. etal, (1981) Natune, 289: 37~41
[128] Walburg, G. etal, (1986) Plant Molec. Biol., 6: 161~169
[129] 吴世宣等(1988) 科学通报, : 480
[130] Gerlach, W. L. etal, (1987) Nature 328: 802~805
[131] Baulcombe, D. C. etal, (1986) Nature 321: 446~449
[132] Sonenberg, N. etal,(1978) Nucleic Acids Res, 5: 2501~2521
[133] 田颖川等(1989) 中国科学(印刷中)
[134] Sylvia, A. M. etal, (1988) Bio/Technology, 6: 61~66
[135] De Block M. etal, (1987) EMBO J., 6: 2513~2516
[136] Botterman, J., etal, (1988) Trends in Genetics, 4: 219~222
[137] Holsters, M. etal, (1978) Mol. Gen Genet., 163: 181~187
[138] Fromm M. etal, (1985) Nat. Acad. Sci. USA, 82: 5824~5828
[139] Klein, T. etal, (1987) Nature, 327: 70~73
[140] Krens, F. A. etal, (1982) Nature, 296: 72~74
[141] Otten, L. etal, (1981) Mol. Gen Genet., 183: 209~213
[142] Andre, H. etal, (1989) Bio/Technology, 7: 273~278
[143] Hoekema, A. etal (1983) Nature 303: 179~180
[144] Powell, A. etal (1986) Science, 232: 738~743
[145] Karp, A. etal (1982) Theor Appl Genet, 63: 265~272
[146] Tumet, T. etal, (1987) EMBO J., 6: 1181~1188
[147] Maria, C. etal, (1988) Bio/Technology, 6: 549~557
[148] Andre, H. etal, (1989) Bio/Technology, 7: 273~278
[149] Amrhein, N. etal, (1980) Plant Physiol., 66: 830~834
[150] Amrhein, N. etal, (1983) FEBS Lett., 157: 191~196
[151] Comai, L. etal, (1985) Nature, 317: 741~744
[152] Schnepf, H. etal, (1981) Proc Natl Acad. Sci USA, 78: 2983
[153] Klier, A. etal, (1982) EMBO J., 1: 791
[154] Honigman, A. etal, (1986) Gene, 4: 69
[155] 田颖川等，(1989) 生物工程学报, 5: 11~18
[156] Fischhoff, D. A. etal, (1987) Bio/Technology, 5: 807~813
[157] Edens, L. etal, (1985) Trends in Biotechnology, 3: 1~4
[158] Frank, F. etal, (1980) J. Bacteri, 3: 1134~1141
[159] Kamada, H. etal, (1986) Plant Cell Reports, 5: 239~242
[160] Lindsey, K. etal, (1987) Plant Mol. Biol, 10: 43~52
[161] Klein, T. etal, (1988) Bio/Technology, 6: 559~563

本文原载：植物杂志. 1974. 1(1): 37-39

植物细胞、组织与器官的培养

胡玉熹　钱迎倩

(中国科学院植物研究所)

总论

植物细胞、组织与器官的各种人工离体培养，目前已成为一种常规的研究方法。它们对于推动植物学的发展，以及在生产实践上的应用都将具有很大的价值。例如在植物生理学方面，应用人工离体培养技术，可以有目的地控制植物生长发育所需要的外界条件，从而研究植物的生长、分化与营养物质、生长激素以及附加有机物质的关系。在植物形态学方面，可以研究形态建成，胚胎发生，分化及反分化等问题，探索植物组织和器官的起源和形成的途径。在植物细胞学方面，可以探明细胞分裂、分化的原因，细胞中生物合成的条件，以及细胞呼吸与酶的活动等问题。

在植物遗传育种学方面，可以通过人工离体培养植物的花粉、幼胚、茎端或单个体细胞得到纯系品种与选育新品种，及缩短育种周期，或克服杂种不孕性等。

植物病理学方面，也可利用植物的无菌培养，对植物病毒和植物肿瘤的研究提供一种新的技术。此外还有助于植物与根瘤菌共生和转移等方面的研究。

目前这些培养技术在生产实践上的应用，多只在试验阶段。例如花药的离体培养(通称单倍体培养)，以诱导花药内小孢子产生单倍体植株，将成为一条快速育种的新途径。又如为复壮被病毒侵染的蔬菜、果树和花卉等而进行的茎端离体培养，最近已取得很大成果，生产上已应用的有草莓、葡萄和马铃薯等。另外，还有人企图利用植物细胞的培养，促进其中有用成分的生物合成(如从颠茄的单细胞培养，获得颠茄碱)，从而为将来工厂大规模生产有用物质提供了可能性。随着有关工业生产和学科理论的不断发展，特别是通过各种人工离体培养的不断实践，今后此等技术将会对农业的增产，制药工业的生物合成及无菌食品的大量生产，甚至可能对人体肿瘤的成因和宇宙飞船中食物的解决等一系列重大问题，作出难以估量的贡献。

关于植物细胞培养的历史，可以追溯到公元1902年，Haberlandt就曾提出人工培养单个植物体细胞的设想，但限于当时的条件，未能将离体的叶肉细胞培养成功。20年后，他的学生 Kotte，培养离体的植物根获得成功。到了三十年代，怀特(White)、高塞雷特(Gautheret)和诺贝考特(Nobecourt)等人，由于改进了培养条件，在综合培养基上成功地培养了番茄离体根和烟草、杨树等形成层组织五十年代后期，斯特瓦德(Steward)等将胡萝卜韧皮部分离成单细胞进行培养，最后得到发育完全的植株，甚至还能开花结果。由于植物单个体细胞的培养成功，使哈伯兰特(Haberlandt)在五十多年前的预言——离体单细胞具“全能性”得到了证实。近10年来，由植物的单细胞培养形成小植株的，已有很多报道。

最近，从单细胞培养又发展到原生质体的培养及细胞杂交的研究，如武部(Takebe, 1971)和甘伯格(Gamberg, 1972)，分别用烟草叶肉细胞和胡萝卜细胞的原生质体进行人工培养，最后都能形成正常的植株。卡尔逊(Carlson, 1972)等进一步用两个不同种的烟草作材料，进行原生质体融合，由此获得的杂交细胞能长成愈伤组织，分化成一完整的杂交植株。

综上所述，近40年来，由于人们在植物的不同器官、组织与细胞的离体培养上，已先后取得了很大的成绩。随着近代分子生物学、细胞生物学、生理学、形态学和遗传学的发展，以及某些先进技术的不断引入，植物的无菌离体培养技术定将得到更大的发展。

我们将陆续地向广大读者介绍：植物原生质体培养，植物单细胞的培养，植物各种组织(如愈伤组织、表皮组织和形成层组织)的培养，植物营养器官(如根尖、茎尖和叶子等)及生殖器官(如花药、果实、种子、胚胎等)的培养等。

I. 植物原生质体培养

本世纪初，有人曾用机械的方法从植物细胞中分离出原生质体。三十年代有人报道可将原生质体进行融合。但由于所得到的原生质体数量少，质量差，难于在实验上应用。直到1960年科金(Cocking)用纤维素酶分离番茄幼苗根尖，得到了大量生活的原生质体。促进了从原生质体培养植株的研究。同时利用植物原生质体进行生物学基础理论研究的报道也不少。如玻纳(Pojnar)等人在1967年首次观察到培养的原生质体再生出细胞壁。接着埃利逊(Eriksson)及武部(Takebe)等又分别能使再生细胞进行细胞核和细胞分裂。1971年武部(Takebe)从烟草叶肉原生质体培养获得完整植株。到目前为止，从原生质体培养生成完整植株的有烟草[7]、烟草单倍体[6]、胡萝卜[5]及矮牵牛[4]等四种植物。近年来我国也有一些单位开展了这方面的研究[1,2,3]。本文将介绍有关原生质体的制备，培养技术及其在理论上和实践上的意义。

植物原生质体的制备

植物原生质体的制备主要有两个过程，即先用果胶酶从植物组织中分离得单个细胞，再用纤维素酶处理细胞，去掉细胞壁；也可将果胶酶与纤维素酶同时混用，从而获得大量处于生活状态的原生质体。

培养过程中为了避免杂菌污染，供试材料须用70%乙醇及饱和漂白粉溶液连续处理。各个程序必须在无菌条件下进行，各种器械须经高压灭菌。供试材料如为叶片，应去掉叶片的下表皮，切下无下表皮的叶片，称所需重量后，即可放入酶液中处理。

酶液要用渗透稳定剂配制，以免在细胞去壁后，由于外界溶液渗透压过低使原生质体吸水膨大而破裂。渗透稳定剂多数用甘露糖醇，也可用山梨糖醇、氯化钾及氯化钠。渗透稳定剂的浓度按供试材料及其生理状态而异。酶液不能高压灭菌，用孔径 0.45μm 的微孔滤器(millipore filter)或用 G5 耐酸过滤漏斗过滤灭菌。调整酶液的氢离子浓度至最适范围。

材料在酶液中作用一定时间后，可取少量在显微镜下检查，当看到大量原生质体时，即停止作用。去壁后的原生质体用尼龙布或不锈钢网过滤，以去掉作用不完善的残片及碎片。待酶液彻底澄清后，就可得到大量原生质体。

为了检查去壁是否彻底，国外普遍采用荧光增白剂(calcofluor white ST)检查。因萤光增白剂是染细胞壁较好的染料，细胞壁经染色后，在荧光显微镜下出现蓝色的荧光。

在显微镜下，生活而优质的原生质体，可看到明显的原生质带及活跃的原生质流动；叶肉细胞的原生质体中则可看到轮廓清晰的叶绿体。

植物原生质体的培养

从原生质体诱导长成植株，一般要经过下列几个程序：首先在合适的培养条件下，从原生质体上长出细胞壁而成再生细胞；然后细胞经过不断分裂成一大团细胞，称为愈伤组织；最后愈伤组织发育和分化成苗及根，长成完整的植株。

原生质体能否长出细胞壁并进行分裂，关键在于培养条件是否适宜。除培养温度、光照强度、光照时间等条件外，足够的原生质体及合适的培养基又至关重要。所用培养基要求含有氮、磷、钾类大量元素，及铁、锰、锌等微量元素。此外还要有为植物利用的碳源(如蔗糖)、为促进细胞生长分裂的激素或细胞分裂素、各种不同成分的有机附加物以及适当浓度的渗透稳定剂。最后，培养基的合适氢离子浓度也是不容忽视的。

原生质体可在液体培养基或固体培养基(加入一定量的琼脂)中培养。液体培养又可在培养皿中作静置培养或在每分钟一转的转床上培养。转床培养在细胞分裂的速度上一般较静置培养快得多。

原生质体在合适的培养条件下，几天内就可再生细胞壁。某些植物如烟草叶肉细胞的原生质体，在培养的第四天就可见到相当数量的细胞进行分裂。一定时间后，就形成了肉眼能见到的愈伤组织。愈伤组织长到一定大小后，即可移入激素和细胞分裂素浓度相对较低的分化培养基中使其进行器官分化。

下面简略地介绍杜兰(Durand)等对矮牵牛原生质体培养的情况：将 4ml 原生质体悬浮液放在直径 5cm 的培养皿中。温度 28℃，光照强度约 700m 烛光，每天照光 16h。第三天，原生质体就合成了新的细胞壁。同时，体积显著增大并成为卵圆形。第 5 天细胞进行第一次分裂，第 10 天可看到幼小的愈伤组织。这时大量不能分裂的原生质体的细胞质收缩变浓，慢慢解体。仅 2%~4%的原生质体能形成愈伤组织。

两周后，用 5ml 培养基(表 1)稀释悬浮液，培养基中的甘露醇改为 2%的蔗糖。再经两周后，将幼小愈伤组织转入固体培养基上(表 2)。愈伤组织迅速生长，4 周后，鲜重可增长 1200%。

表 2 的培养基中，萘乙酸的浓度为 2mg/L，6-苄基腺嘌呤为 0.5mg/L，这样的浓度不仅使愈伤组织迅速生长，并适合于苗的分化。当把所获得的苗移入萘乙酸浓度为

0.1mg/L，而无6-苄基腺嘌呤的培养基中时，就能诱导出根，并成长小植株。表3介绍烟草等四种植物的原生质体制备及培养条件。

表1　矮牵牛原生质体培养基的组成*

A. 无机盐(mg/L)			
NH_4NO_3	270	H_3BO_3	2
KNO_3	1480	$MnSO_4 \cdot H_2O$	5
$MgSO_4 \cdot 7H_2O$	340	$ZnSO_4 \cdot 7H_2O$	1.5
$CaCl_2 \cdot 2H_2O$	570	KI	0.25
KH_2PO_4	80	$Na_2MoO_4 \cdot 2H_2O$	0.1
$FeSO_4 \cdot TH_2O$	27.8	$CuSO_4 \cdot 5H_2O$	0.015
Na_2EDTA	37.3	$CoCl_2 \cdot 6H_2O$	0.01
B. 有机组分(mg/L)			
肌-肌醇	100	盐酸吡哆素	0.7
叶酸	0.4	促生素	0.04
甘氨酸	1.4	2，4-D	1.4
烟酸	4	6-苄基腺嘌呤	0.4
盐酸硫胺素	4	蔗糖	0.05M
		甘露糖醇	0.30M

* 高压灭菌前把pH调整到5.6。

表2　矮牵牛愈伤组织培养基的组成*

A. 无机盐(mg/L)			
NH_4NO_3	825	H_3BO_3	6.2
KNO_3	950	$MnSO_4 \cdot 4H_2O$	22.3
$CaCl_2 \cdot 2H_2O$	220	$ZnSO_4 \cdot 4H_2O$	8.6
$MgSO_4 \cdot 7H_2O$	1233	KI	0.83
KH_2PO_4	680	$Na_2MoO_4 \cdot 2H_2O$	0.25
Na_2-EDTA	37.3	$CuSO_4 \cdot 5H_2O$	0.025
$FeSO_4 \cdot 7H_2O$	27.8	$CoSO_4 \cdot 7H_2O$	0.030
B. 有机成分			
肌-肌醇	100mg/L	6-苄基腺嘌呤	0.5mg/L
盐酸硫胺素	1mg/L	蔗糖	2%
萘乙酸	2mg/L	琼脂	0.6%

* 高压灭菌前将pH调整到5.8。

植物原生质体培养的意义

在研究原生质体培养的同时，有人还提出用不同种植物的原生质体诱导其融合(即体细胞杂交)，从而产生杂种细胞的设想。通过培养杂种细胞而得到杂种植株，使不能有性杂交的植物结合起来。这是其他方法所不能得到的。所以无论在培育新品种，以及在生物学基础理论的研究上都将有很大的意义和价值。科金(Cocking)工作组于 1970 年第一次在实验室中得到燕麦和玉米根部细胞的融合原生质体。卡尔逊(Carlson)等人在 1972 年，再通过融合的原生质体培育出烟草的杂种植株。使体细胞杂交的设想变成现实。

同时已有实验证明，分离的植物原生质体可以吞噬生物大分子(如蛋白质、核酸、病毒)及根瘤菌，这些结果大大开扩了研究领域。人们可以通过在原生质体中引进外源遗传物质来改变植物细胞的遗传组成，通过原生质体培养达到创造植物新品种的目的；同时为研究根瘤菌与大豆细胞间共生固氮关系及固氮菌向非豆科植物转移；病毒侵入寄主的过程；甚至在白化细胞中引入光合效率高的叶绿体，以培育新的高产作物品种等一系列重大的研究课题，开辟了一条新的途径。

植物原生质体又为生物学基础理论研究，如水分平衡、细胞壁形成、细胞膜的结构和特性、细胞核与细胞质的相互关系等许多课题提供了极好的实验材料。因此植物原生质体培养的研究近年来越来越为细胞生物学、遗传学、病理学、生理学等方面工作者重视。

表 3　烟草等 4 种植物原生质体制备及培养对照表

植物材料	取材时期	酶液处理情况						培养条件			培养基	原生质体数
		酶液	渗透稳定剂	pH	温度(℃)	时间	材料/酶液	培养温度	光照时间	光照强度		
烟草伸展叶片	60~100天的叶片	0.5%果胶酶(Macerozyme)	0.7*M* 甘露糖醇	5.8	25	1.5~2h	2g/25ml	28	连续光照	2800m 烛光	参看参考资料[7]	10^4~10^5/ml
		2%纤维素酶(Onozuka CLA623)	0.7*M* 甘露糖醇	5.2	36	2h						
单倍体烟草叶肉组织	叶片达到最大时	0.5%果胶酶(Macerozyme)	0.6*M* 甘露糖醇		27	4次 每次20min	3g/20ml	28	18h	500m 烛光	参看参考资料[6]	每 ml 内含有相当于 250ml 新鲜叶片原生质体数目
		2%纤维素酶(Onozuka)	0.7*M* 甘露糖醇		32	2h						
胡萝卜愈伤组织产生的悬浮培养细胞	参看参考资料[5]	0.5%去盐果胶酶(Serva)+1%去盐纤维素酶(Onozuka P5000)	B5 培养基+0.56*M* 甘露糖醇共 0.6*M*	5.5	25	2h	100mg/2ml	23	连续光照	800~1000m 烛光	参看参考资料[5]	15~20×10^4/ml
矮牵牛幼叶	播种后2~3 月直到开花	0.2%果胶酶(Serva, 31 660)	0.4*M* 甘露糖醇	5.4	35	15min	7g/80ml	28	16h	700m 烛光	参看本文(表 1、2)	10~40×10^4/ml
		2%纤维素酶(Onozuka SS)	0.4*M* 甘露糖醇	5.8	35	25min						

参考资料

[1] 中国科学院植物研究所细胞组, 1973, 植物学杂志, 1(1): 30~31
[2] 中国科学院遗传研究所五室二组, 1973, 遗传学通讯, 1973(4): 7~12
[3] 朱澂, 1973, 遗传学通讯, 1973(4): 43~50
[4] Durand, J., Potrkus and G. Donn, 1973, Z. *Pflanzenphysiol*., 69: 26~34
[5] Grambow, H. J., K. N. Kao, R. A. Miller, and O. L. Ganiborg, 1972, *Planta*, 103: 348~355
[6] Nitsch, J. P. and K. Chyama, 1971, C. R. *Acad*. Sci., D-273: 801~804
[7] Takebe, I., G. Labik, and G., Melchers 1971, *Naturwiss*, 58: 318~320

本文原载：中国科学. 1977. 20(4): 347-354

烟草(*Nicotiana tabacum*)原生质体再生成植株及影响植株分化的某些因素

蔡起贵　钱迎倩　周云罗　吴素萱

(中国科学院植物研究所)

摘　要　从烟草(品种革新一号)单倍体花粉植株的叶和茎产生的愈伤组织，结合悬浮培养，获得的细胞分离出原生质体。在液体培养基中静置培养，12h 后原生质体开始变为卵圆形，细胞壁明显可见，24h 后完成第一次细胞分裂。以后继续分裂形成浅黄色的愈伤组织，在培养四星期后可达 1mm 大小，再放到转床上进行旋转培养 18d 左右，愈伤组织可达 3~4mm 大小。当转移到分化培养基后，分别分化出苗及根，长成完整的植株。

原生质体再生细胞的分裂与分化，不仅受不同器官来源的愈伤组织及其年龄的影响；还受分化培养基的基本成份及所用细胞分裂素的类型等的影响。

为了满足社会主义建设对经济作物在数量及质量上不断提高的需要，寻找克服远缘杂交不亲和性及定向改变植物遗传性状的新途径，以培育出适合要求的优良新品种，一直是生物学工作者努力的一个重要方面。植物原生质体，因其不具备细胞壁而可进行异种间甚至更远亲间的融合，可引进外缘遗传物质，可利用物理、化学因素处理进行人工诱变，以及因其具全能性再生成完整植株等一系列优越性能，从而可能成为遗传基因型的广泛组合和定向诱变的一个极好材料。同时植物原生质体又是从事病毒侵染机理，及细胞生物学、遗传学、植物生理学等基础研究的实验材料，因此引起国内外普遍的重视。

本世纪六十年代，大量产生植物原生质体的技术突破后[1]，近十几年来这方面的工作大量增进，迄今从烟草[2~6]、胡萝卜[7~8]、矮牵牛[9~10]、石刁柏[11]、芸苔[12]、金鱼草[13]、曼陀罗[14]、石龙芮[15]及颠茄[16]的原生质体，通过培养已能再生成完整植株。通过原生质体的融合，烟草也已获得品种间和种间杂种[17~18]。属间、科间直到动植物界间[19]的融合也已有成功的记录。大豆原生质体和大麦原生质体的融合成功，并能分裂产生近 100 个杂种细胞的细胞团，这是远缘结合的很好例子[20]。细胞器、细菌及外源 DNA 引入原生质体的成功，并发现引入的噬菌体基因能在植物细胞中转录和翻译，以及通过原生质体筛选出抗病的突变体[21]等等，都是一些极为可喜的进展。这些进展使我们看到了研究植物原生质体和体细胞杂交的重要意义和前景。

植物原生质体的研究目前面临的重要问题是如何能使更多的植物，特别是在重要的粮食作物上能从原生质体再生成完整植株。我们细胞杂交组在从事水稻原生质体研究[22]

的同时也进行了烟草原生质体再生植株的研究，为今后细胞融合等工作奠定基础。

烟草原生质体再生植株的研究虽已做了一定的工作[2~6]，但原生质体均来自叶片的叶肉细胞。本文报道了从花药培养来源的单倍体植株的叶片及茎段诱导愈伤组织，结合悬浮培养获得游离细胞，从而分离出原生质体，通过原生质体培养再生成完整植株以及探索影响植株分化的某些因素所获得的结果。

一、材料与方法

1. 原生质体的来源：制备烟草(品种革新一号)原生质体所用的原始材料是由本室单倍体育种组提供的花粉植株[23]的叶片和茎段产生的愈伤组织，然后将愈伤组织移到液体培养基中作旋转培养所获得的悬浮细胞。实验步骤如下：①将无菌培养的植株叶片和茎段培养在含有 MS[24]培养基的大量成分、H[25]培养基的微量成分及有机成分，添加 2~6mg/L 2，4-D、1mg/L 激动素、3%蔗糖、pH5.8 的培养基上诱导产生愈伤组织。②将愈伤组织转移到添加 2mg/L 2,4-D，1000mg/L 酵母浸膏及 3%蔗糖、pH5.8 的稍加修改的 H[25]培养基上作继代培养，每隔约两星期转移一次，转移 5~6 次即可使用。③使用继代培养约两年的叶片愈伤组织(简称叶老愈伤组织，下同)及继代培养约三个月的叶片及茎的愈伤组织(简称叶及茎新愈伤组织，下同)。在每次分离原生质体前将 3~5g 愈伤组织移到内盛 25ml 液体培养基(见表 1)的 100ml 三角瓶中，并放到垂直旋转的转床(8 转/分)上进行悬浮培养，培养物在近光源处 6000lx 和远光源处 250lx 的光强度下，每天光照约 10h，白天温度 28℃，夜间约 25℃。培养约 12~14d，此时培养物中有细胞及不同大小的细胞团。

表 1 液体培养基的组成①②

A. 无机盐				B. 有机组分			
大量元素	mg/L	微量元素	mg/L	维生素	mg/L	其他	
KNO_3	2200	$MnSO_4 \cdot 4H_2O$	25	肌醇	100	水解乳蛋白	1000mg/L
NH_4NO_3	600	$ZnSO_4 \cdot 7H_2O$	10	烟酸	5	2，4-D	0.5mg/L
$(NH_4)_2SO_4$	67	H_3BO_3	10	甘氨酸	2		
$CaCl_2$	223						
$MgSO_4 \cdot 7H_2O$	310	KI	0.83	盐酸硫胺素	0.5		
$NaH_2PO_4 \cdot 2H_2O$	85	$Na_2MoO_4 \cdot 2H_2O$	0.25	盐酸吡哆素	0.5		
KH_2PO_4	141	$CuSO_4 \cdot 5H_2O$	0.025				
Na_2-EDTA	37.3			叶酸	0.5	蔗糖	2.5%
$FeSO_4 \cdot 7H_2O$	27.8	$CoSO_4 \cdot 6H_2O$	0.025	生物素	0.05		

① 该培养基的配方由上海复旦大学遗传研究所杨树青同志提供。

② 热压消毒以前调整 pH 到 5.5。

2. 原生质体的分离：在无菌条件下，把旋转培养约 14d 进行旺盛分裂的悬浮培养物倒入 25ml 的量筒中，待较大的悬浮物稍下沉后，即用吸管把较小的悬浮物移入离心管，通过离心处理收集细胞及较小的细胞团。实验证明，几十个细胞以内的细胞团产生的原生质体是合适的。通过微孔滤器(孔径为 0.45μm)过滤灭菌的酶混合液与收集的细胞按约 1.5：1 混合。酶溶液的组成如下：5%(W/v)纤维素酶(Onozuka R-10, Kniki Yakult Mfg. Co., Ltd., Nishinomiya, Japan)，0.8%离析酶(Macerozyme R-10, Kniki Yakult Mfg. Co., Ltd., Nishinomiya, Japan)，0.5%半纤维素酶(Koch-Light Laboratories Ltd., Colnbrook Bucks, England)，0.2%葡聚糖硫酸钾(含硫量 18%)，1*mM*$CaCl_2 \cdot 2H_2O$ 及 0.8*M* 甘露醇；把 pH 调至 5.4。将 10~12ml 酶溶液与 7~8ml 细胞混合后倒进 100ml 三角瓶，在 34℃恒温水浴中静置培养 4~5h(中间轻摇两次)。混合液用孔径 56μm 的不锈钢丝网过滤，除去老细胞及细胞团，通过离心(80 × g，2~5min)，从溶液中将原生质体分离出来，并用含 1*mM*$CaCl_2 \cdot 2H_2O$ 的 0.6*M* 甘露醇溶液洗涤二次，然后用培养基(表 2)洗涤一次。

表 2　原生质体培养基的组成①

A. 无 机 盐				B. 有 机 组 分			
大量元素	mg/L	微量元素	mg/L	维生素	mg/L	其他	
KNO_3	1900	$MnSO_4 \cdot H_2O$	18	肌醇	100	水解干酪素	200mg/L
NH_4NO_3	360			烟酸	1	椰乳②	2%
$(NH_4)_2SO_4$	67	$ZnSO_4 \cdot 7H_2O$	10	甘氨酸	2	2，4-D	0.05mg/L
$MgSO_4 \cdot 7H_2O$	370	H_3BO_3	10	盐酸硫胺素	1	6-苄基氨基嘌呤	0.1mg/L
$CaCl_2$	450	$Na_2MoO_4 \cdot 2H_2O$	0.25	盐酸吡哆素	0.5	蔗糖	10g/L
KH_2PO_4	200					D-葡萄糖	1g/L
Na_2-EDTA	14.92	$CuSO_4 \cdot 5H_2O$	0.025	叶酸	0.5	甘露醇	0.3*M*
$FeSO_4 \cdot 7H_2O$	11.12	$CoSO_4 \cdot 6H_2O$	0.025	生物素	0.01	山梨醇	0.3*M*

① 热压消毒前调整 pH 到 5.6。
② 按 Kao 等(1974)[20]的方法先进行热处理。

3. 原生质体的培养：将 1ml 原生质体悬浮液(密度为 $5 \times 10^4 \sim 10^5$ 原生质体/ml)放在 25ml 有磨口瓶塞的三角瓶中，用纱布及牛皮纸包口。把培养物放在 1250lx 的光强度下，每天光照约 10h，温度 28℃(日)，26℃(夜)。每天早晚各轻轻摇动一次，并用倒置显微镜观察原生质体的发育过程。培养一个月左右，最大的愈伤组织长到约 1ml 时，用约 7ml 没有 D-葡萄糖、甘露醇及山梨醇，而含有 3%蔗糖的同样培养基(表 2)稀释细胞悬浮液，并移进 50ml 的乳头锥形瓶中，放到转床(1r/min)上进行旋转培养，光照和温度与前述细胞的悬浮培养相同。培养约 18d 后，取出较大的愈伤组织转移到分化培养基上，余下的小愈伤组织再加入 3ml 新鲜培养基，在转床上继续培养 10d 左右。

4. 苗的分化：①为了诱导苗的新形成，作了不同分化培养基对愈伤组织分化苗影响的实验，所用过的部分培养基列于表 3。②为了探索不同类型细胞分裂素对愈伤组织分化苗的影响，从表 3 中选择了 N-T3、N-T7、B-MS2 及 K-H1 四种分化培养基，以来自叶的新愈伤组织的原生质体再生的愈伤组织为材料，作细胞分裂素的置换实验。凡原培养基中用 6-苄基氨基嘌呤(6-BA)的改用激动素(kn)或相反，其余成份不变。

表 3 不同分化培养基的组成① (单位：mg/L)

培养基	基本成分	水解干酪素	腺嘌呤	吲哚乙酸	6-苄基氨基嘌呤	激动素	玉米素	蔗糖(%)	琼脂(%)
N-T3	按 Nagata-Takebe[26]	100	—	0.5	1	—	—	2	0.8
N-T5	,,	100	—	0.3	1	—	—	2	0.8
N-T6	,,	100	—	0.1	1	—	—	2	0.8
N-T7	,,	100	—	—	1	—	—	2	0.8
B-MS1	按 MS[24]	100	40	2	2	—	—	2	0.8
B-MS2	,,	100	40	2	1	—	—	2	0.8
Z-BM1	,,	100	40	0.5	—	—	0.2	2	0.8
K-H1	按 H[25]	100	—	0.5	—	1	—	2	0.8

① 所有培养基在热压消毒前均调整 pH 到 5.8。

5. 根的诱导：把已分化的苗移到不加或添加 0.01，0.05，0.1mg/L 吲哚乙酸(IAA)及 2%蔗糖的 White[27]培养基及修改的 H[25]培养基中分化根。H 培养基的修改如下：去掉烟酸，肌醇给为 50mg/L，Fe-EDTA 改为 1mg/L，不加或添加 0.1，0.3，0.5mg/L IAA，pH5.8。

最后把生根的小植株移栽到花盆中。

二、结果

1. 原生质体的分裂：从悬浮细胞或小细胞团刚分离的原生质体一般都呈圆球形，有轻微到中等程度的液泡化，并具数量及大小不等的颗粒内含物，细胞核清晰可见，能看到原生质环流，不同材料来源的原生质体的大小略有不同(图版 I，1~2)。一般不混有未去壁的老细胞。培养 12~20h 后，部分原生质体已不同程度地增大体积，同时细胞核逐渐移向细胞中央，而颗粒内含物则移向并集中在核周围。其中极少数原生质体变为卵圆形，并且再生的细胞壁已明显可见(图版 I，3)。来源于叶老愈伤组织的原生质体培养 24~36h 后，完成第一次细胞分裂，而来源与叶、茎新愈伤组织的原生质体则延迟到约 72h 后才完成。细胞分裂大致可分为两种类型：①均等分裂：分类后形成两个对称的大小相等的半圆形子细胞(图版 I，4)；②不等分裂：分裂后形成各种大小不等的两个子细胞(图版 I，5~6)。子细胞中的细胞核有时位于细胞中央，但多数位于新形成隔壁的两侧。

在这期间还观察到少数原生质体破裂或出芽。培养一星期后，来源于叶老愈伤组织的原生质体已发育成 8~10 个细胞的细胞团，而来源于叶、茎新愈伤组织的原生质体只发育成 4~8 个细胞的细胞团(图版 I，7~9)。培养二星期后，二者分别发育到 20 多个细胞(图版 I，10)及 10 多个细胞(图版 I，11)的细胞团。此外，还观察到另一些分裂类型，如第一次分裂形成两个子细胞后，似乎一个继续分裂而另一个延缓分裂而形成偏向一边分裂的现象(图版 I，8 及 12)，亦有原生质体再生细胞后从两端进行细胞分裂的现象(图版 I，13)。培养三星期后，可形成小愈伤组织(图版 I，14)。培养约一个月后，浅黄色的愈伤组织可达 1mm 左右。此时取样统计分裂频率(两个以上细胞的细胞团及愈伤组织均计在内)，来源于叶老愈伤组织的可达 70%以上，而来源于叶、茎新愈伤组织的则只有约 50%。

当用降低糖浓度的同样培养基稀释培养物，并在转床上作旋转培养后，培养物更活跃地分裂和生长，在原有的小愈伤组织迅速长大的同时还新形成很多小的愈伤组织，在转床上培养约 18d 后，最大的愈伤组织可达约 3~4mm。取出大愈伤组织进行分化，余下的加进新培养基继续旋转培养约 10d 后，最大的愈伤组织又可达到 2~3mm。每个乳头锥形瓶中的培养物通过两次旋转培养后共得到约 1.5~4mm 的愈伤组织 150 块左右。

2. 苗的分化：将约 1.5~4mm 的愈伤组织移到分化苗的培养基(表 3)后，多数都能继续活跃地生长，不同来源及不同年龄的愈伤组织产生的原生质体再生的愈伤组织，在不同或相同的培养基上，苗的分化时间有较大的差异。在 N-T3~N-T7 培养基上，来源于叶老愈伤组织的约需 5~6 星期，来源于叶新愈伤组织的约需 3~4 星期，而来源于茎新愈伤组织的则只需 3 星期左右；在 B-MS1~2 和 Z-MS1 培养基上，出苗的时间相应为 5~6 星期、3~4 星期及 3~4 星期；而在 K-H1 培养基上则相应为约 6 星期、约 5 星期及约 5 星期。

苗分化的途径有二：①按一般正常的分化途径先产生芽，然后形成苗；②按与合子胚分化相类似的发育途径，即通过“球形”、“心脏形”、“鱼雷形”的“胚状体”发育成小苗。“胚状体”形成小苗后，如不及时转移，往往会出现胚根缩短及胚轴变粗等一些不正常现象。叶、茎新愈伤组织来源者在 N-T3~7 及 B-MS1~2 分化培养基上，在同一块愈伤组织上可同时见到以上两种苗分化的途径，其中以 N-T3~7 更为明显。而来源于叶老愈伤组织者同时存在两种苗分化的能力显著降低。甚至不易看到“胚状体”的形成。

(1) 不同分化培养基对愈伤组织分化苗的影响，结果列于表 4。对结果的分析可见：

i. 在各种不同的分化培养基上，一般来源于叶老愈伤组织比来源于叶、茎新愈伤组织的原生质体再生的愈伤组织出苗率低，在 Z-MS1 分化培养基上甚至低于 10 倍以上。同时一块来源于叶老愈伤组织的一般只能分化出 1~10 多颗苗(图版 II，1)，而一块来源于叶、茎新愈伤组织的则可分化出几颗到几十颗苗(图版 II，2~3)。

此外，在 1.5~4mm 范围内，愈伤组织的大小对苗的分化频率没有影响，但对出苗时间及出苗数量则略有影响。

ii. 在 B-MS1 及 B-MS2 两种分化培养基上，来源于叶老愈伤组织及叶、茎新愈伤组织的原生质体再生的愈伤组织，分化苗的频率有明显的差异，来源于叶老愈伤组织的在 B-MS1 培养基上不能分化苗，而在 B-MS2 培养基上则有一定的苗分化率。后二者在这两种培养基上均有较高的苗分化率，而在 B-MS1 培养基上的又比在 B-MS2 培养基上的高。

表 4 不同分化培养基对愈伤组织分化苗的影响

愈伤组织来源	培养基	接种愈伤组织数	分化苗的愈伤组织数	分化苗的愈伤组织占接种愈伤组织(%)①
叶老愈伤组织的原生质体	N-T3	42	21	50.0
	N-T5	10	2	20.0
	N-T6	10	6	60.0
	N-T7	10	4	40.0
	B-MS1	23	0②	0
	B-MS2	39	14	35.9
	Z-MS1	23	1	4.3
	K-H1	17	4	23.5
叶新愈伤组织的原生质体	N-T3	67	59	88.0
	N-T5	24	20	83.3
	N-T6	14	0	0
	N-T7	27	5	18.5
	B-MS1	22	21	95.5
	B-MS2	24	21	87.5
	Z-MS1	26	17	65.4
	K-H1	24	14	58.3
茎新愈伤组织的原生质体	N-T3	44	44	100.0
	N-T5	18	18	100.0
	N-T6	18	18	100.0
	N-T7	16	16	100.0
	B-MS1	18	16	88.8
	B-MS2	17	11	64.7
	Z-MS1	17	10	58.8
	K-H1	17	7	41.2

① 除少数外，均为 2~3 次实验结果的平均数。

② 转移 8 个星期后，未分化出苗，把愈伤组织再转移到 B-MS2 培养基上，在 2 星期内即有八块愈伤组织分化出苗，分化苗的频率为 34.8%。

iii. N-T 组合的四种分化培养基的不同，在于 IAA 的差异(表 3)。试验结果表明，来源于茎新愈伤组织的在这四种培养基上苗的分化率均达 100%；而来源于叶愈伤组织的，不论其继代培养时间的长短，均不如来源于茎愈伤组织的高，其中来源于叶新愈伤组织的又比来源于叶老愈伤组织的高。

(2) 不同类型细胞分裂素对苗分化的影响。细胞分裂素的类型改变后，表 5 的试验结果表明，出现三种情况：i.愈伤组织移到置换了细胞分裂素的培养基后，大多数不但不继续生长，反而颜色逐渐变褐而死亡，只有个别愈伤组织在边缘新产生的小愈伤组织上分化出少量的苗(图版 II，4)。因而引起苗分化的频率大幅度地下降，甚至降低 10 倍以上(比较 N-T3 与 N-T9)。ii.愈伤组织虽能继续生长，但始终没有分化出苗(如 K-MS2 培养基)。iii.置换后苗的分化频率不仅不降低，反而略有提高(比较 K-H1 与 B-H1)。

表 5　不同细胞分裂素对愈伤组织分化苗的影响

培养基	细胞分裂素类型		接种的愈伤组织数	分化苗的愈伤组织数	分化苗的愈伤组织占接种愈伤组织(%)
	原用(mg/L)	改用(mg/L)			
N-T3(对照)	6-苄基氨基嘌呤(1)	—	13	12	90.0
N-T9	—	激动素 (1)	13	1	7.7
N-T7(对照)	6-苄基氨基嘌呤(1)	—	13	5	38.4
N-T10	—	激动素 (1)	13	1	7.7
B-MS2(对照)	6-苄基氨基嘌呤(1)	—	9	7	77.7
K-MS2	—	激动素 (1)	15	0	0
K-H1(对照)	激动素 (1)	—	9	4	44.4
B-H1	—	6-苄基氨基嘌呤(1)	9	5	55.5

3. 根的诱导：在分化培养基上获得的苗一般没有根(通过“胚状体”发育过程形成的小苗除外)，需再转移到诱导根的培养基分化根。来源于叶老愈伤组织的再生的苗，移到 White 及修改的 H 两种组合的培养基后，都很难分化根，只有在 N-T3 分化培养基上获得的苗移到添加 0.5mg/L IAA 修改的 H 培养基上，三星期后个别苗才长根(图版 II, 5)；而来源于叶、茎新愈伤组织的再生的苗，从 N-T3—7 分化培养基上获得的苗移到 White 及修改的 H 两种组合的培养基上，一星期左右便可产生根(图版 II，6)。而从 B-MS1—2，Z-MS1 及 K-H1 获得者，只移到修改的 H 组合培养基上，1~2 星期也都诱导出根(图版 II，7)。有趣的是，在 N-T3~7 分化培养基上，来源于茎新愈伤组织的移到 White 培养基后，不久诱导出正常的根，还能常见到气根及从叶片尖端长根的现象(图版 II，8)。气根是从苗基部 1~4 节间的茎部或叶腋长出，向下长入培养基中。上述现象在相同条件下，从来源于叶新愈伤组织者偶而也能见到。

小植株长成后，移入花盆中并放到温室，就可正常生长(图版 II，9)。

三、讨论

近年来利用单倍体原生质体作为重要的研究材料，已普遍受到植物生物学和植物育种工作者的重视。Ohyama 等[4]用单倍体烟草叶片作材料，而我们用来源于单倍体叶及茎的愈伤组织的悬浮细胞作材料，其优点是：培养条件易于控制，不受季节的影响，原生质体的分裂频率较高，由原生质体再生的供诱导苗的愈伤组织数量较多，实验的重复性好。从1975年12月至1976年7月共进行了二十多次原生质体培养，基本上都获得成功。诚然，愈伤组织继代培养时间过长后，有染色体倍性变化的问题，可出现2*n*，4*n*，8*n*或其他偶数或奇数的多倍体细胞以及分化困难的问题。关于染色体倍性变化问题，林俊朗[28]归纳为由于培养基内加入椰乳或酵母提取物等等原因引起的，因此这问题可在培养基的选择上加以克服。分化困难的问题，我们的实验证明来源于继代培养三个月后的愈伤组织的原生质体再生的愈伤组织，在合适的培养基上苗的分化频率仍达100%，因此也不成为一个障碍。

众所周知，原生质体培养的分裂频率较细胞培养的分裂频率高。从来源于愈伤组织的原生质体，较来源于叶片的原生质体分裂频率高，也已为我们的实验所证明。从单倍体烟草叶片分裂的原生质体，在含蔗糖的培养基上分裂频率为45.9%[4]，而我们来源于愈伤组织的分裂频率高达70%以上。进一步的实验说明，原生质体的分裂频率和速度与不同器官(从叶还是从茎所诱导的愈伤组织)来源的材料无明显的联系，而与材料继代培养的年龄有明显的联系。来源于继代培养二年左右的愈伤组织的原生质体再生细胞后的分裂频率，较继代培养三个月左右的高，前者为70%以上，而后者约为50%；再生细胞的分裂速度快，前者是培养12~20h后原生质体就长壁变形，24~36h后完成第一次分裂，而后者要在约72h后才完成第一次分裂。这是否由于愈伤组织继代培养时间过长引起染色体倍性增加，使细胞增殖更快而引起[28]，值得进一步研究。

很多工作曾指出[28-30]，在组织培养和细胞培养中，随着继代培养时间的延长而苗的分化能力降低。不同年龄的愈伤组织来源的原生质体再生细胞后，是否还符合上述规律？我们积累了一些资料。来源于叶老愈伤组织的原生质体再生的愈伤组织苗的分化频率较低，根的诱导更为困难；而来源于叶、茎新愈伤组织的苗的分化频率高，来源于茎新愈伤组织的可高达100%，同时也容易诱导根。

植物组织在离体培养条件下器官的分化，前田英三[31]曾总结为要注意六个条件：①降低生长素浓度，或从培养基中删除生长素；②以NAA或IAA代替2，4-D；③加入细胞激动素类物质；④不加赤霉素；⑤提高氮素及其他盐浓度；⑥不使用长期继代培养过的愈伤组织。我们的实验结果表明，影响器官分化的因素有内因与外因两方面：①内因方面，除了注意上述的第六个条件即材料的年龄外；不同器官来源的材料之间也存在着差异，表现在来源于叶愈伤组织的原生质体再生的愈伤组织，不论其继代培养时间的长短，均不如茎新愈伤组织来源者高。并且对外源生长素的要求也有差别，如在N-T3~7四种分化培养基上，来源于茎新愈伤组织的苗的分化，在没有外源生长素时仍有100%的最高频率，而来源于叶老及新愈伤组织的，在同样条件下苗分化的效果并不理想(参阅表4及表5)，只在具稍高浓度的生长素(0.3~0.5mg/L IAA)时，才得到较高而稳定的苗的分化率。②外因方面，第一个因素是基本培养基的成分对苗分化的影响是显著的。从表5的实验结果可见，N-T3与B-H1二者的氮素含量差不多，但前者的硫酸镁和磷酸二氢钾的含量却比后者高得多，因而前者矿物盐的总浓度比后者高，而细胞分裂素和生长素则是相同的，结果苗的分化率前者远比后者高。表4的另一些实验也得到类似的结果。第二个因素是细胞分裂素的类型，某一种特定的基本培养基不是用那一种细胞分裂素与之配合使用都能获得好的效果，这从表5的实验结果得到证明。以N-T为基本培养基的 N-T3 培养基在用 6-BA 时，苗的分化率为 90%，改用 Kn(即 N-T9 培养基)后，却降为 7.7%，降低 10 倍以上。苗分化率降低的原因似乎不能仅用细胞分裂素本 6-BA 身活性的大小来进行解释，因为以 H 为基本培养基的 K-H_1 及 B-H_1 培养基。无论使用 kn 或时苗的分化率却差别不大，很可能除了基本培养基的成分外，多种维生素的存在也起作用。此外，在我们的实验条件下，全部的实验结果也说明，6-BA 在苗的诱导方面比 Kn 优越得多，这是否具有普遍意义，尚待更多的实验证明。

参考资料

[1] Cocking, E. C., *Nature* (Lond.), 187 (1960), 962~963
[2] Takebe, I., Labib, G. & Melchers, G., *Natur wisscnschaften*, 58 (1971), 318~320
[3] Nitsch, J. P. & Ohyama, K., *C. R. Acad. Sci.* (Paris), 273 (1971), 801~804
[4] Ohyama, K. & Nitsch, J. P., *Plant and Cell Physiol*., 13 (1972), 229~236
[5] Bajaj, Y. P. S., *Amer. J. Bot*., 59(1972),647
[6] Nagy, J. I. & Maliga, P., Z. *Pflanzenphysiol.*, 78 (1976), 453~455
[7] Grambow, H. J., Kao, K. N., Miller, R. A. & Gamborg, O. L., Planta, 103 (1972), 348~355
[8] Kameya, T. & Uchimiya, H., *Planta*, 103 (1972), 356~360
[9] Durand, J., Potrykus, I. & Donn, G., *Z. Pflanzenphysiol*., 69 (1973), 26~34
[10] Hayward, G., & Power, J. B., *Plant Sci. Lett.*, 4 (1975), 407~410
[11] Bui Dang-Ha, D., Norrcel, D., & Masset, A. L., *Exp. Bot*., 26 (1975), 263~237
[12] Kartha, K. K., Michayluk, M. R., Kao, K. N., Gamborg, O. L. & Constabel, F., *Plant Sci. Lett*., 3 (1974), 265~271
[13] Prat, R., Poirier-Hamon Simone, *Protoplasma*, 86 (1975), 175~188
[14] Schieder, O., *Z. Pflanzenphysiol*, 76 (1975), 462~466
[15] Darion, N., Chupeau, Y. & Bourgin, J. P., *Plant Sci. Lett*., 5 (1975), 325~331
[16] Gosch, C., Bajaj, Y. P. S., & Reinert, J., *Protoplasma*, 86 (1975), 405~410
[17] Mclchers, G. & Labib, G., *Molcc. Gen. Genet*., 135 (1974), 277~294
[18] Carlson. P. S., Samith, H. H. & Dearing, R. D., *Proc. Natl. Acad. Sci.* (USA), 69 (1972), 2292~2294
[19] Jones, C. W., Mastrangclo, I. A., Smith, H. H. & Lin, H. A., *Science*, 193 (1976), 401~403
[20] Kao, K. N., Constabel, F., Michayluk, M. R. Gamborg, O. L., *Planta*, 120 (1974), 215~228
[21] Carlson, P. S., *Proc. Nalt. Acad, Sci*. (USA), 70(1973), 598~602
[22] 中国科学院北京植物研究所细胞杂交组、细胞生化组，中国科学，1975，6，602~605
[23] 郭仲琛、王玉英、钱南芬、顾淑荣、龚明良、徐惠君，植物学报，15 (973), 37~48
[24] Murashige, T. & Skoog, F., *Physiol. Plant*., 15 (1962), 473~497
[25] Nitsch, J. P. & Nitch, C., *Science*, 163 (1969), 85~87
[26] Nagata, T. & Takebe, I., *Planta*, 99 (1971), 12~20
[27] White, P. R., The Cultivation of Animal and Plant Cells. 1963, 2nd Edt. *Ronald Press*, New York
[28] 林俊郎，遗伝，24 (1970), 16~23
[29] Bouharmont, J., *La Cellule*, 69 (1971), 81~109
[30] 王敬驹、孙敬三、朱至清，植物学报，16 (1974), 43~54
[31] 前田英三，日本作物学会纪事，41 (1972), 269~283

图 版 I

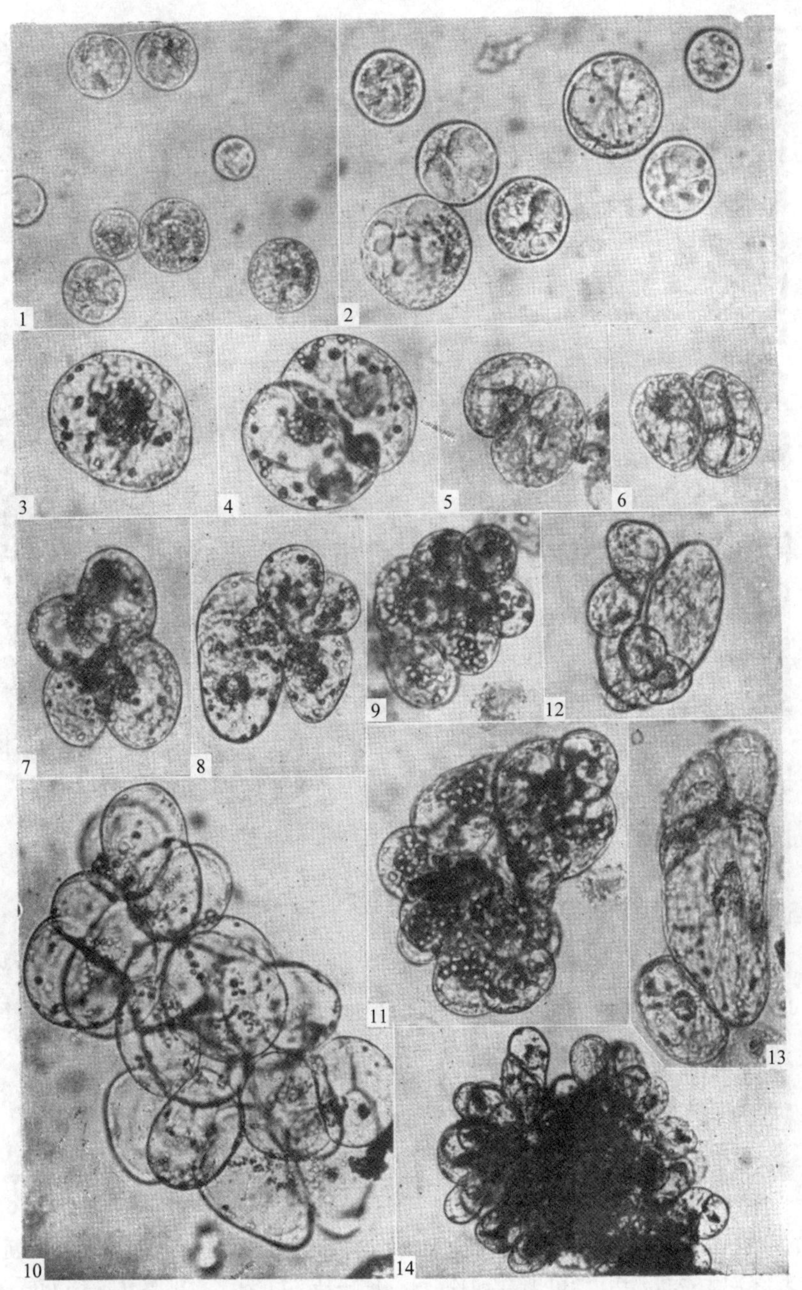

1. 从烟草茎新愈伤组织的悬浮细胞新分离的原生质体；2. 从烟草叶片老愈伤组织的悬浮细胞新分离的原生质体；3. 原生质体体积增大变为卵圆形，细胞壁已明显可见；4. 从一个原生质体起源的 2 个细胞，均等分裂；5~6. 从一个原生质体起源的 2 个细胞，不等分裂；7~8. 从一个原生质体起源的 4 个细胞的细胞团，图 8 示细胞偏向一边分裂；9. 从一个原生质体起源的 8 个细胞的细胞团；10. 从一个原生质体起源的 20 多个细胞的细胞团；11. 从一个原生质体起源的 10 多个细胞的细胞团；12. 从一个原生质体起源的 8 个细胞的细胞团，示细胞偏向一边分裂；13. 从一个原生质体起源的 5 个细胞，从细胞两端进行细胞分裂；14. 从一个原生质体起源的小愈伤组织(×80)；图 1~13 均为×240

图 版 II

1~3. 在 N-T3 分化培养基上再生的苗，1. 来源于叶老愈伤组织的原生质体；2. 来源于叶新愈伤组织的原生质体；3. 来源于茎新愈伤组织的原生质体；4. 在 N-T9 培养基上，细胞分裂素改换后对愈伤组织再生苗的影响(在 N-T3 对照培养基上苗的再生与图 2 相类似)；5. 从叶老愈伤组织原生质体再生的植株；在 N-T3 培养基上再生的苗，转移到添加 0.5mg/L IAA 的修改 H 培养基约 6 星期后照相；6. 从茎新愈伤组织原生质体再生的植株；在 N-T3 培养基上再生的苗，转移到不加生长素的 White 培养基约 6 星期后照相；7. 从叶新愈伤组织原生质体再生的植株；在 Z-MS1 培养基上再生的苗，转移到添加 0.3mg/L IAA 的修改 H 培养基约 2 星期后照相；8. 从茎新愈伤组织原生质体再生的植株，示正常根、气根及叶片尖端长根；9. 移入盆栽的原生质体再生的植株(0.7 倍)；图 1~8 均比原来大小略小

本文原载：植物学报. 1978. 20(2): 97-102

水稻(*Oryza sativa* L.)原生质体分离与培养的进一步研究

蔡起贵　钱迎倩　周云罗　吴素萱

(中国科学院植物研究所)

摘　要　在过去工作[1]的基础上，改进了原生质体的分离技术、培养基及培养条件，成功地获得了大量水稻原生质体再生的愈伤组织。讨论了得到实验重复结果所需要的主要条件。

近年来植物原生质体的研究越来越引起人们的重视，并已有大量的文献详细论述了其在理论上和实践上的重要意义[2,3,5,11, 13,14,16,18]。但迄今能从原生质体长成完整植株的植物种类为数不多。在重要的经济作物中仅棉花和某些豆科植物的原生质体能重复分裂并形成愈伤组织[10,11,13]。为了使原生质体的研究在粮食作物的改良和新品种培育方面发挥作用，世界各国都在大力从事禾本科作物，特别是禾谷类作物原生质体培养的研究，但还未看到有再生成植株的报道。除 Deka 等[15]从水稻叶鞘起源的原生质体再生的愈伤组织能够分化出根外，在多数情况下，原生质体经过培养能膨大、变形、再生细胞壁，并仅在一段时间内保持存活或偶尔发生分裂[11,12,17,22,23,25,28,29]；少数情况下甚至能形成愈伤组织[4,20,21,24,26]，但多数不能进一步生长。

我们于 1975 年曾报道了从水稻单倍体愈伤组织起源的原生质体能再生 30 多个细胞的细胞团[1] ，本文报道近年来我们改进了原生质体的分离技术、培养基及培养条件，成功地获得了原生质体再生大量愈伤组织的结果。

材料与方法

1. 原生质体的来源

制备水稻(品种“廉江密早”)原生质体的程序与制备烟草[6]原生质体的一样，只是某些细节稍有不同，步骤如下：①白花药培养所产生的单倍体愈伤组织[7]是本室单倍体育种组提供的。②将愈伤组织转移到 LB 培养基(表 1)上进行继代培养，获得两种愈伤组织：一种色金黄、质地较紧密；另一种色浅黄、质地稍松。本工作使用了后一种愈伤组织。培养条件为温度 28 ± 2℃、光强约 1300lx、每天光照约 10h，每隔 8d 左右转移一次。③使用了培养 20 个月以后的愈伤组织。在每次分离原生质体前将约 3g 的愈伤组织移进内盛 25ml 细胞悬浮培养基(表 1)的 100ml 三角瓶中，并放到垂直旋转的转床(8 转/分)上，在 28±2℃、不加光照下进行悬浮培养，培养约 8d 即可使用。

2. 原生质体的分离

在无菌条件下，把旋转培养约 8 天进行旺盛细胞分裂的悬浮培养物经离心处理收集，加人约 8ml 通过微孔滤器(孔径为 0.45μm)过滤灭菌的酶混合液后，倒进 100ml 三角瓶中。酶混合液的组成为：4%(W/V，下同)纤维素酶 (Onozuka R-10，Kniki Yakult Mfg. Co., Ltd., Nishinomiya, Japan)，0.6%离析酶(Macerozyme R-10, Kniki Yakulr Mfg. Co., Ltd., Nishinomiya, Japan)，0.2%半纤维素酶(Koch-Light Laborarories Ltd., Colnbrook Bucks, England)，0.2 %葡聚糖硫酸钾(含硫量 18%)，1mM $CaC1_2 \cdot 2H_2O$ 及 0.8M 甘露醇，把 pH 调到 5.4。先在室温下放置约 0.5h，然后在 34℃恒温水浴中静置培育约 3.5h。混合物用 300 目不锈钢丝网过滤，除去残渣。通过离心(80 × g)从混合液中将原生质体分离出来，并用含 1mM $CaC1_2 \cdot 2H_2O$ 的 0.6M 甘露醇溶液洗涤两次，最后用培养原生质体的相应培养基(表 1)洗涤一次。

表 1　愈伤组织、悬浮细胞和原生质体培养基的组成(mg/L)

培养基成分	愈伤组织继代培养基[2)]	细胞悬浮培养基[2)]	原生质体培养基		
			培养基 I	培养基 II	培养基 III
KNO_3	1900	2830	2200	1900	1900
NH_4NO_3	1000	—	—	360	—
$(NH_4)_2SO_4$	—	462	67	—	67
$MgSO_4 \cdot 7H_2O$	35	185	185	370	370
KCl	65	—	—	—	—
$CaCl_2$	—	166	166	450	450
$Ca(NO_3)_2 \cdot 4H_2O$	347	—	—	—	—
KH_2PO_4	300	400	400	200	200
Na_2-EDTA	37.3	37.3	18.7	18.7	18.7
$FeSO_4 \cdot 7H_2O$	27.8	27.8	13.9	13.9	13.9
$MnSO_4 \cdot 4H_2O$	4.4	4.4	4.4	22.3	22.3
$ZnSO_4 \cdot 7H_2O$	1.5	1.5	1.5	10.0	10.0
H_3BO_3	1.6	1.6	1.6	10.0	10.0
KI	0.8	0.8	0.8	—	—
$Na_2MoO_4 \cdot 2H_2O$	0.05	—	—	0.25	0.25
$CuSO_4 \cdot 5H_2O$	0.005	—	—	0.025	0.025
$CaCl_2 \cdot 6H_2O$	0.005	—	—	0.025	0.025
肌醇	20	—	—	—	—
烟酸	0.5	0.5	0.5	0.5	0.5
甘氨酸	2	2	2	2	2
盐酸硫胺素	0.5	1	1	1	1
盐酸吡哆素	0.1	0.5	0.5	0.5	0.5

续表

培养基成分	愈伤组织继代培养基 2)	细胞悬浮培养基 2)	原生质体培养基		
			培养基 I	培养基 II	培养基 III
水解乳蛋白	100	500	250	250	250
椰乳	2.5%(V/V)	—	—	—	—
2, 4-D	2	1	1	1	1
激动素	—	0.1	—	—	—
6-苄基氨基嘌呤	—	—	0.2~0.5	0.5	0.5
甘露醇	—	—	0.4*M*	0.4*M*	0.4*M*
蔗糖	30 000	40 000	10 000	10 000	10 000
D-葡萄糖	—	—	1000	1000	1000
琼脂	10 000	—	—	—	—
pH1)	5.8	5.6~5.8	5.6	5.6	5.6

1) 均为热压消毒前用 1*N* NaOH 调整到的数值。

2) 简称为 LB 培养基。

3) 修改的 N_6[7]培养基。

3. 原生质体的培养及愈伤组织的再生

将 1ml 原生质体悬浮液(密度约为 4 × 10°原生质体/ml)倒进 20~25ml 有磨口瓶塞的三角瓶中，用纱布及牛皮纸包口。培养方法有二：①先把培养物放在光强 1250lx、每天光照约 10h，温度 28℃(日)及 26℃(夜)下静置培养 10~14d，再移到 26℃下不加光照处静置培养；②直接把培养物放在 26℃下不加光照处培养。无论用何种培养方法，培养的头几天每天均需轻轻摇动一次，以防止原生质体黏附在培养瓶底壁。并用倒置显微镜观察原生质体的发育过程。培养后约 6~8 星期，当最大的愈伤组织长到 0.5~1mm 大小时，用 5~6ml 除去甘露醇、D-葡萄糖而蔗糖浓度提高到 3%的相应原生质体培养基稀释原生质体培养物，并移进 50ml 的乳头锥形瓶中，放到转床(1 转/分)上进行旋转培养，培养物在近光源处约为 2000lx 和远光源处约为 170lx 的光强度下，每天光照约 10h，温度为 28±2℃。培养约 5 星期后，取出较大的愈伤组织转移到诱导分化培养基上。余下的小愈伤组织再加入 3~4ml 新鲜培养基，在转床上继续旋转培养 2~3 星期。

结果

1. 原生质体的分裂及愈伤组织的再生

采用水稻单倍体愈伤组织，通过一次悬浮培养后获得的悬浮培养物新分离出来的原生质体，无论在形态或其他性状上都与过去直接用愈伤组织新分离得到的原生质体[1]相类似，但也有差别：①利用悬浮培养物分离获得的原生质体数量远比直接用愈伤组织获得的多，质量也较好(图版 I，1)；②悬浮培养来源的原生质体一般含有稍多及较大的颗粒内含物，故有时不易看到其细胞核；③原生质体群中一般未见到混有未去壁的老细胞。

在培养后的头两星期内，原生质体的发育过程与过去报道[1]的情况差不多，但在此期间除了在变形长壁的再生细胞中有极少数具有浓厚的细胞质而引人注意外，一般既未看到再生细胞产生质壁分离的现象，也不易看到原生质体分裂。原生质体的分裂往往发生在培养两星期以后，第一次分裂一旦发生，分裂便能持续进行下去。无论采用何种培养基和培养方法，一般培养约 4 星期，原生质体便可再生成大小约 0.5ml 的愈伤组织；培养约 6 星期后最大的愈伤组织(在培养基 I 及 III 中)可达约 1ml(图版 I，2)。

当用降低总糖浓度的原生质体培养基稀释培养物，并在转床上作旋转培养后，培养物便活跃地分裂和生长，在原有的小愈伤组织长大的同时还新形成了数以千计的小愈伤组织(图版 I，3)。它们的来源可能有两条途径：①原生质体在静置培养时由其再生的细胞虽能存活但不分裂，经旋转培养后，由于培养条件的适合又能进行分裂而形成；②在旋转培养过程中，有些较大的愈伤组织在生长过程中由于边缘较松，在培养液的轻微冲击下，脱落的小细胞团进一步分裂形成。旋转培养约 5 星期后，最大的愈伤组织可达 2mm 左右，取出 0.5mm 以上的愈伤组织移到诱导分化培养基上(图版 I，4)，余下的加进新鲜培养基继续旋转培养 2~3 星期，最大的愈伤组织又可达到 1mm 左右。

2. 在不同培养基中原生质体再生愈伤组织的比较

实验结果表明，静置培养期间，在培养基 II 中原生质体再生出肉眼可见的愈伤组织最多，达到 60~70 块(最大的 0.5mm 左右)；培养基 III 次之，达到 40~50 块(最大的约 1mm)；培养基 I 最少，只有 20~40 块(最大的超过 1mm)。而在加入降低总糖浓度的同样培养基并移到转床上进行旋转培养期间，虽然都可得到无数各种大小的愈伤组织，但最后获得 0.5mm 以上的、可用于进行诱导分化的愈伤组织数量却与上述情况相反，以在培养基 I 中获得的最多，一般经过两次旋转培养后总共得到 100 块左右，愈伤组织的质地较致密；培养基 III 次之，总共得到约 60~80 块，愈伤组织的质地也较致密；培养基 II 则最少，总共只有约 30~40 块，愈伤组织的质地一般稍松。由此可见，不同的培养基不仅对原生质体再生愈伤组织的数量及大小有影响，并且对其质地也有影响。

讨论

许多资料指出，禾谷类作物原生质体的培养不易发生分裂，更难于再生愈伤组织和植株。这是进行细胞杂交工作的严重障碍。如何克服这一障碍，引起了国内外许多从事原生质体培养工作者的关注，其中 Cocking[13]和 Bhojwani 等[11]提出了一些很有参考价值的建议。我们在过去对水稻原生质体分离和培养的基础上[1]，进行了较大的改进，即采用了烟草[6]原生质体的分离与培养的程序。我们曾指出这一程序具有的某些优点。对水稻原生质体培养获得的结果进一步证明了其优越性。根据多次的实验结果表明，在我们现在的条件下，欲获得可重复的良好结果，以下几点是值得注意的：①要有一个良好的愈伤组织继代培养基，在特定的培养条件下使愈伤组织能稳定而持续地生长；②要有一个较好的细胞悬浮培养基，在旋转培养过程中愈伤组织既要较易于分散(与愈伤组织本身的质地有关)，其细胞又能不断地进行分裂。经过这一步骤的好处是：①细胞易于去壁。在前一报道[1]中，我们是直接将 1~2g 愈伤组织移进 15ml 酶混合液中去壁，所获得的原生质体最多不超过 10^6 个，现在用类似容积(16ml)的酶混合液，分为两半分别加进两瓶细胞悬浮物中(参阅材料与方法)，则获得的原生质体最多时超过 32×10^6 个，两者原生质体的产量相差极大。②许多工作者[2]用叶片细胞分离原生质体时，强调了叶片的预处理对细胞的去壁、原生质体的质量及其后的分裂有很大的、甚至关键性的影响。我们把在琼脂培养基上继代培养的愈伤组织，在每次分离原生质体前经过一次悬浮培养，在某种意义上也可视为一种预处理。实验结果表明，不仅获得的原生质体数量多、质量好，更重要的是它们更能适应以后液体培养的环境。③愈伤组织的继代培养及悬浮培养的条件(如温度、转移及取材时间等)均需保持相对的恒定。如在本文中所描述的条件下，我们所获得的结果是可重复的，但如将愈伤组织在温度为 28 ± 2℃ (日)及约 24℃(夜)下每隔 14d 继代培养一次，最后一次继代培养约 14d 后再移进液体培养基中作旋转悬浮培养，培养 10d 后的悬浮培养物经去壁后获得的原生质体，在形态特征上与在目前条件下培养所获得的原生质体无明显差别，但通过几次培养均失败了。可能是由于培养条件、转移及取材时间的改变影响到细胞的年龄及原生质体的生理状态所造成的结果。这与某些作者[8,9,19]在用叶片作材料时，注意到植株的生长条件、叶片的年龄及其生理状态对原生质体的产量、活力及其分裂有影响的结果基本上是一致的。④需要有极高的原生质体密度(约 4×10^6 原生质体/ml)，才能保证原生质体的持续分裂及再生愈伤组织。⑤要有一个较好的原生质体培养基。

在原生质体培养中关于铵盐对原生质体的影响虽有一些报道，但结果差别很大。如 Upadhya[27]指出，在培养基中即使只含有 100mg/L 的硝酸铵或氯化铵就会导致马铃薯原生质体在 2~3d 内死亡，因而在他的培养基中不加按盐；而 Bhojwani 等[10]则强调在培养基中补加硝酸铵(250mg/L)和氯化钙(最终浓度为 780mg/L)，对棉花原生质体的存活和随后的细胞分裂是必需的。我们在水稻原生质体培养基中作了加入硝酸铵(360mg/L)或硫酸铵(67mg/L)的对比试验(比较培养基 II 与 III)。结果表明，在静置培养期间，硝酸铵对促进原生质体的分裂及愈伤组织再生的效果比硫酸铵好，因前者再生的愈伤组织数量较多。但在旋转培养期间，则发现硝酸铵对愈伤组织的进一步生长有不利的影响，表现在愈伤组织不易长大，因此，以后获得用于诱导分化的愈伤组织数量反而比用硫酸铵的少。其原因并不是硝酸铵抑制愈伤组织的生长，而是它有使愈伤组织质地变松的作用，因此，在旋转培养过程中不断地有小细胞团从大愈伤组织上脱落到培养液中，结果便导致大愈伤组织数量减少，而小愈伤组织却增加到数以千计的原因之一。培养基 I 获得的结果与培养基 III 的差不多(它们的基本培养基成分虽不同，但硫酸铵的含量一样)，这说明在旋转培养的条件下硫酸铵对愈伤组织的生长有好的作用，并且其质地也较致密。

关于诱导分化的工作正在进行中。

参考文献

[1] 中国科学院北京植物研究所细胞杂交组、细胞生化组, 1975: 水稻原生质体的分离和培养. 中国科学, (6): 602~605

[2] 中国科学院北京植物研究所细胞杂交组, 1977: 植物原生质体培养的研究进展. 植物学报, 19(4): 297~305

[3] 中国科学院北京植物研究所细胞杂交组, 1977: 植物体细胞杂交。中国农业科学, (4): 18~25

[4] 兰州大学生物系细胞室, 1977: 黑麦叶肉原生质体的分离、培养与幼小愈伤组织的形成. 遗传学报, 4(3): 242~247

[5] 李向辉, 1975: 体细胞杂交. 遗传与育种，(1): 30~31

[6] 蔡起贵、钱迎倩、周云罗、吴素萱, 1977: 烟草(*Nicotiana tabacum*)原生质体再生成植株及影响植株分化的某些因素。中国科学, (4): 347~354

[7] 朱至清、王敬驹、孙敬三、徐振、朱之垠、尹光初、毕凤云, 1975: 通过氮源比较试验建立一种较好的水稻花药培养基. 中国科学, (5): 484~490

[8] 上海植物生理研究所细胞杂交组, 1977: 烟草叶肉细胞原生质体培养成植株的研究. 遗传学报, 4(3): 233~241

[9] Arnold, S. V. & T. Eriksson, 1976: Factors influencing the growth and division of pea mesophyll protoplasts. *Physiol. Plant*, 36:193~196

[10] Bhojwani, S. S., J. B. Power & E. C. Cocking, 1977: Isolation, culture, and division of cotton protoplasts. *Plant Sci. Lett*., 8: 85~89

[11] Bhojwani, S. S., P. K. Evans & E. C. Cocking, 1977: Protoplast technology in relation to crop plants: Progress and problems. *Euphytica*, 26: 343~369

[12] Brenneman, F. N. & A. W. Galston, 1975: Experiments on the cultivation of protoplasts and calli of agriculturally important plant 1. Oats (*Avena sativa L*). *Biochem. Physiol. Pflanzen*, 168, S. 388

[13] Cocking, E. C., 1977: Plant protoplast fusion: Progress and prospects for agriculture, In: Recombinent molecules: Impact on science and society. Ed. by Beers, R. F. et al., Raven Press, New York

[14] ———, 1976: Fusion and somatic hybridization of higher plant protoplasts. In: Microbial and plant protoplasts, Ed. by Peberdy, J. F. et al., Academic Press

[15] Deka, P. C. & S. K. Sen, 1976: Differentiation in calli originated from isolated protoplast of rice (*oryza sativa* L.) through plating technique. *Molec. gen. Genet*., 145: 239~243

[16] Eriksson, T., H. T. Bonnett，K. Glimelius & A.，Wallin，1974: Technical advances in protoplast isolation, culture and fusion, In: Tissue culture and plant science, Ed. by Street, H. E. Academic Press, London, New York

[17] Evans, P. K., A. G. Keates & E. C. Cocking, 1972: Isolation of protoplasts from cereal leaves, *Planta*, 104 178~181

[18] Gamborg, O. L., F. Constabel, K. N. Kao & K. Ohyama, 1975: Plant protoplasts in genetie modification and production of intergenetic hybrids, In: Modification of the information contend of plant cell, Ed. by Mackham, R. et al., North Holland Publishing Co

[19] Kartha, K. K., M. R. Michayluk, K. N. Kao, O. L. Gambory & F. Constabel, 1974: Callus formation and plant regeneration from mesophyll protoplasts of rape plants (*Brassica napus* L. cv. Zephyr). *Plant Sci. Lett*., 3: 265~271

[20] Koblitz, H., 1976: Isolierung und Kultivierung von Protoplasten aus Calluskulturen der Gerste. *Biochem. Physiol. Pflanzen*, 170: 287~293

[21] Krishnamurthi, M., 1976: Isolation, fusion and multiplication of sugarcane protoplasts and comparison of sexual and parasexual hybridization. *Euphytica*, 31: 1281~1283

[22] Maeda, E., 1971: Isolation of protoplast from seminal roots of rice. *Proc. Crop. Sci. Soc. Jap*., 40: 397~398

[23] ——— & T. Hatwara, 1974: Enzymatic isolation,of protoplasts from the rice leaves and callus cultures. *Proc. Crop; Sci. Soc. Jap*., 43: 68~76

[24] Maretzki, A. & L. G. Nickell, 1973: Formation of protoplasts from sugarcane cell suspensions and the regeneration of cell cultures from protoplasts. *Colloq. Int. Cent. Nat. Rech. Sci*., 212: 51~63

[25] Motoyoshi, F., 1971: Protoplasts isolated from callus cells of maize endosperm: Formation of multinucleate protoplasts and nuclear division. *Exp. Cell Res*., 68: 452~456

[26] Potrykus, I., C. T. Harms H. Lörz. & E. Thomas, 1977: Callus formation from stem protoplasts of corn (*Zea mays* L.). *Molec. gen. Genet*., 156: 347~350

[27] Upadhya, M. D., 1975: Isolation and culture of mesophyll protoplasts of potato (*Solanum tuberosum* L.). *Potato Res*., 18: 438~445

[28] Vasil, V. & I. K. Vasil, 1974: Regeneration of tobacco and petunia plants from protoplasts and culture of corn protoplasts. *In Vitro*, 10: 83~96

[29] Wenzel, G., 1973: Isolation of leaf protoplasts from haploid plants of petunia, rape, and rye, Z. *Pflzücht*., 69: 58~61

图 版 I

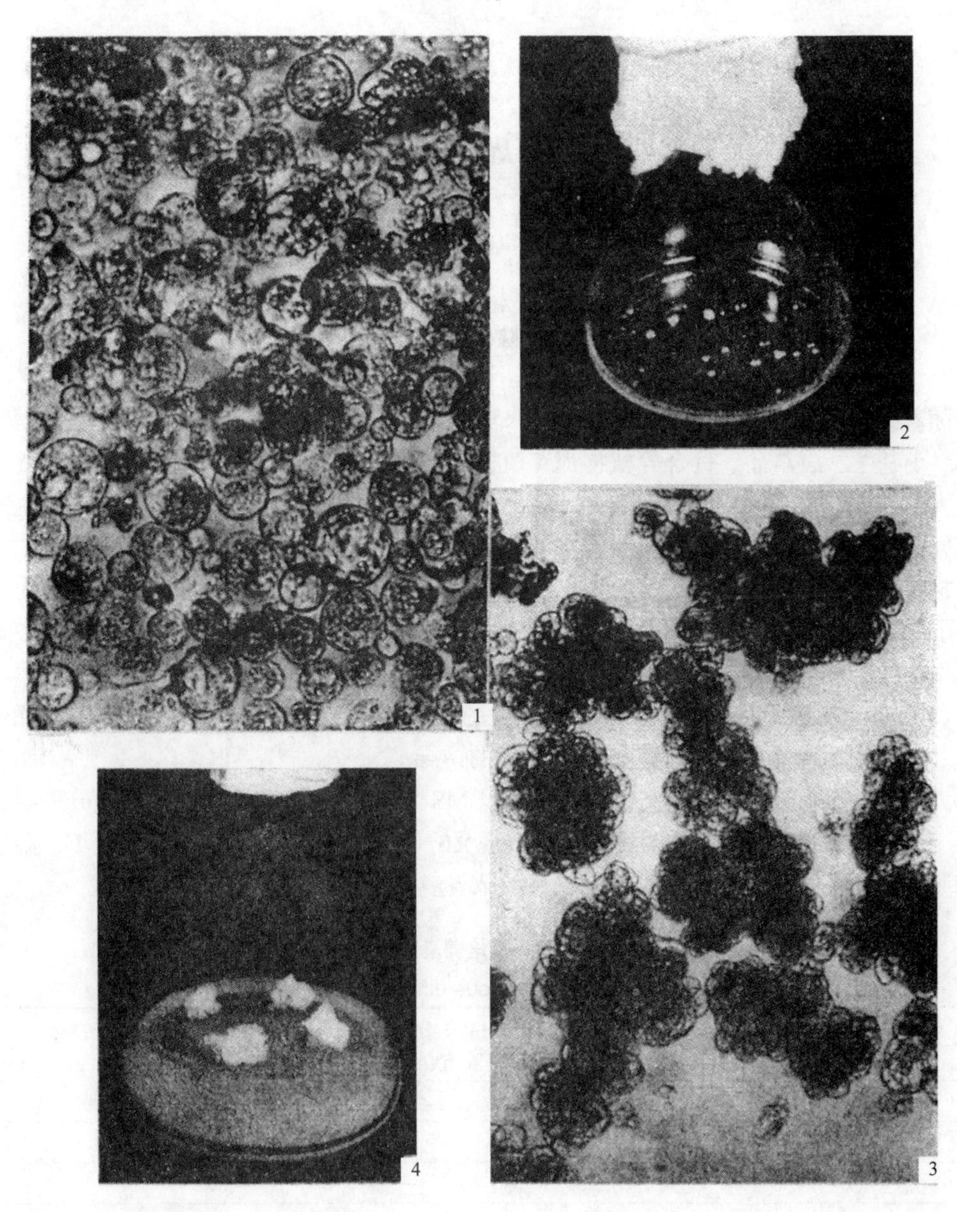

1. 从水稻悬浮细胞新分离的原生质体。×300 2. 在培养基I中培养约6星期后由原生质体再生的愈伤组织。×1.2 3. 经旋转培养后由原生质体再生的小愈伤组织。×120 4. 由原生质体再生的愈伤组织移到诱导分化培养基1个月后的生长情况。×0.7

本文原载：植物学报. 1980. 22(4): 402-403

从大蒜贮藏叶诱导愈伤组织及植株再生

周云罗　钱迎倩　蔡起贵　吴素萱

(中国科学院植物研究所)

随着组织培养技术的进展，70 年代以来鳞茎植物的组织培养也不断有所开展。洋葱、芦荟、小苍兰、唐菖蒲、百合等植物都有植株的再生[3,4]。Havranek 等[1]用贮藏了 4~6 个月的大蒜卷叠在贮藏叶内部的营养叶作为外植体，再生了苗及扁化的畸形根，但再生的器官并无任何联系。本文以大蒜贮藏叶作为外植体，获得了正常生长的再生植株。

材料取自市场的食用大蒜 (*Allium sativum*. L.) 未经萌动的肉质、瓣状小鳞茎在无菌条件下去掉保护叶(大蒜鳞茎形态学参看 Mann[2])，用锋利的解剖刀把贮藏叶切成长、宽和深度各约为 3mm 的小块。然后把小块接到 MS 基本培养基并附加有 500mg/L 水解乳蛋白、1000mg/L 酵母提取物、2mg/L 2，4-D 的培养基上。培养物在 28℃，两根 40 瓦荧光灯，每天约 10h 光照条件下进行愈伤组织的诱导。

为使器官进行分化，把愈伤组织转移到以 MS 为基本培养基(含 5%蔗糖)并分别附加有 6-苄基腺嘌呤、萘乙酸、吲哚乙酸、激动素及酵母提取物的分化培养基上(表 1)。温度及光照条件同上。已分化出苗和根的植株移入花盆中使其继续生长。

表 1　不同分化培养基的组成

Table 1　The components of various differentiation culture media

培养基 Culture Medium	激动素 Kinetin (mg/L)	萘乙酸 NAA(mg/L)	6-苄基腺嘌呤 6-BA(mg/L)	吲哚乙酸 IAA(mg/L)	酵母提取物 Yeast Extract (mg/L)
MS-1	—	—	—	—	—
MS-2	—	0.01	2	—	—
MS-3	—	—	2	0.05	—
MS-4	2	—	—	2	—
MS-5	2	2	—	—	—
MS-6	—	2	0.05	—	—
MS-7	—	—	0.05	1	—
MS-8	—	1	0.05	—	—
MS-9	—	—	0.05	—	800
MS-10	0.5	—	0.05	5	800

为了解球状体的内部结构，对覆盖有球状体的愈伤组织使用1%果胶酶进行了分离，并用石蜡切片法作了组织学的观察。材料用卡诺固定液固定，切片厚度为 10μm，铁矾苏木精染色。主要结果报道如下。

1. 愈伤组织的诱导和球状体的形成

大蒜贮藏叶在上述条件下培养，3d 后就能见到少数外植体开始膨大，10d 左右即有愈伤组织出现。

愈伤组织产生之后不久，其整个表面为许多表面光滑的小球状体所覆盖(图 1)。对球状体的组织切片及用果胶酶分离的产物进行观察，说明了它们是一种内部组织已经很好分化了的愈伤组织。除了可以看到排列整齐的薄壁细胞，及散布在其中的一团团分裂旺盛、细胞质很浓的细胞团(图 2)外，还可看到管状细胞，后者在经果胶酶分离的球状体中尤为明显。这些球状体具分生组织的能力，当把它们作继代培养后，又会长出新的球状体。

2. 苗的分化

当愈伤组织转移到具各种不同激素成分的分化培养基上(表 1)，经过一个月左右，在表 1 所列的 10 种分化培养基上都有苗的分化。MS-l 是不附加有任何激素的基本培养基，大蒜愈伤组织在这样的培养基上也有苗的分化，其分化频率可高达 40%。如果分化培养基中具有适量的细胞分裂素和生长素，并且两者比例配合得合适时(如 MS-2 和 MS-3)，苗的分化频率可高达 80%。在后两种培养基上虽然苗的分化频率一致，但后者的苗却较前者的弱。至于培养物在 MS-4~10 培养基上的情况，虽然它们的分化率都在 40%以下，但在 MS-5，6，7，10 四种培养基上形成的苗要比在 MS-4，8, 9 上的多。

3. 根的分化

在 MS-l，3 培养基上分化的苗一般不易出根。但如果把这些苗转移到 H 培养基[4]并附加有 0.01~0.1mg/L 吲哚乙酸的分化培养基上后，有一部分能分化出根，还有一部分能分化出不正常的鸡爪根。

在 MS-4~10 培养基上，经一个月后，不仅有更多小苗的分化，而且还有很多根的分化。如果把形成的小苗单株分开，并再次转移到 MS-4~10 的培养基上。三周后在 MS-4, 6, 7 培养基上有 40%以上的苗长根(图 3)。而在 MS-5, 8, 9, 10 培养基上却只有 10%的苗有根的分化。将这些分化出苗和根的再生植株移栽花盆后，能继续正常生长(图 4)。

除了正常的再生植株外，我们还可以见到分化出正常的小鳞茎(图 5)，以及各种形态不正常的成瓣状的肉质小鳞片。同时在一个外植体诱导物上可以同时化出有苗、根及不正常的肉质瓣状小鳞片(图 6)。

大蒜储藏叶来源的外植体诱导出愈伤组织后不久，其整个表面被大小不等的球状体所覆盖，这种球状体结构在从营养叶诱导的愈伤组织上曾得到过[3]。Havranek 等认为这种球状体是具分生组织能力、有结构的组织，但它们不会产生任何茎或根的原基，最后停止了发育。而在我们的实验中却发现大量的苗和根都是从球状体上分化出来的(图 7、图 8)，如上所述，在球状体的组织切片上看到的分裂旺盛、细胞质很浓的细胞团，其中的一些可能就是今后分化茎或根的原基。至于是否所有的器官都只能由球状体分化而来,有待进一步的研究。

参考文献

[1] Havránek, P. and F. J. Novák, 1973: The bud formation in the callus cultures of *Allium sativum* L., *Z. Pflanzenphysiol*, 68: s. 308~318

[2] Mann, L. K., 1958: Anatomy of the garlic bulb and factors affecting bulb development, *Hilgardia*, 21: 195~251

[3] Narayanaswary，S., 1977: Regeneration of plants from tissue cultures, In: Applied and Fundamental Aspects of Plant Cell, Tissue, and Organ Culture, Edt. by J. Reinert and Y. P. S. Bajaj, pp. 178~206, Springer-Verlag

[4] Nitsch, J. P., 1969: Experimental androgenesis in *Nicotiana. Phytomorphology* 10: 389~404

图 版 I

Plate I

图 1. 大蒜愈伤组织的表面全部被球状体所覆盖。图 2. 球状体的纵切面，示球状体内部具一团团细胞质浓厚的细胞团(箭头所示)，这就是根或茎的原基。图 3. 完整的再生植株。图 4. 生长在花盆里的大蒜小植株。图 5 . 再生的大蒜小鳞茎。图 6. 在一堆球状体上分化出的根、茎及肉质小鳞片(箭头示根)。图 7. 示苗与根是球状体分化而来的。图 8. 第 7 图右上角的放大

Fig.1 The surface of garlic calli is covered by gloublas. Fig.2 Longitudinal section of globula, a cluster of cells (Arrow shows), which is the Primodium of root or shoot, with dense cytoplasm situate within it. Fig.3 The regenerated plantlet of garlic. Fig.4 Garlic plantlet growing in the pot. Fig.5 Regenerated bulblet of garlic. Fig.6 Root, shoot and succulent clove differentiated from globulas Arrow shows the root. Fig.7 Differentiated shoot and root derived from globulas. Fig. 8 The magnification of the right upper corner of Fig. 7

本文原载：植物学报. 1985. 27(2): 148-150

龙胆叶肉原生质体再生愈伤组织的研究

周云罗[1]　钱迎倩[1]　蔡起贵[1]　张治国[2]　严霄[2]

(1 中国科学院植物研究所；2 浙江人民卫生实验院药物研究所)

摘　要　从龙胆试管苗的叶肉细胞分离得原生质体。培养 4~5d 后能见到第一次分裂，一个月后形成肉眼可见的小愈伤组织。试管苗的低温预处理是龙胆叶肉原生质体能否分裂的重要条件；似乎只有体积小的原生质体能保持持续分裂。获得的愈伤组织正在诱导器官分化。

关键词　原生质体；龙胆

龙胆(*Gentiana scabra* Bunge)是一种常用的清肝胆实火、除下焦湿热的中药。其根和根茎具健胃、降压和保肝利胆等多种效能。近年来，野生资源大量减少，作者之一用组织培养方法快速繁殖龙胆草已做了初步工作[2]。

本研究的目的是试图通过原生质体培养以获得再生植株，从中挑选出药效高的克隆结合快速繁殖能在生产中应用。并为龙胆与其他种进行体细胞杂交作准备，以达到改良药用植物的目的。

材料与方法

1. 试管苗的培育

取龙胆种子在 0.1% L 汞溶液中灭菌 15min，经无菌水冲洗数次后置于培养基上培养。培养基组成如下：MS[6]基本培养基，附加有激动素 5mg/L，萘乙酸 0.25mg/L 和水解乳蛋白 500mg/L，蔗糖浓度为 3%。种子在此培养基中萌发并长成幼苗。再切取无菌苗在改变了激素种类和浓度(0.5mg/L 吲哚乙酸，0.2mg/L 玉米素和附加 0.05mg/L 生物素)的上述 MS 培养基上继代培养。在 28 ± 2℃，1300lx 光照 10h 的条件下获得生长良好的试管苗。

2. 原生质体制备及培养

在分离原生质体前，试管苗先在 4℃左右冰箱内进行预处理。取经过低温预处理约一个月的试管苗的顶端新生幼嫩叶片，去掉下表皮后，放在混合酶溶液内分离原生质体。混合酶液是由 1%纤维素酶 Onozuka R-10 (Kinki Yakult Mfg. Co., Ltd., Japan)，0.8%离析酶 Macerozyme R-10 (Kinki Yakult Mfg. Co., Ltd. , Japan) , 7m*M* $CaCl_2$, $2H_2O$, 0.6m*M*

NaH_2PO_4, 3m*M* MES (2-(N-Morpholino) ethansulfonic acid)——和 0.7*M* 葡萄糖组成，pH5.6。酶液通过微孔滤器过滤灭菌。材料在 30℃条件下处理 14~16h。分离下来的原生质体按常规方法进行收集和洗涤[3]。然后用培养基把原生质体稀释成 1×10^4/ml 的密度。培养基的配方是参考 Durand 等[4]和李向辉等[5]，但加以修改(表 1)。原生质体在温度 25±2℃及漫射光条件下作浅层液体培养。

表 1 原生质体培养基的组成

Table 1 Composition of Culture medium for gentian protoplast

矿质盐 (mg/L)	Mineral salts			
KNO_3	1480,		H_3BO_3	5,
NH_4NO_3	270,		$MnSO_4 \cdot 4H_2O$	0.2,
$CaCl_2 \cdot 2H_2O$	900,		$ZnSO_4 \cdot 4H_2O$	0.3,
$MgSO_4 \cdot 7H_2O$	900,		KI	0.25,
KH_2PO_4	80,		$Na_2MoO_4 \cdot 2H_2O$	0.375,
$FeSO_4 \cdot 7H_2O$	27.8,		$CuSO_4 \cdot 5H_2O$	0.625,
Na-EDTA	37.3,		$CoCl_2 \cdot 6H_2O$	0.5,
维生素 (mg/L) Vitamins				
烟酸 Nicotinic acid 4,			肌醇 Inositol 200,	
盐酸吡哆素 0.7,			盐酸硫胺素 4,	
Pyridoxine. HCI			Thiamine. HC I	
叶酸 Folic acid 0.4,			生物素 Biotin 0.04	
氨基酸 (mg/L) Amino acid,			甘氨酸 Glycine 1.4	
激素(mg/L)Hormones,				
2, 4-D 0.2,		萘乙酸 NAA 1,	玉米素 Zeatin 0.5	
椰乳 (mg/L) 40				
Coconut milk				
葡萄糖 Glucose 0.39*M*				
pH 5.6				

结果与讨论

材料经过酶混合液过夜处理后可以得到大量生活的原生质体。原生质体的大小相互间有很大的差别，直径甚至可有 5 倍之差(图版 I，1)。叶绿体的数量及其分布也是很不一样的。

原生质体在上述培养基上培养 4~5 天后再生细胞进行第一次分裂。一次分裂有等分

(图版 I，2)及不等分(图版 I，3)两种。各种大小原生质体都可以见到有一次分裂。但是往往具中央大液泡的大原生质体在分裂一次后就不能再进行下去，而体积小的原生质体在合适的条件下可持续分裂(图版 I，4)。能持续分裂的细胞的细胞质较浓，内有一些大的颗粒状内含物，很少或不具液泡。两星期左右可以得到小细胞团(图版 I，5)。培养一个月左右，培养物可长成肉眼能见的小愈伤组织(图版 I，6)。

经过大量实验后，龙胆原生质体再生愈伤组织获得成功。在我们的实验条件下，从未经低温预处理的试管苗获得的原生质体，通过培养，不但分裂频率低，并且不能持续分裂。我们觉得，龙胆原生质体分裂，除要求合适的培养基及培养条件外，材料自身的生理状态或对材料进行低温预处理，使材料进入合适的生理状态是很重要的。这已为不少学者注意到了[1]。此外，如上所述，龙胆叶肉细胞的原生质体有大小之别，这涉及原生质体的来源问题，我们推测不能持续分裂的大原生质体，可能来自海绵组织或栅栏组织；而小原生质体数量虽较少，但能持续分裂，估计两者来源不同，并具异质性。究竟来自何种组织，尚须进一步探讨。

目前愈伤组织(图版 I，7)诱导器官分化的工作正在进行中。

参考文献

[1] 中国科学院北京植物研究所细胞杂交组，1977：植物原生质体培养的研究进展。植物学报，19(4): 297~305

[2] 张治国、严霄，1983：用组织培养方法快速繁殖龙胆草。浙江人民卫生实验院院报，总第 34 期，217~218

[3] 蔡起贵、钱迎倩、周云罗、吴素萱，1978：水稻 (Oryza sativa L.)原生质体分离和培养的进一步研究。植物学报，20 (2): 97~102

[4] Durand, J., I. Potrykus, G. Donn, 1973: Plants from protoplasts of petunia. Z. Pfanzenphysiol.. 69: 26~34

[5] Li Hsiang-hui, Yan Qui-sheng, Huang Mei-juan, Sun Yung-ru and Li Wen-bin, 1980: Division of cells regenerated from mesophyll protoplast of wheat. In: Adv. Protoplast Res., pp. 261~267 Budapest

[6] Murashige, T. and F. Skoog, 1962: A revised medium for rapid growth and bioassays with tobacco cultures. Physiol. Plant., 15: 473~497

图 版 I

Plate I

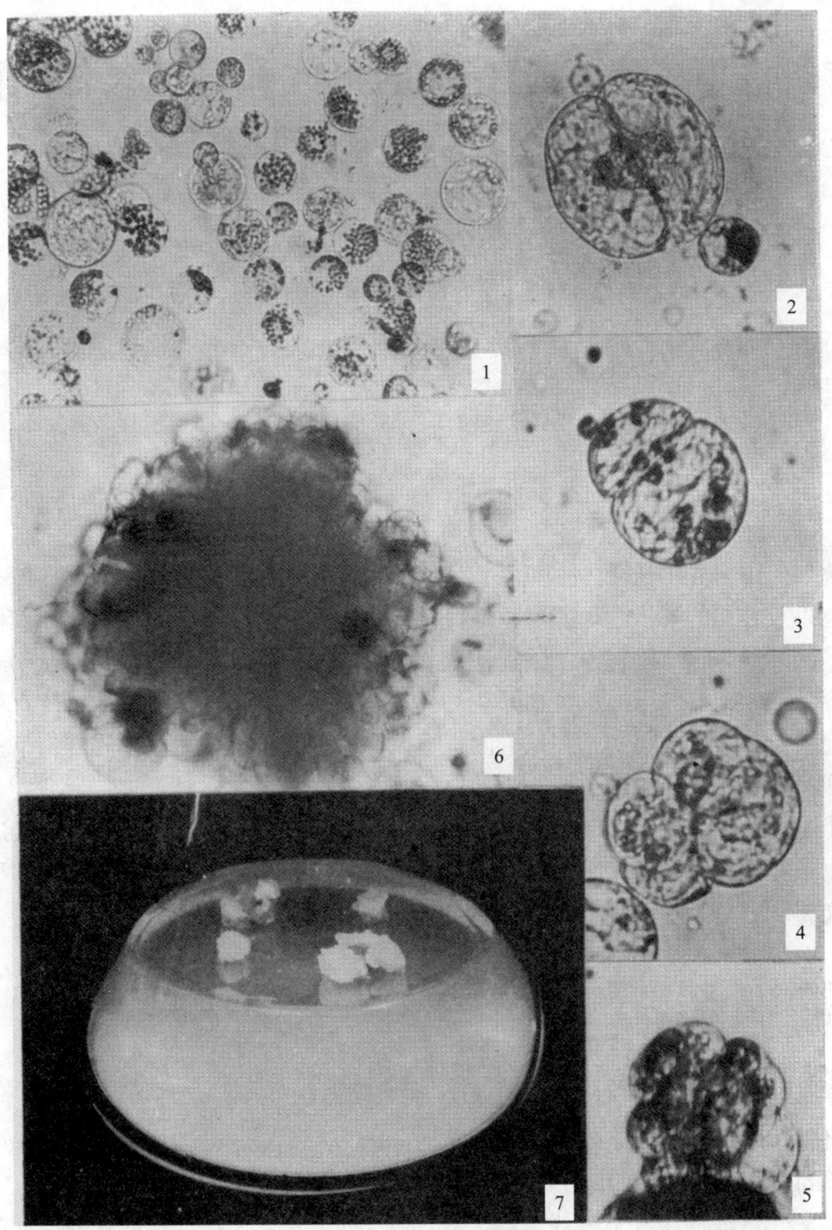

1. 新分离的龙胆叶肉原生质体。2. 龙胆叶肉原生质体第一次等分分裂。3. 龙胆叶肉原生质体第一次不等分分裂。4. 龙胆原生质体再生细胞的第二次分裂。5. 龙胆原生质体来源的小细胞团。6.龙胆原生质体来源的小愈伤组织。7. 正在进行分化的龙胆愈伤组织

Fig.1 Mesophyll protoplasts of gentian isolated freshly. Fig.2 First equal division of gentian protoplast. Fig.3 First unequal division of gentian protoplast. Fig.4 Second division of regenerated cells from gentian ptotoplast. Fig.5 A small cluster derived from gentian protoplast. Fig.6 A samall gentian callus. Fig.7 Gentian calli are being differentiated

本文原载：植物学报. 1987. 29(4): 357-360

离体条件下条叶龙胆花芽的形成和开花条件的研究*

周云罗　钱迎倩　母锡金　蔡起贵

(中国科学院植物研究所)

摘　要　条叶龙胆种子萌发的试管苗，通过快速大量繁殖后，转移到附加玉米素、萘乙酸、激动素及 N-二甲基氨基琥珀酰胺的 MS 培养基上培养。苗端及叶腋可有大量花芽的分化，并能开出蓝紫色的鲜艳花朵，条件合适时，每朵花的花期长达 4 周。经显微技术鉴定，花的雌、雄器官均属正常。

关键词　花芽分化；试管开花；条叶龙胆

植物如何由营养生长转为生殖生长，花器官形成及发育的控制，外界环境条件对它们的影响以及开花的同步性等问题，是植物学工作者长期关注的问题[16]。随着植物组织培养技术的发展，已经得到不少试管开花的植物[1,3,7,8,10~15]，其优越性首先在于离体培养的条件容易控制，有利于揭示植物开花的机理；其次，试管开花的成功，使育种工作者有可能克服自然条件的限制，在试管内进行杂交育种，从而缩短育种周期；第三，试管植物已成为植物快速繁殖的手段，近年来已成为旅游商品[4]。

关于龙胆的快速繁殖及叶肉原生质体培养，已有过报道[2]。这几年我们又进行了离体条件下条叶龙胆花芽分化的研究，并对试管花的形态及雌雄性器官的结构作了初步观察。本文将部分结果作一报道。

材料与方法

(一) 试管苗的快速繁殖

来自种子萌发的条叶龙胆(*Gentiana manshurica* Kitag.)，试管苗*在含有 0.5mg/L 吲哚乙酸，0.2mg/L 玉米素，0.05mg/L 生物素的 MS[9]培养基(培养基 I)上，在温度为 28° ± 2℃，1300lx，每日 8h 光照条件下继代培养。数月后，即可获得大批生长良好的试管苗，以此作为开花实验的材料。

王文铃同志协助制片，特此致谢。

* 种子萌发的试管苗，由浙江医院研究院张治国同志提供。

(二) 诱导开花

把上述材料切成带 2 个叶片的切段，转移到附加 0.4mg/L 玉米素，0.2mg/L 萘乙酸，0.4mg/L 激动素和 2mg/L N-二甲基氨基琥珀酰胺的 MS 培养基(培养基 II)上。并在上述同样的温度、光照条件下培养。当出现花苞后，再次转移到新鲜培养基 II 上，不久即可开花。

(三) 显微技术

开花后，取下花的雌、雄性器官，用纳瓦兴液固定。按石蜡切片法制片。切片厚度为 5~6μm。花药用铁矾苏木精染色，而子房和胚珠用 PAS-苏木精染色。

结果

条叶龙胆试管苗切段，在培养基 II 上经过一个月左右培养后，在切割面上形成了根，并在苗的顶芽和叶腋处或不带顶芽的叶腋处，均可分化出花芽。顶芽处可分化 1~2 个花芽，而叶腋处通常只能分化出 1 个花芽。再经过两个月左右的培养，花芽发育、伸长、露出花苞(图版 I，1)。随着植株的生长，花苞数也不断增加。但在这种情况下，并不利于花苞的开放。此时，只有再次切下具 1~2 个花苞的苗，接种到新鲜的培养基 II 上。此后不久，不仅花苞进一步长大，并可开出鲜艳的花朵(图版 I，2)。正常开花的试管苗，一般很难见到根的分化。个别的出现生根，但具根苗的花苞，生长较缓慢，开花的时间也将延迟。在合适的温度和光照条件下，一朵花可保持开放达 4 周以上。在盛开的花朵中部，可以见到伸长的幼果(图版 I，3)。

条叶龙胆试管花呈蓝紫色，花瓣上带有白色小点，花萼钟状，裂片为三角形，雄蕊 5 个(图版 I，2)。(图版 I，4)显示子房中上部分的纵切面。可以见到柱头和花柱内表面上明显的乳头状突起。所取的材料由于未授粉，因此在柱头表面或花柱沟内均未见到花粉粒。子房为一室，胚珠多数。花药开裂时，花粉普遍为了细胞(图版 I，5)。营养细胞处于退化中，两个精细胞十分清楚。图版 I，6 显示图版 I，4 中单个胚珠成熟胚囊的放大观。由图可见，珠孔端具有一大的卵细胞(E)，极核合并成为大的次生核(Sn)，紧靠在卵细胞的下方。具两个助细胞(不在此切面上)，反足细胞早已消失。

讨论

1964 年前，有关花芽的生长和形态建成方面所积累的资料还是很少的[8,15]。60 年代中期开始，这方面的研究逐步受到重视。至今试管开花的植物已不下 10 种，大致有以下 4 种类型：第 1 类，外植体经过脱分化长出愈伤组织，由愈伤组织分化出试管苗，试管苗长到一定时期转入生殖生长，形成花芽，如石龙芮[7]；第 2 类，外植体经过脱分化长出愈伤组织，无须经过营养生长，而从愈伤组织上直接形成花芽，如风信子[4]；第 3 类，外植体不经过愈伤组织阶段，而直接转入生植生长，长出花茎、花芽，直到开花，如烟草[14]及印度蓝茉莉[11]；第 4 类，利用种子为材料，接种在培养基上，通过培养条件的控制，不使其出现愈伤组织，而直接出苗，试管苗由营养生长转入生殖生长，如蓝花[1]。条叶龙胆的试管开花属于第 4 种类型。

以上 4 种类型，是由于研究的目的不同而出现的，如 Nitsch 等[11]主要是为了研究光周期对花芽及营养芽形成的影响；Tanimoto 等[12]是从植物激素和各种营养成份对花芽形成的角度来进行研究；陆文樑等[3]为了揭露脱分化的细胞，在再分化时，是否可以不从分化的起点开始，而是从分化过程中的某个阶段开始。第 4 种类型是为了能得到容易重复的大量的试管花，和外观秀丽的具花的植株。外植体经过愈伤组织阶段，往往是产生变异的重要因素，因此第 4 类型的试管花，用作试管育种可能是一条可取的途径。

要达到试管育种的目的，必须要求试管花是正常的花。前人在试管花的雌、雄器官的结构，尤其显微结构方面的研究是很少的。Tepfer 等[13]研究了红花耧斗菜(*Aquilegia formosa*)在培养条件下花芽的发育，说明小孢子母细胞过不了前成熟分裂期，心皮内也没有胚珠，说明这不是正常的花。本实验试管花的雌蕊、胚珠、胚囊和花药、花粉的显微结构与 Davis[6]在“被子植物系统胚胎”中，有关龙胆科的描述是一致的。说明条叶龙胆的试管花是正常的花。

最后，试管植株的花芽分化，在种间甚至基因型之间，都有较大的差别。我们除了采用条叶龙胆外，还曾用过龙胆(*G. scabra*)等作实验材料，但是在与本实验完全相同的培养条件下，也未能观察到花芽的分化。

参考文献

[1] 王熊，1984: 兰花快速无性繁殖的研究及花芽分化的探讨。植物生理学报，10: 391~396

[2] 周云罗、钱迎倩、蔡起贵、张治国、严霄，1985: 龙胆叶肉原生质体再生愈伤组织的研究。植物学报，27: 148~151

[3] 陆文樑、郭仲琛、王雪洁、崔澂，1986: 风信子外植体直接再分化花芽的研究 I. 花芽和营养芽形态发生的控制。中国科学 (B 辑)，(5): 491~500

[4] 钱迎倩，1985: 澳大利亚的试管苗工厂化生产。植物杂志，(5): 44~45

[5] Chaouat, L., 1983: Formation de Fleurs a partir de cals chez l'Ail (*Allium sativum* L.), *Bull. Soc. bot. F*, 130: 9~14

[6] Davis. G. L., 1966: Systematic. embryology of the angiosperms, John Wiley and Sons, New York. pp. 126~127

[7] Konar, R. N. and K. Nataraja, 1964: *In vitro* control of floral morphogenesis in *Ranunculus sceleratus* L. *Phytomorphology*, 14: 558~563

[8] LaRue, C. D., 1942: The rooting of flowers in sterile culture. *Bull. Torrey bot. Club*., 69: 332~341

[9] Murashige, T. and F. Skoog, 1962: A revised medium for rapid growth and bioassays with tobacco tissue culture. *Physiol. Plant*., 15: 473~497

[10] Narasimkulu, S. B. and G. M., Reddy, 1984: *In vitro* flowering and pod formation from cotyledons of groundnut (*Arachis hypogaea* L.). *Theor. Appl. Genet*., 69: 87~91

[11] Nitsch, C. and J. P., Nitsch, 1967: The induction of flowering *in vitro* in stem segments of *Plumbago indica* L. II. The production of reproductive buds. *Planta*, 72: 371~384

[12] Tanimoto, S. and H., Harada, 1981: Effects of IAA, zeatin, ammonium nitrate and sucrose on the initiation and development of floral buds in *Torenia* stem segments cultured *in vitro. Plam and Cell Physiol*., 22: 1553~1560

[13] Tepfer, S. S., R. I., Greyson. W. R. Craig, and J. L., Hirdman, 1963: *In vitro* culture of floral buds of *Aquilegia*. *Amer. J. Bot.*, 50: 1035~1045

[14] Tran Thanh Van, M., 1973: Direct flower neoformation from superfical tissue of small explants of *N. tabacum* L. *Planta*, 115: 87~92

[15] Winkler，H, 1908: Uber die Umwandlung des Blattstieles zum Stengel. *Jo wiss. Bot*., 45: 1~82

[16] Zeevart, J. A. D., 1976: Physiology of flower formation, *Ann. Rev. Plant Physiol*., 27: 321~348

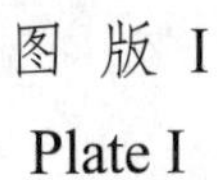

图 版 I

Plate I

1. 示花苞。×0.9 2. 示盛开的花和雄蕊。×1.1 3. 开放 15d 的花和花中部伸长的幼果×0.9 4. 图 3 所示花的子房中上部纵切片，示花柱和胚珠。×32 5. 图 2 所示花药的切片，表现了-细胞成熟花粉，箭头指示精子。×1170 6. 图 4 所示胚珠中胚囊的结构，注意卵细胞(E)和靠近它的合点一端的次生核(Sn)，助细胞不在此切片上，反足器已退化。×1260

E. Egg cell, Sn. Secondary nucleus

Fig. 1. Showing flower buds. ×0.9 Fig. 2. Blooming flower, note tbe anthers in the middle of flower. ×1.1 Fig. 3. A 15-day old flower, showing the elongated young fruit. ×0.9 Fig. 4. Longitudinal section of the middle-upper part of the ovary in the flower of Fig. 3. ×32 Fig. 5. Section of the anther of Fig. 2, showing 3-ce1led pollen grains. ×1170 Fig. 6. Mature embryo sac before fertilization in the ovule of Fig. 4, showing the egg (E) and the secondray nucleus (Sn) adjacent to the chalazal end of the egg (the synergids were not on this section and the antipodal cells had broken down). ×1260

本文原载：云南植物研究. 1988. 10(2): 245-248

香石竹原生质体再生的研究

邹吉涛　钱迎倩

(中国科学院植物研究所)

关键词　香石竹；原生质体培养

香石竹(*Dianthus caryophyllus* L.)是一种受到世界性欢迎的观赏植物。香石竹的快速繁殖已有不少研究报告[1~3]。为了寻找新颖的育种手段，培育新的品种，我们进行了该植物的原生质体培养。米益(Mii, et al., 1682)已对香石竹的原生质体培养作过报道[4]，但他们所用的材料为叶肉原生质体。为期望得到更多变异的再生植株，我们选用愈伤组织作为游离原生质体的材料。

材料和方法

用试管中生长良好的小苗作为材料。在无菌条件下把小苗的叶片切成两半，接种到附加有 2mg/L 2，4-D 的 DPD 培养基上[5]。两星期后，在切口处出现愈伤组织。在同样培养基上转移一次后，将愈伤组织继代到附加有 1mg/L 2，4-D 的 B_5 培养基[6]上。在此培养基上愈伤组织生长很快。继代 4~5 次后，获得大量的愈伤组织。取用愈伤组织上体积小而致密的表层细胞作为游离原生质体的材料。

游离原生质体所用的酶混合液组成如下：1%纤维素酶(Onozuka R-10, Kinki Yakult, Nishinomiya, Japan)，0.3%果胶酶(Macerozyme R-10, Kinki Yakult, Nishinomiya, Japan)，0.5%崩溃酶(Driselase, Kyowa Hakko Kogya, Tokyo, Japan)，0.1%牛血清清蛋白，3%葡聚糖硫酸钾，具 13%(W/V)甘露醇的 CPW[7]盐溶液，pH5.7。25℃黑暗下处理 8h，在处理的最后 2h 放到 60 转/分的转床上旋转振荡。

材料与酶液用 300 目不锈钢网过滤，以除去未被酶解的大块组织。且原生质体的滤液经 $100\times g$ 条件下离心 5min。收集的原生质体用由 900mg/L $CaCl_2\cdot 2H_2O$，200mg/L KH_2PO_4 及 13%(W/V)甘露醇组成的洗液洗涤 2 次，第三次用原生质体培养基(表 1)进行洗涤。以 $1\sim 3\times 10^4$/ml 的密度在直径为 30mm 培养皿中培养。

进行了 B_5，MS[8]及 KM8p[9]等不同基本培养基的比较实验。渗透稳定剂均用 60mg/L

致谢：材料由本所王玉英同志提供。

甘露醇及 30mg/L 蔗糖。原生质体培养的最初几日放在半透明的塑料盒中，27℃散射光条件下。出现分裂后转入同样温度的 1000lx 光照中，光照时间为 8h/d。第二次分裂后，加入不含甘露醇，其他成分相同的细胞培养基。以后加液时细胞培养基的量逐步增加。3 星期后培养物可过渡到在纯细胞培养基中培养。

表 1 香石竹原生质体培养基

Table 1 Medium of protoplast of *Dianthus caryophyllus* L.

基本培养基 B_5 及如下附加物(mg/L, pH 5.7)							
甘氨酸	2	叶酸	0.4	生物素	0.05	椰乳	100 ml/L
L-谷氨酸	100	L-天冬氨酸	100	2，4-D	1	甘露醇	60 g/L
水解酪蛋白	100	NAA	0.1	6-BA	0.2	蔗糖	30 g/L

结果和讨论

愈伤组织细胞的细胞壁成分比较复杂。在我们实验条件下，香石竹愈伤组织如仅采用常规所用的纤维酶及果胶酶，细胞壁不易降解。崩溃酶是必不可少的。崩溃酶是一种降解壁活性强但具多种对原生质体有不利影响(如蛋白酶，脂酶及核酸酶等)的杂酶。实验说明，在酶混合液中加入牛血清清蛋白及葡萄糖硫酸钾是必要的。如酶混合液中无这两种成分，原生质体在收集过程中破碎的数目明显增多，且培养过程中存活率极低。Lai 等[10]在水稻原生质体游离和培养研究中有说服力地指出，牛血清清蛋白不仅提高原生质体的生活力并能阻止细胞器在游离和培养过程中的损坏。葡萄糖硫酸钙可增强原生质体在酶液中的稳定性，也已为不少实验所证明[11,12]。在实验中，由于这两种药品的添加从而得到大量生活的原生质体(图版 I，1)。

香石竹愈伤组织游离得到的原生质体在体积上相差甚大。大原生质体细胞质稀薄，经培养后只见有出芽现象，很少见到分裂。而细胞质致密的小原生质体在 24 小时培养后，就能见到变形，再生了细胞壁，并能持续地分裂下去。

作了不同基本培养基对香石竹原生质体分裂影响的比较。在 MS 培养基上，附加了不同的激素配合，都只能有细胞壁的再生而未见到细胞分裂。在 KM8p 培养基中原生质体再生壁后第一次分裂频率相当高，但绝大多数都不能持续分裂下去，偶尔见到有二次分裂的现象。而在有一系列附加物的 B_5 培养基上(表 1)，培养 3~4d 后观察到第一次分裂。第一次分裂多数是不均等分裂(图版 I，2)。培养 8~10d 后，出现第二次分裂，对香石竹原生质体来说，重要的是此时应开始加细胞培养基，以降低渗透压。细胞培养基添加量为原来原生质体培养基体积的 1/5 左右为宜。过量细胞培养基的加入，因渗透压突然过大的改变，细胞受不了这样的冲击而死亡。此后，细胞培养基的加入量可逐步增加。培养 3 周后可得到细胞团(图版 I，3)。如此 3 周后仍不加新鲜培养基，细胞逐渐变长，衰老，以至死亡。一个月后可形成肉眼可见的愈伤组织(图版 I，4)。

分化植株的工作正在进行，但是较困难。

参考文献

[1] 张丕方, 倪德祥, 玉凯基等. 植物学通报 1985; 6 (5): 49~52

[2] Awad A E, Boundok A, Emara H. Propagation of carnation through tissuc culture, Abstract, VI International Congress of Plant Tissue and Cell Culture. 1986, 238

[3] Hackett W P, Anderson J M. *Proc Am Soc Hort Sci* 1967; 90, 365~369

[4] Mii M, Cheng S-M. Proc 5th Int Cong Plant Tissue and Cell Cultures. Tokyo: IAPTC Maruzen Co, 1982: 585

[5] Durand A, Potrykus I, Donn G. Z. *Pflanzenphysiol* 1973; 69: 26~34

[6] Gamborg O L, Miller R A, O jima K. *Exp Cell Res* 1968; 50: 151~158

[7] Frearson E M, Power J B, Cookong E C. *Dev Biol* 1973; 33: 130~137

[8] Murashige T, Skoog F A. *Physiol Plant* 1962; 15: 473~497

[9] Kao K N, Michayluk M R. *Planta* 1975; 126: 105~110

[10] Lia L-L, Lin L-F. Proc 5th Int Cong Plant Tissue and Cell Cultures. Tokyo: IAPTC Maruzen Co, 1982: 603

[11] Rao I V R, Mehta V, Ram H Y M. Proc 5th Int Cong Plant Tissue and Cell Cultures. Tokyo: LAPTC Maruzen Co, 1982: 595

[12] Sink K C, Niedz R P. Proc 5th Int Cong Plant Tissue and Cell Cultures. Tokyo: IAPTC Maruzen Co, 1982:583

本文原载：遗传学报. 1988. 15(2): 81-85

不同外植体来源和培养条件对拟似棉植株再生的影响*

谭晓连　钱迎倩

(中国科学院植物研究所)

摘　要　对拟似棉的不同器官(叶、叶柄、茎)在离体培养中的反应以及影响植株分化的各种因素(继代培养时间、激素、光、温度)进行了研究。结果表明：茎段作为外植体效果最佳，并且愈伤组织的诱导能力与茎段切口的面积成正比。外植体的方向性，也就是指茎表皮靠着培养基，切口面暴露于空气中为愈伤组织诱导的重要条件。愈伤组织诱导的最适培养基是 MS + 2mg/L IAA + 1mg/L KT，最佳培养条件是强光(10,000lx)、高温(29 ± 1℃)。在 MS + 0.1mg/L NAA + 3mg/L 2 ip + 0.5g/L LH 分化培养基上，在 4,000~5,000lx 的光强，28℃条件下，愈伤组织分化成小苗的频率可达 20%。

关键词：拟似棉(*Gossypium gossypioides*)；组织培养；小植株

棉花是一种重要的经济作物，如何进一步提高产量，增强抗性，正在吸引越来越多的植物细胞和分子遗传学家、育种家进行不懈的努力。近年来，组织培养和遗传工程技术应用于棉花的遗传育种方面，已取得部分成就[2,6,11]。棉花组织培养的器官建成，多集中于栽培种的研究。现已见到通过胚珠[1]、子叶[4]、叶片、叶柄和茎段[3]离体培养诱导形成小苗的报道，也有人描述了 *G. klotzschianum* 体细胞胚状体发生的悬浮培养[9]。

在野生种里具有栽培种中不存在的抗逆性、抗虫、抗病性，以及其他优良性状。通过体细胞杂交或遗传转化等方法有可能把野生种的优良性状转移到栽培种中去。要达到这个目的，棉花的组织培养(包括原生质体培养)再生植株的成功是前提。

拟似棉(*G. gossypioides*)是一种野生棉，具有抗蚜虫、抗红蜘蛛等优良特性。前人对其杂交后代的生物学特性作过一些观察[7]，而对于组织培养方面，国内外均未见有报道。本文首次报道，从成熟的拟似棉外植体诱导愈伤组织，以及不同的外植体来源和培养条件对其植株再生的影响。

材料和方法

(一) 材料

从拟似棉为 6 年生的盆栽苗取材，由植株上取下 1 年生和 2 年生的枝条。

* 实验材料由中国科学院遗传研究所梁正兰教授提供，特此致谢。

(二) 方法

1. 叶片、叶柄和茎段的消毒接种　从枝条上分别取下不同来源的外植体，先用自来水冲洗干净，然后在 70%酒精中洗涤 1~2min，浸入 0.1%L 汞中 10min，取出后用无菌水冲洗 3 次，滤纸吸干，按实验所需切成小块，接入培养基。

2. 培养基　基本培养基为 MS[8]。根据实验的需要附加吲哚乙酸(IAA)、激动素(KT)、萘乙酸(NAA)、异戊基腺嘌呤(2ip)和水解乳蛋白(LH)等，用葡萄糖替代蔗糖，pH 5.8。

3. 培养条件　愈伤组织的诱导和继代培养在 Conviron E7 (Controlled Environments INC Canada)培养箱中进行(温度 29 ± 1℃，光照 15h/d，强度 10,000lx)；器官分化在 NK System Biotron TYPE’LH-200-RD(日本医化器械制作所)培养箱中进行(温度 28℃，光照 12h/d，强度 5,000lx)；同时以常规培养室作为对照(温度为 25 ± 2℃，光照 10h/d，强度 3,200lx)。

结果和讨论

(一) 不同器官在离体培养中的反应

在诱导愈伤组织形成的培养基上(MS + 2mg/L IAA + 1mg/L KT + 3%葡萄糖)，不同的器官在离体培养下的反应均显出差异。

1. 叶片　在培养过程中，不管是老叶(取自 2 年生枝条上的叶片)，还是嫩叶(取自 1 年生枝条上的叶片)，切口端均呈褐色。培养 2d 后，叶片膨大，10d 后长出肉眼可见的白色愈伤组织。但老叶的愈伤组织小，且生长缓慢，幼叶的愈伤组织虽较大，生长速度要快一些。但随着培养时间的增加，到培养 20d 左右，两种愈伤组织都逐渐变褐，最后死亡。

2. 叶柄(取自 1 年生及 2 年生枝条)　在愈伤组织形成过程中，10d 左右的时间，叶柄切口端长出白色疏松的愈伤组织，且能继代培养，但即使转至分化培养基上，也未见任何苗的分化。

3. 茎(取自 1 年生及 2 年生枝条上，从上到下 1~6 个节的部位)　把纵切开的茎段放在诱导愈伤组织的培养基上，当把切口面紧贴培养基面时，外植体变褐或产生生长缓慢，略显淡红色的愈伤组织，这种愈伤组织不能继代培养。而当茎段表皮与培养基接触，切口面暴露于空气中时，10d 内即产生生长迅速的愈伤组织。在整个茎切段面积中，切口面的面积占得越大，诱导愈伤组织的能力越强。这种愈伤组织每两个星期继代培养 1 次，已经继代了 12 个月。当把这种愈伤组织转移到分化培养基上(MS + 0.1mg/L NAA + 3mg/L 2ip + 0.5g/L LH + 3%葡萄糖)，可以诱导芽和根的产生，继而形成完整的小植株(图 1)。

上述实验结果表明，拟似棉叶片和叶柄的细胞在离体培养中虽能诱导脱分化启动，但愈伤组织却不易诱导再分化，而成熟茎的细胞既易于诱导脱分化，愈伤组织也易于再分化。此外，茎切段上愈伤组织的产生几乎完全依赖于外植体切口面的定向。Finer 等在

G. klotzschianum 茎段的离体培养中把外植体的表皮与培养基接触，而让切口面尽可能暴露于空气中，获得了生长迅速、易碎的绿色愈伤组织，从这些愈伤组织中进行悬浮培养，得到了发育于各个时期的体细胞胚胎[5]。本实验结果与他基本一致，清楚地表明了愈伤组织的诱导能力与外植体受伤面积以及切口面定向的关系，即茎段愈伤组织的诱导能力与受伤面积在总面积中所占的比例呈正相关。切口面暴露于空气中又是诱导愈伤组织所必需的条件。2 年生的茎或靠近基部的茎由于粗壮、切口面大。因此所产生的愈伤组织壁 1 年生的茎或幼嫩的茎要好，生长速度要快，并非像其他试验中所出现的幼嫩器官(或组织)在愈伤组织诱导上较老器官(或组织)好得多。

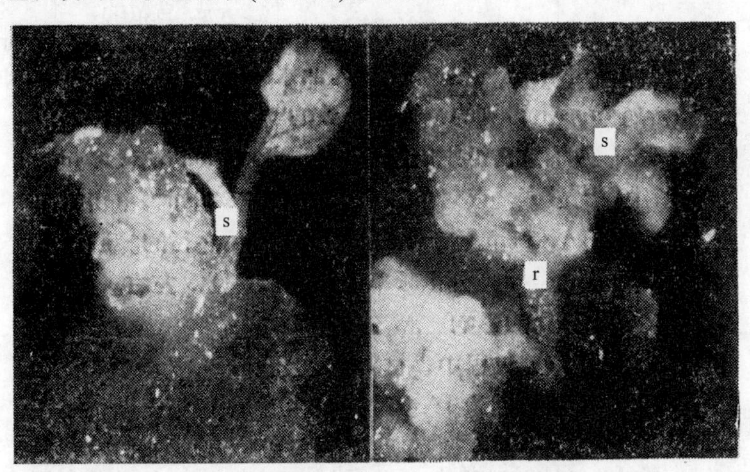

图 1　茎段愈伤组织上分化出的小植株

r: 根；s: 苗

Fig. 1　Plantlets differentiated from calli of stem segments

r：root；s：shoot

(二) 外源激素对愈伤组织的形成、继代和分化的影响

在实验的各个阶段，基本培养基均采用 MS，而只有采用不同的激素浓度配比，方能达到器官分化之目的。

1. 愈伤组织的继代培养　从茎段脱分化形成的愈伤组织质地疏松，且生长缓慢，采用各种激素配比均未见分化。当在基本培养基 MS 上附加 2ip 10mg/L 和 NAA 1mg/L 时，愈伤组织增殖速度大大增加，每隔 2~3 星期继代 1 次，通过半年时间，诱导出了 3 个类型的愈伤组织。第一种类型是白色水渍状的愈伤组织；第二种是生长迅速、疏松的淡绿色愈伤组织；第三种是紧密的深绿色愈伤组织。

2. 器官分化　在合适的激素浓度配比中，经过继代培养的 3 个愈伤组织类型均能进行器官分化，形成芽、根和完整的小植株。试验结果见表 1。

结果表明：①拟似棉外植体诱导产生愈伤组织，既需要 IAA，也需要 KT，且比例为 2∶1 时，效果最佳。在诱导外植体产生愈伤组织中，2,4-D(2.4-二氯苯氧乙酸)是常用的一种激素，但在棉花组培中是一种例外，因为低水平用量就得到不好的结果。这结果与 Smith 等在 *G. arboreum* 上得到的结果是一致的[10]。由此可见，植物激素的作用效果随植物种类而异。②拟似棉愈伤组织需经过较长一段时间的继代培养，方能进行器官分化。③当培养基中缺乏激素，或者单独含有 NAA 或 2ip 时，愈伤组织的分化均不能奏效。④合适配比的 NAA 和 2ip 配合使用，能达到分化之目的。通过实验观察到，使用 NAA 0.1mg/L 和 2ip 3mg/L 时，分化频率最高，可达 20%左右。

表 1 激素对成苗的影响

Table 1 Effect of hormones on plant regeneration

NAA(mg/L)	2ip(mg/L)	接种愈伤组织数(块) No, of calli	形成总苗数(株) No. of plant regeneration	分化频率(%) Frequency of differentiation
1	2	40	2	5
0.5	1	30	1	3
0.1	3	45	8	18
0	3	25	0	0
0.1	0	24	0	0

(三) 光和温度对植株分化的影响

在诱导愈伤组织和继代培养过程中，材料在 Conviron E7 培养箱的强光(10,000lx)、高温(29 ± 1℃)和光照时间为 15h 的条件下，愈伤组织生长很好。而在普通培养室(温度为 25± 2℃，光照为 3,200lx，光照时间为 10h)中，愈伤组织生长缓慢，且继代培养不佳。当转移至分化培养基后，愈伤组织分化植株以在 NK System Biotron TYPE'LH-200-RD 培养箱中为最好。其中尤以光照强度为 4,000—5,000lx，温度为 28℃，光照：黑暗 = 12：12h 结果最佳。结果见表 2。

表 2 光照强度对植株分化的影响

Table 2 Effect of light intensity on plant regeneration

光照强度(勒克斯) Light intensity(lx)	接种愈伤组织数(块) No. of calli	形成总苗数(株) No. of plant regeneration	分化频率(%) Frequency of differentiation
3,200	40	0	0
4,000~5,000	40	8	20
10,000	40	2	5

综上所述，拟似棉组织培养的器官建成以茎作为外植体最佳，愈伤组织诱导的最适培养基为 MS + 2mg/L IAA + 1mg/L KT + 3%葡萄糖，最佳培养条件为强光(10,000lx)，高温(29 ± 1℃)。愈伤组织的分化以 MS + 0.1mg/L NAA + 3mg/L 2ip + 0.59/L LH + 3%葡萄糖作培养基，4,000~5,000lx 的光强，28℃为条件时，分化频率最高。

目前虽已得到分化了的苗和根的小植株，但如何使植物进一步发育、开花结果，尚需我们继续努力工作。

参考文献

[1] 沈增佑等: 1978. 植物生理学报, 4 (2): 183~187
[2] 梁正兰等: 1982. 棉花远缘杂交, 科学出版社
[3] Cateland en Maya: 1975. *Cotton Fibres Trop.*, 30: 373
[4] Davidonis, G. H. et al., 1983. *Plant Sci. Lett.*, 32: 89~93
[5] Finer, J. J. et al., 1984. *Plant Cell Rep.*, 3(1): 41~43
[6] Frydrych D.: 1985. *Cotton Fibres Trop.*, 40: 102~105
[7] Menzel, M. Y. et al., 1955. *Amer. J. Bot.*, 42(1): 49~56
[8] Murashige, J. et al., 1962. *Physiol. Plant,* 15: 473~497
[9] Price, H. J. et al., 1979. *Planta,* 145: 305~307
[10] Smith, R. H. et al., 1977. *In vitro,* 13(5): 329~334
[11] Zhou Guang yu et al., 1983. *In:* Methods in Enzymology, Vol. 101, Ray Wu et al, Edt, Academic Press, pp. 433~481

本文原载：Chinese Journal of Botany. 1990. 2(1): 18-25

Factors Influencing Isolation, Division and Plant Regeneration in Maize (*Zea mays* L.) Protoplast Culture

Zhang Shi-Bo Guo Zhong-Shen Qian Ying-Qian

Qu Gui-Ping Cai Qi-Gui Zhou Yun-Luo

(Institute of Botany, Academia Sinica)

Abstract Factors including different enzyme solutions, sources of material, basic media, nitrogen sources, concentrations of 2, 4-D, schedules of transfer to low osmoticum were studied. Protoplasts in good quality and yield were obtained from light yellow calli, which were subcultured for 8~16 days, and incubated in enzyme solution consisting of 2% Onozuka RS, 1% hemicellulase and 0.1% pectolyase Y-23. Plating efficiency was up to 5% when protoplasts were cultured in the N_6 basic medium supplemented with casein hydrolysate, L-proline, L-asparagine, coconut milk and 1.0mg/L 2, 4-D. The calli derived from protoplasts were transferred to low osmoticum 4 weeks after plating. Step induction was used for embryogenesis and plant regeneration.

Key words Maize; Protoplast culture; Embryogenesis; Plant regeneration

Introduction

Plant regeneration from maize protoplast has been succeeded in various genotypes recently (Rhodes et al., 1988; Shillito et al., 1989; Prioli & Sondahl, 1989; Sun et al., 1989), since the first report from our laboratory (Cai et al., 1987). Significant different medin were used in protoplast culture in the studies, such as N_6, KM, and Rice Protoplast Culture Medium (I), or their modified formulations. Various organic supplements (organic acids, sugar and sugar alcohols, amino acids, casein hydrolysate, coconut milk, etc.), different kinds and concentrations of growth regulators (2, 4-D, Zeatin, Kinein, 6-BA, etc.) were added to culture media. For plant regeneration, different schedules to decrease osmoticum of culture medium were taken. It seems that different culture conditions are required to culture protoplasts from different genotypes of maize.

The present report is an extension of our early work on maize protoplast culture (Cai et al., 1987) and deals with various factors affecting isolation, division and plant regeneration.

Based on the new experiments a more successful culture process was developed.

Materials and Methods

Materials for protoplast isolation was taken from embryogenic calli which were derived from anther culture of F_1 (Hsia o-pa-tang × Shui-pai) and subcultured for two and a half years. Two grams of light yellow calli in fresh weight were added to 10 ml of filter-sterilized enzyme solution. The enzyme solution was kept for 4~5 h in 30℃ incubator, shaked 2~3 times during incubation, then passed through a stainless steel sieve with pore diameter of 56μm. The filtrate was centrifugated at 500 rpm for 6~8 minutes. Protoplasts collected were washed twice with washing solution consisting of 10 mM $CaCl_2 \cdot 2H_2O$ and 0.6 M mannitol and once with protoplast culture medium.

Protoplasts at a final density of 1~2 x 10^5/ml were cultured in petri dish of 5.5cm in diameter containing 2ml of liquid medium. Dishes were scaled with parafilm and kept in dark at 28℃/24℃ (day/night). When regenerated calli were 2~4mm in size, they were transferred to differentiation media and kept under illumination of 1000 lux, 9 h/day, at 25 ℃ /22 ℃ (day/night). Step induction was used for embryogenesis and plant regeneration.

Every experiment was repeated 3 times as usual. After 15 days of culture, the number of clusters formed in 5 fields of microscope for every dish were calculated and the average value was adopted as plating frequency.

Results and Discussion

1. Protoplast isolation

(1) Enzyme solutions

The different combinations of 6 kinds of enzyme including Onozuka R-10 (Yakult Pharmaceutical Industry Co., Ltd., Japan), Onozuka RS (Yakult Pnarmaceutical Industry Co., Ltd., JanPan), Hemicellulase (The Old Brickyard), Macerozyme R-10 (Kinki Yakult Mfg. Co., Ltd., Japan), Pectolyase Y-23 (Seishin Pharmaceutical Co., Ltd., Japan) and Rhozyme HP-150 (Rohm and Hass Co., Ltd., Canada) and different contents were used for is olating maize protoplast (Table 1).

From Table 1 following conclusions could be resched: 1) Solution 1 with the highest concentrations of various enzymes gave the highest harvest of protoplasts, but the plating efficiency of the protoplasts from this solution was low. This may result from protoplast injury in the high concentrations of enzyme solution during the process of isolation. Ishii (1988) reported that essential enzymes for the isolation of rice protoplasts were detrimental,

Table 1 Effect of different enzyme solutions on isolation of maize protoplast* **

Enzyme No.	Onozuka R-10	Onozuka RS	Hemicellulase	Rhozyme	Macerozyme R-10	Pectolyase Y-23	Harvest of protoplast
1		5%	1%		0.8%	0.2%	5×10^5~ 1×10^6
2		2%	1%		0.5%	0.1%	2~8×10^5
3		2%	1%			0.1%	2~5×10^5
4		2%			0.5%	0.1%	3~4×10^4
5		2%		1%		0.1%	3~5×10^5
6		2%	1%				2~4×10^3
7	3%		1%			0.1%	1~5×10^4

* Embryogenic calli were taken from 10 days after subculture.

** Enzyme solutions were incubated under 30℃ for 4 h in dark.

even the use of purified enzymes alone did not greatly enhance the viability of the rice protoplasts. Among the essential enzymes, Onozuka Macerozyme R-10 was more toxic to cells than Onozuka Cellulase RS and Pectolyase Y-23 was the most toxic one (Hahne & Lorz, 1988). 2) Solution 2 was similar to solution 3 in protoplast harvest. In this case, Macerozyme R-10 was shown unnecessary. 3) Hemicellulase was indispensable, which has been shown in the harvest of solution 3 in comparison with solution 4. Carpita (1983) reported that hemicellulasic polymers comprised about 43% of the primary walls of *Zea mays* coleoptiles, and similar contents of hemicellulase were showed in the cell walls of cell suspension culture of some graminaceous species (Carpita et al., 1985). It could be comprehended that there were hemicellulase in the cell wall of maize embryogenic calli. Similar harvest was obtained if Rhozyme substituted for Hemicellulase (solution 3 and 5). 4) The harvest decreased greatly when Pectolyse Y-23 was not used (solution 3 and 6), or Onozuka RS was substituted by Onozuka R-10 (solution 3 and 7). As a result, the optmum combination of different enzymes in our experiments consisted of 2% Onozuka RS, 1% hemicellulase and 0.1% Pectolyase Y-23.

(2) Sources of materials

Embryogenic suspension culture was always used to be the source of material for isolating protoplast in monocots (Kyozuka et al., 1987; Harris et al., 1988; Rhodes et al., 1988). In this report, the source of materials was taken from embryogenic calli subcultured on agar medium for two and a half years. It must be pointed out that the essential step for maintaining the regeneration ability of these calli was selection. On the other hand, calli have been subcultured in suspension culture for some period. Everytime suspension culture cells were transferred to agar solid medium, two types of calli appeared. One was white and slow growing and the other was light yellow and fast growing. Only the latter still maintained the regeneration ability and was used as source of protoplasts.

The question was when the embryogenic calli should be collected after every subculture for obtaining protoplasts with high quality and good harvest. Table 2 showed the optimum time for collecting calli.

Table 2 Effect of subculture days of calli on quality and harvest of protoplast

Subculture days	6~8 days	8~16 days	16~20 days
Harvest of protoplast/g calli	Less than 1×10^4	2×10^5~1×10^6	Less than 1×10^3
Size of protoplast	5~15μm	20~40μm	40~60μm

Results in Table 2 demonstrated that the highest harvest was obtained when embryogenic calli were subcultured for 8~16 days. The protoplasts were more homogeneous in size and more abundant in contents. There were few debris. Most of regenerable protoplasts came from them. Protoplasts derived from 6~8 day old calli were smaller in size, and died after culture for 1~2 weeks. Protoplasts derived from 16~20 days were much more vacuolated. They could swell but not divide and some of them elongated and died eventually. There were numerous debris in the latter two cases, so it could be concluded that light yellow calli subcultured for 8~16 days were the best source of protoplasts.

2. Plating efficiency

(1) Basic medium

As a basic medium N_6 was similar or a little better in plating efficiency (2%~3%) as compared to Rice Protoplast Culture Medium (I) (1%~2%) (Cai et al., 1987). It also could be seen from other successful reports that N_6 or KM-8p, and their modified forms were better than other basic media in maize protoplast culture (Rhodes et al., 1988; Shillito et al., 1989; Sun et al., 1989). Therefore, N_6 was used as basic medium in all of our experiments.

(2) Nitrogen source

Various organic and inorganic nitrogen, and their different combinations were tested. Results were shown in Table 3, 4 and 5 respectively.

Table 3 Comparison of inorganic nitrogen with organic nitrogen* (%)

Nitrogen source	Organic**	Inorganic***	Both
PE	0.1~0.2	0~0.01	3~5

*Protoplast culture medium was composed of N_6 medium with different kinds of nitrogen, 2,4-D 1mg/L,Kn 0.3mg/L, 6-BA 0.1mg/L, mannitol 0.3 M, glucose 0.2 M and sucrose 10g/L, pH 5.8.

**Organic nitrogen: L-P 1,500mg/L + L-A 800mg/L + CH 200mg/L + CM20ml/L

***Inorganic nitrogen: KNO_3 2,830mg/L + $(NH_4)_2SO_4$ 462mg/L.

It was illustrated in Table 3 that both organic and inorganic nitrogen were absolutely necessary in protoplast culture of maize. Plating efficiency decreased greatly in the case of lack of either of them. Organic nitrogen was more effective than inorganic nitrogen in promoting protoplast division. There was even no cell regeneration when inorganic nitrogen was added solely to the medium. It may also be suggested that there was positive interaction between organic and inorganic nitrogen, because the maximum of plating efficiency reached to 5% when both of them were added to the medium.

The second experiment of nitrogen was to compare the effect of different inorganic nitrogen sources on the plating efficiency of maize protoplast. Results were shown in Table 4.

Table 4 Effect of different inorganic nitrogen sources on PE of maize protoplast*

Nitrogen sources	KNO_3	$(NH_4)_2SO_4$	Both
PE	2%~3%	0	3%~5%

*Culture medium was the same as in Table 3 with 4 kinds of organic nitrogen.

This experiment indicated that no cell regeneration occurred when $(NH_4)_2SO_4$ was added solely to the medium, but it had a promoting role when KNO_3 was present simultaneously. Imbrie-Milligan et al. (1987) also reported that nitrate was essential and ammonium inhibited the cluster formation of maize protoplast.

Four kinds of organic nitrogen were examined separately or in different combinations.

Table 5 Effect of organic nitrogen on PE of maize protoplast*

Nitrogen sources	CH	CM	L-P	L-A	CH+ CM	CH+ L-P	CH+ L-A	CM+ L-P	CM+ L-A	L-P+ L-A	L-P+L-A +CH+CM
PE	0.3%~ 0.5%	1.0%~ 1.5%	3.0%~ 4.0%	0%~ 0.01%	0%	0%	0.6%	1.5%~ 2.0	1.0%	2%~ 3%	4%~5%

*Culture medium was the same as in Table 3 with inorganic nitrogen.

It was shown in Table 5 that when 4 kinds of organic nitrogen were tested separately. L-P showed significant effect on protoplast division; CH and CM were less effective; and there was no valuable contribution if L-A was used alone. Negative interaction appeared in combination of any two kinds of organic nitrogen. But plating efficiency reached 4%~5%

when 4 kinds of organic nitrogen were used together. These results were somewhat similar to those of Imbrie-Milligan et al. (1987).

(3) Concentration of 2, 4-D

The plating efficiency in the medium with 2.0mg.L 2, 4-D was similar to that in the one with 1.0mg/ L 2,4-D, and better than that in the one with 0.5mg/L 2, 4-D (Table 6). But according to our experience, differentiation ability of regenerated calli was decreased if regeneration processes were conducted at 2mg/L 2, 4-D level for a long time. So it was thought that 1.0mg/L 2, 4-D was the best.

Table 6 Effect of 2, 4-D on PE of maize protoplast*

Concentration	0.5mg/L	1.0mg/L	2.0mg/L
PE	1%~2%	3%~5%	3%~4%

* Culture medium was the same as in Table 3 with all kinds of nitrogen and different concentrations of 2, 4-D.

(4) Schedule of callus transfer to low osmoticum

The schedule of callus transfer to low osmoticum was also a significant factor affecting plating efficiency.

Table 7 Effect of different schedules of callus transfer to low osmoticum on plating efficiency of maize protoplast*

Duration	1 week	2 weeks	3 weeks	4 weeks
PE	2%	1%	1.5%	4%

*Culture medium was the same as in Table 6 supplemented weith 1.0mg/L 2, 4-D.

The condition that protoplasts were plated for four weeks or the largest calli were 1~2mm in size was the optimum for transfer. This result was somewhat different from those of Imbrie-Milligan et al. (1987) and Rhodes et al. (1988).

It may come to the conclusion from 4 experiments mentioned above that plating efficiency could be increased up to 5% when protoplasts were cultured in the liquid medium consisting of N_6 basic medium supplemented with 1,500mg/L L-P, 800mg/L L-A, 200mg/L CH, 20mg/L CM, 1.0mg/L 2, 4-D, 0.2mg/L Kn, 0.1mg/L 6-BA, 0.3 M mannitol, 0.2 M glucose and 10g/L sucrose, pH 5.8; and the regenerated calli were transferred to low osmoticum medium 4 weeks after plating.

3. Plant regeneration

Plant regeneration could be induced through organogenesis or embryogenesis. Factors influencing embryogenesis of maize callus derived from protoplast were described here.

The protoplast-derived calli of 2~4mm in size were transferred onto the Medium (I) in

Table 8. They grew vigorously in this medium and numerous embryoid structures were emerged on their surface. The frequency of embryogenic callus formation was up to 70%~80% after 2 weeks in culture. They expanded and became ball-like structures if they were not transferred onto Medium (II) in time and no plant regeneration occurred eventually. When these were transferred onto Medium (III) from Medium (I), no plant regeneration occurred as well. But plants were successfully recovered from the embryogenic calli which were transferred onto the medium (III) after cultured on differentiation medium (II) for 2~3 weeks. It was suggested that the embryogenic structures emerged on the medium (I) were not mature enough to develop into plants. In this period, increasing the osmoticum of culture medium was essential. It also has been reported that higher lever of sucrose stimulated embryogenesis in tissue culture of maize (Lu et al., 1983). Among these embryoids, 5% developed into normal plants; only leaves, roots and buds occurred on ca. 70% of them; and others died eventually.

Table 8 Media for plant regeneration in different stages

Culture medium	Proliferation medium(I)		Embryogenesis medium(II)		Plant regeneration medium(III)	
Basic medium	N_6		N_6		N_6	
Organic	CH	200mg/L				
Components	L-P	1,500mg/L	L-P	1,000mg/L		
	L-A	800mg/L				
	CM	20 ml/L			CM	50 ml/L
	Sucrose	40g/L	Sucrose	60g/L	Sucrose	20g/L
	Agar	0.7%	Agar	0.7%	Agar	0.7%
	Activated charcoal	1.0g/L	Activated charcoal	1.0g/L	Activated charcoal	1.0g/L
Phytohormone	2, 4-D	0.5mg/L	2, 4-D	0.3mg/L		
	Kn	1.0mg/L	Kn	1.0mg/L	Kn	1.0mg/L
	6-BA	0.5mg/L	6-BA	0.5mg/L	6-BA	0.5mg/L
pH	5.8		5.8		5.8	

Abbreviations: PE, plating efficiency; L-P, L-proline; L-A, L-asparagine; CH, casein hydrolysate; CM, coconut milk; Kn kinetin; 6-BA, 6-Benzylaminopurine.

References

[1] Cai QG et al., 1987. Plant regeneration from protoplasts of corn (*Zea mays* L.). *Acta Bot. Sin.,* 29 (5): 453~458 (Chinese, Engl. Summ.)

[2] Carpita NC, 1983. Hemicellulosic polymers of cell walls of Zea coleoptiles. *Plant Physiol.,* 72 (2): 515~521

[3] ________, Mulligan JA, Heyser JW, 1985. Hemicellulose of cell walls of proso millet cell suspension culture. *Plant Physiol.* 79 (2): 480~484

[4] Hahne G. Lorz H, 1988. Release of phytotoxic factors from plant cell walls during protoplast isolation. *J. Plant Physiol.,* 132 (3): 345~350

[5] Harris R et al., 1988. Callus formation and plantlet regeneration from protoplasts derived from suspension cultures of wheat (*Triticum aestivum* L.) *Plant Cell Report,* 7(5): 337~340

[6] Imbrie-Milligan C, Kamo KK, Hodge JK, 1987, Microcallus growth from maize protoplasts. *Planta,* 171 (1): 58~64

[7] Ishii S, 1988. Factors influencing protoplast viability of suspension-cultured rice cells during isolation process. *Plant Physiol.,* 88 (1): 26~29

[8] Kyozuka J. Hayashi Y. Shimamoto K, 1987. High frequency plant regeneration from rice protoplasts by nurse culture methods. *Mol. Gen . Genet.,* 206 (3): 408~413

[9] Lu C Vasil V, Vasil IK, 1983. Improved efficiency of somatic embryogenesis and plant regeneration in tissue cultures of maize (*Zea mays* L.) *Theor. Appl. Genet.,* 66 (3/4): 285~289

[10] Prioli I M, Sondahl MR, 1989. Plant regeneration and recovery of fertile plants form protoplasts of maize (*Zea mays* L.) *Bio/technology,* 7 (6): 589~594

[11] Rhodes CA, Lowe KS, Ruby KL, 1988. Plant regeneration from protoplasts isolated from embryogenic maize cell cultures. *Bio/technology,* 6 (1): 56~60

[12] Shillito R D et al., 1989. Regeneration of fertile plants from protoplasts of elite inbrid maize. *Bio/technology,*7 (6): 581~587

[13] Sun CS, Prioli L M, Sondhal M R, 1989. Regeneration of haploid and dihaploid plants from protoplasts of supersweet (sh2sh2) corn. *Plant Cell Reports,* 8 (6): 313~316

本文原载：植物学报.1990. 32(5): 329-336

小偃麦原生质体培养及植株再生

王铁邦[1]　钱迎倩[1]　李集临[2]　屈贵平[2]　蔡起贵[2]

(1 中国科学院植物研究所；2 哈尔滨师范大学生物系)

摘　要　硬粒小麦(*Triticum durum* Desf. AABB)和中间偃麦草[*Elytrigia intermedium* (Host) Nevski BBEEFF]的杂种 F_1——小偃麦的幼穗诱导的胚性愈伤组织继代培养近两年后，转入修改的 MS 液体培养基建成胚性细胞悬浮系。从此悬浮系分离的原生质体在修改的 KM_{8p} 培养基中培养 48h 后出现第一次分裂。15d 后，在液体浅层培养条件下的细胞分裂频率为 2%；而用 1.2%琼脂糖固化进行固体平板培养时，细胞的分裂频率则为 12.14%。20~30d 后，添加渗透压降低的原生质体培养液。当从原生质体再生的愈伤组织长至 2~4mm 大小时，逐步转至生长及分化培养基上再生出完整植株。

关键词　小偃麦；细胞悬浮系；原生质体培养；植株再生

近年来，禾本科的作物如甘蔗(*Saccharum officinarum* L.)[22]、水稻(*Oryza sativa* L.)[23,25]、玉米(*Zea mays* L.)[3,28]和小麦(*Triticum aestivum* L.)[1,2,7]，还有牧草植物鸭茅属(*Dactylis*)[9]、羊茅属(*Festuca*)和黑麦草属(*Lolium*)[5]植物的原生质体已再生出植株。在再生植株的基础上，通过 DNA 直接转化原生质体，水稻(*Oryza sativa* L.)[24,28]、玉米(*Zea mays* L.)[19]和鸭茅(*Dactylis glomerata* L.)[10]、相继获得转基因植株。但转入的基因都是标记性的。小偃麦(*Triticum* sect. *trititrigia* Mackey)是小麦属(*Triticum*)和偃麦草属(*Elytrigia*)的物种通过有性杂交获得的人工多倍体新物种。它在小麦育种和草地植物改良方面起了重要作用。本文报道人工多倍体小偃麦的原生质体能以较高的频率再生出完整植株。

材料和方法

(一) 悬浮培养

硬粒小麦(*Triticum durum* Desf. AABB) × 中间偃麦草(*Elytrigia intermedia* (Host) Nevski BBEEFF) F_1 幼穗诱导的胚性愈伤组织在 MS[17] + 2mg/L 2, 4-D 的培养基上继代培养 18 个月后转至改良的 MS 培养基(CIM)上，CIM 培养基组成如下：MS 无机盐附加 2mg/L 甘氨酸，5mg/L VB_1，0.5mg/L VB_6，0.5mg/L 烟酸，100mg/L 肌醇，100mg/L 水解酪蛋白，200mg/L 谷酰胺，3%蔗糖，2mg/L 2,4-D，0.8%琼脂，pH5.8。材料培养条件是：1300lx 光强度，日照光 9h，白天 25℃夜间 22℃。每 15~20d 继代

培养一次。4 个月后选择生长快、结构松脆[1]具分化能力的淡黄色胚性愈伤组织 1~2g，置于装有 30ml 另一种改良的 MS 液体培养基 S_4 的 100ml 三角瓶中，在 26℃弱散光下，120rpm 旋转式摇床上振荡培养。每 3~4d 继代培养一次。S_4 培养基组成如下：MS 基本成分，附加 300mg/L 水解酪蛋白，200mg/L 谷酰胺，150mg/L 天门冬氨酸，3%蔗糖，2.5mg/L 2，4-D，pH5.6~5.8。2 周后，用镊子把大块愈伤组织尽可能夹碎，并换至 150~200 ml 大三角瓶中培养。约 15d 后，用 80 目尼龙网过滤。滤液用来做继代培养。又二月后得到稳定的悬浮细胞系。以后当培养物体积达到总体积的 1/3 左右时，按 1：5 稀释培养。每月用 80 目尼龙网过滤一次，滤液用来继代培养。在悬浮培养过程中每隔两月用改良的 MS 分化培养基 PR15 测其分化能力。PR15 组成如下：MS 基本成分附加 300mg/L 水解酪蛋白，200mg/L 谷酰胺，3%蔗糖，0.24% Gelrite 固化，pH5.8。在 1300 lx 下光照 16h。温度与愈伤组织继代培养所用的相同。

(二) 原生质体的分离和培养

连续继代培养 4~9 个月(从悬浮培养开始计)的培养物继代培养 2~3d 后用混合酶液分离原生质体。酶液组成如下：1.5% Onozuka RS (Yakult Pharmaceutical Industry Co., Japan)、0.1% Pectolyase Y-23 (Seishin Pharmaceutical Co., Japan)、0.5mmol/L KH_2PO_4、10mmol/l $CaCl_2$、2mmol/L $MgSo_4 \cdot 7H_2O$、0.6mol/L 甘露醇，pH5.6。取静置 2min 自然沉在瓶底的培养细胞 1~2g，投入 10ml 酶液中。在 30rpm，30℃条件下保温 2.5~3h。用 400 目不锈钢网过滤，80 × g 离心 2~3min。然后用 10mmol/L $CaCl_2$ 和 0.6mol/L 甘露醇的等渗液洗二次，原生质体培养基洗一次[3]。收集到的原生质体用三种方法培养：1. 液体浅层培养，分别用改良的 MS 培养基 M_p，改良的 N6 培养基 N_p、改良的 KM_{8p} 培养基 K_p 和改良的 LS 培养基 L_p 培养(表 1)。将原生质体密度调整在 $2 \sim 4 \times 10^5$ 个原生质体/ml。60 × 10mm 的 Falcon 培养皿中加 2ml 培养物，35 × 10mm Falcon 培养皿中加 1ml 原生质体悬液。用 Parafilm 封口。置 26℃下黑暗培养。另有一些样品在弱光下培养。2. 半固体培养：K_p 培养基培养的原生质体用 0.2%琼脂糖(Agarose Sigma Type7)固化。其他同液体浅层培养。3. 固体平板培养；先用 K_p 培养液调整原生质体密度至 $4\text{-}10 \times 10^5$ 原生质体/ml, 再加入同样体积含 2.4%琼脂糖，温度为 40℃左右的培养基。在 60 × 10mm 和 35 × 10mm 的 Falcon 培养皿中分别加 3ml 和 1.5ml 培养物，培养条件同液体浅层培养。培养 48h 后观察细胞壁再生和最早出现的一次分裂。第 15d 统计细胞分裂频率。3~4 周后，液体浅层培养物中加入 1/3 体积的含降低葡萄糖浓度到 0.3mol/l 的同样培养基。置弱光下培养，或继续暗培养。半固体和固体平板培养 4~6 星期后，将整个培养物连同培养基一起平铺到 PS1 培养基(表 2)上。待再生的愈伤组织长至 2~4mm 大小时转至下列一系列分化培养基上进行生长或分化，首先转至 PS2 培养基(表 2)上。培养 15d 后转至 PR6 或 PR10 培养基(表 2)上，以 1300lx，16h 照光培养 2~3 周，然后转至 PR15 培养基(表 2)。10~15d 后分化出完整植株。

表 1　原生质体培养基

Table 1　The media for protoplast culture

培养基 Culture media / 组成 Components	K_P	N_P	M_P	L_P
基本培养基 Basic medium	KM_{8P}[12]	N_6[4]	MS[17]	LS[13]
肌醇 Inositol (mg/L)	100	100	100	100
VB_1(mg/L)	1.0	1.0	0.1	1.0
VB_6(mg/L)	1.0	0.5	0.5	—
烟酸 Nicotinic acid (mg/L)	1.0	0.5	0.5	—
水解酪蛋白 Casein Hydrolysate (mg/L)	100	100	100	100
谷酰胺 Glutamine (mg/L)	100	100	100	100
葡萄糖 Glucose(%)	9.5	9.5	9.5	9.5
蔗糖 Sucrose(%)	0.5	0.5	0.5	0.5
2, 4-D (mg/L)	1.0	1.0	1.0	1.0
激动素 Kinetin (mg/L)	0.2	0.2	0.2	0.2
pH	5.6~5.8	5.6~5.8	5.6~5.8	5.6~5.8

表 2　生长及分化培养基

Table 2　The media for growth and differentiation

培养基 Culture media / 组成 Components	PS1	PS2	PR6	PR10	PR15
大量元素 Major elements	MS	MS	N_6	B_5[6]	MS
微量元素 Microelements	MS	MS	B_5	B_5	MS
维生素 Vitamins	MS	MS	B_5	B_5	MS
水解酪蛋白 (mg/L) Casein Hydrolysate	100	300	300	300	300
谷酰胺 (mg/L) Glutamine		200	200	200	200
椰乳 (%) Coconut milk	2				
2, 4-D (mg/L)	2	1	0.5		

续表

培养基 Culture media / 组成 Components	PS1	PS2	PR6	PR10	PR15
激动素 Kinetin (mg/L)		0.2	0.2	2	
6-BA (mg/L)			0.5	0.5	
IAA (mg/L)			1	1	
蔗糖 (%) Sucrose	3	3	3	3	3
活性炭 (%) Active Charcoal		0.1	0.1	0.1	
琼脂 (%) Agar	0.8	0.8	0.8	0.8	
Gelrite (%)					0.24
pH	5.8	5.8	5.8	5.8	5.8

结果

(一) 悬浮培养

在 MS + 2mg/L 2, 4-D 培养基上继代培养 18 个月的胚性愈伤组织，结构紧密、坚硬，生长缓慢。这种愈伤组织转至液体培养基中，经几次继代培养后褐化死亡。把这种愈伤组织转至 CIM 培养基上，四个月后选择生长快、结构松脆淡黄色的胚性愈伤组织建立了胚性悬浮细胞系(图版 I，1)。在悬浮培养的最初几个星期内生长缓慢，几乎没有量的增加。培养物中除愈伤组织块外就是长而空的老细胞，但没有褐化的愈伤组织块出现。在培养一个月后，愈伤组织明显增长。有些长成 4~5mm 大的愈伤组织块，同时培养物中也出现由 10~100 个球形小细胞组成的胚性细胞团。胚性细胞团的每个细胞都有很浓的细胞质、很薄的细胞壁。用 80 目尼龙网过滤除去大块愈伤组织块后，滤液主要由长细胞组成。此外还有少量胚性细胞团。由于长细胞是不分裂的，所以随着继代次数增加，长而空的老细胞不断减少。相反，胚性细胞团依次增多。再继代培养两个月后，长细胞基本被淘汰。所得悬浮细胞系每 3~4d 增加一倍。在培养过程中仍有大块愈伤组织形成。再用 80 目尼龙网过滤几次后，得到的悬浮细胞系颗粒细密，大小均一。分化测试表明，该悬浮培养物仍具有强的分化能力。

(二) 原生质体的分离和培养

继代培养 2~3d 的悬浮细胞系都能分离到大量有活性的原生质体(图版 I，2)。用本文所述方法，每克鲜重悬浮培养物能分离到 $3\text{~}6 \times 10^5$ 个原生质体。刚分离的原生质体细胞质很浓，大小均匀。在原生质体培养的早期阶段，暗环境是必需的，因为在光下培养的几个样品都没有观察到细胞分裂。

分别用 K_p、N_p、M_p 和 L_p 培养基进行的液体浅层培养实验中，只有 K_p 培养基适合小偃麦原生质体的培养。其细胞分裂频率 2%。在 M_p 和 L_p 培养基中培养的原生质体，10d 后陆续破碎死亡。N_p 培养基上原生质体破碎死亡的频率约为 30%。在一个月的培养时间内未观察到一次分裂。因此，以后的原生质体培养一律采用 K_p 培养基。

用 K_p 培养基进行液体浅层，半固体及固体平板在暗环境培养时，48h 后都能观察到一次分裂(图版 I，3)。液体浅层培养 10h 后，原生质体间相互粘连。用 0.2%琼脂糖的半固体培养及 1.2%琼脂糖的固体平板培养能有效地阻止粘连。半固体法和液体浅层培养法所得到的细胞分裂无明显差别。用 1.2%琼脂糖固体平板培养的细胞分裂频率为 12.14%(图版 I，6)，比液体浅层法及半固体法高 6 倍。培养 5d 后，能见到分裂三次的小细胞团(图版 I，4)。再生细胞在上述的培养基中能持续分裂，15d 后可观察到大细胞团(图版 I，5)。

(三) 原生质体再生愈伤组织的培养及植株再生

培养 3~4 周，当培养基中的渗透压降低后，再生的细胞团迅速长大，成为肉眼可见的小愈伤组织。随后长成 1~2mm 大小白色小硬块状愈伤组织。半固体和固体平板法培养形成的小愈伤组织，随琼脂糖固化的培养基一同转至 PS1 培养基上后，迅速扩增为松脆的愈伤组织。这些愈伤组织当转至 PS2 培养基后，成为结构化的块状愈伤组织。而在液体浅层培养条件下，50d 后能见到大量肉眼可见的愈伤组织(图版 I，7)。当转至 PR6 或 PR10 分化培养基并加强光照后，大多数愈伤组织分化出胚状结构和绿点。当这些已分化的愈伤组织转至无植物生长调节剂的 PR15 培养基后很快再生出小植株(图版 I，8)。其分化频率为 14.5%。除正常苗外，还有无根苗，白化苗和叶片卷缩的畸形苗。正常植株已移栽到土壤中，生长 20d 表现正常。

讨论

固体培养基上继代培养近两年，又在液体培养基中悬浮培养 4~9 个月的胚性细胞系仍能分离收集到大量有全能性的原生质体，并以较高的频率($12.14\% \times 14.5\%$)再生出完整植株。表明这个属间杂种可用来做原生质体水平的遗传转化和体细胞杂交以及细胞分子生物学方面的研究工作。

对小麦来说，虽然几乎所有基因型都能不同程度地被诱导出胚性愈伤组织并分化为植株[1,8,16]，但适于悬浮培养及原生质体再生完整植株的基因型却很有限[1,15]。此外，只有特定类型的胚性愈伤组织才能建立分散好，分化能力强的悬浮细胞系[1,14,21,27]。本文所述四种培养基中只有在 K_p 培养基上获得成功，而这四种培养基的主要差别在于 N 源不同，因此，表明 N 源对原生质体影响极大[1]。经 KM_{8p} 培养基修改简化而来的 K_p 培养基适合于小偃麦原生质体培养。源于 KM_{8p} 的原生质体培养基在甘蔗、水稻、玉米[21]、小麦[1]、鸭茅[9]、羊茅[5]等多种禾本科植物原生质体培养中都获得了成功。葡萄糖作为主要的碳源和渗透压稳定剂，同样具有普遍的适用性。对小偃麦原生质体培养同样适用。

和 Thompson 等(1986)的工作一样[23]，我们发现用 1.2%琼脂糖的固体平板培养可促进培养原生质体的再生及分裂。使细胞分裂频率显著提高。在液体培养条件下，原生质体粘连、出芽和液泡化现象普遍存在。而在固体培养时，原生质体被其周围的胶体所包围而不会发生粘连。此外，可能 1.2%琼脂糖固化的培养基有一定机械强度，对原生质体出芽和液泡化、膜的扩张等有机械性限制作用。同时，这种胶体对保持细胞极性也是有益的。Schnabl 等(1985)证明藻酸盐固化的培养基有效阻止了脂质的过氧化作用，从而增加了原生质体膜的稳定性[20]，可能琼脂糖也有类似的作用。Imbrie-Milligan 等(1987)的实验说明从玉米胚性愈伤组织分离的原生质体只有植入琼脂糖胶体培养基才能分裂[11]。因此，在原生质体培养基中加入琼脂糖，会对难以培养的原生质体的再生及提高植板率起到非常重要的作用。

我们实验中所用的 PS1 培养基中 2, 4-D 的浓度要比原生质体 K_p 培养基中的高出一倍。而由原生质体再生的小愈伤组织转至 2, 4-D 提高的固体培养基后，几乎使小愈伤组织剧增 10~20 倍而不致丧失其分化能力。这说明适当提高生长激素，在短期内对从原生质体再生的愈伤组织的分化能力影响不大。

小麦[1,2]和玉米[3,21]原生质体再生植株的研究表明，生长素如 2, 4-D，IAA 等和细胞分裂素如 KT，6-BA，玉米素的适当配合有利于再生的愈伤组织分化成胚状体或胚状结构。此外，在这一阶段活性炭的加入也有利于分化[2,3]。据此，我们设计了 PR6 和 PR10 培养基，并利用它们成功地从小偃麦原生质体再生的愈伤组织分化成胚状体结构。胚状体的形成是愈伤组织再生植株的重要环节[26]。从胚状体很容易分化出苗。

参考文献

[1] 王海波、李向辉、孙勇如、陈炬、朱祯、方仁、王培, 1989: 小麦原生质体培养——高频率的细胞团形成和植株再生.中国科学(B 辑), 8: 828~835

[2] 任延国、贾敬芬、李名杨、郑国锠, 1989: 小麦幼穗愈伤组织原生质体培养再生植株。科学通报, 9: 693~695

[3] 蔡起贵、郭仲琛、钱迎倩、姜荣锡、周云罗, 1987: 玉米原生质体的植株再生. 植物学报, 29: 453~458

[4] Chu C. C., C. C. Wang, C. S. Sun, C. Hsu, K.C. Yin and C. Y. Chu, 1975: Establishment of an efficient medium for anther culture of rice through comparative experiments on the nitrogen sources. *Sci. Sinica,* 18: 659~668

[5] Dalton S. J., 1988: Plant regeneration from cell suspension protoplasts of *Festuca arundinacea* Schreb. (tall fescue) and *Lolium perenne* L. (perennial ryegrass). *J. Plant Physiol.,* 132: 170~175

[6] Gamborg O. L., R. A. Miller and K. Ojima, 1968: Nutrient requirements of suspension cultures of soybean root cells. *Exp. Cell Res.,* 50: 151~158

[7] Harris R., M. Wright, M. Byrne, J. Varnum, B. Bright well and K. Schubert, 1988: Callus formation and plantlet regeneration from protoplasts derived from suspension cultures of wheat (*Triticum acstioum* L.). *Plant Cell Rep.,* 7: 337~340

[8] He D. G., Y. M. Yang and K. J. Scott, 1988: A comparison of scutellum callus and epiblast callus induction in wheat: the effects of genotype, embryo age and medium. *Plant Sci.,* 57: 225~233

[9] Horn M. E., B. V. Conger and C. T. Harms, 1988: Plant regeneration from protoptasts of embryogenic suspension cultures of orchardgrass (*Dactylis glomerata* L.) *Plant Cell Rep.,* 7: 371~374

[10] Horn M. E., R. D. Shillito, B. V. Conger and C. T. Harms, 1988: Transgenic plants of irchardgrass (*Dactylis glomerata* L.) from protoplasts. *Plant Cell Rep.,* 7: 469~472

[11] Imbrie Milligan C., K. K. Kamo and T. K. Hodges, 1987: Microcallus growth from maize protoplasts, *Planta,* 171: 58~64

[12] Koa K. N. and M. R. Michayluk, 1975: Nutritional requirements for growth of *Vicia hajastana* cells and protoplasts at very low population density in liquid media. *Planta,* 126: 105~110

[13] Linsmaire E. M., and F. Skoog, 1965: Organic growth factor requirements of tabaco cultares *Physiol. Plant,* 18: 100~127

[14] Luhrs R. and H. Lorz, 1988: Initiation of morphogenic cell suspension and protoplast cultures of barley (*Hordcum vulgarc* L.) *Planta,* 175: 71~81

[15] Maddock, S. E., 1987: Suspension and protoplast culture of hexapeoid wheat (*Triticum aestivum* L.) *Plant Cell Rep.,* 6: 23~26

[16] Maddock S. E., B. A. Lancaster, R. Risiott and J. Franklin, 1983: Plant regeneration from cultured immature embryos and inflorescences of 25 cultivars of wheat (*Triticum aestivum* L.). *J. Exp. Bot.,* 34: 915~926

[17] Murashige T. and F. Skoog, 1962: A revised medium for rapid growth ond bioassays with tobacco tissue cultures. *Physiol. Plant.* 15: 473~497

[18] Rhodges C. A., K. S. Lowe and K. L., Ruby, 1988: Plant regeneration from protoplasts isolated from embryogenic cell cultures. *Bio/Technology,* 6: 56~60

[19] Rhodges C. A., D. A. Pierce, I. J. Metller, D. Mascarenhas and J. J. Detmer, 1988: Genetically transformed maize plants from protoplasts. *Science,* 240: 204~207

[20] Schnabl H. and R. J. Youngman, 1985: Immobolisation of plant cell protoplasts inhibits enzymic lipid peroxidation. *Plant Sci.,* 40: 65~69

[21] Shillito R. D., G. K. Carswell, C. M. Johnson, J. J. Dimaio and C. T. Harms, 1989: Regeneration of fertile plants from protoplasts of elite inbred maize. *Bio/Technology,* 7: 581~587

[22] Srinivasan C. and I. K. Vasil, 1986: Plant regeneration from protoplasts of sugarcane (*Saccharum officinarum* L.) *J. Plant Physiol.,* 126: 41~48

[23] Thompson J. A., R. Abdullah and E. C. Cocking, 1986: Protoplast Culture of rice (*Oryza sativa* L.) using media solidified with agarose. *Plant Sci.*, 47: 123~133

[24] Toriyama K., Y. Arimoto, H. Uchimiya and K. Hinata, 1988: Transgenic rice plants after direct gene transfer into protoplasts. *Bio/Technology,* 6: 1072~1074

[25] Toriyama K. and K. Hinata, 1985: Cell suspension and protoplast culture in rice. *Plant Sci.,* 41: 179~183

[26] Vasil I. K., 1988: Progress in the regeneration and genetic manipulation of cereal crops. *Bio/Technology,* 6: 397~402

[27] Vasil V. and I. K. Vasil, 1986: Plant regeneration from friable embryogenic callus and cell suspension cultures of *Zea mays. J. Plant Physiol.,* 124: 399~408

[28] Zhang H. M., H. Yang, E. L. Rech, T. J. Colds, A. S. Davis B. J. Mulligan, E. C. Cocking and M. R. Davey, 1988: Transgenic rice plants produced by electroporation-mediated plasmid uptake into protoplasts. *Plant Cell Rep.,* 7: 379~384

图 版 I

Plate I

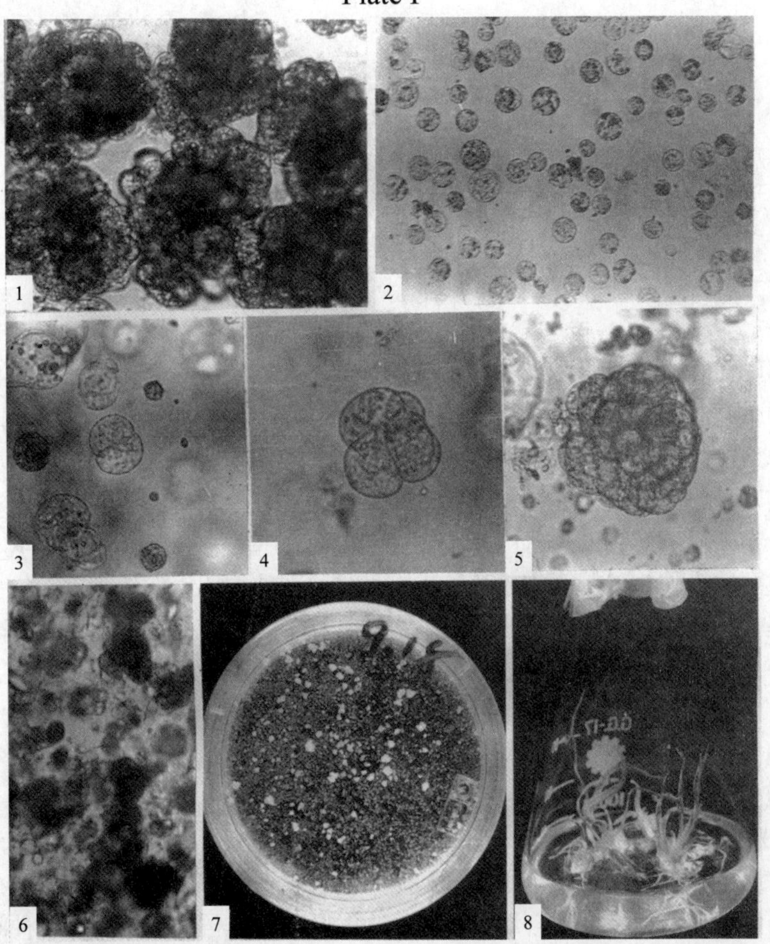

1. 从小偃麦幼穗诱导得到的胚性悬浮细胞系。×240 2. 由胚性悬浮细胞系分离的原生质体。×400 3. 小偃麦原生质体在植板 2d 后的第一次分裂。×400 4. 培养 5d 后，由 8 个细胞组成的小细胞团。×400 5. 培养 15d 后的小愈伤组织。×320 6. 培养 20d 后，在 1.2%琼脂糖固化的培养基中出现大量小愈伤组织。×240 7. 培养 50d 后，在液体培养基中有大量大小不等的愈伤组织。×1 8. 在用 Gelrite 固化的分化培养基上再生的完整植株。×0.8

Fig. 1. Embryogenic cell suspension of *Trititrigia* induced from immature. inflorescence ×240 Fig. 2. Protoplasts isolated freshly from embryogenic cell suspension. ×400 Fig. 3. First division of *Trititrigia* protoplast, 2 days after plating. ×400 Fig. 4. Small cluster consisted of 8 cells after 5 days in the culture. ×400 Fig. 5. Microcalli after 15 days in the culture. ×320 Fig. 6. Numerous microcalli occurred in medium solidified with 1.2% agarose, 20 days after plating. ×240 Fig. 7. Calli, in different size, distributed in liquid medium after 50 days in the culture. ×1 Fig. 8. Whole plants regenerated on differentiation medium solidified with gelrite. ×0.8

本文原载：中国科学院院刊. 1990. 5(4): 336-339

植物原生质体的研究在中国科学院的发展*

袁萍　钱迎倩

(中国科学院生物科学与技术局)

我国科学工作者经过近20年的不懈努力，现已全面突破重要禾本科粮食作物和经济作物原生质体再生植株的难关，进入植物原生质体培养和再生研究的国际先进行列。

植物原生质体是指去除细胞壁，由质膜包被的生活细胞。这种细胞经培养能再生植株，从而实现植物功能的全能性。长期以来，常规的有性杂交在不同种属间难以成功，适于双子叶植物基因转移的Ti质粒载体，不易将目的基因携入禾本科等植物体内，给作物特别是重要粮食作物的基因工程育种带来困难。而植物原生质体为远缘优良性状和基因的转移提供了较理想的受体系统。通过两种具有不同遗传信息的原生质体融合或有用目的基因导入，经人工选择后可创造自然界没有的体细胞杂种或转基因植物，达到改良品种的品质、提高抗性及其他生产性状的目的。植物原生质体还是一个研究细胞壁再生、质膜等细胞骨架的结构和功能以及分离细胞器的良好实验体系，用以深入探索生命科学中有关细胞生物学、遗传学、植物生理学以至分子生物学的基本问题。

从1960年英国诺丁汉大学Cocking教授利用纤维素酶从番茄根尖细胞分离到大量有活力的原生质体以来，植物原生质体培养研究引起了世界各国科学家的极大重视。1971年和1972年世界上第一例来自烟草叶肉细胞的原生质体再生植株和烟草种间原生质体融合的体细胞杂种植物相继问世。此后国际上高等植物原生质体研究迅速发展。人们曾期望的获得地上部结西红柿地下部产马铃薯的杂种植株已不纯属空想。1986年原生质体融合的杂交组合已达80余例。其中，抗病毒病、抗虫、抗寒的马铃薯和番茄，抗除草剂的烟草和油菜，高产优质的脐橙以及胞质不育的水稻等杂种正在大田选育，包心菜和青菜原生质体融合育成的“千宝菜”已进入日本市场。然而植物原生质体培养和再生植株作为体细胞融合、外缘基因导入的基础，其技术的发展经历了一个艰难的过程。1986年以前，80多种再生植株大部分属茄科、伞形科、十字花科、云香料等双子叶植物。单子叶植物的禾谷类和双子叶植物中重要农作物的原生质体培养仍被公认为国际性难题。我国科学家近几年来先后在国际上首次或较早地从玉米、大豆、野生大豆、高粱、谷子、小偃麦、大麦、猕猴桃、哈密瓜、水稻、小麦和棉花的原生质体获得再生植株。中国科学院的原生质体研究在全面攻克难关的过程中进一步得到发展。

---

* 感谢李向辉先生阅稿，并提出宝贵意见。

一、历史的回顾

起步跟踪阶段(1972~1976 年)：70 年代初期，中国科学院遗传研究所、植物研究所和上海植物生理研究所在国内首先开辟了植物原生质体的研究领域。在科研条件不尽如人意的情况下，科研人员自力更生，努力创造实验的基本条件。1973 年遗传所 502 组在国内发表了第一篇关于“几种豆类植物原生质体的游离、培养形成小细胞团”的论文。由于当时选用豆科植物作为研究对象，难度较大，原生质体培养研究的进展缓慢。科研人员及时改用烟草、矮牵牛、胡萝卜等模式植物作为研究对象，在较短的时间内上述 3 个所相继使烟草、胡萝卜、矮牵牛的原生质体再生成植物。1974 年遗传所获得了由小麦和蚕豆原生质体融合形成的细胞团。1975 年植物所以水稻单倍体愈伤组织起源的原生质体获得了再生细胞团和大量愈伤组织,为 80 年代中期主要禾本科作物的原生质体再生植株的突破作了最初的技术贮备。与此同时，以原生质体愈伤组织为基础的体细胞融合技术开始起步。在此阶段，遗传所、植物所、上海植物生理所还在国内积极组织学术交流，于 1974 年和 1975 年分别在北京、上海召开了全国第一届、第二届植物体细胞杂交工作交流会议，讨论解决研究难题的途径和方法。

同步发展阶段(1977~1985 年)：1977 年后，3 所科研人员一方面加速由模式植物转向有经济价值的双子叶植物和重要禾本科粮食作物原生质体的研究。另一方面进一步发展了原生质体融合技术。至 1985 年年底，先后获得了 6 个科的 20 余种植物原生质体再生植株，其中包括茄科、伞形花科、玄参科的一些植物以及不易培养再生的单子叶植物棒头草(禾本科)、洋葱(百合科)等。此外，还获得了水稻、大麦、甘蔗、玉米、大豆、绿豆、草木樨、马铃薯、龙胆、灰藜和猕猴桃等重要植物原生质体的愈伤组织。在原生质体再生的基础上建立了技术体系。1981 年后的 4 年间，共获得烟草与矮牵牛(遗传所、1981 年)等 8 种体细胞融合杂种植株，其中有些植株后代进入大田筛选试验，从而为我国体细胞杂交培育全新的植物品种打下了基础。至此，我国的原生质体研究实现了与国外工作同步发展的转变。我院遗传所、植物所、上海植物生理所、华南植物所、昆明植物所、成都生物所的科学工作者共发表学术论文近百篇。这个阶段组织了国内的第三、四、五次体细胞杂交工作学术交流会议，并于 1984 年 7 月、1986 年 3 月和 4 月先后举办了两期国内、一期亚洲地区国际性原生质体培养、细胞融合技术培训班。

局部领先阶段(1986 年以后)：由于植物原生质体的培养、体细胞的融合技术比较复杂，尚无一定规律可循。1986 年以前的 20 多年，人们一直在探索如何将重要粮食作物和经济作物的原生质体培养成植株。1986 年遗传所、上海植物生理所继法国、日本之后，在国内首先将水稻(粳型)的原生质体再生成植株。1987 年植物所在世界上首次应用杂种玉米的胚性愈伤组织使原生质体再生植株，引起国际上很大反响。1987~1989 年，上海植物生理所突破世界性难关，将 6 个大豆品种和 1 个野生大豆品系的未成熟子叶分离的原生质体再生植株。遗传所于 1988 年几乎与美国同时发表了小麦再生植株的报道。近年来，植物所和上海植物生理所等又在世界上首先成功地将小偃麦、高粱、谷子、猕猴桃、毛白杨、哈密瓜、诸葛菜等植物的原生质体再生成植株。这些成果的取得，使我国在该领域的研究，局部处于世界领先水平，受到国际同行的重视。与美国洛氏基金会、孟山都公司建立了合作关系并得到发展。第七个五年计划期间，3 个所的科学家联合院内外兄弟单位，主持、承担了国家重点科技攻关专题“植物原生质体培养和体细胞融合研究”，“豆科、禾谷类植物转化系统”，“有重要价值的标记基因和受体系统的建立”以及国家高科技研究计划中的“重要粮食作物的原生质体培养、高效成株技术及体细胞融合技术”课题，均较好地完成了计划。

二、技术的进步

E_{A3}-867 纤维素酶的应用在国内原生质体研究中发挥了较大作用。上海植物生理所 1972 年以野生型绿色木霉中选出突变株制成 E_{A3}-867 纤维素酶制剂，酶解细胞壁的效能与日本产的 Onozuka R-10 酶基本相同，且不需配加果胶酶，从而缓解了国内研究工作的急需。至 1976 年，仅该所用 E_{A3}-867 纤维素酶制剂就从 20 多种植物材料中分离出原生质体，并把烟草愈伤组织和叶肉组织分离的原生质体分化成植株。1978 年遗传所在矮牵牛培养基(DPD)的基础上建立了原生质体培养基和分化培养基配合组成的 D_2 培养基，并先后使普通烟草、长花烟草、粉蓝烟草及洋地黄等植物原生质体再生出植株。西德科学家 Meijer 和 Stainbiss 等 1983 年用 D_2 培养基获得了圭亚那柱花草(多年生豆科草)原生质体再生植株。

技术的改进促进了研究工作的发展。虽然 Cocking 1960 年第一次已用酶法游离根的原生质体，但由于根尖细胞壁的组成不同于叶片，采用常规的酶混合液难以获得大量的原生质体。上海植物生理所的科研人员 1981 年在酶溶液中加入较多的 Rhozyme，基本解决了问题，已为国内外广泛采用。植物所在难再生的猕猴桃、玉米、小偃麦原生质体培养研究中，采用以不同组分培养基为特点的分步诱导法，促进了原生质体愈伤组织的繁殖、胚性转移和再化植株的分化。植物所近年来还在世界上较早地进行了水稻、玉米原生质体的超低温保存技术研究，快速化冻后获得再生植株。这项技术的研究成功，提高了原生质体分裂频率，可随时提供遗传转化受体，为研究细胞壁再生和植物细胞的抗性机理，筛选抗寒突变体等基本问题创造了条件。

三、应用的实例

上海植物生理所得到 500 株移栽成活的烟草(草新 1 号)与龙葵野生种原生质体融合的体细胞杂种植株，经与河南省农林科学院烟草研究所合作，现已选育到一个具有生产价值的烟草新品系和一个小叶早熟的新材料。

遗传所将人αD 干扰素分别转到烟草和水稻品种的原生质体中，获得了经分子杂交检测证明有外源基因整合的再生植株。转基因的第二代烟草正在测定对烟草花叶病毒(TMV)的抗性，水稻再生的转化植株已移栽到大田。

遗传所、上海植物生理所已分别以粳稻、糯稻的原生质体再生植株后代中选育到矮秆、抗逆和抗穗颈稻瘟病的一些株系，正在大田试验。其他如猕猴桃、大豆的有益变异株系也正在田间繁殖、筛选之中。

四、问题与展望

目前我国科学家虽然在国际上全面突破了主要农作物再生植株的难关，并较早地开展了实用基因转化原生质体的研究，但仍面临着下述主要问题：①再生成功的主要农作物原生质体的分裂及分化频率还不够高，要使其达到与模式植物(如烟草等)原生质体培养类似的频率，以利于基因转移，还有一段距离；②存在较多难再生的作物品种种类，需进一步研究其再生规律，使培养技术规范化。因此，进一步掌握提高频率的技术，深入研究培养对象的不同遗传型和培养条件、方法以及形态发生能力间的关系，建立原生质体融合的筛选系统和对杂交产物的细胞遗传学分析技术以及分析转化基因的整合规律、后代的遗传稳定性等，将成为我国科学家下一步奋斗的目标。

随着上述目标的实现，我们将努力推进植物原生质体研究和应用的工作，使其进一步发展，并将可能从抗病、优质、高产的体细胞杂种中，从转移抗虫、抗病毒、高蛋白等基因的后代中以及从原生质体再生植株出现的无性系变异材料中，选育一批作物新品系或新材料。

本文原载：植物学报. 1992. 34(11): 822-828

美味猕猴桃原生质体再生植株无性系变异的研究*

蔡起贵[1] 钱迎倩[1] 柯善强[2] 何子灿[2] 姜荣锡[1] 周云罗[1]
叶亚平[1] 洪树荣[2] 黄仁煌[2]

(1 中国科学院植物研究所；2 中国科学院武汉植物研究所)

摘 要 取一雌株美味猕猴桃(*Actinidia deliciosa* line No.26)当年生枝条的茎段再生苗的叶片、细嫩茎段及叶柄分别在培养基上诱导愈伤组织。上述 3 种不同愈伤组织来源的原生质体经培养后，叶片及茎段愈伤组织来源的原生质体再生大量小植株。在 1987~1989 年间，再生小植株通过移栽或嫁接,有 76 株叶片愈伤组织及 21 株茎段愈伤组织来源的原生质体再生植株定植成活。叶片愈伤组织来源的原生质体再生植株中的 3 株，在 1991 年 5 月开花。其中 2 株是雌株，1 株是雄株。经人工授粉后，雌株已结不少果实。从而证实，美味猕猴桃的体细胞再生植株存在性别分化。再生植株的叶片、节间及花的形态上出现大量的体细胞无性系变异。鉴定了 16 株再生植株染色体，其染色体数每株不一样，变动在 116~180。

关键词 美味猕猴桃；原生质体再生植株；体细胞无性系变异

猕猴桃原生质体培养获得再生植株的研究从 1988 年开始已陆续有报道[9,11,12]。除猕猴桃外，多年生水果类的木本或木质藤本攀缘植物的原生质体培养成功的种类还为数不多[1,2,3,7,8,10,13]。而对这些已得到的再生植株，较详细的分析报告至今尚未见到。猕猴桃属共有近 60 个种，其中 57 种原产地在中国。由于其果实维生素 C 含量高，首先由新西兰从美味猕猴桃中选育出“海沃特”品种，以其高的产量及优良的品质作为一种新兴的水果。近年的研究结果表明，猕猴桃还有防癌作用[4]。意大利、智利等国家也相继崛起。培育比“海沃特”更为优质高产的品种已成为国际上共同关心的问题。我们以美味猕猴桃(*Actinidia deliciosa* line No.26)为材料，进行了原生质体培养。已移栽成活的原生质体再生植株中呈现了性别分化和大量的体细胞无性系变异。这些变异可能给猕猴桃提供新的育种材料，也可能对美味猕猴桃的起源、猕猴桃属的分类、甚至植物体细胞性别分化的基础研究有一定价值。本文报道上述体细胞无性系变异的研究结果。

---

* 国家七·五细胞工程资助项目。

李洪钧副教授帮助鉴定原生质体再生植株叶片的形态特征；纵微星同志参加部分染色体制片工作，安和祥及蔡达荣副教授提供 26 号猕猴桃，并在工作过程中进行过有益的讨论，特此致谢。

材料与方法

取生长在中国科学院植物研究所北京植物园的一雌株美味猕猴桃当年生枝条的茎段作为外植体，经培养后得到试管苗。用该苗的叶片、细嫩茎段及叶柄分别在培养基上诱导愈伤组织。从上述3种不同愈伤组织分别分离原生质体。原生质体分离、培养、植株再生的方法及培养基的配方参阅 Tsai(1988)[12]。这里需要说明一点，因猕猴桃属的种名更改较多，1988年发表文章上所用的种名及品种名有误，正确的种名应为 *Actinidia deliciosa* line No.26。

原生质体经培养后，得到大量的试管苗。这些苗都移栽到中国科学院武汉植物研究所植物园中。试管苗首先在花盆中移栽过渡。在1987年间，叶片愈伤组织来源的原生质体再生植株分4批定植或嫁接到中华猕猴桃砧木上。嫁接后，用一玻璃管套住整个嫁接苗以保持温度，待成活后再取下玻璃管。茎段愈伤组织来源的原生质体再生植株由于根系发育不好，因此在培养室中诱导出更多的根系后，于1989年定植于武汉植物所植物园。

为检查原生质体再生植株染色体数目，材料分别取自根尖及茎尖。根尖采用常规压片法制片。上午9时左右取材，用0.1%秋水仙碱溶液在室温下预处理2~3h，然后在无水乙醇：冰醋酸(3：1)固定液中固定20h。根尖在1mol/L HCl中，60℃下解离12min，用铁矾-苏木精染色后压片并作镜检。茎尖的取材时间同上，按照陈瑞阳和宋文芹(1982)[5]的去壁低渗法制片。

结果

(一) 再生植株定植或嫁接后的存活情况

叶片愈伤组织来源的原生质体再生苗49株于1987年分两批定植，成活44株；嫁接

表1　美味猕猴桃原生质体再生植株幼苗期生长情况(cm)*

Table 1　The growth potential of regenerated plants from leaf-derived protoplasts of *Actinidia deliciosa* line No. 26(cm)

嫁接型 Grafting type				生长正常型 Normal growth type				生长缓慢型 Slow growth type			
株号 Strain No.	1987	1988	1989	株号 Strain No.	1987	1988	1989	株号 Strain No.	1987	1988	1989
1	60.0	27.0	249.0	20	21.0	37.5	47.0	21	12.0	13.5	78.0
2	14.3	17.4	58.6	22	21.0	17.0	98.2	23	12.0	7.0	38.0
3	42.0	96.0	178.6	33	26.0	42.0	68.0	24	16.0	11.0	48.0
4	37.0	112.0	189.4	34	21.0	21.0	46.0	30	16.0	21.0	47.0
5	26.0	74.0	138.0	43	42.0	61.0	101.0	31	14.0	8.0	22.0
6	68.0	43.0	59.5	57	25.0	76.0	94.0	32	12.0	7.0	62.0
7	25.0	97.0	126.0	58	37.0	22.4	87.0	35	5.0	4.5	42.0
8	13.2	17.0	48.0	60	25.0	74.2	103.2	39	8.0	7.6	21.0
9	11.2	54.0	78.0	61	50.0	74.0	82.1	46	3.0	5.0	36.5
10	24.0	73.0	95.0	74	38.4	62.1	75.0	47	5.0	11.0	38.5
平均 Average	32.1	61.0	122.1	平均 Average	30.6	53.6	80.2	平均 Average	11.3	9.6	43.3

* 表中数字代表每年增长的高度。

The data in Table 1 are the increasing height (cm) of strains per year.

苗共 36 株也分两批进行，成活 31 株。茎段愈伤组织来源的原生质体再生苗 30 株于 1989 年定植，成活 21 株。上述结果说明，移栽或嫁接的再生植株的成活数量还是较多的，总的成活率达到 84.34％。

(二) 生长情况

从叶片愈伤组织和茎段愈伤组织来源的原生质体都得到了再生植株。但是，从叶柄愈伤组织来源的原生质体仅再生愈伤组织，这些愈伤组织未能获得器官发生。从叶片愈伤组织来源的原生质体再生植株，经移栽或嫁接后，生长情况比茎段愈伤组织来源的原生质体再生植株旺盛得多。后者的生长情况也很不一致，除多数植株能正常生长外，少数植株生长缓慢并出现下面现象，即每年冬天其中一些植株地上部的主干发生死亡，到第二年春天又在近根部再抽出新的主干，这种现象年复一年地出现。

从叶片愈伤组织来源的原生质体再生植株，根据其生长情况可分为 3 种类型：即嫁接、正常生长和缓慢生长型。表 1 说明，在 1987 年和 1988 年时嫁接型和正常生长型之间的平均生长高度相差不多。但是到 1989 年，两者之间有明显的差别，即嫁接型的平均生长速度比正常生长型快 1/3。而 3 种类型之间的生长速度差别则更为显著。它们的差别不仅反映在主干的高度上，同样反映在藤条的多少、长度及株冠的覆盖率上。1989 年后，三者在藤条及株冠之间的差距愈加明显，但已很难以尺度来表示。

表 2 美味猕猴桃原生质体再生植株叶片及节间变异*

Table 2 The variation of leaves and internodes of regenerated plants from leaf-derived protoplasts of *Actinidia deliciosa* line No. 26

株号 Strain No.	叶片大小 (cm) Size of leaves (cm)			叶柄长(cm) Length of petiole(cm)	节间长(cm) Length of internode(cm)	叶片形态特征 Morphological characteristics of leaves
	长 Length	宽 Width	长：宽 Length:Width			
4	10.40	8.20	1.27：1	3.70	3.17	卵圆形，先端突尖，基部亚心形 Ovate, acute at tip and subcordate at base
5	14.30	9.70	1.47：1	3.80	5.29	长卵圆形，先端尖，基部亚心形 Long ovate, acuminate at tip and subcordate at base
6	12.10	6.80	1.78：1	3.30	3.18	倒披针形，先端渐尖，基部楔形 Oblanceolate, acuminate at tip and cuneate at base
12	9.90	9.80	1.01：1	3.70	2.10	圆形，先端突尖具芒刺，基部心形 Round, acute and aristate at tip and cordate at base
13	12.00	10.90	1.10：1	4.40	5.40	卵形，先端尾状渐尖，边缘有刺状小齿，基部心形 Ovoid, acute and tailed off, with echinate denticulate margin with echinate denticulate margin and cordate at base

续表

株号 Strain No.	叶片大小 (cm) Size of leaves (cm)			叶柄长(cm) Length of petiole(cm)	节间长(cm) Length of internode(cm)	叶片形态特征 Morphological characteristics of leaves
	长 Length	宽 Width	长：宽 Length:Width			
19	8.30	7.30	1.14：1	3.91	7.10	扇形，先端截面微凹，基部心形 Flabellate, truncate retuse at tip and cordete at base
21	9.30	7.58	1.22：1	2.30	4.20	椭圆形，先端突尖，基部心形 Ellipticum, acute at tip, cordate at base
43	10.40	8.60	1.20：1	3.90	4.20	椭圆形，先端略尖，基部心形 Ellipticum subacuminate at tip and cordate at base
CK	12.20	13.40	0.91：1	5.17	8.70	多数圆形，先端突尖，基部心形；少数近圆形，先端截形微凹，基部心形 Most of them are near round, acute at tip and cordate at base; Some of them are near round, truncate retuse at tip and cordate at base

* 叶片大小，叶柄长及节间长都是 10 个的平均数。

All data are calculated as the average of 10.

(三) 叶片和节间的变异

原生质体再生植株最显著的变异是表现在叶片上。不仅不同株之间表现出多种多样的叶片形态，甚至在同一株上也反映出叶片的多样性。母株的大多数叶片的形态是圆形、先端突尖，基部为心形；而少数叶片为近圆形、先端截形微凹，基部为心形(图版 I，1)。在再生植株中固然也有像母株形态的叶片，但更多的叶片形态与母株是不一样的。具有明显变异再生植株的叶片及节间的观察结果列于表 2。从表 2 可见，第 6 号植株的叶片形态变异最大，为倒披针形(图版 I，2)。从表 2 号还可看出，在叶片的长度、宽度、叶柄长度及节间长度方面，再生植株都显然比对照母株短。一般来说，再生植株如系雌株，节间变短可能是丰产的特征之一。但是，少数植株突出的变异也表现在节间变得特别短，如第 12 号植株，平均节间长度只有 2.1cm。这种植株呈簇生现象(图版 I，3)，株冠也小，对阳光的吸收显然是不利的。如果是雌株，将对今后果实的长大更为不利。

(四) 雄株和雌株的花器官

叶片愈伤组织来源的原生质体再生植株中的 3 株(均为通过嫁接成活)在 1991 年 5 月中旬开花，其中 1 株是雄株，2 株是雌株。雌、雄株和对照母株的花冠大小、花药数、柱头数和退化花药数的对比见表 3。从表 3 可见，原生质体再生植株除了雌株柱头数略有增加外，其花冠大小、花药数及退化花药数与对照母株相比，均有变小及减少趋势。有趣的是，在两棵雌株中，雌花的形态是不一样的。第 19 号植株所有雌花的花瓣都向后下垂(图版 I，4)，而第 16 号植株的所有花瓣与雄株的雄花一样都是平展的(图版 I，5)。

而母株雌花的花瓣绝大多数是平展的，偶尔也能见到有向后下垂的。再生植株雄花(第 12 号植株)的花药发育正常，用该花的花粉向雌株进行人工授粉几天后，子房就开始膨大，并陆续座果(图版 I，6)，说明其花粉是可育的。1991 年，第 16 号雌株开花 22 朵，结果 14 个；第 19 号雌株开花 114 朵，结果 69 个。

表 3　美味猕猴桃原生质体再生植株雌、雄花的形态*

Table 3　The morphology of pistillate and staminate flowers of regenerated plants from leaf-derived protoplasts of *Actinidia deliciosa* line No. 26

原生质体再生植株 Regenerated plants derived from protoplasts					对照母株 CK(*A. deliciosa* line No. 26)				
12 号雄株(♂) Staminate plant No. 12		19 号雌株(♀) Pistillate plant No. 19			雄株(♂) Staminate plant		雌株(♀) Pistillate plant		
花冠大小 (cm) Size of corolla (cm)	花药数 Number of anther	花冠大小 (cm) Size of corolla (cm)	柱头数 Number of stigma	退化花药数 Number of degenerated anther	花冠大小 (cm) Size of corolla (cm)	花药数 Number of anther	花冠大小 (cm) Size of corolla (cm)	柱头数 Number of stigma	退化花药数 Number of degenerated anther
4.14	149	4.40	29.90	117	5.30	197.40	5.48	25.3	166.40

* 均为 10 朵花的平均数。

All data are calculated as the average of 10 flowers.

(五) 染色体数

美味猕猴桃的染色体数为 174(2n = 6X = 174)[14,15]。但是，原生质体再生植株的染色体数变化很大，绝大多数是非整倍体。从已检查的 16 株再生植株中，染色体数变动在 116~118，而且每一株的染色体数都不一样。其中第 25 号植株的染色体数为 158(图版 I，7)；第 36 号植株的染色体数为 180(图版 I，8)。染色体数这样的不一致，说明了原生质体再生植株的变异是很大的。

讨论

在原生质体再生植株中出现了一定数量的丛生变异株，这是由于这些植株的顶端优势不明显而腋芽很快发育的结果。洪树荣等(1990)[6]报道中华猕猴桃胚乳植株后代中也出现丛生变异株。定植在武汉植物所植物园中的丛生胚乳植株，个别株的丛生、矮化现象比原生质体植株更为严重。定植多年的胚乳植株，始终保持矮化现象，最小的叶片长度只有 5mm 左右。在原生质体再生植株中还未见到有这种现象。

在已开花的原生质体再生植株中，1991 年已出现 2 个雌株及 1 个雄株，说明从同一个雌株叶片愈伤组织来源的原生质体再生植株中有性别分化。猕猴桃属种子起源的籽苗的性别分化是普遍的。洪树荣等(1990)[6]报道了由同一块愈伤组织诱导的胚乳植株后代中也有雌、雄性别的分化。胚乳是一个精子与两个极核融合后的有性过程的产物。而原生质体再生植株中出现雌、雄性植株，说明不经过有性过程的美味猕猴桃的体细胞再生植株也同样存在性别分化，这对从遗传学角度进一步作性别分化的深入研究是很有意义的。

此外，美味猕猴桃原生质体再生植株在叶片形态及染色体数目上的大量变异，可能对今后研究美味猕猴桃种的起源及猕猴桃属的分类有参考的价值；至于今后可能从这些变异株中选择出具优良性状的株系，在猕猴桃育种上的意义就更为明显了。

参考文献

[1] 卫志明、许智宏、许农、黄敏仁，1991：悬铃木叶肉原生质体培养再生植株.植物学报, 33：813~818

[2] 邓秀新, 1991：柑桔原生质体培养与植株再生.植物原生质体培养(孙勇如, 安锡培主编).科学出版社, 北京, 194—201

[3] 李文彬, 1991：木本植物原生质体培养的国内外现状.植物原生质体培养(孙勇如, 安锡培主编).科学出版社, 北京, 116~122

[4] 宋圃菊、徐勇, 1988：中华猕猴桃的防癌作用——(五)阻断大鼠和健康人体内N-亚硝基脯氨酸的合成.营养学报, 10(1)：50~55

[5] 陈瑞阳、宋文芹，1982：植物染色体标本制备的新方法——去壁低渗法及其在细胞学中的应用. 植物染色体及染色体技术(朱澂主编).科学出版社, 北京, 99~114

[6] 洪树荣、黄仁煌、武显维、柯善强、桂耀林、徐廷玉、顾淑荣, 1990：中华猕猴桃胚乳植株后代的观察.植物学通报, 7(4)：31~36

[7] Kobayashi, S., H. Uchimiya and I Ikeda. 1986: Plant regeneration from “Trovita” orange protoplasts. *Japan. J. Brecd*, 33:119~112

[8] ————, 1987: Uniformity of plant regeneration from orange (*C. sinensis* Osb.) protoplasts. *Thero. Appl. Genet*., 74: 10~14

[9] Mii, M. and H. Ohashi, 1988: Plantlet regeneration from protoplasts of kiwifruit, *Actinidia chinensis* Planch. *Acta Hort*., 230: 167~170

[10] Ochatt, S. J., E. C.Cocking and J. B. Power, 1987: Isolation, culture and plant regeneration of colt (*Prunus avium* × *Pseudocerasus*) protoplasts. *Plant Sci*, 50: 139~143

[11] Oliveira, M. M. and M. S. Pais, 1991: Plant regeneration from protoplasts of long-trem callus cultures of *Actinidia deliciosa* var. *deliciosa* cv. Hayward (kiwifruit). *Plant Cell Rep*., 9: 643~646

[12] Tsai, C. K. 1988: Plant regeneration from leaf calli protoplasts of *Actinidia chinensis* Planch var. *chinensis*. *Plant Sci*., 54: 231~235

[13] Vardi, A., P. Spisgel-Roy, and E. Galun, 1982: Plant regeneration from *Citrus* protoplasts: variability in methodological requirement among cultivars and species. *Thero. Appl. Genet*., 62: 171~176

[14] Zhang, J. and T. G. Thorp, 1986: Morphology of nine pistillate and three staminate New Zealand clones of kiwifruit (*Actinidia deliciosa* CA. Cher. C. F. Liang et A. R. Ferguson var. *deliciosa*). *New Zea. J. Bot*., 24: 589~613

[15] Zhang, Z. Y., 1983: A report on the chromosome numbers of 2 varieties of *Actinidia chinensis* Planch. *Acta Phytotax. Sin*., 21: 161~163

图 版 I

Plate I

1. 母株的叶片形态。2. 再生植株倒披针形的叶片形态。3. 叶片愈伤组织来源的矮化和簇生植株。4. 再生植株雌花的形态。5. 再生植株雄花的形态。6. 再生植株结的猕猴桃果。7. 第 25 号再生植株的染色体数为 158 个。8. 第 36 号再生植株的染色体数为 180 个

Fig. 1. Leaf shape of mother plant.Fig. 2. Oblanceolate shape of leaves on regenerated plant.Fig. 3. Dwarf and caespitose plant from protoplasts of leaf-derived calli. Fig. 4. Morphology of staminate flower on regenerated plant. Fig. 5. Morphology of pistillate flowers on regenerated plant. Fig. 6. Kiwifruits beared on the regenerated plant. Fig. 7. Chromosome number (158) of regenerated plant strain No. 25. Fig. 8. Chromosome number (180) of regenerated plant strain No. 36

本文原载：植物学集刊. 1994. 7: 144-157

小麦抗寒力诱导过程中特异性蛋白质的合成*

潘杰　简令成　钱迎倩

(中国科学院植物研究所)

摘　要　通过对小麦抗寒锻炼过程中可溶性蛋白及膜蛋白组分的电泳图谱的分析，主要结果如下：①可溶性蛋白质电泳图谱的分析表明：人工低温锻炼 20d 后，在不同品种中新合成的多肽分子量分别为："郑州 741"是 28kD、73kD；"济南 13 号"是 24kD、28kD 和 73kD；"农大 139"是 28kD、60kD、65kD 和 68kD；田间抗寒锻炼的"燕大 1817"为 15kD、28kD、51kD、60kD、65kD 和 68kD。②经人工低温锻炼 20d 后，不同抗寒品种新合成的膜多肽分别是："郑州 741"为 30kD 和 68kD；"济南 13 号"为 30kD、58kD，68kD 和 81kD；"农大 139"为 18kD、21kD、27kD、32kD 和 56kD。田间锻炼的冬小麦"燕大 1817"为 21kD、29kD、36kD、43kD 和 83kD。③脱锻炼后，抗寒特异性的多肽及与抗寒相关的膜多肽发生减少或完全消失。以上结果进一步表明，在小麦的抗寒锻炼过程中无论是可溶性蛋白还是膜蛋白均确实有抗寒特异性蛋白的新合成，并在各品种间表现出某些共同的特异性多肽，这些新合成的多肽与品种的抗寒性存在密切的关系，品种愈抗寒，特异多肽的种类愈多。这些结果进一步证明，植物抗寒是由多基因控制的。

关键词　抗寒蛋白；植物抗寒性；小麦

近年来，随着植物分子生物学及生物技术的发展，一些研究者开始热衷于研究植物抗寒性诱导的分子机制。研究的最终目的是为了将来能通过基因工程来提高农作物的抗寒性。其研究途径就是通过鉴定、分离抗寒特异性的多肽，以获得氨基酸序列，鉴定其天然的功能以及可能利用其作为探针，筛选出特异的 cDNA 克隆。到目前为止，为这一目标而做过的植物种类有：菠菜、苜蓿、冬小麦和黑麦、油菜、雀麦草、冬油菜悬浮培养细胞，马铃薯苗、拟南芥菜、蒿草和柑桔等(简令成，1992)。这些研究者报道，在他们研究过的材料中，都发现在抗寒锻炼过程中有抗寒特异性蛋白质的新合成。然而在不同植物种类中缺乏普遍性存在的多肽及共同的规律，表明许多问题还有待进一步研究。关于小麦的抗寒机理我们已做过大量的工作(简令成，1986、1990)。基于以上研究动态和我们自己的工作基础，特开展"小麦抗寒力诱导过程中特异蛋白质合成"的研究，旨在探讨：在抗寒力发展过程中，是否真正存在抗寒特异蛋白质的新合成，抗寒性是否是多基因控制的？膜多肽的变化是否与抗寒性相关？以及这些变化在不同抗寒性小麦品种中是否存在共性和可能有的生理功能。为进一步研究抗寒基因的遗传工程提供分子基础。

---

* 北京市自然科学基金资助项目。

现将所获结果报道如下。

材料与方法

1. 材料的培养及处理

采用 4 个不同抗寒性冬小麦品种："郑州 741"，抗寒性较弱；"济南 13 号"，抗寒性中等；"农大 139"，抗寒性强；"燕大 1817"，抗寒性很强。

经清洗过的种子在 24~25℃水中浸 12 小时，然后播种在湿润的滤纸上，于黑暗中，24~25℃萌发 1~2 天。继而，或者①将已萌发的种子仍置于黑暗，24~25℃生长 1~2 天(NA:未经低温锻炼)；或者②转至 2℃黑暗，进行人工低温锻炼 7、14 和 20 天(CA:低温锻炼)；③将锻炼 20 天的幼苗再放在 24~25℃，黑暗中生长 1 或 3 天(DA:脱锻炼)。

"燕大 1817"，于 9 月下旬播种于实验地，至 12 月中旬取材料。期间"燕大 1817"在自然环境中进行了抗寒锻炼。取田间材料(完整植株)的一部分，在培养室 24~25℃下，脱锻炼 3 天。

除了田间和脱锻炼的材料，其余苗均约为 1~2cm 高。

2. 抗寒力的测定

每个样品约 50~60 棵苗，2 个重复。3~15 棵苗用吸水纸包在一起，置于 1.6 × 15cm 试管中。每管加入 1ml 蒸馏水使吸水纸温润饱和，以防止苗脱水。用 Parafilm 封住管口。置于冰冻循环器(Julabo F_{40})中，以 1℃min^{-1} 的速度降至 0℃，而后在 0℃平衡 30min。平衡后，以同样的降温速率降至−6℃，停留 3 小时。处理之后，在 0~2℃的冰浴中化冻过夜，而后转至 24~25℃，黑暗。2 天后，测苗的成活率，膨胀度的维持与是否生长是测定存活率的标准(Guy 等，1987；Mohapatro 等，1987)。

以−6℃下、处理 3 小时后的存活率的高低来表示抗寒力的强弱。

3. 蛋白质的提取及其含量的测定

(1) 蛋白质的提取　取分蘖节以上 1.5cm 左右的部分为材料(田间材料剥去外面老叶)。在液氮中研成粉末，加 1~1.5 倍体积的蛋白质提取缓冲液〔50mmol/L Tris-HCl(pH 8.0), 5mmol/L EGTA , 50mmol/L NaCl, 5mmo1/L β-mercaptoethano1, 5mmol/L DTT, 1mmol/L spermidine, 0. 5 mol/L sucrose 和 1mmol/L PMSF〕。匀浆液在 14 000g [MSE, 12 500 rpm 8×25m1 rotar〕离心 15min, 弃其沉淀, 上清在 156 000g〔日立 70P-72, 8 × 10ml rotar, 50 000rpm; MSE ,8 × 14ml rotar 48 000 rpm〕离心 15min。其上清作为可溶性蛋白质的来源, 分成若干等份, 加入双倍的样品溶剂, 置−20℃保存, 以供电泳分析之用。

156 000g 的沉淀为膜沉淀, 为进行 SDS-PAGE, 在膜沉淀中加入样品溶剂〔62.5mmol/L Tris-HCl(pH6.8), 2.3%(W/V)SDS, 10%(V/V)Glycerol, 5%(V/V) β-mercaptoethano1, 0.1 % (W/V)Bromopheno1 Blue〕, 在沸水中煮 5min, 溶解于样品液中的蛋白为膜蛋白, 可经 100 000g〔日立 70P-72, 8 × 10ml rotar, 35 000 rpm; MSE, 8 × 14m1 rotar, 35 000rpm〕

离心 15min 而获得，弃其沉淀。上清液分成等份，置–20℃保存待用〔Mohapatra 等 1988〕。

(2) 蛋白质含量测定　按 Bradford(1976)的蛋白质—染料结合法，以 BSA 为标准蛋白。

(3) 计算　每克鲜重材料的蛋白质含量= $\frac{\mu g/100\mu l\times 稀释倍数\times 总体积}{克鲜重}$

4. SDS-PAGE 分析蛋白质

分离胶成分的比例按 Laemmli(1970)和 Smith(1984)方法。梯度胶制备主要根据 Walker (1984)方法。所得结果照相和/或用薄层扫描仪进行扫描，个别干胶用于计算机进行图像分析处理并照相。

5. 多肽分子量的确定

采用 Phamasia 生产的 6 种低分子量蛋白质作标准,使之与小麦蛋白一起经电泳法测定。

结果

(1) 不同抗寒品种经低温锻炼后抗寒力的发展

经过 20 天低温锻炼后的麦苗在–6℃处理 3 小时后，4 个不同抗寒品种的存活率分别为："郑州 741"，62%；"济南 13 号"，64%；"农大 139"，100%；"燕大 1817"，100%；"燕大 1817"在田间自然秋冬低温锻炼后，–15℃处理 3 小时，其存活率仍为 100%。各品种所有未经锻炼的麦苗在–6℃处理 3 小时后全部死亡。

低温锻炼后的麦苗经过 1~3 天的脱锻炼，其抗寒力又降至锻炼前水平。

(2) 蛋白质含量的变化

基因表达的最终产物为蛋白质。测定结果表明，4 个不同抗寒性小麦品种在低温锻炼期间，细胞内蛋白质含量均有所增加，以每克鲜重材料所含的毫克蛋白质数量来表示"郑州 741"从未锻炼时的 6.41，锻炼 20 天后增加到 9.42，"济南 13 号"从未锻炼时 5.84，锻炼 20 天后增加到 8.28。"农大 139"未经锻炼的蛋白质含量为 6.94；锻炼 7 天后达 9.10；锻炼 14 天达 11.28；锻炼 20 天后为 14.99。脱锻炼一天后，细胞内蛋白质含量又下降。"郑州 741"降至 5.66。"济南 13 号"降为 6.37。"农大 139"降至未经锻炼水平为 6.96；脱锻炼三天"农大 139"的蛋白质含量又有所回升，为 7.86。

田间自然环境中进行抗寒锻炼的冬小麦"燕大 1817"，其蛋白质含量为 10.47；脱锻炼 3 天后为 9.42。

这些结果表明,不同抗寒品种细胞内蛋白质含量的变化与其品种的抗寒性成正相关。

(3) 抗寒特异性蛋白质的产生

低温锻炼期间，4 个不同抗寒性小麦品种细胞内可溶性蛋白质的变化总结列于表 1。

从电泳扫描图谱 1 和 2 中可见，抗寒性中等的冬小麦"郑州 741"和"济南 13 号"经抗寒锻炼 20 天后，均产生了两条分子量为 28kD 和 73kD 的新带；一条带含量增加(MW:92kD)；一条带消失(54kD)。脱锻炼一天后，新产生的 28kD 在两者中依然存在，

73kD 的多肽在“郑州 741”中消失；92kD 的多肽在两者中的含量又减少；而 54kD 的多肽又重新出现。此外，“济南 13 号”经锻炼 20 天后，还新合成了一条 24kD 的带，并且在脱锻炼一天后消失。

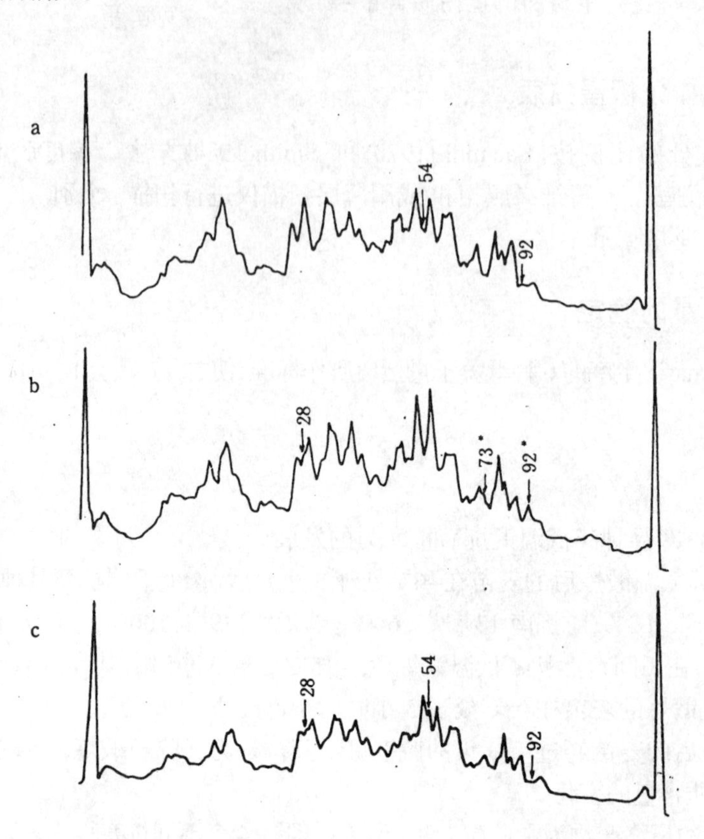

图 1　经 SDS-PAGE(7.5%~15%T; 4.5%T)分离的“郑州 741”可溶性蛋白质的光密度扫描图谱

a. 未经低温锻炼；b. 低温锻炼 20 天；c. 脱锻炼 1 天

Fig. 1　Densitometric tracings of soluble proteins in “Zhengzhou741” which were separated by SDS-PAGE(7. 5%~15%T; 4. 5%T)

a. NA; b. CA20; c. DA1

强抗寒性的冬小麦“农大 139”经抗寒锻炼后，产生四条新带，其分子量分别为 28kD、60kD、65kD 及 68kD，其中 65kD 多肽仅在锻炼 20 天中存在。脱锻炼一天后，65kD 多肽消失，而其余三条带依然存在。此外，分子量为 57kD 的多肽变化引人注目，在锻炼期间其含量增加，脱锻炼后又减少(图 3)。

在自然环境中进行抗寒锻炼的冬小麦“燕大 1817”，其细胞内可溶性蛋白质与脱锻炼三天后电泳扫描图谱比较分析表明：在锻炼期间有三条新合成的带，其分子量为 28kD、60kD 和 68kD；一条带的含量增加(MW：15kD)；一条带含量减少(MW：52kD)；一条带消失(MW：102kD) (图 4)。

计算机图像处理分析结果表明(图 4B)：“燕大 1817”在自然环境的抗寒锻炼过程中，有六条可溶性多肽在脱锻炼后不存在，其分子量为 15kD、28kD、51kD、60kD、

65kD 和 68kD。

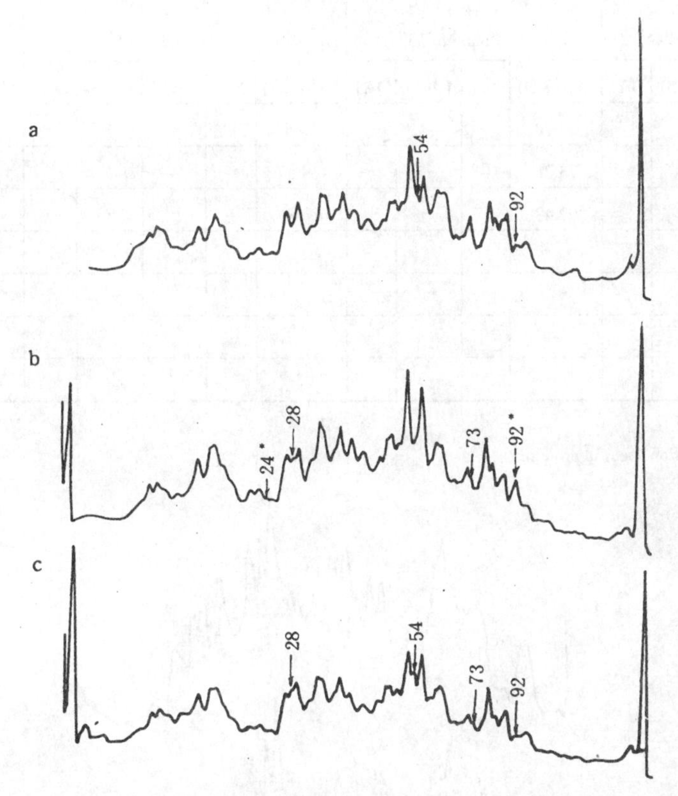

图 2　经 SDS-PAGE(7.5%~15%T;4. 5%T)分离的"济南 13 号"可溶性蛋白质的光密度扫描图谱

a. 未经低温锻炼；b. 低温锻炼 20 天；c. 脱锻炼 1 天

Fig. 2　Densitometric tracings of soluble proteins in "Jinan No.13" which were separated by SDS-PAGE(7.5%~15%T;4.5%T)

a. NA; b. CA20; c. DAl.

综上所述，低温锻炼期间细胞内可溶性蛋白质的变化可分为新产生、消失、含量增加或减少这四种情况。这些变化是否与抗寒性相关，新合成的蛋白质是否是抗寒特异蛋白质，必须结合抗寒力提高与否加以考虑。根据这一标准，低温锻炼期间新合成的分子量分别为 15kD、24kD、28kD、51kD、60kD、65kD、68kD 和 73kD 的多肽，很可能是抗寒特异性的蛋白质(表 1)。

表 1　低温锻炼期间可溶性蛋白质的变化

Tab. 1　Changes in soluble proteins during cold acclimation

"郑州 741" "Zhengzhou741"				"济南 13 号" "Jinan No.13"				"农大 139" "Nongda 139"					"燕大 1817" "Yanda 1817"		
MW(KD)	NA	CA20	DA1	MW(KD)	NA	CA20	DA1	MW(KD)	NA	CA14	CA20	DA1	MW(KD)	CA	DA3
27.54	–	+	+	*23.99	–	+	–	27.9	–	+	+	+	14.8	+++	+
53.70	+	–	++	27.67	–	+	+	56.5	+	++	+++	+	*27.67	+	–

续表

“郑州 741” “Zhengzhou741”				“济南 13 号” “Jinan No.13”				“农大 139” “Nongda 139”					“燕大 1817” “Yanda 1817”		
MW(KD)	NA	CA20	DA1	MW(KD)	NA	CA20	DA1	MW(KD)	NA	CA14	CA20	DA1	MW(KD)	CA	DA3
*73.28	–	+	–	53.70	+	–	++	59.6	–	+	+	+	51.9	+	+++
92.26	+	++	+	73.28	–	+	+	*64.57	–	–	+	–	*60.4	+	–
				92.47	+	++	+	67.61	–	+	+	+	*67.9	+	–
													102.3	–	+
													*14.96	+	–
													*50.7	+	–
													64.57	+	–

* 抗寒特异蛋白。

cold-acclimation specific protein.

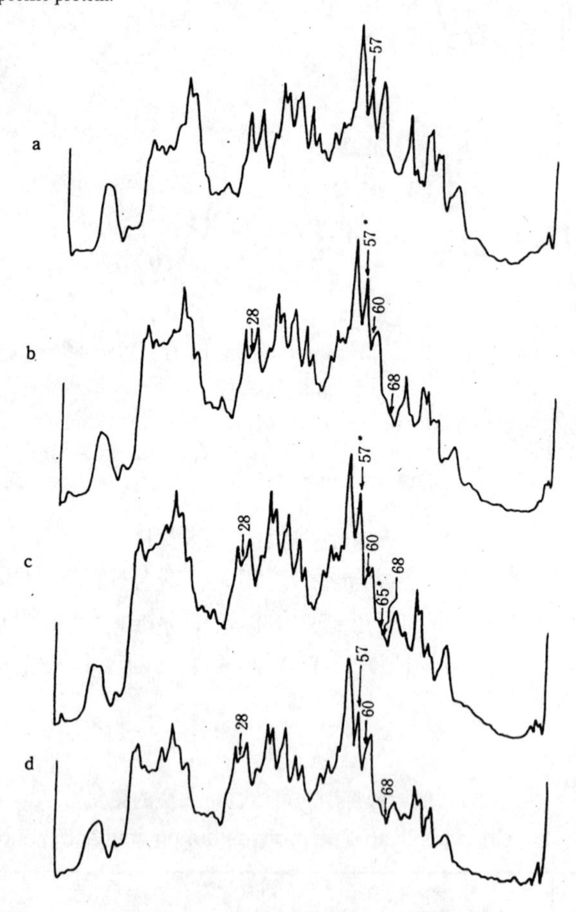

图 3　“农大 139”可溶性蛋白质光密度扫描图谱

a. 未经低温锻炼；b. 低温锻炼 14 天；c. 低温锻炼 20 天；d. 脱锻炼 1 天

Fig. 3　Densitomertric tracings of soluble proteins in “Nongda 139” which were separated by SDS-PAGE

a. NA; b. CA14; c. CA20; d. DA1

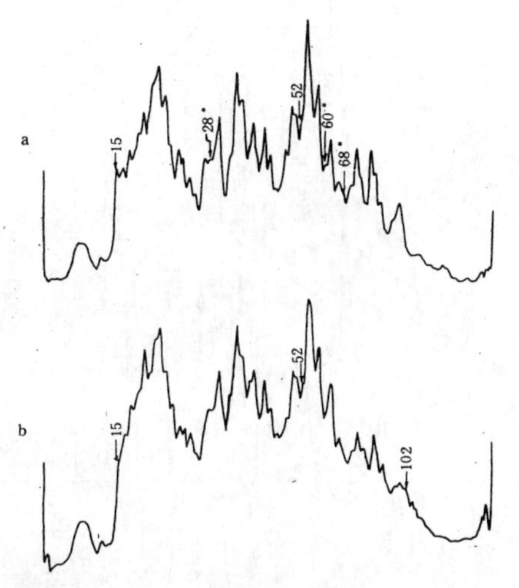

图 4A “燕大 1817”可溶性蛋白质光密度扫描图谱

a. 田间低温锻炼；b. 脱锻炼 3 天

Fig. 4A Densitometric tracings of soluble proteins in “Yanda 1817”which were separated by SDS-PAGE

a. cold acclimated in the field; b. deacclimated for 3days

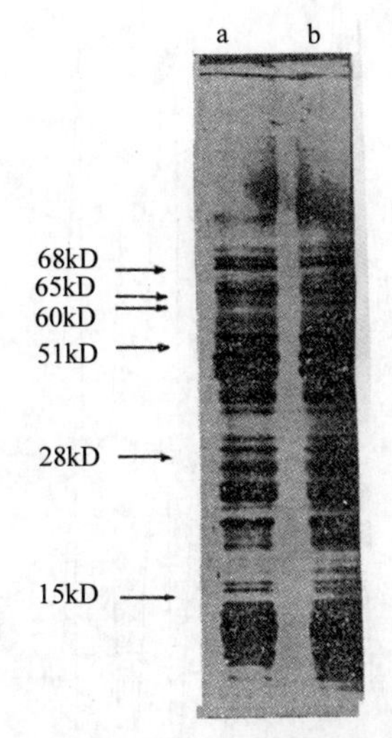

图 4B “燕大 1217”可溶性蛋白电泳图谱计算机图像处理分析结果照片

a. 田间低温锻炼；b. 脱锻炼 3 天

Fig. 4B Computer treatment of electrophoretograms of soluble proteins in “Yanda 1817” which were separated by SDS-PAGE

a. cold acclimated in the field; b. deacclimated for 3days

(4) 膜蛋白的改变

低温锻炼期间，4 个不同抗寒性小麦品种膜蛋白的改变结果总结在表 2 中。抗寒性中等的“郑州 741”和“济南 13 号”锻炼 20 天后均产生分子量为 30kD 和 68kD 的多肽，但脱锻炼一天后，依然存在(图 5、图 6)。此外，“济南 13 号”在锻炼期间，还产生 58kD、81kD 的多肽；25kD 的含量有所增加。脱锻炼一天后，58kD 多肽消失(图 6)。

“农大 139”的电泳图谱的扫描分析(图 7)表明：在抗寒锻炼期间有五条膜多肽产生(MW：18kD、21kD、27kD、32kD 和 56kD)，其中 18kD 的多肽在脱锻炼一天后消失，其余四条带仍存在。此外，52kD 的多肽随着锻炼时间的延长而逐渐减少，脱锻炼后又增加。

“燕大 1817”在自然环境的抗寒锻炼过程中，有五条带(MW：21kD、29kD、36kD、43kD 和 83kD)是未经锻炼和脱锻炼 3 天后不存在的(图 8)。此外，58kD 多肽的含量增加，两条带含量减少(MW：38.5kD、41kD)，一条带消失(MW：15kD)。

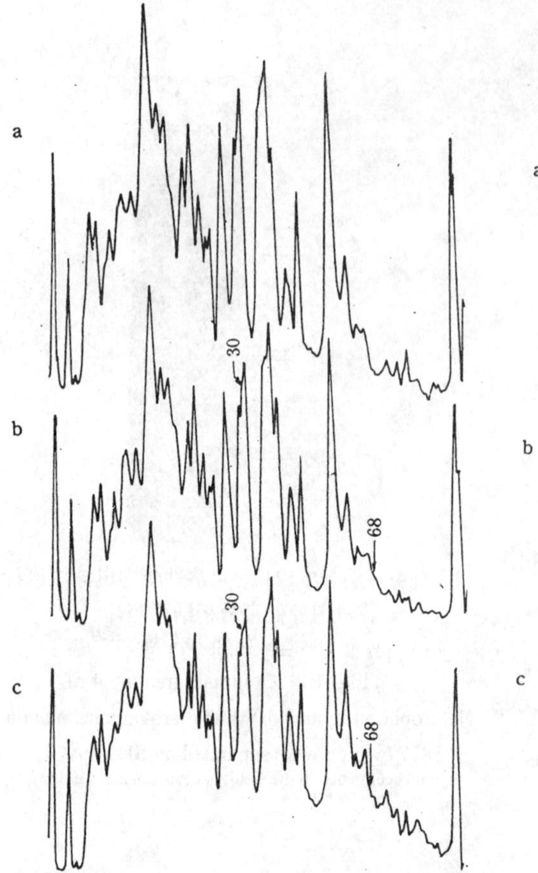

图 5　经 SDS-PAGE(12.5%T; 4.5%T)分离的“郑州 741”膜蛋白电泳图谱的光密度扫描图谱

a. 未经低温锻炼；b.低温锻炼 20 天；c. 脱锻炼一天

Fig. 5　Densitometric tracings of membrane proteins in “Zhengzhou 741” which were separated by SDS-PAGE(12.5%T; 4.5%T)

a. NA; b. CA20; c. DA1

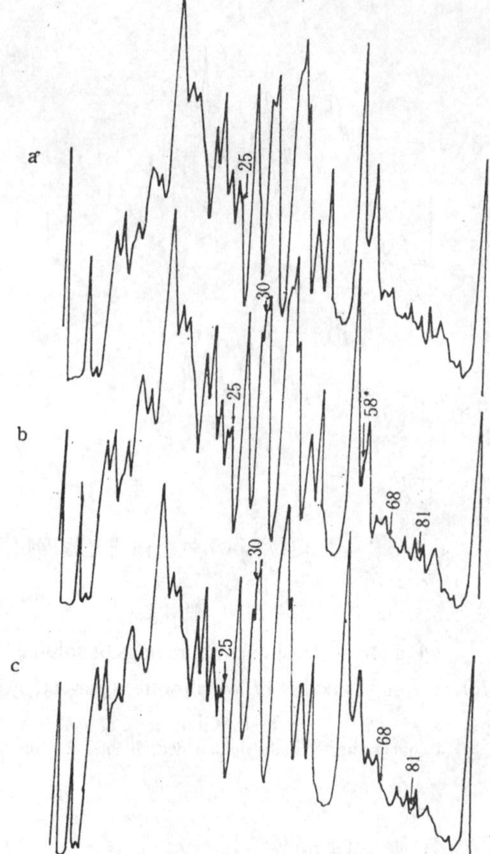

图 6　经 SDS-PAGE(12.5%T; 4. 5%T)分离的“济南 13 号”膜蛋白电泳图谱的光密度扫描图谱

a. 未经低温锻炼；b. 低温锻炼 20 天；c. 脱锻炼一天

Fig. 6　Densitometric tracings of membrane proteins in “Jinan No. 13” which were separated by SDS-PAGE (12. 5%T;4. 5%T)

a. NA; b. CA20; c. DA1

表 2　低温锻炼期间膜蛋白的变化

Tab. 2　Alterations in membrane proteins during cold acclimation

“郑州 741” “Zhengzhou741”				“济南 13 号” “Jinan No.13”				“农大 139” “Nongda 139”					“燕大 1817” “Yanda 1817”			
MW(KD)	NA	CA20	DA1	MW(KD)	NA	CA20	DA1	MW(KD)	NA	CA14	CA20	DA1	MW(KD)	CA	DA3	
30.34	–	+	+	25.12	+	++	++	18.4	–	+	+	–	14.6	+	–	–
68.23	–	+		29.85	–	+	+	20.9	–	+	+	+	20.7	–	+	–
				57.54	–	+	–	26.92	–	+	+	+	28.97	–	+	–
				67.61	–	+	+	32.4	–	+	+	+	35.89	–	+	–
				81.28	–	+	+	51.8	+++	++	+	++	38.46	++	+	–
								55.6	–	+	+	+	40.74	++	+	–
													42.85	–	+	–
													58.21	+	++	+
													83.18	–	+	–

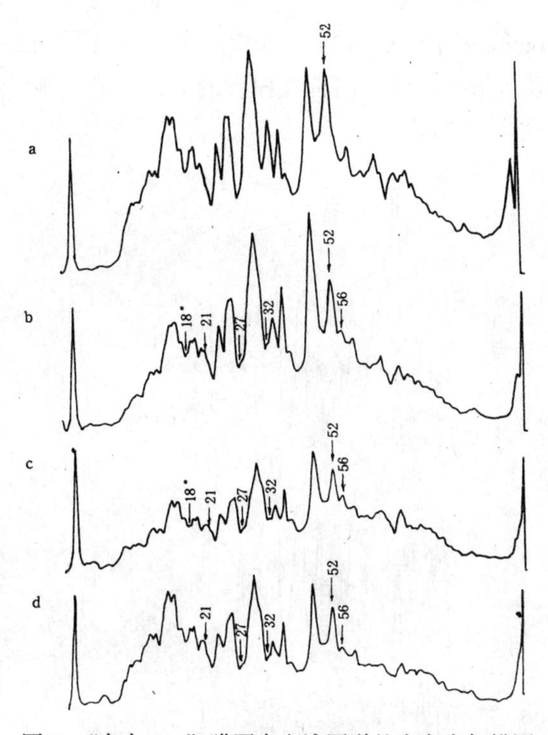

图 7 “农大 139”膜蛋白电泳图谱的光密度扫描图

a. 未经低温锻炼；b. 低温锻炼 14 天；c. 锻炼 20 天；d. 脱锻炼一天

Fig.7 Densitometric tracings of membrane proteins in “Nongda 139” which were separated by SDS-PAGE

a. NA; b. CA14; c. CA20; d. DA1

讨论

1. 蛋白质含量与抗寒性的关系

这方面的研究结果已有许多报道，大部分观测结果指出蛋白质含量与抗寒性成正相关，但也有一些结果说明两者之间并无必然的联系(简令成，1990；Yoshida，1982)。如上所述，我们的测定结果证明蛋白质含量的变化与小麦品种的抗寒性成正相关。蛋白质含量的增加，有助于提高细胞内的束缚水，降低冰点，并可能导致细胞液过冷却的形成(简令成，1990)，从而成为防止细胞内结冰的原因之一。另一方面，我们的测试结果也指出，经过 3 天的脱锻炼，又引起蛋白质含量的增加。这说明，蛋白质含量的增加不仅关系到抗寒性，还与生长发育有关。

2. 植物抗寒特异性蛋白质的发现和证实

已有大量报道指出，生长在寒冷地区的鱼类，适应于环境而产生了一种特异性蛋白——抗冻蛋白质，它在血液中的含量随季节而改变，并在秋季和冬季大量产生。抗冻肽是一类能显著降低血液冰冻点的多肽分子，因而能防止血液的冰冻凝固(简令成，1990)。在一些植物抗寒机理的研究过程中，认为存在着抗寒特异蛋白质(CASP,cold acclimation specific proteins)(简令成，1992)。我们利用 4 个不同抗寒性冬小麦品种，比较了其在低温锻炼期间及脱锻炼后的可溶性蛋白质的变化，进一步证实了经抗寒锻炼的冬小麦中存在抗寒特异性蛋白质(表 1)。

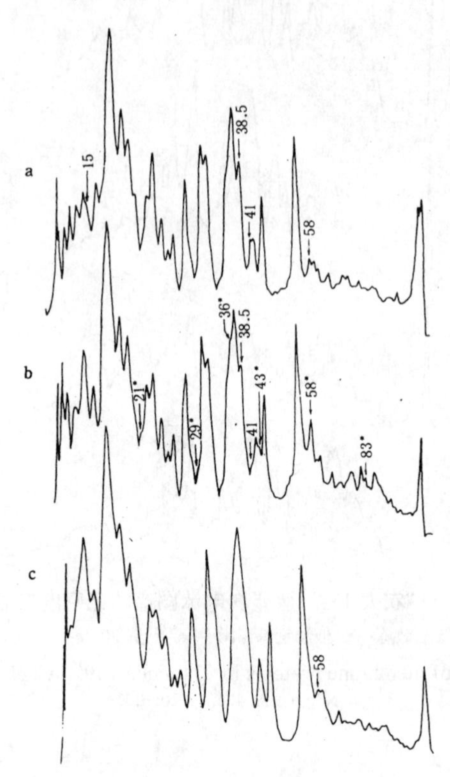

图 8　经 SDS-PAGE(12. 5%T;4. 5%T)分离的“燕大 1817”膜蛋白电泳图谱的光密度扫描图谱

a. 未经低温锻炼；b. 田间低温锻炼；c. 脱锻炼三天

Fig. 8　Densitometric tracings of membrane proteins in “Yanda 1817” which were separated by SDS-PAGE(12.5%T; 4.5%T)

a. NA; b. CA; c. DA3

抗寒性中等的冬小麦“郑州 741”和“济南 13 号”在锻炼 20 天后所达到的抗寒力相似。其可溶性蛋白质的电泳分析揭示了这两者之间存在着一些共性：低温锻炼期间均诱导产生了两条新带(MW：28kD、73kD)。但两者也存在着差异，各自的特异性多肽有所不同：“郑州 741”为 73kD；而“济南 13 号”为 24kD。

在同样锻炼条件下的“农大 139”，其抗寒力比“郑州 741”和“济南 13 号”高。与此相适应，前者在锻炼期间新合成的可溶性多肽也较后两者多。强抗寒性的冬小麦“农大 139”与“燕大 1817”在抗寒锻炼期间可溶性蛋白质的变化也存在着一些共同点，即均新合成分子量为 28kD、60kD、65kD、和 68kD 的多肽，其中 65kD 多肽在“农大 139”脱锻炼一天后消失，脱锻炼 3 天的“燕大 1817”中也不存在。因此 65kD 的多肽很可能是抗寒特异性的多肽。而 28kD、60kD、68kD 的多肽在脱锻炼一天的“农大 139”中依然存在，在脱锻炼 3 天的“燕大 1817”中不存在。所以，此三种多肽在“燕大 1817”中是抗寒特异多肽。鉴于脱锻炼一天只解除锻炼效果的 50%以上，并没有完全除去锻炼效果，因此，此三种蛋白质在“农大 139”中也可能与抗寒基因的表达有关。由于脱锻炼一天后，可溶性蛋白质的含量已降到未经锻炼水平，而抗寒力却同锻炼 7 天的相似。由此推测在细胞内可溶性蛋白质含量较低的情况下，即使存在一些特异的抗寒性的多肽，抗寒力的发展也只在较有限的范围内。

在田间自然环境中进行抗寒锻炼的“燕大 1817”，比实验室条件下锻炼 20 天的“农大 139”抗寒力要高(数据未列出)，并且抗寒特异蛋白质也较后者多。这是因为田间自然环境中锻炼期间除了新合成 28kD、60kD、65kD 和 68kD 的多肽外，还合成了 51kD 的多肽。在锻炼期间“农大 139”中的 57kD 和“燕大 1817”中的 15kD 多肽含量的增加，可能与低温下的代谢调节有关；也可能是产生同样分子量而等电点不同的抗寒特异性的多肽，这需要进一步的证明，此外一些带的消失或减少可能与低温下的代谢调节有关。值得提出的是，以往在菠菜、冬油菜、冬黑麦、冬小麦、苜蓿及马铃薯等植物中发现的抗寒特异性多肽在不同植物间，甚至是同一种植物在不同的实验室中都表现出很大的差异(Singh 等，1988)。然而在我们测试的 4 个冬小麦品种之间，无论是在人工低温或田间自然低温诱导下，均可找到一些共同的特异性多肽，这似乎是一个重要进展。

综上所述，冬小麦经低温锻炼后产生多种抗寒特异性多肽，进一步证明抗寒性是由多基因控制的。

3. 膜蛋白的新合成与抗寒力的发展

低温锻炼期间包括蛋白质的膜物质的增加已有一些报道(Gusta，1972；Mohapatra 等，1988)。Mohapatra 认为膜蛋白增加主要是由于在低温下蛋白质降解的减少而引起的。

然而，关于低温锻炼期间膜蛋白质变化的研究还为数不多(Mohapatra 等，1988；Yoshida 等，1984、1986)。低温锻炼期间膜蛋白变化是否与抗寒力的发展有关，这一问题还不明确。Booz 和 Travis 报道了大豆根中质膜在发育过程中，其多肽组成发生了明显的变化(Booz 等,1980)。如上所述，我们实验中 4 个不同抗寒性小麦品种，在低温锻炼下均诱导产生了一些新多肽，并且，抗寒性愈强的品种新合成的膜多肽愈多；在自然田间环境中锻炼的“燕大 1817”新合成的膜多肽较实验室条件下产生的更多。这说明，膜多肽在低温锻炼期间的变化与抗寒性是密切相关的，它可能起着提高膜稳定性的作用。

参考文献

简令成, 1986, 植物寒害及抗寒性, 黑龙江科学技术出版社, 18~76

简令成, 1990, 植物抗寒性的细胞及分子生物学研究进展, 细胞生物学进展, **2**：296~320

简令成, 1992, 植物抗寒机理研究的新进展，植物学通报, **9** (3)：17~22

简令成、孙龙华、孙德兰, 1986, 几种植物细胞表面糖蛋白的电镜细胞化学及其与植物抗逆性的关系, 实验生物学报, **19** (3)：261~271

Booz M. L. and R. L. Travis, 1980, Electrophoretc comparison of polypeptides from enriched plasma membrane fractions from developing soybean roots, Plant. Physiol. , **66**: 1037~1043

Bradford, M. M. , 1976, A rapid and sensitive method for the quantitation of microgram quantities of protein utilizing the principle of proteindye binding, Anal Biochem, **72**: 248~254

Gusta,L. V. and C. J. , Weiser, 1972, Nucleic acid and protein changes in relation to cold acclimation and freezing injury of Korean boxwood leaves, Plant Physiol., **49**: 91~96

Guy, C. L. , R. L. Hummel and M. Haskell, 1987, Induction of freezing tolerance in spinach during cold acclimation, Plant Physiol. , **84**: 868~871

Laemmli, U. K. ,1970 , Cleavage of structural proteins during the assemdly of the head of bacteriophage T4, Nature, **227**: 680~685

Mohapatra, S. S. , R. J. Poole and R. S. Dhindsa, 1987 , Cold acclimation, freezing resistance and protein synthesis inalfalfa, J.Exp Bot. , **38**(195):1697~1703

Mohapatra, S. S. , R. J. Poole and R. S., Dhindsa, 1988, Alterations in membrane protein-profile during cold treatment of alfalfa, Plant Physiol. , **86**:1005~1007

Mohapatra ,S. S. , R. J. Poole and R. S. Dhindsa, 1988, Abscisic acidregulated gene expression in relation to freezing tolerance in alfalfa, Plant Physiol. , **87**: 468~473

Singh, J. , A. Laroche, 1988, Freezing tolerance in plants: a Biochemical overview, Biochem Cell Biol. , **66**: 650~657

Smith, B. J. , 1984, SDS polyacrylamid gel electrophoresis of proteins. In walker JM ed. Methods in Molercular Biology Vol. I Humama Press Clifton NJ: 41~55

Walker, J. M. , 1984, Gradient SDS-polyacrymide gel electrophoresis. In JM. Walker ed. Methods in Molecular Biology. Vol. I. Humana Press, Clifton NJ 57~61

Yoshida, S. , 1982, Fluorescence polarization studies on plasma isolated from mulderry bark tissues. In PH Li, A Sakai eds. Plantcold hardiness and freezing stress. Mechanism and crop implication, Vol 2, Academic Press, New York, 273~283

Yoshida, S. , 1984, Chemical and biophysical changes in the plasma membrane during cold acclimation of mulberry bark cells (*Morus bombycis* koidz cv Giorji), Plant Physiol. , **76**: 257~265

Yoshida, S. and M. Uemura, 1984, Protein and lipid compositions of isolated plasma membrane from orchard grass (*Dactylis glomerata* L.)and changes during cold acclimation, Plant Physiol. ,**75**: 31~37

Yoshida, S. , 1986, Reverse changes in plasma properties upon deacclimation of mulberry trees *MorusBombysis* cultiver Goroji. Plant Cell Physiol. , **27** (1): 83~90

本文原载：广西科学. 1994. 1(4): 1-5

毛花猕猴桃愈伤组织诱导与植株再生

张远记* 钱迎倩

(中国科学院植物研究所)

摘　要　从毛花猕猴桃(*Actinidia eriantha* Benth)田间生长的茎段、种子无菌条件下萌发的下胚轴及试管苗的茎段和叶片得到愈伤组织。田间来源的茎段诱导愈伤组织较难，愈伤组织生长缓慢；下胚轴及试管苗茎段和叶片容易产生愈伤组织，愈伤组织生长旺盛。消毒时间、接种方法、基因型和培养基都可能影响到田间来源的茎段愈伤组织产生。在MS附加玉米素或6-苄氨基嘌呤(BAP)的培养基上下胚轴来源的愈伤组织不经转代即分化芽和根。试管苗茎段和叶片在附加玉米素或N-(2-氯基-4-吡啶基)-N′-苯基脲(CPPU)的MS培养基上培养一代也分化出芽。试管苗茎段在附加0.0025mg/L CPPU和0.1mg/L吲哚乙酸(IAA)的MS培养基上产生愈伤组织、芽的分化和苗生长都较理想：试管苗叶片则以附加0.025mg/L CPPU和0.1mg/L IAA或0.5mg/L玉米素和0.1mg/L IAA的MS培养基较好，当苗伸长至1cm或以上时切下，转入MS基本培养基(大量元素减半)上后可形成完整植株。

关键词　毛花猕猴桃；愈伤组织；植株再生；猕猴桃

毛花猕猴桃原产我国，果实维生素C含量高，达1 014mg/100g鲜重，而美味猕猴桃著名品种海沃德的维生素C含量仅200~370mg/100g鲜重[1]。且毛花猕猴桃的果实较大[2]，有较大的开发利用价值。

现代生物技术在开发和利用种质资源方面具有重要作用，如体细胞无性系变异，体细胞杂交，遗传转化及超低温种质保存等，可是这些技术都要求建立组织培养系统。毛花猕猴桃组织培养研究尚未见到报道。我们对毛花猕猴桃原生质体进行培养，已经得到再生植株[3]。为了毛花猕猴桃原生质体培养能够顺利地有材料来源并能再生植株，我们对毛花猕猴桃的组织培养进行了比较系统的研究。本文报道毛花猕猴桃不同外植体诱导愈伤组织及植株再生的结果。

1　材料与方法

试验材料由中国科学院植物研究所北京植物园安和祥先生提供。田间生长的一年生茎段采回后先用自来水冲洗干净，然后用75%酒精浸泡30s，再用0.1%$HgCl_2$消毒不同时间，之后用无菌水冲洗4~6次。试管实生苗建立方法如下：自由授粉的毛花猕猴桃果实

---

* 张远记为中国科学院植物研究所博士生；钱迎倩研究员为博士生导师，广西科学院院长(编者注)。

成熟后采回，取出种子。种子用 75%酒精浸泡 1min，然后用 0.1% $HgCl_2$ 消毒 10min，之后用无菌水冲洗 4 次。于无菌条件下解剖出胚，培养在 MS[4]基本培养基(大量元素减半)上，置于 25℃、黑暗条件下直至萌发。然后置于 25℃、12h 光照(光照度 1 250 lx)和 22℃、12h 黑暗条件下培养。伸长的下胚轴和无菌苗茎段(不带腋芽)均切成 1cm 小段、幼叶切成 1cm × 1cm 小块，接种到不同培养基上诱导愈伤组织和芽分化。本试验所用基本培养基为 MS 附加蔗糖 3%和琼脂 0.6%，pH5.6。每处理接种 3 瓶，每瓶接 4~6 块(段)，重复 2 次。培养条件为光照 9h(光照度 1 250 lx)、26℃/黑暗 15h、24℃。

2 结果

2.1 田间来源的茎段诱导愈伤组织

$HgCl_2$ 消毒时间分别为 5、7 和 9min，其中以 7min 最合适，5min 污染严重，9min 则造成材料死亡。对于茎段，消毒后将表皮用解剖刀轻轻刮去,小心切取韧皮薄片(厚约 1mm，大小约 0.5cm × 1.0cm)，垂直插入培养基中。用这种方法较易得到愈伤组织。

材料的基因型对诱导结果也有很大影响。本试验采用白花类型和紫花类型两种基因型的茎段诱导愈伤组织，结果见表 1。白花类型的诱导率较高且生长速度相对较快。但总的来说，田间来源茎段诱导得到的愈伤组织生长速度慢。

以 MS 为基本培养基，分别或配合加入不同浓度的 2，4-D (0.2, 0.5, 1.0, 1.2, 2.0, 4.0, 和 6.0mg/L)、NAA (萘乙酸，naphthaleneacetic acid) (0.05，0.2，0.5，1.0 和 2.0mg/L), BAP(6-苄氨基嘌呤)(0.04, 0.1, 0.2, 0.5, 1.0 和 3.0mg/L)和玉米素(1.0 和 3.0mg/L)共 20 种处理中，以附加 2,4-D 1.2mg/L+BAP 0.04mg/L 和 2,4-D 0.5mg/L+BAP 1.0mg/L 两个组合对愈伤组织诱导的效果较好。但愈伤组织在前者上的质地松软，在后者上较硬(表 1)。

表 1　两种基因型的毛花猕猴桃茎段诱导愈伤组织情况

Table 1　Effects of genotypes of *A.eriantha* on the callus indnction of stem segments

生长调节剂 Growth regulator (mg/L)	基因型 Genotype	诱导率 Frequency of Induction (%)	生长速度 Growth rate	质地 Character
2,4-D 1.2+BAP 0.04	白花 White flower	75.7	++++	松软 Soft
2,4-D 1.2+BAP 0.04	紫花 Purple flower	18.1	+	松软 Soft
2,4-D 0.5+BAP 1.0	白花 White flower	48.6	++	较硬 Solid
2,4-D 0.5+BAP 1.0	紫花 Purple flower	53.0	+	松软 Soft

基本培养基为 MS。2, 4-D：2，4-二氯苯氧乙酸；BAP：6-苄氨基嘌呤，MS was used as basic medium，2，4-D；2，4-dichlorophenoxyacetic acid; BAP：6-benzyl-aminopurine.

2.2 以试管苗为材料的愈伤组织诱导与分化

2.2.1 下胚轴

黑暗下在 MS 基本培养基(大量元素减半)上萌发的胚，在下胚轴伸长到 1cm 时切下以诱导愈伤组织。发现在附加 2,4-D (0.5，1.0mg/L) 配合 BAP(0，0.1，0.5 和 1.0mg/L) 的 MS 培养基上，可得到生长速度快、色泽绿白的愈伤组织。2,4-D 浓度在 2.0mg/L 或以上时,愈伤组织生长不良。上述激素各种不同浓度配合处理的愈伤组织诱导率均为 100%。本试验曾将在附加 2,4-D 1mg/L 的 MS 培养基上诱导的愈伤组织，经一次继代后即可用于分离原生质体。分离的原生质体并能够分裂。在配有其他激素的 MS 培养基上(BAP 0.1mg/L+IAA 0.5mg/L，玉米素 1.0mg/L) (IAA：吲哚乙酸，indole-3-acetic acid)诱导到的愈伤组织体积小，但不经转代即可分化芽和根，进而长成完整植株。

2.2.2 试管苗茎段和幼叶

试管苗的茎段或幼叶接种于具不同激素配比的 MS 培养基上(表 2)，10 天后都明显愈伤组织化，3 周后开始分化芽。不同激素配比的培养基对茎段和幼叶诱导愈伤组织及其芽分化的影响见表 2 和图 1。

表 2 不同生长调节剂对毛花猕猴桃试管实生苗茎段和幼叶诱导愈伤组织及其芽分化的影响(培养 60 天)

Table 2 Effects of growth regulators on the callus induction and bud differentiation of in vitro seedling stem segments and leaves of *Actinidia eriantha* (60 days after inoculating)

生长调节剂 Growth regulator (mg/L)	外植体 Explant	愈伤组织诱导率 Frequency of callus Induction(%)	愈伤组织分化情况 Callus differentiation		
			芽分化频率 Frequency of bud differentiation (%)	苗数 (≥1cm) /愈伤组织 Shoots(≥1cm) /callus	苗生长情况 Shoot growth
CPPU 0.25+IAA 0.1	S	100	83.3	0	慢、芽少 st, f
CPPU 0.25+IAA 0.1	L	100	100	0	慢、芽较多 st, m
CPPU 0.025+IAA 0.1	S	100	100	0.58	稍快、芽多 sl, n
CPPU 0.025+IAA 0.1	L	91.7	81.8	0.86	稍快、芽多 sl, n
CPPU 0.025	S	100	83.3	0.3	较快、芽少 fa, f
CPPU 0.025	L	100	87.5	0.7	较快、芽少 fa, f
CPPU 0.0025+IAA 0.1	S	100	100	2.0	快、芽较多 ft, m
CPPU 0.0025+IAA 0.1	L	75	100	0.2	慢、芽少 st, f
玉米素 0.5+IAA 0.1	S	100	83.3	0.6	较快、芽较多 fa, m
玉米素 0.5+IAA 0.1	L	91.7	100	0.8	较快、芽较多 fa, m
玉米素 1.0	S	100	91.7	0.8	较快、芽较多 fa, m
玉米素 1.0	L	75	100	0.2	慢、芽较多 st, m

MS 为基本培养基，CPPU: N-(2-氯基-4-吡啶基) -N′-苯基脲；IAA: 吲哚乙酸; S: 茎段; L: 叶块。MS was used as basic mediun. CPPU: N-(2-chloro-4-pyridyl) - N′-phenylurea; IAA: indole-3-acetic acid; S: stem segments; L: leaf pieces; st: slowest; sl:slow; fa: fast; ft: fastest; f: few buds; m: many buds; n: numerous buds.

图 1 试管苗茎段和叶块愈伤组织的芽分化情况

Fig. 1 Bud differentiation from calli derived from stem segments and leaves of in vitro seedlings

上排为叶块愈伤组织 (L)，下排为茎段愈伤组织 (S)。从左向右为在 MS 附加如下生长调节剂的培养基上(mg/L): CPPU 0.025+IAA 0.1; CPPU 0.025; CPPU 0.25+IAA 0.1; CPPU 0.0025+IAA 0.1; 玉米素 0.5+IAA 0.1; 玉米素 1.0。Upper row: calli from leaves (L); lower row: calli from stem segments (S). Bud differentiation of the callus on MS medium supplemented with growth regulator (mg/L) (from left to right): CPPU 0.025+IAA 0.1; CPPU 0.025; CPPU 0.25+IAA 0.1; CPPU 0.0025+IAA 0.1; zeatin 0.5+IAA0.1; zeatin 1.0

前面已经提到，我们做毛花猕猴桃组织培养的目的之一是为了研究毛花猕猴桃的原生质体培养。后来在毛花猕猴桃原生质体培养成功后，又返回来，用在原生质体培养中成熟的经验和方法再来丰富毛花猕猴桃组织培养方法。我们曾将毛花猕猴桃原生质体得来的愈伤组织在附加玉米素 0.5mg/L 和 IAA 0.1mg/L 配合的 MS 培养基上分化出苗。本试验中，该培养基对毛花猕猴桃试管苗茎段和叶块的愈伤组织诱导、芽分化和苗形成均有良好的效果，苗生长正常。附加玉米素 1.0mg/L 的 MS 培养基对茎段外植体的培养也较好，苗形成较多且生长正常，但该培养基对叶块的愈伤组织诱导率低，苗生长慢且长出的叶片扭曲。

与玉米素相比，CPPU 在很低浓度就具有较强的效应。为确定 CPPU 的浓度范围，本试验比较了不同浓度的 CPPU (2.5, 0.025 和 0.00 025mg/L，均配合 IAA 0.1mg/L) 对茎段和叶块的培养效果。茎段和叶块在 CPPU 0.00 025mg/L 的培养基上均未产生愈伤组织。在 CPPU 2.5mg/L 培养基上愈伤组织生长慢，芽分化少且生长极慢。CPPU 0.025mg/L 的效果较好、愈伤组织生长快，芽分化多。虽然芽生长也慢并有叶扭曲，但在转入 MS 基本培养基 (大量元素减半) 后形成生长正常的苗。因此进一步比较了 CPPU 0.25 和 0.0025mg/L 两种浓度，发现茎段在 CPPU 0.0025mg/L (配合 IAA 0.1mg/L)上的愈伤组织诱导率和芽分化率均达到100%,形成的苗多 (平均每块愈伤组织有2.0个≥1cm的苗) 且生长健壮。CPPU 浓度过高时(0.025 和 0.25mg/L)，苗生长受到抑制且叶片扭曲。对于叶片外植体，较高浓度 CPPU 有利于芽分化，在具 CPPU 0.025mg/L 的 MS 培养基上芽分化多并有较多的苗形成。在含 CPPU 的几种培养基上，叶片外植体的芽分化率比相应的茎段外植体的多，但苗数目少且生长慢。我们还注意到叶片外植体容易分化根。如在附加有 CPPU 0.025mg/L，CPPU 0.025mg/L 加 IAA 0.1mg/L，CPPU 0.0025mg/L 加 IAA 0.1mg/L 及玉米素 0.5mg/L 加 IAA 0.1mg/L 的 MS 培养基上部分愈伤组织不但分化芽而且有根形成，但茎段外植体仅在附加有 CPPU 0.0025mg/L 加 IAA 0.1mg/L 的 MS 培养基上形成根。另外，CPPU 配合 IAA (0.1mg/L) 有利于芽的分化 (表 2, 图 1)。

将上述培养基上形成的苗转入 MS 基本培养基 (大量元素减半) 中, 长成健壮的小植株(图 2)。

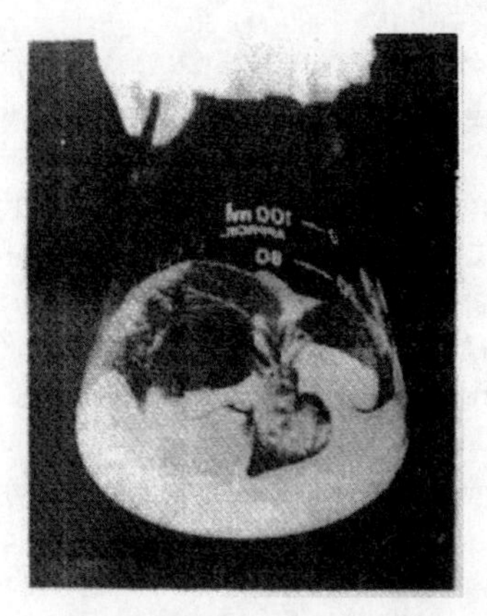

图 2 生根的完整植株

Fig.2 Rooted plant

在另一次试验中，以 MS 附加 2，4-D 0.5mg/L 加 BAP 1.0mg/L，2，4-D 1.0mg/L 及 2，4-D 1.0mg/L 加 BAP 1.0mg/L 三种培养基诱导愈伤组织，结果诱导率均为 100%。在含 2，4-D 1.0mg/L 的两种不同培养基上，愈伤组织在接触培养基处变褐。在附加 2，4-D 0.5mg/L 加 BAP 1.0mg/L 培养基上，愈伤组织为白色，生长速度快，质地较疏松，经长期继代，愈伤组织生长状况稳定。

3 讨论

中华猕猴桃、美味猕猴桃茎段愈伤组织的诱导和分化已有大量报道[1,5~14]。软枣猕猴桃也有报道[14,15]。我们也曾对上述三种猕猴桃茎段诱导愈伤组织进行过研究，很容易地得到了愈伤组织 (未发表)。毛花猕猴桃田间生长的茎段不易产生愈伤组织，本试验虽在改进方法后诱导出愈伤组织，但诱导率不高且生长较慢。然而毛花猕猴桃试管苗茎段、叶片及下胚轴在合适的培养基上愈伤组织诱导率可达到 100%，分化生根也很容易，说明是一种较理想的供试材料。

CPPU 具有强烈的细胞分裂素活性[16]。用 CPPU 处理生长中的猕猴桃果实，可增加果实体积、提早成熟时间[17~19]。CPPU 用于猕猴桃组织培养目前仅见一例报道。Suezawa 等[20]在进行美味猕猴桃细胞悬浮培养物诱导分化时,发现 CPPU 对不定芽形成非常有效，但未说明使用浓度。本试验表明, 对于毛花猕猴桃试管实生苗的茎段和叶片诱导愈伤组织和分化时，很低浓度(0.025~0.0025mg/L) 的 CPPU 具有良好的效果，并且不影响不定根形成。

参考文献

[16] Qian Y Q, Yu D P. Advances in *Actinidia* research in China. Acta Hort, 1991, 297: 51~55
[17] 梁畴芬, 中国猕猴桃属分类志要, 广西植物, 1980, (1): 30~45
[18] 张远记, 母锡金, 蔡起贵等. 毛花猕猴桃叶片原生质体再生植株, 植物学报, 1995, 37: (印刷中)
[19] Murashige T, Skoog F. A revised medium for rapid growth and bioassays with tobacco tissue cultures. Physiol Plant, 1962, 15: 473~497
[20] 桂耀林, 猕猴桃离体茎段愈伤组织的诱导和植株再生, 植物学报, 1979, 21: 339~343
[21] Pedroso M C. Oliveira M M, Pais M S. Micropropagation and simultaneous rooting of *Actinidia deliciosa* var. *delictose* "Hayward". Hort Sci, 1992, 27: 443~445
[22] 林贵美, 叶翠娟. 硬毛猕猴桃组培育苗试验简报. 广西农业科学, 1988, (6): 23~25
[23] Barbieri C. Morini S. Sboot regeneration from callus cultures of *Actinidia chinensis* (cv. Hayward). Acta Hort, 1988, 227: 470~472
[24] Revilla M A, Power J B. Morphogenetic potential of longterm callus cultures of *Actinidia delictosa*. J Hort Sci, 1988, 63: 541~545
[25] Monette P L. Organogenesis and plantlet regeneration fol-Guangxi Sciences, Vol.1 No. 4, November 1994 lowing in vitro cold storage of kiwifruit shoot tip cultures. Sci Hort, 1987, 31: 101~106
[26] 杨增海. 猕猴桃离体培养. 植物生理学通讯, 1985, (3): 25
[27] 林国辉, 郭清平. 中华猕猴桃试管苗培育和栽培技术, 农业科技通讯, 1985, (5): 16
[28] 黄贞光, 谭素英. 猕猴桃的组织培养. 见: 陈正华主编, 木本植物组织培养及其应用. 北京: 高等教育出版社, 1986, 433~443
[29] 洪树荣, 猕猴桃离体茎段和叶愈伤组织的诱导和植株再生, 湖北农业科学, 1981, (9): 28~30
[30] 王际轩, 李淑珍, 李博文等. 猕猴桃的组织培养繁殖. 辽宁农业科学, 1982, (1): 32~34
[31] Huetteman C A, Preece J E. Thidiazuron: A potent cytokinm for woody plant tissue culture. Plant Cell, Tissue and Organ Cult, 1993, 33: 105~119
[32] Lawes G S, Woolley D J, Cruz-Castillo J G. Field responses of kiwifruit to CPPU (cytokinin) application. Acta Hort, 1991, 297: 351~356
[33] Lotter J de V. A study of the preharvest ripening of Hayward kiwifruit and how it is altered by N- (2-chloro-4-pyridyl) -N-phenylurca (CPPU). Acta Hort, 1991, 297: 357~366
[34] Biasi R, Costa G, Giuliani R et al. Effects of CPPU on kiwifruit performance. Acta Hort, 1991, 297: 367~374
[35] Suezawa K, Matsuta N, Omura M et al. Plantlet formation from cell suspensions of kiwifruit (*Actinidia chinensis* Planch, var. chinensis). Sci Hort, 1988, 37: 133~128

本文原载：植物学报. 1995. 37(1): 48-52

毛花猕猴桃原生质体再生植株*

张远记　母锡金　蔡起贵　周云罗　钱迎倩

(中国科学院植物研究所)

摘　要　从毛花猕猴桃(*A ctinid ia eriantha* Benth) 试管培养的实生苗新展开叶片分离的原生质体,培养在液体 M S (除去 NH_4NO_3)附加 2, 4-D 1.0mg/L 和葡萄糖 0.4mol/L 的培养基上。培养 3 周后植板率达到 19.4%。在未添加新鲜培养基的情况下, 原生质体再生的细胞可持续分裂, 并于 3 个月时长成 2mm 大小的愈伤组织。将该愈伤组织转移到附加玉米素 0.5mg/L 和 IAA 0.1mg/L 的固体 MS 培养基上, 分化出苗。试管苗经诱导生根, 长成完整小植株。

关键词　毛花猕猴桃；叶片原生质体；植株再生

猕猴桃为新兴栽培果树，由于人工栽培历史短，在猕猴桃属 (*A ctinid ia*) 60 余种中目前广泛栽培的只有美味猕猴桃(*A. deliciosa*)[1]。一些研究者注意到许多野生种具有优良性状,并将其作为育种材料。目前利用野生种改良栽培种的途径只限于常规有性杂交。但常规杂交常面临两个难题: 一是种间不亲和难以得到种间杂种；二是猕猴桃为雌雄异株植物，对于雄株后代的有关果实性状，如丰产性、果实大小及品质等, 难以预先选择。现代生物技术，如体细胞杂交，不但可克服种间不亲和障碍，而且可望将两雌株的优良性状结合在一起。体细胞杂交的前提是原生质体再生植株。截至目前，猕猴桃原生质体培养再生植株成功的种仅有中华猕猴桃[2, 3]和美味猕猴桃[4-7]。毛花猕猴桃(*A. eriantha* Benth.)是一宝贵的种质资源，其果实维生素 C 含量为 1014mg/100g 鲜重，远远高于中华猕猴桃和美味猕猴桃的含量(分别为 250~300mg/100g 鲜重和 200~370mg/100g 鲜重)[1]。果实大小在猕猴桃属中仅次于中华猕猴桃和美味猕猴桃而列第三位[8]。本文报道毛花猕猴桃实生苗叶片原生质体再生小植株。

1　材料和方法

1.1　材料准备

毛花猕猴桃自由授粉种子由中国科学院植物研究所植物园提供。种子用 75%酒精浸泡 1min，然后用 0.1% $HgCl_2$ 消毒 10min，之后用无菌水冲洗 4 次。于无菌条件下解剖出

* 国家“八五”细胞工程资助项目。

胚，培养在 MS[9]附加玉米素 0.5mg/L、赤霉素(GA) 0.5mg/L 和 IAA 0.1mg/L 的培养基上，置于 25℃、黑暗条件下直至萌发。然后将幼苗转入 MS 培养基(大量元素减半)上于 25℃、12h 光照(光强为 1250lx 或 4000lx)和 22℃、12h 黑暗条件下培养。

1.2 原生质体分离

用解剖刀将新展开的叶片切成 1~2mm 细条或小块，置于酶液中。酶液成分包括 cellulase Onozuka R-10 1.0%，Macerozyme R-10 0.5%和 pectolyase Y-23 0.05%。酶溶于 CPW 溶液[10]中并添加 2-(N-morpholino) ethanesulfolic acid (MES) 3mmol/L 和甘露醇 0.45mol/L，pH 调至 5.6。于 25℃黑暗下酶解 8h。酶解完成后，用 300 目不锈钢丝网过滤，通过离心(40 × g, 2~3min)收集原生质体，并用 CPW(含甘露醇 0.45 mol/L，pH 5.6)洗 3 次，然后用原生质体培养基洗 1 次，最后悬浮于培养基中。以上操作均在无菌条件下进行。用血球计数板统计原生质体产量，并用 EvansBlue (0.1%)染色，检测其活力。

1.3 原生质体培养

将密度为 5×10^4 的原生质体悬浮液 1 mL 移入直径 4.5cm 培养皿中，用 parafilm 封口后在 25℃、黑暗条件下静置培养。所用基本培养基有 MS (除去 NH_4NO_3)、TC-CW[4]、B_5[11]和 KM 8p[12]。基本培养基中均附加下述成分：蔗糖 1%，葡萄糖 0.4 mol/L，水解酪蛋白 100mg/L，椰乳 20mg/L，pH 调至 5.6。2,4-D、NAA 和 IAA 单独或配合加入基本培养基中。

1.4 植株分化

将培养 3 个月后的原生质体所形成的愈伤组织块转移到 MS(含蔗糖 3%和琼脂 0.7%)附加不同激素配比的 3 种培养基上，分别为：(R_1) 2，4-D 0.5mg/L 和 6-BA 1.0mg/L；(R_2) 玉米素 0.5mg/L 和 IAA 0.1mg/L；和(R_3)玉米素 5.0mg/L 和 IAA 0.3mg/L。试管苗分化形成后，按下述方法诱导生根：长度在 1cm 或以上的试管苗在吲哚丁酸(BA)20ppm 溶液中浸泡 2h，然后在无激素的 MS(大量元素减半)的固体培养基上生根[6]。

2 实验结果

毛花猕猴桃叶片原生质体对渗透压敏感，如酶液中甘露醇浓度为 0.5mol/L 即会导致原生质体严重皱缩。叶片组织在含 0.45 mol/L 甘露醇的酶液中酶解 8h 后，原生质体产量可达到 0.7×10^6~1.8×10^6/g 鲜重，原生质体活力在 92%~97%之间(图版 I，1)。两种光照强度下的实生苗叶片在原生质体分离和原生质体形态方面差异不大，但培养结果却不同。来源于强光(4000 lx)条件下的叶片所分离的原生质体，培养在 MS 附加 2,4-D 1mg/L 培养基上不分裂，而弱光条件(1250 lx)的叶片来源的原生质体在同样培养基上，2d 后可见到细胞壁再生，培养 10 d 时发生第 1 次分裂(图版 I，2)。第 2 次和第 3 次分裂分别发生于培养 20 d 和 25 d 时(图版 I, 3、4)，并能持续分裂。培养 21 d 时计算的植板率达到 19.4%。所以其他处理所用材料均来自弱光条件下培养的叶片。在做激素浓度对比实验时，2,4-D 的浓度除 1mg/L 外，还用 0.5、2.0 及 3.0mg/L；也用 NAA、IAA 0.5、1.0、2.0 及 3.0mg/L 4 种不同浓度。结果表明，2,4-D 浓度在 0.5、2.0 和 3.0mg/L 时均不能诱导细胞分裂；在 NAA 浓度为 1.0mg/L 时细胞只分裂 1 次，且植板率较低(5.7%)。而在含其他浓度的 NAA 和所有几个浓度的 IAA 培养基上，细胞均不分裂。3 种不同激素同一浓度(1.0mg/L)对培养的不同影响见表 1。另外，在同时附加有 2,4-D 0.5mg/L 和 NAA 0.5mg/L 的培养基上细胞也不分裂。这些结果说明合适的激素种类和适当的浓度对培养的重要性，这与 Tsai[6,7]，Mii 和 Ohashi[3]，Oliveira 和 Pais[5]及肖尊安等[2]在猕猴桃上的结果是一致的。

表 1 不同植物生长调节物质对毛花猕猴桃原生质体培养的影响 (培养 21d 后)

Table l Effect of different growth regulators on protop last culture of *A ctinidia eriantha* (after 21 days of culture)

生长调节物质种类 Growth regulators (1mg/L)	植板率 Plating efficiency (%)	出芽率 Budding rate (%)	褐化率 Browning rate (%)
2, 4-D	19.4	7.8	22.5
NAA	5.7	21.6	36.4
IAA	0.0	0.0	100.0

Tsai[6]报道用 TCCW 培养基成功地从美味猕猴桃原生质体得到植株。但在本试验中，毛花猕猴桃细胞在 TCCW(附加 2，4-D 1mg/L)培养基上只分裂 2~3 次。而培养在 B_5 和 KM 8p(均附加 2，4-D 1mg/L)培养基上，均未见到细胞分裂。

在 MS 附加 2，4-D 1mg/L 培养基上培养 2 个月后，细胞团的生长开始加速。再培养 1 个月后即有 2mm 大小的愈伤组织块形成(图版 I，5)。此时直接将这些愈伤组织转移到附加不同激素的固体的分化培养基上(表 2)。需要指出的是，在愈伤组织被转入固体培养基之前，一直未向液体培养基中添加新鲜培养基降低渗透压。作为对照，本试验曾于培养 4 周时开始降压，结果细胞停止分裂，最终变褐死亡。

表 2 植物生长调节物质对原生质体来源的愈伤组织芽分化和苗形成的影响

Table 2 Effect of growth regulators on bud differentiation and shoot formation of protoplast-derived calli

培养基 Medium	愈伤组织数目 No. of calli	芽分化 Bud differentiation		试管苗数目 No. of shoots
		愈伤组织数目 No. of calli	百分率(%) Percentage	
R_2	29	25	86.2	15
R_3	12	9	66.7	0
R_1—R_2	29	21	72.4	8
R_1—R_3	10	4	40.0	0

R_1—R_2 和 R_1—R_3 分别表示愈伤组织在 R_1 上培养 1 个周期后转入 R_2 或 R_3 上。

R_1—R_2 and R_1—R_3 represent that calli were cultured on R_1 for one passage before transferring to R_2 or R_3.

愈伤组织在分化培养基上每月继代 1 次。在 R_2 培养基上继代 1 次之后，愈伤组织颜色变绿，质地由疏松变为致密。再继代 1 次即可观察到芽的形成。第 3 次继代后，形成长约 1cm 的苗(图版 I，6)。表 2 的结果取自继代 4 次后，此时在 R_2 培养基上的 29 块愈伤组织中，有 25 块分化芽，分化率达 86.2%，共形成 15 株生长正常的苗(≥1cm)(表 2)。再继代几次则所有愈伤组织均能分化芽，并有大量试管苗生成。在 R_3 培养基上芽分化较慢，因此在第 4 次继代后芽分化率不高(66.7%)，也没有 1cm 高度的苗形成(表 2)。但是继续继代几次后芽分化率也可达到 100%，并形成大量的苗。两种分化培养基上苗的形态及后来诱导生根的效果未见差异。愈伤组织在 R_1 上虽然生长较快，但为淡黄色，质地松软，不分化。若将其转移到 R_2 或 R_3 上，芽的分化推迟。例如直接从液体培养基转移到 R_2 上的愈伤组织，经 2 次继代即能分化，但愈伤组织在 R_1 上先培养 1 个月然后转到 R_2 上，则需要在 R_2 上继代 3 次才分化芽。

在 R_2 培养基上长成的试管苗，偶尔见到其基部有根形成。但大多数苗需诱导生根。BA 处理后，3~10d 开始生根，生根的小植株生长旺盛 (图版 I，7)。目前正在进行试管植株移栽工作。

3 讨论

一般情况下，在原生质体培养中，培养基的渗透压需要逐步降低。个别情况下也有一步降压的[13]。在猕猴桃属原生质体培养成功的几例报道中，在培养 2~7 周后开始降压[2, 3, 5, 6]。本试验未对原生质体培养基降压，而原生质体再生的细胞在高渗透压培养基中培养 3 个月一直保持分裂，原因可能是细胞的快速生长消耗了作为渗透压稳定剂的碳源而使培养基的渗透压自然降低。

为了使中华猕猴桃和美味猕猴桃原生质体所产生的愈伤组织分化植株，Tsai[6]、Mii 和 Ohashi[3]、Oliveira 和 Pais[5]及肖尊安等[2]均采用了分步诱导方法。在他们的方法中，2,4-D 的浓度降低而玉米素浓度升高。Mii 和 Ohashi[3]还特别强调用 NAA 代替 2,4-D 进行过渡培养的重要性。Tsai[6]和肖尊安等[2]则在改变激素配比的同时还使用不同的基本培养基。本试验将愈伤组织直接从原生质体培养基中转到固体分化培养基上诱导分化，成功地得到了植株。

目前猕猴桃原生质体培养成功的报道均采用愈伤组织[2, 5, 6]或悬浮培养物[3]为分离原生质体的材料。与愈伤组织和悬浮培养物相比，叶片为分离原生质体材料具有下列特点：一是未经过愈伤组织阶段，材料的遗传背景相对一致，有利于研究原生质体培养过程中发生的遗传变异；二是材料易于制备且需时较短，而适于分离原生质体的愈伤组织和悬浮培养物难以制备且需花费较长时间。此外，若将叶片原生质体用作体细胞杂交的亲本，与愈伤组织或悬浮培养物来源的原生质体融合，可用肉眼方便地鉴别出异核融合体。

参考文献

[1] Qian Y Q , Yu D P. Advances in *Actinidia* research in China. *Acta Hort*, 1991. 297: 51~55
[2] 肖尊安, 沈德绪, 林柏年, 中华猕猴桃原生质体再生植株, 植物学报, 1992. 34: 736~742

[3] Mii M, Ohashi H. Plantlet regeneration from protop lasts of kiwi fruit, *Actinidia chinensis* Planch. *Acta Hort*, 1988. 230: 167~170

[4] 蔡起贵，猕猴桃原生质体培养与植株再生. 见：孙勇如，安锡培主编，植物原生质体培养. 北京：科学出版社，1991. 190~194

[5] Oliveira M M, Pais M S S. Plant regeneration from protoplasts of long-term callus cultures of *Actinidia deliciosa* var *deliciosa* c v. Hayward (kiwifruit). *Plant Cell Rep*, 1991. 9: 643~646

[6] Tsai C K. Plant regeneration from leaf callus protoplasts of *Actinidia chinensis* Planch. var. *chinensis Plant Sci*, 1988. 54: 231~235

[7] Cai Q K (Tsai C K), Qian Y Q (Chien Y C), Ke S Q *et al*. Regeneration of Plants from Protop lasts of kiwifruit. (*Actinidia deliciosa*). In: Bajaj Y P Seds, Biotechnology in Agriculture and Forestry. Vol 23. Berlin Heidelberg: Springer-Verlag, 1993. 3~17

[8] 梁畴芬，中国猕猴桃属分类志要. 广西植物, 1930. (1): 30~35

[9] Murashige T, Skoog F. A revised medium for rapid growth and bioassays with tobacco tissue cultures. *Physiol Plant*, 1962. 15: 473~479

[10] Power J B, Chapman J V, Wilson D. Laboratory Manual: Plant Tissue Culture Univ of Nottingham, 1984. 125

[11] Gamborg O L, Miller R A, Ojima K . Nutrient requirement of suspension cultures of soybean root cells *Exp Cell Res*, 1968. 50: 151~158

[12] Kao K N, Michayluk M R. Nutritional requirements for growth of *Vicia hajastana* cells and protop lasts at a very low population density in liquid media. *Planta*, 1975. 126: 105~110

[13] Binding H, Gorschen E, Jorgensen J *et al*. Protop last culture in agarose media with particular emphasis to streaky lenses. *Bot Acta*, 1988. 101: 233~239

图 版 I

Plate I

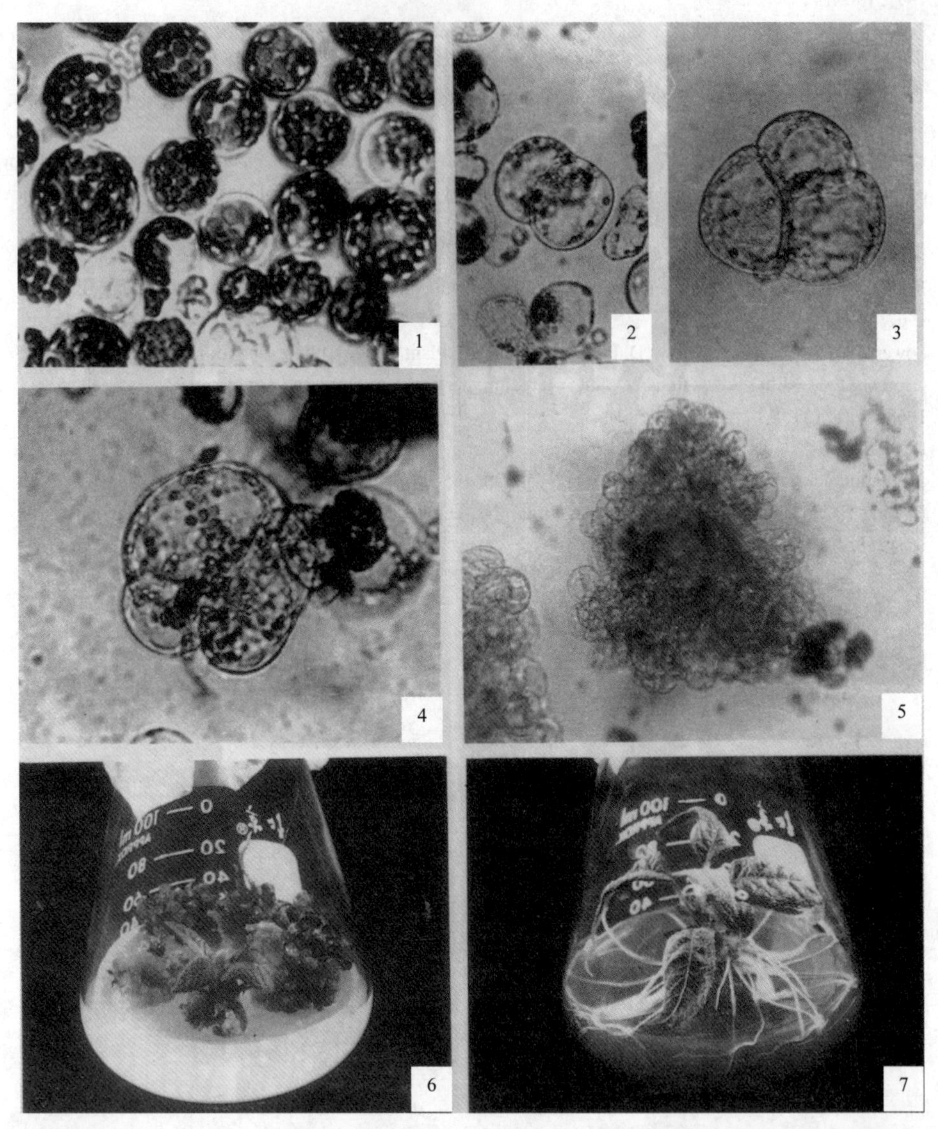

1. 新分离的原生质体。2. 再生细胞第 1 次分裂(培养 10 d)。3. 第 2 次分裂(培养 20 d)。4.第 3 次分裂，叶绿体仍明显可见。5. 培养 3 个月形成的愈伤组织(1~2mm 大小)。6. 原生质体再生的苗。7. 生根后的小植株

Fig.1. Protoplasts newly isolated from seedling leaves. Fig.2. First division of a regenerated cell on 10 days of culture. Fig.3. Second division after 20 days of culture. Fig.4. Third division. Note that chlorop lasts are still visible. Fig. 5. Callus of 1~2mm in size at 3 months of culture. Fig.6. Shoot differentiated on R_2 medium. Fig.7. Rooted plantlet

本文原载：武汉植物学研究. 1995. 13(2): 97-101

美味猕猴桃原生质体再生植株细胞遗传学研究*

I. 体细胞染色体数目的变化

何子灿[1]　蔡起贵[2]　柯善强[1]　钱迎倩[2]　徐立铭[1]

(1 中国科学院武汉植物研究所；2 中国科学院植物研究所)

摘　要　研究了美味猕猴桃叶愈伤组织原生质体再生植株和母株(*Actinidia deliciosa* line No.26)茎尖体细胞染色体数目。结果表明：母株 $2n=6x=174$。所测 29 株再生植株的茎尖体细胞染色体数目差异显著，多为非整倍体类型，占所测植株的 72.4%左右；体细胞染色体数目介于 142~310 条之间，其中 $2n=6x=174$ 约占 20.7%，少于 174 条染色体的植株约占 31.0%，超过 174 条染色体的植株则占 48.3%左右。个别单株部分茎尖体细胞在有丝分裂后期出现染色体桥、断片和落后染色体等异常现象。并对以上现象进行了扼要的讨论。

关键词　美味猕猴桃；原生质体再生植株；染色体数目

原生质体再生植株体细胞无性系变异的研究对该物种的细胞学、遗传学以及细胞工程的发展有着重要意义。迄今为止，已在许多物种的原生质体再生植株中进行了遗传与变异的研究，如甜菜[1]、马铃薯[2,3]、水稻[4]。自 1988 年以来，国内外相继报道了猕猴桃属部分物种从叶愈伤组织[5,6]、茎段细胞[7]、叶柄愈伤组织[8]和子叶愈伤组织[9]的原生质体培养获得再生植株。然而对这些再生植株体细胞无性系细胞遗传学的研究仅有蔡起贵等(1992)对美味猕猴桃叶愈伤组织原生质体再生植株少数植株染色体数目有初步的报道[10]。在此基础之上，本试验对该体细胞无性系大部分植株进行了染色体数目和倍性变化的研究，对个别植株在有丝分裂过程中出现的异常现象进行了观察，对母株染色体数目也进行了观察，还对再生植株的性别和雌株育性等性状与染色体倍性的相关性进行了初步探讨，为体细胞无性系变异以及有用的无性系变异植株的选择提供了细胞学依据。

1　材料和方法

供试材料为雌性美味猕猴桃(*Actinidia deliciosa* No.26)的原生质体再生植株。原生质体来源于该母株的茎段试管苗叶片诱导的愈伤组织。母株茎段由中国科学院植物研究所北京植物园安和祥先生提供。原生质体再生植株定植于中国科学院武汉植物所实验地已

---

* 国家“七五”及“八五”细胞工程资助项目。

7 年，部分植株开花，有雌株与雄株之分。于 1992~1993 年连续 2 年，4~5 月份对供试材料幼嫩茎尖生长点进行细胞学染色体观察。

茎尖体细胞染色体制片技术：母株和再生植株茎尖生长点用 0.2%秋水仙碱预处理，然后分别用酶法去壁低渗火焰干燥制片，Giemsa 染色[11]，用丙酸苏木精染色，常规压片法制片。选取好的细胞分裂中期相拍摄、计数。母株至少观察 10 个分裂相。

2 结果和讨论

2.1 母株体细胞染色体数目

母株雌性，茎尖体细胞染色体数 $2n=6x=174$(图版 I：8)，有丝分裂过程中未观察到异常现象。

母锡金(Mu Xijin)等报道的美味猕猴桃胚和胚乳培养试验所采用母株与本试验母株为同一株系。他们对母株体细胞染色体数目的观察结果与我们获得的结果是一致的，$2n=6x=174$[12]。猕猴桃属(*Actinidia*)大部分物种为二倍体物种，还有一部分物种，如中华猕猴桃(*A. chinensis*)则存在着二倍体、四倍体、六倍体和非整倍体等倍性不同的系列[13,14]。美味猕猴桃(*A.deliciosa*)已确认为六倍体物种，有关染色体数目的报道均为 $2n=6x=174$[15,16]。本试验母株为美味猕猴桃的一个品系(*A. deliciosa* line No.26)。再生植株来源于母株茎段试管苗叶愈伤组织原生质体。检索有关猕猴桃茎段试管苗无性系的资料，未见关于染色体数目和性别发生变异的报道。因此我们以母株作为再生植株的对照，进行遗传分析。

2.2 美味猕猴桃再生植株体细胞染色体数目及性别差异

为了研究美味猕猴桃原生质体再生植株体细胞无性系染色体数目的变化规律，本试验观察了再生植株中 29 个植株体细胞染色体数目，其结果列于表 1。所测再生植株之间染色体数目差异很大，变动在 142~310 条之间，其中有五倍体、六倍体、七倍体和非整倍体，多为非整倍体类型，约占所测植株的 72.4%。表 1 表明 29 株中与母株倍性一致的仅有 6 株(图版 I：3，5)，占所测植株的 20.3%左右；染色体数目低于母株的植株有 9 株，约占所测植株的 31%，其中 1 株为五倍体，8 株为非整倍体(图版 I：1，10)；染色体数目高于母株的植株有 14 株，占所测植株的 48.3%左右，其中 1 株为七倍体，13 株为非整倍体(图版 I：2，6，7，9，11，12)，与李耿光等报道的马铃薯原生质体再生植株染色体数目的变化趋势相似[2]。

表 1 还表明在所测 29 株再生植株中，有 15 株开花，而且性别有差异。其中有 5 株雄株，10 株雌株。染色体数≤174 条的绝大部分植株能开花，有雌株与雄株之分；染色体数目>174 条的 14 株仅有 3 株开花，且均为雌株。所测 5 株雄株染色体数目分别为 174、174、174、168 和 170。可见雄株之间染色体数目差异不大，多为正常六倍体，且染色体数目均未超过 174。

表 1　美味猕猴桃原生质体再生植株的性状

Table 1　The characters of plants regenerated from protoplasts of *A. deliciosa*

项目 Item	染色体数目 Chromosome number				
	$2n<174$		$2n=174$	$2n>174$	
	整倍体 Euploid	非整倍体 Aneuploid	六倍体 Hexaploid	整倍体 Euploid	非整倍体 Aneuploid
植株数 No. of plant	1($2n=5x$)	8	6($2n=6x$)	1($2n=7x$)	13
开花植株数 No. of flowered plants	1	5	6	1	2
开花植株性别 Sex of flowered plants	1(P)	3(P)+2(S)	3(P)+3(S)	1(P)	2(P)
雌株结实习性 Fruit habit of pistillate plant	1 好	2 好+1 未结实	3 好	1 少量结实	1 少量结实+1 未结实

S. 雄株 (Staminate plant); P. 雌株 (Pistillate plant)。

为了研究再生植株雌株类型结实性能与染色体倍性的关系，本试验观察了 10 个雌株体细胞染色体数目及其结实情况，其结果也列于表 1。雌株类型体细胞染色体数目差异很大，变动在 142~277 之间，倍性也不一致，有五倍体、六倍体、七倍体和非整倍体。染色体数为 174 或低于 174 的雌株，雌蕊发育正常，绝大部分能正常结实。仅染色体数为 142 的第 63 号雌株未能结实。染色体数超过 174 的雌株雌蕊大多发育异常，果实畸形或完全不能结实。以上现象表明再生植株开花、结实能力和性别的分化与染色体数目变异拟有一定的相关性，详细情况尚待进一步的研究。

2.3　再生植株不正常体细胞染色体的行为

再生植株中个别植株少数茎尖体细胞在有丝分裂过程中出现落后染色体、染色体桥和断片(图版 I：4)等异常现象，还偶见具双着丝点的染色体、环状染色体等异常染色体。可以推测在此株系中个别染色体的结构发生变异，个别染色体的结构不稳定，个别植株存在混倍体现象。关于染色体结构的变异将另文介绍。

所有再生植株都是来源于遗传性比较一致的同一植株的叶愈伤组织分离的原生质体。但其再生株系却出现高度的染色体变异，表现在染色体数目和倍性的变异以及有丝分裂过程中染色体行为异常。其变异来源可能是多方面的：可能来源于母株茎段试管苗的叶愈伤组织转代培养过程中已有的变异细胞；也可能在原生质体培养过程中发生变异；还可能因为母株是六倍体植物。有学者曾指出高度的细胞学异常可能是多倍体植物在细胞和组织培养中的特点[17]。我们认为还与母株体细胞染色体数目稳定性有关。物种不同，体细胞染色体数目稳定性不同。美味猕猴桃是一个栽培种，新西兰学者 Crowhurst 在 1991 年利用 RFLP 技术证明中华猕猴桃是美味猕猴桃的一个亲本[15]。据报道中华猕猴桃具有倍性不同的系列，其染色体数目明显不同：有 $2n=2x=58$，$2n=4x=116$，$2n=160$[13]，$2n=170$[14]，其多倍体变种表现出染色体数目的不稳定性。猕猴桃属植物染色体极小(约

0.7 微米)，而且很多(染色体基数大，x=29)，不能排除计数困难造成的误差，但也不能排除该属某些多倍体物种体细胞染色体数目的不稳定性。个别染色体的减少或增加对其植株的生长发育影响不大，再生植株中很多非整倍体植株能正常生长发育和开花结实是这一观点的一个佐证。

原生质体培养再生植株发生的遗传变异导致了再生植株出现广泛的表型变异[3,18]，使得该技术在种质保存和良种快速繁殖等领域中的应用受到限制，但也使得原生质体再生植株成为染色体工程和植物遗传与育种的重要变异来源[1]。这些研究结果与我们的实验结果相似。蔡起贵等已报道了部分再生植株在外部形态和生长习性等表型方面的变异[10]，结合本项试验再一次表明猕猴桃原生质体再生植株是一种极其丰富的种质资源，具有培养新品种的巨大潜力，值得进一步的研究和利用。

参考文献

[1] Krens F A, Jamer D *et al*. Transfer of cytoplasm from new beta CM S sources to sugan beet by asymmetric fusion

[2] l. Shoot regeneration from mesopgyll protoplasts and characterization of regenerated plants. *Theor Appl Genet*, 1990, 79: 390~396

[3] 李耿光, 张兰英等. 马铃薯原生质体再生植株表现型变异和染色体数目变化. 植物学报, 1992, 34(9): 712~716

[4] Creissen C, Karp A, Karyotypic changes in potato plants regenerated from protoplasts, *Plant Cell Tiss Org Cult*, 1985, 4: 171~183

[5] 余建明. 水稻原生质体再生植株及后代的性状表现, 遗传学报, 1990, 17: (6): 438~442

[6] 蔡起贵. 猕猴桃. 见: 孙勇如, 安锡培主编, 植物原生质体培养, 北京: 科学出版社, 1991, 190~194

[7] Tsai C-K. Plant regeneration from leaf callus protoplasts of *Actinidia chinensis* Planch var, *chinensis Plant Sci*, 1988, 54: 231~235

[8] Mii M, Ohashi H. Plantlet regeneration from protoplasts of kiwifruit, *Actinidia chinensis* Planch. *Acta Hortic*, 1988, 230, 167~170

[9] Oliveira M M , Pais M S. Plant regeneration from protoplasts of long-term callus cultures of *Actinidia deliciosa* cv, Hayward (kiwifruit). *Plant Cell Rep*, 1991, 9: 643~646

[10] 肖尊安, 沈德绪等. 中华猕猴桃原生质体再生植株. 植物学报, 1992, 34(10): 736~742

[11] 蔡起贵, 钱迎倩, 柯善强, 何子灿等. 美味猕猴桃原生质体再生植株无性系变异的研究. 植物学报, 1992, 34(11): 822~828

[12] 陈瑞阳, 宋文芹. 植物染色体标本制备的新方法——去壁低渗及其在细胞学中的应用. 见: 朱微主编. 植物染色体及染色体技术. 北京: 科学出版社, 1982, 99~114

[13] Mu X-j *et al*, Embryology and embryo rescue of interspecific hybrids in *Actinidia*. *Acta Horti*, 1991, 297: 93~97

[14] 朱道圩, 河南省中华猕猴桃种质资源细胞分裂和染色体数目的研究. 河南农学院学报, 1982, 1: 45~57

[15] Zhang J *et a1*., chromosome numbers in two varieties of *Actinidia chinensis* Planch. *N Z J Bot*, 1983, 21: 161~163

[16] Crowhurst R N *et al.*, The genetic origin of kiwifruit. *Acta Horti*, 1991, 297: 61

[17] Fraser LG, Harvey C F, Kend J. Ploidy manipulatis of kiwifruit in tissue culture. *Acta Horti*, 1991, 297: 109~114

[18] 叶新荣, 余毓君. 小麦再生植株当代(R_1代)的细胞学和形态学变异. 遗传学报, 1989, 16(2): 106~110

[19] Secro G A *et al.*, Variability of protoplast-derived potato clones. *Crop Sci*, 1981, 21: 102~105

图 版 I

Plate I

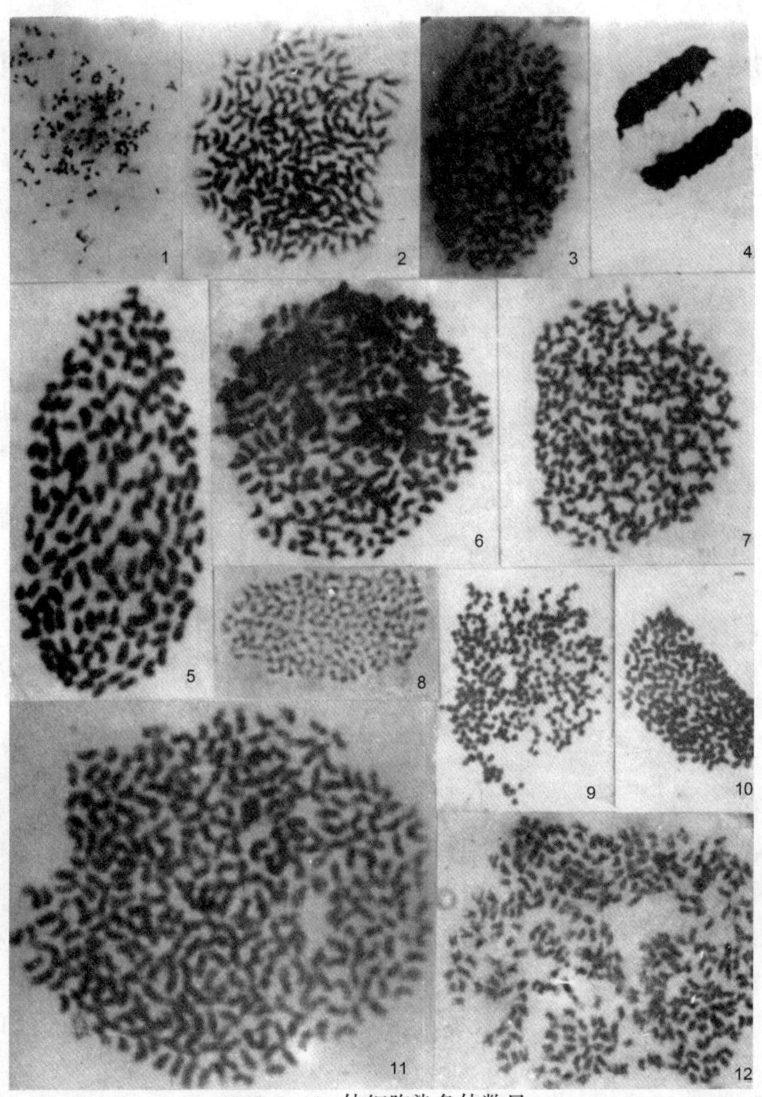

1~3, 5~12, 体细胞染色体数目:

1. 第 24 号雄株 $2n$=168(×1200); 2. 第 76 号雌株 $2n$=178(×1600); 3. 第 72 号雌株 $2n$=174(×1600); 4. 第 5 号植株, 落后染色体和染色体桥(×1200); 5.第 29 号雄株 $2n$=174(×1800); 6. 第 43 号植株 $2n$=231(×1800); 7. 第 10 号植株 $2n$=292(×1400); 8. *A. deliciosa* line No. 26(母株) $2n$=174(×1600); 9. 第 45 号植株 $2n$=287(×1200); 10. 第 13 号雌株 $2n$=170(×1200); 11. 第 36 号植株 $2n$=c.282(×1800); 12. 第 80 号植株 $2n$=c. 310(×1800);

1~3, 5~12. Chromosome number of somatic cell:

1. Staminate plant No. 24, $2n$=168(×1200); 2.Pistillate plant No. 76, $2n$=178(×1600); 3. Pistillate plant No. 72, $2n$=174(×1600); 5. Staminate plant No. 29, $2n$=174(×1800); 6. Plant No. 43, $2n$=231(×1800); 7. Plant No. 10, $2n$=292(×1400); 8. *A. deliciosa* line No. 26(parent) $2n$=174(×1600); 9. Plant No. 45, $2n$=287(×1200); 10. Pistillateplant No. 13,$2n$=170(×1200); 11.Plant No. 36, $2n$=c.282(×1800); 12. Plant No. 80, $2n$=c. 310(×1800);4.Plant No.5, lagging chromosome and chromosome bridge were slown (×1200)

本文原载：武汉植物学研究. 1997. 15(3): 199-207

美味猕猴桃原生质体再生植株细胞遗传学研究*

II. 性别性状变异和小孢子发生及其发育命运

何子灿[1]　蔡起贵[2]　钱迎倩[2]　黄宏文[1]

(1 中国科学院武汉植物研究所；2 中国科学院植物研究所)

摘　要　对美味猕猴桃同一雌株叶原生质体再生植株进行了形态学、细胞学以及育性特性的比较研究，确认该体细胞无性系性别性状发生变异，其中60%雄性再生植株退化的雌蕊仍保留不同程度的雌性化特征，但雌性全不育；小孢子则能发育成有功能的雄配子体，但有一定的功能缺陷。再生雌株中 P_1 组群性状特征与母株相似；P_2 组群花发育畸形，导致雌性不育或育性极差。细胞学研究表明，小孢子母细胞减数分裂时染色体异常行为对小孢子发生的影响不能决定其性别类型；雌株类型小孢子败育过程有受基因调控的细胞学特征。认为雌株和雄株小孢子的发育受控于不同的基因体系，具性别的特异性。再生植株性别性状发生变异可能是性别控制基因或染色体发生结构性变异所致。母株染色体上累积的结构性变异与该遗传基础具易变性密切有关。

关键词　美味猕猴桃；原生质体再生植株；性别性状变异

美味猕猴桃(*Actinidia deliciosa*)植株个体间有遗传上的雄株与雄株之分，是形态上的二性花；但在发育过程中雌蕊群或雄蕊群发生选择性败育，形成功能上的单性花，为雌雄异株型植物[1]。其有性繁殖后代有雌株和雄株，无性繁殖系性别与母株相同，但也不绝对如此。Seal[2]、Messing[3]、Hirsch[4]。在雄性品种芽变系中发现结实的雄株，Bellini[5]在雌性品种芽变系中发现能自花授粉结实的雌株。这些芽变系的出现，表明了在无性系中存在由功能单性花变为功能二性花的可能。但对其遗传基础发生相应变化的研究还未见报道。

1992年，蔡起贵等首次报道了美味猕猴桃同一个雌株(*A. deliciosa* No. 26)茎段试管苗叶愈伤组织原生质体再生植株中有少数植株为雄性[6, 7]，为该物种的无性系性别变异增加一个新的变异类型。在同一个雌性遗传基础上产生的性别差异涉及其体细胞无性系遗传基础发生的相应变化，也涉及该物种的性别决定和性分化。鉴于此种现象的特殊性和可比性，笔者在对该体细胞无性系染色体数目变化与性别和其育性关系进行初步研究基础之上[8]，再对其雌、雄株进行花形态、染色体数目和行为，以及雌、雄性育性的比较研究。鉴于雌株花粉败育而雄株花粉可育，故着重对小孢子的发生和发育进行观察。根

* 国家自然科学基金资助项目。

据小孢子发生和发育的细胞学特征,阐明雌株类型小孢子发生选择性败育的细胞学机理。并探讨了界定该体细胞无性系为雌雄异株系的细胞学、形态学和生物学的依据。

1 材料和方法

1.1 材料

实验采用材料同前[8]，以开花的原生质体再生植株为研究对象，对照(母株)由中国科学院植物研究所安和祥教授提供。

1.2 方法

当再生植株个体发育进入生殖生长状态时，对其雌蕊群和雄蕊群进行观察，将外观具雌性或雄性特征的植株区别开来，结合育性检测，将其划分为雄性组群(记为S组群，简称S)和雌性组群(记为P)。S共有10株；P中能正常结实的7株，记为P_1；不能结实或结实不良的19株为P_2组群，简称P_2。对S、P_1和P_2进行如下比较试验。

(1) 花形态比较：对雌蕊群、雄蕊群的发育进行观察。

(2) 细胞学观察：在再生植株小孢子母细胞(PMC)和小孢子发育各期进行，并辅以茎尖体细胞染色体数目及其行为的观察，其中减数分裂时染色体结构和构型的比较将另文发表。染色体制片方法同前[8]，压片法制片采用醋酸洋红染色，去壁低渗法制片采用Giemsa染色，OLYMPUS显微镜下观察、拍照。

(3) 育性比较：在自由授粉结实情况观察基础上，再进行再生雌雄株间的正反交、自交和与近缘种中华猕猴桃杂交。观察结实能力，统计每果内种子数、种子千粒重和发芽率。花粉育性检查用醋酸洋红染色，显微镜下观察其可染色性，以上实验均以母株为对照。

2 结果

2.1 花形态比较

对照为雌株，常规无性嫁接苗1年后开花结实。子房圆柱形，顶部有花柱-柱头结构。减数分裂(Meiosis)M_1时期，花柱下部就相连呈筒状，上部分离，顶部开始向具V形沟的柱头发育(图版I：1)。开花时柱头高出雄蕊群呈放射状横列，上部微卷(图版I：2)，顶部扩展成具V形沟的柱头，其表面有1层乳突细胞，花药外观正常。

再生植株定植5年后才陆续开花，部分植株至今未有花芽分化，具异常长的童期。形态比较结果列于表1。

P组群雌蕊发达，雄蕊群低于柱头，具雌株类型外观。其中P_1雌蕊发育正常，性状特征与母株相同，此处不再赘述。

P_2花发育畸形，花冠由6~11枚大小和形状均不相同的花瓣组成，部分花瓣出现红色斑纹。蕾期花瓣间不能紧密相靠，使未发育成熟的柱头外露。开花时花柱大多呈长短不一的棒状，无规则地聚集在子房顶部，下部不相连成筒，顶部一般不扩展成具V形沟的柱头(图版Ⅰ：3)，表面乳突细胞极少，基本雌性不育。但有5株雌蕊畸形程度随枝间位置和年份不同而异，受生态环境的影响偶尔结1~2个具粗硬毛的畸形小果。其内十数粒种子无发芽能力，表现出极低的育性。表明P_2植株结实不良主要原因是雌蕊发育畸形。

表1 对照和再生植株不同组群的雌蕊、雄蕊形态

Table 1 Pistil and stamen morphology of CK & different groups of regenerated plants

组别 Group	性别 Sex	植株数 No. of plants	体细胞染色体数 No. of chromosomes in somatic cells	子房 Ovary			柱头 Stigma			雄蕊 Stamen	
				正常 Normal	畸形 Abnormal	退化 Degenerate	正常 Normal	畸形 Abnormal	退化 Degenerate	正常 Normal	异常 Abnormal
P_1	雌	7	156~174	7	0	0	7	0	0	0	7
P_2	雌	19	176~336	19	0	0	5*	14	0	0	19
S	雄	10	168~174	0	3**	7	0	6***	4	10	0
CK	雄	1	174	1	0	0	1	0	0	0	1

* 这些植株中仅部分柱头能正常发育；** 子房具雌性化特征的植株；*** 柱头具雌性化特征的植物。

* Only a part of stigma developed normally in these plants; ** Ovaries with the characteristics of feminization in these plants; *** Stigma with the characteristics of feminization in these plants.

S植株花器具雄性类型特征：雄蕊群发达并高出柱头，雌蕊群随花器发育呈渐进性退化。S植株间柱头退化程度存在差异，如在减数分裂M_1期S-12与母株比较，柱头形态差别不大(图版Ⅰ：4，1)，但开花时，S-12柱头退化呈细丝状(图版Ⅰ：5)；S-29在M_1期柱头就退化呈细丝状，开花时，在退化呈小锥体状的子房顶部，仅有花柱着生部位的痕迹，与自然雄株退化的雄蕊(图版Ⅰ：6)形态相似。S-54开花时柱头仅留退化的痕迹，但子房稍大(图版Ⅰ：7)。总之，60%S植株已退化的雌性器官仍保留不同程度的雌性化特征(表1)。但这些特征并未能改变它们的性别属性，其雌性全不育。形态学的比较表明，再生植株形态上有性别差异。

2.2 细胞学比较

2.2.1 母株小孢子的发生和败育

母株茎尖体细胞染色体数$2n=6x=174$(图版Ⅰ：8)，有丝分裂早中期，可见几条染色体较其余凝缩程度不同(图版Ⅰ：9)。其PMC在减数分裂时染色体行为混乱。凝线期有核穿壁行为。终变期染色体构型复杂，以二价体为主，有H、X、O、∩和棒状各形；并有四价体和六价体呈环状或链状；还时有异形多价体、三价体和单价体出现；也有少数二价体由于凝缩不同步仍呈双线期状态；还有次级配对发生(图版Ⅰ：10)，且这种配对类型

出现率可达10%左右。后$_1$和后$_2$期的落后染色体、染色体桥和断片、微核出现率分别高达72.9%和91.4%，落后染色体数目由0~10不等(表2，图版I：11，12)。四分体时期部分四分体由于细胞质先行解体，细胞核物质浓缩而夭折(图版I：13)。此后小孢子形成，但在早期便停止发育，居中的细胞核物质出现边沿化扩散趋势；伴随核物质扩散未见染色丝进一步形成，反而着色反应减退，表明DNA发生降解，继而核仁核膜消失，随后小孢子中间出现空白区域(图版I：14~16)；再后此区逐步扩大形成空的小孢子，呈有序败育，在时空上具相对的稳定性和一致性，显示出拟受基因调控的细胞学特征，值得进一步研究。

表2 对照和不同组群再生植株细胞学鉴定结果(部分资料)

Table 2 The results of cytological examination of CK & regenerated plants of different groups(Partial data)

材料 Materials	花粉可染性 Pollen stainablity			减数分裂后期1 Anaphase 1 of PMC			减数分裂后期2 Anaphase 2 of PMC			四分体时期 Tetrad Phase
	花粉数 No.of pollen	可染色数 No.of stainable pollen	%	PMC数 No.of PMCs	具异常染色体PMC数 No.of PMCs* with abnormal chromosome	%	PMC数 No.of PMCs	具异常染色体PMC数 No.of PMCs* with abnormal chromosome	%	类型 Type
CK	50	0	0	74	54	72.9	35	32	91.4	四分体
P$_1$-19	50	0	0	75	56	74.7	60	50	83.3	四分体
P$_1$-71	50	0	0	53	35	66.0	53	39	73.6	四分体
P$_2$-10	50	0	0	10	10	100.0	5	5	100.0	多分体
S-12	272	240	88.2	68	40	58.8	29	20	69.0	四分体
S-24	204	180	88.2	37	27	73.0	15	11	73.3	四分体
S-29	192	178	92.7	104	66	63.5	40	32	80.0	四分体

* 异常染色体包括有落后染色体、染色体桥和断片，以及微核等。

* Abnormal chromosome, such as lagging chromosome, chromosome bridge, chromosome fragment and micronucleus *et al*.

2.2.2 P$_1$和P$_2$组群小孢子的发生和败育

(1) P$_1$组群体细胞染色体数在156~174之间，多为174(图版II：17~19)。其Meiosis和有丝分裂过程、染色体行为、小孢子发生及其败育方式都与母株相同，仅M$_1$时期的构型较母株简单，几乎全为二价体(图版II：20)；后$_1$有整条染色体末端呈丝状(图版II：21)；后$_1$和后$_2$染色体异常行为发生率稍低于母株(表2，图版II：22)。P$_1$的非整倍体类型PMC在Meiosis时较整倍体复杂。染色体数与母株相近的，如P$_1$-67体细胞染色体数为170，其PMC染色体数多为整倍体，n=87。这可能与有丝分裂时，由于有落后染色体等原因造成不对称分裂，只有完整染色体组的茎尖生长点才发育成花芽有关；也可能与凝线期核穿壁行为有关，还待深入研究。染色体数与母株相差大的非整倍体类型，如 P_1-16，茎尖体细胞染色体数为 156 及 165，是一株混倍体植株。其体细胞有丝分裂后期有多个落后染色体(图版 II：24)，PMC 在凝线期出现广泛的核穿壁(图版 II：25)，PMC 内染色体数明显不等(图版 II：26)，有多个染色体聚集成团现象(图版 II：27)，还有无核 PMC，此类 PMC 很快夭亡。以上情况严重影响了 PMC 的发育，在 M_1 以前，就观察到近一半的 PMC 夭折。后期$_1$和后期$_2$出现落后染色体、桥、断片、微核等异常现象加剧，四分体时的夭折现象相应增加；小孢子在形成早期同母株一样停止发育，以与母株一样的败育方式形成空的败育花粉。

(2) P_2 组群植株体细胞染色体数在 $174<2n\leqslant336$ 内，多为 300 条左右的非整倍体(图版 II：29，30)。雄性细胞形成早期——造孢细胞时期就出现核穿壁和核物质排出现象(图版 II：31，32)。在形成 PMC 时，细胞核又极易脱落于细胞外形成无核细胞而夭折(图版 III：33)。因此花药内 PMC 量少，且畸形；PMC 内多大小不一的微核，数目不等。凝线期又发生广泛的核穿壁，在整个 Meiosis 时期，每个 PMC 都有染色体行为异常现象，还有严重的纺锤体结构紊乱，造成后期$_1$和后期$_2$有多个分裂中心(图版 III：34，35)，形成的多分体也大小不一、形态各异(图版 III：36)，再形成大小不一空的败育花粉(图版 III：37)。推测它们的大孢子母细胞的发生、发育也可能存在严重异常，可能是其大孢子不育或育性极差的又一重要原因。

2.2.3 S 组群植株小孢子的发生和发育

S 植株体细胞染色体数在 $168\leqslant2n\leqslant174$ 之间，多为 174(图版 III：38，40)，自然雄株 $2n=6x=174$(图版 III：39)。S 植株小孢子的发生过程与母株相似，仅 M_1 染色体构型简单，偶有多价体出现，染色体次级联会形式与母株不同(图版 III：41)。落后染色体、桥和断片、微核等也常出现(图版 III：43~45)。其非整倍体植株的 PMC 在 M_1 期环状、链状多价体以及多条染色体粘连现象增加(图版 III：42)，四分体时期发生的夭折现象也较其整倍体类型的高，表明异常染色体使小孢子的形成受到损害。值得指出的是，S 植株(排除非整倍体植株引起的干扰)在后期$_1$和后期$_2$染色体的异常行为发生率明显低于再生雌株，更低于母株(表 2)，显示了染色体结构重排的可能性。刚形成的小孢子单核居中，细胞层次清晰，染色质着色力强。其后中央大液泡形成使单核靠边，小孢子开始第 1 次有丝分裂(图版 III：47，48)，形成营养细胞和紧靠花粉壁的月牙形生殖细胞，二者之间有细胞壁形成(图版 III：49)。然后生殖细胞脱离花粉壁向花粉中间移动，中间细胞壁消失(图版 III：50)。开花第 1d 的花粉生殖核能被醋酸洋红深染，并由圆形逐渐变成长梭形(图版 III：51)；营养核因水合程度高，折射率与胞质相近，故难以观察。若采用酶法去花粉壁，可见长梭形的生殖核与浅染的营养核贴近。开花第 2d 大部分花粉仍为二细胞；但有少部分开始第 2 次有丝分裂，生殖核分裂形成 2 个精核(图版 III：52)，成三胞花粉。有功能的、发育正常的雄配子体形成意味着 S 植株为雄株类型。表明了 S 植株小孢子与母株和再生雌株的小孢子有完全不同的发育或败育过程，具有两种截然不同的发育命运。

2.3 育性比较

P 组群植株和母株花粉开花时全为空的败育花粉，无着色反应。所有育性实验也表明雄性全不育。S 植株花粉可染色性达 90%左右(表 2)，但不同年份、不同枝间位置差异很大；其退化雌蕊全不育。在雌、雄育性特性上，再生植株具有发生选择性败育的特征。

表 3 P_1-16、P_1-19 × S-12、S-14、S-24、S-29 和中华猕猴桃的种子发芽率、千粒重和平均每果种子数

Table 3 Germination, weight of 1 000 seeds and average number of seeds per fruit in P_1-16, P_1-19 × S-12, S-14, S-24, S-29 and *A. chinensis*

杂交组合 Hybrid combination	发芽率 Germination of seeds (%)	千粒重 Weight of 1 000 seeds (g)	平均每果种子数* Average number of seeds per fruit
对照自由授粉 CK open pollination	9.7	2.125	402.5
P_1-16 自由授粉 P_1-16 open pollination	37.3	1.427	497.5
P_1-16 × S-12	0.3	1.326	611.0
P_1-16 × S-14	0.5	—	542.0
P_1-16 × S-24	0.2	1.917	599.0
P_1-19 自由授粉 P_1-19 open pollination	10.0	1.566	405.6
P_1-19 × 中华猕猴桃 P_1-19 × *A. chinensis*	0.8	0.990	408.5
P_1-19 × S-12	1.0	1.421	169.4
P_1-19 × S-24	0.9	—	433.0
P_1-19 × S-29	5.5	1.230	421.5

* 10 个果实平均数 (All data represent the average of ten fruits)。

用 P_1-16、P_1-19 × S-12、S-14、S-24、S-29、中华猕猴桃，结果表明(表 3)S 植株的花粉确实有使雌株受孕、结实的雄性功能，但形成的种子发芽率一般仅在1%左右。P_1-16 × S-29 种子发芽率虽有 5.5%左右，但仍明显低于对照和 P_1-16、P_1-19 植株自由授粉种子的发芽率(其分别为 9.7%、37.3%，10%)。推测 S 植株雄配子体本身存在一定的功能缺陷。与中华猕猴桃植株杂交成功，则表明了两个物种的近缘关系。

3 讨论

3.1 关于原生质体再生植株性别性状发生变异问题

上述研究结果表明该体细胞无性系不仅是原始型生命的延续，而且在性别性状方面发生了明显的变异。约 28%的已开花再生植株显示其发生性逆转，成为雄株类型(S)；性

别特征与母株相似的 P_1 仅占开花植株 19%；占开花植株 53%的 P_2，性别类型虽未变，但由于染色体数目与母株差异过大，严重损害了雌性器官的发育，使其雌性不育，或育性极低，P_2 内有 1 株(P_2-76)虽染色体数为 176，仅比母株多 2 个染色体，但花器发育畸形，雌性也全不育，推测其染色体组可能极不平衡，仅用染色体数分析倍性具有极大的局限性。通过对 S、P_1 和 P_2 3 个组群的研究，证实该体细胞无性系为一新型雌雄异株系。

对来源于同一个雌性遗传基础的体细胞无性系出现这种性别差异的原因作何解释呢？前人已发现，在美味猕猴桃雄性和雌性无性系中有由芽变而发生雌雄同株现象，证实该物种有在同一个遗传基础上因突变而发生性别性状变异的可能性[2~4]。笔者认为这也是该体细胞无性系能发生性别性状变异的原因之一。Testolin[9]认为美味猕猴桃植株性别是由 XY 性染色体或一对或几对性别控制基因决定的，并对其有性繁殖 F_1 代雄株中，1%~4.2%的植株有不同程度的雌性化特征，解释为与性有关基因“发生轻微改变所致”，但细胞学的证据未有报道。

美味猕猴桃植株染色体既小又多，现有资料表明，该物种 $2n=6x=174$，是异源六倍体栽培种，原始祖先已无从查寻。PMC 在 Meiosis 时，染色体配对方式和行为与二倍体物种相似，M_1 构型以二价体为主，只有 1~2 个环状或链状四价体偶尔可观察到，没有染色体异常行为[9]。笔者通过对母株细胞学的观察，认为该株有遗传上的特异性。其有丝分裂和减数分裂均有少数染色体出现凝集不同步现象，终变期复杂的构型以及后期$_1$、后期$_2$高频率的出现染色体异常现象，表明该植株染色体上累积了许多畸变结构，这一切与染色体易发生结构性变异密切有关。母株遗传基础的不稳定性是其体细胞无性系发生变异的又一原因。

在原生质体诱导过程中，原生质体来源于叶愈伤组织，而后者又来源于叶薄壁细胞，这比来源于分生组织的细胞更具易变性。在培养再生植株过程中，其 DNA 上可能因发生断裂、丢失、增殖、拼接、修复等作用，导致染色体结构的重排和交换，产生结构性变异。在单个细胞内发生的变异通过原生质体的培养得以保存，并在由此形成的再生植株上得到表达。它们的 PMC 在 M_1 期构型的改变和染色体异常行为发生率的比较，显示该体细胞无性系某些染色体确实发生了结构性的变异。与性和性分化有关的染色体或基因(组)发生的结构性变异造成了该体细胞无性系性别性状的变异，这是原因之三。S 组群植株表现出较高频率(60%)的雌性化特征，以及雄配子体功能有一定的缺陷，表明性别性状除受主控基因作用外，还受多个微效基因的调节；同时还由于其雄性遗传基础的形成来源于同一个雌性遗传基础发生的变异，有一定的“返祖”和“先天不足”，有待进一步研究加以确定。

3.2 关于小孢子的发生及其两种不同的发育命运与性别类型关系问题

实验表明 S、P_1、P_2 和母株的 PMC 形成小孢子过程相同。此外，它们在凝线期的核穿壁行为、后期$_1$和后期$_2$高频率出现异常染色体，多条染色体易凝集成团或发生次级配对，以及部分四分孢子由于细胞质先行解体而夭折等方面都相似。小孢子发生过程，不存在与性别类型有关的特异性。它们的非整倍体类型染色体异常行为加剧，小孢子发生过程中夭折现象增加；年份和枝间位置不同对小孢子发生有一定影响。说明染色体的异常行为、染色体数目和倍性，以及外界环境条件对小孢子的形成有着不同程度的影响；但不是雌株小孢子发生选择性败育的原因，与该物种性别类型形成没有相关性。

被子植物的小孢子发育是受许多基因调控的[10]。通过对雌、雄株小孢子具有两种不同的发育途径，并由此产生两种截然不同的发育命运比较，发现美味猕猴桃雌株和雄株的小孢子发育，受控于不同的基因体系，有性别的特异性。雄株小孢子能进行有序的正常发育，形成有功能的雄配子体。雌株则在小孢子形成早期就停止发育，继而有序的败育过程也有受基因调控的细胞学特征。此外，雌株雄蕊群形态上明显不如雄株的发达，表明小孢子所处内环境也存在一定的差异。说明雌株小孢子在小孢子发育早期发生选择性败育是在细胞内、外因子共同作用下，发生的一种有步骤的生理性自行消亡过程，这是关系美味猕猴桃植株性别形成的一个关键问题，具有极高的学术研究价值。

参考文献

[1] 邵宏波. 高等植物性别分化研究的某些进展. 武汉植物学研究. 1994, **12**(1): 85~94

[2] Seal A G & McNeilage M A. Sex and kiwifruit breeding. *Acta Hort*. 1989, **240**: 35~38

[3] Messing R, Vischi N, Marchetti S *et al*. Observations on subdioeciousness and fertilization in a kiwifruit breeding program. *Acta Hort*. 1990, **282**: 377~386

[4] Hirsch A M. Fortune D, Blanchet. Study of diodcism in kiwifruit *Actinidia deliciosa* Chevalier. *Acta Hort*, 1990, **282**: 349~358

[5] Bellini E, Rotondo A, Pilone N. First observations on probable selffertile clones of kiwifruit. *Acta Hort*, 1990, **282**: 349~ 358

[6] 蔡起贵, 钱迎倩, 柯善强等. 美味猕猴桃原生质体再生植株无性系变异的研究. 植物学报, 1992, **34**(11): 822~828

[7] Cai Q G, Qian Y Q, Ke S Q *et al*. Plant protoplasts and genetic engineering. IV. Regeneration of plants from protoplasts of kiwifruit. Biotechnology in Agriculture and Forestry Vol. 23 Berlin Heidelberg: Springer-Verlag, 1993, 1~17

[8] 何子灿, 蔡起贵, 柯善强等. 美味猕猴桃原生质体再生植株细胞遗传学研究. I. 体细胞染色体数目的变化. 武汉植物学研究, 1995, **13**(2): 97~101

[9] Testolin R, Cipriani G, Costa G. Sex segregation ratio and gender expression in the genus *Actindia*. *Sexual Plant Reproduction*, 1995, **8**(3): 129~139

[10] McNeilage M A, Considine J A. Chromosome studies in some *Actindia*. taxa and implications for breeding. *New Zea J Bot*. 1989, **27**: 71~81

[11] Myers J R, Gritton E T, Struckmeyer B E. Genetic nale sterility in the Pea(*Pisum setivam* L.) II. *Cyto Euphytica*, 1992, **63**: 245~256

图版 I

Plate I

1，2. 母株花柱-柱头形状：1. 减数分裂时期；2. 开花时期；3. P_2-10 的畸形花柱；4~7. 雄株退化柱头：4. S-12 减数分裂时期，5. S-12 开花时期，6. 1 个美味猕猴桃雄株，7. S-54 的稍膨大子房，8. 母株 $2n=6x=174$；9. 母株有丝分裂早中期染色体凝缩不同步；10~13. 母株 PMC 的减数分裂：10. 终变期 $2n$=1VI(环状)+1IV(环状)+1III+80II+1 I，b 为 a 的放大，示一晚双线期染色体(箭头)和一个次级配对(短箭头)，11，12 后期$_1$和后期$_2$多个落后染色体、桥和断片；13. 1 个败育的四分体；14~16. 母株小孢子败育过程：14，15. 核物质向边沿扩散，16. 中间出现空白区域

1, 2. The shape of style and stigma of parent plant: 1. At meiosis stage; 2. At blooming stage; 3. Aberrant style of P_2-10; 4~7. Degenerated stigma of staminate plants: 4. At meiosis stage of S-12, 5. At blooming stage of S-12, 6. A staminate plant, 7. Slightly swelled ovary of S-54; 8. Chromosome number of parent plant $2n=6x=174$; 9. Early metaphase of mitosis in parent plant, chromosome concentration is not synchronic; 10~13. Meiotic behaviour of PMC in parent plant: 10. At diakinesis, $2n$=1IV(ring shape)+VI(ring shape)+1III+80II+1 I, b is an enlarged a, showing a late diplonema chromosome (arrow) and a sub-pairing chromosome (short arrow), 11, 12. Showing some lagging chromosomes, chromosome bridges and chromosome fragments at anaphase 1 and anaphase 2; 13. An abortive tetrad; 14~16. Abortive course of microspore in parent plant: 14, 15. Nuclear substance dispersed toward the edge of the cell, 16. Empty area appeared in the middle of a microspore

图版 II
Plate II

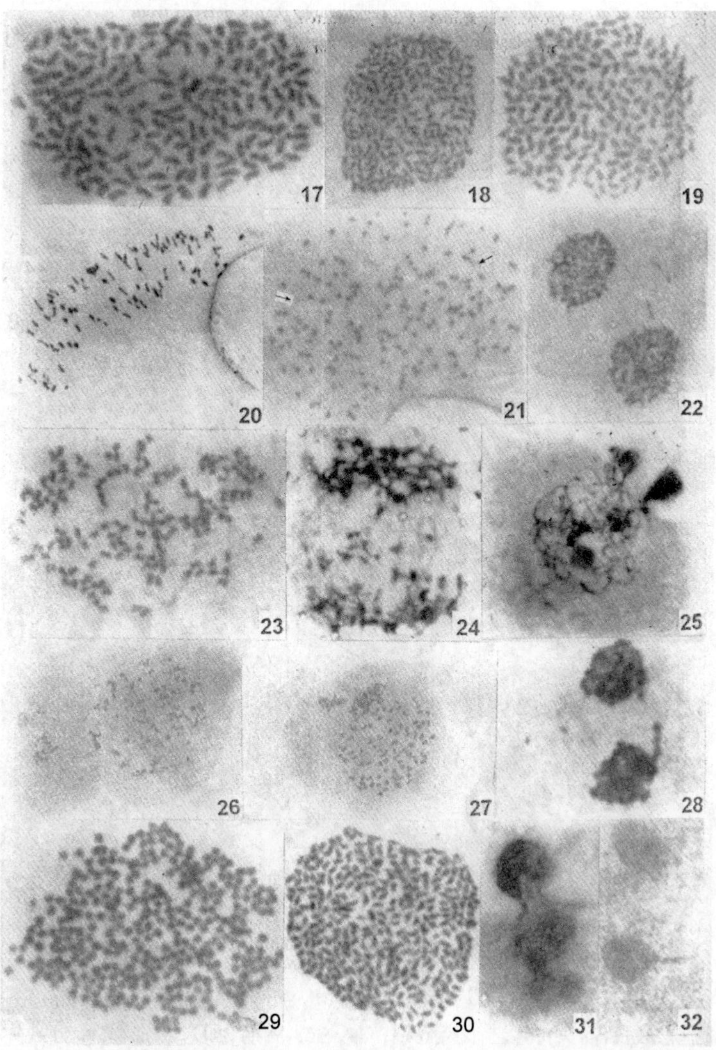

17. P_1-67 $2n$=170； 18. P_1-71 $2n$=$6x$=174； 19. P_1-19 $2n$=$6x$=174； 20~22. P_1-19 PMC 的减数分裂； 20. M_1 $2n$=87II；21. 后期$_1$，示染色体末瑞呈丝状(箭头)；22. 末期$_1$，示落后染色体；23. P_1-16 $2n$=165；24. P_1-16 有丝分裂后期落后染色体； 25~28. P_1-16 PMC 的减数分裂； 25. PMC 间染色质穿壁； 26. PMC 内染色体数目不等；27. 中期$_1$部分染色体聚集在一起；28. 后期$_1$的染色体异常行为；29. P_2-15 $2n$=315；30. P_2-61 $2n$=304； 31~35. 采用酶解压片法观察 P_2-15 的造孢细胞和 PMC； 31. 造孢细胞的核穿壁； 32. 造孢细胞的核物质排出

17, P_1-67 $2n$=170; 18. P_1-71 $2n$=$6x$=174; 19. P_1-19 $2n$=$6x$=174; 20~22. Meiotic behaviour in PMC of P_1-19, 20. Metaphase 1, $2n$=87II, 21. Anaphase 1, 22. Telopohase, showing lagging chromosome; 23. P_1-16 $2n$=165; 24. Mitosis anaphase of P_1-16, showing lagging chromosome; 25~28. Meiotic behaviour in PMC of P_1-16: 25. Chromatin migrated between PMCs, 26. Different chromosome numbers in PMCs, 27. Some chromosomes aggregate together at metaphase 1, 28. Abnormal behaviour of chromosome at anaphase 1; 29. P_2-15, $2n$ = 315; 30. P_2-61 $2n$ = 304; 31~35. Sporogenous cell and PMC of P_2-15 using enzyme squash technique, 31. Nuclear substance migrated in sporogenous cells, 32. Nuclear substance excluding from sporogenous cell

图版 III

Plate III

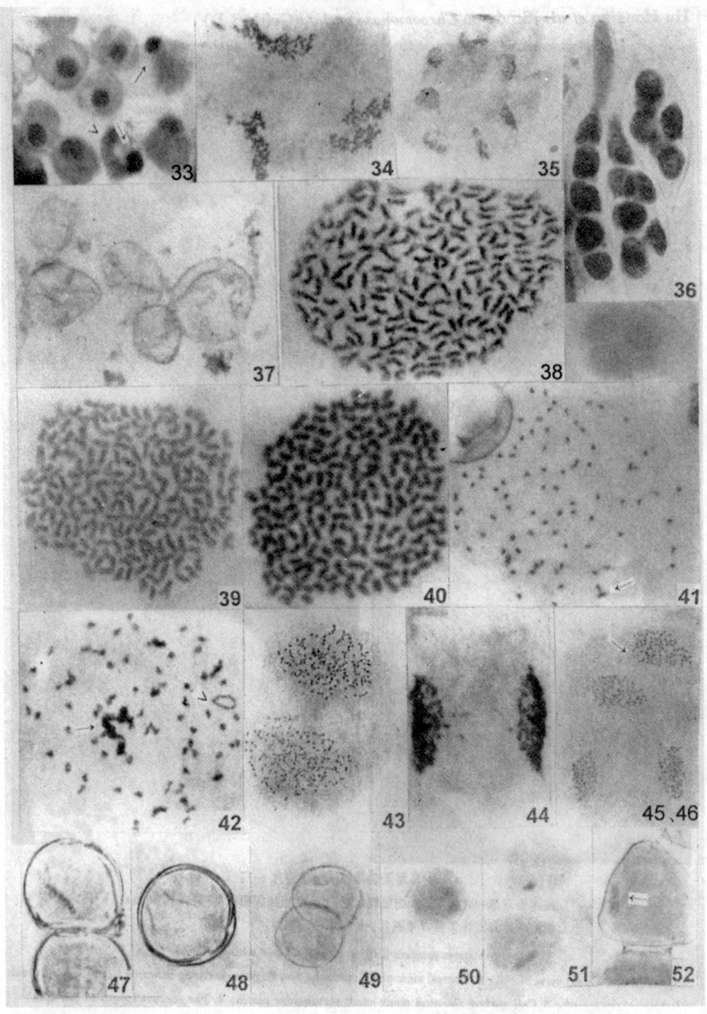

33. 早期PMC细胞核脱落(箭头)和夭折(小箭头)；34，35. 后期$_1$和末期$_2$的多个分裂中心；36. P_2-15的多分体；37. P_2-15空花粉；38. S-24 $2n=6x=174$；39. 1个美味猕猴桃雄株 $2n=6x=174$；40. S-29 $2n=6x=174$；41. S-54 $2n=87II$，示1个次级配对；42. S-41，中期$_1$，示多个染色体粘连在一起(箭头)和多价体(小箭头)；43~46. S-12 PMC的减数分裂：43. 后期$_1$，44. 后期$_1$落后染色体，45. 后期$_2$落后染色体、桥和断片，46. 四分体；47~52. S-12花粉发育的细胞学变化：47，48. 花粉第1次有丝分裂中期、后期，49. 二核早期，50. 二核中期，51. 二核晚期，52. 示生殖细胞沿核的短轴分裂(箭头)

33. Nucleus separated (arrow) and aborted (short arrow) from early PMCs; 34,35. Multt-diviston centre at anaphase 1 and telophase 2; 36. Showing polyad m P_2-15; 37. Empty pollens in P_2-15;38. S-24 $2n=6x=174$; 39. A staminate plant, $2n=6x=174$; 40. S-29 $2n=6x=174$; 41. S-54, $2n=87II$, showing sub-pairing chromosomes (arrow); 42. S-41, Metaphase 1, showing adhesive chromosomes (arrow) and polyvalent ring (short arrow); 43~45. Meiotic behaviour in PMC of S-12: 43. Lagging chromosome at anaphase 1, 44. Lagging chromosome at telophase 1, 45. Lagging chromosome, chromosome bridge and fragment at anaphase 2 (arrow); 46. Tetrad; 47~52. Showing different stages in pollen development of S-12; 47, 48. Metaphase and anaphase at lst mitosis of pollen, 49. Early binucleate phase, 50. Mid binucleate phase, 51. Late binucleate phase, 52. Generative cell divided along short axis of nucleus (arrow)

本文原载：武汉植物学研究. 1999. 17(1): 5-9

美味猕猴桃原生质体再生植株细胞遗传学研究

III. 母株减数分裂前期I染色体配对的光镜观察*

何子灿[1] 蔡起贵[2] 钱迎倩[2] 黄宏文[1] 侯云甫[1]

(1 中国科学院武汉植物研究所；2 中国科学院植物研究所)

摘　要　首次报道在光镜下观察美味猕猴桃(品种：No. 26 原生质体植株的母株)花粉母细胞(PMC)染色体在减数分裂前期的配对，发现其配对和凝缩有明显不同步性。不同细胞间染色体配对形式变化较大，一般以二价联会为主，其次由其他多种配对方式(包括有复合配对、重复配对、着丝点或端粒处联合和多价联会)形成多价体，还有少数未配对或发生内配对(偶见)的单价体和几条二价体之间的次级配对。粗线期观察到少数染色体有缺失(或重复)、倒位、易位和疏松配对等结构性改变。表明该植株是一个复杂的区段异源六位体，少数染色体在结构上累积有变异。还认为该植株是研究减数分裂染色体配对和联会机制的好材料。

关键词　美味猕猴桃；减数分裂；染色体配对

多倍体物种的细胞学行为和遗传规律通常与二倍体不同[1, 2]，然而某些异源多倍体由于各个染色体组之间是非同源的。减数分裂染色体配对如同二倍体物种只形成二价体，被称为二倍化的异源多倍体，如棉花、普通小麦[3]。为了深入了解小麦二倍化的遗传行为，莫兵曾通过对其联会复合体的观察，详细地研究了小麦染色体在减数分裂前期的配对全过程[4]。现有资料认为美味猕猴桃也是一种二倍化的异源六倍体[5, 6]。它的祖先情况不详，染色体多且小，$2n=6x=174$，用一般的制片方法很难观察前期染色体的配对情况，它的二倍化细胞学证据仅见于减数分裂中期 1(M_1)构型。如 MeNeiLage 曾报道除偶见 1~2 个四价体外，均为二价体[6]。

笔者在对原生质体再生植株及其母株的小孢子发育过程的研究中曾报道该母株花粉母细胞第一次减数分裂终变期的染色体凝缩不同步，配对紊乱，构型复杂；对后期 1(A_1)和后期 2(A_2)染色体异常行为观察结果与前人报道也有不同[7]，认为有进一步深入探讨的必要，无论是对该植株体细胞无性系变异规律的研究[8, 9]，还是对促进该物种细胞遗传学的研究都具有重要意义。本研究采用经改进的去壁低渗制片法，首次对其染色体在减数分裂前期配对行为的详细表现进行了直接观察，对染色体组的同源和异源关系提出了新的意见，还对少数染色体的结构变异提供了更精确的细胞学证据。

* 本研究为国家自然科学基金资助项目(批准号：39570508)。

1　材料和方法

材料同前[7]，为原生质体植株的母株(*A. deliciosa* 品种：No. 26)，由中国科学院植物研究所安和祥教授提供。

当 PMC 处于减数分裂前期时取花药，固定于 Famer 氏溶液 24h 后，转入 70%乙醇溶液，置于 6℃冰箱待检。采用改进的去壁低渗法制片，Giemsa 染色，Olympus-BH 光镜观察、摄影。

2　结果

2.1　偶线期染色体配对

呈单一细线状的同源染色体在偶线期开始配对，配对部分染色体发生收缩，染色较深，因染色体太多，造成细线状染色体因密集而不易区分，仅能见部分二价体配对是从一端开始，另一端呈两股细线；有的配对则在染色体全长若干位点同时进行(图版 I：1)；还存在多个染色体之间交替交叉的复合配对。在已配对部分，可辨明为两两相配，遵循配对同源性原则；未能配对的染色体仍呈单一未收缩细线，色浅，表现出染色体凝缩和配对不同步。

2.2　粗线期染色体的配对

此期已联会染色体明显变粗变短，染色加深；但还有染色体继续凝缩和配对不同步。在早粗线期，配对染色体仍较长，与还未配对的细线状染色体相互缠绕，偏于细胞核一侧，呈花束状(图版 I：2)；中粗线期凝缩程度较低的染色体(多为多价体)继续与少数未凝缩的单价体缠绕，集中于染色体图像中间，不易分辨，一些凝缩程度高的二价体多位于图像边沿，易分辨(图版 I：3)，还可见一些单价体向二价体靠拢进行配对。到晚粗线期在 n=87 个成员中，能分辨出约 80 多个成员完成配对(图版 I：4)。

粗线期染色体大多紧密联会，除棒状二价联会外，还能观察到“×”形六价联会，“+”形四价联会，“Y”形三价联会；这些多价体在终变期和 M_1 期可呈环状或链状，如图版 I：6 所示，有环状六价体、环状三价体和链状四价体，此外还有异形二价体之间的次级配对。需指出三价体在该植株 PMC 中经常出现，曾经在 1 个 PMC 中观察到 5 个三价体(图版 I：7)。

此期最值一提的是在少数已联会的二价体上观察到以下几种自发的染色体结构畸变。①缺失或重复(以后讨论)：有中间缺失(图版 II：9，17a)和末端缺失(图版 II：8)。②倒位和易位：有中间倒位、末端倒位(图版 I：5)、易位二价体与易位四价体。易位二价体在易位区不能联会(图版 II：10)，易位四价体在双线期呈∞形，易于辨认(图版 II：11)。③疏松配对：疏松配对区可位于染色体一整条臂上(图版 II：10 细箭头)，也可在臂内部分区域(图版 II：9 细箭头)。后一个图像还显示了该二价体在疏松配对部位染色粒的分布有不对称性，反映了一定的染色体结构变异。

同时，该期 PMC 间配对形式虽无一固定模式，但每一个细胞图像都有多种的配对方式，说明染色体联会是同源染色体之间的随机行为，多倍化增加了它的复杂性。

2.3 双线期配对观察

双细期染色体凝缩更短，已配对染色体开始分离，但于交换处交叉，是研究多价体复杂配对的最佳时期。能观察到由 1 至几条二价体再各与 1 条单价体靠近，重复配对形成三价体，新配上的单价体明显比二价体的长(图版 II：12)。由端粒或着丝粒联合形成的四价体，可见于非核仁染色体(图版 I：5)和核仁染色体(图版 II：13)。在后一个图像中还能初步判断出 2 个同源六价体，1 个为“×”型，另 1 个是由 1 个核仁四价体与 1 个核仁二价体组成的 6 个核仁的染色体。此期有时还见到未联会或环状的单价体，后者显然来源于一等臂染色体的内配对(图版 II：14)。图版 II：15, 16 则显示了多个同源或部分同源染色体在不同同源点上相交、相连地牵连成 1 个复合体情况多处发生。1 个同源 5 价体的配对(图版 II：18)更进一步表现出它们的联会，遵循同源性原则和每 1 个交叉点具有两两相配的特征。晚双线期(图版 II：17)可见到“×”形 6 价体(图版 II：17b)和“+”形四价体，而其他多价体的配对形式已不易辨认。该图像中可见 1 个二价体上大的自身折叠(图版 II：17a)，可能源于缺失、重复或外源片断的插入。总之此期图像因配对情况复杂，凝缩并不同步，对相互重叠和缠绕的染色体配对情况仍不易判断。

3 讨论

本研究结果显示美味猕猴桃品种：No.26 的 PMC 染色体配对始于偶线期，染色体的配对和凝缩不同步。除发生二价联会外，还有其他多种配对形式(如重复、复合、端粒或着丝粒联合、多价联会等)形成多价体(有六价体、五价体、四价体、三价体)。这些多价体的形成源于同源染色体配对还是同祖染色体配对呢？莫兵[4]通过对小麦联会复合体的发育过程观察，认为小麦(二倍化异源六位体物种)偶线期的确有同祖染色体配对形成的多价体，但在粗线期被消除，只见到二价体；而且在偶线期，同祖多价体的出现频率也远低于同源配对形成的二价体。这些情况显然与我们在本实验观察到的结果有所不同。后者在双线期时染色体复合配对普遍存在，其他形成多价体的配对形式也常见，直到终变期和 M_1 仍有各种类型多价体存在。再结合所观察到的同源六价体和同源五价体情况，有理由认为美味猕猴桃品种：No.26 的基本染色体组 29 个染色体成员中，至少有 2 个或更多一点的成员具有同源群，每个同源群的 6 个染色体同源，且可形成多种形式的同源多价体。因为从理论上推测，6 个同源染色体在配对过程中，由于它们所处的位置不同和任何同源区段只能有 2 条染色体的联会等原因，有可能出现：1VI 或 3II，2III 或 1IV+1II，1III+1II+1I 或 1V+1I……等情况。综上所述，认为该植物并非像前人所描述的那种二倍化异源六倍体。当然我们也认为可能有同祖染色体存在，如异形二价体之间的次级联会是因其之间有“残余吸引”[10]，同时在第 1 次减数分裂前期时的染色体复合配对多处发生，均反映了部分同质染色体的同源性[8]，也可能就是有同祖性，需进一步确证。

然而一直持续到终变期的染色体配对和凝缩不同步，配对紊乱，以二价联会为主，有未能配对的单价体等现象，可能源于种间染色体结构差异所致。为此，笔者又认为美味猕猴桃还具有种间杂种的细胞学特征。Crow hurst[11]采用 RFL P 技术后认为至少有 2 个物种与它的形成有关。杂交和异源多倍体的形成是物种形成的一个重要途径[12]，异源多倍体物种的细胞学行为取决于它的几个原始物种之间的系统和分类关系。美味猕猴桃原始祖先虽不知，但它的细胞学行为显然暗示其原始祖先们的染色体组之间，具有一定的同源性程度。根据 Stebbins[13]对多倍体类型的划分，它应属于复杂的区段异源多倍体；该染色体组中只有某些成员与其他染色体组成员同源，而其他成员不同源或部分同源(同祖)。并推测该物种在形成过程中，可能有染色体结构的畸变，其中稳定下来的变异具有重要的进化意义。对它在 M_1 时所反映的多价体不及前期多的现象，笔者认为是由于其染色体太小，配对时交叉少，再随着交叉端化的分离进程，这些多价体被提早消除，或是由于“联会消失”的缘故；当然还有一部分是同祖染色体的配对消失造成。因而，以 M_1 的构型研究这种小染色体的配对情况有一定的局限性和不确切性。

环状三价体和环状单价体的存在表明有完全的等臂染色体，其来源有深究价值。

本研究还表明，双线期能很好进行配对情况的观察，粗线期能研究染色体上累积的结构性变异。有些变异具有遗传上的不稳定性，也为 A_1 和 A_2 时期出现高频率的染色体异常行为所证实[7]。

被试材料的复杂和丰富的配对形式是研究减数分裂染色体配对和联会机制的好材料。但染色体的配对、联会和分离是一个多步骤的复杂过程，受着复杂的多种因素影响。本研究虽观察到一些现象，但还需采用更多的方法来促进该项研究向更深层次发展。

参考文献

[1] 李竞雄, 宋同明. 植物细胞遗传学. 北京: 科学出版社, 1993. 188

[2] 桂建芳, 梁绍昌, 蒋一珪等. 人工三倍体水晶彩鲫雌性型间性体减数分裂的染色体行为. 中国科学(B 辑), 1991(4): 388~396

[3] 沈大棱. 遗传学基础. 北京: 化学工业出版社, 1988. 145~146

[4] 莫兵, 施立明. 普通小麦联会复合体发育过程的电镜观察. 遗传学报, 1990, 17 (5): 369~372

[5] FraserL G, Harver C F, Kaut J. Plcidy manipulations of kiwifruit in tissue culture. *Acta Hor*, 1992, **297**: 104~114

[6] McNeilage M A, Considine J A. Chromosome studies in some *A ctinidia* taxa and implications for breeding *New Z J Bot*, 1989, **27**: 71~81

[7] 何子灿, 蔡起贵, 钱迎倩等. 美味猕猴桃原生质体再生植株细胞遗传学研究 II 性别性状变异和小孢子发生及其发育. 武汉植物学研究, 1997, **15**(3): 199~209

[8] 蔡起贵, 钱迎倩, 柯善强等. 美味猕猴桃原生质体再生植株无性系变异的研究.植物学报, 1992, **34**(11): 822~828

[9] 何子灿, 蔡起贵, 钱迎倩等. 美味猕猴桃原生质体再生植株细胞遗传学研究 I 体细胞染色体数目的变化. 武汉植物学研究, 1995, **13**(2): 97~101

[10] 蓝译蘧, 梁学礼主编. 遗传学实验原理和方法. 成都: 四川大学出版社, 1990. 183~184

[11] Crowhruse R N, Whittaker D, Gardner R C. The genetic origin of kiwifruit. *Acta Hor*, 1992, **297**: 61

[12] 洪德元. 植物细胞分类学. 北京: 科学出版社, 1990

[13] Stebbins G L. 植物的变异与进化. 复旦大学遗传学研究所译. 上海: 科学出版社, 1963. 254~271

图版 I
Plate I

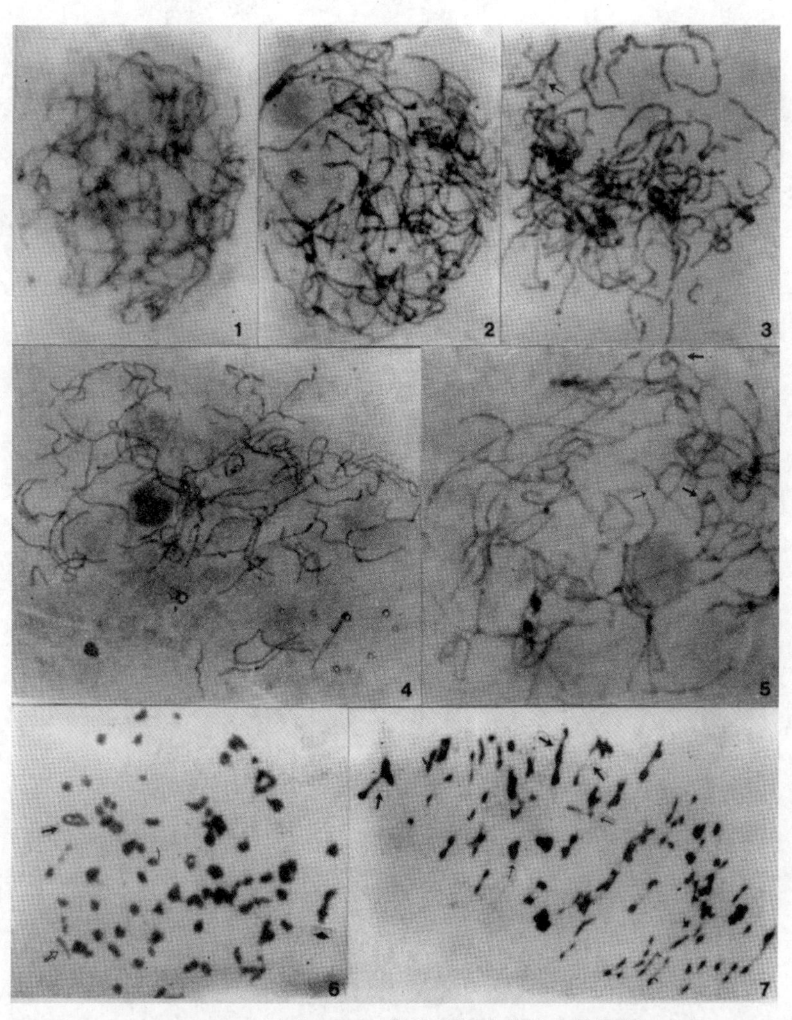

A. deliciosa 品种: No.26 花粉母细胞的染色体图像

1. 偶线期示同源染色体的配对(箭头); 2.早粗线期, 呈花束状; 3.中粗线期示单价体(箭头); 4. 晚粗线期图像; 5. 粗线期局部图, 示 1 个三价联会(细箭头), 2 个二价体的端粒联合(空心箭头)和末端倒位(粗箭头); 6. 中期 1, 示 1 个环状六价体(粗箭头)、1 个环状 3 价体(细箭头)、1 个链状四价体(空心箭头)和 1 个次级联会(短箭头); 7. 晚 M_1 期, 示异形三价体(粗箭头)、三价体(细箭头)

The chromosome figures of PMCs in *Actinidia deliciosa* No. 26.

1. Pairing (arrow) of homologous chromosomes in zygotene; 2. Bouquet-like chromosomes in early pachytene; 3. Mid pachytene, showing univalent(arrow); 4. A figure of late pachytene; 5. A partial figure of pachytene, showing a trivalent synapsis(thin arrow), the association area of the teloemers and centromeres of two bivalents(hollow arrow) and terminal inversions(thick arrow); 6. Metaphase I, showing a loop-like hexavalnent(thick arrow), another loop-like trivalen I(thin arrow), a chain-like quadrivalent (hollow arrow), and a secondary pairing(short arrow); 7. A figure of late M_1, showing trivalents (thin arrow), heteromorphic trivalents(thick arrow)

图版 II
Plate II

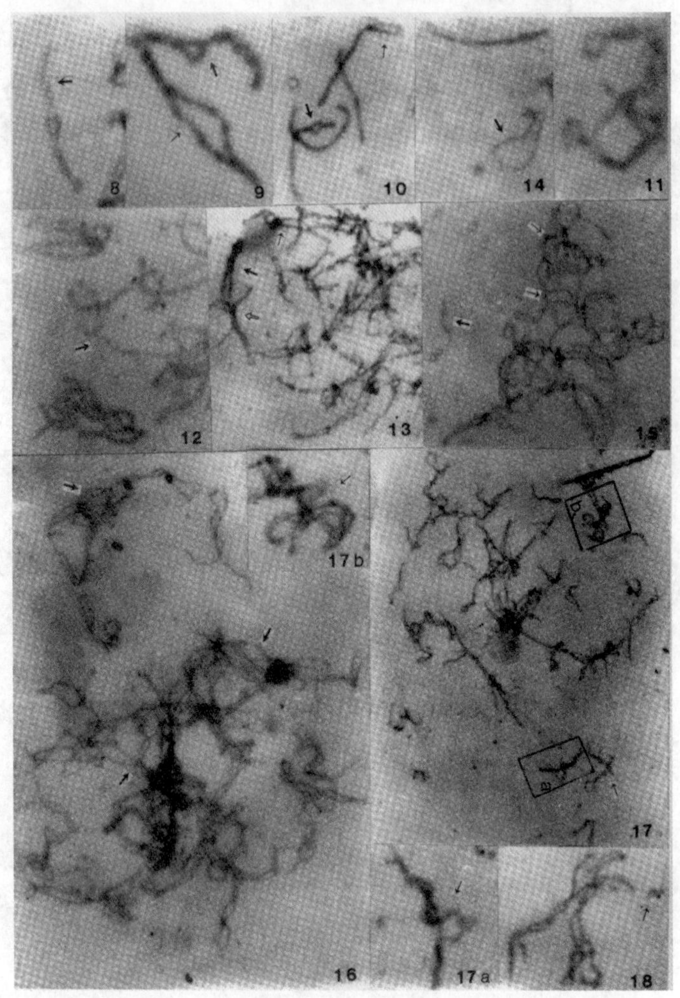

8~11. *A. deliciosa* 品种: No.26 染色体结构的畸变; 12, 13, 15~18. 双线期图像. 8. 1 个末端缺失; 9.已配对区的缺失环(粗箭头)和疏松配对(细箭头); 10. 1 个易位二价体(粗箭头)、1 个疏松配对(细箭头); 11. 1 个易位四价体; 12. 示重复配对(箭头); 13. 示 1 个核仁四价体(细箭头)、1 个核仁二价体(空心箭头)和 1 个六价联会(粗箭头); 14. 1 个环状单价体; 15. 示未配对的单价体(粗箭头)和复合配对(细箭头); 16. 双线期局部图像, 示复合配对(箭头); 17. 晚双线期, 示四价体(细箭头); 17a. 为 17 图像中 a 的放大, 示缺失环(箭头); 17b. 为 17 图像中 b 的放大, 示六价体(箭头); 18. 1 个同源 5 价体和断片(箭头)

8~11. The aberration of chromosoms in *A. deliciosa* No.26, and 12, 13, 15~18. some figures of diplotene. 8. A terminal deficiency; 9. A deficiency loop in paired region(think arrow), and a loosepairing(thin arrow); 10. A translocation bivalent (thick arrow), and a loose pairing bivalent(thin arrow); 11. A translocation quadrivalent; 12. Showing a repeated pairing(arrow); 13. Showing a nucleolar quadrivalent (thick arrow), a nucleolar bivalent(thin arrow), and a hexavalent synapsis(hollow arrow); 14. A loop-like univalent; 15. Showing the unpaired univalent I(thick arrow), and complex pairing (thin arrow); 16. A partial figure of diplotene, showing lomplex pairings(arrow); 17. A figure of late diplotene, showing a quadrivalent (arrow); 17a. A enlarged figure of a in Fig. 17, showing a deficiency loop(arrow); 17b. A enlarged figure of b in Fig.17, showing a hexavalent(arrow); 18. An autopentavalent and fragments (arrow)

本文原载：西北植物学报. 1996. 16(2): 137-141

软枣猕猴桃试管苗叶片和茎段的愈伤组织诱导及植株再生

张远记　钱迎倩

(中国科学院植物研究所)

摘　要　从软枣猕猴桃 [*Actinidia argula* (Sieb. et Zucc.) Planch. ex Miq.]试管苗茎段和叶片诱导出愈伤组织并得到再生植株。茎段外植体容易愈伤化，但其愈伤组织难以分化，叶片外植体不易愈伤化，但其愈伤组织容易分化。MS 培养基分别附加 BAP (0.5，1.0 和 2.0m/L)、Kin (0.5, 1.0 和 2.0mg/L)、TDZ (0.0001, 0.01 和 1.0mg/L)或 CPPU (0.00025、0.025 和 2.5mg/L，配合 IAA 0.lmg/L)都不能诱导芽的分化，而 MS 附加玉米素 (0.5，1.0，2.0 和 3.0mg/L)能有效地诱导芽分化，其中以 2.0mg/L 玉米素效果最好。

关键词　猕猴桃；软枣猕猴桃；组织培养；植株再生

猕猴桃栽培始于本世纪初。1904 年新西兰科学家从美味猕猴桃一批实生后代中，选育出著名品种“Hayward”。此后猕猴桃栽培便在新西兰发展起来。虽然现在猕猴桃已成为许多国家的栽培果树，但主栽品种仍是 Hayward。单一的品种构成难以适应不同国家栽培地区的气候、地理、栽培条件和消费者的需求。因此，新品种的培育已受到各国育种工作者的重视。在猕猴桃属 60 余种中，许多种具有优良性状，如高维生素 C 含量，果面无毛及抗性强等。这些野生种是培育新品种的重要资源。利用种间杂交结合胚拯救技术在引进外源种质方面已取得相当进展[10]。其他生物技术如快速繁殖、超低温种质保存、体细胞无性系变异、体细胞杂交和遗传转化等在种质资源保存、开发利用等方面具有很大潜力。这些技术都要求建立组织培养系统。目前，组织培养已成功的种包括中华猕猴桃、美味猕猴桃、毛花猕猴桃、软枣猕猴桃、狗枣猕猴桃和葛枣猕猴桃[2,3,7,9]。

软枣猕猴桃具有许多优良性状，如果面无毛、抗寒能力极强等，即可作为培育新品种的种质资源，也可直接进行栽培，还可用作生产上的抗寒砧木。因此，软枣猕猴桃的开发利用受到了一些研究者的重视。赵淑兰等(1994)[4]选育成功软枣猕猴桃新品种“魁绿”，Mu 等(1992)[10]利用胚拯救技术得到软枣猕猴桃和美味猕猴桃种间杂种，其果实较大，果皮绿而无毛。王际轩等(1982)[1]以软枣猕猴桃成熟胚和生长枝顶芽为外植体，对组织培养繁殖作了研究。以软枣猕猴桃组织或器官为外植体，通过诱导愈伤组织和芽分化而再生植株的研究目前报道很少。洪树荣(1981)[3]以软枣猕猴桃叶片和茎段为材料，对愈伤组织诱导和植株再生作了研究，发现软枣猕猴桃愈伤组织诱导率不高(茎段外植体的为 50%)。愈伤组织分化率低(仅 11.5%)。芽分化系数也低(每块愈伤组织一般仅分化一个苗)。

为了解决组织培养中存在的这些问题，我们对软枣猕猴桃不同外植体、不同生长调节剂对愈伤组织诱导和芽分化的影响作了研究，得到了较理想的结果。

1　材料和方法

材料由中国科学院植物研究所植物园安和祥先生提供。将软枣猕猴桃成年雌株当年生枝取回后，用自来水冲洗干净，然后用 0.1% $HgCl_2$ 消毒 10min，再用无菌水冲洗 4~5 次。在无菌条件下将枝条切成带芽茎段，插于培养基中。所用培养基为 MS 附加 1.0mg/L 玉米素、3.0%蔗糖和 0.6%琼脂。腋芽萌发后每 4 周继代一次。培养得到的试管苗叶片和茎段(不带腋芽)分别切成 1cm × 1cm 和 1.0cm 大小，接种于附加 3.0%蔗糖、0.6%琼脂和不同生长调节剂的 MS 培养基上，pH 调至 5.6~5.8。每瓶接种 10 块(段)，每处理接种 4 瓶，重复二次。在诱导培养基上培养一月后转入分化培养基上诱导分化。分化培养基除注明外，均为 MS 附加蔗糖 3%、琼脂 0.6%和玉米素 2.0mg/L。培养条件均为 25℃、1250lx 光照 10h/22℃、14h 黑暗。

分化出的苗在生长到 1cm 以上高度时，切下插入附加 IAA 1.0mg/L 的 MS 培养基上诱导生根。

2　结果与讨论

2.1　茎段和叶片外植体的愈伤组织产生和芽分化

2.1.1　外植体

茎段较叶片容易产生愈伤组织。如在培养基 2(表 1)上，茎段培养约二周即完全愈伤化，而叶片则需培养约四周时间才能完全愈伤化。在培养基 3 上，茎段外植体在培养 10d 时已完全愈伤化，叶片则要求 20d 时间。表 1 所列三种培养基上二种外植体在培养 30d 时愈伤组织诱导率均达到 100%。洪树荣(1981)以田间生长的茎段和叶片为材料，在与本试验培养 3 相同的培养基上诱导愈伤组织，结果叶片的诱导率为 93.3%，而茎段的诱导率仅为 50%，与本试验的结果是不一致的，原因可能是所用材料不同所致，本试验采用的是试管培养材料。二种外植体所产生的愈伤组织在分化能力方面有显著差别。叶片愈伤组织容易分化，表现在分化起始时间早，每块愈伤组织分化芽多。分化的苗生长快。而茎段愈伤组织则与此相反。如在培养基 3(表 1)上得到的叶片愈伤组织，在分化培养基上培养约三周开始分化芽，但在同一培养基上诱导的茎段愈伤组织在分化培养基上培养三代(90d)后，愈伤组织仍为白色，没有芽的分化。在毛花猕猴桃组织培养中也发现叶片愈伤组织较茎段愈伤组织容易分化的现象[2]。

2.1.2　诱导培养基中不同生长调节剂的效果

诱导培养基中添加 1mg/L 玉米素则外植体难以完全愈伤化，得到的愈伤组织质地紧密，色绿，无褐化现象。这些愈伤组织容易分化芽，在愈伤组织诱导后不继代即能分化出芽(图 1. A)。外植体在培养基 2 和 3(表 1)上培养一代都能完全愈伤化，愈伤组织生长快，较松软，并有不同程度的褐化现象。这些愈伤组织在转入分化培养基之前不能分化，而且茎段愈伤组织转入分化培养基也很难分化。

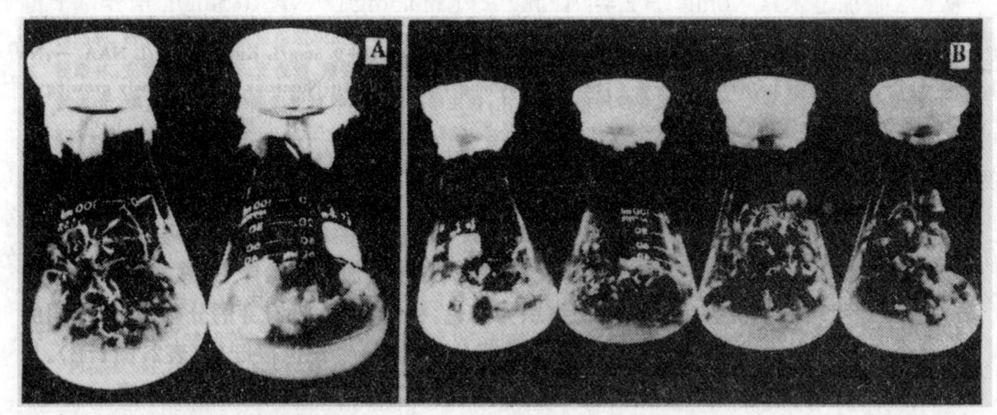

图 1　A. 不同外植体在 MS 附加 1.0mg/L 玉米素培养基上不经继代即分化出芽。左为叶片外植体，分化芽多；右为茎段外植体，分化的芽少。B. 叶片外植体在诱导培养基 3 上培养 30d，然后转入不同的分化培养基上(基本培养基为 MS)培养 60d。从左向右分别为：玉米素 0.5mg/L；1.0mg/L；2.0mg/L 和玉米素 1.0mg/L+Kin0.5mg/L

*Explants were cultured on the callus induction medium for 30 days and then transferred to the bud differentiation medium on which the calli were cultured for 2 passages (60 days). MS medium supplemented with 3% sucrose and 0.6% agar was used as basal medium. Induction medium No.1.2 or 3 was basal medium added with 1.0mg/L zeatin; 0.5mg/L zeatin+0.5mg/L 2,4-D; or 1.0mg/L zeatin+1.0mg/L 2,4-D+0.5mg/L NAA. –: No browning; ++: Sightly browning; ++++: Serious browning; f: Few buds; n: Numerous buds. s: Slowly growing; f: Fast growing.

表 1　不同生长调节剂对茎段和叶片外植体愈伤组织产生及芽分化的影响*

Table 1　Effects of growth regulators on callus production from stems and leaves and on bud differentiation

诱导培养基 Induction medium	外植体 Explant	愈伤组织 Callus			芽分化 Bud differentiation	
		色泽 Color	生长速度 Growth rate	褐化程度 Browning	分化率(%) Frequencies	苗生长 Shoot growth
1	茎段 Stem	绿 Green	慢 slow	–	27.5	芽少，生长慢 f. s
1	叶片 Leaf	绿 Green	慢 slow	–	95.0	芽多，生长快 n. f
2	茎段 Stem	浅绿 Greenish	快 fast	++	0.0	
2	叶片 Leaf	浅绿 Greenish	快 fast	++	45.0	芽多，生长快 n. f
3	茎段 Stem	白 White	快 fast	++++	0.0	
3	叶片 Leaf	白 White	快 fast	++--	87.5	芽多，生长快 n. f

* 外植体在不同诱导培养基上培养 30d 后转入同一分化培养基上继代二次(60d)。基本培养基为 MS 附加 3%蔗糖和 0.6%琼脂。诱导培养基 1、2 和 3 分别添加玉米素 1.0mg/L；玉米素 0.5mg/L+2, 4-D 0.5mg/L；玉米素 1.0mg/L+2, 4-D 1.0mg/L+Kin0.5mg/L+NAA0.5mg/L，分化培养基为 MS 附加玉米素 2.0mg/L。–：无褐化；++：褐化轻；++++：褐化重。

* Explants were cultured on the callus induction medium for 30 days and then transfered to the bud differentiation medium on which the calli were cultured for 2 passages (60days). MS medium supplemented with 3% sucrose and 0.6% agar was used as basal medium. Induction medium No.1.2 or 3 was basal roedium added with 1.0mg/L zeann; 0.5mg/L zeatin +0.5mg/L 2,4-D; or 1.0mg/L zeatin +1.0mg/L 2,4-D+0.5mg/L Kin+0.5mg/L NAA. –: No browning; ++: Slightly browning; ++++: Serious browning. r: Few buds; n: Numeous buds. s: Slowly growing; f: Fast growing.

2.2　芽分化中生长调节剂的作用

从MS附加玉米素1.0mg/L+2,4-D1.0mg/L+Kin0.5mg/L+NAA0.5mg/L培养基上得到的叶片愈伤组织分别转入MS附加下列激素的培养基上诱导分化：玉米素、BAP或Kin，均使用三个浓度：0.5,1.0和2.0mg/L。在添加不同浓度BAP或Kin的分化培养基上继代培养二次(60d)时，愈伤组织为白色，褐化严重，没有芽的分化。与此不同的是，在含三种浓度的玉米素培养基上有大量芽分化，苗的生长也很旺盛(表2；图1，B)。从表2看出，芽分化随玉米素浓度增加而增加，玉米素2.0mg/L对分化最好，玉米素1.0mg/L+Kin0.5mg/L也有良好效果。本试验表明，玉米素对软枣猕猴桃愈伤组织的芽分化效果最好，这与其他人在中华猕猴桃和美味猕猴桃上的试验结果是一致的[5,6,8]。

表2　软枣猕猴桃叶愈伤组织在含玉米素的培养基上的芽分化(培养60d)

Table 2　Bud differentiation of leef callus of *A. arguta* on zeatin-presented media (at 60 days of culture)

生长调节剂 Growth regulators(mg/L)	芽分化率 Bud Differentiation Frequencies(%)	苗数(≥1cm)/愈伤组织 Shoot number (≥1cm)/Callus
Zeatin 0.5	66.7	0.33
Zeatin 1.0	70.8	0.96
Zeatin 2.0	95.8	1.54
Zeatin 1.0+Kin 0.5	91.7	1.13

注：基本培养基为MS

Note: MS medium was used as basal medium.

在另一次实验中，从MS附加玉米素0.5mg/L和2，4-D 0.5mg/L培养基上诱导的叶片愈伤组织，转移到MS附加玉米素3.0mg/L和MS附加玉米素2.0mg/L+IAA0.3mg/L二种培养基上，结果发现玉米素3.0mg/L抑制芽分化，芽分化率仅为5%；而在有IAA的培养基上，芽分化率为52.5%。同样来源的愈伤组织在MS附加玉米素2.0mg/L培养基上芽分化率为45%(表1)。我们还对TDZ(0.0001，0.01及1.0mg/L)和CPPU(0.00025，0.025及2.5mg/L，均配合IAA0.1mg/L)的效果作了初步研究，发现上述浓度的TDZ和CPPU均未能诱导分化。但Suezawa等(1988)[11]发现TDZ和CPPU对美味猕猴桃悬浮培养物的芽分化效果很好，我们在毛花猕猴桃组织培养中也发现CPPU具有强烈促进分化的作用[2]。

分化的小苗在生根培养基上培养二周左右开始长出新根，继续培养一段时间后形成发达的根系。

参考文献

[1]　王际轩，李淑珍，李博文，任思瀛. 猕猴桃的组织培养繁殖. 辽宁农业科学，1982；(1)：32~34

[2]　张远记，钱迎倩. 毛花猕猴桃愈伤组织诱导与植株再生. 广西科学，1994；1(4)：1~5

[3] 洪树荣，猕猴桃离体茎段和叶愈伤组织的诱导和植株再生. 湖北农业科学，1981；(9)：28~30

[4] 赵淑兰，袁福贵，马月申，赵井才，杨金茹. 软枣猕猴桃新品种—魁绿. 园艺学报，1994；21(2)：207~208

[5] 桂耀林. 猕猴桃离体茎段愈伤组织的诱导和植株再生. 植物学报，1979；21(4)：339~344

[6] 桂耀林，安和祥，蔡达荣，王俊儒. 猕猴桃的组织培养. 科学通报，1979；(4)：188~190

[7] 黄贞光，谭素英. 猕猴桃的组织培养. 见：陈正华主编，木本植物组织培养及其应用. 北京：高等教育出版社，1996: 432~443

[8] Barbieri C, Morini S. Shoot regeneration from cultures of *Actinidia chinensis* (cv. Hayward). Acta. Hort., 1988; 227: 470~472

[9] Kovac J. Micropropagation of *Actinidia kolomikta*. Plant Cell Tissue Organ Cult., 1993; 35 (3): 301~303

[10] Mu X J. Tsai D R, An H X, Wang W L. Embryology and embryo rescue of mterspecific hybrids in *Actinidia*. Acta Hort.,1991; 297: 93~97

[11] Suezawa K. Yamamoto N, Tanaka O. Plantlet formation from cell suspensions of kiwifruit (*Actinidia chinensis* Planch. var. *chinensis*). Sci. Hortic.,1988; 37: 123~128

[12] Sugawara F. Yamamoto N, Tanaka O. Plant regeneration *in vitro* culture of leaf, stem and periole segments of *Actinidia polygama* Miq., Plant Tissue Culture Letters, 1994; 11(1): 14~18

本文原载：植物学报. 1997. 39(2): 102-105

Somaclonal Variation in Chromosome Number and Nuclei Number of Regenerated Plants From Protoplasts of *Actinidia Eriantha*[*]

Zhang Yuan ji[1] Qian Ying qian[1] Cai Qi gui[1] Mu Xi jin[1]
Wei Xiao ping[2] Zhou Yun luo[1]

(1 Institute of Botany, Chinese Academy of Sciences; 2 Beijing Plant Cell Bioengineering Laboratory)

Abstract By counting the chromosome number of root tip cells in 18 regenerated plants derived from protoplasts of *Actinidia eriantha* Benth., the authors found 12 euploid plants and 6 mixoploid plants. Of the 12 euploid plans, 6 were diploid ($2n=2x=58$) and the other 6 were tetraploid ($2n=4x=116$). The chromosome numbers of the mixoploid plants varied from 59 to 203. Multinucleate phenomenon was also observed in the interphase cells of 10 protoplast-derived plants. Cells with binuclei or trinuclei were common and cells having heptanuclei were also seen occassionally. Multinucleate phenomenon did not occur in the control, i.e., the donor plant, where the chromosome number was $2n=2x=58$.

Key words *Actinidia eriantha*, Protoplast- derived plants, Chromosome number, Multinucleate phenomenon

Actinidia eriantha Benth. is a species native to China.The fruit of this species contains high content of vitamin C, i. e., up to 1014mg/100g fresh weight, an amount three times as high as that of the famous cultivar "Hayward"[1]. The fruit size ranks third in the genus *Actinidia*[2]. Numerous papers have been reported on the somaclonal variation generated from cell and tissue cultures since the first paper by Larkin and Scowcroft[3] was published in 1981. Hirsch *et al*[4] pointed out that somaclonal variations, expressed by the use of tissue culture methods, were a useful tool in kiwifruit breeding programme. In genus *Actinidia*, plant regeneration from protoplasts of *A. deliciosa*[5~7], *A. chinensis*[8] and *A. eriantha*[9] has been reported. Plants derived from protoplasts of *A. deliciosa* Clone No. 26 were transplanted into the field. After 8 years, observation on the plants, Cai *et al*[10, 11] found that these regenerated plants exhibited a wide range of variations in leaf and flower morphology, length of internode, vegetative growth habit, and sex differentiation. Cytological study showed that the chromosome number of 29 plants examined varied greatly, with the range from 142 to

* This research was supported by chinese National "The Eighth Five-Year-Plan" Key Project-New Crop Cultivar Breeding Through Cell Bioengineering.

310[12].The root tip cells of 18 protoplast-derived *A. eriantha* plants without detectable morphological difference were cytologically examined in this study. The variation of chromosome number and multinucleate phenomenon are reported in this paper.

1 MATERIALS AND METHODS

The regeneration of plantlets from protoplasts of *Actinidia eriantha* Benth. and induction of roots were described in our previous paper[9]. When roots elongated to about 1cm, root tips were sampled at 5 p. m., 8 to 10 days after rooting and pretreated with saturated parachlorobenzene at room temperature for 90min. They were then fixed in Camoy' s fixative (absolute ethanol: glacial acetic acid = 3 : 1) at 4℃ for 24h. They were stained with 1% aceto-carmin for at least 4h, boiled up for 30s in the flame of an alcohol burner and then squashed gently with acetic acid. Chromosome number at mitotic metaphase and nucleus number at interphase were examined under a microscope. The donor plants for protoplast culture were used as the control.

2 RFSULTS AND DISCUSSION

2.1 Chromosome number of protoplast-derived plants

The chromosome number of the control plants was $2n=2x=58$ (Table 1; PI. I: 1), which was consistent with the observation on *A. eriantha* by Deng and Sun[13]. Among 18 protoplast-derived plants examined, the chromosome number of 6 plants was $2n=58$ (plant No. 1, 7, 10, 13, 16 and 18), that of another 6 plants was $2n=116$ (plant No. 2, 3, 4, 9, 14 and 17) (PI. I: 2), and the rest 6 plants were mixoploid (plant No. 5, 6, 7, 11, 12 and 15) (Table 1). He *et al*[12] reported that 72.3% of the regenerated plants from protoplasts of *A. deliciosa* clone No. 26 were aneuploid, while most of those derived from protoplasts of *A. eriantha* were euploid (66.7%). One possible reason was the different genetic background of the source materials used for protoplast culture. Protoplasts were isolated from cultured calli by Tsai[5] while that from seedling leaves in our experiment[9].Leaf cells were genetically homogeneous in contrast with callus cells. Another possibility was the ploidy difference between *A. deliciosa* clone No. 26 ($2n=6x$)[10,12] and *A. eriantha*. Plants of high ploidy show a tendency of more frequent and wider variation during tissue culture[14].

For the 6 mixoploid plants, the chromosome numbers varied from 59 (PI. I: 3) to 203. It was interesting that 6 different chromosome numbers were found in a single plant (plant No. 6), and the numbers were 88, 90, 96, 100, 110 and 112, respectively. In addition to aneuploid cells, euploid cells could also be seen in mixoploid plants (Table 1; PI. I: 5, 6), e. g. $2n=116$ in plant No. 8 and $2n=174$ in plant No. 15 (PI. I: 4). Another phenomenon also occurred in mixoploid plants was that there were more cells with a certain chromosome number than those with other chromosome number (s) within one plant. For example, among 125 cells in plant No. 11, 59 chromosomes existed in 113 cells whereas 116 in the other 12 cells (Table 1). Twenty-eight root tips were examined from 6 mixoploid plants, the chromosome number in cells of one root tip was consistent in 26 root tips. Exception was found only in one root tip of plant No. 5 and another in plant No. 6, in which the chromosome number was different, i. e., 104 and 112 in the former and 96 and 110 in the latter, respectively.

Table 1 Chromosome number (metaphase) and nuclei number (interphase) of root-tip cells of plants derived from protoplasts of *Actinidia eriantha*

No. of plant	Root-tips observed (cells observed)	Chromosome number (cell number)	Nuclei number
1	4 (33)	58 (33)	1
2	3 (11)	116 (11)	1
3	1 (36)	116 (36)	1, 2, 3, 5
4	3 (11)	116 (11)	1
5	4 (31)	102 (18), 104 (6), 112 (6), 114 (1)	1, 2
6	6 (60)	88 (7), 90 (6), 96 (2), 100 (2) 110 (15), 112 (28)	1, 2, 3, 4, 5, 6, 7
7	2 (4)	58 (4)	1
8	5 (29)	100 (2), 110 (5), 116 (12)	1, 2
9	2 (21)	116 (21)	1
10	3 (22)	58 (22)	1
11	6 (125)	59 (113), 116 (12)	1
12	4 (18)	108 (7), 110 (1), 116 (9),203 (1)	1, 2, 3, 4, 5
13	2 (12)	58 (12)	1
14	3 (14)	116 (14)	1, 2, 3
15	3 (67)	160 (27), 174 (40)	1, 2, 3
16	3 (16)	58 (16)	1, 2, 3
17	2 (11)	116 (11)	1, 2, 3, 4, 5
18	3 (6)	58 (6)	1, 2
Control	3 (31)	58 (31)	1

In addition to protoplast-derived plants of *Actinidia*, the variation of chromosome number in the course of tissue culture of the genus was also reported[15, 16]. The instability of chromosome, number resulted from tissue culture of other woody trees such as apple, poplar and *Hevea* was described by Mu and Liu[17], Lu and Liu[18] and Chen *et al*[19]. In addition, Chen *et al*[20] found that after transplantation of the anther-derived tree of *H. brasiliensis* into the field, the chromo some number increased gradually along with the growth of the tree. Therefore, further study is needed to determine whether the variation described in this paper will remain stable as the growth of the trees continues.

2.2 Multinucleate phenomenon at metaphase cells

All the cells observed in the control were mononucleate. But 10 out of 18 protoplast-derived plants contained some multinucleate cells as well as mononucleate cells (Table 1; PI. I: 7, 8). Binuclei and trinuclei cells were common, and even heptanuclei cells was occassionally found in plant No. 6 (Table 1). In general, the larger the nucleus number the cells had, the lower the frequency the oells would appear. In plant root tips with multinucleate cells, however, mononucleate cells were still the dominant cells over multinucleate ones. For example, of 558 cells from plant No. 14 examined, there were 528 mononucleate cells (94.6%); 24 binucleate cells (4.3%); and 6 trinucleate cells (1.1%). It seemed that there was no correlation among multinucleate phenomenon, chromosome number, and mixoploidy of the plant. As few papers concerning multinucleate phenomenon in somatic cells have been available so far, it is hard to estimate the significance of the phenomenon to genetics and to the improvement of this tree.

At present, all plants are growing vigorously except plant No.5 which was died. Theoretically, the variation of chromosome number and multinucleate phenomenon should be expressed in phenotype. Therefore, further observation is needed. As a reasonable deduction, chromosome number may be unreliable in the identification of hybrids of *Actinidia* via somatic hybridization, owing to the wide variation of chromosome number in protoplast-derived plants, as demonstrated in this paper and papers by Cai *et al*[10, 11] and He *et al*[12].

REFERENCES

[1] Qian Y Q, Yu D P. Advances in *Actinidia* research in China. *Acta Hort*, 1991. **297**: 51~55

[2] Liang C F. Outline of taxonomy on *Actinidia* in China. *Guangxi Plants*, 1980. (l): 30~45

[3] Larkin P J, Scowcroft W R. Somaclonal variation, a good source of variability from cell cultures for plant improvement. *Theor Appl Genet*, 1981. 60: 197~214

[4] Hirsch A M, Fortune D, Xiao X G *et al.* Somaclonal variation related to kiwifruit micropropagation, study of fruitful male plants and use of peroxidase as an early sex marker. *Acta Hort*, 1992. 297: 123~132

[5] Tsai C K. Plant regeneration from leaf callus protoplasts of *Actinidia chinensis* Planch. var. *chinensis*. *Plant Sci*, 1988. 54: 231~235

[6] Mii M, Ohashi H. Plantlet regeneration from protoplasts of kiwifruit, *Actinidia chinensis* Planch. *Acta Hort*, 1988. 230: 167~170

[7] Oliveira M M, Pais M S S. Plant regeneration from protoplasts of long-term callus cultures of *Actinidia deliciosa* var. *deliciosa* cv. Hayward (kiwifruit). *Plant Cell Rep*, 1991. 9: 643~646

[8] Xiao Z A, Shen D X, Lin B N. Plant regeneration from protoplasts of *Actinidia chinensis* Planch. *Acta Bot Sin*, 1992. 34: 736~742

[9] Zhang Y J, Mu X J, Cai Q G *et al.* Plantlet regeneration from protoplasts of seedling leaves of *Actinidia eriantha* Benth. *Acta Bot Sin*, 1995. 37: 48~52

[10] Cai Q G, Qian Y Q, Ke S Q *et al*. Studies on the somaclonal variation of regenerated plants from protoplasts of *Actinidia deliciosa*. *Acta Bot Sin*, 1992. 34: 822~828

[11] Cai Q G, Qian Y Q, Ke S Q *et al*. Regeneration of plants from protoplasts of kiwifruit (*Actinidia deliciosa*). In: Bajaj Y P S ed., Biotechnology in Agriculture and Forestry. Vol. 23. Plant Protoplasts and Genetic Engineering IV. Berlin: Springer-Verlag, 1993. 3~17

[12] He Z C, Cai Q G, Ke S Q *et al*. Cytogenetic studies on regenerated plants derived from protoplasts of *Actinidia deliciosa*. I. Variation of chromosome number of somatic cells. *J Wuhan Hot Res*, 1995. 13: 97~101

[13] Deng X X, Sun H M. Observation on chromosome number of *Actinidia*. *Acta Bort Sin*, 1986. 13 (2): 80

[14] Skirvin R M, McPheeters K D, Norton M. sources and frequency of somaclonal variation. *Hort Sci*, 1994. 29: 1232~1237

[15] Gui Y, Hong S，Ke S *et al*. Fruit and vegetative characteristics of endosperm-derived kiwifruit (*Actinidia chinensis* F) plants. *Euphytica*，1993. 71(1/2): 57~62

[16] Fraser L G, Harvey C F, Kent J. Ploidy manipulations of kiwifruit in tissue culture. *Acta Hort*, 1992. 297: 109~114

[17] Mu S, Liu S. Cytological observations on calluses derived from apple endosperm cultured *in vitro*. In: Proceedings of Symposium on Plant Tissue Culture. Beijing: Science Press，1978. 507~510

[18] Lu Z H, Liu Y X. Studies on anther culture of poplar and the ploidy of pollen-derived tree. In: Chen Z H ed., Tissue Culture of Woody Tree and Its Application. Beijing: Higher Education Publishing House, 1986. 158~178

[19] Chen Z H, Xu X E，Pang R S. Studies on anther culture and pollen-derived plants of *Hevea*. In: Chen Z H ed., Tissue Culture of Woody Tree and Its Application. Beijing: Higher Education Publishing House, 1986. 481~500

[20] Chen Z H, Qian C F, Cen M *et al*. Recent advances in anther culture of *Hevea brasiliensis* Muell-Arg. *Theor Appl Genet*, 1982. 62: 103~107

Plate I

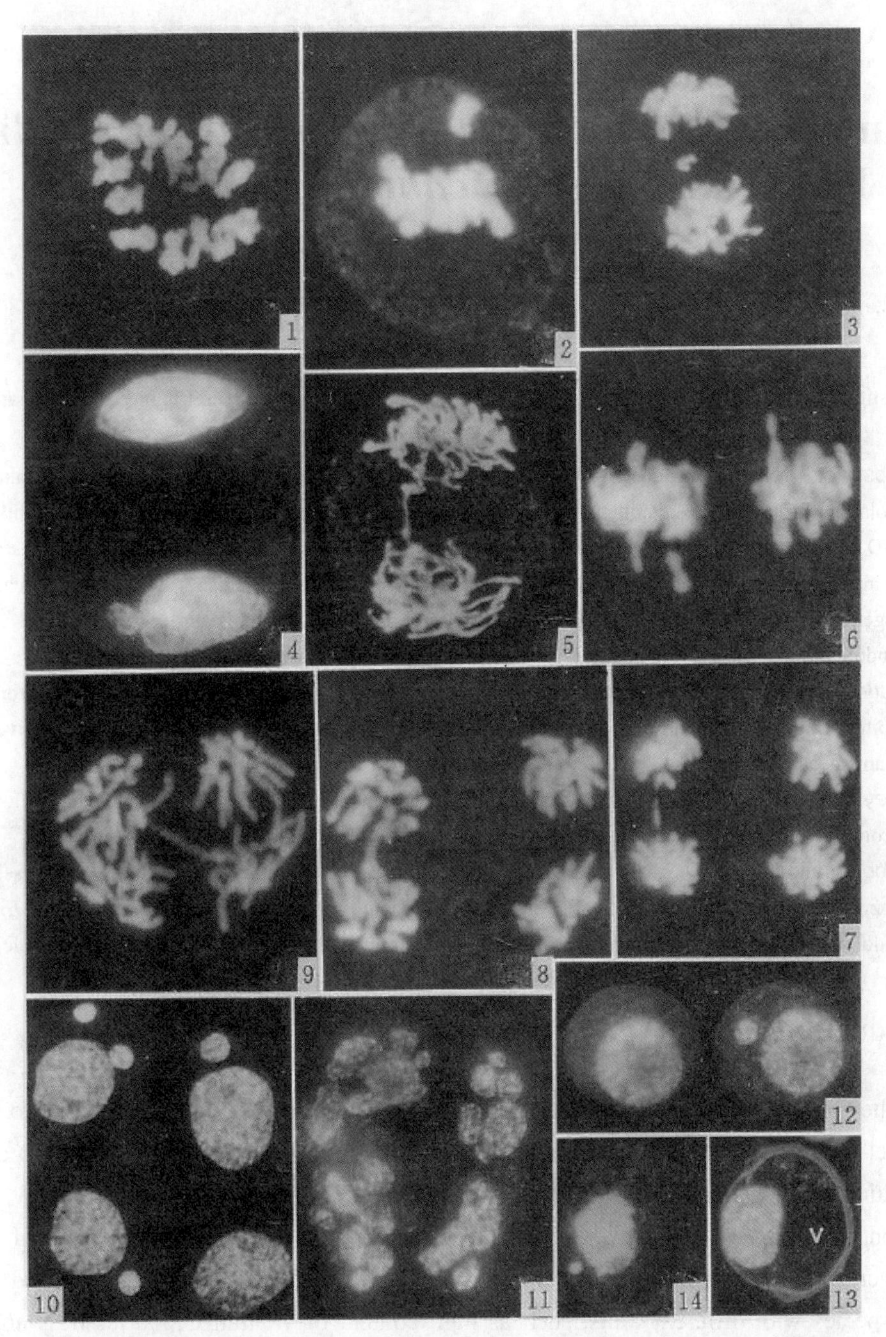

Fig.1. Chromosome number of donor plant, $2n$=58. Figs. 2~6. Chromosome numbers of plants regenerated from protoplasts, $2n$=116,59,174,104 and 114, respectively. Fig.7. One cell with an additional mininuclei. Fig.8. Multinuclei cell (arrow)

本文原载：Plant Cell Reports. 1998. 17: 819-821

Plant regeneration from *in vitro*-cultured seedling leaf protoplasts of *Actinidia eriantha* Benth

Y. J. Zhang[1] Y. Q. Qian[1] X. J. Mu[1]
Q. G. Cai[1] Y. L. Zhou[1] X. P. Wei[2]

(1 Institute of Botany, Chinese Academy of Sciences; 2 Beijing Plant Cell Bio Engineering Laboratory)

Abstract Newly expanded *in vitro* leaves of *Actinidia eriantha* were used for protoplast isolation. Protoplasts were cultured in liquid MS medium (lacking NH_4NO_3) supplemented with 2, 4-D (2, 4-dichlorophenoxyacetic acid) and 0.4*M* glucose. The plating efficiency after 3 weeks of culture was 19.4%, and calli were recovered without addition of fresh medium. These calli regenerated shoots on transfer to MS medium containing 2.28 μ*M* zeatin and 0.57 μ*M* IAA (indole-3-acetic acid). Regenerated shoots were rooted by immersion in 20ppm IBA (indole-3-butyric acid) solution before culturing on half-strength MS medium lacking growth regulators. Somaclonal variation, in terms of chromosome number and nuclei per cell of protoplast- derived plants, was estimated.

Key words *Actinidia eriantha*; Chromosome number; Multinucleate cells; Plant regeneration; Protoplast culture

Abbreviations 2,4-*D* 2,4-Dichlorophenoxyacetic acid *BA* 6- benzylaminopurine. *CH* casein enzymatic hydrolysate. *f. wt.* fresh weight. GA_3 gibberellic acid. *IAA* indole-3-acetic acid. *IBA* indole-3-butyric acid. *MES* 2-(*N*-morpholino) ethanesulphonic acid. *NAA* 1-naphthalene acetic acid

Introduction

The genus *Actinidia* consists of more than 60 species, most of which are native to China. The well-known cultivar 'Hayward' was selected by a New Zealand nurseryman from a small population of *A. deliciosa.* Kiwifruit industries are being developed rapidly globally and in addition to *A. deliciosa*, *A. chinesis* is cultivated in parts of China (Qian and Yu 1991). However, only a small part of the genetic resources of the genus has been exploited. Many other species with different traits, such as high content of vitamin C, hairlessness and cold hardiness, are also of value in breeding. Attempts to introduce useful genes from wild species into cultivated ones have so far been limited to sexual hybridization. Breeders often face two difficulties: one is that interspecific hybrids can be difficult to produce; the other is that

---

Communicated by S. Gleddie.

Actinidia is a dioecious genus, which makes it hard to estimate the breeding value of characters of the staminate plant, such as fruit size and quality. Methods have been established for kiwifruit that may help breeding, such as endosperm culture (Gui *et al.* 1982) and embryo rescue (Mu *et al.* 1992). Somaclonal variation may also be useful in kiwifruit breeding (Hirsch *et al.* 1992), while somatic hybridization may not only provide new approaches for overcoming interspecific incompatibility but may also allow for the combination of valuable traits of two pistillate plants. The successful regeneration of whole plants from protoplasts is a prerequisite for this approach, and to data, whole plants have only been regenerated from protoplasts of *A. chinesis* (Mii and Ohashi 1988; Xiao *et al.* 1992) and *A. deliciosa* (Tsai 1988; Oliveira and Pais 1991).

The species *A. eriantha* is valuable breeding material, as the vitamin C content of the fruit is 1013.98mg/100g f. wt., which is much higher than that of *A. deliciosa* (200~370mg/100g f. wt.) and *A. chinesis* (250~300mg/100g f. wt.) (Qian and Yu 1991), and its fruit size is the third largest for species in this genus (Liang 1980). This paper describes plant regeneration from leaf protoplasts of *A. eriantha.*

Materials and methods

Material preparation

Seeds derived from open pollination of *A. eriantha* were kindly provided by Prof. H. X. An (Botanical Garden, Institute of Botany, Chinese Academy of Sciences). They were sterilized by immersion in 75% (v/v) ethanol for 1min, followed by immersion in 0.1% (v/v) aqueous $HgCl_2$ solution for 10min, and then rinsed four times with sterile distilled water. Embryos were then excised aseptically and cultured on MS medium (Murashige and Skoog 1962) supplemented with 2. 28 μ*M* zeatin, 1. 45 μ*M* GA and 0. 57 μ*M* IAA and solidified with 0.6% (w/v) agar (Sigma) in the dark at 25℃, until germination. Seedlings were grown on solidified MS medium with halfstrength macrominerals in a growth chamber kept at 22℃ (night) to 25℃(day) and a 12- h photoperiod (17 or 50 μmol m^{-2} s^{-1}).

Protoplast isolation

Newly expanded seedling leaves were excised and cut into 1-to 2-mm-thick slices. Protoplasts were isolated by enzymatic digestion in a solution containing 1% (w/v) Cellulase R-10, 0.5% (w/v) Macerozyme R-10, 0.05% (w/v) Pectolyase Y-23 and 3m*M* MES dissolved in CPW salts solution (Power et al. 1984) containing 0.45 *M* mannitol at pH 5. 6. Incubation was carried out in the dark, at 25℃, for 8h. After filtration through a 200- mesh (127μ*M* pore), the protoplasts were centrifuged (50g, 3min). The supernatant was removed and 10ml CPW salts solution (containing 0. 45 *M* mannitol) was slowly added to the pellet, which was then centrifuged. Protoplasts were washed three times with CPW 0.45 *M* mannitol and resuspended in culture medium. Viability was determined with 0.1% (w/v) Evans Blue staining.

Protoplast culture

Protoplasts were cultured in 4.5-cm-diameter petri dishes, either in liquid medium at a density of 5×10^4 protoplasts ml^{-1} liquid medium or in agarose- solidified [0.75%(w/v)] streaky lenses (Binding et al. 1988). MS basal medium (without NH_4NO_3), TCCW (Tsai 1988), B5 (Gamborg et al. 1968) or KM8P media (Kao and Michayluk 1975) were used. All media were supplemented with 1% (w/v) sucrose, 0.4 *M* glucose, 100mgl^{-1} CH and 20mgl^{-1} coconut milk. The pH was adjusted to 5. 6. Growth regulators, including 2, 4-D, NAA, IAA, zeatin or BA, were added to the basal media separately or in combination. Cultures were maintained at 25℃ in the dark.

Plant regeneration

After 3 months of culture, the colonies were transferred to MS medium [containing 3% (w/v) sucrose and 0.7% (w/v) agar] supplemented with either 2.26 μ*M* 2, 4-D and 4.44 μ*M* BA or 2.28 μ*M* zeatin and 0.57 μ*M* IAA and kept at 25℃ and 12-h photoperiod to promote callus growth and shoot regeneration. The rooting of shoots longer than 1cm were induced by immersing the roots in 20ppm IBA solution for 2h and then placing them vertically on half-strength, solidified MS medium lacking growth regulators (Tsai 1988). The rooted plants were removed from the culture vessels, washed thoroughly to remove the nutrient medium and transplanted in pots. These pots were placed at 25±2℃ with a 16-h photoperiod and initially covered by polyethylene bags for 1 week.

Cytological observation

When the roots of *in vitro*-maintained plants attained a length of about 1.0cm, root tips were sampled (at 5p.m.) and pretreated with saturated parachlorobenzene at room temperature (20℃) for 90min, then fixed in Carnoy fixative (absolute ethanol: glacial acetic acid=3 ∶ 1) at 4℃ for 24h. They were stained with 1% (w/v) acetocarmine for at least 4h, boiled for 30s above an alcohol burner and then squashed with glacial acetic acid. Chromosome number at mitosis and at interphase nuclei were observed microscopically.

Results and discussion

Growth regulators and culture methods

Leaf tissues gave protoplast yields of 0.7~1.8×10^6/g f. wt. and with a viability of

92%~97%. Although leaf-protoplast yields from leaves of seedlings from the two regimes showed no difference, protoplasts from seedlings kept at the highest light level did not divide when cultured in liquid MS (NH_4NO_3) with 4. 52μ*M* 2,4-D. Conversely, those from seedling leaves under the lower light regime regenerated cell walls after 2days, and entered division after 10days of culture; the second and third division took place at 20 and 25days, respectively, leading to colony and callus formation. The plating frequency was 19.4% at 3 weeks. Leaves from seedlings under the lower light conditions were therefore used routinely.

Division was not observed if a different concentration (up to 4.52 μ*M*) of 2,4-D was included in the MS medium (without NH_4NO_3). Similarly, NAA (at 2.69, 10.74 or 16.11 μ*M*), a combination of 2,4-D (2,26 μ*M*) and NAA (2.69 μ*M*) or combinations of auxins (4.52 μ*M* 2,4-D, 5.37 μ*M* NAA or 5.71 μ*M* IAA) in the presence of 4.56 μ*M* zeatin did not support division. On the other hand, in the presence of 5.37 μ*M* NAA, cells divided once with a 5.7% lower plating efficiency than on the optimum medium, i.e. with 4.52 μ*M* 2,4-D. This role of 2.4-D for successful culture concurs with other reports on *Actinidia* protoplasts (Mii and Ohashi 1988; Tsai 1988; Oliveira and Pais 1991; Xiao et al. 1992). Tsai (1988) reported the successful culture of callus-derived protoplasts of *A. deliciosa* on TCCW. In our experiments, protoplast division stopped at the fourto eight-cell stage on this medium (supplemented with 4.52 μ*M* 2,4-D). Cells failed to divide on B5 (with 4.52 μ*M* 2,4-D) and KM8P media.

After 2 months of culture on MS medium (without NH_4NO_3) supplemented with 4.52μ*M* 2,4-D, the growth rate of clusters accelerated. With an additional month, calli (2mm in diameter) had formed and were transferred directly to the regeneration medium. Gradual addition of low osmotic medium [MS (without NH_4NO_3) supplemented with 4.52μ*M* 2,4-D and 3% (w/v) sucrose] to the original liquid culture, beginning after the third cell division, caused division to stop and the cells to die. It was found that cells could undergo sustained division without diluting the original liquid medium. Therefore, the procedure of dilution was not followed.

After one monthly passage on MS with 2.28μ*M* zeatin and 0.57μ*M* IAA, calli turned green and became compact. Bud formation took place in a further subculture, and a month later the buds grew into shoots of 1cm or longer. Subculturing for six passages brought about 100% callus differentiation coupled with prolific shoot formation. Calli cultured on MS with 4.44 μ*M* BA and 2.26μ*M* 2,4-D were yellowish and friable and did not differentiate. Moreover, these calli, upon transfer to medium with 2.28μ*M* zeatin and 0.57μ*M* IAA, were slower to regenerate buds and needed one additional subculture passage to produce buds comparable with those transferred from liquid medium directly onto the same differentiation medium.

Adventitious roots emerged within 8~10days in the rooting medium, and the rooted plantlets were successfully potted.

Mii and Ohashi (1988), Oliveira and Pais (1991), Tsai (1988) and Xiao *et al.* (1992) applied step-wise induction methods to obtain plant regeneration from protoplast culture of

Actinidia. Our results show that it is possible to regenerate plants using simpler procedures. These authors isolated protoplasts from calli (Tsai 1988; Oliveira and Pais 1991; Xiao *et al*. 1992) and suspension cultures (Mii and Ohashi 1988). Our protocol for leaf protoplasts provides an alternative which takes less time for preparation of the source material. Protoplast isolation from leaves may also facilitate somatic hybridization in *Actinidia*.

Chromosome number and nuclei of protoplast-derived plants

The chromosome number of the control plant was $2n=2x=58$, consistent with the observation by Deng and Sun (1986). Of 18 protoplast-derived plants examined, 6 plants had $2n=58$, 6had $2n=116$ and the remaining 6 plants were mixoploid. Euploid plants accounted for 66.7% of the plants examined. For the 6 mixoploid plants, the chromosome number varied from 59 to 203. Chromosome counts showed that the cells from the same root tip of a mixoploid plant usually had the same chromosome number.

Multinucleate cells were found in 10 out of 18 protoplast-regenerated plants. Binucleate and trinucleate cells were common, and even heptanucleate cells were occasionally found in 1 plant root tip. There appeared to be no association between multinucleate cells, chromosome number variation and mixoploidy of the plants. All the cells observed from the control were mononucleate.

In protoplast culture of *A. deliciosa*, Cai *et al*. (1992, 1993) reported considerable variation in chromosome number, morphological characters, sex differentiation, and vegetative growth of protoplast-derived plants, indicating the possibility of producing new breeding resources by protoplast culture in kiwifruit. Our cytological observation revealed somaclonal variation in chromosome and nucleus number. Further investigation is needed to determine if fur ther somaclonal variation will occur at the whole plant level.

Acknowledgements

The authors wish to thank Dr. A. Seal, HortResearch, New Zealand for reading the manuscript. This research was funded by the Chinese National Key Project-Crop Breeding by Means of Cell BioEngineering.

References

Binding H, Gorschen E, Jorgensen J, Krumbiegel-Schroeren G, Ling H Q, Rudnick J, Sauer A, Zuba M, Mordhorst G (1988) Protoplast culture in agarose media with particular emphasis to streaky lenses. Bot Acta 101: 233~239

Cai Q G, Qian Y Q, Ke S Q, He Z C, Jiang R X, Zhou Y L, Ye Y P, Hong S R, Huang R H (1992) Studies on the somaclonal variation of regenerated plants from protoplasts of *Actinidia deliciosa*. Acta Bot Sinica 34: 822~828

Cai Q G, Qian Y Q, Ke S Q, He Z C (1993) Regeneration of plants from protoplasts of kiwifruit (*Actinidia deliciosa*). In: Bajaj YPS (ed) Biotechnology in agriculture and forestry, vol 23. Plant protoplasts and genetic engineering IV. Springer, Berlin Heidelberg New York, pp 3~17

Deng X X, Sun H M (1986) Observation on chromosome number of *Actinidia*. Acta Hort Sinica 13: 80

Gamborg O L, Miller R A, Ojima K (1968) Nutrition requirement of suspension cultures of soybean root cells. Exp Cell Res 50: 150~158

Gui Y L, Mu S K, Xu T Y (1982) Studies on morphological differentiation of endosperm plantlets of Chinese gooseberry in vitro. Acta Bot Sinica 24: 216~221

Hirsch A M, Fortune D, Xiao X G, Blanchet P (1992) Somaclonal variations related to kiwifruit micropropagation, study of fruitful male plants and use of peroxidase as an early sex marker. Acta Hortic 297: 123~131

Kao K N, Michayluk M R (1975) Nutritional requirements for growth of *Vicia chajastana* cells and protoplasts at a very low population density in liquid media. Planta 126: 105~110

Liang C F (1980) Outline of taxonomy on *Actinidia* in China. Guangxi Plants 1: 30~45

Mii M, Ohashi H (1988) Plantlet regeneration from protoplasts of kiwifruit, *Actinidia chinensis* Planch. Acta Hortic 230: 167~170

Mu X J, Tsai D R, An H X, Wang W L (1992) Embryology and embryo rescue of interspecific hybrids in *Actinidia*. Acta Hortic 297: 93~97

Murashige T, Skoog F (1962) A revised medium for rapid growth and bioassays with tobacco tissue cultures. Physiol Plant 15: 473~497

Oliveira M M, Pais M S S (1991) Plant regeneration from protoplasts of long-term callus cultures of *Actinidia deliciosa* var '*deliciosa*' cv 'Hayward' (kiwifruit). Plant Cell Rep 9: 643~646

Power J B, Chapman J V, Wilson D (1984) Laboratory manual: plant tissue culture. Nottingham

Qian Y Q, Yu D P (1991) Advances in *Actinidia* research in China. Acta Hortic 297: 51~55

Tsai C K (1988) Plant regeneration from leaf callus protoplasts of *Actinidia chinensis* Planch. var '*chinensis*'. Plant Sci 54: 231~235

Xiao Z A, Shen D X, Lin B N (1992) Plant regeneration from protoplasts of *Actinidia chinensis* Planch. Acta Bot Sinica 34: 736~742

生物安全与分子生态学研究

本文原载：生物多样性研究的原理与方法. 1994. 钱迎倩，马克平主编. 北京：中国科学技术出版社，217-224

生物技术与生物多样性的保护和持续利用

钱迎倩

(中国科学院植物研究所)

1 引言

1992年5月22日由世界很多国家参加在内罗毕召开的会议上通过了全球《生物多样性公约》。随后，同年6月5日在巴西里约热内卢举行的联合国环境与发展大会上有153个国家首脑在该《公约》上签了字。《公约》要求缔约国的政府的批准，并按第36条规定，在第30个缔约国政府批准并递交加入书后的三个月才正式生效。李鹏总理代表我国政府在《公约》上签了字，在第七届全国人民代表大会常务委员会第28次会议上又讨论并批准了《公约》，这样我国已正式成为生物多样性公约缔约国。中国是在国际上批准《公约》较早国家之一。到1993年11月已有包括亚洲的中国、日本、蒙古，大洋洲的澳大利亚、新西兰等绝大多数国家，欧洲的丹麦、德国、挪威，北美的加拿大，非洲的几内亚、毛里求斯、津巴布韦，拉丁美洲的墨西哥、秘鲁等等31个国家的政府的批准，并递交了加入书。蒙古人民共和国在1993年9月30日是第30个批准的国家，因此《公约》生效的日期是1993年12月29日。

《公约》生效后，按照第6条的规定每一缔约国要为保护和持续利用生物多样性制定国家战略、计划和方案，并可能将生物多样性的保护和持续利用纳入有关的部门或跨部门的计划、方案和政策中去，从而实现《公约》所规定的目标。《公约》第一条“目标”的内容如下：“本公约的目标是按照本公约有关条款从事保护生物多样性、持续利用其组成部分以及公平合理分享由利用遗传资源而产生的惠益；实现手段包括遗传资源的适当取得及有关技术的适当转让，但需顾及对这些资源和技术的一切权利，以及提供适当资金”。

《公约》目标中两处提到技术的问题，在《公约》的条款中有十多处都谈到技术，并明确指出技术是包括生物技术。其中16条则论述“技术的取得和转让”，第18条论述“技术和科学合作”，第19条又是专门论述“生物技术的处理及其惠益的分配”。《公约》中提到的生物技术与其目标和内容中涉及到的遗传资源、技术转让、利益分享以及知识产权密切相关。此外与生物技术有关的还涉及到由生物技术改变的任何活生物体(例如转基因生物等)的释放、安全转让、处理和使用，这些在《公约》中也都有叙述(马克平等，1994)。以上种种说明了生物技术与生物多样性的保护和持续利用有着密切的关系。

2　生物技术对生物多样性的依赖

在《公约》的第 2 条“术语的使用”上，对生物技术有专门的定义，即“生物技术是指使用生物系统、生物体或其衍生物的任何技术应用，以制作或改变产品或过程以供特定用途”。实际上，生物技术本身早就不是什么新鲜事物，上千年来人类一直在对有机体进行操作，最初是进行动、植物的选种、育种，利用微生物进行发酵，如酱油等豆类加工产品，以及面包或奶酪等等。这些传统的技术在世界上某些地区、农村或在某些领域上，一直沿袭到现在还在应用。近几十年来，生物技术有了很大的发展，例如组织培养、细胞融合、胚胎移植以及重组 DNA 技术等等新技术不断涌现。技术的发展已可以使单个植物细胞或者原生质体通过人工培养再生成完整的植株；两个不同种亲本的细胞在实验室里进行融合，可以创造出具有双亲性状的杂种；具有极高经济价值的动物胚胎通过移植在一般的动物中进行发育等等。此外，结合了重组 DNA 技术在酶工程和发酵工程方面也有了很大的突破。生物技术的内容繁多，但其中最重要的领域或当今人们最关心的领域是从 20 世纪 70 年代开始的重组 DNA 技术、细胞融合技术和转基因动、植物等类的基因工程技术。人们通过重组 DNA 技术已可能鉴定和分离特有的基因，把它们增强并插入到其他有机体的遗传物质中，从而改变这些机体的遗传组成。在实践上这个技术第一次得到应用是把分离到的人胰岛素基因插入到普通大肠杆菌工程菌中，通过发酵而大量生产出人胰岛素。发达国家中 2/3 的糖尿病患者正是使用重组 DNA 技术所产生的人胰岛素来进行治疗。中国科学院生物化学研究所科学家采用酵母表达胰岛素系统已成功地大批量、低成本生产出人胰岛素。

至今很多治疗疾病的药物是在投资巨大的反应器重发酵，然后经过提取、纯化等一系列的生产过程来进行生产的，生物技术的发展使科学家想到是否可以用基因工程的途径得到转基因动物来生产药物。这些转基因动物就成为所谓的“生物反应器”。目前这种设想已成为现实，例如英国爱丁堡医药蛋白公司已培育出一种转基因绵羊，其奶中含有一种 α—1—抗胰蛋白酶(AAT)，缺少这种酶的人易导致肺穿孔，喝了这种羊奶就可以治疗该症。又如美国加利福尼亚生物技术公司通过基因工程将人的基因转移到牛的体内已取得成功，并且由转基因公牛授精的母牛产下 5 头健壮的牛犊，这些小牛犊均携带有人的 HLF 基因。再一个明显的例子是红细胞生成素(EPO)是人体内最重要的造血生长因子，若肝脏受损就不能产生这种因子而导致贫血，尿毒症患者只能定期血透和输血。目前南京军区军事医学研究所等单位用基因工程方法获得人的红细胞生成素基因片段并插入哺乳动物细胞内，在体外大量繁殖，得到了与人 EPO 结构和功能完全相同的纯蛋白，目前已进入中试阶段。在渔业生产方面，例如人们也在利用分离的抗冻基因转入罗非鱼，目的是使罗非鱼能向北移，在更低的温度下养殖。

在农业生产上人们期望得到优质、高产、抗逆、抗病虫、少用农药、少施肥的作物品种。基因工程研究的进展已获得了一批从各种转基因植物中筛选出来的具优良性状的植株或后代。例如，利用苏云金杆菌的 Bt 杀虫蛋白基因转入烟草及番茄，得到抗虫率较高的抗虫转基因烟草和番茄；培育出抗多种除草剂、抗烟草花叶病毒、抗黄瓜花叶病毒、抗马铃薯Y病毒、抗马铃薯X病毒以及抗鳞翅目和鞘翅目害虫的转基因植物，其中包括含苏云金杆菌基因的转基因棉花，这个基因能控制烟青虫、棉铃虫、红铃虫和其他毁坏棉花的鳞翅目幼虫；得到了能增加马铃薯淀粉含量的转基因马铃薯；为了使番茄能耐储藏，得到的转基因番茄只有在外加乙烯条件下才能成熟；从烟草中分离到毡绒层专一表达的基因 TA29，通过一系列技术转化到烟草、油菜等作物中得到了雄性不育的植株；从不为人们所重视而只作为观赏用的仙人掌中分离得抗旱基因，企图能得到抗旱的转基因植物；从萤火虫中分离得萤火虫的发光基因，导入烟草后已可使再生的烟草植株的叶片发光，当然目前光还太弱。技术的改进将使萤火虫发光基因更明显地发挥作用后导入圣诞树，让圣诞树在黑暗条件下也能发光。

综上所述，基因工程尽管在理论上和技术上还存在许多有待解决的问题，但技术本身已经成熟到一定的程度，使其在农业、林业、医药及环境保护等等方面展现了极其广阔的应用前景。另一方面说明要获得各种各样的转基因动、植物，将大大依赖于生物多样性。从长远看，人类将要大量利用尚未为人们所认识的具重要经济性状的物种多样性及遗传多样性。也就是说，基因工程在人类的经济与社会发展上已起到或即将起到的重大作用已经非常明显，但是以抗虫基因为例，人们所用的基因还非常有限，绝大多数局限于苏云金杆菌，而存在于其他各种生物体内的基因的作用尚未被认识，更谈不上利用。地球上可能存在500万~5000万种生物，而已定名的仅140万种。

但是，摆在人类面前一个严峻的现实是人类对赖以生存的地球却在肆无忌惮地加以利用、加以破坏，带来的后果是对生物多样性的毁灭。据世界自然基金会(WWF)一个报告中指出，世界热带森林栖息着世界半数以上的物种。由于人类对木材的需求、经济发展的需要以及对生物多样性永续利用知识的贫乏，热带雨林已遭到大量的砍伐，估计每年有奥地利国土面积大小的热带雨林遭到毁灭。在热带海洋中，清晰、温暖的浅海水体促成了珊瑚礁的形成。由于有持续的营养供应和温暖稳定的条件，使这个生态系统中存在着可与热带潮湿雨林相比拟的多样性。研究资料说明，珊瑚礁生态系统中的生物多样性将为人类的未来提供治疗疑难疾病的药物来源。但由于用炸药来捕鱼以及收集珊瑚用于装饰或建筑材料，使珊瑚礁遭到大面积的破坏，有些地方已经灭绝。在国内，捕食野生动物的情况极为严重并屡禁不止。有资料说明，我国海南岛海口市1993年每月消耗的野生动物约有18吨之多，其中包括国家及省级保护动物。据1992年时海南省林业局调查，国家一级保护动物长臂猿50年代时有2000多只，现仅存10余只；国家二级保护动物黑熊全岛仅存50多只。

美国全球2000年报告预测，到2000年，地球上所有物种的15%~20%将会丧失。按保守估计现存物种为300万~1000万种，那么到时我们将失去45万~200万物种。IUCN植物中心的保守估计，到2050年，6万种植物将要灭绝或濒临灭绝。如按一种植物供养10~30种动物计，到2050年物种灭绝的总数将为66万~186万种。这个数字要比自然状态下物种灭绝的速度至少高25 000倍。国际上一些比较权威的一些机构及知名科学家还有一些预测，例如1990年时美国哈佛大学的E. Wilson等三位科学家提出警告，按目前人口和工业发展的增长率，在今后50年内，人类将毁灭地球上二分之一的动、植物物种。Wilson还认为，即使作出努力来保护世界的生物多样性，物种的四分之一仍将在100年内灭绝。英国剑桥的世界保护监测中心(WCMC)在 1993 年指出，全世界有 2.5 万种植物面临灭绝的威胁，另有 1 万种植物已经消亡。

以上的材料或数字尽管不完全准确，但令人确信无疑的是：自然进化赋予人类大量的生物多样性财富正以惊人的速度遭到毁灭；大量的物种或基因在尚未知道其用途前就已在地球上灭绝。因此，从要发挥生物技术巨大潜力的角度来看，保护生物多样性也已经成为生物技术科学工作者的紧迫任务。

3 生物技术在生物多样性保护和持续利用上的作用

上面一节谈的是生物技术对生物多样性的依赖，但是反过来看，生物技术也为生物多样性的迁地保护，特别是遗传资源的保存提供了可靠的保证。植物优良种质的器官、组织、细胞或原生质体都可在超低温(–196℃)条件下加以保存，技术的发展并可保证一旦需要时它们能再生成完整的植株。动物的胚胎或精子也都可以利用这种技术来保存。此外，生物技术中的 DNA 指纹技术可以进行新生子代的鉴定，勇于繁殖行为的研究。分子标记可以研究不同基因型花粉竞争和更精确地估计种群的遗传多样性。至于生物技术上已常规在使用的 RFLP(限制长度片段多态)、RAPD(随机扩增多态 DNA)技术也在生物多样性保护研究中，特别是遗传多样性研究中应用。

生物技术在生物多样性的持续利用方面也能发挥作用，例如广义的植物组织培养是生物技术的各种技术中相当成熟的一种技术。一些珍稀、濒危而具重要经济价值的植物，则可用极少量的器官、组织甚至细胞、原生质体再生成完整植株，并结合快速繁殖技术进行大量的繁殖，为人类所利用。

所谓的微观生物学和宏观生物学之间的距离正在缩小。美国国家科学基金会和能源部近年来召开了一系列小型讨论会，目的是在促进分子生物学家和生态学家之间的对话。《分子生态学(Molecular Ecology)》刊物在近年来已面世。这些都说明了依赖于近代分子生物学进展而发展起来的生物技术与生物多样性保护与持续利用之间的关系是越来越密切了。

4 生物技术改变的活生物体的使用、释放及安全转让

所谓由生物技术改变的活生物体往往指的是用基因工程的技术获得转基因生物。在不同的文献中也有的人称工程生物或经遗传修饰的有机体，但都是同一个含义。有关生物技术改变的活生物体的使用释放问题在《公约》第 8 条，就地保护的(g)款上专门有叙述，“制定或采取办法酌情管制、管理或控制由生物技术改变的活生物体在使用和释放时可能产生的危险，即可能对环境产生不利影响，从而影响到生物多样性的保护和持续利用，也要考虑到对人类健康的危险”。其实《公约》第 8 条中所提到的问题早在 70 年代初期，即分离特种基因并将它们导入到其他有机体技术发展的早期，一些科学家已对与重组 DNA 研究有关的潜在生物学和生态学危险以及释放到环境中所带来的潜在危害表示担心。归纳起来大概有下列几点：

(1) 有人担心当某种生物的遗传组成经过修饰或它们的基因组与其他生物体交换而演变成有毒的病原体；

(2) 转基因作物的基因有可能自然转移到这个作物的野生和杂草近亲中去，特别是当它们被释放到该作物的遗传多样性中心或接近该中心时，其后果更是难以预料的；

(3) 以抗虫转基因作物来说，目前绝大多数是集中在使用苏云金杆菌的基因。在许多作物上广泛地应用如此狭窄的抗性来源，会使作物变得非常脆弱，害虫和病原体一旦克服如此单一的抗性来源，将造成作物的大面积减产；

(4) 释放经过遗传修饰的微生物是一个更为复杂的问题。目前绝大多数的微生物尚未得到鉴定、定名或研究，但对于微生物不同种属之间的自然基因转移比较频繁，这一点人们是知道的。新插入的带有明显选择优势的基因会在整个微生物界传播，这会造成对某一些经遗传修饰的微生物的长期影响的评估带来困难。

关于生物技术产物或经遗传修饰生物的释放等是人们普遍关注的问题，在由世界资源研究所(WRI)、国际自然与自然资源保护联盟(IUCN)、联合国环境规划署(UNEP)联合主持出版的《全球生物多样性策略》中专栏 13，专门谈到最大限度地减小生物技术对社会和生态的潜在危险。其中指出了八个方面的准则，目的在于克服在新的生物技术发展、检测和使用过程中，如不很好地加以调节可能存在的潜在负效应。专栏 13 中并提出要求，“在国家、地区及国际水平上建立更为详细的准则是 90 年代的优先重点”。

转基因生物对整个生态系统将会带来什么样的长期影响，这方面尚未积累是以说明问题的科学依据。但是，尽管不是转基因生物，盲目引入外来种对某个生态系统以及生物多样性都会造成破坏。因此在《公约》第 8 条“就地保护(h)防止引进、控制或消除那些威胁到生态系统、生境或物种的外来物种。”造成损失的在国内外都不乏例子。突出的例子登载在 1990 年 10 月 22 日中国农牧渔业报上，黄舟维撰写的“谁能除掉大米草”一文中提到，福建省霞浦县东吾洋沿岸 14 万亩滩涂，1983 年时从美国引进大米草，认为可护提、喂牛并可作燃料。原先该滩涂生态系统中有 200 多种生物，其中自然生长的鱼类多种，又是全国养对虾、贝类的实验基地。引进大米草后，由于大米草繁殖力强，生长茂盛，盘根错节，海水涨潮时滩涂生物被冲进草丛而无法逃生，以至蛏、蛤、章鱼、跳鱼等许多水产品濒临绝迹。浮游生物附着滞留在草丛中，致使人工养殖的牡蛎、对虾因海水缺乏营养而产量锐减，不仅破坏了滩涂的生态系统，造成生物多样性的灭绝，并带来不可估量的经济损失。另一个很能说明问题的例子是 60 年前，美国政府为了排干沼泽地带的水，从澳大利亚引进了吸水量极大的白千层属乔木，并在沼泽地带广泛种植。但这树种生长得非常快，可达 20 米高，繁殖力和生命力也都极强，因此这树种在沼泽地带发展的速度也十分惊人。据估计，如不采取措施进行制止，到 2000 年时，整个国家公园将变成白千层属的乔木公园。造成的后果是沼泽地的水是排掉了，但凡生长这种树的地方，其他植物均无法生存，整个沼泽生态系统遭到破坏。在夏威夷，大约 86 种引种植物严重地危害了当地的生物多样性；一种引进树种现在已经取代了超过 3 万英亩的当地森林(世界资源研究所等，1993)。

上述大米草的例子是在引进 7 年后发现的问题，而白千层属的例子说明盲目引进外来种的后果要几十年的时间才为人们所重视。转基因生物的使用时间还很短，释放后对人类健康的影响以及会给整个生态系统带来的长期影响的科学根据还不足，因此一些国际组织对此予以很大的关注。例如联合国粮农组织(FAO)1991 年 4 月在罗马召开的植物遗传资源委员会第四届会议所发放的文件—“生物技术和植物遗传资源以及生物技术守则的内容”、“经遗传修饰生物体的处理和释放”一节中有较多的篇幅提到准则与法规的问题。在此报告中提到的多数发达国家已经制定或正在制定国家准则，由于各个国家对生物技术潜在的风险的认识和关心的程度不一样，各国的法规在许多方面又有不同。一些发展中国家也有活跃的国家生物技术计划，但多数还没有制定法规。按报告上说，“也缺乏实施法规的能力”。人们还希望有国际上都能接受的生物安全标准，由于经遗传修饰的生物体是没有政治边界的，具潜害性状的生物体在一个国家释放、增殖后有可能把它们的基因传播到另一个国家的植物中去；另外，法规不健全的国家可能被用作其他国家所禁止的试验场所。为此，由 UNEP、WHO、UNESCO 及 FAO 在 1985 年联合组织成立了一个非正式的关于生物技术安全的特别工作小组，至今只是回顾了生物安全的现状，还没有提出任何建议。此外，如世界银行与洛克菲勒基金会等一些机构也正在考虑发展中国家的一些特殊需要。国际农业研究磋商小组(CGIAR)于 1989 年设立了一个“生物技术工作组”(BIOTASK)，其主要任务是法规和环境释放的问题。

前面提到发达国家对经遗传修饰生物体释放的大致情况，下面介绍美国科学院外事秘书 James B. Wyngaarden(1992)在“健康和技术”的报告中所提到的情况。在 1982 年前后美国公众对转基因生物的释放或大田试验后对环境影响的问题非常关注，到 1987 年国家专门制订了环境政策条例。条例要求对转基因生物释放的所有主要活动都要做出对环境的评价。此后，美国农业部接受了第一个大规模大田试验的申请。可是到 1989 年时美国白宫科技政策办公室的生物技术科学协作委员会还是提出要建立一个机构。这个机构按照“我们对有机体的特性以及有机体准备释放进去的环境的特性是否熟悉？我们能否确定或有效地控制这些有机体？如果引入的有机体或遗传性状比原先想象的持续时间更长，或者引入到了不是想要引入的环境中去时将会对环境产生什么样的影响？”这样的标准去评价危险地可能性。从本文前面提到引入外来种对生物多样性的破坏的事实来看，白宫提出建立一个机构的标准看来是正确的。事情发展到 1992 年 2 月，美国科技政策办公室总统执行办公室公布了一个称为“Scope 文件”。这个文件抵制了下列观点，即由生物技术，如重组 DNA 等新方式生产的产品必然或固有的比由老技术，如杂交育种更危险。国际著名杂志“自然”(Nature)的一个评论中称赞 Scope 政策是“与真的科学相协调的”和是一个“白宫的清楚思路”的产物。从而美国农业部接受作大田试验的数量迅速增加。到 1992 年 4 月累计已接受 314 项申请，其中 234 项已签发了许可证。据报告介绍，当一种实验植物或微生物已建立了一种当地的生态小生境时，还没有一个有害的例子。

与美国相反的是包括欧洲一些国家在内的其他国家持不同的态度。他们提出对新生物技术的产品和工序要加强特殊的规章控制。德国制定了许多规则来控制重组有机体在实验室和工业中的使用，奥地利也颁布一项与德国相类似的法律。总之，转基因生物释放看来还是一项很复杂的问题，不仅要看它们对包括生物多样性在内的环境的近期影响，还应注意到长远影响。发达国家和美国国内是反反复复，而德国、奥地利等国则持慎重的态度。

有关对由生物技术改变的任何活生物体的安全转让、处理、使用以及引进等问题，《公约》第 19 条“生物技术的处理及其惠益的分配”有明确的说明。第 19 条第 3 款上规定,“缔约国应考虑是否需要一项认定书，规定适当程序，特别包括事先知情协议，适用于可能对生物多样性的保护和持续利用产生不利影响的生物技术改变的任何活生物体的安全转让、处理和使用，并考虑该议定书的形式”。第 4 款的规定是“每一缔约国应直接或要求其管辖下提供以上第 3 款所指生物体的任何自然人和法人，将该缔约国在处理这种生物体方面规定的使用和安全条例的任何现在资料以及有关该生物体可能产生的不利影响的任何现有资料，提供给将要引进这些生物体的缔约国”。

在发展中国家中我国在生物技术的研究方面还是比较先进的，已获得不少数量的转基因植物，可以或已经进入大田试验，个别的甚至已接近可推广的水平。我国又是《生物多样性公约》缔约国之一。但对转基因生物的使用、处理、释放、安全转让及引进等都还未见到有关法规的发布。政府有关主管部门应该根据《公约》第 8 条，(g)款及第 19 条第 3 款、第 4 款的规定制定有关的法规，公诸于众。

5 生物技术与《公约》其他有关问题的关系

在 DNA 双螺旋结构论文发表 20 年后，在 70 年代初美国旧金山加利福尼亚大学分子生物学家郝伯特·博耶与斯坦利·科恩等利用重组 DNA 技术从哺乳动物基因组中切割了一个基因，将它插入大肠杆菌获得成功。这一巨大的突破意味着可以克隆动物基因，很快就被风险资本家鲍勃·斯旺森抓住机遇，说服了博耶成立了世界上第一个利用重组 DNA 技术制造蛋白质用于治疗人体疾病的公司。同时生物技术作为一个产业从此诞生了。

生物技术作为一种产业并不是一帆风顺，经过了 70 年代和 80 年代的专利战，临床试验失败等考验以及世界市场的波动等等原因，使投资者对生物技术时而支持，时而不支持。造成生物技术产业长期徘徊甚至亏损。随着技术不断地完善，这一局面已扭转，生物技术产业开始进入盈利和兴旺发展时期。生物技术作为一种高技术，需要高的投入，也必然有高的产出，如文中提到转基因绵羊生产药物 AAT。羊奶每升中含 AAT70 克，每克市场售价 100 美元，有人形容羊奶成了“液体黄金”。在 1993 年时美国的遗传技术公司(Genetech) 营业额已达 5 亿多美元。预计 90 年代世界市场将出现生物技术产品销量的黄金时期。按保守的估计，美国 5 年后生物技术产品的销售额将达到 60 亿美元，10 年后可达到 200 多亿美元。

到了 90 年代,生物技术产业已经到兴旺发展的时期,这一点已成为世界各国的共识。因之，各个国家以至与生物技术有关的各个公司都关注生物技术以及与生物技术有关的内容如何反映到《公约》上。《公约》当然主要是政府间谈判的一个产物，国际上各种有影响的非政府组织也召开与《公约》内容有关的各种会议。由于《公约》会对发达国家中很多私营公司起到制约的作用，这些公司关心《公约》的每一条款、每一措辞是必然的，他们提出不少建议，这些建议对《公约》的产生起到重要的作用。联合国环发大会结束后不久瑞士 Giba—Geigy 公司农业部、种子分部的专利和法规经理 Duesing 博士撰文谈了《公约》对生物技术研究的影响一文。

读了 Duesing 博士文章后，知道这个《公约》是有几千份建议书的递交，包括 100 个以上的团体或国家的参加，经过多少次各种各样会议讨论后的一个产物。发展中国家与发达国家之间有很大的争议，争议的焦点与生物技术直接有关的涉及到遗传资源、技术转让、利益分享和知识产权等敏感问题。发展中国家往往是遗传资源丰富的国家，而发达国家则是掌握先进技术的国家。发展中国家关心的是不该把遗传资源无偿地给发达国家利用，而提供国却得不到利益，可是发达国家所关心的是《公约》将对生物技术工业的发展有负影响。最后，经过持续四年时间的争论、谈判，对绝大多数国家来说，以上四个敏感问题取得了大家可接受的结论。这些在《公约》的第 15 条“遗传资源的取得”，第 16 条“技术的取得和转让”，第 19 条“生物技术的处理及其惠益的分配”及其他有关条款中都有了充分的论述。即使这样，还有一部分包括美国在内的国家在环发大会期间还是未在《公约》上签字。直到 1993 年上半年美国政府首脑最终还是签了字。

这些条款的内容概括起来大致包括如下几个方面：

(1) 确认各国对其自然资源拥有的主权权利，因而可否取得遗传资源的决定权属于国家政府，并依照国家法律行使；

(2) 每一缔约国应酌情采取立法、行政和政策措施，让提供遗传资源用于生物技术研究的缔约国，特别是其中的发展中国家，切实参与此种研究活动；可行时，研究活动宜在这些缔约国中进行；

(3) 每一缔约国应采取一切可行措施，以赞助和促进那些提供遗传资源的缔约国，特别是其中的发展中国家，在公平的基础上优先取得基于其提供资源的生物技术所产生的成果和惠益。此种取得应按共同商定的条件进行；

(4) 每一缔约国认识到技术包括生物技术属于专利和其他知识产权的范围时，这种取得和转让所根据的条件应承认且符合知识产权的充分有效保护；缔约国认识到专利和其他知识产权可能影响到本公约的实施，因而应在这方面遵照国家立法和国际法进行合作，以确保此种权利有助于而不违反本公约的目标。

上述几点概括地说明了《公约》之所以能为包括发达国家与发展中国家的世界各国接受的条件。一个拥有遗传资源但缺乏技术的缔约国，当他的某个遗传资源被另一个缔约国利用时，他可以通过利用这个资源参与研究工作，获得利用这个资源的技术以及遗传材料或资源作商业开发后得到财政利益的分享。而拥有技术又缺乏遗传资源的缔约国也可以从获得某种特定的遗传资源、技术转让以及共同商定条件的利益分享中得到惠益。而在知识产权问题上，《公约》第 16 条第 2 款中又有明确的规定，即“此种技术属于专利和其他知识产权的范围时，这种使用和转让所根据的条件应承认且符合知识产权的充分有效保护”。这也就解除了对发达国家的生物技术工业的发展起到不利影响的顾虑。

80 年代后期开始，生物多样性的保护与持续利用已逐步引起我国科学工作者及政府有关部门的关心。已有不少的出版物出版(汪松等，1990；陈灵芝等，1993；钱迎倩，1992，1994；Duesing，1994)，其中有少数文章介绍过生物多样性与生物技术的关系(钱迎倩，1994；Duesing，1994)。我国作为《公约》的缔约国之一，将会陆续制定国家级的生物多样性保护和生物资源持续利用的策略和计划。

参考文献

马克平，钱迎倩. 1994.《生物多样性公约》简介. 中国科学报，1994 年 4 月 29 日，第三版
汪　松，陈灵芝(主编). 1990. 中国科学院生物多样性研讨会会议录. 北京：中国科学院生物可续与技术局世界资源研究所等. 1992. 中国科学院生物多样性委员会译. 1993. 全球生物多样性策略. 北京: 中国标准出版社
陈灵芝(主编). 1993. 中国的生物多样性——现状及其保护对策. 北京：科学出版社
钱迎倩. 1992. 生物多样性的保护与永续利用. 科技导报，(5): 36~38
钱迎倩. 1994. 生物多样性与生物技术. 中国科学院院刊，(2): 40~44
Duesing, J. 1992. 王静译. 1994. 《生物多样性公约》及其对生物技术研究的影响. 生物多样性，2(2): 118~124
FAO. 1991. *Biotechnology and Plant Genetic Resources and Elements of a Code of Conduct for Biotechnology*. Rome: Commission on plant genetic resources, Fourth Session, 15~19, April Wyngaarden, J. B. (袁萍译). 1992. 健康和技术. 生物工程进展，(5)：33~39

本文原载：自然资源学报. 1995. 10(4): 322-331

生物技术与生物安全

钱迎倩　马克平

(中国科学院植物研究所)

摘　要　本文通过大量的实例介绍了国内外生物技术，特别是基因工程的进展。继而从伦理道德、对人类的健康和环境的影响等方面阐述了生物技术对人类生存安全可能带来的威胁。最后就生物安全的立法等问题提出了建设性意见。

关键词　生物技术；遗传修饰的生物体；生物安全；生物多样性

在 1992 年召开的联合国环境与发展大会上由 153 个国家首脑签字的《生物多样性公约》(以下简称《公约》)的第 2 条，“用语”对生物技术作了下述的定义：“生物技术”是指使用生物系统、生物体或其衍生物的任何技术应用，以制作或改变产品或过程以供待定用途。此外，在《公约》第 8 条，就地保护的(g)款有如下的叙述：制定或采取办法酌情管制、管理或控制由生物技术改变的活生物体在使用和释放时可能产生的危险，即可能对环境产生不利影响，从而影响到生物多样性的保护和持久使用，也要考虑到人类健康和危险。这一段叙述密切关系到当前国际社会普遍关注的所谓“生物安全”(biosafety)问题。本文仅就当前生物技术的巨大进展，由生物技术改变的活生物体的使用、释放可能带来的各种危机以及为生物安全应做好立法工作等方面作一介绍。

1　当代生物技术的巨大进展

国内习惯把生物技术划分为基因工程、细胞工程、酶工程、发酵工程以及生化工程等几个领域，本文要涉及的主要是基因工程。经过生物技术操作后得到的产物，国际上较普遍的采用了两个名词，一个是经遗传修饰的生物体(GMO)，另一个是基因工程的生物体(GEO)。GMO 的含义似乎更广泛一点，一切经过遗传操作其基因得到修饰的生物体都包括在内，但目前似乎更多的还是指经基因工程操作后的生物体。

1.1　国际上生物技术的进展

20 世纪 80 年代后期以来，基因工程的研究得到了突飞猛进的发展，不少成果已不局限在实验室水平，某些产物已达到商业化的程度。按 J.Rissler 和 M.Mellon(1993)的报道[9],在美国正在开发的转基因植物已涉及到禾谷类、纤维类、牧草、森林植物、水果、油料、花卉、蔬菜以及其他类似烟草等的作物。其中重要的包括主要的粮食作物水稻、玉米、纤维作物棉花；油料作物大豆、花生、油菜以及例如黄瓜、土豆、南瓜等经常食用的蔬菜。到去年底，数量已远不止这些，至少还包括小麦、香蕉、菠萝、甜椒等等。例如美国DNA植物技术公司(DNAP)正和英国Zeneca集团合作研究生产成熟慢,且口味好的香蕉。

发达国家由澳大利亚、比利时、加拿大、丹麦、法国、德国、荷兰、挪威、日本、西班牙、瑞士、英国和美国等14个成员国组成的经济合作和发展组织(OECD)已批准在1986~1992年间对具6种性状的转基因作物作小规模田间试验。性状及所占比例如表1。表1中的质量性状包括油和蛋白质成分以及水果成熟期等。例如，正在试验中的一种转基因马铃薯，其淀粉含量要比普通马铃薯高60%。用这种马铃薯炸制马铃薯条或片时吸油更少，食用这种条或片将更有利于健康。已达到商业化水平的值得提出的有两种作物，即西红柿和南瓜。转基因西红柿是位于美国加州的一个生物技术公司Calgene用了8年时间花费2000万美元得到的。这种转基因西红柿被称为保味西红柿(flavor-save tomato)。西红柿成熟、老化是由于多聚半乳糖醛酸酶的作用，这是乙烯合成途径中的一种关键酶，Calgene 的科学家把这种酶的基因分离出来，然后再反方向地插入到染色体组中。促使西红柿在成熟过程中只产生少量的这种酶，以延长其成熟的时间，继而延长其在货架上的时间。西红柿可在大田藤蔓上成熟变红的时间更长，口味更好，运到超级市场时还是很硬，色泽保持鲜艳。转基因西红柿已于1994年5月间为美国食品和药物管理局(FDA)批准，在10月份推向市场。英国生物种子公司Zeneca集团也准备用转基因西红柿制成酱，目前正在就出售这种新型西红柿酱同超级市场进行最后谈判，有可能今年在英国超级市场的货架上出现。转基因南瓜是在美国Upjohn化学公司中的Asgrow种子公司研制成功的。这种转基因南瓜被称为抗病长弯颈南瓜新品种ZW-20。这个品种抗夏南瓜黄斑纹病毒和西瓜斑纹病毒，可提高单位面积产量，也可使农民少施农药。1990年以来已在美国10个州46个农庄做过田间试验。目前已经美国农业部(USDA)批准，预期不久的将来，可与消费者见面。

表1 具6种性状转基因作物及所占比例[9]

Table 1 The transgenic crops with six traits and their percentage

性状	百分比
抗除草剂	57
抗病毒	13
抗虫	10
质量性状	8
雄性不育	5
抗其他病害	4

转基因动物方面也有很大的进展。例如有报道阿根廷首都布宜诺斯艾利斯展出一种转基因的矮种牛。两岁半的牛才高67cm，重45kg，是世界上最矮小的牛。最值得提出

的是转基因猪。插入人生长激素的转基因猪，其体形和出肉量都比正常猪高出一倍，据报道，澳大利亚已有转基因猪肉出售。研究转基因猪的目的远不止提高出肉量而是用于人类的医疗目的。一是利用转基因猪的血红蛋白。至今，人类需要的血红蛋白都从人血红细胞中取得。但是用人的血红蛋白存在着供应不足、价格昂贵的问题。更为严重的是所输的人血中往往带有病毒，甚至艾滋病病毒。科学家已可能把人血红蛋白基因插入猪的血红细胞，转基因血红细胞中有15%人血红蛋白。而猪血红蛋白与氧结合的能力与人很相似，人们希望今后能利用转基因猪的血红蛋白作为人的血红蛋白补充物。更诱人的是转基因猪的器官作为今后人器官移植的来源，由于猪的 DNA 与人十分接近，猪的器官尺寸与人又基本相称，其肾、心脏、肝、肺甚至血管都有可能作为人器官移植的供体。目前正在进行免疫基因工程改造试验，使猪的免疫类型能与人一致，不至于造成器官移植后的排异反应。这种实验在美国和英国已获得初步成功。

转基因酵母的研制也早已成功，并已用于制作面包、酿酒和奶酪。在美国、瑞士和意大利市场上都可买到用转基因技术制造的奶酪。

此外，基因工程技术用于药物生产，治疗人体各种疾病也已取得很大的进展。如德国科学家在吸血蝙蝠唾液中分离到一种防止血液凝固的基因，用此制造能化掉心肌梗塞和脑血栓血块的药。人体本身能产生约 8 万种蛋白质以维护身体的各种机能。目前用基因工程的手段已能生产其中的 30 种，如防止血液凝固的制剂、生长激素和胰岛素等。还有 300 种蛋白正在开发中，有的正在做临床试验。又如美国加州希尤公司生产的名为 Betaseron 的β干扰素在美国已为 FDA 批准使用。拜耳公司生产的抗体已在 36 名类风湿关节炎患者身上试用。利用转基因动物或转基因植物作为“生物反应器”来生产药物已有很多的尝试，并已取得不少成功的例子。Calgene 公司将人的基因转移到牛的体内，由转基因公牛授精的牛已产下 5 头健壮的带有人的 HLF 基因的小牛犊。

1.2　国内生物技术的进展

我国的生物技术研究至少在“六・五”期间已经开始。以广义的生物技术领域论，经过 10 多年的研究已硕果累累,其中特别值得提出来的是花药培养方面不仅研究的深度和广度在国际领先，而且已应用于作物的育种，并已大面积地在生产上应用。花药培养与染色体工程结合，至少已得到不少好的种质。在原生质体培养方面，玉米，大豆等重要作物的植株再生在国际上都是首先成功[2]。在快速繁殖方面，为解决马铃薯块茎退化，从无病毒的茎尖培养开始得到无毒植株。用快繁技术，一株苗一年能繁殖到 100 万株。在国内 20 个以上省市已大面积推广，在这一点上，水平达国际领先是无疑的。

正像今年初德国《明镜》周刊的一期上登载的，国际上已打破了“基因殖民地化”。与其他发展中国家相比，我国在基因工程方面的工作已走在前面，并已引起发达国家的重视。在转基因植物方面，先后已得到了抗除草剂、抗病毒、抗虫、耐盐的作物[1]。例如抗除草剂的大豆已繁殖到第五代。抗烟草花叶病毒烟草特别是抗烟草花叶病毒和黄瓜花叶病毒的双抗转基因烟草在河南省1992年已达到 8000hm^2 的大田面积，是当时国际上转基因植物释放面积最大的作物[10]。按 Krattiger(1994)报道[7]，世界上只有中国和美国两个国家已批准为了商业化目的，大规模释放转基因植物。中国的转基因抗病毒烟草的释放已接近100万 hm^2(注：原著是这样报道的，但面积肯定被大大地扩大了)，或占整个烟草种植面积的 5%。虽然报道面积大大地被扩大了，但抗病毒烟草确实是在生产上大面积获得应用，并是抗病性状表现良好的第一个例子。把抗虫基因导入欧洲黑杨，得到的转基因欧洲黑杨可使舞毒蛾和扬天蝼死亡率高达100%。从豇豆子叶中分离到豇豆胰蛋白酶抑制剂基因，这种基因插入烟草后，转基因烟草具有良好的抗棉铃虫和烟青虫的特性。此外，在进行田间试验的还有转基因甜椒、马铃薯以及西红柿。在亚洲发展中国家中，除泰国在 1993 年开始有西红柿的田间试验外，中国是唯一进展得最早(1989 年)最快的国家[7]。

在转基因动物方面，我国在国际上率先开展了转基因鱼的育种研究，用人生长激素基因导入鲤鱼受精卵，转基因鱼生长速度比对照快。用乙肝表面抗原基因导入兔受精卵，通过借腹怀胎获得转基因兔。此外，我国还在国际上首次报道获得含酶性核糖核酸基因的转基因兔。

在基因工程药物方面我国的进展也是十分喜人的。人α型基因工程干扰素已进入产业化阶段。乙型肝炎表面抗原基因工程疫苗，1991 年已完成中试，已形成年产 100 万人份的生产能力。基因工程白细胞介素-2 与新型白细胞介素-2 的工艺及得率都达到国际先进水平，并已经卫生部新药评审委员会批准进行临床试验。此外，在人生长激素、猪生长激素、α-干扰素、表皮生长因子等基因工程药物在实验室研究已完成，有的已进入中试。

总之，在全世界范围内生物技术发展迅速。到 1993 年的 20 年左右时间，基因工程公司仅在美国就发展到 1000 多家，各种基因工程产品不断推出，美国的年总销售额达 40 多亿美元。特别是 90 年代以来，生物技术发展的势头预计更会加速，以转基因作物为例，目前美国正在进行田间试验的已有 1400 次。仅 1994 年一年进行田间试验的次数就超过 1987 年到 1993 年的总和。田间试验如果顺利的话，转基因马铃薯、玉米、棉花、大豆、小麦、甜椒、香蕉、菠萝、西瓜、甘蔗等等都将陆续上市，估计在今后 5 年内美国市场上至少会推出 50 种像转基因西红柿这类的转基因农产品。到本世纪末，通过转基因技术生产的销售额可能达到 1000 亿美元。生物技术正以其巨大的活力改变着传统的生产方式和产业结构，迅速向经济和社会各领域渗透和扩散，人类面临的粮食、能源、环境、人口、资源等五大危机以及人类的各种疾病有可能得到相当程度的缓解。

2 生物技术可能带来的危险

有关生物技术的进展及其在食品、新的药物、种质改良等等方面可能给人类带来巨大的效益，这在前面已经作了比较详细的介绍。但这项高新技术像原子能一样，在造福于人类的同时也会给人类带来严重的危险。生物技术改变的活生物体或者说是经过遗传修饰的生物体的使用和释放可能会对环境产生不利的影响，从而影响到生物多样性的保护和持续利用；也可能对人类健康带来威胁；此外在伦理道德方面已引起一场争论。实际上，在 70 年代初期(即这项技术发展的早期)，已分离到特种基因并将其导入其他生物体，这在科学界已开始有争论。有人对与重组 DNA 研究有关的潜在生物学和生态学危险以及释放到环境后可能带来的潜在危险表示担心。随着生物技术迅速的发展，伦理道德问题也随之提出来。

2.1　有关伦理道德的争论

随着基因工程的进展，人胰岛素基因在大肠杆菌中、在酵母中都可表达；人生长激素和人干扰素基因插入到细菌中早已成功，这些都已形成产品，先后在80年代就已投放市场；人生长激素基因在鱼、猪、牛等高等动物中也都能成功地表达；人促红细胞生成素(EPO)、组织血纤维蛋白溶酶原激活剂(TPA)等等都已接近生产阶段或已投入市场。此外，用人的血清蛋白基因转入马铃薯，这种转基因马铃薯能生产人血清蛋白。以上的例子说明人的不同基因已经插入到不同的微生物、真菌、动物、植物中。据不完全统计，目前至少有24种人体基因已引入到各种生物体内。而实际上，目前技术的进展几乎可做到将包括人体在内的各种生物来源的基因转移到任何其他一种生物体中去。由于人体的基因在不同生物体中任意的转移，有人提出了下列一系列问题：人类是否有权任意把任何数量的人体基因转移到其他生物体去？消费者是否愿意食用带有人体基因的食品？用人类基因做转基因工作有没有一个法定限度？人体基因任意的转移会不会出现“弗兰肯斯坦”那样的科学怪人，而使人类遭受灾难[①]。

发达国家中生物技术迅速发展的一个重要推动因素是一些公司以其先进的技术追逐高额利润。以转基因作物为例，据统计，1987年至1993年夏，549家向美国农业部申请进行转基因作物田间试验的申请者中占最大比例的是化学公司，占到申请者中的46%。其中包括孟山都(Monsanto)、杜邦(Dupont)、西巴—盖奇(Ciba-Geigy)等等著名的大公司，而孟山都又在化学公司中占到52%的比例。其次是大学，占申请百分比中的17%。实际上，在美国不少大学中科学家的经费来源于一些大的化学公司。上面表2中说明了美国在转基因作物方面抗除草剂的占了整个的57%，这就意味着美国的农业更趋向于而不是离开化学农业。抗除草剂的作物将使农民更多地依赖化学除草剂，这样实际上增加了生产除草剂的化学公司的收入。孟山都公司与杜邦公司都是生产化学除草剂的大公司。因此国际上也有人提出，为了获取利润，把整个生物界的遗传结构加以混合或加工是否合法？

美国马哈里希国际大学(Maharishi International University)的一位被国际公认的DNA研究者，由康奈尔大学培养出来的分子生物学家，1994年时46岁的John Fagan博士，1994年11月17日在美国首都华盛顿举行一个新闻发布会，他站在伦理道德的立场上基于遗传工程的巨大危险而反对遗传工程。他本人放弃掉从美国国立卫生研究院(NIH)得到的60万美元以上的科研资助，同时他还放弃掉了从其他来源争取到的125万美元的资助。他认为他的研究成果会对有害的基因工程应用作出贡献；他呼吁人们对种系(germ-line)的遗传操作暂停50年。所谓种系的操作，即是把新的基因引入到精子、卵或非常早期胚胎的DNA中去。导入到这些生殖细胞中引起的改变将一代代地传下去。这种被他称为

---

① 所谓“弗兰肯斯坦”是恐怖小说《弗兰肯斯坦》一书中的主人公，一个用尸体制造怪人的医生。

事故及其不可预料的副作用将无限期地存下去。此外，1993 年国际上成立了由 50 人组成的国际生物伦理学委员会。该委员会是由从 32 个国家来的 4 位诺贝尔医学奖获奖者、律师、遗传学家、生物学家、哲学家、社会学家、人口学家、政治学家等等人员组成。他们将对有关遗传学研究的各个方面予以注意,目标是在 1995 年之前起草一个有关保护人类基因组的国际公约。遗传学的迅速发展，在给人类疾病的治疗、预防等等带来喜人的前景的同时也带来许多问题。该委员会的任务是把遗传学进展可能带来的问题让公众知道并传播有关的知识。

2.2 对人类健康的影响

遗传工程实验室的操作及其释放到环境，尤其是转基因生物作为食品对人体的健康可能带来的影响，一直是人们关心的问题。科学界以及新闻媒介都不断有各种各样的报道。其中难免存在一定程度的讹传。但即使是潜在的危险，也应引起人们足够的重视。1994 年 5 月“文摘报”曾转载过“中国中医药报”的报道。美国的转基因西红柿释放后使厨师在制作菜肴过程中过敏难受，他们称这种食品为“弗兰肯食品”。更令厨师不安的是有些顾客吃了他们餐馆的这类食物后病倒了。因而他们表示不再卖基因食品，并在他的菜单上、餐馆门上表明了拒绝基因食物的立场。有关转基因猪作为食品在 1994 年 8 月德国“星期日图片报”也有报道，提到插入人生长激素的转基因猪比正常猪大一倍，出肉量也多一倍，但它却百病缠身。患有肿瘤、肺炎、心力衰竭和关节畸形。吃下这类食品后对人体会有什么影响，目前人们全然不知，不知道风险有多大。在同一篇报道中德国自然保护和环境联合会的基因专家卡策克指出,美国 Monsanto 农产品公司生产的转基因豆子能抗杀虫剂，但这种豆子产生一种类似雌性激素的物质，男人吃了这些豆子后，乳房会反常地增大。

在转基因作物实验过程中往往需要用标记基因，大多数的实验用抗生素抗性基因来作为标记基因，以此来选择转基因植物。因此引起人们担心的是这些抗药性是否可能转嫁给吃了这类转基因食品的人体。对人体是否有害，尤其这些效应可能不是在短时间内为人们所观察到的。

2.3 对环境可能带来的危险

转基因生物能达到商业化并为人类所利用,这就意味着他们已在环境中大量地释放。某一种生物一旦这样大量地释放，将来要在环境中消灭他们将不仅要花费大量的资金，甚至可以说将是不可能做到的，因此更应引起人们的重视。转基因作物释放后对环境的危险归纳有下列几点。

2.3.1 转基因作物本身将可能变为杂草

不少作物已被人类驯化到不依赖于人的耕作就生存不了的程度，如玉米、小麦、香蕉就是明显的例子。Clowell[6]认为这类作物不管怎么通过生物技术来改良，在生态学范畴内不会变成具杂草化特征的植物。而另一些栽培植物，例如某些狗尾草或高粱属的种在某种意义上来说本身就是杂草，而在另外的场合下它们又是作物。这类作物当插入一个例如抗病或抗虫的基因时，可能会把本来在某些地区很安全的作物，但由于改变了其平衡而趋向于杂草化。再如有另一些作物如甘蔗、水稻、马铃薯、番薯、油菜、向日葵和麦燕等，它们本来就有很近的杂草性的近缘种。其中某些作物，它们的不少性状与它们的杂草化的祖先是共同的，因此某些遗传上的改变就可能使作物的本身形成杂草。例如高度抗盐的转基因水稻品种本身就可能侵入到港湾中去大量繁殖起来。

2.3.2 转基因作物使野生近缘种变为杂草

自然界的不少作物的野生近缘种由于自然的制约，目前并不以杂草的形式存在于自然界。但是一旦某一个转基因作物通过花粉的传播，把转基因作物的花粉引入野生近缘种，使这种近缘种能大量繁殖而变成杂草。在美国，野葫芦之类的南瓜的进缘植物是很普遍的，可是这些野葫芦目前并未形成杂草。南瓜在美国东南部是土生土长的，这地区野葫芦也是很普遍的。正在进行实验，观察南瓜是否有可能与野葫芦自然杂交或通过渐渗(introgression)而起用。如果大自然的相互制约和平衡一旦遭到破坏，野葫芦就很可能变成一种杂草。病毒的存在很可能是对野葫芦发展的一种制约，但美国有人担心，目前培育成的抗病毒南瓜的基因流入野葫芦，就会使原来对黄瓜斑纹病毒和西瓜斑纹病毒敏感的绿皮密生西葫芦(一种美洲野生南瓜)变成抗这两种病毒，从而大量繁殖起来而成为严重的杂草。又如威尔斯大学的群体遗传学家对三个栽培甜菜亚种、野生种和杂草种的DNA 分析结果说明，在遗传图谱上杂草种介于栽培种和野生种之间。因此，有可能由于栽培种与野生种之间花粉的传播而产生杂草。他们预言抗除草剂的转基因甜菜大面积种植后，由于花粉作为基因流的传播者，而使抗除草剂基因转到野生种内而造成抗除草剂的杂草。杂草这个术语是包括在农田、草坪、路边和未管理的生态系统中的不受欢迎的植物。据报道，美国在 1991 年为控制杂草就花掉 40 亿美元。

2.3.3 转基因生物可能作为有害的外来种

转基因生物是人类创造的、自然界本来不存在的一种生物。对一个生态系统来说，转基因生物的本身就是一种外来种。外来种的引入，历来非常普遍，有起好的作用，也确实不乏大量的例子说明外来种的引入对整个生态系统的破坏并造成了不可估量的经济损失。在前面的文章中[3, 4]，已举例了我国引入大米草及美国引入千层叶属树种，给当地的生物多样性的保护及经济建设造成巨大的影响的例子。这里还可举出两个有说服力的例子，昆明的滇池是全国有名的景点，也是昆明人民用水的主要来源。但由于近年来水源的污染、水质的富营养化，造成水葫芦(凤眼莲)已覆盖了整个滇池的 80%，成为一大公害。又据报道，越南在 1986 年从国外引进一种作为食品的金蜗牛，农民饲养后可增加收入。这种蜗牛繁殖极快，逸出的蜗牛已严重威胁到湄公河三角洲水稻种植区。已有 1440hm^2 水稻田遭到破坏，其蜗牛密度已高达每平方米 5~10 只。越南政府于 1994 年 10 月发起运动来消灭这种蜗牛，但收效不大。这例子再一次说明，一种生物一旦引入某个生态系统后，要消灭它是非常困难又耗巨资的。

英国的一些科学家指出，要是听任转基因生物不加控制地进入自然环境中，最后会有一天人工物种可能会取代天然物种。自然界的生物多样性，尤其是目前的一些珍稀濒危物种将在地球上消失。

2.3.4 形成新的病毒的可能性

1993 年上半年美国 Arizona 大学的科学家报道，整合到植物基因组内的病毒外壳蛋白基因可以和其他病毒发生重组，因此，存在着产生超病毒(super virus)的潜在危险。类似的报道来自 Michigan 大学植物学系的实验，他们把花椰菜花叶病毒外壳蛋白的基因插入豇豆，从而得到抗病毒的豇豆。他们进一步又把缺失外壳蛋白的病毒接种到转基因豇豆上。实验结果发现 125 株豇豆中有 4 株又染上了花叶病。因此，他们推测，为使作物获得对病毒的抗性而被转入植物中的病毒可能与再接种病毒的遗传物质结合，从而形成新的病毒。或者是转基因植物如含有病毒颗粒的话，植物可能会促进新的病毒的产生。这种新病原体如再侵入到其他重要经济作物的话，造成的危害或控制它的费用会更大。

2.3.5 对生态系统中其他种的危害

上面已提到“生物反应器”的概念，即人们已经可以利用转基因植物有目的地生产某些药物。转基因植物如能表达潜在的有毒物质(如苏云金杆菌毒素)的话，这些植物将对其他的生物产生危害。例如，生产药物的转基因植物在玉米田里被鸟吃了，造成鸟的中毒而死亡。

2.3.6 更为严重的化学药剂的污染

上文提到了发达国家的一些如 Monsanto 等大的化学公司投入大量的资金，做抗除草剂的作物，目的是为了使该公司的除草剂的销路更大，创造更多的利润。从另一个角度来看，令人担心的是大量抗除草剂作物的培育成功将促使农民更多地去使用除草剂或其他化学药剂。从而造成更为严重的环境污染。

3 生物技术、生物多样性、生物安全与持续农业

当前我国与世界都面临着一系列的危机。对中国来说，可能最根本的还是人口与粮食两大问题。因此，1994 年全国人大着重提出省长要抓“米袋子”、市长要抓“菜篮子”的问题。人大会议一结束，立即又召开了主要中央领导人都出席的计划生育会议。世界人口的爆炸问题也是十分尖锐的，Beversdorf(1994)报道[5]，国际人口统计学家预计到 2060 年全球人口可能会达到 100 亿~160 亿。地球能不能养得了这么多的人口？持续农业看来是目前国际的潮流，也是解决不断膨胀的人口之温饱问题的唯一出路。持续农业的发展受到制约或影响的因素是很多的，至少有土地面积的限制、不可再生资源如燃料、鳞、钾等等的限制以及全球气候变化的影响等等。专家们预计由于全球气候变化会对下一世纪农业生产的稳定性产生冲击。当然农业问题还会受到政治的影响，在世界范围内如关贸总协定(GATT)的影响，我国国内也直接受到农业政策的影响。

从生物学的角度来看，持续农业与生物多样性、生物技术与生物安全的关系也是十

分密切的。从“科学是第一生产力”的角度看，后三者可能又是持续农业的决定性制约因素。本文第一节列举大量事实说明生物技术对今后世界粮食问题或食品问题的解决能起到的关键作用及美好前景。但目前生物技术也确实存在不少的问题，例如基因工程中抗虫转基因作物，绝大多数是集中地采用了苏云金杆菌毒素(Bttoxin)基因。在许多作物上广泛地使用如此狭窄的抗性来源，必然会使作物变得非常脆弱。害虫或病原体一旦克服如此单一的抗性来源，将会造成作物大面积的减产。这问题可能要从三个方面来找到解决的答案，亦即生物多样性。遗传学的进展不断推出新的生物技术以及生物安全。就以抗虫基因来说，人们必须从自然界的生物多样性中广泛地去寻找新的抗虫基因。但当今世界的生物多样性以惊人的速度在消失，人们谈不上了解某些物种的形状，甚至来不及知道其名字，这些物种已在地球上消失，保护生物多样性的重要性及紧迫性就显而易见了。其次是要求遗传学不断有新的进展，使生物技术随着有不断的发展，使这项技术在保持环境资源，也就是在保护环境中的水、空气、营养物以及绿色空间、生物多样性等方面作出新的贡献。保持好的生态环境对持续农业的发展是非常关键的。此外，还应通过研究及立法来解决本文第 2 节中提到的由于生物技术带来的一系列生物安全问题。

4　生物安全的立法问题

《公约》第 8 条，就地保护(k)款中规定：制定或维持必要立法和/或其他规范性规章，以保护受威胁物种和群体；第 19 条，生物技术的处理及其惠益的分配第 3 款提出：缔约国应考虑是否需要一项议定书。规定适当程序，特别包括事先知情协议，适用于可能对生物多样性的保护和持久使用产生不利影响的由生物技术改变的任何生物体的安全转让、处理和使用，并考虑该议定书的形式。

4.1　国际上有关生物安全立法的情况

有关遗传工程、重组 DNA 分子等从 70 年代后期以来，如美国、德国等发达国家就发布指南。80 年代后期以来基因工程的发展迅速到某些成果已达到商业化的程度，促使有关经遗传修饰的生物体(GMO)的释放及生物安全在大多数发达国家都已有法规。OECD 在 1986 年和 1992 年持续地发布有关重组 DNA 安全问题和生物技术安全问题的文件。如法国为对 GMO 的评价和立法成立了两个专门委员会。第一个是遗传工程委员会，成立于 1975 年，任务集中于实验室的重组 DNA 的研究。到 1986 年时又成立了生物分子工程委员会(Biomolecular Engineering Committee)，它的任务是评价 GMO 的大田试验、释放以及它们的商业化。发达国家大致上也就像法国这种情况，90 年代以来各种具体的法规与条例在一些发达国家不断地发布。在发展中国家中，1990 年印度的科学和技术部也颁发了重组 DNA 安全指南。此外，联合国的有关组织，如粮农组织(FAO)、环境规划署(UNEP)等也十分关注生物安全的问题。世界银行也出版了“生物安全：生物技术在农业和环境中安全使用”专著。

《生物多样性公约》缔约国的第一次大会1994年10月在巴哈马召开，这次大会的主要议程之一就是讨论怎样制定有关生物安全在国际上生效的议定书。会议上不同的国家从各自利益出发采取各自的立场，尽管有很大的争论，但最后还是一致同意成立由10个国家参加的“生物安全专家小组”来商讨“生物技术安全的国际技术指南”。这次专家小组会议于1995年5月在埃及举行。

题为“经遗传修饰的植物和微生物大田试验生物安全的结果”的国际会议已开过三次，第一次是1990年11月在美国召开，第二次是1992年5月在德国举行，第三次是1994年11月，还是在美国召开。此外，小型的讨论会及国际会议也十分频繁[8]。凡此种种说明有关生物安全的课题，国际上已做了大量的研究。研究的内容涉及到转基因作物释放的危险评估，转基因植物释放后对生物多样性和种群水平的影响，对土壤动物区系的影响，转基因植物与生物地球化学循环以及生物安全数据库建立等。这些研究的成果也就是建立生物安全程序和法规的基础。

4.2 我国生物安全的有关情况

我国有关生物安全的第一个法规是针对基因工程药物的，即1990年制定的“基因工程产品的质量控制标准”。按标准规定，基因工程药物的质量必须满足安全性的要求。对基因工程产品普遍适用的是1993年12月24日由国家科委第17号令发布的《基因工程安全管理办法》(下称《办法》)。《办法》规定了我国基因工程工作的管理体系，按潜在危险程度，将基因工程工作分为四个安全等级，并规定了分级审批权限。从可操作性考虑，农业部还将于今年内发布对一切与农业有关的转基因工作适用的、更为具体的法规。这些法规的出台将是十分重要的。当然转基因生物释放的潜在危险可能要有相当长的一段时间才能为人们所认识。一是要针对生物安全进行系统的科学研究，另一点是需要时间的考验。国内在有关生物安全方面的科研工作进行得还很不够。在第九个五年计划中应引起足够的重视，作出应有的安排。转基因生物释放后的效应还需要有长期的监测。我们应做到既能充分发挥生物技术积极的作用，又能充分了解GMO可能带来的危险，再进行研究，克服这些危险，真正造福于人类。

参考文献

[1] 张树庸. 基因工程研究的二十年. 科技导报, 1994, (6): 39~42
[2] 袁　萍, 钱迎倩. 植物原生质体的研究在中国科学院的发展. 中国科学院院刊, 1990, (4): 336~339
[3] 钱迎倩. 生物多样性与生物技术. 中国科学院院刊, 1994, (2): 40~44
[4] 钱迎倩. 生物技术与生物多样性的保护和持续利用. 见: 钱迎倩, 马克平主编. 生物多样性研究的原理与方法. 北京: 中国科学技术出版社, 1994, 217~224
[5] Beversdorf W. D. The importance of biotechnology to sustainable agriculture. In Krattiger, A. F. et al(eds.). Bilsafety for sustainable agriculture. ISAAA/SEI. 1994, 29~32
[6] Colwell R. K. Potential ecological and evolutionary prlblems of introducing transgenic crops into the environment.In: Krattiger A. F. et (eds.). Biosafety for sustainbale agriculture. ISAAA/SEI. 1994, 33~46
[7] Krattiger A. F. The field testing and commercialization of genetically modified plants: A review of worldwide data (1986 to 1993/94). In: Krattiger A. F. et al(eds.). Biosafety for sustainable agriculture. ISAAA/SEI. 1994, 247~266

[8] Leicester T. B. et al. Ecological implications of transgenic plant rclease.Molecular Ecology, 1994, 3(1)
[9] Rissler J. and M. Mellon. Perils amidst the promise-ecological risks of transgenic crops in a global market. Union of Concerned Scientists. 1993
[10] Zhou Ruhong, Fang Rongxiang et al. Large-scale field performance of transgenic tobacco plants resistant toboth tobacco mosaic virus and cucumber mosaic virus (in press). 1995

本文原载：保护中国的生物多样性. 1996. 汪松等主编. 北京：中国环境科学出版社, 152-156

生物安全的现状与对策

钱迎倩　马克平　魏伟　裴克全

(中国科学院植物研究所)

自从美国政府 1994 年在国际上第一个批准延迟成熟期的转基因番茄商品化种植以来，转基因作物种植的面积发展得非常迅速，到 2000 年时已达到 4420 万 hm^2。其中美国种植面积占 63%，阿根廷占 23%，加拿大占 7%，中国占 1%左右。被批准作商品化种植的作物，美国已有 11 种以上，但主要的还是抗除草剂转基因大豆、抗虫转基因棉花、抗虫转基因玉米，以及抗除草剂转基因油菜等几种。美国转基因大豆的面积在 1999 年时已占其整个种植面积的 55%，抗虫转基因棉花(主要是 Bt 棉花)，占整个棉田的 50%左右，而抗虫转基因玉米占玉米田的 30%。因在国内外产品的销路问题，特别受到欧洲国家的抵制，近年来面积没有过多增加，有的甚至可能有所减少。

1　对 GMOs 持截然不同的观点

所谓的 GMOs(Genetically modified organisms)，是指经遗传修饰了的生物体。转基因作物就是 GMOs 中的一种。目前在国际上对 GMOs 存在下列截然不同的观点。

一种是赞同大力发展 GMOs 的观点，其理由是基于下列几点。

(1) 具有明显的经济效益

下面有几个数字能说明问题。如美国，1996 年时 70%的转基因 Bt 棉花不再喷洒杀虫剂，产量提高 70%，每公顷节约 140~180 美元；美国原来每年约有一半的玉米田(3200 万 hm^2)受棉铃虫危害，丧失金额达 10 亿美元，但种植转基因 Bt 玉米后，产量提高 9%，而经济效益 1996 年是 190 万美元，1997 年达 1900 万美元；在加拿大，在 1996 年种植了 1200 万 hm^2 耐除草剂油菜后，产量提高 9%，经济效益达 600 万美元；中国种植转基因抗虫棉花，从 1997~2000 年的 4 年，总的经济效益达 3 亿 3 千 7 百万美元。全世界 2000 年转基因作物产品的价值为 30 亿美元，预计到 2010 年时价值可达 300 亿美元。由此可见，经济效益是十分明显的。

(2) 解决发展中国家人民的饥饿问题

世界人口，特别在发展中国家，会不断增长是肯定的，而粮食如何能随着增长的人口同时增加，是一个全世界关心的严重问题。不少人认为，基因工程技术，特别是转基因技术，将是解决 21 世纪不断增加人口对粮食需求的唯一途径。1999 年，在英国皇家学会曾召开过一次世界上有关科学院共同讨论 GMOs 问题的会议，会议上一个发展中国家科学院院长认为："我们与欧洲的一些发达国家不一样的是他们国家人口少，已经有足够的粮食，可以不发展转基因技术。而我们是发展中国家、人口多，需要大力发展转基因技术来解决我国的粮食问题"。转基因技术不仅能提高粮食或作物的产量，并可提高其品质。全球每年由于维生素 A 缺乏症导致 50 万人失明，100 万儿童死亡，这类事件多数是发生在以稻米为主食的发展中国家的贫困人口中，特别是非洲。瑞士科学家 Ingo Petrykus 领导的研究组用基因工程技术培育出一种称为"金稻"的水稻，这是一种具高含量维生素 A 原物质的水稻，有可能解决维生素 A 缺乏症问题。

(3) 可能大大缩短作物生长期

西班牙科学家从拟南芥菜中提取一种基因插入柑橘树中，使原来要 5~6 年才能成熟的柑橘树，在一年内就开花结果(Pena *et al*., 2001)；又如德国科学家培育的马铃薯在栽种后 15 周就能收获马铃薯，比普通马铃薯块茎收获时间要提早 7 周之多，这种新品种并能产生一种细菌酶，可以把能使马铃薯萌芽的蕉磷盐酸分解而阻止其出芽(Farre *et al*., 2001)。

2001 年 7 月联合国开发计划署(UNDP)发布的第 12 期《2001 年人类发展报告》中对基因改良技术的可利用性的一面也是充分肯定的。《报告》指出，尽管充满争议，基因改良生物(GMOs 是一种翻译方式)可能成为发展中国家的突破性技术。在承认需要面对基因改良技术所带来的环境和健康等方面风险的同时，仍要注意到这一技术在生成抗病毒、抗旱和富有营养的作物方面具有的独特潜力，这些作物能够大幅度减少目前仍困扰着全球 8 亿人口的营养不良现象。《报告》认为基因改良生物带来的风险可以得到控制。

另一种观点是全面对 GMOs 持否定的态度。特别是"绿色和平组织"等一些非政府组织，他们不仅游行、抗议，有时甚至采取行动。2001 年 8 月 28 日中央电视台新闻 30 分节目中播出了法国的反对 GMOs 的群众，拿起了镰刀大量的砍除已长得很大的转基因玉米，因为法国食品安全机构在递交给政府的一份报告中说，"在受测试的玉米种子中，大概 41%的样品含有转基因物质成分。此外，一小部分油菜种子和大豆种子也含有转基因物质"报告还指出，"我们观察到的一些现象使我们得出结论，常规食品含有转基因物质的现象并不仅限于我们所研究的种子。现在常规谷物的种子或作物含有微量转基因物质的可能性已成为现实"。

绿色和平组织在对一片赞扬声中上述的"金稻"也持截然相反的立场。当然他们对任何转基因产品都是反对的，他们认为转基因技术存在着不可预测、不精确、和不可逆转等问题。与其他基因工程技术一样"金稻"没有解决根本的安全问题，对环境有潜在的威胁。他们引用营养学家的意见说，贫困人口的饮食结构中缺乏脂肪，为之才影响了他们吸收大米中维生素A。因此“金稻”解决不了维生素A缺乏症。从营养学角度考虑，转基因技术能够解决饥荒的理论是没有充分依据的。他们甚至认为不论是在发达国家或是发展中国家，想仅仅凭借某一种技术力量解决复杂的社会和经济问题是不可能的。

对上述能使传统产品大大缩短生长期的转基因技术，环境保护主义者也持强烈反对的态度，他们认为这些作物对环境和健康的长期影响还不得而知。在他们的强烈反对下，西欧目前实际上禁止对转基因作物作商品化的种植。

2 转基因作物的潜在生态风险

关于转基因作物的潜在生态风险早在1992年公布的《生物多样性公约》条款中就已明确提出来，要求制定或采取办法酌情管制、管理或控制由生物技术改变的活生物(LMO或GMO)在使用和释放时可能产生的危险，即可能对环境产生不利影响，从而影响到生物多样性的保护和持续利用，也要考虑到对人类健康的危险。对环境产生不利的影响，包括了对农田生态系统的影响，以及自然生态系统的影响，影响是多方面的，我们已有文章报道(钱迎倩等，1998)，在Kjellsson(1997)的基础上列了表1。

表1中所列的不少是生态风险，转基因作物因为是人工制造的品种，我们可以把这些品种看作为自然界原来不存在的外来种。一般说来，外来种对环境或生物多样性造成威胁或危险会有一段较长的时间。有时需10年的时间，或更长的时间。转基因作物商品化种植至今最长也就是5~6年的时间，一些潜在危险在这么短的时间内不一定能表现出来。可是有些风险在实验室水平上已经证实。如Mikkelsen等证实抗除草剂转基因油菜的抗除草剂基因可以通过基因流在一次杂交、一次回交的过程已转到其野生近缘种中(Mikkelsen *et al.*,1996)。这就是表中所指出的在农田生态系统中可能产生新的农田杂草。没有预料到的是转基因作物自身变为杂草成为现实的时间来得如此之快。根据2001年8月的报道，在加拿大主要的转基因作物是耐除草剂的GM油菜，但它们正在变成杂草。农民们正在与他们农田里的一种新的有害植物作斗争。因为在他们农田里已出现了未种植过的GM油菜，而这种植物能抗常规使用的除草剂，要杀死它们还比较困难。曼尼托巴大学的植物科学家Martin Entz说，“GM油菜传播的速度要比我们想到的要快很多，而要控制它是绝对不可能的”。加拿大食品检验署已劝告农民们用另外的药剂来杀死他们。可是其他的药剂能把农民种的作物杀死，在某些情况下，GM油菜对这些药剂却具有抗性。这些GM油菜真正成为所谓的“超级杂草”。

再举一个例子是GMOs对生物多样性的影响。Losey等(Losey *et al.*,1999)的实验结果在*Nature*上发表后引起了很大的轰动。他们在实验室中用加有Bt玉米花粉的马利筋叶片来喂饲大斑蝶幼虫，加普通玉米花粉及不加玉米花粉的马利筋叶片作为对照，结果说明喂饲加有Bt玉米花粉的马利筋的幼虫第二天死亡10%以上，4天后死亡44%，而对照全部存活。此外，对加有Bt玉米花粉的马利筋摄取量小，幼虫生长缓慢，重量只有喂饲无花粉叶片的幼虫的一半。从另外一角度也可能威胁大斑蝶的生存，在无转基因抗除草剂作物前，除草剂一般只能在作物种子萌发前喷洒一次。在种植抗除草剂作物后，就可在作物生长期多次喷洒除草剂，杀死杂草而对作物无威胁，随着多次除草剂的喷洒，马利筋就大量减少。由于大斑蝶的惟一的食物是马利筋，随着马利筋大量减少，也就威胁到大斑蝶的物种的生存。大斑蝶是一种非常漂亮的蝴蝶，深受美国人民的喜爱。还有另外几个对生物多样性造成威胁的例子，已在另外文章中报道了(钱迎倩等，2001)。GMOs对环境的其他方面影响，我们也作过报道(钱迎倩、马克平，1998)，国际上近年来普遍重视生物安全的研究工作，随着时间的推延，会不断有新的报道。

表 1 转基因植物释放到环境后潜在的风险

对环境有害的影响		造成影响的过程
农田生态系统 Agro-ecosystem	增加杀虫剂的使用	抗性的选择和转运到可相容的其他植物中
	产生新的农田杂草	基因流和杂交
	转基因植物自身变为杂草	插入性状的竞争
	产生新的病毒	不同病毒基因组和转基因作物的病毒外壳蛋白的重组
	产生新的作物害虫	病原体——植物相互作用 食草动物——植物相互作用
	对非目标生物的伤害	食草动物的误食
自然生态系统 Natural ecosystem	侵入到新的栖息地	花粉和种子的传播 干扰 竞争
	丧失物种的遗传多样性	基因流和杂交 竞争
	对非目标物种的伤害	改变了互惠共生关系
	生物多样性的丧失	竞争 环境的胁迫 增加的影响(基因、种群、物种)
	营养循环和地球化学过程的改变	与非生物环境的相互作用 (如转基因植物与 N_2 固定系统)
	初级生产力的改变	改变了物种的组成
	增加了土壤流失	增加的影响(与环境、物种组成的相互作用)

顺便也要提到关于对人体健康问题，据报道，美国市场上已有千种以上的食品是从GM作物来源的，因为至今还没有一个实验证据证明被政府批准作商品化种植的GM产物对人身健康造成危害。即使这种情况，美国农业部对某些GM产物还不允许作为人类的食物，只能作为牲口饲料。2000年美国曾发生一事件，StarLink公司培育的抗虫的Bt玉米，农业部担心一部分人可能对这种玉米内含有Cry9C蛋白质而引起过敏反应，因此只允许作为动物饲料。但是StarLink公司却把这种玉米出售给生产人类食品的工厂，从而在杂货店的食品架上就出现了含转基因玉米成分的煎玉米卷、玉米点心和其他玉米食品。美国农业部发现后，不仅迫使这些食品从货架上收回，把去年生产的所有玉米都作为转基因玉米来处理。因为转基因玉米的价格要比常规玉米的低，因此造成种植常规玉米的农民及中间商蒙受损失，也影响到整个玉米出口量下降。

上面提到法国食品安全机构在普通玉米种子种已检测到转基因物质，其含量通常不超过0.1%，安全机构负责人声称，“食用这些谷类生产的食品对消费者造成危险的可能性非常小”。

3 拟采取的对策

生物技术这门高新技术在解决医药、农业、环境等各个方面问题确实是一条重要的途径，并会带来巨大的经济效益和社会效益，这一点是不容置疑的。但 GMOs 对环境及人体健康的安全性也是不能忽视的。UNDP《2001 年人类发展报告》呼吁，人们应对基因改良生物的长期影响做进一步研究，并提倡对基因改良产品做标记，以便使顾客做出知情的选择。《报告》并指出，生物技术和食品安全问题往往是政策欠妥、法规不当和缺乏透明度的结果。

提出下列几点对策：

(1) 2001 年 5 月 23 日国务院总理朱镕基签署第 304 号中华人民共和国国务院令，公布了《农业转基因生物安全管理条例》，规定了国务院农业行政主管部门负责全国农业转基因生物安全的监督管理工作，并建立农业转基因生物安全部际联席会议制度；还规定列入农业转基因生物目录的农业转基因生物，由生产、分装单位和个人负责标识、未标识的，不得销售。农业转基因生物标识应当载明产品中含有转基因成分的主要原料名称等等。《条例》的颁布，为转基因作物及其产品的安全使用打下了重要的基础。下一步有两个重要的工作可能应该重视的，一个是转基因作物的安全问题涉及的部门多，部门之间的合作与协调是一个重要而复杂的问题；第二个是宣传、教育、贯彻落实问题，转基因作物将涉及到广大农民，目前中国农民对什么是转基因作物、转基因作物可能带来的潜在风险，为什么要采取标识制度等等方面的教育十分重视。

(2) 切实加强生物安全的科学研究工作。发达国家，尤其是欧洲一些国家，在生物安全方面较早就开展了研究，而中国在这方面还处于刚起步或尚未开始的阶段。对农田及自然生态系统中一系列的生态风险的研究如何起步，如何切入，得到的结果往往既有正面效应、又有负面影响。对此又如何作分析等等一系列问题有待研究。在对人体健康影响问题，可能与生态效应一样，得到结论有一个时间问题。可能在短期内得不到结论。这些问题都是在考虑生物安全科研时可供思考的问题。

(3) 提高粮食产量，解决饥饿问题有一个创新的问题。前面已经肯定，转基因技术是解决粮食短缺的一条重要途径，但应该说不是唯一的途径。中国育种家袁隆平培育出来的“超级稻”最高亩产可达 1139kg，他的杂交水稻提高的产量可解决 5000 万人的吃饭问题。因此研究新的提高粮食产量及品质的途径，走创新之路是非常重要的。

(4) 切实加强正确的全民宣传活动。尤其要注意媒体的报道。2000 年 12 月，北京一个发行量很大的媒体作了如下的报道，题目为“本报记者驱车百余里，寻找转基因草”。记者在北京近郊见到 6.67hm^2 由某农业科技有限公司从美国引进的转基因草，在宣传这草的一系列优点外，最后一句话是：“转基因，让小草也‘疯狂’。”这里最少有两个问题：一是任何转基因植物种植这么大面积，必须经过政府有关部门的批准，可报道上并未提到一点；二是我们虽然不知道这种转基因草是什么种，它在北京近郊是否有亲缘关系很近的近缘种？一旦这种小草真的“疯狂”起来，上面我们提到的加拿大转基因油菜问题很快在北京近郊就会发生，有可能通过种子传播到大量的农田里成为杂草，如有近缘种，还可能通过杂交，让本来不是杂草的近缘种也到处“疯狂”起来。

(5) 不能让中国的大地成为发达国家的实验场所。现在在一些发达国家，虽然进行大量的生物技术，包括 GMOs 的研究，但不允许作商品化的种植。如挪威等欧洲一些国家，GMOs 作商品化种植要经过国王或国会的批准。目前国际上实验室已经成功的转基因作物是大量的，但真正被各国政府批准能作商品化种植的还极少。已有迹象表明一些发达国家通过各种途径把实验室的成果拿到中国来作大田试验，甚至大面积的种植，而我们多数人还缺乏这方面的知识。上述“转基因草”可能是一个很好的双方都愿意接受的例子。但如果大面积种植后真出现严重的生态负效应，后果将不可收拾。

参考文献

Farre, E. M *et al.* 2001. Acceleration of potato tuber sprouting by the expression of a bacterial pyrophosphatase, ***Nature Biotec***., 19(3): 268~272

Losey, J. E. *et al.* 1999. Transgenic pollen harms monarch larvae. ***Nature***, 399: 214

Mikkelsen, T. R. *et al*. 1996. The risk of crop transgene spread. ***Nature***, 380: 31

Pena, L. *et al*. 2001. Constitutive expresson of *Arabidopsis* leafy or APETALA, genes in citrus reduces their generation time. ***Nature Biotec***., 19(3): 263~267

钱迎倩, 马克平. 1998. 经遗传修饰生物体的研究进展及其释放后对环境的影响. 生态学报, 18(1): 1~9

钱迎倩, 田　彦, 魏　伟. 1998. 转基因植物的生态风险评价. 植物生态学报, 22(4): 289~299

钱迎倩, 魏　伟, 桑卫国, 马克平. 2001. 转基因作物对生物多样性的影响. 生态学报, 21(3): 337~343

本文原载：植物生态学报. 1998. 22(4): 289-299

转基因植物的生态风险评价

钱迎倩[1]　田彦[2]　魏伟[3]

(1 中科学院植物研究所；2 中国科学院基础研究所；3 中国农业大学生物技术系)

摘　要　自从 1983 年第一株转基因植物诞生以来，至今各种类型的转基因植物进入大田试验的已不计其数，近 10 种转基因作物的产物已经商品化。与此同时，转基因植物向环境释放后可能带来的生态风险问题也越来越受到人们的重视。关于转基因植物的生态风险或对环境的危害，科学家提出了不同的概念和测试方法。生态毒理学的经验以及 80 年代发展起来的，为作环境决策用的生态风险评价的经验可以借鉴以作转基因植物生态风险的评价。本文介绍了转基因植物对农田生态系统和自然生态系统可能带来的危害以及从基因、基因组、个体、种群以至生态系统等各级水平上危害测试的方法。对风险的判断作了详细的论述，对风险的管理也作了概略的介绍，并对生态风险评价当前发展的水平进行了讨论。

关键词　转基因植物；大田试验；生态学风险评价

20 世纪 70 年代，科学家已经成功地从生物体中鉴定和分离特有的基因，把它们增强并插入到其他生物体的遗传物质中去，从而改变这些生物体的遗传组成，这就是重组 DNA 技术。自从 1983 年第一株转基因植物诞生以来，世界上各种类型的植物进入大田试验的已不计其数，如种子、果实、叶片等等转基因作物的产物已经作为商品上市的至少已有 10 种，这些在前面的文章中以作过报道(钱迎倩，1995；1997；钱迎倩等，1998)。说明了基因工程飞跃的发展,并已向人们展示了其在解决 21 世纪人类所面临挑战中的潜力。另一方面，也就在重组 DNA 技术发展的早期，另外一些科学家就提出对这一技术潜在的生物学和生态学的风险，以及一旦释放到环境中去后可能带来的潜在危险，因此要对重组 DNA 技术进行生态风险评价问题早就提出来了(Colwell，1994；Rissler *et al.*,1993；Tiedje *et al.*，1989)。

美国自从 1994 年第一次批准延迟成熟的转基因番茄上市以来到 1997 年底，转基因植物或产物已经出现了各种各样的问题。例如，到 1997 年，转基因番茄在市场上已经消失，其原因是目前的产品还是经受不了采、收、包装及运输的整个过程，很多番茄在到目的地时已经软化或碰伤，失去了商品的价值；另一方面是推出来的品种在生长的地区，其产量及抗病性状上都达不到商品的要求。能抗两种病毒的转基因黄色弯颈南瓜是 1995 年被批准上市的，但就是当年出售了少量种子，1996 年就不再出售。据开发这种转基因南瓜的公司发言人说，在培育出能抗 3 种病毒前，这种南瓜种子暂时停止出售。美国 Monsanto 公司开发的耐除草剂甘膦转基因油菜中的一个品种推销到加拿大，由于种子繁殖时质量控制失败而未被加拿大权威机构批准上市。上述涉及到的问题，可能是工作上的失误或者研究的结果还未能到达商品化程度，这些问题的本身可能并不构成生态风险或对环境或人类健康的威胁。

此外，Monsanto 公司培育的抗虫转基因棉花 1995 年被批准为商品化，商品名为 Boll-gard，1996 年种植面积达 80 万 hm^2，占美国全国棉花种植面积的 12%。但其中有 800hm^2 遭到失败，出现了大量存活的棉铃虫，一些科学家认为，这一结果会使棉铃虫能耐这种毒素,加速了昆虫的抗药性。Monsanto 公司开发的另一种商品名为 Roundup Ready 的抗除草剂草甘膦转基因棉花，1996 年被批准商品化，1997 年第一年大规模种植。到秋季时，在棉花产区 Delta 地区这种转基因棉花在收获前大量出现落铃或畸形棉桃，面积达 1.2 万 hm^2。有人认为棉桃脱落和畸形的问题是由于“基因走向疯狂”，并认为除草剂草甘膦可能已进入到种子内，而其中有一部分种子还正在作食用油利用。此外，转基因植物还可能出现其他一系列生态风险，这些在早些时候的文章中已作过报道①(钱迎倩，1994；钱迎倩等，1995；闻大中，1992)。因此，从安全的角度，从风险管理的角度，对转基因作物进行生态风险评估是完全必要的。

1 对环境影响或生态风险的概念

本文主要介绍由 Goy 和 Duesing(1996)提出的“潜在的环境影响”的概念和由 Kjells-son(1997)介绍的“风险”概念。虽然对 Goy 等提出的概念已遭到反对，下文将专门会对此作评论，但还是值得提出来供参考的。Kjellsson 介绍的概念似乎比较成熟，本文将作重点介绍。

1.1 Goy 等提出的“潜在的环境影响”概念

Goy 等认为转基因植物的释放或作大田试验，对环境最主要的潜在的负影响是基因转移到野生近缘种中去，为之列于下列的公式.即：

转移的可能性 × 转移的结果=潜在的环境影响

这里,“转移的可能性”是根据作物生殖特性，存在潜在的与野生近缘种有性可育性，这些野生近缘种的种群密度以及种子的持久性。他们根据欧洲的情况，参考了 Raybould 等(1994)的分类法，把作物分成 3 个组：第Ⅰ组诗“与野生近缘种的基因流有最小的可能性”，这组的作物有例如马铃薯、烟草和玉米，它们或者是没有野生近缘种，或者与它们的野生近缘种是有性不育的；第Ⅱ组是“与野生近缘种基因流有低的可能性”，如栽培作物中的油菜与莴苣，在同一地理区域里与野生近缘种有性可育性是有限的；第Ⅲ组则是“与野生近缘种基因流有高的可能性”，如甜菜、苜蓿和杨树，与附近的野生近缘种具生殖可育性。他们把“转移的后果”的含义定为工程遗传性状如果一旦转移了，根据通过授予野生近缘种选择有利性(Selective advantage)而提高竞争性的潜在能力大小，按此

① 钱迎倩、马克平，1998：有关经遗传修饰生物体的讨论(待发表)。

又分为三类：第一类是性状授予的有利性很小，称为“最小有利性类”，这一类例如标记基因和授予的是不利的性状。例如雄性不育或延长成熟的；第二类又基于是否具选择压而又分为两个亚类；有选择压的称为“第二类 b”，其中包括有对虫害、病害、病毒和胁迫的抗性；没有选择压的称为“第二类 a”，如具耐除草剂性状；而第三类则是称“高的有利性类”，包括的形状有促进生长和成活的状况，这种性状在任何条件下可授与一种有利性。潜在的环境影响就是转移的可能性与转移的结果的积。

1.2 Kjellsson 的“危险”概念

在环境科学研究中或在作环境决策时，从 80 年代开始生态风险评价就是经常被利用的一种手段，如在生态毒理学中很多涉及到有毒化合物释放后对环境的风险。这些经验或其方法学在一定程度上可以借用来作转基因植物释放后潜在生态风险的分析。Kjellsson 就借用了有毒化合物释放后对环境风险的概念而列出了下列的公式，即：

$$\text{风险}=\text{发生的事件}\times\text{危险}$$

这里“发生的事件”是指着会引起伤害的事件发生的概率；而“危险”是指着对环境具有负后果的影响，或者说是受伤害的总的情况。他把“风险”定义为“将成为现实的一种危险的结果所造成损害的潜势”。因此，用于转基因植物时，对其作生态风险评价时有两个中心问题：一个是转基因植物或其后代是否会让环境受到危险；二是转基因物质是否会转到其他生物体中去，而这些生物又可能使环境受到危险。

2 生态风险判断的程序

按照 Kjellsson 的概念，我们首先要对危险与发生的事故进行分析。从这两方面分析的结果再进行影响的分析。根据上述各方面的分析以及与收集到的必要的资料进行综合，就可能对生态风险有一个比较正确的判断。

2.1 危险分析

已有不少文献专门讨论了转基因作物向环境释放后可能存在的潜在危险，例如由于插入的基因(如抗除草剂基因等)通过花粉或种子传播造成的基因流而产生了新的杂草；或者转基因作物由于插入了某些性状在一定的时空条件下本身可能变为杂草；作为生物反应器以生产药物的转基因作物被食草动物的误食；以及营养循环和地球化学过程的改变等等方面可能对农田生态系统或自然生态系统造成各种危险。有关这方面已发表过大量的报道，也召开过多次国际会议。在 90 年代才兴起的学科“分子生态学”，以它来命名 1992 年才创刊的杂志，在 1994 年第 3 卷中有一期专刊为“转基因植物释放的生态影响”国际会议的论文集(Burke *et al.*，1994)。我们综合了其他有关文献，在表 1 上相当全面地列出了转基因植物释放到农田生态系统及自然生态系统中后可能带来的影响以及对造成影响的过程进行分析(见表 1)。

表 1　转基因植物释放到环境后潜在的风险[1]

Table 1　Ecological risks brought about by the release of transgenic plants

对环境有害的影响 Harmful effects on the environment		造成影响的过程 Affecting Processes
农田生态系统 Agro-Ecosystem	增加杀虫剂的使用	抗性的选择和运输到可兼容植物中
	产生新的农田杂草	基因流和杂交
	转基因植物自身变为杂草	插入性状的竞争
	产生新的病毒	不同病毒基因组和蛋白质衣壳的转衣壳
	产生新的作物害虫	病原体-植物相互作用 食草动物-植物相互作用
	对非目标生物的伤害	食草动物的误食
自然生态系统[2] Natural Ecosystem	侵入到新的栖息地	花粉和种子的传播 失调[3] 竞争[3]
	丧失物种的遗传多样性	基因流和杂交 竞争[3]
	对非目标物种的伤害	改变了互惠共生关系
	生物多样性的丧失	竞争[3] 环境的胁迫 增加的影响(基因、种群、物种)
	营养循环和地球化学过程的改变	与非生物环境的相互作用[3] (如转基因植物与 N_2 固定系统)
	初级生产力的改变	改变了物种的组成[3]
	增加了土壤流失	增加的影响(与环境、物种组成的相互作用)

① 此表是综合了文献 Falk et al. (1994). Kjellsson(1997), 钱迎倩等(1988)而成 Based on related papers-Falk *et al*., 1994; Kjellsson, 1997; Qian Y. Q. *et al*., 1988.

② 在自然生态系统中的影响在农田生态系统中也会发生 Including those effects mentioned in Agro-eccsyseems.

③ 详细的可参考文献 Kjellsson 等(1994)和 Kjellsson 等(1997)) For details see Kjellsson's (1994; 1997a).

由于 Kjellsson 的概念是从生态毒理学借鉴来的。生态毒理学上有一个终端定义(Endpoint defintiton),“终端”这个术语含义是涉及到变量(Viariables)的评价，这变量是用于各种影响的测定。在生态毒理学实验中是用死亡率程度(LD_{50})、作用浓度(EC)以及没有观察到的作用浓度(NOEC)，以这些来测定生物体的生存、生长和繁殖等生活史的形状。而把终端定义，或者说测定影响的变量用于转基因植物的风险评价时，其内容可包括：适合度(Fitness)的测定(例如，生存、生物量累积和结籽)，种群增加速度，在某个定植转基因植物栖息地中的遗传多样性或生物多样性等等。

在危险分析中，还应该对环境进行描述。在这里的环境指的是将要作为转基因植物释放的地方，或者转基因植物可能入侵的栖息地。对环境要从下列有关方面进行描述：栖息地类型、转基因植物释放的范围、当地的生物多样性(动、植物)、植被覆盖密度、自然或人为干扰情况、主要的相互过程(食草动物、传粉者-植物、竞争关系)以及气候和土壤条件等方面进行描述。生物体之间相互作用的反馈环在一定程度上决定生态系统的稳定性，尤其对关键种的干扰将会使一连串的物种受到影响，因此必须要考虑到环境风险评价中去。

在生态毒理学中有一个“源条件”(Source terms)的问题，这是指着一种化学物质释放的时间和空间格局，例如一种杀虫剂从某一种点源的喷施或散发。这种释放条件的概念放在转基因植物的风险评价上时，可以包括下列的内容：释放的地点、释放的数量和覆盖的面积、转基因植物的量、释放的时间等等。这些信息如果已经在有关数据库或地理信息系统(GIS)中的话、则转基因的转移和杂交等潜在的风险可能可以掌握得更为有效。

2.2 发生事件的分析

在生态毒理学作化学物质的风险评价时，对人及动、植物的目标种和非目标的伤害的情况是风险评价的主要内容。对伤害分析的主要涉及到化学物质分布的途径、通过生态系统后化学物质的降解的整个过程所需的时间。而对转基因植物而言，发生的事件的概念涉及到的因子有如基因转移、杂交和植物是否分布到新的区域内，也就是入侵能力。这就意味着转基因植物一次释放后，插入基因逃逸的可能性以及在环境中这些植物和插入性状的最后的命运。因此，为基因转移、传播和入侵建立模型对预测入侵能力是会有价值的。上述因子主要对大田试验时为阻止基因扩散作安全测量时是重要的，而在作商业化释放的风险评价时，Kajeiva 等(1994)提出逃逸的可能性要接近于 1，并必须要长期的监测其对环境的负效应。

2.3 影响分析

生态毒理学作影响分析时要定量地去分析有害物质的伤害增加程度，例如进行剂量-反应关系的分析。进行生态风险评价的影响分析，有些报道主要集中在物种水平上做的，可是还应该在种群和生态系统水平上来作分析，这样做或许更有用。表 2 列出了在不同层次上对转基因植物的测试项目以及有关的实验方法。

表 2 不同层次上对转基因植物的测试项目及实验方法①

Table 2 Items and methods for measuring transgenic plants at different levels

层次 Level	测试项目 Measuring items	实验方法② Testing methods
基因和基因组 Gene and genome	染色体结构的改变	基因图构成 核型分析：染色体数、大小和形式
	插入检测、遗传标记 (标记基因)	形态特性分析 多聚酶链式反应(PCR) Southern 和 Northern 杂交

续表

层 次 Level	测试项目 Measuring items	实验方法[2] Testing methods
个 体 Individual	异花授粉，自花授粉	在柱头上的花粉：花粉数和捻性 种子发育分析 空间自相关分析
	交配系统，不亲和性	(Diallel 杂交)双列杂交 实验授粉 花粉萌发试验
	传粉者活性	传粉者吸引力：化学提示，直观提示 传粉者觅食行为
	植物竞争	叶面积 相对生长速度 2 个物种混合物
种 Population	种群动态，补充 (Recruitment)	萌发试验 半存留期 Leslie 矩阵模型 种子埋藏处理 有效种群-大小 Ne
	花粉传播	父系(来源)分析 花粉计数 花粉收集 花粉生活力试验
	基因流，杂交，渐渗	扩增片段长度多型性(AFLP) DNA 测序 F-统计 单模标本统计 减数分裂分析：染色体配对和重组 形态特性分析 蛋白质电泳：同功酶分析 随机扩增多型性 DNA(RAPD) 限制性片段长度多态性(RFLP)
	遗传稳定性，遗传多样性，遗传漂变，非亲缘交配	适合性测量 遗传距离 遗传领域-大小 (Genetic neighbourhood-size) 自交和非亲缘交配率
生态系统 Ecosystem	入侵，入侵能力	生物地理测定和监测 地区适应分析 外来植物的繁殖 移植实验
	生物多样性，群落结构	多样性指标 取样程序；植被分析 空间格局分析

① 引自文献 Kjellsson(1997)。 Cited from Kjellsson(1997).

② 具体测定方法在文献 kjellsson 等(1994)及 kjellsson 等(1997)上都有详细说明。 Detailed descriptions could be seen in kjellsson *et al*.(1994; 1997).

2.3.1 个体水平的试验

个体水平的试验一般是在实验室里或温室里进行。不管是化学物质或转基因植物的毒性试验已在一些容易培养的如藻类、弹尾目昆虫和小鼠上已做过了。从单个物种试验所得到的数据，用各种统计的方法推断到属一级或更高的分类级别上去，这样做应该要很小心。个体水平风险分析可测量传粉者的活性、花粉传播、异花或自花授粉、基因流、杂交以及植物竞争等项目。因此可把转基因植物在竞争能力，胁迫耐受情况以及繁殖产量等方面与正常的非转基因植物来作比较。

2.3.2 种群水平的试验

进行一些发育试验和种群大小波动试验(包括建模)可以提供影响分析有价值的参数。表 2 中指出的测试项目如种群动态、补充、交配系统、遗传多样性、遗传稳定性、遗传漂变和渐渗都是重要的。

一个物种能成功地入侵到一个群落中去的阈值是要求种群的繁殖率>1，如果一种转基因植物已获得选择有利性，则将有利于其入侵力。在一个已知的群落中繁殖率代表了物种的竞争能力、耐胁迫和繁殖成功的一个总的量度。

2.3.3 生态系统水平试验

除非事先已采取了严格的预防措施，并特别小心，从环境保护角度出发并不希望在某个生态系统中做实验，可是在这里做实验却可为风险评价提供最直接和整套的信息。有关物种相互作用和生态系统的反应的信息很有用，但这些数据却很难分析、因为太复杂了、何况每年在时空上都有变化。因此尽可能在一个能有较高程度控制条件下的生态系统里来做试验，近代发展了一种微型或中等水平宇宙(Mesocosm)的控制系统，已被用来作为陆生生态系统中植物生命活动观察和测试的场所。(Kjellsson，1997；Stokey *et al.*,1994)。受控环境设施(CEFs)已被用作于研究陆生生态系统的环境改变，并来模拟在生态系统过程中影响生物多样性的丧失(Lawton，1995)。用 CEFs 做转基因植物的试验是昂贵的，但是可能的。在大田中做转基因植物与非转基因植物的比较试验，把它们种在不同类型的生境中就可得到所需要的数据。当然作大田试验可能会要某些安全措施，而有些安全措施又可能使植物的生命活动难以表现或难以收集数据。

2.3.4 等级试验系统

Kjellsson(1997)把生态风险分析的程序分为三个层次，也即第一层分析是基于对生物体可用的一些资料或从文献上收集的资料，例如亲缘关系、插入性状与生活史等等。第二层次是基于基因、个体及种群试验得到的数据，而第三层次的数据是从生态系统试验中得到的。因此第一层次的信息主要是定性的，而第二、第三层次的数据是定量的。每一个层次只要信息或者数据足够时，都可以作出“否定”或“接受”的决策。当不够时再往下做下去。当然这里有一个决策标准的问题，在定量测试时，转基因植物与非转基因植物比较在统计学上无重大的偏离，这才是“安全”的，如果转基因植物与非转基因植物的测试值相等，或在同一实验条件下转基因植物表现得稍好一些，这就没有价值。

一般的舆论都认为重要的是对转基因植物风险评价有一个长期影响的资料。当然，多少年才算是长期的界限的限定是困难的，一般认为 5~10 年可能是合适的，然而，这要根据转基因植物的生活周期和当地环境的演替速率，Parker 等(1996)提出为转基因植物的释放要求建立一个检测程序，包括例如转基因植物的扩散、转基因向野生近缘种的转移以及可能引起生态系统的改变等等。转基因植物向各种作物的起源中心释放时(如南美的马铃薯)应该特别考虑到成杂草种的直接影响以及对原始基因库的长期保护的影响。

2.3.5 影响机理的鉴别

欧洲的“环境和自然栖息地保护和管理执行委员会”1992 年时有一个文件，题目是“经遗传修饰生物体的生态影响，文献、指南和法规的概论”(CDPE，1992)内容中涉及到发生过一次危险后，是可能进行对生态系统影响机理的鉴别的，他们称之回顾性的风险评价。从事这样鉴别可从下列三个层次上来进行：a.摸清形成这些影响的生态学的相互作用；b.摸清形成生态学相互作用的生物体的表型或生理特征；c.摸清导致生物体表型或生理特性的遗传特性。这种从 c~a 的倒顺序的鉴别将可应用到正常的、预测性的风险评价上去。很多生物学案例支持了这样的观点。

2.4 风险的判断

根据发生事件可能性的数据和从转基因植物释放的影响试验得到的数据，参考着表 3 列出的有关资料或数据，对风险进行判断。

表 3 作转基因植物生态风险评价所需要的背景资料和试验数据[①]

Table 3 Review data and test data needed for evaluating ecological risks brought about by transgenic plants

涉及的方面 Aspects	要求的资料 Data needed
受体生物体(植物)	遗传组成 分类学 进化历史 生活史特性 竞争能力(杂草化) 授粉和基因转移 繁殖 移植和栖息地选择
转基因(插入的性状)	性状的类型
生物技术方法和稳定性	技术的精确度 所用生物载体的本质 拷贝数和位点数
转基因植物	插入基因的表达(表型) 转基因产物或代谢的毒性 改变了的生活史特性

续表

涉及的方面 Aspects	要求的资料 Data needed
考虑释放的条件	位置的特性 性状设计 限制措施
转基因的命运	基因转移和杂交 种子传播和存活(种子库，Seed bank) 种群的建立
生态学的影响	见表 1

① 此表引自 Kjellsson(1997)。 The table was cited from kjellsson(1997).

2.4.1 背景资料和试验数据

表 3 是总结了作物转基因植物生态风险评价时所要求的背景资料和试验数据。这些条目是从工业、研究和特殊环境风险分析中总结出来的，并已成为一些发达国家的权威机构对大田试验和商业性释放作决策的依据。

2.4.2 影响的概率和程度

把上述各方面的资料与数据综合起来，才可能搞清风险的特性和作出影响程度的判断。这就需要用描述和用图解或模型的形式来表示发生事件的影响间或者事件和影响间的关系。风险常常用或然率的术语来表达，虽然这种表达的方式是理想的，但常常难以做到，特别是如对生态系统的影响这一类复杂的情况下作分析时更难做到。然而，并入一些主要参数来做模型可能可用来包括随机成分在内的危险程度的判断。

3 生态风险的管理

生态风险管理的目的是希望转基因植物释放后把危险能减小到最小，因此风险管理应包括在决策中。管理涉及到社会问题，实践时的谨慎态度以及恢复措施。在一些发达国家，他们不仅从科学上考虑问题，还从公众的娱乐活动、美学价值等方面来评价，而这些方面还要平衡地来考虑。分析程序中还可能要包括价值-惠益(Cost-benefit)，因此风险管理者与风险分析者科学家之间需要有很好的交流。

转基因植物作大田释放的风险管理应涉及到两个主要问题：一是按已知的生物体和插入的性状，要有相应的使用安全条件；二是在作试验期间和试验后的有效的监测程序。在做基础研究及转基因植物培育过程中，应考虑到防止危险的程序。对大田试验的要求，经济合作与发展组织(OECD)根据过去的经验制定了一些该组织成员要共同遵守的原则(Teso，1993)。这些原则涉及到根据生物体特性，研究地点和好的实验条件的设计所要求的安全因素等。

4 讨论

科学家之间对问题的认识往往是很不一致的，对问题分析的结论也不同，甚至有很大的差别。本文前面介绍的，按 Giba-Geigy 公司的 Goy 和 Pioneer H;-Bred 公司的 Duesing 的定义和方法，对 1993 年前在欧洲进行的 391 次大田试验作了分析，得出了如下的结论：在 391 次大田试验中，91%的试验对环境无潜在影响，如果有也是最小的，而余下的 9%的试验对环境只有低的潜在影响。文章发表后反应非常迅速，3 个月后在同一杂志上两位丹麦科学家就提出了可认为是彻底否定的见解。其中一位是 Aarhus 大学生态和遗传系的 Landbo 和 Risϕ 国家实验室植物遗传部的 Mikkelsen(1996)。首先，他们反对 Goy 等把油菜放在“低的转移可能性”一类里。因为 Jϕrgensen 等(1994)的实验已经证实，当大田的油菜附近有杂草近缘种 *Brassica campestris* 时，萌发的后代种子中，有 93%证实是种间杂种，说明了人们对作物和野生近缘种基因交换的知识还是很不足的。甚至在基因交换很少发生的情况下，进化的历史告诉我们，低的转移可能性确确实实是在发生的，并有很大的影响。它们还对 Goy 等的分析，没有把转基因杂种和转基因野生近缘种区别开来，认为这就涉及到对渐渗这一术语的理解问题。

对 Goy 等提出的“转移的后果”，Landbo 等认为我们对这个问题还缺乏知识，还不了解是什么因子限制了野生近缘种的分布。因此，很难预言一个特殊基因转移到一个野生近缘种去后将会有哪些预料不到的生态学后果。他们也反对 Goy 等对侵入力(Invasiveness)问题的预言，因为 Bergelson(1994)的研究说明，具产生劣质种子基因型的拟南芥菜可以令人惊讶地像一个野生型基因型同样地侵入到自然栖息地中去。对 Goy 等把对昆虫、病害、病毒和胁迫等抗性列入到“低有利性类”里表示不能理解。最后，对 Goy 等把一种严重后果与一种极少转移可能性的结合，其结果都是对环境极小的潜在影响的解释也表示异议。以上的例子似乎向人们提示了下面两点：在公司工作的科研人员与在国家研究室和大学工作的科研人员，他们对科学问题的认识是不一致的；在实验分析时，从起始的指导思想、分类或取样的不一致，最后可以得出截然相反的结论。

正如本文一开始就提出来的，从重组 DNA 这项技术提出来开始，就有生物学家提出其对环境问题可能的风险，随着技术的成熟，在短短近 20 年时间内，重组 DNA 的成果已在医学、药物、农业等等方面得到了应用。与此同时，像转基因植物释放后对环境造成的生态风险评价问题，从理论上、概念上直到方法学上，在国际上也都已有了相应的发展。评价已发展到从分子、个体、种群、群落直到生态系统的水平。本文就当前在这方面的进展作一综述，显然对我们在开展转基因作物的评价研究，在思想方法上及具体操作上都有很好的参考价值。但是是否可以认为，目前的进展从理论上或概念上已经相对地成熟，但在方法学及对结果的分析上还有待进一步完善，尤其是在生态系统水平上，因为生态系统是一个非常复杂的系统，应该抓住哪些主要的参数还有待摸索。人们对大自然还远远没有认识，有些问题由于人们的知识所限，还未被认识到，这些都有待于今后进一步的研究。

参考文献

钱迎倩, 1994, 生物多样性与生物技术, 中国科学院院刊, 2: 134~138

钱迎倩(钱迎倩、马克平主编), 1995. 生物技术与生物多样性的保护和持续利用, 生物多样性研究的原理与方法, 北京: 中国科学技术出版社, 217~224

钱迎倩、马克平, 1995. 生物技术与生物安全, 自然资源学报, 10(4): 322~331

钱迎倩(蒋志刚等主编)、1997. 生物安全. 保护生物学，杭州：浙江科学技术出版社, 168~175

钱迎倩、马克平, 1998. 经遗传修饰生物体的研究进展及其释放后对环境的影响. 生态学报, 18(1): 1~9

闻大中，1992. 基因工程生物的生态影响及其评价，应用生态学报, 3(4): 371~377

Bergelson J., 1994, Changes in fecandity do not predict inrasireness: A model study of transgenic plants. Ecology. 75(1): 245~252

Burke T, *et al*., 1994. Ecological implications of transgenic plant release. Mol Ecol., 1~89

Colwell R. K., 1994, Potential ecological and evolutionary problems of introducing transgenic crops into the environment. In: *Biosafety for sustainable agriculiure*: Sharing biotechnology regulatory experiences of the western hemisphere. (eds. by Krattiger, A. F.*et al*.), ISAAA &. SEI. Stockholm, 33~46

CDPE., 1992, Ecological impact of genetically modified organisms. A survey of literature. guidelines and legislation. Steering committee for the conservation and management of the enviroment and natural habitat. *Council of Europe*, Strasbourg, 1~89

Falk B. W. *et al*., 1994, Will transgenic crops. generate new viruses and new diseases? *Science*, 263: 1395

Goy P, A. &. Duesing J. H.. 1996. Assessing the environmental impact of gene transfer to wild relatives. *Bio/Tech*. 14: 39~40

JØrgensen R. B. &. Andersen B., 1994, Spontaneous hybridization between oilseed rape (*Brassica napus*) and weedy B. *Campestris* (Btsddivsvrsr): A risk of growing genetically modified oilseed rape. Amer. *J. Bet*. 81, 1620~1626

Kareiva P. & Stark L., 1994: Environmental risks in agricultural biotechnology. *Chem. Ind*. (London). 2: 52~55

Kjellsson G. & Simonsson V. 1994. *Methods for risk. asessment of transgenic plants*. I. Competition. establishment and ecosystem effects. Brikhauser Verlag. 1~214

Kjellsson G., 1997, Principles and procedures for ecological risk assessment of transgenic plants. In: *Methods. for risk assessmtent of transgenic plants*. II. Pollination. gene · tran.sfer and population impacts. (eds. by Kjellsson, G. *el al*.) Bnkhauser Velag. 221-237

Kjellsson G. *et al*., 1997, *Methods. for risk assessment of transgenic plants*. II. Polination. transfer and population impacts. Brikhauser Verlag. 1~308

Landbo L. & Mikkelsen R., 1996. Risk assessment made (too) simple? *Nature Brtctech*. 14: 406

Lawton I. H., 1995. Ecological experiment with model systems. *Science*. 269: 328~331

Parker I. M. & Bartsch D., 1996. Recent advances in ecological biosafety research on the risk of transgenic plants. A trans-continental perspective. In: *Transgenic or gantsms: Biological and social implications*. (eds. Tomiuk. J. *et al*.), Birkhauser Verlag. 147~161

Raybould A F. & Gray A J., 1994, Will hybrid of genetically modified crops invade natural cornmunities? Trends *Ecol. Evol*., 9: 85~89

Rissler J. & Mellon M., 1993. *Perils amidst the promise. Ecalogical risks of transgenic crops in a global market*. Union of Concemed Scientists

Stockey A. & Hunt R., 1994, Predicting secondary succession in wetland mesocosms on the basiS of autecological information on seeds and seedlings. *J. Appl. Ecal*. 31: 543~559

Teeso B., 1993. OECD *intenational principes for biotechnology safety. Agro Food Industry Hi-Tech*. 4: 21~31

Tiedje. J. M. *ed al*., 1989: The planned introduction of grnetically engineered organisms, Ecological considerations and recommendatons. Ecology. 70: 298~313

本文原载：生态学报. 1998. 18(1): 1-9

经遗传修饰生物体的研究进展及其释放后对环境的影响*

钱迎倩　马克平

(中国科学院植物研究所)

摘　要　80 年代以来，以基因工程为代表的生物技术突飞猛进，转移不同性状的转基因作物在美国被批准进入大田试验的有 40 个以上的作物，包括小麦、玉米和水稻等 4 种谷类粮食作物，主要的纤维作物棉花、蔬菜种类 10 种以上，水果 9 种、其他还有油料作物，牧草和花卉等。到 1996 年 6 月已被批准进入市场的已有 18 种，还有一批有待批准商业化。今年 2 月，美国农业部已第一次批准一种喂饲其他螨的转基因螨进入大田试验。第一个转基因线虫也正在申请向环境释放。已至少有 25 个发展中国家，10 个以上作物转基因成功，GMOs 作大田释放的总数在 160 次以上。基因工程能带来巨大的经济效益和社会效益。但是有不少数量的科学家或如“有关科学家联盟”等一些非政府组织指出基因工程的产物向环境释放会可能带来生态或环境危险。发达国家中，美国与欧洲国家的政府对 GMOs 批准释放的态度也是一样的，后者要比前者慎重得多。最近丹麦科学家已证实转基因油菜中的抗除草剂基因已经转入杂草中；由美国一种子公司开发的转基因大豆被证实对人体过敏而其产品决定不向市场投放。

要有充分的科学实验，自然科学家与社会科学家相结合，对经遗传修饰生物体可能带来巨大经济效益和造成环境或生态危机进行充分的评估。在这基础上作出权衡、供政府决策者能作出正确的决策。这不仅在中国而是在全世界范围内已到了一个关键时刻。因此，生物安全问题是每次《生物多样性公约》缔约国会议的主要讨论议题。

关键词　经遗传修饰生物体；大田试验；商业化；危机评估；生物安全

生物技术与生物多样性的关系。在 1992 年联合国环境与发展大会签署的《生物多样性公约》[1](下称《公约》)有关条款中有明确的叙述。第 2 条“用语”中的生物技术就作为《公约》的一个专门用语来加以说明。在第 8 条“就地保护”的(g)款中作如下的叙述：“制定或采取办法以酌情管制、管理或控制由生物技术改变的活生物体在使用和释放时可能产生的危险，即可能对环境产生不利影响，从而影响到生物多样性的保护和持续利用。也要考虑到对人类健康的危险”。实际上，在 70 年代初期，即重组 DNA 研究发展的初期就有一部分科学家对其在生物学和生态学上的危险以及释放到环境后可能带来的危险表示担心。到 1992 年时世界各国，尤其是发达国家已有不少产物已进入中试或田间

---

* 国家“八五”重大基础研究项目“中国生物多样性保护生态学基础研究(PDSS-31)”的一部分。

试验。当时虽还未大规模释放或进入商业化，科学家们要求对其进行管制、管理及控制的呼声越来越高，《公约》第19条第(3)款又提到“缔约国应考虑是否需要一项议定书，规定适当程序，特别包括事先知情协议，适用于可能对生物多样性的保护和持续利用产生不利影响的由生物技术改变的任何活生物体的安全转移、处理和使用，并考虑该议定书的形式”。有关生物安全议定书的拟定从此作为届次缔约国大会的主要讨论内容。并为此还专门成立了“特设专家工作组”，多次召开会议，其任务是草拟文件供每次缔约国大会上讨论。与此同时，联合国环境署(UNEP)也十分关注生物安全问题，在1995年组织起草了《国家生物技术安全技术准则(草案)》(下称《准则》)，经过几次有关会议讨论，同年12月对《准则》进行了最后定稿。该《准则》将作为一临时机制和技术文件，与拟定好的“生物安全议定书”互为补充。议定书既有科学性、技术性，又更具有政治性。从世界范围来划分，就是涉及到发达国家与发展中国家的利益问题。可是对每一个国家内部来说，生物安全更应看作是一个环境问题，对人类健康攸关的问题，应密切关注，予以重视，开展必要的科学研究。

在《公约》中有关生物技术所涉及到的还有拥有遗传资源的发展中国家向发达国家提供遗传资源用于生物技术研究今后技术转让的优惠政策问题，以及生物技术的专利和知识产权等问题。本文不可能涉及到这么多问题，仅围绕着生物技术产物，目前一般是用基因工程手段得到的经遗传修饰生物体(GMO)或经修饰的活生物体(LMO)，释放后对环境可能带来的危险及对人体健康带来的危险进行讨论。

1 基因工程将可能是21世界的希望

读完前言部分，给人的感觉似乎生物技术给人带来的是各种各样的危险，但实际上这仅是问题的一个方面。另一方面，生物技术将可能或已经提供治疗人体疾病的药物及治疗手段，可能解决21世纪大大膨胀的人口的粮食问题以及其他环境问题。此外，生物技术这门高技术，既要求高投入，更会产出巨额的利润。

1.1 与人体健康的关系

首先该提出的是应用基因工程技术生产药物。基因工程技术第一次在实践上得到应用是把分离到的人胰岛素基因插入到大肠杆菌工程菌中,通过发酵大量生产出人胰岛素。据估计，发达国家中目前三分之二糖尿病患者治疗所用的胰岛素来自基因工程产物[2]。还有不少生产药物的例子，在前文[3,4]中已经提到，这里不再列举。

此外，科学家已发现了不少人体疾病的基因，如肠癌、乳腺癌基因，侏儒基因，诱发躁狂抑郁症，精神分裂症、成人糖尿病基因等等。英国科学家还在一种生活在土壤中的虫子中发现了“长寿基因”。这种虫子经毒物污染、高温或低温以及紫外线辐射后，受损细胞能很快恢复。此基因有修复受伤或衰老细胞的能力，科学家希望能进一步找到人类长寿的基因。美国有3个不同的科研组同时发现了一种“减肥蛋白”，它能在短期内减去动物体内的脂肪。给胖老鼠每天注射一种称为OB的蛋白，一个月后体重由65g下降到 40g，其作用一是降低食欲，二是促使机体内储存的脂肪迅速消耗，但这种蛋白有无副作用尚待研究。上面所提到的都是当代人类的一些顽症，有可能下一步用基因工程手段来治疗。

1.2 转基因动物的进展

研究转基因动物的目的是多种多样的。希望动物个体能比正常的大，使出肉量增加，如澳大利亚等国科学家已成功的转基因猪就是这个目的。用转基因生物作为“生物反应器”生产药物又是另一种目的。较新的资料提到以色列科学家用人体血清白蛋白基因注射到羊受精卵细胞核中，再把受精卵植入母体，从而得到世界上第一头带有人体血清白蛋白基因的转基因羊。血清白蛋白是人体血浆中一种主要成分，可用以治疗休克、烧伤或补偿血液损失，白蛋白过去是从人体血液中分离得到。可是人血价值昂贵，人体血清白蛋白国际市场每公斤约 2000~2500 美元。整个国际市场交易可达 10 亿美元以上，而一升羊奶可提出 10g 白蛋白，一头羊每年可创造 10kg 白蛋白，价值达 2~2.5 万美元，经济效益是可观的。此外，目前人血中常常带有各种病毒，更提高了转基因羊的价值。

转基因猪是另一种引起科学家重视的动物。英国剑桥大学科学家将人的基因植入猪卵细胞，这种转基因的心脏中含有人的基因。将转基因猪的心脏移植到猴子体内，实验说明猴子几乎未产生排异反应，平均能存活 40d。1995 年时科学家预言到 1996 年底，能把猪的器官用到人体的器官移植上。由于猪的 DNA 与人的十分接近，猪器官的尺寸与人又基本相称，其肾、心脏、肝、肺甚至血管都有可能作为人体器官移植的供体。1996 年 12 月 17 日中央电视台午间新闻 30 分报道了英国已用转基因猪的器官成功地用于人体的器官移植，画面上显示着医生正在进行移植手术。

蚊子本来是传染疟疾的昆虫，在德国的欧洲分子生物学实验室正在研究转基因蚊子，用它来消灭疟疾病。科学家从老鼠体内分离得一种抗体基因，它能附着在疟原虫体上，阻止其进入蚊子的消化道。如能成功地把这种抗体基因移植到蚊子体内，就可能培养出“反疟疾蚊子”。科学家们还在寻找一种“弹跳基因”，这基因能在几代遗传中迅速扩展到所有后代上。如把抗体基因和“弹跳基因”合起来，就能迅速繁殖出大批“反疟疾蚊子”。

佛罗里达大学的科学家向美国农业部(USDA)申请要求释放第一个转基因的节肢动物——螨，这种螨是草莓和花卉害虫——蜘蛛螨的饲料。1996 年 2 月底已批准其释放作大田试验[5]。1995 年冬，USDA 已收到第一个遗传工程线虫向环境释放的要求[6]。此外，转基因鱼及水生贝壳类动物，在不少国家正在蓬勃地开展着。

1.3 转基因植物的进展

自从 1983 年第一株转基因植物诞生以来[7]，转基因作物不断地走出实验室，进入大田的中间试验。1994 年以来有不少数量已达到商业化的阶段。1994 年时，世界上已有两种转基因作物大规模释放[8]。一个是经 USDA 和美国药物和食品管理署(FDA)批准的，由 Calgene 公司推出的转基因番茄，商品名为 Flavr Savr，性能是能延长成熟时期。另一个是中国的抗病毒转基因烟草，按 Krattiger 报道，从 1992 年起中国的抗病毒转基因烟草已用于烟草工业，到 1994 年时转基因烟草种植面积已接近全国烟草种植面积的 5%。根据 USDA 的资料，美国各种不同的转基因作物进入中试的已超过 40 种[9]。其中包括了如水稻、小麦、玉米等粮食作物，纤维作物棉花，大豆，花生，油菜等油料作物，南瓜、马铃薯、豌豆等蔬菜，以及杨树、云杉等木本树种。作大田试验的转基因作物种类的增长很快，不到两年种类数量增加近一倍，但大多数增加的是水果和蔬菜类的小作物。其他发达国家的进展也是非常迅速的，如英国科学家已成功地把去除木质素的基因插入到白杨树的种子里，已正在种植的转基因白杨目的是用此木材造纸，这种木材很容易从纤维素中去除木质素，从而达到节省漂白剂、减少能耗的目的。

基因工程农产品要商业化，在美国要经过 3 个政府部门的审批，即 USDA，FDA 和环境保护署(EPA)。以 1996 年 5 月为限，经批准或无异议的能步入商业化的转基因作物已有 7 种，由于由不同公司或改变的性状不同，总数为 14 个种次(见表 1)。此外还有 1 种抗除草剂的转基因油菜，1 种雄性不育转基因油菜，2 种抗除草剂玉米，1 种抗钻心虫玉米和 1 种抗除草剂玉米，1 种抗除草剂棉花，1 种抗病毒木瓜，1 种抗除草剂大豆，1 种抗 3 种病毒南瓜等都已提出要求商业化的申请，正在审批中。

表 1　经美国政府部门批准商业化的转基因农产品(至 1996 年 5 月)

产品	公司	改变的性状	商品名	产品	公司	改变的性状	商品名
油菜	Calgene	改变油的成分——高月硅酸	1995Laurical	玉米	Mycogen Calgcne/	抗玉米钻心虫(Bt 毒等)	1995 Nature Card
玉米	Ciba-Gegy	抗玉米钻心虫(Bt 毒等)	1995 Maximizer	棉花	Rhone Poulent	抗除草剂溴苄腈	1995 BXN Cotton
棉花	Monsanto	抗除草剂草甘膦	1996Round up Ready	马铃薯	Monsanto	抗科罗拉多马铃薯甲虫(Bt 毒等)	1995 New Leaf
棉花	Monsanto	抗棉铃虫和鳞翅目幼虫(Bt 毒素)	1995 Bollgard	大豆	Monanto	抗除草剂草甘膦	1995 Round Ready
南瓜	Asgrow	抗两种病毒	1995 Freedom11	番茄	Calgene	延迟成熟期	1994 Flavr Savr
番茄	(cher-Agritope)	改变成熟期	1996 尚不知名	番茄	DNA Plant Technology	延迟成熟期	1995 Endless Summer
番茄	Monsanto	同上	1995 尚不知名	番茄	Zeneca/ Peto-Seed	皮增厚改变果胶	1995 尚不知名

以上概略地介绍了能代表国际水平的基因工程进展情况。仅 1994 年 1 年 GMO 进入大田试验的次数就超过 1987~1993 年的总和。按 1996 年 GMO 商业化的发展进度，如大田试验顺利的话，有人预计到本世纪末美国市场上至少会推出 50 种转基因农产品，通过转基因技术产品的销售额可达到 1000 亿美元。基因工程巨大的活力将可能是 21 世纪的希望。

2　发达国家和发展中国家的进展

2.1　发达国家的进展

2.1.1　基因工程的进展

总体上看美国在实验室、中试及商业化等各个水平上在世界是领先的。上文所提到的绝大部分是美国在基因工程方面的进展。

2.1.2　欧洲发达国家的进展也是很快的

1991~1994 年，从递交的报告被批准释放的遗传工程生物体共 311 个(见表 2)[10]

表 2　按欧共体法律，1991~1994 年被释放的遗传工程生物体数

植物	291			微生物	20
油菜	95	甜瓜	2	Pseudomonas	7
玉米	58	大豆	2	Rhizobium	5
马铃薯	41	向日葵	2	Autographica californica	2
甜菜	36	胡萝卜	1	Bacillus	2
番茄	17	菊花	1	Pseudorabies 疫苗	2
菊苣	16	桉树	1	Azospirllum	1
烟草	12	杨树	1	噬菌体 M13	1
菜花	3	小麦	1		
苜蓿	2				
总数	311				

表 3　转基因植物在发展中国家释放的情况

区域	国家	被批准释放的总数	释放的总数
南美洲	阿根廷	43	43
	玻利维亚	1	5
	智利	9	17
	秘鲁	2	2
中美洲	伯利兹	—	4
	哥斯达黎加	6	8
	危地马拉	2	3
	墨西哥	20	20
加勒比	古巴	13	13
	多米尼加共和国	1	1
	波多黎各	21	21
亚洲	埃及	1	1
	印度	2	3
	泰国	1	1
非洲	南非共和国	17	17
总计		139	159

注：此外还有南美的巴西、哥伦比亚、委内瑞拉、亚洲的印度尼西亚、马来西亚、巴基斯坦、菲律宾和非洲的肯尼亚、尼日利亚和津巴布韦未得到有关释放的文件。

欧洲发达国家大多数是欧共体成员，共有15个国家组成。这些国家的GMO向环境释放要根据欧共体下设的欧洲专门事务委员会会签的“GMO 审慎地向环境释放”的指令，而GMO要商业化必须经过大多数成员国的同意。到1995年底只有4份申请报告被批准，其中3个是疫苗，1个是抗除草剂烟草，还有若干个GMO或是被否定或是有待批准。GMO释放的311总次数中，释放量最大的是法国，占93个，其他依次为比利时59、英国50、荷兰44等，其中德国仅占12次。

2.2 发展中国家的进展

2.2.1 除中国以外发展中国家的情况

发展中国家的情况。Krattiger在1994年时曾有过详细的报道[8]。Kathan报道了除中国之外至1996年9月的最新进展[11]。发展中国家的国名及释放的次数见表3。

这些国家主要释放的转基因作物是玉米、大豆、棉花、番茄和马铃薯。这5种作物占整个释放总数159中的81%。另外30次释放的是其他的一些作物。引入基因的性状最主要的是抗除草剂，占释放总数的近一半，其他依次为抗虫、提高品质及抗病毒等等。说明发展中国家在基因工程方面已经给予了很大的关注，并已取得很可观的进展。

2.2.2 我国发展情况

除前文[2,3]已提到的外，在转基因作物方面，已成功地把Bt基因转入棉花主栽品种，获得抗虫能力在80%以上的转基因棉花品系13个；转基因抗病小麦有的品种已进入大田试验；抗青枯病转基因马铃薯已筛选到抗性提高1~3级的株系3个[12]。黑龙江水产研究所将牛、羊的生长激素基因移植到普通鲤鱼，得到生长速度提高20%的第一代转基因鱼，又将大马哈鱼的生长激素基因向第一代转基因鱼进行基因转移，目前后代已有上万尾转基因鱼，正在进入有控制的中试阶段。由湖北省农业科学院畜牧兽医研究所承担的转基因猪作为器官移植供体的研究已取得很大进展。

上述情况说明，发展中国家近十年来在生物技术方面确有长足的进步，但与发达国家相比还相差甚远。从总体上看，发展中国家是属于自然资源拥有的国家，而发达国家则是资金及技术拥有的国家。《公约》第15条“遗传资源的取得”与第19条“生物技术的处理及其惠益的分配”中所涉及到的“自然资源拥有的主权权利”、“切实参与提供遗传资源用于生物技术研究活动”以及“在公平的基础上优先取得基于其提供资源的生物技术所产生的成果和惠益”等等条款都是发展中国家与发达国家谈判得到的结果。

3 GMOs释放给环境带来的风险

缔约国1995年11月在雅加达举行第二次会议时，秘书处提供了一份“实施《公约》第6条和第8条的有关做法和经验”的文本，其中第54点指出：“从《公约》的角度来看，生物技术产生的经修饰的活生物体(LMO)引起的有关问题涉及的范围很广。它们包括植物基因的稳定性、对非针对对象产生的影响、对生态系统过程的不利影响、基因改变植物潜在脆弱性等问题；基因改变、控制基因表现、预定和非预定的改变等问题；供体生物体的表现特征，例如竞争性、致病性和毒性等问题；对人类健康产生有害影响等问题。这一段说明对 GMO 已有实验证实的或潜在的风险作了相当完善的概括。说明在对生物技术作为 21 世纪希望的同时，还不能忽视其可能带来的一系列危机。

已有相当多的文献、论文集或专著[13~15]讨论 GMOs 释放的生态危机对人类影响问题。期刊“分子生态学”(Molecular Ecology)1994 年第 3 卷出专集[6]讨论基因植物释放的生态学影响。此外题为“经遗传修饰的植物和微生物大田试验生物安全结果”的国际会议，从 1990 年起每两年举行一次，至今已有三次出版了论文集[17~19]。第一次是 1990 年 11 月在美国 Kiawah 岛召开，被称为 Kiawah Island Conference。两年后在德国 Goslar 举行了第二次会议，这次会议的内容不仅讨论到 GMOs 大田试验中释放问题，并已有文章涉及商业化后的生物安全问题。第三次会议 1994 年 11 月在美国召开。从这 3 次会议参加的国家数与到会人数说明世界各国对生物安全重视程度逐渐增加。第一次会议仅 10 个国家 130 个代表；第二次 22 个国家 200 位代表；第三次会议则已有 32 个国家 225 位代表，发展中国家参加第二、第三次会议的科学家越来越多。

在 1994 年第三次会议上法国科学家 Deshayes 报告中指出[20]，从 1986~1994 年间全世界已有 1500 个 GMO 释放做大田试验，但对 GMOs 向环境释放后其生态学风险和对人类健康影响确切的回答却很少，他强调了风险评估的长期性，尤其要注意的是目前可作没有影响的回答并不能保证经过一段时间的考验后还是正确的。对 GMOs 释放后的生态学、生物学以及对人体健康的风险，过去多数是预见性的评估，在提法上多数提的是潜在的风险。可是近年来，特别是 1996 年在 Nature[21]等著名杂志上登载了 GMOs 释放的风险的文章，一方面是对一部分风险的证实，另一方面说明生物安全问题的确要引起人们足够的重视。

3.1 对环境潜在的风险

3.1.1 上文已经提到了美国政府有关审批机构已经批准了转基因螨释放

实际上，美国国内有反对释放的呼声。一个称为“有关科学家联盟”(Union of Concerned Sctentests(UCS))的组织，他们密切关注着生物安全问题，并有一系列的出版物。该组织及其他科学家迫切要求 USDA 推迟批准，要求在批准前的一个公众充分参与对风险评估的过程，并要求有 90d 的时间可供广泛的质疑，让科学家及其他有兴趣的团体一起来讨论评估转基因节肢动物危机的原则。UCS 提出美国已有相当数量的转基因节肢动物正在研究或准备提出申请，其中包括有地中海果蝇、蚊子、蜜蜂以及棉铃虫等昆虫。他们认为这些转基因节肢动物存在巨大的潜在环境风险，因为它们繁殖得快、数量又大，它们起到一系列例如作为害虫、有益的食肉动物和传粉等重要的生态学作用；而不少节肢动物还非常小、能移动的距离却相当长，一旦确证风险的存在，是不可能从环境中收回的，但 USDA 不顾 UCS 和其他人的反对批准了。

3.1.2 Rissler 等[13]和 Kathen[11]等文献中都谈到转基因作物本身可能变为杂草

这里首先讨论有关杂草的生物学特性，杂草有旺盛而顽固的生命力，从营养生长到开花这段时间可以非常短，如是多年生植物，往往有旺盛的营养繁殖或能在从断片中再生的能力；花是自交的，但往往不是专性的自花授粉、而异花授粉的花粉是通过虫媒或风媒来传播；种子存活期能保持很长，只要生长条件许可植物可连续不断、大量地并在很大的环境范围内产生种子。

部分栽培植物，命名如一些高粱属的种，在一定环境下本身就是杂草，而在某些条件下它又可是作物，这类作物当插入一个例如抗病、抗虫基因，或转基因作物中基因逃逸时，可能会把本来在某些地区很安全的作物，由于改变了其平稳而趋向于杂草化。又如甘蔗、水稻、马铃薯、油菜和燕麦等作物，它们本来就有其很近的杂草性的近缘种，因某些遗传上的改变就可能使作物成为杂草。

3.1.3 某些转基因作物具抗杀虫剂的性能或者是作为生物反应器来生产药物

这一类转基因作物可能会对其他自然界的生物产生反效果，这就称为“非目标效应”。因为很少有哪一种杀虫剂能选择来杀死某一种害虫，而往往带有一定的广谱性，何况目前多数用的都是 Bt 基因，因此插入到作物中的杀虫或杀真菌的基因也可能对其他非目标生物起到作用，从而杀死了环境中有益的昆虫和真菌。带有 Bt 抗虫基因的植物，当它们的遗传在土壤中被土壤昆虫降解时，也可能使这些昆虫受到毒害。此外，例如带有几丁质酶的抗真菌的转基因作物，其遗传分解时可能减少土壤中菌根的种群。菌根是一种真菌，对植物的主要作用是众所周知的。由于几丁质酶可以消化掉带有几丁质的菌根的细胞壁。细胞壁一旦破坏，个体就自然死亡。从而土壤中的凋落物不可能被分解，营养流被中断，整个生态系统的功能被阻滞。

目前人们期望通过转基因作物作为生物反应器来生产人类及动物所用的药物、激素和疫苗，以及工业用的酶、油及其他化学品。这些转基因作物不仅对土壤生物产生影响，还可能被其他食草动物或其种子被鸟类摄食而起到相反的作用。

3.1.4 转基因作物还可能使其野生近缘种变为杂草

由于自然界的制约，不少作物的野生近缘种虽然目前未被人类利用，但并不以杂草形式存在。可以是一旦接受到某个 GMO 逃逸的基因，在一定条件下使其大量繁殖起来而变成杂草。在美国有人反对已被 USDA 和 FDA 批准的转基因南瓜上市，就因为在美国野葫芦一类的南瓜近缘种植物是普遍存在的。这些野生近缘种由于有黄瓜斑纹病毒和西瓜斑纹病毒而不能大量繁殖，如果抗多种病毒的转基因南瓜基因通过基因流转入野葫芦，后果将不堪设想。

Mikkelsen 等[21]作了芸苔(*Brassica napus*)的基因渐渗到其杂草近缘种野油菜(*B. campestris*) 中的研究，芸苔染色体 $2n=38$，野油菜染色体 $2n=20$，但两个种能自发地杂交，在自然种群中能发现杂种。当耐除草剂 glufosinate 的转基因芸苔与野油菜杂交后得到的种间杂种与野油菜种在一起时，早在回交第一代就能发现形态上完全像野油菜，染

色体也是 $2n$=20 的高度能育的耐除草剂转基因野油菜。在刚杂交和回交两代后就出现了能育的转基因杂草状的植物，说明了芸苔的基因可能快速地向野油菜传播。这个实验是 GMO 的转基因会向野生近缘种自然转移的一个确切的证明。

3.2 转基因作物可能产生新的病毒或新的疾病

1994 年，美国密歇根州立大学科学家把花椰菜花叶病毒外壳蛋白的基因插入豇豆，得到抗病毒的豇豆。当他们把缺少外壳蛋白的病毒再接种到转基因豇豆上时，发现 125 株豇豆中有 4 株又染上了花叶病。由此，他们认为插入转基因作物中的病毒可能与再接种病毒的遗传物质结合而形成新的病毒。或者说，GMO 中的病毒 RNA 有能力再组成很多新的形式。为此，Falk 等[22]在 Science 刊物上发表了题为“转基因作物将产生新病毒和新疾病?”的文章。据报道，1996 年又有实验证据说明至少在实验室条件下，原来准备作为抗病疫苗的黄瓜花叶病毒(CMV) 自发地突变。这种新的突变不仅仅不能抗 CMV，反而更加剧了这种病毒对烟草的危害。闻大中[23]也列举了改变某些动物病原体的基因，可使该病原体的毒性增强，或增加其对农药和抗菌素的抵抗力，或者因基因的改变可使与动、植物共生的微生物具有致病力的例子。

目前在发达国家转基因微生物已少数被批准释放。但应该认识到，转基因微生物的释放更是一个复杂的问题。因为目前绝大多数微生物尚未得到鉴定、定名或研究。微生物不同种、属之间的自然基因转移比较频繁，而所插入的带有明显选择优势的基因有可能在大范围的微生物界传播,这会造成对某一些转基因微生物长期影响作评估带来困难。

3.3 对人体健康的影响

转基因生物作为食品对人体健康是否会带来风险一直是人们所关心的问题。过去的报道多数是由各种新闻媒体发出的，其中当然难避讹传的可能，但有一点应该是肯定的，作为美国第一个释放上市的转基因番茄是 1994 年 6 月，至今还只有两年多一点的时间，长期效应如何及风险又可能有多大等问题是目前人们全然不知，要有相当长的时间考验。

可就是在 1996 年科学期刊上发表了“在转基因大豆中对巴西果过敏原的鉴定”的文章[24]，说明基因工程大豆对人体是过敏的。这是美国 Proneer Hi-Bced 种子公司的成果。因巴西果的蛋白质含有对人和动物营养最主要的一种氨基酸，蛋氨酸。这种蛋白质加到大豆中去是为了改良其营养组成。可是有一部分人对巴西果敏感，与人体血清有反应。实验证明当用对巴西果过敏的人的血清与转基因大豆与巴西果作试验时，反应是一样的，说明转基因大豆包含有巴西果的过敏原，不同的人对巴西果过敏反应不一样，从很轻例如心脏作无规律的跳动，直到心脏病严重发作，以至死亡。由此 Proneer Hi-Bced 公司决定已不能作为上市的产品。

此外，新闻媒体报道，美国 Monsanto 公司研制的抗除草剂转基因大豆向欧共体出口，其中载有 4 万多吨的转基因大豆货船抵达德国汉堡，引起环保组织的抗议活动，绿色和平组织也发起和领导抵制这种大豆进口的宣传活动。

3.4 对生物多样性的影响

转基因生物本身是自然界不存在的人工制造的生物，释放到任何一个生态系统中都是外来种，引入外来种历来是被普遍采用的，不乏起好作用的例子，但也确实有大量由于外来种引入后，破坏了原来的生态系统，使该生态系统的物种大量消灭的例子[2, 3]。

中国在栽培作物和家养动物方面是具有丰富的遗传多样性资源的国家之一。为满足人口压力对粮食及食品的要求，迫使近代工农业向单一化的优质高产品种发展，这在客观上已经自然淘汰了大量具有一定优良遗传性状的农家品种及其他遗传资源，造成遗传多样性不可挽回的损失。GMO 的释放，如果处理不当可能更加剧了品种的单一化，使农业进一步处于脆弱的状态。

4 加强生物安全的措施

生物安全的措施要从风险评估的科研工作、立法以及教育与培训 3 个方面来加强。

4.1 风险评估的科研工作

发达国家出于种种原因或者说出于公众的压力对风险评估的科研工作是比较重视的，正像本文提到的近 1~2 年来，对 GMO 释放的风险评估已不仅停留在预测上而已开始有研究的论文发表。只有经过科学的证实，找到原因，才可能进一步找到克服危机的方法。

进行风险评估，研究经费的投入是重要的。以美国为例，USDA 对农业上的 GMO 的生态学风险研究的投资从 1992~1995 年间共计 640 万美元。按报道[25]，是在下列 9 个领域投资过 40 个课题。其中抗病毒转基因作物占 33%，转基因流向野生植物占 20%，工程植物和细菌的非目标效应占 13%，转基因鱼占 9%、与微生物相关的工程植物占 7%、昆虫抗 Bt 作物占 6%、工程动物疫苗占 6%、工程昆虫病毒占 3%、工程真菌占 2%、可见 60%以上的投资是放在转基因植物的风险评估研究上。即使这样，风险研究的投资只占到同一期间 USDA 给农业生物技术研究投资的 1%。也就是说，1992~1995 年间，USDA 为农业生物技术拨的研究经费为 6 亿 4 千万美元。

4.2 立法

不同的发达国家对 GMO 释放的风险的认识是不一样的，总体上欧共体国家要比北美国家更为严格。欧共体内部尤以德国最严格，使一些德国的 GMO 产物到加拿大去申请释放。发展中国家一般说来在实际行动中尤为放松一点，考虑得更多的是投资后的近期效应。

在看到生物技术带来可观的经济效益和社会效益的同时，不应忽视其潜在的或已被实验证实的危机，更应对其长期可能产生的效应，对子孙万代可能带来的后果有充分的考虑。为之，要立充分具操作性的并行之有效的法律是重要的，立法后的执法更应严格。

当然法律的制定应立足于科学研究的基础上，随着科研工作的深入，立法逐步完善。《公约》生物安全议定书一旦制定，就应严格执行议定书的规定。

4.3 教育与培训

GMOs 从研究—中试、大田试验—生产，中间涉及不同文化水平、不同职务或职位的人物。他们中对生物安全的认识及知识参差不齐。为了使 GMO 释放后尽可能减少对环境和对人体健康的负影响，采取不同方式和不同水平的教育和培训是必须要强调的。

5 结束语

包括基因工程在内的生物技术是高科技，这类高科技往往会在造福于人类的同时，在一定时间、一定范围内带来祸害或灾难。核技术就是最好的例子，在军事上，民用上核技术会越来越显示其重要作用,但也会出现 1986 年前苏联乌克兰境内的切尔诺贝利核电站的核泄漏事故。生物技术的命运应该是同样的，转基因产物的释放并走向商业化是必然的趋势，也是不以人们意志为转移的。而对其带来的负效应，对生物安全问题又必须引起高度的重视。

参考文献

[1] Convention on Biological Diversity UNEP, 1994
[2] 钱迎倩, 生物多样性与生物技术. 中国科学院院刊, 1994. 2: 134~138
[3] 钱迎倩，生物技术与生物多样性的保护和持续利用. 钱迎倩, 马克平主编. 生物多样性研究的原理与方法. 北京: 中国科学技术出版社, 1995.217~224
[4] 钱迎倩等, 生物技术与生物安全 自然资源学报, 1995. 10(4): 322~331
[5] Anomnous. First release of engineered arthropod. *The Gene Exchange*, 1996, 6 (4): 7
[6] Anomynous. First proposed release of trangenic nematode. *The GeneEx change.*1996, 6 (4): 1
[7] Zambryske P, *et al*., Tiplasmid vector for the introduction of DNA into plant cells without alteration of their normal regulation capacity. *EMBO J.*, 1983, 2: 2143
[8] Krattiger A F. The field testing and commercialization of genetically modified plant; A review of world wide data (1986) to 1993/94. In Krattiger A F. *et al*., eds. *Biosafety for sustainable agriculture*. *ISAAA/SEI*, 1994, 247~266
[9] Anomynous Field testing of over 40 different transgenic crops. *The Gene Exchange* 1996, 6 (4): 11
[10] Anomynous Around the world: European Union. *The Gene Exchange*, 1995, 6(2&3): 12~13
[11] Kathen A. The impact of transgenic crop releases on biodiversity in developing countries. *Biotec.Developm. Monitor* 1996, 28: 10~15
[12] 徐新来. 我国生物技术快速发展的十年. 生物工程进展, 1996, 16(3): 2~3
[13] Rissler J, *et al*., Perils amidst the promise, Ecological risks of transgenic crops in a global market. *Union Concerned Scientists*, 1993. 1~92
[14] Krattiger A F *et al*., Biosafety for sustainable agriculture, Sharing biotechnology regulatory experiences of the western hemisphere.1994, *ISAAA/SEI*, 1~278
[15] Tzotzos G T. Genetically modified organismes. A guide to biosafety UNIDO, UNEP, CAB International 1995. 1~213
[16] Burke T, *et al.* ed. Ecological implications of transgenic plant release. *Mol Ecol* 1994, 3
[17] Makenzie D R *et al. The biosafety results of field test of genetically modified plant and microorganisms*. Maryland U.S.A. 1990. 1~301

[18] Casper R *et al*., *The biosafety results of field tests of genetically modified plants and microorganisms*. Proceedings of 2nd International Symposium. Goslar, Germany, 1992. 1~296

[19] Jones D D. The biosafety results of field tests of genetically modified plants and microorganism, Proceedings of the 3rd International Symposium, California. U.S.A. 1994, 1~558

[20] Deshayes A F. Environmental and social impacts of GMO's: What have we learned from the past few years? In: *The biosafety results of field test of genetically modified plant and microorganisms*. Proceeding of the 3rd International Symposium. Jones D D, ed. California, U.S.A. 1994. 5~19

[21] Mikkelsen T R *et al*. The risk of crop transgene spread, *Nature*, 1996. 380: 31

[22] Falk B W *et al*. Will transgenic crops generate new viruses and new deseases? *Science*, 1994. 263: 1395~ 1396

[23] 闻大中. 基因工程生物的生态影响及其评价. 应用生态学报, 1992. 3(4): 371~377

[24] Nordlee J, *et al*. Identification of a Brazil-nut allergen in transgenic soybeans. *The New England J. Medic*., 1996. 334: 688~692

[25] Anomynous. USDA biotechnology risk assessment research. *The Gene Exchange*, 1995. 5(4)

[26] Anomynous. USDA biotechnology risk assessment. *The Gene Exchange*, 1995. 6(1): 5

本文原载：生物技术通报. 1999. 5: 7-11

转基因作物的利弊分析*

钱迎倩

(中国科学院植物研究所)

摘　要　1995年后转基因作物的商品化种植迅猛发展。优良的农艺性状和巨大的经济效益，日益显示出转基因作物是解决21世纪不断膨胀人口对食物需求的主要途径之一。转基因作物的潜在生态风险及对人体健康影响的争论随着转基因作物的商品化也日趋尖锐。为保护转基因作物知识产权发展起来的“终止子技术”引起第三世界国家的强烈反对。《生物多样性公约》缔约国对生物安全有关问题斗争激烈,迟迟达不成协议。围绕转基因作物的斗争已不仅是科学技术之争，已发展到经济领域,甚至政治领域的斗争。本文对转基因作物的发展与生物安全的研究提出几点建议。

关键词　转基因作物；生态风险；生物安全；“终止子技术”；“特殊性状的遗传利用限制技术”

从70年代重组DNA技术创建，到1983年第一株转基因烟草获得以来，国际上对转基因作物就存在着截然不同的观点。随着技术日趋成熟，转基因作物由实验室进入大田中试，不少作物已向商品化发展。与此同时，转基因作物的生态风险，可能带来的环境问题、转基因产品作为食品对人体健康问题、产品贴标签问题、运输问题、国际贸易问题、知识产权问题等已引起世界性的所谓“生物安全”的论战。拥护者以各种形式进一步促进其更快地发展。反对者则以示威游行，甚至毁坏大田实验等各种行动来进行抵制。1992年在巴西召开的环发大会上通过《生物多样性公约》后，专门设立了“生物安全特设工作组”，致力于在上述一系列问题上各缔约国取得共识。“特设工作组”1999年1月在哥伦比亚召开第6次会议，事先作了争取达成协议的充分准备，事与愿违，矛盾尖锐不欢而散。转基因技术实际上已由学术观点分歧，发展到知识产权问题、环境问题、经济问题甚至政治问题。本文对此作一分析。

1　转基因作物的优越性

目前国际国内已大面积商品化生产的转基因作物主要是以提高作物抗性(如抗病、抗虫、抗除草剂)和改良作物的性状为主。以抗虫转基因棉花为例，其优越性是十分明显的。它不仅可以抵抗棉铃虫等害虫的危害，提高棉花产量，而且因大量减少了农药的使用量

---

* 本课题为“九五”国家重点科技项目(攻关)计划(97-925-02-04-05)资助。

而节省了费用，减少了农药对棉农的毒害及对天敌的杀害，保护了环境。

从转基因作物所得到的效益也是非常明显的。以美国为例，1996年全国得到的净利为9200万美元，其中Bt棉花占6100万美元，Bt玉米占1900万美元，抗除草剂大豆为1200万美元。到1997年时，全国的净利已达3.15亿美元。其中Bt玉米为1.19亿美元，抗除草剂大豆为1.09亿美元，Bt棉花为8100万美元，抗除草剂棉花为500万美元，Bt马铃薯少于100万美元。加拿大得益明显的是抗除草剂转基因油菜，1996年时全国净利为500万美元左右；1995年上升为4800万美元，另外加拿大Bt玉米得益500万美元，全国估计共达5300万美元。

从全球角度看，1995年到1998年4年间转基因作物销售收入增加20倍。1995年时仅为7500万美元；1996年翻三番达2.35亿美元，1997年又再翻了近3番，达6.7亿美元；1998年在12~15亿美元之间。预计世界市场到2000年时会达到30亿美元；2005年达60亿；到2010年时将达到200亿美元。

1.1 国际转基因作物的研究进展

中国是国际上第一个商品化种植抗黄瓜花叶病毒(CMV)和抗烟草花叶病毒(TMV)双价转基因烟草的国家。由国家科学技术委员会第一次发布的《基因工程安全管理办法》颁布以前，1992年双价转基因烟草已发展到8600公顷，但后劲不足，其他国家，尤其是美国很快就赶上来，1996年后以惊人的速度发展。据Krattiger[1]道，1994年转基因作物当时在国际上只有中国及美国有商品化生产，当时中国转基因烟草面积已达100万公顷。James[2]的报道数字把中国的产量排除在外。1996年全世界转基因作物生产的面积为170万公顷，1997年达到1100万公顷，其中美国就占810万公顷；1998年总面积翻了一番，已达到2780万公顷，其中美国占2050万公顷。其次是阿根廷占430万公顷；加拿大占280万公顷；澳大利亚、墨西哥、西班牙、法国及南非都仅有10万或10万公顷以下的面积。

转基因作物中发展得最快的是大豆，全球1997年为510万公顷，到1998年猛增到1450万公顷。其他依次为转基因玉米、棉花、油菜，转基因马铃薯仅占很小一部分面积。以转基因的性状而论，发展得最快的是抗除草剂转基因作物，1997年全球面积为690万公顷，1998年猛增1290万公顷，达到1980万公顷，其次是抗虫转基因作物，由1997年的400万公顷发展到770万公顷，此外抗虫与抗除草剂双价转基因作物也有所发展。

1.2 我国转基因作物的研究进展

我国是世界上转基因作物第一个商品化种植的国家。美国一烟草公司一直收购河南烟叶，但当知道进口烟草中有转基因烟草后，他们停止了向中国进口。由于大量烟草积压，河南省有关部门发文停止了转基因烟草的种植。

目前经农业部审查并经全国基因工程安全委员会批准商品化生产的作物已有我国自行研制开发的抗虫转基因棉花(Bt棉及Bt + C*p TI*棉)、美国Monsanto公司开发的有Bt棉、延迟成熟期的转基因番茄、抗CMV转基因番茄、抗CMV转基因甜椒及转查尔酮合酶(CHS)基因矮牵牛，但除转基因抗虫棉已经大面积生产外，后几种作物面积仅在 1 公顷左右。

由中国农科院生物工程中心开发的 Bt 棉在全国 9 个主要产棉区到 1999 年已种植 16 万公顷左右。减少农药用量 80%，并减少用工 150 个/公顷，以上两者每公顷节省 1500 元/公顷。Bt 棉的棉种价格比对照要高 3~5 倍，深受棉农的欢迎。最近他们又开发了 Bt+*Cp TI* 抗虫棉，已推广 400 公顷，明年可达 1 万公顷。

Monsanto 的 Bt 棉在安徽省固镇县 1998 年时种植 1000 亩，最高产量可达 395.7 公斤/亩，平均为 218 公斤/亩，比对照增产 24.2%。1999 年全县已种 4 万亩。

双价转基因烟草的抗性达到 60%，产量比对照增加 15%，产值增加 20%，1992 年每亩增产 200 元。遗憾的是现已不推广。

2 转基因作物的潜在风险

80 年代后期以来对转基因作物可能存在的风险不断有报道。随着转基因作物商品化的迅猛发展，认为转基因作物商品化不存在风险或风险不大的报道日益增多。世界银行 1997 年曾邀集一批学者，以世界银行的名义对转基因作物有一专门报告[3]，这报告对转基因作物商品化基本肯定。欧洲一些国家对转基因作物的态度与北美国家截然相反。国际权威性刊物如 Nature 等也陆续有转基因作物存在风险的实验报道[4,5]，有关转基因植物风险评估方法学至少已有两本专著[6,7]。

有关转基因作物潜在生态风险，我们曾作过报道[8,9,10]，这里除提纲挈领地提一下外，主要对未作过介绍的作一些补充。

2.1 转基因作物的潜在风险

2.1.1 转基因作物本身可能变为杂草；

2.1.2 转基因作物通过基因流可使野生近缘种变为杂草；

2.1.3 可能产生新的超级病毒或新的病害；

2.1.4 作为人工制造的转基因作物，可能成为自然界原来不存在的外来品种，若干年后可能对环境造成破坏；

2.1.5 对非目标生物有伤害，对生物多样性形成威胁。

这方面有几篇新的报道，Hilbeck[11]用转基因 Bt 玉米喂饲欧洲玉米钻心虫(ECB)，并以它作为草蛉的饲料，GN 喂饲一般玉米的作为对照。实验结果，转基因 Bt 玉米组死亡率 60%以上，而对照组 40%以下。该作者认为，较高死亡率是与 Bt 有关的因子直接有关，存活的草蛉中喂 Bt 玉米组成熟的时间平均比对照要晚 3 天。Birch[12]的实验是用喂饲转基因马铃薯的蚜虫作为瓢虫的饲料，与喂一般马铃薯作对照。喂转基因马铃薯雌蚜虫的卵比对照组的减少 1/3。用喂转基因马铃薯长大的雄蚜虫与对照组雌蚜虫交配，所得未受精卵的数量多 4 倍。喂饲转基因马铃薯蚜虫的已受精卵在未孵化前比对照组死亡率高近 3 倍，以转基因马铃薯蚜虫为食物的雌瓢虫的存活时间比对照组少一半。虽然以上仅是实验室的结果，如大田试验结果相类似的话，则大规模种植转基因抗虫作物将可能会减少有益昆虫的种群。最近美国康奈尔大学 Losey[5]等报道，在一种植物马利筋叶片上撒上转基因 Bt 玉米花粉后，一种称之为黑脉金斑蝶的幼虫对叶片就吃得少，长得慢，死得快。4 天后幼虫死亡率达 44%，而对照(饲喂不撒 Bt 玉米花粉的叶片)无一死亡。这结果在美国新闻报道后环境保护者担心今后会有更多的灾难接踵而至。

2.2 转基因作物作为食品的安全性问题

转基因作物在实验室阶段经常要用抗生素作为抗性标记进行筛选，这是人们担心的问题。目前已找到了替代物，应逐步淘汰对抗生素抗性标记的使用已成为共识。最近英国一科学家在未发表论文前向公众宣布实验用的大鼠在食用转基因马铃薯后，免疫系统受到削弱，因之被迫退休。21 位著名科学家为其呼吁要求恢复他的工作，但英国皇家学会对此事专门组织科学家调查研究后，认为，该科学家的实验从设计、执行到分析，多方面都有缺陷，不应过早得出结论。认为喂转基因马铃薯与对照所得的数据虽然看上去有一些差异，但因受到实验技术的限制和不正确的利用统计学，这些差异说明不了问题。

转基因作物的安全性是一个重要而复杂的问题，应谨慎对待，不要急于下结论。当前有的转基因食品已经上市，应该在上货架时对该食品要贴标签，让公众对是否愿意购买食用转基因食品有选择的自由。

3 转基因作物的专利保护

国外出售的玉米种子都是杂交种，只能种一年，由于第二年会发生大量分离而收获的种子不能作种用，农民每年得向种子公司购买种子。这本身也就起到了专利保护的作用。而其他如水稻、大豆、棉花、小麦卖的都不是杂交种，应用高技术得到转基因作物种子的农民可以把收获到的种子留作种用，这样，遗传工程技术公司就赚不到高额的利润。为此，Delta and Pine Land(DPL)公司和美国农业部联合申请了一个称为“终止子技术”的专利[13]，并于 1998 年 3 月获得美国专利局的批准。该专利技术可使作物种植后得到的种子是不育的，虽然收获了种子，但不能留作种用。这项技术的大致程序是，科学家用遗传工程的技术把终止子基因插入到作物中得到转基因作物的种子；种子公司在种子出售前再加上一种诱导剂，农民播种后长出正常的植株，收获成熟的种子。这种种子在油脂、蛋白质等各方面分都是完全正常的，但不能种用。因为在诱导剂的作用下，加入的毒素基因启动产生了毒素，在种子成熟收获前就杀死了胚胎，因此这种种子不能发芽当生产用种。

终止子技术获得专利后引起国际很大的反响。1998 年 10 月国际农业研究磋商小组(CGIAR)在华盛顿召开会议，明确提出 5 点：农民留种的重要性，特别对贫穷的农民尤为重要；终止子技术对遗传多样性的影响；为了发展持续农业农民育种的重要性；由于外观上分不清终止子技术生产的种子，可能出售或交换不能发芽的种子，播种后对生产造成不可弥补的损失；通过花粉非故意传播造成生物安全的风险。为了保护对世界食品的保障，要求禁止终止子技术。国际农业促进基金会(RAFI)和一些非政府组织赞同 CGIAR 的政策，动员公众反对这项技术，要求停止会对农民、生物多样性和世界食品保障都受损害的终止子技术专利，并要用 CGIAR 的政策来影响联合国生物多样性议程。

联合国生物多样性公约的科学顾问们提出了一项既能保护知识产权又相对缓和得多的技术，称“特殊性状的遗传利用限制技术”(T-Gurt)[14]。T-Gurt 种子也和终止子种子一样是由美国的 Monsanto 和英国的 Astra Zeneca 等类似公司来开发的。T-Gurt 种子是科学家经过基因遗传修饰后产生特殊的，例如耐盐或耐旱的性状。如农民需要这种种子则必须到有关公司去买专卖的化学品去喷洒种子活化这种性状。与终止子技术根本不同的是种子本身还是活的，1999 年 6 月，在加拿大蒙特利尔召开的生物多样性公约有关会议上，欧盟、拉丁美洲和东南亚国家代表对 T-Gurt 持谨慎欢迎的态度，而非洲国家科学家则人力劝阻公约科学顾问们，在他们满意地认为 T-Gurt 不会对人体健康和环境带来伤害之前，不要去认同这个技术。

4 几点建议

4.1 加强优质、高产及提高各种抗逆性转基因作物的研究

到 2030 年，中国人口将达到 16 亿。生产农艺性状良好优质高产的转基因作物是解决不断增加的人口对粮食需求的重要途径之一。从目前内外的形势来看，必须加速转基因作物的研究。虽然我国转基因作物商品化在国际上首先进行，但由于基础、经费及人才等种种原因而造成后劲不足。美国很快就赶上来，远远将我们抛在后面。针对我国国情，加强优质、高产及提高各种抗逆性，特别是提高抗旱及抗盐碱能力的转基因作物研究将是发展的重点。此外，按照转基因作物释放的法规，加快商品化生产的速度也是一个重要的方面，这里涉及到体制问题。从实验室到商品化整个环节上，大学与研究所应做些什么？哪些工作或哪些环节应放到企业去发展？也是应着重研究的。白书农的观点[15]是值得参考的。

4.2 加强“生物安全”问题的研究

转基因作物商品化的历史还非常短。世界上第一个 90 年代初商品化生产的转基因烟草由于销路问题已停止推广。1994 年美国第一个批准商品化的延迟成熟期的转基因番茄也因种种原因停止了生产。从 1995 年至今才不到 5 年的时间，应该说人们对转基因作物的不少方面还知之甚少，转基因作物作为人工制造的外来品种对环境影响如何，转基因作物的安全性如何，现在下结论还为时尚早，当前应该加强“生物安全”的研究。

4.3 建立“生物安全”的监测制度

加强生物安全的首要方面是要建立临测制度。建立法规，对进行商品化释放的每一种转基因作物进行长期监测。组织多学科的科研人员制定“生物安全”科研计划，并及时组织科学研究。这里有一个问题值得提出，科研工作切忌主观、片面。我们曾经注意到[16]，在生物工程公司工作的科研人员与在国家研究室或大学工作的科研人员，对同一问题的结论是完全相反的。例如在 Ciba -Geigy 公司工作的 Goy 和在 Pioneer Hi-Bred 公司工作的 Duesing 曾共同发表文章[17]，对转基因油菜的结论是“在 391 次大田试验中，91 %的试验对环境无潜在影响，如果有也是最小的，而余下 9%的试验说明对环境只有低的潜在影响。”但是 3 个月后，在同一期刊上两位丹麦科学家提出了彻底否定的见解[18]。这里不仅涉及到学术观点问题，更主要的是无视前人的研究，对研究材料的分类或取样有主观性，故同一试验得出截然相反的结论。

4.4 利用基因工程技术保护知识产权

利用基因工程技术保护农作物产品(新品种)知识产权，这已成为国际发展趋势之一。美国农业部发言人明确声称，终止子技术的初衷就是针对第二世界和第三世界的。在发展转基因技术的同时，我们也必须重视这方面技术的研究，并采取对策。

致谢：农业部方向东、李宁先生、中国农科院生物工程中心郭三堆先生、中国科学院微生物研究所方荣祥先生提供国内发展情况，在此一并致谢。

参考文献

[1] Krattiger AF. The field testing and commercialization of genetically modified plants: A review of worldwide data (1986 to 1992/94), In: Biosafety for sustainable agriculture：Sharing biotechnology regulatory experiences of the Western hemisphere, eds. Krittiger, AF *et al.*, ISAAA/ SEI,247~266

[2] James C. Global review of commercialized transgenic crops: 1998, ISAAA Briefs No. 8. ISAAA: Ithaca, 1998

[3] Kendall HW, Beachy R, Eisiner T, *et al.* Bioengineering of Crops, Report of the World Bank Panel on Transgenic Crops. 1997, Washington, USA.: The World Bank,1997, 1~30

[4] Mikkelsen TR. The risk of crop transgene spread Nature, 1996, 380: 31

[5] Losey J E, Rayor LS,Carter ME. Transgenic pollen harms monarch larvae. Nature, 1999, 399: 214

[6] Kjellesson G, Simonsson V. Methods for risk assessment of transgenic plants. I. Competition,establishment and ecosystem efforts. Brikhauser Verlag, 1994, 1~214

[7] Kjellesson G,Simonsson V. Methods for risks assessment of transgenic plants. II. Pollination,transfer and population impacts.Brikhauser Verlag, 1997, 1~308

[8] 钱迎倩, 马克平. 经遗传修饰生物体的研究进展及其释放后对环境的影响. 生态学报, 1998, 18(1): 1~9

[9] 魏伟, 钱迎倩, 马克平. 转基因作物与其野生亲缘种间的基因流. 植物学报, 1999, 41(4): 1~5

[10] 魏伟, 钱迎倩, 马克平. 害虫对转基因 Bt 作物的抗性及其管理对策. 应用与环境生物学报, 1999, 5(2): 215~228

[11] ilbeck A. Effect of transgenic Bacillus thuringiensis corn- fed prey on mortality and development time of immature Chrysoperla carnea (Neuroptera: Chrysopidae). Environ Entomol, 1998, 27: 480~487

[12] Birch A. Interactions between plant resistance genes,pest aphid populations and beneficial aphid predators, 1996/7, Scottish Crop Res. Inst. Annual Report, Dundee, 68~72

[13] 钱迎倩, 马克平, 桑卫国, 等. 终止子技术与生物安全. 生物多样性, 1999, 7(2): 151~155

[14] Masood E, Compromise sought on ‘Terminator’. Nature, 1999, 399: 721

[15] 白书农. 农业生物技术产业的发展与社会资源配置的策略. 欧美同学会会刊, 1999, 2: 14~15

[16] 钱迎倩, 田彦, 魏伟. 转基因植物的生态风险评估. 植物生态学报, 1998, 22(4): 289~299

[17] Goy PA, Duesing J H. Assessing the environmental impect of genetransfer to wildveletives. Bio/Tech, 1996, 14: 39~40

[18] Lando L, Mikkelson R. Risk assessment made (too) simple? Nature Bio-tech, 14: 406

本文原载：应用与环境生物学报. 1999. 5(4): 427-433

转基因作物在生产中的应用及某些潜在问题*

钱迎倩[1]　魏伟[2]　田彦[3]　马克平[1]

(1 中国科学院植物研究所；2 中国农业大学生物技术系；3 中国科学院基础研究局)

关键词　转基因作物；商品化；潜在风险
中图法分类号　Q788，S51

1997年，经修饰的活生物体，尤其是转基因作物，得到了突飞猛进的发展，但同时转基因作物在商品化过程中也出现了一系列问题，对转基因生物潜在风险一直有不同的观点，本文就上述几方面问题作一综述。

1　1997年全球转基因作物的进展

转基因生物目前在国际、国内的书籍、刊物、各种媒体上使用的名词太多了，各种名词含义虽然不尽完全相同，但都可包括转基因生物，常见到的有经遗传修饰的生物体[GMOs(Genetically modified organisms)]、遗传工程生物体[GEOs(Genetically engineered organisms)] 、生物技术改变的活生物体[LMOs(Living modified organisms resulting from biotechnology)](注：此为《生物多样性公约》用语，目前国内常翻成改性活生物体，确切的含义是经修饰的活生物体)、经修饰的生物(modified organisms)以及工程生物(engineered organisms)。

1.1　1997年全球转基因作物商品化情况

70年代初，对农作物遗传工程的研究一开始就有争论，出于不同社会和经济目的，有的人认为转基因作物将造福于人类，另一部分人则认为转基因作物将可能给人类带来环境、人体健康及生态危险，双方的争论随着时间的推进，由于转基因作物的成功、走向商品化以及反对者的科学实验的不断积累，使争论更加深化，并还会持续地进行下去。但是受到 21 世纪人口膨胀压力等因素的驱动，生物技术特别是转基因作物将成为解决21世纪食物保证的重要措施之一，这一点已越来越成为共识，转基因作物 1997 全球年种植面积比 1996 年的面积增加 4.5 倍就足以说明这一趋势。

---

* “九五”国家重点科技项目(攻关)计划(97-925-02-04-05)资助。

1996 年，全球转基因作物商品化种植面积为 2.8×10^6hm^2，到 1997 年面积猛翻到 12.8×10^6hm^2，增加 4.5 倍。转基因作物从中试向大田释放的国家已经很多，但是主要是各国政府对转基因作物作大面积商品化释放的各种风险认识的不一致,到 1997 年作商品化释放的主要仅限于美国、中国、阿根廷、加拿大、澳大利亚及墨西哥等国家[1](见表 1)。表 1 说明这些国家种植的绝对面积都有增加，但美国、阿根廷与加拿大上升的趋势尤其明显。我国转基因作物大面积释放是世界上最早的国家，1992 年时，抗烟草花叶病毒和黄瓜花叶病毒的双抗转基因烟草在河南省已达到 8×10^3hm^2 的面积[2]。按 Kraltiger 报道，1994 年时，我国转基因烟草释放面积已达 1×10^6hm^2，当时国际上仅仅美国有大面积种植的延迟成熟期的转基因番茄，而且释放面积远不如我国大[3,4]。到 1997 年时，我国转基因作物大面积释放至少已包括有烟草、番茄等作物[5]，面积在国际上还占第 2 位，但从发展速度来看已远不如美国。整个发展中国家转基因作物商品化种植的面积在 1996 年几乎占全球一半(43%)，可到 1997 年仅占 1/4(见表 2)[6]。发达国家面积增长的速度几乎是发展中国家的 4 倍。

表 1　不同国家 1996 年和 1997 年商品化转基因作物面积

Table 1　The area of commertialized trangenic crops in 1996 and 1997 in different countries

国家 Country	1996	1997
	$A/10^6$hm^2(%)	$A/10^6$hm^2(%)
美国 USA	1.5 (51.0)	8.1 (64.0)
中国 CHN	1.1 (39.0)	1.8 (14.0)
阿根廷 ARC	0.1 (4.0)	1.4 (11.0)
加拿大 CAN	0.1 (4.0)	1.3 (10.0)
澳大利亚 AUS	<0.1 (1.0)	0.1 (<1.0)
墨西哥 MEX	<0.1 (1.0)	<0.1 (<1.0)
总数 Total	2.8 (100)	12.8 (100)

表 2　发达国家和发展中国家 1996 年和 1997 年商品化转基因作物面积

Table 2　The area of commertialized transgenic crops in 1996 and 1997 in developed and developing countries

地区 Area	1996	1997
	$A/10^6$hm^2(%)	$A/10^6$hm^2(%)
发达国家 Developed countries	1.6 (57)	9.5 (75)
发展中国家 Developing countries	1.2 (43)	3.3 (25)
总数 Total	2.8 (100)	12.8 (100)

1.2 全球 1997 年与 1996 年相比转基因作物面积的差异

按 James(1998)的报道[6]，以全球已大面积释放的转基因烟草、棉花、油菜、番茄、马铃薯、大豆和玉米等 7 种作物为例，绝对释放面积在一年内都有增加，而不同作物增长的速度却大不一样。面积相对减少的有番茄(由 4%减到 1%)、烟草(由 35%减到 13%)

及棉花(由 28%减到 11%)，而大豆、玉米与油菜却大幅度的增加，其中尤其是转基因大豆由 1996 年的 18%一下跃到占 40%。美国种植转基因大豆与玉米两种作物所增加的面积占到全球转基因作物增产面积的 5%。按媒体报道，1997 年，美国已有大量的耐除草剂转基因大豆输出到德国及其他国家。

1.3 1996 年与 1997 年不同性状转基因作物种植面积的变化

目前，已商品化的转基因作物的主要性状不外乎是耐除草剂、抗虫、抗病毒以及如延缓成熟期番茄或改变油质量的转基因油菜等改变质量性状，改变质量性状所占的面积少于 1×10^5hm^2，1996 年与 1997 年相比没有太大的变化，不一样的是 1997 年又增加了具抗虫及耐除草剂双重性状的转基因棉花[1,6]。其他性状虽然绝对面积都有增加，但是抗病毒的转基因作物种植面积由 1996 年所占的 40%猛跌到 1997 年的 14%。而耐除草剂性状的转基因作物由 23%增到 54%，翻了一番还多.抗虫性状基本持平，1996 年占 37%而 1997 年占 31%。

总之，1997 年与 1996 相比：①美国的耐除草剂转基因大豆面积大大增加，阿根廷虽面积不如美国大，但是也有增加；②在北美抗虫玉米有较大的发展；③耐除草剂油菜种植面积在加拿大有大量的增长。

2 转基因作物的经济效益及存在的问题

到 1997 年底，转基因作物的种植已得到明显的经济效益，但在国外也已出现各种各样的问题，按许智宏在 1995 年[7]时的提法是“植物基因工程还是一个新生儿”，到 1997 年底作为“新生儿”的产物大面积商品化种植才 2 ~ 3 年，在技术、经验、评估、检测等各方面都还有不少问题。

2.1 转基因作物的效益

按 James 报道[6]，美国 1996 年有 70%的抗虫转基因棉花(Bt 棉花)没有再喷杀虫剂，而产量提高了 7%。Bt 棉花节约的杀虫剂费用每 hm^2 高达 140 ~ 280 美元。美国种植的 32×10^6hm^2 玉米中的 50%受到欧洲玉米钻心虫的侵袭，估计每年损失达 10 亿美元，而种植抗钻心虫转基因玉米后，在 1996 及 1997 两年平均产量都提高 9%。经济效益 1996 年达 19×10^6 美元，1997 年已到 19×10^7 美元。由于种植了耐除草剂转基因大豆，1996 年少施了 10%~40%除草剂，其结果是控制了杂草及土壤湿度、提高了产量、没有了除草剂的残留物并且在作物的农艺管理上的灵活性大得多了。1996 年时，抗虫转基因马铃薯(Bt 马铃薯)也有效地控制了科罗拉多甲虫。

在转基因油菜种植较多的加拿大，1996 年由于耐除草剂转基因油菜的种植减少了对除草剂的依赖，并提高产量 9%，12×10^4hm^2 面积经济效益为 6×10^6 美元。与此同时，土壤的湿度能较好地保持，无除草剂的残留物，农艺管理的灵活性得到改善，级别高的油菜也比以前多了[6]。

在我国，抗病毒转基因烟草增加了烟草叶片的产量 5%~7%，并节约了 2%~3%杀虫剂的用量[6]。

总之，某些转基因作物在北美的表现比较好，经济效益也是明显的，1996 年种过转基因作物的很多农民 1997 年时还愿意再种，但由于转基因作物种子供应不足，本来还可发展的转基因作物 1997 年时未能做到[6]。

2.2 转基因作物存在的问题

转基因作物存在的问题可归为两类，一类是转基因作物商品化的利用刚处于萌芽阶段，各方面的经验不足或由于其他原因造成的；另一类则是转基因作物的潜在风险，这问题将在下一节另作讨论。

按 Kaiser 报道[8]，美国最大的研制转基因作物的 Monsanto 公司，1996 年时，栽种转基因抗虫棉的面积达到 $8 \times 10^5 hm^2$，但在东得克萨斯(Taxas)有 $8 \times 10^3 hm^2$Bt 棉不抗虫，受到棉铃虫危害。消息传出，使 Monsanto 公司占股份的专营棉花种子的 Delta 和 Pine Land 公司的股票一天内下跌 18.5%.Monsanto 公司一面采取措施，劝告从俄克拉荷马(Oklahoma)州到佐治亚(Georgia)州的棉农准备喷洒杀虫剂，以免受更大损失，一方面对此事件作出由于当年气温高所引起等解释.环境活动家和部分科学家担心 Bt 棉不抗虫，又鼓励棉农再喷洒杀虫剂，这样做会加速棉铃虫对 Bt 毒素产生抗性。Mellon[9]也作了类似的报道。

美国有一称为 Union of Concerned Seientists 的组织，所办的一个不定期类似“通讯”的出版物，1997 年报道了下列三条消息[10]：第 1 条是有关 1994 年美国第一个批准商品化的延迟成熟期转基因番茄到第 3 年，即 1997 年时在市场上已经消失，其原因是这种西红柿经不起采收、包装及运输的整个过程，很多番茄运到目的地时已经软化或碰伤，失去了商品的价值；另一个原因是推广的番茄品种在产量及抗病性状上都达不到商品的要求。第 2 条是有关能抗两种病毒的转基因黄色弯颈南瓜，此南瓜是经很长时间争议后在 1995 年才批准上市的，当年出售了少量种子，但第 2 年就停止出售。据开发这种转基因南瓜公司的发言人说，在培育出能抗 3 种病毒前，这种南瓜种子暂时停止出售。第 3 条是有关 Monsanto 公司开发的耐草甘膦除草剂转基因油菜，其中一个品种推销到加拿大，未能被加拿大政府管理机构批准，据 Monsanto 公司发言人说，错误是出在种子繁殖时质量失控的结果。这 3 条消息说明，转基因作物虽然已走上商品化的应用，但是在实验室阶段到中试阶段没有出现，或者由于时间、空间差异而一时未表现的问题是难以预料的。

Fox 曾报道[11],Monsanto 公司抗除草剂草甘膦转基因棉花(商品名为 Roundup Ready)大量落铃及棉桃畸形问题。这种转基因棉花经美国政府部门 1996 年批准商业化，1997 年第 1 年大规模种植。密西西比流域是美国主要种棉区，到秋天时，Delta 地区 40 个以上农民向美国农业部上诉，有 $1.2 \times 10^4 hm^2$ 这种转基因棉花在收花前大量落铃或棉桃畸形，损失达 5×10^5 美元。农业部官员调查后，证实了这情况，有些农场表现还很广泛。对此现象有种种解释，有人认为是由于“基因走向疯狂”，有人认为严重的是草甘膦可能已进入棉花种子内，而这棉种还在榨油作为食用。当然尚不可能一下子得出结论。

总之，萌芽状态的转基因作物即已出现明显的经济效益，但问题也已初露端倪。

3 转基因作物潜在的问题

正如本文一开始就提到的，对重组 DNA 技术或转基因生物的肯定和否定的争论至少已有 20 年以上的时间了，已发表的文章及专著已经很多[12~17]，召开过有关生物安全的国际会议也已不计其数，出版物也不少[18~21]，涉及生物安全的文章至少近千篇，本文引用的仅是作为代表性的沧海一粟，即使如此，人们对生物安全问题还知之甚少。转基因作物大面积释放仅有几年的时间，对转基因作物的生态风险评价，从理论上、概念上直到方法学上，在国际上虽然都已有相应的发展，但在方法学及对结果的分析上还有待进一步完善，尤其是在生态系统水平上，因生态系统是一个非常复杂的系统，应该抓住那些主要的参数还有待摸索[22]。

世界银行对全世界的环境问题、持续发展问题、人口、资源等一系列问题，有专门的总称为“环境和社会持续发展”的会议录系列，以及研究和专著系列。1997 年 10 月出版了题为“作物的生物工程，世界银行专家组对转基因作物的报告”(专著系列第 23)的专著[23]。参加撰写的有遗传育种、生物工程、生态学、化学生态学、昆虫学、种子科学、植物学等各领域国际著名的专家，报告完成后又邀请了一批国际有关专家提意见并作修改，应该说对转基因作物的观点相对比较公正。报告在充分肯定生物工程在提高作物产量及质量方面、在解决环境保护的一些问题以及人类健康问题上的巨大潜力的同时也有专门一章论及可能存在的问题。在报告中著者们也指出，他们企图对科学家和环境主义者所提出的有关的问题和风险，根据目前的知识作出一种不偏不倚的评论，本文着重按世界银行报告的论点来作介绍。

3.1 由于基因流引起的作物变为杂草问题

世行报告(以下简称“报告”)对这一点是充分肯定的。“报告”指出，正如已详细研究了 50 年的原理已清楚地表现,存在于栽培作物或其他植物中的任何基因可通过杂交而转移到其野生或半驯化种中去。能在近缘品系中提高竞争能力的一个或几个基因将可能被选择发生转移，这样转移的结果，在特定条件下，将增强某些植物杂草化的特性。当然，未必任何单个基因转移到如玉米、棉花这类已高度驯化了的作物中就能使它们变成有害的杂草，而一些还未十分驯化的如直播植物苜蓿和一些商品化的松树品种容易出问题。某些转基因(transgenes)可以增强它们在野外的适合度(fitness)，例如，一棵抗吃种子害虫的转基因松树可能由于种子抗虫而大量的保留下来而潜在地使它们能竞争过当地其他物种，一旦这种情况发生时，森林群落将遭到破坏。

田波的文章中也指出，常规育种培育的品种在某些地区种植后成为了野生植物，一种油用油菜在英国种植后不仅变成野生杂草，并成为花粉气喘过敏症的过敏原，并指出转基因作物也有成为野生杂草的可能[24]。

3.2　转基因作物的转基因通过基因流转移到野生植物

“报告”中例举野生稻的例子来说明这问题，转基因水稻如与起源的野生种同在一个区域内时，水稻中的转基因会转移到野生稻中去。在某些条件下，某些作物的近缘种是危害很大的杂草(例如野生稻和阿拉伯高粱)。如果一种野生植物被一种转基因或能抗拒自然发生病虫害的其他基因提高适合度的话，这种植物就可能变成极坏的害草，或者可破坏自然植物群落的生态平衡。杂草常常通过自然进化的过程而进化出对病害或其他性状的抗性，如澳大利亚大量使用除草剂草甘膦已使杂草产生抗性了，而从转基因作物来的基因转移可加速这个过程。如在转基因水稻田里的野生稻得到了抗除草剂转基因水稻来的抗除草剂基因，则野生水稻危害更大，因此，报告指出在作生物技术项目投资前要考虑到这种类似的基因转移的问题。

此外，有报道指出，反对已被美国农业部(USDA)和食品和药物管理署(FDA)批准的转基因南瓜上市的原因，就因为美国较普遍存在野葫芦一类的野生南瓜近缘种。如能抗多种病毒的转基因南瓜中的抗病毒基因一旦转入这些对黄瓜斑纹病毒和西瓜斑纹病毒敏感的野生种，野生种具有了抗性后果将是严重的[25]。

3.3　有关对含有编码病毒序列基因的转基因作物释放问题

对这个问题是人们普遍关注并有争议的问题，本文既介绍“报告”的观点，也介绍“报告”发表后国际上有关这个问题研究工作进展的情况。

3.3.1　有关病毒蛋白引起过敏反应问题

“报告”认为，对有人提到有关病毒蛋白引起过敏反应的问题已不值得一提了，因为自然界很多谷物本来就受到植物病毒侵染，人们食用后并未见有过敏反应。贾士荣也持同样观点，认为“水果或蔬菜(如番茄)均会系统感染病毒，因此人们生食水果或蔬菜，实际上每天都在摄入病毒外壳蛋白”[26]。因此转基因植物中含病毒外壳蛋白基因是没问题的。

3.3.2　有关杂草化问题

对有人提出的抗病毒转基因植物在大田中与杂草杂交后会增加其在自然界的竞争性以及杂草化问题，“报告”也持否定态度，认为至今还缺乏数据来说明这个问题的重要性。

3.3.3　有关病毒重组问题

大田作物中转基因病毒序列的存在，就有可能与侵染该植物的其他病毒进行重组，从而提高了产生新的病毒的可能性。“报告”确认了这个事实，即很多作物同时可被多种病毒浸染，以及已有少数例子证实了不同病毒之间有遗传重组。此外还认为，在类病毒与病毒株系间有重组证据的话，可还没有证据说明在转基因作物中会比正常情况重组发生的频率要高，因此，“报告”的结论是，已有的证据还不足以支持病毒的重组将引起生态问题的论点。可是，1997 年 8 月的 *New Scientist* 杂志上报道了 McGrath 题为“致命的杂种使丰收无望”的短文[27]。引述了周雪平等报道的实验证明，在乌干达木薯中发现非洲木薯花叶病毒（ACMV)和东非木薯花叶病毒(EACMV)在植物体内发生重组而形成新的流行性的杂种病毒[28]。这种杂种病毒正在毁灭整个乌干达木薯，损失已达 6×10^6 美元。McGrath 文章指出，这是国际上第一次说明植物病毒种间重组后杂种病毒造成严重流行病的例子，目前这种新病毒已向肯尼亚和苏丹等国蔓延。1998 年，周雪平等又在巴基斯坦棉花曲叶病毒中发现重组现象并形成杂种病毒[29]。这两个例子已有力地说明，不同种的病毒确实可在植物体内重组，新的杂种病毒会发生流行，并给作物带来毁灭性的打击。至于抗病毒转基因作物的情况又如何呢？在美国 Iowa 州立大学工作的植物病毒学家 Miller 指出，转基因植物中的病毒基因在所有细胞和所有时间内都存在，从而提高了重组的风险，因此当转基因作物释放面积达到上百万英亩，这些作物又都在表达病毒基因时，将会出现什么问题谁都不能作出预料[30]。

3.3.4 有关产生更有害病毒株问题

有关由转基因作物产生的病毒外壳蛋白可以和自然界的病毒的结合而产生更为有害的病毒株，“报告”的结论是产生这样病毒株理论上是可能的，但以此来评估作为转基因作物的风险则是太低了。

3.4 转基因植物产生的杀虫剂对非靶生物的影响

目前已商品化应用的抗虫转基因作物仅局限于能产生杀虫剂的 Bt 抗虫转基因作物。“报告”指出产生的毒性蛋白是高度特化的，有一组毒性蛋白仅影响到鳞翅目的一些种，另一组蛋白仅对一些有限的甲虫有毒性，这些蛋白还没有对有益昆虫或对吃害虫物种有大的破坏影响的报道。另外，这些蛋白在阳光下降解的也很快，即使是在植物体内的残留物也还是要被降解掉。“报告”还提到，用人的消化系统的酶做研究，结果说明这些 Bt 蛋白很快就消化了，并不会引起对人体的伤害作用。

3.5 对生态系统的破坏

应该说，“报告”对生态系统的破坏这一节讨论的问题太少，仅仅谈论了与土壤有关的问题。实际上，对生态系统的问题是一个最复杂的问题，也是人们对此了解得最少的问题，却又是一个极为重要的问题，不是短时间，而是少则五六年，多则几十年才能作判断的问题。我们可以把转基因作物作为一个引入生态系统的外来种，因为这样的作物自然界不存在，完全是人工制造的。对外来种的问题，近年来越来越受到国际上的重视，国际科联环境问题科学委员会(SCOPE)会同其他国际组织专门有一个称为全球外来种项目(GISP)。外来种有的对全球的经济和环境是有益的，很多种既无益也无害，而又有大量的外来种是有害的。由于它们的引入造成生态系统严重的破坏。它们会成为带来病害的生物体、农业的杂草、破坏性的昆虫以及其他威胁到生产力、生产稳定性、生物多样性和人类社区的健康。而全世界的人类和自然生态系统正面临着日益增长的破坏性外来种的包围。转基因作物大面积释放的物种数，实际数量及释放到环境中的时间，可能都还来不及对此作出是有益的、既无益也无害或是有破坏性外来种的结论，但是不能不考虑到这个问题。

“报告”认为，目前对有关遗传信息从植物如何向微生物流动知道得很少，因此对植物基因扩散到土壤微生物中的情况不了解，难以对风险作评估。土壤微生物，尤其是细菌能从周围环境中摄入被土壤颗粒束缚住的 DNA，从而有人假设植物植株释放出的 DNA 可被土壤颗粒束缚住，而后再被土壤微生物摄入。“报告”认为这样的假设是不可能的，任何这样一种转移的潜在风险可被排除。有人还推测，基因可能转移到土壤中生存的真菌(霉菌)中去；而“报告”认为，一般来说，基因转移到真菌中比转移到细菌中更为困难。

在美国，转基因线虫及转基因节肢动物(如螨、蜜蜂等)都已成功，1997 年已在向政府有关部门申请作环境释放[4]。这类转基因无脊椎动物在生态系统功能中的作用显然是极为重要的。与植物不一样的是，相对来说植物是较固定的，而蜜蜂等节肢动物在基因流动上起到重要作用又是能自由飞动，因此必然会引起公众的极大关心。

3.6 对遗传工程作物代价-惠益的评估

“报告”提出，对一个作物遗传工程的投资前，必须调研清楚准备转移的基因是否在准备释放的地理区域内能发挥重要的功能；另一个问题是这个基因发挥的功能能持续多长时间。

3.6.1 在释放地理区域发挥功能问题

对某种特定的如棉花或玉米等作物，不同地理区域的害虫是不一样的，如美国南部棉区的害虫主要是两种鳞翅目昆虫，棉铃虫和蚜虫，而中美洲棉区害虫却主要是秋天的粘棉铃象虫。Monsnato 开发的含 Bt 毒蛋白的转基因棉在美国南部有效而对中美洲是无效的。另一个问题是在发达国家能行的在发展中国家未必可行。如不少公司出售的耐除草剂转基因玉米的种子内只含一个拷贝的抗除草剂基因，是由转基因玉米亲本与一个不含这个转基因的亲本杂交得到的，这种种子只能种一年，所有植株都抗除草剂。在美国就是运用这种保护知识产权的体制，而在大多数发展中国家行不通，“报告”例举了萨尔瓦多农民因为种子很贵，每 3 年只买一次这样的种子。由于后代的遗传分离，到第 2 年只有 3/4 到第 3 年只有 1/2 左右的玉米能抗除草剂，从而造成很大的经济损失。

3.6.2 基因的功能持续多长的问题

某些害虫经过一年或两年在某些情况下就可能进化出耐高浓度的 Bt 毒性，美国的 EPA 对含 Bt 棉花种子采取限制出售的方法，保证每一个美国的农场有一定面积种不含产生 Bt 蛋白的品种。目的是使两种土地上的昆虫交尾后，冲淡抗 Bt 蛋白昆虫的频率，而导致更持续的抗性，这就是所谓避难所策略[31]，这种在昆虫中描述过的相类似的适应问题在转基因抗病及耐除草剂作物中也同样存在，“报告”提出，对一些如草甘膦类的除草剂原来考虑对杂草的适应是“免疫”的，但不清楚当除草剂大量使用时是否还是“免疫”的。

3.7 其他

对可能存在的问题，“报告”从以上提到的4个方面作了叙述。但在某些问题上叙述的范围显得过于狭窄，尤其在生态系统破坏的问题上，我们在这些问题上有另文介绍[22]。此外，有关对人体健康以及伦理道德这些相当多人关心的问题，在“报告”中也未涉及。

对转基因作物商品化的生态风险持不同意见的人大致有下列几个观点：

(1) 至今对转基因作物释放风险的根据都来自生产的公司自己做的实验，未必很客观；

(2) 近年来发达国家尽管针对生物安全，开始已拨出专门经费安排了一定的实验，但时间还太短，结果还太少；

(3) 评估得到的结论均是从小范围的大田释放得到的，这结论是否符合商品化生产的情况还是问题；

(4) 商品化生产的时间还很短，大面积释放后的监测，特别是在自然生态系统中积累的数据还太少。我们同样持这种观点，因之我们认为现在对一系列问题作结论显然还为时尚早。

参考文献

[1] James C. Global status of tansgnicc crops in 1997. ISAAA Briefs NO. 5., ISAAA: I thaca, NY, USA: ISAAA

[2] Zhou R, Zhang ZC, Wu Q, Fang RX, Mang KQ, Tian YL, Wang GL.Large-scales perforce of transonic tobacco Plants resistant to both tobacco motoic virus and cucumber mosaic virus. In: Jones DD ed. The biosafety results of field test of genetically modified plant and microorganisms. California: The University of California, 1994, 49~56

[3] Krattiger AF. The field testing and commercialization of genetically modified plants; A review of worldwide data (1986 to 1993/94). In: krattiger, AF *et al* ed Biosafety for unobtainable agriculture. ISAAA / SES, 1994, 247~266

[4] Qian YQ(钱迎倩), Ma KP(马克平). On biotechnology and biosafety, *J Nature Ressour* (自然资源学报).1995, 10(4): 322~331

[5] Stone R.Large plots are next text for transgenic crop safety, *Science*. 1994, 226:1471~1473

[6] James C. Global status and distribution Of commercial transgenic crops in 1997. Biotech Develp Monitor. 1998, 35: 9~12

[7] 许智宏．植物生物工程.序.见：田波，许智宏，叶寅主编.植物生物工程．济南：山东科学技术出版社, 1995, 1~2

[8] Kaiser J. Pests overwhelm Bt cotton crop *Scienc*.1996, 273: 423

[9] Mellon M. Resistance management. *Science*.1996, 274: 704

[10] Anonymous. Post-approval blues. *The Gene Exchange*.1997. Fall1997: 11

[11] Fox JL. Farmers say Monsanto's engineered cotton crop bolls. *Nature Biotech*. 1997, 15(12): 1233

[12] Wen Dz (闻大中).Ecological effect of genetic engineered organism and its assessment. *Chin J Appl Ecol* (应用生态学报). 1992, 3 (4): 371~377

[13] Qian YQ (钱迎倩). Biodiversity and biotechnology. *Bull Chin Acad Sci*(中国科学院院刊). 1994. 2: 134~138

[14] Qian YQ(钱迎倩), Ma KP(马克平). Progress in the studies on genetically modified orgasnisms, and the impact of its release on environment. *Acta Ecol Sin*(生态学报). 1998, 18 (1): 1~9

[15] Krattiger AF, Rosemarin A. Biosafety for sustainable agriculture, Sharing biotechnology regulatory experiences of the Western hemisphere. Ithaca, U. S. A, and Stockholm, Sweden: ISAAA/SEI, 1994, 1~278

[16] Tzotzos GT. Genetically modified organisms, A guide to biosafety. Wallingford, UK: CAB International, 1995, l~213

[17] Rissler J, Mellon M. The ecological risks of engineered crops.London, England: The MIT Press, 1996, l~168

[18] Burke T, Seidler R, Smith H. Ecological implication of transgenic Plant release. *Mol. Ecol* 1994, 3(l): l~89

[19] Mackenzie DR, Henry SC. The biosafety results of field test of genetically modified plant and microorganisms. November 27~30, 1990, Kiawah Island, southn Carolina: Agricultural Research Institute, Maryland U.S.A. 1990, l~301

[20] Capers R, Landsmanu J. The biosafety results of field test of genetically modified plant and microorganisms. Proceeding of 2nd International Symposium May 11~14, 1992, Goslar, Germany: Bioligische Bundesanstalt fur land-und Forstwirtschaft, Braunschweig, Germany, 1992, l~296

[21] Jones DD. The biosafety result of field test of genetially modified plant and microorganisms, Proceeding of 3nd International symposium November 13~16, 1994. Monterery, California: University of Califoria, 1994, l~558

[22] Qian YQ (钱迎倩), Tian Y (田彦), Wei W(魏伟).Ecological risk assessment of transgenic plant. *Acta Phytoecol*(植物生态学报). 1998, 22 (4): 289~299

[23] Kendall HW, Beachy R, Eisner, T. Bioengineering of Crops, Report of the World Bank Panel on Transgenic Crops. 1997. Washington, U.S.A.: The Worldbank, 1997, l~30

[24] 田波. 植物基因工程: 机会和问题. 见: 田波, 许智宏, 叶寅主编. 植物基因工程. 济南：山东生物技术出版社, 1998, 1~7

[25] Kling J. Could transgenic supercrops one day breed supersedes Science, 1996, 274: 180 ~181

[26] 贾士荣, 曹冬孙. 转基因植物. 见: 荆玉祥, 匡廷云, 李德葆主编. 分子生物学: 成就与前景. 北京: 科学出版社, 1995, 254~267

[27] McGrath P. Lethal hybrid decimates harvest. *New Science*. 1997, 155 (2097): 8

[28] Zhou XP. Liu YL, Calvert L, Munoz C, Otim-Nape GW, Robinson DJ, Harrison, BD. Evidence that DNA—A of a germinivirus associated with sever cassava mosaic disease in Uganda has arisen by interspecific recombination. *J Gen Virol.* 1997, 78: 2101~2111

[29] Zhou XP, Liu YL, Robinson DJ, Harrison BD. Four DNA—A variants among Pakistan isolates of cotton leaf curl virus and their affinities to DNA—A of gemini virus isolates from okra. *J Gen Virol*.1998, 79: 915~923

[30] Kleiner K. Fields of genes. *New Scient*. 1997, 155(2095): 4

[31] Wei W(魏伟), Qian YQ (钱迎倩), Ma KP (马克平). Pests, resistance to transgenic Bt crops and their management strategies. Chin J Appl Environ Biol(应用与环境生物学报). 1999, 5(2): 215~228

本文原载：生物多样性. 1999. 7(2): 151-155

终止子技术与生物安全*

钱迎倩　马克平　桑卫国　魏伟

（中国科学院植物研究所）

摘　要　终止子技术是美国 Del ta and Pi ne Land 种子公司和美国农业部联合申请、经美国专利局1998年3月批准的一项专利。整个过程可叙述为遗传工程师在转基因作物中加入了由3个基因组成的终止子基因；得到的转基因作物的种子由种子公司加上一种诱导剂；经诱导剂的作用及终止子基因间的相互作用，在种子胚胎发育的后期产生一种毒素；这种毒素杀死了发育后期的胚胎；最后得到的是成熟但不育的种子。专利获得后，引起国际上巨大反响。国际农业研究磋商小组指出，终止子技术必须禁止，不然将给全球食品保障带来影响。原因是这项技术会使农民无法留种、对遗传多样性有负影响，由于农民不再育种影响到持续农业的发展，可能出现出售或交换不能发芽的种子以及通过花粉非故意的传播造成生物安全的风险。第三世界国家认为这项技术是“种子的灾难”、“农业上的中子弹”。虽然转基因作物产生不育种子可能在解决转基因逃逸带来的生态风险上有益处，但这个收获与终止子技术可能给全球食品保障带来危机相比，两者就不能等量齐观了。从另一角度看，这项技术可能又是遗传工程带来的另一种生物安全危机。

关键词　终止子技术；不育种子；基因保护；“种子的灾难”；生物安全

用遗传工程手段得到的经修饰活生物体(LMO)向环境释放后可能产生一系列生态风险其中已被实验证明了的风险是转基因的逃逸[1, 2]，从而可能使转基因作物的野生近缘种成为杂草。但由美国的 Delta and Pine Land (DPL)种子公司(该公司现已被 Monsanto 公司购买)和美国农业部联合申请的一个称为“终止子技术”的专利，该专利技术可使作物种植后得到的种子是不育的，从而解决转基因物质从一种作物向其他物种或作物野生近缘种的扩散，提高了 LMO 的安全性。尽管这项技术在解决生物安全方面有如此的优点，但在美国国内、一些国际 组织、尤其是在第三世界国家已经引起了强烈的反响与争论。本文首先对该项技术作一介绍，并对国际上争论的核心问题以及与生物安全的关系作简短的讨论。

1　终止子技术介绍

在国外，出售的玉米种子都是杂交种，杂交种只能种一年，第二年再种就开始大量分离，因此种子收获后不能用作留种，农民每年都要向种子公司购买杂交种。转基因玉米由于高技术的加入可卖到更高的价格，投资者不仅收回了投资，并能获取高额利润，

* 九五国家重点科技项目(攻关)计划(97-925-02-04-05)资助。

可是小麦、水稻、大豆以及棉花等作物都不是卖的杂交种，转基因作物出售一次后，农民可以继续留种，不存在每年都要再买种子问题，投资者运用了遗传工程的手段创造了“终止子技术”[4]，使作物第一年种后得到的种子是不育的，不能留种作为第二年再种的种子。实际上，终止子技术是一项用遗传工程的手段对遗传工程技术中基因保护的一种措施。

终止子技术已于1998年3月经美国专利局批准，美国专利号为5723765名称为“植物基因表达的控制”[3]。这项技术大致的程序是遗传工程师把终止子基因插入到作物中得到转基因作物的种子；种子公司在种子出售前，在种子中加入一种诱导剂；农民把这些种子播下去后，长出正常的植株，并能收获成熟的种子，这种种子在油脂、蛋白质等各个部分都是完全正常的，就是胚胎已被杀死，因此农民不能把这样的种子作留种用。DPL 公司称这项专利谓“技术保护系统”。而国际农业促进基金会(RAFI)称这项专利为“终止子技术”[4]。一般把用这项技术获得的种子称为“终止子种子”。

2 终止子技术作用原理

这项技术的成功是依赖于一种受控的序列。这个序列控制着拼接进去的3 个基因之间的相互作用，最后的工程基因在种子发育的很晚期才进入角色。公司在种子出售前要加入诱导剂(可能是四环素)，当一个特殊的开关在诱导剂控制下把基因打开后，使这个基因产生毒素，毒素把成熟种子中的胚胎杀死。基因相互作用有多种途径，这些途径都已申请了专利，下面介绍一种途径(见图 1)。

<table>
<tr><th>终止子基因在不存在诱导剂时</th><th>终止子基因加上诱导剂后</th></tr>
<tr><td colspan="2">基因 I：抑制子</td></tr>
<tr><td>一种抑制子基因产生一种抑制子蛋白</td><td>与左方一样，产生同样的抑制子蛋白</td></tr>
<tr><td colspan="2">基因 II：重组酶
一种重组酶基因受到一种启动子控制，在启动子和这个基因之间，科学家又放上一个 DNA 片段，而这个 DNA 片段就成为基因 I 抑制子的结合部位。</td></tr>
<tr><td>当不存在诱导剂时，抑制子结合到接合部位，植物就不产生重组酶蛋白。这种重组酶可以切掉这 DNA 片段</td><td>受诱导剂的干扰，抑制子结合不到结合部位上，这样就使基因 II 产生重组酶</td></tr>
<tr><td colspan="2">基因 III：毒素
一种毒死胚胎的基因(毒素基因)是受到一种迟生启动子(late promoter, LP)所控制，在胚胎发育过程中，到种子发育的后期 LP 才有活性。在 LP 和毒素基因中间科学家又放了一小片段 DNA，称之阻断子(blocker)。阻断子干扰了启动子启动基因的能力。</td></tr>
<tr><td>没有诱导剂，就没有重组酶去切去阻断子

阻断子存在时，不产生毒素

种子公司可以通过不加入诱导剂而使胚胎保持存活，一代一代地生产活的种子</td><td>基因 II 来的重组酶切去了阻断子，并到种子发育季节的后期使迟生启动子启动了毒素基因
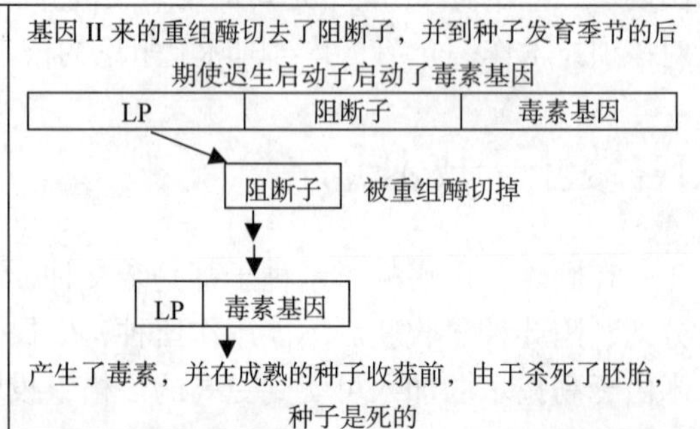
产生了毒素，并在成熟的种子收获前，由于杀死了胚胎，种子是死的</td></tr>
</table>

图 1 终止子技术中 3 种基因相互作用的途径[5]

Fig. 1 The ways of interactions of three genes in terminator technology

3 终止子技术存在的问题

终止子技术获得专利后，国际上反响很大，1998 年 10 月在华盛顿世界国际农业研究磋商小组(CGIAR)召开会议，明确提出为了保护对世界食物的保障，禁止终止子技术[6]。CGIAR 是 16 个国际农业研究中心的全球网络，在全球农业及粮食方面有相当的权威性。该组织明确提出下列 5 点：

(1) 农业留种的重要性，特别对贫穷的农民尤为重要

(2) 对遗传多样性的负影响

(3) 为了发展持续农业，农民育种的重要性

(4) 可能出售或交换不能发芽的种子用于播种

(5) 通过花粉非故意的传播造成生物安全的风险

以上 5 点深刻地指出了终止子技术存在的问题，终止子技术的目的就是要让农民不能留下当年收获的种子作下年播种用。但是众所周知，每一种品种是不可能适合各种温度、气候、土壤等各种环境条件的，一个农场或一个农民得到了适合当地的优质、高产品种后，得到的种子却不能留种用，对贫穷的农民来说他们付不起每年大量购买高价留种的种子的金额。农民得不到好的产量，是对全世界粮食保障的一种破坏。世界上有一半以上的农民是贫穷的，但他们生产了世界的 15%~20%的粮食，他们至少直接养活了世界 14 亿人口，其中 10 亿在亚洲、1 亿在拉丁美洲、3 亿在非洲。这些农民多少年来世世代代一直是用他们自己的育种技术来培育适应他们自己土地上的品种，因此 CGIAR 提出，保证农民育种是发展持续农业的重要部分。

种植具终止子基因作物后，携带终止子基因的花粉会随着各种媒介而侵入到农民的土地中去，不管这些农民是拒绝或无能力买这技术都有可能得到这样的花粉。其后果是一方面造成农民使用品种成为不育的，而影响到遗传多样性的降低。另一方面受携带终止子基因花粉影响的作物，当年是见不到影响的，农民不可能去识别哪些种子是不育的，哪些是可育的，都留种作为来年播种用，当发现某些种子是不育时已为时过晚，造成减产。如果这技术是通过隐性基因传递时，则会可能出现以后若干年无规律的收成，从而造成当地农村社区食物保障的受损。

此外，CGIAR 的政策会深刻影响到联合国生物多样性公约的科学组织即将举行的会议。该组织会要审查终止子技术的影响。《公约》的代表曾参加 CGIAR 会议，并表示《公约》应很仔细地考虑 CGIAR 的政策，目前全球已有不同的政府、科学界和民众团体明确地反对，这技术又无任何可信赖的能促进生物多样性的阐明，而却对全球粮食保障有影响，应该禁止。

4 对终止子技术所持态度

在 CGIAR 召开的会议上发展中国家乌干达、津巴布韦和印度代表以及发达国家中的英国和荷兰的代表都态度明朗地反对终止子政策，美国政府代表保持沉默希望能抵挡

住，但在公众舆论压力下，美国农业部作出决定，不用这项技术制成的种子卖给美国农民。美国农业部发言人明确表示，终止子技术的初衷是针对第二世界和第三世界的，主要的作物包括有水稻、小麦、高粱和大豆。但反对者认为矛盾并未解决，进一步向美国农业部提出为何既然承认这项技术释放给美国农民是不可取的，另一方面又把专利的权利交给 Monsanto 公司作商业发展；为何这项技术对美国农民不适用，而对世界上其他国家又是合适的呢?

RAFI 和其他的非政府组织赞同 CGIAR 的政策，他们要求禁止终止子技术，采取了不少行动，1998 年 11 月前来自 57 个国家的 2400 人利用了 RAFI 的 Website 向美国农业部长表达了下列 3 点要求美国政府停止与 Monsanto 公司谈判发放终止子执照的问题;要求美国农业部放弃这项技术所有专利用到其他 87 个国家去；在美国禁止应用这项技术，其他国家禁止应用时美国政府也不要去干预。RAFI 动员公众都起来反对这项技术，让这项会对农民、对生物多样性和世界食品保障都会受损害的专利停止掉。此外，RAFI 还要用 CGIAR 的政策来影响联合国生物多样性议程。

Monsanto 公司与印度的 Mahyco 公司合作开发其 Bollgard^{TM} (Bt) 转基因抗虫棉花，到 1998 年已是第 3 年了，印度农民知道了终止子技术后曾在他们国内出现把 Bt 棉花连根拔掉并烧掉的事件。Monsanto 公司为之专门出告示，一方面宣传其转基因抗虫棉的能抗棉铃虫的优点，并宣传这种棉花已在美国、澳大利亚、南非和中国种植，大大减少了虫害、让农民增加了产量。另一方面又说明了目前 Bt 棉中没有用终止子技术，终止子技术还需要用几年的时间花几百万美元来做研究才能作商业化的利用。印度到 1998 年 12 月前在其“经济新闻”等媒体上大肆宣传，呼吁政府要对终止子种子紧闭大门，不许进口会永久严重危害印度农业的含终止子基因的种子。认为“终止子种子”会迫使农民每年都要重新买种子，会使传统的作物品种逐渐灭绝。尽管目前终止子基因还仅仅在烟草和棉花上应用，但通过花粉的传播，可能影响到印度的其他植物，因此是一种“种子的灾难”会给整个第三世界国家带来巨大的危机。

目前掌握专利的人声称，终止子技术对所有的作物都有用，但实际上终止子技术只在烟草和棉花上作过应用，在其他作物不一定可行或者可能表现得不稳定。希望它失败不如禁止它的使用更为有效。何况终止子基因还有可能从烟草或棉花上进行扩散。即使是某种作物偶尔发生种子不能萌发的情况，由于这样的偶尔发生的事件，已足够让农民惊吓得不敢留种。智利的一个称为教育和技术中心(CET)组织要求禁止终止子技术，把这技术称为“农业的中子弹”。

5 结束语

CGIAR 已把终止子技术的问题分析得很清楚，其初衷明显地是为了对其开发的转基因作物的知识产权保护服务的，但是带来的后果是严重的。尽管可能会在解决转基因作物由于转基因逃逸所带来的生态风险问题，但这项技术所带来的严重后果将与转基因逃逸是不可相比的。从另一个角度考虑，这可能又是由于遗传工程引起的一种新的生物安全的问题。

参考文献

[1] Mikkelsen T R, Andersen B, JØrgensen R B. The risk of crop transgene spread. *Nature*, 1996,380: 31

[2] 钱迎倩，马克平. 经遗传修饰生物体的研究进展及其释放后对环境的影响. 生态学报, 1998, 18(1): 1~9

[3] Crouch M L. How the Terminator terminates: an explanation for the nonscientist of a remarkable patent for killing second generations seeds of crop plants, http://www.bio.indiana. edu/people. terminator. html

[4] Anonmynous. Terminating food security? http://www.rafi.org/pr/release15.html, 1998

[5] Anonmynous. Terminator technology. The Gene Exchange, 1998, Fall/Winter, 1998, 4

[6] Anonmynous. Terminator seeds rejected by global network of agriculture experts. http://www.rafi.org/pr/release23.html, 1998

本文原载：生态学报. 2001. 21(3): 337-343

转基因作物对生物多样性的影响

钱迎倩　魏伟　桑卫国　马克平

(中国科学院植物研究所)

摘　要　转基因作物对生物多样性的影响是重要的环境问题之一，近年来，已有这类实验的报道。夏敬源等的研究说明大田种植转基因 Bt 抗虫棉花对棉铃虫优势寄生性天敌齿唇姬蜂(*Campoletis chlorideae*)和侧沟绿茧蜂(*Microplitis* sp.)的寄生率、羽化率和蜂茧质量造成严重的危害。国际上一些昆虫学家也做了很好的工作，尤其 1999 年 5 月 Losey 等在 *Nature* 上发表转基因 Bt 抗虫玉米在实验室水平上引起大斑蝶死亡报道后，世界范围内引起极大的反响。在有关经遗传修饰生物体(*GMOs*)的潜在生态风险和人体健康影响的问题上美国始终抱抵制的强硬态度，这次也开始有所松动。两个有影响的美国玉米加工公司宣布不再接受欧盟拒绝进口的转基因玉米品种。欧盟宣布在进一步研究得到结论前冻结转基因作物产品进口的审批。欧盟所属有关国家有的禁止进口，有的反对欧盟审批。科技界及公众众说纷纭。建议我国政府要加强 GMOs 潜在生态风险及对公众健康的研究及商业化生产后的监测。

关键词　转基因作物；大斑蝶；生态风险；生物多样性

经遗传修饰的生物体(Genetically modified organisms(GMOs))中的转基因作物在大田作大规模释放最早的是中国。抗烟草花叶病毒和黄瓜花叶病毒双抗的转基因烟草 1992 年在河南就发展到 8600hm^2[3]，按 Krirtlger 报道 1994 年中国转基因烟草已发展到 100 万 hm^2[2]。美国有的烟草公司一直进口大量河南烟草，后得知中国出口烟草中有转基因烟草后，停止了进口。由于不能大量出口，影响了转基因烟草的种植，可是美国的转基因作物近年来以势似破竹的速度迅猛发展，按 James 报道，全世界(不包括中国在内)，转基因作物种植面积达 2780 万 hm^2[3]，以美国为例，被批准能大面积生产的作物有转基因油菜、菊苣、玉米、棉花、木瓜、马铃薯、大豆、南瓜以及番茄，共计 34 个品种。

对 GMOs 及其产物的生态风险及对人体健康的影响，不同国家政府及不同阶层公众的观点历来是不同的，甚至截然相反的[4,5]。GMOs 对生物多样性或说对非目标生物的影响早几年虽已提出来，但实验证据还不多。近年来，昆虫学家做了一些出色的工作[6~8]。特别是 Losey 等有关转基因玉米花粉对大斑蝶(*Danaus plexippus*)幼虫伤害的报告发表以来，世界各国引起很大的反响，包括美国在内的有关政府部门在一定程度上调整了对转基因作物及其产物的政策，当然对这报告也有持不同观点的。本文将作全面报道，并阐明自己的观点。

基金项目：“九五”国家重点科技攻关(97-925-02-04-05)资助项目。

1 几个案例

随着美国政府 1995 年后陆续批准转基因 Bt 玉米和棉花及抗除草剂大豆商品化生产后，有相当数量的 GMOs 产物作为食用或农用销往欧盟及包括我国在内的亚洲、南美等地。一些发达国家对 GMOs 生物安全问题的科研工作也不断深入，下面是几个案例。

1.1 转基因玉米的花粉伤害大斑蝶幼虫

转 Cry1A(b)基因抗虫 Bt 玉米的毒素是在花粉中表达的：Losey 等[6]在实验室水平上做了一个很简单但影响深远的实验。他们用一种大斑蝶，也称君主斑蝶(*Danaus plexippus*)作为实验对象，这种蝴蝶的唯一食物是马利筋属的杂草，包括马利筋(*Asclepias curassavica*)。由于这种杂草田内或田边有大量分布，玉米扬花时花粉可随风飘 60m 远。在杂草叶片表面上撒落有相当密度的花粉。作者以撒有与自然界同样密度的转基因 Bt 玉米花粉的马利筋叶片喂饲大斑蝶，并以同样条件的正常玉米花粉和不加花粉的马利筋作为对照。每张叶片上放 5 条 3 日龄的幼虫、每个实验重复 5 次。4d 后记录马利筋叶片的消耗量、虫子的成活率及幼虫的重量。

喂有 Bt 玉米花粉马利筋叶片的幼虫第 2 天就有 10%以上死亡，4d 后死亡 44%。而两个对照全部存活。幼虫对不同处理的马利筋叶片摄取量也明显不同；摄取不加花粉的叶片量最大，而加 Bt 花粉的叶片摄取量少了很多，由于叶片摄取量少，幼虫生长就缓慢，实验结束时摄食 Bt 花粉叶片的幼虫重量平均只有无花粉叶片的一半。

作者认为这虽是实验室的结果，但有深层的内涵。因有成亿数量的大斑蝶每年从美国的东北部经过中西部到墨西哥中部 Oyamel 森林中越冬。这一点最近已被用稳定性同位素的实验证明了[9~13]。中西部是美国的玉米种植带，大斑蝶迁移经过的时间是 6 月晚些时候到 8 月中，此时是蝴蝶幼虫叶片喂饲阶段，又是玉米扬花季节。如果实验结果能适用于大田的话，则对大斑蝶物种生存将可能造成重大的威胁。

几乎与 Losey 等的工作同时，美国 Iowa 州立大学的昆虫学家 J. Obrycni 和 L. Hansew 在网上公布了类似的大田实验的结果。他们用的马利筋叶片是玉米田内或田边收集的，用的大斑蝶的幼虫是刚孵化出来的。实验结果说明用 Bt 玉米花粉处理的 48h 后就有 19%死亡，而非玉米花粉处理的幼虫无一个死亡的。而没有花粉处理的对照死亡率为 3%[12]。

1.2 转基因玉米对有益昆虫绿草蛉的死亡和发育的影响

世界很多农业系统范围内，捕食其他动物的普通草蛉(*Chrysoperla carnea*)的幼虫是重要的害虫天敌。在生物防治中起到很大的作用。所以在作杀虫剂的副作用时常常是以普通草蛉的幼虫为对象。Hilbeck 等[7]的实验是用了两种食草昆虫。即鳞翅目的目标害虫欧洲玉米螟(*Ostrinia nubilalis*)和棉贫夜蛾(*Spodoptera littoralis*)，分别喂以转基因 Bt 玉米和正常的玉米(对照)。观察绿草蛉幼虫吃了这两种经不同处理的虫子后，对其发育和死亡率的影响。结果说明绿草蛉幼虫喂饲吃 Bt 玉米长大的欧洲玉米螟的死亡率为 62%，而对照的死亡率为37%。欧洲玉米螟和海灰翅夜蛾两者间的死亡率没有明显的差别。作者认为较高的死亡率是与Bt直接有联系的。在绿草蛉幼虫发育方面，喂饲吃Bt玉米的欧洲玉米螟者发育时间延长，成虫时间比对照平均要慢3d，但在海灰翅夜蛾上未看到不同。作者认为发育时间的延长，是由于Bt和病了的玉米螟营养不良造成的综合效应。

1.3　瓢虫喂饲食转基因马铃薯的蚜虫出现生殖力及存活力问题

蚜虫是温带作物中的重要害虫。估计仅在英国每年造成作物的损失达1亿英镑。而瓢虫是蚜虫的天敌。Birch等的实验[8]发现瓢虫(*Adaliu bipunctata*)喂以食转基因马铃薯的蚜虫者出现生殖的问题，并死亡得比对照要早。实验用的转基因马铃薯是插入编码有雪花莲植物凝集素(*Galanthus niualis agglutinin*-GNA)的抗虫基因。这种凝集素能有效地抑制蚜虫进食、生长和繁殖，但尚未发现有致死效应。温室实验说明，种植这种转基因马铃薯大大地减少了马铃薯的蚜虫。

实验观察到，一旦瓢虫交配后，喂饲吃含GNA马铃薯蚜虫(处理组)的雌性瓢虫的生殖力要比喂词吃正常马铃薯蚜虫(对照组)降低38%。卵出生后1星期，孵化率也有很大差别，不能孵化卵子处理组要比对照组高3倍。喂以处理组蚜虫的雄性瓢虫与对照组雌性蚜虫交配后，所得的未受精卵数量是雌雄都喂对照组蚜虫的4倍。此外，喂食处理组蚜虫存活时间也要比对照组少一半。

1.4　转基因Bt棉对优势寄生性天敌有严重危害

夏敬源等[13]应用中国科学院植物所培育的转基因Bt抗虫棉品种中国棉花研究所(简称中棉所)29和中棉所30做大田实验，结果说明Bt棉对优势寄生性天敌造成严重的危害，中棉所30中棉铃虫幼虫寄生性天敌齿唇姬蜂(*Campoletis chlorideae*)和侧沟绿茧蜂(*Microplitis* sp.)的百株虫量分别较常规棉对照减少79.2%和88.9%。用Bt抗虫棉饲养的棉铃虫中寄生的齿唇姬蜂的寄生率和出蜂率分别较常规棉对照减少91.4%和37.5%，茧重和蜂重分别减轻54.0%和11.1%；侧沟绿茧蜂的寄生率较对照减少57.1%，蜂茧重减轻44.2%，且其茧不能出蜂。可见，Bt抗虫棉对棉铃虫幼虫优势寄生性天敌的寄生率、羽化率和蜂茧质量造成严重危害。

1.5　抗除草剂转基因作物对大斑蛛造成威胁

美国Kansas大学昆虫学家Taylor发表文章[9]认为如此快速地大面积种植抗除草剂转基因大豆和玉米，将会造成大田中马利筋种群的减少。由于马利筋是大斑蝶类蝴蝶幼虫唯一的食物来源，因而会对大斑蝶的生存造成威胁。

例如用草甘膦等除草剂以常规方式来除掉玉米或大田草中的杂草。只能在下种前来喷洒，这种方式还可让大量的马利筋照常生存。如Monsant等公司开发了抗除草剂转基因作物。在作物发芽并生长后还要喷洒除草剂，从而大量杀死马利筋及其他难以除掉的杂草。在美国，1999年已有近一半的大豆面积已种植抗除草剂转基因大豆。如此大量种植后。将使马利筋群丛大大地减少，随之而来就会威胁到大斑蝶的生存。第1案例中已提到 Wassenaar 等[10]已发现到墨西哥越冬的 50%的大斑蝶是来源于中西部 Nebraska 和 Ohio 间。这地区是美国玉米和大豆的主要产地。

2 不同结果和不同意见

上一部分的几个案例谈到的是转基因作物对生物多样性有不利的影响，但也有实验得到了影响不大甚至有利的结果。此外，对于转基因作物的生态风险及其对人体健康影响，科技界及公众的不同阶层、不同的人可能持完全不同的意见。

2.1 Bt 棉能有效地保护增殖捕食性天敌

夏敬源等[13]的大田实验结果说明转基因 Bt 棉对优势寄生性天敌有严重危害，但却能有效地保护增殖捕食性天敌。与对照相比，Bt 中棉所 29 品种的百株七星瓢虫(*Cocinella septempunctata*)数量减少 14.0%、龟纹瓢虫(*Propylaea japonica*)减少 8.5%、草蛉(*Chrysopa* sp.)增加 14.0%、小花蝽(*Orius mintus*)减少 1.6%、草间小黑蛛(*Erigonidium graminicolu*)增加 15.9%，差异均不显著；Bt 中棉所 30 品种棉田的龟纹展虫数量增加 11.8%、小花蝽减少 30.4%、草蛉减少 20.0%、草间小黑蛛减少 3.6%，作者认为差异均不显著。但两种转基因棉田的捕食性天敌总量均较相应的对照明显地增加，说明种植 Bt 棉能有效地保护增殖捕食性天敌。作者又做了饲养试验，结果说明龟纹瓢虫、七星瓢虫、草间小黑蛛和大眼长蝽(*Geocoris pallidipennis*)对用 Bt 棉叶片饲喂 1.2h 棉铃虫初孵幼虫的日最大捕食量为对照的 1.5~3.0 倍，处理1头猎物的时间为对照的 33.3%~66.2%，瞬间攻击率为对照的 1.1~1.4 倍。说明用 Bt 棉饲喂棉铃虫后能提高天敌对棉铃虫的捕食率。

2.2 Cornell 大学生态和农业科学教授 Pimental 和 Missouri 植物园主任 Raven 对 Losey 等的工作发表了截然相反的意见①

他们认为目前能得到高产农业的重要原因是因为大量使用杀虫剂、除草剂、杀菌剂和化肥。这些化学物对作物有利外也杀死了有益的昆虫、鸟、鱼，也污染了水并引起其他环境和公众健康问题。在美国，由于使用杀虫剂而引起环境和公众损失总值每年达 90 亿美元。农民通常就是通过斩草除根，用除草剂或改变耕作方式来除掉马利筋等杂草，并且农业上所用的杀虫剂和除草剂不仅威胁到大斑蝶，同时也威胁到有用的益虫，每年要杀掉 10%左右在农田生活的鸟类(在美国约 6700 万只鸟)。面对这么严重的问题不顾，而去推测马利筋叶片由于污染了 Bt 玉米花粉而成为使大斑蝶种群受到威胁的一个主要原因，他们认为是一种极端的无根据的结论。他们也承认 Bt 抗虫蛋白对蛾子和蝴蝶是有损害的，并提出是否可让转基因植物的花粉中不表达毒蛋白、或转基因植物产生其他抗虫蛋白来替代 Bt 抗虫蛋白。他们也主张不管是喷洒 Bt 毒蛋白还是转基因植物表达 Bt

① Pimental D., Raven PH. Monarch betterflies farmers and conservation, 1999 年英国皇家学会会议上散发的未发表论文。

毒蛋白的环境效应的测试和评估应该继续做下去。

2.3 有关的生物工程公司对 Losey 等的实验是持不同意见的

Monsanto 公司发言人认为这项发现并不十分重要，由于多数马利筋不生长在玉米地附近，所以多数的大斑蝶不会受到有毒 Bt 花粉的侵害。而 Novartis 公司认为尚需进一步的证实转基因抗虫 Bt 玉米是否真会对大斑蝶或其他物种构成真正的威胁。

由于美国 EPA 在批准转基因抗虫 Bt 玉米时只要求公司做对蜜蜂及草蛉的影响，而未要求做对大斑蝶及其他蝴蝶或蛾子的影响，因此，环境保护和消费组织联盟、有机农业生产者组织和个体有机农业生产者联合向 EPA 控诉。控诉针对以下 3 个方面：即昆虫对 Bt 抗性的增强、Bt 基因向其他植物的转移以及 Bt 作物对有益的非目标昆虫的影响等的环境风险缺乏严格的评估，以及他们的注册对有机农业生产者的影响。控诉要求在对环境风险和对有机农业生产者的经济影响有合适的评估以前，EPA 要撤消所有现有的注册，并且拒绝今后对 Bt 作物的批准，参加控告的有 70 个以上的绿色和平组织和在 100 个国家具 650 个成员的国际有机农业运动联盟以及环境保护组织等等。

3 以上案例对有关政府的冲击

3.1 美国政府对农业生物工程策略有了变化

《生物多样性公约》1992 年在巴西的环发大会上通过后，专门成立了“生物安全特设工作组”。针对转基因作物的生态风险、转基因作物产品作为食品对人体健康影响、产品贴标签、运输和知识产权等一系列所谓“生物安全”问题进行研讨，力争让“公约”缔约国取得共识。在 1999 年 1 月哥伦比亚召开的第 6 次特设工作组会议上，美国虽非“公约”缔约国。却在一系列问题上态度强硬，与发展中国家及欧盟的一些国家持相反的立场：上述案例特别是转基因 Bt 作物花粉对大斑蝶的影响引起国内公众对 GMOs 反对呼声的高潮以及欧盟国家抵制美国转基因作产物的进口将给美国农民带来几亿美元的损失，从而美国农业部长作为政府最高官员在 1999 年 7 月第一次宣布，为了消除消费者对遗传工程食品的恐惧，贴标签是必须的。针对公众批评 Bt 玉米在批准释放时，没有对蝴蝶的风险进行鉴定，他要求美国农业部对生物技术批准过程要有一个独立的科学评估，并准备和美国环境保护署(EPA)一起对转基因作物及其产品长期效应的监测建立地区中心。

由于“终止子技术(Terminacor technology)”[12]是美国农业部和 Delta and Pine Land 种子公司共同申请的专利。在公司产品是由农业部批准这一点上受到公众的批评。农业部长也表示要采取措施拉开农业部与工业界的距离，宣布成立新的生物技术咨询委员会，要求工业界要关心农民和消费者的利益，不能只顾追求利润。

当然，他最后还是重申了他相信农业生物技术在解除饥饿和解决现代农业所引起的困窘的环境问题上有”巨大潜力”的观点[14]。

3.2 日本为保护环境严格了对 GM 作物的法规

日本的 GMOs 是由农林水产省(MAFF)负责管理，过去更多地集中在 GMOs 对人体健康的风险问题，已提出要求对 GMOs，食品贴标签[16]，Bt 玉米对大斑蝶影响报道的发表，引起政府很大的重视。虽然日本没有这种蝴蝶，但他们担心当地的蛾子和蝴蝶也会处于危机之中，从而对 GMOs 的生态风险也立即作出反响[17]。MAFF 在文章发表后一个月就申明他们的 GMOs 委员会计划在年底前提出修订的安全评估程序，对这类作物的安全性建立新的评估标准。在新标准实现前，对用作农业目的的 Bt 作物停止审批：日本目前已批准从美国 Monsanto 公司进口的 6 种用作食品的 Bt 玉米，但对用作农业目的的 Bt 玉米尚未批准。这是日本政府为减少 GM 作物潜在的生态风险采取的第一个重要步骤[17]。

3.3 其他国家的态度

欧洲只有西班牙有很小的大斑蝶种群，但 Lasey 等的报告发表后，英国宣布要等 3 年后再审批 Bt 玉米，法国最高法庭维持暂时停止栽种 Bt 玉米的决定；奥地利、卢森堡和挪威不顾欧盟当时对 Bt 玉米的批准而禁止栽种这种玉米；希腊根本反对欧盟的审批；而欧盟在 Losey 等文章发表的第 2 天就宣布在进一步研究前冻结一切审批[18]。

4 讨论

4.1 本文介绍的几个案例中有两个是以大斑蝶为实验对象

目前在美国大斑蝶还并不是一个濒危物种。但 Losey 为首文章的第二作者昆虫学教师 Rayor 说“大斑蝶可考虑作为一种旗舰种(Flagship species)来加以保护”[18]。所谓的旗舰种是指那些一般为人们喜爱的、具巨大魅力的物种，这种物种可以是一种象征并激励着人们的保护意识和行动[19]。而大斑蝶确是美国人最喜欢的昆虫，由于它们有大的体积和惹人注目的色彩，经常被人们作为自然和生物多样性的象征。美国的蛾子和蝴蝶在濒危和受威胁物种的名单上有 19 种。这些种都有可能受 Bt 有毒花粉的影响。因此以大斑蝶作为研究对象能够激励人们对濒危或受威胁物种的保护。

4.2 《中国生物多样性国情研究报告》指出

“国外文献中还常提到存在价值，即伦理或道德价值”意思是：每种生物都有它自已的生存权利，人们没有权利伤害它们，使它们趋于灭绝[20]。人们可以不从生存权利来理解，从几个案例中就可看到的确应该保护生物多样性。马利筋本身是一种有毒的杂草，应该说在农田生态系统中不是有益的植物，它却是大斑蝶唯一的食物来源。有人形容人类常用的植物是 200 种，再缩小一点范围是 20 种，在全世界最常用的仅 3 种，即水稻、玉米和小麦。绝大多数物种人们尚不了解其利用价值。事实已告诉人们杂草的重要用途，没有李必湖在水沟边偶然发现一株花粉败育的野生稻(简称野败)[21]。就不会有袁隆平的杂交水稻的伟大成就。更多的事实告诉人们，野生近缘种是作物育种重要的种质资源。第5个案例给人们的启示是种了Bt作物后，由于除草剂使用时间的不同，可能造成马利筋生存的威胁。当然对人们尚不知道其利用价值的其他植物，同样会造成威胁。因此，从总体上考虑转基因作物今后大规模种植后对生物多样性可能会造成什么影响，不能不说是应该列入重要议程的一个问题。国际上对此问题极为重视[22]。

4.3 本文专门有一段落谈到不同结果与不同看法

这种不同结果与不同看法在现阶段是绝对正常，就是在今后也是不可避免的，大规模种植转基因作物是最近几年的新生事物，对GMOs早在70年代初，重组DNA技术发展早期，一些科学家已对与重组DNA研究有关的潜在生物学和生态学危险以及释放到环境中所带来的潜在危害表示担心[23]，GMOs尤其是转基因作物商品化生产后，导致不同看法或不同观点的因素已不仅局限于科学技术观点不同，而是已深深地陷入到经济利益之争，也必然发展到政治斗争。不同的结果是由于有的是实验室的结果，有的是大田试验的结果。即使是大田试验的结果也会由于种种原因，如实验条件不同、外界因素不同等而得到不同的结果，这在目前GMOs大规模释放初期，或实验研究还不太多情况下是必然的。事实上人们已经有了可供参考的厚厚的风险评估的方法学的书籍[24~26]，或者已有一些有关转基因作物释放后如何监测的文章[27]。目前人们所缺少的还是大量可得到结论的研究或监测结果的第一手资料。这已引起一些发达国家的重视，正像文中提到的日本政府已要求在1999年年底前要提出转基因作物商品化生产后安全评估的程序:夏敬源等[28]的工作虽然不是专门从事转基因Bt抗虫棉大田释放后的监测工作，他们所报道的某些实验结果，已提供了一些可贵的监测资料。

4.4 生物多样性保护研究在国内还应更加重视

21世纪还会有大量物种遭到灭绝或受到威胁。最近国际鸟类保护组织的一份报告指出，下一世纪将会有1200种鸟类灭绝，600~900种鸟也将处于濒临灭绝境地。其中受灭绝威胁的鸟中国就有82种。世界昆虫物种数还是未知数，灭绝或受威胁的物种情况更是无知，在各类生态系统的结构和功能中，在整个食物链中，鸟类和昆虫都起着重要的作用，可是人类在这方面的知识就更为贫困。近年来自然界中又加入了一个新的GMOs，它们对非目标生物的影响、对生物多样性的影响应该考虑到并值得重视。

4.5 GMOs商品化生产在国际范围内至多才5~6年的历史

其生态风险及对人体健康影响远不到明朗化程度。世界上不少国家对这一新生事物反映非常灵敏。正像Pimental和Raven文章中指出，Losey等的报告在*Nature*上一发表，美国国内几乎每一报纸都头版报道，电视新闻中广泛宣传：又如“终止子技术”在国际上有广泛反响[12]，印度政府和公众强烈反对。为唤起科技界和公众重视，为保护环境和人体健康，应鼓励科技界加强这方面报道。政府有关主管部门应及时掌握国际动态并在政策上作出反应。

4.6 建议加强我国在 GMOs 生态风险及人体健康影响的研究

安排好经费，从实验室到 GMOs 释放后大田监测有足够的科研工作。

参考文献

[1] Zhou R, *et al*. Large scale performance of transgenic tobacco plants resistant to both tobacco mosaic virus and cucumber mosaic virus. In; Jones DD ed. *The biosafety results of field test of genetically modified plant and microorganisms*. California, The University of California, 1994, 49~56

[2] Krattinger AF.The field testing and commercialization of geneucally modified plants; A review of worldwide data (1986~ 1993/1994). In: Krittiger AF. *et al*. ed. *Biosafety for sustainable Agriculture*.ISAAA/SES, 1994, 247~266

[3] Jarnes C. Global review of commerriahzed transgenic crops: 1998, ISAAA Briefs No.8 ISAAA. Ithaca, 1998

[4] 钱迎倩, 马克平. 经遗传修饰生物体的研究进展及其释放后对环境的影响. 生态学报, 1998. 18(1): 1~9

[5] 钱迎倩, 魏 伟, 田 彦, 等. 转基因作物在生产中的应用及某些潜在问题. 应用与环境生物学报. 1999. 5(4): 427~433

[6] Losey JE, *et al*. Transgenic pollen harnis monarch larvae. *Nature*. 1999. 399: 214

[7] Hibeck A, *et al*. Effect of transgenic *Bacillus thuringiensis* corn fed prey on mortality and development time of immature *Chrysoperla carnea* (Naeuroptera; Chrysopidae). *Enuiron. Entomol*., 1998, 27(2): 480~487

[8] Birch ANE, *et al*. Interactions between plant resistance genes, peat aphid populations and beneficial aplud predators. *Scouish Crop Res, inst Annual Report* Dundee, 1998/7, 68~72

[9] Taylor C. Monarch butterflies may be threatened in their North American range. *Environ. Review*, 1999. 6(4): 1~9

[10] Wassenaar LI, *et al*. Natual origins of migratory monarch butterflies at wintering colonies in Mexico: New isotopic evidence *Proc. Natl. Acad. Sei*. USA. 1998, 95: 15436~15439

[11] Holden C, Monarchs and their roots. *Science*, 1999. 283: 17

[12] Http://www. Pme. iastste.Edu/info/monarch.htm

[13] 夏敬源. 崔金杰, 等. 转 Bt 基因抗虫棉在害虫综合治理中的作用研究. 棉花学报, 1999. 11(2): 57~64

[14] Union of Concerned Scientists.USDA announces new biotech policies. *The Gene Exchange*, April-August, 1999.13

[15] 钱迎倩. 马克平. 桑卫国, 等. 终止子技术与生物安全. 生物多样性, 1999. 7(2): 151~155

[16] Saegusa A. Japan May require labels on genetic food, *Nature* 1998. 395: 628

[17] Saegusa A, Japan tighten rules on GM crops to protect the environment. *Nature*, 1999. 399: 719

[18] Anomynous. Possible threat to monarch butterfly posed by Bt corn set off alarms for environmentalists,farmers and seed industry. *Diversity*. 1999. 15(1): 17~18

[19] UNEP. Gjobal Biodiiversity Assessment.Cambridge University Press, 1995. 1104~1119

[20] 《中国生物多样性国情研究报告》编写组, 中国生物多样性国情研究报告. 北京：中国环境科学出版社. 1998. 11~12

[21] 李竟雄, 周洪生主编. 高产不是梦. 长沙：湖南科学技术出版社, 1995. 83~112

[22] Anornynous. Assessing the threat to biodiversity on the farm. *Nature*. 1999. 398: 645~656

[22] 钱迎倩. 生物多样性与生物技术. 中国科学院院刊, 1994, (2): 134~138

[23] Kjellsson G, *et al*. Methods for risk assessment of transgenic plants I. Competition, establishment and ecosystem effects. Brikhauser Verlag, 1994, 1~214

[24] Kjellsson G, *et al*. Methods for risk assessment of transgenic plants, II. Pollunation, transfer and population impacts. Brikhauser Verlag, 1994, 1~308

[25] Scientists Working Group on Biosafety.Manual for assessing ecological and human health effects of genetially engineered organisms.Part one: Introductory materials and supporing text for flowcharts, Part Two: Flowcharts and worksheets, 1998, 1~245. The Edmonds Instute. 1998. 1~158

[26] 钱迎倩, 田 彦, 魏 伟. 转基因植物的生态风险评价. 植物生态学报. 1998. 22(4): 289~299

本文原载：科学对社会的影响. 2002. (4): 23-28

对生物安全问题的思考

钱迎倩　魏伟　马克平

(中国科学院植物研究所)

摘　要　2001 年墨西哥本土的玉米品种资源受到进口转基因玉米的基因污染。该国是玉米的起源国及品种资源的中心，该事件引起了国际上极大的关注。加拿大转基因油菜造成基因污染早在 1998 年已有报道。我国是水稻和大豆的起源地，野生近缘种也极为丰富，该两种转基因作物在我国的大面积商业化生产要极为慎重。转基因作物的各种生态风险以及对转基因食品安全性的研究要调动生物工程、生态学、植保、育种、生物多样性保护等各领域科技人员的积极性，多学科共同攻关研究，使生物工程这项高新技术在 21 世纪能更好地造福于人类。

关键词　生物安全；转基因作物；基因污染

生物技术是 21 世纪高新技术中一种重要的技术，重组 DNA 技术又是生物技术中的核心技术之一。人们希望通过该项技术得到优质、高产、抗逆的农作物以及家禽和家畜品种。以转基因植物为例，在实验室和中试水平已经成功的估计有 35 科 120 种左右，包括粮食、蔬菜、水果、和林木等。转基因的性状有抗病、抗虫、品质改良、抗逆、抗除草剂、发育调控以及药物生产等。已经商品化的转基因作物主要有抗除草剂转基因大豆、抗虫转基因玉米、抗除草剂转基因油菜以及抗虫转基因棉花等。产值也逐年增高，转基因作物全球总产值 1995 年为 0.75 亿美元，1998 年达 16.4 亿美元，预计到 2010 年可增值到 200 亿美元。

但是转基因作物也会给环境带来生态风险及可能影响人体健康。这个问题在世界各国政府尚未批准转基因作物大规模商品化生产前，在 1992 年联合国环境与发展大会上，由各国政府首脑共同签署的《生物多样性公约》中明确提出了。《公约》条文中要求每一个缔约国制定或采取办法管制、管理或控制由生物技术改变的活生物体在使用和释放时可能对环境和人体健康产生的不利影响，并要求缔约国防止引进，控制或消除那些威胁于生态系统、生境或物种的外来物种。当然转基因植物，现在虽然还谈不上是一个新的物种，但是由人工制造的外来品种应是无疑的。《公约》条文所提及的也就是本文要讨论的所谓“生物安全”问题。

有关转基因作物可能带来的生态风险，过去仅是实验室或田间的小试水平的工作，

基金项目：“九五”国家重点科技攻关(97-925-02-04-05)资助项目。

谁也没料到转基因作物商品化释放才几年的时间，墨西哥玉米由于基因流出现了基因污染事件，证实了有关实验室得到的结果，从而引起国际上极大的重视。

墨西哥玉米受转基因污染事件的争论

每一个农作物都有它的原产地。玉米的原产地在墨西哥。从该国的平原到 2700 米高度的各种地区分布有 300 多个玉米品种，遗传多样性非常丰富。此外，野生玉米类玉蜀黍属在墨西哥国土上也有广泛的分布。虽然墨西哥生产的玉米足够本国的消费，但自从 1994 年北美自由贸易协定实施后，美国玉米由于得到政府高价补贴，价格比墨西哥低，使墨西哥从美国进口的玉米逐年上升，在进口玉米中至少有 25%是转基因玉米。政府没有对转基因玉米与国内传统玉米采取隔离措施。直到 1998 年，墨西哥政府规定禁止转基因玉米的田间试验和商品化生产，但仍然只是防止进口的转基因可能被种植的措施。墨西哥政府曾进口200吨玉米分送到2300个社区作为救济食品出售，可是没人告知购买者，这些玉米是禁止种植的。到 2001 年 9 月 18 日，墨西哥政府环境保护部公布了墨西哥玉米已受基因污染的研究报告。在 Oaxaca 州受调查的 22 个社区中，有 15 个社区的传统玉米中发现有转基因，污染程度在 3%~10%[1]。(1)由政府发到上述社区的救济玉米的样品中，环境部发现有 37%的玉米是转基因玉米。2001 年 11 月美国加拿大学柏克莱分校的科学家 Quist 和 Chapala 在 *Nature* 上报道了墨西哥玉米受到基因污染的分子基础，也发现在上述救济粮的玉米样品中有转基因玉米。文章还指出这种基因污染可能会蔓延到更广阔地区，更为严重的是可能会影响到玉米的野生近缘种，并呼吁墨西哥政府需采取紧急措施，以消除基因污染的源头[2]。(2)到 2002 年 1 月 23 日，墨西哥政府和环境部门提供了新的信息，完善了 2001 年 9 月的研究数据，确认墨西哥玉米受转基因污染的事实。此后，大约 80 位科学家、学者和育种家联合发表了公开信，呼吁各国政府，特别是墨西哥政府要采取一切措施来制止基因污染。

事情并未到此结束，2001 年 4 月 11 日出版的 *Nature* 上针对墨西哥玉米污染事件发表了一系列的文章。其中有 *Nature* 杂志的声明，对发表 Quist 和 Chapela 等人的证据不足的文章表示后悔；也有 Metz 和 Futterer 以及 Kaplinsky 等对 Quist 等的研究方法提出质疑，认为墨西哥玉米的转基因污染是一种人工赝象。同一期上也发表了 Quist 和 Chalepa 的回答，给出了 DNA 杂交的证据，再次肯定了转基因在墨西哥玉米中的存在。2002 年 4 月 23 日墨西哥政府再次确认了本土玉米品种受转基因污染这一事实。国家生态研究所所长 Ezcurra 指出，污染率平均是 8%，有的地方甚至超过 10%。

2002 年 6 月 27 日的 *Nature* 上又发表了一批科学家的通讯。Suarez 对 *Nature* 发表了 Quist 等文章后，又发表声明对该文证据不足的做法提出批评，认为科学就是源于假设和对假设的检验，随着科学的进步这些假设可能的结果是得到验证、或者进一步修正，也可能遭到否定，科学杂志的任务就是为它们提供一个公平的论坛，而不应该对其研究结论作出明确的取舍，尤其涉及经济和政治有关问题时，更不应该在发表一篇文章后又去发表撤回该文的声明。在 Suarez 的通讯后又有十几位科学家签名表示赞同。Worthy 等人的观点更直截了当，他们提出 *Nature* 已受到 Novartis 和 Astra Zeneca 等一些生物技术公司的左右。由于意识到 Quist 等的文章可能会对正在进行国际谈判的“生物安全议定书”产生潜在影响，*Nature*2002 年 4 月 11 日的声明及多位科学家对 Quist 等人批评文章的发表都抢在 UNEP 负责召开的生物多样性公约讨论生物安全议定书之前发表。并指出 8 位批评 Quist 等的科学家中有 7 位曾受到 Novartis 公司的资助,另一位 Futterer 也与 Novartis 间接有关。Metz 和 Futterer 等人承认他们得到过 Novartis 的资助，但反驳说他们仅是对 Quist 等的实验数据提出质疑，这里不存在商业资助的因素。并指出 Chapela 本人曾是 Novartis 公司的雇员，这次对 Novartis 攻击是报私人恩怨。Kaplinsky 更尖锐地提出，Chapela 是反对 GMOs 一个组织的成员，这才是他持不同意见的真正原因。对上述事件魏伟等[3]已经有过概述，下面是我们对这事件提出的几点思考。

Nature 上针对某一个事件连续多期发表众多科学家参与的多篇文章和通讯恐怕为数不多，这可理解为有关生物安全问题的本身已经成为国际关心的热点问题之一。墨西哥玉米事件的前前后后，反映了以下几个方面的问题：

首先，围绕着转基因作物(或笼统说 GMOs)的争论，至今不仅仅是一个科学技术问题的争论，已涉及学风问题、经济问题、贸易问题、甚至由此而引起的政治斗争问题。而对科学家来说，由于各人所处的情况不同也会自觉、不自觉地有各人的立场。

第二，尽管有科学家批评 *Nature* 杂志反悔等的做法，但应该说 *Nature* 对整个事件的立场还是公正的，敢于把各种不同的观点、意见、甚至是批评自身的意见都公之于众。我们不去讨论，因为不了解情况也无法去讨论批评 *Nature* 的意见是正确还是错误的，甚至可能带有攻击性的。*Nature* 的做法是值得提倡的，这也就是我们长期在提倡的百家争鸣，把各种不同的观点有机会都能放到桌面上来，让读者们去自辨。

第三，对于墨西哥玉米事件，我们可以撇开 *Nature* 上发表的实验报告、质疑、答复以及它自身的表态，有一点似乎是可以坚信无疑的，即墨西哥本土的传统玉米已经被外国进口的转基因玉米的转基因通过基因流而污染，这可以从墨西哥政府有关部门及研究所发表的报告得到证实。

生物安全的其他方面

“墨西哥玉米事件”作为生物安全事件不是唯一的，只是因为影响太大，才引起国际广泛的重视。实际上，转基因抗除草剂油菜早在 20 世纪后期在加拿大已多次发现由于基因流造成的基因污染，Alberta 省在 1998 年转基因油菜田里就发现有自生自长的能抗草甘膦、固杀草及保幼酮等三种除草剂的转基因油菜。抗草甘膦等前两种抗性性状来自转基因油菜，而保幼酮抗性则来自传统育种培育的抗性油菜。到 1999 年，Saskatchewan 省的 11 个田块中也证实了有自生自长的抗多种除草剂性状的油菜[4]，甚至与油菜田相邻的小麦田中也发现了这种自生自长的抗多种除草剂的油菜[5]。这种抗多种除草剂的油菜已经很难被一般除草剂杀死的杂草。Hall[6]及 Beckie 等[7]分析了这种基因流是花粉由于风、虫或其他动物的传播或种子的传播造成的。转基因的任意扩散会使加拿大种植传统油菜的农民难以保证其出售的油菜种子是无转基因的(GM-free)。

转基因生物的另一个生态风险是对环境中的非目标生物的影响。Losey 等实验室水平的工作早已说明转基因抗虫玉米的花粉会对大斑蝶的幼虫造成危害[8]，也就是转基因抗虫玉米除了能杀死目标害虫外，可能同样会杀死环境中的非目标生物，从而对生物多样性带来影响。我国目前已大面积种植的转基因作物是转基因抗虫棉花(Bt 棉)。中国农业科学院棉花研究所的科学家在 2 万亩种植 Bt 棉的示范区中，由于全年减少施药 5~8 次，用药量减少 60%~80%，从而每公顷降低成本 600~1200 元，并减少了对环境的污染。棉花平均增产 17%~20%，每公顷增加收入 1000~1200 元，减少用 60~80 个劳动田，此外，捕食性天敌总量增加 24%~26.9%。经济、社会和生态效益是明显的。他们从 1994 年也开始进行生物安全方面的研究。值得注意的是，在大田试验中发现棉铃虫的优势寄生性天敌的数量明显减少；实验室研究表明，Bt 棉对棉铃虫的优势寄生性天敌的寄生率、羽化率和蜂茧质量造成严重损害，而用 Bt 棉饲喂棉铃虫后能提高捕食性天敌对棉铃虫的捕食率[9]。另一点是在单作 Bt 棉田中，对目标害虫棉铃虫得到控制的同时，棉蚜、棉叶螨、棉盲蝽、白粉虱和棉叶蝉等刺吸性害虫的发生和为害呈加重趋势①。大田的环境比较复杂，数据往往会受到地区、各种农业措施、气候及其他环境因子的影响，规律性的结论有待长期的监测和研究。转基因作物的其他生态风险及转基因食品的安全性问题，由于篇幅有限这里不再叙述。

两点思考

1. 墨西哥玉米事件之所以引起国际关注是因为调查的 Oaxaca 州是玉米起源中心，也是遗传多样性极为丰富地区，这事件对自然基因库造成了基因污染的后果。转基因逃逸如不断发生，会导致当地遗传多样性的丧失，造成遗传冲刷(genetic erosion)。遗传多样性在防止人类发生饥荒上的重要性是难以估量的，此外，农作物与其野生近缘种也往往是可以互相杂交的，转基因可以通过杂交转移到其野生近缘种中去，并得到可育的后代，从而可能造成一些野生近缘种或稀有种的灭绝。而野生近缘种也经常被育种学家作为远缘杂交的重要遗传资源。因此，采取措施防止转基因造成基因污染而导致遗传多样性或某些物种的丧失是必要的。

我国是水稻的原产地，不仅遗传多样性丰富，品种资源多，野生近缘种也分布很广。卢宝荣报道②，栽培稻与野生稻都具有基因相互交流的时空条件，而大多数含 AA 基因组的稻属近缘种都与栽培稻有较高的杂交亲和性。异交发生的可能性非常高。我国转基因水稻的研究已取得很好的成果，有媒体介绍已接近商品化生产的水平。此外，也不能排除瑞士科学家培育成功的改良品质的转基因“黄金水稻”在我国的试种的可能性。对转基因水稻的大面积商品化生产的批准应该持慎重的态度。

另一个重要的作物是大豆。常如镇③指出中国是大豆的原产地和多样性集中地，拥有 90%的大豆资源。大豆虽然是自花授粉的植物，但采集到的野生种质在种植后出现分

① 崔金杰, 转 Bt 比基因抗虫棉生物安全性研究进展及研究设想, 国外生物安全, 2002, 第 4 期, 5-7.
② 卢宝荣, 转基因逃逸及生态风险, 国外生物安全信息, 2002, 第 5 期, 1-4.
③ 常如镇, 大豆：不可重蹈覆辙, 国外生物安全信息, 2002, 第 1 期, 8.

离，说明天然杂交是存在的。野生大豆在中国从北到南全国分布，野生大豆与栽培大豆没种的隔离，外源基因很容易逃逸到野生大豆中去。遗传多样性和种质资源一旦遭到破坏，会严重威胁到粮食安全。近年来，我国从美国进口的大豆逐年增长，去年已远远超过1000万吨，其中大部分都是转基因抗除草剂大豆。严重的是有的单位把进口的抗除草剂转基因大豆分发到其他单位试种。为之，常如镇’呼吁，中国的大豆不重蹈墨西哥玉米的覆辙。综合各种因素考虑，为保护我国的大豆资源，应该禁止转基因大豆的种植。

有关遗传资源的重要性，洪德元曾有过报道①。1978年后美国人从中国收集到大量的野生大豆资源，经过常规育种的杂交，选育出的品种能在贫瘠、干旱的土壤上生长，从而产量大增。使美国由过去大豆的进口国一跃而成大豆出口国。此外，自花授粉的大豆能通过基因流形成天然杂种，日本科学家最近也有报道[10]，实验说明栽培大豆的花粉可以很容易地传播到野生大豆上去造成天然杂种，杂交率可高达17.4%。从有关方面获悉，我国的商品大豆由于含油量略逊于美国大豆而造成滞销，是否也应该效仿美国为保护农产品的出口政府对农业实行高价补贴的做法，从科研、育种、种质资源保护直到销售等各个方面采取果断的综合措施来保护我国大豆丰富的遗传资源与大豆产业。

2. 生物安全的问题已经引起科技界和各界的广泛重视。政府有关部门对转基因生物的研制、释放制定了有关条例或法规，规定转基因产品要在2002年3月起采取贴标签的措施，已立项开展生物安全领域的研究。生物安全关系到潜在的生态风险和人体健康问题，会涉及各学科领域的研究，如生物技术、生态学、植物保护、育种、生物多样性保护以及食品安全等方面。因此要调动各学科科技人员的积极性、有足够的科研经费共同攻关。逐步明确涉及生态风险及人体健康的有关问题，研究解决问题的各种途径，采取必要的安全措施，认生物技术、转基因生物在21世纪更快地发展，造福于人民。

参考文献

[1] Dalton. R. Transgenic con found growing in Mexico. Nature. 2001, 413: 337

[2] Quist. D. I. H. Chapela. Transgenic DNA introgressed into tradifional maize landrarances in Mexiro. Natrue. 2001. 414: 541~543

[3] 魏伟、马克平. 如何面对基因流和基因污染. 中国农业科技导报, 2002. 4 (4): 10~15

[4] Http://www producer. com /articles / 20000210 / news /

[5] CBC News Online-Manitoba. GM seeds blowin in the wind,Jun 21 200l

[6] Hall, L. K. Topinka, *et al.*, Pollew flow between herbicide-resistant Brassica napus is the cause of multiple-resislant B. napus volunteers. Weed Science, 2000, 48; 688~694

[7] Beckie, H. J., L. M. Hall etal. Jmpact of herbicide-resistant crops as weeds in Canada,In: Proceedings of Brighton Crop protection Council Conference-Weeds, 2001, 135~142

[8] Losey, J E. *et al.*, Transgenic Pollen harms monarch larvae. Nature. 1999, 399: 214

[9] 夏敬源、崔金杰等, 转Bt基因抗虫棉在害虫综合治理中的作用研究, 棉花学报, 1999, 11(2): 57~64

[10] Nakayama. Y H. Yamaguchi,Natural hybridization in wild soybean (Glycine max subsp. soya) by pollen flow from cultivated soybean (Glycine max subsp. max) in a designed population.Weed Biology and Management, 2002, 2(l): 25~30

① 洪德元, 傅立国, 我国植物的重要地位和面临的危机, 见: 汪松、杜学浩(主编), 中国科学院生物多样性研讨会会议录, 北京: 中国科学院生物科学与技术局, 1990, 40-44。

本文原载：中国生物多样性保护与研究进展: 第五届全国性生物多样保护与持续利用研讨会论文集. 2004. 陈宜瑜主编. 北京: 气象出版社, 117-121

墨西哥发生基因污染事件的新动态

钱迎倩　魏伟　马克平

(中国科学院植物研究所)

摘　要　墨西哥是世界玉米的起源中心。最近进行调查分析的结果说明，在全国 31 个州中已有 9 个州，也即在其国家的南部、中部和北部都已有基因污染的事件发生。而且实际情况比想象中的要严重得多。这一事实再一次提醒人们，要非常慎重地对待转基因作物的商品化大面积释放，尤其是在作物起源地的发展中国家。

关键词　墨西哥；转基因玉米；基因污染

墨西哥是世界玉米的起源中心，政府为了保护玉米的遗传多样性不受威胁，1988 年就已规定在墨西哥本土不允许转基因玉米的种植。可是 2001 年 9 月国际知名刊物 *Nature* 上报道了当年 9 月 17 日墨西哥环境部公布的研究结果，说明在墨西哥的 Oaxaca 和 Puebla 两个州的 22 个地区中有 15 个地区已经发现有转基因玉米(Dalton，2001)。同年 11 月，美国加利福尼亚大学伯克利分校的 Ouist 和 Chapela 也在 *Nature* 刊物上发表了题为“转基因 DNA 渐渗到墨西哥 Oaxaca 传统玉米地方品种中”的文章(Ouist 等，2001)。在分子水平上证实了墨西哥玉米的地方品种中已经受到基因污染，这篇文章可谓是一石掀起千层浪，持反对观点者认为实验数据不足，对这实验报告进行质疑。*Nature* 编辑部也出来表示对发表这个实验报告作了反悔，接着 Quist 等再次发表文章提供数据答复反对观点者，随后又有一批科学家起来批评 *Nature* 编辑部。看来，对待转基因作物是否影响农作物起源地遗传多样性问题是一个非常敏感的问题。从广义上讲，转基因作物涉及的已远远不仅是科学技术问题，而且涉及重大的经济、社会甚至政治问题。不仅科技界关心，社会上各阶层人士甚至政府首脑也十分关注转基因作物及其产物(魏伟等，2002；Pearce，2002)。

由于事件发生在墨西哥，墨西哥是玉米的起源中心，遗传多样性非常丰富，墨西哥政府继 2001 年的研究报告后，于 2002 年 1 月国家环保部门公布了由环境与资源部、国家生态研究所和国家生物多样性委员会联合的研究报告。报告再一次确认了墨西哥玉米的品种已经遭到转基因玉米的基因污染，在 Oaxaca 州和 Puabla 州某些村落基因污染率甚至高达到 35%。

事件发生后，墨西哥的各类研究中心、协会等有关单位对墨西哥本土的相关州的玉米基因污染作了更为广泛的调查并开展了研究工作。2003 年 10 月 9 日，在墨西哥城召开了记者招待会。出席这次记者招待会的有墨西哥农村改变中心(CECCAM)，当地慈善机构中心(CENAMI)，侵蚀、技术和精选行动中心(ETC Group)，社会分布、信息和公众培训中心(CASIFOP)，瓦哈卡 Sierra Juarez 组织联盟(UNOSJO)，支持当地团体 Jaliscan 协会(AJAGI)，以及来自 Oaxaca、Puebla、Chihuahua、Veracruz 的当地村落和农场的代表，他们分别通报了各自独立研究的结果(Lim Li Lin 等，2003) 。

1　调查分析

(1) 在 138 个当地社区和农场中，采集了 411 组样品，并对样品中的 2000 株左右植株进行了分析。所有 138 个点都是社区的农田或小规模的农场，他们利用的都是家庭劳动力，没有或者仅少量利用化学药物；生产玉米的目的仅仅是为了解决家庭的粮食自给，因此播种面积就在 1~2hm^{2}之间；所用的玉米种子都是自己粮库里用作留种的当地品种；大多数社区的地理位置都远离城市中心。

(2) 每一个参与本次研究的社区的样品都按规定大小，植株的选择是随机的，并规定一律从每个样田的几个角和中心来进行取样。

实验室测试内毒素用的是 ELISA 技术，商业试剂盒由 Agdia 公司生产。使用酶标仪读数吸收光波长为 620nm。测试共进行了两轮。第一轮是在墨西哥国立自治大学(UANM)生物学家的技术指导和支持下，由各社区和机构自己完成的。第二轮的测试则是由 Fumigaciones y.Mantenimiento de Plantas S.C.实验室进行的。实验条件和试剂盒与第一轮一致。

(3) 分析结果与 Quist 和 Chapela 报道的以及与墨西哥国立生态学研究所(INE)和国家生物多样性委员会(CONABTO)的分析结果是一致的，再一次证明墨西哥的当地玉米品种已被转基因污染。第一轮在 2003 年 1 月进行，分析了 Puebla、Veracruz、Chihuahua、SanLuis、Potosi、MexicoState 和 Morelos 等 6 个州的样品。从 53 个社区的 95 个样块中取得 520 株植株分成 105 组进行分析。测得植株叶片中所存在的外源转基因蛋白共有 5 种。其中 4 种是 Bt 毒素中的 Bt-Cry1Ab/1Ac，Bt-Cry9C，Bt-CrylC 和 Bt-Cry2a，另外一个是耐除草剂的 CP4EPSPS。转基因蛋白呈阳性的占整个测试样品的 48.6%。其中只测出一种蛋白阳性的占 18.6%；有两种的占 13%；有 3 种的占 17%。在整个样品中，检测到有 Bt-Cry1Ab/1Ac 的占 21%，有 Bt-Cry9C 的占 26.67%，有 CP4EPSPS 的占 34%。

第二轮实验是在 2003 年 8 月进行的。从 Oaxaca、Puebla、Chihuahua、Durango、Veracruz 和 Tlaxcala 州等 6 个州的 101 个社区中取样。从 1500 株植株中组成 306 个样品组。测试结果中有 32 个样品的转基因蛋白呈阳性，占整个测试样品的 10.45%。其中有 1%的样品出现 Bt-Cry9C；有 3.6%的样品出现耐除草剂的 CP4EPSPS；有 4.9%样品同时出现 2 种或 3 种不同的转基因产物；有 3.9%样品出现 3 种转基因产物，其中 2 种是 Bt 毒素中的 Bt-Cry9C 和 Bt-Cry1Ab/1Ac，另一种是耐除草剂的 CP4EPSPS；有 0.65%样品有 2 种外源转基因蛋白，即 Bt-Cry9C 和 Bt-Cry1Ab/1Ac；此外，还有 0.33%样品呈现 CP4EPSPS 和 Bt-Cry9C 阳性。

按第二轮分析的结果统计，不同地块的污染率从 1.5%~33.2%。在 Oaxaca 和

Chihuahua 两个州的田块中还发现有畸形的植株。这些植株经过测试说明转基因的产物都呈阳性。

2 讨论

(1) 墨西哥共有当地原产的玉米品种 300 个以上，这些当地品种在中部和北部的分布更加密集。可是从图 1 中我们可以看到从南部的 Chihuahua 州到最北部的 Oaxaca 州共 9 个州的当地玉米品种都已发生了基因污染。实际上这次反对图中所指的 9 个州进行调查，其中 Chihuahua、Puebla 和 Veracruz 三个州经过两轮调查，而且都是小部分的抽样分析，结果样品都呈阳性。此外，有相当部分的植株还发现有 2 种、3 种甚至 4 种不同转基因在一株植物内。这现象说明基因污染已经发生多年了，这些污染了的玉米在小农场中已经交叉授粉了好几代，在它们的基因组中已含有这些转基因的各种不同性状了。以上这些都已足够说明问题已远比想象的严重得多。人们可以预见墨西哥当地玉米品种的基因污染远远不仅发生在这 9 个州。

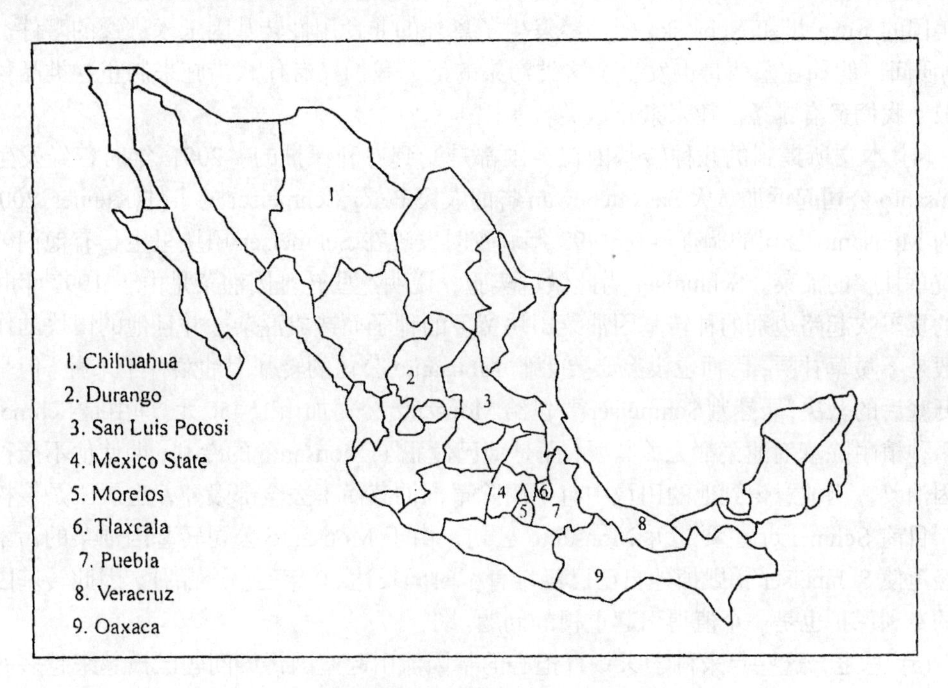

图 1 墨西哥国家地图及 31 个州的分布图

从南到北的 9 个州经过调查分析,当地玉米品种在不同程度上都已发生基因污染

(2) 这次所发现的 4 种转基因都是美国公司的产物。其中 Bt-cry1Ab/1Ac 为 3 个公司所有，即 Monsanto 公司研制的，品牌名为 YieidGard，有 Novartis 公司(现归 Syngenta 所有)的，品牌名为 Knockout，以及 Mycogen 公司的，品牌名为 Nature Gard；Bt-Cry1C

* Collin，M.,2002，墨西哥玉米品种受基因污染，国外生物安全信息，4, 25~25

是 Mycogen 公司的品牌产品；Bt-Cry9C 是 Aventis 公司(现归 Bayer 所有)的，品牌为 StarLink；还有 Monsanto 公司研制的品牌名为 Roundup Ready 的 CP4EPSPS 表达产物。应该注意的是其中由 Aventis 公司研制的为 StarLink(星联)玉米。由于可能会引起部分人产生皮疹、腹泻以及呼吸系统的过敏反应，并且还有潜伏效应，美国政府环境保护署 1998 年在批准可进行商业化生产时，规定其产品仅作为动物饲料用，而不允许作为人类的食品。可是在 2000 年 9 月间，在美国超市货架上以玉米为原料的某些食品中测试到 Bt-Cry9C 杀虫蛋白，在美国曾引起一场很大的风波(钱迎倩，2003)。这种在美国本土不能作为人类食品的玉米居然已到了墨西哥，将会造成双重的危害。不仅仅使墨西哥的人民可能会受到星联玉米的害处，更严重的是使世界玉米原产国——墨西哥的当地品种资源通过基因流而被污染。

(3) 美国研制转基因玉米产物是很广泛的，远远不仅是把玉米作为粮食或饲料来利用，而是把转基因玉米作为生物发应器来生产如塑料、黏合剂、杀精子剂以及堕胎药物等。如果没有严格的措施使这些转基因不造成扩散的话，将给人类食用的粮食造成严重的威胁。2003 年 10 月在墨西哥召开的记者招待会上，ETC 小组的 Silyia Ribeiro 警告说，在美国的 Iowa 州和 Nebraska 州已经发生了意外的非食用性转基因玉米逃逸的事件。他(她)质问，假如在墨西哥也发生了这类污染的话，我们又有什么措施来制止这类品种的扩散？我们又有哪条法律来禁止这类转基因玉米？

(4) 本文所提到的几种转基因在美国都是受到专利保护的。2001 年时曾经发生过 Monsanto 公司起诉加拿大 Saskatchewan 省的农民 Percy Schmeiser 的事件(Kleiner，2001)。因为 Monsanto 公司的调查员在 1998 年调查时发现在 Schmeiser 田块里生长有他们公司的抗草甘膦的油菜。Schmeiser 为此做过实验，说明这些转基因油菜是由于 1997 年时过路的货车吹起路边别的种转基因油菜田块留下的种子而造成混杂，并且他的田块的作物一般是不喷草甘膦，因而也没有必要去偷 Monsanto 公司的转基因油菜种子来种。但是法庭开庭后的裁决，居然判 Schmeiser 要付给 Monsanto 公司加币 15450 元。理由是 Schmeiser 是否种植耐除草剂油菜都无关紧要，而是他已侵犯了 Monsanto 的专利；即使他不想种转基因油菜，当他意识到他的田块中有了耐除草剂油菜而不去全部毁掉，也属于是侵权行为。目前 Schmeiser 也要起诉 Monsanto 公司，由于 Monsanto 公司转基因油菜的污染，已经迫使 Schmeiser 销毁掉他自己已经培育了时间长达 50 年的一个品种。因此转基因作物的专利保护也是一个值得引起重视的问题。

(5) 总之，这些年来科学家一直担心的基因流引起基因污染问题已被越来越多的事实所证实。在世界几个重要粮食作物及其他经济作物的起源地国家种植该种的转基因品种是一个非常值得引起重视的问题。农作物遗传多样性的丧失直接威胁到世界粮食的安全。中国是大豆、水稻和小麦等主要起源地，遗传多样性非常丰富。中国有六千余份野生大豆品种资源，占到世界的 90%以上；野生稻分布也相当广；小麦的野生近缘种有 110 种，其中有 97 种分布在中国的西部，76 种还是中国的特有种。这些宝贵的资源都需大力保护，切勿遭到转基因的污染。

总之，墨西哥玉米基因污染事件的动态再一次提醒人们对转基因作物商业化大面积种植应慎之又慎。

参考文献

魏伟, 马克平. 2002. 如何对待基因流和基因污染, 中国农业科技导报, **4** (4): 10~15

钱迎倩. 2003. 再论生物安全, 广西科学, **10** (2): 126~134

Dalton R.2001.Transgenic corn found growing in Mexico, *Nature*, 413: 337

Quist D, Chapela I H 2001.Transgenic DNA introgressed into traditional maizelandraces in Mexico, *Nature*, **44**: 541~543

Pearce F. 2002.Genetic contamination, New Scientist, 15 June 2002. 14~16

Lim Li Lin and Chee Yoke Heong. 2003. Contamination by GM maize in Mexico much worse than feared, http://www. Twnside. org.sg/title/ service82.htm

Kleiner K.2001.Blowing in the wind, http://www.newscientist.com/news/news.jsp?id=ns9999586

本文原载：应用与环境生物学报. 1999. 5(2): 215-228

害虫对转基因 Bt 作物的抗性及其管理对策*

魏伟　钱迎倩　马克平

(中国科学院植物研究所)

摘　要　至今为止，已经有 26 种植物成功地转入了 Bt 毒蛋白基因，它们将在防治害虫中发挥重要作用。Bt 作物释放的潜在风险是害虫的抗性进化。害虫对 Bt 毒蛋白产生抗性的机制包括行为躲避、生理生化机制及遗传机制。抗性等位基因的初始频率和抗性的遗传稳定性等特性影响着抗性管理对策的实施和效用。抗性管理对策包括 Bt 作物的轮作、转入多个杀虫基因、Bt 毒蛋白高剂量表达、低剂量表达和目标特异表达以及避难所策略等，它们是互为补充的。其中，“高剂量/避难所”策略受到广泛的重视。但是，这些策略来自理论数学模型和实验室数据，其有效性尚需要田间实验的检验并得到进一步完善。

关键词　Bt 作物；Bt 抗性；抗性机制；对策

中国法分类号 S433.1=Q789

世界范围内，大约有 67 000 种害虫危害农作物，其中约 9 000 种是昆虫和螨类；如果不使用杀虫剂或其他非化学控制策略，损失将接近作物产量的 70%[1]。例如，仅玉米螟给美国玉米带来的损失每年可达 10 亿美元[2]。自从施用化学农药防治农业害虫以来，曾经取得了良好的效果。然而，有 500 多种昆虫和螨类对化学农药产生了抗性[3]。并且人们逐步认识到化学农药给环境和人类健康带来的危害。于是生物防治受到广泛的重视，其中来源于苏云金杆菌(*Bacillus thuringiensis*)的生物杀虫剂(Bt)由于其专一性强，对环境无害并且对人、畜安全，已在许多国家和地区推广使用。但是 Bt 杀虫剂也有其局限性：这种杀虫剂的生产比较昂贵；它的应用需要农业机械；每个生长季一般都需要重复喷洒若干次，太阳光可以降低 Bt 杀虫剂有效成份；降水或露水会冲洗掉植株上的杀虫蛋白，从而缩短 Bt 杀虫剂的效用时间[1]。另外，在 70 年代晚期和 80 年代中期，人们发现一系列的 Bt 产品对防治烟芽夜蛾(*Heliothis virscens*)等棉花的害虫效果并不好，经过研究，原因是 Bt 制剂只能喷到作物表面，而这类害虫在花和棉铃内部生活的时期比较长，并且 Bt 毒蛋白只有被害虫食用后才有毒效[4]。随着基因工程技术的飞速发展，将 Bt 毒蛋白基因转入植物则在很好地控制害虫的同时，使得 Bt 制剂在应用中的弊端迎刃而解。目前，许多植物都已经成功地转入了 Bt 毒蛋白基因，并且一些主要的转基因农作物如玉米、棉花等已经获得批准进入市场。

如同化学农药的命运一样，昆虫对 Bt 杀虫剂也发生进化而产生了抗性[5]。迄今为止，

* 九五国家重点科技项目(攻关)计划：专题生物安全研究(97-925-02-04-05)。

在田间和实验室研究中已经发现有十多种昆虫对 Bt 杀虫毒蛋白产生了抗性[6]。由于转 Bt 作物能够持续地高水平表达单一的杀虫毒蛋白，因而 Bt 作物的释放将会加速昆虫的抗性进化。“自然界中的生物体对遗传工程作物的进化反应将使这类作物的优势消失殆尽”[7]。然而，转 Bt 基因作物具有很高的经济价值[1,8]，其商业化释放势在必行，而害虫对 Bt 作物的抗性是不可避免的，因此现在我们应该做的工作应该是研究如何延缓害虫 Bt 抗性的进化。在提出针对性的对策之前研究抗性发生的机制是非常必要的。虽然，前人对抗性机制和抗性管理的有关问题进行了综述，如 McGaughey 和 Whalon(1992)[9]、Tabashnik (1994)[10]、Bergvinson 等(1997)[6]等。但是，这些文献的侧重点各有不同。并且转 Bt 基因植物的种类不断增加，抗虫作物的释放面积从 1996 年至 1997 年增加了 3.8 倍[8]，其中主要是转 Bt 基因作物。1996 年，美国南部 8 000hm^2 Bt 棉失去了对害虫的控制，虽然 Mansanto 公司认为怀疑害虫对 Bt 毒蛋白产生了抗性是没有科学依据的，但人们开始重新提起害虫的抗性进化这一议题，并对那些通过理论和模型推算出来的抗性管理策略展开讨论[11,12]，这一点将在后文作详细介绍。因而，有必要根据新的进展就害虫的 Bt 抗性及其评价以及各种抗性管理对策的利弊进行全面的论述，为害虫的抗性管理增添新的内容并为寻求合理可行的抗性管理对策提供必要和有力适时的理论依据。

1 转 Bt 内毒素基因植物概况

由于植物种类的不同，害虫抗性产生的机制不同，因而管理对策也就可能因植物和害虫种类的不同而有所不同。所以本文在探讨害虫对 Bt 作物的抗性风险及其管理对策之前，首先概括介绍世界范围内转 Bt 基因植物的概况。

文献中，一般用 Cry 表示 Btδ-内源毒蛋白的晶体状态，cry 表示编码这个蛋白的基因 *Bt* 毒蛋白和它们的基因一般被分为四类：CryⅠ(鳞翅目特异)、CryⅡ(鳞翅目和双翅目特异)、CryⅢ(鞘翅目特异)和 CryⅣ(双翅目特异)[13]。Feitelson 等(1992)又增添了两类 CryⅤ和 CryⅥ[14]。CryⅤ对鳞翅目和鞘翅目昆虫及线虫特异，CryⅣ对线虫特异，Koziel 等(1993)列出了目前的 Btδ-内毒素以及它们的杀虫谱[15]。

第一例转 Bt 植物是抗烟草天蛾(*Manduea Sexta*)的转基因烟草[16]。至 1997 年早些时候，在大约已经或即将被批准上市的 80 种转基因作物中，有 21 种是转 Bt 作物，其中 11 种是玉米(转 *cry*ⅠA(b)或 *cry*Ⅰ(c))、5 种是马铃薯(转 *cry*ⅢA(a))、另外 5 种是棉花(转 *cry*ⅠA(a)或 *cry*ⅠA(c))[1]。其他还有 20 余种成功转 Bt 植物的例子(表 1)，有的只是田间试验，有的仅仅是获得了转基因植株，它们的上市只是一个时间问题，其商业化释放不能够回避 Bt 抗性进化这个问题。表 1 列出了迄今为止主要的转 Bt 植物以及它们的目标害虫，为探讨害虫对 Bt 作物的抗性进化提供了背景资料。

2 害虫对转基因 Bt 作物的抗性

2.1 Btδ-内毒素蛋白的杀虫机理

为了探讨害虫对 Bt 抗性产生的机制，首先应该了解 Bt 毒素的杀虫机理。

害虫摄食 Bt 杀虫剂中的杀虫晶体蛋白(insecticidal crystal proteins，ICPs)后，在中肠碱性条件下二硫键打开，在胰道胰蛋白酶的作用下激活形成抗蛋白酶的毒性核心片段，才有活性[48]。在转基因植物体中，为了提高表达量，所转入的基因都是经过修饰的，所表达的 Bt 毒蛋白是已被活化的蛋白[49,50]。活性毒素与中肠上皮的刷状缘膜囊(brush border membrane vesicles, BBMV)上的中肠受体蛋白结合，研究表明，毒素活性与其对 BBMV 结合的能力呈正相关[51]。

Bt 活性蛋白与中肠上皮细胞结合后，有毒性的α-螺旋穿透细胞质膜形成一个离子通道(孔)，依 pH 的不同，这些孔具有选择性(仅 k^+可通过)和非选择性(Na^+和阴离子可通过)。由于鳞翅目昆虫的中肠是碱性的，因而这些孔很有可能有 K^+渗漏，这种阳离子通道损坏了膜电势，细胞膨胀并裂解，导致中肠坏死，围食膜和上皮退化变性，肠壁受损后，中肠的碱性高渗内含物进入血腔，血淋巴 pH 升高而导致昆虫麻痹死亡。害虫死后由毒素导致了细菌败血病[6,48]。

表 1　转 Bt 基因作物概况*

Table 1　List of Major Transgenic Plants with Bt Genes*

作物 Grops	Bt 基因 Bt genes	目标害虫 Target Pests	作物 Grops	Bt 基因 Bt genes	目标害虫 Target Pests
烟草 Tabacco	*cry* I A(a) *cry* I A(b)	烟草天蛾(*Manduca Sexta*)[17] 甜菜夜蛾(*Spalaptera exigua*)[15,18~19] 棉铃虫(*Heliothis zea*)[15,18~19]	白花三叶草 White Clover	*cry* I A(b)	*Orocramhus flexuosellus*[41]
				cry I B	*Porina moth*(*Wiseana spp.*)[41]
			花生 Peanut	*cry* I A(c)	南美玉米苗斑螟(*Elasmopalpus lignosellus*)[38]
	cry I A(c)	烟芽夜蛾(*H.virescens*)[20~21]	花茎甘蓝 Bracoli 卷心菜 Cabbage	*cry* IA(c)	小菜蛾(*Plutella xylastella*)[42]
	cry I C(a)	甜菜夜蛾(*Spaloptera exigua*)[22]			
	*cry*ⅢA	马铃薯甲虫(*Leptinctarsa decemillineata*)[23]			
番茄 Tomato	*cry* I A(b)	烟草天蛾(*Mandua Sexta*)，棉铃虫(*H*, *zea*)，番茄蠹蛾(*Keiferia lycopersicella*)[24~25]			
	cry I A(c)	鳞翅目昆虫(*Lepidoptera*)[26]	甘蓝型油菜 Oilsee drape /canola	*cry*IA(c)	棉铃虫(H. *zea*), 粉纹夜蛾(*Trichoplusia ni*), 小菜蛾(*P. xylastella*), 甜菜夜蛾(*S. exigua*)[43]
马铃薯 Potato	*cry* I A(b)	马铃薯麦蛾(*Phthorimaea operculella*)[27]			
	cry I A(c)	烟草天蛾(*Monduca Sexta*)[28]	芜菁甘蓝 Rutabaga	*cry*IA(a)	菜粉蝶(*Pieris rapae*)[44]
	cry ⅢA	马铃薯甲虫(*Leptinctarsa decemilineata*)[29~30]			
茄子 Eggplant	*cry* I A(b)	茄白翅野螟(*Leucincdes orbonalis*)[31]	苹果 Apple	*cry*IA(a) *cry*IA(c)	鳞翅目害虫(*Lepidoptera*)[26]
	cry ⅢA	鞘翅目昆虫(*Coleoptera*)[26]			

续表

作物 Grops	Bt 基因 Bt genes	目 标 害 虫 Target Pests
棉花 Cotton	*cry*IA(b) *cry*IA(c)	烟芽夜蛾(*Heliothis virescens*), 棉铃虫(*Heliothis zea*), 等鳞翅目(*Lepidoptera*) 害虫[26,32–33]
	cry ⅡA	鳞翅目害虫(*Lepidoptera*)[26]
玉米 Maize/corn	*cry* I A(b)	巨座玉米螟(*Diatraea grandiosella*), 小蔗螟(*D. saccharalis*)[6]
	cry I A(b)	欧洲玉米螟(*Ostrinia nubilalis*)[34]
	cry I A(c)	亚洲玉米螟(*O.turnacalis*)[35]
	*Prt*A	鳞翅目害虫(*Lepidoptera*)[26]
	cry I H	鞘翅目害虫(*Coleoptera*)[26]
水稻 Rice	*cry* I A(b)	二化螟(*Chilo supperessulis*), 稻纵卷叶螟(*Cnaphalocrosis medinalis*)[36]
	cry I A(b)	三化螟(*Scirpophaga incertulas*), 二化螟、稻纵卷叶螟和 *Marasmia patnalis*[37]
	cry I A(c)	鳞翅目害虫(*Lepidoptera*)[26]
苜蓿 Alfalfa	*cry* I C(a)	海灰翅夜蛾(*S. littoralis*), 甜菜夜蛾(*S. exigua*)[20]
	cry ⅥA	鞘翅目害虫(*Coleoptera*)[26]
大豆 Soybean	*cry* I A(b)	黎豆夜蛾(*Anticarsia gemmatalis*)[39]
	cry I A(c)	烟芽夜蛾(*H .virescens*), 黎豆夜蛾(*A. gemmatalis*), 棉铃虫(*H.zea*), 大豆夜蛾(*Pesudoplusia includens*)[40]

作物 Grops	Bt 基因 Bt genes	目 标 害 虫 Target Pests
酸果蔓 Cranberry	*cry*IA(a)	鳞翅目害虫(*Lepidoptera*)[26]
葡萄 Crapevine	*cry*IA(c)	鳞翅目害虫(*Lepidoptera*)[26]
山楂 Hawthorn	Bt**	苹果蠹蛾(Laspeyresia *pomonella*)[1]
唐棣 Juneberry	Bt**	鳞翅目害虫(*Lepidoptera*)[1]
梨 Pear	Bt**	苹果蠹蛾(*L. pomonella*)[1]
甘蔗 Sugarcane	*cry*IA(c)	小蔗螟(*D. saccharalis*)[1]
草莓 Strawberry	*cry*IA(c)	鳞翅目害虫(*Lepidoptera*)[1]
杨树 Poplar	*cry*IA(a)	森林天幕毛虫(*Malacosoma disstria*), 舞毒蛾(*Lymantvia dispar*)[45–46]
胡桃 Walnut	*cry*IA(c)	鳞翅目害虫(*Lepidoptera*)[1]
白云衫 White Spruce	*cry*IA	枞色卷蛾(*Chorisoneura fumiferana*)[47]

* 按照 Hofte 和 Whiteley(1989)[13]对 Bt 基因的分类 According to the classification of Bt genes by Hofte and Whiteley (1989)[13]

** 一种 Bt 基因，名称未知 A Bt gene whose name is unknown

2.2 害虫对转基因 Bt 作物的抗性

抗性是一个种群对一种杀虫剂敏感度的降低，这种降低是以遗传为基础的。抗性使得种群中等位基因的频率发生变化,所以可以定义为一种进化现象[10]。1983 年,Georghiou 等首先从五带淡色库蚊(*Culex quinquefasciatus*)中检测到了它对 Bt ICPs 和其商品制剂的抗性[48]。培养 32 代后,发现五带淡色库蚊的 LC_{50} 仅有 8 倍的增长[10]。1985 年,McGaughey

在实验室条件下进行抗性筛选，发明印度谷螟(*Plodia interpunctella*)选择两代后抗性增长近 30 倍，15 代以后比对照增长 100 倍[5]。Tabashnik(1994)总结了在实验室选择条件下迄今对 Bt 产生抗性的害虫[10]：鳞翅目——烟芽夜蛾，甜菜夜蛾，海灰翅夜蛾，粉纹夜蛾，小菜蛾，地中海粉螟(*Anagasta kuehniella*)，粉斑蛾(Cadra cautella)，向日葵斑螟(*Homoeosoma electellum*)，印度谷螟，枞色卷螟(*Choristoneura fumiferana*)；鞘翅目——黑杨叶甲(*Chrysomela scripta*)，马铃薯甲虫；双翅目——埃及伊蚊(*Aedes aegypti*)，五带淡色库蚊，黄猩猩果蝇(*Drosophila melanogaster*)，家蝇(*Musca domestica*)。欧洲玉米螟在实验室选择条件下也表现出了对 Bt 的抗性[52]。其中，只有一种害虫——小菜蛾在田间进化出对 Bt 的抗性[53]，并且从夏威夷、佛罗里达、纽约，到菲律宾、泰国和马来西亚的田间种群以及日本的温室种中群中都报道了小菜蛾对 Bt 的抗性[10]。中美洲的小菜蛾田间种群也报道了对 Bt 的抗性[3]。其他 15 种害虫仅是在实验室选择的条件下发现了对 Bt 的抗性。而且 Tabashnik 等(1990)认为，由于 Bt 毒蛋白和传统杀虫剂的作用方式不同，因而 Bt 抗性的产生是由 Bt 的本身的选择压力引起的，而不是来其他杀虫剂(如化学农药)的交叉抗性[52]。如此多的害虫可以对 Bt 杀虫剂产生抗性，那么人们就不能不考虑种植转 Bt 作物而导致害虫抗性的风险。转 Bt 棉在美国南部的失败[11,12]，更加重了人们的这种担心。国内的一项研究表明，抗 Bt 杀虫剂的棉铃虫品系同样对转 Bt 棉也有抗性[55]。

与 Bt 杀虫剂相似，高度抗虫的转基因植物也会导致类似的选择压力[7]，由于单一的杀虫毒素的持续表达，转 Bt 植物的选择压力甚至比 Bt 杀虫剂还要高，因而在此较高的选择压力下，害虫很有可能以更快的速度进化出对 Bt 的抗性。当害虫对 Bt 作物的抗性一旦产生，不但 Bt 作物对害虫失去控制，而且那些 Bt 杀虫剂也将变得毫无价值。

3 害虫对 Bt 抗性的机理及抗性的评估

一般来讲，抗性产生的机制总体上可分为生理、生化、行为三方面的因素[48]。但这几方面的机制应该是在与遗传控制因素紧密联系的[56]。Heckel(1994)认为转 Bt 作物与传统的化学农药和杀虫剂情况不同，它有些类似于植物与食草动物之间的协同进化：植物可能会进化出一种新的化学防御的方法来逃避食草动物，而食草动物则能够产生共进化，设计出一种机制，来适应抗食草动物的植物[56]。食草动物的适应受以下因素的影响：选择强度、适应的等位基因初始强度、显性、上位性以及适应的生态学和生理学代价等[7]。将害虫和转 Bt 作物的关系与食草动物和植物的关系相提并论，将有助于我们理解和评价害虫对 Bt 作物潜在抗性的机制。

3.1 害虫 Bt 抗性的生理生化机制

生理与生化机制密切相关，因此我们将它们放在一起讨论。目前对抗性机制研究的重点集中在蛋白质水解作用和结合位点的变化上[56]。许多研究表明，抗性的增加与 BBMV 上可能受体与毒素特异性结合的降低有关[57~59]。另外，在 Bt 毒素作用途径的许多步骤上都可以产生抗性机制。抗性机制的发生可能仅局限于 Bt 对昆虫杀伤途径上某些作用因子的量变，而非整套特异的作用机制的突变[48]。我们将 Heckel(1994)所列出的可能产生抗性机制的毒素发生作用的各个阶段以及抗性的生理生化机制[56]略加改动，用于阐述害虫对 Bt 作物的抗性机制(表 2)。显然，毒素的溶解和活化对于 Bt 杀虫剂的效力是至关重要的。然而，对于 Bt 作物来说，由于转入的 Bt 基因都是经过修饰或人工合成的，其表达产物可能并不需要激活作用而直接与靶受体结合而发挥毒效。虽然如此，为了对问题有个较全面的认识，我们还是将原毒素的溶解作用和激活作用保留在表 2。

表 2 害虫 Bt 抗性可能的生理生化机制及其特性*

Table 2 Some potential Bt resistance mechanisms in pests and their likely properties*

受影响的阶段 Steps affected	抗性的本质 Nature of interference	保护程度[a] Protection	交叉抗性[b] Cross-resistance	是否隐性[c] Recessive	代价[d] Cost
1.溶解[e] Solubilization	失去作用 Failure	M	+	+	H
2.激活[e] Activation	未完全蛋白质水解 Deficient proteolysis	M	+	+	H
3.激活 Activation	蛋白质过度水解 Over–proteolysis	M	+	–	M
4.接近靶受体 Access to target	竞争性抑制 Competitve inhibition	M	–	–	M
5.靶位点结合 Target binding	靶位点初级结构变化 Change in primary structure of target	H	–	+	M
6.靶位点结合 Target binding	靶位点修饰(糖基化作用) Change in target modification (glycosylation)	H	–	+/–[f]	H
7.孔的形成 Pore formation	阻碍 Hindered	M	+	+	?
8.孔的功能 Pore function	堵塞 Plugged	H	+	–	L
9.中肠上皮损伤 Loss of midgut epithelium	生理学克服 Physiological coping	L	+	?	?
10.自我剂量测定[g] Self–dosing	行为变化 Behavioral changes	L	+	?	?

注：a 对最初选择毒素的抗性：分 L(低)、M(中等)、或 H(高). Relative degrees of protection conferred against the primary selective toxin: L(Low), M(medium)or H(high). b 该机制是否有交叉抗性? +：有交叉抗性，-：无交叉抗性. Is substantial cross – resistance to other toxins also conferred by the mechanism? +: cross-resistunce; - : no cross-resistance. c 该机制是否隐性? + ：隐性；- ：非隐性，? ：表示未知. Is the resistance mechanism likely to be recessive? + : recessive; - : notrecessive; ? : Unknown. d 撤去毒素后抗性机制的相对适应代价：H(高)、M(中等)或 L(低)，? ：表示未知. Relative fitness cost of the resistance mechanism in the absence of toxin: H(High), M(Medium)or L(Low); ? : Unknown. e 对 Bt 作物来说可能不起作用. It may have no function for Bt crops. f 如果由正常的糖基化作物的失败而引起就是隐性，如果由一个新的糖基化作物引起就是非隐性. Recessive if due to failure of a normal glycosylation pathway; Not recessive due to prescence of a novel glycosylation activity. g 对 Bt 作物来讲，害虫主要采用在时空上转变宿主对策. Pests avoid toxins by shifting hosts spatially and temporally for Bt crops.

*来自文献[46]，略加改动。According to reference[46]with a little modification.

3.2 害虫 Bt 抗性的行为机制

Gould(1991)曾讨论过食草动物对植物抗性的行为适应[60]，如果时空上 Bt 毒素的浓度有差异，那么行为上尽量减少摄食将会构成一种抗性机制。表 2 中第 10 个机制既是一种行为抗性。对害虫和 Bt 作物的关系来说，害虫可以进化成只是避免有毒植株或有毒的部分。Gould 在 1988 年就提出一个问题，棉铃虫是以棉花和大豆为食的，如果突然面对大面积的能够导致 80%死亡的抗性棉花(比如 Bt 棉)，棉铃虫是在生理上产生适应而是抗性棉(Bt 棉)失去价值，还是在行为上适应转而去以大豆为食，而对大豆的取食仅会导致较少的损失并且易于控制[7]。这个问题很难回答。实际上生理生化抗性机制和行为抗性机制可能同时存在,哪种机制为主要依具体情况而定。在 CIMMYT 的 Bt 玉米种,CryIA(a)的表达需要光的条件由 PEP 羧化酶启动子启动。由于心叶见光少，害虫就可能能够忍受低量表达的 Bt 毒素，所以，研究发现，害虫一般都在心叶中生活[6]。

3.3 害虫 Bt 抗性的遗传机制

抗性的产生应该是以遗传为基础的[10]。害虫 Bt 抗性的生理生化机制是与遗传机制紧密联系的[56]。受体分子结构的变化将使毒素与受体的结合能力降低(表 2，机制 5,6)是抗性遗传机制最直接的证据。至于害虫的行为抗性机制可能是一种生活习性改变的结果，有无遗传基础尚无定论。

Tabashnik 等(1997)研究表明,小菜蛾中一个抗性基因的存在可以提供对四种 Bt 毒素的抗性，当然还需要进一步的研究来确定提供这种多毒素抗性的遗传因素是一个位点，还是几个紧密连锁的位点，他们指出这个证据排除了这样一个观点—这些毒素的抗性需要各自独立的分离位点上的突变[61]。在对小菜蛾的大多数实验室选择和田间选择的研究中发现，昆虫对 Bt 的抗性是半隐性或完全隐性的[3,10]。

害虫快速适应一种杀虫剂的风险主要依靠田间野生种群中的初始抗性等位基因频率[62]。目前广泛应用的抗性频率是 10^{-2}~10^{-3},它是基于突变—选择理论的一个估计值[63]。Crow 和 Kimura 的这个理论认为：有利选择前，任何一个等位基因的频率由都是由突变产生的新等位基因和对杂合体的选择之间的平衡保持在种群中[64]。当然选择也应该作用于纯合个体，但由于稀少而被 Crow 和 Kimura(1970)忽略不计。然而，实际情况并不像人们用理论模型来预测的那样。Tabashnik 等(1997)发现小菜蛾中的初始抗性等位基因频率为 0.12,10 倍于目前所广泛引用的感性群体中初始抗性等位基因频率的估计值[61]。Gould 等(1997)通过采自美国 4 个州的烟芽夜蛾的雄性与实验室的抗 Bt 的雌蛾杂交，并观察 F_1 和 F_2 代对 Bt 毒蛋白的忍受能力，估计到田间抗性等位基因的初始频率为 1.5×10^{-3}，并指出他们的这种技术能够提高检测隐性抗性等位基因的频率的能力[62]。Tabashnik(1997)[3]高度评价了这个技术[62]，认为隐性纯合个体存在的概率是 P^2(P 为隐性抗体等位基因频率)，远远小于杂合个体存在的频率 $2 \times P \times (1-P)$，能够检出隐性纯合体意味着敏感度提高了 2000 倍。而这样做对确定隐性抗性等位基因的初始频率是非常重要的。前人，如 Crow 和 Kimura(1970)[62]，根据遗传学模型估计抗性基因的初始频率时将抗性隐性纯合体忽略不计，这个错误导致低估了隐性抗性等位基因的初始频率。

昆虫害虫的 Bt 抗性的遗传机制比较复杂，例如，马铃薯甲虫对 CryⅢA 的抗性与一个以上的位点有关[65]。为了使问题简化，从前的工作认为抗性是受一个单一位点上的一个稀有的初始等位基因控制。为了更好地研究害虫 Bt 抗性的遗传机制，建立 Bt 抗性与标记位点的连锁作图是一个比较有用的方法。我们可以用连锁作图来研究复杂的 Bt 抗性机制。它有如下用途[56]：1)能够明确地检出不同的抗性机制；2)用标记来帮助鉴定和分类抗性位点，这一点在抗性发生在几个特异位点上时特别重要；3)可以允许位点特异显性评估，也就是确定抗性位点的显隐性；4)检测出若干个位点以后，这些标记可以用来研究这些位点是如何相互作用提供抗性的；5)用于交叉抗性的分析；6)用于特异性等位基因适应代价(fitness cost)的细致研究。由于烟芽夜蛾的所有 31 条染色体上的具有标记位点的连锁图已经完成，因而适于进行标记位点和 Bt 抗性连锁作图的研究[66]。Heckel 等(1997)[66]通过研究烟芽夜蛾对 Bt CryIA(c)的抗性发现，连锁群 9 由同工酶 MPI 位标记，是在烟芽夜蛾中发现的影响抗性的第 4 个连锁群，称为 BtR-4，提供烟芽夜蛾抗性品系(YHD2)对 CryIAc80%的抗性。这个发现具有很大的意义：1)抗性品系 YHD2 是最近由田间获得的，BtR-4 位点上的抗性等位基因在田间种群存在着不容忽视的频率，并将由于 Bt 棉的商业性释放而进一步增大；2)首次发现了昆虫中一个主要的 BtR 抗性位点与一个遗传标记的连锁，检测到 MPI 与 Bt 抗性间的连锁是揭示昆虫对相同选择压力(Bt)共同进化的第一步；3)BtR-4 的连锁对于建立烟芽夜蛾中 Bt 的抗性机制也是很重要的一步。

3.4 害虫 Bt 抗性的评估

目前，许多抗性选择试验是在实验室里进行的，而实验室选择结果往往不能代表田间情况。特别是当实验室种群的遗传变异与田间相比比较有限时，实验室选择不能产生抗性并不意味着田间选择条件下也没有抗性的发生[10]。我们需要一个标准的方法来分析报道实验室的研究结果，并将其用于抗性的风险评价中。Tabashnik(1992，1994)为我们提供了可以用来评价抗性对不同选择程度响应的现实遗传力这样一个参数的估计方法[67,70]。现实遗传力 h^2 为：

$$h^2=R/S \tag{1}$$

这里 R 是选择响应，S 是选择差。其中，

$$R=\frac{\left\{\ln(\mathrm{LC}^{\mathrm{f}}_{50})-\ln(\mathrm{LC}^{\mathrm{i}}_{50})\right\}}{n}/n \tag{2}$$

这里 $\mathrm{LC}^{\mathrm{f}}_{50}$ 是选择 n 代以后后代的最终半致死浓度，$\mathrm{LC}^{\mathrm{i}}_{50}$ 是 n 代选择以前亲本世代的初始半致死浓度；

$$S=\mathrm{i}\sigma_p \tag{3}$$

这里 i 是选择的强度，用文献[68]的附录 A 由选择的存活率 P 估计得出；σ_p 是表型标准

偏差：

$$\sigma_p=[1/2(K_i+K_f)]^{-1} \tag{4}$$

K_i(初始斜率)和 K_f(最终斜率)分别是选择前亲本和 n 代选择后子代概率回归线的斜率。

将公式(1)改换一下可以用来评价抗性对选择压力的反应：

$$R=h^2S \tag{5}$$

当抗性选择停止后，不同昆虫(种或品种)对 Bt 抗性的稳定性是不相同的。例如，对印度谷螟选择 9 代后，抗性群体用不加 Bt 的饲料喂养，7 个世代中抗性并没有下降，表明抗性选择了一个纯合的抗性品系，或者抗性并没有什么显著的繁殖不利[5]。

在小菜蛾中，当选择停止时，其 Bt 抗性缓慢降低[69]。而对于马铃薯甲虫来说选择压力撤去 5 个世代以后其抗性水平下降，12 个世代以后抗性水平不再下降[65]。当去掉选择压力后，抗性水平下降的原因可能是提供 Bt 抗性的遗传变化在没有 Bt 的选择条件下会给害虫造成一个适应代价，当选择停止时，这个代价会引起混合种群中抗性的下降[10]。然而，基因流(感性个体的迁入和抗性个体的迁出)、突变和遗传漂变同样也会降低种群中抗性个体的频率[69]。

用于估计抗性响应的参数 R 可以用来定量选择停止后 LC_{50} 的变化，也就是抗性的稳定性。这时，公式(2)中的 LC_{50}^{f} 和 LC_{50}^{i} 分别代表选择停止 n 代后和 n 代前的 LC_{50}，若 R 是页值则表示 LC_{50} 的降低，即抗性水平的下降。R 的倒数是 LC_{50}10 倍变化所需要的世代数。

4 害虫对 Bt 作物抗性的管理对策

前文已讲述，害虫对 Bt 毒素的抗性是不可避免的，我们所要做的是采取一系列有效的策略或对策来延迟抗性，延长转 Bt 作物或 Bt 杀虫喷剂的效用时间。害虫对 Bt 作物的抗性管理对策的制定一是要从化学农药和 Bt 杀虫剂的抗性管理中吸取经验，二是要结合转 Bt 作物的具体情况。

抗性管理应该是遵循综合害虫管理(IPM)基本原理的一项对策，后者就是将害虫种群密度控制在能导致经济损失的域值以下，同时尽量减小由施用杀虫剂而造成的社会经济和环境的负面影响。抗性管理来源 4 个基本对策：①不要使害虫仅受一种致死机制的选择，使致死原因多样化；②降低每种主要致死机制的选择压力；③通过避难所(refuges)或迁入来提供感性个体；④通过应用诊断工具，监测和模型来估计和预测抗性过程[9]。依照这些原则，延迟害虫对 Bt 作物抗性的管理策略主要有以下几种：Bt 作物的轮作、开发新的毒素基因、避难所、毒素高剂量表达、毒素低剂量表达、转入多种杀虫基因以及毒素在时空上的特异表达，它们在实际应用中应该是互为补充，相辅相成的。

4.1 Bt作物的轮作

McGaughey和Whalon指出[9]，Bt毒素与其他毒素，杀虫剂或者耕作防除或生物控制策略的轮作或变换可以用来管理抗性。虽然与Bt杀虫剂不同，Bt作物一般具有持续的毒素表达，但是Bt作物的轮作，即与含有不同Bt毒素基因的作物或非转基因作物间的轮作，将会有助于害虫抗性的延迟。这个策略的有效性依赖于当选择压力不连续或者变化至另外一种毒素时，害虫种群对该选择压力敏感性的恢复。害虫的抗性稳定性在前文(3.4 部分)已作了详细讨论，虽然印度谷螟在不存在选择压力的情况下，抗性将持续较长的时期[5]，但大多数情况下，选择的早期抗性比较不稳定，并当选择不连续时抗性水平会下降[9]。另外，当用含有不同杀虫毒素基因的作物进行轮作时，要注意交叉抗性的问题。当然轮作的周期、面积等尚需根据害虫的不同、转基因作物的不同而进行细致深入的研究。

4.2 建立避难所策略

避难所是指在转 Bt 作物附近种植一定面积的非转基因作物，来保证感性昆虫的存活，并与潜在的抗性个体交配，从而降低抗性基因频率增大的可能性。许多理论模型的预测证明，避难所能够延迟害虫对 Bt 作物的抗性[74~77]。还有很多文献论述了避难所的应用[1,3,6~7,9~10,78]。

避难所有时间上还有空间上的，它在每种害虫与植物相互作用关系上都是独特的，避难所可以位于一特定植株(不同部分和不同发育阶段)上，也可以存在于不同植株上(混合种子)或不同的种植地中[6,9]。一般地，避难所和高剂量方法是结合在一起应用的。Peferoen(1997)详细地说明了高剂量策略和避难所策略的结合的基本原理[78]：消除抗性基因最有效的方法是将目标定在携带杂合抗性基因的害虫上，原因是种群中大多数抗性基因是以杂合状态存在，杂合抗性昆虫和纯合的感性昆虫都可以被高剂量表达的Bt作物杀死；在提供感性昆虫存活的一个避难所的条件下，纯合抗性个体和纯合感性个体间的交配导致杂合后代的产生，而杂合后代对Bt作物是敏感的；所以，现在的重点是如何设计一个避难所驱使纯合抗性个体和纯合感性个体进行交配。在这个策略中，由于在避难所中使用非转基因作物，害虫的危害可能会比较严重，造成一定的经济损失。为了改进这个策略，Alstad和Andow(1994)设计一种改进型“高剂量/避难所”策略[74]，他们在转基因作物地中使用一种对欧洲玉米螟有吸引力的Bt玉米品种，吸引6月蛾到Bt玉米地中产卵，避免了避难所中由于使用非转基因作物而造成的损失，很好地控制了害虫对 Bt 作物和非Bt作物的危害。然而，如果在选择压力下害虫在行为上产生逃避这种有引力的Bt作物的抗性，这种方法的实用性尚需进一步的研究。

表3列出了为了延迟抗性，在美国上市的5个Bt作物品种所需要的避难所的最小面积。然而，1996 年夏天 Monsanto 公司的棉花在美国南部控制棉铃虫的失败[11,12]，使人们对这种避难所策略产生了怀疑。但是Monsanto公司的发言人认为没有迹象表明害虫进化出了抗性，昆虫的大发生只是由于异常干燥的气候。McGaughey 指出，当具有较高昆虫大发生的压力时，平时100%的杀虫剂量也会失去作用，异常的温度也会影响 Bt 毒素

的合成和表达[11]。Monsanto 的 Bt 棉的目标害虫是烟芽夜蛾[61,62]和棉红铃虫[11]。Gould 认为，4%的避难所(或 20%的喷药的避难所)对于控制棉花主要的害虫—烟芽夜蛾是合适的，这种害虫对 Bt 非常敏感。然而，棉铃虫对 Bt 有较低的敏感性，所以对棉铃虫应用“高剂量/避难所”的方法是错误的。对于 Bt 不敏感的害虫需要较大面积的避难所来延迟抗性[11]。

表 3　不同 Bt 作物中延迟抗性的最小避难所面积[1]

Table 3　Mininum refuge areas for different transgenic crops to delay the likelihood of inselt resistance III

公司 Company	产品名称 Product	作物 Crop	避难所面积 Minimun refuge areas
Monsanto	Bollgard™	棉花 Cotton	25%面积的非转基因棉花(如果需要，可以用任何杀虫剂，但不包括与转基因棉相同的 Bt 杀虫剂措施) 或 4%的非转基因棉花(不用任何的杀虫措施) 25% of unprotected cotton(non-transgenic)as a refuge using conventional insect controls if desired or 4% of unprotected cotton(non-transgenic)as a total refuge using no insect control whatsoever
	Nature Gard™	玉米 Corn	使用对欧洲玉米螟有 99%以上水平的致死高剂量对策；并且建议使用 5%~50%面积的非转基因玉米 High-dose strategy with levels exceeding the LC_{99} for European corn borer; proposing to plant 5%~50% of unprotected corn(non-transgenic)
	Newleaf™	马铃薯 Potato	20%的非转基因马铃薯(若需要，可用任何杀虫剂) 20% of non-transgenic potatoes as a refuge using conventional insect controls if desired
Novartis	Maximizer™	玉米 Corn	使用对欧洲玉米螟有 99%致死量水平的高剂量对策；并且建议种植 5%~50%面积的非转基因玉米 High-dose strategy with levels exceeding the LC_{99} for European corn borer; proposing to plant 5%~50% of non-transgenic corn
Mycogen	Yield Gard ™	玉米 Corn	5%面积的非转基因玉米，避难所中不用任何杀虫剂 5% of non-transgenic corn as a total refuge using no insect control whatsoever

在通常情况下，玉米也是棉铃虫的宿主，玉米田可以作为 Bt 抗性管理的避难所，但当 Bt 玉米商业化以后，这种情况就可能不复存在了。同时，为了避免棉铃虫抗性的加速，美国国家环保局已严令禁止 Bt 棉与 Bt 玉米邻近种植。

4.3　转入多个杀虫基因

在转基因抗虫作物研究中，除了开发新的 Bt σ-内毒素蛋白基因外，尚可利用其他的抗虫基因，如蛋白酶剂基因，包括豇豆胰白酶抑制剂(CpTi)基因、马铃薯蛋白酶抑制剂-Ⅱ(PinⅡ)基因和水稻疏基蛋白酶抑制剂基因，淀粉酶抑制剂基因，外源凝集素基因等[70,71]。可以将它们与 Bt 基因一起转入作物，具有不同结合位点的两种以上的 Bt 基因也可同时转入同一作物，用于提高转基因抗虫作物延迟害虫抗性的能力。然而这个策略的应用需要避难所的协助[72]，其中一个原因就是防止交叉抗性[1]。

4.4 高剂量方法

高剂量方法就是使基因转作物的毒素表达量在一个高水平上(大于 LC_{99},即超过 99%的致死量)，在理论上，昆虫克服这种毒素需要很长的时间。这个方法假设大多数或全部的抗性是隐性的或处于最差的加性状态，并且大多数的抗性携带者是杂合的，甚至预计抗性纯合体也将被高水平表达的毒素杀死[1]。同样，高剂量方法也必须与避难所结合起来应用。如果没有避难所的同时存在，这个方法必须满足 6 个方面的假设：① 抗性因子的遗传方式；② 抗性因子的生态学代价；③ 害虫幼虫和成虫对毒素的行为响应；④ 幼虫在植物株之间的移动；⑤ 成虫散布和交配行为；⑥ 表达和不表达这些毒素宿主植株的分布[73]。当多种 Bt 作物和多种害虫分布在同一地区，并且作物受到两种以上的害虫的侵害，而这几种害虫对毒素的敏感程度不同，同时同一害虫能够以两种以上的作物作为宿主时，问题就变得比较复杂，结果就更加难于预测。

4.5 低剂量方法

一般地，我们可以这样假设，一种植物抗性因子降低食草动物适应的程度愈低，食草动物适应这个抗性因子的速度愈慢[7]。低剂量的毒素表达的目的是降低选择压。亚致死的剂量将会降低害虫种群的育性和生长，并且使得受到影响的害虫易于被捕食和寄生[1]。然而，如果昆虫开始就暴露于低剂量的毒素之下，表 2 中第 9 个抗性机制—使损伤的中肠上皮得到修复，就有可能形成。并且，从商业的角度来看，低剂量毒素表达导致的作物的损失不能被接受，因此这种方法已被有关公司弃用[1]。

4.6 Bt 毒素的目标表达

这个策略就是在作物某一部分或作物发育的特定时期特异地表达 Bt 毒素。研究表明，棉花需要防护的最重要部分是幼棉铃，使抗性因子仅在幼铃中表达，幼虫就会依赖其他部分，引起较少的损失[7]。这个方法将允许很多感性昆虫正常地生长和繁殖，因而增加了它们的捕食者和寄生者的数量，同时，在主要的部分或生活史阶段能够免受损失[1]。然而，也有不同意见，如果组织特异性启动导致 Bt 在一些组织中高量表达，在另外一些组织中低量表达，那么害虫的抗性将会被加速而不是延迟，这是因为害虫将会由不同生活史阶段利用的组织的不同而被分化选择[9]。

随着对基因调控的深入了解，这一策略将作为避难所和高剂量策略的补充有可能得到广泛应用。

4.7 建立数学模型对抗性管理的评估

由于在田间检验上述策略比较困难，所以现在一般用实验室数据[75]和数学模型来评价延迟抗性的策略。

Mallet 和 Porter (1992)用数学模型比较了避难所策略(转基因作物和非转基因作物种

植在不同的农田中)和种子混合策略(转基因和非转基因植株种植在同一农田中)或组织特异表达策略(避难所在同一植株上)对于延迟害虫 Bt 抗性的作用[76]。Tabashnik(1994)[77]则用 Mallet 和 Porter(1992)提供的模型[76]评价了种子混合、避难所、种子混合+避难所与纯转基因农田对昆虫抗性的影响。

这个模型有几个假设：① 害虫对 Bt 毒素的抗性由单一位点控制；② 昆虫幼虫有两个生活史阶段，每个阶段上抗性的选择是独立的；③ 在两个生活史阶段上，摄食不含毒素植株幼虫的适合度为 1；④ 幼虫在两个生活史发育阶段之间并不迁入和迁出避难所；⑤来自含毒素和不含毒素植株的成虫以及不同基因型的成虫之间的交配是随机的，表达毒素和不表达毒素的植株上的产卵是随机的[76,77]。

该抗性位点上有两个等位基因：A_R 为抗性等位基因，A_S 为感性等位基因。于是，害虫种群中有三种基因型：A_SA_S——感性的；A_RA_R——抗性的；A_RA_S——杂合的。

首先根据假设定义各种参数。种子混合对策中，不表达毒素植株的比例定义为 V。幼虫从阶段 1 到阶段 2，从一株植物到另一株植物的迁移比例定义为 M。避难所中不表达毒素植株的比例定义为 C。假设在第一个生活史阶段上，摄食 Bt 作物幼虫的选择系数为 S_1，遗传显性系数为 h_1，因而 A_SA_S、A_RA_S 和 A_RA_R 的相对适合度分别为 $1-S_1$，$1-(1-h_1)S_1$ 和 1；同样，在第二个生活史阶段上，摄食 Bt 作物的幼虫群体中 A_SA_S、A_RA_S 和 A_RA_R 的适合度分别为 $1-S_2$，$1-(1-h_2)S_2$ 和 1.如果不用避难所，A_{SS} 和 A_{RS} 总的适合度分别为：

$$\mathrm{W_{SS}}=1-(1-V)(S_1+S_2)+\{1-V[1+M(1-V)]\}S_1S_2 \tag{6}$$

$$\mathrm{W_{RS}}=1-(1-V)[(1-h_1)S_1+(1-h_2)S_2]+\{1-[1+M(1-V)](1-h_1)S_1(1-h_2)S_2\} \tag{7}$$

A_{RR} 总的适合度是 1，总的选择系数 $S=1-W_{SS}$，总的显性系数 $H=1-(1-W_{RS})/S$，这样就得到一个标准的遗传学模型：

$$W_{SS}=1-S,\ W_{RS}=1-(1-H)S,\ W_{RR}=1 \tag{8}$$

如果使用避难所：

$$W_{SS}=1-(1-\mathrm{C})S,\ W_{RS}=1-(1-C)(1-H)S,\ W_{RR}=1 \tag{9}$$

然后计算出昆虫种群中抗性等位基因 A_R 的频率，将以上数据代入孙儒泳(1992)提供的公式[79]得：

$$P_{(\mathrm{R},T+1)}=\frac{P_{(\mathrm{R},T)}{}^2+P_{(\mathrm{R},T)}P_{(\mathrm{S},T)}W_{\mathrm{RS}}}{P_{(\mathrm{R},T)}{}^2+2P_{(\mathrm{R},T)}P_{(\mathrm{S},T)}W_{\mathrm{RS}}+P_{(\mathrm{S},T)}W_{\mathrm{SS}}} \tag{10}$$

其中，$P_{(\mathrm{R},T+1)}$为 T+1 世代，抗性等位基因的频率；$P_{(\mathrm{R},T)}$和 $P_{(\mathrm{S},T)}$分别为 T 世代抗性等位基因和感性等位基因的频率。

当抗性等位基因的频率即 $P_{(\mathrm{R},T+1)}$达到或超过 0.5 时，说明种群对 Bt 作物进化了抗性，(T+1)则为抗性进化所需的世代。从而可以比较各种策略下昆虫种群进化出抗性所需世代数，用以说明它们各自在延迟昆虫抗性中的作用。

5 讨论

5.1 转基因抗虫作物展望

随着转 Bt 基因棉花，玉米和马铃薯的上市，标志着 Bt 作物成为抗虫转基因工程的主流。但是，害虫对 Bt 作物抗性的进化的潜在风险不容忽视。除了在 Bt 转基因作物释放后，在种植策略方面尽量延迟害虫的抗性，还可以在进行转基因操作时进行一些改进，如组织特异和发育阶段特异表达以及采用一些别的害虫较难适应的抗虫基因，如蛋白酶抑制剂等(见前文)。Estruch 等(1997)将这类转基因作物称为第一代杀虫植物[80]。

Bt 内毒素的杀虫活性仅需要在饲料中的质量浓度达到 50~500ng/ml 即可[15]，而蛋白酶抑制剂、几丁质酶和凝血素等的活性则要求有 mg/mL 数量级的含量[81]。前者的杀虫活性是急性的，后者则是慢性的，慢性的杀虫蛋白往往在转基因植物中得不到高量表达而达不到合适的杀虫效果[80]。

现在发现包括 Bt 毒素在内的杀虫蛋白对某些害虫也是束手无策。于是，科学家们又在寻求新的杀虫蛋白。来自 *Bacillus* 营养生长的杀虫蛋白(vegetaive insecticidal proteins, VIPs)以及来自链霉菌培养物滤液的胆甾醇氧化酶(cholesterol oxidase，CO)具有很好的杀虫效果[80]，表现这两类杀虫蛋白的第二代转基因作物将为害虫的综合防治提供新的方法和策略。

5.2 Bt 作物的风险评价

害虫的抗性进化是一个长期的过程，而 Bt 作物的商业化释放为抗性进化提供了很好的选择条件。因而对于抗性的评价是一个长期而艰巨的任务。目前，虽然已经有了一些抗性管理策略，但这些策略的有效性大部分来自数学模型的预测和来自小规模的试验。这样的结果不能够代替田间试验[3]。由于田间试验抗性管理策略是很困难的，人们还是需要借助于那些用模型预测和小规模测试得来的抗性管理策略。这就要求我们在进行室内实验或小规模测试时，一定要尽量选择能够代表田间种群遗传多样性的害虫群体来实行抗性选择。如果与田间种群相比，实验室群体的遗传变异比较有限，那么在实验室选择条件下没有抗性反应，并不能排除田间抗性产生的可能性[10]。而且，实验室选择和田间选择抗性的产生的因素各不相同，实验室抗性与多种基因有关，而田间抗性则可能与单纯的主效基因有关[63]。

前文(2.2)总结了迄今为止报道的在田间或实验条件了对 Bt 制剂产生抗性的 17 种害虫，在这些害虫中，有很大一部分是目前转基因作物的目标害虫(表 1)。沈晋良等(1998)[55]发现，棉铃虫对 Bt 生物农药与转 Bt 植株间存在着交互抗性，并指出在棉铃虫对 Bt 农药产生早期抗性的地区应用转 Bt 棉时，可能会直接影响到其抗虫效果和使用寿命。因而，我们在释放其目标害虫已经检测或选择出抗性的 Bt 抗虫作物，要特别谨慎，更要仔细研究和实施其抗性管理策略。

Bt 作物释放的风险除了害虫抗性进化的风险外，还包括 Bt 作物本身变成杂草的风险、Bt 毒蛋白基因通过基因流动逃逸到其野生亲缘种中的风险以及对非目标生物体的负面影响的风险。Stewart 等(1996)在将 *cry*IAc 基因转入甘蓝型油菜(*Brassica napus* L.)获得转基因植株时，就注意到 Bt 基因提高了转 Bt 植株的适合度的同时有使其杂草化的可能，并且 Bt 基因可能通过基因渐渗从转基因甘蓝型油菜进入其野生亲缘种的基因组，从而提高该野生亲缘种的适合度[43]。并且 Bt 基因提高转基因植株适合度已在田间得到证实[82]。有关转基因通过基因流动进入其野生亲缘种的风险评价，我们已经专门撰文讨论过①，在这里不再重复。

Sims 和 Holden (1996)发现，Bt 玉米收获后，其残留组织中的杀虫蛋白 CryIA (b)需要 1447d 的消散时间(dissipation time，DT_{90})[83]。非目标生物体就有可能接触到这些残留的杀虫蛋白。虽然，Bt 棉和 Bt 马铃薯的杀虫蛋白对于一种弹尾虫和一种奥甲螨没有产生负面影响[84]，但是，Bt 杀虫蛋白对非目标生物影响的潜在风险不容忽视。瑞士联邦农业生态与农业研究站的科学家们研究了 Bt 玉米对一种益虫—绿草蛉(*CHRY SOPER CARNEA*)的间接影响[85]。绿草蛉是以欧洲玉米螟为食的，研究者用分别取自 Bt 玉米和非转基因玉米的欧洲玉米螟喂食绿草蛉，发现食用采自 Bt 玉米的玉米螟的绿草蛉与对照相比，其死亡率较高，发育也比较延迟。

参考文献

[1] Krattiger AF. Insect resistance in crops: a case study of *Bacillus thuringiensis* (Bt) and its transfer to developing countries (ISAAA Briefs No.2). Ithaca, NY: ISAAA, 1997

[2] Dutton G. Agbiotech companies' technologies lead the way toward a carbohydrate-based economy. *Genetic Engineering News*. 1997, June 15: 1, 6, 39

[3] Tabashnik BE. Seeking the root of insect resistance to transgenic plants. *Proc Natl Acad Sci USA*. 1997, **94**: 3488~3490

[4] Beegle CC, Yamamoto T. History of *Bacillus thuringiensis* Berliner research and development. *Can Ent*. 1992, **124**: 587~616

[5] McGanghey WH. Insect resistance to the biological insecticide *Bacillus thuringiensis*. *Science*. 1985, **229** :193~194

[6] Bergvinson D, Willcox M, Hoisington D. Effcacy and deployment of transgenic plants for stemborer management. *Insect Sci Applic*. 1997, **17**(1):157~167

[7] Gould F. Evolutionary biology and genetically engineered crops. *BioSeience*. 1988, **38**:26~33

[8] James C. Global status of transgenic crops in 1997(ISAAA Briefs No. 5). Ithaca, NY:ISAAA, 1997

[9] McGanghey WH, Whalon ME. Managing insect resistance to *Bacillus thuringiensis toxins*. *Science*. 1992, **248**: 1441~1444

[10] Tabashnik BE. Evolution of resistance to *Bacillus thuringiensis*. *Annu Rev Entomol*. 1994, **39**: 47~79

[11] Fox JL. Bt cotton infestations renew resistance concerns. *Nat Biotech*. 1996, **14**: 1070

[12] Kaiser J. Pests overwhelm Bt cotton crop. *Science*. 1996, **273**: 423

[13] Hofte H,Whiteley HR. Insecticidal crystal protein of *Bacillus thuringiensis*. *Microbiol Rev*. 1989, **53**: 242~255

[14] Feitelsom FS, Payne J, Kim L. *Bacillus thuringiensis*: Insects and beyond. *Bio/Technology*. 1992, **10**: 271~275

① 魏伟，钱迎倩，马克平. 转基因作物与其野生亲缘种间的基因流动. 植物学报(印刷中)。

[15] Koziel MG, Carozzi NB, Currier TC, Warren GW, Evola SV. The insecticidal crystal proteins of *Bacillus thuringiensis*: Past, present and future uses. Biotechnol. Gen Engin. Rev. 1993, **11**: 171~228

[16] Vaeck M, Reynaerts A, Hofte H, Jansens S, de Beuckeleer M, Dean C, Zabeau M, van Montagu M, Leemans, Leemans J. Transgenic plants protected from insect attack. *Nature*. 1987, **328**: 33~37

[17] Barton KA, Whiteley HR,Yang N-S. *Bacillus thuringiensis* δ-engotoxin expressed in transgenic *Nicotiana tabacum* provides resistance to Lepidopteran insects. *Planr Physiol.* 1987, **85**: 1103~1109

[18] Carozzi NB, Warren GW, Desai N, Jayne SM, Lotstein R, Rice DA, Evola S, Koziel MG. Expression of a chimeric CaMV35s *Bacillus thuringiensis* insecticidal protein gene in transgenic tobacco. *Plant Mol Biol.* 1992, **20**:539~548

[19] Warren GW, Carozzi NB, Desai N, Koziel MG. Field evalnation of transgenic tobacco containing a *Bacillus thuringiensisi* insecticidal protein gene. *J Econ Entomol.* 1992, **85**:1651~1659

[20] Adang MJ, Firoozabady E, Kein J, DeBoer D, Sekar V, Murray E, Rocheleau TA, Rashka K, Sraffeld G, Stock C, Suton D, Merio DJ.Applocation of a *Bacillus thuringiensis* crystal protein for insect control. In: Amtzen CJ, Ryan C ed. Molecular Strategies for Crop Protection. New York: Alan, R Liss, 1987. 345~353

[21] McBride KE, Svab Z. Schaaf DJ, Hogan PS, Stalker DM, Maliga P. Amplification of a chimeric *Bacillus* gene in chlroplasts leads to anextraordinary level of an insecticidal protein in tobacco. *Bio/Technology*. 1995,**13**:362~365

[22] Strizhov N, Keller M, Mathur J, Koncz-Kalman Z, Bosch D, Prudovsky E, Schell J, Sneh B, Koncz C, Zilerstein A. A synthetic *cry*IC gene, encoding a *Bacillus thuringiensis* δ-endotoxin confers *Spodoptera* resistance in alfalfa and tobacco. *Proc Narl Acad Sci USA.* 1996,**93**:15012~15017

[23] Sutton DW, Havstad PK, Kemp JD. Synthetic cryIIIA gene from *Bacillus thuringiensis* improved for high expression in plants. *Transgenic Res.*1992,(5):228~236

[24] Fishhoff DA, Bowdish KS, Perlak FJ, Marrone PG, McCrmick, Niedermeyer JG, Dean DA, KusanoKretzmer K, Mayer Ej, Rochester DE, Rogers SG, Fralay RT. Insect tolerant transgenic tomato plans. *Bio/Technology*. 1987,**5**:807~813

[25] Delannay X, Lavallee BJ, Proksch RK, Fuchs RL, Sims SR, Greenplate JT, Marrone PG, Dodson RB, Augustine JJ, Layton JG, Fischhoff DA. Field performance of transgenic tomato plans expressing the *Bacillus thuringiensis var. kurstaki* insect control protein. *Bio/Technology.* 1989.**7**:1265~1269

[26] Schuler TH, Poppy GM, Kerry BR, Denholm I, Insect-resistant transgenic plants. *TIBTECH.* 1998, **16**: 168~175

[27] Jansens S, Cromelissen M, de Clercq R. *Phthorimaea operculella* (Lepidoptera; Gelechiidse) resistance in poato by expression of yhe *Bacillus thuringiensis* CryIA(b) insecticidal crystal protein. *J Econ Entomol.* 1995, 88(**5**): 1469~1476

[28] Cheng J, Bolyard MG, Saxena RC, Sticklen MB. Production of insect resistant potato by genetic transformation with a delta-endotoxin from *Bacillus thuringiensis var. Kustaki. Plant Sci*. 1992, **81**: 83~91

[29] Perlak FJ, Ston TB, Muskopf YM, Petersen LJ, Parker GB, Mcpherson SA, Wyman J, Love S, Reed G, Biever D, Fishhcff DA. Genetically improved potatoes : protection from damage by Colorado potato beetles. *Plant Mol Biol.* 1993, **22**: 313~321

[30] Adang MJ, Brody MS, Cardiineau G, Eagan N, Roush RT, Shewmaker CK, Jones A, Oakes JV, McBride KE. The reconstruction and expression of a *Bacillus thuringiensis cry* III A gene in protoplasts and potato plants. *Palnt Mol Biol.* 1993, **21**: 1131~1145

[31] Kumar PA, Mandsokar A, Sreenibasu K, Chakrabarti SK, Bisaria S, Sharma SR, Kaur S, Sharma RP. Insect-resistant transgenic brinjal poants. *Moleculor Breeding.* 1998, **4**: 33~37

[32] Perlak FJ, Deaton RW, Armstrong TA, Fuchs RL, Sims SR, Creenplate JT, Fischhoff DA. Insect resistant cotton plants. *Bio/Technology*. 1990, **8**:939~943

[33] Benedict JH, Sachs ES, Altman DW, Deaton WR, Kohell RJ, Ring DR, Berberich SA. Field performance of Cottons expressing transgenic CryIA insecticidal prcteins for resistance to *Heliothis virescns* and *Helicoverpa zea* (Lepidoptera: Noctuidae). *J Econ Entomol*. 1996, **89**: 230~238

[34] Koziel MC, Beland GL, Bowman C, Carozzi NB, Grenshaw R, Crossland L, Dawson J, Desai N, Hill M, Kadwell S, Launis K, Lewis K, Maddox D, McPherson K, Meghji MR, Merlin E, Rhodes R, Warren GW,Wright M, Evola SV. Field performance of elite transgenic maize plants expressing an insecticidal protein derived from *Bacillus thuringgiensis*. *Bio/Technology*.1993,**11**:194~200

[35] Wang GY(王国英), Du TB(杜天兵), zhang H(张宏), Xie YJ(谢友菊), Dai JR(戴景瑞), Mi JJ(米景九), Li TY(李太源), Tian YC(田颖川), Qiao LY(乔利亚), Mang KQ(莽克强). Transfer of Bt-toxin protein gene into maize by high-velocity microprojectile bombardments and regeneration of transgenic plant. *Science in* China(中国科学)(Series B).1995,**25**(1):86~92

[36] Fujimoto H, Itoh K, Yamamato M, Kyozuka J, Shimamoto K. Insect resistant rice generated by introduction of a modified δ-endotoxin gene of *Bacillus thuringiensis. Bio/Technology*. 1993,**11**:1151~1155

[37] Wunn J, Kloti A, Burkhardt PK, Biaswas GCG, Launis K, Iglesias VA, Potreykus I. Transgenic indica rice breeding line IR48 expressing a synthetic *cry*IA(b) gene from *Bacillus thuringiensis* provides effective insect pest control. *Bio/Technology*. 1996,**14**:171~176

[38] Singsit G, Adang MJ, Lynch RE, Anderson WF, Wang A-M, Cardineau G, Ozias-Akins P. Expression of a *Bacillus thuringiensis cry*IA(c) gene in transgenic peanut plants and its efficacy against lesser cornstalk borer. *Transgenic Res*. 1997,**6**(2):169~176

[39] Parrott WA, All JN, Adang MJ, Bailey MA, Boerma HR, Stewart CN Jr. Recovery and evaluation of soybean plants transgenic for a *Bacillus thuringiensis* var. *kurstaki* insecticidal gene. *In vitro Cell Dev Biol*. 1994, **30**P: 144~149

[40] Stewart CN, JR, Adang MJ, All JN, Boerma HR, Cardineau G, Tucker D, Parrott WA. Genetic transformantion, recovery, and characterization of fertile soybean transgenic for a synthetic *Bacillus thuringiensis cry*IAc gene. *Plant Physiol*. 1996, **112**:121~129

[41] Voisey CR,White DWR, Wigley PJ, Chilcott CN, McGregor PG, Woodfield DR, Hokkanen HMT. Release of transgenic white clover plants expressing *Bacillus thuringiensis* genes: an ecological perspective. *Biocontrol Sci Technol*. 1994,**4**(4):475~481

[42] Metz TD, Dixit R, Earle ED. *Agrobacterium tumefaciens*-mediated transformation of broccoli(*Brassica oleravea var italita*) and cabbage (*B.oleracea var. capitata*). *Plant Cell Rep*. 1995,**15**:287~292

[43] Stewart CN Jr., Adang MJ, All JN, Raymer PL, Ramachandran S, Parrott WA. Insect control and dosage effects in transgenic canola containing a synthetic *Bacillus thuringiensis cry*IAc gene. *Plant Physiol*. 1996,**112**:115~120

[44] Li X-B, Mao H-Zh, Bai Y-Y. Transgenic Plants of rutabaga(*Brassica napobrassuca*) tolerant to a pest insect. *Plant Cell Rep*. 1995,**15**:97~101

[45] Kleiner KW, Ellis OD, Mccown BH, Raffa KF. Field evaluation of transgenic poplar expressing a *Bacillus thuringiensis* CryIA(a)d-endotoxin gene against forest tent caterpillar (Lepidoptera: Lasiocampidae) and gypsy moth (Lepidoptera: Lymantriidse) following winter dormarry. *Environ Entomol*.1995,**24**:1358~1364

[46] McCown BH, McCable DE, Russell DR, Robinson DJ, Barton KA, Raffa KF. Stable transformation of *Populs* and incorporation of pest resistance by electric discharge particle acceleration. *Plant Cell Rep*.1991,**9**:590~594

[47] Ellis DD, McCable DE,Mclnnis S, Ramachandran S, Russell DR, Wallace Km, Martinell BJ, Roberts DR, Raffa KF, McCown BH. Stable transformation of *Picea glauca* by particle acceleration. *Bio/Technology*.1993,**11**:84~89

[48] Yu JX(余健秀), Yu RJ(余榕捷), Pang Y(庞义), Xu JM(徐建敏), Li JH(李建华).Advances in studies on insect resistance to *Bacillus thuringiensis* (I): Characteristics and mechanisms of resistance. *Natutal Enemies of insects*(昆虫天敌).1997, 19(4):173~179

[49] Perlak FJ, Fuchs RL, Dean DA, McPherson SL, Fishhoff DA. Modification of the coding sequence enhances plant expression of insect control protein genes. *Proc Natl Acad Sci USA*. 1991,**88**:3324~3328

[50] Mang KQ(莽克强). A discussion on the biosafety of transgenic plants. *Prog Biotechnol* (生物工程进展).1996,**16**(4):2~6

[51] Gill SS, Cowles EA, Pietrantonio PV. The mode of action of *Bacillus thuringiensis* endotoxins. *Annu Rev Entomol*.1992, **37**:615~636

[52] Huang F, Higgins RA, Buschman LL. Bsaeline susceptility and changes insusceptibility to *Bacillus thuringiensis* subsp. *Kurstaki* under selection pressure in European com Borer (Lepidoptera: Pyralidae). *J Econ Entomol*.1997, **90**(5): 1137~1143

[53] Tabashnik BE, Cushing NL, Finson N, Johnson MW. Field development of resistance to *Bacillus thuringiensis* in diamondback moth(Lepidoptera: Plutellidae). *J Econ Entomol*. 1990, **83**: 1671~1676

[54] Perez CJ, Shelton AM. Resistance of *Plutella xylostella* (Lepidoptera: Plutellidae) to *Bacillus thuringiensis* Berliner in Central America. *J Econ Entomol*.1997,**90**(1):87~93

[55] Shen JL(沈晋良), Zhou WJ(周威君), Wu YD(吴益东), Lin XW(林祥文), Zhu XF(朱协飞).Early resistance of *Helicocerpa armigera* (Hubner) to *Bacillus thuringienst*s and its relation to the effect of transgenic cotton lines expressing Bt toxin on the insect. *Acta Entomol Sinica* (昆虫学报). 1998, **41**(1): 8~14

[56] Heckel DG. The complex genetic basis of resistance to *Bacillus thuringiensis* toxin in insects. *Biocontrol Sci Technol.* 1994,**4**(4):405~417

[57] Van Rie J, McGaughey WH, Jonhson DE, Barnett BD, Van Mellaert H. Mechanism of insect resistance to the microbial insecticide *Bacillus thuringiensis. Science.* 1990,**247**:72~74

[58] Ferre J, Real MD, van Rie J, Jansens S, Peferoen M. Resistance to the *Bacillus thuringiensis* bioinsecticide in a field population of *Plutella xylostella* is due to a change in a midgut membrane receptor. *Proc Natl Acad Sci USA.* 1991,**88**:5119~5123

[59] Tabashnik BE, Finson N, Groeters FR, Moar WJ, Jhonson MW, Luo K, Adang MJ. Reversal of resistance to *Bacillus thuringiensis* in *Plutella xylostella. Proc Natl Acad Sci USA.* 1994,**91**:4120~4124

[60] Gould, F. Arthropod behavior and the efficacy of plant protectants. *Annu Rev Entomol.* 1991,**36**:305~330

[61] Tabashnik BE, Lin Y-B and Finson N, Masson L, Heckel DG. One gene in diamondback moths confers resistance to four *Bacillus thuringiensis toxins. Proc Natl Acad Sci USA.* 1997,**94**:1640~1644

[62] Gould F, Anderson A, Jones A, Sumerford D, Heckel DG, Lopez J, Micinski S, Leonard R, Laster M. Initial frequency of alleles for resistance to *Bacillus thuringiensis* toxins in field populations of *Heliothis virescens. Proc Natl Acad Sci USA.* 1997,**94**:3519~3523

[63] Roush RT, Mckenzie JA. Ecological genetics of insecticide and acaricide resistance. *Annu Rev Entomol.* 1987,**32**:361~380

[64] Crow JF, Kimura M. An introduction to population genetics theory. New York: Harper & Row, 1970

[65] Rahardja U, Whalon ME. Inheritance of resistance to *Bacillus thuringiensis* spp. *tenebrionis* CryIIIA δ-endotoxin in Colorado poatao beetle (Coleoptera: Chrysomelidae). *J Econ Entomol.* 1995,**88**:21~26

[66] Heckel DG, Gahan LG, Gould F, Anderson A. Identification of a linkage group with a major effect on resistance to *Bacillus thuringiensis* CryIAc endotoxin in the tobacco budworm (Lepidoptera: Noctuidae). *J Econ Entmol.* 1997,**90**:75~86

[67] Tabashnik BE. Resistance risk assessment: realized beritability of resistance to *Bacillus thuringiensis* in diamondback moth (Lepidoptera: Plutellidae), tobacco budworm (Lepidoptera: Noctnidae), and Colorade potato beetle (Colcoptera: Chysomelidae). *J Econ Entomol.* 1992, **85**:1551~1559

[68] Falconer DS. Introduction to quantitative genetics. 3rd ed. New York: Longman, 1989

[69] Tabasshnik BE, Finson N, Johnson MW. Managing resistance to *Bacillus thuringiensis*: Lessons from the diamondback moth (Lepidoptera: Plutellidae). *J Econ Entomol,* 1991,**84**:49~55

[70] Zhou ZL(周兆斓), Zhu Z(朱祯). Advances in the genetic engineering of insect_resistance plant. *Prog Biotechnol*(生物工程进展). 1994,**14**(4):18~24

[71] Kjellsson G, Simonsson V, Ammann K. Methods for risk assessment of transgenic plants; II. Polination, transfer and population impacts. Basel: Birkhauser Verlag,1997

[72] Roush RT. Managing pests and their resistance to *Bacillus thuringiensis*: can trangtic crops be better than sprays? *Biocontrol Sci Technol*. 1994,**4**:501~516

[73] Gould F. Potential and problems with high-dose strategies for pesticidal engineered crops. *Biocontrol Sci Technol.* 1994,**4**:451~461

[74] Alstad DN, Andow DA. Managing the evolution of insect resistance to transgenic plants. *Science.* 1995,**268**:1894~1896

[75] Lin Y-B, Tabashnik BE. Experimental evidence that refuges delay insect adsptation to *Bacillus thuringiensis. Proc R Soc Land B.* 1997.**264**:605~610

[76] Mallet J, Porter P. Preventing insect adapation to insect-resistant crops: are seed mixtures or refugia the best strategy? *Proc R Soc Lond B*. 1992, **250**: 165~169

[77] Tabashnik BE. Delaying insect adaptation to transgenic plants: seed mixtures and refugia reconsidered. *Proc R Soc Lond B.* 1994, **255**: 7~12

[78] Peferoen M. Progress and prospects for field use of Bt gens in crops. *TIBTECH.* 1997, **15**:173~177

[79] Sun RY(孙儒泳). Principles of Animal Ecology. 2nd ed. Beijing: Beijing Normal University Press. 1992

[80] Estruch J J, Carazzi NB, Desai N, Duck NB, Warren GW,Koziel MG. Transgenic plants: An emerging approach to pest control. *Nat Biatech.* 1997,**15**:137~141

[81] Boulter D. Insect pest control by copying nature using genetically engineered crops. *Phytochemistry*. 1993, **34**:1453~1466

[82] Stewart CN Jr., All JN, Paymer PL, Ramachandran S. Increased fitness of transgenic insecticidal rapeseed under insect selection pressure. *Mol Ecol.*1997,**6**:773~779

[83] Sims SR, Holden LR. Insect bioassay or determining soil degradation of *Bacillus thuringiensis* ssp. *kurstaki* CryIa(b) protein in corn tissue. *Environ Entomol.* 1996,**25**:659~664

[84] Yu L, Berry RE, Croft BA. Effects of *Bacillus thuringiensis* toxins in transgenic cotton and potato on *Folsomia candida* (Collembola: Isotomidae) and *Oppia nirens* (Acari: Orbatidae). *J Econ Entomol.* 1997,**90**(1):113~118

[85] Union of Concerned Scientists(UCS). Risk research: transgenic insect-resistant crops harm beneficial insects. The Gene Exchange. 1998,summer:4

本文原载：植物学报. 1999. 41(4): 343-348

转基因作物与其野生亲缘种间的基因流*

魏伟 钱迎倩 马克平

(中国科学院植物研究所)

关键词 转基因；逃逸；基因流；转基因作物

随着基因工程技术的突飞猛进,许多主要的农作物经过遗传修饰获得了优良的性状,并被批准进入市场。在美国，到 1996 年 5 月为止，经政府批准商业化的转基因作物已有 7 种；而在欧共体，仅在 1991~1994 年被释放作大田试验的转基因植物就达 291 个[1]。对于转基因作物释放可能导致的生态风险要进行评估已引起科学家们的共识。目前来看，相当多转基因作物风险评价的研究是集中在转基因逃逸(transgene escape)所造成的转基因作物与其野生亲缘种间的基因流动以及转基因产物进入土壤后对土壤生物多样性的影响问题上[2]。目前转入作物的插入特性(inserted traits)以抗除草剂的为多，其次是抗虫和抗病毒，然后是抗逆[3]。当这些转基因通过基因流逐渐在野生种群中定居(establishment)后就使得作物的野生亲缘种具有了获得选择优势的潜在可能性[4~6]。这样，作物本身及其野生亲缘种就有可能成为杂草[1]。如果获得选择优势的野生亲缘种本身就是杂草，那么就会为该杂草的控制增加很大的困难。也有学者认为，转基因在野生种群的固定将导致野生等位基因的丢失而造成遗传多样性的丧失①。转基因作物与其野生亲缘种间的基因流动是转基因作物释放后可能带来风险的重要方面。为了阐明基因流动的风险评估和管理的理论依据，本文将就转基因花粉的传布、转基因作物和其野生亲缘种间杂种的形成以及风险评价的方法和可能解决途径作简要论述。

1 转基因花粉的传布

一般认为，转基因花粉的传布是转基因在空间上逃离的主要渠道，也是转基因作物与其野生亲缘种间基因流动的主要原因。虽然控制转基因花粉逃逸在农业中是一个新的课题，但是，植物育种学家对如何保护作物不受外来花粉污染的研究已经进行了半个世纪，如今我们所知道的有关作物基因流动和花粉传布的知识来源于那些为保证种子的基

* 九五国家重点科技项目（攻关）计划(97-925-02-04-05)。

因纯度而进行的有关隔离距离的研究[7]①。主要的农作物大都进行了传粉隔离距离的研究。小萝卜[8,9]、玉米[10,11]、棉花[12~15]、甘蓝型油菜②、小麦[16,17]、甜菜[10]、黑麦[18,19]、芸苔[8,20]和苜蓿[21,22]等。上述作物的转基因品种有的已经上市，有的彼此之间是亲缘种，在合适条件下可以进行基因流动。对作物传粉隔离距离的研究结果为转基因花粉传布的研究奠定了坚实的基础，并提供了宝贵的研究思路和方法。

关于转基因作物的传粉距离，已经积累了一些研究成果。在这些研究中，转基因通过传粉在空间上逃逸的程度是由不同方向的不同距离上转基因花粉与非转基因作物杂交的频率来确定的。随着距离的增加，杂交的频率降低。转 Bt 毒蛋白基因棉花的花粉在 7m 远处的杂交频率从 5%将至小于 1%，在 25 m 处小于 1%的杂交偶尔发生[23]。在另外一个研究中，杂交频率在离转基因油菜样方 12 m 处陡然降至 0.02%，在 47 m 处，10^7 粒非转基因油菜种子中只有 33 粒种子携带转基因[24]。10 m 处转基因马铃薯花粉传布的频率为 0.017%，到 20 m 的距离时则接近零[25]。

对于同一作物，不同试验所估测的隔离距离有很大的变异性③。例如，在英国，原来对转基因马铃薯隔离距离的估计达到 600m，而现在只不到 50m[26]。这种隔离距离的变异，部分是由于统计强度不够造成的，也可能是由于这种变异性是特定作物的生物学传粉特性。对传粉生物学的许多研究已经证明，至少昆虫传粉的作为是这样，除了作物本身，其他因素包括周围植被的类型和密度、其他植物的开花期以及气象条件都会影响转基因传粉的距离③。

转基因作物释放的面积也可能会影响到转基因的传粉距离。在转基因油菜的研究中，Scheffler 等[24]释放转基因油菜的面积只有 $75m^2$，47m 处转基因传粉频率就降到 0.00033%；在 Scheffler 等[27]另外一次释放中，转基因油菜的面积 $400m^2$，200m 处的传粉频率为 0.0156%，400m 处为 0.0038%。而在一次较大规模的释放中(转基因油菜面积达 10 ha)，360m 处花粉的密度只降到释放地边缘花粉密度的 10%，在 1.5km 处，仍计数到 22 粒/m^3 的花粉[28]。这种差异除了可能存在上一段所提到的传粉距离易变形的原因外，释放的规模显然是一个决定因素。Dale 等[26]认为，从小规模转基因作物释放所获得的传粉距离的资料对于大规模商业性释放的参考价值比较有限。换句话说，大田试验所得的数据不能作为商业性释放的依据。

2 转基因作物与其野生亲缘种间杂种的形成

转基因作物与其野生亲缘种之间的杂交是转基因逃逸的主要形式，也是转基因作物与其野生亲缘种间基因流动的证据。

---

① Gaggiotti O E. Potential Evolutionay and Ecological Consequences of the Release of *GMOs* into the Wild. The Workshop on Transgenic Organisms in the New Millenium: Risks and Benefits, Italy, Dec 1~5, 1997.

② Stringam G R, Downey R K. Effectiveness of isolation distance in seed production of rapeseed (*Brassica napus*). *Agron Abst*, 1982, 136~137.

③ Gliddon C, Boudry P, Walker S. Gene flow-a review of experimental evidence. The Workshop on Transgenic Organisms in the New Millenium: Risks and Benefits, Italy, Dec . 1~5, 1997.

许多栽培作物都驯化自野生植物。在自然界中，这些农作物都存在自己的野生亲缘种。玉米的野生亲缘种为玉米草(teosinte)(产于墨西哥和中美洲)[29]。这里玉米草是玉米的不同野生亲缘类群的统称，包括 *Zea diplopernnis*、*Z. perennis*、*Z. luxurians*、*Z. mays* ssp. *mexicana*、*Z. mays* ssp. *parviglumis* 和 *Z. mays* ssp. *huehuetenangensis*，并且除了 *Z. perennis* 外，所有的玉米草都可与栽培玉米形成杂种[30]。水稻可与其野生亲缘种红水稻[31]和 O. perennis[29]杂交。

转基因作物与其野生亲缘种间杂交的可能性依赖于许多因素：作物和其野生亲缘种必须是有性亲和的，必须生长在同一地点，需要在同一时间开花并且它们之间必须有传粉的途径。其中的有性亲和性是特别重要的一个方面[4]。在马铃薯的原产地——南美，它可与茄属的野生双倍体种类杂交；但在欧洲，没有发现它与两种普遍分布的杂草龙葵(*Solanum nigrum*)和蜀羊泉(*S. dulcamara*)杂交的证据[25]。相反，甘蓝型油菜(*Brassica napus*)可与很多的亲缘种，如芜菁(*B. rapa*)，*B. adpressa*，*Sinapis arvensis*，野生小萝卜(*Raphanus raphanistrum*)等进行杂交[32]。而且在截止 1992 年所报道的转基因植物的 400 例释放中，有 80 例是转基因甘蓝型油菜的释放[33]。所以，关于转基因甘蓝型油菜与其野生亲缘种间基因流动的研究报道很多[24,32,34~36]。

转基因作物与其野生亲缘种杂交后，转基因就可能在自然界获得存留的机会。Dale[5]总结了决定作物与其野生亲缘种的杂种在农田生态系统中或自然界中成为定居者的因素(表 1)，并认为研究传统育种作物和其野生亲缘种之间的杂种的效应是研究转基因对杂种影响的基础。

在表 1 所列诸因素中，种子库的特性是比较重要的一个方面。作物种子与其野生亲缘种的种子相比，具有较短的休眠、存活期以及较差的萌发反应。而作物与野生亲缘种的杂种就可能具有比较适合存留的种子库。而且，如果杂种的母本是野生种，那么母本效应就使种子库更加有利于存留[37]。转基因可以通过种子库在时间上逃逸，通过转基因作物与其野生亲缘种的杂交种在自然界中存留。在存留的过程中，在适合的条件下，转基因作物与其野生亲缘种的杂交种可以与其野生亲本不断回交。转基因进入野生亲本的遗传背景，完成了其在时间上的逃逸。

通过杂交种的形成，不可避免地会发生转基因作物与其野生亲缘种之间的基因流动，因而现在需要做的工作应该是评价杂交种中转基因表达的稳定性和其影响以及杂种的命运。Scheffler 和 Dale[35]认为转基因甘蓝型油菜 *B. napus* 与其亲缘种的杂种具有较低的存活能力和较高的不育性，因而意味着其杂种和其杂种的后代可能不会在农田或自然生境中存活。然而，Chevre 等[38]获得转基因 *B.napus* (抗除草剂)与野生小萝卜(作为父本)的杂交种以后，研究了随后的 4 个世代的可育性，他们发现，由于杂(回)交母本用的是转基因 *B. napus*($2n = 38$)，所以在随后的 4 个世代中，染色体数目逐渐降低，逐步接近父本野生小萝卜的染色体数目($2n = 18$)，在这个过程中，每一世代的可育性不断增加，而转基因的传递(transmission)频率都在第一世代以后的几个世代中降低。他们同时指出，这种属间的基因流动可在合适的条件下缓慢地低频率发生；但当转基因 *B. napus* 作父本时，这种现象的发生就更加罕见。

表 1 决定作物与其野生亲缘种的杂种在农田或自然生境中定居可能性的因素[5]

Table 1 Factors determing the likelihood of hybrids between crop plants and related species becoming established in agricultural or natural habitats[5]

I	The production of viable hybrid seeds.
1	Compatibility of the two parental genomes (mitotic and gentic stability).
2	Ability of the endosperm to support hybrid embryo development.
3	Direction of the cross: one parent may support embryo and seed development better than the other.
4	Number and viability of hybrid seeds.
II	Establishment of hybrid plants from seeds in soil.
5	Seed dormancy.
6	Vigour of the hybrid plant.
7	Direction of cross: maternal effects influencing seedling vigour.
8	Nature of habitat: wild, semi-wild or agricultural.
9	Nature of competition from other plants.
10	Influence of pest, diseases and animal predator.
III	Ability of the hybrid to propagate vegetatively and sexually.
11	Method of vegetive propagation.
12	Persistence of vegetative propagules in agricultural habitats.
13	Dissemination of vegetative propagules.
14	Invasiveness of vegetative propagules in natural habitats.
15	Sexual breeding system: cross compatible, self compatible, ability to cross to either parental species.
16	Male and female fertility: meiotic stability and chromosome pairing.
17	Seed number and viability.
18	Seed dormancy.
19	Nature of habitat : wild, serni-wild or agricultural.
20	Nature of competition from other plants.
21	Influence of pest, diseases and animal predator.

3 转基因作物与其野生亲缘种间基因流动的风险评价方法

3.1 转基因花粉散布的测度方法

Kjellson[39]总结了测度转基因花粉散布的主要研究方法，包括父本分析、花粉计数、花粉收集以及花粉活力测试等。父本分析的目的是分辨出特定基因型母株所产种子的可能父本(即可能的花粉供体)用以鉴定基因流动的存在。花粉计数可以用来估计花粉的产量等。在转基因花粉散布的研究中，与花粉收集相结合可以用来测度花粉的释放。Timmons 等[28]用设在离地面 10 m 的花粉采收器来评价长距离的花粉移动，收集器可以旋转 360°，并配一装置使其正对风向，计数每 24 h 每立方米上花粉粒的数量。花粉的活力影响着传粉的效果，研究花粉活力的一个直接的方法是实验性授粉，种子或果实的形成作为花粉粒活力的测度。

研究转基因花粉散布的例子在文中第一部分已经列举了很多，其研究方法大都是亲本分析，比较注重转基因作物的栽培设计。一般是在实验地中心设一个转基因作物样方，周围种植非转基因作物或其亲缘种，于作物成熟期在不同方向的不同距离上取一定面积的样方或一定数量的植株或种子(果实)，分析成熟种子或果实中转基因存在的频率，作为转基因传粉的频率。

3.2 鉴定转基因存在的方法

在上述实验设计中，非转基因作物或其亲缘种的后代中转基因的存在是转基因逃逸的测度，也是转基因作物与其亲缘种之间基因流动产生杂交种的证据。一般来讲，采用向后代的幼苗喷洒除草剂的方法，能够筛选出带有抗除草剂转基因的杂种后代。然而对于其他类型的转基因，基因流动的鉴定可以采用形态学特征分析、细胞学方法(如减数分裂和染色体配对分析)、蛋白质及同工酶电泳分析、DNA 分子标记技术(包括 AFIP，PCR、RAPD、RFLP 以及 DNA 测序等)以及统计分析方法(如 F-统计)等[39]。

一般地，这些分析方法在研究工作中是相辅相成的。Doebley[30]将形态学、同工酶和叶绿体 DNA 分析结合起来研究玉米与其野生亲缘种间的基因流动。Kerlan 等[34]结合 PCR 技术，用染色体计数的方法研究了转基因甘蓝型油菜与其亲缘种间的基因流动。Metz 等[36]则用流式细胞光度分析法说明了杂交种的核 DNA 含量明显地位于两个亲本之间。转基因存在的直接鉴定一般是用特定引物扩增转基因片段或者用特定探针与可能含有转基因的总 DNA 进行 Southern 杂交。

3.3 评价基因流动的数学模型

Bateman[40]给出了距离对风媒和虫媒传粉作物花粉污染影响的 3 个方程式，并将它们近似地合并成一个：

$$F = ye^{-KD}/D \tag{1}$$

这里，F 是花粉污染的比率，D 是距离，y 是零隔离距离时的污染。

Manasse[41]给出了评价基因流动的指数模型，他的模型类似于方程(1)，然而更加完善，适合于评价转基因作物与其野生亲缘种间的基因流动。Manasse 在研究中发现，随着植物丛或个体间距离的增加，一年中基因传播的平均距离也在增加。这就意味着伴随着长距离隔离，一个罕见的长距离传粉事件会增加转基因逃逸的风险。

Kareiva 等[7]给出了一个与 Manasse 的指数模型[41]类似的可靠性函数(reliability

function)：

$$R(x)=\exp\left(-ax^{b}\right) \tag{2}$$

$R(x)$是花粉传布到距离 x 的可能性，其平均数等于$1/a\Gamma(b+1)/b$，变异等于$1/a^{2}\left[\Gamma(b+2)/b-\Gamma^{2}(b+1)/b\right]$。当 b=1 时，这个可靠性函数为：

$$R(x)=\exp(-ax) \tag{3}$$

成为一个指数函数。

由于植物可以接受各种来源(包括自身)的花粉，因而来自转基因植物的花粉可能只是柱头上总花粉的一小部分，所以可以用异交的数据来估计一个参数 c，也就是离转基因作物零距离的污染的估计。

获得一个含转基因的种子的概率与 $R(x)$成比例：

$$L=\prod_{k=1}^{N}\binom{S_k}{M_k}\left[cR(x)\right]^{M_k}\left[1-cR(x)\right]^{S_k-M_k} \tag{4}$$

其中：S_k＝第 k 个取样点采集的种子数：M_k＝S_k中含有转基因的种子数；N＝取样点的数量。

对于风险评价来说，需要的不是在某一距离上的传粉频率，而是描述一个转基因在一个或几个方向上传布到某一特定距离以外的可能性，这就是累积密度函数(cumulative density function. c. d. f.)①：

$$c.d.f.=\Gamma(\alpha,\beta)/\Gamma(\beta) \tag{5}$$

这里，α为 ax^{b}；β为 $1/b$(一个方向)或 $2/b$(所有方向)；$\Gamma(\alpha,\beta)$是不完全迦马函数，$\Gamma(\beta)$是完全迦马函数。

4 讨论

4.1 Goy 和 Duesing[42]把马铃薯、烟草和玉米划为“与野生亲缘种间基因流有最低可能性”的一组，把油菜等划为“与野生亲缘种间基因流有低的可能性”的一组，把甜菜等划为“与野生亲缘种间基因流有高的可能性”的一组，然后经过一系列的分析，得出结论：在 391 次大田试验中，91%对环境无潜在影响，如果有的话也是最小的，而 9%的对环境只有低的潜在影响。文章一发表，马上遭到 Landbo 和 Mikkelson[43]的反驳，钱迎倩等[44]对此进行了讨论。从前文的论述来看，玉米、油菜等作物与其野生亲缘种间有着较为频繁的基因流动，Goy 和 Duesing[42]将其划入与野生亲缘种间的基因流有最小或低的可能性显然是不合适的，因而其结论也就很难成立。

从目前的研究来看，转基因在时空上的逃逸不可避免，这就需要较好的技术方法来

① Gliddon C, Boudry P, Walker S. Gene flow-a review of experimental evidence. The Workshop on Transgenic Organisms in the New Millenium: Risks and Benefits, Italy, Dec. 1~5, 1997.

控制和管理转基因作物与其野生亲缘种间的基因流动。除了用距离来隔离转基因作物外，也可以用其他的方法，比如去掉转基因作物的花，移去与作物有性亲和的种类，调整开花时间以及在其周围种植同种的非转基因作物作为缓冲区[45]。Metz 等[36]发现，如果转基因整合到 *B. napus* 的C型基因组的染色体上就能降低杂种与亲缘种 *B. rapa* 和 *B. juncea* 回交时转基因转移的频率，但可能会增加转基因向 *B. oleracea* 和 *B. carinate* 转移的风险[36]。

用物理隔离来实现完全的牵制似乎不可能，这时就可以用雄性不育的品种来阻止转基因花粉的逃逸[7]。虽然雄性不育品种在阻止转基因花粉传布方面是非常有效的，但是，种植雄性不育的转基因作物果真就能阻止它与其野生亲缘种之间的基因流动吗？答案是否定的。一般认为，转基因作物的花粉传布是转基因逃逸的主要渠道，然而，也有另外一种情况，如果转基因作物作为其野生亲缘种花粉的受体，形成的杂种种子在土壤中存留，通过与其亲本的回交也会造成转基因的逃逸。而且，如果不是采用传统育种法，转基因雄性不育品种的释放同样也可能会导致风险。

在前文提到的 Chevre 等[38]对转基因甘蓝型油菜与野生的小萝卜间基因流动的研究中，他们用的是雄性不育的转基因油菜，并将其用作母本进行杂交，随着几个世代的回交，杂种的可育能力逐渐提高，接近野生小萝卜。虽然转基因的传递在第 2 个世代以后逐渐降低，但其风险是不容忽视的。再次证明了转基因作物与其野生亲缘种间的基因流不可避免。

4.2 迄今为止，大约有 2000 个转基因植物的大田释放[3]。它们的大部分是小规模的作大田试验的释放，再加上细致的管理，因而还没有转基因作物的释放导致严重的生态学风险或者导致对环境产生恶劣的影响的报道。然而，许多影响是长期的风险。当这些转基因作物进入市场在农业中广泛推广应用时，就需要对转基因作物的大规模释放的风险评估进行细致研究。那么，那些小规模释放的研究结果到底对大规模释放的风险评估有多大价值呢？到我们有机会直接对比小规模和大规模释放的风险时，才有可能回答这个问题。

由于除了一些特殊的作物(如用于工业原材料或药物提取材料的转基因作物)可以应用遗传隔离的办法来实行完全的隔离外，用距离或缓冲作物区来隔离商业化了的转基因农作物的办法一般是不切实际和不可能的，因而小规模释放获得的距离数据对大规模释放来说可能意义不大[26]。虽然如此，小规模的释放可以提供有关转基因或转基因植物特性的重要信息，可以用来指导大规模的转基因作物的释放。例如，有关有性亲和的数据可以用来推断大规模释放的情况——当大规模释放转基因作物时，有性不亲和提供了最有效的阻断基因流动的手段。从小规模释放的研究中，我们知道杂交的成功不仅与植物的种类有关，而且与特定的基因型和环境有关，这就促使我们在一个大的地理范围上大规模释放转基因作物前，认真考虑这些问题。

转基因逃逸如此难于阻断，我们最好还是着手研究转基因逃逸以后的命运和影响[7]。于是我们又面临着评价转基因入侵(invasiveness)风险的任务。如果我们要阻止或评价转基因在野生种群中的散布，就必须具备来自小规模释放的有关基因流动和杂交的信息。

参考文献

[1] Qian Y-Q(钱迎倩), Ma K-P(马克平). Progress in the studies on genetically modified organisms, and the impact of its release on environment. *Acta Ecol Sin* (生态学报), 1998, **18**: 1~9 (in Chinese)

[2] Wei W(魏伟). A review on molecular ecology. In: Ji W-Z(季维智)ed. The Principle and Approach of Genetic Diversity. Hangzhou: The Science and Technology Press of Zhejiang Province, 1998, in press. (in Chinese)

[3] Kjellsson G, Simonsen V, Ammann K eds. Methods for Risk Assessment of Transgenic Plants: II Pollination, Gene-Trans-fer and Population Impacts. Basel: Birkhauser Verlag, 1997, 1~308

[4] Dale P J. Spread of engineered genes to wild relatives. *Plant Physiol*, 1992, **100**: 13~15

[5] Dale P J. The impact of hybrids between genetically modified crop plants and their related species: general considerations. *Mol Ecol*, 1994, **3**: 31~36

[6] Dale P J, Irwin J A. The release of transgenic plants from containment, and the move towards their widespread use in agriculture. *Euphytica*, 1995, **85**: 425~431

[7] Kareiva P, Morris W, Jacobi C M. Studying and managing the risk of cross-fertilization between transgenic crops and wild relatives. *Mol Ecol*, 1994, **3**: 15~21

[8] Bateman A J. Contamination of seed crops: I. Insect pollination. *J Cenet*, 1947, **48**: 257~275

[9] Crane M B, Mather K. The natural cross-pollination of crop plants with particular reference to radish. *Ann, Appl Biol*, 1943, **30**: 301~308

[10] Bateman A J. Contamination of seed Crops: II. Wind pollination. *Heredity*, 1947, **1**: 235~246

[11] Paterniani E, Stort A C. Effective maize pollen dispersal in the field. *Euphytica*, 1974, **23**: 129~134

[12] Afzal M, Khan A H. Natural crossing in cotton in Westem Punjab: II Natural crossing under field conditions. *Agron J*, 1950, **42**: 89~93

[13] Afzal M, Khan A H. Natural crossing in cotton in Westem Punjab: III. Methods of checking natural crossing. *Agron, J*,1950, **42**: 202~205

[14] Green J M, Jones M D. Isolation of cotton for seed increase. *Agron, J*, 1953, **45**: 366~368

[15] Simpson D M, Duncan E N. Cotton pollen dispersal by insects. *Agron, J*, 1956, **48**: 305~308

[16] Vries A P de. Wheat (*Triticum aestivum* L.): 4. Seed set on male sterile plants as influenced by distance from the pollen source, pollinator: male sterile ratio and width of the male sterile strip. *Euphytica*, 1974, **23**: 601~622

[17] Khan M N, Heyne E G, Arp A L. Pollen distribution and the seedset on *Triticum aestivum*, L. *Crop Sci*. 1973, **13**:223~226

[18] Copeland L O, Hardin E E. Outcrossing in the ryegrass (*Lolium*, spp.) as determined by fluorescence tests. *Crop Sci*, 1970, **10**: 254~257

[19] Griffiths D J. The liability of seed crops of perennial ryegrass (*Lolium perenne*) to contamination by wind-borne pollen. *J Agr Sci*, 1950, **40**: 19~38

[20] Stringam G R, Downey P K. Effectiveness of isolation distance in tumip rape. Can, *J PLanL Sci*, 1978, **58**: 427~438

[21] Bradner N R, Frakes R V, Stephen W P. Effects of bee species and isolation on possible varietal contamination in alfalfa. *Agron, J*, 1965, **57**: 247~248

[22] Pederson M W, Hurst R L, Levin M D, Stoker G L. Computer analysis of the genetic contamination of alfalfa seed. *Crop Sci*, 1969, **9**: 1~4

[23] Umbeck P F, Kenneth B A, Nordheim E V, McCary J C, Parrott W A, Jenkins J N. Degree of pollen dispersal by insects from a field test of genetically engineered cotton. *J Econ, EntomoL*, 1991, **84**: 1943~1950

[24] Scheffler J A, Parkinson R, Dale P J. Frequency and distance of pollen dispersal from transgeric oilseed rape (*Brassica napus*). *Transg Res*, 1993, **2**: 356~364

[25] McPartlan H C, Dale P J. An assessment of gene transfer by pollen from field-grown transgenic potatoes to non-transgenic potatoes and related species. *Transg Res*, 1994, **3**: 216~225

[26] Dale P J, Scheffler J A, Irwin J A. The transition from the small-scale field release of transgenic crop plants to their widespread use in agriculture. In: Jones D D ed. Proceedings of the 3rd International Symposium on the Biosafety

Results of Field Tests of Genetically Modified Plants and Microorganisms. Oakland, California, USA: University of California, Division of Agriculture and Natural Resources, 1994. 57~67

[27] Scheffler J A, Parkinson R, Dale P J. Evaluating the effectiveness of isolation distances for field plots of oilseed rape (*Brassica napus*) using a herbicide-resistance transgene as a selectable marker. *Plant Breeding*, 1995, **114**: 317~321

[28] Timmons A M, O'Brien E T, Charters Y M, Dubbels S J, Wilkinson M J. Assessing the risks of wind pollination from fields of genetically modified *Brassica napus* ssp. *oleifera*. *Euphytica*, 1995, **85**: 417~423

[29] Barrett S C H. Crop mimicry in weeds. *Econ Bot*, 1983, **37**: 255~282

[30] Doebley J. Molecular evidence for gene flow among *Zea* species. *Bioscience*, 1990, **40**: 443~448

[31] Langevin S A, Clay K, Grace J B. The incidence and effects of hybridization between cultivated rice and its related weed red rice (*Oryza sativa*). *Evolution*, 1990, **44**: 1000~1008

[32] Kerlan M C, Chevre A M, Eber F, Baranger A, Renard M. Risk assessment of outcrossing of transgenic rapeseed to related species: I. Interspecific hybrid production under optimal conditions with emphasis on pollination and fertilization. *Euphytica*, 1992, **62**: 145~153

[33] Dale P J, Irwin J A, Scheffler J A. The experimental and commercial release of transgenic crop plants. *Plant Breeding*, 1993, **111**: 1~22

[34] Kerlan M C, Chevre A M, Eber F. Interspecific hybrids between a transgenic rapeseed (*Brassica napus*) and related species: cytogenetical characterization and detection of the transgene. *Genome*, 1993, **36**: 1099~1106

[35] Scheffler J A, Dale P J. Opportunities for gene transfer from transgenic oilseed rape (*Brassica napus*) to related species. *Transg Res*, 1994, **3**: 263~278

[36] Metz P L J, Jacobsen E, Nap J P, Pereira A, Stiekema W J. The impact on biosafety of the phosphinothricin-tolerance trans gene in inter-specific B. *rapa* × B. *napus* hybrids and their successive backcrosses. *Theor Appl Genet*, 1997, **95**: 442~450

[37] Linder C R, Schmitt J. Assessing the risks of transgene escape through time and crop-wild hybrid persistence. *Mol Ecol*, 1994, **3**: 23~30

[38] Chevre A M, Eber F, Baranger A, Renard M. Geneflow from transgenic crops. *Nature*, 1997, **389**: 924

[39] Kjellson G. Ptinciples and procedures for ecological risk assessment of transgenic plants. In: Kjellsson G, Simonsen V, Ammann K eds. Methods for Risk Assessment of Transgenic Plants: II . Pollination, Gene-transfer and Population Impacts. Basel:Birkhauser Verlag, 1997. 221 ~ 237

[40] Bateman A J. Contamination in seed crops: III. Relation with isolation distance. *Heredity*, 1947, **1**: 303~336

[41] Manasse R. Ecological risks of transgenic plants: effects of spatial dispersion on gene flow. *Ecol Appl*, 1992, **2**: 431~438

[42] Coy P A, Duesing J H. Assessing the environmental impact of gene transfer to wild relatives. *Bio/Tech*, 1996, **14**: 39~40

[43] Landbo L, Millelsen R. Risk assessment made (too) simple? *Nature Biotech*, 1996, **14**: 406

[44] Qian Y-Q(钱迎倩), Tian Y(田彦), Wei W(魏伟). Ecological risk assessment of transgenic plants. *Acta Phytoecol Sin*, (植物生态学报), 1998, **22**: 289~299 (in Chinese)

[45] Dale P J, McPartlan H C. Field performance of transgenic potato plants compared with controls regenerated from tuber discs and shoot cutting. *Theor Appl Genet*, 1992, **84**: 585~591

本文原载：生物多样性. 1999. 7(4): 312-319

遗传修饰生物体(GMOs)生态风险的监测*

魏伟　钱迎倩　马克平　桑卫国

(中国科学院植物研究所)

摘　要　遗传修饰生物体(GMOs)释放的生态学风险往往要在相当长的时期内才表现出来，因而必须对其进行长期监测。监测的内容和方法依对象的不同而有所不同。在短期和长期监测中，数学模型具有重要的作用。本文就监测的内容、原则和方法进行了全面的论述。

关键词　遗传修饰生物体(GMOs)；监测；数学模型

1　导言

目前，各国政府都制定了相应的制度来管理遗传修饰生物体(GMOs)的释放，即遗传修饰生物体(GMOs)及其产品上市以前都经过了严格的评审和论证。然而，其生态学后果是长期的，也就是说，既使遗传修饰生物体(GMOs)的短期释放在有效的管理措施的保证下是安全的，也不能忽视其长期释放可能带来的生态学风险[1~5]。1996 年美国南部的 Bt 棉失去对害虫的控制[6~7]，1997 年抗除草剂转基因棉花在密西西比河流域大规模种植后发生大量落铃和棉桃畸形现象[8]，这些都是现实发生的生态学风险。

对于遗传修饰生物体(GMOs)释放的风险评价的结果及后果必须通过长期的监测才能获得。这种监测的结果能够为其他 GMOs，尤其是为类似 GMOs 的释放提供有用的信息，减少不必要的重复劳动，并且监测能够帮助我们避免发生与上一次释放时同样的错误，了解那些不可预见的事件。因此，必须监测任何一次转基因生物体等遗传修饰生物体(GMOs)的释放。

2　监测的内容

2.1　转基因生物的入侵(invasion)风险

我们可以用外来种入侵的经验来评价转基因生物体对自然生境的入侵风险[9,10]。针对入侵，有的学者总结出了一个粗放的 10%~10%规律，适用于所有的动植物，即 10%的外来物种定居成功，10%的定居者成为有害生物。对于转基因生物体的入侵来讲，这

---

* 本文为第三届全国生物多样性保护与持续利用研讨会大会报告之一。

个规律意味着其大多数不能够定居，而大部分的定居者不会产生生态学影响，然而很小部分的有害定居者将产生显著的生态学效应，而那些没有成为有害生物的定居者在某些方面或某些地点可能仍然是不利的[10]。

很多人认为，栽培作物的生长要依赖于人类的培育，在自然界中不能够独立生存。实际上这是不正确的[10]。在邻近耕作地的同一地区，栽培作物可以生长得很好，更不要说获得了优良性状的转基因作物了。已有证据表明，Bt 基因提高了转基因甘蓝型油菜在田间的适合度[11]。导致新物种入侵的主要因素是人为干扰[9]，在这种情况下，转基因生物体通过杂草策略入侵，这种策略增加了转基因生物体在不稳定环境中存留的可能性。

2.2 转基因逃逸(escape)的风险

许多栽培作物都驯化自野生植物，在自然界中，这些作物都存在自己的野生近缘种[12~16]。通过转基因作物与其野生近缘种间的基因流动所造成的转基因逃逸是转基因作物释放后可能带来风险的重要方面[4]。转基因可以通过传粉在空间上逃逸，也可以通过种子库在时间上逃逸，并通过转基因作物与其野生近缘种的杂交种在自然界中存留。在存留的过程中，在适合的条件下，转基因作物与其野生近缘种的杂交种可以与其野生亲本不断回交，转基因进入野生亲本的遗传背景，从而完成了转基因在时空上的逃逸。

目前，转入作物的特性(inserted traits)以抗除草剂的为多，其次是抗虫和抗病毒，最后是抗逆[17]。当这些转基因逃逸后并逐渐在野生种群中固定下来以后，就使得作物的野生近缘种具有了获得选择优势的潜在可能性[18~20]。如果获得选择优势的野生近缘种本身就是杂草，那么就会为该杂草的控制增加很大的困难。也有学者认为，转基因在野生种群中的固定将导致野生等位基因的丢失而造成遗传多样性的丧失[21]。从目前的研究来看，转基因在时空上的逃逸不可避免，因而需要监测、控制和管理转基因作物与其野生近缘种间的基因流动。

2.3 从抗病毒转基因作物产生新的病毒的风险

含有病毒基因的转基因抗病毒作物所释放的最受关注的一个风险就是转基因有可能会与其他病毒重组，从而产生新的、甚至是更为恶劣的病毒。在实验室外和田间条件下，已有了转基因与其他病毒基因重组产生新的病毒的例子，并且会使非病原病毒转变成病原病毒[22~27]。

2.4 转基因作物释放对土壤生态系统及生物地球化学循环的影响

转基因作物对土壤生物的影响，不仅包括初级基因产品，也包括来自生物和非生物反应所产生的次级产品的影响[28]。土壤中的生物体通过捕食、竞争、对抗或共生而发生相互作用，一旦环境由于转基因产品的释放而发生改变，一些敏感生物体快速发生反应，达到一定程度后，其他生物也发生反应，从而影响到整个土壤生态系统[29]。

转基因植物及其产物进入土壤以后，可能会与土壤微生物发生相互作用，影响到一些微生物的活动过程，而微生物对生物地球化学循环有着重要的贡献，从而转基因植物对生物地球化学循环产生了重要影响[30]。转基因植物对生物地球化学循环的影响依赖于土壤类型和质地、气候条件以及转基因植物的种类等因素。

2.5 害虫对转 Bt 抗虫植物的抗性风险

由于转 Bt 基因植物能够持续地高水平表达单一的杀虫毒蛋白，因此 Bt 植物对害虫造成的选择压力甚至比 Bt 杀虫剂还要高，Bt 植物的释放将会加速害虫的抗性进化。在迄今为止所报道的在田间或实验室条件下对 Bt 杀虫剂产生抗性的 17 种害虫中有很大一部分是目前转基因植物的目标害虫[5]。

2.6 转基因植物产生的杀虫剂对非目标生物的影响的风险

目前已经商品化的抗虫转基因植物就是能够产生 Bt 杀虫蛋白的转基因作物。Bt 杀虫蛋白对非目标生物影响的潜在风险不容忽视[31]。

2.7 GMOs 对于人类和其他生物体的致病性

包括 GMOs 导致的疾病的传染性、感染剂量、宿主范围及改变的可能性、在人宿主以外生存的可能性、传播媒介的存在或者传播的方式、生物学稳定性、抗体的抗性模式、毒性、致敏性、非活性 GMOs 以及它们代谢产物的毒性或致敏性影响、代谢产物的危险性[32]。

还应该监测 GMOs 的释放对受体环境中的任何植物、动物和生态系统，包括关键的、稀有的、濒危的或特有的种、潜在竞争生物体的潜在影响；以及潜在受体环境中任何生物体接受释放生物体基因的潜在可能性，以及它们可能对被释放生物体产生排斥性和耐受性等不良反应的可能情况。

3 GMOs 环境监测

3.1 总则

3.1.1 监测要按照案例逐个进行的原则，不同的 GMOs 以及不同的用途要用不同的方法和程序来满足特殊的监测需求，这些需求与以下几个方面有关：所监测的生物体或其遗传修饰构成、释放的类型、释放地点的特征、对环境潜在的影响等。

3.1.2 必须监测任何一次 GMOs 的释放，环境监测应该贯穿释放过程中和释放结束后，监测所需的时间依赖于 GMOs 的生活周期，以及其所处生境的演替速率，一般为 5~10 年。

3.1.3 监测可以是简单的观测，也可以是全面而细致的研究，但一定要满足监测的要求；监测可以由 GMOs 的使用者或是独立的官方机构、组织和团体来进行，但一定要置于监督机制的管理之下。

3.1.4 有效的监测需要遗传学方法和生态学方法的同时参与；需要遗传标记时，要最先选择最廉价的、易于操作的并且是容易获得的标记，以保证监测能够在足够大的尺度上进行，从而获得可靠的统计重复性。

3.1.5 监测的方法要从以下几个方面进行考虑——灵敏性、可靠性、应用性、实用性、重复性、特异性、所需投资、取样的方便及可能性以及其限制性等；监测的设计要以有关监测对象的知识、释放的环境以及释放方案为基础。

3.1.6 在监测实施项目的过程中或监测项目实施的后效时，要如实记录各项指标的结果，在被要求时要如实上报，并根据需要永久保存记录。在监测过程中，一旦发生了对人类健康或环境意外或有害的影响时，必须及时地采取一切可能的有效措施，并及时地向上级主管部门提供有关信息。

3.2 遗传修饰植物体释放的环境监测的原则和方法

3.2.1 原则

(1) 遗传修饰植物体的受体植物的生物学特性必须指示着需要进行田间监测，并足以证明所付出的努力和耗费是值得的；

(2) 在考虑监测的手段和方法时，首先要考虑在特定的条件下，监测某一遗传修饰植物体是否台适；

(3) 监测的试验设计必须保证所获得的监测数据能够进行统计分析，并且最好向统计学家咨询；

(4) 试验设计必须能够提供所需的灵敏水平，所能达到的检测灵敏水平必须在一开始就确定；

(5) 遗传修饰作物释放后，由于某些基因插入可能导致向环境中释放一些蛋白和其他物质，它们可能会对随后种植的作物产生直接或间接的影响，这种影响依赖于插入基因的性质、释放的产物、在环境中的存留以及作物的轮作制度，监测必须要考虑到这一点；

(6) 检测出转基因植物与其他植物间的基因流并不一定意味着某一基因将在受体种群中固定，或者其环境影响将随后发生。

3.2.2 监测的方法

包括直接观察的方法、用生物学或物理学手段阻断花粉逃逸进行取样和鉴定的方法以及间接研究的方法。在释放前和释放后的监测中，直接观察采取对释放地点采样进行鉴定、记录，或者在必要时移去这种植物或其亲缘种的方法，并且必须考虑这种植物的繁殖生物学习性。用直接观察的方法进行检测所释放植物的明显形态学特征应该是稳定遗传和表达的，并且有别于当地植物和该种作物的野生种群的，这些特征包括形态学标记(种子的颜色和形状、植物及花的形态等)、生理学标记(抗病性、抗啃食性、除草剂耐受性、抗生素抗性)，另外还有生物化学标记(二次代谢产物、蛋白、同工酶、抗体)以及分子生物学标记(核 DNA、核外 DNA、遗传修饰所构建的 DNA)。

为了大大减少工作量，监测的对象最好是完美设计的取样而不是对释放地点及其周围的彻底调查。可以在一种转基因作物周围或者邻近种植非转基因作物用来取样并测度花粉的运动。用来测度转基因花粉运动的非转基因植物根据用途的不同可以分为两类：①与转基因植物完全杂交亲和，并且其开花特性尤其是开花时间和持续时间尽量相同，用来测度花粉的移动距离；②与转基因植物应是相同属或族中非常近缘的物种，用来确定转基因作物与其近缘种特别是杂草间基因流发生的可能性，在这种情况下，细胞学检查也是用来鉴定潜在杂种的一种方法。

用于捕捉花粉的植物基因型应该在一些特征方面有别于所监测植物，并且这些特征(见前文)是稳定遗传和表达或者是能够检测出的，它们存在于四个水平上：①形态学、②生理学、③生物化学、④分子水平。

也可以用间接的方法来估计转基因的扩散，这些间接的方法基于这样一种概念，就是种群中基因型的分布可以用来推断基因流潜在的模式。

3.3 遗传修饰动物体释放环境监测的原则和方法

3.3.1 原则

(1) 必须能够标记动物；

(2) 所监测动物需要能够被重捕；

(3) 由于遗传修饰动物体的活动性比较强，监测时应该强调其在意外事故中逃逸的可能性；

(4) 对于昆虫来说，一般应监测其活动性比较强的时期，即成虫阶段，但对拟寄生等，最好监测其幼虫阶段。

3.3.2 方法

监测的方法分为取样、检测遗传修饰动物或其插入基因、确定其生物学或环境影响三个步骤：

取样就是在自然界捕获一定数量的自然种群，用以检测遗传修饰动物体逃逸或修饰基因构成逃逸的情况，诱捕的方法有很多，诱捕昆虫的方法有：光诱捕(适于鞘翅目、半翅目和双翅目的昆虫)、诱饵诱捕(适于某些昆虫)、性激素(适于鳞翅目的昆虫)、胶黏、陷阱、电力抽吸、捕虫网等。

为了鉴定遗传修饰生物体或转基因，必须要对其进行标记，标记的方法大体上分为人为的和生物体或修饰基因构成本身的。人为的标记方法有以下几种：无线电发射机、颜色标记、标签、在动物身上用剪刀剪出标记(如鱼鳍)等。生物体或修饰基因构成本身的遗传学标记有以下几种：形态学的、生理学的、生物化学的、分子遗传标记。这些遗传学标记必须是稳定表达和遗传的。

3.4 遗传修饰微生物体环境释放监测的方法

可以用平板计数法、最大可能数量(MPN)法、显微镜检技术进行数量动态监测。也可以用标记基因如生物发光基因、乳糖基因、抗生素抗性基因、重金属抗性基因、*xyl*E 抗性基因等监测它们的存在，所用到的核酸技术包括 PCR 的目标特异扩增、直接杂交、用寡核苷酸探针检测细胞核糖体 RNA 等。

4 遗传修饰生物体(GMOs)环境释放影响监测的数学模型

4.1 监测转基因逃逸的数学模型

4.1.1 Bateman给出了距离对风媒和虫媒传粉污染影响的三个方程式，并将它们近似地合并成一个：

$$F = (y\mathrm{e}^{-kD})/D \tag{1}$$

这里，F 是花粉污染的比率，D 是距离，Y 是零隔距离时的污染[33]。

4.1.2 Manasse 给出了评价基因流动的指数模型[34]，他的模型类似于方程(1)，然而更加完善，适合于评价转基因作物与其野生亲缘种间的基因流动。Manasse 在研究中发现，随着植物丛或个体间距离的增加，一年中基因传播的平均距离也在增加。这就意味着伴随着长距离隔离，一个罕见的长距离传粉事件会增加转基因逃逸的风险。

Kareiva 等给出了一个与 Maraasse 的指数模型类似的可靠性函数(reliability function)[35]：

$$R(x) = \exp(-ax^b) \tag{2}$$

$R(x)$是花粉传布到距离 x 的可能性，其平均数等于 $1/a\Gamma(b+1)/b$，变异等于 $1/a^2[\Gamma(b+2)/b-\Gamma^2(b+1)/b]$。

4.1.3 由于植物可以接受各种来源(包括自身)的花粉，因而来自转基因植物的花粉可能只是柱头上总花粉的一小部分，所以可以用异交的数据来估计一个参数 C，也就是离转基因作物零距离时污染的估计。

获得一个含转基因的种子的概率与 $R(x)$成比例：

$$L = \prod_{K=1}^{N} \binom{S_k}{M_k} \left[cR(x)\right]^{M_k} \left[1 - cR(x)\right]^{S_k - M_k} \tag{3}$$

其中：S_k = 第 k 个取样点采集的种子数；M_k = S_k 中含有转基因的种子数；N = 取样点的数量。

对于风险评价来说，需要的不是在某一距离上的传粉频率，而是描述一个转基因在一个或几个方向上传布到某一特定距离以外的可能性，这就是累积密度函数(cumulative density function，c.d.f.)[36]：

$$\text{c.d.f.} = \Gamma(\alpha,\ \beta)/\ \Gamma(\beta) \tag{4}$$

这里，a 为 ax^b ；β 为 $1/b$(一个方向)或 $2/b$(所有方向)；$\Gamma(\cdot,\ \cdot)$是不完全迦马函数，$\Gamma(\cdot)$是完全迦马函数。

4.2 监测转基因入侵的数学模型

4.2.1 Kareiva 等[37]认为可以用 Lotka-Volterra 竞争模型来预测转基因入侵的后果。他们将有关的参数定义以后，用来预测一种(缺失突变)遗传修饰微生物体 *Pseudomoas syringae* 品系同其野生品系间的竞争：

$$dN^+ / dt = r^+ N^+ (1 - N^+ / K^+ - \alpha_{-+} N^- / K^+) \tag{5}$$

$$dN^- / dt = r^- N^- (1 - N^- / K^- - \alpha_{+-} N^+ / K^-) \tag{6}$$

N^+和 N^-分别是遗传修饰生物体和自然种群的种群密度，r^+和 r^-分别是遗传修饰生物体和自然种群的种群内禀增长率，K^+和 K^-是各自的环境容纳量，。a_{+-}和 a_{+-}则分别是各自的竞争系数。

4.2.2 转基因生物体进入自然系统中以后，将会与多种生物而不仅与一种生物发生竞争作用，特别是对于高等植物来说，都一样需要光、CO_2、水和营养物这些少数资源，资源利用出现分化的可能性比较小，因而研究起来困难较大。而 Tilman 的竞争模型能够提供解决途径[38]，可以利用 Tilman 的竞争模型来研究转基因生物体入侵对群落的影响。Andow[39]根据 Tilman 模型建立了一个数学理论模型来预测转基因生物体释放对群落结构的改变。在这个模型中，Andow 用一个参数(R^*)来描述一个物种的最低资源需求，一个物种的 R^*愈低，其竞争能力就愈强。当群落中初级消费者消耗植物比较大时，转基因抗性就能够降低植物的 R^*，这种转基因植物就可能会影响到群落的结构；当植物的竞争能力差(高的 R^*)时，并且转基因性状对 R^*没有影响时，这种转基因植物就不会影响到群落的结构。

4.2.3 Crawley 等[40]研究了一种抗除草剂转基因甘蓝型油菜入侵自然生境后的生态学后果。他们用一个有限增长率(λ)来指示转基因入侵后的命运。

$$\lambda_1 = (1 - d_1 - g) + g(1 - d_2)F \tag{7}$$

d_1 是一年中种子失活的比例，g 是第一年春天种子萌发的比例，d_2 是冬天种子失活的比例，F 是每个萌发种子结实种子的平均数量。$\lambda>1$ 时，表示转基因植物种群数量将增大，$\lambda<1$ 时，表示转基因植物将会消亡。

公式(7)计算出的λ值是在种子的生活史开始于一个没有竞争的农田生境中，因而可能有些偏高。当考虑到种子萌发一开始就会有自然植被的竞争时，λ值可以这样估算：

$$\lambda_2 = \text{第二代的幼苗} / \text{第一代的幼苗} \tag{8}$$

4.3 监测昆虫对抗虫作物抗性的等位基因频率的数学模型

$$P_{(R,T+1)} = \frac{P_{(R,T)}^{\ 2} + P_{(R,T)}P_{(S,T)}W_{RS}}{P_{(R,T)}^{\ 2} + 2P_{(R,T)}P_{(S,T)}W_{RS} + P_{(S,T)}W_{SS}} \tag{9}$$

$P_{(R,\ T+1)}$为 T+1 世代抗性等位基因的频率，$P_{(R,\ T)}$和 $P_{(S,\ T)}$分别为 T 世代抗性等位基因和感性等位基因的频率，W_{SS} 和 W_{RS} 分别为纯合感性个体和杂合个体的适合度。当抗性等位基因的频率即 $P_{(R,\ T+1)}$达到或超过 0.5 时，说明种群对 Bt 作物进化出了抗性，T+1 则为抗性进化所需的世代数[5]。

5 结束语

本文的主要目的是论述对遗传修饰生物体(GMOs)的释放进行监测的原理与方法，为开展 GMOs 释放的监测工作提供依据，使遗传修饰生物体(GMOs)及其产品更好更安全地为人类服务。目前，国内国际上尚无此类文献，因而撰写这样一篇文章是非常及时而有益的。

参考文献

[1] 钱迎倩, 田彦, 魏伟. 转基因植物的生态风险评价. 植物生态学报, 1998, 22(4): 289~299

[2] 钱迎倩, 马克平. 经遗传修饰生物体的研究进展及其释放后对环境的影响. 生态学报, 1998, 18(1): 1~9

[3] 钱迎倩, 魏伟, 田彦, 马克平. 转基因作物的进展及可能存在的问题. 应用与环境生物学报, 1999, 5(4): 427~433

[4] 魏伟, 钱迎倩, 马克平. 转基因作物与其野生亲缘种间的基因流动. 植物学报, 1999, 4l(4): 343~348

[5] 魏伟, 钱迎倩, 马克平. 害虫对转基因 Bt 作物的抗性及其管理对策. 应用与环境生物学报, 1999, 5(2): 215~228

[6] Fox J L, Bt cotton infestations renew resistance concems. *Nat. Bwtech*, 1997, 14: 1070

[7] Kaiser J . Pests overwhelm Bt cotton crop. *Science*,1996, 273: 423

[8] Fox J L. Farmers say Monsanto's engineered cotton crop bolls, *Nat. Bwtech*, 1997, 15: 1233

[9] Kjellsson G, Simonsen V. Methods for risk assessment of transgenic Plants. I. Competition, establishment and ecosystem effects, Basel: Birkhauser Verlag, 1994, 1~214

[10] Williamson M, Community response to transgenic plant release: predictions from British experience of invasive plants and feral crop plants. *Mol, Ecol*, 1994, 3(1): 75~80

[11] Stewart C N Jr, All J N, Paymer P L et al. Increased fitness of rransgenic insecticidal rapeseed under insect selection pressure, *Mol Ecol*, 1997, 6: 773~779

[12] Barrett S C H. Crop mimicry in weeds. *Economic Botany*, 1983, 37: 255~282

[13] Doebley J Molecular evidence for gene flow among Zae species. Bioscience, 1990, 40: 443~448

[14] Kerlan M C, Chevre A M ， Eber F et a1.Risk assessment of outcrossing of transgenic rapeseed to related species: I. Interspecific hybrid production under optimal conditions with emphasis on pollination and fertilization.*Euphytica*, 1992, 62: 145~153

[15] Dale P J, Irwin J A, Scheffler J A. The experimental and commercial release of transgenic crop Plants. *Plant Breeding*, 1993, 111: 1~22

[16] Kendall H W, Beachy R, Eisiner T et a1. Bioengineering of Crops, Report of the World Bank Panel on Transgenic Crops Worldbank, 1997, 1~30

[17] Kjellsson G, Simonsen V, Ammann K(eds.). Methods for Risk Assessment of Transgenic Plants: *II*, Pollination, Gene-transfer and Population Impacts, Basel: Birkhauser Verlag, 1997, 308

[18] Dale P J. Spread of engineered genes to wild relatives, *Plant Physiol*, 1992, 100: 13~15

[19] Dale P J. The impact of hybrids between genetically modified crop plants and their related species: general considerations. *Mol. Ecol*, 1994,3: 31~36

[20] Dale P J,Irwin J A. The release of transgenic plants from containment, and the move towards their widespread use in agriculture. *Euphytica*, 1995, 85: 425~413

[21] Gaggiotti O E. Potential evolutionary and ecological consequences of the release of GMO's into the wild. The workshop on transgenic organisms in the new millenjum: risks and benefits, Italy, Dec 1~5,1997

[22] Allison R F, Schneider W L, Greene A E. Recombination in plants expressing viral transgenes. *Virol*,, 1996, 7: 417~422

[23] Zhou X P, Liu Y L, Calvert L et al. Evidence that DNA-A of a genmivirus associated with severe cassava mosaic disease in Uganda has arisen by interspecific recombination, *J. Gen. Virol*, 1997, 78: 2101~2111

[24] McGrath P. Lethal hybrid decimates harvest. *New Scientist*, 1997, 2097: 8

[25] Harrison B D, Zhou X P, Otim-Nape G W et al. Role of a novel type of double infection in the geminivirus-in-duced epidemic of severe cassava mosaic in Uganda. *Ann. Appl. Biol*, 1997, 131: 437~448

[26] Zhou X P, Liu Y, Robinson D J et al.Four DNA-A Variants among Pakistani isolates of cotton leaf cirl virus and their affinities to DNA-A of geminivirus isolates from okra. *J. Gen. Virol*, 1998, 79: 915~923

[27] Kleiner K, Fields of genes. *New Scientist*,1997, 2095:4

[28] Morra M J. Assessing the impact of transgenic plant products on soil organisms. *Mol. Ecol*., 1994, 3:53~56

[29] Angle J S. Release of transgenic plants:biodiversity and population level considerations. *Mol. Ecol*., 1994, 3: 45~50

[30] Trevors J T, Kuikman P, Watson B. Transgenic plants and biogeochemical cycles. *Mol. Ecol*., 1994, 3: 45~50

[31] Union of Concerned Scientists(UCS). Risk research: transgenic insect-resistance crops harm beneficial insects. *The Gene Exchange*,1998, Summer: 4

[32] OECD. Industrial products of modern biotechnology intended for release to the environment. Pans,1996, 130

[33] Bateman A J. Contamination in seed crops: III. Relation with isolation distance. *Here dity*, 1947, 1: 303~336

[34] Manasse R. Ecological risks of transgenic plants:effects of spatial dispersion on gene flow. *Ecol. Appl*., 1992, 2: 431~438

[35] Kareiva P, Morris W, Jacobi C M. Studying and managing the risk of cross-fertilization between transgenic crops and wild relatives. *Mol. Ecol*., 1994, 3: 15~21

[36] Gliddon C, Boudry P,Walker S.Gene flow – a review of experimental evidence. The workshop on transgenic organisms in the new millennium: risks and benefits, Italy, Dec 1~5, 1997

[37] Kareiva P,Parker I M. Pascual M. Can we use experiments and models in predicting the invasiveness of genetically engineered organisms? *Ecology*, 1996, 77: 1670~1675

[38] 孙儒泳. 动物生态学原理(第二版). 北京: 北京师范大学出版社, 1992, 1~511

[39] Andow D A, Community response to transgenic plant release: using mathematical theory to predict effects of transgenic plants. *Mol. Ecol*., 1994, 3: 65~70

[40] Crawley M J, H ails R S, Rees M et al. Ecology of transgenic oilseed rape in natural habitats. *Nature*, 1993, 363: 620~623

本文原载：自然资源学报. 2001. 16(2): 184-190

转基因食品安全性评价的研究进展*

魏伟　钱迎倩　马克平　裴克全　桑卫国

(中国科学院植物研究所)

摘　要　转基因食品的安全性问题在世界范围内倍受关注，国内外尤其国外已经开展和正在开展许多的研究工作。实质等同性原则在转基因安全性评价中得到广泛应用，但存在一定的局限性。目前已经进行了转基因马铃薯、大豆、番茄、棉花、西葫芦、水稻、烟草以及芦笋的食用安全性评价，积累了一些研究经验和方法，得到一些有意义的研究结果，但也存在着一定的争论。文中将从评价的方法、原则和结果等几个方面报道和讨论转基因食品安全性评价的研究进展，并且指出评价中存在的问题，对转基因食品的安全性问题作了一个相对全面而客观的报道，并且总结了转基因食品安全性评价中应该注意的几个问题，对开展安全性评价工作有一定的参考价值。

关键词　转基因食品；安全性；实质等同性；致敏性；全食物饲喂

中图分类号　Q—1　**文献标识码**　A

最近，苏格兰Rowett研究所(RRI)的一项研究表明，一种抗虫转基因马铃薯所产生的雪花莲外源凝集素能够对大鼠的内脏器官和免疫系统产生损伤，而对于人类来讲，类似的影响可能会导致癌症发病率和死亡率的大幅上升[1]。虽然有关科学家及科学团体在此项研究的实验设计和结果分析上存在很大分歧，但其研究结果经媒体公布后产生的负面的社会影响非常大，其主要研究责任人Arpad Pustztai被迫提前退休。另外的一个研究发现，美国Pioneer Hi-Bred种子公司的一种表达2S种子贮藏蛋白的转基因大豆会使对巴西坚果过敏的人群产生过敏反应，因此公司决定不让它上市[2,3]。那么，迄今为止上市的转基因食品是否会对人类健康产生不利的影响，并且如何对其进行安全性评价?这些都是颇受关注，并且迫切需要回答的问题。国内虽然有大量的即将和已经上市的转基因食品，但尚无针对此类问题的专门的文献报道。为了推动国内转基因食品安全性评价的研究工作，本文将针对这些问题详细论述国内外转基因食品评价的研究进展，以及存在的问题和可行的评价方法。

* 基金项目：国家重点基础研究发展规划项目(G2000046803)资助。

1 评价的原则与方法

1.1 实质等同性原则

1993年，OECD(经济合作与发展组织)提出了食品安全性评价的原则——实质等同性(substantial equivalence)原则[4]。即如果一种转基因食品与现存的传统同类食品相比较，其特性、化学成分、营养成分、所含毒素以及人和动物食用和饲用情况是类似的，那么它们就具有实质等同性。实质等同性的确定说明了这种新食品与非转基因品种在有益健康方面可能是相似的[5]。

若仅仅因为一种新的转基因食品同一种现存的对应食品不存在实质等同性并不意味着它就是不安全的。如果进行安全测试，就必须要以这种新食品的特性为基础。依照其化学成分以及对其熟知的程度，可以推断是否需要动物实验和离体研究，并不是所有的转基因食品都需要进行动物实验的，评价必须以个案的原则为基础。如果需要用转基因食品或其成分进行动物实验，那么实验目的也必须是明确的，设计是严谨的[5]。

1.2 评价方法

1.2.1 Monsanto 公司的评价方法

在美国，有很多的基因公司，Monsanto 公司是最大的一个，该公司的资本已经渗入到许多拥有商品化转基因食品的公司里。该公司在食品安全评价方面的经验值得借鉴。Monsanto 公司根据实质等同性原则将评价的内容分为 3 个方面：

(1) 插入基因所表达蛋白的安全性评价；

(2) 用选择性和特异性的分析检验来进行非预期(多效性的)影响，转基因食品的重要营养成分要与相应的非转基因品系以及其亲本的进行比较，分析结果要与现有的数据进行比较，以确定其营养水平在正常的范围之内，抗营养成分也要与现有数据和其对照比较以确认内源毒素没有发生有意义的变化，食品加工产品各种成分也应进行分析，以保证所测定的参数在可接受的范围之内；

(3) 健康显示(Wholesomeness)测试的选择性应用，一般地，为模拟商业化的饲喂实践，这些饲喂实验用家畜家禽进行。对于人类食用的食品来讲，就将这种新食品用 25 倍于人类最大估计摄入量去饲喂大鼠，实验用每组每种性别的大鼠进行 4 周以上。全食物(Whole food)饲喂实验时，动物对食物的微小变化不敏感，健康显示测试的参数包括每日健康观察、每周体重、食品消耗等，4 周后进行全面的尸检，如果在尸检中发现任何异常，这些组织就要进行显微镜检。这种 2Bd 的急性毒理学研究通常用来评价是否在饲喂待检食品过程中，有任何不利的影响表现出来，在尸检中，应该观察器官重量、血液学、临床化学以及组织病理学等方面的变化[7]。

1.2.2 数据库的应用

数据库可以提供有关食品成分的基底信息，用来评价转基因食品中主要的营养和毒素是否有显著性变化。当然也应考虑到这些主要的营养和有毒成分有一定的变动范围，另外必须保证数据的质量，并且必须发展有效的方法来定量这些主要的成分[8]。

1.2.3 活体(in vivo)和离体(in vitro)动物模型

可以用活体或离体的动物模型来评价转基因微生物食品的安全性，丹麦食品部的毒理学研究所已经建立了若干个哺乳动物消化道模型[9]。其中，大鼠模型建立的最齐全，可能是研究中应用大鼠模型较多的缘故。无菌大鼠模型除了可以研究细菌的存活和移殖外，还可以研究微生物间遗传物质的转移。如果将携带质粒 pAMβ_1的供体菌系和受体菌喂服无菌的大鼠，几天后在大鼠的排泄物中就会发现 DNA 接合转移的产物。

1.2.4 转基因食品致敏性的评价方法[10]

如果转基因食品中所含蛋白是已知来源的，就用 SDS—PAGE 作点免疫反应后，进行放射性致敏吸着剂抑制反应测试(RAST—inhibition)，如果结果是阳性的，就不需要进一步的试验而下结论认为这种转基因食品对人类是致敏的；如果结果是阴性的，那么接着进行皮刺测试和双盲、安慰剂对照的食品免疫试验(DBPCFC，double-bhnd, placedbo-controlled food challenges)，如果结果仍是阴性的，那么就可以下结论，对消费者来说，这种转基因食品没有风险。如果转基因食品所含蛋白是非食品来源，或来源于不常见食品，那么就不能用过敏个体或者他们的血清进行测试，在这种情况下，就将这种蛋白的特性与已知的食品过敏原进行对照。

1.2.5 PCR 检测的方法

目前，转基因植物的构建经常会用到来自花椰菜花叶病毒(CaMV)的 35s 启动子。对 35s 启动子的 PCR 检测是欧盟新食品管理的依据。最近欧盟修改了其食品管理策略，GMO(遗传饰生物体)含量大于 5%的食品必须进行标签，于是由定性 PCR 转向定量 PCR，其中数量竞争性 PCR(QC—PGR，quantitative competitive PCR)的方法特别有用[11]。

2 结果与分析

2.1 马铃薯

继公开在电视上宣布转雪花莲外源凝集素(GNA)基因马铃薯对大鼠的内脏器官有损害后[1]，Ewen 和 Pusztai 于 1999 年正式发表了它们的研究结果 。他们研究了转 GNA 基因抗虫马铃薯对大鼠胃肠道不同部分的影响，实验分别用含有转基因马铃薯、非转基因的马铃薯亲本以及非转基因马铃薯加上 GNA 的 3 种膳食来饲喂实验大鼠。结果发现，胃黏膜、腔肠绒毛以及肠道的小囊(Crypt)长度均有不同程度的变化。经过比较探讨，他们得出结论是，胃黏膜的加厚主要是由 GNA 基因表达的后果，而小肠和盲肠的变化主要是由遗传操作或、和转基因构成引起的，GNA 基因表达的影响只占很小的一部分。Fenton 等[13]的研究发现，GNA 能够与人类的白细胞结合，虽然这并不能说明什么，但增加了对人类健康产生影响的风险。已有实验证明 Bt 毒蛋白对人畜是安全的，并且一种转 Bt 基因马铃薯与其对应的非转基因品种间具有实质等同性[14]。对于一种转基因抗除草剂马铃薯来说,与相应的非转基因亲本品系非常接近[15]。

2.2　番茄

研究表明，Calgene 公司的 FLAVR SAVR™ 延迟成熟番茄的主要营养成分(如 V_A 和 Vc)没有改变，番茄碱等天然毒素没有显著变化，也没有发现有害的多效性，在一个 7d 的大鼠饲喂实验中，没有发现不良影响[16]。对一种转基因抗虫番茄的食品安全研究中 [17,18] ,用相当于一个人日耗2000KgBt番茄量的Bt蛋白饲喂Brown Norway雄性大鼠、小鼠和兔子，未产生全身不良反应。在对一种抗烟草花叶病毒(TMV)转基因番茄的食品安全性评价中，转基因和非转基因番茄相比，糖碱、糖类、有机酸、多酸类都没有明显变化，诱变性上也没有差别。

2.3　大豆

Nordlee 等[3]评价了一种转巴西坚果 2S 清蛋白基因大豆的食品安全性，在研究中他们取了 9 个对巴西坚果有过敏史的人的血清，RAST 研究表明，转基因大豆提取物可有效地与来自生巴西坚果的蛋白提取物竞争性地结合过敏人群血清中的 IgEC(免疫球蛋白)。而用与之遗传上相对应的非转基因大豆的蛋白提取物观察到抑制现象；SDS—PAGE 研究表明，转基因大豆中出现了一种新的蛋白质带(约 9KD)，巴西坚果也有这条带，并且与部分纯化的 2S 清蛋白有相同的迁移率，而非转基因大豆中都无这样一种相对应的带；免疫点杂交研究表明，9 份血清的 8 份能识别部分纯化的 2S 清蛋白，也能与巴西坚果提取物中的 9KD 的蛋白产生免疫反应，9 份血清中的 7 份能识别上述转基因大豆中与巴西坚果 2S 清蛋白有共同迁移率的 9KD 的蛋白质，没有血清与非转基因大豆中低分子量的蛋白反应，来自对照的血清不与任何大豆或巴西坚果的蛋白发生反应，因此可以肯定这种转基因大豆中存在与巴西坚果类似的过敏原。

根据 Fuchs 等[19,20]的研究结果，Monsanto 公司的抗除草剂的转基因大豆与市场上的相对应的非转基因大豆具有实质等同性。

2.4　棉花

Monsanto 公司的 Bt 棉表达的 Bt 毒蛋白可被哺乳动物很快地消化，与非转基因棉相比,其棉籽和棉籽油的质量以及抗营养成分没有显著的改变,并且分别用含有 5%~10 %、10%和 20%棉籽的饲料喂养大鼠、鹌鹑和鲇鱼 28d、8d 和 10 周，也没有发现有任何显著的变化，证明这种 Bt 棉是安全的[2] 。

陈松等[22]用棉籽粉喂养大鼠28d、喂养鹌鹑8d的动物实验表明，转基因各组动物的体重、食物利用率与对照相比，无显著差异，受试动物生长发育及行为正常、无死亡：对大鼠的肝、肾、胃、盲肠、结肠、小肠及睾丸进行组织切片检查，均未见病理性改变，大鼠肝、肾、睾丸的重量比，以及血液中谷丙转氨酶活性和尿素氨水平均在正常范围内，转基因与对照组相比无明显变化，因此这种Bt棉与常规棉有实质等同性。

2.5 其他

一种抗病毒的转基因水稻[23]，抗病毒的转基因西葫芦品系ZW20[24]，抗病毒的转基因烟草[25]及一种转基因芦笋[26]与其对应的非转基因亲本间没有发现显著的区别[26]。

3 讨论与结论

3.1 实质等同性的概念局限性

实质等同性的概念体现了这样一种思路.就是可将作为现时用作食品或食品来源的生物体作为比较的基础来评价一种来自生物技术的食品或食品成分的安全性。然而，实质等同性这个概念也有它的局限性，比如说，虽然一种新的食品与一种已知食品有99%的相同，即除含有一种新的毒素外，二者具有实质等同性，但是这种食品可能需要进一步细致的检验；而既使一种新食品与其对应的现存食品只有70%的相同，特别是当营养成分的不同可被一种混合膳食替代时，这种新食品也可能仅需要很小程度的检验测试[27]。因此，用实质等同性这个概念并不能完全预测新食品是否需要动物实质性毒性实验。

而且，科学家还不能令人信服地用已知的有关转基因食品的化学成分来预测转基因食品的生化或毒理学效应。一种转基因食品在化学成分上与其自然存在的对应食品相似，并不能够说明人类食用该转基因食品是安全的[28]。有的科学家认为，一种转基因抗除草剂大豆与其对应的非转基因大豆具有实质等同性。而Millstone等[28]则认为，这个结论是建立在这样一个假设的基础上的，即假定已知的遗传和生化差异并不具有显著的毒理学差异。实际上，即使不施用除草剂，这种转基因抗除草剂的大豆与其相对应的所有品种的化学成分也不相同。在农业生产上实际应用这种抗除草剂的大豆时，必然会经常地用降草剂处理，而用除草剂处理大豆，必然会导致其化学成分发生显著性的变化，这一点已够证实。而在得出实质等同性的结论的实验中，所用的转基因大豆是未经除草剂经常处理的，并且比较的仅是部分化学成分，因此并没有什么实际意义。

3.2 全食物(Whole food)饲喂研究的局限性

前面已经提及，许多的转基因食品安全性评价工作都用整个的转基因食品进行急性实验动物毒理实验。然而，用全食物饲喂动物的实验有一定的局限性，它很难检测出食品中的微小变化，食品学家和营养学家比较反对在进行转基因食品安全评价时使用全食物饲喂研究的方法。国际食品生物技术委员会(IFBC)指出，一般情况下不推荐使用这个方法评价转基因食品的安全性，如果确实需要，那么全食物饲喂研究的实验设计要十分小心和谨慎，并且持续时间不能太长，以避免因营养不平衡等因素的影响而对动物产生不利影响，从而掩饰了转基因食品的安全性[7]。

实际上，上述经验和结论来自对辐照食品安全评价的实验结果。当时，不了解以某种食物过量饲喂实验动物会导致营养的不平衡，对动物的健康产生不利影响。Hammond等[0]总结了一些这样的例子，可能对转基因食品的评价工作有较高的参考价值。

3.3 有关转 GNA 基因马铃薯安全性的争论

Pusztai 一经公布他和同事们的转 GNA 基因马铃薯会损伤大鼠的消化和免疫系统的研究结果，其实验设计和实验结果马上遭到多方批评。前面已提过。相应的研究论文投到国际著名杂志 *THE LANCET* 后，也引起诸多争议，*THE LANCET* 编辑部认为，虽然 Pusztal 及其同事的这项研究有一些不足，但是该论文提供了一项研究结果，是一个争论的开端，并且有必要让公众了解事实，以增强公众对科学的信任感，因此，*THE LANCET* 还是于 1999 年公开发表了这篇论文[24]。对于该篇论文中存在的问题，Kuiper 等[30]认为有以下几点：① 论文中没有介绍饲喂大鼠的不同膳食的成分，虽然 Pusztal 等在网上公布了部分细节，转基因马铃薯中的淀粉、多聚葡萄糖、外源凝集素、胰蛋白酶和糜蛋白酶与其余亲本品系不同，但这种不同是由转基因引起的还是由品系不同而引起的尚未可知；② 大鼠膳食中仅含 60%的蛋白质，容易造成饥饿反应，从而导致其他的一些不利影响；③ 实验设计不严密，每个饲喂组的大鼠个体数太少，而且缺少膳食对照，比如一个含 15 %蛋白的标准的啮齿动物膳食，以及包含“空白”载体的马铃薯的对照膳食；④ 研究中没有观察到一致性的变化，很难说明实验中大鼠消化道的变化是转基因马铃薯影响的结果。摄食马铃薯本身也会导致消化道适应变化[6]。支持 Kuiper 等的批评。英国皇家学会经研究讨论后也持类似观点[33]。

3.4 转基因食品安全性评价中应注意的问题

(1) 由于实质等同性的尺度不好掌握，因此实质等同性这个概念比较模糊，其应用价值随转基因食品的不同而不同；

(2) 全食物饲喂动物有一定的缺陷，因此最好不用或少用，使用时一定要谨慎设计实验；

(3) 目前来讲，除了转巴西坚果基因大豆有致敏性，转 GNA 基因马铃薯的安全性有争议外，其他许多的转基因食品已被现在的研究结果证明是安全的，但转基因食品的长期效应有待探讨，能够批准一种新的转基因食品的指标体系还有待进一步完善；

(4) 转基因食品安全性评价的程序基本上包括这样几个方面：① 新基因产品的特性的研究；② 分析营养物质和已知毒素含量的变化；③ 潜在致敏性的研究；④ 转基因食品与动物或人类的肠道中的微生物群进行基因交换的可能及其影响；⑤ 活体和离体的毒理和营养评价。

参考文献

[1] Dommelen A van. Scientific requirements for the assessment of food safety [J] *Biotechnology and Development Monitor*. 1999, 38: 2~ 7

[2] 钱迎倩.马克平. 经遗传修饰生物体的研究进展及其释放后对环境的影响[J] 生态学报.1998, 18(1)：l~9

[3] Nordlee J A, Taylor S L, Townsed J A, *et al.* Investigations of the a1lergemcity of Brazil nut 2S seed storage protein in transgenic soybean [A] In: OECD.Food Safety Evaluation[C] Paris：OCED, 1996, 151~155

[4] OECD Safety Evaluation of Foods Derived by Modern Biotechnology：Concepts and principles[C] Paris：1993.

[5] OECD Food Safety Evaluation[C] Paris OCED, 1996.

[6] Hammond B, Rogers S G, Fuchs R L. Limitations of whole food feeding studies in food safety assessment[A].OECD. Food Safety Evaluation[C] Paris: OCED, 1996. 85~97

[7] Hattan D Evaluation of toxicological studies on flavr savr tomato[A] OECD. Food Safety Evaluation[C] Paris：OCED. 1996.58~ 60

[8] Gry J, Sϕborg T, Knudsen L. The role of databases：the example of a food plant database[A]. OECD. Food Safety Evaluation[C]. Paris：OCED, 1996 118~129

[9] Jaoobsen B L. The use of in vivo and in vitro models in the testing of microorganisms [A]. OECD.Food Safety Evaluation[C]. Paris：OCED, l996. 130~134

[10] Taylor S L. Evaluation of the allergenicity of foods developed through biotechnology[A]. Jones D D Proceeding of the 3rd International Symposium on the Biosafety Results of Field Tests of Genetically Modified Plants and Microorganisms[C] Oakland.California：The University of Calrfonia.1994. 185~ 198

[11] Hubner P.Studer E.Luthy J Quantitation of geneticalty modified organisms in food[J]. *Nature Biotechnology*. 1999. 17: 1137~1138

[12] Ewen S W B, Pusztai A. Effect of diets containing genetically modified potatoes expressing Galanthus nivalts lectine on rat small intestine[J]. *The LANECT*. 1999. 354：1353~ 1354

[13] Fenton B, Stanley K, Fenton S, Bolton-Smith C. Differential binding of the insecticidal Jectin GNA to human blood cells[J] *The LANCET*, 1999, 354: 1354~1355

[14] 贾士荣, 吕群燕, 张长青. 转基因植物的安全性评价[A]. 朱守一. 生物安全与防止污染[C].北京：化学工业出版社. 1999. 30~53

[15] Conner A J-Biosafety assessment of transgenic potatoes environmental momtoring and food safety evaluation[A] Jones D Proceeding of the 3rd International Symposium on the Biosafety Results of Field Tests of Genetically Modified Plants and Microorganisms[C] .Oakland, California：The University of California. 1994. 245~262.

[16] Mitten D H, Reden baugh M K, Sovero M, Kramer M G. Safety assessment and commercir lization of transgenic fresh tomato food products, transgenic cotton products and transgenie rapeseed oil produets[A]. Casper R.Landsmann J. Proceeding of the 2nd International Symposium on The Biosafety Results of Field Tests of Genetically Modified Plants and Microorganisms[C]. Braunschweig, Germany：Biologische Gundesanstalt FurLan-und Forstwirtschaft. 1992. 179~184

[17] Kuiper H A, Noteborn HPJM. Food safety assessment of transgenic insect-resistant Bt tomatoes[A] OECD. OECD Food Safety Evaluation[C]. Paris: OCED, 1996. 50~57

[18] Noteborn HPJM Kuiper H A. Safety assessment strategies for genctically molified plant products：a case study of Bacillus turingiensis-toxion tomato[A]. Jones D D. proceeding of the 3rd Internstional Sympostom on the Biosafety Results of Field Tests of Genetically Modified Plants and Microorganisms[C] Oakland, California: The University of California. 1994, 199~207

[19] Fuchs R L, Re D B, Rogers S G, *et al.* Safety evaluation of gtyphosate-tolerant soybeans[A]. OECD. Food Safety Evaluation[C]. Paris OCED, 1996. 1996 61~70

[20] Fuchs R L, Re D B, Rogers S G, *et al.* Commercialization of Soybeans with the Roundup ReadyTM gene[A] jones D D Proceeding of the 3rd International Symposium on the Biosafety ResuJts of Field Tests of Genetieally Modified Plants and Microorganisms[C]. Oakland, California: The University of Caifornia, 1994. 233~244

[21] Fuchs R L. Berberich S A, Serdy F S. The biosafety aspects of commercialization insect resistant cotton as a case study[A] Casper R. Landsmann J.Proceeding of the 2nd International Symposium on The Biosafety Results of Field Tests of Genetically Modified Plants and Microorganisms[C]. Braunschweig, Germany：Biologische Gundesanstalt fur Lan-und Forstwirtschaft 1992. 171~178

[22] 陈松，黄骏麒，周宝良，等. 转 Bt-基因抗虫棉棉籽安全性评价——大鼠，鹌鹑毒性试验[J] 江苏农业学报，1996, 12(2)：17~22

[23] Yahiru Y, Kimura Y, Hayakawa T Biosafety results of transgentic rice plants expressing rice stripe virus-coat protem gene[A]. Jones D D. Proceeding of the 3rd lnternational Symposium on the Biosafety Results of Field Tests of Genetically Modified Plants and Microorganisms[C]. Oakland, Cahforma: The University of California 1994. 23~36

[24] Quemada H Food. afety evaluation of a transgenle sguashfA]. OECD. Food safety evatuation[C] Paris：OCED, 1996: 71~79

[25] Zhou R-H. Zhang ZCh.Wu Q, *et al*. Large-seale perfolTnanee of transgenic tobacco plants resistant to both tohacoomosaic viras and cuculmber mcoaic virus[A1 Jones D D Proceeding of the 3rd Internationa] Symposiumon the Biosafetv Results of FieId Tests of Genetically Modified Plants andMicroorganisms [C1.Oakland, California: The University of California. 1994: 49~55

[26] Conner A J. Biosafety evaluation of transgenlc asparagus[A1 Jones D D. Proceeding of the 3rd International Symposimn on the Biosafety Results of Field Tests of Genetlcally Modified Pants and Microorganisms [C]. Oakland California. The Universlty of California, 1994 363~369

[27] Lazarus N The concept of suhstantialequivalence: toximtegieal testing of novel foods [Al. OECD Food Safety Evaluation] C1 Paris: OCED, 1996 98~106

[28] MillstoneE, Brunner E, Mayer S. Beyond ‘Substantial equivalence’ *Nature* 1999, 401: 525~526

[29] Harton R Genetically modified foods: “absurd” concern or Welcome dialogue” [J] *The LANCET*. 1999, 354: 1314-1315

[30] Kurper H A, Noteborn HPJM , Peijnenhurg AACM.Adequacy of methods for testing the safety of genetieally modified foods [J]. *THE LANCE* 1999.354 1315~1316

[31] The Royal Society. Review of data on possible toxicity of GM potatoes[A]. Statement [R] London: The Royalsociety.1999 1~4

本文原载：生物多样性科学：原理与实践. 2001. 陈灵芝，马克平主编. 上海：上海科学技术出版社，191-217

生物技术与生物多样性

魏伟 钱迎倩

(中国科学院植物研究所)

1 生物技术进展

生物技术的发展与生物多样性密不可分，生物多样性是生物技术创新的源泉，发展生物技术则是保护生物多样性的必要手段和重要目的。

《生物多样性公约》对生物技术有专门的定义——生物技术是指使用生物系统、生物体或其衍生物的任何技术应用，以制作或改进特定用途的产品或工艺过程。生物技术的内容繁多，但其中最重要的领域或当今人们最关心的领域是从 20 世纪 70 年代开始的重组 DNA 技术、克隆技术、细胞融合技术和动植物基因工程技术[1]。

1.1 植物基因工程进展

世界范围内已经大面积释放的转基因作物有烟草、棉花、油菜、番茄、马铃薯、大豆和玉米等。1996 年全球转基因作物商品化种植面积为 170 万公顷，到 1997 年面积猛增到 1100 万公顷，到 1998 年时，又比 1997 年翻了一倍多，达到 2780 万公顷。要说明的是这里不包括中国的面积，James 估计中国仅达 10 万公顷，占全球转基因作物面积不到 1%，主要作物是棉花[2]。虽然全球绝对释放面积增加了，但不同作物释放面积增长的速度却不一样。面积相对减少的有番茄、烟草及棉花，而大豆、玉米与油菜却大幅度增加，增加最多的是转基因大豆，全球转基因作物增加面积的 75%是大豆和玉米。转基因作物作为中试向大田释放的国家已经很多，但由于各国政府对转基因作物大面积商品化释放的风险的认识不一致，到 1997 年进行商品化释放的仅限于美国、中国、阿根廷、加拿大、澳大利亚及墨西哥等主要的一些国家，1998 年又增加了西班牙、法国和南非。从 1996 年到 1997 年，这些国家种植转基因作物的绝对面积都有增加，其中美国、阿根廷与加拿大上升的趋势尤其明显。

我国可能是世界上最早大面积释放转基因作物的国家[2]。1992 年，我国抗烟草花叶病毒和黄瓜花叶病毒的双抗转基因烟草在河南省种植面积已达 8000 公顷。1994 年，我国转基因烟草释放面积已达 100 万公顷。其时，国际上仅美国有大面积种植的延迟成熟的转基因番茄，其释放面积远不如我国大[3]。虽然，1997 年我国转基因作物大面积释放面积在国际上还占第二位，但从发展速度来看已远不如美国。整个发展中国家转基因作物商品化种植的面积在 1996 年尚占全球释放面积的近一半，可到 1997 年仅占到 1/4。发达国家转基因作物商品化释放面积增长的速度几乎是发展中国家的 4 倍，1998 年，前者占全球面积的 84%，后者仅占 16%[2]。

虽然国内转基因烟草的释放面积已经远远地超出了环境释放的所允许的范围，但没有进行正式商品化生产的报批程序。另一方面，虽然华中农业大学的转基因耐贮藏番茄，北京大学的转查尔酮合酶基因矮牵牛、转基因抗黄瓜花叶病毒甜椒和转基因抗黄瓜病毒番茄已经获得农业部的批准，可以进行商品化生产，但并没有进行实际上的商品化释放。中国农科院生物技术研究中心的转基因 Bt 棉已经获得在国内商品化生产的许可，1997 年的释放面积为 15 万公顷。另外，美国孟山都公司的一种 Bt 保铃棉也被批准进入中国市场，并在河北省进行了事实上的商品化释放。

转基因作物的经济效益是明显的。在美国，1996 年有 70%的转基因 Bt 抗虫棉没有再喷杀虫剂，而产量提高了 7%。抗虫棉节约的杀虫剂每公顷达 140~280 美元。美国玉米由于欧洲玉米螟而遭受的损失每年达 10 亿美元，种植转基因抗虫玉米后，1996 年和 1997 年两年的平均产量都提高了 9%，经济效益在 1996 年达 1900 万美元，1997 年已到 1 亿 9 千万美元。由于种植了耐除草剂转基因大豆，1996 年少施了 10%~30%除草剂，结果控制了杂草及土壤温度，提高了产量，没有了除草剂的残留物，并且在作物的农艺管理上的灵活性大得多了。1996 年转基因 Bt 抗虫马铃薯也有效地控制了科罗拉多甲虫。

在加拿大，1996 年由于耐除草剂转基因油菜的种植，产量提高了 9%，减少了对除草剂的应用，12 万公顷面积的转基因油菜的经济效益为 600 万美元。在我国，抗病毒的转基因烟草增加了烟草叶片产量 5%~7%，并节约了 2%~3%的杀虫剂用量。

转基因作物的应用除了能够节省费用外，还能够提供方便。抗虫作物可以减轻管理工作的强度，例如可以降低对监视害虫的需求，并杜绝或减少杀虫剂的使用。种植耐除草剂的作物可以使农户简化除草剂的使用程序，而且减少了化学农药的应用。但另一方面，随着耐除草剂作物的增多，农户必须随时关注哪种除草剂可以用于或者哪种除草剂不能用于某一特定作物[4]。

虽然转基因作物带来的惠益是明显的，但是决不能忽视转基因作物所带来的生态风险[2, 5~7]。关于这点，本文将在后面进行论述。

1.2　药物基因工程进展

据丁锡申(1998)报道[8]，至 1997 年 7 月止，美国食品与药物管理署(FDA)已批准上市的基因工程药物、疫苗和注射用单克隆抗体达 39 种，分为 17 类：胰岛素、人生长激素、干扰素、白细胞介素 2、粒细胞集落刺激因子、粒细胞巨噬细胞集落刺激因子、红细胞生成素、组织溶纤原激活剂、生长激素、促生长素、抗血友病因子Ⅷ、葡糖脑苷酯酶、脱氧核糖核酸酶、乙型肝炎疫苗、甲型肝炎疫苗、体内用单克隆抗体、鼠单克隆抗体等。日本共批准上市的基因工程药物 24 种，分为 9 类：干扰素、集落刺激因子、红细胞生成素、肿瘤坏死因子、胰岛素、人生长激素、组织溶纤原激活剂、心钠素和乙型肝炎疫苗。我国已经批准 12 种基因药物和疫苗上市，其中干扰素 5 种，人细胞介素 2 两种，粒细胞集落刺激因子、粒细胞巨噬细胞集落刺激因子、链激酶、红细胞生成素和碱性成纤维细胞生长因子各 1 种。

1.3 动物克隆技术与动物基因工程进展

许多动物如小鼠、绵羊、山羊、牛、猪、马、兔等，都已经用胚胎分割、胚胎嵌合和胚胎干细胞核移植等技术进行了成功的克隆。最近，英国科学家用体细胞克隆了绵羊，打破了只能使用胚胎干细胞克隆动物的传统，是划时代的成果。由于体细胞核移植可以无限制地克隆动物，为培养良种家畜、生产药物、提供能被人体接受的移植器官、建立实验动物模型等开辟了新的途径。

在转基因动物方面，基因工程定向育种、大动物生物反应器研制、人类疾病模型构建以及异体器官移植等方面取得重大进展[9]。1982 年，Palmiter 等成功地将大鼠生长激素重组基因导入小鼠受精原核中。1984~1985 年，Hammer 等得到转基因兔、羊和猪，朱作言等首次将人生长激素基因导入鲤鱼受精卵获得成功；澳大利亚的学者用分离出的猪生长激素基因注入猪的受精卵中，获得了“超级猪”；美国学者将人的基因转移到牛体中，并由转基因公牛授精的母牛生下 5 头健壮的牛犊，这些牛犊均携带有一个人类的基因(HLF)。1987 年，Simons 等将羊β乳球蛋白基因在鼠乳腺中高效表达，Wilmut 等将人的α_1-抗胰蛋白酶基因在羊乳腺中表达。转基因动物模型的出现，为深入研究基因表达调控机制提供了重要途径。在癌基因功能、肿瘤发生以及人类遗传疾病研究中，近年来已建成肌肉营养障碍症、莱-纳二氏综合征及恶性肿瘤发生等多种人类疾病的转基因动物模型，它们是实现基因疗法的重要基础。在异体器官移植研究中，将人类免疫系统有关因子的基因如补体激活调节基因转移至受体动物中，或从受体动物中剔除与人类免疫系统不相容因子的基因，从而用转基因动物建立人类器官移植治疗的组织器官库。

1.4 微生物基因工程进展

至少有下列几种抗虫的、提高固氮能力的或作为狂犬病疫苗的转基因细菌或病菌在 1997 年已经商品化了：苏云金杆菌(*Bacillus thuringien-sis*)、荧光假单孢菌(*Pseudomonas fluorescens*)、苜蓿根瘤菌(*Sinorhizobium melioti*)、牛痘病毒疫苗。

2 生物多样性是生物技术的基础

世界上的动物、植物和微生物等的基因是生物技术尤其是重组 DNA 技术的基础，生物技术依赖于这些基因分子，这些基因分子来源于生物多样性。目前，生物技术的发展和应用一般是这样的：首先是收集和筛选有用的生物资源，找出其基因资源来，或者是直接应用，或者经过修饰或改造后应用。著名学者 E. O. Wilson (1988)指出，对于生物多样性的开发利用是生物技术创新的最重要的源泉。

据报道，世界上有数亿人感染了由活生物引起的疾病，每年有数十亿美元用于应付这些疾病所导致的社会负担[10]。在这些疾病中主要有最严重的三类：由原生动物寄生引起的疟疾、由血吸虫寄生引起的血吸虫病和由 HIV 病毒引起的艾滋病。来自有花植物的药品的销售额达到数十亿美元。与 250 000 种有花植物相比，微生物的多样性程度更高，可成为药物和其他生物技术产品的主要来源[11]。前面已讲过，基因工程带来的经济惠益是明显的，而基因工程的研究和应用将大大地依赖于生物多样性，而且人类将要大量利用尚未被人们所认识的具有重要经济性状的物种多样性和遗传多样性，因而，生物多样性对于生物技术的发展和应用是至关重要的。

然而，摆在人类面前一个严峻的现实是人类对赖以生存的地球肆无忌惮地利用和破坏，它带来的后果是对生物多样性的毁灭。美国全球 2000 年报告指出，2000 年地球上所有物种的 15%~20%丧失。按保守估计现存物种为 300 万~1000 万种，那么到时我们将失去 45 万~200 万物种。据 IUCN 植物中心的保守估计，到 2050 年，6 万种植物将要绝灭或濒临绝灭。如按一种植物有 10~30 种其他生物依赖其生存计，到 2050 年物种绝灭的总数将为 66 万~186 万种，这个数字比自然状态下物种绝灭的速度至少高 25 000 倍。有的科学家预测，按目前人口和工业发展的增长率，在今后 50 年内，人类将毁灭地球上二分之一的动植物物种，即使作出努力来保护世界的生物多样性，物种的四分之一仍将在 100 年内绝灭。WCMC(世界保护监测中心)1993 年指出，全世界有 2.5 万种植物面临绝灭的威胁，另有 1 万种植物已经消灭[1]。自然进化赋予人类大量的生物多样性财富正以惊人的速度遭到毁灭，大量的物种或基因在尚未知道其用途前就已经在地球上绝灭。因此，从发展并发挥生物技术巨大潜力的角度来看，保护生物多样性也应该成为生物技术工作者的紧迫任务。

3 生物技术在生物多样性保护和持续利用中的作用

尽管现在我们已经拥有抗生素、疫苗以及良好的卫生条件和饮食，然而，许多从前已经消灭的疾病又在复发，而且新的疾病又不断出现，很多从前被认为是非病原菌的生物，现在发现是病原菌[10]。因此，需要应用生物技术去寻找新的遗传多样性并开发和研究基因资源，获得有效的药物和治疗方法。生物技术可以帮助我们降低对生物资源的需求[12]，例如可以种植高品质的作物，在不增加对资源需求的同时提高产量；通过生物技术还可以对工业产品进行再循环利用并减少工业产品对环境的污染，降低对自然资源的消耗，达到保护生物多样性的目的。生物技术在生物多样性保护和持续利用中的作用将分以下几点进行论述。

3.1 检测生物多样性，并对未知物种进行定名和描述

迄今为止，我们所知道的已经定名的物种仅仅是现存物种的一小部分[11](表 1)。要预测生物多样性的未来，并保护和持续利用生物多样性，必须对地球上的生物多样性进行

完整的调查。然而，面对如此多的未知物种和如此复杂的生物多样性，普通的分类手段往往力不从心，这就需要现代生物学技术的介入。生物技术在检测生物多样性并对未知物种进行定名和描述中的作用表现在以下几个方面。

表 1　地球上已知物种和估计物种的数量[11]

类　群	已知物种	估计的总的物种	已知物种所占百分比
病毒 Viuses	500	13 万	4
细菌 Bacteria	4760	4 万	12
真菌 Fungi	69 000	150 万	5
藻类 Alga	40 000	6 万	67
苔藓植物 Bryophytes	17 000	2.5 万	68
裸子植物 Gymnosperms	750		
被子植物 Angiosperms	250 000	27 万	93
原生动物 Protozoa	30 800	10 万	31
海绵动物 Porifera	5000		
刺胞动物 Cnidaria	9000		
线虫 Nemarodes	15 000	50 万	3
甲壳纲 Crustacea	38 000		
昆虫 Insects	800 000	600 万~1000 万	8~13
节肢动物/小无脊椎动物 Arthropod/minor inverrtebrates	132 460		
软体动物 Molluscs	50 000		
棘皮动物 Echinoderms	6100		
两栖动物 Amphibians	4184		
爬行动物 Reptile	6380		
鱼类 Fishes	19 000	2.1 万	90
鸟类 Birds	9198		约 100
哺乳动物 Mammals	4170		约 100

1. 系统分类学

(1) 分子系统分类，通过 DNA 碱基对差异的研究，可以将形态上类似但遗传上不同的品种分开。

(2) 化学系统分类，就是对整个生物体或细胞进行生物化学成分的分析，达到分类和鉴定的目的。

2. 对微生物体的培养和筛选

(1) 对人类有用途的微生物资源都是从自然界收集和分离而来，需要用生物技术将它们进行培养和筛选，以达到应用的目的。

(2) 借助微生物分类和鉴定的进展并结合药物筛选程序的要求，可以发展新的选择培养基来培养稀有的、不常见的或新的微生物体，特别是放线菌纲的微生物体[11]。另外，许多极端环境中的微生物，在实验室条件下根本就不能够培养，更谈不上对它们的定名和描述了，因而迫切需要发展生物技术来解决这一技术难题。

3. 揭示生物的遗传多样性

(1) 基于 RNA 分子标记技术，应用基于 5S、16S 和 23S rRNA 的探针并结合 RNA 分子的提取、分离和测序，可以用来确定新的系统发育亲缘关系[11]。Woese 等(1990)利用 16S rRNA 划分了一个界(Kingdom)以上的分类单位——域(Domain)，并认为，按照 16S rRNA，地球上的生命可以分为三个域，即细菌域(Bacteria)、原核生物域(Arehaea)和真核生物域(Eukaya)。一旦选择了合适的 rRNA 探针，就可以在域、界、门、属或种的水平上分析群落的组成[11]。

(2) 基于 DNA 的分子标记技术，可分为以下几类：

① 以传统的 DNA 杂交为基础的分子标记技术：限制性片段长度多态性(RFLP)、单链构象多态性 RFLP(SSCP-RFLP)和变性梯度凝胶电泳 RFLP (DGGE-RFLP)。

② 以聚合酶链反应(PCR)为基础的分子标记技术：随机扩增多态性 DNA(RAPD)、标记位点测序(STS)、扩增片段测序(SCAR)、随机引物 PCR(AP-PCR)、单链构象多态性 PCR(SSCR-PCR)、小寡核苷酸 DNA 分析(SODA)、DNA 扩增指纹(DAF)和扩增片段长度多态性(AFLP)等。

③ 以重复序列为基础的标记技术：卫星 DNA、简单重复序列(SSR)、可变数量串联重复(VNTR)等。

以上标记技术可以用来区分形态上类似但遗传上不同的品种，在检测遗传多样性方面用处极大。

3.2 生物技术在生物多样性迁地保护中的作用

迁地保护是生物多样性保护的重要方面，生物技术在其中发挥着巨大的作用。Conway(1989)[13]列出了适用于动物迁地保护的生物技术，例如人工授精、选择性育种、胚胎移植、胚胎切割、克隆、短期圈养繁殖和再引入自然以及长期圈养繁殖等，并且给出了适用某种生物技术进行保护的动物，如金丝小绢猴、印度豹、红狼、美洲和欧洲野牛、阿拉伯长角羚羊、游隼、加拉帕哥斯陆地鬣蜥等应使用短期繁殖和再引入的生物技术进行保护，而人工授精技术适用于鳄鱼、大熊猫、黄狒狒、曲角羚羊、大羚羊和红褐色美洲驼等的保护，胚胎移植技术则适用于非洲旋角大羚羊、摩弗伦羊、斑马和狨等的保护。

有人提出来[14]，将现在受威胁的生物体冷冻起来以保存生物多样性，以便在将来应用。这一方法的最大好处就是直接尽最大可能地取样，而不必考虑哪些物种更有用。现代生物技术的发展，使得这个设想变得更加现实和更加有意义。虽然在植物种子保存及动物的胚胎移植和冷冻方面还存在许多问题，但是已有数十种鸟类、哺乳类的生殖细胞冷冻取得成功。

3.3 解决外来种问题

外来种已经产生并将继续产生对农业、商业、环境和生物多样性的不可估量的危害[15]。例如，由于一种外来鱼种的引入，巴拿马 Gatun 湖中 8 个普通鱼种有 6 种消亡，种群骤减了 1/7，使食物链遭到严重破坏。现代生物技术，特别是分子生物学和免疫生物学使我们在了解生物的遗传结构和抗病方面取得巨大的进展，及时地借助它们并结合相关领域的方法，我们会找到解决问题的方法。运用雄性不育产品、基因工程产品、特定宿主的病原体、人工诱导遗传负荷、抑制免疫性、调控繁殖的遗传基础和性引诱剂等，可能会在 10 年内消除大多数的外来种。

3.4 解决小种群中遗传变异的丧失和有害突变固定的问题

在小种群中，遗传变异的丧失和有害突变的固定是不可逆且不可避免的。经过插入和诱导遗传突变，可以补偿由遗传漂变而造成的后果[15]。用生物技术可以克隆并将这种用途的基因转移到生物体中，也可以在发育的早期阶段去除或替代“坏”的基因。因而，应用生物技术能够阻止基因的有害突变，并恢复遗传多样性。

4 生物技术与生物安全

4.1 《生物多样性公约》与生物安全

生物技术改变的活生物体[注：改变的活生物体在《生物多样性公约》英文文本上是 Living modifed organism(LMO)，确切的含义是经过遗传修饰的活生物体]或其产品的释放，它是人们普遍关注的问题。对于这个问题，《生物多样性公约》第 8 条“就地保护”的 g 款写道：“制定或采取办法酌情管制、管理或控制由生物技术改变的活生物体在使用和释放时可能产生的危险，即可能对环境产生不利影响，从而影响到生物多样性的保护和持续利用，也要考虑到对人类健康的危险”。为了最大限度地减小生物技术的社会和生态的潜在危险，世界资源研究所(WRI)等扼要给出了使用生物技术的行为准则[12]：

(1) 各国应在发展和检测新的生物技术之前，首先提高监测和控制它们的能力。

(2) 对释放遗传修饰生物体可能存在的危险进行仔细评估，对于遗传多样性丰富的地方尤要如此。

(3) 各国对进口遗传修饰生物体等材料应严加管理。

(4) 严格控制生物技术，以防止由于利用新技术而使得动、植物品种过分单一化，如植物材料的克隆繁殖和转移家畜胚胎的方法。

(5) 禁止发展、试验和应用生物技术用于军事目的，例如不得用来制造生物武器。

(6) 在国家和国际水平上建立补偿机制，以支持受损害的农业社区和国家，而这种损害是由于利用生物技术创造的新作物取代原有作物造成的。

(7) 应建立早期预警网络，以监测生物技术对社会与经济带来的压力及其对生物多样性的影响，防止一些小型的农场被迫迁至更边远地区。

(8) 应制定生物技术的国际行为准则，以在各层次管理生物技术。

有关对生物技术改变的活生物体的安全转让、处理、使用以及引进等问题，《生物多样性公约》第19条“生物技术的处理及其惠益的分配”中有明确的说明。第19条第3，款上指出：“缔约国应考虑是否需要一项议定书，规定适当程序，特别包括事先知情协议，适用于可能对生物多样性的保护和持续利用产生不利影响的生物技术改变的任何活生物体的安全转让、处理和使用，并考虑该议定书的形式。”第4款规定“每一个缔约国应直接或要求其管辖下提供以上第3款所指生物体的任何自然人和法人，将该缔约国在处理这种生物体方面规定的使用和安全条例的任何现有资料以及有关该生物体可能产生的不利影响的任何现有资料，提供给将要引进这些生物体的缔约国。”此后，生物安全议定书的拟定就成为生物多样性公约缔约国大会一项重要工作内容，到1998年8月已召开了四次关于生物安全议定书的“特设专家工作组”会议，并给出了议定书的初稿，供特别缔约国大会讨论，计划到1998年12月底，最迟不晚于1999年2月底，完成生物安全议定书，并召开“议定书”实施大会。但是议定书内容涉及一系列的政治与经济利益问题，部分发达国家和大部分发达国家与发展中国家(主要是以美国为首的迈阿密集团)间存在很大分歧，至1999年2月底议定书并未达成协议。

按照1992年签署的《生物多样性公约》的规定，需要建立生物技术改变的活生物体安全管理的国际性统一准则，1994年缔约国第一次大会一致同意成立生物安全专家小组，先商讨制定“国际生物技术安全的技术准则”。1995年12月，联合国环境规划署(UNEP)在开罗发布了《国际生物技术安全管理的技术准则》[16]，这个技术准则包括6部分的正文，即导言、总则、风险评价和管理、安全管理的国家级和区域机制、安全管理的国际性机制以及能力建设，另外还有7个附录。

4.2 遗传修饰生物体的安全问题

基因工程是生物技术领域中的重要组成部分，近年来飞速发展，已向人们展示了其在解决21世纪人类面临挑战中的潜力，这在前文已有论述。然而，就在重组DNA技术发展的早期，一些科学家提出这一技术潜在的生物学和生态学风险，需要对该技术及其产品的释放进行认真的评估。遗传修饰生物体释放可能带来的生态学风险大致可以分为以下几个方面。

4.2.1 转基因生物的入侵风险

我们可以用外来种入侵的经验来评价转基因生物体对自然生境的入侵风险[17]。前文

3.3 提到了外来种会对生物多样性造成危害,为了更好地获得有关转基因生物体入侵风险的经验，在这里首先讨论一下外来种对自然生态系统的入侵。为了控制另外一个引入种，Moorea 岛引入了一种蜗牛，结果使当地六种蜗牛几乎全部消失。1988 年，来自加勒比的螺旋蝇(screwworm)传入利比亚，它携带着其寄生菌传播了 10 万公里，在北非，它威胁了 7000 头牲畜的生命，并且可能已传到非洲的亚撒哈拉地区、中东、欧洲和南亚[12]。在大不列颠，主要有 14 种入侵者成为有害植物，虽然其中的加拿大眼子菜的危害程度已有所降低[17]。外来种入侵对生态系统造成破坏的原因可能是它们在入侵地缺少天敌。

针对入侵，有的学者总结出了一个粗放的 10%~10%规律，适用于所有的动植物，即 10%的外来物种定居成功，10%的定居者成为有害生物。对于转基因生物体的入侵来讲，这个规律意味着其大多数不能够定居，而大部分的定居者不会产生生态学影响，然而很小部分的有害定居者将产生显著的生态学效应，而那些没有成为有害生物的定居者在某些方面或某些地点可能仍然会产生不利影响[17]。

很多人认为，栽培作物的生长要依赖于人类的培育，在自然界中不能够独立生存。实际上这是不正确的[17]。在邻近耕作地的同一地区，栽培作物可以生长得很好。更不要说获得了优良性状的转基因作物了。已有证据表明，Bt 基因提高了转基因甘蓝型油菜在田间的适合度[18]。而且导致新物种入侵的主要因素是人为干扰，在这种情况下，转基因生物体以杂草性策略入侵,这种策略增加了转基因生物体在不稳定环境中存留的可能性。

4.2.2 转基因逃逸的风险

通过转基因作物与其野生亲缘种间的基因流动所造成的转基因逃逸是转基因作物释放后可能带来风险的重要方面[7]。转基因可以通过传粉在空间上逃逸，也可以通过种子库在时间上逃逸，并通过转基因作物与其野生亲缘种的杂交种在自然界中存留。在存留的过程中，在适合的条件下，转基因作物与其野生亲缘种的杂交种可以与其野生亲本不断回交，转基因进入野生亲本的遗传背景，完成了转基因在时空上的逃逸。

许多栽培作物都驯化自野生植物，在自然界中，这些作物都存在自己的野生亲缘种[7]。例如，玉米(*Zea mays* ssp., *nays*)的野生亲缘种为玉米草(teosinite)(产于墨西哥和中美洲)，这里玉米草是玉米的不同野生亲缘类群的统称，包括 *Zea diplopemis*、*Z.perennis*、*Z. luxurioas*、*Z. mays* ssp. *mexicana*、*Z.mays* ssp. *parviglumis* 和 *Z. mays* ssp. *huehuetenangensis*。除了 *Z. perennis* 外，所有的玉米草都可与栽培玉米形成杂种。甘蓝型油菜(*Brassica napus*)可与很多的亲缘种，如芜菁(*B. rapa*)、*B. adpressa*、*Sinpisarvensis* 和野生小萝卜(*Raphanus raphanistrum*)等杂交，而且截止于 1992 年所报道的转基因植物的 400 例释放中，就有 80 例是转基因甘蓝型油菜的释放，因此应当引起对甘蓝型油菜转基因逃逸问题的重视。栽培水稻(*Oryza sativa*)则可与其野生亲缘种红水稻和 *O.perennis* 杂交。世界银行的一份报告[2]也列举了野生稻的例子来说明转基因逃逸的问题。“报告”指出，转基因水稻如与起源的野生种同在一个区域时，水稻中的转基因会转移到野生稻中去。

在某些条件下，某些作物的近缘种是危害很大的杂草(例如野生稻和阿拉伯高粱)。如果一种野生植物被能抗拒自然发生病虫害的转基因提高适合度的话，这种植物就可能变成极坏的害草，可以破坏自然群落的生态平衡。一般来讲，杂草常常通过自然进化的过程而进化出对病虫害或其他性状的抗性。例如，在澳大利亚，大量使用除草剂草甘膦已使杂草产生了抗性，而来自转基因植物的转基因逃逸可加速这个过程。如果商品化稻田里的野生稻得到了来自抗除草剂转基因水稻的抗除草剂基因，则野生稻的危害更大[2]。又如，在美国，普遍存在野葫芦一类的野生南瓜近缘种，如果能抗多种病毒的转基因南瓜的抗病毒基因一旦转入那些对黄瓜斑纹病毒和西瓜斑纹病毒敏感的野生种，后果将是严重的。因而有许多学者反对美国农业部(USDA)和 FDA 批准这种转基因南瓜上市。

目前，转入作物的特性(inserted traits)以抗除草剂的为多，其次是抗虫和抗病毒，最后是抗逆。当这些转基因逃逸且逐渐在野生种群中固定下来以后，就使得作物的野生亲缘种具有了获得选择优势的潜在可能性。如果获得选择优势的野生亲缘种本身就是杂草，那么就会为该杂草的控制增加很大的困难。也有学者认为，转基因在野生种群中的固定将导致野生等位基因的丢失而造成遗传多样性的丧失[19]。从目前的研究来看，转基因在时空上的逃逸不可避免，因而需要控制和管理转基因作物与其野生亲缘种间的基因流动。目前比较常用的是物理隔离的方法，但用物理隔离来实现完全的牵制(containment)似乎不可能，这时就可以用雄性不育的品种来阻止转基因花粉的逃逸[20]。虽然，雄性不育品种在阻止转基因花粉传播方面是非常有效的，但是仍然不能够阻断转基因作物与其野生亲缘种间的基因流动[10]。例如，在一个对转基因甘蓝型油菜与野生小萝卜间基因流动的研究中，Chevre 等(1997) [21]用雄性不育的转基因油菜作为母本与野生小萝卜进行杂交，随着几个世代的回交，杂种的可育能力逐渐提高，接近野生小萝卜，虽然转基因的传递在第 2 个世代以后逐渐降低，但其风险是不容忽视的。

4.2.3 抗病毒转基因作物可以产生新的病毒

目前广泛应用的抗病毒基因来自植物病毒本身。在过去 10 年间，转基因作物试验了不少转基因，最广泛试验的是能产生病毒外壳蛋白的基因，其中一些转病毒外壳蛋白基因植物在美国已被批准可以进行商品化释放，关于这一点前文已有论述，在这里不再重复。含有病毒基因的转基因抗病毒作物释放的最受关注的一个风险就是转基因有可能会与其他病毒重组，从而产生新的、甚至是更具毒性的病毒。在实验室内和田间条件下，已有了转基因与其他病毒基因重组产生新的病毒的例子，并且会使非病原病毒转变成病原病毒[2]。世行的报告承认很多作物同时可被多种病毒侵染，但认为不同病毒之间发生遗传重组的例子很少，并认为即使在类病毒与病毒株系间有重组证据，但没有证据表明转基因作物中的重组会比正常情况下发生重组的频率高。所以最终的结论是已有的证据还不足以支持病毒的重组将引起生态风险。

周雪平等(1997)第一次在乌干达木薯中证实非洲木薯花叶病毒(ACMV)和东非木薯花叶病毒(EACMV)能重组形成杂种病毒[2]。这是国际上第一个植物病毒种间重组形成杂种病毒造成严重流行病的例子，这种杂种病毒正在毁灭整个乌干达的木薯，损失已达 6000 万美元。目前这种新病毒已向肯尼亚和苏丹等国蔓延。随后的一篇报道中，Harrison 等(1997)将这种由 ACMV 和 EACMV 重组形成的杂种病毒称为乌干达变种(UgV)。他们发现，由于 UgV 能够侵染已被 ACMV 侵染过的植株，因而在 UgV 和 ACMV

间又发生重组形成又一种新的杂种病毒，其影响要比ACMV严重得多。1998年，周雪平等又在巴基斯坦棉花卷叶病毒中发现重组现象并形成杂种病毒。这三个例子有力地说明了不同种的病毒确实可在作物体内重组，新的杂种病毒可能引发流行病，并给作物带来毁灭性的打击。由于转基因作物中的病毒基因在所有细胞和所有时间内都存在，从而提高了重组的风险，因此当转基因作物释放面积达到上百万亩，这些作物又都在表达病毒基因时，后果将难以预料[22]。含有病毒基因的转基因抗病毒作物释放的风险可以归结为以下几个方面[2]：

(1) 人们普遍担心食品中的病毒蛋白可能会引起过敏反应。但世行报告中指出，不必再担心这个问题了，因为很多用来制作食品的作物都会受到植物病毒的侵染，这么多年来人们食用后并没有不良反应。比如，水果或蔬菜均会感染病毒，人们生食水果或蔬菜，实际上是每天都在摄入病毒外壳蛋白。

(2) 抗病毒植物在大田中可能会表现出竞争有利性，与杂草杂交后会增加其竞争性和使其杂草化。

(3) 由转基因作物产生的病毒外壳蛋白可以和自然界的病毒结合而产生更为有害的病毒株，产生这样的病毒株在理论上是可能的，但在评价转基因作物中，它的风险真是太低了。

(4) 除外壳蛋白基因以外，其他病毒基因可以引起较大的安全问题。不产生蛋白质但能提供抗性的编码RNA的基因容易得到批准，因为它们没有产生风险的科学依据。但不清楚其他的基因是否会得到批准。能减少被一种病毒侵染的可能性，但却提高了被其他病毒侵染的那些病毒基因可能是得不到批准的，除非把它们突变了并只能在防护状态下起作用。

4.2.4 转基因作物释放对土壤生态系统及生物地球化学循环的影响

转基因作物对土壤生物的影响，不仅包括初级基因产品，也包括来自生物和非生物反应所产生的次级产品的影响。土壤中的生物体通过捕食、竞争、对抗或共生而发生相互作用，一旦环境由于转基因产品的释放而发生改变，一些敏感生物体快速发生反应，达到一定程度时，其他生物也发生反应，从而影响到整个土壤生态系统[23]。转基因产品进入土壤有许多途径，其中最重要的途径是作物收获后，其残留物回到土壤中。其次，还可以随着根的分泌物进入根际的土壤生物圈。土壤生物群受转基因产品引入影响的程度依赖于很多因素，其中最重要的是土壤生态系统的复杂性和稳定性。那些简单并缺少生物多样性的生态系统容易受到进入土壤的转基因产品的影响。种植单一作物的农业生态系统相对比较简单，因而对于干扰比较敏感。相反，森林生态系统多样性程度高，相对比较稳定，因而其土壤生物群就不太容易因转基因产品的进入而发生迅猛的变化。土壤生物群因转基因产品引入而发生的一个微妙而重要的变化是土壤生物多样性的变动。生态系统中的多样性可以用种、属成分来测定，也可以应用分子生物学手段和数量分类的方法。对生物多样性的评价要包括好些对生态系统变化敏感以及对转基因产品敏感的每一种类，然后用多样性指数来确定多样性的变化。Angle(1994)[23]综述了土壤中病毒、细菌、真菌、藻类、地衣、原生动物、微动物群、中型动物群和大型动物群可能对转基因产品发生的反应，并建议了测度其多样性的方法。Widmer 等(1996)发现，重组 DNA 进入土壤后，有一定的存留期[24]。在实验条件下，无论烟草叶子 DNA 还是质粒 DNA 进入土壤后的降解开始都比较快，但仍有少量 DNA 能够抵抗降解并且几个月内都能检出它们的存在，其原因可能是这些 DNA 被土壤颗粒吸收了，这样能够保护它们被完全降解[24]。重组 DNA 在土壤中能够存留较长的一段时间，增加了转基因产物进入土壤后向土壤生物体进行基因转移的生态风险性[25]。

转基因植物及其产物进入土壤以后，可能会与土壤微生物发生相互作用，影响到一些微生物的活动过程，而后者对生物地球化学循环有着重要的贡献，从而转基因植物对生物地球化学循环产生了重要影响。转基因植物与土壤微生物间可能的相互作用的例子如下[25]：

(1) 转基因植物中的 DNA 转移到土壤中自然生长的微生物体内。

(2) 重组事件使得一些细菌的固氮能力丧失。

(3) 长期持续种植转基因作物所导致的重组事件，将会改变微生物的代谢途径。

(4) 重组 DNA 和基因产物(蛋白质)会流入作为饮用水源的地下水中。

(5) 转基因植物材料进入土壤将会刺激植物病原微生物具有比非病原体更强的竞争力。

转基因植物对生物地球化学循环的影响依赖于土壤类型和质地、气候条件以及转基因植物的种类等因素。需要检验对土壤地球化学循环可能产生影响的转基因植物有：① 增进对植物营养的吸收的；② 改变了直接或间接产物，或者是对营养元素的利用的(如固氮、光合)；③ 对特异植物病原微生物有毒性的或抗土壤微生物降解作用的；④ 其利用痕量元素作为辅助因子的酶类被修饰了的。Trevors 等(1994)[25]给出了简单的研究实验方法：选择一些简单的容易测度的微生物过程(活动)，研究转基因植物材料及基因产物对这些过程(活动)的影响，并且一个过程(活动)受到影响有可能会间接地影响另外的过程。这些过程可以包括酶的活性(如脱氢酶、磷酸酶、几丁质酶、过氧化氢酶和纤维素酶等)，二氧化碳放出，氧消耗，氢消耗，硝化作用，反硝化作用，需氧的、厌氧的及非共生的固氮作用(共生的固氮作用比较难于估测)，甲烷发生，各种基质的矿化作用(C、N、S、P)，硫氧化作用。也可以研究转基因植物一次或多次释放对土壤生物过程(如硝化作用)的影响，以对照转基因存在和不存在时土壤生物地球化学过程的变化。

4.2.5　害虫对转 Bt 抗虫植物的抗性风险

迄今为止，在实验室选择条件下对 Bt 产生抗性的害虫有[6]：鳞翅目(Lepidoptera)——烟芽夜蛾(*Heliothis virescens*)、甜菜夜蛾(*Spaloptera exigua*)、海灰翅夜蛾(*S. littoralis*)、粉纹夜蛾(*Trichoplusia ni*)、欧洲玉米螟(*Ostrinia nubilalis*)、地中海粉螟(*Anagasta kuehniella*)、粉斑螟(*Cadra cautella*)、向日葵斑螟(*Homoeosoma electellum*)、印度谷螟(*Plodia interpunctella*)、枞色卷蛾(*Choristoneura funiferana*)，鞘翅目(Coleoptrea)——黑杨叶甲(*Chrysomela scripta*)、马铃薯甲虫(*Leptinctarsa decemilineata*)，双翅目(Diptera)——埃及伊蚊(*Aedes aegypti*)、五带淡色库蚊(*Culex quinquefas-clatus*)、黄猩猩果蝇(*Drosophila melanogaster*)、家蝇(*Musca domestica*)。其中，只有一种害虫——小菜蛾在田间进化出了

对 Bt 的抗性。

由于转 Bt 基因植物能够持续地高水平表达单一的杀虫毒蛋白，因此 Bt 植物对害虫造成的选择压力甚至比 Bt 杀虫剂还要高，Bt 植物的释放将会加速害虫的抗性进化。至 1997 年的早些时候，在已经或即将被批准上市的大约 80 种转基因作物中，有 21 种是转 Bt 作物，其中 11 种是 Bt 玉米，Bt 马铃薯和棉花各 5 种，其他还有 20 余种成功转 Bt 毒蛋白基因的例子[6]。有的只是田间试验，有的仅仅是获得了转基因植株，但它们的商业化释放只是一个时间问题。在迄今为止所报道的在田间或实验室条件下对 Bt 杀虫剂产生抗性的 17 种害虫中，有很大一部分是目前转基因植物的目标害虫[6]。沈晋良等(1998)发现，棉铃虫对 Bt 生物农药与对 Bt 植株间存在着交互抗性，并指出棉铃虫对 Bt 农药产生早期抗性的地区，种植 Bt 棉时，可能会直接影响到其抗虫效果和使用寿命[26]。

害虫快速适应一种杀虫剂的风险主要依赖于田间野生种群中的初始抗性等位基因频率[27]。目前广泛使用的抗性等位基因的初始频率值是 10^{-2}~10^{-13}，它是基于突变——选择理论的一个估计值。Crow 和 Kimura 的这个理论认为：有利选择前，在种群中任何一个等位基因频率的保持，都是由突变产生新等位基因和对杂合体进行选择两者之间平衡作用的结果[28]。当然，选择也应该作用于纯合个体，但由于稀少而被 Crow 和 Kimura 忽略不计，这个错误导致低估了隐性抗性等位基因的初始频率，其结果是低估了害虫对 Bt 作物产生抗性的风险。Tabashnik 等(1997)发现小菜蛾中的初始抗性等位基因频率为 0.12, 10 倍于目前被广泛引用的感性群体中抗性等位基因初始频率的最大估计值[29]。Gould 等(1997)采用一种较新颖的实验设计，确定了隐性纯合个体存在的频率[27]，能够检测出隐性纯合个体，意味着灵敏度提高了 2000 倍，这对正确估计田间条件下，感性种群中隐性抗性等位基因的初始频率是至关重要的，获得了正确的估计，对害虫的抗性风险也就可能有了正确的认识和评价。

4.2.6 转基因植物产生的杀虫剂对非目标生物的影响的风险

目前已经商品化的抗虫转基因植物就是能够产生 Bt 杀虫蛋白的转基因作物。Sims 和 Holden(1996)发现，Bt 玉米收获后，其残留组织中的杀虫蛋白需要 15~ 47 天的消散时间[30]。非目标生物体就有可能接触到这些残留的杀虫蛋白。虽然，Bt 棉和 Bt 马铃薯的杀虫蛋白对一种弹尾虫和一种奥甲螨没有产生负面影响[31]。但是，Bt 杀虫蛋白对非目标生物影响的潜在风险不容忽视。瑞士联邦农业生态和农业研究站的科学家们研究了 Bt 玉米对一种益虫——绿草蛉(*Chrysoperla cama*)的间接影响[32]。绿草蛉是以欧洲玉米螟为食的，研究者用分别取自转基因 Bt 玉米和非转基因玉米的欧洲玉米螟喂食绿草蛉，发现食用采自 Bt 玉米的玉米螟的绿草蛉，与对照相比，其死亡率较高，发育比较延迟。

5 转基因生物体释放的生态学风险评价

生态学风险可被定义为释放一种新的生物材料引起非目标生物体种群大量死亡或缩减等有害影响的可能性，这种可能性是由于对生殖的影响或对生态系统功能的破坏所引起的。对于转基因生物体的生态学风险评价可以借助于有关生态毒理学中有毒化合物释放对环境风险评价的经验和方法[5]。转基因生物体释放的生态学风险评价思想可以抽象为下列公式：

$$风险=危险的严重性\times可能发生的概率 \quad (1)$$

对于风险的评价需要一定的程序，在基因组、个体、种、生态系统的不同水平上进行[33]。并且对于转基因生物体释放风险的评价，必须随释放或评价对象的不同以及规模的不同而有所不同。这里的释放规模一般包括中间试验、环境释放和商业化生产等几个阶段。下面就一些主要的备受关注的转基因生物体释放风险的评价作简要论述。

5.1 转基因逃逸风险的评价

5.1.1 转基因花粉传播的测度方法

一般认为转基因花粉的传播是转基因在空间上逃逸的主要渠道，也是转基因作物与其野生亲缘种间基因流动的主要原因。测度转基因花粉传播的研究方法主要包括亲本分析、花粉计数、花粉收集及花粉活力测试等[33]。亲本分析的目的是辨出特定基因型母株所产种子的可能父本，也就是可能的花粉供体用以鉴定基因流动的存在。花粉计数可以用来估计花粉的产量等，与花粉收集相结合可以用来测度花粉的传播。花粉的活力影响着传粉的效果，研究花粉活力的一个直接的方法是实验性授粉，结实情况作为花粉粒活力的测度。在转基因花粉传播的研究中，转基因作物的栽培设计比较重要。一般是在实验地中心设一个转基因作物的样方，周围种植同一品种的非转基因植株或其亲缘种，于作物成熟期在不同方向的不同距离上取一定面积的样方或一定数量的植株或种子(果实)，分析成熟种子或果实中转基因存在的频率，作为转基因传粉的频率。

5.1.2 鉴定转基因存在的方法

在上述实验设计中，非转基因作物或其亲缘种的后代中转基因的存在是转基因逃逸的测度，也是转基因作物与其野生亲缘种之间基因流动产生杂交种的证据。一般来讲，采用向非转基因作物或其野生亲缘种后代的幼苗喷洒除草剂的方法，能够筛选出带有抗除草剂目的基因或标记基因的杂种后代，以鉴定转基因逃逸的存在。然而，对于其他类型的转基因，只能应用间接的方法确定转基因的存在，包括形态学特征分析、细胞学分析(如减数分裂和染色体配对分析)、蛋白质及同工酶电泳分析、DNA 分子标记分析(AFLP、PCR、RAPD，RFLP 以及 DNA 测序等)以及统计分析(如 F-统计)等[33]。当然这些分析方法在研究工作中是互为补充的。目前，转基因存在的鉴定方法一般是用特定引物扩增基因片段或者用特定探针与可能含有转基因的总 DNA 进行 DNA 杂交。

5.1.3 评价转基因逃逸的数学模型

Bateman(1947)给出了距离对风媒和虫媒传粉污染影响的三个方程式，并将它们近似地合并成一个：

$$F=\left(Ye^{-kD}\right)/D \quad (2)$$

这里，F 是花粉污染的比率，D 是距离，Y 是隔离距离为零时的污染[34]。

Manasse(1992)给出了评价基因流动的指数模型[35]。他的模型类似于方程(2)，然而更加完善，适合于评价转基因作物与其野生亲缘种间的基因流动。Manasse (1992)在研究中发现，随着植物丛或个体间距离的增加，一年中基因传播的平均距离也在增加。这就意味着伴随着长距离隔离，一个罕见的长距离传粉事件会增加转基因逃逸的风险。

Kareiva 等(1994)给出了一个与 Manasse (1992)的指数模型类似的可靠性函数(reliability function)[20]：

$$R(x)=\exp\left(-ax^{b}\right) \tag{3}$$

$R(x)$ 是花粉传播到距离 x 的可能性，其平均数等于 $1/a\Gamma(b+1)/b$，变异等于 $1/a^{2}\left[\Gamma(b+2)/b-\Gamma^{2}(b+1/b)\right]$。当 $b=1$ 时，这个可靠性函数为：

$$R(x)=\exp(-ax) \tag{4}$$

成为一个指数函数。

由于植物可以接受各种来源(包括自身)的花粉，来自转基因植物的花粉可能只是柱头上总花粉的一小部分，所以可以用异交的数据来估计一个参数 c，也就是离转基因作物零距离时污染的估计。

获得一个含转基因的种子的概率与 $R(x)$ 成比例：

$$L=\prod_{k=1}^{N}\binom{S_k}{M_k}\left[cR(x)\right]^{M_k}\left[1-cR(x)\right]^{S_k-M_k} \tag{5}$$

其中：S_k=第 k 个取样点采集的种子数；

$M_k=S_k$ 中含有转基因的种子数；

N=取样点的数量。

对于风险评价来说，需要的不是在某一距离上的传粉频率，而是描述一个转基因在一个或几个方向上传播到某一特定距离以外的可能性，这就是累积密度函数(cumulative density function, *c. d. f.*)[36]：

$$c.d.f.=\Gamma(\alpha,\beta)/\Gamma(\beta) \tag{6}$$

这里，α 为 ax^{b}，β 为 $1/b$(一个方向)或 $2/b$ (所有方向)，$\Gamma(\alpha,\beta)$ 是不完全伽玛函数，$\Gamma(\beta)$ 是完全伽玛函数。

5.2 转基因生物体入侵的风险评价

5.2.1 转基因生物体与自然种群竞争的风险评价

转基因生物体进入自然界后，其最主要的风险是它可能会与自然种群发生竞争作用，尤其是那些获得了选择有利优势的转基因生物。这种竞争可以用群落中的种间竞争来描述。

20 世纪 20 年代中期，Lotka 和 Voltena 分别独立地提出了 Lotka-Volterra 竞争模型。

Kareiva 等(1996)[37]认为可以用 Lotka-Voltena 竞争模型来预测转基因入侵的后果。他们将有关的参数定义以后，用来预测一种(缺失突变)遗传修饰微生物体 *Pseudomonas syringae* 品系同其野生品系间的竞争：

$$\mathrm{d}N^{+}/\mathrm{d}t = r^{+}N^{+}\left(1 - N^{+}/K^{+} - a_{-+}N^{-}/K^{+}\right) \tag{7}$$

$$\mathrm{d}N^{-}/\mathrm{d}t = r^{-}N^{-}\left(1 - N^{-}/K^{-} - a_{+-}N^{+}/K^{-}\right) \tag{8}$$

这里，N^+ 和 N^- 分别是野生型和缺失型的种群密度，r^+和r^- 分别是野生型和缺失型的种群内禀增长率，K^+和K^- 是各自的环境容纳量，a_{-+}和a_{+-} 则分别是各自的竞争系数。

模型预测结果发现，通过竞争，缺失型不可能替代野生型。但研究者同时也指出，在其他有利于缺失型的物理或者说生物条件下会得出不同的结果。

转基因生物体进入自然系统中以后，将会与多种生物而不仅与一种生物发生竞争作用，特别是对于高等植物来说，都一样需要光、CO_2、水和营养物这些资源，资源利用出现分化的可能性比较小，因而研究起来困难较大，而 Tilman 的竞争模型能够提供解决途径。可以利用 Tilman 的竞争模型来研究转基因生物体入侵对群落的影响。Andow(1994)[38]根据 Tilman 模型建立了一个数学理论模型来预测转基因生物体释放对群落结构的改变。在这个模型中，Andow 用一个参数(R^*)来描述一个物种的最低资源需求，一个物种的 R^*值愈低，其竞争能力就愈强。当群落中初级消费者消耗植物比较大时，转基因抗性就能够降低植物的 R^*值，这种转基因植物就可能会影响到群落的结构；当植物的竞争能力差(高的 R^*值)，并且转基因性状对 R^*没有影响时，这种转基因植物就不会影响到群落的结构。

5.2.2 转基因甘蓝型油菜入侵的风险评价

Crawley 等(1993)[39]研究了一种抗除草剂转基因甘蓝型油菜入侵自然生境后的生态学后果。他们用一个有限增长率(λ)来指示转基因入侵后的命运。$\lambda > 1$ 时，表示转基因植物将增大种群数量；$\lambda < 1$ 时，表示转基因植物将会消亡。

$$\lambda_1 = \left(1 - d_1 - g\right) + g\left(1 - d_2\right)F \tag{9}$$

这里 d_1 是一年中种子失活的比例，g 是第一年春天种子萌发的比例，d_2 是冬天种子失活的比例，F 是每个萌发种子结实种子的平均数量。这些参数都可通过独立的试验估算出来。公式(9)等号右边第一项指从一年到下一年的活种子存留，第二项计数那些种子萌发后在与自然植被竞争中生长植物的结实。

公式(9)计算出的 λ 值是在种子的生活史开始于一个没有竞争的农田生境中，因而可能有些偏高。当考虑到种子萌发一开始就会有自然植被的竞争时，λ 值可以这样估算：

$$\lambda_2 = \text{第二代的幼苗/第一代的幼苗} \tag{10}$$

即使如此，Crawley 等也没有发现转基因油菜能够入侵无干扰的自然生境，并且没有发现转基因油菜比它的同类传统品种对干扰后生境有更强的入侵和存留能力。

然而，Kareiva 等(1996)[37]的研究指出，转基因生物体的入侵对环境条件特别敏感。

由于年度之间环境条件变化比较明显，因此对于油菜的研究来说，取样的年度数远远比取样的样点数重要，任何少于 3 年的数据都不能很好地反映油菜种群的增长率。因而现在下结论说这种转基因油菜没有入侵风险尚为时过早。

5.3 害虫对转 *Bt* 基因作物抗性进化的风险评价

转 Bt 毒蛋白基因作物释放的主要潜在风险是害虫的抗性进化，这在前文已有讨论。

目前，许多抗性选择试验是在实验室里进行的，而实验室的选择结果往往不能代表田间情况。特别是当实验室种群的遗传变异与田间相比比较有限时，实验室选择不能产生抗性并不意味着田间选择条件下也没有抗性的发生[40]。Tabashnik (1992、1994)提供了根据实验室的研究结果来评价害虫抗性风险的方法[40]，他用到了现实遗传力(h_2)这样一个参数，用来评价抗性对不同选择强度的响应。

$$h_2 = R/S \tag{11}$$

这里 R 是选择响应，S 是选择差。

$$R = \left[\ln\left(\mathrm{LC}_{50}^{\mathrm{f}}\right) - \ln\left(\mathrm{LC}_{50}^{\mathrm{i}}\right)\right]/n \tag{12}$$

这里 $\mathrm{LC}_{50}^{\mathrm{f}}$ 是选择 n 代以后后代的最终半致死浓度，$\mathrm{LC}_{50}^{\mathrm{i}}$ 是 n 代选择以前亲本世代的初始半致死浓度。

$$S = i/\sigma_p \tag{13}$$

这里 i 是选择的强度，用《数量遗传学导论》的附录 A 由选择的存活率 P 估计得出。σ_p 是表型标准偏差：

$$\sigma_p = 1/\left(1/2\left(S_{\mathrm{i}} + S_{\mathrm{f}}\right)\right) \tag{14}$$

其中，S_{i} 和 S_{f} 分别是选择前亲本和 n 代选择后子代概率回归线的斜率。

将公式(11)变换一下可以用来评价抗性对选择压力的反应：

$$R = h^2 S \tag{15}$$

用于估计抗性响应的参数可以用来定量选择停止后半致死浓度(LC_{50})的变化，也就是抗性的稳定性。这时，公式(12)中的 $\mathrm{LC}_{50}^{\mathrm{f}}$ 和 $\mathrm{LC}_{50}^{\mathrm{i}}$ 分别代表选择停止 n 代后和 n 代前的 LC_{50}，若 R 是负值则表示 $\mathrm{LC}_{50}R$ 的降低，即抗性水平的下降。R 的倒数是 LC_{50}10 倍变化所需要的世代数。

6 遗传修饰生物体释放风险的监测

6.1 监测的必要性

目前，各国政府都制定了相应的制度来管理遗传修饰生物体的释放，即遗传修饰生物体及其产品上市以前都经过了严格的评审和论证。然而，其生态学后果是长期的，也就是说，即使遗传修饰生物体的短期释放在有效的管理措施的保证下是安全的，也不能忽视其长期释放可能带来的生态学风险。1996 年美国南部的 Bt 棉失去对害虫的控制，1996 年批准上市的抗除草剂转基因棉花，1997 年在密西西比河流域大规模种植后发生大量落铃和棉桃畸形现象。这些也许仅仅是自然界对我们发出的警告[2]。

对于遗传修饰生物体释放的风险评价的结果及后果必须通过长期的监测才能获得。而且这种监测的结果还能够为其他转基因生物体，尤其是类似转基因生物体的释放提供有用的信息，能够减少不必要的重复劳动。例如美国 USDA-APHIS 对转基因植物的备案制管理规定，如果新的遗传修饰生物体与以前已确定为非管制的生物十分相似，则可全部或部分解除管制。并且监测能够帮助我们避免发生与上一次释放同样的错误，了解那些不可预见的事件。因此，必须监测任何一次转基因生物体等遗传修饰生物体的释放。

6.2 监测的内容

监测的内容应当包括遗传修饰生物体释放可能带来生态学风险的方方面面：

(1) 转基因生物入侵的风险。

(2) 转基因逃逸的风险。

(3) 抗病毒的转基因作物产生新病毒的风险。

(4) 转基因作物释放对土壤微生物及生物地球化学循环产生影响的风险。

(5) 害虫对转 Bt 基因抗虫植物产生抗性进化的风险。

(6) 转基因生物体对非目标生物影响的风险。

(7) 转基因生物体的相互作用可能导致的风险，例如棉花和玉米都是棉铃虫的宿主，Bt 棉和 Bt 玉米的邻近种植可能会加速害虫的抗性进化等。

当然，最重要的监测内容应当是那些可能会对人类健康及自然环境带来极大危害的风险。

6.3 监测的方法

监测的方法要依监测对象及其可能带来风险的不同而不同，并且最重要的是要保证监测的认真执行和及时交流。

为了延迟害虫对 Bt 作物的抗性进化，在美国上市的 5 个 Bt 作物品种采用了避难所策略[9]。但对这些策略的有效性需要进行长期监测。美国政府要求所有种植 Bt 作物的公司和农户要随时监测田间昆虫的抗性。对于害虫的抗性进化情况可用抗性等位基因的频率来衡量，魏伟等[6]给出了估算抗性等位基因频率的公式：

$$P_{(\mathrm{R},T+1)}=\frac{P_{(\mathrm{R},T)}{}^{2}+P_{(\mathrm{R},T)}P_{(\mathrm{R},T)}W_{\mathrm{RS}}}{P_{(\mathrm{R},T)}{}^{2}+2P_{(\mathrm{R},T)}P_{(\mathrm{R},T)}W_{\mathrm{RS}}+P_{(\mathrm{S},T)}W_{\mathrm{SS}}} \tag{16}$$

这里 $P_{(\mathrm{R},T+1)}$ 为 T+1 世代抗性等位基因的频率，$P_{(\mathrm{R},T)}$和$P_{(\mathrm{S},T)}$ 分别为纯别为 T 世代抗性等位基因和感性等位基因的频率，W_{SS} 和 W_{RS} 分别为纯合感性个体和杂合个体的适合

度。当抗性等位基因的频率即 $P_{(R, T+1)}$ 达到或超过 0.5 时，说明种群对 Bt 作物进化出了抗性，$T+1$ 则为抗性进化所需的世代数。

7 结束语

本文在结束时想用 Colwell 在 1994 年作过的一个报告的题目——“生物多样性与生物技术：一对新的伙伴关系”来表明两者之间的关系[10]。Colwell 在文章中用较多的篇幅说明了生物多样性的潜在的经济利益是巨大的，特别是与生物技术结成伙伴后更是如虎添翼，会发展出更多新的产品、新的工艺，甚至新的工业。而本文则阐明了近年来生物技术的飞速发展及其所产生的巨大经济效益，更证实了生物技术的巨大作用。此外，本文又从相反的角度来看生物技术特别是转基因生物可能带来的潜在的生态风险，从而影响或威胁到生物多样性，更深一层次地对这一对新的伙伴关系作了说明。

我们认为生物技术的发展是势不可挡的，会给 21 世纪的经济、农业、甚至环境保护的一些方面带来巨大的效益，但对它的潜在风险又不能忽视。应加强研究，掌握规律，尽可能缓解或克服这些风险，让这对新的伙伴关系更好地发挥作用。

参考文献

[1] 钱迎倩, 生物技术与生物多样性的保护和持续利用, 见：钱迎倩, 马克平主编, 生物多样性研究的原理与方法, 北京：中国科学技术出版社, 1994, 217~224

[2] 钱迎倩, 魏伟, 田彦, 马克平. 转基因作物在生产中的应用及某些潜在问题. 应用与环境生物学报, 1999, **5**(4): 427~433

[3] 钱迎倩, 马克平. 生物技术与生物安全. 自然资源学报, 1995, **10**(4): 322~331

[4] Riley P A, Hoffman L, Ash M.U Sfarmers are rapidly adopting biotech crops. *Agricultural Outlook*, 1998, **8**: 21~24

[5] 钱迎倩, 田彦, 魏伟, 转基因作物的生态风险评价. 植物生态学报, 1998, **22**(4): 289~299

[6] 魏伟, 钱迎倩, 马克平, 害虫对转 Bt 基因作物的抗性进化及其管理对策. 应用与环境生物学报, 1999, **5**(2): 215~228

[7] 魏伟, 钱迎倩, 马克平, 转基因作物与其野生亲缘种间的基因流动. 植物学报, 1999, **41**(4): 343~348

[8] 丁锡申. 基因工程药物的过去、现在和未来, 生物工程进展, 1998. **18**(3): 2~6

[9] 朱作言, 汪亚平, 转基因动物. 见：孟广震主编, 中国科学院生物技术研究进展. 北京：科学出版社, 1998. 41~45

[10] Colwell R R.Biodiversity and biotechnology: a new partnership. In: Peng Ch-I, Chou Ch-Heds. Biodiversity and Terrestrial Ecosystems: Proceeding of the International Symposium on Biodiversity and Terrestrial Ecosysterns, Taipei, April 17~20, 1994

[11] Bull A T, Goodfellow M, Slater J H. Biodiversity as a source of innovation in biotechnology. In: *Annu Rev Microbiol*, 1992, **46**: 219~252

[12] 世界资源研究所(WRI)等(1992). 中国科学院生物多样性委员会译. 全球生物多样性策略. 北京：中国标准出版社, 1993

[13] Conway, W G. The prospects for sustaining species and their evolution. In: Western D, Pearl M C eds. Conservation for the Twenty-first Century. New York: Oxford University Press, 1989. 199~209

[14] Benford G. Saving the “library of life”. *Proc Natl Acad Sci USA*, 1992, **89**: 11098~11101

[15] Soule M E. Conservation biology in the twenty-first century: summary and outlook. In: Western D, Pearl M C eds. Conservation for the Twenty-first Century. New York; Oxford: Oxford University Press, 1989. 297~303

[16] United Nations Environment Programme(UNEP). UNEP International Technical Guidelines for Safety in Biotechnology, 1995.1~31

[17] Williamson M. Community response to transgenic plant release: Predictions from British experience of invasive plants and feral crop plants. *Mol Ecol*, 1994, **3**(1) : 75~80

[18] Stewart C N Jr. , All J N, Paymer P L, *et al*. Increased fitness of transgenic insecticidal rapeseed under insect selection pressure. *Mol Ecol*, 1997, **6**: 773~779

[19] Gaggiotti O E. Potential evolutionary and ecological consequences of the release of GMO's into the wild. The workshop on transgenic organisms in the new millenium: risks and benefits, Italy, Dec 1~5, 1997

[20] Kareiva P, Morris W, Jacobi C M. Studying and managjng the risk of cross-fertilization between trans-genic crops and wild relatives. *Mol EcoL*, 1994, **3**: 15~21

[21] Chevre A-M, Eber F, Baranger A, *et al*. Ceneflow from transgenic crops. *Nature*, 1997, **389**: 924

[22] Kleiner K, Fields of genes. *New Scientist*, 1997, **2095**: 4

[23] Angle J S, Release of transgenic plants: biodiversity and population level considerations. *Mal EcoL*, 1994, **3**: 45~50

[24] Widmer F, Seidler R J, Watrud L S. Sensitive detection of transgenic plant marker gene persistence in soil microcosms. *Mol Ecol*, 1996, **5**: 603~613

[25] Trevors J T, Kuikman P, Watson B. Transgenic Plants and biogeochemical cycles. *Mol Ecol*, 1994, **3**: 57~64

[26] 沈晋良, 周威君, 吴益东等. 棉铃虫对 Bt 生物农药早期抗性及与转 Bt 基因棉抗虫性的关系. 昆虫学报, 1998. **41**:8~14

[27] Gould F, Andersion A, Jones A, *et al*. Initial frequency of alleles for resistance to *Bacillus thuringiensis* toxins in field *Heliothis virescens. Proc Natl Acad Sci USA*, 1997. **94**: 3519~3523

[28] Crow J F, Kimura M. An introduction to population genetics theory. New York: Harper & Row, 1970

[29] Tabashnik B E, Liu Y-B, Finson N, *et al*. One gene in diamondback moths confers resistance to four *Bacillus thuringiensis* toxins. *Proc Natl Acad Sci USA*, 1997, **94**: 1640~1644

[30] Sims S R, Holden L R. Insect bioassay for determining soil deggradation of *Bacillus thuringiensis* subsp. *kurstaki* CrylA(b) protein in corn tissue. *Environ Entomol*, 1996, **25**: 659~664

[31] Yu L, Berry RE, Croft B A. Effects of *Bacillus thuringiensis* toxins in transgenic cotton and potato on *Folsomia candida* (Collembola: Isotomidae) and *Oppia nitens* (Acari: Orbatidae). *J Econ Entomot*, 1997, **90**: 113~118

[32] Union of Concerned Scientists(UCS). Risk research: transgenic insect-resistance crops harm beneficial insects. *The Gene Exchange*, 1998, Summer: 4

[33] Kjellsson G. Principles and Procedures for ecological risk assessment of transgenic plants. In: Kjellsson C, *et al*. eds. Methods for risk assessment of transgenic plants. 11. Pollination, gene-transfer and population impacts. Basel: Birkhauser Veriag, 1997. 221~237

[34] Bateman A J. Contamination in seed crops: III. Relation with isolation distance. *Heredity*, 1947, **1**: 303~336

[35] Manasse R. Ecological risks of transgenic plants: effects of spatial dispersion on gene flow. *Ecol Appl*, 1992, **2**: 431~438

[36] Gliddon C. Boudry P, Walker S. Cene Flow—a review of experimental evidence. The workshop on transgenic organisms in the new millenium: risks and benefits. Italy, Dec 1~5, 1997

[37] Kareiva P, Parker I M, Pascual M. Can we use experiments and models in predicting the invasiveness of genetically engineered organisms? *Ecology*, 1996, **77**: 1670~1675

[38] Andow D A, Community response to transgenic plant release: Using mathematical theory to predict effects of transgenic plants. *Mol Ecol*. 1994, **3**: 65~70

[39] Crawley M J, Hails Rs, Rees M, *et al*. Ecology of transgenic oilseed rape in natural habitats. *Nature*, 1993, **363**: 620~623

[40] Tabashnik B E. Evolution of resistance to *Bacillus thuringiensis. Annu Rev Entomol*, 1994, **39**: 47~79

本文原载：植物生态学报. 2002. 26(增刊): 127-132

转 *Bt* 基因棉花生态风险评价的研究进展

魏伟　裴克全　桑卫国　钱迎倩　马克平

(中国科学院植物研究所)

摘　要　转 *Bt* 基因抗虫棉(*Gossypium* spp.)是目前国内释放面积最大的转基因作物，其生态风险问题从一开始就受到密切的关注。从生态风险评价的角度，分转基因棉花中 *Bt* 杀虫蛋白的时空表达及其对害虫的控制效果、*Bt* 基因通过花粉传播而扩散的风险、害虫对 *Bt* 棉花抗性的进化风险、*Bt* 棉花对非目标生物体影响的风险等几个方面，综述了 *Bt* 棉安全性评价的最新研究进展，为生物安全管理提供咨询意见，并提出了目前针对 *Bt* 棉亟待研究的内容。期望本文能够为推动生物安全的研究和生物技术的发展做出一定的贡献。

关键词　*Bt* 棉；生态风险；转基因逃逸；抗性进化；非目标效应

自从 Perlak 等(1990)首次成功地将苏云金杆菌(*Bacillus thuringiensis*)的杀虫基因转入棉花(*Gossypium hirsutum*)获得抗虫植株以后，有很多实验室随后也成功地用不同的方法将 *cryIA* 基因转入棉花(*Gossypium* spp.)(Fitt *et al.*，1994；Benedict *et al.*，1996；谢道昕等，1991)。从 1996 年开始，*Bt* 棉开始在美国大面积种植，1997 年起，中国也开始大面积释放 *Bt* 棉，*Bt* 棉的全球种植面积逐年上升。虽然在 2000 年，全球转基因棉花的种植品种中抗除草剂的棉花比较多(210 万 hm^2)，但是兼抗除草剂的转 *Bt* 基因棉花以及抗虫转 *Bt* 基因的棉花仍然占大多数，分别为 170 万 hm^2 和 150 万 hm^2(James，2000)。2000 年国内转基因棉花的面积约为 50 万 hm^2，2001 年仅国产 *Bt* 棉就达 60 多万 hm^2，加上孟山都公司的转 *Bt* 基因棉花总计 150 万 hm^2，比 2000 年增加了 100 万 hm^2 (James，2001)。最近出版的一部“863”生物高技术丛书——《转基因棉花》较系统地介绍了国内转基因棉花研究的进展(贾士荣等，2001)。*Bt* 棉带来的效益是明显的，据报道，国产 *Bt* 棉能够减少农药使用量 80%左右，每亩增加净收益 120 元以上(方宣钧等，1999)。然而，在享受 *Bt* 棉的惠益的同时，不能忽视 *Bt* 棉所带来的潜在的生态学风险。1996 年，美国南部 *Bt* 棉失去对害虫的控制，虽然原因是多方面的，但对 *Bt* 棉释放后的生态风险评价的研究迫在眉睫(Fox，1996；Kaiser，1996；Mellon & Rissler，1999)。转基因 *Bt* 棉花的生态风险主要有 4 个方面的内容：① 转基因棉花中 *Bt* 杀虫蛋白的时空表达及其对害虫的控制效果，② *Bt* 基因通过花粉传播而扩散的风险，③ 害虫对 *Bt* 棉花抗性的进化风险，

基金项目：中国科学院院长基因和国家重点基础研究发展规划项目(G2000046803)。
感谢陶氏益农(DowAgrosciences)中国有限公司的 Zhai Emi 提供棉花农药的中文译名。

④ *Bt* 棉花对非目标生物体影响的风险。本文将就这几个方面的内容综合介绍一下国内外转基因 *Bt* 棉的生态风险评价的研究进展概况。

1 转基因棉花中 *Bt* 杀虫蛋白的时空表达及其对害虫的控制效果

目前转基因棉花中广泛应用 CaMV 35s 作为转基因启动子，该启动子能够在大多数植物组织中启动转基因的表达，它也能引导转基因在除成熟花瓣和花粉外所有的棉花组织中的表达。有很多的研究发现，转基因在不同植物品种和不同组织及部位有不同的表达量(Schuler *et al.*，1998)。由于转基因 *Bt* 棉花最早在美国和澳大利亚商品化生产的面积比较大，因而，两国科学家对棉花中 *Bt* 蛋白表达情况的研究开展的比较早。Sachs 等(1998)发现 *Bt* 蛋白的表达受遗传(插入位点、基因构成、遗传背景的基因型、遗传上位性、体细胞突变)和环境(温度、湿度等)因素影响。并且在整个生长季节中，*Bt* 棉花的杀虫功效是不断变化的，生长的中间阶段往后，可以在田间发现存活的害虫(Fitt *et al.*，1998)。*Bt* 蛋白的表达水平在整个生长季节中呈下降的趋势(Holt，1998)、*cryIA* 基因的 mRNA 转录的不稳定性(Murray *et al.*，1991)、棉花体内丹宁浓度的变化(Olsen.，1998)以及植物/毒素间的相互作用(Olsen & Daly，2000)等因素都可以影响 *Bt* 棉花的杀虫效率。

国内的实验室也针对国产的 *Bt* 棉开展了此类研究工作，研究发现杀虫蛋白的表达量在棉花发育过程中有明显的时空动态变化(张永军等，2001；邢朝柱等，2001)。在室内进行的生物测定实验发现棉铃虫(*Helicoverpa armigera*)幼虫校正死亡率与其杀虫蛋白表达量高度一致。但是，在田间，由于受多种因素的影响，田间表现与 *Bt* 杀虫蛋白含量有一定的差异。

2 *Bt* 基因逃逸的风险

虽然控制转基因花粉的逃逸是我们面临的一个新课题，植物育种学家对如何保护作物不受外来花粉污染的研究已经进行了半个世纪，但是，如今我们获得的有关作物基因流动和花粉传播的知识来源于那些为保证种子的基因纯度而进行的有关隔离距离的研究(Kareiva *et al.*，1994)。根据 Pope 和 Simpson (1994)的研究，单纯在棉田间种植若干行玉米是不足以保护棉花品种之间不进行杂交的，Pope 等指出，在他们的实验条件下，至少需要 1 英里(1609m)以上的距离才能实现完全的保护。Afzal 和 Khan(1950)则指出，100 英尺(约 33m)的隔离距离是完全安全的。

张宝红等(2000)用对害虫抗性为指标，发现 50 米的隔离距离足以使花粉的传播距离降到零，同时他们以是否具备除草剂抗性的表型指标研究了一种抗除草剂转基因棉花的转基因花粉散布的距离，认为 50 m 的隔离距离已经足够使转基因逃逸的概率降为零。他们的研究结果同张长青等(1997)对同一种抗 2，4-D 的转基因棉花的花粉扩散频率的结果相差不大，后者认为 100 m 的隔离距离可以使转基因逃逸的频率降为零。但是，他们同时都忽略了很重要的一点：除多种环境因素外，转基因作物释放的面积也可能会影响到转基因花粉的传播距离(魏伟等，1999a)。如今国内外转基因棉花的释放面积都是非常大的，50 m 或 100 m 的隔离距离恐怕不足以控制转基因花粉的扩散。虽然，澳大利亚的研究人员认为 20 m 的非转基因棉花的缓冲带足够限制转基因花粉的传播，但也同时指出，这个数字仅适用于小面积的释放(Llewellyn & Fitt，1996)。Green 和 Jones(1953)指出，风力和风向在棉花花粉扩散过程中并不重要，多个关于隔离距离的研究结果的差异在于该地区昆虫种群的差异以及棉花种植面积的差异。

以上转基因棉花花粉传播距离的数据是以实际产生杂交后代的频率而得出的，实际上，更准确的结果应该建立在对扩散花粉的收集和鉴定上(Kjellson *et al.*，1997)。许多传播的花粉可能是由于没有雌性受体接受或有受体接受但没有产生种子而被忽视，从而可能低估转基因花粉的散布距离。

3　目标害虫对 *Bt* 棉花产生抗性进化的风险评价

在世界范围内已经有 500 多种昆虫和螨类对化学农药产生了抗性，经验表明，它们也会对 *Bt* 蛋白产生适应性(Tabashnik，1994)。而且害虫摄食苏云金杆菌杀虫制剂中的 *Bt* 杀虫晶体蛋白后，在中肠碱性条件下二硫键打开，在胰蛋白酶的作用下激活形成抗蛋白酶的毒性核心片段，才有活性。目前转基因棉花所使用的 *Bt* 基因都是经过人工改造过的，能够持续高效地表达单一的杀虫晶体蛋白，并且所表达的 *Bt* 蛋白是已经具有活性的毒蛋白，由于长期暴露于表达高浓度 *Bt* 蛋白之下，*Bt* 作物的释放将可能会比 *Bt* 杀虫剂更能促进害虫的抗性进化(魏伟等，1999b)。所以，对转基因 *Bt* 棉花的释放而可能造成的害虫适应性必须予以重视。

针对害虫对 *Bt* 作物进化出抗性风险的管理，McGaughey 和 Whalon(1992)提出了 4 个原则：① 不要使害虫仅受一种致死机制的选择，使致死原因多样化；② 降低每种主要致死机制的选择压力；③ 通过避难所(Refuges)或害虫的迁移来提供敏感性个体；④ 通过应用诊断工具，监测和模拟来估计和预测抗性过程。依照这些原则，延迟害虫对 *Bt* 作物抗性的管理策略主要有以下几种(魏伟等，1999b)：*Bt* 作物的轮作、开发新的毒素基因、避难所、毒素高剂量表达、毒素低剂量表达、转入多种杀虫基因以及毒素在时空上的特异表达，它们在实际应用中应该是互为补充，相辅相成的。

在田间释放中，广泛推荐的策略是避难所策略，*Bt* 棉花也是一样。美国环保局推荐的 *Bt* 棉避难所管理策略有两个选择(Gould & Tabashnik，1998)：① 每种植 100 hm^2 的保铃棉，需要种植 25 hm^2 的可以用杀虫剂(除苏云金杆菌亚种 *Kurstaki* (Bt k)的杀虫产品以外)管理的不携带 *Bt* 基因的棉花，这些杀虫剂用来控制烟蚜夜蛾(*Heliothis virescens*)，美洲棉铃虫(*Helicoverpa zea*)和棉红铃虫(*Pectinophora gassypiella*)；② 每种植 100 hm^2 的保铃棉，需要种植 4 hm^2 的非保铃棉，这个避难所不能用以下农药——双甲脒、硫丹、灭多威、丙溴磷、合成的拟除虫菊酯、棉铃虫核多角体病毒、多杀霉素、硫双威、乙丙硫磷、吡咯、用来杀灭烟蚜夜蛾、棉铃虫和棉红铃虫的 Btk 杀虫剂以及胡椒粉和大蒜杀虫喷剂，但可以用每次不超过每公顷 0.5 磅的乙酰甲胺磷活性成分。这个非保铃棉田必须采取与保铃棉田相似的管理对策(包括肥料、杂草控制及其他害虫管理)。

很多生态学和遗传学因素影响着害虫对 *Bt* 植株进化出抗性的速率(Gould &

Tabashnik，1998)。这些因素包括：① 每年中暴露于转基因作物中或杀虫剂中 *Bt* 蛋白的害虫的世代数，② 每一世代中，害虫种群暴露于转基因作物中或杀虫剂中 *Bt* 蛋白的百分比，③ 由 *Bt* 蛋白引起的害虫杂合个体的死亡率，④ 成虫活动和交配的模式，⑤ 幼虫的移动，⑥ 害虫种群中抗性等位基因的初始频率，⑦ 在 *Bt* 蛋白存在和不存在的条件下，携带抗性等位基因害虫个体的适合度。所以避难所策略的成功与否也依赖于这些因素。目前广泛应用的田间野生种群中的初始抗性等位基因频率是 10^{-2}~10^{-13}，Gould 等(1997)通过采自美国 4 个州的烟芽夜蛾的雄性与实验室的抗 *Bt* 的雌蛾杂交，并观察 F_1 和 F_2 代对 *Bt* 蛋白的忍受能力，估计到田间抗性等位基因的初始频率为 1.5×10^{-3}，并指出他们的这种技术能够提高检测隐性抗性等位基因的频率的能力。何丹军等(2001)用单雌系 F_2 代法检测了河北邱县转基因 *Bt* 棉(新棉 33B)棉田中棉铃虫的抗性等位基因的频率，发现仅仅种植一年 *Bt* 棉，棉铃虫自然种群中的抗性等位基因频率已达 5.8×10^{-3}，已经略大于避难所策略所假设的害虫初始抗性等位基因频率($p < 10^{-3}$)。这就对避难所策略的实际效果提出了疑问。

避难所策略的另一个假设是，害虫对 *Bt* 蛋白的抗性基因是隐性的，如果这一假设成立的话，就为早期发现抗性增加了困难。有的科学家认为如果能对害虫的抗性基因本身进行研究，获得一种简易的 DNA 方法来检测抗性基因的存在，就能够为农民提供一个早期预报工具，使农民能够及时停止种植转基因 *Bt* 作物而改用一段时间的化学杀虫剂，从而有效地延迟抗性的进化(Stokstad，2001)。Griffitts 等(2001)在一种线虫体内克隆了抗 *Bt* 蛋白 Cry5B 的抗性基因，而在毒性区域，Cry5B 与目前商品化的 Cry1Ac(Monsanto 公司转基因棉花的表达产物)等杀虫蛋白有 24%的同源性。Gahan 等(2001)则在棉花的主要害虫——烟蚜夜蛾中发现了由反转座子介导的突变导致了对 *Bt* 蛋白 Cry1Ac 的抗性，而由反转座子插入引起的突变很容易检测，这样就使建立以 DNA 为基础的方法检测隐性基因来筛选抗性杂合子成为可能。

在国内，由于各种农作物的种植基本上是小规模的和个人行为的，因此，有的专家就提出来，除新疆棉区外，全国其他棉区在种植转 *Bt* 基因抗虫棉花时不需要单独种植非转基因棉花作为避难所，其他的农作物如玉米、大豆等可以作为害虫的天然避难所。这种做法受到国际上特别是来自欧洲的有关专家的批评(Freudling，1999)。虽然根据目前的调查研究，没有发现害虫的抗性进化，并且，谭声江(2001)根据玉米和蓖麻田中的棉铃虫种群能够与 *Bt* 棉田种群随机交配的实验证据认为这些作物在田间能起到避难所的作用。但是我们认为对玉米、蓖麻等作为避难所的作物来说，在推行这种天然避难所策略以前，应该客观评价由于棉花害虫造成的损失或者由于防治害虫而增加的投入。

经过多年的研究，我国学者在对转基因抗虫棉的抗性管理和治理上也积累了相当多的研究成果。如吴孔明教授(2001)通过调查 *Bt* 抗虫棉田中棉花害虫的发生规律，提出了 *Bt* 抗虫棉田中棉花害虫的控制技术，以及适合于国情的棉田综合防治技术。

4 *Bt* 棉花对非目标生物体影响的风险

转基因作物释放到环境中去以后，除了对目标生物体发生作用外，还可能对非目标生物体产生一定的作用，从而有可能影响到生态系统的生物多样性。自从 Losey 等(1999)在自然杂志上发表了 *Bt* 玉米(*Zea mays*)的花粉能够影响大斑蝶(*Danaus plexippus*)的生长和发育的文章，对于抗虫转基因作物所产生的非目标效应的研究已经成为生物安全评价的一个焦点。Birch 等(1998)的实验发现，当用饲喂转基因抗虫马铃薯的蚜虫(*Myzus persicea*)喂养瓢虫(*Adalia bipunctata*)时，瓢虫出现生殖问题，并且死亡比对照要早。Hilbeck 等(1998)分别用转基因 *Bt* 抗虫玉米和非转基因玉米喂养两种食草害虫——欧洲玉米螟(*Ostrinia nubilalis*)和棉蚜夜蛾(*Spodoptera littoralis*)，然后再用这两种害虫饲喂草蛉(*Chrysoperla carnea*)，发现与对照相比，其发育迟缓，死亡率较高。但是，Dutton 等(2002)的实验说明，草蛉食用以 *Bt* 玉米为食的蚜虫(*Rhopalosiphum padi*)和螨虫(*Tetranychus urticae*)没有影响。

以上研究大都是针对现象的，现在国际上研究发展的趋势是进行非目标生物体受影响或不受影响的机理研究。Schuler 等(1999)在一个种群水平上的实验室内的研究表明，当以转 *Bt* 基因油菜(*Brassicanapus*)的植株在培养笼里培养小菜蛾(*Plutella xylostella*)时，由于小菜蛾的 *Bt* 敏感品系比耐性品系生存的时间要短，所以小菜蛾的寄生蜂(*Cbtesia plutella*)倾向于寄生并杀死 *Bt* 抗性品系，而寄生蜂本身并不受影响。在接下来的实验中，在从摄食 *Bt* 蛋白的小菜蛾幼虫体内孵化出来的寄生蜂体内没有检测到 *Bt* 蛋白的存在，从一个角度解释了寄生蜂不受转基因油菜影响的机理(魏伟等，未发表数据)。在上述 Hilbeck 等(1998)和 Dutton 等(2002)的不同结果的研究中，如果能够揭示转基因产物在食物链中的转移及其在不同营养级水平上的存留，则可能有助于理解其实验结果的不同。

目前转 *Bt* 基因棉花的释放面积比较大，在田间，转基因抗虫棉的害虫存在很多的寄生性天敌和捕食性天敌，*Bt* 棉可能会通过影响其害虫而影响到昆虫天敌。夏敬源等(1999)利用他们本所的转基因抗虫棉进行大田实验，发现棉铃虫的优势寄生性天敌的数量明显减少，捕食性天敌的数量减少不明显。实验室的研究表明，*Bt* 抗虫棉对棉铃虫幼虫的优势寄生性天敌的寄生率、羽化率和蜂茧质量造成严重危害，而用 *Bt* 棉饲喂棉铃虫后能提高捕食性天敌对棉铃虫的捕食率。魏国树等(2001)则对比了转 *Bt* 基因棉田与非转基因棉田中节肢动物群落的构成与结构，提出转 *Bt* 基因棉田应该采取与常规棉不同的害虫防治策略。

转基因生物对土壤生物的影响，不仅包括初级基因产品，也包括来自生物和非生物反应所产生的次级产品的影响。转基因产品进入土壤有许多途径，其中最重要的途径是作物收获后，其残留物回到土壤中。其次，还可以随着根的分泌物进入根际的土壤生物圈。土壤中的生物体通过捕食、竞争、拮抗或共生而发生相互作用，一旦环境由于转基因产品的释放而发生改变，一些敏感生物体快速发生反应，达到一定程度时，其他生物也发生反应，从而可能会影响到整个土壤生态系统(Angle，1994)。土壤生物群受转基因产品引入影响的程度依赖于很多因素，其中最重要的是土壤生态系统的复杂性和稳定性，那些简单并缺少生物多样性的生态系统容易受到进入土壤的转基因产品的影响。种植单一作物的农业生态系统相对比较简单，因而对于干扰比较敏感。Widmer 等(1996)发现，重组 DNA 进入土壤后，有一定的存留期，在实验条件下，无论烟草叶子 DNA 还是质粒 DNA 进入土壤后的降解开始都比较快，但仍有少量 DNA 能够抵抗降解并且几个月内都能检出它们的存在，其原因可能是这些 DNA 被土壤颗粒吸收了，这样能够保护它们不被完全降解。重组 DNA 在土壤中能够存留较长的一般时间，增加了转基因产物进入土壤后向土壤生物体进行基因转移的生态风险性(Trevors *et al.*，1994)。

土壤生物群因转基因产品引入而发生的一个微妙而重要的变化是土壤生物多样性的变动。土壤微生物对环境变化最为敏感，而土壤微生物多样性对土壤生态系统的结构和功能有着重要作用(Trevors *et al.*, 1994)。有的学者已经将核糖体小亚基 RNA 基因的分析用于研究转基因作物对土壤微生物多样性的影响上。裴克全(2001)首次采用对原核生物核糖体小亚基 16s rDNA 全序列分析的方法，研究转基因抗虫棉根际土壤微生物的多样性。试验刚刚进行 2 年，虽然没有发现转基因棉田与非转基因棉田间有显著的差异，但是已经获得了一些有意义的数据，为进一步深入的研究奠定了良好的基础。

5 结束语

转基因 *Bt* 抗虫棉释放后，其生态后效是长期的，需要对其生态风险进行长期的研究和监测。很多方面都需要认真研究，但目前针对 *Bt* 棉，最迫切需要开展的研究工作有以下 3 个方面：① 转基因棉花中 *Bt* 基因产物的表达、稳定性以及转基因表达 *Bt* 蛋白的检测；② 转基因棉花对非目标生物体的影响，这里，非目标生物体主要指目标害虫的昆虫天敌和土壤中的根际微生物，并且应着重评价 *Bt* 蛋白在食物链中的传递和累积，理解转基因作物对非目标生物体影响的机理和机制，为安全管理提供理论依据；③ 棉铃虫等害虫对 *Bt* 棉花的抗性进化以及抗性等位基因频率的监测，评价在国内现行田间管理对策下，作为害虫的天然避难所的玉米等农作物由于棉花害虫造成的损失或者由于防治害虫而增加的投入。

近年来，生物安全研究得到愈来愈大的重视，国家有关部门已经计划拨出专门款项资助转基因生物体释放的生物安全的研究。目前，从事转基因生物研究的生物技术工作者与注重环保的生态学研究人员在对待生物安全问题上有很大的意见分歧，其原因是看待问题的出发点不同，生物技术工作者更注重转基因产品本身的效益，而环境工作者对其释放后而导致的潜在的生态学风险更加警惕。其实，二者没有本质的区别，其目的都是为了保护中国的生物技术产业和促进人们的生活和健康水平的提高。然而，不同的观点可能会促使研究者采取不同的方法从而可能会导致截然不同的研究结果和结论。因此，目前最重要的是生物技术工作者与生态学研究人员的相互交流与共同协作，一起承担生物安全的研究工作，为推动我国生物技术的产业化发展和人们的生活水平而共同努力。

参考文献

Afzal, M. & A. H. Khan. 1950. Natural crossing in cotton in western Punjab. II. Natural crossing under field conditions. Agronomy Journal, **42**: 89~93.

Angle, J. S. 1994. Release of transgenic plants: biodiversity and population level considerations. Molecular Ecology, **3**: 45~50.

Benedict, J. H., E. S. Sachs, D. W. Altman, W. R. Deaton, R. J. Kohel, D. R. Ring & S. A. Berberich. 1996. Field performance of cotton expressing CryIA insecticidal proteins for resistance to *Heliothis virescens* and *Helicoverpa zea* (Lepidoptera: Noctuidae). Journal of Economic Entomology, **89**: 230~238.

Birch, A. N. E., I. E. Geoghegan, M. E. N. Majenus, C. Hackett & J. Allen. 1998. Interactions between plant resistance genes, pest aphid population and beneficial aphid predators. Dundee: Scottish Crop Research Institute Annual Report. 68~72.

Fang, X. J. (方宣钧) & S. R. Jia(贾士荣). 1999. Progress of commercialization of transgenic cotton in China. Biotechnology Information(生物技术通报), **1**: 39~40(in Chinese).

Fitt, G. P., J. C. Daly, C. L. Mares & K. Olsen. 1998. Changing efficacy of transgenic *Bt* cotton-patterns and consequences. In: Zalucki, M. & R. Drew eds. Pest management-future challenge. Proceeding of the 6th Australian Applied Entomology Conference, Brisbane. Vol. 1. 189~196.

Fitt, G. P., C. L. Mares & D. J. Llewellyn. 1994. Field evaluation and potential ecological impact of transgenic cottons(*Gossypium hirsutum*) in Australia. Biocontrol Science and Technology, **4**: 535~548.

Fox, J. L. 1996. *Bt* cotton infestations renew resistance concerns. Nature Biotechnology, **14**: 1070.

Freudling, C. 1999. Chinese *Bt* cotton need resistance management. Biotechnology and Development Monitor, **38**: 22~23.

Gahan, L. J.. F. Gould & D. Heckel. 2001. Identification of agene associated with *Bt* resistance in *Heliothis virescens*. Science. **293** : 857 ~ 860.

Gould, F., A. Anderson. A. Jones, D. Summerford. G. G. Heckel. J. Lopez, S. Micinski. R. Leanard & M. Laster. 1997. Initial frequency of alleles for resistance to *Bacillus thuringiensis* toxins in field populations of *Heliothis virescens*. Proceedings of the National Academy of Sciences of the USA. **94**: 3519 ~ 3523.

Gould. F. & B. Tabashnik. 1998. Bt-cotton resistance management. In: Mellon, M. & J. Rissler eds. Now or never: serious new plans to save a natural pest control. Cambridge: Union of Concerned Scientists.67~106.

Green, J. M. & M. D. Jones. 1953. Isolation of cotton for seed increase. Agronomy Joumal, **45**: 89~93.

Griffitts, J. S. J. L. Whitacre. D. E. Stevens & R. V. Aroian. 2001. *Bt* toxin resistance from loss of a putative carbohydrate modifying enzyme.Science. **293**: 860~864.

He. D. J. (何丹军). J. L. Shen (沈晋良). W. J. Zhou (周威君) & C. F. Gao(高聪芬). 2001. Using F2 genetic method of isofemale lines to detect the frequency of resistance alleles to *Bacillus thuringiensis* toxin from transgenic *Bt* cotton in cotton bollworm(Lepidoptera : Noctuidae). Acta Gossypii Sinica (棉花学报). **13** (2): 105~108. (in Chinese).

Hilbeck. A., M. Baumgartner, P. M. Fried & F. Bigler. 1998. Effect of transgenic *Bacillus thuringiensis* corn fed prey on mortality and development time of immature *Chrysoperla carnea* (Naeuroptera: Chrysopidea). Environmental Entomology, **27**: 480~487.

Holt. H. E. 1998. Season-long quantification of *Bacillus thringiensis* insecticidal crystal protein in field grown transgenic cotton. *In*: Zalucki. M. & R. Drew eds. Pest management-future challenge. Proceeding of the 6th Australian Applied Entomology Conference.Brisbane.Vol. 1. 215~222.

James, C. 2000. Global status of commercialized transgenic crops: 2000 ISAAA Briefs.No. 21. Ithaca. NY : ISAAA.

James. C. 2001. Global review of commercialized transgenic crops: 2001 ISAAA Briefs. No. 24. Ithaca, NY: ISAAA.

Jia, S. R. (贾士荣). S. D. Guo (郭三堆) & D. C. An (安道昌). 2001. Transgenic cotton. Beijing: Science Press. **281**. (in Chinese)

Kaiser, J. 1996. Pests overwhelm *Bt* cotton crop. Science, **273**: 423.

Kareiva, P., W. Morris & C. M. Jacobi. 1994. Studying and managing the risk of cross-fertilization between transgenic crops and wild relatives. Molecular Ecology, **3**: 15~21.

Kjellson, G., V. Simonsen & K. Ammann. 1997. Methods for risk assessment of transgenic plants. II. Pollination, gene-transfer and population impacts.Basel: Birkhauser Verlag.

Llewellyn, D. & G. Fitt. 1996. Pollen dispersal from two field trials of transgenic cotton in the Nami Valley, Australia. Molecular Breeding, **2**: 157~166.

Losey, J. E., L. S. Rayor & M. E. Carter. 1999. Transgenic pollen harms monarch larvae.Nature, **399** : 214.

McGaughey, W. H. & M. E. Whalon. 1992. Managing insect resistance to *Bacillus thuringiensis* toxins. Science, **258**: 1451~1455.

Mellon. M. & J. Rissler. 1998. Now or never: serious new plans to save a natural pest control. Cambridge: Union of Concemed Scientists. 149.

Murray, E. E., T. Rocheleau, M. Eberle. C. Stock. V. Sekar & M. Adang. 1991.Analysis of unstable RNA transcripts of insecticidal ciystal protein genes of *Bacillus thuringiensis* in transgenic plants and electroporated protoplasts. Plant Molecular Biology, **16**: 1035 ~ 1050.

Olsen. K. M. & J. C. Daly. 2000. Plant-toxin interactions in transgenic *Bt* cotton and their effect on mortality of *Helicoverpa armigera* (Hübner) (Lepidoptera : Noctuidae).Journal of Economic Entomology, **93**: 1293 ~ 1299.

Olsen. K. M., J. C. Daly & C. J. Tanner. 1998. The e. ffect of cotton condensed tannin on the efficacy of the CrylAc δ-endotoxin of *Bacillus thuringiensis*. In: Proceeding of the 9th Australian Cotton Conference. **337**~342.

Pei, K. Q.(裴克全).2001.Biosafety information construction and preliminary study of molecular ecology of transgenic cotton thizospherical microbes. Postdoctoral report. Beijing: Institute of Botany, CAS.

Perlak, F. J., R. W. Deaton. T. A. Armstrong, R. L. Fuchs, S. R. Sims, T. J. Greenplate & D. A. Fischoff. 1990. Insect resistant cotton plants.Bio/Technology, **8** : 939 ~ 942.

Pope, O. A. & D. M. Simpson. 1944. Effect of corn harriers on natural crossing in cotton. Joumal of Agricultural Research. **68**: 347 ~ 361.

Sachs, E. S., J. H. Benedict. D. M. Stelly, J. F. Taylor, D. W. Altman. S. A. Berberich & S. K. Davis. 1998. Expression and segregation of genes encoding CryIA insecticidal proteins in cotton. Crop Science, **38**: 1~11.

Schuler. T. H..R. P. J. Potting, I. Denholm & G. M. Poppy. 1999. Parasitoid behaviour and *Bt* plants. Nature, **400**: 825 ~ 826.

Stokstad. E. 2001. First light on genetic roots of Bt resistance. Science. **293**: 778.

Tabashnik. B. E. 1994. Evolution of resistance to *Bacillus thuringiensis*. Annual Review of Entomology, **39** : 47 ~ 79.

Tan, S. J. (谭声江).2001. A study on resistance of *Helicoverpa Armigera* (Hubner) (Lepidoptera: Noctuidae) to transgenic *Bt* cotton and resistance management strategies. Ph. D. dissertation of Institute of Zoology of the Chinese Academy of Sciences.

Trevors, J. T., P. Kuikman & B. Watson. 1994. Transgenic plants and biogeochemical cycles. Molecular Ecology, **3**: 57 ~ 64.

Wei. W. (魏伟), Y. Q. Qian(钱迎倩) & K. P. Ma(马克平). 1999a. Gene flow between transgenic crops and their wild related species. Acta Botanica Sinica(植物学报), **41**: 343~348. (in Chinese)

Wei. W. (魏伟), Y. Q. Qian(钱迎倩)&K. P. Ma(马克平). 1999b. Pests resistance to transgenic *Bt* crops and its management strategies. Chinese Journal of Applied&Environmental Biology(应用与环境生物学报), **5**: 215~228. (in Chinese)

Wei. G. S. (魏国树), L. Cui(崔龙), X. M. Zhang(张小梅), S. Liu(刘顺), N. Lü(吕楠)&Q. W. Zhang(张青文). 2001. Arthropod community structures in transgenic *Bt* cotton fields. Chinese Journal of Applied Ecology(应用生态学报), **12**: 576~580. (in Chinese)

Widmer, F., R. J. Seidler&L. S. Watrud. 1996. Sensitive detection of transgenic plant marker gene persistence in soil microcosms. Molecular Ecology, **5**: 603~613.

Wu. K. M. (吴孔明). 2001. The dynamic of main pests in the field of *Bt* cotton and their management. In: Jia. S. R. (贾士荣), S. D. Guo(郭三堆)&D. C. An(安道昌). Transgenic cotton. Beijing: Science Press. 218 ~ 224. (in Chinese)

Xia, J. Y. (夏敬源), J. J. Cui(崔金杰), L. H. Ma(马丽华), S. L. Dong(董双林)&X. F. Cui(崔学芬). 1999. The role of transgenic Bt cotton in integrated insect pest management. Acta Gossypii Sinica(棉花学报), **11**(2): 57~64. (in Chinese)

Xie. D. X. (谢道昕), Y. L. Fan(范云六), W. C. Ni(倪万潮) &J. Q. Huang(黄骏麒). 1991. Transgenic cotton plant containing an insecticidal crystal protein gene derived from *Bacillus thuringiertsis*. Science in China(Series B)(中国科学 B 辑), **4**: 367~373. (in Chinese)

Xing, C. Z. (邢朝柱), S. R. Jing(靖深蓉), X. F. Cui(崔学芬), L. P. Guo(郭立平), H. L. Wang(王海林)&Y. L. Yuan(袁有禄). 2001. The spatio-temporal distribution of Bt (*Bacillus thuringiensis*) insecticidal protein and the effect of transgenic Bt cotton on bollworm resistance. Cotton Science (棉花学报). **13**(1): 11 ~ 15. (in Chinese)

Zhang, B. H. (张宝红)&T. L. Guo(郭腾龙). 2000. Frequency and distance of pollen dispersal from transgenic cotton. Chinese Journal of Applied and Environmental Biology(应用与环境生物学报). **6**: 39~42. (in Chinese)

Zhang, C. Q. (张长青) , Q. Y. Lü(吕群燕), Z. X. Wang(王志兴) & S. R. Jia(贾士荣). 1997. Frequency of 2. 4-D resistant gene flow of transgenic cotton. Scientia Agricultura Sinicae(中国农业科学), **30**(1): 92 ~ 93. (in Chinese)

Zhang, Y. J. (张永军) , K. M. Wu(吴孔明)&Y. Y. Guo(郭予元). 2001. On the spatio-temporal expression of the contents of *Bt* insecticidal protein and the resistance of Bt transgenic cotton to cotton bollworm. Acta Phytophylacica Sinica(植物保护学报), **28**(1):1~6. (in Chinese)

本文原载：高技术通讯. 2002. 12(4): 100-105(59)

基因工程树的现状、生态风险与对策

沈孝宙[1]　钱迎倩[2]　张树庸[3]

(1 中国科学院动物研究所; 2 中国科学院植物研究所; 3 中国生物工程学会)

摘　要　应用基因工程技术改良树种，具有巨大的经济潜力和社会效益。林业生物工程将可能是继农业生物工程之后又一个热潮。目前，无论是阔叶树种还是针叶树种的转基因都已获得成功，已有几十种转基因树在北美、欧亚大陆、澳洲和非洲释放到野外进行田间试验。尽管当前转基因树木尚未大面积推广种植，人们却已对其生态安全性展开了广泛的争论。这是因为转基因树木可能是迄今所有转基因生物中最具生态风险的种类。其主要的生态风险表现在对周围环境中野生树种可能造成基因污染以及转基因树种作为一类新的外来种入侵，威胁现今已十分脆弱的地球森林生态系统。一些研究转基因树木的主要国家和实验室已开始注意到应从基因水平上采取防范对策，趋利避害，以防止或减少转基因树木对自然环境造成不可逆转的污染和破坏。

关键词　树木；基因工程；生态风险；生殖不育

引言

20 世纪 90 年代，就在生物工程向农业大举进军并取得辉煌成果的时期，林业生物工程也随之悄然兴起。但树木的转基因比农作物难度大，因为树木有其自身的特殊性，这包括：①树木的类型复杂，涉及被子植物和裸子植物，而农作物则单纯是被子植物；②树木的基因组非常大，相当于人类基因组的 10 倍，研究困难；③树木生命周期长，种植周期也长，即使对于人工林，一般也在十年以上。导入的外源基因长期表达的稳定性，需要经过多年观察，因此研究速度缓慢。此外，树木的分子生物学和发育生物学研究远比农作物薄弱，缺乏开展林业生物工程所必需的树木基因结构与调控以及个体发育与分化机制等基础科学资料。尽管如此，过去 10 年来林业生物工程也有不少长足进步。主要开展了基因导入的方法学研究；树木的基因定位(Mapping)和功能分析；已开始进行首例树木(杨树)基因组分析；分离与鉴定了一些树木的基因；自 1988 年第一种转基因树木——耐除草剂转基因杨树在比利时进行田间实验以来，10 年间至少有 116 种转基因树木(多数都是在 1995 年以后)研究成功，其中已有几十种转基因树在北美、欧亚大陆、澳洲和非洲陆续释放到野外进行田间试验。今天这个数字肯定又增加了很多。但目前只有一种基因工程树——抗病毒番木瓜已在美国正式批准进行商业化种植。尽管基因工程树木的研究还处在萌芽时期，是一个尚不发达的生物工程领域，但却引起人们的深切的疑虑和广泛的争论。毫无疑问，生物技术可以为树种品质的改良提供强有力的工具，能够克服物种间不可逾越的遗传屏障，实现任意基因及相应性状的转移。生物技术也为林业带来前所未有的商机。因而国际上已有 10 多家大财团纷纷投入巨资发展林业生物工程。雄厚的资金无疑将加速基因工程树的商品化进程。而与此同时，在各国和国际间有关基因工程树的安全操作规程又相对滞后和不健全。于是，大财团的介入，更加剧了公众的担心。

因此，我们认为有必要审视国际上基因工程树木的研究现状，并在此基础上引述目前人们如何分析基因工程树的生态危险性以及介绍目前国外学者为解决这类问题所提出和采取的对策，供有关方面参考。

1 树木转基因的类型

目前树木已有多种类型的转基因，具有人类所期望的各种品质，其中包括耐除草剂、抗虫、抗病、抗环境胁迫(Stress)、改良木质素和快速生长等。

1.1 耐除草剂基因工程树

最初耐除草剂转基因杨树是沿用耐除草剂基因工程作物所采取的一种经过诱变的细菌 *aroA* 基因[1]。该基因编码 5-烯醇丙酮酸莽草酸-3-磷酸合成酶，能降解除草剂草甘膦。对杂交杨树进行转 *bar* 基因(编码草丁膦-N-乙酰转移酶)或转 *als* 基因(编码乙酰乳酸合成酶)也都已获得成功，能分别降解草丁膦或磺酰脲类除草剂。后来的改进是使 *aroA* 基因能在叶绿体表达，因为草甘膦的作用位置就在叶绿体[2]。耐除草剂基因工程针叶树(如落叶松 *Larix*)也已研究成功。这对于苗圃和经济林除草，以防止杂草与树苗和林木争夺空间、水分和养料，提高树木存活率和生物量，降低管理费用均有很大作用。

1.2 抗虫基因工程树

由于林木易遭受虫害，抗虫基因工程树木的研究一直受到各国林业部门的重视。目前已有多种杨树、榆树以及欧洲落叶松和白云杉均成功地转移了苏云金杆菌δ-内毒素(*Bt*)基因[3]。获得的这些转基因杨树能抗鳞翅目害虫的攻击，效果显著。此外，蛋白酶抑制剂肽类对树木抗虫也特别有价值。许多植物都存在这类小分子多肽物质，当叶片受损伤或被昆虫咬噬后，植物能在创伤组织周围积累这些物质。蛋白酶抑制剂多肽基因受控于 pin 2 启动子，可被创伤作用诱导。当该基因导入杨树后，仍能保持其可诱导性[4]，其生物安全性也高，因为外源基因在一般情况下是不表达的。所以在阔叶树种抗虫基因工程操作上很有前途。还值得提及的是：最近从水稻分离的半胱氨酸蛋白酶抑制肽基因，在导入杨树后所产生的转基因树有非常强的抗甲虫幼虫侵害能力[5]。这对解决某些树种历来遭受鞘翅目昆虫严重危害问题将提供新的途径。

1.3 抗真菌病基因工程树

一些重要树种特别易染真菌病，如栗树枯萎病和荷兰榆树病(DED)。后者是欧洲和北美榆树的主要病害。近年国外实验室已陆续发现一些与抗 DED 有关的基因，如植物抗毒素基因、抗真菌毒素基因、几丁质酶基因和β-1，3 葡聚糖酶基因。将这些基因导入榆树，都能使其增强抗真菌病的能力[6]。

1.4 抗细菌病基因工程树

许多阔叶树种如杨树极易感染冠瘿病，系农杆菌感染所致。用农杆菌致瘤基因、激素 IAA 基因或细胞分裂素基因的反义 RNA 技术，都能获得抗冠瘿病的基因工程杨树[7]。另一种策略是在树木中导入各种抗菌肽的基因，也能获得抗细菌病的基因工程树种。

1.5 抗胁迫基因工程树

这是一类包括抗逆性的基因工程树种，如获得耐霜冻、耐干旱、耐盐碱、抗污染等品质，这对治理贫瘠土地、改善环境具有重大意义。目前国外在抗胁迫基因工程树方面研究最深入的是抗氧化物。像臭氧这类光化学氧化物是对树木产生胁迫作用的主要根源。臭氧毒性可降低树木的生长速度，使叶绿素降解，破坏 Rubisco 加氧酶，导致光合作用受损。已证明一种抗氧化剂谷胱甘肽还原酶基因导入杨树，可使杨树对氧化胁迫作用具有很强的耐受性，而且还可以抵抗光合作用过程中产生的过氧化物自由基引起的光化学抑制效应[8]。

1.6 改造木质素的基因工程树

对木质素进行基因改造可能是一项非常有意义的工程。树的木质素占木材干重的 1/4，极难与木纤维分离，而后者又是造纸木材纸浆的主要成分。为去除木质素，需要大量的化学试剂和能源。例如在美国，每年加工纸浆木纤维达 6400 万吨，须去除木质素 2000 万吨。这个过程需 1600 万吨氢氧化钠和 600 万吨硫酸钠，耗电 800 万 kW/h。这些化学试剂造成环境极大的污染。因此若能明显降低木材中木质素含量或改变木质素的性质，则能大幅度降低制浆成本，减少环境污染。针叶树种的木纤维较长，质地优良，是造纸工业首选的原料。但针叶树的木质素结构致密，属于邻甲氧苯基木质素(G-木质素)。

而阔叶树的木质素是 G-木质素与大量的丁香醇基木质素(S-木质素)聚合而成。这种 G/S-木质素质地较松软，制浆过程所需化学原料和能源要少得多。目前含 G/S-木质素的基因工程针叶树在美国已研究成功[9]。另一种降低木质素含量的方法是通过反义 RNA 技术抑制与木质素生物合成相关酶系(如肉桂醇脱氢酶和 5-羟阿魏酸-O-甲基转移酶)的基因表达，或者抑制与木质素单体聚合成多聚体的漆酶(Laccase)基因的表达。现正在对几种杨树、桉树和云杉进行这类实验[10]。

1.7 快速生长的基因工程树

植物的生长与发育受激素调节，特别是一类赤霉素起着关键的作用。从拟南芥(*Arabidopsis thaliana*)中已分离出赤霉素生物合成的调节基因，包括赤霉素—20—氧化酶的编码基因。将该基因转移到杂交杨树，生长速度显著提高[11]。导入细菌编码生长调解剂的基因，也可以改变植物的生长速度。例如用农杆菌的一些基因，能够调整植物生长索与细胞分裂素的比率，达到改变植株生长速度的目的。此外，不育性也可以提高树木的生长速度 14%至 38%，因为不育可以使树木节省开花和结实的代谢消耗，将能量用在生长上。另一方面，缩短树木幼苗期在某种意义上也相当于加快树木生长。在拟南芥已鉴定出 *LEAFY* 和 APETALA1 两种基因对诱发开花期具有非常重要的作用。已证明这两种基因导入柑橘能明显缩短幼苗期，使柑橘一年即可开花结果[12]。

1.8 除污基因工程树

利用基因工程树清除土壤和空气环境中毒性化学物质的污染，受到人们的重视。现今创用了一个新名词来描述这个过程，称为“植物治疗法”(Phytoremediation)。据新近报道，细胞色素 P450 2E1 基因导入杂交杨树，能清除土壤中积累的各种工业化学物质，如三氯乙烯、苯、苯乙烯等[13]。

1.9 不育基因工程树

主要目的是为了防止基因漂流造成天然森林基因库的污染。将在下面详细讨论。

2 进入田间试验的基因工程树种

据世界野生动物基金会(WWF)公布的资料[14]，在 1999 年之前，世界各国释放到田间进行试验的基因工程树种包括多种杨树(杨树、山杨、三角叶杨、黑杨、颤杨等)，其基因工程操作是相当成功的，已成为阔叶树转基因的模型树种。这是因为杨树对农杆菌非常敏感，又很易进行无性繁殖，再生效率很高。同样，落叶松也具有这两种特性，所以它是针叶树转基因的模型树种。其他已研究成功的转基因针叶树种还有黑云杉、挪威云杉、欧洲赤松、辐射松等。一些转基因的桉树(如赤桉、蓝桉和大桉)、果树(如苹果、李树、柑橘、樱桃)以及坚果类树木(如黑胡桃、欧洲栗和美洲栗)也都相继释放到野外进行田间试验。

我国转基因树木的工作是 20 世纪 80 年代后期开始的。已研究成功的树种主要是各种杨树，包括欧洲黑杨、毛白杨、欧美杨等。目的是通过基因工程手段培育出抗虫、抗病、抗逆及雄性不育的转基因树种。但研究工作比较成熟或已作大田试验的集中在抗虫方面。早在 1991 年我国成功地将 *Bt* 毒蛋白基因用根癌农杆菌导入欧洲黑杨，获得转基因植株，杀虫率高达 76%以上。此外还得到 *Bt* 转基因欧美杨。豇豆胰蛋白酶抑制剂基因(*CPTI*)导入毛白杨，获得的转基因植株也已进入大田试验。

3 基因工程树的生态风险

直到 1999 年，尽管上百种转基因树在研究着，还有几十种释放到野外进行试验，但并未引起人们注意。1999 年 7 月在英国牛津大学召开了一次令人瞩目的林业生物技术会议，遭到一群环保人士的抗议，示威者砍倒了牛津大学转基因杨树的试验地，此后这股反基因工程树的浪潮在欧洲声势浩大的反基因工程作物运动的背景下，迅速蔓延到北美。加拿大和美国的一些转基因树试验基地也不断遭到焚烧和砍伐的破坏。非同寻常的是世界野生动物基金会在 2000 年提出一份措词十分严厉的报告，强烈呼吁世界各国应对基因工程树的危险性进行更深入的研究，并要求推迟基因工程树的商业化[15]。一个国际性的组织对某项生物工程的研究与开发提出警告，这似乎还没有过先例。可见基因工程树向自然界的释放已引起广泛的关注与担心。

基因工程树可能产生的生态危险性表现在以下几方面：

3.1 树木转基因的长期稳定性方面的不确定性

在多年生树木漫长生命过程中，有关外源转基因的稳定性问题，人们所积累的知识还极少。插入到树木庞大基因组上的外源基因，在树木几十年的生命活动中，在各种各样的内外环境条件下，是否会发生沉默或者发生失控？是否会在某个时刻开始影响树木的其他基因的表达，从而改变树木的个体发育？这些问题至今无人能给予确切的回答。因为至今没有任何一种实验模型可以代替“时间”这个变数。而一年生转基因作物的外源基因稳定性研究难以作为多年生转基因树木稳定性研究的依据。

3.2 树木的转基因可能通过基因漂流(Gene flow)污染天然森林的基因库

这种称之为“基因污染”(Gene pollution)的过程是通过有性生殖的花粉进行转播的，一般叫做基因的垂直转移。据分析，转基因树比起转基因作物更易对天然种群的基因库造成污染。这有以下几方面原因：

(1) 树的驯化程度很低。几乎所有人工栽培的树种还只能算是属于半驯化状态，不同于完全驯化、并有明显变异的栽培作物。因此易于和野生种群交配，使转基因发生垂直转移。

(2) 绝大部分栽培树种在其种植区都存在同类的天然野生种群，成为转基因漂流的通道。

(3) 有许多树种在同一属内能发生种间杂交。就以现在已经进行转基因的树种为例：如阔叶树的杨树属(*Populus*)、桉树属(*Eucalyptus*)和针叶树的落叶松属，其属内多数物种之间就能够进行杂交[16]，这就使基因漂流变得更为复杂。

(4) 有些树木的花粉可飞扬 600 km 以外的地方，其影响面极广。

(5) 树木是多年生的，一经释放到野外，对周围环境的正反面作用都是长期的、持续的。

应该看到，国外从事树木转基因研究的植物分子生物学家对基因工程树的基因漂流问题也是十分关注的。他们利用杂交杨树进行基因漂流的模型实验，发现野生杨树种子中约 0.4%含有来自杂交杨树的 DNA[17]。诚然，对于具有极强繁殖力的树种，0.4%的基因污染并非是一个小数目。事实上，在世界野生动物基金会的一份调查报告上已经指出：目前释放到野外进行田间试验的有些基因工程树，其转基因已逃逸到自然界[14]。

3.3 对自然生态系统的生物多样性可能产生负面影响

基因工程树的大规模种植，对自然生态系统可能发生有害作用，主要反映在对生物多样性的负面影响。这有以下几方面原因：

(1) 基因工程树是比人工林更强的单一性种植。事实证明单一性种植已对生物多样性产生巨大破坏。例如：引起毁灭性的病虫害；导致结构简单和贫乏的生物群落等，这都是过去营造单一人工林众所周知的教训。

(2) 基因工程树以自身的各种特性影响生物多样性。例如抗虫基因工程树对非靶昆虫和动物(包括一些益虫和害虫的天敌)具有直接或间接的有害作用；快速生长的基因工程树在短时期内过度耗损土壤水份和养料，加剧林地生产力下降和恶化[14]；耐除草剂基因工程树可能发生转基因的漂流，使野生同类或相近种获得抗除草剂性能而成为杂草[18]。降低木质素含量的基因工程树，其花粉若与野生同类树种杂交，则被污染树种的树干抵御强风袭击的能力减弱，对这类树木是毁灭性的灾难。不育性基因工程树不能产生花粉、花或果实，这就影响一大批以花粉、花或果实为生的昆虫、鸟类和哺乳类动物的生存，而昆虫的减少又直接影响食虫鸟类的数量，继之影响哺乳类的数量，然后反过来又影响猛禽的数量。这些地区森林生态系统的生物链被拆毁，最终走向消亡。

(3) 基因工程树可能成为新的入侵外来种。外来种入侵(alien invasion)是指来自其他分布区的物种对本土种及其栖息地的生态系统产生的威胁作用。外来种入侵问题已引起国际社会的严重关注。根据美国、印度和南非向联合国提出的报告，这三个国家因外来种入侵造成的经济损失分别为 1500 亿、1300 亿和 800 亿美元。值得人们警觉的是，多数造成严重问题的外来种入侵，最初基本上都是从经济利益考虑的人为大量引种。在多少年后，其结果却是适得其反。还应该特别提及的是，树木可能是所有入侵生物中最危险的种类，因为它们躯干巨大，寿命长，繁殖力强，其入侵后的生态后果在很长时间后才能显露出来[16]。可以举出许多例子，如引进南半球造成本土生态系统破坏的松树已到了声名狼藉的程度[18]。对于基因工程树而言，它们均具有一些特殊的功能，如抗虫、耐寒、快速生长等，赋予某些种类的转基因树更强的环境“适合度”(Fitness)，使它们可能成为超级入侵种，这对地球生态系统和生物多样性带来的危害将大大超过今天普通树木引种发生入侵所造成的危害。

(4) 与上述情况相反，有些基因工程树则对野生种群产生“遗传同化”(Genetic assimilation)作用。通过基因工程树与野生树种交配，发生“远缘杂交衰退”，就是一种遗传同化。这可能引起杂交后代对环境适应性减弱，造成小种群的消亡。国外林学界对出现这种危险性已有广泛共识[18]。在栽培植物方面，已发现至少有 6 种相关的野生亲缘种与驯化的植物发生杂交后消亡，其中包括一种野生的树种——印度黑胡桃(*Juglans hindsii*)[19]。

(5) 转基因通过水平转移发生扩散。转基因以非有性生殖方式进行传播，学术界称其为基因的水平转移。其中非常重要的是通过微生物发生的水平转移。几乎所有的木本植物的根部都与土壤真菌发生很强的共生作用，两者形成一种所谓的菌根(Mycorrhiza)，为双方提供养分。问题在于一种真菌可以与许多非常不同的木本植物在各种生态环境下共生。而这类真菌种类又很多。因此，转基因树木通过共生的各种真菌发生基因水平转移的可能性很大，而且经过真菌媒介，又可将转基因传到其他树种，其中包括远缘的树种。事实上，在温室中已观察到转基因卡诺那油菜和霉菌(*Aspergillus niger*)之间确实能发生基因的水平转移[20]。

4 关于防止基因工程树对环境造成污染的对策

许多人都认识到基因工程树对环境野生树种可能会造成基因污染，于是相继有不少学者提出一些对策。基本策略是设置生物屏障或物理屏障。将基因工程树造成不育，这样可以防止转基因向自然界扩散，这就是生物屏障。国外多数林业生物工程专家均接受了这个基本观点，所以不育问题成为基因工程树木主要的研究方向之一。但是，至今有关控制树木生殖过程的分子生物学研究资料还很缺乏，这为转基因树木的不育性研究带来困难。业已证明，有众多的基因参与植物生殖的调控[21]。对农作物的研究发现：在花发育过程中存在重要作用的基因至少有 6 种，目前已利用这些基因在杨树上进行不育试验。实施这类研究的依据是：杨树与作物同属被子植物，存在进化上的同源性。在过去几年，与树木开花有关的基因研究也有初步进展[22]。但针叶树种生殖调控基因的研究可能更加困难，因为针叶树在进化上与阔叶树分离已有 3~3.5 亿年之久[10]，控制裸子植物球果发育的分子机制可能与被子植物花的发育明显不同。现已鉴定出与黑云杉球果发育相关的两种 MADS 盒基因[23]。找出与树木生殖配子发育相关的那些基因后，研究人员就可以采用多种途径控制雄蕊或雌蕊的发育，达到使树木不育的目的。其中一个途径是沿用在抗病转基因作物方面较成功的反义 RNA 技术。例如利用苯基苯乙烯合成酶的反义 RNA 抑制类黄酮产生，使花粉败育[24]。另一途径则是通过导入一类嵌合基因，它们可以特异地在花组织开启一种所谓的“自杀基因”(例如 RNA 酶基因可充当这类功能)，抑制花的发育。用这种技术已能做到基因工程植株的雄花不育[25]。基因工程植株的雌花不育也获成功，这是通过改变同源异形基因(Homeotic gene)的表达[22]。这类基因最初是在拟南芥菜中鉴定的，如 LEAFY，AGAMOUS 和 DEFICIENS 等同源异形基因，在杨树也存在[25]。正如前面提到的，无花或无种子的基因工程树可能会影响整个森林的食物生态链。因此有学者提出应该针对改造植物生殖后期相关的基因，这样可以做到依然能产生花瓣和花蜜，甚至还能产生无种子的果实[26]。此外，为了制作不育转基因树而引入外源单基因时，外源基因可能发生基因沉默化作用(Gene silencing)，致使转基因树不能达到预期的不育效果。为了使转基因不育达到更为可靠的程度，目前建议采用所谓“多重不育系

统 (Redundant sterility system)[27]，也就是使用多种不育基因或不同的遗传机制，后者包括仅在雌雄异株树(如杨树)的雌性植株上进行基因转移，其转基因也就不会扩散。当然，无花粉的转基因树却有另一个优点，就是可以大量减少花粉过敏原的产生，对人体健康有利。有的学者认为：最可靠的不育方法还是将那些与树木繁育相关的基因进行永久性的定位诱变，使这些基因的正常功能丧失。但对于树木来讲，目前还没有足够的研究基础能做到这一步。还应当提及树木的转基因可以在染色体外遗传系统中进行，如线粒体和叶绿体。线粒体在所有植物为母系遗传，而叶绿体在大多数植物也为母系遗传。在这些染色体外遗传系统中进行转基因，具有许多优点，如它们的基因组比较简单，可以控制外源基因插入的位置；不会影响染色体遗传系统；能防止基因通过有性生殖扩散到非转基因同类树种。但目前有关这个领域的研究还不多。

还有一些简易的方法也能在一定程度上控制基因工程树的转基因漂流到自然界。其中一种方法是在基因工程树周围用与之性不亲和的相近种隔离。例如在基因工程杨树、山杨树周围种植不能与之交配的三角叶杨。远离可杂交的相近种也不失为一种方法。这些方法就属于前述的物理屏障。

除人们重点研究的基因工程不育树种外，针对某种转基因树可能造成的负面影响，也在研究一些具体的防范对策。例如在抗虫 *Bt* 基因工程树方面，最令人担心的是昆虫抗性的产生，而昆虫生态学家已经发现存在这种可能[15]。为此提出了两种策略：一是像 *Bt* 作物那样，在 *Bt* 基因工程树附近种植一定面积的同类非转基因树作为所谓的庇护区(Refuse)，用以保留少数对 *Bt* 毒性敏感的昆虫种群，以延缓昆虫抗性的产生[18]。另一策略是发展多抗性基因的转基因树，因害虫难以对多种毒性基因同时产生抗性。对于有争议的抗菌素抗性标记基因问题，尽管目前尚无定论，但国外不少实验室已经开始换用其他标记基因。事实上现在已有许多方法对转基因植物进行选择，而无需依赖抗菌素。例如可通过染色、激发荧光或营养互补的基因等，以选择那些转化的细胞或组织，甚至也可在转基因成功后对抗菌素抗性基因进行删除。

5　结论

在可预见的未来，基因工程树将成为地球人工林景观的重要组成部分。但人们是不愿看到一片毫无生机的仅仅为人类眼前利益而存在的“工程林”。如果真是那样，人类不可避免将再一次演绎着 20 世纪工业革命对自然掠夺所造成的灾难。森林令我们如此倍加关注，不独是它与人类的生存息息相关，也因为历史上它被毁坏得太多，存留的又太脆弱。而且在所有栽培植物品种中，种植的人工林树种又几乎都没有经过明显的驯化而属于“半野生”状态，因而，如对人工林树种进行基因改造，则相应的野生树种天然基因库就很易被污染。此外，树木又是具有几十年甚至上百年漫长存活期的生命，至今我们还没有足够的时间来认真考察和分析对它们进行基因“手术”会有什么样的长期后果。凡此种种，比起生活周期短到只有几个月的多数农作物来讲，对树木进行基因工程改造必然面临着更多的不确定性。因而在向自然界释放基因工程树时，我们没有理由不万分谨慎!

还应该看到，基因工程树基本上是用于营造各种人工林。但人工林在我国历来是“树种单一，结构极不合理，森林病虫害和地力衰退问题比较严重”[28]。可以设想，如果不研究相应对策和采取有力措施，大面积推广基因工程人工林所造成的问题只能会更为严重。有些技术革命与发明在出现时曾受到热烈欢迎和普遍接受，但多少年后却发现它们严重损害了人类的根本利益而最终被抛弃。在近代发明史上，不乏这类教训。上世纪中叶号称具有革命创新性并荣获诺贝尔奖的 DDT 化学杀虫剂就是其中一例。这种化学毒物在过去几十年对人类和畜禽所造成的遗传损伤，至今还无法消除由于大规模释放基因工程树而招致的任何天然森林树种的基因污染，或者在某些地区可能作为一类新的外来种入侵，所造成的生物多样性的衰竭将永远无法恢复，尽管它不是发生在今天。

21 世纪人类将进入更为理智、对自身行为更为规范的时代，这是人类社会的可持续发展的需要。国际上“有机农业”的兴起，林业纳入 EMS-ISO 14 000 国际质量论证体系的轨道[29]等，均显示人类正在以前所未有的勇气告别对自然资源利用的那种混乱无序甚至肆意掠夺的年代。为此我们支持下述观点，即：“……在开发和使用现代生物技术的同时亦采取旨在确保环境和人类健康的妥善安全措施，则此种技术可为人类福利带来巨大的惠益”[30]。

参考文献

[1] Parsons T J. et al. *Bio/Technology*. 1986. 4: 533

[2] Riemenschneider D E. Haissig B E. In: Ahuja M R, ed. Biotechnology of woody plants. New York: Plenum Press,1991. 247

[3] Montgomery M E. Wallner W E. In: Berryidan A A. ed. Dynamics of forest insect populations, New York: Plenum Press, 1988, 353

[4] Ryan C A. *Ann Rev Phytopathol*. 1990, 28: 425

[5] Leple J C, et al. *Molecular Breeding*, 1995. 10: 1

[6] Kamosky D F. *Environ Cons*, 1979. 6: 311

[7] Neale D B. et al. *Plant Cell*, 1990, 2: 673

[8] Overhaugh I M. Fall R. *Plant Physiol*. 1985, 77: 437

[9] Tillman D A.In: Forest products: advanced technological and economic analyses. New York: Academic Press,1985 133

[10] Tsai C J, et al. *Plant Physiol*. 1995. 107: 1459

[11] Eriksson M E, et al. *Nature Biotechnology*，2000, 18:784

[12] Doty S L. et al. *Proc Natl Acad Sci* USA, 2000. 97 (12): 6287

[13] Owusu R A. GM technology in the forest sector. A scoping study for WWF. http: //www. panda. org/ressources/ publications/forest /gm/gm- overview. html. 1 999

[14] Kaiser J. *Science*. 2001. 292 (5514): 34

[15] Richardson D M.*Conservation Biology*. 1998, 12: 18

[16] DiFazio S P. 2000 Progress Report-EPA Grant Number: U 91522. 2000

[17] Strauss S H, et al. The *Forestry Chronicle*, 2001, 77(2): 271

[18] Ellstrand N C, et al. *Annual Review of Ecology and Systematics*, 1999, 30: 539

[19] Hofmann T, et al. *Current genetics*, 1994. 27: 70

[20] Rutledge B. Producing Sterile Trees. Canadian Forest Service Report, 1998

[21] Strauss S H. et al. *Molecular Breeding*, 1995. 1: 5
[22] Weigel D. Nilsson O. *Nature*. 1995, 377: 495
[23] van der Meet I M, et al. *Plant Cell*, 1992, 4: 253
[24] Mariana C. et al. *Nature*. 1991, 347: 737
[25] Varoquax F, et al. *Trends in Biotechnology*, 2000. 18:233
[26] Bell A C. et al. *Science*, 2001, 291: 447
[27] 成林, 中国环境与发展评论(第 1 卷). 社会科学文献出版社, 2001. 135
[28] Strauss S H, et al. *International Forestry Review*, 2001, 3(2): 85
[29] 生物多样性公约卡塔赫纳生物安全议定书. 2000

本文原载：植物学报. 1997. 39(1): 34-42

盐渍条件下野大豆群体的遗传分化和生理适应：同工酶和随机扩增多态 DNA 研究*

王洪新　胡志昂　钟敏　陆文静
魏伟　恽锐　钱迎倩

(中国科学院植物研究所)

摘　要　黄河三角洲野大豆(*Glycine soja* Sieb.et Zucc.)盐渍群体的耐盐性高于附近的正常群体。群体内个体间耐盐能力差别很大。盐渍群体有比最耐盐的栽培大豆(*G.max* (L.)Merr.)品种耐盐能力高得多的个体，也有对盐相当敏感的植株。同工酶分析表明群体内高水平多态性，但酶谱与抗性没有相关性。盐渍与正常群体间的遗传一致性高达 0.96。用改良的随机扩增多态 DNA(RAPD)方法，10 个引物扩增得出群体内多态位点百分数为 68/188= 0.36。看来，绝大多数位点与耐盐能力无关。上述资料说明，盐渍条件下野大豆自然群体的高度遗传多样性和发育变通性，可能是对盐胁迫强度随时随地变化的环境的适应。

关键词　野大豆；自然群体；耐盐性；分子标记；遗传多样性；发育变通性

土壤盐渍化是世界农业所面临的越来越严重的问题。大多数作物，特别是豆类对盐敏感[1]。麦类和番茄近缘野生种高耐盐资源筛选和利用的成功经验[2]，促进了自然群体耐盐性及其进化潜力的研究。例如广泛栽培的白三叶草(*Trifolium repens* L.)品种在 50 mmol/L NaCl (0.3%)条件下，生长减少近一半[1]，而 Ab-Shukor 等[3]报道盐沼泽的野生群体能在 150~200 mmol/L NaCl(0.9%~1.2%)中生长良好。在理论上自然群体耐盐性研究也为探讨生物如何适应变化着的环境这个生态学中心议题提供了资料。本文报道黄河三角洲野大豆盐渍和正常群体的耐盐性、同工酶和随机扩增多态 DNA(RAPD)的遗传分化，探讨适应的机理。

1　材料和方法

1.1　材料收集和生境

取样的野大豆(*Glycine soja*　Sieb.et Zucc.)群体位于山东省垦利县。群体 1 位于县城黄河

---

*中国科学院重点研究项目。
美国农业部大豆和苜蓿研究所 P B Cregan 博士提供栽培大豆品种。山东省垦利县张日震、赵清华和顾杰夫对野大豆采集提供指导和帮助，一并致谢。

胜利大桥下，采集了 11 个单株的种子；群体 2、3、4 均位于黄河 1976 年改道后形成的新黄河三角洲的入海口，分别采集了 12、15、23 个单株的种子。群体 3、4 生长在积水或湿润的芦苇丛中，水分状况类似群体 1，而群体 2 分布在高出地面 5m 左右的台地上。黄河三角洲的滨海地区，海陆交接地区 5~10 km 范围内，土壤平均含盐量均大于 1%[4]。群体 2、3、4 正是处于这类区域内。群体 1 距海远，不受海潮影响，河水矿化度远小于海水，平均在 0.15~0.30 g/L，河流两侧地下水及土壤含盐量一般均较低[4]。所以确定群体 1 为正常非盐渍群体，其他为盐渍群体。

1.2 耐盐性测定

1.2.1 耐盐指数

自然群体耐盐性研究的多数报道，采用 Hannon 和 Bradshaw[5]的方法。将盐溶液中植株的最长根的平均长度除以对照溶液中植株的最长根的平均长度定义为耐盐指数。野大豆盐渍群体结实率很低，所以群体耐盐指数的测定是用人工种植后以群体为单位收获的种子。具体步骤是各群体任取种子 50 粒，破种皮后播在泡沫塑料上[5]，悬浮于 5 L Johnson 等[6]的培养液中。真叶出现后外加 NaCl 达到 0.5%，为盐处理。2~3 周后测量各株最长根的长度，并测量地上部的高度和鲜重。根据 PantaloneⅢ和 Kenworthy[7]，用 0.5% NaCl 处理能最大限度地显示栽培大豆及其野生近缘种在耐盐性上的差别。

1.2.2 从盐害出现的时间测定耐盐系数

自然群体各单株收获的种子在培养皿中萌发后，在加有 Johnson 培养液的大塑料盘中水培到第一对真叶展开。其后每 5d 加一次 NaCl，使其浓度从 0.2%逐级上升到 0.8%。植株真叶叶缘出现青枯斑为盐害症状。以盐害症状出现前在不同浓度 NaCl 中生长的天数乘以百分比浓度的总和为耐盐系数。例如，栽培大豆品种“Jackson”在加 0.2% NaCl 中生长 3d 后即出现盐害，其耐盐系数 $0.2\times3=0.6$。品种“Morgan”在 0.2%、0.4%、0.6% NaCl 中相继各生长 5d 后，在 0.8% NaCl 中生长 2d 后才出现盐害。其耐盐系数 $0.2\times5+0.4\times5+0.6\times5+0.8\times2=7.6$。

1.3 种子蛋白和同工酶

基本上按照我们以前报道的方法[8]，但用 Kadlec 等[9]的方法制备提取液。种子蛋白用考马氏蓝 R-250 染色。同工酶染色基本上用 Vallejos[10]的方法。酸性磷酸酯酶(ACP)、酯酶(EST)和脲酶(URE)的显色是电泳后先将胶板在显色所用缓冲液中浸泡 15~30min。分析的酶系统还有乙醇脱氢酶(ADH)、淀粉酶(AM)、黄递酶(DIA)、谷氨酸脱氢酶(GDH)和亮氨酸氨基肽酶(LAP)。ACP 染色用 Düring[11]的方法。

1.4 RAPD

用我们改良的方法，基本步骤是用 Stewart[12]的方法纯化水培幼苗叶的 DNA。用

Williams 等[13]的方法进行扩增，扩增产物用 Bassam 和 Caetano-Anolles[14]的聚丙烯酰胺凝胶电泳分离和银染。

2 结果和讨论

2.1 自然群体的耐盐性

鉴定植物的耐盐性有各种各样的方法，但较可靠的是测量盐胁迫下的生长或盐害症状出现的时间[15]。

2.1.1 耐盐指数 0.5% NaCl 处理对群体内个体生长的影响见表 1

表 1 中显示，从所测各项生长指标的平均值看，群体 3 平均耐盐能力最强，群体 4 次之，群体 1、2 互有上下。而从所列各项生长指标的最低和最高值看，群体内各个体间无论是植株高度、地上部分鲜重或最长根的长度变化都很大。实验重复两次，得到类似结果。说明广泛应用于评价多年生、以营养繁殖为主的禾草群体耐盐性的方法并不适用于一年生完全有性繁殖的野大豆，因为后者群体内在生长速度上有高得多的变异。

表 1 NaCl 对各群体幼苗生长的影响

Table 1 Influence of Nacl on growth of seedling

群体 Population		植株高度 Height(cm)			地上部鲜重 Fresh weight of shoot(mg)			最长根长度 Length of the longest root(cm)		
		最低 Min	平均 Average	最高 Max	最低 Min	平均 Average	最高 Max	最低 Min	平均 Average	最高 Max
1	NaCl	9	28.32	55	64	197.13	349	5	10.04	16
	Control	6	32.85	54	39	280.56	584	6	9.03	13
2	NaCl	6	23.89	44	72	193.38	537	5	9.80	15
	Control	4	29.11	54	52	254.53	648	5	9.10	20
3	NaCl	6	25.63	50	43	192.33	463	6	11.36	17
	Control	8	25.08	46	68	222.15	825	6	9.54	25
4	NaCl	6	28.26	42	81	191.53	352	5	10.32	16
	Control	9	28.92	53	93	228.35	521	5	8.77	16

2.1.2 耐盐系数

根据所计算的各群体内不同个体的耐盐系数，绘制了各群体不同耐盐系数植株的百分比图(图 1)。为了直接反映野大豆的耐盐水平，我们同时测定并计算了已知最耐盐的栽培大豆品种“Morgan”和敏感品种“Jackson”[16]的耐盐系数并标于图 1。可以看出正常群体的耐盐性分布较窄，均在栽培大豆抗性范围内。而群体 3、4 中有对盐较敏感的，但都有少数植株耐盐性大大超过品种“Morgan”的，表现出极为广泛的变异。上述结果与 Kik[17]的报道比较接近，即盐渍群体平均耐盐性高于正常群体，主要是因为盐渍群体有更多耐盐个体以及存在正常群体所没有的高耐盐的植株。

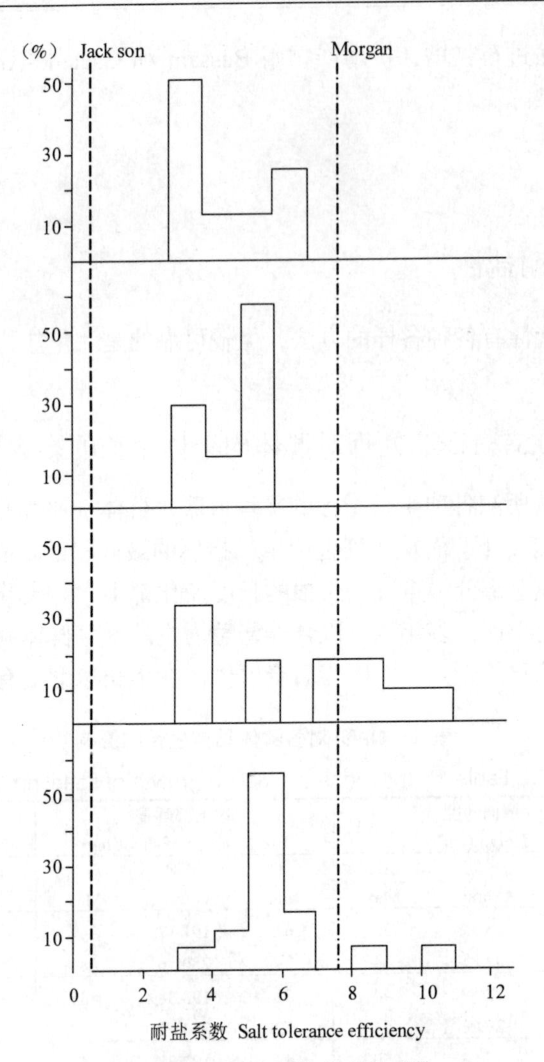

图 1　野大豆自然群体的耐盐系数

Fig.1　Salt tolerance coefficient of natural populations Glycine soja

各群体的平均耐盐系数：群体 1 为 4. 66，群体 2 为 4.76，群体 3 为 6.46，群体 4 为 5.85。与多数报道一致，盐渍群体的平均耐盐性高于正常群体。群体 2 耐盐性偏低，可能与测定方法有关。水培的条件与群体 1、3、4 的生境类似，却不能代表群体 2 土壤比较干燥和通气良好的状况。Kik[17]曾讨论过测定耐盐性所用的水培方法可能低估了匍茎剪股颖(*Agrostis stolonifera*)砂丘群体的耐盐潜力。我们也用砂培方法对各群体一些个体进行逐株的耐盐性测定，得到与水培类似的结果。只是重复样品之间耐盐性波动较大，不如水培的稳定。水培条件下，各植株根系暴露在离子浓度十分一致的条件下。而砂内盐分状况要复杂得多。

2.2　同工酶

种子蛋白电泳基本上没有检测到遗传变异。用 Davis[18]系统所分离的各种同工酶谱与 Kiang 和 Gorman[19]，Doong 和 Kiang[20]报道的基本相似，因此他们的遗传分析可以应用于我们的结果。表 2 列出群体 1 和群体 4 各等位的频率。

有关大豆成熟子叶的 GDH 研究很少。仅 Broue 等[21]报道用淀粉胶电泳分离澳洲多年生野大豆的 GDH，得到快慢不同的 3 条谱带。我们用 Davis 系统共检测到 9 条带，其中电泳最快的 3 条没有多态性。淌度最小的 4 条带，每个植株只有其中 1 条，也有少数植株在这个区域 1 条带也没有。因此我们推测是 1 个位点(Gdh1)编码的 a、b、c、d 和零等位的产物。中间两条带活性最高，快慢不同，1 个植株只有 1 条，推测是另 1 个位点(Gdh2)两个等位 a、b 的产物。

群体 1 和 4 的 EST、URE 和 Ti(胰蛋白酶抑制剂)没有发现多态性。

群体 1 和 4 的平均基因多样性(或群体杂合性)分别为 0. 326 和 0.245，远大于自交植物的平均值 0.124 和全部植物的平均值 0.149[22]。同是野大豆，该数值也大于韩国的任一野大豆群体，甚至大于该国总的野大豆多样性值 0. 215[23]，两群体之间的平均遗传一致性 I= 0.957，遗传距离 D=0.045。我们[24]报道野大豆在自然条件下是严格自交的，后得到 Yu 和 Kiang[23]证实，自交有利于群体间遗传分化。但本研究所得到的两群体间的遗传距离，远小于 Yu 和 Kiang[23]报道的韩国野大豆任意两群体之间的距离(0.066~0.193)。群体 4 位于群体 1 下游，而且在 1976 年黄河最后一次改道后所形成的新三角洲内。所以群体 4 有可能是群体 1 少数耐盐个体通过奠基者效应(founder effect)所形成的。但是群体 4 有比群体 1 更广泛的耐盐性分化、很高水平的同工酶多样性，这与一般意义上的奠基者效应不同，下面将详细进行讨论。

表 2　野大豆盐渍群体 4 与正常群体 1 同工酶频率

Table 2　Isozyme frequencies of saline and normal populations of *Glycine soja*

位点 Locus	等位 Allele	频率(%) 群体 1 Pop.1	频率(%) 群体 4 Pop.4	位点 Locus	等位 Allele	频率(%) 群体 1 Pop.1	频率(%) 群体 4 Pop.4
Adh1	+	0.38	0.15	Am^3	a	0.03	0.08
	–	0.62	0.85		b	0.97	0.92
Adh2	+	0.30	0.00	Gdh1	a	0.05	0.13
	–	0.70	1.00		b	0.25	0.20
Adh3	+	0.03	0.13		c	0.10	0.20
	–	0.97	0.87		d	0.30	0.20
Adh4	+	0.15	0.08	Gdh2	–	0.30	0.27
	–	0.85	0.92		a	0.15	0.20
AP	a	0.05	0.21		b	0.85	0.80
	b	0.95	0.68	Lapl			
	c	0.00	0.11		a	0.10	0.00
dia2	a	0.50	0.18		b	0.25	0.08
	b	0.50	0.82		c	0.65	0.92
dia3	a	0.25	0.00	Lap2	+	0.10	0.08
	b	0.75	1.00		–	0.90	0.92

Pop. Population.

我们也比较了不同耐盐水平植株的同工酶谱。无论是从 4 个群体或其中任一群体看，酶的组成和耐盐性没有相关性。对于任一耐盐植株，总能找到一个有相同酶谱的盐敏感植株；而同是耐盐的或同是敏感的植株之间也都有不同的酶谱。在群体耐盐性研究中，Ab-Shukor 等[3]的报道是唯一提到进行同工酶研究的，他们也未发现盐渍群体有特别的同工酶基因型。

2.3 RAPD

表 3 分别列出 10 个引物所扩增的群体 4 各植株 RAPD 位点数及多态位点百分数。表中只统计 2.3 kb 以下的片段。2.3 kb 以上还有很多片段，例如用引物 OPJ 04 就有大于 2.3 kb 的 26 条带。但在我们的实验条件下，这些带很集中，很难确定有否淌度的差异。

从表3可以看出:① 用我们改良的RAPD方法揭示出野大豆群体内有高水平的DNA多样性；② 扩增产物数以及多态位点百分数均随引物而异。其中引物 OPJ 04 扩增多态位点百分数最高，达 65.4%。表 4 以 OPJ 04 为例列出多态位点在各群体某些代表植株里的分布。可以看出除 3-1 和 3-3 之间、3-7 和 4-19 之间有同样 RAPD 谱外，其他植株都有其特有的谱。更多引物的筛选结果表明，4 个群体内所检测的全部个体在基因型上都有其唯一性(uniqueness)。有的位点是植株专一的，例如表 4 中的 OPJ 04_{360} 仅出现于 3-11。我们推测植株基因型的唯一性不仅仅是某些序列成分不同组合而已，很可能有新的 DNA 序列。这有待今后序列分析来证实。

表 3 野大豆群体 4 RAPD 位点

Table 3 DNA diver sity detected by RAPD for population No.4 of *Glycine soja*

引物 Primer	RAPD 位点 RAPD locus			
	总数 Total	单态位点数 Monomorphic	多态位点数 Polymorphic	多态位点百分数 P
OPD 01	39	25	14	35.9
OPD 03	13	9	4	30.8
OPD 04	16	6	10	62.5
OPD 05	13	11	2	15.4
OPD 07	15	12	3	20.0
OPD 11	12	7	5	41.7
OPD 15	24	21	3	12.5
OPD 18	13	13	0	0
OPD 20	17	7	10	58.8
OPJ 04	26	9	17	65.4

与同工酶相比，RAPD 有高得多的多态性。已有的结果表明盐渍群体的 DNA 多样性高于正常群体。我们已经鉴定到个别高耐盐个体所特有的 RAPD 位点，如 OPJ 04_{360}。

正在进一步研究这些位点是否与耐盐性紧密连锁。但是必须指出，和全部同工酶位点一样，RAPD 的绝大多数位点与耐盐性无关。

表 4 OPJ 04 引物 RAPD 多态位点分布

Table 4 RAPD patterns of wild soybean populations by using primer OPJ04

产物 Product (bp)	植株编号①Plant code①														
	1-2	1-3	1-8	2-1	2-4	3-1	3-3	3-5	3-7	3-11	3-13	3-14	4-17	4-18	4-19
1700								+				+	+		
1300								+							
1200	+	+	+		+	+	+			+	+	+	+		
1010						+	+		+	+	+	+	+	+	+
980		+		+	+	+	+	+	+	+	+	+			+
960	+							+					+	+	
930		+													
800		+		+	+	+	+		+	+	+		+	+	+
760													+	+	
720													+	+	
680	+	+	+	+	+	+	+		+	+	+	+	+	+	+
660	+	+		+	+			+						+	
590								+				+			
540									+				+		
500					+								+	+	
380					+							+	+	+	
360										+					

①植株编号分前后两个数字，前一个数字是群体号，后一个数字为群体内植株的采集号。

①Plant code consists of two numbers, the first ones are the number of population, the second ones the sapling number.

2.4 适应机理

野大豆盐渍群体的平均耐盐能力高于正常群体，而且存在正常群体所没有的高耐盐个体。这两点比较容易理解，也和国外的很多报道一致。植物自然群体抗逆性的研究，早期集中于铜等重金属的抗性。有的植物能很快地侵入废弃的重金属矿区形成抗性植物群体。Gartside 和 McNeilly[25]测定了很多种植物的耐铜能力，发现那些有抗性群体的种类如剪股颖属和鸭茅(*Dactylis glomerata*)的正常群体里有极少数(0.08%)个体有和抗性群体一样强的充分的耐铜能力。其他种类如多年生黑麦草(*Lolium perenne*)和长叶车前(*Plantagolanceolata*)没有抗性变异，不能形成抗性群体。由此提出了抗性是预先就存在的理论。进化过程是非污染土壤上正常群体里很低频率预先存在的抗性或部分抗性的个体通过选择快速形成抗性群体。Walley 等[26]用重金属废矿渣筛选细弱剪股颖(*Agrostis tenuis*)正常群体，一次就得到能在废矿区生长的抗性植株，证明了上述理论。后来进行的自然群体耐盐研究取得了类似的结果。其中少数提到进行了同工酶和蛋白质电泳。或曰抗性群体没有专一的同工酶基因型[3]，或显示盐渍群体比正常群体有更多蛋白质电泳基因型[17]，似乎不符合抗性群体由正常群体中的极少数抗性个体通过奠基者效应形成的假说。一般认为奠基者效应决定了抗性群体基因型少于正常群体[27]。我们认为，从文献[3，17]看，正常群体和盐渍群体都有很多蛋白电泳基因型。很可能与本报道一样，盐敏感植株的所有电泳型，耐盐植株都有。因此，针对耐盐性所产生的奠基者效应并不反映在同工酶多样性的减少上。事实上，迄今为止关于盐胁迫或盐适应条件下基因表达变化的大量报道，没有一个是涉及群体遗传学研究中常用的同工酶位点；负责环境应答的是另外一些基因群[28]。不仅是同工酶位点，本文报道的RAPD位点绝大多数也与耐盐无关，个别高耐盐植株专一的位点是否涉及耐盐还有待遗传分析。通过耐盐与盐敏感品种之间的杂交和后代分离实验，Abel[29]证明大豆耐盐性是由一个显性的氯排斥基因位点控制的。Dvorak 等[30]用异源附加系和异源替换系证明长穗偃麦草(*Lophopyrum elongtum*=*Elytrigia elongata*)耐盐主基因分别定位在3E、4E和7E 3对染色体上，表现出加性遗传效应。提出偃麦草高耐盐性是在逐渐适应土壤盐渍化过程中逐步固定了这些相互独立位点的显性突变。因此不难理解，为什么高耐盐植株只出现在盐渍群体的缘故。

出乎意料的是在野大豆盐渍群体里有和正常群体一样的对盐相当敏感的植株，这是与前人不同的结果。自Hannon和Bradshaw[5]以来，Wu[31]、Ashraf等[32]等都发现无论是植物盐渍群体还是正常群体，群体内都有耐盐性的分化。Venables和Wilkins[33]早就用杂交试验证明抗性是可遗传的，而且耐盐性是显性，并得到Humphreys[34]、Ashraf等[35]的证实。但是他们报道的群体内耐盐能力的遗传分化程度都不大。盐渍群体内每个个体的耐盐能力都大于正常群体的任何植株[31]。也就是说盐渍群体和正常群体的耐盐谱相互不重叠。Kik[17]报道了他研究的盐沼匍匐剪股颖群体与非盐渍草甸群体之间个体耐盐谱的重叠现象，但在盐沼群体内没有发现草甸群体所特有的对盐最敏感的植株。为什么野大豆的盐渍群体里会出现对盐敏感的植株呢？我们认为有两个原因：① 野大豆是一年生自花授粉只行有性生殖的植物，不同于国外报道的多年生以营养繁殖为主的植物；② 黄河三角洲的盐渍度不稳定[4]，而国外报道的盐渍群体有稳定的生境[5]。

野大豆作为自交植物，群体内不断自发产生的遗传变异很容易保存下来。本文报道的群体内个体间生长速度、耐盐系数、同工酶位点和RAPD的高度遗传多样性充分证明了这一点。野大豆是一年生植物。野外调查和人工栽培的实践表明它可以在2~3个月内完成从种子到种子的整个生活史。对盐敏感的个体在夏季多雨土壤淋溶情况下有避开高盐渍生境的可能。野大豆另一个重要的生物学特征是种皮不透水性，一个植株所结的种子可以休眠不同时间，几年内不丢失发芽力。这些特点造成了土壤中存在不同年份成熟的由不同基因型组成的极其复杂的种子库。黄河三角洲的盐渍状况不稳定[4]，主要是年降雨集中在夏季，海水入侵不规律，土壤蒸发量很大。随时随地变化的盐渍状态允许不同耐盐性的种子在其适当的地点和时间萌发和生长。很低的群体密度并不构成剧烈的竞争，多数植株很快进入开花结实。

国外群体耐盐研究全用以多年生营养繁殖为主的植物。威尔士海边的盐渍状况很稳定[5]，因为降水年分配均匀，海水入侵十分规律，而土壤蒸发量不大。这种盐渍条件下只有耐盐的个体能够长期存在。对盐敏感的个体即使进入，也不能保存下来。

野大豆等一年生自交植物以其高水平遗传多样性和发育变通性对随时随地变化着的环境多样性灵活做出应答，不失为适应的范例。这也解释了华北沿海分布的植物偏向一年生生活型的原因。

3 结论

① 野大豆盐渍群体的平均耐盐性高于正常群体，是因为盐渍群体存在着正常群体所没有的高耐盐植株，其耐盐能力远大于已知最耐盐的栽培大豆品种。② 群体内各植株的生长速率，耐盐性差别均很大，盐渍群体尤甚。很难用简单的奠基者效应来解释。③ 同工酶分析表明群体内的高水平遗传多样性。盐渍和正常群体有类似的遗传结构，很少遗传分化。④ 没有发现同工酶变异与耐盐性有相关性。⑤ RAPD 分析证实野大豆群体内的高度遗传多样性。DNA 水平多样性高于同工酶。并显示野大豆群体各植株 DNA 成分的唯一性。⑥ 绝大多数 RAPD 产物与耐盐性无关，但发现有的高耐盐个体有其特征性的 RAPD 产物。⑦ 高水平遗传多样性和发育变通性是野大豆群体对盐渍强度随时随地变化的环境的适应。

参考文献

[1] Lauchli A. Salt exclusion: An adaptation of legumes for. crops and pastures under saline conditions. In: Stapes R C, Toenniessen G T eds., Salinity Tolerance in Plants. New York: John Wiley & Sons, 1984. 171~187

[2] Epstein E, Norlyn J D, Rush D W *et al*. Saline culture of crops: A genetic approach. *Science*,1980. **210**: 399~404

[3] Ab-Shukor N A, Kay Q O N, Stevens D P *et al*.Salt tolerance in natural populations of *Trifolium repens* L. *New Phytol*,1988. **109**: 483~490

[4] 中国科学院土壤及水土保持研究所，水利电力部北京勘测设计院土壤调查总队，华北平原土壤. 北京：科学出版社. 1961.

[5] Hannon N, Bradshaw A D. Evolution of salt tolerance in two coexisting species of grass. *Nature*, 1968. **220**: 1342~1343

[6] Johnson C M, Stout P R, Broyer T C *et al.* Comparative chlorine requirements of different plant species. *Plant Soil,* 1957. Ⅷ **4**: 337~353

[7] Pantalone Ⅲ V R, Kenworthy W J. Salt tolerance in *Glycine max* and perennial *Glycine Soybean Cenetics Newsl*, 1989. **16**: 145~146

[8] 胡志昂，王洪新.检测大豆种子蛋白 Sp1、Ti 两基因位点各等位酶方法的改进.植物学报, 1983. **25**: 532~536

[9] Kadlec M, Stejskal J, Letal J *et al.*Screening of enzyme systems. *Soybean Cenetics Newst,* 1994. **21**:92~96

[10] Vallejos E. Enzyme activity staining. In: Tanksley S D, Orton T J eds., Isozymes in Plant Genetics and Breeding. Amsterdam: Elsevier. 1983. part A, 469~516

[11] Düring K. Ultrasensitive chemilluminescent and colorigenic detection of DNA, RNA and protein in plant molecular biology. *Anal Biochem*, 1991. **196**: 433~438

[12] Stewart Jr C N. Soybean DNA isolation procedure using fresh tissue. *Soybean Cenetics Newsl*. 1994. **21**:243~244

[13] Williams J G K. Kubelik A R. Livak J *et al.*DNA polymorphisms amplified by arbitrary primers are useful as genetic markers. *Nucleic Acids Res*.1990. **18**: 6531~6535

[14] Bassam B J, Caetano-Anolles G.Silver staining of DNA in polyacrylamide gels.*Appl Biochem Biotechn*, 1993. **42**: 181~188

[15] Munns R.Physiological processes limiting plant growth in saline soils: Some dogma and hypotheses. *Plant Cell Environ*, 1993.**16**: 15~24

[16] Ragab A S, PantaloneIII V R, Kenworthy W J *et al*. Salt tolerance of soybean in solution culture experiments: II. Reacton of 19 genotypes. *Soybean Genetic Newsl*, 1994. **21**: 277~279

[17] Kik C.Ecological genetics of salt resistance in the clonal perenial, *Agrostis stolonifera* L. *New Phytol*, 1989. **113**: 453~458

[18] Davis B J.Disc electrophoresis: Method and application to human serum proteins. *Annals N Y Acad Sci*, 1964. **121**: 404~427

[19] Kiang Y T, Gorman M B. Soybean. In:Tanksley S D, Orton T J eds., Isozymes in Plant Genetics and Breeding. Amsterdam: Elsevier. 1983. part B, 295~328

[20] Doong J Y H, Kiang Y T. Cultivar identification by isozyme analysis. *Soybean Genetics Newsl*, 1987. **14**: 189~226

[21] Broue D, Marshall D R, Muller W J. Biosystematics of subgenus *Glycine isozymatic* data. *Austr J Bot*, l977. **25**: 555~566

[22] Hamrick J L, Godt M J W. Allozyme diversity in plant species. In: Brown A D H et al. eds., Plant Population Genetics, Breeding, and Genetic Resources, Sunderland: Sinauer Associates Inc, 1990. 43~ 64

[23] Yu H, Kiang Y T.Genetic variation in South Korea natural populations of wild soybean(*Glycine soja*).*Eupytica*, l993. **68**: 213~221

[24] 胡志昂, 王洪新, 北京地区野大豆天然群体遗传结构.植物学报, 1985. **27**: 599~604

[25] Gartside D W, McNeilly T.The potential for evolution of heavy metal tolerance in plants. II. Copper tolerance in normal populations of different plant species. *Heredity*, 1974. **32**: 335~348

[26] Walley K A, Khan M S I, Bradshaw A D *et al.*The potential for evolution of heavy metal tolerance in plants. I. Copper and zinc tolerance in *Agrostis tenuis*. *Heredity*, l974, **32**: 309~319

[27] Warwick S I.Black L D.Electrophoretic variation in trazine resistant and susceptible populations of *Amaranthus retroflexus*. *New Phytol*. 1986. **104**: 661~670

[28] 胡志昂, 王洪新, 植物抗旱耐盐基因研究进展.见: 荆玉祥, 匡廷云, 李德宝等编, 植物分子生物学.北京: 科学出版社.1995. 204~ 213

[29] Abel G H.Inheritance of the capacity for chloride inclusion and chloride exclusion by soybean.*Crop Sci*, l969. 9: 697~698

[30] Dvorak J, Edge M, Ross K *et al.*On the evolution of the adaptation of *Lophopyrum elongatum* to growth in saline environments. *Proc Natl Acad Sci USA*, 1988. **85**:3805~3809

[31] Wu L. The potential for evolution of salinity tolerance in *Agrostis stolonifera* L. and *Agrostis tenuis* SiBth. *New Phytol*, 1981. **89**: 471~486

[32] Ashraf M. McNeilly T, Bradshaw A D *et al.*The potential for evolution of salt (NaCl) tolerance in several grass species. *New Phytol*. 1986. **103**: 299~309

[33] Venables A V.Wilkins D A.Salt tolerance in pasture grasses, *New Phytol*, 1978. **80**: 613~622

[34] Humphreys M O. The genetic basis of tolerance to salt spray in populations of *Festuca rubra* L. *New Phytol*, 1982. **91**: 287~ 296

[35] Ashraf M, McNeilly T, Bradshaw A D *et al*. Selection and heritability to sodium chloride in four rorage species. *Crop Sci*, 1987. **27**: 232~234

本文原载：植物学报. 1998. 40(2): 169-175

北京东灵山辽东栎种群DNA多样性的研究*

恽锐　钟敏　王洪新　魏伟　胡志昂　钱迎倩

(中国科学院植物研究所)

摘　要　在同工酶研究基础上，利用随机扩增多态性DNA(RAPD)及DNA扩增指纹(DAF)方法，从生态学观点分析了北京东灵山区辽东栎(*Quercus liaotungensis* Koidz.)种群的遗传结构和多样性。对12个引物扩增产生的205个产物(部分)，经Shannon信息指数分析，结果表明：辽东栎种群内部存在丰富的遗传变异，中央种群的遗传多样性高于边缘种群的遗传多样性。总遗传多样性的95%发生在种群内，只有5%发生在种群间。两种群在个别位点上存在差异。不同年龄组辽东栎的分析结果表明：人为干扰对辽东栎的遗传结构有一定影响。
关键词　辽东栎；同工酶；RAPD；遗传分化；遗传多样性

同工酶技术是六、七十年代发展起来的，利用同工酶技术对多种栎属植物进行了研究[1, 2]，但同工酶检测的位点相对较少。80年代产生的聚合酶链式反应(PCR)技术为DNA水平的研究开辟了广阔的前景。随机扩增多态性DNA(RAPD)[3]和DNA扩增指纹(DAF)[4]技术利用极少量的植物材料即可检测极丰富的DNA序列变化的信息，是有效的检测植物种群多样性的分子技术[5,6]。近年来，利用RAPD方法对多种植物进行了种内、种间变异及遗传分化的研究[7~10]。虽然栎属DNA方面的工作已做了许多，但用RAPD、DAF标记检测种群内和种群间的遗传多样性还未见报道。本文应用同工酶及RAPD和DAF方法，分析了北京东灵山辽东栎种群的遗传分化，探讨其与环境的关系，以期为该生态系统的恢复提供遗传资料和科学依据。

1　材料和方法

1.1　研究地点的自然概况

样品取自中国科学院北京森林生态系统定位研究站。其地理位置位于北纬39°58′，东经115°41′附近。有关该地区的自然概况已作过报道[11]。

经野外考察，结合前人工作，共选择4个样地：样地1、2分别为钟敏等[12]报道的标准样地和崖口。为进一步研究不同年龄组同工酶的频率分布，增加了样地3和样地4，样地3位于标准样地对面的东南坡，海拔1200 m左右；样地4位于定位站侧面的东南

---

* 中国科学院重大项目的一部分。

坡，海拔 1300 m 左右。

1994 年 10 月中旬采集辽东栎(*Quercus liaotungensis* Koidz.)冬前芽，方法同钟敏等[12]的报道。每个样地随机采集植物样品，1、2 样地各 60 株，3、4 样地各 30~40 株。采芽的同时记录树的胸径和高度。

1.2 同工酶的提取、电泳及统计分析方法

详情见钟敏等[12]。年龄结构的研究：将 4 个样地的样品混合按年龄分为 3 组：A 组(10 ~ 26 龄)，B 组(26 ~ 34 龄)，C 组(34 ~ 50 龄)。A 组样品数为 48 株，B 组为 32 株，C 组为 64 株。本实验所用 3 种酶见表 1。

表 1　3 种同工酶系统的名称及所用电泳系统

Table 1　Three isozyme system abbreviations and buffer systems used in the electrophoretic analysis

Isozyme	Abbreviation	Buffer system	E.C.No.
Peroxidase	PER	DAVIS	E.C.1.11.1.7
Esterase	EST	LIOH	E.C.3.1.1.1
Phosphorylase	PHO	DAVIS	E.C.2.4.1.1

The three kinds of isozymes chosen from eleven what Zhong *et al*.[12] did have large variation.

1.3 DNA 样品的提取、扩增、电泳、分析统计方法及引物序列

1.3.1 DNA 提取

每个样地各取植物 12 株，共 24 株。采用 2%的十六烷基三甲基溴化胺(CTAB)方法[13]从辽东栎植物冬芽中提取总 DNA。

1.3.2 PCR 反应及电泳

总体积为 25 μL，包含 50 ng 的总 DNA。RAPD 参考文献[3]，其中连接温度改为 35 ℃，DAF 参考文献[4]。详情见胡志昂等[14]。扩增产物均采用 3.2%的聚丙烯酰胺凝胶电泳，银染法染色[15]。

1.3.3 统计分析方法

采用 Shannon 信息指数[16]计算表型多样性：

$$H_O = -\sum Pi\log_2 Pi$$

式中，Pi 示 i 带的表型频率，H_O 示表型多样性。

1.3.4 引物及序列

随机引物为 Operon 公司生产的 9 种 10 个碱基的引物及 ABI 合成仪合成的 3 种 8 个碱基的引物，所用引物及序列见表 2。

表 2 随机引物及序列

Table 2 Random oligonucleotide primer sequence

Primer	Sequence	Primer	Sequence
OPD-02	GGACCCAACC	OPH-08	GAAACACCCC
OPD-03	GTCGCCGTCA	OPJ-04	CCGAACACGG
OPD-04	TCTGGTGAGG	OPJ-06	TCGTTCCGCA
OPD-07	TTGGCACGGG	8.6L	GTAACCCC
OPD-08	GTGTGCCCCA	8.7B	GCTGGTGG
OPD-12	CACCGTATCC	8.9A	CGCGGCCA

2 结果和分析

2.1 辽东栎 3 个年龄组的同工酶变异

表 3 列出了辽东栎种群 3 个年龄组 3 种同工酶 11 个可能位点的等位基因频率。

表 3 辽东栎取样种群 3 个年龄组的基因频率分布

Table 3 Allele frequences of three age groups of sampling populatcons of Liaodong oak

Locus	Allele	Age groups			Locus	Allele	Age groups		
		A	B	C			A	B	C
PER-1	a	0.08	0.00	0.05	EST-1	a	0.38	0.45	0.47
	b	0.92	1.00	0.95		b	0.23	0.34	0.39
PER-2	a	0.45	0.32	0.40		c	0.39	0.21	0.15
	b	0.55	0.68	0.60	EST-2	a	0.18	0.31	0.23
PER-3	a	0.50	0.50	0.50		b	0.50	0.21	0.29
	b	0.50	0.50	0.50		c	0.32	0.48	0.48
PHO-1	a	0.015	0.00	0.02	EST-3	a	0.14	0.18	0.04
	b	0.985	1.00	0.98		b	0.86	0.82	0.96
PHO-2	a	0.20	0.32	0.32	EST-4	a	0.03	0.23	0.00
	b	0.80	0.68	0.68		b	0.27	0.39	0.22
PHO-3	a	0.27	0.13	0.28		c	0.58	0.32	0.78
	b	0.73	0.87	0.72		d	0.12	0.06	0.01
					EST-5	a	0.99	0.97	1.00
						b	0.01	0.03	0.00

从表 3 可见,A、C 两组在部分位点上频率很接近,仅在个别位点上(如 PHO-2、EST-1)基因频率在两组间差异较大。而 B 组则与 A、C 两组差异稍大。总的来说，3 组在各项变异指标上的差异均不大(表 4)，说明它们的变异水平相近。

根据表 3 的数据我们计算了 A、B、C3 组的遗传距离：D_{AB}=0.0307，D_{AC}=0.0192，D_{BC}=0.0292。它们两两之间的遗传距离均很小，表明 3 组间分化程度很低。3 个年龄组 11 个位点的 G_{ST} 平均值为 0.0118，即 3 组间的变异仅占总变异的 1%左右，大多数变异存在于 3 组内部。

2.2 两个种群 DNA 多样性

我们对两个种群(种群 1 和 2)12 个引物扩增产生的 205 个扩增产物进行了分析(表 5，图 1)。图 1 清楚地显示了辽东栎两个种群的谱带(箭头所示在 562、589、692、708……等位点上均有变化)。

表 4 辽东栎取样种群 3 个年龄组的遗传变异参数值

Table 4 Genetic diversity values of three age groups of the sampling populations of Liaodong oak

Age groups	Average sample size per locus	Percentage of polymorphic loci	Average No.of alleles per locus	AverageNo. of effective alleles	Average effected heterozygosity perlocus
A	4.36	100%	2.36	1.76	0.362 5
B	2.82	81.8%	2.18	1.82	0.355 1
C	5.82	90.9%	2.18	1.67	0.328 1
Average	4.33	90.9%	2.24	1.75	0.348 6

表 5 用 12 个引物检测的辽东栎两个种群的多态位点及多态位点百分率

Table 5 Polymorphic loci detected with twelve primers for two populations of Liaodong oak (proportion of poplymorphic loci)

Primer	Number of loci	Population 1 (A)	Population 2 (B)	Total number of polymorphic loci
OPD-02	9	5(0.56)	6(0.67)	6(0.67)
OPD-03	19	17(0.89)	17(0.89)	17(0.89)
OPD-04	9	9(1.00)	9(1.00)	9(1.00)
OPD-07	9	8(0.89)	8(0.89)	8(0.89)
OPD-08	16	12(0.75)	10(0.63)	12(0.75)
OPD-12	16	15(0.94)	13(0.81)	15(0.94)
OPH-08	23	18(0.78)	18(0.78)	19(0.83)
OPJ-04	17	13(0.76)	13(0.76)	13(0.76)
OPJ-06	25	22(0.88)	23(0.92)	23(0.92)
8.6 L	23	17(0.74)	17(0.74)	17(0.74)
8.7 B	12	4(0.33)	6(0.50)	6(0.50)
8.9 A	27	17(0.63)	16(0.59)	17(0.63)
Average		0.77	0.76	0.79
Total	205	157	156	162

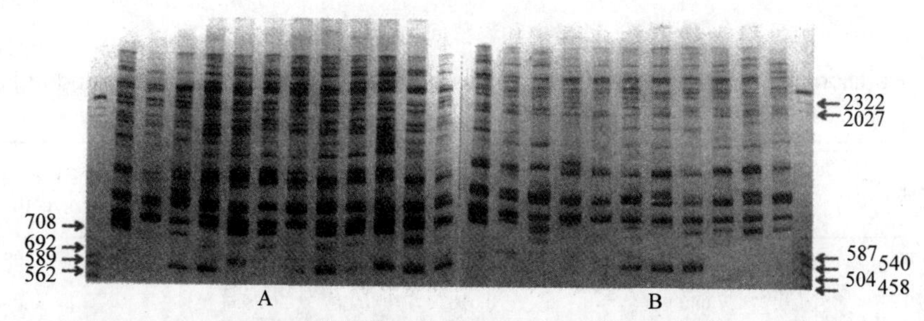

图 1 用 OPJ-06 引物扩增的两个种群的 DNA 谱带(A.种群 1；B.种群 2)

Fig. 1 DNA amplification profiles of two populations with primer OPJ-06 (A.Population 1, B. Population 2)

从表 5 可见：12 个引物检测的位点数从 9 到 27 不等(我们仅统计了 2kb 以下的部分位点)。总的多态位点百分率变化从 50%～100%，随引物和种群而变化。但引物间变化较大，而种群间变化较小。例如，引物 OPD-04 检测了 9 个位点，全部为多态的，多态位点百分率达 100%，而引物 8.7 B 检测了 12 个位点，只有一半为多态的，多态位点百分率仅为 50%。12 个引物中，OPD-03、OPD-04、OPD-07、OPH-08、OPJ-06、8.6 L 在两个种群的多态位点百分率相同。用 Shannon 信息指数对 12 种引物检测的 2 个种群的表型频率进行了计算，结果见表 6。

表 6 辽东栎两个种群内基因多样性的估测值

Table 6 Estimates of genetic diversity within populations for Liaodong oak from two locations

Primer	Population 1	Population 2
OPD-02	2.000	2.592
OPD-03	7.588	7.703
OPD-04	3.807	3.587
OPD-07	3.408	2.913
OPD-08	4.249	4.318
OPD-12	6.192	5.346
OPH-08	7.172	6.548
OPJ-04	5.748	5.456
OPJ-06	8.153	9.146
8.6 L	6.290	6.454
8.7 B	0.866	1.345
8.9 A	5.929	4.738
Average	5.116 8	5.034 7

从表 6 可见：种群 1 显示了相对较大的种群内变异。这可能与种群 1 的气候较湿润、对辽东栎的生长更为适合有关。加之种群 1 样地位置较种群 2 低，种群 2 植物的花粉很容易被吹到样地 1，使之变异加大。本文 DNA 的结果和以前报道[12]的同工酶数据一致。

Shannon 信息指数的表型多样性通常又被分为种群内和种群间两部分(表 7)。

表 7 种群内和种群间的遗传多样性

Table 7 Partitioning of the genetic diversity between and within populations of Liaodong oak for twelve random oligonucleotide primers

Primer	Genetic diversity within populations	Total genetic diversity	Percentage of diversity within populations	Genetic differentiation coefficient
OPD-02	2.296	2.374	0.967	0.033
OPD-03	7.646	8.018	0.954	0.046
OPD-04	3.697	3.985	0.928	0.072
OPD-07	3.161	3.201	0.987	0.013
OPD-08	4.284	4.516	0.949	0.051
OPD-12	5.769	6.210	0.929	0.071
OPH-08	6.860	7.453	0.920	0.080
OPJ-04	5.659	5.892	0.960	0.040
OPJ-06	8.983	9.523	0.943	0.057
8.6 L	6.372	6.653	0.958	0.042
8.7 B	1.106	1.139	0.971	0.029
8.9 A	5.334	5.723	0.932	0.068
Average	5.097 3	5.390 6	0.950	0.050

从表 7 可见，OPJ-06 检测了最高的多样性，而 8.7 B 检测了最低的多样性。总的来说，大多数的变异发生在种群内(95%)，而仅有 5%的变异发生在两个种群间。当然，引物不同所占百分率也不同，如：OPD-04 引物检测了群体内的变异为 92.8%，而 OPD-07 则高达 98.7%。

为进一步说明两个种群的分化程度，我们利用 Nei 的相似指数[17]计算了两个种群的遗传距离为 D = 0.044，说明它们的分化程度是相当小的。

3 讨论和结论

3.1 精确地估计多样性是建立优化模式和保护树种基因资源的先决条件。通过对辽东栎取样种群不同年龄组的遗传结构所做的进一步分析，证实 A、C 组基因频率接近，而与 B 组有一定差别，这与钟敏等[12]对东灵山两个种群年龄结构的研究相符。但分析三组的遗传距离，我们看到它们两两间的遗传距离均很小，表明其分化程度很低，大多数的变异存在于三组内部。我们以前认为该现象可能与砍伐有关[12]。只有对不曾砍伐的 B 年龄组做进一步研究，才能阐明基因频率变化的原因，这有待我们做进一步的工作。

3.2 通过 RAPD 及 DAF 的研究，我们发现种群 1 和种群 2 的 DNA 在个别位点上存在差异，OPD-12(1230)、OPH-08(955)、OPJ-06(912)、8.7B(955)、8.7B(832)、8.9A(724)在种群 1 为单态的，在种群 2 为多态位点。OPD-08(1202)、OPD-08(1047)、OPD-12(324)、OPD-08(575)则相反，OPD-12(513)，8.9A(330)在种群 1 为多态的，在种群 2 未检测到；反之，OPD-06(550)则在种群 1 未检测到，在种群 2 为多态的，两种群的平均多态位点百

分率相差不大。每个种群都有一些全部植株共有的单态位点，还有某些扩增产物为两种群共有，但是没有发现种群专一的扩增产物。DNA多样性表现为中央种群略高于边缘种群，说明在水分和基质条件较好的情况下种群具有较高的遗传变异水平。我们认为这与两个种群对不同生境的适应有关。种群2(边缘种群)相对于种群1(中央种群)生态条件恶劣，它紧临荒山，而且其地理位置较高，处于阳坡顶部的风口，有可能是这种边缘效应造成的基因流不正常，致使个别基因丢失，这还有待于进一步的研究。

3.3 通过实验还发现，种群内、种群间的遗传多样性在不同引物间也有很大差别，不同引物产生显著不同的带谱数据表明，每个植株都有其专一的DNA扩增片段的组成，证明生物个体组成的唯一性。种群1的多样性从8.6 B引物检测的0.866变化到OPJ-06的8.132，种群2则从1.345变化到9.416。遗传分化系数则从OPD-07的0.013变化到OPH-08的0.080。总的来说，辽东栎种群DNA总变异的95%产生于种群内，远远大于种群间(5%)的变异，这与钟敏等[12]所做的同工酶水平的遗传多样性G_{ST}结果吻合。

总之，通过同工酶、DNA水平的研究，我们发现东灵山辽东栎种群具有较高的遗传变异水平。这同Hamrick[18]所得的结论相一致。他认为异交、木本、生活史长的植物有较高的变异水平，而且大多数的变异是在种群内。这就为辽东栎成为群落的优势种或建群种提供了遗传证据，也为该生态系统的恢复发展提供了充分的遗传基础。

参考文献

[1] Manos P S, Fairbrothers D E. Allozyme variation in populations of six Northeastern American red oaks (Fagaceae: *Quercus G. Erythrobalanus*). *Syst Bot*, 1987, **12**: 365 ~ 373

[2] Hokanson S C, Isebrands J G, Jensen R J, Hancock J F. Isozyme variation in oaks of the Apostle Islands in Wisconsin: Genetic structure and levels of inbreeding in *Quercus rubra* and Q. *ellipsoidalis* (Fagaceae). *Amer J Bot*, 1993, **80**: 1349 ~ 1357

[3] Williams J G, Kubelik A R. Livak K J. Rafalski J A, Tingey S V. DNA polymorphisms amplified by arbitrary primers are useful as genetic markers. *Nucleic Acids Res*, 1990, **18**: 6531 ~ 6535

[4] Caetano-Anolles G, Bassam B J. DNA amplification fingerprinting using arbitrary oligonucleotide primers. *Appl Biochem Biotechnol*, 1993, **25**: 189 ~ 200

[5] Anderson W R, Fairbanks D J. Molecular markers: important tools for plant genetic resource characterization. *Diversity*, 1990, **6**: 51~53

[6] Waugh R. Powell W. Using RAPD markers for crop improvement. *Trends Biotechnol*, 1992, **10**: 186 ~ 191

[7] Dawson I K, Chalmers K J, Waugh R, Powell W. Detection and analysis of genetic variation in *Hordeum spontaneum* populations from Isreal using RAPD markers. *Mol Ecol*, 1993, **2**: 151 ~ 159

[8] Chalmers K L, Waugh R, Sprent J I. Simons A J, Powell W. Detect of genetic variation between and within populations of *Gliricidia sepium* and *G. maculata* using RAPD markers. *Heredity*, 1992, **69**: 465 ~ 472

[9] Russel J R. Hosein F, Johnson E, Wauch R, Powell W. Genetic differentiation of coca (*Theobroma cacao*) populations revealed by RAPD analysis. *Mol Ecot*, 1993, **2**: 89 ~ 97

[10] Soren B, Crawford D J, Stuessy T F. Ribosomal DNA and RAPD variation in the rare plant family Lactoridaceae. *Amer J Bot*, 1992, **79**: 1436 ~ 1439

[11] Ma Ke-Ping(马克平), Huang Jian-Hui (黄建辉), Yu Shun-Li(于顺利), Chen Ling-Zhi(陈灵芝). Plant community diversity in Dongling Mountain, Beijing, China: II Species richness, evenness and species diversity. *Acta Ecol Sin* (植物生态学报), 1995, **15**: 268 ~ 277 (in Chinese)

[12] Zhong Min (钟敏), Wang Hong-Xin (王洪新), Hu Zhi-Ang (胡志昂). Qian Ying-Qian (钱迎倩). A preliminary study on genetic structure of Liaodong oak (*Quercus liaotungensis*) populations in dry and moist habitats and its adaptive implications. *Acta Bot Sin* (植物学报). 1995, **37**: 661 ~ 668 (in Chinese)

[13] Doyle J J. Doyle J L. Isolation of plant DNA from fresh tissue. *Focus*, 1990,**12**:13 ~ 15

[14] Hu Zhi-Ang (胡志昂), Yun Rui (恽锐), Zhong Min (钟敏), Dong Fu-Gui (董夫贵), Wang Hong-Xin (王洪新), Qian Ying-Qian (钱迎倩). Comparison and improvement of polymorphism amplification methods used for detecting DNA diversity of plants. *Acta Bot Sin* (植物学报), 1997, **39**: 144 ~148 (in Chinese)

[15] Bassam B J, Caetano-Anolles G. Silver staining of DNA in polyacrylamide gels. *Appl Biochem Biotechnol*, 1993, **25**: 181~ 188

[16] King L M, Schaal B A. Ribosomal DNA variation and distribution in Rudbckia missouriensis. *Evolution*, 1989, **43**: 1117 ~ 1119

[17] Nei M. Genetic distance between populations. *Amer Nat*, 1972, **106**: 283 ~ 292

[18] Hamrick J L. Isozymes and the analysis of genetic structure in plant populations. In: Soltis D E. Soltis P M eds. Isozymes in Plant Biology. London: Chapman and Hall, 1990. 87 ~ 105

本文原载：植物学报. 1998. 40(11): 1040-1046

蒙古栎、辽乐栎的遗传分化：从形态到DNA*

恽锐　王洪新　胡志昂**　钟敏　魏伟　钱迎倩

(中国科学院植物研究所)

摘　要　通过植物群落结构、壳斗、叶脉形态特征、同工酶及DNA等多方面调查与测定，分析了帽儿山的蒙古栎(*Quercus mongolica* Fisch.)和东灵山、关帝山的辽东栎(*Q.liaotungensis* Koidz)的遗传分化及多样性。各种水平的研究一致说明：两种植物的遗传分化较小，东灵山种群是典型蒙古栎、辽东栎种群的中间类型。确切地说，从东北到山西组成一个地理渐变群，存在大范围、强大的双向基因流。

关键词　栎树；形态学；同工酶；RAPD；DAF；遗传分化

有关蒙古栎、辽东栎的形态特征[1]早已为分类学家所描述。但由于栎树本身高的多态性，频繁的种间杂交及二者的表型可塑性，形态特征并不能提供令人满意的分类依据。一些植物学家，如Borzi[2]、Burger[3]怀疑生物种这个概念是否能应用在栎属中。VanValen[4]则建议：属应为一个分类单位，不应设种。为研究栎属种间关系，关于形态、数量分析、同工酶及DNA方面已做了大量工作[5~11]，但利用RAPD及DAF作为标记探讨种间关系的报道极少。东灵山地处蒙古栎、辽东栎分布的交界处，长期以来在东灵山分布的是蒙古栎还是辽东栎尚在争论之中。本文通过植物形态、生态结合同工酶、DNA方法对典型地区的蒙古栎(帽儿山)、典型地区的辽东栎(关帝山)及东灵山的辽东栎进行了比较分析。

1　材料和方法

1.1　植物材料采集

为研究蒙古栎(*Quercus mongolica* Fisch.)、辽东栎(*Q. liaotungensis* Koidz.)的遗传分化及多样性,选择黑龙江省东北林业大学帽儿山实验林场、北京东灵山中国科学院北京森林生态系统定位研究站和山西省关帝山庞泉沟自然保护区为采样地。帽儿山实验林场位于黑龙江省尚志市境内，其地理位置为北纬45°20′~45°25′，东经127°30′~127°34′。样地平

* 中国科学院重大项目资助。Supported by a project of Eighth Five Years Major Program of the Chiese Academy of Sciences.

均海拔300m，坡度30°①。东灵山北京森林生态系统定位研究站，其地理位置位于北纬39°58′，东经115°41′附近。有关该地区的自然概况马克平等[12]已有详细报道。样地平均海拔1300 m左右。坡度60°。关帝山庞泉沟自然保护区地处山西省文城、方山县交界处，其地理位置为北纬37°45′~37°55′，东经111°22′~111°33′之间。样地海拔1600~17 00m之间。坡度75°②。

植物材料分别于1995年9月26~28日采自帽儿山老爷岭(蒙古栎)1995年10月17~18日采自东灵山小龙门林场：1995 年 10 月 11 日~12 日采自关帝山庞泉沟(辽东栎)。将采集的冬前芽立即放入装有湿润滤纸的塑料袋中，存放于荫凉处，再转入 4℃冰箱中。每个样地各随机采集植物30株。

1.2 同工酶的提取、电泳及统计分析方法

详见钟敏等[13]，所用的酶及电泳系统见表1

表1 5种同工酶系统的名称及所用电泳系统

Table 1 Five isozyme systems (including their abbreviations) and buffer systems used in electrophoretic analysis

Lsozyme systems	Abbreviation	Buffer system	E.C.No.
Peroxidase	PER	DAVIS	E.C.1.11.1.7
Esterase	EST	LIOH	E.C.3.1.1.1
Phosphorylase	PHO	DAVIS	E.C.2.4.1.1
Glutamate oxaloacetate transaminase	GOT	DAVIS	E.C.2.6.1.1
Leucine-aminopeptidase	LAP	DAVIS	E.C.3.4.11.1

1.3 DNA样品的提取、扩增、电泳

所做样品数：帽儿山6株，东灵山4株，关帝山6株。采用2%的CTAB方法[14]从植物冬芽中提取总DNA。

DNA多样性检测方法详见胡志昂等[15]。RAPD参考Williams等[16]，其中退火温度改为35℃，DAF参考Caetano-Anolles等[17]，扩增产物均采用3.2%的聚丙烯酰胺凝胶电泳分离，银染法染色[18]。

1.4 系统分析方法

采用Shannon信息指数[19]。$Ho=-\Sigma Pi\log_2 Pi$，式中，*Pi*示表型频率，*Ho*示表型多样性。

1.5 引物及序列

随机引物为Operon公司生产的9种10个碱基的引物及用ABI公司的DNA合成仪

① 东北林业大学主编. 东北林业大学帽儿山实验林场基础资料，1984.

② 山西省林业局主编. 庞泉沟自然保护区基础资料，1994.

合成的 3 种 8 个碱基的引物，所用引物及序列见表 2。

表 2 随机引物及序列

Table 2 Random oligonucleotide primer sequence

Primer	Sequence	Primer	Sequence
OPD-02	GGACCCAACC	OPH-08	GAAACACCCC
OPD-03	GTCGCCGTCA	OPJ-04	CCGAACACGG
OPD-04	TCTGGTGAGG	OPJ-06	TCGTTCCGCA
OPD-07	TTGGCACGGG	8.6 L	GTAACCCC
OPD-08	GTGTGCCCCA	8.7 B	GCTGGTGG
OPD-12	CACCGTATCC	8.9 A	CGCGGCCA

2 结果和分析

2.1 植物群落特征

对 3 个地点成长的植物及生境进行了调查。帽儿山的生境特点为湿而冷，土壤比较肥沃，群落中生长有北五味子(*Schizandra chinensis*)、蕨菜(*Pteridium aquilinum*)、苔藓(bryopyta)等，环境比较荫蔽。关帝山生境特点相对较干，土壤瘠薄，生长一些沙棘(*Hippophaerhamnoides*)、黄刺玫(*Rosa xanthina*)等耐旱的植物，群落郁闭度相对较小。东灵山介于两者之间。

2.2 形态特征

通过分析壳斗突起、叶脉数目可知：帽儿山蒙古栎壳斗包坚果的 1/2，苞片具瘤状突起，而关帝山辽东栎壳斗包坚果不足 1/3，苞片无瘤状突起，东灵山的介于两者之间。东灵山栎树的叶脉数目为 5 ~ 11 对，而帽儿山的蒙古栎为 7 ~ 11 对，关帝山的辽东栎为 5 ~ 8 对。

2.3 同工酶的多样性

表 3 列出了 3 个地点蒙古栎、辽东栎的变异系数。

表 3 蒙古栎、辽东栎变异水平一览表

Table 3 Genetic diversity values at three locations of Mongolia oak and Liaodong oak

Location	Percentage of polymorphic loci	Average No.of alleles per locus	Effective No.of alleles per locus	Average expected heterozygosity
Maoer Mountain (*Quercus mongolica*)	92.3	2.08	1.596	0.3202
Dongling Mountain (*Q. liaotungensis*)	92.3	2.15	1.908	0.3833
Guandi Mountain (*Q. liaotungensis*)	84.6	2.08	1.636	0.3345
Average	89.7	2.10	1.713	0.3460

所分析的 5 种酶受 13 个可能位点控制，其中 PER-2 在 3 个地点都是单态的。GOT-2 在关帝山为单态的，其余位点为多态的。

从表 3 数据我们可以看到：我们研究的 3 个地点的栎树的 5 种同工酶几个指标变异均不大，说明它们在变异水平上相近。只是东灵山的辽东栎各指标相对高一些，说明它的变异要大一些。

我们利用基因频率计算了 3 个地点的遗传距离：

$$D(\text{帽、东}) = 0.0182；D(\text{东、关}) = 0.0704；D(\text{帽、关}) = 0.0976$$

可见 3 个地点的分化程度还是较低的，进一步分析可见，帽儿山与关帝山的栎树差异相对大一些。

2.4 DNA 的多样性

在同工酶研究的基础上，我们进一步采用 RAPD 及 DAF 方法研究了 DNA 水平上的变异。我们研究了 172 个产物，并对其多态位点百分率进行了统计(表 4)。

表 4　12 个引物检测的 3 个地点的栎树的多态位点及多态位点百分率

Table 4　Polymorphic loci detected with twelve for three locations of Menggu oak and Liaodong oak (proportion of polymorphic loci)

Primer	Loci number	*Quercus mongolica* (Maoer Mountain)	*Q. liaotungensis* (Dongling Mountain)	*Q. liaotungensis* (Guandi Mountain)
OPD-02	14	11(0.79)	6(0.43)	8(0.57)
OPD-03	16	10(0.63)	12(0.75)	13(0.81)
OPD-04	12	10(0.83)	8(0.67)	10(0.83)
OPD-07	8	5(0.63)	7(0.88)	8(1.00)
OPD-08	16	6(0.38)	7(0.44)	6(0.38)
OPD-12	18	11(0.61)	14(0.78)	11(0.61)
OPH-08	24	12(0.50)	14(0.58)	17(0.71)
OPJ-04	15	8(0.53)	10(0.67)	7(0.47)
OPJ-06	13	11(0.85)	11(0.85)	11(0.85)
8.6 L	12	2(0.17)	3(0.25)	1(0.08)
8.7 B	15	4(0.27)	1(0.07)	3(0.20)
8.9 A	9	3(0.33)	6(0.67)	5(0.56)
Average		0.54	0.59	0.59
Total	172	93	99	100

从表 4 可见：12 个引物检测的谱带(部分)从 8~24 不等。多态位点百分率变化从 7%～100%不等，随引物及种群而变化。除 OPJ-06 引物 3 个地点多态位点百分率相同外，其余均不同。而且 DAF 检测的多态位点百分率明显低于 RAPD 检测的多态位点百分率。3 个地点的平均多态位点百分率相差并不大。利用 Shannon 信息指数，我们对 3 个地点的表型频率进行了计算，结果表明：变异主要存在于种群内部，而种群间的变异占总变异的 15%左右，是东灵山两个种群变异(5%)的 3 倍[20]。

表 5 DNA 扩增产物频率的地理渐变群

Table 5 Geographical cline of DNA amplification products

DNA bands	*Q. mongolica* (Maoer Mountain)	*Q. liaotungensis* (Dongling Mountain)	*Q. liaotungensis* (Guandi Mountain)
$OPD\text{-}02_{1096}$	0.50	1.00	1.00
$OPD\text{-}02_{1350}$	0.33	0.00	0.00
$OPD\text{-}03_{562}$	0.50	0.00	0.00
$OPD\text{-}03_{1514}$	1.00	1.00	0.83
$OPD\text{-}04_{550}$	1.00	1.00	0.33
$OPD\text{-}04_{1514}$	1.00	0.50	0.50
$OPD\text{-}08_{434}$	0.00	0.50	1.00
$OPD\text{-}12_{324}$	0.50	1.00	1.00
$OPD\text{-}12_{1288}$	1.00	0.75	0.33
$OPH\text{-}08_{398}$	1.00	0.75	0.33
$OPH\text{-}08_{447}$	1.00	0.75	0.67
$OPH\text{-}08_{537}$	0.00	0.00	0.50
$OPH\text{-}08_{603}$	1.00	0.75	0.33
$OPH\text{-}08_{891}$	1.00	0.75	0.50
$OPH\text{-}08_{1698}$	0.67	1.00	1.00
$OPJ\text{-}04_{661}$	0.33	0.50	1.00
$OPJ\text{-}04_{1047}$	0.33	1.00	1.00
$OPJ\text{-}04_{1175}$	0.00	0.50	0.67
$OPJ\text{-}04_{1318}$	1.00	0.50	0.33
8.61_{589}	0.33	0.00	0.00
$8.7b_{562}$	0.33	0.00	0.00
$8.7b_{832}$	0.83	1.00	1.00
$8.9a_{562}$	0.00	0.25	0.67

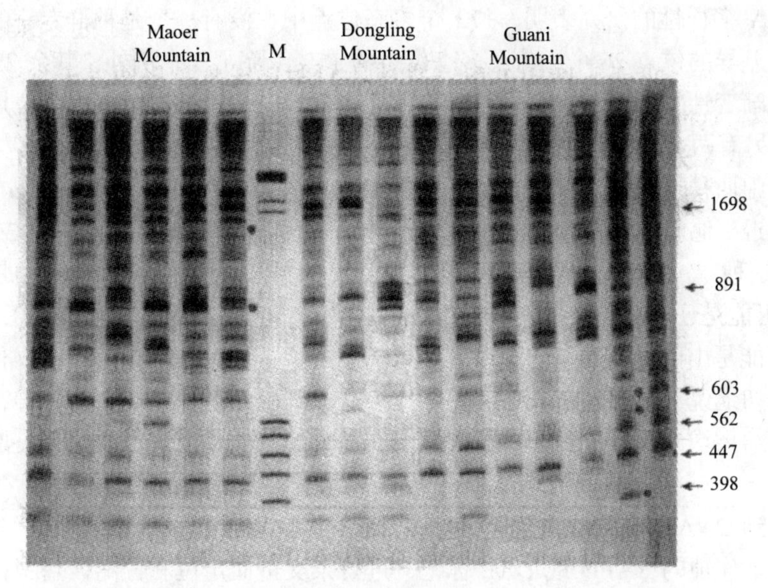

图 1 三个地区栎树 OPH-08 的 DNA 扩增谱

Fig.1 DNA amplification profiles of quercus from 3 location using OPH-08

M. DNA molecular markers including *λ/Hind* III (bands≥4kb, 2.3kb, 2.0kb)and pBR322/Hae III (587, 540, 504, 458, 434bp)

图 1 为用 OPH-08(B)引物扩增的 3 个地点的 DNA 谱带。

进一步统计 3 个种群每个扩增产物的频率。172 个多态位点中，26 个表现出显著频率变化，其中 23 个表现出地理渐变群(cline)性质，列于表 5。可以看出没有一个位点是种群专一的。只有一个扩增带 $OPJ\text{-}08_{434}$ 可能是辽东栎专一的，通过渐渗杂交进入东灵山种群。一些位点，如 $OPD\text{-}12_{1288}$，$OPJ\text{-}04_{1175}$，$OPJ\text{-}04_{1318}$，$OPH\text{-}08_{891、603、447、398}$，$8.9A_{562}$ 表现出东灵山种群的中间性质。而 $OPD\text{-}02_{1350、1096}$，$OPD\text{-}03_{562}$，$OPD\text{-}12_{324}$，$OPH\text{-}08_{1698}$，$OPJ\text{-}04_{1047}$,$8.6L_{589}$,$8.7B_{832、562}$ 带着谱则表现为东灵山种群的与关帝山种群的一致，与帽儿山差异较大。$OPD\text{-}03_{1514}$，$OPD\text{-}04_{550}$，$OPH\text{-}08_{537}$ 等带谱则为帽儿山的与东灵山的一致，与关帝山的有差异。

3 讨论和结论

3.1 从帽儿山的蒙古栎到关帝山的辽东栎,无论在它们的生境上、植物群落的结构上、叶子及果实的大小与形态上还是树的高矮上都有连续性变化。东灵山的辽东栎占有中间位置，正如它本身的地理位置一样。辽东栎曾被看作蒙古栎的变种，也说明它们的相似性。

3.2 同工酶的分析表明，东灵山的各项变异指标均较帽儿山与关帝山的为高，平均杂合度分别高出 16%和 13%，它同帽儿山及关帝山的遗传距离较之帽儿山与关帝山为小。说明东灵山与帽儿山、关帝山的栎树差别较小，而帽儿山与关帝山的栎树差别较大。但遗传距离数值均不足 10%。

3.3 DNA 多样性的研究表明，172 个多态位点中，没有一个是种群专一的。种群间频率有显著差异的位点 26 个，占总多态位点的 15%。除了 3 个例外，其余 23 个表现出明显的地理渐变性(cline)。13 个位点频率，北京种群接近山西种群，8 个位点上接近黑龙江种群。另有两个位点，北京种群的频率是两翼的平均值。因此，DNA 多样性上北京种群更接近山西种群。这个结果与 Bodenes 等 1997[21]两种近缘栎树 *Q. petraea* 和 *Q. robur* 的报道很接近，他们统计的 2800 个 RAPD 位点，两种间频率有差别的只占 2%，没有一个 RAPD 是种专一的。还没有其他植物自然种群的类似报道。值得注意的是我们发现 $OPD\text{-}08_{434}$ 可能是辽东栎专一的，在山西种群频率为 100%，黑龙江种群为 0，北京种群为 50%，可能是山西种群的基因渐渗的结果。总之蒙古栎和辽东栎是近缘物种，或互为变种，更确切地说从形态到 DNA 都证明从黑龙江到山西是一个地理渐变群，各种水平标记的研究结果均说明两个种间存在大范围的强大的双向基因流，表明其长期连续分布的历史。

从形态到 DNA 有其内在的联系，进一步的工作就是通过 RAPD 及 DAF 分析找出与编码形态特征连锁的 RAPD 或 DAF 标记，进行杂交进而定位和分离该基因，这样遗传变异能在 DNA 序列这一最终水平上予以阐明。由于本文所做的植物的样本数较少，容易造成偏差，进一步的工作还要加大取样数目，才可得到更令人信服的结论。

致谢 本工作得到中国科学院植物研究所陈灵芝研究员、马克平研究员、北京森林生态系统定位站的各位先生，本实验室周永刚硕士，东北林业大学聂绍荃教授、崔国富博士、钟秀丽博士，山西大学张金屯教授、邱扬硕士的热情支持与帮助，谨致谢忱。

参考文献

[1] He Shi-Yuan(贺士元), Xing Qi-Hua(邢其华), Yin Zu-Tang(尹祖棠). Flora of Beijing, Vol. 1, Beijing: Beijing Press, 1984. 100~104 (in Chinese)

[2] Borzi A. Le querce della flora Italiana. *Boll Reale Orto Bot, Giardino Colon Palermo*, 1911, **10**: 41~66

[3] Burger W C. The species concept in *Quercus. Taxon*, 1975, **24**: 45~50

[4] Van Valen L. Ecological species, multispecies, oaks. *Taxon*, 1976, **25**: 233~239

[5] Rushton B S. Artificial hybridization between *Quercus robur* L. and *Quercus petraea*(MTT.). *Liebl Watsonia*, 1977, **11**: 229~236

[6] Knops J F, Jensen R. Morphological and phenotypic variation in a three species community of red oaks. *Bull Torrey Bot Club*, 1980, **107**: 418~428

[7] Mariani C P, Chiesura L F,Grigoletto F. Pollen grain morphology supports the taxonomical discrimination of Mediterranean oaks(*Quercus*, Fagaceae). *Pl Syst Evol*, 1983, **141**: 273~284

[8] Olsson U. Peroxidase isozymes in *Quercus pecraea* and *Quercus robur*. *Bot Not*, 1975, **128**: 408~411

[9] Edward E B, Hamrick J L. Spatial and genetic structure of two sandhills oaks: *Quercus laevis* and *Quercus margaretta*(Fagaceae). *Amer J Bot*, 1994, **81**: 7~14

[10] Guttman S I, Weight L A. Electrophoretic evidence of relationships among *Quercus*(oaks)of eastern North America. *Can J Bot*, 1989, **67**: 339~351

[11] Bellarosa R, Delre V, Schirone B, Maggini F. Ribosomal RNA genes in *Quercus* spp.(Fagaceae). *Pl Syst Evol*, 1990, **172**: 127~139

[12] Ma Ke-Ping(马克平), Huang Jian-Hui(黄建辉), Yu Shun-Li(于顺利), Chen Ling-Zhi(陈灵芝). Plant community diversity in Dongling Mountain, Beijing, China: II Species richness, evenness and species diversity. *Acta Ecol Sin*(生态学报), 1995, **15**: 268~277(in Chinese)

[13] Zhong Min(钟敏)，Wang Hong-Xin(王洪新)，Hu Zhi-Ang(胡志昂)，Qian Ying-Qian(钱迎倩). A preliminary study on genetic structure of Liaodong oak(*Quercus liaotungensis*)populations in dry and moist habitats and its adaptive implications. *Acta Bot Sin*(植物学报), 1995, **37**: 661~668(in Chinese)

[14] Doyle J J, Doyle J L. Isolation plant DNA from fresh tissue. *Focus*, 1990, **12**: 13~15

[15] Hu Zhi-Ang(胡志昂)，Yun Rui(恽锐)，Zhong Min(钟敏)，Dong Fu-Gui(董夫贵)，Wang Hong-Xin(王洪新)，Qian YingQian(钱迎倩). Comparison and improvement of polymorphism amplification methods used for detecting DNA diversity of plants. *Acta Bot Sin*(植物学报), 1997, **39**: 144~148(in Chinese)

[16] Williams J G, Kubelik A R, Livak K J. Rafalski J A, Tingey S V. DNA polymorphisms amplified by arbitrary primers are useful as genetic markers. *Nucl Acids Res*, 1990, **18**: 6531~6535

[17] 17 Caetano-Anolles G, Bassam B J. DNA amplification fingerprinting using arbitary oligonucleotide primers. *Appl Biochem Biotechnol*, 1993, **25**: 189~200

[18] Bassam B J, Caetano-Anolles G, Gresshoff P M. Fast and sensitive silver staining of DNA in polyacrylamide gel. *Anal Biochem*, 1991, **80**: 81~84

[19] King L M, Schaal B A. Ribosomal DNA variation and distribution in *Rudbckia missouriensis*. *Evolution*, 1989, **43**: 1117~1119

[20] Yun Rui(恽锐)，Zhong Min(钟敏)，Wang Hong-Xin(王洪新)，Wei Wei(魏伟)，Hu Zhi-Ang(胡志昂)，Qian Ying-Qian(钱迎倩). Study on DNA diversity of Liaodong oak population at Dongling mountain region, Beijing. *Acta Bot Sin*(植物学报), 1998, **40**: 169~175(in Chinese)

[21] Bodenes C, Joandet S, Laigret F. Detection of genomic regions differentiating two closely related oak species *Quercus petraea*(Mutl.)Liebl and *Quercus robur* L. *Heredity*, 1997, **78**: 433~444

本文原载：植物学报. 1998. 40(5): 412-416

野大豆群体DNA随机扩增产物的限制性内切酶消化*

魏伟 钟敏 王洪新 恽锐 胡志昂** 钱迎倩

(中国科学院植物研究所)

摘 要 为了提高RAPD方法检测野大豆(*Glycine soja* L.)群体DNA多态性的能力，随机扩增产物用限制性内切酶(*Msp*I、*Hinf* I、*Taq*I、*Eco*RI、*Sal*I、*Dra*I和*Hae*III)消化，通过聚丙烯酰胺凝胶电泳分离后用银染法检测酶切产物，结果发现：1.有的限制性内切酶能够消化野大豆群体DNA的随机扩增产物，有的却不能。2.有的限制性内切酶消化无RAPD个体的扩增产物后能够产生多态性DNA片段，有的内切酶不能产生。3.有的引物的无RAPD个体的扩增产物经限制性内切酶消化后能够产生多态性的DNA片段；有的引物的扩增产物虽然可被内切酶消化，但不能够产生多态性DNA片段。实验证明，用限制性内切酶消化扩增产物，确实能够提高RAPD方法检测野大豆群体DNA多态性的能力。

关键词 随机扩增多态性DNA；限制性内切酶；多态性DNA片段；野大豆群体

目前，检测植物群体遗传多样性的分子标记主要有限制性片段长度多态性(RFLP)以及基于DNA扩增技术的随机扩增多态性DNA(RAPD)、随机引物PCR(AP-PCR)和DNA扩增指纹(DAF)等。RFLP是利用限制性内切酶能够识别专一的碱基序列这一特点，DNA序列变异导致酶切位点的消失或增加，因而表现在限制性片段长度的变化上。Caetano-Anollés[1]将那些基于DNA扩增技术的分子标记概括为多种随机扩增谱(MAAP)，认为用多种限制性内切酶消化模板DNA或随机扩增产物可以显著增加MAAP的DNA多态性。可以说，Caetano-Anollés的这种方法是RFLP标记和MAAP标记的有机结合。前文[2]报道了野大豆群体RAPD的研究。有的引物的扩增产物DNA多态性很低甚至是单态的。我们试图通过限制性内切酶消化这些随机扩增产物来提高RAPD标记检测野大豆群体DNA多态性的能力，以便更好地研究野大豆群体的遗传分化。

1 材料和方法

1.1 材料

用前文[2]研究中所提取的野大豆(*Glycine soja* L.)基因组DNA及其随机扩增产物。

* 中国科学院“八·五”基础性研究重点课题资助。

** 通讯联系人。

1.2 扩增产物限制性内切酶消化

根据前文[2]随机扩增产物的检测结果，选取无多态位点即没有 RAPD 个体的扩增产物作为酶切对象。限制性内切酶包括 *Msp*I(10 U/μL)、*Hin*f I(10 U/μL)、*Taq*I(10 U/μL)、*Eco*RI(10 U/μL)、*Sal*I(20 U/μL)、*Dra*I(16 U/μL) 和 *Hae*III(16 U/μL)。酶切参考 Caetano-Anollés 等[3]的方法，略加修改。酶切反应液总体积为 20μL，其中扩增产物 2μL、限制性内切酶 1μL(10~20 U/μL)、相应的 10 倍反应缓冲液 2μL，以及 15μL 去离子水，混匀后，37℃水浴保温 1.5~3 h (保温时间依酶的不同而有所不同)。

1.3 酶切结果的检测

同前文[4]，用聚丙烯酰胺凝胶电泳分离后银染显示。

2 结果和分析

我们选取引物 OPD03、OPD05、OPD04、OPD07、OPD11、OPD15 和 OPD18 的随机扩增产物作为酶切对象，选择无 RAPD 个体(表 1)的扩增产物酶切后与酶切前对照。本实验所用到的几种限制性内切酶如表 2 所示，它们在上述 7 种引物中没有切口。

表 1 扩增引物序列及无 RAPD 的个体

Table 1 Sequences of arbitrary primers and individuals of non-RAPDs

Primer	Sequence	Individuals of non-RAPDs
OPD03	5′-GTCGCCGTCA-3′	①[1)]4-14,4-16,4-19[2)]；②4-1,4-3,4-8,4-9,4-10
OPD05	5′-TGAGCGGACA-3′	4-9,4-10,4-12,4-14,4-15,4-19,4-20
OPD04	5′-TCTGGTGAGG-3′	①4-8,4-17；②4-10,4-11,4-12,4-14
OPD07	5′-TTGGCACGGG-3′	4-1,4-3,4-5,4-8,4-11,4-17,4-18
OPD11	5′-AGCGCCATTG-3′	4-8,4-12,4-11,4-17
OPD15	5′-CATCCGTGCT-3′	①4-8,4-18；②4-10,4-11,4-14,4-17
OPD18	5′-GAGAGCCAAC-3′	4-8,4-9,4-11,4-12,4-14

1) A group of individuals that have no RAPD; 2) Symbols for individuals.

根据酶切结果看，*Taq*I、*Dra*I 没有消化扩增产物，其他 5 种酶都较好地消化了扩增产物，说明扩增产物中可能没有 *Taq*I 和 *Dra*I 的识别序列，而具有其他 5 种限制性内切酶的识别序列。

各种限制性内切酶消化扩增产物产生新的片段数量不一样，这与该种扩增产物中各种内切酶的识别序列存在的情况有关。一般来讲如果源 DNA 是环状的(如脊椎动物的线粒体基因组)，消化片段的数量等于限制性位点的数量。但是，实际情况往往不是这样，限制性位点数目的真实统计要通过对限制性位点作图来完成。通常，如果所研究的序列是完整的，那么我们就可以通过产生消化片段的数目来统计限制位点的数目[5]。由于随机扩增产物一般是线性的，我们可以做这样一个假设，本实验所研究的限制性位点的数目等于新产生限制性消化片段的数目减 1。根据实验结果，我们给出了扩增产物中存在各种内切酶识别序列的情况(表 2)。从表 2 可以看出，限制性内切酶 *Hae* III 对野大豆群体 DNA 的随机扩增产物的识别为点最多(平均 10 个)，*Sal* I 较少(平均 1 个)，*Taq* I 和 *Dra* I 则没有(为零)。

表 2　本实验所用到的几种限制性内切酶及其识别序列

Table2　The restriction endonucleases and its recognition sequences

Restriction endonucleases	Recognition sequences	Mean of numbers for recognition loci
Dra I	TTT↑AAA	0
Eco R I	G↑AATTC	6
*Hae*III	GG↑CC	10
Hinf I	G↑ANTC	9
Msp I	C↑CGG	8
Sal I	G↑TCGAC	1
Taq I	T↑CGA	0

野大豆群体中无 RAPD 个体的扩增产物经 5 种限制性内切酶(*Eco* RI、*Hae* III、*Hinf* I、*Msp*I 和 *Sal*I)消化后的变化见表 3。在表 3 中，引物 OPD07 和 OPD18 的扩增产物经多种限制内切酶消化后虽然也有 DNA 片段的消失和出现，但不能产生多态性的 DNA 片段。另外几种引物(OPD03、OPD04、OPD05 和 OPD15)的扩增产物经一定的内切酶消化后却能够产生多态性的 DNA 片段。

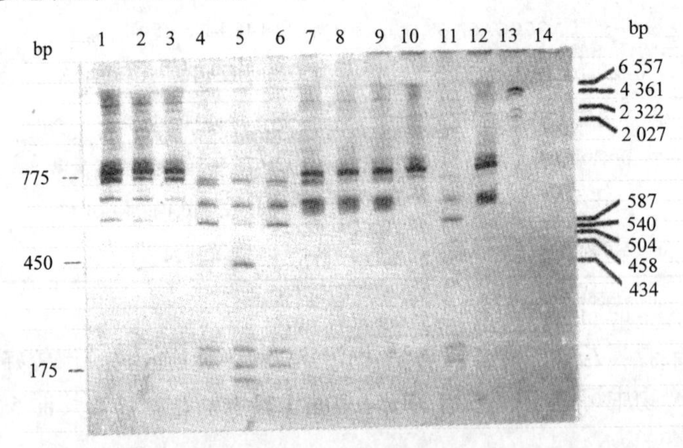

图 1　引物 OPD11 的无 RAPD 个体扩增产物被内切酶消化的结果

Fig.1　The restriction endonuclease digestion of non-RAPD amplification products generated by primer OPD11 1~3. The amplification products of individuals 4~8, 4~12 and 4~17 by primer OPD11, respectively; 4~6. The digested products of lane 1~3 by *Hae* III; 7~9. The digested products of lane 1~3 by *Dra* I; 10. The amplification products of individual 4~11 by primer OPD11; 11. The digested products of lane 10 by *Hae* III; 12. The digested products of lane 10 by *Hae* III; 13. λDNA/*Hind*III marker; 14. PBR-332/*Hae* III marker.

引物 OPD03、OPD04、OPD05 和 OPD15 的扩增产物被有的限制性内切酶消化后一些片段消失了，出现了另外一些片段，但没有产生多态性的 DNA 片段；然而，它们的扩增产物经另外的限制性内切酶消化后，伴随一些片段的消失和出现，产生了多态性的 DNA 片段。例如，引物 OPD03 的扩增产物经限制性内切酶 *EcoR*I 消化后，没能产生多态性的 DNA 片段；但是经 *Msp* I 和 *Hinf* I 消化后分别产生了多态性的 DNA 片段。

扩增产物经限制性内切酶消化，通过聚丙烯酰胺凝胶电泳分离后银染检测 DNA 多态性的一个例子见图 1。图 1 中，引物 OPD11 的无 RAPD 个体的扩增产物，用内切酶 *Dra*I 消化后看不出多态性的变化(槽 7~9 和 12)；但是用 *Hae* III 消化后，较大扩增片段消化得比较完全，新出现了 775 bp、450 bp、224 bp、198 bp 和 175 bp 的消化片段，其中 450 bp 和 175 bp 的片段只出现在个体 4-12 的 *Hae* III 消化产物中(槽 5)，775 bp 的片段则出现在 4-8、4-11、4-17(槽 4、11、6)的 *Hae* III 消化产物中。所以在 *Hae*III 消化产物的电泳谱上，775 bp、450 bp 和 175 bp 这 3 个位点是多态的。

表 3 限制性内切酶消化扩增产物后的变化

Table 3 The changes of digested amplification products by restriction endonuclease

Primer	Restriction endonuclease	Disappeared fragments (bp)	New emerged fragments (bp)	Polymorphic fragments (bp)
OPD03	*Msp* I	*	341,372,250,234,217,205,173,155,146,311,117,50,45,38	341,173,146
	Hinf I	*	732,540,288,234,217,205,173,146,138,131,117,110,109,70,61	288,109
	EcoR I	846,657	450,268,260,142	Non
OPD04	*Hae* III	*	627,629,587,497,455,370,344,310,306,267,242,235,221,209,98	209,98
	EcoR I	*	697,648,527,520,442,399,370,360,297,268,242,213,209,191,180,170,119,98,84	Non
OPD05	*Msp* I	*	630,438,406,349,139,124	Non
	Hinf I	*	323,311,220,182,134	Non
	EcoR I	833,502,341	434,473,321,124,362	362
OPD07	*Hae* III	1856,703,465	594,555,426,273,229,175,157,115	Non
	EcoR I	640,483	310,192,184,153,140,123	Non
	*Sal*I	*	476,261	Non
OPD11	*Hae* III	842,485,379,330	775,450,224,198,175	775,450,175
OPD15	*Hae* III	*	685,625,537,434,408,340,315,213,184,163,156,124,105,80,64	213
	EcoR I	*	762,786,739,521,505,315,305	Non
OPD18	*Hae* III	*	625,517,503,476,405,394,325,317,265,205,160	Non
	EcoR I	*	546,427,334	Non
	Msp I	861,836,680,621,507,434	810,690,587,457,173,149,129	Non
	Hinf I	700,680,621,507,434	406,394,303,246,168,151,145,124,113,93	Non

* Fragments that have not been kept count of.

3 讨论

Caetano-Anollés 等[3]用限制性内切酶 *Hae* III、*Sau* 3A 消化大豆的随机扩增产物后，与酶切前相比较，只是几条扩增片段的消失以及几条消化片段的出现[3]，电泳谱的基本模式没有改变。与之稍有不同，当我们用限制性内切酶 *Hae* III、*Eco* RI 和 *Sal* I 消化野大豆群体 DNA 的随机扩增产物后，较长的 DNA 扩增片段变化不大，主要变化表现在较短扩增片段(<860 bp)的消失和出现。然而，当我们用内切酶 *Hinf* I 和 *Msp* I 消化野大豆群体 DNA 的随机扩增产物(引物为 OPD03 和 OPD05，消化结果见表 3)后，较长的扩增片段消失了，出现了许多高浓度、短的消化片段，电泳谱的模式完全被改变了(没有照片)，与 Caetano-Anollés 等[3]的描述完全不同。这种不同可能与所用限制性内切酶的量有关，本实验用 10~20 单位的内切酶消化 2 μL 的扩增产物，而 Caetano-Anollés 等[3]仅用 4 个单位的内切酶来消化 2 μL 的扩增产物。具体的原因和机理有待于进一步研究探讨。

从表 2 可以看出，扩增产物被识别 4 碱基的内切酶消化后新产生的限制性片段最多(如 *Hae* III 消化新产生 11 个片段)，被识别 6 碱基的内切酶消化后，新产生的限制性片段最少(如 *Sal* I 消化后仅新产生 2 条片段)。其原因可能是由于 6 碱基内切酶的一般酶切几率是每 4 kb 才有一个切点(4^6=4 kb)，而 4 碱基的酶切几率是每 256 bp 有一切点(4^4=256 bp)。

一般来讲，酶切前后消失了的扩增片段长度总和与新出现的消化片段总和应该相等。但本文中除个别情况下消失的扩增片段与新出现的消化片段长度相差不大(图 1；表 3)外，消失的扩增片段长度与新出现的片段长度总和有较大的差距。这可能有两方面的原因：① 没有统计较长的扩增片段的消失以及较长消化片段的出现，其中后者尤为重要；② 短的消化片段在电泳谱上没有检测到，或者新出现的消化片段的高浓度可以补偿扩增片段和消化片段间长度的差别，即许多较短的消化片段在凝胶上具有相同的迁移率，银染显色后形成高浓度的带。上述第一点可以通过认真统计较长片段在酶切前后的变化而得到改正；第二点可以通过改进电泳方法，提高电泳的分辨率而使问题得到解决。

文中的方法和思路也见于某些 RFLP 的研究中。Williams 等[6]根据水稻的基因组克隆序列，合成了成对的引物，进行 PCR，然后用若干个识别 4~6 个碱基序列的限制性内切酶消化 PCR 产物，来检测不同品种间的碱基变化或小的插入和缺失，取得了满意的结果。这个方法的主要优点在于它能够避免繁琐的 Southen 杂交，节约基因组 DNA，而且还可以检测出用 Southern 杂交所不能检测的 DNA 多态性。在扩增前用限制性内切酶消化模板 DNA 或在扩增后用内切酶消化扩增产物可以提高 MAAP 检测 DNA 多态性的能力[1,3]。后者在本文中得到证实。这种 MAAP 和 RFLP 的巧妙结合，除在遗传多样性的研究中有重要作用外，它还将用在不必了解基因组 DNA 序列的有关信息以及不必消耗大量基因组 DNA 的条件下进行抗性基因、植物繁育系统以及濒危物种保护的研究中。

致谢　中国科学院植物研究所徐卫辉博士在洗印照片方面给予热情帮助，特致谢忱。

参考文献

[1] Caetano-Anollés G. MAPP: A versatile and universal tool for genome analysis. *Plant Mol Biol*, 1994, **25**: 1011~1026

[2] Wang Hong-Xin (王洪新)，Hu Zhi-Ang (胡志昂)，Zhong Min (钟敏)，Lu Wen-Jing (陆文静)，Wei Wei (魏伟)，Yun Rui (恽锐)，Qian Ying-Qian (钱迎倩). Genetic differentiation and physiological adaptation of wild soybean

(*Glycine soja*) populations under saline conditions: isozymatic and random amplified polymorphic DNA study. *Acta Bot Sin* (植物学报)，1997, **39**: 34~42 (in Chinese)

[3] Caetano-Anollés G, Bassam B J, Gresshoff P M. Enhanced detection of polymorphic DNA by multiple arbitrary amplicon profiling of endonuclease-digested DNA: indentification of markers tightly linked to the supernodultion locus in soybean. *Mol Gen Genet*, 1993, **241**: 57~64

[4] Hu Zhi-Ang (胡志昂)，Yun Rui (恽锐)，Zhong Min (钟敏)，Dong Fu-Gui (董夫贵)，Wang Hong-Xin(王洪新)，Qian Ying-Qian (钱迎倩). Comparison and improvement of polymorphism amplification methods used for detecting DNA diversity of plants. *Acta Bot Sin* (植物学报), 1997, **39**: 144~148 (in Chinese)

[5] Hoelzel A R, Bancroft D R. Statistical analysis of variation. In: Hoelzel A R eds. Molecular Genetic Analysis of Population.London: IRL Press, 1992

[6] Williams M N V, Pande N, Nair S *et al*. Restriction fragment length polymorphism analysis of polymerase chain reaction products amplified from mapped loci of rice(*Oryza sativa* L.)genomic DNA. *Theor Appl Genet*, 1991, **82**: 489~498

本文原载：生态学报. 1999. 19(1): 16-22

毛乌素沙地柠条群体分子生态学初步研究：RAPD证据*

魏伟　王洪新　胡志昂**　钟敏　恽锐　钱迎倩

(中国科学院植物研究所)

摘　要　毛乌素沙地柠条群体是一个杂种带。为了进一步阐明分子变异和基因流与生境或生态过渡带的联系，应用RAPD标记开展了柠条群体的分子生态学研究。根据RAPD数据利用Shannon信息指数估计了6个柠条群体的遗传多样性，发现大部分的分子变异存在于柠条群体之内(82.4%)，只有少部分的分子变异存在于群体之间(17.6%)，又利用Nei指数统计了RAPD数据，也证实了大部分的遗传变异存在于群体之内。柠条锦鸡儿群体与中间锦鸡儿群体的遗传分化系数和遗传距离都很小，以上结果都肯定了柠条群体间和种间的基因流动，无论是从多态位点比率还是群体的遗传多样性来看，硬梁和硬梁覆沙群体是最小的，滩地覆沙群体则具有较高的水平。某些RAPD扩增片段的频率在柠条群体间有规律的变化也许具有着特殊的生态学意义，更可能是中性突变的随机固定。根据以上研究可以得出下列结论：①通过比较Shannon指数和Nei指数的统计结果，可以认为，对于异交植物来讲，Shannon指数在统计RAPD数据方面有用。②毛乌素沙地柠条群体之间存在着强大的基因流，物种的杂交性与生态过渡性一致。

关键字　毛乌素沙地；生态过渡带；RAPD标记；分子生态学；基因流；Shannon指数；Nei指数；柠条群体

自从*Molecular Ecology*杂志1992年问世以来，分子生态学受到越来越多的重视。一些分子标记特别是RAPD标记在分子生态学中有着广泛的应用[1~3]。RAPD标记在分子生态学中的应用主要集中在研究分类学上的同一属的不同种之间，同一种内的不同亚种之间以及同一种内不同无性系或群体之间分子的遗传变异，以及这些分子变异与其生境或生态学之间的联系[4~8]。

毛乌素沙地是具有特殊地理景观的生态过渡带[9]。柠条则是该地区常见的固沙植物。根据柠条群体的形态学及种子蛋白多态性的研究，可以认为该地区的柠条可能是小叶锦鸡儿(*Caragana microphylla*)和柠条锦鸡儿(*C. korshinskii*)的杂种带[10,11]。为了在分子水平上探讨毛乌素沙地柠条群体的高度杂交性与生态过渡带的关系，阐明柠条群体可能存在的过渡性以及柠条群体分子变异与生境间的关系，本文应用RAPD标记初步研究了毛乌素沙地柠条群体的分子生态学特征。

---

* 国家科委攀登资助助目。

野外工作中得到中国科学院植物研究所孔令韶、陈旭东、董学军及鄂尔多斯沙地草地实验站阿拉腾宝的支持与帮助，数据处理得到中国科学院植物研究所刘成刚的帮助，谨致谢忱。

** 通讯联系人。

1　材料和方法

1.1　野外取样

取样均在鄂尔多斯沙地草地生态站附近进行。选取生长在沙丘(population on sand dune,PSD,编号 7)、滩地覆沙(population on lowland with sand-covered, PLS,编号 2)。硬梁覆沙(population on hard ridge with sand-covered,PHRS,编号 4-1)，硬梁(population on hard ridge,PHR,编号 4-2)和软梁覆沙(population on soft ridge with sand-covered,PSR,编号 5)等典型景观上的柠条群体作为研究对象，来探讨生境对柠条基因频率的选择作用，并选取种子来自伊盟西北的柠条锦鸡儿(*C.korshinskii*)的人工纯林(俗称毛条群体，population of *C.korshinskii*，PCK，编号 6-2)作为对照来研究生态过渡带与柠条分子变异间的关系。由于本文与文献[10,11]属于同一研究系列，所以各群体的取样和编号是一致的，生境条件及各群体的地理位置均见文献[10]。随机取样，每群体 9~13 株，采集幼叶，−30℃贮存备用。

1.2　基因组 DNA 提取

采用 Doyle & Doyle 的方法[12]提取叶子 DNA，每株用量 50mg 左右，得 DNA1μg 左右，存于−20℃冰箱备用。

1.3　随机扩增引物

随机引物采用 Operon 公司生产的引物系列 H 和 D，选择能够获得稳定扩增产物的引物对各个群体的基因组 DNA 进行随机扩增。

1.4　随机扩增

参考 Williams 等[13]的方法，并略加改动。本实验中，随机扩增及反应液的总体积 25μL，包括 100 mM Tris-HCl (pH 8.3)，50 mM KCl，1.5 mM $MgCl_2$，0.001% (w/v)明胶，100 μM dATP，dCTP，dGTP，dTTP，1). 2 μM 引物，25ng 左右的基因组 DNA，1.5 单位的 Tag DNA 聚合酶，混匀后加 1 滴矿物油进行以下温度循环(45 个)：94℃ 1 min，35℃ 1 min，72 ℃ 2 min。

1.5　随机扩增产物的分离及显色

用作者实验室改良的方法[14]进行聚丙烯酰胺凝胶电泳分离随机扩增产物，银染检测。

1.6　RAPD 数据的统计方法

1.6.1　多态位点比率

多态位点比率是指其绝大多数等位基因的频率小于或等于 0.99 的位点所占比率。

假设一个 RAPD 位点上有两个等位基因，用 Kongkiatngam 等的方法[15]估测 RAPD 位点上的显、隐性等位基因频率，然后用 Shannon 指数和 Nei 指数估算群体的遗传结构参数。

1.6.2 Shannon 信息多样性指数

$$H = -\sum P_1 \log_2 P_i$$

P_1:等位基因频率，H 可以估算两种水平的多样性：群体内平均多样性(H_{pop})和种内多样性(H_{sp})。

1.6.3 Nei 的遗传分化指数

总群体的基因多样性(H_T)，包括群体内基因多样性(H_s)和群体间基因多样性(D_{ST})，群体的基因分化系数：$G_{ST}=D_{ST}/H_T$。群体间的遗传距离：$D=-\text{loge}\, I$ 或 $D=-\text{In}I$.

具体的计算方法详见文献[10~15]。

2 结果与分析

2.1 柠条群体 RAPD 数据的统计分析

本实验共用引物 5 个，其序列如表 1 所示。由这 5 个引物获得的 RAPD 标记的重复性很好①，说明实验中 RAPD 标记检测群体遗传多样性的可靠性和可信性。表 2 列出了 5 个引物检测柠条各群体 RAPD 位点数及多态位点比率。表中只统计 2kb 以下的扩增片段，2kb 以上还有很多片段，但在本实验的条件下，这些带很集中，难以确定这些扩增片段是否有迁移率上的差别。5 个引物在 6 个柠条群体中共检测出 154 个位点，其中 153 个是多态的，总的多态位点比率为 0.994。硬梁群体由 5 个引物检测出的多态位点比率最小(0.796)，软梁覆沙群体和滩地覆沙群体最大(分别为 0.9143 和 0.9137)。按所检测的多态位点比率排列各群体顺序为：硬梁群体<沙丘群体<硬梁覆沙群体<毛条群体<滩地覆沙群体<软梁覆沙群体。

为了进一步研究柠条群体内及群体间的变异以及这些分子变异与生境的联系。应用 Shannon 指数和 Nei 的遗传分化指数估算了群体的遗传多样性。

2.1.1 Shannon 多样性指数

根据统计结果，硬梁群体的遗传多样性最低(16.112，表 3)，滩地覆沙群体最高(17.671)按顺序排列如下：硬梁群体<硬梁覆沙群体<沙丘群体<软梁覆沙群体<毛条群体<滩地覆沙群体。柠条群体内和群体间遗传多样性所占比例分别为 82.4%和 17.6%(表 3)，遗传变异大部分存在于群体之内。有的引物甚至检测出只有 9.3%的遗传变异存在于群体间。

① 魏伟等. 1996. 检测柠条群体遗传多样性时 RAPD 标记的重复性，见生物多样性与人类未来(第二届全国生物多样性保护与持续利用研讨会论文摘要集)。

2.1.2　Nei 的遗传分化指数

仍用估测等位基因频率，根据 Nei 的遗传分化指数估算柠条群体分子变异，由 Nei 指数估算各引物检测到的基因多样性中(表 4)，硬梁群体最低(0.233)。滩地覆沙群体最高(0.262)。5 个引物所检测出的各群体基因多样性按顺序排列如下：硬梁群体<硬梁覆沙群体<沙丘群体<软梁覆沙<毛条群体<滩地覆沙群体。

根据 Nei 指数计算的 6 个柠条群体间的遗传分化系数为 0.0403。即群体间的分子变异只占群体总的基因多样性的 4.03%。大部分的遗传变异(95.97%)存在于群体之内(表 4)。表 5 是 6 个柠条群体间的遗传距离矩阵。各群体间的遗传距离从 0.0534 到 0.0949 不等，平均为 0.0707 ± 0.0107，硬梁覆沙群体和硬梁群体与滩地覆沙群体间的遗传距离较大，分别为 0.0778 和 0.0781。

表 1　实验中所用到的随机引物序列

Table 1　Sequences of five arbitrary primers (Operon) used to generate RAPD markers in *Caragana* spp.

引物 Primer	序列 Sequence
OPH04	5′-GGAAGTCGCC-3′
OPH05	5′-AGTCGTCCCC-3′
OPH18	5′-GAATCGGCCA-3′
OPH19	5′-CTGACCAGCC-3′
OPD20	5′-ACCCGGTCAC-3′

2.2　各群体 RAPD 表型频率的变化

随机扩增后电泳，银染后的 RAPD 谱上一些位点的表型频率的变化在各群体之间是有规律可循的。这 6 个柠条群体的 RAPD 谱之间具有着共同的扩增片段以及在柠条锦鸡儿群体和中间锦鸡儿群体之间存在差异的扩增片段(表 6)。在中间锦鸡儿各群体之间，也有一些扩增片段的频率有规律的变化。这些群体的生境是有一定梯度的，硬梁的基质是侏罗纪或白垩纪粉红色、灰绿色砂层，土壤层较薄，地下水位较深(>10 m)；硬梁覆沙由硬梁经覆沙后形成，覆沙能够防止水分蒸发利于植物生长；软梁的基质是第 3 系或第 4 系冲击或洪积物，地下水位较高(6.5 m)覆沙后形成软梁覆沙；滩地覆沙则是在湿滩地上覆沙形成，地下水位较高(2~5 m)，水分条件较好[19]。由于硬梁和硬梁覆沙与滩地覆沙之间有着水分和基质的差异，而且其上分布的中间锦鸡儿群体之间的遗传距离也较大，所以本文在讨论 RAPD 表型频率在 5 个中间锦鸡儿群体间的规律变化时，着重分析了在硬梁群体和硬梁覆沙群体与滩地覆沙群体之间有差异的扩增片段(表 7)。

表 2　各引物检测柠条群体多态位点的数量(括弧里是多态位点的比率)

Table 2　Polymorphic loci detected with five primers for six populations of *Caragana* spp. (proportion of polymorphic loci)

引物 Primer	毛条群体 PCK	沙丘群体 PSD	软梁覆沙群体 PSR	硬梁覆沙群体 PHRS	硬梁群体 PHR	滩地覆沙群体 PLS	总的多态位点 Total loci
OPH04	24(0.923)	22(0.88)	24(0.923)	24(0.923)	22(0.846)	25(0.962)	28(1.0)
OPH05	27(0.9)	27(0.9)	26(0.897)	27(0.9)	23(0.821)	26(0.867)	29(0.967)
OPH18	28(0.933)	23(0.885)	24(0.923)	26(0.929)	24(0.828)	29(0.935)	31(1.0)
OPH19	24(0.774)	24(0.828)	30(0.938)	24(0.85)	19(0.704)	26(0.929)	34(1.0)
OPD20	26(0.929)	23(0.821)	24(0.889)	23(0.821)	21(0.778)	21(0.875)	31(1.0)
总的位点数 Total loci (总多态位点比率)	129(0.89)	119(0.862)	128(0.914)	124(0.886)	109(0.796)	127(0.9137)	153(0.994)

表 3　由 Shannon 信息指数估计的柠条各群体的遗传多样性

Table 3　Genetic diversity for *Garagana* spp. populations estimated by Shannon diversity index

引物 Primer	OPH04	OPH05	OPH18	OPH19	OPD20	平均 Mean
毛条群体 PCK	16.503	18.971	19.146	14.822	17.522	17.393
沙丘群体 PSD	14.088	19.195	16.252	17.875	16.399	16.760
软梁覆沙群体 PSR	16.802	18.367	15.255	17.685	18.635	17.349
硬梁覆沙群体 PHRS	13.735	18.094	15.743	17.685	16.048	16.358
硬梁群体 PHR	14.540	17.419	17.591	16.684	14.326	16.112
滩地覆沙群体 PLS	17.976	18.128	19.397	16.844	16.010	17.671
群体内遗传多样性 H_{pop}	15.665	18.387	17.289	16.844	16.590	16.955
总群体的遗传多样性 H_{sp}	18.291	20.267	20.628	23.073	21.087	20.669
群体内遗传多样性比率 H_{pop}/H_{sp}	0.856	0.907	0.838	0.730	0.787	0.824
群体间遗传多样性比率$(H_{sp}-H_{pop})/H_{sp}$	0.144	0.093	0.162	0.270	0.213	0.176

表 4　由 Nei 指数估算的群体的基因多样性

Table 4　Gene diversity for six populations of *Caragana* spp. estimated by Net's index

引物 Primer	OPH04	OPH05	OPH18	OPH19	OPD20	平均 Mean
毛条群体 PCK	0.264	0.283	0.281	0.194	0.262	0.257
沙丘群体 PSD	0.220	0.288	0.239	0.239	0.242	0.246
软梁覆沙群体 PSR	0.273	0.274	0.216	0.239	0.277	0.256
硬梁覆沙群体 PHRS	0.208	0.268	0.223	0.237	0.243	0.236
硬梁群体 PHR	0.229	0.259	0.252	0.224	0.203	0.233
滩地覆沙群体 PLS	0.292	0.272	0.281	0.224	0.241	0.262
群体内基因多样性 H_s	0.247	0.275	0.249	0.225	0.246	0.248
总的基因多样性 H_T	0.288	0.303	0.297	0.307	0.309	0.301
群体间基因多样性 D_{sr}	0.0415	0.0283	0.0475	0.0819	0.0629	0.0524
遗传分化系数 G_{ST}±SE	0.0322	0.0217	0.0336	0.0627	0.0481	0.0403±0.0157

表 5　6 个柠条群体间的遗传距离矩阵

Table 5　Matrix based on genetic distance for six *Caragana* spp. populations

	PCK	PSD	PSR	PHRS	PHR	PLS
毛条群体(PCK)	0					
沙丘群体(PSD)	0.0628	0				
软梁覆沙群体(PSR)	0.0661	0.0677	0			
硬梁覆沙群体(PHRS)	0.0762	0.0798	0.0571	0		
硬梁群体(PHR)	0.0631	0.0617	0.0797	0.0949	0	
滩地覆沙群体(PLS)	0.0708	0.0697	0.0534	0.0788	0.0781	0

表 6　6 个柠条群体共同具有的扩增片段以及柠条锦鸡儿与中间锦鸡儿之间有差异的扩增片段

Table 6　The applification fragments shared among six *Caragana* spp. populations and the fragments differed between *C. korshinskii* population and *C. intermidia* population

	共有的扩增片段 Shared fragments			差异的扩增片段 Differed fragments		
	OPH05	OPD20	OPH04	OPH04	OPH19	
	C220	C2027	C2000	C1940	C525	C465
柠条锦鸡儿群体①	1.0	1.0	1.0	0.90	0.17	0.25
中间锦鸡儿群体②						
沙丘群体③	1.0	1.0	1.0	0.27	0.09	0.09
软梁覆沙群体④	1.0	1.0	1.0	0.5	0	0
硬梁覆沙群体⑤	1.0	0.92	1.0	0.17	0	0
硬梁群体⑥	1.0	1.0	1.0	0.33	0	0
滩地覆沙群体⑦	1.0	1.0	0.92	0.38	0	0

① PCK，② Populations of *C.intermidia*，③ PSD，④ PSR，⑤PHRS ，⑥ PHR，⑦ PLS。

表 7　扩增片段频率在 5 个中间锦鸡儿群体间的变化

Table 7　Frequencies of special fragments varying among *C. intermidia* populations

	OPH04		OPH05		OPH19		OPD20	
	C670	C1240	C870	C670	C350	C330	C320	C280
滩地覆沙群体 PLS	0.38	0	0.08	0	0.42	0	0	0.17
沙丘群体 PSD	0.73	0.11	0.09	0	0.73	0	0.18	0.91
软梁覆沙群体 PSR	0.7	0.1	0.1	0.1	0.6	0	0.4	0.8
硬梁覆沙群体 PHRS	0.83	0.33	0.25	0.09	0.82	0.25	0.42	0.75
硬梁群体 PHR	1.0	0.22	0.44	0.44	1.0	0.11	0.67	1.0

从表 7 可以看出，有的扩增片段不存在于滩地覆沙群体中，却存在于硬梁和硬梁覆沙群体中(如 OPD20-C320)，或存在于所有其他柠条群体(如 OPD20-C320 和 OPH40-C1240)。有的扩增片段的滩地覆沙群体中有较低的频率，如 OPD20-C280 在滩地覆沙群体中的表型频率为 0.17。而在其他柠条群体中的表型频率均大于 0.75，甚至在硬梁群体中达到 1.0。

3　讨论

3.1　由于柠条的杂交性倾向很明显[10,11]，所以 RAPD 谱中一条扩增产物的存在并不能区别与之相关的位点是纯合的还是杂合的，需要确定位点的杂合性时，就必须要借助另外的实验手段来补充检验，这不是本文所能解决的问题。本文只能根据 Kongkiangam 等[15]的方法估算等位基因的频率。结果表明 Nei 指数和 Shannon 指数估算的柠条各群体的遗传多样性的大小顺序相同，并且由这两个指数估测的群体间群体内遗传变异的分布是一致的。但是由 Nei 指数估算的群体间遗传多样性占 4.03%(表 4)，与 Shannon 指数估算的 17.6%相去很多。这可能是因为 Nei 指数的计算需要严格的显、隐性等位基因的频率。而 Shannon 指数就不同了，虽然说 Shannon 表型多样性指数较 Nei 指数来说缺乏生物学意义，但正是由于它没有很明确的生物学意义从而在一定程度上避免了对 RAPD 扩增位点显隐性的讨论。所以对于异交植物来说，应用 Shannon 信息指数估算遗传多样性是可行的。

3.2　无论是 Nei 指数还是 Shannon 指数统计 RAPD 数据的结果都显示出大量的分子变异存在于柠条群体之内，只有少量的分子变异存在于群体之间(表 3 和表 4)，说明 6 个柠条群体之间具有很相似的基因频率。梅里尔认为，如果邻近群体有相似的基因频率，可能只是表明它们具有相同的选择压力而并不能证明有基因流动[20]。本文所选的生境是比较有代表性的，从硬梁到硬梁覆沙，然后是软梁覆沙和沙丘，最后是滩地覆沙。这 5 个生境是一定梯度的，硬梁的水分和基质条件最差，滩地覆沙最好，生境选择压力相同的可能性很小。柠条形态学、种子蛋白的研究[10~11]以及同工酶的研究①都认为群体之间具有强大的基因流动。

从群体之间的遗传距离上也说明问题。柠条锦鸡儿和中间锦鸡儿在分类学上本应是两个种，但是柠条锦鸡儿群体(PCK)与中间锦鸡儿每个群体间遗传距离最大的是 0.0762，最小的只有 0.0628，后者比中间锦鸡儿群体之间的遗传距离都小(表 5)。另外，柠条锦鸡儿群体与中间锦鸡儿群体之间遗传分化系数为 0.0287(限于篇幅，该数据没有给出)，也要小于 6 个群体间的遗传分化系数(0.0403)。说明在分类学上两个不同种之间也存在明显而强大的基因流动。这也许是生态过渡带物种分子变异的重要特征。

3.3　硬梁和硬梁覆沙群体与滩地覆沙群体间的遗传距离都较大(分别为 0.0781 和 0.0788，表 5)，一种可能是由于生境选择的压力，硬梁群体和硬梁覆沙群体与滩地覆沙群体在遗传上产生了较大的分子变异，某些扩增片段的频率在这些群体中的变化(表 7)也说明了这个问题，例如扩增片段 OPD20-C280 的表型频率在滩地覆沙群体中为 0.17，而在其他所有群体中的频率均大于 0.75，在硬梁群体中为 1.0；又如片段 OPD20-C320 在滩地覆沙群体不存在，而在硬梁和硬梁覆沙群体中以较高的频率存在。另一种可能解释是繁育系统变化的结果，与选择无关。根据周永刚的研究，发现滩地覆沙群体的异交率 100%，而硬梁群体的异交率较低(53%)，随着生境变旱，异交率降低。近交导致个别基因在群体中的固定，而一定程度的外交则可能导致个别基因的扩散。这同样能够解释表 7 中一些扩增片段的表型频率总是在硬梁和硬梁覆沙群体中以较高频率存在，而在滩地覆沙群体中以较低频率存在甚至为零。

3.4　硬梁和硬梁覆沙群体由 RAPD 标记检测的 DNA 多态性位点比率最低(分别为 79.6%和 88.6%表 2)，滩地覆沙群体的 DNA 多态位点比率则较高(91.37%，表 2)，仅低

① 周永刚，1997，柠条同工酶，种子蛋白的遗传分析和繁育系统(硕士毕业论文)，中国科学院植物研究所。

于软梁覆沙群体的(91.4%)。而根据群体遗传多样性的检测结果，无论是 Shannon 指数还是 Nei 指数，都是滩地覆沙群体的最高，硬梁和硬梁覆沙群体的最低。一般认为较高的遗传变异能够较从容地应付环境的变化和选择。

3.5 根据以上研究结果，可以认为毛乌素沙地柠条群体间强大的基因流可能与其生境的过渡性和群体的异交性有关。但是得出这个结论的研究对象——5 个典型景观上的柠条群体都选自这个生态过渡带内，似乎不足以说明群体异交性与生态过渡性间的联系。然而，根据陈旭东的研究结果①，水分是鄂尔多斯高原生态系统的最大限制因子，降雨是生物群区转换即生态过渡带的最大驱动因子，生物群区发展的最大限制因子是水分，锦鸡儿属植物在水分梯度上的物种替代较为明显。而硬梁、硬梁覆沙、软梁覆沙和滩地覆沙几个景观或生境是有一定水分梯度的，以这个小尺度来研究大尺度是一种尝试，也是合理的。进一步的工作将是选择一个合适的水分梯度，研究和对照包括典型草原区、典型荒漠区及过渡带的几种锦鸡儿植物在分子水平上与生境的联系，也许能从更大的尺度和更深的层次上理解生态过渡性与植物物种遗传结构过渡性的联系。

参考文献

[1] Bachmann K. Tanstey review no. 63—Molecular markers in plant ecology. *New Phytal*. 1994. **126**: 403~418

[2] Burke T. Rainy W E and White T J. Molecular variation and ecological problems. In Berry R J *et al*(ed.)*Genes in Ecology*. Oxford.Blackwell Scientific Publications. 1992. 229~254

[3] Hadrys H. Blick M and Schierwater B. Application of random amplified polymorpbic DNA(RAPD)in molecular ecology. *Molecular Ecology*. 1992. **1**: 55~63

[4] Dawson 1 K. Chalmers K T and Waugh R. *et al*. Detection and analysis of genetic of genetic variation in *Hordeum spontaneum* population from tsraet using RAPD markers. *Molecular Ecology*. 1993. **2**: 151~159

[5] Bucci G and Menozzi P. Segregation analysis of random amplified polymorphic DNA(RAPD)markers in *Picea abies* Karst.*Molecular Ecology*. 1993. **2**: 227~232

[6] 王洪新，胡志昂，钟敏. 等. 盐渍条件下野大豆群体的遗传分化和生理适应：同工酶和随机扩增多态 DNA 研究. 植物学报, 1997. **39**: 29~34

[7] 恽锐，钟敏，王洪新. 等. 北京东灵山辽东栎种群 DNA 多样性的研究. 植物学报. 1998, **40**: 169~175

[8] Keil M and Griffin A P. Use of random amplified polymorphic DNA(RAPD)Markers in the discrimination and verification of genotypes in *Eucalyptus.Theor. Appl. Genet.* 1994. **89**: 442~450

[9] 张新时，毛乌素沙地的生态背景及其草地建设的原则与优化模式. 植物生态学报. 1994. **18**(1): 1~16

[10] 王洪新，胡志昂，钟敏. 等. 毛乌素沙地锦鸡儿(*Caragana*)种群形态变异.生态学报. 1994. **14**(4): 366~371

[11] 王洪新，胡志昂，钟敏. 等. 毛乌素沙地锦鸡儿种群种子蛋白多样性及其生物学意义. 生态学报. 1994. **14**(4): 372~380

[12] Doyle J J & Doyle J L. lsolation of plant DNA from fresh tissue *Focus*. 1990. **12**(1): 13~15

[13] Witliams J G K. Hanafey M K and Rafalski J A.*et al*.Genetic analysis using random amplified polymorphic DNA markers.*Methods in Enzymology*. 1993. **218**: 704~740

[14] 胡志昂，恽锐，钟敏. 等. 检测植物 DNA 扩增多态性方法的比较和改进. 植物学报. 1997. **39**: 138~144

[15] Kongkiaingam P.Waterway M J.Fortin M G.*et.al.*Genetic variation within and between two cultivars of red clover (*Trifolium pretense* L.): Comparisons of morphological.isozyme.and RAPD markers *Euphytica*. 1995. **84**: 237~246

[16] Lewontin RC.The apportionment of human diversity.In Dobzbansky T ed. *Evolutionary Biology*.Appleton Century Crofts.New York. 1972. **6**: 381~398

① 陈旭东，1996. 鄂尔多斯高原生物多样性的研究(博士毕业论文)，中国科学院植物研究所。

[17] Nei M.Analysis of gene diversity in subdivided populations. *Proc. Natl. Acad. Sci. USA*. 1973. **70**: 3321~3323
[18] Nei M.*Molecular population genetics and evolution*.North Holland Publisbing Company. 1975
[19] 陈仲新, 谢海生. 毛乌素沙地景观生态类型与灌丛生物多样性初步研究. 生态学报. 1994. **14**(4): 345~354
[20] 梅里尔 D J. 黄瑞复等译. 生态遗传学. 北京: 科学出版社. 1991

本文原载：植物学报. 1997. 39(2): 144-148

检测植物DNA扩增多态性方法的比较和改进*

胡志昂　恽锐　钟敏　董夫贵　王洪新　钱迎倩

(中国科学院植物研究所)

摘　要　以辽东栎(*Quercus liaotungensis* Koidz.)、锦鸡儿(*Caragana* ssp.)和野大豆(*Glycine soja* (L.) Sieb. et Zucc.)为材料，比较了随机扩增多态DNA(RAPD)和DNA扩增指纹(DAF)方法。用RAPD的琼脂糖胶电泳和溴乙锭染色，RAPD和DAF谱一般不足10条带。用DAF的变性聚丙烯酰胺凝胶电泳(PAGE)和银染，极大地提高了RAPD的灵敏度和分辨率，多达20~40个产物。用3′末端完全相同的引物，RAPD和DAF有同样的扩增谱，说明两种方法有相似的机理。降低胶的浓度可提高RAPD和DAF的分辨率，达40~80条带。琼脂糖电泳分离的溴乙锭显示的单荧光带，用PAGE和银染可分辨出多个片段。分子克隆证实单荧光带的分子量异质性。在用Taq DNA多聚酶的条件下，RAPD和DAF的再现性均良好。

关键词　随机扩增多态DNA；DNA扩增指纹；植物自然群体；DNA多样性；聚丙烯酰胺凝胶电泳；银染

近年来DNA随机扩增片段长度多态性的发现，极大地提高了检测生物自然群体DNA多样性的能力。其中随机扩增多态DNA(RAPD)[1]方法简便、迅速，得到广泛应用。类似的有Caetano-Anolles等[2]的DNA扩增指纹(DNA amplification fingerprinting, DAF)。两者有几点不同[3]：RAPD通常用10核苷引物，更短的引物得不到扩增产物；DAF提高引物浓度，用更短的7至9核苷引物可以得到扩增产物。二是DAF用聚丙烯酰胺凝胶电泳(PAGE)和银染。三是DAF的产物远多于RAPD。本文报道以3种植物为材料，包括乔木、灌木和草本；包括远交和自交的；交替使用RAPD和DAF方法，探讨两者在机理上的异同，从中推出一种改良的RAPD方法。

1　材料和方法

1.1　植物材料

辽东栎(*Quercus liaotungensis* Koidz.)的冬芽采自北京市门头沟区小龙门林场。锦鸡儿(*Caragana* ssp.)的种子采自内蒙伊克昭盟伊金霍洛旗。野大豆(*Glycine soja*(L.)Sieb. et Zucc.)采自山东省垦利县黄河入海口。

* 本研究是国家科委攀登项目的一部分，还得到中国科学院重大和重点项目的资助。

1.2　DNA 纯化

辽东烁的冬芽和锦鸡儿一年生苗的幼叶 DNA 用 Doyle 和 Doyle[4]的方法纯化。野大豆 DNA 采用 Stewart[5]的方法从幼苗的幼叶纯化。

1.3　DNA 扩增

RAPD 按 Williams 等[1]的方法，退火温度改为 35℃。引物购自美国 Operon 技术公司。DAF 按 Caetano-Anolles 和 Bassam[6]及 Bassam 和 Caetano-Anolles[7]的方法，但胶的浓度降为 4%、3.5%或 3.2%。RAPD 和 DAF 都用北京华美生物工程公司的 Taq DNA 多聚酶、扩增缓冲液和核苷三磷酸底物。DAF 的引物用 ABI 公司的 DNA 合成仪合成，其序列见 Eskew 等[8]。扩增在军事医学科学院生产的 PTC-51B 型热循环仪中进行。

1.4　DNA 克隆用 Boehringer Mannheim 公司的 pUC 克隆试剂盒并按其说明书操作

羟基毛地黄苷标记探针和杂交也用该公司的 DIG DNA 标记和检测试剂盒。其他分子操作如从琼脂糖胶中电洗脱 DNA 等均按 Sambrook 等[9]。

2　结果和讨论

2.1　扩增产物的琼脂糖电泳和溴乙锭染色

虽然随植物种类和引物而变，但 RAPD 的产物通常不足 10 个，和大多数报道一致。DAF 的产物用琼脂糖电泳分离和溴乙锭染色，数目略多些，最多的是辽东栎 DNA，用引物 8. 9a(CGCGGCCA)扩增可分辨出 16 条带。Ceatano-Anolles[3]也报道这种条件下 DAF 只有少数几个产物。为了获得足够强的荧光谱，RAPD 和 DAF 都必须加 10~20μL 扩增产物。

2.2　PAGE 和银染

虽然产物的数目和分子量随模板 DNA 和引物而异，但这种方法分辨的 RAPD 一般可达 20~40 条带(图 1)。每次电泳只要加 1μL 扩增产物。DAF 谱通常比 RAPD 复杂些。最多的如辽东栎 DNA 用 8.9a 引物时的 DAF 谱用 3.2% PAGE 可分辨出约 80 个成分(图 2)。银染的高灵敏度也为研究工作提供了一次扩增可进行多次电泳显示的机会。Caetano-Anolles[3]评论中强调产物数目是 RAPD 与 DAF 主要不同点。我们和他本人的实验都说明决定两者产物数目主要是电泳分离和染色方法。RAPD 与 DAF 的差别并不像以前认为的那么大。当然，DAF 用了更短的引物，因而能在模板上引发更多的扩增子(amplicon)，结果产生更多更短的扩增片段。虽然 DAF 多用 Taq DNA 多聚酶的 Stoffel 片段[2, 6, 8]，但在本实验室用 Taq DNA 多聚酶的条件下，RAPD 和 DAF 的实验重复性均良好(图 3、图 4)。用同一个模板，以 7.7a(CGAGCTG)引物所得 DAF 谱和以 OPA-02(10 mer 引物，序列为 TGCC-GAGCTG，3'端的 7 个碱基就是 7.7a 引物)为引物所得 RAPD 谱完全一样，进一步说明两种方法有相似的机理，也证明 3'末端序列的重要性[10]。

将 RAPD 或 DAF 的产物先用 1%低熔点琼脂糖电泳分离和溴乙锭染色，然后切下各荧光带在 70℃或 95℃下熔化直接进行 PAGE 和银染。从图 5 可以看出随着荧光带分子量下降，其 PAGE 和银染的片段分子量也下降。更重要的是每个荧光带都由数个不同分子量的片段组成。再电泳的结果还显示荧光带之间共享某些 DNA 片段。

用 pUC 克隆试剂盒克隆从琼脂糖电泳分离并电洗脱纯化的番茄 HindIII酶切的 3.5kb 片段。从随机挑选的 JM109 白色转化菌落中，其质粒的 HindIII酶切片段除 2686bp 的 pUC19 片段外，插入的番茄 DNA 分子量变化很大，包括 0.6、2.5、3.5、4.0kb 不等(图 6)。证明琼脂糖电泳溴乙锭染色的单带是不同分子量片段的混合物。也曾将 pNP24 质粒(美国 NPI 赠送的 pUC19 的 EcoRI 位点有 NP24 蛋白 cDNA 插入[11])经 EcoRI 酶切后用 20cm 长的 1%琼脂糖胶进行电泳分离，pUC19 与 943 bp 插入间隔若干厘米，中间没有任何荧光带。切下 943 bp 片段再用 1%琼脂糖电泳和溴乙锭染色证明没有其他 DNA 片段。电泳洗脱纯化后，943 bp 片段用羟基毛地黄苷标记为杂交探针。EcoRI 酶切的 pNP24 电泳分离后用上述探针进行 Southern 杂交，膜上的 943 bp 片段在碱性磷酸脂酶染色的最初几分钟即出现强紫色，其他区域无染色。染色过夜后，2.7 kb 附近出现浅紫色。已知 943 bp 插入与 pUC19 并无同源性，弱杂交信号只能解释为探针里带有 pUC19。很多实验室也有类似的经验，即不论是用毛地黄苷一类非放射性标记或放射性标记，常常出现探针不纯的现象。估计是琼脂糖电泳的问题。

RAPD 和 DAF 的产物在用琼脂糖电泳和溴乙锭染色后，切下跑在荧光带后的凝胶块，经 PAGE 和银染，发现有分子量大于λDNA/HindIII的 6557 bp 的产物。表明在 RAPD 和 DAF 谱中大分子量扩增产物并非人为效应，只是含量低而溴乙锭不能显示出来。

Bachmann[12]在评论中指出："最保险而简单的方法是用琼脂糖电泳分离而且只注意那些无疑而重复性高的带"。我们同意实验方法的再现性是极其重要的。PAGE 和银染有极高的分辨率和灵敏度，更可能出现实验误差。从我们的结果及 Gresshoff 和 McKen-zie[13]的详细研究可看出在 RAPD 和 DAF 中应用 PAGE 和银染的可行性和稳定性。尤其是对于大豆和野大豆一类遗传变异水平较低的种类，高灵敏度尤为必要。

PAGE 和银染所揭示的高信息量的 DNA 扩增多态性，可以加快分子标记的鉴定过程。特别有利于提高基因定位、标记辅助育种和基因定位克隆[14]的效率。

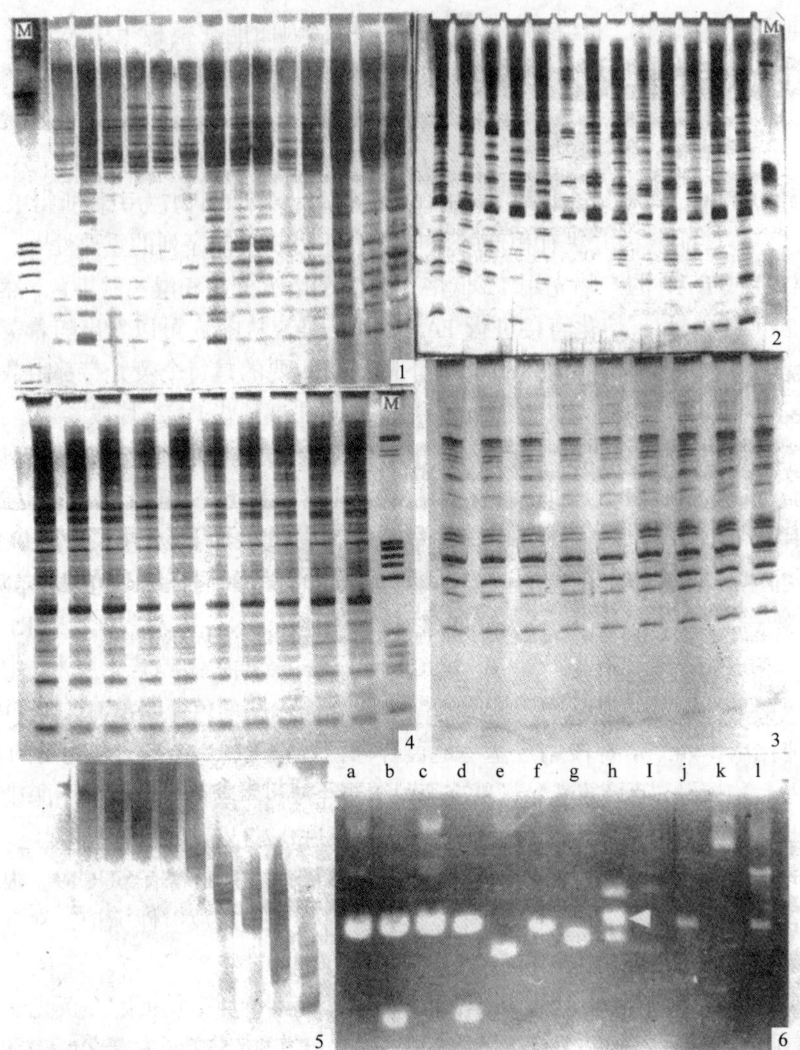

图 1　野大豆群体不同植株的 RAPD 谱(引物 OPD-01，PAGE 分离和银染)。M. DNA 分子量标准，λ DNA/Hind III (6557+4361，2322，2027bp)和 pBR322/Hae III (587，540，504，458，434;267，234，213，192，184；124+123,109,89bp)。图 2　不同辽东栎植株的 DAF 谱(引物 8.9a)。M.DNA 分子量标准，同图 1。图 3　辽东栎植株 183 号 DNA 平行扩增的 RAPD 谱(引物 OPJ-06，PAGE 分离和银染)。图 4　辽东栎植株 183 号 DNA 平行扩增的 DAF 谱(引物 8.9a)。M.DNA 分子量标准，同图 1。图 5　琼脂糖电泳分离、EB 染色的各 DNA 片段的 PAGE 再电泳谱。图 6　带番茄 DNA 的 pUC19 的琼脂糖电泳。a、c、e，g、i、k，带插入的 pUC19；b、d、f、h、j、l. Hind III 酶切的带插入的 pUC19。箭头示 2686bp 的 pUC19 DNA

Fig.l　PAGE-separated and silver-stained RAPD profiles of wild soybean (*Glycine soja*) populations by using primer OPD-01. M. DNA marker, λ DNA/HindIII (6557+ 4361, 2322; 2027bp) and pBR322/ Hae III (587, 540, 504, 458, 434; 267, 234, 213, 192, 184; 124+123, 109, 89bp). Fig. 2　DAF profiles of different liaodong oak tree (*Quercus liaotungensis*) population by using primer 8.9a. M. marker DNA, same as in Fig.1. Fig.3 RAPD profiles from parallel amplifications of the liaodong oak tree No. 183 by using primer OPJ-06. Fig.4 DAF profiles of parallel amplifications of the liaodong oak tree No. 183 by using primer 8.9a. M. marker DNA, same as in Fig.1. Fig.5 PAGE re-electrophoretic patterns of DNA fragments separated by agarose gel electrophoresis and EB-staining. Fig 6. Agarose gel electrophoresis of pUC19 DNA-cloned tomato DNAs. A, c, e, g, i, k. pUC19 with inserts; b, d, f, h, j, l. HindIII digested pUC19 DNA with inserts. The arrow showed pUC19 DNA (2 686 bp)

参考文献

[1] Williams J G K, Kubelik A R, Livak K J *et al*. DNA polymorphisms amplified by arbitrary primers are useful as genetic markets. *Nucl Acid Res*, 1990. **18**: 6531~6535

[2] Caetano-Anolles G, Bassam B J, Gresshoff P M *et al*. DNA amplification fingerprinting using very short arbitrary oligonucleotide primer. *Bio/Technlogy*, 1991. **9**: 553~557

[3] Caetano-Anolles G. MAAP: A versatile and universal tool for genome analysis. *Plant Mol Biol*, l994. **25**: 1011~ 1026

[4] Doyle J J, Doyle J L. Isolation of plant DNA from fresh tissue. *Focus*, 1990. **12**: 13 ~15

[5] Stewart Jr C N. Soybean DNA isolation procedure using fresh tissue. *Soybean Genet Newsl*, 1994. **21**: 243 ~244

[6] Caetano-Anolles G, Bassam B J. DNA amplification fingerprinting using arbitrary oligonucleotide primets. *Appl Biochem Biotechnol*, 1993. **25**: 189~200

[7] Bassam B J, Caetano-Anolles G. Silver staining of DNA in polyacrylamide gels. *Appl Biochem Biotechnol*, 1993. **25**: 181~188

[8] Eskew D L, Caetano-Anolles G, Bassam B J *et al*. DNA amplification fingerprinting of the *Azolla-Anabaena* symbiosis. *Plant Mol Biol*, 1993. **21**: 363~373

[9] Sambrook J. Fritsch E F, Maniatis T. Molecular Cloning. 2nd ed. New York: Cold Spring Harbor Laboratory Press, 1989. 6.28~6.35

[10] Caetano-Anolles G, Bassam B J, Gresshoff PM. Primer-template interactions during DNA amplification fingerprinting with single arbitrary oligonucleotides. *Mol Gen Genet*, 1992. **235**: 157 ~165

[11] King G J, Victoria A, Turner C E *et al.* Isolation and characterization of a tomato cDNA clone which codes for a salt-induced protein. *Plant Mol Biol*, 1988. **10**: 401~412

[12] Bachmann K. Molecular markers in plant ecology. *New Phytol*, 1994. **126**:403~418

[13] Gresshoff P M, McKenzie A K. Low experimental variability of DNA profiles generated by arbitrary primer based amplification(DAF)of soybean. *Chinese J Bot*, 1994. **6**:1~6

[14] Miksche J P. The USDA-ARS Plant Genome Research Program. Washington DC: USDA ARS, 1994

生物多样性保护研究

本文原载：科技导报. 1992. (5): 36-38

生物多样性的保护和永续利用

钱迎倩

(中国植物学会)

当今世界面临着人口、粮食、资源、环境与能源五大危机，这五大危机的解决都与生物多样性有着密切的关系。人口，又包含着人口无限制地膨胀与人类的健康两大问题。我国政府提倡计划生育的政策无疑是非常正确的。要做好计划生育，除手术及避孕器具方法之外，人类将从生物多样性的生物物种中寻找高效而对人体无害的化合物来达到目的。根据世界卫生组织的统计，发展中国家有 80%的药物依靠传统的自然药物来进行疾病的治疗，发达国家 40%以上的药物依靠自然资源，中药中的药用植物有 5000 种以上，其中 1700 种为常用药物。例如，近年来我国科学家在一个菊科的蒿类植物中提出青蒿素，目前已证明它是一种比奎宁更有效的治疗疟疾的药物；癌症与艾滋病是国际上的两大顽症，科学的发展使人们认识到中药天花粉(栝楼的根)的蛋白质不仅能治愈绒毛膜皮癌，而且可能还是治疗艾滋病的良药。

由于人口不断的增长，迫使人们努力去提高粮食的产量。要提高单位面积的产量，灌溉、施肥及其他农业措施固然重要，良种的培育却是首要的要素。良种大面积的推广，在粮食大丰收的同时也潜伏着很大的危机。由于品种的单一，遗传物质基础狭窄而极易遭受病虫的危害，可能使粮食产量急剧下降，提高抗病虫害能力的唯一途径是从生物多样性中寻找有抗逆能力的品种或野生近缘种进行杂交，或者应用现代基因工程方法，把抗逆基因导入作物品种。例如，美国有人在十年前从我国的东北带走了长有白毛的野生大豆的一个类型，用以与美国的栽培大豆杂交，培育出抗旱的新品种，比原有栽培品种节水 15%，并能在较贫瘠、干旱的土地上栽培，扩大了种植面积，从而使美国代替我国成为大豆最大的出口国。人们谈到资源，往往想到的是石油、矿藏等不可再生的资源，此类资源的危机固然严重，但殊不知这些被人们忽视的生物多样性的资源，一旦受到威胁，遭到灭绝，对当今的人类，对一个国家的经济发展，对我们的子孙万代又有多么密切的关系。

中国原始森林砍伐的速度是非常惊人的。仅以西双版纳为例，50 年代时，当地原始森林覆盖率为 55%，而现在还留下的已不到 28%。全国的森林覆盖率 12%左右。森林大面积消失，不仅造成严重的水土流失，并使整个气候发生变化。50 年代长江的水基本是清的，而 40 年后的今天已快成为中国第二条“黄河”，这就是自然生态系统被破坏的后果。海南岛与西双版纳等中国的热带地区原始森林砍伐后，大量种植橡胶林。当然橡胶的种植有其重大的政治意义及经济意义，但是从环境的角度来看，单一的人工生态系统并不能替代自然生态系统的功能，对环境的恶化还是严重的。根据我国热带地区有关研究所在海南岛尖峰岭林区的观察，森林破坏后短短一年内，地表径流量增加 5~6 倍，水土流失量为 105 立方米/公顷，为有林地的 7 倍，径流含沙量为有林地的 20 倍，有 2 厘米的表土被冲走。云南西双版纳的植胶区，由于单一的人工林替代了天然林，据 20 年资料分析，温度的年变化幅度增加 1~1.5℃。冬季温度降低，暖季温度升高，年雨量减少 100~200 毫米，雾日减少 20~30 天，大风日增加 6~8 天，雷暴天气增加 10~60 天。不仅如此，原有自然生态系统中的动、植物、微生物的种类十分丰富，一旦变成农田或单一的经济林后，原来不少生物由于丧失其栖息地而灭绝。对农田来说，原来丰富的生物多样性中存在很多虫害的天敌，由于天敌无栖息地而灭绝，造成害虫大量繁殖。环境的破坏，对人类粮食生产带来的恶果是显而易见的。最后，众所周知，人类目前所利用的绝大多数能源，例如石油、煤等都是由几百万年前的森林或其他生物储藏的几百万年前的太阳能所提供，全世界一年内消耗的煤炭便相当于消耗一万年所储存的太阳能。这些不可再生的能量资源总有一天将为人类耗尽。人们必须，也已经在生物多样性中开发新的油脂植物。现代工业生产也需要从生物多样性中开发更多更新的生物资源，为各种工业生产提供新型的能源。

综上所述，保护生物多样性的重要性已是不言而喻。为之，举世瞩目的将于今年 6 月在巴西召开的联合国环境与发展大会(UNCED)上生物多样性将是会议的主要议题之一。

生物多样性的概念

根据化石的考证，地球上出现低级形式的生命(例如细菌和蓝藻)起源于 40 亿年以前。经过几十亿年的缓慢进化与分化，逐渐出现多种多样的千变万化的生命形式，形成了生物多样性。换句话说，生物多样性就是地球上存在的所有动物、植物和微生物，它们每个个体所拥有的基因，以及由此形成的错综复杂的生态系统。一个地区生物多样性的丰富度一般来说是指该地区物种数量的多少。但是，一个物种内的不同个体绝对不是完全一样的。在物种之下，还有变种，亚种，品种以及生理小种等等。此外，不同的物种又往往是聚集在一起形成群落，它们与环境在一起又组成了不同的生态系统。因此，讨论生物多样性通常包含有三个层次的概念，这就是物种多样性、遗传多样性和生态多样性，多样性是这三个层次的固有特性。

一个物种是指某一类生物，它们之间的遗传特性十分相似，能够通过交配繁殖出有繁殖能力的后代。例如白狗与花狗虽然外形不一样，颜色不一样，它们能交配，并后代还有繁殖能力，因此是一个物种。马与驴经交配得到的骡子没有繁殖能力，马与驴就是两个物种。白人与黑人虽然都属同一物种——人，但是他们的肤色不一样，这意味着他们是不同的人种，拥有不完全相同的基因，说明物种下有不同的遗传多样性。在某一环境内，生存着丰富多彩的动物群落、植物群落、微生物群落，群落与群落之间以及它们与所栖息的环境之间形成了具有一定相互关系的不同生态系统，不同的地理及气候条件构成了各种各样的环境，不同的环境下又有千姿百态的生物，它们又组成了生态系统多样性。

生物多样性的现状

有人形容，数百年来，人类像对付一部租来的汽车一样地对待地球。不仅不关心这颗星球，而且刻薄地、肆无忌惮地加以利用，使它正在我们眼前毁灭。人类大量砍伐森林，工业的发展带来大量废气、废物污染了环境，破坏了自然。不仅大量的生物物种被消灭，也造成了很多物种由于没有了栖息地而死去。再由于人口的膨胀，大量地消耗自然资源，造成了更多的物种的灭绝。世界的热带森林栖息着世界半数以上的物种，但每年有像奥地利国土面积大小的热带雨林遭到破坏。有人估计，目前的世界，每天有一个种正在消灭，热带地区每天有100个种正在灭绝。如果人类的消费模式和破坏作用仍不改变的话，到2000年，地球上所有物种的15%~20%将会消失。在自然情况下，物种一方面在进化，一方面也在自然灭绝，但由于人类破坏的干扰，物种灭绝的速率是自然灭绝速率的1000倍。按估计，世界上现有1000万个物种(有人估计有3000万种)，但已为人们定名的仅140万种。很多物种连名都未定下来，用途更不知道的情况下正在不断地从地球上消失。一个物种一旦消失，不可能在地球上再出现，这对人类本身来说，又是多么悲惨的现实呵!

总之，对生物多样性保护的重要性日益为人们所认识。生物多样性与全球变化的关系已引起人们的重视，人类要利用生物多样性才能生存，但又必须合理地利用，持续地利用，这也成为科学家的一个研究课题。总之，生物多样性的保护及持续利用已成为近年来国际社会重点关注的问题之一。

1980年发表的《世界自然保护大纲》就生物多样性保护的问题进行了专题论述；世界自然保护基金会1989年就这问题发表了声明；联合国环境规划署将它列为全球关注的问题之一；世界银行和亚洲开发银行为此已提供了大额贷款与部分赠款；由联合国环境规划署组织、国际自然保护联盟起草的《全球生物多样性保护公约》正在磋商中(我国政府也已参加)；美国国务院及世界许多有关组织和科研机构(例如美国的Keystone Center和世界资源研究所)召开了一系列研讨会；南美洲的哥斯达黎加成立了生物多样性研究所；一系列国际组织，如联合国教科文组织、国际生物科学联盟等，都把它列入重要的议事日程。列举这些已足以说明对生物多样性保护及持续利用的关注已成为国际上的历史趋向。在这种情况下，“保护动物就是保护人类自己”，“拯救植物就是拯救我们自己”的口号在世界上被响亮地提出来了。

我国的情况又是怎样呢?地质年代第四纪冰川期，东亚、欧洲、北美由于地理条件的不同而有着完全不同的遭遇。由于冰川的来临，北美的南面是墨西哥湾和墨西哥沙漠，生物向南退却的后路被切断而遭绝灭；欧洲南部横着一条阿尔卑斯山，使北欧、中欧及阿尔卑斯山几乎全被冰川覆盖，仅少数生物在避难所里保存下来。而东亚，由于不存在上述障碍，生物可随冰川前进而向南退却。而东亚地区的冰川活动又较弱，因此遭灭绝的生物较少，保留了大批第三纪及第三纪以前就有的古老植物。以植物为例，中国的银杏就是典型的已生存一亿多年的活化石。此外水杉、银杉都是中国所特有。我国植物的特有属超过200，特有种超过一万。

此外，我国气候从热带直至寒温带，这种气候带的多样性是世界上唯一的。我国从东面沿海到世界屋脊的青藏高原有三级台阶，从地平面，甚至地平面以下到海拔 8884 米，地形的复杂性也是世界之最。多样的气候和复杂的地理条件为生物多样性创造了极大地丰富度，我国的生物多样性占世界的第八位。我国的国土面积虽仅占世界总面积的 6.4%，可是高等植物和脊椎动物种类却占世界总数的 1/10。

尽管我国有如此得天独厚的优越条件，生物多样性如此之丰富，但它却面临着严重的危机。近 30 年来我国毁林的速度十分迅速。例如海南岛，50 年代初期森林面积占 25.7%，现在仅存 7.2%，每年递降率为 2.7%；此外，沿海的红树林、珊瑚礁也遭到严重的破坏。50 年代科学工作者采到的标本，很多已在我国灭绝。有几个数字是触目惊心的，1987 年从我国走私到日本的麝香达 700 多公斤，而采集 700 公斤麝香需 10 万多头麝。我国到底还有多少头野生麝?麝这个种正处于灭绝的过程。我国某些公司要求出口 1 万条蟒蛇皮以及大批眼镜蛇及眼镜王蛇，甚至成吨出口珊瑚，而生活在珊瑚礁中的许多海洋生物极可能成为解救人类心脏病和癌症的关键药物，珊瑚礁的破坏使这些海洋生物失去了它们的栖息地，生存受到了严重的威胁。而目前我国生物多样性消亡的情况是无人能提出一个估计数字的、亟待研究的课题。

从另一角度看，我国已建立了近 600 个自然保护区，占国土面积的 3%，其中长白山、鼎湖山、卧龙、武夷山、梵净山、锡林郭勒和博格达峰等 7 个自然保护区先后加入"国际生物圈保留地网";收集主要粮食作物的品种及野生近缘种已是近几个五年计划中的国家攻关项目，并已建立了品种资源库；某些珍稀濒危物种的保护，如大熊猫和白暨豚的保护，已为政府部门及国际上所重视；大量的科研单位，尤其是中国科学院，解放以来对我国生物资源的调查也十分重视，科学家已陆续写就关于生物的《红色名录》及《红皮书》;《自然保护纲要》已出版，《中国植物志》、《中国动物志》、《孢子植物志》也在相继出版。凡此种种，说明了我国进行生物多样性的研究已有了较好的基础，同时也反映了国家对生物多样性的保护及永续利用的问题已开始重视。但是，从总体角度来看，工作还是零散的，很不完整。面临的现状十分严峻，大量的工作急待进行研究。生物多样性保护的重要性有待进行全民教育，有效的政策措施有待制定。

保护生物多样性应采取的措施

这里仅提纲挈领地提出几个要点。

1. 生物多样性的调查及生物编目(Bioinventory)

中国的生物多样性如此之丰富，但至今除高等植物及脊椎动物调查比较清楚外，大量的生物，尤其是昆虫还未查清，更有大量的标本尚未定名。在调查的基础上还必须利用现代信息处理的方法进行生物编目。

2. 生物多样性的就地保护及迁地保护

建立自然保护区是生物多样性就地保护国际上目前普遍采用的好方法。但不少我国的珍稀、濒危物种必须进行迁地保护。植物园、动物园及野生动物饲养场是迁地保护的优良场所。迁地保护后还必须让这些生物回归大自然。

3. 生物多样性的经营管理

世界上不少国家及国际组织都在实施生物多样性的行动计划，并十分重视生物多样性的经营及管理问题。我国尽管已经建立了约600个自然保护区，但经营管理上还存在着大量亟待解决的问题。

4. 基础研究

生物多样性的就地保护及迁地保护，自然生态系统的恢复，把生物多样性作为全球变化的指示进行长期监测，直至物种内遗传变异通过物理特征或生物化学的实验测定等一系列课题有待进行基础研究。

5. 宣传与教育

生物多样性这个术语的本身至今还鲜为人知。保护生物多样性的重要性，及其与人类的生存与发展的密切关系还必须进行大量的宣传、教育。

6. 政府要制定或修订一系列有关法规，履行国际公约

为了真正保护生物多样性，单靠宣传教育是不够的。政府必须制定切实可行的法规，其中包括生物资源国际贸易的法规等等。

本文原载：现代化. 1992. 14(7): 5-7

历史的责任：保护生物多样性

钱迎倩

(中国科学院植物研究所)

概念

根据化石的考证，地球上出现低级形式的生命(例如细菌和蓝藻)是40亿年以前，经过几十亿年缓慢的进化与分化，逐渐呈现多种多样千变万化的生命形式，形成了生物的多样性。换句话说，生物多样性就是地球上存在的所有动物、植物和微生物，它们每个个体所拥有的基因，以及形成的错综复杂的生态系统。一个地区生物多样性的丰富度一般来说是指该地区物种数量的多少，但是，一个物种内的不同个体绝对不是完全一样的。在物种之下，还有变种、亚种、品种以及生理小种等等。此外，不同的物种又往往是聚集在一起形成群落，它们与环境一起又组成了不同的生态系统。因此，讨论生物多样性通常包含有三个层次的概念，这就是物种多样性、遗传多样性和生态多样性。多样性是这三个层次的固有特性。

一个物种是指某一类生物，它们之间的遗传特性十分相似，能够通过交配后繁殖出有繁殖能力的后代。例如白狗与花狗虽然外形不一样，颜色不一样，它们能交配，其后代还有繁殖能力，因此是一个物种。马和驴经交配后得到的骡子，它们没有繁殖能力，马和驴就是两个物种。白人与黑人虽然都属同一物种：人，但是他们的肤色不一样，这意味着他们是不同的人种，拥有不完全相同的基因，说明了物种下有不同的遗传多样性。在某一环境内，生存着丰富多彩的动物群落、植物群落、微生物群落，群落与群落之间

以及它们与所栖息的环境之间形成了具有一定相互关系的不同生态系统。不同的地理及气候条件构成了各种各样的环境，不同的环境下又有千姿百态的生物，它们又组成了生态系统的多样性。

现状

有人形容，这数百年来，人类像对付一部租来的汽车一样地对待地球。不仅不关心这颗星球，而且刻薄地、肆无忌惮地加以利用，使它正在我们眼前毁灭。人类大量的砍伐森林，工业的发展带来大量的废气、废物，污染了环境，破坏了自然。不仅大量的生物物种被消灭，也造成了很多物种因没有了栖息地而死去。再加上由于人口的膨胀，大量地消耗自然资源，造成了更多的物种的灭绝。热带森林栖息着全世界半数以上的物种，但每年有像奥地利国土面积大小的热带雨林遭到破坏。有人估计，目前的世界，每天有一个物种正在消灭，热带地区每天有 100 个物种正在灭绝。如果人类的消费模式和破坏作用仍不改变的话，到 2000 年，地球上所有物种的 15%~20%将会消失。在自然情况下，物种一方面在进化，一方面也在自然灭绝，但由于人类破坏的干扰，物种灭绝的速率是自然灭绝的 1000 倍。按估计，世界上现有 1000 万个物种(有人估计有 3000 万个)，但已人们定名的仅 140 万种。很多的物种，在连名字都未定下来，用途更不知道的情况下正不断地从地球上消失。一个物种一旦消失，就不可能在地球上再出现，这对人类本身来说是多么悲惨的现实啊!

因此，生物多样性保护的重要性日益为人们所认识，生物多样性与全球变化的关系已引起人们的重视，人类要利用生物的多样性才能生存，但又必须合理地利用，持续地利用，这已成为科学家的研究课题。总之，生物多样性的保护及持续利用已成为近年来国际社会重点关注的问题之一。

地质年代第四纪冰川期，东亚、欧洲、北美由于地理条件的不同而有着完全不同的遭遇。由于冰川的来临，北美的南面是墨西哥湾和墨西哥沙漠，生物向南退却的后路被切断而遭灭绝；欧洲南部横着一条阿尔卑斯山，使北欧、中欧及阿尔卑斯山上几乎全被冰川覆盖，仅少数生物在避难所里保存了下来。东亚，由于不存在上述障碍，生物可随冰川前进而向南退却，而东亚地区的冰川活动又较弱，因此遭灭绝的生物较少，保留了大批第三纪及第三纪以前就有的古老植物。以植物为例，中国的银杏就是典型的已生存 1 亿多年的活化石。此外，水杉、银杉都是中国所特有。我国植物的特有属超过 200，特有种超过 1 万。

此外，我国气候从热带直至寒温带，这种气候带的多样性是世界上唯一的。我国从东面沿海到世界屋脊的青藏高原有三级台阶，从地平面，甚至地平面以下到海拔 8884 米，地形的复杂性也是世界之最。多样的气候和复杂的地理条件为生物多样性创造了极大的丰富度，我国的生物多样性居世界第 8 位。我国的国土面积虽仅占世界总面积的 6.4 %，但高等植物和脊椎动物种类却占世界总数的 1/10。

尽管我国有如此得天独厚的优越条件，生物多样性如此之丰富，但却面临着严重的危机。近 30 年来我国毁林的速度十分迅速。例如海南岛，50 年代初期森林面积占 25.7 %，现仅占 7.2%，每年递降率为 2.7%；此外，沿海的红树林、珊瑚礁也遭到严重的破坏。50 年代科学工作者采到的标本很多已在我国灭绝。有几个数字是触目惊心的：1987 年从我国走私到日本的麝香达 700 多公斤，而采集 700 公斤麝香需 10 万多头麝，我国到底还有多少头野生麝？我国某些公司要求出口 1 万条蟒蛇皮以及大批眼镜蛇及眼镜王蛇，甚至成吨出口珊瑚，而生活在珊瑚礁中的许多海洋生物极可能成为救治人类心脏病和癌症的关键药物，珊瑚礁的破坏使这些海洋生物失去了它们的栖息地，生存受到了严重的威胁。而对目前我国生物多样性消亡的情况，竟无人能提出一个估计数字。

从另一角度看，我国已建立了近 600 个自然保护区，已占国土面积的 3%，其中长白山、鼎湖山、卧龙、武夷山、梵净山、锡林郭勒和博格达峰等 7 个自然保护区先后加入“国际生物圈保留地网”；收集主要粮食作物的品种及野生近缘种已是近几个五年计划中国家科技攻关的项目，并已建立了品种资源库；某些珍稀濒危物种的保护，如大熊猫和白暨豚的保护已为我国政府部门及国际上所重视；很多的科研单位，特别是中国科学院，建国以来对我国生物资源的调查也十分重视，科学家们已陆续写就生物的《红色名录》及《红皮书》；《自然保护纲要》已出版，《中国植物志》、《中国动物志》、《孢子植物志》也正相继出版。凡此种种，说明了我国进行生物多样性的研究已有了较好的基础，同时也反映出国家对生物多样性保护及永续利用的问题已开始重视。但是，从总体角度来看，工作还是零散的、不完整的，面临的现状仍十分严峻，大量的课题急待进行研究。生物多样性保护的重要性有待进行全民教育，有效的政策措施有待制定。

对策

(1) 生物多样性的调查及生物编目(Bioinventory)　中国的生物多样性如此之丰富，但至今除高等植物及脊椎动物调查得比较清楚外，大量的生物，尤其是昆虫还未查清，更有大量的标本尚未定名。在调查的基础上还必须利用现代信息处理的方法进行生物编目。

(2) 生物多样性的就地保护及迁地保护　建立自然保护区是生物多样性就地保护国际上目前普遍采用的好方法。但我国不少珍稀、濒危物种必须进行迁地保护，植物园、动物园及野生动物饲养场是迁地保护的优良场所。迁地保护后还必须让这些生物回归大自然。

(3) 基础研究　生物多样性的就地保护及迁地保护，自然生态系统的恢复，把生物多样性作为全球变化的指示进行长期监测，直至物种内遗传变异通过物理特征或生物化学的实验测定等一系列课题有待进行基础研究。

(4) 宣传与教育　生物多样性这个术语本身至今还鲜为人知。保护生物多样性的重要性，与人类生存发展的密切关系还必须进行广泛深入的宣传、教育。

(5) 政府要制定或修订一系列有关法规，履行国际公约　必须制定切实可行的法规，其中包括生物资源国际贸易法规等。

本文原载：生物多样性研究进展. 1995. 钱迎倩，甄仁得主编. 北京：中国科学技术出版社. 15-23

我国生物多样性保护与持续利用中存在的问题及对策

钱迎倩[1]　马克平[1]　王晨[2]

(1 中国科学院植物研究所；2 中国科学院生物学部办公室)

摘　要　生物多样性保护与持续利用在中国已受到政府有关部门的重视，并采取了一定的措施。但在实践中还存在很多问题。本文对此进行了分析，并提出了以下建议：①切实加强自然保护区的建设；②加强对公众的宣传教育，提高全民生物多样性保护的意识；③进一步用好对外开放政策，大力开展国际合作；④积极履行《生物多样性公约》中规定的义务；⑤建立全国生物多样性权威机构，使保护、管理、教育、科学研究和持续利用等协调进行。
关键词　生物多样性；保护；问题；对策

尽管与生物多样性有关的工作在国内已开展了几十年，但生物多样性这个术语及其内涵在 80 年代后期才开始逐步为人们所理解并接受。1990 年初面世的《中国科学院生物多样性研讨会会议录》是国内第一本生物多样性方面的论文集。中国政府积极参与了由联合国环境规划署组织制定的保护世界生物多样性法律文书的起草、修订和谈判会议，这就是后来形成的《生物多样性公约》。1992 年 6 月在巴西召开的联合国环境与发展大会上通过了《公约》，李鹏总理代表中国政府在《公约》上签了字。1992 年 11 月 7 日我国全国人民代表大会常务委员会第 28 次会议批准了中国政府加入该《公约》，成为世界上首先批准公约的六个国家之一。在全球环境基金(GEF)的资助下，由国家环保局牵头，10 个以上部委的代表及中外专家参加，于 1992 年开始《中国生物多样性保护行动计划》的编制工作，1994 年 6 月发布并开始实施。此外，《中国 21 世纪议程》的制订，生物多样性作为其中重要内容之一。以上种种事实都说明对生物多样性的保护及其持续利用已得到我国政府的相当重视。在行动方面，我国自然保护区数量已达 763 个(截止到 1993 年)，总面积 6818.4 万 ha，约占国土面积的 6.8%(国家环保局，1994)。动物保护有：大熊猫保护工程，海南坡鹿拯救工程，保护和发展扬子鳄工程以及麋鹿、野马、高鼻羚羊重返故里；东北虎及朱鹮等的人工繁殖；对珍稀濒危植物迁地保护主要基地—植物园全国已达到 110 个左右；在教育方面，东北林业大学成立了野生动物资源学院，以及利用电视、广播等宣传媒介的科普教育；科研方面，在“八五”期间国家科委、国家自然科学基金委员会、中国科学院及各部委对基础及应用基础开始投资；以上种种也在实践上说明了生物多样性保护在我国正在迅速地发展。

但是中国还是一个发展中国家，全民对生物多样性的保护意识相对较差，对野生生物的滥捕、乱杀、滥挖并未有效地得到制止，生物多样性还在继续遭到严重的破坏；自然保护区由于经费不足、管理不善以及科学研究开展得不够，还未真正起到应有的积极作用；边境贸易中的非法贸易也使《濒危野生动植物种国际贸易公约》规定的物种以及国家一级、二级保护动物不断受到威胁；科研方面由于投资不够、经费短缺，特别是基础研究面临危机，与国际差距甚远。以上种种说明我国面临的问题还是十分严峻的。本文准备从生物多样性保护及其持续利用健康发展的角度，针对当前存在的某些问题谈些认识，与各界共同商榷。

1　切实加强自然保护区的建设

建立自然保护区对生物多样性进行就地保护是生物多样性保护的最佳途径，这不仅成为全世界的共识，并已为实践所证实。各种不同的生态系统以及各种生态系统内的物种多样性及遗传多样性都可以得到有效的保护。我国已建立了近 800 个自然保护区，成效是明显的。生态环境已开始改善，在保护区范围内的森林火灾，乱砍、滥伐，乱捕现象明显下降。以云南省为例，原已干枯的龙潭又重新流出清泉(陈念祖，1993)，环境也已有明显的改善。

美国哈佛大学标本馆鲍夫德博士(David E. Boufford)今年经过林业部批准去河南宝天曼国际级自然保护区工作一段时间，回国后给笔者来信。既说明了我们国家大自然的可爱，也可以反映我国自然保护区存在问题的一个侧面。来信是这样写的：宝天曼自然保护区物种非常丰富与多样化，这里的鸟、蝴蝶及动物的物种和变种数量之多是他多次到中国不少地方所没有见到过的。有猫头鹰、鹰及尾巴极长的鸟，这些鸟整天在歌唱，让你不能不听到鸟的叫声，还有三种猫科动物，其中包括一种豹，还有数量很大的松鼠与兔子……当地政府领导人对外来的人非常开放、热情，非常希望进一步与外界接触和合作，这保护区内只有一个人去外省—哈尔滨东北农业大学学习过，还有一个去过河南农业大学学习。有一个女孩，她中学没有毕业，但对自然有极强的兴趣，在昆虫方面可以说是自学成才。河南省有记录的蝴蝶 225 种，她除了昆虫针之外，一切用自制的器材至今已收集到 190 种蝴蝶……但这地方非常穷，不少当地农民年收入才 300 元(少于 40 美元)，当地小学校长月薪是 50 元。宝天曼年轻工人月薪是 120 元，但他每月的食品及房子就付掉近 100 元……宝天曼自然保护区的维持费是不够的，正在砍伐保护区周围的树，实际上是用保护区内的树来补差……我们到过一个地区是准备皆伐的地区，但这里的优势种是山白树(*Sinowilsonia henryi*)，树的高度达 25m，甚至更高，胸径 50cm，这些树比以前报道的山白树要大得多。我们提了意见，认为这可能是以山白树为优势种森林的幸存者。提意见后，从当地政府领导到保护区主任都立即保证这个地方要保护起来。不幸的是在低海拔多样性最丰富的地区森林基本上已砍光了，而海拔最高的地区，几乎是清一色的栎树(*Quercus* spp.)，其森林、亚林冠层及草本层发育得非常差的地方却处于绝对保护状态……保护区经费的另一个来源是养蘑菇及把山茱萸的果实干燥后做成类似茶叶，这种茶叶有药效，并可外销往香港。由于养蘑菇，要砍掉很多直径大约 20cm 的栎树。伐到的木材只可养三年蘑菇，砍掉这么多树来养蘑菇，自然更新可绝对没有这么快。在保护区内散居着看守保护区的护林人。几年前他们已得到通知，保护区不再给他们付工资了，他们只能靠山吃山，这就意味着他们将要砍更多的树来养蘑菇，采中草药或对森林起破坏作用的其他事……宝天曼保护区的赤字每年工资 10 万人民币，其他费用也是 10 万人民币，这些赤字意味着工作人员不可能增加工资，他们的生活会更困难……

上面信中的内容不一定全面、真实、但很有参考价值。值得我们去认真思考。借此，对我国自然保护区管理谈几点看法。

(1) 目前有部分自然保护区不仅有大学毕业生，并已获有得硕士学位的工作人员，但可以自我开展大量研究工作的保护区为数不多。自然保护区应成为生物多样性长期监测的理想场所，但除少数保护区外，目前普遍存在着家底不清或者还不了解哪一些应该重点保护的问题。正像鲍夫德博士信中提到的当地政府官员及保护区领导知道他们这儿还有这么好的一批山白树的幸存者，他们就会立即同意绝对保护。摸清家底是最基本的基础工作。云南省林业厅已有很好的经验，他们省由林业部门牵头，邀请科研、教学单位，先后对西双版纳、哀牢山、高黎贡山三个国家级自然保护区作了综合科学考察；利用昆明动物研究所的科技力量对滇金丝猴、野象资源作了调查并作了生态研究。这就掌握了保护区现状，为加强资源的保护管理提供了依据。这例子说明要依靠科技，要依靠科技人员，依靠专家的重要性。

提高劳动者素质也确实是加强自然保护区建设的一个关键方面。当然素质包括科学文化素质和管理素质。科学文化素质的提高除了派人去大学深造外，更主要的是采取培训班的形式，这种短期培训的方式是行之有效的，也是能做到的。中国科学院植物研究所已经办过几次这种类型的培训班。有的省林业厅如云南省也很重视培训工作，主动委托高教及科研单位，甚至与世界自然基金会合作开办了多次培训班。

(2) 根据国家经济情况，有计划、有步骤地发展自然保护区，发展一批、巩固一批，从个别点上取得经验，在面上推广，使已建立的自然保护区切实发挥作用后再建新的。按蒋明康等(1992)报道，世界发达国家自然保护区面积约占国土面积 10%以上。最近几年来发展的确很快，按国家环境保护局自然保护司编的“自然保护区有效管理论文集”(1992)中提到 1979 年我国自然保护区 59 处，占国土面积的 0.17%，到 1989 年底时全国有 600 多个自然保护区，而目前已发展到 900 多个(季维智，1995，个人通讯)，发展的速度相当快。但总体来看，“论文集”“前言”中提到的存在着资金严重不足、机构人员不落实、政策法规不完善等问题和困难。看来鲍夫德博士信上描述的情况还是有相当的可靠性。

更值得总结的是被称为我国保护拯救珍稀濒危野生动物的龙头工程“保护大熊猫及其栖息地工程”,按 1994 年 8 月 6 日中国环境报李瑞农撰文说这是一个非常宏伟的计划，但目前面临重重困难，甚至有骑虎难下之势。最大难题是保护区及栖息地内已建和新建保护核心区至少有 5000 ~ 7000 人需要迁出安置，这些工作将耗去工程总投资 2/3，林业企业存在转产，农户搬迁安置都加大了资金缺口。安置等问题得不到妥善处理，带来的可能是第二轮甚至第三轮采伐，目前对大熊猫这样的大项目来说，国内筹资是极其有限，因大熊猫出国展出被禁，在国外捐款也受到严重影响。这典型事例的教训教育了我们，要让自然保护区真正能发挥作用，除周密设计科学管理外，第一重要的还是要根据国力情况而定。

(3) 办好一些事业离不开资金，自然保护区的建设也是一样，上面的例子已透彻地说明了国家有关管理部门已尽了很大努力，但国家财力有限，还不可能短期内有很大好转，这些都是明显的。自然保护区如按鲍夫德博士信上说的方法来维持不该算是正常运转途径。除国家或地方政府在可能条件下增加一定投资外，开展生态旅游可能是一条能在一定程度上自我运转的途径。

众所周知，自然保护区应该分为三个部分，第一部分即所谓的核心区，区域应是原生性的相对好的部分，这部分应严格保护，可以作为科学研究的基地或生物多样性长期监测的所在地；第二部分是缓冲区，这个区域处于核心区的周围。设立缓冲区的目的是使科学工作者，或一般游人能够看到这个自然保护区生态系统的类型，物种多样性的丰富度等等。同时由于核心区是绝对保护，一般旅游者不得进入，缓冲区就起到缓冲的作用，这个区的生物资源也是不允许开发的。最外面的一圈即经营区，在这个区域则可搞一定规模的动物饲养，药材或其他经济作物，经济林木的栽培，所得收益用以补偿自然保护区收入的不足。而生态旅游只能局限子缓冲区，必须设置一定的路线，并且类似现在一些著名的旅游点一样，设立导游。既向群众讲解本自然保护区的各种生态系统，当地主要的特有物种等科学知识，还结合着宣传生物多样性保护的重要意义。这种形式的生态旅游在发达国家(如澳大利亚)及发展中国家(如印度)都已经普遍地采用了。生态旅游不仅增加了自然保护区的经济效益，同时也是教育群众、宣传群众的一个重要的场所。

(4) 要非常重视自然保护区周围土地合理经营，以及在保护区的经营区中辟一定的试验区进行当地生物多样性持续利用的试验，并不断把成果向周围群众推广，使当地居民能够在他们的土地上得到必需的生活资料，并逐渐富裕起来，这样才可能减少或消除对自然保护区的索取。

2 加强对公众的宣传教育，提高全民生物多样性保护意识

要能够做好对我国生物多样性的保护，并使它能为子孙万代持续地得到利用。根据我国国情来加强对公众宣传教育，提高全民对生物多样性保护意识是另一个极为重要的方面。

本文上面已提到了最近几年来，我国政府已开始注意了这方面的工作，除东北林业大学成立了野生动物资源学院外，还不时在报刊杂志上报道一些保护野生生物的消息，并利用在中国已相当普及,深入到千家万户的极为有效的宣传媒介——电视来进行教育。电视《动物世界》系列片不仅仅是给予人们很多动物知识，同时也增加了热爱动物以及热爱动物栖息地的意识。在此基础上中央电视台又组织了《人与自然》栏目，介绍国外保护动物的人和事以及我国在维护生态平衡、保护大自然的成绩，收到了很好的效果。北京通县一个普通农民刘宝元一家把在潮白河边捡到的一只受伤的秃鹫抱回家，精心用肉喂养，半年时间伤愈后送到松山林场让它回归自然。这例子生动的说明宣传教育的有效性，使一般农民也已有了保护野生动物的意识。此外，陕西电视台摄制的电视纪录片《最后栖息地的朱鹮》，在日本举行的1993年度世界野生动物映象节上获得了“环境保

护奖”等三项大奖。

我们不得不承认，发达国家人民大众保护自然，保护生物多样性的意识远比我们强，这与这些国家对群众长期的宣传、教育，针对不同年龄的人进行不同内容的教育是密切相关的。以美国为例，国家级、国际及各个州的政府和非政府组织从事保护工作的机构和个人有近2000个。不包括学报级的刊物，以上这些机构的各种各样的出版物就有1650种左右。全国最大、最主要的一个组织是国家野生生物联盟(National Wildlife Federation)，其任务是教育、鼓励和帮助各种组织、机构甚至个人来保护野生生物和其他自然资源以及环境。在全国51个州中，波多黎各和维尔京群岛有530万会员、支持者和分支机构。这联盟本身有四种出版物：对其会员有双月刊的保护杂志，“国家野生生物”(National Wildlife)和“国际野生生物”(International Wildlife)；对6~12岁的儿童有月刊，一种介绍自然的杂志，称为“Ranger Rick”;为学龄前儿童则有一套自然系列丛书，称为“你们的大后院”(Your Big Backyard)。联盟下设多个部门，开展多种多样的教育、服务及其他活动。每年出版一本“保护指南”(Conservation Directory)，去年已是第38版，说明这联盟至少已有38年的历史。

与此相比，从历史和投资情况来看，我国目前仅仅是起步，我们还非常缺乏对不同年龄层次的公众进行系统教育的工作。计划生育已成为我国的国策，对生物多样性的保护也应该成为我国的国策。应该看到我们这么庞大的人口数字，生物多样性得不到保护或者说继续以现在的速度锐减，直接威胁到国家与人民的生存与发展。因此两者可看作为一个事物的两个方面。根据我国国情，中央到地方各级政府要像抓计划生育一样来抓生物多样性保护。

中国科学院过去几年在这方面做过不少工作，前面提到的1990年出版了《中国科学院生物多样性研讨会会议录》。以后，为迎接1992年联合国环境与发展大会，宣传我国在生物多样性保护方面的成就，中国科学院生物多样性委员会出版了《Biodiversity in China》小册子带到大会上散发。以后陆续又出版了《中国的生物多样性—现状及其保护对策》以及翻译了《全球生物多样性策略》及《生物多样性译丛》(一)等书籍。最近又出版了《生物多样性研究的原理与方法》并准备在近期内出版系列的生物多样性研究专著。此外，中国科学院生物多样性委员会又主办了《生物多样性》(Chinese Biodiversity)中英文期刊，在全国主办多次讲习班，研讨会。以上这些都为生物多样性在中国的教育、普及起到了良好的作用。

3 进一步用好对外开放的政策，大力开展国际合作

我国是一个发展中国家，对生物多样性的保护及持续利用历史还很短，经验不足。此外，更重要的是对生物多样性保护从总体上说是一项耗资的事业，我们还严重地感到资金短缺。因此，进一步用好对外开放的政策，大力开展国际合作，不管是从汲取国外先进的技术和经验，通过合作研究培养提高我们人员的水平，以至到能够获得国外的资助、贷款等方面是大有益处的。

近10年左右时间，我们通过国际合作受益的已不乏例子，如1985年，我国接受了

英国贝福特公爵送来的原来在我国较广泛分布，但已在我国绝迹的麋鹿，让它们重返故里——北京南苑。1986年，又从英国伦敦动物学会返回一批麋鹿，生活在江苏大丰大片海滩沼泽人工林的保护区内。目前它们都已繁衍生息，数量成倍增长。此外，受世界关注的珍稀濒危动物，国宝大熊猫在保护及科学研究方面通过与世界野生动物基金会等单位的合作，我国也得益不少。在植物方面，中国科学院植物研究所在都江堰市支持下的华西亚高山植物园与英国爱丁堡植物园合作获得英国达尔文基金在世界野生资源保护项目方面的资助，把英国从本世纪以来收集的中国杜鹃花种苗近400种返回对杜鹃花生长极为理想的栖息地。华西亚高山植物园得到的这笔基金包括种苗及有关资料及器材的运输费用以及为植物园去爱丁堡植物园培养两名工作人员。杜鹃花是全世界有名的花卉，不少国家都成立有杜鹃花协会。华西亚高山植物园本来已收集了以生长在横断山山区为主的一百多种杜鹃花，爱丁堡植物园这批杜鹃花的回归故里，将使这个植物园不仅可成为国内杜鹃花的科研基地，生态旅游的主要项目内容，并在国际上起到很大的影响。

全世界生物多样性灭绝的速度已达到惊人的程度。据德国自然保护联盟警告说，全世界每天灭绝的动、植物物种数竟达160 种之多。如这一趋势得不到控制，在今后25 年中将有150 万个物种告别人类。为此发达国家为保护世界野生生物，拯救野生生物设立有各种各样的基金，例如美国的麦克阿瑟基金与福特基金，国内已有一些单位得到过资助。

此外，利用深化改革，更加开放的大好形势，在生物多样性的保护方面我们还可以学习工业与外商合资的途径来吸引国外资金，建立适应中国条件的各种各样的基金会。在发展中国家不乏范例，在印度马德拉斯近郊离一豪华旅馆 Fisher-man's Cove 不远处有一个鳄鱼基因库，占地面积数公顷。目前世界上尚存21种鳄类，在这个库里饲养并保存有世界各国15个以上的种或变种。包括生长在海水及淡水中的物种。每个种或变种占有一个大小不等的池塘，每池数量由约10条至近百条不等，并都树有牌子对此物种加以说明。这个鳄鱼库的经费除印度政府资助一小部分外，主要来源于国外资助，其中最主要的是美国的 Smithsonian 研究院及世界野生生物基金(WWF)。此外，在粮食作物方面很多国际上的遗传资源中心就分布在发展中国家。如众所周知的国际水稻所在菲律宾，在墨西哥有世界小麦、玉米遗传资源中心等，这些机构在这些国家的设立对该国受益匪浅。此外，云南省林业厅在中国科学院昆明动物研究所等单位参与下与国外合作在西双版纳建立起我国第一个热带雨林地区的空中索桥，对于该地区作为一个定位站进行生物多样性长期监测研究起到很好的作用。

目前不少高等院校用香港影业界巨头邵逸夫的捐赠款建立起不少的以邵逸夫名字命名的图书馆和体育馆等。我们认为在自然保护区建设方面，国外如有愿意资助的，我们应该抱欢迎的态度，愿意树碑立传的，也应该像“邵逸夫馆”一样予以允许。本文上面提到的 Boufford 博士给著者信的后面提到他愿意到美国去找有关人士出资建立一个基金，由这基金来支付宝天曼国家级自然保护区每年维持费的缺额。他信中提到，有了这笔基金就可以不再去砍树。并且他甚至愿意个人出钱来培养保护区内一位工作非常出色的搞昆虫的女孩子，让她能继续上学，并让她到中国科学院动物研究所的标本馆学习标本的制作与管理。

总之，国际合作的途径是非常广阔的，只要我们能充分用好开放的政策，我国生物多样性保护资金来源的一部分是可以通过国际合作的途径来解决的。

4 积极执行联合国《生物多样性公约》中规定的条款

我国已成为联合国《生物多样性公约》的缔约国。这就意味着我们要认真地履行《公约》规定的义务。《中国生物多样性保护行动计划》已经在 1994 年 6 月正式发布。根据我国国情要执行好《公约》，特别应该强调立法及执法问题，这问题在我国的《行动计划》中就已提到。前言中提到需要注意解决的关键问题的第一条就是“生物多样性保护的法规和法制需要得到健全、完善并加以执行”。第二章和第四章中也都提到“政策法规”和“立法和政策保证”。

《行动计划》第二章中列出了近 10 年来，我国已颁布的与生物多样性保护有关的法规，如《森林法》、《野生动物保护法》及《土地法》等有关法规 13 种以及有关条例 11 种，并指出对生物多样性保护和自然资源保护的立法缺乏系统和完善性以及对已有的法规常常没有得到执行或没有严格执行。执法部门对已发现的犯罪者处理不严。第四章中对“立法与政策”有更详细的叙述。

《行动计划》已经得到国务院环境保护委员会的批准，它将成为中国生物多样性保护的纲领性文件。《行动计划》的出台是我国执行《公约》的具体行动，但似乎以下几点还是应该值得注意的。

(1) 首先是《行动计划》执行的时间缺乏一个比较具体的规定。其次，在某些方面，例如第四章中的“科学研究”已明确规定了建议的执行单位。但在立法方面，例如综合性的生物多样性保护法、珍稀与濒危物种保护法和自然保护区管理条例也应该建议由政府哪个部门来制定，何时制定，但遗憾的是没有一个明确的规定。根据全世界和中国生物多样性灭绝的速度来看，这些法规或条例的制定是刻不容缓的。

(2) 中国正处于经济建设大高潮的时期，也是由过去的计划经济向社会主义市场经济过渡的时期，对综合性的生物多样性保护法不能不考虑到这个时代背景。例如中国的红树林本来已经所存无几，目前广西境内红树林分布的面积在全国占第一位，但由于经济发展的需要，广西将成为大西南出海口的大通道。钦州湾一带是广西红树林分布较大的区域，由于要建港口，已有相当数量的红树林遭到砍伐，余下的是否能健康地保留下来，还是个问题。《行动计划》第四章中规定“谁开发谁保护，谁破坏谁恢复，谁利用谁补偿”的政策是否能够执行，这就应该通过立法、执法来解决。

(3)《行动计划》第四章中提到“现有政策都是针对现实中发现的紧急的具体问题制定的，因此，政策的整体性、系统性和相互协调性不够”。过去制定的法规同样存在这个问题，甚至不同法律法规之间衔接不好，相互矛盾，造成执法困难。1994 年 8 月 11 日中国环境报登载着一个明显的例子，内蒙古大兴安岭林业管理局反映《森林法》、《草原法》和《土地法》之间衔接不顺，在有些地区既发林权证，又发土地证，致使林区部分地区毁林开荒十分严重，仅大杨树地区十几年内已开荒 10 多万 ha，部分地区林缘已后退 50~100km。立法的不顺造成人为的林农争地，林牧争地，毁林开荒，造成生物多样性的丧失，这是值得注意的。

(4) 执法不严问题应该引起足够的重视

乱捕乱杀滥伐野生生物以及非法边境贸易问题，虽然已引起政府的重视。但由于执法不严，在我国，尤其在沿海或边境口岸一带还是相当触目惊心的。根据李义明等(个人通讯，1964)介绍，广西从1954~1993年野生动物贸易涉及的鱼类、鸟类、两栖类和爬行类动物91种，其中35种是国家重点保护的野生动物，包括兽类21种、鸟类8种、爬行类6种。中、越野生动物边境贸易涉及39个物种，其中包括穿山甲、巨蜥等国家重点保护动物。本文作者也去过东兴口岸，目睹此类现象，虽然并不合法，却无人制止。

报刊上也经常可以看到我国目前存在的权大还是法大，以及由于地方保护主义使有一系列法律法规执行不下去的现象，这些都是现实生活中应该引起足够重视的问题。

5　建立全国生物多样性权威机构，使保护、管理、教育、科学研究、持续利用等全面协调地进行

中国成为《生物多样性公约》缔约国以后，国家成立了中国环境与发展国际合作委员会，这是一个旨在加强环境与发展国际合作和向国务院提出具体建议的高层次机构。在该委员会下面有一个工作组专门负责生物多样性的有关事宜。在1993年5月该委员会第二次会议上有一报告“中国生物多样性保护亟待采取的行动”,其中主要建议之一是：建立一个全国生物多样性权威机构。建议政府建立一个高层次的国家生物多样性计划与协调机构来协调各有关部门和全国生物多样性综合保护计划和各个方面的主管权威机构。

另一方面，国际著名的植物生物学家，中国科学院生物多样性咨询委员会成员Peter H. Raven博士在给生物多样性委员会的信中也提到他准备向宋健国务委员和其他官员建议建立一个国家级的生物多样性委员会。该委员会旨在协调有关生物多样性各个领域的工作，其中包括对生物多样性的持续利用。他认为正像其他很多国家一样，在生物多样性的知识、管理、持续发展、经济开发、教育和保护之间要建立起紧密的联系，使之成为一体，这样才能使中国在这个领域将会有良好的发展。我们认为上述两方面的意见是非常中肯并有非常明确的针对性。以我国现有管理体制为例，近800个自然保护区的大的主管部门至少有林业部、国家环保局、农业部、国家海洋局以及有关地方政府。各部门为保护我国的自然资源和自然环境的确做了大量贡献。但多头管理带来的问题是缺乏全国统一的管理规范，影响部门间科技协作、信息交流、人才培养等等。甚至个别部门间有相护对立、争夺地盘的现象。1994年9月2日国务院第24次常务会议已原则上通过了《中华人民共和国自然保护区条例(草案)》解决了，在一定程度上解决了自然保护区管理问题。近年来，生物多样性保护与其持续利用问题在国内已为各部门所重视。但由于所涉及的部门较多，没有一个权威机构的统一规划、协调，同样会出现各种不协调的问题。正像Peter H. Raven博士所强调的，有一个国家级的生物多样性委员会，他把生物多样性的科学研究、管理、持续发展、经济开发、教育和保护看作一个整体，打破部门的界线，全国一盘棋，统一部署才能充分调动各方面的积极性。

生物多样性的保护及其持续利用的问题在国际上大约是在 80 年代前后开始得到重视。在国内起步较晚，大量的科学研究的基础工作有待加强。例如近年来国内很重视保护濒危物种，重视在自然保护区的就地保护，还重视在植物园中的物种迁地保护。但是正像《行动计划》第 22 页中指出的存在着保护的种群不能满足多基因采集法技术的要求；一个物种迁地保护的数量应以种群生存能力分析为理论依据，这样才能保证有足够的遗传多样性。又如对生物多样性的持续利用就必须开展利用价值的研究。草原的适度放牧，森林的适度采伐，适度到何种强度才能维持生物多样性，才能使生态系统不退化，这些都是重要的基础研究问题。“科学研究”在《行动计划》第 52~55 页，有很详细的叙述。在“主动多样性研究的现状与发展趋势”(马克平等，1994)一文中也作了说明。 目前的问题是各个方面，包括，课题，资金等的落实。在第九个五年计划对生物多样性的投资应大大多于第八个五年计划，使“八五”期间刚刚开始的科研工作能得到继续，一大批跨世纪的学科带头人能够成长起来。

总之，在全国权威机构的统一领导及部署下，投入足够的资金，协调好生物多样性的保护及持续利用的各个方面，把力量充分调动起来，我们就可以有足够的信心，到本世纪末，在理论与实践方面会得到较大的发展。

参考文献

陈念祖. 1993. 云南自然保护区的现状及今后对策. 见吴征镒(主编). 云南生物多样性学术讨论会论文集. 昆明： 云南科技出版社，232~235

国家环境保护局自然保护司(编辑). 1992. 自然保护区有效管理论文集. 北京：中国环境科学出版社. 1~226

国家环境保护局. 1994. 1993 年全国环境状况公报. 北京：中国环境科学出版社

蒋明康，张更生，薛达元，吴晓敏. 1992. 我国自然保护区建设现状与发展设想. 见国家环境保护局自然保护司(编辑). 自然保护区有效管理论文集. 北京：中国环境科学出版社. 1~6

马克平，钱迎倩，王晨. 1994. 生物多样性研究的现状与发展趋势. 见钱迎倩，马克平(主编). 生物多样性研究的原理与方法. 北京：中国科学技术出版社，1~12

生物多样性工作组. 1993. 中国生物多样性保护亟待采取的行动. 生物多样性，1(1): 26~29

“中国生物多样性保护行动计划”总报告编写组. 1994. 中国生物多样性保护行动计划. 北京：中国环境科学出版社，1~121

本文原载：自然资源学报. 1995. 10(4): 322-331

生物技术与生物安全

钱迎倩　马克平

(中国科学院植物研究所)

摘　要　本文通过大量的实例介绍了国内外生物技术，特别是基因工程的进展。继而从伦理道德、对人类的健康和环境的影响等方面阐述了生物技术对人类生存安全可能带来的威胁。最后就生物安全的立法等问题提出了建设性意见。

关键词　生物技术；遗传修饰的生物体；生物安全；生物多样性

在 1992 年召开的联合国环境与发展大会上由 153 个国家首脑签字的《生物多样性公约》(以下简称《公约》)的第 2 条，“用语”对生物技术作了下述的定义：“生物技术”是指使用生物系统、生物体或其衍生物的任何技术应用，以制作或改变产品或过程以供待定用途。此外，在《公约》第 8 条，就地保护的(g)款有如下的叙述：制定或采取办法酌情管制、管理或控制由生物技术改变的活生物体在使用和释放时可能产生的危险，即可能对环境产生不利影响，从而影响到生物多样性的保护和持久使用。也要考虑到人类健康和危险。这一段叙述密切关系到当前国际社会普遍关注的所谓“生物安全”(biosafety)问题。本文仅就当前生物技术的巨大进展，由生物技术改变的活生物体的使用、释放可能带来的各种危机以及为生物安全应做好立法工作等方面作一介绍。

1　当代生物技术的巨大进展

国内习惯把生物技术划分为基因工程、细胞工程、酶工程、发酵工程以及生化工程等几个领域，本文要涉及的主要是基因工程。经过生物技术操作后得到的产物，国际上较普遍的采用了两个名词，一个是经遗传修饰的生物体(GMO)。另一个是基因工程的生物体(GEO)。GMO 的含义似乎更广泛一点，一切经过遗传操作其基因得到修饰的生物都包括在内，但目前似乎更多的还是指经基因工程操作后的生物体。

1.1　国际上生物技术的进展

20 世纪 80 年代后期以来，基因工程的研究得到了突飞猛进的发展，不少成果已不局限在实验室水平，某些产物已达到商业化的程度。按 J. Rissler 和 M. Mellon(1993)的报道[9]。在美国正在开发的转基因植物已涉及禾谷类、纤维类、牧草、森林植物、水果、油料、花卉、蔬菜以及其他类似烟草等的作物。 其中重要的包括主要的粮食作物水稻、玉米；纤维作物棉花；油料作物大豆、花生、油菜以及例如黄瓜、土豆、南瓜等经常食用的蔬菜。到去年底，数量已远不止这些。至少还包括小麦、香蕉、菠萝、甜椒等等。例如美国 DNA 植物技术公司(DNAP)正和英国 Zeneca 集团合作研究生产成熟慢，且口味好的香蕉。

发达国家由澳大利亚、比利时、加拿大、丹麦、法国、德国、荷兰、挪威、日本、西班牙、瑞士、英国和美国等 14 个成员国组成的经济合作和发展组织(OECD)已批准在 1986~1992 年间对具 6 种性状的转基因作物作小规模田间试验。性状及所占比例如表 1。表 1 中的质量性状包括油和蛋白质成分以及水果成熟期等。例如，正在试验中的一种转基因马铃薯，其淀粉含量要比普通马铃薯高 60%。用这种马铃薯炸制马铃薯条或片时吸油更少，食用这种条或片将更有利于健康。已达到商业化水平的值得提出的有两种作物，即西红柿和南瓜。转基因西红柿是位于美国加州的一个生物技术公司 Calgene 用了 8 年时间花费 2 000 万美元得到的。这种转基因西红柿被称为保味西红柿(flavor-save tomato)。 西红柿成熟、老化是由于多聚半乳糖醛酸酶的作用，这是乙烯合成途径中的一种关键酶，Calgene 的科学家把这种酶的基因分离出来，然后再反方向地插入到染色体组中。促使西红柿在成熟过程中只产生少量的这种酶，以延长其成熟的时间。继而延长其在货架上的时间。西红柿可在大田藤蔓上成熟变红的时间更长，口味更好，运到超级市场时还是很硬，色泽保持鲜艳。转基因西红柿已于 1994 年 5 月间为美国食品和药物管理局(FDA)批准。在 10 月份推向市场。英国生物种子公司 Zeneca 集团也准备用转基因西红柿制成酱，目前正在就出售这种新型西红柿酱同超级市场进行最后谈判，有可能今年在英国超级市场的货架上出现。转基因南瓜是在美国 Upjohn 化学公司中的 Asgrow 种子公司研制成功的。这种转基因南瓜被称为抗病长弯颈南瓜新品种 ZW-20。 这个品种抗夏南瓜黄斑纹病毒和西瓜斑纹病毒，可提高单位面积产量，也可使农民少施农药。1990 年以来已在美国 10 个州 46 个农庄做过田间试验。目前已经美国农业部(USDA)批准，预期不久的将来，可与消费者见面。

表 1 具 6 种性状转基因作物及所占比例[9]

Table 1 The transgenic crops with six traits and their percentage

性状	百分比
抗除草剂	57
抗病毒	13
抗虫	10
质量性状	8
雄性不育	5
抗其他病害	4

转基因动物方面也有很大的进展。例如有报道阿根廷首都布宜诺斯艾利斯展出一种转基因的矮种牛。两岁半的牛才高 67cm，重 45kg，是世界上最矮小的牛。最值得提出

的是转基因猪：插入人生长激素的转基因猪，其体形和出肉量都比正常猪高出一倍。据报道，澳大利亚已有转基因猪肉出售。研究转基因猪的目的远不止提高出肉量而是用于人类的医疗目的。一是利用转基因猪的血红蛋白。至今，人类需要的血红蛋白都从人血红细胞中取得。但是用人的血红蛋白存在着供应不足、价格昂贵的问题：更为严重的是所输的人血中往往带有病毒，甚至艾滋病病毒。科学家已可能把人血红蛋白基因插入猪的血红细胞。转基因血红细胞中有15%人血红蛋白。而猪血红蛋白与氧结合的能力与人很相似，人们希望今后能利用转基因猪的血红蛋白作为人的血红蛋白补充物：更诱人的是转基因猪的器官作为今后人器官移植的来源，由于猪的 DNA 与人十分接近，猪的器官尺寸与人又基本相称，其肾、心脏、肝、肺甚至血管都有可能作为人器官移植的供体。目前正在进行免疫基因工程改造实验，使猪的免疫类型能与人一致，不至于造成器官移植后的排异反应。这种实验在美国和英国已获得初步成功。

转基因酵母的研制也早已成功，并已用于制作面包、酿酒和奶酪。在美国、瑞士和意大利市场上都可买到用转基因技术制造的奶酪。

此外，基因工程技术用于药物生产，治疗人体各种疾病也已取得很大的进展。如德国科学家在吸血蝙蝠唾液中分离到一种防止血液凝固的基因，用此制造能化掉心肌梗塞和脑血栓血块的药。人体本身能产生约 8 万种蛋白质以维护身体的各种机能。目前用基因工程的手段已能生产其中的 30 种，如防止血液凝固的制剂、生长激素和胰岛素等。还有 300 种蛋白正在开发中，有的正在做临床试验。又如美国加州希尤公司生产的名为 Betaseron 的β干扰素在美国已为 FDA 批准使用。拜耳公司生产的抗体已在 36 名类风湿关节炎患者身上试用。利用转基因动物或转基因植物作为“生物反应器”来生产药物已有很多的尝试，并已取得不少成功的例子。Calgene 公司将人的基因转移到牛的体内，由转基因公牛受精的牛已产下 5 头健壮的带有人的 HLF 基因的小牛犊。

1.2 国内生物技术的进展

我国的生物技术研究至少在“六・五”期间已经开始。以广义的生物技术领域论，经过 10 多年的研究已硕果累累,其中特别值得提出来的是花药培养方面不仅研究的深度和广度在国际领先，而且已应用于作物的育种，并已大面积地在生产上应用。花药培养与染色体工程结合，至少已得到不少好的种质。在原生质体培养方面，玉米、大豆等重要作物的植株再生在国际上都是首先成功[2]。在快速繁殖方画，为解决马铃薯块茎退化，从无病毒的茎尖培养开始得到无毒植株。用快繁技术，一株苗一年能繁殖到 100 万株。在国内 20 个以上省市已大面积推广，在这一点上，水平达国际领先是无疑的。

正像今年初德国《明镜》周刊的一期上登载的，国际上已打破了“基因殖民地化”。与其他发展中国家相比，我国在基因工程方面的工作已走在前面，并已引起发达国家的重视。在转基因植物方面，先后已得到了抗除草剂、抗病毒、抗虫、耐盐的作物[1]。例如抗除草剂的大豆已繁殖到第五代。抗烟草花叶病毒烟草特别是抗烟草花叶病毒和黄瓜花叶病毒的双抗转基因烟草在河南省 1992 年已达到 8000 hm^2 的大田面积，是当时国际上转基因植物释放面积最大的作物[10]。按 Krattiger (1994)报道[7]，世界上只有中国和美国两个国家已批准为了商业化目的，大规模释放转基因植物。中国的转基因抗病毒烟草的释放已接近 100 万 hm^2(注:原著是这样报道的,但面积肯定被大大地扩大了)，或占整个烟草种植面积的 5%。虽然报道面积大大地被扩大了，但抗病毒烟草确实是在生产上大面积获得应用，并是抗病性状表现良好的第一个例子。把抗虫基因导入欧洲黑杨，得到的转基因欧洲黑杨可使舞毒蛾和扬天蝼死亡率高达 100%。从豇豆子叶中分离到豇豆胰蛋白酶抑制剂基因，这种基因插入烟草后，转基因烟草具有良好的抗棉铃虫和烟青虫的特性。此外，在进行田间试验的还有转基因甜椒、马铃薯以及西红柿。在亚洲发展中国家中，除泰国在 1993 年开始有西红柿的田间试验外，中国是唯一进展得最早(1989 年)最快的国家[7]。

在转基因动物方面，我国在国际上率先开展了转基因鱼的育种研究，用人生长激素基因导入鲤鱼受精卵，转基因鱼生长速度比对照快。用乙肝表面抗原基因导入兔受精卵，通过借腹怀胎获得转基因兔。此外，我国还在国际上首次报道获得含酶性核糖核酸基因的转基因兔。

在基因工程药物方面我国的进展也是十分喜人的。人α型基因工程干扰素已进入产业化阶段。乙型肝炎表面抗原基因工程疫苗，1991 年已完成中试，已形成年产 100 万人份的生产能力。基因工程白细胞介素-2 与新型白细胞介素-2 的工艺及得率都达到国际先进水平，并已经卫生部新药评审委员会批准进行临床试验。此外，在人生长激素、猪生长激素、α-干扰素、表皮生长因子等基因工程药物在实验室研究已完成，有的已进入中试。

总之，在全世界范围内生物技术发展迅速。到 1993 年的 20 年左右时间，基因工程公司仅在美国就发展到 1000 多家，各种基因工程产品不断推出，美国的年总销售额达 40 多亿美元。特别是 90 年代以来，生物技术发展的势头预计更会加速，以转基因作物为例，目前美国正在进行田间试验的已有 1400 次。仅 1994 年一年进行田间试验的次数就超过 1987 年到 1998 年的总和。田间试验如果顺利的话，转基因马铃薯、玉米、棉花、大豆、小麦 、甜椒、香蕉、菠萝、西瓜、甘蔗等都将陆续上市，估计在今后 5 年内美国市场上至少会推出 50 种像转基因西红柿这类转基因农产品。到本世纪末，通过转基因技术生产的销售额可能达到 1000 亿美元。生物技术正以其巨大的活力改变着传统的生产方式和产业结构，迅速向经济和社会各领域渗透和扩散，人类面临的粮食、能源、环境、人口、资源等五大危机以及人类的各种疾病有可能得到相当程度的缓解。

2 生物技术可能带来的危险

有关生物技术的进展及其在食品、新的药物、种质改良等方面可能给人类带来巨大的效益，这在前面已经作了比较详细的介绍。但这项高新技术像原子能一样，在造福于人类的同时也会给人类带来严重的危险。生物技术改变的活生物体或者说是经过遗传修饰的生物体的使用和释放可能会对环境产生不利的影响，从而影响到生物多样性的保护和持续利用；也可能对人类健康带来威胁；此外在伦理道德方面已引起一场争论。实际上，在 70 年代初期，(即这项技术发展的早期)，已分离到特种基因并将其导入其他生物体，这在科学界已开始有争论。有人对与重组 DNA 研究有关的潜在生物学和生态学危险以及释放到环境后可能带来的潜在危险表示担心。随着生物技术迅速的发展，伦理道德问题也随之提出来。

2.1 有关伦理道德的争论

随着基因工程的进展，人胰岛素基因在大肠杆菌中、在酵母中都可表达；人生长激素和人干扰素基因插入到细菌中早已成功，这些都已形成产品，先后在 80 年代就已投放市场；人生长激素基因在鱼、猪、牛等高等动物中也都能成功地表达；人促红细胞生成素(EPO)、组织血纤维蛋白溶酶原激活剂(TPA)等都已接近生产阶段或已投入市场。此外，用人的血清蛋白基因转入马铃薯，这种转基因马铃薯能生产人血清蛋白。以上的例子说明人的不同基因已经插入到不同的微生物、真菌、动物、植物中。据不完全统计，目前至少有 24 种人体基因已引入到各种生物体内。而实际上，目前技术的进展几乎可做到将包括人体在内的各种生物来源的基因转移到任何其他一种生物体中去。由于人体的基因在不同生物体中任意的转移，有人提出了下列一系列问题：人类是否有权任意把任何数量的人体基因转移到其他生物体去？消费者是否愿意食用带有人体基因的食品？用人类基因做转基因工作有没有一个法定限度？人体基因任意的转移会不会出现“弗兰肯斯坦”那样的科学怪人，而使人类遭受灾难[①]。

发达国家中生物技术迅速发展的一个重要推动因素是一些公司以其先进的技术追逐高额利润。以转基因作物为例，据统计，1987年至1993年夏，549 家向美国农业部申请进行转基因作物田间实验的申请者中占最大比例的是化学公司，占到申请者中的46%。其中包括孟山都(Monsanto)，杜邦(Dupont)、巴西—盖奇(Ciba-Geigy)等著名的大公司,而孟山都又在化学公司中占到52%的比例。其次是大学，占申请百分比中的17%。实际上，在美国不少大学中科学家的经费来源于一些大的化学公司。上面表2中说明了美国在转基因作物方面抗除草剂的占了整个的57%，这就意味着美国的农业更趋向于而不是离开化学农业。抗除草剂的作物将使农民更多地依赖化学除草剂，这样实际上增加了生产除草剂的化学公司的收入。孟山都公司与杜邦公司都是生产化学除草剂的大公司。因此国际上也有人提出，为了获取利润，把整个生物界的遗传结构加以混合或加工是否合法?

美图马哈里希国际大学(Maharishi International University)的一位被国际公认的 DNA 研究者，由康奈尔大学培养出来的分子生物学家,1994 年时 46 岁的 John Fagan 博士，1994 年 11 月 17 日在美国首都华盛顿举行一个新闻发布会，他站在伦理道德的立场上基于遗传工程的巨大危险而反对遗传工程。他本人放弃掉从美国国立卫生研究院(NIH)得到的 60 万美元以上的科研资助，同时他还放弃掉了从其他来源争取到的 125 万美元的资助。他认为他的研究成果会对有害的基因工程应用作出贡献；他呼吁人们对种系(germ-line)的遗传操作暂停 50 年。所谓种系的操作，即是把新的基因引入到精子、卵或非常早期胚胎的 DNA 中去。导入到这些生殖细胞中引起的改变将一代代地传下去。这种被他称为

① 所谓“弗兰肯斯坦”是恐怖小说《弗兰肯斯坦》一书中的主人公，一个用尸体制造怪人的医生。

事故及其不可预料的副作用将无限期地存在下去。此外，1993 年国际上成立了由 50 人组成的国际生物伦理学委员会。该委员会是由从 32 个国家来的 4 位诺贝尔医学奖获得者，律师、遗传学家、生物学家、哲学家、社会学家、人口学家、政治学家等人员组成。他们将对有关遗传学研究的各个方面予以注意,目标是在 1995 年之前起草一个有关保护人类基因组的国际公约。遗传学的迅速发展，在给人类疾病的治疗、预防等带来喜人的前景的同时也带来许多问题。该委员会的任务是把遗传学进展可能带来的问题让公众知道并传播有关的知识。

2.2 对人类健康的影响

遗传工程实验室的操作及其释放到环境，尤其是转基因生物作为食品对人体的健康可能带来的影响，一直是人们关心的问题。科学界以及新闻媒介都不断有各种各样的报道。其中难免存在一定程度的讹传。但即使是潜在的危险，也应引起人们足够的重视。1994 年 5 月“文摘报”曾转载过“中国中医药报”的报道。美国的转基因西红柿释放后使厨师在制作菜肴过程中过敏难受，他们称这种食品为“弗兰肯食品”。更令厨师不安的是有些顾客吃了他们餐馆的这类食物后病倒了。因而他们表示不再卖基因食物，并在他的菜单上、餐馆门上表明了拒绝基因食物的立场。有关转基因猪作为食品在 1994 年 8 月德国“星期日图片报”也有报道，提到插入人生长激素的转基因猪比正常猪大一倍，出肉量也多一倍，但它却百病缠身。患有胃肿瘤、肺炎、心力衰竭和关节畸形。吃下这类食品后对人体会有什么影响，目前人们全然不知，不知道风险有多大。在同一篇报道中德国自然保护和环境联合会的基因专家卡策克指出,美医 Monsanto 农产品公司生产的转基因豆子能抗杀虫剂，但这种豆子产生一种类似雌性激素的物质，男人吃了这些豆子后，乳房会反常地增大。

在转基因作物实验过程中往往需要用标记基因，大多数的实验用抗生素抗性基因来作为标记基因，以此来选择转基因植物。因此引起人们担心的是这些抗药性是否可能转嫁给吃了这类转基因食品的人体。对人体是否有害，尤其这些效应可能不是在短时间内为人们所观察到的。

2.3 对环境可能带来的危险

转基因生物能达到商业化并为人类所利用,这就意味着他们已在环境中大量地释放。某一种生物一旦这样大量地释放，将来要在环境中消灭他们将不仅要花费大量的资金，甚至可以说将是不可能做到的，因此更应引起人们的重视。转基因作物释放后对环境的危险归纳有下列几点。

2.3.1 转基因作物本身将可能变为杂草

不少作物已被人类驯化到不依赖于人的耕作就生存不了的程度，如玉米、小麦、香蕉就是明显例子。Colwell[6]认为这类作物不管怎么通过生物技术来改良，在生态学范畴内不会变成具杂草化特征的植物。而另一些栽培植物，例如某些狗尾草或高粱属的种在某种意义上来说本身就是杂草，而在另外的场合下它们又是作物。这类作物当插入一个例如抗病或抗虫的基因时，可能会把本来在某些地区很安全的作物，但由于改变了其平衡而趋向于杂草化。再如有另一些作物如甘蔗、水稻、马铃薯、番薯、油菜、向日葵和燕麦等，它们本来就有很近的杂草性的近缘种。其中某些作物，它们的不少性状与它们的杂草化的祖先是共同的，因此某些遗传上的改变就可能使作物的本身形成杂草。例如高度抗盐的转基因水稻品种本身就可能浸入到港湾中去大量繁殖起来。

2.3.2　转基因作物使野生近缘种变为杂草

自然界的不少作物的野生近缘种由于自然的制约，目前并不以杂草的形式存在于自然界。但是一旦某一个转基因作物通过花粉的传播，把转基因作物的花粉引入野生近缘种，使这种近缘种能大量繁殖而变成杂草。在美国，野葫芦之类的南瓜的近缘植物是很普遍的，可是这些野葫芦目前并未形成杂草。南瓜在美国东南部是土生土长的，这地区野葫芦也是很普遍的。正在进行实验，观察南瓜是否有可能与野葫芦自然杂交或通过渐渗(introgression)而起用。如果大自然的相互制约和平衡一旦遭到破坏，野葫芦就很可能变成一种杂草。病毒的存在很可能是对野葫芦发展的一种制约，但美国有人担心，目前培育成的抗病毒南瓜的基因流入野葫芦，就会使原来对黄瓜斑纹病毒和西瓜斑纹病毒敏感的绿皮密生西葫芦(一种美洲野生南瓜)变成抗这两种病毒，从而大量繁殖起来而成为严重的杂草。又如威尔斯大学的群体遗传学家对三个栽培甜菜亚种、野生种和杂草种的DNA分析结果说明，在遗传图谱上杂草种介于栽培种和野生种之间。因此，有可能由于栽培种与野生种之间花粉的传播而产生杂草。他们预言抗除草剂的转基因甜菜大面积种植后，由于花粉作为基因流的传播者，而使抗除草剂基因转到野生种内而造成抗除草剂的杂草。杂草这个术语是包括在农田、草坪、路边和未管理的生态系统中的不受欢迎的植物。据报道，美国在1991年为控制杂草就花掉40亿美元。

2.3.3　转基因生物可能作为有害的外来种

转基因生物是人类创造的、自然界本来不存在的一种生物。对一个生态系统来说，转基因生物的本身就是一种外来种。外来种的引入，历来非常普遍，有起好的作用，也确实不乏大量的例子说明外来种的引入对整个生态系统的破坏并造成了不可估量的经济损失。在前面的文章中[3,4]，已例举了我国引入大米草及美国引入千层叶属树种，给当地的生物多样性的保护及经济建设造成巨大的影响的例子。这里还可举出两个有说服力的例子。昆明的滇池是全国有名的景点，也是昆明人民用水的主要来源。但由于近年来水源的污染、水质的富营养化，造成水葫芦(凤眼莲)已覆盖了整个滇池的80%，成为一大公害。又据报道，越南在1986年从国外引进一种作为食品的金蜗牛，农民饲养后可增加收入。这种蜗牛繁殖极快，逸出的蜗牛已严重威胁到湄公河三角洲水稻种植区。已有1400hm^{2}水稻田遭到破坏，其蜗牛密度已高达每平方米5~10只。越南政府于1994年10月起发起运动来消灭这种蜗牛，但收效不大。这例子再一次说明，一种生物一旦引入某个生态系统后，要消灭它是非常困难又耗巨资的。

英国的一些科学家指出，要是听任转基因生物不加控制地进入自然环境中，最后会有一天人工物种可能会取代天然物种。自然界的生物多样性，尤其是目前的一些珍稀濒危物种将在地球上消失。

2.3.4 形成新的病毒的可能性

1993 年上半年美国 Arizona 大学的科学家报道，整合到植物基因组内的病毒外壳蛋白基因可以和其他病毒发生重组，因此，存在着产生超病毒(super virus)的潜在危险。类似的报道来自Michigan大学植物学系的实验，他们把花椰菜花叶病毒外壳蛋白的基因插入豇豆，从而得到抗病毒的豇豆。他们进一步又把缺失外壳蛋白的病毒接种到转基因豇豆上。实验结果发现125株豇豆中有4株又染上了花叶病。因此，他们推测，为使作物获得对病毒的抗性而被转入植物中的病毒可能与再接种病毒的遗传物质结合，从而形成新的病毒。或者是转基因植物如含有病毒颗粒的话，植物可能会促进新的病毒的产生。这种新病原体如再侵入到其他重要经济作物的话，造成的危害或控制它的费用会更大。

2.3.5 对生态系统中其他种的危害

上面已提到“生物反应器”的概念，即人们已经可以利用转基因植物有目的地生产某些药物。转基因植物如能表达潜在的有毒物质(如苏云金杆菌毒素)的话，这些植物将对其他的生物产生危害。例如，生产药物的转基因植物在玉米田里被鸟吃了，造成鸟的中毒而死亡。

2.3.6 更为严重的化学药剂的污染

上文提到了发达国家的一些如 Monsanto 等大的化学公司投入大量的资金,做抗除草剂的作物，目的是为了使该公司的除草剂的销路更大，创造更多的利润。从另一个角度来看，令人担心的是大量抗除草剂作物的培育成功将促使农民更多地去使用除草剂或其他化学药剂。从而造成更为严重的环境污染。

3 生物技术、生物多样性、生物安全与持续农业

当前我国与世界都面临着一系列的危机。对中国来说，可能最根本的还是人口与粮食两大问题。因此，1994 年全国人大着重提出省长要抓“米袋子”、市长要抓“菜篮子”的问题。人大会议一结束，立即又召开了主要中央领导人都出席的计划生育会议。世界人口的爆炸问题也是十分尖锐的，Beversdorf(1994)报道[5]，国际人口统计学家预计到 2060 年全球人口可能会达到 100 亿~160 亿。地球能不能养得了这么多的人口？持续农业看来是目前国际的潮流，也是解决不断膨胀的人口之温饱问题的唯一出路。持续农业的发展受到制约或影响的因素是很多的，至少有土地面积的限制、不可再生资源如燃料、磷、钾等的限制以及全球气候变化的影响等等。专家们预计由于全球气候变化会对下一世纪农业生产的稳定性产生冲击。当然农业问题还会受到政治的影响，在世界范围内如关贸总协定(GATT)的影响，我国国内也直接受到农业政策的影响。

从生物学的角度来看，持续农业与生物多样性、生物技术与生物安全的关系也是十

分密切的。从“科学是第一生产力”的角度看，后三者可能又是持续农业的决定性制约因素。本文第一节列举大量事实说明生物技术对今后世界粮食问题或食品问题的解决能起到的关键作用及美好前景。但目前生物技术也确实存在不少的问题，例如基因工程中抗虫转基因作物，绝大多数是集中地采用了苏云金杆菌毒素(Bttoxin)基因。在许多作物上广泛地使用如此狭窄的抗性来源，必然会使作物变得非常脆弱。害虫或病原体一旦克服如此单一的抗性来源，将会造成作物大面积的减产。这问题可能要从三个方面来找到解决的答案，亦即生物多样性。遗传学的进展不断推出新的生物技术以及生物安全。就以抗虫基因来说，人们必须从自然界的生物多样性中广泛地去寻找新的抗虫基因。但当今世界的生物多样性以惊人的速度在消失，人们谈不上了解某些物种的性状，甚至来不及知道其名字，这些物种已在地球上消失，保护生物多样性的重要性及紧迫性就显而易见了。其次是要求遗传学不断有新的进展，使生物技术随着有不断的发展，使这项技术在保持环境资源，也就是在保护环境中的水、空气、营养物以及绿色空间、生物多样性等方面作出新的贡献。保持好的生态环境对持续农业的发展是非常关键的。此外，还应通过研究及立法来解决本文第2节中提到的由于生物技术带来的一系列生物安全问题。

4　生物安全的立法问题

《公约》第 8 条，就地保护(k)款中规定：制定或维持必要立法和/或其他规范性规章，以保护受威胁物种和群体；第 19 条，生物技术的处理及其惠益的分配第 3 款提出：缔约国应考虑是否需要一项议定书。规定适当程序，特别包括事先知情协议，适用于可能对生物多样性的保护和持久使用产生不利影响的由生物技术改变的任何生物体的安全转让、处理和使用，并考虑该议定书的形式。

4.1　国际上有关生物安全立法的情况

有关遗传工程、重组 DNA 分子等从 70 年代后期以来，如美国、德国等发达国家就发布指南：80 年代后期以来基因工程的发展迅速到某些成果已达到商业化的程度，促使有关经遗传修饰的生物体(GMO)的释放及生物安全在大多数发达国家都已有法规。OECD 在 1986 年和 1992 年连续地发布有关重组 DNA 安全问题和生物技术安全问题的文件。如法国为对 GMO 的评价和立法成立了两个专门委员会。第一个是遗传工程委员会，成立于 1975 年，任务集中于实验室的重组 DNA 的研究。到 1986 年时又成立了生物分子工程委员会(Biomolecular Engineering Committee)，它的任务是评价 GMO 的大田试验、释放以及它们的商业化。发达国家大致上也就像法国这种情况，90 年代以来各种具体的法规与条例在一些发达国家不断地发布。在发展中国家中，1990 年印度的科学和技术部也颁发了重组 DNA 安全指南。此外，联合国的有关组织，如粮农组织(FAO)、环境规划署(UNEP)等也十分关注生物安全的问题。世界银行也出版了“生物安全：生物技术在农业和环境中安全使用”专著。

《生物多样性公约》缔约国的第一次大会1994年10月在巴哈马召开。这次大会的主要议程之一就是讨论怎样制定有关生物安全在国际上生效的议定书。会议上不同的国家从各自利益出发采取各自的立场，尽管有很大的争论，但最后还是一致同意成立由10个国家参加的“生物安全专家小组”来商讨“生物技术安全的国际技术指南”。这次专家小组会议于1995年5月在埃及举行。

题为“经遗传修饰的植物和微生物大田试验生物安全的结果”的国际会议已开过三次，第一次是1990年11月在美国召开，第二次是1992年5月在德国举行，第三次是1994年11月，还是在美国召开。此外，小型的讨论会及国际会议也十分频繁[8]。凡此种种说明有关生物安全的课题，国际上已做了大量的研究。研究的内容涉及转基因作物释放的危险评估，转基因植物释放后对生物多样性和种群水平的影响，对土壤动物区系的影响，转基因植物与生物地球化学循环以及生物安全数据库建立等等。这些研究的成果也就是建立生物安全程序和法规的基础。

4.2 我国生物安全的有关情况

我国有关生物安全的第一个法规是针对基因工程药物的，即 1990 年制定的“基因工程产品的质量控制标准”。按标准规定，基因工程药物的质量必须满足安全性的要求。对基因工程产品普遍适用的是 1993 年 12 月 24 日由国家科委第 17 号令发布的《基因工程安全管理办法》(下称《办法》)。《办法》规定了我国基因工程工作的管理体系，按潜在危险程度，将基因工程工作分为四个安全等级，并规定了分级审批权限。从可操作性考虑，农业部还将于今年内发布对一切与农业有关的转基因工作适用的、更为具体的法规。这些法规的出台将是十分重要的。当然转基因生物释放的潜在危险可能要有相当长的一段时间才能为人们所认识。一是要针对生物安全进行系统的科学研究，另一点是需要时间的考验。国内在有关生物安全方面的科研工作进行得还很不够。在第九个五年计划中应引起足够的重视，作出应有的安排。转基因生物释放后的效应还需要有长期的监测。我们应做到既能充分发挥生物技术积极的作用，又能充分了解 GMO 可能带来的危险，再进行研究，克服这些危险，真正造福于人类。

参考文献

[1] 张树庸，基因工程研究的二十年，科技导报，1994，(6)：39~42.

[2] 袁萍，钱迎倩. 植物原生质体的研究在中国科学院的发展. 中国科学院院刊. 1990，(4)：336~339.

[3] 钱迎倩. 生物多样性与生物技术. 中国科学院院刊，1994，(2)：40~44.

[4] 钱迎倩. 生物技术与生物多样性的保护和持续利用. 见：钱迎倩，马克平主编. 生物多样性研究的原理与方法. 北京：中国科学技术出版社，1994，217~ 224.

[5] Beversdorf W. D. The importance of biotechnology to sustainable agriculture. In Krattiger, A. F. et al (eds.) Biosafety for sustainable agriculture. ISAAA/SEI. 1994. 29~32.

[6] Colwell R. K. Potential ecological and evolutionary problems of introducing transgenic crops into the environmern. In：Krattiger A. F. et al(eds.). Biosafety for sustainable agriculture. ISAAA/SEI. 1994, 33~460.

[7] Krattiger A. F. The field testing and commercialization of genetically modified plants：A review of worldwide data (1986 to 1993/94.) In: Krattiger A. F. et. al(eds.). Biosafety for sustainable agriculture. ISAAA/SEI. 1994, 247~266.

[8] Leicegter T. B. et al. Ecological implications of transgenic plant release. Molecular Ecology, 1994, 3(1).

[9] Rissler J. and M. Mellon. Perits amidst the promise-ecological risks of transgenic crops in global market. Union of Concerned Scientists. 1993.

[10] Zhou Ruhong, Fang Rongxiang et al. Large-scale field periormance of transgenic tobacco plants resistant toboth tobacco mosaic virus and cucumber mosaic virus(in press). 1995.

本文原载：广西植物. 1996. 16(4): 295-299

生物多样性研究的几个国际热点

钱迎倩　马克平

(中国科学院植物研究所)

摘　要　DIVERSITAS 是国际上生物多样性研究的主要项目，到 1995 年时，这项目发展到一个新的阶段，研究内容由过去 4 个方面发展到目前代表 DIVERSITAS 核心的 5 个主要项目组成部分及 4 个交叉项目组成部分。系统学作为生物学的一门分支学科，它的重要任务之一就是要研究生命的多样性。为了世界性地提高对系统学研究重要性的认识，加强系统学基础设施和人才资源，国际上制定了 2000 年系统学议程项目。此外，本文还介绍了 IUBS 组织的物种 2000 项目。

关键词　生物多样性；DIVERSITAS；2000 年系统学议程；物种 2000

生物多样性及其栖息地是人类赖以生存的基础。近几十年来，由于世界人口无节制的膨胀及人类的经济活动，导致人类自己把赖以生存的基础肆无忌惮地加以破坏。据估计，生物多样性正以自然灭绝 1000 倍的速度在消亡着。80 年代以来，生物多样性的保护与持续利用的研究兴起。90 年代特别是 1992 年联合国环境与发展大会上《生物多样性公约》被批准后，与生物多样性密切相关的重要问题及基础学科蓬勃展开。本文介绍几个重要的研究热点。

1　DIVERSITAS[1]

1991 年在荷兰阿姆斯特丹国际生物科学联盟(IUBS)第 24 次全体会议上提出一个重要的研究项目，即“生物多样性的生态系统功能”。到 1992 年这项目扩大并发展，与环境问题科学委员会(SCOPE)和联合国教科文(UNESCO)合作，把项目名称改为 DIVERSITAS。从此，这项目的研究发展为从遗传到生态系统水平的地球上所有有生命的生物。研究包括了生物多样性的起源、组成、功能、保持和保育(conservation)。开展 DIVERSITAS 项目的目的是确定关键的科学问题，并通过国际合作以促进这些科学问题的合作研究。1994 年时国际微生物科学联盟(IUMS)参加到该项目中。到 1995 年时 DIVERSITAS 进入到一个新的阶段，又增加了两个新成员，即国际科学联盟委员会(ICSU)和国际地圈、生物圈项目/全球变化和陆生生态系统(IGBP/GCTE)。由 1992 年时研究主题，即① 生物多样性的生态系统功能；② 生物多样性的起源和保持；③ 生物多样性的编目和监测；④ 家养种的野生近缘种的生物多样性等 4 个[2]扩大为 9 个组成方面，并分为主要项目及交叉项目两个部分(图 1)。

第一部分即主要项目组成方面，也是生物多样性研究的关键领域，即：

(1) 起源、保持和丧失

(2) 生态系统功能

(3) 编目、分类和相互关系

(4) 评估与监测

(5) 保育、恢复与持续利用

第二部分称为交叉(cross-cutting)项目组成方面。下列 4 个方面是由于它们的重要性和迫切需要而列出的：

(6) 生物多样性的人类影响范围(human dimensions)

(7) 土壤和沉积物的生物多样性

(8) 海洋生物多样性

(9) 微生物生物多样性

生物多样性对人类的影响范围之所以是交叉的项目组成方面因为是涉及多学科的，强调人类社会从很多的方面去了解、影响和利用生物多样性。后面 3 个，即土壤和沉积物、海洋和微生物生物多样性所以是交叉的是由于必须以多学科的途径去研究极为重要的栖息地；提出对系统学迫切的需要；考虑到生物多样性的保育、起源和保持方面的主要问题。DIVERSITAS 也非常重视对有关的生物类群的系统学的研究，因为这是开展上面 9 个项目组成部分研究的基础。

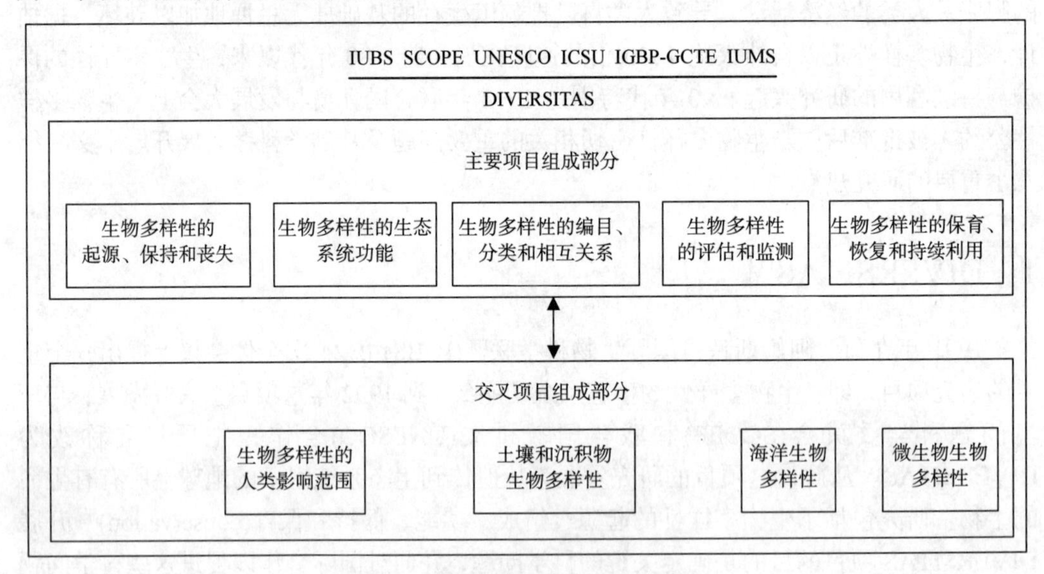

图 1　生物多样性科学的国际项目

下面对上述 9 个项目组成方面作进一步的介绍。

1.1 生物多样性的起源、保持和丧失

这个项目的研究目的是去了解人类如何能保持一个丰富的生命世界。

一个物种对它所在环境发生变化后的反应是根据物种的遗传、生理、物种间相互关系和生活史等参数而异。本项目研究是在物种内的遗传和种群水平上进行以及研究物种形成和物种灭亡的过程和机制。去探索、了解种群和遗传过程导致生物的多样化和丧失，然后利用这些知识来发展保持生物多样性的有效的策略。

1.2 生物多样性的生态系统功能

这个项目是研究生物多样性是如何为人类服务作贡献的。

本项目主要说明两个基本问题：(a)物种多样性如何影响到系统的稳定性和恢复以及全球变化如何影响这些关系?(b)生物多样性(基因、物种和景观)在例如生产、分解和营养循环等生态系统过程起到什么样的作用，包括反馈以及全球变化(气候变化、土地利用变化和生物入侵)全过程。通过评估和直接进行实验，这个项目将定量化地来说明生态系统是如何为下列各方面服务或起作用的，例如水质和水量、土壤肥力、空气质量的维持以及了解气候变化对以上这些方面的影响。生物多样性功能性的知识可以被综合起来，并有助于设计一个实验性研究方案去与其他相关的国际性项目接轨。

1.3 生物多样性的编目、分类和相互关系

这个项目企图说明生物多样性的现状以及如何信息化后为所有的国家可利用。

本项目将发展一种为国际上一致能接受的，对全世界物种的系统学的编目方法和优先领域；把从全球获得的信息分析和综合成能反映生命史的具有推断性的分类；并去促进把这种知识组织成为世界各国都能得到的一种有效的、有推断性的数据库。同时还要反映出在系统学方面基础设施和人才资源的匮乏，以致世界性地妨碍了对生物多样性特性的描述与了解。

这个项目与下面要谈到的第2个问题“2000年系统学议程”(Systematics Agenda 2000)是一致的。下文将稍加展开加以叙述。

1.4 生物多样性的评估和监测

这个项目是研究生物多样性的分布以及它们又如何在迅速地变化着。

要对全球生物多样性调查和保持以及缓和它们丧失的影响作出政策和管理的决定必须基于对自然、物种数和物种相互作用改变的程度以及从遗传到生态系统水平上所造成后果的了解。这个项目将发展出有效的和标准化的监测方法和优先领域。这样做可促进快速积累有关生物多样性现状和未来状态的资料，从而得到地球不同位置之间作比较和监测活动的一个更可靠、更具预测性的框架。第4个项目应与第3个项目有紧密的联系。

1.5　生物多样性保育、恢复和持续利用

这个项目是研究生物多样性如何保育、恢复和持续利用。

生物多样性的保育和它组成部分的持续利用对保持全球的稳定性起决定性的作用。这个项目在保育策略上对生物多样性和其内涵的动态增加了科学的了解。特别强调对栽培植物和驯养动物野生近缘种遗传多样性的保育。与项目 1 一致的地方是，从生态系统和种群动态研究得到的知识将有助于保育政策制定和生物资源的持续管理。另一个重点研究领域则是强调对退化生态系统的恢复，了解在恢复过程中种群统计和遗传过程，以及在恢复过程中提高生物多样性保育所需要的不同方案。

1.6　生物多样性的人类影响范围

这个项目要了解生物多样性与人类健康、幸福间的关系。

人类的很多活动，例如通过生产食物、纤维、盖房子和娱乐等来改善生活质量，可是其后果往往对生物多样性是不利的。由于人类在改变生态系统过程中起到关键的作用，所以重要的是在保育和持续管理生物多样性时，要将人类活动综合到这些生态系统功能中去考虑。本项目从下列各个方面获得并综合到的科学信息，可起到一种催化剂的作用：在了解社会文化特征和其相应对生物多样性的科学理解之间的关系；在评估人口压力和生物多样性动态之间的关系，这个关系是指对人类健康、幸福的影响；分析传统的与现代的人类社会，即过去如何管理和现在正在管理生物多样性的这些高度复杂的管理方法；以及保证在生物多样性的保育和持续管理生物资源上，对人民参与的策略进行评估等方面。

1.7　土壤和沉积物生物多样性

这个项目是研究人类了解得极少的土壤和沉积物中的生物在生态系统中起什么作用。

土壤和淡水水体及海洋系统的沉积物中的生物在重要的生态系统过程(包括营养循环的控制和它们对温度、气体的影响等)中起关键的作用。虽然对土壤和沉积物的生态系统功能和主要分类类群已有了一个粗放的和一般性的了解，但非常需要在物种水平上有协调的信息，进一步去发现物种组成和群落结构如何影响生态系统功能的细节。了解保持肥沃的土壤和沉积物的生物学基础将是一个重点研究问题。要为评估和监测土壤和沉积物建立数据库及标准的方法，以及开展定量化的实验去了解土壤和沉积物中的生物在生态系统功能中的作用。本项目要与 DIVERSITAS 其他项目的活动协调进行。

1.8　海洋生物多样性

这个项目是研究海洋和海岸带的生物多样性是如何被人类活动所影响。

人们常常把海洋生态系统看作是全球共有的，对这个生态系统的保育将要求对控制海洋生物多样性的模式和过程要有更广泛的了解。海洋是如此之大，相对难以接近，其

混合、扩散和输导的过程等等向研究海洋生物多样性的学者提出了大量科学和保育方面的挑战。人类对海洋生物多样性丧失的模式和过程也了解得非常之少。因此，这项目将研究海洋生物多样性如何受到渔业作业、富营养化作用、物理栖息地的变动、外来种入侵以及其他人类活动影响。这个项目将在大量有兴趣的研究单位间建立网络共同来对生物多样性的起源、保持和生态系统功能等方面的问题加以阐明。

1.9 微生物生物多样性

这个项目是研究微生物的活动如何影响到生态系统的功能。

微生物具有巨大的遗传多样性，在食物链和生物地球化学循环中它们作为基本组分起到极为重要和不可替代的作用。虽然这么重要，可是全球微生物已描述过的少于5%。本项目要建立方法和技术以加速微生物多样性的发现和描述，要开发一个数据库机制去收集和交换微生物生物学特性的信息。

2 2000年系统学议程

系统学是一门发现、组织和解释生物多样性的学科。为解释全世界物种的特性，用系统学的知识通过建立一种概念性的框架，把生物学的一切领域都统一成一体。一切企图进行生物多样性保育和持续利用的人们，必须要掌握系统生物学的知识。系统学是研究生物多样性的基础[4]。

2000 年系统学议程最早是在 1994 年由美国植物分类家学会、系统生物学学会和Willi Hennig 学会等 3 个国际系统学会与系统学收集馆协会合作，由美国国家科学基金资助而制定出版的。到 1995 年时又成为 IUBS 的一个国际性项目，称为 The Systematics Agenda 2000 International Programme(SA2000／I)。其主要目的是企图把国际级和国家级的系统学学会以及例如博物馆和植物园等研究和培训机构组织成一个大的网络。对所有国家，尤其是物种丰富的国家强调系统学基础设施和人才资源的建设。在下列 3 个方面进行国际合作研究：① 全世界物种的编目；② 对生命的多样性进行系统发育的研究，最后归入分类系统内；③ 把获得的系统学的各种各样信息组织成一种有效的、计算机化可查询的形式， 以满足科学和社会各方面的需要。

3 物种2000

这是在 1994 年 9 月 IUBS 第 25 次全体大会上决定的一个新的项目。这项目与 ICSU 的科学和技术数据委员会(CODATA)和 IUMS 合作进行。

物种 2000(Species 2000)项目的目的是把地球上所有已知的动、植物、真菌和微生物列举出来，作为研究全球生物多样性的基础性的数据库，其总的目的是要创造一个全球重要物种数据库，增加现有的数据库间的合作，在合适的时候还可建立新的系统。

建成后可起到下列的作用：成为各国为履行《生物多样性公约》所必需的信息的重

要组成部分；为制备生物多样性的概况和编目提供支持；可作为有关生物资源和它们利用及保育进行全球性交流的共同媒介。

参考文献

[1] Anonymous，International Union of Biological Sciences, Statutes, Organization and Activities, 1995, 5~6
[2] 马克平，钱迎倩，王晨．生物多样性研究的现状与发展趋势, 钱迎倩, 马克平主编: 《生物多样性研究的原理与方法》, 北京: 中国科学技术出版社, 1994, 1~12
[3] The Committes of Systematics Agenda 2000. Systematics Agenda 2000；Charting the Biosphere, 1994. 1~34
[4] 马克平, 王恩明. 生物多样性监测研讨班在美国举办．生物多样性，1994，2(3): l84~186

本文原载：植物学通报. 1998. 15(5): 1-15

生物多样性的几个问题*

钱迎倩

(中国科学院植物研究所)

摘　要　本文从生物多样性的现状、存在的问题及应采取的措施等三个方面比较全面地叙述了我国生物多样性的情况。“生物安全”是《生物多样性公约》签订后每次缔约国会议都要讨论的中心议题之一。为之，本文也用一定的篇幅作了较详细的介绍。现状部分从物种多样性、遗传多样性及生态系统多样性等三个方面作了介绍，又从自然因素以及由于人类活动造成栖息地的丧失、环境恶化、偷猎走私、过度捕捞和水产养殖、高新技术发展、全球气候变化以及外来种引入等两个方面对生物多样性造成严重威胁作了相当详细的分析。在应采取措施部分，不仅是根据我国目前所存在的问题，还介绍了国外值得借鉴的、可取的经验，以及正在开展的有关项目。使读者对我国生物多样性的情况及应采取的对策有了比较明确的了解。此外，对什么是“生物安全”，为什么要提出生物安全的问题以及应重视的问题也给出了答案。

关键词　生物多样性；《生物多样性公约》；经遗传修饰生物体；生物安全；DIVERSITAS

地球经过近 40 亿年的进化，生存着几千万种包括动物、植物、微生物在内的生物。家养的、野生的各种形形色色的物种构成了物种多样性。在物种之下还有很多品种、变种等，例如猪我国就有上海荡脚猪、河南项城猪、明光小耳猪以及保山猪等；栽培作物中小麦、水稻等都有数不清的品种，品种的不同是由于存在着不同的基因，或者说遗传类型是不一样的。这就构成了遗传多样性。在一定的空间内的动物、植物、微生物和它们赖以生存的居住环境(或者说包括光、空气、土壤、水、矿物质在内的栖息地)之间，通过能量流动与物质循环的相互作用、相互影响而构成一个综合体。这综合体又称生态系统。陆地上、水体中，不同的气候带、不同的地理环境存在着多种多样的生态系统，这就形成了生态系统多样性。因此，生物多样性就是指包括动物、植物、微生物的所有生物和它们所拥有的基因，以及由它们及其环境构成的生态系统，形成的千姿百态的生物世界。生物多样性又包括三个层次，即物种多样性、遗传多样性以及生态系统多样性。

1　我国生物多样性现状

我国幅员辽阔，气候类型多样、地貌类型丰富，西南部有青藏高原的隆起，为各种

* 本文为国家科委“八五重大基础项目”，中国生物多样性保护生态基础研究部分内容。

生物种类的产生和繁衍提供了各种各样的环境，从而使我国成为世界上生物多样性特别丰富的国家之一。下面首先对我国的物种多样性、遗传多样性和生态系统多样性的现状作一介绍。

1.1　中国的物种多样性

1.1.1　物种多样性概况

经过分类学家和系统学家近 200 年的努力，人类对地球上生物的知识还是微乎其微。仅以最基本的命名来说，科学家最多仅对地球的 1/10 的生物进行了命名，估计已描述的物种大概不足 150 万种。一类大型的生物还是近 10~20 年内才发现的，例如世界上目前还存活有 80 种鲸类，其中 11 种是本世纪才发现的，最近的一种是 1991 年才定的名；在过去的 10 年中植物学家在中美和南墨西哥所发现新的植物定了三个新的科；在 1993 年时，还为动物界定了一个新的门，称为 Loricifera(王晨，1996)。地球上还有数以万亿计的物种有待去探索，去认识(表 1)。

表 1　中国及世界已描述以及世界有待发现的物种数的估计

类别	中国已描述的物种数(万)	世界已描述的物种数(万)	有待发现物种的估量(万)
病毒	0.04*	0.5	约 50
细菌	0.05*	0.4	40~300
真菌	0.80*	7.0	100~150
原生动物	-	4.0	10~20
藻类	1.14**	4.0	20~1000
植物	3.00*	25.0	30~50
脊椎动物	0.60**	4.5	5
线虫	0.065**	1.5	50~100
软体动物	0.35**	7.0	20
甲壳动物	0.38**	4.0	15
螨、蜘蛛	0.70**	7.5	75~100
昆虫	3.40**	95.0	800~10 000

* 数字引自陈灵芝(1993)。
** 数字引自“中国生物多样性国情研究报告”(《中国生物多样性国情研究报告》编写组，1998)。
无星号的数字引自 Systematic Agenda 2000(Anonymous, 1994).

我国由于有上述的优越条件，南北跨越寒、温、热三带，高原、山地占 80%，孕育了丰富的物种，在世界物种多样性中占很高的比例数(表 1)。此外，我国具有独特的自然历史条件，特别是自第三纪各期以来，大部分地区未受冰川覆盖影响，使我国的动、植物区系保留了许多在北半球其他地区早已灭绝的古老孑遗和残遗的种类和一些在发生上属于原始的或孤立的特有属或特有种。例如单种属银杉(*Cathaya argyrophylla*)只生长在中国中南部，白暨豚(*Lipotes vexillifer*)只生长在洞庭湖及长江下游，大熊猫(*Ailuropoda melanoleuca*)仅局限于中国川、甘、陕相邻的山区。中国的特有属和特有种是非常丰富的(见表 2)。根据世界野生生物基金会(WWF)资料，中国特有的维管束植物、哺乳动物和鸟类的物种数，仅次于印度尼西亚，居亚洲第二位。高等植物特有种在一万种以上，约占中国高等植物总种数的 57%以上(陈灵芝，1994)。

1.1.2 物种多样性现状

虽然我国物种多样性在国际上占有特殊的地位，但是由于人口压力、栖息地破坏等人类活动的影响，当然也包括一部分或少部分的自然灭绝，大量物种已处于不同等级的濒危状态，有的甚至已经灭绝。1996 年在北京召开的世界自然保护联盟(IUCN)物种生存委员会中国成员会议上,我国研究各生物类群的专家分别分析了各类群生物物种的现状。这资料是比较正确地反映到 1996 年的现状。

张树义报道我国灵长类有 3 科、5 属、19 种，其中白眉长臂猿(*Hylobates hoolock*)、白颊长臂猿(*H.leucogenya*)、白掌长臂猿(*H. lar*)和倭蜂猴是处于极危状态，数量少于 150 只；豚尾猴(*Macaca nemestrina*)、黑长臂猿(*H. concolor*)、戴帽叶猴和黔金丝猴等 4 种处于濒危状态，数量在 150~1000 只；其中黔金丝猴为我国特有；蜂猴(*Loris tardigradus*)、熊猴(*Macaca assamensis*)、黑叶猴(*Presbytis francoisi*)、滇金丝猴等 4 种为易危种，数量在 1000~10 000 只，其中滇金丝猴为我国特有；短尾猴(*Macaca arctoides*)、藏酋猴(*M. thibetana*)、灰叶猴(*Presbytis pileatus*)和川金丝猴等 4 种处于低危状态，数量为 10 000~20 000 只,其中川金丝猴为我国特有。此外,台湾猴(*Macaca cyclopis*)和长尾叶猴(*Presbytis entelus*)数量不详。仅有猕猴(*Macaca mulatta*)这一种数量丰富。在亚种水平上，一些我国特有的亚种如海南黑长臂猿只留下 50~200 只，云南白长臂猿 10 只，白头叶猴(*Presbytis leucocephalus*)不足 1000 只，数量都极稀少，亟待保护。

胡锦矗报道我国大熊猫在秦岭数量约 200 只，岷山和崃山各约 350 只，相岭不到 50 只，凉山不到 100 只，整个数量约 1000 只。栖息地面积约 10 000 km^2,但已分割成 20 多块小区。这些斑块彼此隔离，其中有 14 块数量已减少到 40 只以下，加速大熊猫局部绝灭和总体衰败进度，处于极危状态。目前国内外迁地保护共约 130 只，从种群的性比和年龄结构看，属增长型种群。20 年后可望增加到 200 只。

高行宜等报道了我国马科动物，目前野生的有 3 种，西藏野驴(*Asinus kiang*)有 2 亚种，即 *A. k. kiang* 和 *A. k. holderei*。估计总数在 200 万头以上；蒙古野驴(*A. hemionus*)总数在 3000 头左右，属易危种；野生野马(*Equus prezewalskii*)在我国境内要有也是所存无几了。但按报道，在新疆建立的野马繁殖培育中心已有十几年的历史，目前已建立了野马的基本种群，正在进行野化训练。

马建章报道我国现存熊类有棕熊(*Ursus arctos*)、黑熊(*Selenarctos thibetanus*)和马来熊(*Helarctos malayanus*)3 种，过去在我国季风区蒙新高原区和青藏高原区这三大自然地理区域中均有分布。但 94 年报道的全国资料调查结果说明熊类分布区已不能连续成片，中间出现大片分布的空白地带，熊类数量大幅度减少，三种熊栖息地面积只有 259 万 km^2，数量仅有 48 386 头左右，其中主要是黑熊，为 46 528 头，而棕熊仅有 1483 头，临近濒危，而马来熊已仅有 375 头，已处于濒危状态。马逸清等认为近 10 年来活熊取胆汁，城乡各地养熊取胆事业一时曾出现高潮，给野生种群带来很大的压力。

表 2　中国动、植物部分类群特有种(或属)

类群名称	已知种(或属)	特有种(或属)	特有种(或属)占总数(或属)百分数
哺乳类	581 种	110 种	18.93
鸟类	1244 种	98 种	7.88
爬行类	376 种	25 种	6.65
两栖类	284 种	30 种	10.56
鱼类	3862 种	404 种	10.46
苔藓植物	494 属	13 属	2.63
蕨类植物	224 属	6 属	2.67
裸子植物	34 属	10 属	29.41
被子植物	3123 属	246 属	7.88

注：引自"中国生物多样性国情研究报告"(《中国生物多样性国情研究报告》编写组，1998)。

马逸清和谢钟报道虎的近况，虎的种群近百年来种群数量急剧减少，有的亚种(*Panthera tigris virgata*)已灭绝。我国有 4 个亚种虎的总数量估计为 100~200 只，分散隔离在很有限的林区，处于极端濒危状态，华南虎很有可能会灭绝，目前总数不会超过 20 只。迁地保护的华南虎在 1985~1995 年期间种群增长率接近于零。近年来加强了野生动物的保护，东北虎在牡丹江一带频频出现，中俄美专家组成的调查组在中俄边境每天都能见到虎、豹的活动踪迹。

王应祥等报道我国豹猫除少数地区外，全国都有分布，有 5 个亚种，栖息地也较广泛。用毛皮收购数测算，全国豹猫 1992 年资源储量为 106.5 万只。濒危野生动植物国际贸易公约(CITES)和 IUCN 把豹猫列为附录I或附录II，我国未把豹猫列入国家重点保护野生动物名单，但在管理和经营方面目前处于混乱状态。

吴家炎报道我国羚羊亚科(*Antilopinae*)4 属 6 种的近况。高鼻羚羊(*Saiga tatarica*)可能已经灭绝，普氏原羚(*Procapra prezewalskii*)已处于濒危状态，藏原羚(*P. picticaudata*)、藏羚(*Pantholops hodgsonii*)及鹅喉羚(*Gazella subgutturosa*)在资源分布、保护管理方面问题不少；只有黄羊(*Procapra gutturosa*)虽大量的被猎杀，但还有一定的种群数。罗宁等对新疆等 8 个代表性区域的盘羊(*Ovis ammon*)的种群作了研究，估算新疆境内盘羊资源储藏目前已发展到 7 万头，建议不再定为 2 类保护动物，而可作一定的利用。但应根据物种现状与发展态势，对不同亚种与生态地理群确立相应的保护等级，采取加强禁猎或者通过合理利用，促进资源保护与发展。

周开亚和王丁报道了我国鲸类现状，已知的鲸类 31 种，其中须鲸类 8 种，齿鲸类 23 种，除白暨豚和长江江豚(*Neophocaena phocaenoides*)外,其他鲸类现状都缺少研究，种群情况都不明。白暨豚种群数量可能已不足 100 头，已濒临灭绝，就地保护已不可能，为此国家建立了湖北天鹅洲国家级白暨豚半自然保护区。长江江豚的种群数量约 2700 头，数量还在迅速减少，应提高其保护等级，并加强就地、迁地和人工繁殖研究。

李欣海报道朱鹮目前仅存一个种群，1981 年发现至今一直在 20 只左右波动，做过大量专门研究，从种群生存力分析显示在 100 年后绝灭的可能性是 22%。

王岐山报道长江中下游越冬鹤类的现状，丹顶鹤、白头鹤、白枕鹤、白鹤和灰鹤等 5 种总数约 8000~10 000 只在这里居留或过境。在长江中下游越冬的鹤类占中国野生鹤类总数的一半，但其分布面积和占据面积都很小，而且局限于几个保护区内，受到开发滩涂、芦苇塘改为农田、非法捕鱼等影响而使鱼类及水产资源枯竭，还受到猎杀、围捕、剧烈农药毒杀等人类活动的威胁。

郑光美报道，我国是世界雉类(*Phasianini*)资源最丰富的国家，共 27 种，占世界总种数(51 种)的 53%，但受威胁雉类有 11 种，近危 10 种，分别占世界受威胁及近危种类的 40%及 70%。目前国内在鸡形目鸟类分布数据库、西南部受威胁雉类调查、绿尾红雉、褐马鸡、白颈长尾雉、白冠长尾雉、绿孔雀的生态与保护研究方面正按照 WPA-China 和 SSC 雉类专家组在 1995~1999 世界雉类研究和保护行动计划进行研究工作。丁平等对我国特产种、世界濒危种和国家一级保护动物白颈长尾雉(*Synmaticus ellioti*)作了专题报道。在 19 个已知的自然保护区中，多数国家级保护区(如梵净山、武夷山和乌岩岭自然保护区等)栖息地保护较好，基本禁止了捕猎。但其他保护区问题较多，如雷公山保护区，栖息地已成 8 个不连续的片段，并正不断在加剧。1991~1993 年该保护区被捕猎的白颈长尾雉达 161 只，目前面临较严重的受胁状态。

杨岚报道占全国鸟类种数 63.5%(共 793 种)的云南鸟类保护现状，珍稀保护鸟类中，已绝迹的种类有斑嘴鹈鹕(*Pelecanus phitippensis*)、白头鹮(*Myctena leucocephalus*)、黑头白(*Pseudibis papillosa*)、马来渔(*Ketupa ketupu*)等 5 种，白琵鹭(*Platalea laucorodia*)、黑冗鹫(*Sarcogyps calvus*)、赤颈鹤(*Grus antigone*)等 3 种处于极度濒危。其他罕见的计有 34 种，占珍稀保护种类的 23%；稀有的计 77 种，占 52%，而常见的只有 30 种，占 20%。绿孔雀在 15 个县还存在一定种群数量，估计整个云南现存野生种群数为 800~1100 只。但栖息地破坏严重，现存种群形成小家族群落状隔离分布状态。有 7 个迁地保护单位，但总计才 50 余个个体。此外，许维枢报道了海鸟及何芬奇报道了鹑类等鸟类都在不同程度处于受威胁的状态。

熊郁良等报道了我国蛇类的现状。中国蛇类 180 余种(亚种)，分属 50 属，7 科，其中有毒蛇类约 50 种(亚种)，占总数的 1/3 左右。我国对蛇类的利用非常广，除食用外，蛇毒、蛇胆作药用的多达 40 余种，蛇油、蛇皮都有广泛用途。因此各种合法的、非法的贸易导致蛇类资源急剧减少，其中眼镜蛇(*Naja naja atra*)、扁颈蛇(*Ophiphaqus hanna*)、金环蛇(*Bungarus fascictus*)、银环蛇(*B. multisictus*)、滑鼠蛇(*Ptyas mucosus*)、五步蛇(*Agkistrodon acutus*)数量的锐减尤为明显。中国出口的蛇为 1500~1800 吨。为利用目的我国建有蛇饲养场近 200 个，其中问题不少。按陈壁辉报道，蛇类养殖场仅安徽省就有 11 个，名义上是养殖场实质上多为收购暂养场，能初步繁殖成功者寥寥无几。他认为这种养殖场起着加速野生种群数量锐减的作用。

袁德成报道中国蝴蝶已知种约为 1300 种，约占世界已知种的十分之一。特有性也很高，如凤蝶科全世界已知近 15%的种类为中国特有，如一些珍贵的种类，金带喙凤蝶(*Teinopalpus imperialis*)、金斑喙凤蝶(*T. aureus*)、二尾褐凤蝶(*Bhutanitis mansfieldi*)、三尾褐凤蝶(*B. thaidina*)以及中华虎凤蝶(*Luehdorfia chinensis*)和长尾虎凤蝶(*L. longicaudata*)。

近10年来蝴蝶资源作为商品，对珍稀种类商业化规模的采集严重危及了种群的生存。此外，面临最大的威胁是栖息地的改变和破坏，新闻媒体多次报道云南以大量蝴蝶出现而著名的蝴蝶泉已见不到蝴蝶。

病毒、细菌和真菌方面，数十年来对具重要经济价值、社会效益和生态意义的物种进行过较系统的调查，目前菌种保藏机构在国内有权威的是中国科学院微生物研究所。按统计目前保藏有放线菌36属，450种，1332个菌株；Frankia-共生固氮放线菌我国有6属，44种树木与放线菌共生结瘤固氮，其中19种是国际上未报道的新种。我国保藏有病毒600余株，其中动物病毒146株，植物病毒151株，昆虫病毒214株，噬菌体91株。除大型真菌外，病毒、细菌类的微生物在我国甚至全世界的物种多样性是远远不清楚的，因此对受威胁情况就无从谈起。当然对一些大型真菌的威胁是显而易见的，尤其是具食用及医用价值的野生菌，过度采收，资源枯竭的问题是相当严重的，如冬虫夏草(*Cordyceps sinensis*)，分布区相当狭窄，50年代时每年能产20 000 kg以上，但目前因遭严重滥采而资源枯竭；口蘑也由于过度放牧，乱采滥收，1991年在内蒙古已经到了几乎收购不到的程度。利用价值越高，濒危程度也相应地高，甚至灭绝。

我国的微生物、植物也和动物一样，物种受到不同程度的威胁，有些也已经灭绝，以下的资料多数引自“中国生物多样性国情研究报告”(简称“国情报告”)。

我国的淡水藻类已发现的约9000种，海藻2458种。淡水红藻和褐藻尤为珍贵，它们是海、陆演变过程中残留在淡水中的孑遗生物。具分布狭窄及一定封闭性的特点。不少是珍稀种，有的仅采集到一次，在我国共12种。如淡水褐藻类中的层状破藻(*Lithoderma zonatum*)、红藻类中的绞纽串珠藻(*Batrachospermum intortum*)、中华串珠藻(*B. sinense*)、中华链珠藻(*Sirodotia sinica*)、中华鱼子菜(*Lemanea sinica*)等。由于这些藻类都生长在泉水、井水和溪水中，由于人类活动以及气候干旱、泉水区水源枯竭而使这些珍稀物种已处于极危状态，有些淡水褐藻已经灭绝。过去很丰富的淡水红藻如外果串珠藻(*Batrochospermum ectocarpus*)和美芒藻(*Compsopogon spp.*)由于旅游区开发已几乎绝迹。此外，由于水体污染及高度富营养化，藻类群落物种多样性被破坏，一些有害蓝藻如微囊藻(*Microcystis spp.*)和鱼腥藻(*Anabaena spp.*)等大量繁殖，在淡水中形成水华，海洋中形成赤潮，进一步恶化水质，危及渔业生产，水华的严重发生甚至危及沿江地区的工业生产及居民生活。

我国苔藓植物有2200种，占世界物种总数的9.1%，特有类群丰富，占总数的2.2%。另一特点是在系统发生上居关键位置的类群多，如藻苔(*Takakia lepidozloides*)和角叶藻苔(*T. ceratophylla*)。中国的苔藓以热带及亚热带成分占优势。但由于森林砍伐，大气污染及其他人类活动影响，苔藓植物也面临严重威胁，估计濒危及稀有苔藓植物约36种。证实已灭绝的至少有耳坠苔(*Ascidiota blepharophylla* var. *blepharophylla*)和拟短月藓(*Brachymeniopsis gymnostoma*)等5种。有些苔藓植物在药用及检测环境污染的指示性方面都具有相当的重要性，过去重视很不够。

蕨类植物在我国有2200~2600种，占世界种数的22%左右。我国的蕨类植物具极高的多样性，拥有的科属数几乎占世界的95%，特有种有500~600种，占已知种25%左右。如松叶蕨(*Psilotum nudum*)、天星蕨(*Chistensenia*)等是在探讨物种进化系统问题上具十分重要意义的种类，很多种是传统中药和民间草药，占全部种类的 10%，如贯众(*Cyrtomium fortunei*)、骨碎补(*Davallia barometz*)等。出口需求量也很大，其他在食用及作为肥料等亦具一定的利用价值。但目前濒危状况也很严重，占我国蕨类总数的 30%，其中重要的有 101 种急需保护。

裸子植物因受到第四纪冰期影响小，基本上保持了第三纪的成分，因此我国的裸子植物其区系种类丰富，起源古老，残遗、孑遗特有的成分多，针叶林类型多等特点。另一特点是物种数虽仅为被子植物种数的 0.8%，可是形成针叶林面积却略高于阔叶林面积，占森林总面积的 52%。裸子植物由于树干直，材质优良，出材率高，针叶林就成为优先被采伐的对象，因之破坏严重。最大的东北大、小兴安岭及长白山区天然林 80%已被采伐，横断山区的 70%天然林也相继被伐，目前仅于交通不便的深山河谷和山坡陡壁及自然保护区内尚有天然针叶林保存。已绝灭的种有崖柏(*Thuja sutchuanensis*)，仅有栽培无野生植株的有苏铁(*Cycas revoluta*)等多种，极危种有柔毛油杉(*Keteleeria pubescens*)、康定云杉(*Picea montigena*)等 14 种。濒危和受威胁的有 63 种，占总数的 28%，其中百山祖冷杉(*Abies beshanzuensis*)和台湾穗花杉(*Amentotaxus formosana*)已被列入世界最濒危植物。

被子植物是人类主要食用的植物，是我国大多数人作为药用的植物，此外与人类的衣、食、住、行息息相关。因此也是物种多样性丧失最严重的类群之一。我国被子植物物种处于濒危或受威胁状态的物种估计占总数的 15%~20%，达 4000~5000 种。而且数目可观的植物已经绝灭，如喙毛红豆、毛叶坡垒、毛叶紫树、锯叶竹节树、锈花茜、异叶玉叶金花、双蕊兰、无喙兰等数十种经多年考察已无踪迹，估计都已绝灭。更多的植物只剩下一株或少数几株，如浙江的普陀鹅耳枥、海南的滕柄木、园籽荷、猪血木、琼棕等，按估计 200 种植物会在近期内绝灭(洪德元，1990)。

从上述各种生物类群现状的概述，可说明我国物种多样性已面临很严重的危及。

1.2 中国的遗传多样性

1.2.1 遗传多样性保护及持续利用的重要性

董玉琛(1993)对遗传多样性作如下的说明，以作物为例，作物遗传多样性是作物品种、品系及其野生基因源携带的遗传信息的总和。遗传信息实质上是基因的信息，而基因存在于遗传资源之中，所以讨论作物遗传多样性问题首先就要讨论作物遗传资源问题，或称基因资源问题、种质资源问题。这个概念可把家畜、家禽等等的遗传多样性的含义都包括了。《生物多样性公约》中有很大的部分是涉及遗传资源的问题。首先《公约》第一条目标，“本公约是按照本公约有关条款从事保护生物多样性、持续利用其组成部分以及公平合理分享由利用遗传资源而产生的惠益；实施手段包括遗传资源的适当取得及有关技术的适当转让，但需顾及对这些资源和技术的一切权利；以及提供适当资金”。第 2 条用语，对“遗传材料”、“遗传资源”等款项都有专门的解释；第 15 条“遗传资源的取得”，以及在其他条款中多处涉及到遗传资源的问题。《公约》的用语中对“遗传资源”的解释是：“是指具有实际或潜在价值的遗传材料”，而对“遗传材料”的解释是：“是指来自植物、动物、微生物或其他来源的任何含有遗传功能单位的材料”。在含义上显然更为广泛一些，但与董玉琛的理解是没有矛盾的，由于遗传资源在生物多样性保护和持续利用中的重要位置，因此在第三次缔约国大会上农业生物多样性保护和持续利用作物重要议题之一。这次大会审议了与《公约》第一条目标(见上述的三项目标)有关的农业生物多样性保护的文件和联合国粮农组织(FAO)保护和使用植物资源促进粮食和农业生产的进展情况报告。大会最后并通过了“保护和持续利用农业生物多样性”的决定。这一段说明遗传多样性在《公约》中所占的位置以及对其保护与持续利用的重要性。

1.2.2 我国遗传多样性的概况

尼古拉·伊·瓦维洛夫早在本世纪 30 年代根据各种作物在各地的种和种内多样性的程度提出作物起源中心学说，其中指出中国是世界主要作物起源地之一。新中国成立后 50 年代农业合作化高潮时期，就在全国农村作过作物品种普遍征集，以免推广优良品种造成地方品种灭绝。70~80 年代又在边远地区对小作物作过全国性的补充征集。70 年代后期还作了一系列旨在收集作物遗传资源的考察活动，对饲用植物资源、野生稻、猕猴桃、大豆、小麦及在重要地区如云南、西藏、海南岛等地收集了 4 万份以上的材料。

大量作物的遗传资源是起源于中国或中国是起源地之一(董玉琛，1993；1994)。首先是谷类作物，我国是起源地之一的有水稻(*Oryza sativa*)、粟(*Setaria italia*)，荞麦(*Fagopyrum esculenicum*)；只起源于中国的有稷(*Panicum miliaceum*)，裸燕麦(*Avena nuda*)、裸大麦及蜡质种玉米等。中国还是小麦(*Triticum aestivum*)和高粱(*Sorghum kaoliang*)的次生起源地；豆类作物中大豆是中国起源，不论在栽培种(*Glycine max*)还是野生种(*G. soja*)方面，遗传资源都很丰富；薯类作物起源于中国的有山药(*Dioscorea batatas*)、芋(*Colocasia esculenta*)、紫芋(*C. tonoimo*)、麻芋(*Hydrosme konjac*)等；油料作物方面，白菜型和芥菜型油菜(*Brassica spp.*)、苏子(*Perilla nankinensis*)和油茶都是起源于中国；纤维作物中萱麻(*Boehmeria nivea*)和青麻是中国起源，而大麻(*Canabis sativa*)和罗布麻是起源地之一；茶(*Camellia sinensis*)和桑(*Morus alba*)均起源于中国；蔬菜方面，萝卜、白菜、芥菜、莴笋、茄子、丝瓜等等的一些种(或类型)起源于中国；有 10 余种果树原产中国，其中包括有猕猴桃(*Actinidia spp.*)、樱桃(*Prunus pseudocerasus*)、梅(*P. mume*)、扁桃(*Amygdalus communis*)、黄皮(*Clauseua lansium*)、香榧(*Torreya grandis*)、海棠(*Malus prunifolia*)、柑橘(*Citrus*)、枇杷(*Eriobotrya*)、荔枝(*Litchi*)、龙眼(*Dimocarpus*)、杏(*Armeniaca*)等。此外，还有 10 余种果树的某些品种起源于中国；花卉方面，从 16 世纪开始，各国植物学家纷纷来华收集观赏植物资源，种质资源的丰富被西方誉为中国是“世界园林之母”。中国的花卉开遍了世界许多国家。按“国情报告”中列举中国原产的观赏植物至少占 30 个属中的不同的物种数，最少的如腊梅属 6 个种，全部原产中国，多至马先蒿属中有 329 个种原产中国。

在家畜、家禽方面，中国各种家畜的地方品种(类型)就有 200 多个，其中猪就有 100 个品种左右。远在 2000 年前，罗马帝国就已经引进中国猪种育成罗马猪。18 世纪英国引进中国华南猪育成大约夏克、巴古夏猪。其他如多产性的太湖猪、金华猪、寒羊、湖羊、耐湿热的滇南小耳猪、耐寒冷和粗放饲料的藏猪，都具有特殊的遗传基础。正像上面提到的，中国幅员辽阔，在一些边远交通不便的地区有不少优良品质的家畜品种，如云南省，由于独特的地理位置和复杂多样的气候和地形地貌，地理隔离以及众多少数民族特有经济、文化活动，保留有不少地方品种和类型，如文山黄牛、邵通黄牛、德宏水牛、大理马、腾冲马、保山猪、明光小耳猪、云岭山羊、丽江绵羊等。西双版纳还分布有不少家养动物的祖型或近缘种如原鸡、马来西亚野牛、爪哇野牛以及很可能驯化为小家畜的热带动物，如麂鹿，在滇西西北高山峡谷中，除保留古老的地方品种如藏猪、藏羊外，还有大额牛。

1.2.3 我国动、植物遗传多样性的现状

目前全国共有各种作物的遗传资源总数约达 35 万份以上，其中禾谷类 20 万份，豆类 5.5 万份，棉、麻、油、糖、烟等经济作物 3.1 万余份，蔬菜 1.8 万余份，果树 1.1 万余份、牧草、绿肥及其他 1.5 万余份(董玉琛，1993)。这些遗传资源 80%以上是原产，这些遗传资源绝大部分保存在中国农科院国家作物种质库和在全国各地建立的 25 个作物种质圃内。遗传资源的收集和保存的目的是为了利用。因此必须对这些资源作研究和鉴定。目前已对收入国家作物种质库和种质圃的约 27 万份材料都进行了初步农艺性状的鉴定，对其中 15 万份材料作了抗病、抗逆和产品品质的初步鉴定并建立了国家作物资源数据库，对一部分野生种、特有种和亚种也进行了细胞学鉴定。但在作物遗传多样性方面还存在以下几个问题：一是还有大量有用的作物种植资源尚未收集或收集得不系统；二是已有大量的农家品种由于推广优良品种而丧失掉；三是作物的野生种和野生近缘种的原地保存几乎还是空白，有一些非常重要的野生种或野生近缘种已灭绝。高立志(1996)等报道，中国分布有三种野生稻，即普通野生稻(*Oryza rufipogon*)，药用野生稻(*O. officinalis*)和疣粒野生稻(*O. meyeriana*)均被列为国家二级保护植物。近年来随着人口膨胀，农业生产系统现代化和农田城市化，野生的生境遭到毁坏，遗传多样性大量丧失。其中尤以普通野生稻最为严重。他们呼吁如不抓紧抢救，按目前消失速率继续下去，野生稻在中国的灭绝将为期不远了。由于上述原因，也同样造成其他作物遗传多样性的大量灭绝。如山东垦利县黄河入海口附近，原有数万亩野生大豆，由于开采石油和开垦农田，野生大豆只零星可见，黑龙江省三江平原的野生大豆情况亦类似。

从家养畜禽方面，按“国情报告”报道，由于 70 年代后期，以承包责任制为主体的农户经济，使马、驴、牛、驼等大牲畜数量锐减，当地品种大量灭绝。80 年代中后期猪和鸡的配合系又取代本地猪、鸡品种和新培育品种。按普查资源，猪、牛、羊、鸡等不少品种如上海的荡脚猪、河南的项城猪、湖北的枣北大尾羊、甘肃的临兆鸡等都已灭绝。不少已处于濒危状态，如河西猪只留 48 头、五指山猪只留 16 头，并没有成年的公猪，北京西鸡仅留下 1000 只左右。据统计，近年来有 60 余个大、中城市和工矿区的本地种已灭绝，并有一批驴、马、牛、猪、羊、鸡等种质资源已处于濒危。此外，目前家养昆虫的种质保存完全处于无人过问的状态。

1.3 我国的生态系统多样性

1.3.1 我国生态系统多样性概况

按陈灵芝(1994)报道，出现在北半球的各种生态系统在中国均有出现。森林生态系统可分为① 寒温性针叶林，主要有多种落叶松(*Larix* spp.)、云杉(*Picea* spp.)林、冷杉(*Abies* spp.)林和松(*Pinus* spp.)林。它们均分布在凉冷、湿润的生境内，林内有野生动物约200多种；② 温带针阔叶混交林，以红松(*Pinus koraiensis*)阔叶混交林为代表，这类森林破坏后，常被落叶阔叶林所替代，林内野生动物约有360种；③ 温湿带落叶阔叶林和针叶林，阔叶林的栎(*Quercus* spp.)林和栎与多种阔叶树混交林为代表。针叶林主要有油松(*Pinus tabulaeformis*)林、赤松(*P. densiflora*)林、白皮松(*P. bungeana*)林和侧柏(*Platycladus orientalis*)林等。野生植物种类约2000多种，脊椎动物约200多种，属国家保护动物有20种。落叶阔叶林破坏十分严重，次生中龄林呈岛屿状分布，老龄林已经基本消失；④ 亚热带常绿阔叶林和针叶林，中国的亚热带是世界上亚热带面积最广阔的区域，自然地理条件特别优越，是地中海、中亚、南亚次大陆、日本西南部、北美佛罗里达半岛及澳洲南部和西南沿海的狭小亚热带地区所不可比拟。中国的亚热带以常绿阔叶林为代表，并有多种针叶林，常绿阔叶林主要出壳斗科、樟科、木兰科、山茶科植物所组成。针叶林在东部以马尾松(*Pinus massoniana*)林为代表，在西部以云南松(*P. yunnanensis*)林、华山松(*P. armandii*)林为主，还有第三纪活化石植物构成的森林如银杉(*Cathaya argyrophylla*)、金钱松(*Pseudolarix kaempferi*)林、水杉(*Metasequoia glyptostroboides*)林和秃衫(*Taiwania flousiana*)林等，种子植物有2674属，14 600种以上，野生动物种类也十分丰富，脊椎动物达1000多种，属国家重点保护动物有80多种，如大熊猫、金丝猴等是中国的特有种。⑤ 热带季雨林、雨林，中国热带森林面积只占国土面积的0.5%，却拥有全国物种总数的25%。主要分布在云南南部和西南部、海南岛、广西南部和西藏东南部，拥有的植物种类占全国植物总数的15%，动物种类占全国总数的27%，其中黑长臂猿(*Hylobates consolor*)是中国特有种。

草原生态系统可分为温带草原、高寒草原和荒漠区山地草原三类。温带草原分布于内蒙古、黄土高原北部和松嫩平原西部。从东到西随气候逐渐的变干而分化为草甸草原、典型草原和荒漠草原。草甸草原以贝加尔针茅(*Stipa baicalensis*)、羊草(*Aneurolepidium chinense*)和线叶菊(*Filifolium sibiricum*)为群系代表；典型草原以大针茅(*Stipa grandis*)和克氏针茅(*S. krylovii*)群系为主；荒漠草原以小针茅(*S. klemenzii*)和小半灌木草原为代表。温带草原中的野生动物主要有黄羊、狐和啮齿类等。南寒草原为青藏高原所特有，东部半湿润地区为高寒草甸，以蒿草(*Kobresia spp.*)建群而西部半干旱区为高寒草原，代表群系有紫花针茅(*S. purpurea*)草原及硬苔草(*Carex moorcroftii*)草原，野生动物主要为藏羚、雪豹和啮齿类。荒漠区山地草原主要分布在一定海拔高度的阿尔泰、天山、昆仑山等高大的山系上。植物以针茅(*S. capillata*)群系为主，动物主要有鹅喉羚(*Gazella subgutturosa*)，狍(*Capreolus capreolus*)和岩羊(*Pseudois nayaur*)。

荒漠生态系统

中国的荒漠主要分布在中国的西北部，占国土面积的 1/5，沙漠和戈壁面积共约 100 余万 km^2。可分为小乔木荒漠、灌木荒漠、半灌木与小半灌木荒漠和垫状小半灌木荒漠等 4 个类型。植物优势种有梭梭(*Haloxylon ammodendron*)、白梭梭(*H.persicum*)、木霸王(*Zygophyllum xanthoxylon*)和驼绒藜(*Ceratodes* spp.)等，动物中蜥蜴种类和数量较多，还有大沙鼠(*Rhombomys opimus*)、野驴(*Equus hemoinus*)等。

农田生态系统

中国耕地面积占国土的 11%，主要分布在东南部，由于中国农业历史悠久，农田生态系统类型复杂，粮食作物 30 多种，蔬菜 200 多种，果树约 300 种。除各种作物的农田生态系统类型外还常见玉米田中套种豆类、水稻田中种绿肥。此外，林木、果树与作物间作构成多种类型农林复合生态系统。此外，茶园、桑园、果园与橡胶园也是重要的农田生态系统。

湿地生态系统

主要包括浅水湖泊、河流和沼泽，面积在 $50km^2$ 以上的大中型湖泊主要分布在青藏高原、蒙新地区、云贵高原、江汉平原和三江平原，数量很多。水生生物有浮游生物、底栖动物和水生维管束植物、淡水鱼类 770 种和亚种以上，其中土著鱼类有 690 多种。中国的大多数湖泊与河流相通，因此生物种类有很多相似处。中国沼泽总面积约 1400 万余 km^2，集中在三江平原、东北山地、若尔盖高原等地。以苔草、禾草沼泽和多种落叶松泥炭沼泽为主，湿地水禽多数为候鸟，一些特有水禽在这些湿地上越冬、繁殖和栖息。

海岸与海洋生态系统

海域跨暖温带、亚热带和热带三个温度带，受沿岸流、黑潮暖流和上开流等多种流系影响，海岸滩涂和大陆架面积广阔，1500 余条大、中河流入海，具海岸滩涂生态系统和河口湾生态系统、海岸湿地生态系统、红树林生态系统、珊瑚礁生态系统、海岛生态系统和大洋生态系统等。黄海和渤海是暖温带生态系统，冬季有岸冰，生物季节变化明显，许多温带种如斑海豹(*Phoca largha*)、鳕(*Gadus macrocephalus*)和紫贻贝(*Mytilus edulis*)等在此出现。东海和南海沿海除亚热带生态系统，已有珊瑚和红树林出现。中国著名的长江、珠江和黄河等河口湾生态系统，海南岛以南和台湾东南的广大海域属热带生态系统，物种丰富，热带海洋生物占绝对优势，有 185 种连礁珊瑚，发育良好。

1.3.2 我国生态系统的现状

可是中国森林特别是天然森林大幅度下降，1971~1975 年天然林面积为 9817 万 km^2，到 1981~1985 年下降为 8635 万 km^2。以海南岛为例，1956 年时天然林覆盖率为 25.7%，64 年时减少到 18.1%，83 年时仅留下 7.2%。草原地带占国土面积约 1/3，近 20 年来，产草量已下降 1/3~1/2，北方半干旱地区草场，超载放牧，毁草开荒及鼠害等退化尤为严重，草原生态系统面临严重衰退局面，沙漠化面积大幅度增加。如鄂尔多斯 50 年代时沙化面积仅 2000 万亩，80 年代初已达 6000 多万亩，还有 4000 多万亩水土流失极为严重的草原。其他各种生态系统都遭受不同程度或相当严重的破坏，如红树林已由 50 年代初的 5 万 km^2 下降到目前仅剩 2 万 km^2。海南岛沿岸 80%珊瑚礁资源破坏，海水生态系统由于兴建大型水利、电力工程及围湖造田也受到严重破坏；湖北号称“千湖之省”，目前仅剩下湖泊 326 个，湖面面积由 1250 万亩减至 355 万亩。

总之，整个中国各种生态系统由于受到各种灾害，主要还是人类活动严重影响，已在不断被破坏并恶化。由于森林锐减，草原退化，农田土地沙化和退化，招致水土流失，沿海水质恶化，淡水中的水华、海洋中的赤潮频频发生，经济资源大量减少，自然灾害加剧。

2　经遗传修饰生物体释放后的生态风险及生物安全

在《公约》第 2 条“用语”中有专门一款“生物技术”；在第 8 条“就地保护”的(g)款作如下叙述：“制定或采取方法以酌情管制、管理或控制由生物技术改变的活生物体在使用和释放时可能产生的危险，即可能对环境产生不利影响，从而影响到生物多样性的保护和持续利用，也要考虑到对人类健康的危险”。生物技术和生物多样性的关系在《公约》条款上已作了充分的说明，而实际上，在 70 年代初期，即重组 DNA 研究发展的初期就有一部分科学家对其在生物学和生态学上的危险以及释放到环境后可能带来的危险表示担心。到 1992 年时世界各国，尤其是发达国家已有不少产物进入中试或田间试验，当时虽还未大规模释放或进入商业化，科学家们要求对其进行管制、管理及控制的呼声越来越高。为之《公约》第 19 条第(3)款又提到“缔约国应考虑是否需要一项议定书，规定适当程序，特别包括事先知情协议，适用于可能对生物多样性的保护和持续利用产生不利影响的由生物技术改变的任何活生物体的安全转移、处理和使用，并考虑该议定书的形式”。有关生物安全议定书的拟定从此作为历次缔约国大会的主要讨论内容，专门设立了“特设专家工作组”，草拟文件供每次缔约国大会上讨论。此外，联合国环境署(UNEP)也十分关注生物安全问题，在 1995 年组织起草了《国家生物技术安全技术准则(草案)》(下称《准则》)，同年 12 约对《准则》进行了最后定稿。《准则》将作为一临时机制和技术文件，与拟好的“生物安全议定书”互为补充。目前国际上通常对由生物技术改变的活生物体，用下列 3 个名词，即经遗传修饰的生物体(GMOs)、基因工程生物体(GEOs)和经修饰的活生物体(LMOs)，这 3 个名词含义基本是一样的。

2.1　GMOs 在国内外的发展

生物技术经过 20 多年的发展，已经展示了它巨大的社会效益和经济效益，它可能或已经提供治疗人体疾病的药物及治疗手段，还可能解决 21 世纪大大膨胀的人口的粮食问题以及其他环境问题(高立志，1996)。科学家已经通过转基因微生物的发酵及转基因生物来生产如胰岛素，促红细胞生成素(EPO)、干扰素等等药物，有的已在临床上应用；发现了不少人体疾病的基因，为今后基因治疗打下了基础；突出的在动物方面是转基因猪的成功，英国已经成功地可用转基因猪的器官作为人体器官移植的脏器，但由于在伦理道德方面遭到反对而尚未在临床上应用。在转基因农作物方面已在一大批禾谷类、纤维类、果蔬类、豆类、花卉、牧草作物方面取得成功。早已走出实验室进入大田作中间试验，并从 1994 年以来不少数量已达到商业化的阶段，番茄是美国在 1994 年第一个批准上市的转基因作物，这两年来商业化了的转基因作物数量迅速增长。在玉米、棉花、大豆、马铃薯、油菜等具不同性状的转基因作物都已上市。

我国的生物技术研究至少在“六五”期间已开始部署，至今与其他发展中国家相比，在基因工程方面成就并不落后。在转基因作物方面，先后已得到了抗除草剂、抗病毒、抗虫、耐盐的作物(钱迎倩，1995；1998)。例如抗除草剂的转基因大豆已繁殖到第五代，抗烟草花叶病毒，特别是抗烟草花叶病毒和黄瓜花叶病毒的双抗转基因烟草在河南省 1991 年已达到 8000km^2 的大田面积，成为当时国际上转基因植物释放面积最大的作物。此外已成功地 Bt 基因转入棉花主栽品种，获得抗虫能力在 80%以上的转基因棉花品系 13 个；转基因抗病小麦有的品种已进入大田试验；抗青枯病转基因马铃薯已筛选的抗性提高 1~3 级的株系 3 个。在转基因动物方面，黑龙江水产所将牛、羊的生长激素基因移植到普通普通鲤鱼，得到生长速度提高 20%的第一代转基因鱼，又将大马哈鱼的生产激素基因向第一代转基因鱼进行基因转移，已有上万尾转基因鱼的后代据报道正在进入有控制的中试阶段。由湖北省农科院畜牧兽医研究所承担的转基因猪作为器官移植供体的研究已取得很大的进展。从上述现状来看，中国在基因工程方面的成就以及 GMOs 向环境的释放都已达到一定的程度。

2.2 GMOs 释放给生态环境带来的风险

《公约》缔约国 1995 年 11 月在雅加达举行第二次会议时，秘书处提供了一份“实施《公约》第 6 条和第 8 条的有关做法和经验”的文本，其中第 54 点指出：“从《公约》的角度来看，生物技术产生经修饰的活生物体(LMO)引起的有关问题涉及的范围很广。它们包括植物基因的稳定性、对非针对(目标)对象产生的影响、对生态系统过程的不利影响、基因改变植物潜在脆弱性等问题；基因改变、控制基因表现、预定和非预定的改变等问题；供体生物体的表现特征，例如竞争性、致病性和毒性等问题；对人类健康产生有害影响等问题”。这一段说明对 GMOs 已有试验证实的或潜在的风险作了相当完善的概括。我们在看到生物技术给人类带来巨大效益的同时，还不能忽视其可能带来的一系列危机。对 GMOs 释放后的生态学、生物学以及对人类健康的风险，过去多数是预见性的评估，在提法上多数提的是潜在风险。可是近年来，特别是 1996 年两篇证实有风险的科学论文在 Nature 等著名杂志上登载后(Krattiger, 1994; Mikkelsen 等，1996)，更说明了生物安全问题的确要引起人们足够的重视。

2.2.1 对环境潜在的风险

转基因作物本身可能变为杂草，一部分栽培植物，例如一些高粱属的种，在一定环境下本身就是杂草，而在某些环境下它又可以是作物，这类作物当插入一个例如抗病、抗虫基因，或转基因作物中基因逃逸时，可能会把本来在某些地区种植很安全的作物，由于改变了其平衡而趋于杂草化。

转基因作物还可能使其野生近缘种变为杂草，由于自然界的制约，不少作物的野生近缘种虽然目前未被人类利用，但并不以杂草形式存在，可能一旦接受到某个 GMO 逃逸的基因，在一定条件下使其大量繁殖起来而变成杂草。如在美国，有一部分科学家反对政府批准转基因南瓜上市，就因为在美国野葫芦一类的南瓜近缘种植物是普遍存在的，本来这些野生近缘种由于有黄瓜斑纹病毒和西瓜斑纹病毒而不能大量繁殖起来，一旦抗多种病毒的转基因南瓜基因通过基因流转入野葫芦，后果将不堪设想。Mikkelsen 等(1996)作了芸苔(*Brassica napus*)的基因渐渗到其杂草近缘种野油菜(*B. campestris*)中的研究。芸苔染色体 $2n$=38,野油菜染色体 $2n$=20，但两个种能自发地杂交，在自然种群中能发现杂种，当耐除草剂 glufosinate 的转基因芸苔与野油菜杂交后得到的种间杂种与野油菜种在一起时，早在回交第一代就能发现形态上完全像野油菜，染色体也是 $2n$=20 的高度能育的耐除草剂转基因野油菜，说明芸苔的基因已快速地向野油菜传播，这个实验说明了 GMO 的转基因会向野生近缘种自然转移的一个确切的证明。

某些转基因作物或者是已具抗杀虫剂的性能或者是作为生物反应器来生产药物，这一类转基因作物可能会对其他自然界的生物产生反效果，这就是所谓的“反目标效应”。很少有哪一种杀虫剂能选择地杀死某一种害虫，而往往带有一定的广谱性，何况目前我们多数用的都是 Bt 基因。因此插入到作物中的杀虫或杀真菌的基因也可能对其他非目标生物起到作用，从而杀死了环境中有益的昆虫和真菌。此外，带有 Bt 抗虫基因的植物，当它们的遗体在土壤中被土壤生物降解时，也可能使这些生物受到毒害。例如带有几丁质酶的抗真菌的转基因作物的遗体分解时，可能会减少土壤中菌根的种群，由于几丁质酶可以消化掉带有几丁质的菌根的细胞壁，细胞壁一旦破坏，个体就自然死亡。从而土壤中的凋落物不可能被分解，营养流被中断，整个生态系统功能受阻滞。

目前美国政府已批准一种转基因螨的释放而遭到相当大的指责，因为已有相当数量的转基因节肢动物正在研究或准备提出申请向环境释放，其中包括有地中海果蝇、蚊子、蜜蜂以及棉铃虫等昆虫，因为这些节肢动物繁殖得快，数量又大，它们起到一系列例如作为害虫、有益的动物和传粉等重要的生态学作用。相当一部分节肢动物还非常小，能够动的距离还相当长，一旦确证风险的存在，要从环境收回这些转基因节肢动物将是不可能的。

2.2.2 转基因作物可能产生新的病毒或新的疾病

1994 年，美国密歇根州立大学科学家把花椰菜花叶病毒外壳蛋白的基因插入豇豆，得到抗病毒的豇豆，当他们把缺少外壳蛋白的病毒再接种到转基因豇豆上时，发现 125 株豇豆中有 4 株又染上了花叶毒。由此，他们认为插入转基因作物中的病毒基因可能与再接种病毒的遗传物质结合而形成新的病毒。Falk 等(1994)为此曾在 Science 上发表了题为“转基因作物将产生新病毒和新疾病？”的文章。1996 年又有实验证据说明至少在实验室条件下，原来准备作为抗病疫苗的黄瓜花叶病毒(CMV)自发地发生突变，这种新的突变，不仅不能抗 CMV，反而更加剧了这种病毒对烟草的危害。

2.2.3 对人体健康的影响

转基因生物作为食品对人体健康是否会带来风险一直是人们所关心的问题，过去的报道多数是由各种新闻媒体发出的，当然难避讹传的可能。但是有两点是值得深思的，作为美国第一个释放上市的转基因番茄是 1994 年 6 月，至今才有两年多一点的时间，其长期效应如何？风险又可能有多大？目前人们全然不知。第二点是按 Krittiger 报道中国从 1992 年起抗病毒转基因烟草已用于烟草工业，到 1994 年时转基因烟草种植面积已接近全国烟草种植面积的 5%(Nordlee 等，1996)。过去美国 Marlboro 烟草公司大量收购中国烟草，由于已有这样大面积的转基因烟草而不再收购，可见美国人对转基因作物的态度。

1996 年在科学刊物上，Nordlee 发表了“在转基因大豆中对巴西果过敏原的鉴定”的文章。说明基因工程大豆对人体是过敏的。巴西果的蛋白质内含有蛋氨酸，对人和动物营养是很重要的，把这种基因插入大豆目的是为了改良其营养组成，可一部分人对巴西果敏感，可与人体血清反应。实验证明当用对巴西果过敏的人的血清与转基因大豆与巴西果作试验时，反应是一样的。当然不同的人对巴西果过敏反应不完全一样，严重的可死亡，因此这家公司已放弃了将这一成果投放市场。

近来新闻媒体不断有关于欧洲共同体抵制美国 Monsanto 公司研制的抗除草剂转基因大豆进入欧洲，美国政府颁布命令禁止把动物器官移植到人体内的报道，这是针对转基因猪器官向人体移植成功而发布的，说明转基因生物对人体健康产生的效应是人们特别关注，又必须要非常慎重对待的问题。

2.4.4 对生物多样性的影响

转基因生物本身是自然界不存在的人工制造的生物，释放到任何一个生态系统中都是引入外来种。引入外来种历来是被普遍采用的，当然不乏起好作用的例子，但也确实可能引起当地生物多样性大量的灭绝。突出的例子登载在 1990 年 10 月 22 日中国农牧渔业报上，黄舟维撰写的“谁能除掉大米草”一文中提到，福建省霞浦县东吾洋沿岸 14 万亩滩涂，1983 年时从美国引进大米草(*Spartina anglica*)，认为可护堤、喂牛并可作燃料，原先该滩涂生态系统中有 200 多种生物，其中自然生长的鱼类多种，又是全国养对虾、贝类的试验基地。引进大米草后，由于大米草繁殖力强，生长茂盛，盘根错节，海水涨潮时滩涂生物被冲进草丛而无法逃生，以至蛏、蛤、章鱼、跳鱼等许多水产品濒临绝迹。浮游生物附着滞留在草丛中，致使人工养殖的牡蛎、对虾，因海水缺乏营养而产量锐减，不仅破坏了滩涂的生态系统，造成生物多样性的灭绝，并带来不可估量的经济损失。这类事例不胜枚举。

此外，上面已提到中国在栽培作物和家养动物方面是具有丰富遗传多样性的国家之一，为满足人口压力对粮食及食品的需求，迫使近代农业向单一化的优质高产品种发展，这在客观上已经自然淘汰了大量具有一定优良遗传性状的农家品种及其遗传资源，造成遗传多样性不可挽回的损失。GMOS的释放，如果处理不当可能更加剧了品种单一化，使农业进一步处于脆弱的状态。

本文原载：植物学通报. 1998. 15(6): 1-18

生物多样性的几个问题(续)*

钱迎倩

(中国科学院植物研究所)

摘　要　从生物多样性的现状、存在的问题及应采取的措施等三个方面比较全面地叙述了我国生物多样性的情况。“生物安全”是《生物多样性公约》签订后每次缔约国会议都要讨论的中心议题之一。为之，本文也用一定的篇幅作了较详细的介绍。现状部分从物种多样性、遗传多样性及生态系统多样性等三个方面作了介绍，又从自然因素以及由于人类活动造成栖息地的丧失、环境恶化、偷猎走私、过度捕捞和水产养殖、高新技术发展、全球气候变化以及外来种引入等两个方面对生物多样性造成严重威胁作了相当详细的分析。在应采取措施部分，不仅是根据我国目前所存在的问题，还介绍了国外值得借鉴的、可取的经验，以及正在开展的有关项目。使读者对我国生物多样性的情况及应采取的对策有了比较明确的了解。此外，对什么是“生物安全”，为什么要提出生物安全的问题以及应重视这问题也给出了答案。
关键词　生物多样性；《生物多样性公约》；经遗传修饰生物体；生物安全；DIVERSITAS

1　我国生物多样性存在的问题

我国的生物多样性无论在生态系统层次上或是在物种多样性、遗传多样性方面都面临着严重的问题。按照国际上一般的提法是由于人类活动影响导致生物多样性的灭绝是自然灭绝速度的1000倍。中国又是什么样的情况，目前恐怕无人能对这个问题作出明确的答复。虽然具体数字不可能回答，但对存在的问题必须要有明确的认识，并在履行《公约》过程中不断地予以解决。

1.1　自然因素对生物多样性的威胁

中国是一个自然灾害多发的国家，由于人类活动的影响，往往可能加重了自然灾害的危害性，或者甚至可能诱发某些灾害。对自然灾害造成的危害，人们所关心的是带来多大的人及牲畜的丧亡或者造成多大经济损失，还顾不及去仔细研究对生物多样性造成的严重后果。对于目前人们还没有认识有经济价值或社会效益的各种层次上的生物多样性，很少有人去研究造成多大的威胁或灭绝。因此当今在中国，生物多样性自然灭绝的资料是无法得到的。国际上可见到例如每年有4万种生物正走向灭绝，按此速度，到2000年，从地球上消灭的生物达到 50~100 万种等等，这种报道的数字也仅是一个大致的估

* 本文为国家科委“八五重大基础研究项目中国生物多样性保护生态学基础研究”部分内容。

计数。

新闻媒体上时而也能见到一些地区自然灾害的报道，例如，1996年4月新疆南部的雪灾，巴音布鲁克天鹅自然保护区，塔什库尔干自然保护区和托木尔峰自然保护区积雪厚达40~80cm。使保护区内的雪豹、天鹅、北山羊、雪鸡、岩牛、盘羊等野生动物因无处觅食而死亡，发现的死亡天鹅达470只左右。

虫灾对树木及作物的危害也是很严重的，如天牛是危害树木很严重的害虫，它可把一颗树干蛀得千疮百孔，如长春市绿色覆盖率曾达到38.3%，但从80年代中期后由于天牛对糖槭树及杨树的危害，只能成千上万株地砍掉病树。不时还发生倒树造成人亡、交通堵塞等事故。广西壮族自治区偏僻山区近万亩宝贵的原始金刚木在一个夏天树叶几乎全部被吃光。此外，松毛虫、松突园蚧对南方马尾松的危害更带来巨大的经济损失。

其他每年在我国发生的火灾、水灾对生物多样性造成的危害就很难有详细的资料可查了。

1.2 人类活动对生物多样性的威胁

中国人口基数过大，虽然政府采取有效的计划生育措施，但目前还在呈增长的趋势；中国还是一个贫穷的国家，各方面对包括生物资源在内的各种资源的需求量大；此外还由于群众对生物多样性保护的不重视等因素造成了不符合自然规律或者破坏自然活动的出现。这些都是造成对中国生物多样性严重威胁或大量灭绝的主要原因。下面对人类活动对生物多样性的威胁作详细的分析，所列举的事例都可见诸于报端。

1.2.1 栖息地的丧失

栖息地的丧失可能是造成大量动物、植物以至微生物受威胁或大量灭绝的首要原因，栖息地丧失的因素是很多的，例如森林大量砍伐、森林或农田城市化、修建公路、机场，围海造田，过度放牧及其他等原因。

中国全国的原始森林已基本上见不到，近几十年来，有几次错误的政策造成全国性森林大面积的丧失。解放后全国造林面积虽不少，特别是近十年来全国建立起近800个自然保护区以来，森林得到相当程度的保护。但是从生物多样性保护观点来看，前途还是不容十分乐观的。以中国特有的滇金丝猴为例，目前仅存的滇金丝猴被分割成从西藏兰康到云南丽江完全隔离的13个种群，总数仅存1000多只。有一群200多只生活在施坝林区内，但该林区正是被计划要砍伐的区域。林区所属的德钦县主要是依靠森工企业的“木头财政”，木材是唯一的财源。经11年的采伐，采伐范围已高达海拔3900m。经过全国性的呼吁，这次预定的砍伐事件暂时平息，但问题远没有解决，如果没有办法解决当地居民的生活问题，隐患是始终存在的。下面还有更可悲的例子，据中国环境报1996年12月14日报道，在云南森林资源日益枯竭、森工企业面临危机时，云南省林业厅决定与西藏自治区林业局联合开发西藏东南部森林资源，合作砍伐怒江和金沙江水系的大片森林，并准备建立一个40万m^2的储木场，准备存放从藏东南砍伐下来的木头。这个地区一方面是中国尚存仅有的少数原始森林中的一片，又是怒江、澜沧江和金沙江三江并流之地。三江流域的森林不仅在保护生物多样性的栖息地方面有重要意义，并对涵养水源、保持水土具有更为重要的作用。对于长江上游防止水土流失、保护三峡大坝、控制长江中、下游水量的作用更为巨大。这反映了很多实际矛盾以及如何来对待、处理好这些矛盾的问题，同时反映出对待森林保护、尤其是称得上原始或相对原始森林、涵养水源的水源林保护的迫切性。西双版纳是我国仅有的少数热带地区之一，占全国总面积的比例很小。但由于当地居民传统的刀耕火种以及橡胶林等经济林的大量发展(目前橡胶林的面积已达 200 万亩)，西双版纳森林覆盖率已由 50 年代的 60%降到目前的 30%左右。每年以 25 万亩的速度递减，由于热带森林大面积的破坏，使丰富的生物多样性受到严重威胁或灭绝。据估计，自 1957 年以来，处于灭绝和濒危的植物可能有 500~800 种。此外，中国仅有的其他热带地区如海南岛等都遭同样的命运。专家们呼吁，照此下去，我国有限的热带雨林将从“中国植被图”上消失掉。

草原生态系统是很多野生动物和野生植物的栖息地，但是中国草原的破坏也是惊人的。以黑龙江西部草原为例，松嫩平原地区过度放牧已使松嫩平原的实际载畜量达到理论载畜量的 4.7 倍。该地区的沙化、碱化、退化面积已达 2200 万亩。目前每年还以 200 万亩的速度扩展。由于沙化、碱化，草原原有种类成分发生很大变化，生物多样性的变化也可以估计到，草原退化问题在国内是十分普遍的。造成草场严重破坏的另一个原因是为了发财、用资源换取外汇。如宁夏地区连续三次滥挖甘草的高潮。据报道，马儿庄 53 万亩草场有 40 万亩遭劫；盐池 180 万亩草场遭劫的达 150 万亩，其中全沙化的已有 20 万亩。自 80 年代至今，在宁夏仅仅挖甘草一项，直接或间接毁坏的草场地共达 800 万亩。栖息地沙漠化的问题在我国是十分严重的，各种各样的生态系统都在不断地沙漠化。首先是农业生态系统面对世界上最严重的水土流失及沙漠化的威胁，最大的塔克拉玛干沙漠与古尔班通古特等大沙漠一起形成了绵亘万里的西部风沙线，直接危害着 260 个县的耕地。塔克拉玛干沙漠南缘，以每年 5m 的速度南移。个别区域甚至达到 100m。在卫星云图上，中国西部风沙线已入侵到使北京、天津、沈阳等城市处于沙漠前沿的包围之中。例如辽宁省康平县包括林地、水面在内的 320 万亩地域中，已沙化或半沙化的土地为 108 万亩。人类的破坏是造成沙漠化最大的危害。如海南万宁县，原先天然植被与人工防护林的覆盖率达 50%~60%，后因发现了钛矿，至 1985 年 5 月，为开矿而砍掉了 2 万亩防护林，25 公里长的珍贵青梅林自然保护区也遭到严重的破坏，现已到发出海南沙漠化警报的时候了；云南省沙化面积已达 7 万多公顷，解放初期云南省森林覆盖率为 50 %左右，长期以来乱砍滥伐，过度放牧开垦等原因，风沙化土地已分布到全省的 100 个县市，分布较为集中的 31 个县就有风沙化土地 7 万多公顷；祁连山森林覆盖率已由 50 年代的 22.4%减少到 15.45%。1990 年以来，由于开矿、采金、放牧、挖药材等活动，大面积的灌木林地被破坏。如肃南县境内的文殊沟滩至堡子滩，每年秋冬季有大量群众进山挖麻黄，致使 50km^2 的植被重度退化，失去蓄水保土、防风固沙的作用；天祝县哈溪双龙沟、肃南县隆畅河林区的白泉门，每天有上万人进山采金；河滩灌木林严重破坏；河南省民权县林木砍伐严重，防沙固沙林带遭到破坏，导致 1983 年前已得到治理的 10 多万亩土地重新沙漠化，气候为之越来越恶化。1996 年 5 月底敦煌地区连续 13h 的狂风沙暴，速度达每秒 25km，直径 30cm 的白杨连根拔起。棉花等作物、牲畜大量失踪。生物多样性受威胁，以致灭绝又知多少呢?

1990 年以来各种各样的开发区也是造成各种生态系统破坏的重要原因之一。如海南岛从 1990 年以来共征用林地 14 万余亩，珍贵植物群落青皮(*Vatica mangachapoi*)林已减少 30% 以上。近年来，海南各市、县平均每年征用林地 3.5 万余亩，大面积次生林被毁。按 1994 年报道，近 10 年来，我国耕地减少的速度惊人。1985 年减少 2300 万亩；开始实行土地法的 1987 年，当年减少 1200 万亩；1988 年以后，其状况继续恶化，尤其是在开发区热和房地产热中，破坏更为严重，建国以来中国耕地每年平均净减少 700 多万亩，相当于一个北京市。1983 年后全国平均每年减少耕田 1135 万亩。再以红树林生态系统来看，近 10 年来，红树林破坏十分严重，从原有的 4.7 万公顷减少到目前的 1.4 万公顷。海南的三亚牙龙湾的清眉港原有高大茂盛的红树林，由于 10 多年来的乱砍滥伐，目前残存不足 27 公顷，且均为 1m 以下的次生灌丛，覆盖率不及原有面积的 20%。深圳福田红树林自然保护区近年来由于筑路、盖房、建厂等原因，红树林生态系统遭到严重破坏，鸟类减少七成以上。其他如围海造田，围垦养殖等都是导致我国红树林不足过去三分之一的重要原因。

1.2.2 环境恶化

近年来，随着气候变化和人类活动的加剧，气候干旱少雨，气温上升，青海湖流域内蒸发量大于降水量，湖水位持续下降。从 1958~1990 年，青海湖共下降 3.2m。水位下降，影响了土壤的湿度，干燥的气候导致植被逐年退化。水分不足、过度的放牧，植物变得低矮稀疏，甚至枯死。该流域内有退化草场 6898km^2，占草场总面积的 35.65 %，植被严重退化，鼠虫害迅速加剧，沙化面积已达 756km^2，并以每年约 10km^2 的速度增加。青海湖鸟岛，每年夏季斑头雁、棕头鸥等多达 10 余万只，可是随着湖水位下降，湖岸线退缩，鸟岛已与陆地相连接，候鸟数减少，现每年已不足 5 万只，流域内西北几条河流均受到不同程度的污染，使青海湖水质受到影响，加之湟鱼产卵场所不断的丧失，湟鱼遭到严重破坏，年产量已由最高时 2 万吨下降到目前不足 2 千吨。

酸雨会对生物及土壤造成严重的威胁，陕西省环保局经 10 余年监测发现，陕西省不仅出现了酸雨，并已形成了以西安为中心的较为严重的三角形酸雨区。降水的 pH 值在 4.85~5.30。位于三角形区域内的秦岭山脉已受到酸雨的危害。秦岭因生物多样性极为丰富，被誉为“生物基因库”。处于腹地的略阳县和商州市酸雨频率加大，酸度加重，对秦岭的生物多样性以及农业生产已造成重大损失，酸雨的危害已不仅在陕西省，在其他省区也是一个严重的威胁。

此外水域的污染造成珍贵鱼种的绝灭也是值得注意的问题。淮王鱼是生长在淮河中游，安徽省凤台县境内的稀有鱼种。此鱼品质优良，但自 80 年代后期至今，淮河污染日益严重，使淮王鱼失去生存条件而灭绝。乡镇企业的短期行为是导致环境严重污染的重要原因。上海大学已有课题组对我国从南到北几个大的水系；如珠江、长江、黄浦江、黄河和松花江的水源水和自来水反复采样测试，发现这些地区的水源水和自来水的污染都相当严重，其中最严重的是淮河流域，污染源是流域内几千个小造纸厂和近万家小皮革厂。

1.2.3 偷猎走私

中国有一句古话，称为靠山吃山、靠海吃海。狩猎是一部分山区、林区群众或一部分少数民族的传统，利用野生动、植物作为药物来治病也是中国历史的遗产。在过去人口少，资源量大时，不仅是合理的，并对世界的医药学作过重大贡献。与近十多年来的偷猎、滥挖有本质的区别。随着市场经济的发展，野生动、植物的偷猎、滥挖走私行为越来越严重，成为生物多样性受威胁、甚至灭绝的非常重要的原因之一。偷猎走私行为所涉及的野生动、植物遍及全国以及各个生物类群。只要有可赚钱的均在遭灭之列。江西省吉安县破获从广西资源县潜入境的非法狩猎团伙，在东固林区非法猎到国家一级保护的珍稀动物山鹿以及 3 头野牛等动物。1980 年至今，东固有 8 只虎、豹，40 多只山鹿，近千只山麂等珍稀的动物被猎杀；广西是我国西南的门户，与越南有近 2000km 长的边境线，边贸交易中珍稀野生动物成为最活跃的商品，其中包括国家一、二级和地方重点保护动物，如巨蜥、穿山甲、山瑞、沙鲨、合龟、懒猴、虎斑蛭、斑鹫等。据自治区林业公安处测算，仅弄尧一个边贸点，一年就走私、倒卖各类野生动物 13.2 万头(只)，各种龟鳖 6.84 万 kg。可可西里地区有多种国家一级保护野生动物，如野牦牛、藏野驴、藏羚羊、雪豹、黑颈鹤、岩羊、盘羊、雪鸡等，为此这地方成为捕杀珍稀野生动物武装犯罪团伙猖狂的场所。1994 年治多县委副书记兼治多县西部工委书记杰桑·索南达杰与犯罪团伙搏斗不幸以身殉职。非法野生动物交易已成为国际社会继武器和毒品走私后的第三大走私活动，根据 CITES 的数据，仅濒危动物的交易额每年达 50 亿美元。隼，是飞禽中的骄子，飞行速度快，能从空中捕捉飞翔的猎物，能大量捕食害虫和鼠类。在生态平衡中起重要作用，是国家二级保护动物。在青海境内，1994 年查处到从巴基斯坦和我国境外偷猪者 60 多人，1995 年 9 月一个月竟查获境外偷猎者 118 人。这批外国偷猎者是利用隼来贩运千克以上的海洛因等毒品。一只猎隼在境外价格高达 30 万元，偷猎者直接转卖牟取暴利。

野生动物偷猎走私的严重几乎遍及全国各省，按新闻媒体报道，“云南野生动物面临灭顶之灾”。马龙县马过河是经营野味的“王国”。1996 年云南省将打击非法猎杀、倒卖、加工、走私野生动物列入“严打”内容。一个月内各地林业厅查获非法经营野生动物 1715 只(条)。其中国家一级保护动物巨蜥 24 条、懒猴 9 只、蟒 2 条、大象皮 1 张；国家二级保护动物穿山甲 70 只、红腹锦鸡 7 只、眼镜蛇 188 条、爪陆龟 1 只、豹骨 1 架、豹皮 2 张。问题的严重在于享受野味的竟是领导。1996 年昆明一大饭店 4 只孔雀被杀后上宴，赴宴者竟是数十位参加社会活动的各界名流。

偷捕偷猎的面涉及各种生物类群，只要有钱可赚都有铤而走险者，新疆天山深处的天然公园巩乃斯的棕熊、雪豹、马鹿被偷猎，名贵中草药雪莲、党参、贝母等也遭破坏性采挖。有私贩子开专车收购雪莲，等候卖雪莲的人群蜂拥而上。广东湛江市东风市场随意摆卖益鸟，虽经登报批评，但却变本加厉。每个市场售出的各种益鸟多达六七百只。生物类群中也包括蝴蝶。据报道，中科院一个研究员与一投机商合作筹办所谓中国珍稀昆虫保护协会，在广东、福建、湖北一带大量捕捉贩卖蝴蝶，非法牟利数十万元。日本人在云南偷捕过价值 70 万元的蝴蝶。在第 19 届世界昆虫学大会在北京召开之际，竟然有一些不法蝴蝶商乘机搞起蝴蝶标本的公开买卖。

中国的偷捕、偷猎所以屡禁不止原因是多方面的，其中有群众的无知、上层社会各界名流缺乏保护意识，还包括其他要解决的问题，例如，野生动物如此丰富的青海省，负责保护工作的林业公安人员却仅有 270 人，平均每 $2600km^2$ 以上才有一人；地方财政措施极为不利，林业公安的装备极为落后；此外还有有关部门对盗猎分子打击不力，如 1991 年发生青海湖毁岛案件中，6 名盗猎分子竟公然在青海湖野生动物自然保护区核心区三块白岛上拣鸟蛋、毁鸟窝、大肆捕杀斑头雁，鸬鹚等水禽，被有关部门抓获后，竟以每人罚款 300 元后全部释放。

1.2.4 过度捕捞和水产养殖

中国海域辽阔、跨越热带、亚热带和温带 3 个气候带，有渤海、黄海、东海和南海四大海域，其中渤海是中国的内海。海岸线长达 1.8 万 km 左右，分布有平原型、山地丘陵型和生物型等多种类型的海岸，海域内岛屿星罗棋布，浅海滩涂面积约为 $13.4km^2$，以上形成了各种不同类型的生态系统。因此中国的浮游生物、潮间生物、浅海底栖生物等都非常丰富，如海洋鱼类就有 1694 种，其中软骨鱼类 175 种、硬骨鱼类 1519 种。过去一到鱼汛季节，大量的海产生物丰收，大黄鱼、小黄鱼等海产品消费不完，渔民们做成腌鱼、鱼干等保存起来。随着人口增长，消费量随之大量增长，海产生物资源日益枯竭。以胶东沿海为例，原来盛产刀鱼、鲅鱼、黄花鱼、牙片鱼、其他各种鱼及贝类，目前资源量已经很小，收购价格飞涨，造成所谓的“海鲜王国吃鱼难”。渤海湾的有些地方甚至到虾、蟹难觅的地步。如河北黄骅拥有 55km 长海岸线，渔区面积达 $116km^2$，目前渔民下一次海仅能捕获几十公斤、几公斤海产品，甚至有时放空，原因是自从 1986 年以来，渤海湾地区就出现冬季或早春就捕蟹，并是用耙子无限制地灭绝式捕捞，使海蟹及其他海产品已濒临灭绝。造成海产资源匮乏的重要原因一是由于沿岸每天都有大量的污水排入沿海，造成水质长期污染，严重影响水产资源生存环境，产量逐年下降；其次是个体捕捞渔民逐年增多。他们中的大多数使用自制网具，网扣标准达不到国家有关规定，个体渔民不顾是否封海进行非法灭绝式捕捞；第三是由于渔政部门人员较少、装备落后，管辖的海域面广，执法力度又不够，导致长年的非法滥捕。海洋生物多样性中的不少物种已濒临灭绝的危险。

在淡水方面，主要有长江、黄河、黑龙江、珠江等为代表的水系。流域长度大于 100km 的河流有 50 000 多条，全国大小湖泊 24 800 多个，总面积达到 $83\,400km^2$，因此水生生物资源极为丰富。与海洋一样，浮游生物、底栖生物和鱼类的物种多样性在世界上都在前列的，各地都还有各自的特有种，尤其云、贵一带特有种尤其丰富。在生物资源中，与人民生活关系最密切，经济价值最大的应算鱼类资源，可是也遭到海洋同样的命运。由于过度捕捞，自然资源已大幅度下降，不少地区的物种已经灭绝。目前中国食用鱼类主要靠淡水养殖，青鱼、草鱼、鲢鱼和鳙鱼四大名鱼世界闻名，养殖的产量也占世界第一位。

淡水情况基本与海洋一样，生态环境日益恶化，管理体制不顺，乱捕滥捞造成不少流域与湖泊水产资源枯竭，如著名的洞庭湖，从事渔业生产的渔船有一万多艘，大多数用害具、害法来捕鱼，如拦江网、布围子、泥围子、密网、电船、甚至用炸药、毒药来捕鱼，这样的捕法能把大鱼、小鱼一网打尽。一艘一般的电动捕鱼船能将3~4m深，3~4m宽水域内的大小鱼全打光。每年5~8月，平均被电船残杀的幼尾可达800万尾。据沅江市渔政站统计，甲鱼、乌龟、才鱼、黄鳝、洞庭华鳅等特种水产，过去产量可达8000吨，现不足1000吨。近年来，沅江市外湖鲜鱼年捕捞量为7万多担，其中约70%是害业捕捞的，整个生物多样性受到严重的威胁。湖泊是这样，大江中的特种鱼类有的已到了灭绝的边缘，如长江鲥鱼(*Macrura reeuesii*)以其肉质鲜嫩而闻名，但这种特有种已基本绝迹。中华鲟(*Acipenser sinensis*)这白垩纪留下来的孑遗种、活化石也已受到很大威胁。又如世界裂腹鱼中的珍稀物种，我国特有种新疆大头鱼是国家一级保护物种，50年代开始年产量年年增加，到70年代中期，大头鱼已十分少见，到80年代已几乎绝迹。上面提到的青海鳇鱼(*Huso dauricus*)也几乎遭到同样的命运。泸沽湖裂腹鱼有3个品种，是云南省宁县泸沽湖的特有种，是省级自然保护区泸沽湖“三宝”之一。1993年时省科委曾下达“宁县泸沽湖裂腹鱼保护繁殖”科研项目，但直到1995年都难以寻到种鱼，说明这种珍稀鱼已濒临灭绝，或者已经绝种。专家们分析造成的原因是由于电站拦断了回游路线，乱捕滥炸使湖内越冬的洞穴被破坏、水土流失和水污染使鱼产卵场所被破坏，另一个原因可能是鱼子大多数被杂鱼吃掉，生存艰难。

不法分子不仅破坏渔业资源还大肆破坏湖泊。如内蒙的呼伦湖，也称达赉湖，水面达23万公顷。由于滥捕乱捞，近十年来，渔业资源发生很大变化，优质鱼产量急剧下降。在1992年，来自黑龙江、吉林、河北、山东等11个省区的无业人员近700人，动用200多条船在“嘎拉达白辛”核心保护区进行捕鱼、猎鸟、拣蛋、捣巢，甚至点燃芦苇，大火持续3天3夜，核心区内3600多公顷的芦苇被焚，在这里繁殖的大、小天鹅、白天鹅、丹顶鹤等40多种国家重点保护珍禽和100多种水禽的栖息环境被毁于一旦，同年10月达赉湖被确定为国家级自然保护区，但达赉湖自然保护区水域至今没有统一的机构来管理。

由于自然资源破坏严重，政府对海产及淡水养殖予以特殊的重视以满足人民对水产品日益增长的需要。目前中国水产品中，不管海洋还是淡水，养殖所得产量占总产量中的很大比例。但最近报道，海产养殖若管理不善会给生态环境造成破坏，首先渔业养殖可能对海洋沿岸的水草地和原始峡湾等环境造成破坏，如鲑鱼和虾类的养殖已给生态环境造成非常严重的影响，其中虾类养殖对草滩和茂密的矮树丛造成的破坏尤为严重，而草滩、树丛能为热带和亚热带地区海洋生物的生长提供大部分营养及减缓海潮对海岸的冲击力。一般虾类产品是在海岸附近挖掘的池塘里养殖的，养虾池可以不受海潮侵袭，但却对海岸侵蚀严重，其破坏的力量是不可低估的。此外，高密度养殖会使疾病蔓延，病原体沉入死虾和饲料形成的淤泥中，使虾池得停止养殖了3~6年后才能再用，于是养殖者只能另觅草滩和稻田挖新的池养虾，给环境造成严重的破坏。在国际上养虾造成沿海环境的破坏，养殖鲑鱼对海底造成污染已屡见不鲜。由于喂鱼的饲料是鱼粉，造成惊人的浪费，大部分鱼粉同鱼类一起沉入海底，可使一些海湾发出类似养猪场的臭味。每到夏季由于海藻和细菌大量繁殖，一些海湾的水变成淡红色。此外疾病也会由此迅速传播。细菌感染的网箱养殖鱼从网箱中逃脱，会很容易把疾病传播到野生鱼群中。

以上这些都是造成水生或海洋生物多样性严重受威胁，甚至灭绝的主要原因，但威胁或灭绝到何种地步，要有定性和定量的结论还有待做详细的研究。

1.2.5　高新技术发展的影响

在上文中已有专门一节讨论生物技术，尤其是 GMOs 释放后对环境的影响，也已讨论过我国 GMOs 释放的情况，应该说我国存在的问题还是比较多的。

首先要建立起切实可操作的法规，并且执法要严。我国有关生物安全的第一个法规是针对基因工程药物的，即 1990 年制定的“基因工程产品的质量控制标准”。按法规规定，基因工程药物的质量必须满足安全性的要求。对基因工程产品普遍适用的是 1993 年 12 月 24 日由国家科委第 17 号令发布的《基因工程安全管理办法》。《办法》规定了我国基因工程工作的管理体系，按潜在危险程度，将基因工程分为四个安全等级，并规定了分级审批权限。应该说，这《办法》太原则，可操作性不强，约束力不强。农业部在 1996 年 7 月 10 日发布了第 7 号令，即“农业生物基因工程安全管理实施办法”。这是一个具体、可操作性强的法规。当然，对中国的情况来说更重要的是执法要严。另一个问题是 GMOs 释放的危机要让人们有真正的认识可能还有相当一段时间，更重要的是针对生物安全进行系统的科学研究，要针对中国的国情作出科研的具体安排；并对已释放的 GMOs 对环境影响，对人类健康的影响进行长期的监测。

信息高速公路是本世纪 90 年代前后才发展起来的新技术，对它的构想与启动曾赢得一片赞扬，的确可为人们的信息传递和经济与军事等各个领域带来巨大的贡献。但为时不久，国内环境界的一些人士已经把高速信息公路看作将是 21 世纪初期最大的环境破坏技术。未来学家预测在未来的一二十年内，信息高速公路将使残留的森林、荒野、植物、动物更快地绝灭，原因是“在家上班”使人口向乡间疏散。随着信息高速公路的建设，人口向大城市流动的趋势将被逆转。人们可到拥有蓝天、绿树的广大农村或原野去建别墅，在那边他们可以享受到过去在城市所能享有到的一切。过去数百年中，尽管世界人口不断剧增，但只是高度集中在占地球陆地面积 20% 的城镇里。有人以美国为例，如果每户人家都在城市以外建造一个理想住宅而占用几英亩土地的话，那么整个美国大陆的森林和空地行将毁坏。

1.2.6　全球气候变化的影响

世界三大环境热点是酸雨、臭氧层破坏和温室效应，由于 CO_2 浓度提高导致全球气候变暖。最近美国一些科学家经过长期研究后认为，地球上众多的白蚁和地球升温和臭氧层耗损有着某种直接的关系。科学家们在危地马拉热带雨林中发现许多树上筑满了巨大的蚁巢，用口袋收集，很快袋子里充满了甲烷。在非洲肯尼亚有同样的实验证明。据估算，每年全世界白蚁释放出的甲烷约 1 亿多吨，占释放到大气中甲烷量的 25%~30%。

此外，牛科动物在打嗝时也会排出甲烷气体，而牛科动物平均每 40 秒钟打一次嗝，积少就会成多。科学家认为目前南极上空臭氧层形成的巨大空洞是亿万年以来一点一点形成的，一些动物也是危害臭氧的元凶。20 世纪以来工业严重污染只是使这个空洞迅速扩大而已。此外，还有科学家认为森林也会污染大气，森林本身会产生各类挥发性物质并不断向大气排放。其排放量相当可观，如青冈栎和白杨所产生的异戊二烯量，可达到该树种经光合作用所得到的碳量的 2%，森林排放的大量挥发性物质，可扩散到森林附近的城市与城市大气中的氮氧化物结合而生成臭氧，从而污染大气环境。植物在气温越高的条件下异戊二烯的排放量就越大。

上面谈到的是由于动物和植物的因素造成全球气候变化，而人类活动的影响又是怎样呢？实际上这问题已不仅仅是一个科学的问题，而是带有政治性质的问题。由 100 多个国家 2500 多名科学家、气候学家组成“气候变化政府间工作组”。在 1990 年工作组第一次报告中，专家们虽然提出人为产生的 CO_2 和 CH_4 等温室气体增加，但还隐讳地表示，确定上几个世纪以来全球平均温度的上升是否由此引起还为时过早。到 1995 年 11 月工作组在马德里召开会议时，工作组第一次正式承认全球性的气候变化是由人为因素造成的。报告指出，温室气体浓度在持续升高，最近几年已成为 1860 年以来气温最高的年份，与会代表已同意人类影响气候这一说法，但沙特阿拉伯、科威特等石油大国反对“人类影响全球变暖”的看法，因为石油国家的炼油业向空气排放大量温室气体必将成为指责对象。报告的措辞也是争论的问题，经多方的平衡能达成的措辞是“多方面的证据显示，人类对地球气候有一定影响”。

尽管这样，还有一些科学家认为全球变暖不仅仅是由于温室气体引起的，人类对气候变暖的成因还有许多不解之谜。不久前格陵兰冰川研究所提供的证据表明，早在 8200 年前，地球气温突然下降大约 4℃，持续 200 年后又突然变暖，其原因显然与人类活动无关，而是地球系统存在着某些自发振荡现象。一位美国科学家根据对冰川的研究认为，中高纬度地区变暖的原因，也许在于被称为“北大西洋振荡”的气候自然波动。在过去 130 年里，这种因暖洋流使大气获得额外能量而形成的“自然振荡”曾经发生过两次。一次在 1900~1930 年，另一次是从 70 年代后期至今，中高纬度地区因此而变暖。一位从事树木年轮学研究的美国气候学家对古树桩残迹研究发现，美国加利福尼亚在遥远的过去也曾经经历过极严酷的“热浪”袭击，分别发生在 1112 年前和 1350 年前，这年代与史载的全球变暖巧合。一些从事太阳活动研究的科学家最近指出，太阳黑子活动周期长度变化与全球冷暖相吻合，地球气候曲线总是紧随太阳黑子活动周期长短的变化而起伏，20 世纪 30、40 年代及 80 年代以来，太阳黑子周期最短(9.6 年)，因此全球气候变暖。这些研究不仅较好地解释了历史上地球经受多次“热浪”侵扰的原因，同时表明，人类活动造成的温室效应不是影响气候变化的唯一因素，还有太阳活动等自然因素。

不少科学家指出，气候变暖，南极地区一些冰山的脆性也随之增加，结果导致飘浮的冰山在海洋不断出现，并使海平面在较短时间内上升了将近 6m。挪威科学家对最近 17 年来所收集的大量资料进行分析后得出结论：北极地区的结冰表面正一天天地缩小。1978~1987 年期间，该地区每年春夏两季融化的积冰面积都在 3.2km^2 左右，而最近几年都达到 35.4 万 km^2。由于海平面上升，潜在的威胁可使岛屿及沿海大片陆地将渐渐沉没在海中，还会加剧风暴潮灾害，使现有江海堤防工程的减灾防御能力不断减弱，洪涝威胁不断增大。此外还会出现盐水入侵，土壤盐渍化，对海岸带的侵蚀加重等灾害。由于气候变暖，干旱、热浪等自然灾害频发，有人曾预言，假如气温上升 4℃，我国干旱区将平均每年增加近万平方公里，而湿润地区将每年减少 1 万多 km^2，几乎整个中国北部将趋于干旱化，从而导致我国缺水形势更加严峻。我国的海平面上升速度还比全球平均上升速度快。近 50 年来，我国近海海平面上升速率为 1.2~2.0mm，大于全球海平面 1.1~1.7mm 的上升速率。按专家们实测，天津沿海、珠江三角洲、长江口区的相对海平面上升率较大，这与沿海经济发达地区，抽用地下水超量，这些地下水经使用后排放到江河入海，造成地面下沉，增加排入大海的排水量有关。

但是，科学家也发现，气候变暖也是人类自身发生发展所不可缺少的环境条件，大约 1 万年前，地球结束了漫长的冰河期逐步走向温暖期，人类才从冰川中“解脱”出来。大约 6000 年前，地球进入近万年以来最温暖的时期之一，人类生存环境获得空前改善，埃及、巴比伦、印度及中国的四大文明发祥地才相继诞生。据科学家考证，当时我国大部分地区气温比现代偏高 1~4℃，东部海面比现在高出 1~3m，沿海发生过大范围海侵现象。但是，我国大部分地区侵水量都有增无减。我国干旱、沙漠面积比现在都小得多。有关研究还表明，在 3400 年前的殷商时代、春秋战国及盛唐等我国历史上几个重要社会经济发展时期，也与我国乃至全球气候变暖相吻合。

至于气候变暖多数人都看作是灾难，对人类的生存与发展造成威胁，对生物多样性的影响从看到的报道也是不利的，如奥地利生态学家发现，由于全球变暖，阿尔卑斯山寒冷环境下纤弱的小型植物的生存范围正在缩小，所有植物都日渐向高处迁徙，其中的 40~50 种植物可能因上升到太高的海拔高度而无法适应环境，一批高寒物种面临灭绝。还有报道，近 40 年来，由于加利福尼亚太平洋沿海海水温度的升高，导致这里的海洋浮游生物减少 80%。认为如果地球变暖持续下去，将对海洋生物的生长带来灾难性的影响。同样，科学家发现近年来从大西洋回游到英国河流中产卵的大马哈鱼越来越少，原因是随着全球变暖，西北大西洋水的温度分布发生了变化，其北部水温因北极冰山融化后大量冷水流入湾中而下降。南部水温则因全球变暖而上升，这种变化破坏了大马哈鱼的生存环境，至于全球变暖对生物多样性的影响将是肯定的。由于各个物种对气候变化的适应性，遗传忍耐力的差异以及繁殖与散布能力的差异各不相同，估计会有一部分物种灭绝，但也同时会有新种产生。

1.2.7　外来种引入的影响

外来种的入侵，特别是具杂草性的植物种或是对作物造成毁灭性灾害的一些节肢动物的入侵对当地生物多样性的威胁以及造成当地农业、林业或其他各方面经济损失以及人类健康的影响是相当严重的。在国内外都有很多的例子，突出的例子是从国外引入的一种认为它能使污染的水体净化又能作为猪喂料的植物——水葫芦。水葫芦也是一种杂草性的植物，新闻媒体曾经报道，云南滇池本来是美丽而具多样性生物的有名的高海拔湖泊。但近年来 80%的水面已被水葫芦所覆盖，并且很难或需花很大的投资才能去掉。

由于它大面积的覆盖，湖泊中的阳光及氧都为它所占，对其他生物造成很大的威胁。

豚草，包括普通豚草(*Ambrosia artemissifolia*)及三裂叶豚草(*A. trifida*)起源于北美洲Soniran地区，分别在30年代和50年代传入我国并迅速扩散，现已扩散到东北、华北、华东、华中地区15个省市。严重发生地区每平方米可达1686株，种子量极大，达每株结3000~62 000粒，并具三次休眠性，植株高大，存活力强，适于不同环境中生长，在被人类开垦过的地带，很快可被它占领成为单一的群落，是对农田、农牧业生产以及城市绿化严重危害的一种恶性杂草。国家环保局及中国农科院生防所谢红等(1997)曾发表文章研究了其在沈阳的危害性及所造成的经济损失，他们从农作物减产、阻碍交通及影响人体健康等角度来评估其环境经济价值。首先是对农作物的影响方面，由于豚草的恶性杂草性质，不采取措施可能成为农田的优势种而导致农作物减产，并耗竭很大地力使土地越来越贫瘠。据调查在1993年共侵入8400亩农田，减产18%，按每亩140元产值计，损失21.2万元；豚草的疯长会影响到公路、铁路的正常通行甚至恶性交通事故。还是以1993年计,共投入95个人/月的劳力来清除豚草来计算造成交通损失费为9.3万元；豚草的花粉是人类变态反应症，即枯草热或花粉热的主要致病原，造成花粉过敏者大量眼睛流泪、咳嗽、哮喘、皮炎甚至到不能工作。沈阳市发病率达1.52%，1993年时沈阳市人口以450万计，发病人数达6.84万，豚草造成健康损失费为803.7万。这三种损失费的总数为834.2万元。由于其杂草特性对生物多样性威胁或灭绝所造成的损失和对景观的破坏由于数据资料不足暂时还无法计算。

2 保护生物多样性已采取的及应采取的措施

我国生物多样性的保护和持续利用存在着上述7个方面的问题，可能是一个比较全面的论述。这些问题的解决不外乎从下列3个方面着手：第一首先重要的是加强各级领导以及广大群众对生物多样性保护及持续利用的认识，使他们真正认识到保护动物就是保护人类自己，保护植物就是保护人类自己的道理；第二是针对上述问题采取有关措施，重要的是立法和加强执法；第三是要使生物多样性能真正保护起来，并做到持续利用就应该加强科学研究。让各级领导及广大群众知道如何做才能把生物多样性保护好，如何做才能让生物多样性被子孙万代持续利用下去。

2.1 已采取的措施

针对上述三个方面，我国政府确实已采取了不少措施。首先是我国在国际上相当早地成为《生物多样性公约》的缔约国之一，国际上自1995年起，每年12月29日定为“生物多样性日”的活动开展以来，我国政府每年都举办活动。此外，通过新闻媒体及其他渠道揭露我国在生物多样性保护及持续利用方面所存在的问题并介绍、宣传在这方面执行得好的单位及个人，以及开展爱鸟周、在电视中开辟“人与自然”等栏目来对群众进行宣传教育。政府已颁布了与生物多样性保护密切相关的法规，例如“野生动物保护法”、“全国人民代表大会常务委员会关于惩治捕杀国家重点保护的珍贵、濒危野生动物犯罪的补充规定”、“中华人民共和国自然保护区条例”、“森林和野生动物类型自然保护区管理办法”、“国务院关于禁止犀牛角和虎骨贸易的通知”、“中国自然保护区发展规划纲要”以及“中国21世纪议程”中专门有关生物多样性的一章等。在科学研究方面，在于生物多样性有关的科研我国长期来有所积累，在“八五”期间，国家有关部门及中国科学院都针对生物多样性的研究立了项目。尽管如此，生物多样性的保护及持续利用的科研方面应该说仅处于起步的阶段，要解决好上述问题，还有大量的工作要做。

2.2 今后应采取的措施

2.2.1 加强教育

首先重要的是切实加强对各级领导的教育。有计划地对从中央到地方的各级领导加强教育，印度的经验是值得借鉴的(季维智等，1996)。印度有一个国家级的野生生物研究所，是全国唯一专门从事野生生物保护的研究所。这研究所主要有两个任务，除从事研究工作外，还要为各级有关领导及全国自然保护区的干部在自然保护及野生动物保护方面进行培训。国家拨给经费中的40%专门用于培训，该研究所为培训人员的工作配备有专门的设施及食宿条件。从野生动物生物学、野生动物健康、种群和栖息地管理、自然保护区规划和管理以及促进保护意识等方面进行系统的授课和野外实习的培训。对国家公园的管理干部进行9个月授予毕业文凭的野生生物管理训练。这种班同时强调理论和实践的训练，另一种班的培训对象是森林管理官员，这班是3个月的野生生物管理培训，结业后也发给证书，对这样的干部强调的是实践的培训。研究所同时还不断地举办一些1~4星期的短训班或研讨班。这种班可以侧重在某一个专题或技术方面，例如野生生物的普查、栖息地的评估等。这种培训的对象则是针对资深的森林管理官员、动物园管理人员、各级行政官员以及非政府组织人士等。这个研究所对加强各级行政官员对生物多样性保护的意识，对各类从事生物多样性保护，特别是自然保护区各级管理人员的培训，对印度野生动物的有效保护以及自然保护区的有效管理都起到积极的作用。正如我们在参观印度 Sariska 老虎保护区时，当地 Rajasthan 邦负责森林和野生动物保护的副长官就非常熟悉当地野生动物的情况，知道豹出没的途径，傍晚时刻听到猴群不寻常的叫声，就知道豹不久就会从这里附近经过(钱迎倩等，1996b)。

生物多样性保护和持续利用的教育要从学龄前儿童开始抓起，在小学、中学的教科书中由浅入深地加入生物多样性的内容。全国众多出版社中的一部分，应有专门的人员从事这方面的编辑工作，从出版社不同性质出发出版适合各种年龄层次，或者不同业务水平的各种出版物。这方面也有可参考的资料(钱迎倩，1995b)。以美国为例，国家级、国际及各个州的政府和非政府组织从事保护工作的机构和个人有近2000个。不包括学报级的刊物，以上这些机构的各种各样的出版物就有1650种左右。全国最大、最主要的一个组织是国家野生生物联盟(National Wildlife Federation)，其任务是教育、鼓励和帮助各种组织、机构甚至个人来保护野生生物和其他自然资源以及环境。在全国51个州，加上波多黎各和维尔京群岛共有530万会员、支持者和分支机构。这联盟本身就有4种出版物：首先是该联盟的会员有双月刊的保护杂志，“国家野生生物”(National Wildlife)和“国际野生生物”(Internalional Wildlife)；对 6~12 岁的儿童有月刊，一种介绍自然的杂志，称为“Ranger Rick”；为学龄前儿童则有一套自然系列丛书，称为“你们的大后院”(Your Big Backyard)。联盟下设多个部门，开展多种多样的教育、服务和其他活动。每年出版一本“保护指南” (Conservation Directory)，1994 年已是第 38 版，说明已有很长的历史。

计划生育已成为我国的国策，对生物多样性的保护也应该成为我国的国策。应该看到我国这么庞大的人口数字,如果生物多样性得不到保护或者说继续以现在的速度锐减,就会直接威胁到国家与人民的生存与发展。我们可以把生物多样性保护和计划生育看作为一个事情的两个方面，根据我国国情，中央到地方各级政府应该要像抓计划生育一样的来抓生物多样性的保护。

2.2.2 加强立法、严肃执法

在存在问题这一段落里可以看到我国在自然环境破坏及生物多样性受威胁程度乃至灭绝的情况，虽然已立下了不少法，出台了不少措施，但仍呈发展的趋势。正像王丙乾同志指出的:“生态环境破坏的范围在扩大，程度在加剧。环境污染和生态破坏已经成为制约一些地区经济发展、影响改革开放和社会稳定的重要因素”。究其原因，王灿发曾发表长篇文章“论自然保护立法存在的问题及完善途径”(王灿发，1996)，作过专门的论述，其中很多意见是针对国情提出来的，很有参考的价值。结合我本人的观点，综述如下：

我国的自然保护法体系不健全。我国虽在 1987 年颁布了《中国自然保护纲要》，但还缺乏一部综合性的自然保护法。有关法律散见于污染防治法、自然资源法和其他有关法律、法规中，使各种立法之间缺乏协调和配合。甚至不同法律、法规之间衔接不好，相互矛盾，造成执法困难。1994 年 8 月 11 日中国环境报登载着一个明显的例子，内蒙古大兴安岭林业管理局反映《森林法》、《草原法》和《土地法》之间衔接不顺，在有些地区既发林权证，又发土地证，致使林区部分地区毁林开荒十分严重，仅大杨树地区十几年已开荒 10 多万公顷，部分地区林缘已后退 50~100km。立法的不顺造成人为的林农争地，林牧争地，毁林开荒，造成生物多样性的丧失。在野生植物保护、湿地保护、生物多样性保护等方面，不仅没有相应的法律，而且连行政法规都没有，这就使得对这些自然环境及经济和社会发展水平很不平衡。一个法律或法规不可能顾及全国各地方的特殊情况，应该还有专门的自然保护地方性法规。

体制不完善。生物多样性的保护不是孤立的，至少涉及自然保护区的建立和管理、野生动物的贸易、迁地保护等各个方面的问题，这就涉及许多管理部门的事业，作为环境保护中一个组成部分的生物多样性保护，虽然国家明确履行《生物多样性公约》的牵头单位是国家环保总局，可是没有一个法律明确把生物多样性保护置于环境保护行政主管部门的统一监督管理之下，如野生动物保护法这一涉及物种保护的法律，也没有赋予环境保护行政主管部门任何监督管理职责。由于管理体制不顺，各有关行政主管部门的职责分工不明确，相互交叉过多，再加上缺乏统一监督管理的协调机制，结果有的问题几个部门同时在管，互相扯皮，争论不休；有的方面则无人负责，互相推诿，造成漏洞。

缺乏行之有效的管理制度。法律的规定是通过法律中的一些制度和措施来体现的。没有一定的制度和措施，只有笼统规定的法律或法规是很难得到实施的，或者说不具可操作性的。我国与生物多样性有关的某些法律或法规就存在这类的问题。例如野生动物保护法规定的受害补偿制度、草原法规定的防止过量放牧制度等，都没有具体的实施办法，结果使一些因保护野生动物而受到损害的当事人得不到应有的补偿，使草原的过牧状况得不到扭转。又如草原法中笼统地规定“国家保护草原生态系统”，渔业法规定采取措施“保护和改善渔业水域的生态环境”，水法规定“国家保护水资源，采取有效措施，保护自然植被，种树种草，涵养水源，防治水土流失，改善生态环境”。究竟采取什么措施，怎样保护和改善生态环境，则没有具体的措施。这些规定是难以得到有效实施的。再如上文中提到 GMOs 释放的问题，国家科委令第 17 号“基因工程安全管理办法”中例如分为四等的安全等级中的低度、中度、高度危险的标准是什么就没有明确的规定，由于这标准不明确，第三章中的审批部门就随着一起不明确。上文中指出在 GMOs 释放的面积上，我国在国际上是名列前茅的，但是又是否经过第八条中规定的“应当进行安全性评价，评估潜在危险，确定安全等级，制定安全控制方法和措施”以及按第十一条规定的“从事遗传工程体释放，应当对遗传工程体安全性，释放目的，释放地区的生态环境，释放方式，监测方法和控制措施进行评价，确定释放工作的安全等级”来实施呢？似乎都还缺乏有效的管理制度。

尽快出台“生物多样性保护法”。按照目前我国生物多样性面临威胁或者说已有相当一部分物种已经灭绝的情况，尽早出台“生物多样性保护法”是非常必要的。这个法律或法规的内容应克服上述的弊病外，应考虑到我国目前的国情，即一是我国正处于经济建设大高潮的时期以及生物多样性在我国丰富的地区往往是贫困的地区，法律或法规的条款应考虑到当地群众的生存问题，即如何能持续利用生物多样性的问题。

我国目前正处在由过去的计划经济向社会主义市场经济过渡的时期，要制定生物多样性保护法不能不考虑到这个时代背景。例如中国的红树林本来已经所存无几。广西境内红树林分布面积占全国第一位。但由于经济发展需要，广西将成为大西南出海口的大通道。广西钦州湾一带是自治区内红树林分布面积较大的区域，由于建设港口的需要，已有相当数量的红树林遭到砍伐，余下的是否能健康地保留下来，还是严重的问题。“中国生物多样性行动计划”第四章中规定，“谁开发谁保护，谁破坏谁恢复，谁利用谁补偿”(《中国生物多样性保护行动计划》总报告编写组，1998)的政策必须要有具体措施来实现，不要成为一纸空文。

至于当地居民的生存问题也必须要考虑到，特别是建立自然保护区的地区一般来说也是相对贫穷落后的地区。没有具体的措施，由于自然保护区职工工资及建设资金不到位，不仅是当地居民会破坏当地的生物多样性，自然保护区的职工也会参加到破坏的行列中。

执法不严问题应引起足够的重视，要制止由于人类活动引起的生物多样性遭受威胁以至灭绝。立法虽然重要，严格执法更为重要，特别对于各级领导违法更应严惩。报刊上经常可以看到我国当前存在着类似权大还是法大以及地方保护主义等报道，使一系列的法律、法规无法执行下去，应该引起足够的重视。

2.2.3 加强科学研究

生物多样性的科研工作，在国内最早是由中国科学院开始的。1989年底中国科学院成立了生物多样性工作小组。于1990年3月召开了“生物多样性研讨会”，这也是国内有关生物多样性方面第一次科学讨论会。目的在于组织院内的研究力量制订和推动今后这方面的研究计划。在这次会上，当时的中国科学院副院长李振声教授以三个实例说明了：“一个基因可以影响一个国家的兴衰”；“一个物种可以左右一个国家的经济命脉”，以及“一个优良的生态群落的建立不仅可以改善一个地区的生态环境，而且可以使生产与经济向着良性循环的方向发展”，从而在生物多样性三个层次的科研成果上强调了科学研究的重要性(李振声，1990)。当时的中国科学院生物科学与技术局在综述了国际、国内生物多样性现状的基础上，又分析了中国科学院过去的基础及科研力量，强调指出生物多样性是一个亟待研究的课题(钱迎倩，1990)。从而在“八五”期间，在国家科委和中国科学院领导的支持下，生物多样性正式立项，经过5年左右的研究，已经取得一批可喜的成果。

在80年代初期，生物多样性的研究在国际上已开始。国际生物科学联盟(IUBS)在1983年开始的热带10年计划(Decade of the Tropics)中就开展了“热带生态系统的物种多样性及其重要性”研究项目。并在1991年第24次全体会议上提出了“生物多样性的生态系统功能”研究项目。到1992年时，研究内容扩大到研究生物多样性的起源、组成、功能、保持和保护。研究的角度是从遗传到生态系统水平的地球上所有生活的生物体。研究主题发展为4个：即“生物多样性的生态系统功能”；“生物多样性的起源和保持”；“生物多样性的编目和监测”；以及“家养种的野生近缘种的遗传多样性”。同年，环境问题科学委员会(SCOPE)和联合国教科文组织(UNESCO)等两个国际组织参加进来，共同合作把此项目正式定名为DIVERSITAS。

1994年时马克平等根据当时国际上生物多样性研究发展的趋势提出7个方面的研究热点：①生物多样性的调查、编目及信息系统的建立；②人类活动对生物多样性的影响；③生物多样性与生态系统功能；④生物多样性的长期动态监测；⑤物种濒危机制及保护对策的研究；⑥栽培植物与家养动物及其野生近缘种的遗传多样性研究；⑦生物多样性保护技术与对策。这些热点实际上也是综合了国际发展与国外专家的意见，成为在制定“九五”生物多样性研究项目的指导思想。

但是生物多样性研究所涉及的面非常宽，与其他学科交叉的地方很多。国内不少专家提出应明确生物多样性本身是否一门科学，它的内涵与外延又是什么?为之，这课题成为“香山会议”的讨论议题。也正在这段时间里，在1995年DIVERSITAS这一生物多样性全面研究唯一的项目又增加了新的成员，即国际微生物科学联盟(IUMS)、国际科学联盟委员会(ICSU)和国际地圈生物圈计划全球变化和陆地生态系统(IGBP/GCTE)。DIVERSITAS发展到新的阶段；进一步确认了其目的是为了明确生物多样性关键的、前沿的科学问题；促进、加速和催化生物多样性起源、组成、功能、保持和保护等方面的科学研究；为各方面提供生物多样性的状况与地球上生物资源利用的可持续的正确的信息和预测模型。研究主题由 4 个扩大到 9 个组成方面，并用图解分为主要项目及交叉项目两个部分来表示(钱迎倩等，1996a；赵士洞等，1996)。主要项目也就是生物多样性研究的关键领域，是由 5 个方面组成，即：①起源、保持和丧失；②生态系统功能；③编目、分类和相互关系；④评估和监测；⑤保护、恢复与持续利用。另一部分称为交叉项目，是根据问题的重要性和迫切需要而列出的 4 个方面，即：⑥人类的影响范围(human dimensions)；⑦土壤和沉积物的生物多样性；⑧海洋生物多样性；⑨微生物多样性。

为了完善这一新的阶段的项目，1996 年 4 月 22 日 IUBS 又草拟了一个“操作计划”草案,提供 1996 年 7 月在英国伦敦皇家植物园召开的第一届科学指导委员会全体会议以及 1996 年 8 月 23~24 日在匈牙利布达佩斯举行的 IUBS 执行委员会上讨论。这次提出的草案有两个重大的发展，首先是对 1995 年时提出的 9 个方面有了新的提法，重要的对前面 5 个方面有了新的提法，称为核心组分(core elements)，这 5 个方面也不是并列地提出来，而是用图解说明了 5 个方面的相互关系(图 1)。从图 2，1 可以理解为在 5 个核心组分中最后一个方面“生物多样性的保护、恢复和持续利用”既是一个研究方面，又是要想达到的最后目标，前面 4 个组分是为这个研究方面或最后目标服务的。“生物多样性对生态系统功能的作用”又是其中的中心环节，其重要性也就显而易见了。而“起源、保持和变化”“系统学：编目和分类”以及“监测”等三个组成方面是用三个箭头指向“生物多样性对生态系统功能的作用”的研究，说明这三个方面是后者开展研究的基础，其中尤其是处于中间位置的系统学：“编目和分类”，箭头尤其粗，更说明是基础的基础。对 4 个 STARs，“操作计划”草案中说明它们是 5 个核心组分之间的重要交叉领域，对这些领域的知识，过去经常被忽视或者说过去仅得到有限的重视。由于其重要性，被专门提了出来。在“操作计划”草案中对 9 个方面的内容作了更为详细的叙述，其他国际组织在这些方面的考虑也作了说明。在草案的文本上已提出了第 10 个方面，即淡水生物多样性，但当时尚未展开来谈。

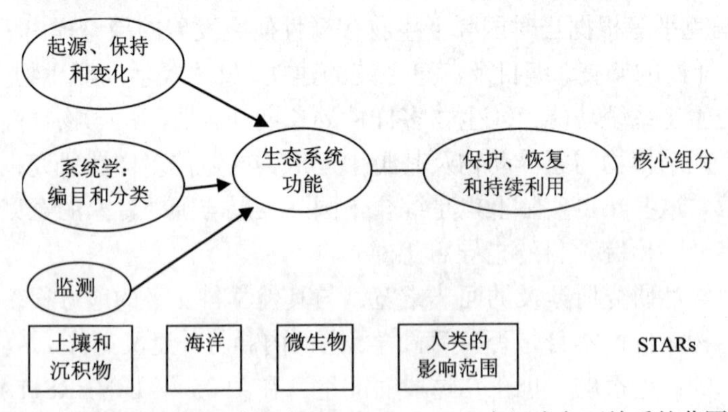

图 1　“操作计划”草案中 DIVERSITAS 9 个组成方面关系的草图

经过 IUBS 执委会讨论后，提出了 1996 年 DIVERSITAS“操作计划”的最后文本(陈灵芝等，1997)。在这个文本中，DIVERSITAS 有 10 个组成方面，淡水生物多样性已正式作为一方面提了出来。对这 10 个研究方面的相互关系，在草案基础上又作了最后的修订，用图解方式在图 2 上表示出来。

这里值得一提的是图 1 和图 2 与 1995 年的图解(钱迎倩等，1996a)上的提法有三处不同。第一，原来提法是“生物多样性的起源、保持和丧失”，而最后定稿时改为“生物多样性的起源、保持和变化”；第二，“生物多样性的生态系统功能”改为“生物多样性对生态系统功能的作用”；第三是增加了“淡水生物多样性”。此外，图 2 中又把四个方面编了号，其间的相互关系更为密切。把“生物多样性对生态系统功能的作用”位置未作变动，编号编为第 1 号。这一方面实际上是 1991 年第 24 次全体会议上已提出的一个唯一的方面，即进一步强调这一研究方面在生物多样性研究中的重要位置。

生物多样性对生态系统功能的作用，归结起来有 7 个大的方面，即：

(1) 生产力和生物量

(2) 土壤结构、养分和分解作用

(3) 水分的分布、平衡和质量

(4) 大气性质及反馈

(5) 生物世代 / 物种相互关系

(6) 景观及流域的结构

(7) 微生物活动

这 7 个方面在 Heywood 等(1995)编著的“全球生物多样性评估”一书中有详细的阐述。

对我国生物多样性研究的几点认识：

(1) 履行《生物多样性公约》当然是各缔约国的政府行为，但是要履行好《公约》，必须有科学研究作为基础，《公约》条款中也明确了科学研究与培训作为履约的主要任务。DIVERSITAS 的研究项目作为生物多样性科学的前沿，必须是符合《公约》条款的要求，科学研究就是为履约服务的，我国是《公约》缔约国之一，科学研究就必须要为履约服务，不同的部门或单位，应根据各自的性质和任务分别在应用、应用基础及基础研究不同角度进行工作。

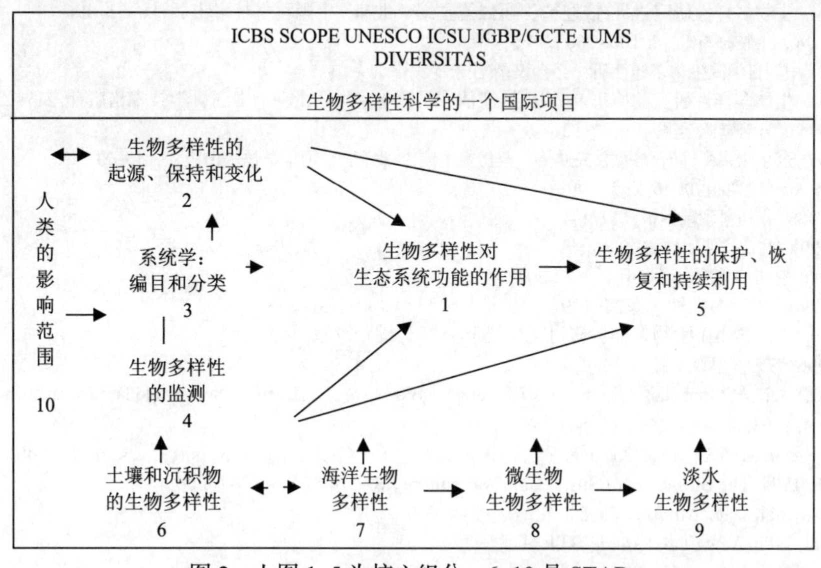

图 2　上图 1~5 为核心组分，6~10 是 STARs

(2) 我国生物多样性丧失是非常严重的，在第一部分从物种、遗传及生态系统三个方面分析我国生物多样性现状的资料都是从已发表的资料中收集到的，但这仅仅是反映了一个小的部分，真实的现状是怎么样？按目前的国情其发展趋势又是如何?政府的决策者必须要掌握这些真实的数据及趋势。中国的各种生态系统的破坏也是惊人的，根据当地自然条件下能使生物多样性恢复的生境恢复也是亟待解决的。这些研究工作应在哪里进行？应该按中国国情从有代表性的优先地区，从不同的角度加以考虑。当然也必须考虑到研究工作及人员的基础。人类的生存就是依赖于地球上的生物多样性，对一些野生动物的养殖，或对一些药用或其他有用植物的栽培当然是持续利用的手段之一，但如何合理持续利用野生的生物多样性，既是主要而经济的途径，也是重要的研究方面。“中国生物多样性保护行动计划”在生物多样性的科研以及各方面的行动都已作了明确的叙述，应该在科研的组织领导、项目的落实以及资金的到位方面都作出明确的安排。

(3) DIVERSITAS 本身是一个国际项目，又是当前一个比较完善的包括了生物多样性研究各个方面的项目。下一步的研究项目的安排除“行动计划”已提出的内容外，应尽可能地与 DIVERSITAS 接轨，这样做既能开展国际合作，又能较快地提高我们的研究水平。

参考文献

王晨等, 1996. 生命科学, **8**: 1~4
王灿发, 1996. 中国环境报, 7 月 6 日, 第三版
陈灵芝, 1993. 中国的生物多样性—— 现状及其保护对策(陈灵芝主编)，科学出版社, 北京, 5
陈灵芝, 1994. 生物多样性研究的原理与方法(钱迎倩、马克平主编)，中国科学技术出版社, 北京, 13~35
阵灵芝等, 1997. 生态学报, **l7**: 565~572
《中国生物多样性国情研究报告》编写组, 1998. 中国生物多样性国情研究报告, 北京: 中国环境科学出版社, 1~430
《中国生物多样性保护行动计划》总报告编写组, 1994. 中国生物多样性保护行动计划, 北京: 中国环境科学出版社, 47~62
洪德元等, 1990. 中国科学院生物多样性研讨会会议录(汪松等编), 北京, 40~44
马克平等, 1994. 生物多样性研究的原理与方法, 北京: 中国科学技术出版社, 1~12
董玉琛, 1993, 生物多样性, **1**: 35~39
董玉琛, 1994. 生物多样性研究进展(钱迎倩、甄仁德主编), 北京: 中国科学技术出版社, 491~496
高立志等, 1996. 生物多样性, **4**: 160~166
钱迎倩, 1990. 中国科学院生物多样性研讨会会议录(汪松等编), 北京, 3~5
钱迎倩, 1994. 生物多样性研究的原理与方法(钱迎倩、马克平主编), 北京: 中国科学技术出版社, 217~224
钱迎倩等, 1995a. 自然资源学报, 10: 322~331
钱迎倩等, 1995b. 生物多样性研究进展(钱迎倩、甄仁德主编)，北京: 中国科学技术出版社，15~23
钱迎倩等, 1996a. 广西植物, **16**: 295~299
钱迎倩等, 1996b. 广西科学院学报，**12**: 1~7
钱迎倩等, 1998. 生态学报, **18**: 1~9
谢红等, 1997. 中国环境报, 1 月 30 日，第 3 版
赵士洞等, 1996. 生物多样性, **4**: 125~129
李振声, 1990. 中国科学院生物多样性研讨会会议录(汪松等编), 北京, 1~2
季维智等, 1996. 广西科学院学报, **12**: 8~15
Anonymous, 1994. In “Systematics Agenda 2000: Charting the Biosphere”，American Society of Plant Taxonotnists et al，pp 16
Falk B W et al, 1994. *Science*, **263** : 1395~1396
Heywood V R et al , 1995. Global Biodiversity Assessment, UNEP, Cambridge University Press, pp. 1~1140
Krattiger A F, 1994. The Biosafety for Sustainable Agriculture, ISAAA/SEI, pp. 247~266
Mikkelsen T R et al, 1996. *Nature*, **380**: 31
Nardlee J et al, 1996. *New Engl J Medie*, **334**: 668~692

本文原载：生物多样性. 1994. 2(1): 54-57

《生物多样性公约》的起草过程与主要内容

马克平　钱迎倩

(中国科学院生物多样性委员)

《生物多样性公约》是生物多样性保护与持续利用进程中具有划时代意义的文件。这是因为：①它是第一份有关生物多样性各个方面的国际性公约；②遗传多样性第一次被包括在国际公约中；③生物多样性保护第一次受到全人类的共同关注。目前已有 150 多个国家在《公约》上签了字。这一文件为全球生物多样性的保护及生物资源的持续、合理的利用奠定了坚实的基础。鉴于目前许多从事生物资源保护、利用和管理的人员以及对此有兴趣的人士还不熟悉或不甚了解该《公约》的现状，有必要对《公约》的产生和主要内容等予以介绍。

1　《公约》的由来

《生物多样性公约》于 1992 年 5 月 22 日在内罗毕讨论通过。继而有 150 多个国家在巴西的里约热内卢联合国环境与发展大会上签署了这份文件。此后，又有中国、美国等国家签署了《公约》。然而，在由联合国环境规划署主持的对该《公约》的起草和进行的政府间谈判开始之前，国际上已有许多专家提出了拟定全球《生物多样性公约》的想法，并积极促进该《公约》的形成。

世界自然与自然资源保护联盟(IUCN)始终致力于《公约》的起草工作，特别是在 1984~1987 年间该联盟探索了形成这一《公约》的可能性，并于 1984~1989 年多次起草和修改《公约》所包括的条款。这份由世界自然与自然资源保护联盟的环境法中心起草的《公约》草案得到了无数专家特别是 IUCN/WWF 植物咨询组的帮助。该草案旨在提出在物种、基因和生态系统水平的生物多样性保护所需的行动。集中在保护地内或保护地外的就地保护。它还包括提出财政资助机制，以在发达国家与发展中国家之间合理分配保护的负担。

1987 年，联合国环境规划署(UNEP)执行委员会，认识到需要增加保护生物多样性的国际努力。因此，由该组织成立了一个特别工作组，调查和形成《公约》框架，以鼓励该领域正在开展的保护活动。同时，提出应该包括在该《公约》之内的其他领域。

该小组于 1988 年底举行的第一次会议认为：已制定的有关生物多样性保护的《公约》只包括生物多样性保护的特殊问题，不能满足全球性的保护生物多样性的需要。就全球而言，已形成的《公约》仅仅涉及了诸如具有全球意义的自然地点(世界遗产公约)、濒危物种贸易的特殊威胁(CITES)和特定的生态系统(拉姆萨尔或湿地公约)。此外，还有一些区域性的自然与自然资源保护公约。总而言之，这些国际公约不能保证全球生物多样性的保护。因此，该组织认为，需要制定一个全球性的法律文件。

人们很快认识到，形成一个包括已有公约的统一的松散公约的想法在法律和技术上都是不可能的。到1990年初，该特别工作组已经认识到迫切需要一个新的全球生物多样性保护公约。该公约是一个建立在已有公约基础上的框架文件。在讨论公约的范围时，人们很快意识到许多国家不仅仅考虑狭义的保护。同时，也有一些国家不准备把讨论仅仅局限于野生资源。因此，公约的范围逐步扩大到包括生物多样性的各个方面，即野生与家养物种的就地和迁地保护；生物资源的持续利用；遗传资源的获取以及相应的技术，包括生物技术的利用和由这些技术得到的惠益的分配，与经遗传修饰的生物(即转基因生物)有关的各种活动的安全性，以及新的财政支持的渠道。

依据IUCN起草的公约草案和后来由世界粮农组织(FAO)起草的草案以及由联合国环境规划署进行的一系列研究，该特别工作组提出大量可以包括在全球生物多样性公约中的条款。UNEP秘书处在这些条款的基础上，起草了《公约》的第一稿。

正式的谈判过程始于1991年2月。此时，该特别小组被指定为《生物多样性公约》政府间谈判委员会(INC)。该委员会，召开了5次专门会议，进行了充分协商。于1992年5月22日《公约》在内罗毕通过而告结束。为了消除《公约》中存在的许多冗余和矛盾，将主要的有争议的问题分为两组，逐条进行讨论。第一组处理概括性的问题，如基本原则、承担的义务、就地和迁地保护的措施以及与其他法律文件的关系。第二组处理有关遗传资源与技术的获得、技术转让、技术援助、财政资助机制和国际合作。此时，距离于1992年6月召开的签署《公约》的联合国环境与发展大会已经很近了，时间十分紧迫。

谈判经常于拂晓结束，就在5月22日这最后一天，甚至在最后的时刻，该《公约》能否被通过，仍然没有把握。如果联合国环境与发展大会召开的日期没有确定的话，该《公约》是不可能在那一天被通过的。尽管如此，6月5日在里约热内卢，在该公约上签字的国家的数目还是空前的。

2　《公约》的主要特点

《生物多样性公约》是一个框架文件，为每一个缔约国如何履行《公约》留下了充分的余地。对于保护的承诺大多以总体目标和方针的形式表达，而不是像有些公约，如国际濒危物种贸易公约(CITES)那样的硬性规定。也不像近来通过的欧共体生境、植物和动物区系的规定那样，确定具体指标。相反，《生物多样性公约》旨在将主要的决策权放在国家水平，不列全球性的清单。

侧重于国家水平的行动，并强调了两个关键条款：条款1说明缔约国同意的目标；条款6要求每个缔约国都要制定国家的生物多样性保护和生物资源持续利用的策略和计划。这一国家策略或计划经常比《公约》规定的义务更具体、深入，并与条款提出的总体目标相一致。

通过包括遗传资源的获取和利用以及技术转让和生物安全即转基因生物释放的安全等议题，该《公约》试图阐述生物多样性的所有细节。通过创造为发展中国家提供资助的机制，以帮助他们履行《公约》，缔约国认识到需要新的更多的资金从发达国家流向发展中国家。结果是该《公约》试图达到一种平衡，即发达国家和发展中国家之间付出与获得的平衡(从这个意义上说，该《公约》与大多数其他保护公约不同，其他公约大多没有这样的意愿去平衡成员国之间的需求)。

3 《公约》的主要内容

3.1 国家主权与人类共同关心的问题

生物多样性应视为人类“共同财富”或“人类遗产”的提法，在早期就遭到反对。因为它意味着人类共同拥有对这一资源以及由此获得的惠益的支配权。相反，强调了对生物资源的主权，而且认识到生物多样性是人类“共同关心”的议题。“共同关心”意味着对生物多样性共同承担着责任，而不意味着自由的或无限制的获取。

国家对于其自然资源的主权权力在序言中提出，在正文中又提到两次。条款 3 原原本本地引用了斯德哥尔摩宣言的第 21 条原则即国家拥有按照其自己的环境政策开发其资源的主权权力。有关遗传资源获取的条款 15 再一次申明国家对其自然资源拥有主权权力，并有权决定对遗传资源的获取。

然而，对于国家主权的强调可以由下列两点得到平衡：①主权本身要求承担的责任；②生物多样性是整个国际社会共同关心的财富这一点所引发的义务。事实上，序言首先强调了“生物多样性保护是人类共同关心的议题”，接着又一次重申国家拥有对其生物资源的主权权力。

《公约》还强调了国家对其生物资源应承担的责任。例如，在条款 3 中，国家必须保证在其自己管辖区内的活动不能危害其他国家或其管辖区以外地区的环境，序言中已经申明各缔约国有责任保护他们的生物多样性并且以可持续的方式利用生物资源。文中还就此阐释了具体的责任和义务，例如，条款 6(保护和持续利用的一般措施)，条款 8(就地保护)和条款 10(生物多样性组分的持续利用)。

3.2 保护和持续利用

《公约》包括一系列有关生物多样性保护与持续利用的义务。如前所述，在政策规划方面，《公约》规定了如下的义务：制定国家策略和规划，把生物多样性保护和持续利用不仅结合到国家水平的决策中，而且结合到相关的部门或跨部门的规划和政策中去(条款 6)。

为了使各种活动依据坚实的科学基础，每个成员国都应确定生物多样性的重要部分，确定需要特别保护措施或具有最大的持续利用潜力的优先重点。同时也要确定和监测对生物多样性保护和利用且有十分不利影响的活动的过程和等级(条款 7)。

《公约》强调就地保护的重要性。其涉猎的范围非常广泛，既包括保护地系统的建立；又包括退化生态系统的恢复；濒危物种的拯救；自然生境的保护和自然生境中物种最小存活种群的维持(条款 8)。迁地保护主要用以弥补就地保护的不足(条款 9)。

有关生物资源持续利用的义务在若干条款中都有所体现,条款 10 对其进行了集中表述。《公约》成员国承担协调和管理生物资源的保护和持续利用以及鼓励创造持续利用途径的责任。

土著民族或地方居民在保护生物多样性中具有重要作用，与此相关的知识和实践经验应得到保护。最后,《公约》要求各缔约国不仅要采取研究、培训、教育和宣传措施，而且采取技术和应付突发情况的措施以支持国家水平的政策。

关于上述义务有 4 点需要说明：

3.2.1 《公约》对把保护和持续利用两个概念明确区分开来这个问题还存在争议，有些人认为广义的保护应该包括持续利用在内。但为了叙述方便，还是把持续利用作为一个独立概念在条款 2 中予以定义，以强调持续利用的重要性。相反,《公约》中没有对保护进行定义，有时用其广义的，有时用其狭义的概念。总体而言，尽管《公约》中有关保护的概念有些含糊，但还是基本上反映了当今的保护概念。《公约》不仅一直认为生物资源和生态系统的持续利用是生物多样性保护的前提，而且阐明了生物多样性的某些组分应给予特殊考虑的必要性。因此，有关保护和持续利用的规定反映了《公约》总体目标的各个方面。

3.2.2 《公约》的义务通常是关于具体的生物资源，而不是多样性本身。虽然全球生物多样性的保护是《公约》的核心内容，但这一点只能通过对其不同组分(生态系统、物种和基因)或生物资源的有关规定实现。生物资源可以看作是生物多样性的产物。通过对生物多样性组分的关注,《公约》阐述了生物多样性丧失的原因而不仅仅是现象。同时，也为持续发展提供了依据。这种超过生物多样性本身的整体途径，使得该《公约》对于每一个国家都具有重要意义。

3.2.3 《公约》在谈及保护和持续利用的义务时，在大多数条款前都有一段限制其应用范围的句子。其目的在于使《公约》的履行与各缔约国的能力相联系。有时明确指出发展中国家与发达国家在承担义务方面的不同。有关保护和持续利用的一般措施的条款 6 和有关资金机制的条款 20 就是例子。这些限定也受到了一些批评。但是，人们早已认识到了区分发达国家与发展中国家能力的差异的必要性。海洋公约法率先对这一区分的可能性、必要性和实践意义等进行了阐述。

3.2.4 《公约》特别强调发挥各缔约国的作用，开展国家水平的行动。其原因有三：①只有在国家或地区水平上生物多样性才能得以有效的保护，生物资源才能得到有效的管理；②各缔约国最有可能重视在国家水平上确定的优先重点，而不是主要考虑全球意义而确定的优先重点；③生物多样性保护和生物资源的持续利用是如此的复杂，以至于具体任务的完成只能依靠国家甚至地区水平的工作。同时《公约》也注意到了另一种可能出现的倾向,即如果各国都按自已的意愿和标准开展生物多样性保护和持续利用工作，必然会出现与国际水平上确定的总体目标不一致的情况。这样,《公约》的履行及其总体目标的实现就可能受到影响。这个问题可以通过财政机制得以协调和缓解。

3.3 有关获取(Access)的议题

这是《公约》谈判中争议最大的议题。为了讨论并履行《公约》的义务，发展中国家提出了自己的观点。他们不仅要求把《公约》变成实用性更强的文件，而且在《公约》中要规定对遗传资源、有关的技术(包括生物技术)和惠益的获取的途径和对此应承担的义务。

直到《公约》谈判的时候，有关遗传资源自由获取的原则一直沿用 1983 年 FAO 植物遗传资源承诺的规定。然而这是在对遗传资源的控制的争议不断增长的背景下形成的一份没有法律效率的文件。自 80 年代早期以来，有几个发展中国家通过了限制获取其所辖遗传资源的法律。而且发展中国家控制其遗传资源的呼声越来越高。在《生物多样性公约》谈判期间，这种观点占居主导地位，最后，条款 15 规定对遗传资源获取的决定权归缔约国政府所有，而且受其国家法律的约束。

这一点很好理解。没有理由把遗传资源与其他受国家主权控制的自然资源分离出来，而不受国家主权的制约。另外，一个很现实的原因是：对遗传资源获取的控制为条款 15 第 7 点的谈判成功提供了可能。即公平合理地分享研究和开发的成果以及利用这些资源所产生的惠益。

最后，有关技术转让和生物技术惠益获取的规定受到条款 15 第 3 点的限制。条款 15 第 3 点的限制不包括保存在基因库和其他迁地保护设施中的遗传资源。

3.4 资助

资金从发达国家流向发展中国家以满足完成《公约》的各种目标的需要。这一点在整个《公约》谈判的过程中始终是没有争议的。在《公约》谈判的早期阶段人们提出了几条途径，包括基于利用生物资源特别是遗传资源征收的费用在发达国家建立国际基金。其他的如：在谈判过程中考虑过的创建国际公司，《公约》成员国可以通过购买该公司股份进行投资。最后，参加谈判的各方选择创立较为经典的财政资助机制即由发达国家成员提供资金，由发展中国家成员专用。按有关财政来源的条款 20 的规定，这些资金将是新增款项，而且用于提高发展中国家成员的财力以补偿他们履行《公约》义务所造成的额外支出。额外支出将由每个发展中国家成员与负责管理财政机制的机构的双边谈判来确定。

额外支出的计算还存在一些尚未解决的问题。尽管有关臭氧耗竭的公约成功地使用了额外支出的概念，但生物多样性与臭氧耗竭的情况不同。对《生物多样性公约》而言，额外支出的确定是非常困难的。但这又是个不能回避的问题。条款 20 的第 2 点对于财政义务的规定还是比较实际的。

《公约》始终对发展中国家和发达国家区别对待。具体说，《公约》主要要求发展中国家缔约国履行《公约》中规定的保护和持续利用的义务，而发达国家缔约国主要承担提供资金和技术转让的义务。《公约》同时也阐述了《公约》的履行还要考虑到经济和社会发展以及摆脱贫困是发展中国家第一位的、压倒一切的大事这样一个事实。

缔约国会议确定定期需要的资金数量。为了履行《公约》的义务，捐献必须考虑预测性、准确性和资金定期流动的需要。这个问题是个争论的热点并在发达国家间引起了他们对开放型财政资助的恐惧。而且，几乎导致《公约》在最后时刻不被通过。

条款 21 中规定的财政机制可以保证向发展中国家提供资金。该过程在缔约国会议的指导下进行。条款 39 指定全球环境基金(GEF)为财政机制的执行机构。发展中国家感到 GEF 不像条款 21 第 1 点规定的那样以透明和民主的方式进行管理，因此，他们不太情愿接受这样的决定。

(本文主要根据 IUCN 环境法中心，1993，The Convention on Biological Diversity：An Explanatory Guide 摘编。)

本文原载：科技导报. 1995. (1): 27-30

生物多样性研究的现状与发展趋势

马克平　钱迎倩　王晨

(中国科学院)

生物多样性是地球上生命经过几十亿年发展进化的结果，是人类赖以生存的物质基础。然而，随着人口的迅速增长，人类经济活动的不断加剧，作为人类生存最为重要的基础的生物多样性受到了严重威胁。

在过去的2亿年中自然界每27年有一种植物物种从地球上消失，每世纪有90多种脊椎动物灭绝。随着人类活动的加剧，物种灭绝的速度不断加快，现在物种灭绝的速度是自然灭绝速度的1000倍!很多物种未被定名即已灭绝，大量基因丧失，不同类型的生态系统面积锐减。无法再现的基因、物种和生态系统正以人类历史上前所未有的速度消失。如果不立即采取有效措施，人类将面临能否继续以其固有的方式生活的挑战。生物多样性的研究、保护和持续、合理地利用亟待加强、刻不容缓。

中国是生物多样性特别丰富的国家之一。据统计，中国的生物多样性居世界第八位，北半球第一位。同时，中国又是生物多样性受到最严重威胁的国家之一。由于生态系统的大面积破坏和退化，使中国的许多物种已变成濒危种和受威胁种。高等植物中濒危种高达4000~5000种，占总种数的15%~20%。在“濒危野生动植物种国际贸易公约”列出的640个世界性濒危物种中，中国就有156种，约为总数的1/4，形势是十分严峻的。

凡此种种，都要求我们必须立即开展有关的应用基础研究，为有效的保护行动和持续利用措施提供可靠的依据。这将不仅有利当代人，而且造福于子孙后代，既有重要的理论意义，又可产生巨大的社会效益；既是中国持续发展的需要，又是国际社会极为关注，并为之努力工作的重点。

生物多样性的概念

生物多样性是生物及其与环境形成的生态复合体以及与此相关的各种生态过程的总和。它包括数以百万计的动物、植物、微生物和它们所拥有的基因，以及它们与生存环境形成的复杂的生态系统。因此，生物多样性是一个内涵十分广泛的重要概念，包括多个层次或水平。其中，研究较多，意义重大的主要有遗传多样性、物种多样性、生态系统多样性和景观多样性四个层次。

1. 遗传多样性

遗传多样性是指种内基因的变化，包括种内显著不同的种群间和同一种群内的遗传变异，亦称为基因多样性。种内的多样性是物种以上各水平多样性的最重要来源。遗传变异、生活史特点、种群动态及其遗传结构等决定或影响着一个物种与其他物种及其环境相互作用的方式。而且，种内的多样性是一个物种对人为干扰进行成功反应的决定因素。种内的遗传变异程度也决定其进化的潜势。

遗传多样性的测度是比较复杂的，主要包括四个方面即形态多样性、染色体多态性、蛋白质多态性和 DNA 多态性。染色体多态性主要从染色体数目、组型及其减数分裂时的行为等方面进行研究。蛋白质多态性一般通过两种途径分析：一是氨基酸序列分析，二是同工酶或等位酶电泳分析，后者应用较为广泛。DNA 多态性主要通过 RFLP(限制片段长度多态性)、DNA 指纹、RAPD(随机扩增多态 DNA)和 PCR(聚合酶链式反应)等技术进行分析。此外，还可应用数量遗传学方法对某一物种的遗传多样性进行研究。虽然，这种方法依据表型性状进行统计分析，其结论没有分子生物学方法精确，但也能很好地反映遗传变异程度，而且实践意义大，特别对于理解物种的适应机制更为直接。

2. 物种多样性

此处的物种多样性是指物种水平的生物多样性，与生态多样性研究中的物种多样性不同。前者是指一个地区内物种的多样化，主要是从分类学、系统学和生物地理学角度对一定区域内物种的状况进行研究；而后者则是从生态学角度对群落的组织水平进行研究。物种多样性的现状(包括受威胁现状)、物种多样性的形成、演化及维持机制等是物种多样性的主要研究内容。物种水平的生物多样性编目(即物种多样性编目)是一项艰巨而又亟待加强的课题，是了解物种多样性现状包括受威胁现状(及特有程度等)的最有效的途径。然而，目前我们甚至不能将地球上的物种估计到一个确定的数量级，其变化幅度为 500 万至 3000 万种，甚或 200 万至 1 亿种。即使是目前已定名或描述的物种数目也不十分清楚，一种说法为 140 万种，一种说法为 170 万种。要想搞清这些问题，困难相当大。此外，物种的濒危状况、灭绝速率及原因、生物区系的特有性、如何对物种进行有效的保护与持续利用等都是物种多样性研究的内容。

3. 生态系统多样性

生态系统多样性是指生物圈内生境、生物群落和生态过程的多样化以及生态系统内生境差异、生态过程变化的惊人的多样性。此处的生境主要是指无机环境，如地貌、气候、土壤、水文等。生境的多样性是生物群落多样性甚至是整个生物多样性形成的基本条件。生物群落的多样性主要指群落的组成、结构和动态(包括演替和波动)方面的多样化。从物种组成方面研究群落的组织水平或多样化程度的工作已有较长的历史，方法也比较成熟。生态过程主要是指生态系统的组成、结构与功能随时间的变化以及生态系统的生物组分之间及其与环境之间的相互作用或相互关系。这是生物多样性研究中非常重要的方面。

4. 景观多样性

景观多样性指由不同类型的景观要素或生态系统构成的景观在空间结构、功能机制和时间动态方面的多样化或变异性。

景观是一个大尺度的宏观系统，是由相互作用的景观要素组成的、具有高度空间异质性的区域。景观要素是组成景观的基本单元，相当于一个生态系统。依形状的差异，景观要素可分为嵌块体、廊道和基质。嵌块体是景观尺度上最小的均质单元，它的起源、大小、形状和数量等对于景观多样性的形成具有十分重要的意义。廊道是具有通道或屏障功能的线状或带状的景观要素，是联系嵌块体的重要桥梁和纽带。按照来源的不同，廊道可以分为干扰廊道、栽植廊道、更新廊道、环境资源廊道和残余廊遭。不同的廊道适合不同的景观类型。例如，防火隔离带和传输线等干扰廊道适于森林景观，而防护林带和绿篱等栽植廊道则适于农业景观。基质是相对面积大于景观中嵌块体和廊道的景观要素，它是景观中最具连续性的部分，往往形成景观的背景。基质具有三个特点：相对面积比景观中的其他要素大；在景观中的连接度最高；在景观动态中起最重要的作用。由于能量、物质和物种在不同的景观要素中呈异质分布，而且这些景观要素在大小、形状、数目、类型和外貌上又会发生变化，这就形成了景观在空间结构上的高度异质性。

景观功能是指生态客体即物种、能量和物质在景观要素之间的流动。自然干扰、人类活动和植被的演替或波动是景观发生动态变化的主要原因。近年来，特别是自 70 年代以来，森林的大规模破坏造成的生境的片段化、森林面积的锐减以及结构单一的人工生态系统的大面积出现严重地影响了景观的变化过程，形成了极为多样的变化模式。其结果是增加了景观的多样性，给生物多样性的保护造成了严重的障碍。

景观多样性的研究越来越受到人们的重视，特别是在景观格局与生物多样性保护、生境(特别是森林)的片段化对生物多样性的影响、景观的异质性与景观多样性的测度，以及人类活动对景观多样性的影响和景观规划与管理等方面都引起了广泛的关注。

国内外研究现状与发展趋势

1. 生物多样性的调查、编目及信息系统的建立

至今没有一个人能对世界上生物的物种有一个确切的数字。说明在世界范围内生物的调查、定名的工作远远没有做完。其中昆虫尤为突出，估计全世界昆虫可能高达 3000 万种，但已描述的仅 75.1 万种。我国约占 1/10，但目前已记载的仅 4.2 万种。从中国科学院动物研究所昆虫标本馆收藏标本的范围来看，全国被考察过的面积仅 1/3 左右。

编目工作包括有物种、生态系统以及遗传资源的信息，主要是建立数据库。在此基础上建立生物多样性信息系统，包括数据库、图形库、模型库以及专家系统库。信息系统的目的主要在于利用系统中各种数据库建立有关生物多样性监测和评估模型、生物多

样性空间分布及其形成机制模型、重要物种长期种群动态模型、系统的演替模型等。为了提高建模工作效率，缩短建模周期，信息系统应建立一个分析、建模的硬件和软件环境。这些模型和建模环境共同构成信息系统的模型库。从各种理论模型结果到将其用于具体的、实际的生物多样性保护和持续利用活动，一般需要结合大量专家的经验性知识。这是生物多样性保护与生物资源持续利用的专家系统。同样，这些专家系统和专家系统软件环境构成信息系统的专家系统库。

美国内务部专门成立了直属其下的第一个生物调查委员会，开展生物调查编目工作。很多国际机构在这方面已有大量的工作积累，也建有规模较大的生物多样性信息系统。

2. 人类活动对生物多样性的影响

人类活动不断加剧，致使生物多样性受到的威胁日益严重。被誉为“物种宝库”的热带雨林正以每年 20 万 km^2 的速度锐减，天然草场以每年 10 万 km^2 的速度荒漠化。昔日连绵不断的森林景观，现已多是残斑缺部。这种生境片段化或岛屿化的现象是当前生物多样性大规模丧失的主要原因。戴蒙德(Diamond 1989)在分析物种灭绝的原因时总结了四点，他称其为“灾祸四重奏”，即生境的破坏或片段化；过度掠取动物和植物；外源种的引入；由上述三个原因导致的次生灭绝效应。这“灾祸四重奏”中每一个因素无一例外地都源于人类活动。据估计，在过去的几十亿年中物种的自然灭绝速率大约是每年 1 种，而现在由于人类活动所引起的物种灭绝速率至少 1000 倍于此。美国“全球 2000 年度总统报告书”中指出，人类若不采取有效措施，在 1980 至 2000 年的 20 年中将会有 150~200 万种生物(占物种总数的 15%~20%)从地球上消失。鉴于这种严峻的现实，人类活动对生物多样性影响的研究已引起国际社会的广泛关注。

这方面的研究主要包括探讨个体、种群、生态系统对人类干扰方式、强度和频度的反应；土地和水资源利用方式的变化对物种多样性和生态学过程的影响；人类引起的和其他环境变化对物种进化的影响；生态系统的片段化对生物多样性和生态学过程的影响；全球变化对生物多样性的影响；退化生态系统的恢复等方面。其依据的理论基础主要是岛屿生物地理学、恢复生态学和保护生物学等。

3. 生物多样性与生态系统功能

生态系统生态学着眼于不同时空尺度上系统对能量和物质的获取、贮存和传递过程。在研究生态系统功能与环境之间的关系时，只注重生态过程而非物种组成。然而，事实上物种组成或物种多样性和基因多样性对于相应的生态系统功能的发挥是十分重要的。

景观改变造成的物种、生物群落和生态系统的大量丧失，迫使人们重视生物多样性与生态系统功能关系的研究。特别是国际生物科学联合会(IUBS)、环境问题委员会(SCOPE)和联合国教科文组织(UNESCO)联合组织的全球性生物多样性研究项目把“生物多样性的生态系统功能”作为其项目的四个主题的第一项。IUBS 早在 1983 年开始的“热带十年计划”的“热带生态系统的物种多样性及其重要性”研究中就开展了这方面的研究工作。上述三个组织分别于 1989 年和 1991 年召开了以“生物多样性的生态系统功能”

为主题的学术讨论会，并正式出版了《从基因到生态系统》和《生物多样性与生态系统功能》两本专著。

这一领域研究的问题主要有：生物多样性怎样影响生态系统抵御不利环境的能力，或者说生物多样性与生态系统维持或稳定的关系如何?景观的改变如何通过影响不同水平生物多样性的变化而影响生态系统功能?物种之间相互关系怎样影响生态过程，继而影响生态系统功能?生态系统的关键种及其作用如何?生态系统中是否存在物种冗余?不同类群的生物怎样影响生态系统功能?

4. 生物多样性的长期动态监测

生物多样性的动态监测工作始于 80 年代初叶。主要是美国的一些研究机构(如 Smithsonian Institution 和 Nature Conservancy 等)在南美洲开展的若干生物多样性动态监测项目。他们选择了不同类型和不同区域的热带雨林设立固定监测样地，组成监测网络。尽管这些项目在网络建设、组织协调等方面还不够完善，但是迈出了可喜的第一步。近年来，某些国际组织，如国际生物科学联合会、环境问题委员会和联合国教科文组织等，正在积极努力，筹建世界生物多样性研究网络。开展“生物多样性的编目和监测”国际合作计划，为全球生物多样性的保护与持续利用提供基本的科学依据。

5. 物种濒危机制及保护对策的研究

据国际自然与自然资源保护联盟的物种保护监测中心估计，全球有 10%的物种面临灭绝，到本世纪末，将有 15%~20%的物种从地球上消失，如果不采取有效措施，灭绝速率可能超过 20%，形势十分严峻。更为严重的是我们对于濒危物种知识的贫乏(见下表)。

保护所面临的严重局面

了解程度不同的物种数目	数量级
1988 年估计存在的物种数目	10^7
已经描述的物种数目	10^6
生态与行为上了解的物种数目	10^4
遗传上了解的物种数目	10^3
可以用科学方法管理的物种数目	10^2

“保护物种就是保护人类自己”，“一个基因关系到一个国家经济的兴衰，一个物种影响一个国家的经济命脉”已不是科学家们的宣传口号，而是被多个实例证明的事实。然而，贫乏的物种生物学知识严重地影响了物种保护行动。近年来，世界各国有关的科学家都在开展这方面的研究工作。特别是 1985 年以来，保护生物学的创立与发展大大促进了这一领域的研究。其内容主要包括：濒危物种生殖生物学研究，濒危物种群体遗传学与生态遗传学研究，濒危物种种群生存力分析，以及在此基础上进行濒危物种保护对策的研究等。

6. 栽培植物与家养动物及其野生近缘的遗传多样性研究

这些遗传变异是物种进化的重要元素储备，一个物种的遗传变异愈丰富对环境变化的适应性就愈强。反之，遗传多样性贫乏的物种通常在进化上的适应性就弱。也就是说，群体内的遗传变异反映了物种的进化潜力。从保护生物学的角度对物种遗传多样性的了解。有助于物种濒危原因的探讨以及对物种“命运”的预测。这就是制定合理保护对策的科学依据。家养动物和植物的遗传多样性在某种意义上也就是宝贵的遗传资源。因此，对遗传多样性的深入了解，不但是现代动植物遗传育种的基础，也是为适应未来人类需求的变化培育相应的品种作准备。特别是随着当代生物技术的迅猛发展，基因转移技术的日益成熟，这种研究更具现实意义。

众所周知，到目前为止，对物种水平的多样性我们还远非都了解，而述及遗传多样性，情况就更令人失望了。据伍德拉夫(Woodruff 1989)统计，仅有约几千个物种对之进行过遗传学研究，只占已描述物种的很小一部分。面对这种状况，唯一的出路在于确定优先重点。目前，国际上遗传多样性研究最多的生物类群就是家养动物与栽培植物及其野生近缘。国际生物科学联合会-环境问题委员会-联合国教科文组织的生物多样性合作研究项目也把“栽培种野生亲本的生物多样性”列为四大主题之一。

这方面的研究可为遗传资源保存、品种改良以及生物生产力提高提供重要理论依据。

7. 生物多样性的保护管理

这方面的研究包括：自然保护区及国家公园的布局、规划、设计及管理；对特有或濒危物种保护区外的保护；各种迁地保护的方法以及生物技术在生物多样性保护上的应用；对某一个地区生物多样性持续利用的方法及策略以及迁地生物重返自然，等等。

近十年来，国际上出现了一门新兴的学科——保护生物学。应该说，保护生物学是生物多样性保护的理论与实践的基础，其主要目的在于：明确保护的问题；建立正确的程序；在科学和管理之间建立一个桥梁，使科学家熟悉保护的问题，管理工作者熟悉生物学的问题；提供科学的保护与管理。保护生物学的发展很快，美国 1985 年成立了保护生物学学会。目前已有 4000 多会员，并专门出版一本杂志，名称是《保护生物学》(*Conservation Biology*)。并于 1994 年 6 月 7~12 日在墨西哥举行了第八届年会。

结语

综上所述，生物多样性的保护与持续利用研究已受到国际社会的普遍关注，成为当今人类环境与发展领域的中心议题之一,并已引起各国政府和有关国际组织的高度重视，在进行生物多样性保护实践的同时，开展了大量的基础研究工作，为生物多样性的有效保护奠定了基础。

我国由于种种原因，这一领域的研究起步较晚，基础薄弱。虽然已开展了多次大规模的生物资源普查，但目前仍处于家底不清的状态。过去的工作多集中于高等植物及大型动物，而对其他类群则了解甚少，对于生态系统和基因水平的生物多样性研究更嫌不足。随着经济的发展，人口的增加，给生物多样性造成的压力越来越大。生态系统遭受破坏的过程尚在继续，大批物种正在急剧减少乃至绝灭。然而，我们对于生物多样性受威胁的程度、原因等又缺乏了解，生物多样性动态变化的监测几近空白。因此，组织有关部门的研究力量，将不同类群与不同水平的研究有机结合起来，设立系统性、科学性强的重大项目，全面、深入地开展中国生物多样性的保护生物学等基础研究已成为当务之急。无论是从我国的实际需要考虑，还是从缩小与国际同类研究的差距着想，都是十分必要而紧迫的。

本文原载：生命科学. 1996. 8(5): 1-4

系统学与生物多样性

王晨[1] 钱迎倩[2] 马克平[2]

(1 中国科学院学部联合办公室；2 中国科学院植物研究所)

摘 要 系统学家 200 多年的努力，地球上最多仅有 1/10 生物被命名。至今，系统学却被误认为已是古老学科，基础设施和人才走向没落。1992 年《生物多样性公约》被批准后，对系统学重要性有了重新认识。1994 年国际上提出了“2000 年系统学议程”。本文对“议程”提出的发现生物多样性、了解生物多样性及管理系统学知识等三大任务及每个任务的优先领域作了介绍。明确了系统学是保护和持续利用生物多样性的重要基础。应把系统学研究提到应有高度加以支持。

关键词 生物多样性；系统学；“2000 年系统学议程”；生物分类学

自从 18 世纪中叶瑞典科学家林奈对生物物种提出双名法以来，分类学、系统学逐步得到发展，成为生物科学的一门基础学科。随着生物科学的发展，特别是近 20 多年来分子生物学突飞猛进的发展并向生命科学其他分支学科的渗透，系统学在人们的心目中已成为一门古老而不足以引起重视的学科。其基础设施得不到加强，人才越来越匮乏，已成为世界性的问题。生物系统学家发现，经过近 200 年分类学家、系统学家的努力，人类对地球上生物的知识还是微乎其微，仅以最基本的命名来说，科学家最多仅对地球的 1／10 的生物进行了命名。不少有识之士惊呼，必须彻底改变目前人们对系统学的认识，大力加强系统学的研究。1992 年联合国环境与发展大会上《生物多样性公约》被批准后，人们对系统学重要性的认识进入一个新的阶段。1994 年，“2000 年系统学议程”(Systematics Agenda 2000)[1]面世。该“议程”有三大任务，即发现生物多样性、了解生物多样性及管理系统学的知识，目的都是为了持续利用生物多样性。系统学为保护和持续利用生物多样性提供了重要的基础。“议程”呼吁要重视系统学研究外，还应加强基础设施及人才培养。要使“议程”成为国际性的共同行动，加强国际合作来迎接 21 世纪的挑战。

“2000 年系统学议程”对系统学作了如下的解释，即系统学是生物学的一个分支学科，是建立在分类学(发现、描述和划分物种或物种类群的科学)、系统发育分析(发现某一物种类群间的进化关系)和分类(按照进化关系将物种最终归为类群)等三项工作之上的科学。系统生物学家已描述的物种大概不足 150 万种。Raven 和 Wilson(1992)[2]列举了不少例子说明一些大型的生物还是近 10~20 年内才发现的，例如世界上目前还存活的鲸类有 80 种，其中 11 种是本世纪才发现的，最近的一种是 1991 年定的名，并在东太平洋还有一个种因为未捕捉到而未定名；在过去的10年中植物学家在中美和南墨西哥发现新的植物定了三个新的科；在1993年时，还为动物界定了一个新的门，称为Loricifcra。地球上还有数以千万计的物种仍有待去探索、去认识。(附表)

本文将结合我国的情况，对“议程”的框架作一介绍，以期对我国系统生物学的发展有所推动。

附表　全世界已描述及可能存在的物种数

类　别	已描述物种的数量	有待发现物种的估量
病毒	0.5万	约50万
细菌	0.4万	20万~300万
真菌	7.0万	100万~150万
原生动物	4.0万	10万~20万
藻类	4.0万	20万~1000万
植物	25.0万	30万~50万
脊椎动物	4.5万	5万
线虫	1.5万	50万~100万
软体动物	7.0万	20万
甲壳动物	4.0万	15万
螨、蜘蛛	7.5万	75万~100万
昆虫	95.0万	800万~10 000万

1　系统生物学议程的三大任务

“议程”确定了以下三项研究任务；第一项任务，发现、描述和把全球生物多样性进行编目；第二个任务，从这个全球计划获得的信息进行分析，并将其汇入成一个能体现生命史的推测性分类系统；第三个任务，把这个全球计划获得的信息整理成为一种有效的、可查询的形式，以最大限度地满足科学和社会的需求。以上三项任务的完成，将会对科学和社会发生如下巨大的作用：①新发现的物种将扩充社会有用资源的编目；② 各国的保护学家、政策制定者及生物资源管理人员可用新的系统学的资料来持续利用他们本国的物种多样性；③物种多样性知识将有助于新产品的发现，并将指导农作物和药物新品种和改良品种的选择；④获得的基本资料可用于监测全球气候及生态系统的变化，其中包括物种灭绝速度，生态系统退化以及外来的、引起病害和虫害生物体的传播等。

2　对三个任务主要内容的介绍

2.1　第一个任务

发现、描述和全球多样性的编目。人类对全球环境的破坏已迫切要求我们尽快掌握世界生物多样性的知识。今后的几十年中，地球上估计有 1/5 的物种行将灭绝。但目前对全球生物资源编目还远远不够，难以提供物种多样性全面的信息。

本项任务中，应优先考虑以下几个方面的工作：①调查海洋、陆地和淡水生态系统，获得全球物种多样性的综合性的知识；②确定这些物种的地理分布和时间分布；③发现、描述和编目受威胁及濒危生态系统中生存的物种；④针对了解最少的生物类群体作为目标；⑤对能够维持全世界各种生态系统的功能及完整性、促进人类健康、改善人类食物来源的关键类群。

建国以来，我国在这方面虽做了不少工作。曾由中国科学院为主，组织全国有关单位和专家学者对我国生物资源进行了十余次大规模调查，目前已收藏生物标本1000多万号。但与国际差距还很大，我国尚有许多重要地区和重要生物类群没有进行调查。特别是近些年来，由于经费短缺，已经多年没有开展具有规模的野外生物资源考察，馆藏标本数量几乎没有太多的增加。以昆虫为例，据张广学，尹文英估测，按中国约占世界种类(800~1000万)的1/6估算，素有"昆虫王国"之称的中国现存昆虫物种数应为130~160万种，其中已知种应该有16万种。但是，实际查清的仅有4.5万种，距最低标准尚有2/3的差距[3]。

2.2　第二项任务

分析从全球获得的信息，并将其汇入一个能反映生命史的推测性分类系统。人们如果仅仅掌握一份物种的名录是远远不够的。系统学家要与其他生物学分支学科如解剖学、遗传学，分子生物学、古生物学及生物地理和其他分支学科结合，通过了解物种间血缘关系或系统发育关系而产生出分类系统，也就是把以上掌握的知识整理出一个推测性的框架。

本项任务中，应优先考虑以下几个方面的工作：①确定主要类群的系统发育关系，为基 础生物学和应用生物学提出一个总体理论框架；②发现对应用生物学至关重要的物种类群的系统发育关系，重点放在对人类健康、粮食生产、全世界各种生态系统保护等有重要作用的物种上；③发现对基础生物学至关重要的物种类群的系统发育关系，比如与实验科学有广泛联系的学科，或者对维持生态系统功能及完整性必不可少的学科；④继续探索对分析系统学数据更有效的技术和方法。

通过系统发育研究而产生的分类系统或称推测性框架，对持续利用生物多样性上的作用是非常明显的。对癌症有特效的紫杉醇的寻找是一个很好的例子。紫杉醇最早是在短叶紫杉(*Taxus brerifolia*)的树皮中发现的，但树皮中含量太低，更严重的是树皮剥掉后树也就死了。由于掌握了短叶紫杉的进化关系，从它的近缘种浆果紫杉(*T. baccata*)的叶子中也提取到了紫杉醇，这就解决了可不使树死亡并持续利用的问题。进一步还从短叶紫杉的树皮中发现了一种真菌的新种(*Taxomyces andreanac*)，这种真菌也能产生紫杉醇，这将对今后紫杉醇的生产指出光明的前途。我国目前正在研究通过含量高物种的细胞培养来进行紫杉醇的生产。如果能利用真菌发酵，将大大降低生产成本。另一个例子是大豆，中国是大豆的原产地，也是传统的出口产品。1978年后，美国科学家在中国找到了具抗旱等性状的野生近缘种。与其栽培品种杂交后，使美国由大豆的进口国一跃而成出口国。[4]

系统发育分类还有下列几方面的作用：可建立一套测定物种灭绝速率和全球变化模式的框架;为了解形成当今生命多样性的物种形成、灭绝、适应等过程提供科学基础等。

2.3 第三项任务

整理从全球获得的信息，使之成为一个有效的、可查询的系统，以最大限度地满足科学和社会的需求。

本项任务中，应优先考虑以下几方面的工作：①以世界自然历史标本存储机构收藏的标本为基础，建立物种信息的系统学、生物地理学和生态学数据库；②综合系统学标本存储机构的数据和地理信息系统(GIS)数据库中的信息，为监测过去和现在全球变化对物种的分布和灭绝造成的影响提供条件；③建立各数据库间的联系，使各种分类单元及其分布区所有有用的信息可有效地被查询；④建立和采用一套信息系统，便于国际用户使用；⑤编撰所有系统学数据库必需的，包括分类名称、地理分布及其他信息内容的数据字典；⑥出版手册、图解、电子动植物志、专著等数据产品；⑦通过持续提供软件和硬件的支持以建立维持和更新数据库及信息网络的机制。

我国在这方面也做了大量工作，特别是“八五”期间，在国家和各有关单位的支持下开始建立了地理信息系统(GIS)、生物物种数据库、生物多样性信息系统。但只是起步，离一个有效的、可查询的系统，以最大限度地满足科学和社会的需求还相差甚远。

3 系统学知识及生物多样性的价值

对于试图了解生命多样性、为子孙后代保护和管理生命多样性的基础科学和应用科学研究人员来说，系统学知识乃为基础的基础。它将为人类生存做出更多的贡献。

3.1 人类健康

纵观世界上所有的疾病，目前让人深恶痛绝的有三种：导致疟疾的原生动物、引发日本血吸虫病的血液蠕虫及造成艾滋病的 HIV 病毒。此外还有其他各种寄生虫、细菌引起的疾病等。如果没有系统学这门科学，就不可能得到对付这些疾病的进展。系统学家能够认识、区分并说明影响人类健康的非病原体及病原体的特征。仅仅了解可能引发疾病的生物还不够，还要把一个类群中的所有已知物种区别开来，以便加强对新发现物种的了解，确定某个已知的品系或物种本为非病原体是否已转变成病原体。掌握致病有机体的进化对提高人类健康水平起着关键的作用。

3.2 物种经济学

历史表明，新种的发现伴随着其特性研究往往会带来重大的经济效益。1970 年我国育种工作者采集到一棵野败的不育系，使我国在杂交水稻上取得巨大的成功就是一个很好的例子[5] 。

3.3 药物

据世界卫生组织统计，人类为药用目的而利用的植物有两万多种。发展中国家有80 %的人仍然依靠传统药物作为主要的疾病治疗。这些药物大部分来自野外采集的植物。实践证明，在筛选有药效成分时，如果选用传统药物所利用的物种，其成功机遇比选用同一地区植物大得多。

3.4 农业

从世界范围看，发达的农业体系正朝着减少杀虫剂、化肥和除草剂的施用量，加强生物防治、害虫综合管理和持续性农业的方向发展。以上技术强烈依赖于有关害虫类群、害虫的植物寄生及害虫的天敌的系统学知识。系统学信息是农业管理的语言和预测基础，由于系统学信息的不足而造成失败的项目多不胜数。

3.5 与农业同样重要的遗传资源、林业、渔业等，系统学的知识对其都具有重要作用。

3.6 了解和保护地球的生命支持系统

系统学知识在监测地球变化方面起到最基本的作用。收藏的标本是生物群落和生态系统的变更见证，记载着长时间内环境对所受压力的反应。同样是这些标本，由于包含不同的物种存在和鉴定的基本科学证据，因此也是物种灭绝的最可靠记载。对下个世纪物种灭绝的推测，主要依靠森林砍伐和生境破坏方面的综合信息。没有物种存在和分布的完整记录的科学知识，就没有生态变化和物种灭绝的准确评估。只有系统学才能可靠地衡量生物多样性的危机程度。

正确鉴定物种对监测地球变化也十分重要，所有的生物群落都包含一些对环境变化特别敏感的物种。为此，科学家已越来越多地利用这些指示种来考察全球变化对自然群落的影响，从而实现监测全球变化的目的。

系统学对自然资源的管理和保护同样有重要作用。保护区生物多样性的保护管理人员需要对物种作鉴定并了解其地理分布，为有效管理策略的制定和实施提供依据。系统学则为物种的鉴定、多样性的评价以及需要特别保护的物种的确定提供理论基础。此外，系统学信息与保护区和开发区的选址及规划、它们与地方和国家法规的关系的评估，都有着密切的联系。有效管理动、植物种国际贸易也同样需要精确的系统学资料。这些资料还直接有利于一些像濒危野生动植物种国际贸易公约(CITES)的国际性条约和公约的执行和实施。

综上所述，系统学知识与生物多样性的关系是如此的密切、如此之重要、系统学家面临的任务又如此之艰巨。McNeely 撰文列举了系统学与《生物多样性公约》有关条款的关系[6],可是当今的社会对系统学又是如此之冷漠，这也是“2000 系统学议程”诞生的重要背景。“议程”最早是由美国植物分类学家学会、系统生物学家学会和 Willi Hennig 学会与系统学收藏馆协会共同合作，由美国国家科学基金会资助的一个产物。初稿是由各方面机构来的 300 位以上科学家参加共同完成，并经美国国内和国际科学家和有关学会、协会审阅。“议程”发表后引起国际上广泛的重视。1995 年成为国际生物科学联盟(IUBS)的一个重要项目，称为 Systematics Agenda 2000／International (SA2000／I)[7]。

参考文献

[1] Anonymous Systematics Agenda 2000: Charting the Biosphere. American Society of Plant Taxonomists *et al*, 1994. 1~34

[2] Raven P H and Wilson E O. Science, 1994, 238: 1099~1100

[3] 张广学, 尹文英. 应加强昆虫分类学研究, 中国科学报, 1994 年 11 月 14 日

[4] 洪德元, 傅立国. 我国植物的重要地位和面临的危机. 中国科学院生物多样性研讨会会议录, 北京, 1990, 40~44

[5] 李竞雄, 周洪生主编. 高产不是梦——粮棉油雄性不育杂种优势的基础研究. 1995，85

[6] McNcely J A. Keep all the pieces: Systematics 2000 and world conservation. biodiversity and conservation. 1995, 4: 510~519

[7] Anonymous. International Union of Biological sciences, Statutes. Organization and Activities, IUBS, 1995, 6

本文原载：生态学报. 1997. 17(6): 565-572

生物多样性科学前沿*

陈灵芝　钱迎倩

(中国科学院植物研究所)

摘　要　由国际生物科学联盟(IUBS)在 1991 年首先提出，至今已由其他 5 个重要国际组织或项目(SCOPE，UNESCO，ICSU，IGBP-GCTE 及 IUMS)共同主持的 DIVERSITAS 是迄今生物多样性科学研究唯一的国际性项目。1996 年 7 月，科学指导委员会草拟了本阶段新的操作计划，并于同年 8 月在 IUBS 执行委员会上讨论。操作计划详述了 10 个组成方面的内容。其中 5 个为核心组成部分，其他 5 个为特别目标研究领域(STARs)。“生物多样性对生态系统功能的作用”是最核心的组成方面，也是 1991 年提出的唯一的研究内容。生物多样性的保护，恢复和持续利用既是重要的研究内容又是研究所要达到的最后目的。特别目标研究领域包括了土壤和沉积物、海洋、淡水和微生物生物多样性等重要而过去未引起足够重视的领域。

DIVERSITAS 的研究内容与《生物多样性公约》中的有关条款十分吻合，说明科学研究就是为履行《公约》服务的。明确研究的指导思想，按中国国情选择好有代表性的优先地区以及开展国际合作，逐步与国际接轨是下一步开展生物多样性研究应考虑到的几个方面。

关键词　DIVERSITAS；生物多样性；生态系统功能；《生物多样性公约》；优先地区

世界人口无节制地增长、工业化进程不断地加速、人类消费水平无约束地提高，带来了森林大量砍伐、生物多样性急剧减少、大气 CO_2 浓度不断提高、不少发展中国家粮食短缺等等各种各样的恶果。因此，生物多样性保护、全球变化以及可持续发展已成为国际关注的 3 个热点。这 3 个问题的研究又相互联系、相互交叉，例如农业问题，就与 3 个方面都有密切的相关。此外，这 3 个问题也为各种不同的国际组织共同关心，列为这些组织的研究前沿或共同支持的项目或课题。

生物多样性的保护及持续利用问题自从 1992 年联合国环境与发展大会上《生物多样性公约》签署后，已引起世界各国政府及各界人士的重视。涉及生物多样性的科学研究，历史上有些部分从不同的角度已长期分别地在进行着，有的已有很长的历史，例如其中一个组成部分—— 系统学的研究已有 200 年左右的历史。但是从来没有像今天这样把生物多样性作为一门科学全面地加以考虑并进行研究。国际上一些知名的研究机构或学术团体都分别在某些领域内开展了工作，例如美国 Smithsonian 研究院在生物多样性的测定和监测方面已进行了一定的研究，并且和人与生物圈(MAB)合作在这方面每年举办国际

* 国家“八五”重大基础研究项目“中国生物多样性保护生态学基础研究(PD85-31)”的一部分。

性的培训班；又如由美国植物分类学家学会、系统生物学学会等组织在1994年为加强系统学的研究提出了系统学议程2000(Systematics Agenda 2000)等等。但都不如国际生物科学联盟(IUBS)等组织把生物多样性研究的各个方面系统地加以组织，取名DIVERSITAS，并推动国际性的合作。

1 DIVERSITAS发展的两个阶段

IUBS对生物多样性问题早就予以重视，并在1991年第24次全体会议上提出了“生物多样性的生态系统功能”研究项目，这是在生物多样性研究上的核心问题。到1992年时，研究内容扩大到研究生物多样性的起源、组成、功能、保持和保护。研究的角度是从遗传到生态系统水平的地球上所有生活的生物体。研究主题发展为4个：即“生物多样性的生态系统功能”；“生物多样性的起源和保持”；“生物多样性的编目和监测”；以及“家养种的野生近缘种的生物多样性”。同年，环境问题科学委员会(SCOPE)和联合国教科文组织(UNESCO)等两个国际组织参加了进来，把此项目正式定名为DIVERSITAS。国际微生物科学联盟(IUMS)在1994年也参加到这个项目中去。以上就是DIVERSITAS发展的第一阶段。

在第一阶段，DIVERSITAS逐步成为政府间和非政府组织共同的合作伙伴，其目的是要明确生物多样性关键的、前沿的科学问题；促进、加速和催化生物多样性起源、组成、功能、保持和保护等方面的科学研究；为各方面提供生物多样性的状况与地球上生物资源利用的可持续的正确的信息和预测模型。

1995年DIVERSITAS项目在上述4个国际组织的基础上又增加了两个新的成员，即国际科学联盟委员会(ICSU)和国际地圈生物圈计划全球变化和陆生生态系统(IGBP/GCTE)。研究主题由4个扩大到9个组成方面，并用图解分为主要项目及交叉项目两个部分来表示[1,2]。主要项目也就是生物多样性研究的关键领域由5个方面组成，即：①起源、保持和丧失；②生态系统功能；③编目、分类和相互关系；④评估与监测；⑤保护、恢复与持续利用。另一部分称为交叉项目，是根据问题的重要性和迫切需要而列出的，有下列4个方面，即：⑥人类的影响范围(human dimensions)；⑦土壤和沉积物的生物多样性；⑧海洋生物多样性；⑨微生物多样性。这样的安排是不断完善、深入发展得出的。按IUBS的提法，DIVERSITAS已进入到下一个时期，或称为第二个阶段。至于上述9个方面研究目的及具体说明请参见钱迎倩、马克平[1]的报道，这里不再赘述。

为了完善第二个阶段的项目，1996-04-22草拟了一个“操作计划”草案，提供1996-07在英国伦敦皇家植物园召开的第一届科学指导委员会全体会议以及1996-08-23~1996-08-24在匈牙利布达佩斯举行的IUBS执行委员会上讨论。这次提出的草案有两个重大的发展，首先是对1995年时提出的9个方面有了新的提法，更重要的是对前面5个方面不是平列地提出，而是用图表说明了其中的相互关系(见图1)；其次是对9个方面作了更为详细的叙述，各个方面间的相互联系以及其他有关国际组织对这些方面的考虑也作了说明。再一点是在草案文本上已提出了第10个方面，即淡水生物多样性，但当时尚未展开。

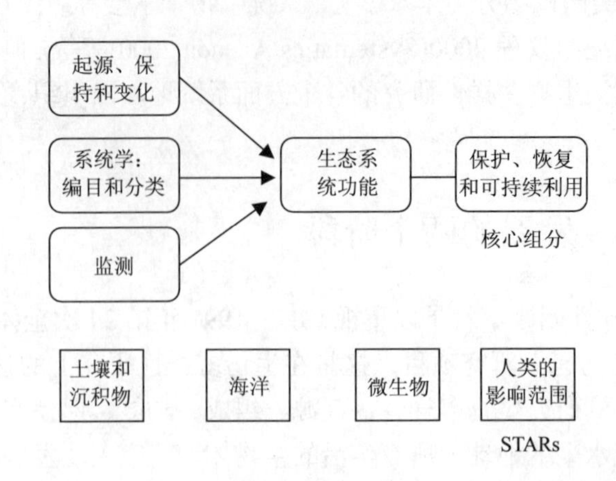

图 1　“操作计划”草案中 DIVERSITAS 9 个组成方面关系的草图

Fig.1　The relationship between 9 programme elements of DIVERSITAS in the draft of “operational plan”

“操作计划”草案把 9 个方面分为两个部分的新提法是核心组分(core elements)以及特殊目标研究领域(special target areas of research)简称 STARs，9 个方面的提法也稍有变化。

从图 1 可以理解为在 5 个核心组分中最后一个方面“生物多样性的保护、恢复和持续利用”既是一个研究方面，又是要想达到的最后目标。前面 4 个组分是为这个研究方面或最后目标服务的。“生物多样性对生态系统功能的作用”又是其中的中心环节，其重要性也就显而易见了。“起源、保持和变化”，“系统学：编目和分类”以及“监测”等 3 个组成方面用 3 个箭头指向“生物多样性对生态系统功能的作用”的研究，说明这 3 个方面是后者开展研究的基础，其中尤其是处于中间位置的“系统学：编目和分类”，更是基础的基础。系统学研究的重要性，近年来又再次为国际社会所强调，提出“系统学议程 2000”这一重要报告。系统学与生物多样性之间的密切关系，王晨等已有专门的介绍[3]。对 4 个 STARs，“操作计划”草案中说明了它们是 5 个核心组分之间的重要交叉领域 。对这些领域的知识，过去经常被忽视或者仅得到有限的重视。由于其重要性，被专门提了出来。

经过最近这次 IUBS 执委会讨论后，提出了 1996 年当前 DIVERSITAS“操作计划”的最后文本[4]。在这个文本中 DIVERSITAS 有 10 个组成方面，淡水生物多样性已被正式提了出来。对这 10 个研究方面的相互关系，在草案的基础上又作了最后的修订(见图 2)。

这里值得一提的是图 1 与图 2 与 1995 年的图[5]上的提法有 3 个不同之处，第一，原来提法是“生物多样性的起源、保持和丧失”，而最后定稿时改为“生物多样性的起源、保持和变化”；第二，“生物多样性的生态系统功能”改为“生物多样性对生态系统功能的作用”；第三是增加了“淡水生物多样性”。

因为“淡水生物多样性”是新提出的同题，有必要在这里作些补充说明，由于各种不同的环境，隔离的水体和极为丰富的动、植物区系，使淡水生物多样性的研究有其特殊的科学和保护意义。对很多国家来说，淡水生态系统的保护和管理是要解决的主要问题之一。下列的原因已引起淡水生物多样性发生了很大的变化，其中主要的有：出于各种不同的用途而过量的采水，各种水体生境自然的改变，化学污染和富营养化，过度捕捞鱼类及其他水产品，外来种的入侵以及包括酸雨、气温上升和荒漠化在内的全球变化，造成湖泊内环流和营养供给的变化。上述这些因素都在深刻地影响着生态系统内的淡水生物多样性，要通过考察与在各种实验基础上提出的结论相结合，最后得到淡水生态系统功能的预测模型及其基本理论。

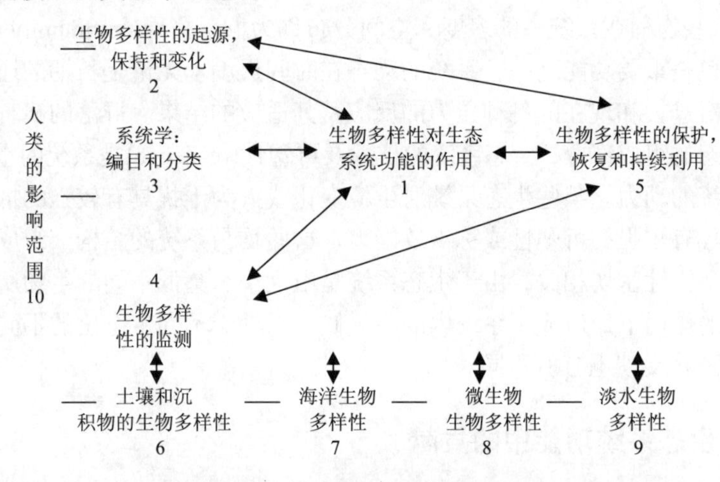

图2 生物多样性科学的一个国际项目——
DIVERSITAS 的 10 个组分；其中 1~5 为核心组分，6~10 是特殊目标的研究领域

Fig.2 Ten programme elements of DIVERSITAS——
an international programme of biodiversity science; Core programme elements are number 1 to 5, and special target areas of research (STARs) are numbered 6 to 10

2 生物多样性对生态系统功能作用的几个问题

生态系统功能亦称生态系统过程或简称生态过程。它是组成系统内生物体与外界环境相互作用的过程，也是系统内部生物之间以及生物与栖息地生境之间相互影响、相互作用的过程。生态系统内生物的种类、数量及其不同的生物学、生态学特征，必然对生态系统功能起到深刻的作用。生态系统多样性的保护、功能的正常运行，对人类生存与发展至关重要。生态系统内生物多样性为人类提供各种资源，为人类生存环境提供多种生态效益，因此生物多样性对生态系统功能的作用无疑是生物多样性保护的核心。但是它又必须与物种多样性和遗传多样性保护密切结合，才能解决生物多样性保护、恢复和持续利用的问题。

2.1 生态系统的主要功能

生态系统的功能在生态系统水平上主要是指 CO_2 吸收和丧失，能量的固定、分配与消耗、养分的获得、保持、归还和流失，水分的获得、分配和平衡，生产力和生物量等等。这些功能是组成生态系统的生物与外界环境条件相互影响、相互作用的结果。另一方面，在生态系统中的生物与非生物组分中的水分、能量、养分的数量及构件(configuration)，称之谓生态系统格局(ecosystem patterns)。

生态系统功能还包括系统的内部功能，主要有物种之间的特有相互关系。如系统内各营养级之间生物捕食的与被捕食的关系，植物、动物与微生物之间的关系，以及生物之间的互惠共存关系等等。这些生物之间相互作用的过程也称之为群落过程(community processes) 。这些物种在系统中的多度和空间分布称为群落格局(community patterns)；生态系统的动态也是重要功能之一，系统的动态在时间尺度上无论是长期的还是短期的，都是组成生物对过去和现在的各种压力的反应及其适应的结果。群落的演替及林窗动态是生态系统动态的组成部分，生态系统的抗性及可塑性(resilence)是系统的重要功能，也是维持生态系统的动力。某些生态系统对生境变化或人为干扰具有较强的抵抗能力，或在生境改变后具有较强的可塑性或称恢复能力。这些均与系统的结构、组成系统的物种多样性及遗传多样性密切相关；由于生态系统是由大小、高低不同的生物所组成，在生物与外界环境的作用下，形成了系统内的小气候。而处于不同生态位的不同物种，对受小气候的作用及其反馈也有所不同。

2.2 物种在生态系统功能中的贡献

生态系统的功能是受生物多样性的影响，关于组成生态系统的物种对系统功能贡献大小是否相同的问题，不同学者各抒己见，从而在组成物种的功能作用上有如下几个假设：

2.2.1 关键种(keystone species)假设

Paine[5,6]在海洋生态系统中对捕食生物首次用了关键种的概念。关键种是指一些物种由于它们的多度和作用对维持生态系统的完整性和稳定性具有重要作用。关键种的丢失，可能导致生态系统发生重大变化，以至破坏。关键种假设已受到很多学者重视。他们对关键种进行了分类，主要有捕食动物关键种；草食动物关键种；病原体生物关键种；竞争生物关键种；互惠共生生物关键种；其中还包括有资源生物、传播生物和授粉生物关键种；地下活动的生物如土豚(食蚁兽)、兔子、鼹鼠、白蚁以及形成小丘的蚂蚁，它们对某些生态系统的维持具有十分重要的作用，因此也存在着地下生物关键种；对维持各种生态过程有重要影响的关键种，是维持生态系统功能的关键[7]，关键种假设提出后,不少学者认为对生物多样性保护,首先要着重于关键种的保护。

2.2.2 冗余假设(redundancy hypothesis)

这假设是由 Walker[6]和 Lawton 和 Brown[9]所提出的，也有人建议称为功能补偿假设(functional compensation hypothesis)。这假设认为某些物种在生态功能上有相当程度的重叠，因此其中某一个种的丢失不会对生态功能发生影响。

2.2.3 铆钉假设(rivet hypothesis)

该假设认为每一个物种都好像飞机上的一个铆钉，任何一个物种丢失，同样都存在使群落或生态系统过程发生改变的概率。这一观点是认为系统中的每一物种具有同样重要的功能。随着发展，这一假设有所变化，认为某些物种可以假设为是飞机上重要部位的铆钉，它比其他物种具有重要的作用。确定重要部位铆钉的依据是某些物种的数量，它们所占据的位置及其对相邻物种的影响。这种观点或多或少相似于关键种假设。

这几种假设欲阐明生物多样性对生态系统功能的作用，必须研究不同物种在系统中的贡献、它们的数量及其变化对生态系统功能的作用。这些假设必须通过观察和实验手段加以论证。关于关键种问题不少学者已在进行实验

2.3 物种多样性变化与生态系统功能的关系

要了解物种的入侵和灭绝对生态系统功能的作用,应从以下5个方面进行重点研究。

2.3.1 生态系统中物种的数量，也就是物种的丰富度

物种数量无疑会影响生态系统稳定性及其某些生态过程：我们现在还不知道在一个系统中应有多少物种数量才可以维持系统的相对稳定性;对于各类不同的生态系统过程,物种的数量与生态系统某一过程速率之间关系的形式是怎样的；在哪一个点上，这种关系可以达到饱和。因为这种关系达到饱和后，物种的增加或减少都可能会产生很大影响。这种现象在物种比较少的生态系统中可能会出现，特别是在岛屿上。

2.3.2 必须要测定物种的多度

在生态系统中物种的多度往往是不同的，有优势种、常见而数量不多的物种以及数量很少的物种，它们在生态系统中的贡献是不同的。多度最大的物种、在生物量、生产力、养分和水分循环中占有重要比重。可以预见，系统中优势种的灭绝比多度少的稀有物种的丢失对生态系统的某些过程会产生更大的影响。

2.3.3 对每一个物种功能的探讨也是重要的方面

有一些物种和另外一些物种具有相似的功能，这些属于相似的物种可归属于同一功能群，在功能群中有的物种的消失对生态系统功能的影响较小。关于功能群的研究已受到重视。在生态系统中生产者、消费者和分解者3个主要组分中都可划分出不同的功能群，如根据植物生活型、生活史策略、叶子的结构、根系的深度、共生体、气体交换特征、对光周期的敏感性和抗水性等特性，可把具共同特性的一些物种归属于同一功能群；又如在生态系统中植物和植物器官的空间排列，具有水平和垂直的结构，如林冠的顶部、灌木丛、下木层、土表植物、根系在土壤中占有不同深度的植物，均可形成不同的功能群；植物的物候学特征也可作为划分功能群的标准；如幼苗与成熟个体，夏季一年生植物与冬季一年生植物，演替早期的物种与演替后期的物种均可构成不同的功能群；此外，

还可根据生理特性分为 C_3、C_4、CAM 植物功能群等。关于功能群的划分，以及它们的功能作用还需要有实验的验证。功能群的研究在生物多样性对生态系统功能的作用中具有重要意义。

2.3.4 生物的某些性状对生态系统功能比起其他性状会有更大的影响

Vitousek[10]和 Chapin 等[11]认为物种改变生态系统过程,最初是影响环境中的资源有效性,影响了水分和养分的供给和周转;又如引入具有固氮能力的物种,将会改变系统的生产力和营养元素循环，也可能改变系统的结构和物种组成;引进深根植物可以增加水分和养分的获得；增加了维持生态系统生产力的资源库的有效性；某些物种的特性会控制对资源的消耗，如食物链中处于高营养级水平的物种常常有此现象，就是所谓的高级-低级的控制(topdown contro1);也有一些物种的特征会影响土壤资源库的水分、养分供应速率，如固氮作用、凋落物的养分含量及其分解速率等；再如土壤微生物群落中，不同物种对硝化和反硝化速率的影响，这过程就是所谓的低级-高级的控制(down-top contro1)，即营养级低的生物对高级生物的控制；从生物对资源的消耗而论；生物个体的高度或大小及其生物量相对生长速率都是预测生物对资源消耗的最重要特征。以植物为例，高大的植物种增加了对光能的获得，深根可以从基质中获得更多水和养分资源，以上这些都是物种的某些性状对生态系统功能作用的几个范例。

2.3.5 间接影响的物种

有的物种对生态系统功能作用很小，但是它们的间接影响却又很大。它们往往影响着生态系统过程有直接影响的物种多度，例如某些种子传播生物和授粉生物，它们在生态系统过程中影响较小，但是对某些优势种的繁育，又必须依靠它们进行授粉或种子迁移、传播。有的树种的种子必须通过某种生物的作用才易于发芽、更新。类似这类生物的变化，将间接地对生态系统功能产生重要作用。

综上所述，生物多样性对生物系统功能的作用，归结起来有 7 个大的方面：

① 生产力和生物量； ② 土壤结构、养分和分解作用；
③ 水分的分布、平衡和质量； ④ 大气性质及反馈；
⑤ 生物世代／物种相互关系； ⑥ 景观及流域的结构；
⑦ 微生物活动。

这 7 个方面在 Heywood 等[12]编著的“全球生物多样性评估”一书中有详述的阐明。

3 DIVERSITAS 与《生物多样性公约》之间的关系

履行生物多样性公约当然是各缔约国的政府行为，但是要履行好《公约》必须有科学研究作为基础。《公约》条款中也明确了科学研究与培训作为履约的主要任务。DIVERSITAS 的研究项目作为生物多样性科学的前沿，必须要符合《公约》条款的要求，科学研究就要为履约服务。

从 DIVERSITAS 项目来说，除了明确当前科研 10 个组成方面外，还规定了要举办研讨班、会议以及出版各类型出版物以适应不同层次的各方人士的需要，这些措施就是为了达到《公约》第12条上有关研究和培训的规定及13条上有关公众教育和向公众宣传的要求，实际上DIVERSITAS所有的组成方面都与第14条“影响评估和尽量减少不利影响”有关联，并且有益于生物多样性科学的基础设施和人才的建设。当然，DIVERSITAS项目中的每一个组成方面所得的研究成果又分别有助于履行《公约》某些条款所规定的任务。现分别叙述如下：

项目组成1　生物多样性对生态系统功能的作用

这方面研究与《公约》第1条中的为生物多样性保护和持续利用所制定的国家政策、计划、各项项目提出有密切关系；它为第8条就地保护和第9条迁地保护服务；也为第10条(a)款，在国家决策过程中考虑到生物资源的保护和持续利用、(b)款采取有关利用生物资源的措施，以避免或尽量减少对生物多样性的不利影响、(d)款在生物多样性已减少的退化地区资助地方居民规划和实施补救行动等服务。

项目组成2　生物多样性的起源、保持和变化

为《公约》第1条，第6条保护和持续利用方面的一般措施，以及第8条，第9条和第10条服务。

项目组成3　系统学：生物多样性的编目和分类

为第7条查明与监测，第8条(j)款所涉及的地方社区的参与能力建设服务。

项目组成4　生物多样性的监测

为第7条，特别是(a)款中提到的已查明对保持和持续利用生物多样性至关重要的生物多样性组成部分的监测和(b)款中提到的要建立和评估抽样调查和监测所用的标准方法服务。

项目组成5　生物多样性的保护、恢复和持续利用

为第6条，第8条，第9条和第10条服务。

项目组成6　土壤和沉积物中的生物多样性

为第6条，第8条，第9条和第10条服务。

项目组成7　海洋生物多样性

为第6条，第7条，第8条，第10条和第16条技术的取得和转让以及第17条信息交流和第18条技术和科学合作服务。

有关海洋生物多样性的研究项目，1995年在印度尼西亚召开的《公约》缔约国大会上和《公约》第25条所规定的科学、技术和工艺咨询事务附属机构(SBSTTA)于1995年在法国召开的会议上都强调指出，正在制定本国的海岸和海洋生物多样性的国家级科研项目的国家数量不断在增加，因此在DIVERSITAS中对海洋生物多样性这个STAR可以处在一个辅助的位子上。

项目组成8　微生物生物多样性

为第7条，第9条，第10条和第15条遗传资源的取得服务

项目组成9　淡水生物多样性

为第1条，第7条和第10条服务

项目组成10　人类的影响范围

为第 8 条，第 9 条，第 10 条与第 11 条服务

DIVERSITAS 与《公约》的密切联系在“操作计划”上作了上述详尽的交代。

4 几点商榷意见

DIVERSITAS 项目这 10 个研究方面的每一个既有其独立研究的内容和意义又相互有密切的联系。其中最核心的组成方面是“生物多样性对生态系统功能的作用”。在 1991 年 IUBS 在讨论生物多样性研究领域时首先提出这个问题，发展到第二阶段，经过若干次的反复讨论而趋于成熟时，在图表说明中又把这问题放在核心的位置上。因此，本文对这个问题专门展开了讨论。

DIVERSITAS 项目 10 个研究方面，其每一个在历史上的研究基础以及目前的进展都是很不平衡的。例如系统学，虽然已经研究了近 200 年，可是仅以世界物种的发现和描述来看，完成的数量还只占一小部分，随着其他科学技术发展的渗透或借鉴，可能研究进展会加快，但任务还是非常艰巨。再以生物多样性的监测来说，发达国家在监测方法标准化上还未统一，未完全解决。此外，世界是如此之大，生态系统又是如此之多，哪些地区具有代表性或是监测的优先领域，监测结果能否反映一个地区，一个国家甚至是全球生物多样性的状况，对这问题还有不同观点。至于土壤和沉积物生物多样性，微生物生物多样性以及海洋生物多样性等方面都是最近才提出来，研究的任务是非常繁重的。因此，生物多样性的研究在国际上还处于很不完善的地步、发展的初级阶段。对我国生物多样性研究提出几点商榷的意见。

4.1 指导思想问题

目前我们所处的情况与 80 年代末，制定第八个五年计划时不同。1992 年《公约》已签订。我国已是缔约国成员之一，科学研究就必须为履约服务；要为我国甚至世界的生物多样性的保护、恢复和持续利用做出贡献。不同的部门或单位，应根据各自的性质和任务分别在应用、应用基础及基础研究不同角度进行工作。

4.2 代表性及基础问题

我国生物多样性的丧失是非常严重的，真实的现状是怎么样?按目前的国情其发展趋势又是如何?政府的决策者必须掌握这些真实的数据及趋势。此外，中国的各种生态系统的破坏也是惊人的。根据当地自然条件下能使生物多样性恢复的生境恢复也是亟待解决的。这些研究工作应在哪里进行?应该按中国国情从有代表性的优先地区，从不同角度加以考虑。当然也必须考虑到研究工作及人员的基础。人类的生存就是依赖于地球上的生物多样性，对一些野生动物的养殖，或对一些药用或其他有用植物的栽培当然是持续利用的手段之一，但如何合理持续利用野生的生物多样性，可能也是一个极为重要而经济的途径，也是一个重要研究方面。

4.3 与国际接轨问题

DIVERSITAS 已为我们提出了比较完善的生物多样性研究的各个领域。另外 DIVERSITAS 项目的本身也是一个国际项目，促进国际合作的项目。因此我们下一步的研究内容,尽可能与 DIVERSITAS 接轨,这既能提高我们的研究水平又能开展国际合作。此外，应熟悉国际上与生物多样性有关的国际动态。钱迎倩、马克平[1]已对物种 2000(Species 2000)作过一些介绍。根据新的资料介绍，物种 2000 项目已被 UNEP1996~1997 的生物多样性工作项目(Biodiversity Work Programme)所批准，并与《公约》的情报交换所机制(Clearing House Mechanism)相联系。1996 年 3 月在菲律宾马尼拉召开的研讨会上,这项目已为 18 个分类学数据库组织所正式采纳。由于刚起步，当前只包括下列生物类群：病毒、细菌、珊瑚、软体动物、甲壳纲、双翅目、黄蜂、蛾类和蝴蝶、甲虫、鱼类、鸟类、哺乳类、菌物(fungi)、仙人掌类、棕榈类、豆类、伞形花类和古植物。物种 2000 项目已于 1996 年 10 月 1 日起正式实施，这项目也设想每年都有一个年度清单(annual checklist)，作为一年一次的参考资料，并在 CD-ROM 和 Internet 上都合用。我国在分类学上已有很好的基础，在“八五”期间也都分别建立了数据库。为了与国际接轨，还应该加入这项目，将对下一步系统学的开展会有益处。Species 2000 表示热情地愿与世界范围的任何生物类群的全球物种数据库管理者们取得联系。(Species 2000 秘书处的地址：Species 2000 Secretariat, School of Biological Sciences, University of Southampton, Southampton, SO16 7PX. U. K.)

最后应提出的是，我们已有“八五”生物多样性研究的基础，在“八五”基础上，对生物多样性的认识与研究内容又有了新的认识，“九五”一定会有长足的进步。

参考文献

[1] 钱迎倩, 马克平. 生物多样性研究的几个国际热点. 广西科学, 1996, **16**: 295~299

[2] 赵士洞, 郝占庆. 从“DIVERSITAS 计划新方案”看生物多样性研究的发展趋势. 生物多样性, 1996, **4**: 125~129

[3] 王晨, 钱迎倩, 马克平. 系统学与生物多样性. 生命科学, 1996, **8**: 1~4

[4] IUBS, SCOPE, UNESCO *et al. DIVERSITAS, An Internationan Programme of Biodiversity Science, Operational Plan*, 1996

[5] Paine R T. Food web complexity and species diversity. *American Naturalist*. 1996, **100**: 65~75

[6] Paine R T. A note on trophic complexity and community stability . *American Naturalist*. 1969, **103**: 91~93

[7] Schulze E-D, Mooney H A. *Biodiversity and Ecosystem Function*. Springer-Verlag, Berlin, 1993

[8] Walker, B. H. Biodiversity and ecological redundancy. *Conservation Biology*, 1992, **6**: 18~23

[9] Lawton J H and Brown. V K. Redundancy in ecosystem. In: Schulze E-D and Mooney H A. eds. Biodiversity and Ecosystem Function. Springer-Verlage. Berlin. 1993. 255~270

[10] Vitousek P M. Biological invasions and ecosystem processes: Towards and integration of population biology and ecosystem studies. *Oikos*, 1990, **57**: 7~13

[11] Chapm F S I, Reynolds H L, Antonio C D′ *et al*. The functional role of species in terrestrial ecosystems. In, Walker B. *Global Change in Terrestrial Ecosystem(In press)*, 1996

[12] Heywood V H, Watson R T . *Global Biodiversity Assessment*. UNEP, Cambridge University Press. 1995

本文原载：应用与环境生物学报. 1998. 4(1): 95-99

生物多样性保护及其研究进展

马克平　钱迎倩

(中国科学院植物研究所)

摘　要　由于人口的增长和人类经济活动的加剧，致使生物多样性受到了严重的威胁，引起国际社会的普遍关注。生物多样性是生物及其与环境形成的生态复合体以及与此相关的各种生态过程的总和。具有十分重要的价值，是人类生存的物质基础，各国政府和有关的国际组织积极投入到保护生物多样性的全球行动中。为了促进保护工作，国内外都开展了相关的研究工作，综观该领域的研究现状，可以看出以下 7 个方面已成为当前生物多样性研究的热点：①生物多样性的调查、编目及信息系统的建立；②人类活动对生物多样性的影响；③生物多样性的生态系统功能；④生物多样性的长期动态监测；⑤物种濒危机制及保护对策的研究；⑥栽培植物与家养动物及其野生近缘的遗传多样性研究；⑦生物多样性保护技术与对策。结合我国的具体情况，建议优先考虑以下 4 个方面的研究：①生物多样性的调查、编目与动态监测；②物种濒危机制及保护对策的研究；③生物多样性的生态系统功能与生态系统管理；④栽培植物与家养动物及其野生近缘的遗传多样性研究。

关键词　生物多样性；保护；研究；进展

中图法分类号　Q145 + X171

生物多样性是地球上数十亿年来生命进化的结果，是生物圈的核心组成部分，也是人类赖以生存的物质基础。然而，随着人口的迅速增长与人类活动的加剧，生物多样性受到了严重的威胁，成为当前世界性的环境问题之一，受到国际社会的普遍关注。[1]

1　生物多样性的概念及其价值

生物多样性(biological diversity 或 biodiversity)是生物及其与环境形成的生态复合体以及与此相关的各种生态过程的总和，包括数以百万计的动物、植物、微生物和它们所拥有的基因以及它们与其生存环境形成的复杂的生态系统，是生命系统的基本特征。生命系统是一个等级系统(hierarchical system)，包括多个层次或水平：基因、细胞、组织、器官、种群、物种、群落、生态系统、景观。每一个层次都具有丰富的变化，即都存在着多样性。但理论与实践上重要，研究较多的主要有基因多样性(或遗传多样性)、物种多样性、生态系统多样性和景观多样性。[2]现在，人们往往把生物多样性视为生命实体本身，而不仅仅看作生命系统的重要特征之一。人类文化的多样性也可被认为是生物多样性的一部分。正如遗传多样性和物种多样性一样，人类文化(如游牧生活和移动耕作)

的一些特征表现出人们在特殊环境下生存的策略。同时，与生物多样性的其他方面一样，文化多样性有助于人们适应不断变化的外界条件。文化多样性表现在语言、宗教信仰、土地管理实践、艺术、音乐、社会结构、作物选择、膳食以及无数其他的人类社会特征的多样性上。[3]

生物多样性包括不同的水平，每个水平的多样性都有各自的特点，很难用统一的方法和标准予以测度。物种丰富度(species richness)可以用于物种水平的多样性，即用一定面积内的物种数目表示。更精确的方法是考虑物种之间的关系，即测度分类学多样性(taxonomic diversity)。例如一个有 2 种蛇和 1 种鸟的岛屿的多样性高于一个只有 3 种蛇的岛屿。生物群落多样性测度的方法相对比较成熟，除物种丰富度外，还有物种相对多度(species abundance)、物种多样性指数(species diversity index)和均匀度(evenness)等。[4] 常用的物种多样性指数主要有 Shannon-Wiener 指数和 Simpson 指数等。生态系统水平多样性测度的难度较大，主要是生态系统的边界不确定，本身的结构又比较复杂。但是，如果用一系列的标准来定义生态系统，其数量和分布还是可以测定的，也有人从种间关系或营养结构的角度构造生态系统多样性指数。[5-6]遗传多样性的测度要困难的多。形态上判定的遗传多样性如作物或家养动物的品种可以参照物种水平的方法测度，而染色体、蛋白质和 DNA 水平的遗传多样性的测度则很困难，目前还没有确定很好的测度公式或指标。但群体遗传学中等位基因频率、遗传一致性和遗传距离等的计算方法是很有参考价值的。[7]

生物多样性是人类赖以生存的物质基础，其价值可以从下列两个方面得以了解。第一，直接价值，从生物多样性的野生和驯化的组分中，人类得到了所需的全部食品、许多药物和工业原料，同时，它在娱乐和旅游业中也起着重要的作用；第二，间接价值，间接价值主要与生态系统的功能有关，通常它并不表现在国家核算体制上，但如果计算出来，它的价值大大超过其消费和生产性的直接价值，生物多样性的间接价值主要表现在固定太阳能、调节水文学过程、防止水土流失、调节气候、吸收和分解污染物、贮存营养元素并促进养分循环和维持进化过程等 7 个方面。随着时间的推移，生物多样性的最大价值可能在于为人类提供适应当地和全球变化的机会。[8] 生物多样性的未知潜力为人类的生存与发展显示了不可估量的美好前景。

2 生物多样性受到的威胁

近年来，物种灭绝的加剧，遗传多样性的减少，以及生态系统特别是热带森林的大规模破坏，引起了国际社会对生物多样性问题的极大关注。生物多样性丧失的直接原因主要有生境丧失和片段化、外来种的侵入、生物资源的过度开发、环境污染、全球气候变化和工业化的农业及林业等。但这些还不是问题的根本所在。根源在于人口的剧增和自然资源消耗的高速度、不断狭窄的农业、林业和渔业的贸易谱、经济系统和政策未能评估环境及其资源的价值、生物资源利用和保护产生的惠益分配的不均衡、知识及其应用的不充分以及法律和制度的不合理。总而言之，人类活动是造成生物多样性以空前速度丧失的根本原因。[9]

中国是生物多样性特别丰富的国家(mega-diversity countries)之一。据统计，中国的生物多样性居世界第八位，北半球第一位。同时，中国又是生物多样性受到最严重威胁的国家之一。中国的原始森林长期受到乱砍滥伐、毁林开荒等人为活动的影响，其面积以每年 $0.5\times104km^2$ 的速度减少；草原由于超载过牧、毁草开荒的影响，退化面积达 $87\times104km^2$。生态系统的大面积破坏和退化，不仅表现在总面积的减少，更为严重的是其结构和功能的降低或丧失使生存其中的许多物种已变成濒危种(endangered species)和受威胁种(threatened species)。高等植物中有 4000~5000 种受到威胁，占总种数的 15%~20%。在“濒危野生动植物种国际贸易公约”列出的 640 个世界性濒危物种中，中国就占 156 种，约为其总数的四分之一，形势是十分严峻的。[10]

生物多样性保护关系到中国的生存与发展。中国是世界上人口最多人均资源占有量低的国家，而且是 85%左右的人口在农村的农业大国，对生物多样性具有很强的依赖性。中国是近年来经济发展速度最快的国家之一，在很大程度上加剧了人口对环境特别是生物多样性的压力。如果不立即采取有效措施遏制这种恶化的态势，中国的持续发展是不可能实现的，甚至会威胁到世界的发展与安全。

3 生物多样性保护的重要行动

鉴于生物多样性面临的严峻局面，有关的国际组织或机构以及许多国家政府都纷纷采取措施，致力于生物多样性的保护与持续利用工作。联合国环境规划署在 1987~1988 年起草的 1990~1995 年联合国全系统中期环境方案中提出了保护生物多样性的目标、策略以及实施方案。1992 年 6 月在巴西里约热内卢召开的联合国环境与发展大会(UNCED)通过了 1994~2003 年为国际生物多样性十年(International Biodlversity Decade)的决议。同时，通过了《生物多样性公约》。当时有 150 多个国家的首脑在《公约》上签字。《公约》于 1993 年 12 月 29 日正式升效。截止 1996 年 8 月 28 日，已有 144 个国家或地区批准了该《公约》。《生物多样性公约》的宗旨是保护生物多样性、持续利用生物多样性以及公平共享利用遗传资源所取得的惠益(benefit)。《公约》主要包括国家主权与人类共同关心的问题、保护和持续利用、有关获取(aecess)的议题和资助机制 4 个方面的内容。该《公约》是一个框架文件，强调国家水平的行动，为各缔约国如何履行公约留下了充分的余地。《公约》还试图平衡缔约国之间的需求，区别对待发展中国家和发达国家。具体说来，《公约》要求发展中国家缔约国履行保护和持续利用的义务，而发达国家缔约国承担提供资金和技术转让的义务。《生物多样性公约》的履行必将有力地促进全球生物多样性保护与持续利用的进程。为了纪念《生物多样性公约》生效，更好地宣传和履行《公约》，联合国大会于 1994 年 12 月 29 日通过 49/119 号决议，决定从 1995 年起，每年的 12 月 29 日为“国际生物多样性日”。

4 研究的现状与趋势

国际科学联合会(ICUS)所属的国际生物科学联合会(IUBS)自 1983 年始，在热带 10

年计划(Decade of the Tropics)中就开展了“热带生态系统的物种多样性及其重要性”研究项目。并于1989年6月与联合国环境问题委员会(SCOPE)一起召开了“生物多样性的生态系统功能研讨会”。继而，这两个组织与联合国教科文组织(UNESCO)一起于1992年10月联合召开了“生物多样性编目与监测研讨会”，同时联合发起了一个全球性的生物多样性合作研究项目，即DIVERSITAS。目前，该项目的组织者已发展到由6个生物与环境领域最有影响的国际组织和机构组成。研究内容也大大拓宽，由原来的4个方面增加到现在的10个领域，包括5个核心领域：①生物多样性的生态系统功能；②生物多样性的起源、维持和丧失；③生物多样性的编目与分类；④生物多样性的监测；⑤生物多样性的保护、恢复和持续利用。5个交叉领域：①土壤和沉积物中的生物多样性；②海洋生物多样性；③微生物多样性；④淡水生物多样性；⑤人类对生物多样性的影响。DIVERSITAS是生物多样性领域内最大的国际合作研究项目。目前，各项准备工作基本就绪，即将付诸实施。[12]此外，世界保护监测中心(WCMC)长期以来对物种的濒危程度、濒危原因以及世界范围内自然保护区的现状及动态趋势进行监测。美国的Smithsonian研究院、自然保护组织(The Nature Conservancy)等也都开展规模较大的生物多样性研究项目。纵观该领域的研究现状可以看出以下7个方面已成为当前生物多样性研究的热点[10]：①生物多样性的调查、编目及信息系统的建立；②人类活动对生物多样性的影响；③生物多样性的生态系统功能；④生物多样性的长期动态监测；⑤物种濒危机制及保护对策的研究：⑥栽培植物与家养动物及其野生近缘的遗传多样性研究；⑦生物多样性保护技术与对策。此外，遗传修饰生命体释放对环境和人类健康可能产生的影响以及外来种效应等也受到国际社会的广泛关注。[13]

八五期间在有关部门的支持下，由中国科学院主持了三个生物多样性方面的重大研究项目，即国家科委支持的“中国生物多样性保护生态学基础研究”(执行期为1992~1996年)。国家自然科学基金委员会支持的“中国主要濒危植物保护生物学研究”(执行期为1993~1997年)和中国科学院支持的“生物多样性保护与持续利用的生物学基础”(执行期为1991~1995年)等项目，取得了一批可喜的研究成果。初步明确了重要森林、草原、淡水和珊瑚礁生态系统的受损现状及其原因；通过种群生存力分析、DNA序列分析等保育生物学新方法，评估了重要濒危物种的受威胁状态及其机制，为生物多样性保育，特别是重要物种和生态系统的保育提供了科学依据。已在国内外重要刊物发表大量有影响的研究论文，并正式出版了数本专著。

5 研究展望

根据国际上生物多样性保护研究的现状与发展趋势，并结合中国的具体情况，我们认为下列几个方面应做为本领域优先考虑的研究内容。

5.1 生物多样性的调查、编目与动态监测

至今没有一个人能对世界上生物的物种有一个确切的数字。[11] 说明在世界范围内

生物的调查、订名的工作远远没有做完。其中昆虫尤为突出，估计全世界昆虫可能高达3000 万种，但已描述的仅 75.1 万种。[14]我国约占 1/10，但目前已记载的仅 4 万多种。这种家底不清的局面，严重地影响着生物多样性的保护与持续利用。为此，很多国家和组织成立了专门机构或设立专门的研究计划。刚启动的国际性项目如“2000 年系统学议程”和“物种 2000 年”等。[15]

生物多样性监测与生物多样性编目有着密切的联系。可以认为，生物多样性监测就是在不同时刻对生物多样性组成部分的编目。前者旨在了解生物多样性在某一段时间内的变化过程，而后者则在于了解某一时刻生物多样性的状态。生物多样性监测主要在三个水平上进行：①物种及其种下等级的监测，选择受到严重威胁的物种、具有重要经济价值的贸易物种和重要作物或家养动物的品种及其野生近缘种等，对其种群动态和主要影响因素进行监测；②对重要生态系统的监测，选择重要的生态系统类型，在其典型地段建立一定面积的固定观测样地，对生态系统的组成、结构、关键物种、受威胁物种和主要的生态学过程进行监测。生态系统水平的生物多样性监测应在野外定位研究站、自然保护区、国家公园等设施和基地的基础上，采取网络化途径，建立监测系统。并使这一工作与自然保护地(protected area)的管理实践相结合；③对景观多样性的监测，选择一定的区域，利用遥感手段(卫星照片和航空照片等)和地理信息系统等计算机技术对景观格局和过程及其影响因素进行监测。由此获得的信息可以为区域规划、持续发展和生物多样性保护等的宏观决策提供科学依据。

利用上述三个层次监测获取的信息不断地更新相应的数据库和图形库，并据此做出规划和决策。使得生物多样性保护与持续利用实践建立在科学的基础之上，使其真正变成有效的行动。

5.2 物种濒危机制及保护对策的研究

据国际自然与自然资源保护联盟的物种保护监测中心估计，全球有 10%的物种面临灭绝，到本世纪末，将有 15%~20%的物种从地球上消失；如果不采取有效措施，灭绝速率可能超过 20%，形势十分严峻。更为严重的是我们对于濒危物种知识的贫乏。[16]研究内容主要包括物种受威胁等级的评价、濒危物种生殖生物学研究、濒危物种群体遗传学与生态遗传学研究、濒危物种种群生态学研究以及在此基础上进行濒危物种保护对策与措施的研究等。

5.3 生物多样性的生态系统功能与生态系统管理

生态系统生态学着眼于不同时空尺度上系统对能量和物质的获取、贮存和传递过程。在研究生态系统功能与环境之间关系时，只注重生态过程而非物种组成。然而，事实上物种组成抑或物种多样性和基因多样性对于相应的生态系统功能的发挥是十分重要的。由于人文因素的影响，生态系统退化严重。如何从生物多样性的生态系统功能的机制出发，对受损生态系统进行恢复与重建受到人们的高度重视。[3, 17]

这一领域研究的问题主要有：生物多样性怎样影响生态系统抵御不利环境的能力或

者说生物多样性与生态系统维持或稳定的关系如何？景观的改变如何通过影响不同水平生物多样性的变化而影响生态系统功能？物种之间相互关系怎样影响生态过程，继而影响生态系统功能？生态系统的关键种及其作用如何？生态系统中是否存在物种冗余(Species redundancy)？不同类群的生物怎样影响生态系统功能等。[18~20]

5.4 栽培植物与家养动物及其野生近缘的遗传多样性研究

遗传信息储存在染色体和细胞器基因组的 DNA 序列中。虽然动植物和其他生物一样，都能准确地复制自己的遗传物质 DNA，将自己的遗传信息一代一代地遗传下去，保持遗传性状的稳定性，但有许多因素能影响 DNA 复制的准确性。这些影响因素有的是来自外界的，有的是本身的。可能引起的变化是多种多样的，小的可能是一个碱基对的变化，大的可能由于 DNA 片断的倒位、易位、缺失或转座而引起多个碱基对的变化，从而导致不同程度的遗传变异。随着遗传变异的不断积累，遗传多样性的内容也就不断地得到丰富。

众所周知，物种水平的多样性到目前为止我们还远非了解。[9]述及遗传多样性，情况就更令人失望了。据 Woodruff 统计，[21]仅有约几千个物种进行过遗传学研究，后者仅占已描述物种的很小一部分。而对这种状况，唯一的出路在于确定优先重点。目前，国际上遗传多样性研究最多的生物类群就是家养动物和栽培植物及其野生近缘。[10]这方面研究可为遗传资源保存、品种改良以及生物生产力提高提供重要理论依据。

参考文献

[1] Wilson EO. Francis MP ed. Biodiversity Washington D.C.: National Academy Press, 1988
[2] 马克平. 试论生物多样性的概念, 生物多样性. 1993, 1(1): 20~22
[3] Heywood VH. Watson RT ed. Global biodiversity assessment. Cambridge: Cambridge Universoty Press, 1995
[4] 马克平. 生物群落多样性的测度方法, 见：钱迎倩, 马克平主编. 生物多样性研究的原理与方法. 北京：中国科学技术出版社, 1994, 141~165
[5] Zhou, J *et al* An index of ecosystem diversity. *Ecological Modelling*. 1991, **59**: 151~163
[6] 赵志模, 郭依泉. 群落生态学原理与方法. 重庆：科学技术文献出版社重庆分社，1990
[7] 胡志昂, 王洪新. 研究遗传多样性的原理和方法. 见：钱迎倩, 马克平主编. 生物多样性研究的原理与方法. 北京：中国科学技术出版社, 1994, 117~122
[8] 陈灵芝主编. 中国的生物多样性：现状及其保护对策. 北京：科学出版社，1993
[9] 世界资源研究所(WRI)等著. 中国科学院生物多样性委员会译. 全球生物多样性策略. 北京：中国标准出版社, 1993
[10] 马克平, 钱迎倩, 王晨. 生物多样性研究的现状与发展趋势. 见：钱迎倩, 马克平主编. 生物多样性研究的原理与方法. 北京：中国科学技术出版社, 1994, 1~12
[11] May RM. How many species are there on earth？*Science*. 1988, 241：1441~1449
[12] DIVERSITAS. DIVERSITAS: An international programme of biodiversity science. operational plan. DIVERSITAS. Paris, 1996
[13] 钱迎倩, 马克平. 生物技术与生物安全. 自然资源学报. 1995, 10(4):322~331
[14] McNeely JA 著. 李文军等译. 保护世界的生物多样性. 见：中国科学院生物多样性委员会编. 生物多样性译丛(一). 北京：中国科学技术出版社, 1992, 1~164
[15] 钱迎倩, 马克平. 生物多样性研究的几个国际热点. 广西植物. 1996, 16(4): 295~299

[16] Ehrlich PR, Wilson EO. Biodiversity studies: science and policy. *Science*. 199l, 253: 758-762
[17] Schulze E-D，Mooney HA ed. Biodiversity and ecosystems function. Berlin: Springer-Verlag, 1993
[18] Lawton J. 1994. what do species do in ecosystems. *Oikos*. 1994, 71(3): 367~374
[19] Moffat AS. Biodiversity is a boon to ecosystems, not species. *Science*. 1996, 271: 1497
[20] Tillman D, Wedin D, Knops J. Productivity and sustainability influenced by biodiversity in grassland ecosystems. Nature. 1996, 379: 718~720
[21] Woodruff DS. The problems of conserving genes and species. In: Western D. Pearl MC ed. Conservation for the twenty-first century Oxford: Oxford University. Press, 1989, 76~88

科学普及与考察见闻

本文原载：农村科学实验. 1978. (6): 2-3

这已经不是幻想

——介绍植物体细胞杂交

钱迎倩

(中国科学院植物研究所)

十几年前，有人就提出来要培育什么“豆小麦”，还有什么“番茄薯”。如果真有了地上结番茄、地下长薯块这样的奇异植物，的确是件大好事。可是，这在过去不过是种美好的幻想，现在通过体细胞杂交，再接再厉，这种幻想就有可能成为现实。

体细胞杂交是怎么回事呢?

奇异的“全能性”

高等植物的细胞与高等动物的细胞有一个很大的不同，这就是，经过人工培养，单个的植物细胞能够长成一棵完整的植物，动物细胞就办不到。植物细胞的这种本领，人们叫它为“全能性”。实践证明，不仅植物的细胞有全能性，就连没有细胞壁的原生质体也有这种全能性。

原生质体在合适的培养条件下，会长出细胞壁，还会按一分二、二分四这样进行细胞分裂，结果或长成一团没有一定形状的细胞堆，称为“愈伤组织”；或长成一个类似小胚胎的一团细胞，称为“胚状体”。愈伤组织被移到另一个合适的培养条件下，就可以长出根和苗，成为一棵小植物。胚状体通过不断地发育。也能成为一棵小植物。

像烟草、胡萝卜、矮牵牛、油菜、颠茄等十几种植物，现在已经能够从原生质体起源，长成为完整的植株了。

图1　番茄薯

酶的妙用

怎样得到原生质体呢?

植物的细胞与细胞之间，靠一种叫果胶质的东西相互连结，并且在各式各样的细胞外面，还包有一层主要由纤维素构成的细胞壁。

人们通过一种叫果胶酶的蛋白质处理植物，可以将连在一起的细胞一个个拆散；然后再用一种叫纤维素酶的蛋白质处理整个细胞，就会脱去细胞外面穿着的厚厚“外衣”。就这样，靠着酶的帮助，人们就得到了大量裸露出来的原生质体。

目前，人们利用这种方法，已经能从植物的根、叶、根瘤、胚芽鞘、子叶、果实、果皮和花瓣等各个不同部位，得到大量具有生活力的原生质体了。

由“媒人”撮合

有性杂交，是通过受精作用来完成的。体细胞杂交，则是由“媒人”从中撮合，才能把不同的原生质体融合到一起。这个“媒人”就是融合诱导剂。

早期的融合诱导剂，用的是硝酸钠。只因它的诱导率太低，近来才又被一种叫聚乙二醇的药物，结合高钙高氢离子浓度的办法所代替，获得了比较理想的效果。

目前，通过这种“媒人”的撮合，已经能够把大豆与大麦，大豆与豌豆，胡萝卜与大麦，以及大豆与烟草等的原生质体融合到一起了。因为这种原生质体来源于不同属、不同科的植物，它的融合体就叫做异源融合体。

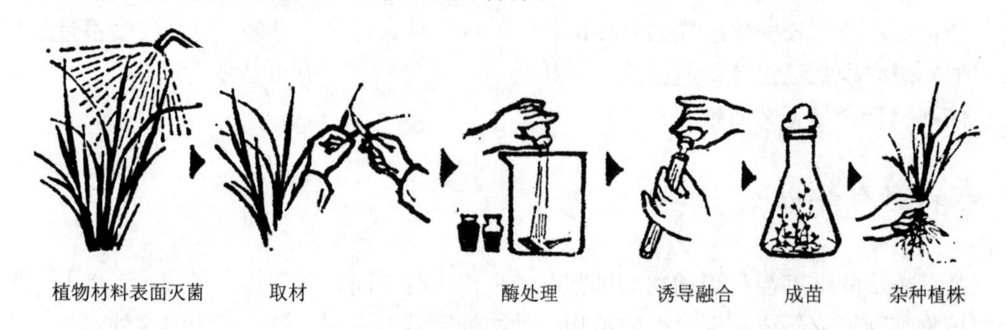

图 2　植物体细胞杂交过程示意图

巧法挑选

不过，两种原生质体经诱导融合后，不仅有甲与乙融合而成的异源融合体，也有甲与甲或乙与乙融合而成的同源融合体；既有经融合的融合体，还有未经融合的原生质体。那么，如何从成千上万的混合体中，把人们所需要的那种异源融合体挑选出来呢？

人们知道：不同的原生质体对培养基的营养要求不同，对某种药物的抵抗能力也不一样。从这两点出发，如果能设计一种培养基，让它只满足甲原生质体生长所需的营养，可又具有乙原生质体能够抵抗的药物，这样，把经过诱导融合的混合体，都放在这种培养基上培养，结果成活下来的必定是具有甲乙两种原生质体遗传物质的融合体。这种互补选择法，看来还是一种比较有希望的好办法。

接着，存活下来的异源融合体中的两个细胞核，进一步融合成一个核，并重新长出新的细胞壁。这时的融合体，就可以叫做“杂种细胞”了。

可喜的收获

体细胞杂交进展的情况如何呢?

除了在烟草属、矮牵牛属中的不同种间，通过体细胞杂交的途径，已经获得了杂交种植株以外，更可喜的是：有人用大豆与大麦的原生质体融合，它的杂种细胞已经分裂，并得到了近一百个细胞的细胞团；也有人用矮牵牛与爬山虎的原生质体融合，或用大豆与烟草的原生质体融合，它们的杂种细胞也都发育成了愈伤组织。

可以设想，由于体细胞杂交的初步成功，只要再接再厉，今后高光效作物与低光效作物的杂交，甚至把叶绿体、固氮细菌和兰绿藻等引进原生质体中去的一天，已经不会太远了。

本文原载：植物杂志. 1978. (3): 24-26

植物组织培养的培养基

钱迎倩

(中国科学院植物研究所)

植物组织培养要获得成功，有两个特别重要的因素，一个是培养组织的材料来源(或称外植体的来源)；另一个是培养基。下面我们着重讲讲有关培养基的一些知识。

培养基的成分

在植物组织培养中所用的大多数培养基是由无机营养物、碳源、维生素、生长调节物质和有机附加物等五类物质组成(表 1、2)。

无机营养物 它包括大量元素和微量元素两部分。一般情况下，培养基中至少含有各为 25 毫克分子，浓度的硝酸盐和钾。一般来说，铵的含量超过 8 毫克分子时就会对培养物有毒害作用，但对正规的愈伤组织培养和细胞悬浮培养来说，硝酸盐加铵的浓度可以提高到 60 毫克分子，这说明铵可能对某些培养物有重要作用。通常，钙、硫、镁的浓度在 1~3 毫克分子比较合适。微量营养物包括碘(Ⅰ)、硼(B)、锰(Mn)、锌(Zn)、钼(Mo)、铜(Cu)、钴(Co)和铁(Fe)，其中碘可能不太重要。

碳源和能源 大多数细胞对蔗糖浓度的需要范围是 2%~4%。蔗糖可用葡萄糖、果糖来代替，其他糖类作碳源不够理想。m-肌醇可能不太重要，但一般培养基中都加它，因为它有增强愈伤组织生长的作用。

维生素 谈到维生素，只有盐酸硫胺素是必需的，而烟酸和盐酸吡哆素对生长只起促进作用。

氨基酸和有机附加物 一般来说，氨基酸并非必需，但在摸索一个新的细胞培养时，如果感到培养基中的无机营养物对培养物的生长不太适宜时，最好是加入 0.05%~0.1% 的水解干酪素。经过几次继代后，可加入 L-谷酰胺(2~10 毫克分子)来代替水解干酪素。在以后多次继代后，甚至把有机氮删掉。

激素 附加的激素有两类：一是生长素类，常用的有 2,4-D、萘乙酸(NAA)、吲哚乙酸(IAA)等；另一类是细胞分裂素类，常用的有激动素(K)、玉米素、6-苄基嘌呤等。在大多数情况下，诱导愈伤组织只用 2,4-D(10^{-6}~10^{-5} 克分子)即可获得成功。当然，加入一种细胞分裂素(10^{-6}~10^{-7} 克分子)可能更好。而诱导分化植株时，则用 NAA 与 6-苄基嘌呤、玉米素或异戊烯嘌呤中的任一种的组合可能比较好。用 2,4-D 诱导细胞分裂，有抑制形态发生的趋势。NAA 可由 IAA 代替，但 IAA 应该过滤灭菌，以防止高温高压对 IAA 的破坏。另外，IAA 也可以被细胞中的酶降解。对谷物来说，用 2,4-5-三氯苯氧乙酸(2,4-5-T)诱导愈伤组织效果较好。

培养基的制备

水和药品 配制培养基用的蒸馏水最好是用玻璃器皿重蒸馏的去矿质盐的蒸馏水。所用药品要求比较纯的。生长调节物质在应用前如果有可能最好进行重结晶。蛋白质水解物有用酸水解的及酶水解的两种方法，最好是用酶水解的，因为这样可以使氨基酸保持在自然状态中保存。

母液 在制备培养基之前，先配制一系列母液。大量矿质盐(NO_3^-、NH_4、P、Mg、Ca 和SO_4^{2-})可配制成 10 倍浓度的母液；微量矿质盐和维生素可配制成 1000 倍的浓度，两者都贮存在冰箱里。把钙盐和碘化钾从母液中分出来比较好。对于 NAA 2, 4-D 和类似的化合物，要先用少量的乙醇来溶解，然后加水至 2~3 毫克分子浓度。细胞分裂素则先加少量的 0.5N 盐酸(HCl)，并加微热来溶解，然后加水至 1~2 毫克分子的浓度。这些化合物也可在二甲亚砜中溶解。

高压灭菌和保存 将全部矿质盐加维生素配制成 10 倍浓度进行保存，而蔗糖、激素和其他要素则在制备培养基时再加。pH 调整在 5.5~6.2 之间。制备好的培养基在 120℃下高压灭菌 15~20 分钟。培养基中，除 IAA 和 L-谷酰胺外，大多数成分都经得住高压灭菌。此外，盐酸硫胺素经高压灭菌后，可能有一定的损失。灭菌后的培养基可在室温下(最合适的温度是 10℃)保存。

几种常用的培养基

在早期，多采用 White 培养基。它含有植物细胞需要的营养。但是，要使愈伤组织(或悬浮培养物)在这种培养基中不断而快速地生长，其中氮和钾的量就不合适了，应补充酵母提取物、蛋白质水解物、氨基酸、椰乳或其他有机附加物。

MS(Murashigc-Skoog)培养基，原来是为培养烟草细胞设计的。目前它应用的范围较广泛，如在固体培养条件下培养愈伤组织；在液体培养条件下作细胞悬浮培养；还用在形态发生的研究方面，都得到好的结果。这种培养基中无机营养物的数量和比例都较合适，足以满足很多培养细胞在营养和生理上的要求，在一般情况下不必加入氨基酸、水解干酪素、酵母提取物或椰乳等类有机附加物。MS 培养基中硝酸盐、钾和铵的含量比其他培养基高，这是它的明显特点。

ER(Eriksson)培养基与 MS 是非常相似的，但其中磷酸盐的量比 MS 的高一倍，而微量营养物浓度则比 MS 低得多。它对某些细胞的培养是合用的。

B_5 培养基的主要特点是铵的含量较低，因为铵对不少培养物来说有抑制其生长的作用。有人用 B_5 与 MS 和 ER 作过比较培养实验，发现有些植物的愈伤组织和细胞培养物在 MS 中长得比在 B_5 和 ER 中好一些，有的植物则相反。

SH (Schenk 和 Hildebrandt)培养基与 B_5 相类似，其矿质盐的量稍高一点，铵和磷酸盐是作为一种化合物来提供的。

HE(Heller)培养基在欧洲得到广泛应用。它的盐含量比较低，并含有一些不必要的化合物。这种培养基中的钾和硝酸盐是通过不同的化合物来提供的。镍盐和铝盐可能不必要。其中没有钼盐，但是按植物营养的需要说来，培养基中应该有钼盐。

N_6 培养基是中国科学院植物研究所的科研人员自行设计的，在国内已经广泛用在花药和花粉的培养上。这种培养基适用于禾谷类植物花药和花粉的培养。其成分与 B_5 相似，但也不含钼盐。

讨论不同培养基的相似性，主要是比较它们的矿质盐的成分，因为培养基中维生素、激素和其他附加物是随着不同种的植物和不同的研究目的而异的。过去曾经报道过不少新的培养基，往往认为由于加入了有机附加物，满足了细胞对氮和其他营养物的需要，适宜细胞的生长。而得到好的结果。但是在很多情况下，这种需要可以通过增加无机盐的浓度，特别是提高氮、蔗糖和维生素的浓度而得到同样的效果。

介绍上述培养基，是为了在不同目的的组织培养研究中，以此为起点，进一步发展新的培养基或者进一步摸索对某些细胞所特需的激素或有机附加物。

几个问题的讨论

怎样设计一种新的培养基？要了解某一种新的植物细胞在营养上和生长上的要求，应作系统的实验。还要研究这种植物细胞对特殊营养化合物的特殊要求，并且还要了解加入这些化合物后与其他化合物有什么结合效应。这种实验应当采用 MS 培养基中的矿质盐作对照。MS 中的维生素、蔗糖和肌醇的量也可以作为一种起点。用 2，4-D 与某种细胞分裂素配合作为这个实验中的激素比较好。如要加有机氮(例如水解干酪素)，应该作一系列的浓度试验。有机氮不一定必要，但有提高生长速度的效果，特别当愈伤组织在起动时更是如此。在作加维生素实验时，应该有一个对照，就是只加盐酸硫胺素，因为已经知道盐酸硫胺素对某些植物细胞是必需的。

表 1　6 种植物组织和细胞培养基中矿质盐含量的比较

盐　类 大量矿质盐	MS		ER		B_5		SH		HE		N_6	
	mg/l	mM	mg/l	mM	mg/l	mM	mg/l	mM	mg/l	mM	mg/l	mM
硝酸铵 (NH_4NO_3)	1650	20.6	1200	15.0							463	5.8
硝酸钠 (KNO_3)	1900	18.8	1900	18.8	2500	25	2500	25			2830	28.0
氯化钙 ($CaCl_2 \cdot 2H_2O$)	440	3.0	440	3.0	150	1.0	200	1.4	75	0.5	166	1.1
硫酸镁 ($MgSO_4 \cdot 7H_2O$)	370	1.5	370	1.5	250	1.0	400	1.6	250	1.0	185	0.75
磷酸二氢钾 (KH_2PO_4)	170	1.25	340	2.5							400	3.0
硫酸铵 [$(NH_4)_2SO_4$]					134	1.0						

续表

盐类 大量矿质盐	MS		ER		B_5		SH		HE		N_6	
	mg/l	mM	mg/l	mM	mg/l	mM	mg/l	mM	mg/l	mM	mg/l	mM
磷酸铵 ($NH_4H_2PO_4$)							300	2.6				
硝酸钠 ($NaNO_3$)									600	7.0		
磷酸钠 ($NaH_2PO_4 \cdot H_2O$)					150	1.1			125	0.9		
氯化钾 (KCl)									750	10.0		
微量矿质盐	mg/l	μM	mg/l	μM	mg/l	μM	mg/l	μM	mg/l	μM	mg/l	μM
碘化钾 (KI)	0.83	5.0			0.75	4.5	1.0	6.0	0.01	0.06	0.8	4.8
硼酸 (H_3BO_3)	6.2	100	0.63	10	3.0	50	5.0	80	1.0	16.2	1.6	26.0
硫酸锰 ($MnSO_4 \cdot 4H_2O$)	22.3	100	2.23	10					0.1	0.5	4.4	19.7
硫酸锰 ($MnSO_4 \cdot H_2O$)					10	60	10	60				
硫酸锌 ($ZnSO_4 \cdot 7H_2O$)	8.6	30			2.0	7.0	1.0	3.5	1.0	3.5	1.5	5.2
Zn、维尔烯酸盐			15	37								
钼酸钠 ($Na_2MoO_4 \cdot 2H_2O$)	0.25	1.0	0.025	0.1	0.25	1.0	0.1	0.4				
硫酸铜 ($CuSO_4 \cdot 5H_2O$)	0.025	0.1	0.0025	0.01	0.025	0.1	0.2	0.8	0.03	0.12		
氯化钴 ($CoCl_2 \cdot 6H_2O$)	0.025	0.1	0.0025	0.01	0.025	0.1	0.1	0.4				
氯化铝 ($AlCl_3$)									0.03	0.22		
氯化镍 ($NiCl_2 \cdot 6H_2O$)									0.03	0.13		
三氯化铁 ($FeCl_3 \cdot 6H_2O$)									1.0	3.7		
螯合剂钠盐 $Na_2 \cdot EDTA$	37.3	100	37.3	100	37.3	100	20	55			37.3	100
硫酸亚铁 ($FeSO_4 \cdot 7H_2O$)	27.8	100	27.8	100	27.8	100	15	55			27.8	100
蔗糖	30(g/l)		40(g/l)		20(g/l)		30(g/l)				50(g/l)	
pH	5.7		5.8		5.5		5.8				5.8	

表2　5种培养基中所用的维生素，激素和附加物的种类和数量

化合物	MS mg/l	ER mg/l	B_5 mg/l	SH mg/l	N_6* mg/l
肌醇	100		100	10000	
菸酸	0.5	0.5	1.0	5.0	0.5
盐酸硫胺素	0.1	0.5	10.0	5.0	1.0
盐酸吡哆素	0.5	0.5	1.0	0.5	0.5
甘氨酸	2.0	2.0			2.0
吲哚乙酸 (IAA)	1-30				0.2
萘乙酸 (NAA)		1.0			
激动素	0.04-10	0.02	0.1		1.0
2, 4-D			0.1-1.0	0.5	2.0
P-氯苯氧基醋酸 (P-CPA)				2.0	

* 诱导愈伤组织时加入 2, 4-D，诱导分化时加入 IAA 和激动素。

表 3　6 种培养基中无机营养物的浓度

大量营养物(mM)	MS	ER	B_5	SH	HE	N_6
钾 (K)	20	21.3	25	25	10	31
硝态氮 [$N(NO_3)$]	40	33.8	25	25	7.0	34
铵态氮 [$N(NH_4)$]	20	15.0	2.0	2.6		5.8
镁 (Mg)	1.5	1.5	1.0	1.6	1.0	0.75
磷 (P)	1.25	2.5	1.1	2.6	0.9	3.0
钙 (Ca)	3.0	3.0	1.0	1.4	0.5	1.1
硫 (S)	1.5	1.5	1.0	1.6	1.0	0.75
钠 (Na)			1.1		7.9	
氯 (Cl)	6.0	6.0	2.0	2.8	0.11	2.2
微量营养物 (μM)						
碘 (I)	5.0		4.5	6.0	0.06	4.8
硼 (B)	100	10	50	80	16	26
锰 (Mn)	100	10	60	60	0.5	19.7
锌 (Zn)	30	37	7.0	3.5	3.5	5.2
钼 (Mo)	1.0	0.1	1.0	0.4		
铜 (Cu)	0.1	0.01	0.15	0.8	0.12	
钴 (Co)	0.1	0.01	0.1	0.4		
铝 (AI)					0.22	
镍(Ni)					0.13	
铁 (Fe)	100	100	100	55	3.7	100

如何鉴别一种新培养基效果的优劣？一方面要看是否有好的重复性，同时还要与现有的培养基作比较。必须有三次以上的继代培养，每次都定量测定其生长速度，并有一个标准培养基作对照，才能肯定其优点。另外，当细胞转移到一个新培养基中以后，要注意在第一、第二次继代培养时，因细胞没有适应新的环境前，往往生长速度减缓。因此，只有经过 2~3 次继代培养后才能正确的评价某一种培养基是否适宜于某种材料的生长。

如何快速有效地建立起一个组织培养系统呢？除了要了解每一种植物一般的营养和环境条件要求之外，还必须研究适合其生长的各种精确的条件。其中包括有激素和材料的来源。想要使培养物快速生长(如要求在 24~36h 就产生一个细胞世代的话)，不仅要有合适的培养基和生长条件，继代培养的时间也很重要。此外，还有细胞的选择问题。不注意这几点，就会化很长的时间去研究一种新的培养系统，或者会增加一些不必要的变化因素而造成今后分析的困难。

最后一个问题是如何解释培养细胞的行为。在文献中可能出现使人误解或矛盾的结论，这往往是由于没有很好的分析具体的培养条件所造成的。从慢速生长的愈伤组织细胞所获得的生化、结构或遗传稳定性方面的数据，就不能与从快速生长的悬浮培养细胞所得到的数据相比较。同样，生长在加有某些抽提物(其详细成分还不清楚)的复杂培养基中培养的细胞也不可能与培养在简单培养基中的细胞一样。此外，要肯定细胞的某一种特殊的行为，必须有一个合适的对照实验。例如，早期的研究认为培养的胡萝卜细胞要求有胚胎发生，需要培养基中加椰乳和某些激素，但是当作了简单的对照试验后，说明加这些物质并不需要。

本文原载：植物杂志. 1977. (6): 27-29

植物细胞

——植物细胞的基本结构

朱至清　钱迎倩

(中国科学院植物研究所)

细胞是生物的结构和生命活动的基本单位,除病毒和噬菌体这类最简单的生物以外，现存的所有生物都是由细胞构成的。细胞的发现是生物学上的一件大事，它使人们对于生命本质的认识前进了一大步。伟大导师恩格斯曾经高度评价了细胞学说，把它和能量转化规律与进化论并列为十九世纪自然科学的三大发现。恩格斯指出：**“第一是发现了细胞，发现细胞是这样一种单位，整个植物体和动物体都是从它的繁殖和分化中发育起来的。由于这一发现，我们不仅知道一切高等有机体都是按照一个共同规律发育和生长的，而且通过细胞的变异能力指出了使有机体能改变自己的物种并从而能实现一个比个体发育更高的发育的道路。”**在这里恩格斯不仅把细胞看做生命的结构单位，并且深刻地指出细胞又是生物个体发育和系统发育的基础。研究细胞的构造和机能对于认识生命和改造生物具有重要的意义。

植物细胞在一些基本方面和动物细胞是一致的，但它又有独自的特点。植物细胞具有细胞壁和特殊的细胞器——叶绿体。重要的是植物细胞还能在实验条件下从一个细胞再生出完整的有机体。利用植物细胞的这一特点，我们采用花粉培养、原生质体培养、细胞融合及核酸分子导入等新技术有可能开辟改造植物的新途径。正因为如此，近年来植物细胞方面的研究十分活跃，进展也较快。要想系统地了解植物细胞，首先必须认识细胞的构造，这里我们简略地介绍植物细胞的基本构造。

根据细胞内部结构的复杂程度可以把细胞分为两大类，即原核细胞和真核细胞。原核细胞处于细胞进化的原始阶段，在这种类型中只有一个膜系统，即质膜及其衍生物，其他的内膜则是直接与质膜相连或是由质膜起源的。在原核生物中有核物质，但这些核物质没有形成一定形态结构的细胞核。最简单的植物是细菌和蓝藻，它们均属于原核细胞。真核细胞是较原核细胞进化的类型，具有细胞核和各种特化的细胞器，细胞中有如几个膜系统。

现在我们以蓝藻为例来说明原核细胞的基本构造(图 1)。蓝藻细胞的最外面是一层胶质鞘，鞘内有细胞壁，其成分为纤维素及果胶质。蓝藻细胞的质膜为一单层膜，厚度为 75~100 埃[10 000 埃(Å)=1 微米(μ)]。细胞质中有光合作用片层(或称束片)，其上附着有叶绿素 a 和藻蓝素。光合作用片层和质膜是连续的。在细胞中央区域分布着核物质，它与细胞质之间不存在界膜，通常叫类细胞核。此外在细胞质中还分布着核糖体、糖原颗粒和类脂颗粒。蓝藻和细菌的细胞是相当小的，一般长约几微米，直径 1 微米或更小。从结构上看它们比真核细胞简单得多，但在生物化学上它们还是极为复杂的。蓝藻和光合细菌可以在只有无机盐和水的环境中生存，它们利用太阳能把这些简单的物质合成它生存所必需的各种复杂的高分子化合物(核酸、蛋白质、类脂和碳水化合物等)。

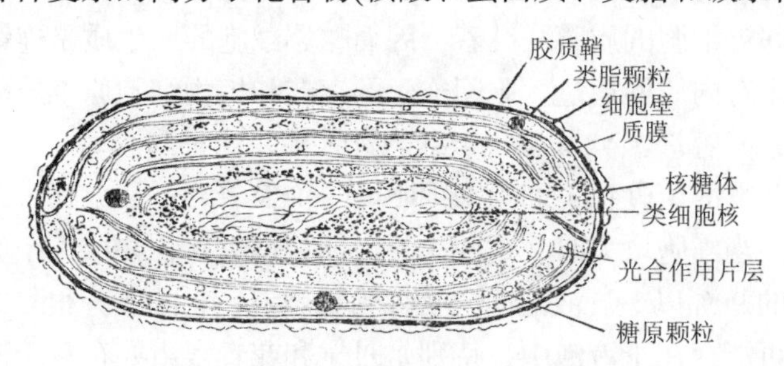

图 1 蓝藻的结构示意图

除细菌和蓝藻外，其他植物(绿藻、真菌、苔藓、蕨类和种子植物等)的细胞均为真核细胞。高等植物是多细胞的有机体，植物体由各种组织和器官组成，而每一种组织以至同一种组织中细胞均分化为许多特化的类型。尽管如此，各种植物细胞的基本构造单位仍然是相似的。为了叙述的方便，我们利用图 2 说明真核植物细胞的内部结构。

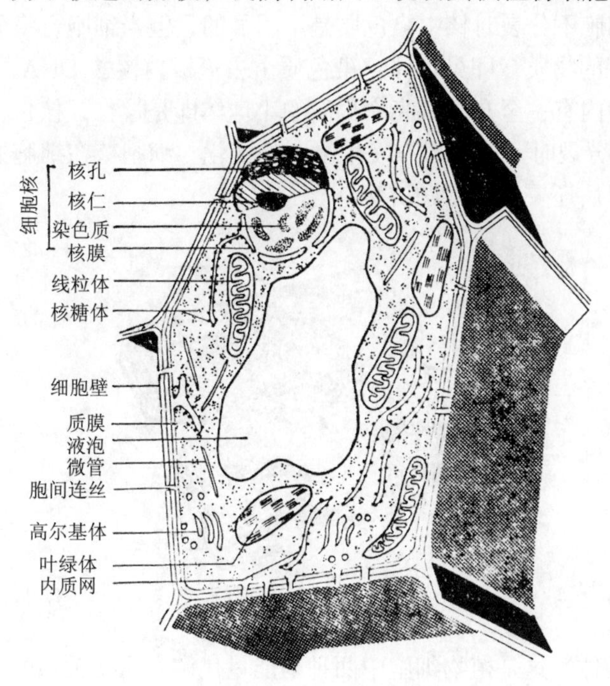

图 2 真核植物细胞模式图

细胞壁 细胞壁是植物细胞的外壳。壁的中部为果胶质构成的中层，它在细胞之间起连结和缓冲作用。中层的两侧为初生壁，主要由纤维素和半纤维素组成。在某些特化的细胞中，初生壁向外加厚形成次生壁。细胞壁构成支持植物体的骨架。

质膜和胞间连丝　质膜是原生质(或细胞质)外面的一单层膜，厚度是 70~100 埃，在光学显微镜下是看不到的。细胞和外界以及细胞之间的物质交换通过质膜进行，质膜具有选择性吸收的能力，同时它还可以通过本身的内陷把外部的物质包裹起来而转移到细胞内部，这种现象叫做胞饮现象。在质膜上除了胞间连丝所在的位置外没有其他形态学上的孔。胞间连丝是植物细胞特有的构造。通过电子显微镜可以看到，在胞间连丝中，一个细胞的质膜和邻近细胞的质膜联结着，因而相邻细胞的原生质是连续的，有时还可以看到在胞间连丝中有内质网通过。胞间连丝的存在和植物细胞原生质的连续性有利于细胞间的物质转运，并容许大分子从一个细胞进入另一个细胞。

液泡和液泡膜　液泡是分化了的植物细胞的一个显著的特征。在未充分分化的细胞中含有许多小液泡，当细胞增大时，这些小液泡体积增大并合并成一个大液泡，其体积可以占到整个细胞的 90%以上。液泡内含物称为细胞液，它的成分很复杂，细胞产生的任何可溶性物质都可能存在于液泡中，特别是丹宁和花青素主要存在于液泡中。液泡是植物细胞的储藏器和排泄器，一方面，一些营养物质(如蔗糖、无机盐和可溶性蛋白质)可以贮存在液泡中，另一方面，植物新陈代谢形成的不能再利用的物质(如丹宁、草酸钙等)也排泄到细胞液中去。液泡的外膜为一单层膜，它选择透性的能力比质膜还强一些。

细胞核和核仁　细胞核是细胞的重要成分。在细胞分裂间期，核为一圆球体。核表面是核膜，它是双层膜，膜上均匀分布着直径约 400~700 埃的核孔(图 3)。细胞核的主要成分是染色质。细胞不分裂时核中染色质是不明显的，但当细胞行将分裂的时候，染色质浓缩成为着色深的物质，即染色体。染色质由去氧核糖核酸(DNA)、组蛋白和少量的酸性蛋白组成。核内有一至几个折光率很高的小球体即是核仁，核仁含有大量的核糖核酸(RNA)。在细胞分裂时，核的形态发生复杂的变化。细胞核在细胞的遗传和代谢上都是极其重要的，以后还要进行专题讲解。

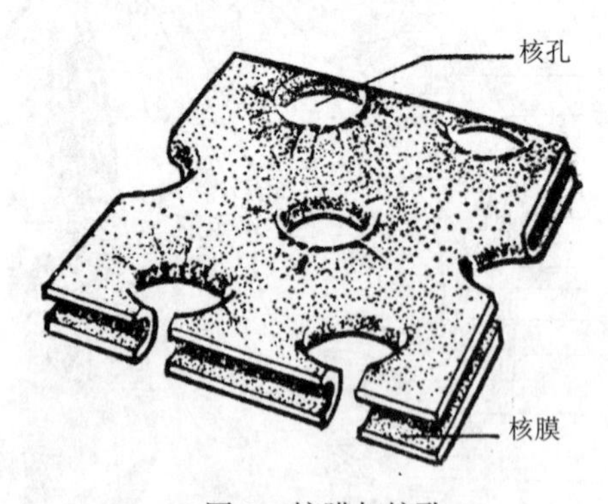

图 3　核膜与核孔

叶绿体和线粒体　这是植物细胞中两种与能量代谢有密切关系的细胞器。叶绿体由前质体发育而来，它有着复杂的片层构造。叶绿体的主要功能是进行光合作用。线粒体的内部结构也相当复杂。它的主要功能是进行呼吸作用。这两种细胞器的结构与功能在下期再作详细介绍。

内质网和核糖体 内质网在细胞质中到处都有分布，它也是双层膜构造，其立体构造如图 4。在超薄切片上呈现为沟状和小泡状，内质网常常与核膜相接，可能是由核膜起源的。内质网的形状和数量因细胞的类型和环境条件而有变化。在内质网的表面上通常覆盖有直径大约 200 埃的球状细胞器，这就是核糖体。附有核糖体的内质网称为粗糙型内质网，而不附有核糖体的内质网叫做平滑型内质网。核糖体可以附着在内质网上，也可以游离在细胞质中。核糖体由大致等量的蛋白质和核糖体核糖核酸(rRNA)组成。rRNA 是在核仁中合成，然后输送到核糖体上。在多数情况下，几个核糖体呈螺旋状或圆圈状成簇地存在，在簇外并有信息核糖核酸(mRNA)分子与其相连，这种与信息核糖核酸连在一起的成簇的核糖体称为多聚核糖体。核糖体是细胞的一个极重要的成分，是合成蛋白质的主要场所，而内质网则作为蛋白质合成的原料和最终产物的通道。叶绿体和线粒体中也有核糖体。

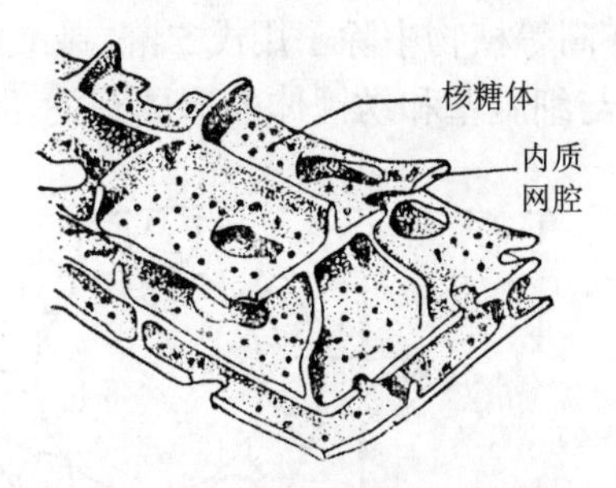

图 4　内质网的立体模型图

高尔基体 高尔基体由很多小盘组成，每一小盘为单层膜所包围，它们的末端往往膨大，在盘的四周有一排排的小泡(图 5)。随着细胞的活动，盘和小泡在大小和数量上是有变化的。当把细胞放在用放射性同位素标记的果胶质和半纤维素中培养时，通过放射自显影可以看到这些化合物首先出现在高尔基体及其四周的小泡中，以后小泡和质膜融合。这时放射性化合物便转移到细胞壁上。因此，可以认为壁物质的沉淀和积聚是通过高尔基体进行的。关于高尔基体的起源目前还不清楚。

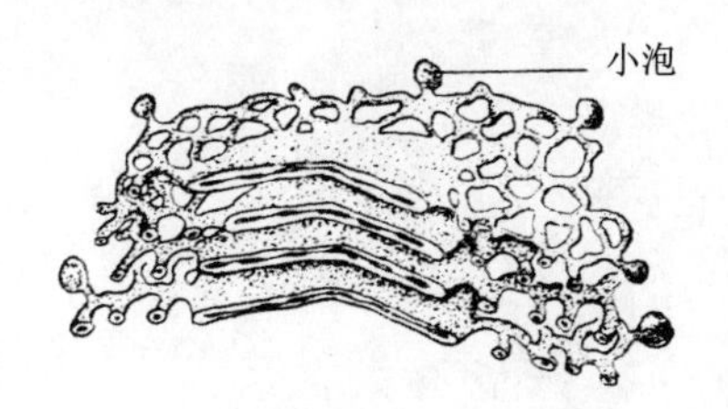

图 5　高尔基体立体模型图

溶酶体、微粒体和圆球体 这三种细胞器存在的真实性及其功能近几年才搞清楚，以上图中没有表示出来。当用分级离心法制备线粒体时，发现有一种在大小与形状上与线粒体完全一致的，但又含有不同酶的细胞质颗粒，这就是溶酶体。溶酶体的大小和线粒体一样，但结构不同，它只有一单层外膜，内部没有膜状结构。溶酶体含有大量的各种水解酶，这些酶在溶酶体中是不活动的，但当溶酶体外膜破裂时，这些酶便释放出来，并且活化，结果引起细胞解体，在植物维管细胞成熟时可以看到这种现象。微粒体是一种体积较小(直径 0.5~1.5μm)为单层膜包围的球状或杯状颗粒。在电子显微镜下微粒体内部比周围的细胞质要黑一些，有些还含有蛋白质结晶。近年来查明，微粒体内含有大量氧化酶，它们和植物细胞中的许多特殊的生化作用有关。根据微粒体的生化功能可将其再分为几种类型，例如在贮藏油脂的种子萌发时，其细胞中存在一种叫做乙醛体的微粒体，它们能将油脂转化成碳水化合物。在叶片中有一种叫做过氧化体的微粒体，它们和氨基酸的合成及光呼吸有关。圆球体比微粒体更小些，由于它在固定的细胞中保存不好，因此，关于它的功能及发生尚未完全查清，有人认为它们是由内质网断裂形成的。

微管　细胞质中的微管直径为 230~270 埃，长度还不清楚。管壁厚约 70 埃，在横切面上可以看到管壁是由很多亚单位组成的(图 6)。在间期细胞中，微管一般靠近质膜平行排列，在分裂的细胞中，细胞周缘的微管消失，在纺锤区出现在结构上类似的微管，它的直径约 150~200 埃。在高等植物中除了用戊二醛–锇酸固定者以外，纺锤区微管不能很好保存下来。微管可能与细胞壁和纺锤体的形成有关。

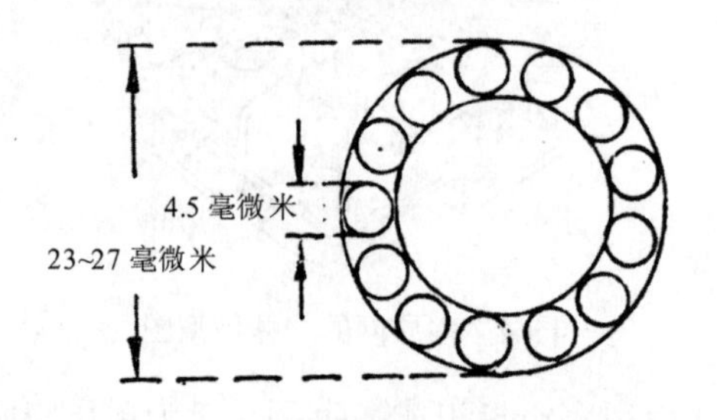

图 6　微管的横切面图

1 毫微米(mμ)=10 埃(Å)

本文原载：植物杂志. 1978. (6): 19-20

植物细胞

——细胞核

钱迎倩

(中国科学院植物研究)

细胞内，细胞核在控制植物体的遗传性状方面起着主导作用，因此，自19世纪中叶发现细胞核以来，人们对它已进行了大量的研究。

高等植物的所有细胞都有细胞核。少数细胞(如成熟的筛管分子)中没有核，但它幼年时期细胞中都有核。一般情况下，一个细胞中只有一个核，但也有多核的，在菌、藻植物中这种现象更常见。此外，当植物细胞经过低温或化学药剂处理后，也有双核现象出现。

间期核的结构和功能

一个不处于分裂时期的细胞核，称为间期核(图1)。间期核的形态多数近圆形，可是在某些花粉细胞中的营养核则是成无定形，而生殖核又是呈纺锤状。在高等植物的分生组织细胞中，核占整个细胞的3/4，而在较老的细胞中，核只占细胞的一个小部分，并被挤到液胞和细胞壁之间。在一个器官内，核的体积随着细胞年龄的增长而增大。有人指出，豌豆根尖细胞的核体积一般比根尖生长点细胞的核体积大2~3倍。同时每个核中去氧核糖核酸(DNA)的含量也随着年龄的增长而增多。多倍体的核要较二倍体的核大。间期核一般具有核膜、核质、核仁等几个部分。

1. 核膜

它使细胞核与细胞质之间有一明显界限。在电子显微镜下，核膜是由两层膜组成。这两层膜与细胞中的内质网相连接。核膜上有很多核孔。核孔的开、闭可能与植物的生理活性有密切的关系，如有的实验证明，小麦在分蘖盛期核膜上呈较大的核孔，这就给核和细胞质的物质交换提供了通道。到冬天，抗寒品种小麦的核孔随温度降低而逐渐关闭(放大倍数不高，核孔不明显)。

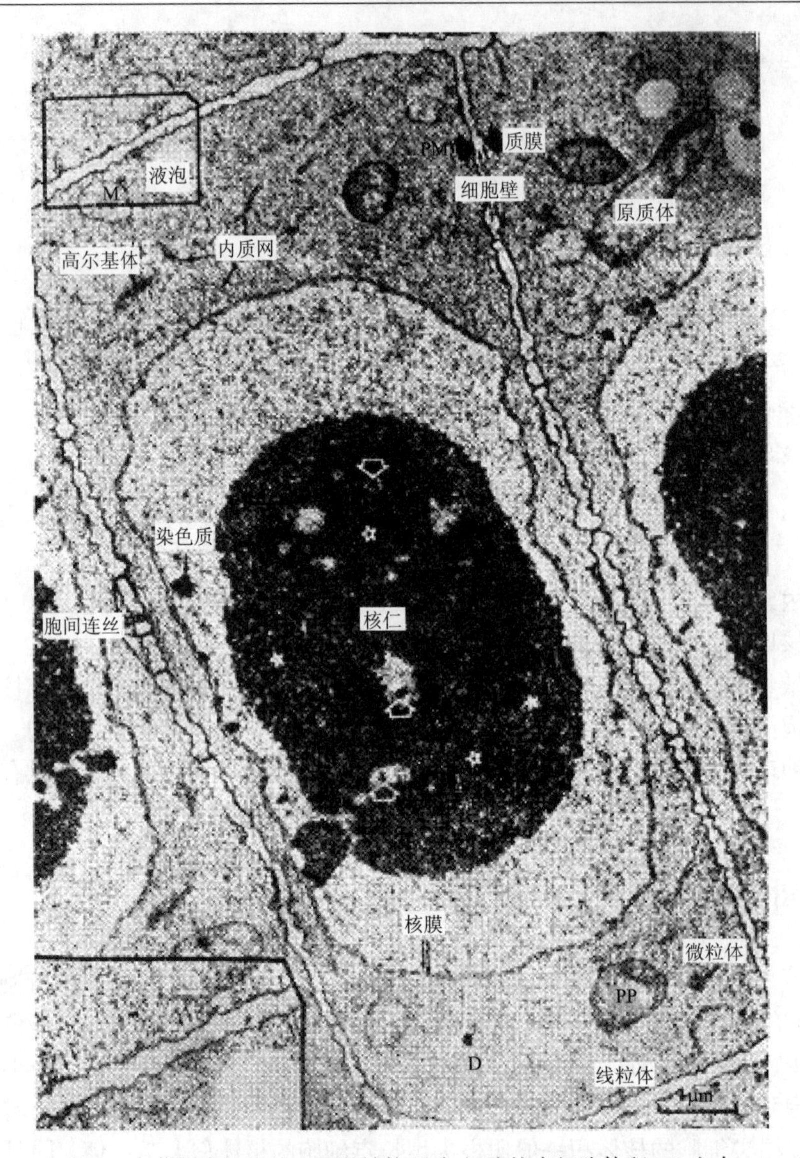

图 1　水芹根尖细胞的亚显微结构照片(细胞核占细胞体积 3/4 左右)

2. 核质

它充满了核内大部分的空间(也可以称为核液)。核内主要的部分是染色质。在间期核中，即使用染色技术进行处理，也很难看到染色体。经过染色后，可以看到网状结构的染色质。染色质又可分为染色深的异染色质与染色浅得多的常染色质。常染色质是代表了染色质的非凝聚区域。异染色质部分的染色质在间期时保持凝聚状态。它们的分子组成紧密地聚集在一起，常常可以在核膜附近找到它们。

染色质内主要成分是 DNA 和蛋白质。

3. 核仁

这是在间期细胞核中，不用染色就能看到的结构。一般在一个核中有一个到几个核仁。它是圆而致密的实体。核仁内除含 DNA 外，大部分是由核糖核酸(RNA)及蛋白质组成，但其主要成分是蛋白质。在不同类型细胞中，RNA 与蛋白质的比例有很大变化。用电镜观察研究，表明核仁有两个区域，一个是纤维状的，另一个是颗粒状的。这两个区域都是由 RNA 与蛋白质相结合而形成的。核仁外围没有膜的存在。核仁的功能还研究得不太清楚。目前认为一种可能是合成核糖核蛋白体 RNA(rRNA)，另一种可能是具有传递信息的功能。有人发现，如果细胞核中没有核仁，遗传信息就不能从核中传递到细胞质中去。此外，有人认为核仁又是合成核内蛋白质的活跃场所。

当细胞核进入分裂时期，染色质逐步浓缩而成为着色很深的染色体。有人推测，在间期核中染色体也是存在的，它的结构如图 2 所示。染色体是一种长的纤维状结构，它上面有大小不等、按不等的间隔分布的致密区域。这些区域称为染色粒。核仁与染色体上的特定部位相结合，这个特定的部位称为核仁组织者。

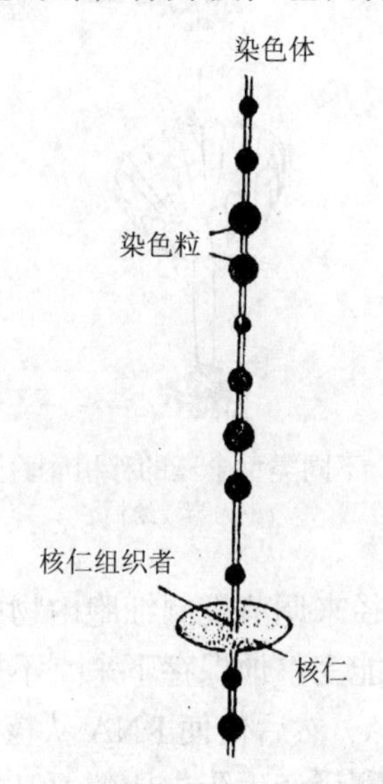

图 2　间期染色体的图解

染色体中除 DNA、RNA 外，还有相当大量的两种蛋白质与它们相结合。这两种蛋白质就是碱性蛋白——组蛋白和酸性蛋白。此外，还有少量的别种蛋白质。组蛋白中含比例很高的赖氨酸和精氨酸。而酸性蛋白可能含有大量的二羧基氨基酸。这两种蛋白质与 DNA 结合通常称为核蛋白。组蛋白与 DNA 相互作用，阻碍了 DNA 合成 RNA 的模板作用，从而抑制了基因的表现，起到“面罩”的作用。而细胞核内的酸性蛋白可能又起到消除这种抑制的作用。

细胞核的主要功能是控制植物体的遗传性状以及调节和控制细胞内物质代谢的途径，从而“指导”细胞的发育。有一个实验很能说明细胞核的功能：伞藻(一种绿藻)的每一个藻体就是一个细胞，形状像伞。它具有藻柄，柄的顶端有一帽状的膨大部分。这个细胞的细胞核是在柄的近基部。如果把上部的帽状部分切掉的话，柄部又可再长出一个新的帽子。如果用甲乙两种帽子形状不同的伞藻作实验，把甲伞藻的柄及伞都切掉，留下含有核的假根，然后接上一段不带核的乙伞藻的柄。我们可以看到，不久以后乙藻柄上再生的帽子不再是乙藻类型的帽子，而是甲藻类型的了(图 3)。这个实验证明了形成一个再生帽子的遗传信息是存在于细胞核中的。

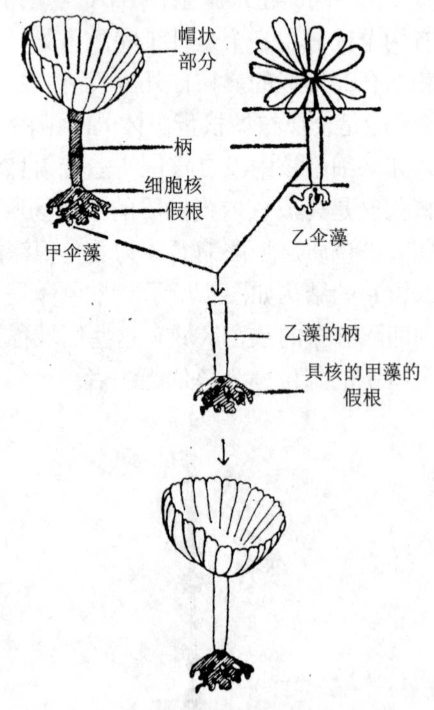

图 3　不同类型伞藻的移植实验图解

(王秀琴　绘)

至于遗传信息是通过何种途径来调节控制细胞内物质代谢呢？我们都知道，遗传信息是存在于核内的 DNA 中，并能完整地保存下来，不加改变地从一代传到下一代。以 DNA 为模板，通过转录产生 RNA，然后信使 RNA 从核中转到细胞质中，并在细胞质中以其核苷酸的顺序为基础，经过翻译产生蛋白质的氨基酸顺序，最后产生不同的蛋白质产物。这就是所谓的中心法则。但是，目前已知道，细胞质内的信息也可被传回到细胞核中去。

原核细胞和真核细胞

由于生物化学与亚显微结构研究的进展，人们逐步认识到细菌和蓝藻的染色质类物质的周围没有膜与细胞质隔开。它们的 DNA 结构、核仁的有无等等都与其他高等生物有很大的差异。后来，有人又发现两者在细胞质部分也有明显不同，从而把细菌和蓝藻的细胞称为“原核细胞”，而把比它们高等的生物细胞称“真核细胞”。下表说明原核细胞与真核细胞的主要差异。

	原核细胞	真核细胞
核 膜	无	有
DNA	不与蛋白质结合，大多形成单独封闭的环，直接附着在细胞膜的内膜上	与蛋白质相结合，并成线状，存在于二条以上的染色丝中，并绞在一起，成股地被包在核膜内
RNA	不与 DNA 连结在一起	与 DNA 连结在一起
核 仁	无	有
分裂方式	无丝分裂	有丝分裂或减数分裂
线粒体	线粒体内没有呼吸和光合作用的酶	线粒体内有呼吸和光合作用的酶
叶绿体	无	植物细胞中有
转录与翻译	出现在同一时间与地点	出现在不同时间与地点

本文原载：科学世界. 1998. (6): 12-14

保护地球的生物多样性

钱迎倩

(中国科学院植物研究所)

90年代以后，在报刊杂志上经常能看到“生物多样性”这一术语。1992年在巴西里约热内卢召开的联合国环境与发展大会上，签订了《生物多样性公约》，包括我国在内的一百多个国家首脑在《公约》上签字，成为《公约》的缔约国。那么，什么是“生物多样性”呢？本文就什么是生物多样性和为什么要保护好生物多样性作一介绍。

什么是生物多样性

地球上生存着几千万种包括动物、植物和微生物在内的生物。每一种生物，例如家养动物狗、猪，栽培作物中的水稻、玉米都称为一个物种。这些包括家养及野生在内的形形色色的物种构成了物种多样性。在物种之下还有很多品种、变种等。例如猪在我国就有保山猪、明光小耳猪、上海荡脚猪、河南项城猪等；栽培作物例如玉米、水稻、小麦都有数不清的品种。品种与品种的不同是由于生物体内存在基因的不同，或者说遗传类型是不一样的。这就构成了遗传多样性。在一定的空间内的动物、植物、微生物和它们赖以生存的居住环境(或者说包括光、空气、土壤、水、矿物质在内的栖息地)之间，通过能量流动和物质循环的相互作用、相互影响而构成一个综合体。这综合体又称为生态系统。在陆地上、淡水及海洋中都可有不同的综合体。不同的气候带，不同的地理环境就有不同的生态系统。这就形成了生态系统多样性。

因此，生物多样性是地球上40亿年来生物进化的结果。地球上包括动物、植物、微生物的所有生物和它们所拥有的基因，及其环境构成的生态系统，形成了千姿百态的生物世界。而生物多样性又有三个层次的概念：即物种多样性、遗传多样性和生态系统多样性。

为什么要保护生物多样性

下面从四个角度来谈保护生物多样性的重要性。

1. 生物多样性与人类的关系极为密切

人类的衣、食、住、行没有一项能脱离生物多样性。以食物为例，人类历史上大约有 3000 种植物被用作食物，估计有 75 000 种植物可作食用。这说明了物种多样性的重要性。尽管如此，目前人类所需营养的 75%仅来自 7 个物种，也就是小麦、水稻、玉米、马铃薯、大麦、甘薯和木薯，而前 3 种提供的营养占到 50%以上。而且往往由于追求高产，用的是遗传基础狭窄的单一品种。世界上每年由于作物品种单一导致病害而造成的损失超过 250 亿美元。提高抗病能力或提高其他抗逆能力的途径，是与有抗逆能力的品种或野生品种杂交，或者应用基因工程手段把抗逆基因导入作物品种中去。从中，保存遗传多样性的重要性就显而易见了。

再以人类健康为例说明生物多样性的重要性。我国传统医学所利用的中草药越来越为世界各国所重视，有记载的药用植物至少在 5000 种以上，其中常用的药物为 1700 种。在发达国家中传统药物也起着举足轻重的作用。除植物外，海洋及陆栖动物的医疗作用也不能忽视。至今约有 119 种取自高等植物的纯化学物质在世界医疗事业中得到广泛应用，而这些化学物质仅来自不到 90 种植物。实际上，人类在探索生物的药用价值方面仅刚刚开始。大量动、植物的药用价值有待开发，而微生物的药用价值可比喻为才开始开垦的处女地。

2. 生物多样性与人类面临的五大危机

人类正面临着人口、粮食、环境、资源及能源等五大危机。这五大危机的解决无一不与生物多样性有密切的关系。人口问题是包含着人口无限制地膨胀与人类健康两大问题。要做好计划生育，人们将从生物物种中去寻找高效且对人体无害的化合物来达到目的。在药物开发方面，近年来我国科学家从一种菊科的蒿类植物中提取了青蒿素，目前已证明它是一种比奎宁更有效的治疗疟疾的药物。此外，癌症与艾滋病是国际上两大顽症，科学的发展使人们认识到中药天花粉的蛋白质不仅能治疗绒毛膜皮癌，还有可能是治疗艾滋病的良药。

在粮食方面除了上面提到的外，有一个很好的例子说明保护遗传多样性的重要性。中国是野生大豆资源极为丰富的国家，在 80 年代早期，美国有人从我国的东北带走了长有白毛的野生大豆中的一个类型，并用此类型与美国的栽培大豆杂交，培育出抗旱的新品种。此品种比原有栽培品种节水 15%，并能在较贫瘠、干旱的土地上种植，从而扩大了种植面积，使美国代替我国成为大豆最大的出口国。

森林为人类提供木材，并且贮藏了百万年前的太阳能，为今天提供了原油、煤和天然气。世界上一年内消耗的煤量相当于消耗一万年所贮藏的太阳能量。因此，要从今天的植物材料中获取太阳能的一条捷径是快速并持续聚集大量的“生物量”，才可能满足人类持续的需要。

所谓环境的破坏也就是一个好的生态系统的破坏。要维护或恢复一个被破坏的生态系统，就要通过科学研究，了解到过去该生态系统中曾经有过的动物、植物、微生物，它们之间的相互关系，它们在生态系统中所发挥的作用，及其与环境中其他因子的相互作用，再通过实践才可能恢复或重建。

3. 物种与遗传资源的灭绝、生态系统的破坏

《生物多样性公约》正式生效已近 5 年的时间。但至今总的来说，环境还在进一步恶化，森林、耕田面积锐减，淡水匮乏。根据联合国粮农组织报告，近年来全世界每年约有 1130 万 hm^2 的森林遭到毁灭性破坏。1990~1995 年的 6 年内，全世界共有 6510 万 hm^2 森林遭到破坏。其中 5630 万 hm^2 在发展中国家，880 万 hm^2 在发达国家。热带雨林是世界上生物多样性最丰富的地区，但每年还有 1800 万 hm^2 的热带雨林遭到破坏。据联合国环境规划署文件指出，全球已有约 1/4 的陆地面积受到荒漠化的威胁。由于荒漠扩散，每年全球造成的损失达 420 亿美元，仅在亚洲的损失是 210 亿美元。此外，水体生态系统的状况也令人堪忧。水体污染问题并未好转，今年我国广东、香港一带由于水体严重的富营养化造成的赤潮，不仅使海水养殖的贝类、鱼、虾大量死亡，并造成生物多样性的大量丧失。

由于生态系统大量破坏，使动物、植物、微生物物种栖息地丧失，物种大量灭绝。造成物种灭绝的因素还有野生生物的非法买卖，非本地物种的入侵，甚至高新技术发展的影响，如基因工程研制的转基因生物向环境释放后可能带来的生态风险以及信息高速公路的发展，都可能给生物多样性造成巨大的威胁。联合国环境规划署在 1996 年世界地球日发表的报告说，全世界已有 12%的哺乳动物和 11%的鸟类濒临灭绝。每 24 小时有 150~200 种生物物种从地球上消失。有报告指出，全球范围内已知的 233 种灵长类动物正面临生存挑战，一半以上的猿类、狐猴、猕猴和濑猴处于灭绝的边缘。我国物种灭绝的情况也是很严重的。本文已谈到遗传多样性在解决粮食问题上的重要性，但我国的遗传资源至少面临三大问题：一是还有大量有用的作物、家禽、家畜遗传资源尚未收集或收集得不系统；二是大量的农家品种由于推广优良品种而丧失掉；三是农作物的野生种和野生近缘种的原地保护几乎还是空白。

4. 人类对绝大多数的物种尚处于无知状态

地球上动物、植物、微生物到底有多少物种呢？说法不一，但一般的估计是在 3000 万种左右。虽然经过分类学家及系统学家近 200 年的努力，但地球上的物种已定名的仅 150 万种左右，保守的估计是仅有 1/10 的物种被定了名。其中高等植物和脊椎动物的分类学研究得比较透彻，但即使这样，还有不少大型的生物还是近 10~20 年内才发现的，例如：世界上目前还存活的鲸类有 80 种，其中 11 种是 21 世纪才发现的，在 1991 年还发现了一个新品种。根据地球上物种灭绝的速度，意味着人们对大量的生物根本谈不上知道它们的用途，甚至还来不及给它们定一个名之前，这些物种已经在地球上消失了。

有人统计，1997 年时，发展中国家人口为 46 亿，年增长率为 1.9%；发达国家人口为 12 亿，年增长率为 0.1%；全球人口 58 亿，平均增长率为 1.5%。到 21 世纪末时，全球人口可能达到 100 亿。要维持全球人口在衣、食、住、行的需要，满足人类对优良的生存环境及文化娱乐的需要，采取一切可采取的措施来保护及持续利用生物多样性的重要性就不言而喻了。

本文原载：大自然. 2002. (2): 13-15, 16

从湟鱼陈尸论青海省的环境

钱迎倩

(中国科学院植物研究所)

湟鱼又名青海湖裸鲤，是仅生长在青海湖的特有鱼种。2001 年 9 月笔者有机会到西宁出差，8 月时就已听到关于青海湖湟鱼产卵难的消息，到西宁后找到 8 月出版的当地报刊，实际情况比当初了解的要严重得多。问题还得从青海湖说起。

青海湖坐落在青海省刚察县，面积 4300km^2，湖面海拔 3196m，是我国最大的内陆微咸水湖。1975 年被划为省级自然保护区，1997 年 12 月又被批准为国家级野生动物类型的自然保护区。

青海湖水源来自南面和北面山区冰雪融化所形成的 108 条淡水河流，其中较大的有布哈河、沙柳河、泉吉河、哈尔盖河、黑马河等。从 20 世纪 60 年代初开始，青海湖周围的草地陆续被开垦为农田，造成当地的环境逐年恶化，环湖的草场沙漠化程度日趋严重。草场被开垦为农田后，流入青海湖的河流上也筑起了拦水坝、修建了农用灌溉渠，大量水源用于农田灌溉。由于受到青藏高原气候变干的影响，流入青海湖的水量逐年减少，导致青海湖面积逐年缩小，湖水水位每年下降 10~12cm。按 1996 年资料显示，湖深由原来的 31m，下降到 27m 左右。1997 年环保局调查数据显示，当年青海湖地区耕地面积已达 2242hm^2，农作物面积占 1509 万 hm^2，共有 27 个环湖农牧场，大部分农牧场都使用了水利灌溉。致使青海湖周围的入湖河流数量严重减少，严重程度已达到由过去入湖河流 108 条减少为 5 条，其他河流均已干涸。

灾难终于发生了。青海省《西海都市报》2001 年 8 月 8 日发表题为“湟鱼陈尸沙柳河”的报道。报道说：“7 月 3 日，这是青海湖湟鱼灾难性的一天，成千上万的产卵亲鱼死在沙柳河河道内，在沙柳河拦河坝上下一段长约 200m 的河道内，死鱼形成一条约 50cm 厚的鱼道”。原因是湟鱼亲鱼有洄游的行为，每年到产卵期时亲鱼会向淡水河流溯流而上。7 月 3 日当天，成千上万产卵亲鱼拥进仅有的几条缺水的河流中。刚察县渔政局长事发后赶到现场，看到所有的死鱼都聚集在河道中的 40 几个洼坑内，每个洼坑内的死鱼约有 50cm 厚，最大洼坑内的死鱼至少也有 20 多吨。死去的产卵亲鱼每尾均在 150~200g 左右，按每条鱼产卵后能成活十几尾鱼计，这次死鱼给青海湖湟鱼资源带来的损失无法估计。据渔政局长称，湟鱼成批死亡事件并非是第一次，在 20 世纪 80 年代末河水曾断流过一次，死鱼达 1m 厚。

从有关资料中得知，青海湖现有的湟鱼资源量约为 7500 吨，已不足开发初期的十分之一。而鸟岛栖息的各种鸟类每年要吞食近千吨的湟鱼。由于水源补充逐年减少，青海湖水的含盐量已由 1962 年的 12.49g/L 上升到目前的 16g/L。平均 pH 值已由过去的 9 上升到 9.2 以上，有的水区高达 9.5。青海湖水的盐碱化对水生饵料生物和鱼类的生存及繁衍也造成严重威胁，湟鱼生长缓慢，个体小型化，繁殖力下降。湟鱼资源的再生能力与资源量已到了最低临界线。因此青海省政府对青海湖实施了封湖育鱼措施已有多年，禁止捕捞湟鱼，但是至今湖周围偷捕湟鱼现象并未得到有效控制。

由于过度捕捞，与原始状态相比湟鱼资源量已减少 90%，到产卵季节产卵亲鱼又大批死亡，从最悲观估计，湟鱼这个物种有可能灭绝已不再是耸人听闻了。湟鱼一旦灭绝，各种候鸟、留鸟与旅鸟由于找不到食物，青海湖就不再可能成为它们的栖息地，驰名中外的青海湖鸟岛这一旅游胜地也就不复存在。

2001 年 7 月 3 日湟鱼大批惨死事件再次警告人们，从速解决湟鱼生育繁衍的问题，从根本上说是如何解决青海湖及其有关生境的生态良性循环问题。

笔者认为，仅仅从青海湖及其周边环境的角度来考虑解决各种生态系统严重退化的问题，从根本上来说是难以奏效的。而把青海省作为一个整体，从该省在我国所占有的重要地位和该省的环境严重恶化的角度思考，由中央政府与地方政府协调配合才可能解决。除青海湖外，青海省还有面积为 5868km^2 的中国第一盐湖——察尔汗盐湖。更重要的是青海省是我国三条主要河流：长江、黄河与澜沧江的发源地，素有“中华水塔” 之称。三江源头是世界上江河最多、海拔最高、面积最大的湿地地区，也是世界上高海拔地区生物多样性最集中的区域。目前包括三江源头地区在内的整个青海省各种生态系统都有进一步恶化的趋势：如湟水河是黄河在青海省境内的一级支流，《2000 年度青海省水资源质量年报》表明，湟水河水质污染到了快成为“龙须沟”的境地；属德令哈市管理的尕海湖每年都有两三万人去湖内图发财而滥捕滥捞，《西宁晚报》报道“尕海湖要‘死’了”。可可西里的藏羚羊由于其绒毛能在国外被织成妇女用的披肩，每年遭到成万头的残杀；可可西里自然保护区旧伤未疗又添新伤， 因沿海养虾缺饵料，每年有成万的民工涌人保护区大肆捕捞卤虫卵，环境遭到严重破坏；更令人担忧的是黄河源头本有的星罗棋布的高原湖泊现正在迅速消失。以上例子说明各种生态系统已严重恶化，青海省的环境已出现千疮百孔的情况，并有进一步恶化的趋势。

原因：首先是自然因素。根据青海省气象局近 40 年来的气象资料分析，青藏高原平均每 10 年温度升高 0.16℃，比过去世界 100 年平均气温仅上升 0.7℃高出不少。进入 90 年代以来，全年降水量有所减少，气候变暖变干。实际上从六、七十年代开始就已经出现冰川萎缩、河流水量补给量减少、湖泊干涸、荒漠化进程加剧、大面积优质草场退化、水土流失加重、河流含沙量逐年加大的趋势。专家分析，预计到 21 世纪末，青藏高原将比 20 世纪的平均气温上升近 3℃。这种自然因素造成的恶化当前还不是人力所能克服，但对未来应有一个正确的预计却是十分重要的。

另一重要的因素是人类活动造成的结果。人类活动在这个地区主要是过度放牧、非法猎杀野生动物、草场改为农田、无序的黄金开采和冬虫夏草的采挖，以及非法或过度捕捞等。从而导致植被严重破坏、荒漠化加剧、沙尘暴天气增加、水资源日益枯竭、生物多样性遭受严重威胁、珍稀特有物种濒临灭绝，经济损失惨重。

黄河源头玛多县的遭遇就是一个很好的例子。1988~1996年9年间，黄河源头地区水量比正常年份减少23.3%，1997年出现断流，全县4000多个湖泊已有2000个干涸。据1998年统计，退化草地面积已占全县草地面积的70%，沙化面积占全县草地面积的35%，退化、沙化面积每年还以20%的速度在扩展。草场退化造成鼠害肆虐，鼠害面积已占全县草地面积的65%。国家一类保护动物野牦牛、藏羚羊、盘羊等珍稀野生动物越来越少。牧业收入本来是当地牧民的生活保障，到1999年人均占有牲畜仅37.8头，比最高年份下降65.7%。牧民生活日趋困难，已有38%的牧民生计无着，他们离开沙化了的草场，赶着牛羊远去他乡。严重退化了的生态系统使沙尘暴天气增加，仅1999年因沙尘暴天气导致死亡的各类牲畜达5.47万头，使65户325口人当上了“生态难民”而无家可归，直接经济损失达到1072.14万元。上面虽举的是青海湖湟鱼及玛多县的例子，但是否可以认为这是青海省环境现状的缩影呢？

我们也看到了好消息的报道。自从执行了中央关于“退耕还林、退耕还草”政策后，三江源头的环境已开始有所好转；有关部门对青海湖已开始使用“三S系统”(即遥感、地理信息系统及全球定位系统)来进行动态监测。1998 年青海省领导亲自率队赴京与有关部委领导和专家共商三江源头与青海省的环境保护及建设，计划用 53 年时间，使全省的环境明显改观，最终恢复各类生态系统使之能有良性循环。2000 年三江源头已批准建立省一级的自然保护区，并在不久的将来批准为国家级的自然保护区。这一系列举措说明省一级直到国家对青海省的环境保护已有足够的重视。

青海全省人口 500 多万，60%人口又集中在湟水河流域。三江源头及省内重要的各类生态系统内居住人口虽少，但他们的活动加剧了各种已很脆弱生态系统的破坏。对这些地区采取移民政策应该提到议事日程上来。重庆市巫山县已有先例。近年来由于环保意识加强，环境好转， 野猪、黑熊、猴子、羚羊等野生动物大量繁衍。巫山县政府决定，利用国家退耕还林政策，将 10 万多深受野生动物“骚扰” 的农民从深山里迁出，把山林还给野猪、黑熊。当然青海省与巫山县条件不尽相同，但指导思想是一致的。为了保护“中华水塔”以及青海省的关键生态系统，移民政策的实施是十分必要的。

本文原载：福建教育. 2003. (4):1(16)

试谈基础教育

钱迎倩

(中国科学院植物研究所)

我长期从事科研工作，也兼职担任相当一段时间的科研管理工作，应该说对教育是一窍不通。教育学本身就是一门科学，本人不懂教育学，现在年事已高，已没有机会也没有精力专门学习，因此只能从个人的经历与平时对社会现象片面的了解与观察，来谈谈我对我国基础教育的意见。要说明的是本人所理解的基础教育，应该是包括德智体在内的基础教育，并且本文仅仅局限于讨论中小学阶段的基础教育问题。

德智体全面发展的方针不是新鲜事物，早在50年代建国初期已经提出来。在这个方针指导下，几十年来我国培养出一批又一批建设祖国的人才，其中也不乏栋梁之才，成绩是肯定的、主要的。可是我国的基础教育，尤其在当前新形势下德智体方面都还存在着一定的问题。20世纪五、六十年代，学校对学生德的教育十分重视，除课堂教育外党团活动也十分活跃。学生们普遍地以高的道德标准来要求自己，朝气蓬勃，有理想，热爱祖国。在这阶段已为大学毕业后“祖国的需要就是自己的志愿”打好基础。文化大革命把全民的思想搅乱了，目前我国又正经历从计划经济到市场经济转轨的阶段，社会风气远不如当年，青少年犯罪率上升并有向低龄化发展的趋势。德的教育方面确实要比建国初期难做得多。当前，国家在经济飞跃发展的同时，十分迫切地要求迅速提高全民的道德素质。而道德素质的提高必须从娃娃抓起，这就给中小学德的基础教育提出了更高的要求，急需有一批教育家潜心研究在当前新形势下德的标准是什么？如何有效地开展中小学德方面的基础教育？使培养的中学毕业生至少能达到解放初期德的水平，这是关系到国家百年大计的大事。

在智的方面偏向似乎也十分明显。我国有一句古话“学会数理化，走遍天下都不怕”，这句话已经有重理轻文的嫌疑，但总还是把理科的知识较全面地提出来了。而现在从小学低年级开始就偏数学，各种各样的数学班，学校的“奥校”、区一级的“奥校”、还有“华校”等。数学到底不能替代物理、化学及其他科学。生命科学是21世纪的前沿科学，解密人类基因组不仅需要有好的数学基础，还需要有扎实的生物学、物理、化学以及其他科学的基础。当然，没有好的外语基础，要想与国际接轨、赶超国际水平只能是空谈。因此，让学生花大量的时间去钻数学某些领域解的技巧或其他专门问题，显然对全面打好各种基础知识的基础是无益的。强调基础知识的全面教育，还应注意实践，注意学用结合，要创造实践的条件及学用结合的环境。

在体的方面，中小学阶段是孩子们的长身体的阶段，让孩子们有充分的睡眠时间是重要的。目前，中小学生负担过重的问题有待于进一步解决，应让孩子们少一点学校布置的作业，多一点符合他们自己兴趣的包括体育在内的各种活动。我国人口众多，城市中绝大多数中小学校的体育场面积及各种体育设施远远满足不了全体学生体育锻炼的需要。如何从有条件的学校开始逐步加强，是一个值得重视的问题。

最后，有关基础教育还有三个问题提出来商榷。

第一，要加强基础教育已是共识，可是对什么是基础教育、基础教育的内容是什么、如何才能加强基础教育等一系列问题的见解是不可能一致的。世界本来是丰富多彩的，人们对各种事物的认识也是多种多样的，在基础教育问题上也应该是百花齐放的。在总的教育方针确定的情况下，要允许不同类型、不同条件的学校按各自的理解努力去办好基础教育，切忌一刀切。几十年来，包括教育在内的各条战线由于一刀切而尝到的苦果已经够多，包括经济、时间、人才等各种各样的损失已经够大，只有百花齐放才能调动群众的聪明才智，才能结出丰硕的果实。

第二，由于在校学生过多，不少学校把学生分为尖子班(实验班)及普通班两类。学校把重点放在实验班上，对多数的普通班没有精力潜心办好。本人认为按学生水平分班教育确有好处，但对普通班要花更大的力气办好。普通班的学生是多数，学校有责任尽一切可能为国家培养出更多合格的人才。提高中小学教师的地位及待遇，把大批优秀的大学毕业生、研究生充实到中小学教师队伍中去。中小学期间受到优良的德智体基础教育，毕业后不管在哪个岗位上都会起到重要的作用。这是全民素质提高的关键所在。

第三，青少年是国家的希望，基础教育的成功不仅是学校的任务，也是每个家庭的任务、全社会的任务。因此，社会、学校、家庭应该配合，达成共识，共同努力，不断提高我国的基础教育，把每个学生都培养成国家的栋梁，这是基础教育最终的目的。

本文原载：生命世界. 2006. (2): 40-47

“转基因热”背后的冷思考

钱迎倩

(中国科学院植物研究所)

在超市里购买大豆色拉油的时候，只要你稍微留心一下，十有八九都会在原料一栏看见“转基因大豆”这几个不起眼的小字。2005 年，中国从国外进口转基因大豆 2142 万吨，占世界转基因大豆总产量的 30%，它们中的绝大部分被用作豆油生产的原料。据农业部统计，中国目前转基因棉花的种植面积已经达到 500 万公顷，占所有棉田的 80%。可以毫不夸张地说，现在人们吃的是转基因的油，穿的是转基因的棉……

当“转基因”不知不觉进入人们日常生活领域之时，对公众而言，它就不再是学术殿堂中一个抽象的科学概念了。如同主妇洗菜时可能会考虑到农药残留问题一样，公众在知道购买的是转基因生物产品时，也可能会产生一丝疑问，“转基因是什么？”“它安全吗？”……这些恰恰是科学家在生物技术与生物安全领域所要解答的问题。

转基因技术的科学与现实

生命科学的重要性已经毋庸置疑，而生物技术无疑是将科学转化为现实的直通车。转基因技术其实只是生物技术中很小的一部分，但却是 21 世纪科学技术发展的重点。

什么是转基因技术呢？以目前在国内推广的最多的转基因抗虫棉为例，科学家发现一种名叫苏云金杆菌的细菌，它的遗传物质内有一种毒素基因(简称 Bt 基因)。毒素基因表达的蛋白可以杀死棉铃虫。在实验室中把这种细菌的 DNA 提取出来，经过切割、拼接后把毒素基因重组起来，通过各种途径将具有毒素基因的重组 DNA 导入并整合到棉

本文图片由许永松提供。

花细胞的细胞核中，经过这样再培育成功的棉花，就是转基因抗虫棉。棉铃虫如果吃了转基因抗虫棉的叶片和棉桃会死亡。农民种植这样的棉花就可以不喷洒或少喷洒农药专吃棉花叶片和棉桃的棉铃虫会造成棉花的大量减产，棉花田中的农药投放曾经占据我国农药投放的70%。

抗病虫害、抗旱、抗寒、抗除草剂、耐盐碱、耐重金属污染、高产、营养成分高、易储存……我们希望农作物具有的这些优良性状其实都是由生物基因决定的，可以用转基因抗虫棉同样的技术来培育出具有各种优良性状的转基因作物。也许你会问，为什么要用转基因技术呢？提高作物产量不是还有传统的杂交育种手段吗？没错，科学家想方设法培育新的优良品种，提高农作物产量，降低生产成本。但是传统育种方式只能在同类作物间进行杂交，如水稻与水稻、大豆与大豆，却无法结合水稻与大豆的优良特征。此外，传统育种是把兼具双方不同优点的作物进行杂交，从其后代中挑好的再育种，指望其基因重组产生出兼具双方优点、性状稳定的品种，但这往往要花费很长时间、很大精力。而转基因技术则把由"自然选择"产生的基因重组过程转变为直接由人掌握，而且从理论上来说动物、植物、微生物的基因可以"一锅烩"，省时省力，发挥的余地要大得多。转基因作物正式问世十几年来，国际上已经培育出至少120种转基因植物。

此外，转基因技术在医药方面也得到了实践上的应用。1982 年美国食品与药品管理局批准了世界上第一例基因药物重组天胰岛素的正式生产以来，以基因工程药物为主的各种基因工程产品陆续实现商品化生产。科学家把人体内能够表达胰岛素蛋白的基因分离出来，重组到大肠杆菌遗传物质内，用发酵罐大量培养并摄取这种转基因大肠杆菌，就能得到大量而廉价的胰岛素，用于治疗糖尿病，促红细胞生成素能促进红细胞的生成，它对肿瘤化疗等红细胞减少症状有积极的疗效，但在人体内含量有限。目前，科学家已经成功培育出一种促红细胞生成素的转基因牛，仅从这种转基因牛的奶中就可以提取促红细胞生成素。如果将来科学足够发达，将转基因技术与克隆技术结合起来，克隆这种有价值的转基因牛的体细胞，就可以得到许多廉价的转基因牛，进而便宜地得到大量促红细胞生成素。虽然科学研究会遇到许多困难，但生物技术给我们展示的前景无疑是非常美好的。

从不同转基因作物种类看，转基因大豆发展最快。到2002年全球转基因大豆面积第一次超过大豆种植总面积的一半(51%)，达到3650万公顷

转基因作物的发展非常迅速。从 1983 年科学家通过基因工程首次获得转基因植物，只经过短短的 10 多年时间，转基因技术已取得举世瞩目的成就。1986 年转基因作物在美国和法国首次进入大田试验，到 1997 年底全世界转基因作物的田间试验已达 25 000 例。1994 年美国批准了转基因延熟番茄的商品化

生产，到1997年底，全世界共有51种转基因植物产品被正式批准投入商品化生产，其中抗虫、抗病、抗除草剂的转基因大豆、玉米、油菜、棉花、马铃薯等已有较大面积的推广。1996年全球种植转基因作物的面积仅有170万公顷，但到2003年这个数字就达到了6770万公顷，增长了40倍。它们目前分别种植在18个国家，其中美国、阿根廷、加拿大占了近95%的面积，中国占4%(虽然我国在水稻、西红柿、玉米、小麦、棉花、大豆、甜椒、杨树等转基因植物的研究方面都已经取得成功，但是被农业部批准商品化种植的作物仅有转基因抗虫棉花、转基因耐储存西红柿、转基因甜椒和矮牵牛等6种转基因作物，种植面积最大的就是转基因抗虫棉花)，1996年全球转基因作物的市场价值仅3亿美元，可是到2003年已经达到45亿~47.5亿美元，占全球农作物市场310亿美元的15%和全球种子市场300亿美元的13%。

统计表明，2002年全球3400万公顷棉花中转基因棉花有680万公顷。我国2005年转基因棉花的种植面积已经达到500万公顷，占所有棉田的80%

转基因技术不仅在农业及医药上得到应用，在食品、能源以及净化环境等各方面的应用也都具有十分广阔的前景。

转基因作物与食品安全

转基因技术前景如此美好，但是20世纪90年代后期却出现了一些“不和谐”的声音。

1999年英国发生了转基因马铃薯事件。科学家普兹塔依(Pusztai)和他的同事在电视上公布了他们的实验，发现转雪花莲外源凝集素基因的抗虫马铃薯喂饲大鼠后，对大鼠的消化和免疫系统有损害。事件公布后他遭到了不公平待遇，但他事后还是发表论文坚持其研究结果的正确性。

2000年9月，美国《华盛顿邮报》报道在超市货架上发现卡夫食品公司生产的一种玉米饼中含有星联玉米的杀虫毒蛋白。星联玉米是美国一种转基因玉米，它的转基因抗虫玉米毒蛋白的表达是其他转基因抗虫玉米的50~100倍。美国政府为避免引起人体的过敏反应，批准星联玉米只能做动物饲料，而不能做人类食品。事发后相关公司蒙受近10亿美元的损失，并严重影响了美国玉米的出口贸易。

2002年10月，美国农业部在内布拉斯加州刚收获的大豆中发现混入了少量的转基因玉米的茎叶，因为该玉米是作为植物反应器用于生产胰岛素蛋白的，所以政府将被污染的大豆全部销毁，并要求有关单位保证不再发生类似事件。

美国先锋种子公司为了改良大豆的营养组成，从巴西坚果中提取表达蛋氨酸的基因并插入大豆中，但是研究结果却发现该转基因大豆对一部分人群会产生过敏反应，公司从而放弃了这种转基因大豆的商业化生产。

《生物多样性公约》中指出转基因技术“在使用和释放时可能产生危险，即可能对环境产生不利影响，从而影响到生物多样性保护和持续利用，也要考虑到对人类健康的危险”。这里提出了两点，即转基因生物可能对环境及人体健康的潜在风险问题。这其中，公众最关心的就是转基因食品的安全性问题(用转基因作物为原料制成的食品即转基因食品)。

全球玉米面积为1400万公顷，转基因玉米面积占9%，美国、巴西、阿根廷等是转基因玉米种植大国

转基因食品产生潜在健康影响可能的原因有预期和非预期两种情况。现在人们比较关注，同时科学界争议较大的主要是转基因食品对健康影响的非预期效应。

可能导致非预期效应产生的原因与生命体的遗传特性有关。在一些转基因生物中，外源基因的随机插入有可能导致该生物自身的基因发生改变，进而影响到基因的表达。由转基因产生的新蛋白质其毒性也是人们的健康关注之一。转基因植物中可能会出现没有安全食用历史的非蛋白物质，可能会影响人体健康。转基因过程还可能使一些转基因植物在代谢产物方面发生改变，植物的代谢产物可能在食物中积累并对人体健康产生影响。

转基因过程还可能会改变传统食品与加工有关的一些特性。转基因作物(食品)加工方式与传统对等物或基因供体加工方式的不同可能会产生一些安全性方面的新问题。转基因植物中的外源基因被摄入人体后，是否会水平转移至肠道微生物或上皮细胞，从而对人体产生不利影响？这方面可能性虽然很小，但是仍然需加以考虑。

截至目前为止，科学界尚未对转基因食品安全定论。在科学上，对一种没有表现短期毒性和安全问题的食品，如果怀疑其可能存在隐患，则必须观察其远期毒性和安全问题是否存在，这种远期跟踪监测通常需要一二十年。因此，在没有拿到足够确凿的证据之前，相当长的一段时期内，这样的争论还会一直存在

世界卫生组织(WHO)对转基因食品安全性问题一直持谨慎态度。2004 年 10 月，该组织副总干事克斯廷·莱特(Kerstin Leitner)在一次新闻发布会上说：“当前，我们没有证据表明食用含有转基因成分的食品是危险的。但是我们也不清楚这些食品是否会带来危害。因此，我们必须承认我们现在不清楚转基因食品对人类健康的危害性。”

虽然已有的事例尚不能作为科学上的证据证明转基因食品对人体健康存在安全性问题，但是至少可以说明转基因食品在安全方面还存在着一些尚无定论的内容。在科学没有定论的今天，政府给公众以知情权，让公众可自行取舍就显得非常必要。

转基因生物与环境安全

除了食品安全，转基因生物的环境安全问题(即生态风险)同样值得我们关注。这里生态风险指的是转基因生物对环境和生物多样性影响的风险问题。转基因生物的生态风险首先涉及到基因流的概念。在生物安全研究中，基因流是指外源基因在转基因生物与其同一物种个体之间或与其有亲缘关系的生物之间的交流。这种基因的交流主要存在两种途径：一种是转基因植物的花粉通过风媒或虫媒来传播，如果找到受体并形成可育或不可育的杂交后代，就完成了转基因向环境中的释放；另一种是转基因作物的种子可能散落到周围或其他环境中，这种散落的转基因作物的种子开花后可与当地同种的作物或其野生近缘种杂交，如果它所携带的基因在生存选择上具有优势，那么该植株就有可能大量繁殖而成为杂草。简单地说，基因流就是基因发生逃逸。

由于基因流的存在，就必然会产生基因污染的后果，也就是说转基因生物的外源基因，通过基因流转入并整合到其他生物的基因组中，使其他生物及其植物的种子或产品中混杂有转基因成分，进而造成自然界基因库的混杂和污染。

1998 年，加拿大阿尔伯塔省转基因油菜田间发现了能抗三种除草剂的自生自灭的“超级”油菜，其中两种抗性来自转基因油菜，另一种则来自常规育种的抗性油菜，说明由于基因流导致了基因污染。由于多种除草剂都杀不死它，这种自生自灭的油菜生命力很强，甚至可能演变为超级杂草。一旦如此，加拿大油菜种植就很难保证他们所种的非转基因的油菜的种子内不含转基因。目前，国际市场上转基因油菜的价格普遍偏低，并且受到一些进口国家的抵制。

2001 年 9 月，墨西哥政府报告称该国瓦哈卡州的玉米受到一种没有被批准在墨西哥种植的转基因抗虫玉米的污染，该州 22 个村的玉米样品中有 15 个污染率在 3%~10%。墨西哥是世界玉米的起源中心，玉米遗传资源极为丰富，并有多种玉米草(能与玉米自然杂交的野生近缘种)。墨西哥玉米受污染事件在《自然》杂志报道后引起国际重视。从长远看，基因污染有可能导致玉米遗传多样性的减少，而玉米作为世界粮食供应的主要农作物之一，它的遗传多样性在育种方面具有不可估量的价值。

此外，转基因作物还可能带来其他生态效应，比如 Bt 毒素有可能毒死一些本来不该毒死的生物，从而导致生物多样性的丧失，科学上将转基因作物的这种生态效应称作“非靶标效应”。转基因作物的产品随着根的分泌物进入土壤，可能对土壤生态系统及土壤中的生物产生影响。还有其他一些生态风险由于篇幅所限不可能详细一一介绍。

转基因生物的环境风险主要在于转基因DNA的移动性，即这种DNA是否会转至生态系统中，因而引起环境及生态问题

由于世界经济的一体化，农业的利益明显下降。在这样的背景下，转基因技术天翻地覆地改变了传统育种方法，不善于在农业“绿色革命”之后可能引发的一场“蓝色革命”。转基因作物所描绘出的美景很容易吸引人。辩证地去思考转基因生物所代表的新兴科技、新兴产业和新兴模式，我们可以发现，转基因生物带来的的确是一个前所未有的挑战，它涉及了社会生活的各个层面

中国是油菜等芸苔属作物的生产大国，也是芸苔属植物起源地之一，存在着不少野生近缘种。芸苔属植物间非常容易进行杂交，种子又小，在收割或运输过程中很容易扩散。加拿大是耐除草剂转基因油菜生产大国，大量转基因油菜出口，我国也有少量进口。这种转基因也就很容易通过基因流扩散，会对农业生产造成危害。

同时，中国也是水稻的起源中心之一，除栽培水稻的遗传多样性丰富外，野生稻分布也很广，这些都是保证我们培育新品种的遗传资源。实验证明栽培水稻与普通野生稻可以通过基因流自然发生杂交。因此，虽然国内转基因水稻已经培育成功，从生物安全考虑，农业部至今尚未批准其商业化生产。

另一个应受到关注的作物就是大豆。中国是大豆的起源中心，种质资源十分丰富，野生大豆分布范围也很广。虽然大豆在遗传上是严格自交的植物，但栽培大豆与野生大

豆以及不同野生大豆间的自然杂交都是存在的。为了保护中国大豆资源的遗传多样性，虽然国内转基因大豆也已培育成功，农业部并未批准转基因大豆的商业化生产。可是我国每年进口上千万吨的转基因大豆，很难保证老百姓不会去种这种转基因大豆，尤其在我国大豆的主要产地东北。保护大豆遗传资源不受转基因的污染将是我们重要的任务。

从 20 世纪 80 年代以来，国际上开始有转基因技术生物安全研究论文的报道。进入 20 世纪 90 年代后，这方面的研究工作大幅增加，国内这方面的研究也逐步多起来。目前国内主要种植的转基因作物是抗虫棉，所以这方面有关生物安全的研究相应多一些，其他领域的研究也都在逐步开展。

生物安全问题的提出虽然已有 10 多年的历史，但人们的认识还处于初期阶段。随着转基因生物更广泛的应用及基础研究的深入，人们对转基因技术的生物安全会得到一个更为客观的认识。任何事物都存在正、反两面，科学技术也不例外。用科学的方法和理论去思考科学技术潜在的负面影响，是非常有意义和必不可少的。

本文原载：科技潮. 2007. (5): 24-25

防治外来物种入侵北京

钱迎倩

(中国科学院植物研究所)

外来物种是指在某个生态系统或某个国家原先没有这种物种，而是通过各种途径从国外进入的物种。绝大多数的外来物种对世界各国的生态系统是有利的，比如我们日常吃的粮食(如玉米)、蔬菜(如马铃薯)、花卉(如郁金香)等，有相当数量的物种是外来种，对百姓的生活，对政府在经济、社会甚至政治上都起到重要的作用。但确有一小部分外来种一旦在某个生态系统或自然条件合适的地区定居下来后，对当地环境、经济、人体健康带来恶劣的影响。这部分如入侵者一样的外来种被人们称为外来入侵种。目前入侵北京的植物已超过 50 种，入侵动物超过 18 种。据农业部统计，入侵我国的外来种动、植物已达 400 种左右，每年对农林牧渔等行业造成的经济损失达 198.6 亿元，对生态系统、物种和遗传资源造成的间接经济 1000.2 亿元。总经济损失达 1200 亿元。

作为外来入侵种往往有适应性强，繁殖速度快等特点。目前我国内陆水体存在程度不同的富营养化，正适合水葫芦在短期内大量泛滥

外来入侵种不仅会造成重大经济损失，还会使各种生态系统失去生态平衡，使生物多样性丧失，引起当地物种濒危、甚至灭绝，也会给人体健康带来严重的危害，显然也威胁到 2008 年在北京举办的奥运会。有一种可能直接威胁到奥运会的外来入侵种，就是美国白蛾。美国白蛾 1979 年从国外传播到辽宁丹东一带，由于它是一种林木、行道树、果树、农作物、野生植物都食的杂食性昆虫，繁殖能力极强，扩散速度又快，早几年已扩散到北京。2006 年不仅在京郊 12 个区县有发现，并已扩散至北京核心区域，天坛公

园和龙潭公园都已有发现。虽然有关部门已采取了紧急措施，可是今年是一个暖冬，过冬的虫卵不易冻死，因此如果措施不力，2007 年在北京有大暴发的可能。如果各种树木成片成片的没有了叶子，行道树叶子也被吃成光杆司令，这将严重威胁到 2008 年的奥运会，后果不堪设想。

福寿螺又名大瓶螺，原产亚马逊河流域，作为高蛋白食物，1981 年被引入广东。作为经济动物繁殖，并很快传扩到其他省份。由于肉质不好被当地遗弃。福寿螺繁殖力强、食量大，对水稻等作物危害大。体内有广州管圆线虫等寄生虫。在北京发生过 17 名食福寿螺患者向蜀国演义饭店索赔百万事件

外来种的入侵主要有三条途径，即有意引入、无意传入及自然侵入。有意引入是指人们出于经济、改善环境、观赏以及作为宠物或特殊礼物等目的有意的引入某些动植物物种。我国有意引入种在外来入侵种中占的比例是相当大的，最典型的例子是在我国南方泛滥成灾的水葫芦。它造成河道堵塞、威胁当地物种生存、破坏水体生态系统，并造成重大的经济损失。无意传入是指藏在包装材料或运输工具中随着货物的运输传入，货船在压舱水中的物种以及旅客通过海陆空途径传入的外来入侵种。在经济全球化的今天，外来入侵种中无意传入比例相当大。2008 年奥运会有几十万国外游客入境参赛或观看比赛，将会大大增加外来入侵种传入的机会，应引起有关责任部门的重视。此外，一些植物种子、微生物或病毒都可能随着风和河流自然侵入我国国境。鸟类的迁栖也可能造成自然入侵。禽流感目前在全球流行，有专家认为鸟类迁飞是造成世界性传播的原因之一。虽然由自然侵入带来的外来入侵种的比例相对较少，但已造成的如禽流感全球性发生的后果应引起人们足够的重视。

入侵北京的外来种已近百种，为迎接“绿色奥运”，杜绝外来入侵种已迫在眉睫。当然，杜绝外来入侵种不仅是为了迎接奥运，而是为了整治我们国家的环境，恢复各种生态系统，保护当地物种，保护生物多样性以及保障人民的健康。积极防治是首要的措施，如对目前最具威胁的美国白蛾，北京市各有关部门已采取了一系列措施：生物防治是首选，北京已联合天津、河北大量繁殖天敌周氏啮小蜂来消灭美国白蛾；在近期已由相关职能部门联合科研单位、大专院校成立了首都生态圈外来入侵种监测研究中心，将在全市设立 100 个监测点，定期进行系统调查；建立数据库和相应网站，及时通报疫情，沟

通信息，制定相应措施。对全国来讲，目前国家缺少一个全国统一的防范管理部门，也还没有一部统一的相关法规，建议前两者应尽快地建立。通过法规及管理部门的管理、执行，可更加强检疫、监控，建立预警机制，预先确定防范重点，制定防范规划以及加强宣传工作，提高全民的防范意识。还应加强生物入侵的科学技术研究，提出快速有效的方法，以及研究如何综合利用，变废为宝。通过前面的措施，外来入侵种是可防可治的。

巴西龟，已成为全球性的外来入侵种，作为宠物。我国从南到北几乎所有宠物市场上都有出售，已被世界自然保护联盟列为世界最危险的100个入侵种之一。巴西龟也是疾病传播的媒介

豚草和同一属的三裂豚草，原产北美洲，除华南外几乎全国都已扩散。北京的顺义、门头沟等6个区县都有分布，面积达3万余亩。生命力强，适应性强，与农作物和其他植物争水，肥，光。能产生大量有毒花粉，引起花粉过敏、枯草热症、过敏性哮喘、鼻炎、皮炎，还可并发肺气肿、心脏病

小龙虾学名克氏原螯虾，原产南美洲，20世纪30~40年代从日本作为食物和宠物引进，我国南方各省有庞大的自然种群，作为食品到处销售。此物种食性广泛，扩散能力强，在湿地生态系统中对鱼类、甲壳类、水生植物都具有威胁，食取水稻根系造成灾害，还能在堤坝中打洞，威胁堤坝设施

椰子树由于遭到外来入侵种椰心叶甲的危害，叶片都已脱落枯死，2006年海南全省染椰心叶甲的椰树317万株，其中重度受害38万株，中度受害57万株

美国白蛾，原产北美洲，适应范围广，危害各种树木、农作物300多种。繁殖力强，一次产卵300多粒，每年可以向外扩散35~50km，目前不仅已扩散到河北、天津、山东、陕西等地，已扩散到北京，严重威胁2008年奥运会

本文原载：植物学报. 1979. 21(1): 88-91

第四届国际植物组织、细胞培养会议简介

钱迎倩

(中国科学院植物研究所)

第四届国际植物组织、细胞培养会议于 1978 年 8 月 20~25 日在加拿大卡加立大学召开。共有来自 42 个国家的 550 多名科学家。我国派了 8 名科学家第一次参加了这个领域的国际会议。中国科学院遗传研究所所长胡含在会上作了“中国花药培养的部分研究工作”的报告，引起了与会科学家的重视与兴趣。

这次会议内容相当丰富，涉及 18 个方面，共提出综述报告 48 篇，研究成果 320 篇(表1)。下面分四个方面向读者作一简介。

表 1　综述与墙报的内容和数量

Table 1　The contents and amounts of lectures and poster demonstrations

内　容 Contents	综　述(篇数) Amount of lectures	墙　报(版数) Amount of poster demonstration
形态建成 Regulation of morphogenesis	4	44
遗传操作 Genetic manipulation	4	6
花药培养 Anther culture	3	17
原生质体 Protoplasts	1	11
体细胞杂交 Somatic hybridization	2	19
同步生长和生化调节 Synchronous growth & biochemical regulation	3	11
次生代谢 I　Sccondary metabolism I	3	20
细胞结构 Cell structure	2	6
植物与病毒的相互作用 Plant/Virus interaction	2	4
细胞与器官培养 Cell and organ culture	2	15
遗传稳定性 Genetic stability	1	6
细胞贮藏 Cell preservation	1	8
生长调节 Growth regulation	3	22
次生代谢 II　Secondary metabolism II	3	26
植物与微生物相互作用 Plant/Microbe interaction	2	6
突变发生 Mutagenesis	2	34
应用的形态建成 Applied morphogenesis	4	48
初生代谢 Primary metabolism	4	17
大会报告 All congress symposium	2	
总　计　Total	48	320

植物组织培养在农业上的重要性

美国著名植物组织培养学家，MS 培养基创建人之一 Murashige 在全体大会上作了“植物组织培养在农业上的重要性”的报告。他把植物组织培养在农业上的应用归纳为三点：①培养植物新的杂种；②复壮特殊的无病系；③快速的无性繁殖。50 多年来，植物杂交工作者通过胚胎、胚珠和子房培养已经获得了一些稀有的杂种。近年来利用单倍体育种在我国已培育出品质优良的烟草、水稻、小麦等新品种。加拿大在大麦、油菜的单倍体育种方面也作得相当出色。但正像瑞士的 Thomas 指出的，今后如果把遗传变异与有效的细胞选择结合起来，将会使植物组织培养在农业上起更有效的作用。也就是说，要有更多的具重要经济价值的作物，能够从单细胞或单细胞愈伤组织无性系去诱导其形态建成。这次会议上有不少的展出说明，玉米、小麦、黑麦等二倍体愈伤组织的分化问题已经解决，但总的看来困难还很多。外植体的组织来源，其生理—发育状态，基因型和培养基的组成都会影响培养物的发育和分化。而对禾谷类来说，培养组织的年龄，基因型的稳定性和激素的相互关系等也直接影响其植株的再生。

利用体外培养方法消除植物病害，在农业生产上已收到显著的效果。我国在通过分生组织培养解决马铃薯退化问题是成功的。目前国际上通过愈伤组织和原生质体培养也可以根除病毒。采用培养前和培养中的温度、生长素和细胞分裂素等因子的作用来控制病毒的失活。其中尤其是利用温度这个因子，采用高温处理或高低温双周期处理结合组织培养，可以提高病毒活性的丧失。

至于无性系快速繁殖方向，世界上大概有 100 个实验室在进行这方面的工作。其中以观赏植物做得最多，国际上有试管商品出售，这次大会亦有商品展出。具重要经济价值的优秀树种的培养，近年来发展亦很快。尽管目前能达到商品规模的繁殖还不多，但大多数的木本植物可在实验室中进行苗的培养，促进其发生不定芽或腋枝。通过这种称为“微繁殖”技术来解决森林树种无性繁殖的困难，以及用以去除病毒，早期选择质量、产量和抗病性。近年来，诱导茎、叶、根或胚胎外植株的再生亦开始成功。这次会议上有一些松、云杉、冷杉组织培养的报告。但是，在诱导愈伤组织或悬浮培养细胞的植株再生方面，目前还有很大的困难。美国 Banks 报告了采用长春藤的体外培养，来研究多年生木本植物的幼态相和成熟相之间的差异。从幼态相和成熟相植物来源的茎形成层，通过培养都能形成愈伤组织。前者的愈伤组织生长得比后者快得多，并且分化的叶子是卵形或浅裂，而后者则分化为完整的胚胎。这结果对树木的无性繁殖可能有一定的参考意义。

近年来，还有应用组织培养方法来进行除草剂的预先筛选，及研究除草剂在植物中的作用，其作用形式和除草剂的“解毒”作用和代谢关系，以及探索通过培养物来分离抗除草剂的谷物等方面的工作。

细胞或组织在−196℃液氮里冰冻贮藏是近年来发展的保存种质的一种新方法。一般采用二甲亚砜和葡萄糖结合聚乙二醇作为保护剂起到好的效果。目前在技术上和其他方面尽管还存在不少问题，但细胞或组织在保存一段时间后，经过化冻能继续生长并分化植株。

有关细胞工程的研究

细胞工程的研究既有其基础的研究，又为作物的改良创造新的途径。这次大会从综述报告及研究成果来看，似乎看不到有重大的突破，但亦有一定的进展。

细胞器和微生物由于原生质体的内吞作用而被引入成功，这已不是近年来的新成果。但由于给体在新细胞的细胞质内很快解体，造成对引入的细胞器的生理活性、复制等研究的困难。这次会上美国 Uchimiya 的研究报告说明，他确认 *Nicotiana gossei* 的叶绿体已引入 *N. tabacum* 的白化原生质体中。但根据微量免疫电泳的分析，无证据能说明外源遗传信息在部分 I 蛋白的大、小亚基的多肽上有任何的翻译。

DNA 引入萌发种子、苗、组织、培养细胞、原生质体的研究也已有近 10 年的历史，至今争论还很大。某些研究者主张外源 DNA 不仅可被受体细胞吸收，可并入到受体的基因组内，还可进行复制。而另一部分研究者却既看不到并入，更看不到复制。其原因正如加拿大的 Pelcher 等的研究报告说明的，细胞可吸收 DNA，但可能进入细胞内的大多数只是简单的 DNA 的降解产物。美国 Matthews 在技术上的革新值得注意，他用人造脂体(liposome)把大肠杆菌 RNA 包裹起来，然后在作原生质体引入。证明 4S 和 16SRNA 受到保护，而未用人造脂体保护的 RNA，引入后全部降解了。

关于突变发生的研究，国际上研究得颇为热闹。通过辐射和化学药物处理促使植物细胞发生突变，产生一系列抗病、抗盐、抗冻、抗药、生长素自养型营养缺陷型等细胞株。除直接在农业上应用外，还可作为遗传标记结合细胞器转移和体细胞杂交进行细胞工程的研究。会议上美国的 Pittenger 报道用链霉素处理玉米、高粱和小麦种子可容易地获得白化和花斑苗，以及 Pandey 等报道用 ^{60}Co 照射 *Haworthia mirabilis* 愈伤组织导致植物肿瘤发生的工作，可能对今后白化和植物肿瘤发生的研究会有帮助。

至于原生质体和体细胞杂交的研究，在方法学上反映新成就的不多。瑞典 Eriksson 用化学药品 Cytochalasin B 处理加上离心后，可把原生质体分为无核原生质体和细胞核外包有少量细胞质和质膜，他们称为微原生质体两个部分。从而开辟了去掉植物细胞核甚至单个染色体的新途径，这工作值得注意。通过体细胞杂交途径，匈牙利的 Dudits 得到了伞形科的属间杂种植株，加拿大 Gamborg 等得到烟草与西红柿的杂种植株，印度的 Brar 得到高粱与玉米的杂种细胞。有意思的是苏联的 Gleba 把拟南芥菜和 *Brassica campestris* 原生质体融合后，得到的杂种细胞系至少在 30 个细胞周期内，杂种细胞内的双亲染色体没有丢失的现象。采用雄性不育系得到细胞质杂种，法国的 Belliard 等利用两种烟草已得到第四代的后代。此外，在动植物细胞融合方面，英国诺丁赫姆大学工作组最近把胡萝卜原生质体与蟾蜍细胞融合成功，其优点是两栖类细胞生长的温度要求与植物原生质体是一致的，都是 25℃。

体细胞杂交的应用前途又是如何呢?我们从一美籍华人处了解到，国外已把产生重要药物的植物原生质体与真菌融合，企图把高等植物的基因并入真菌基因组内，然后通过真菌发酵的途径生产药物。他乐观地估计 2~3 年后，体细胞杂交就可在生产上见到分晓。

植物组织培养的基础研究

有关细胞分裂生长、分化、形态建成和它们的调节，以及细胞结构、遗传稳定性等基础研究。占到整个会议内容 1/3 以上，反映了国际上对基础研究的重视。要对这些问题有深刻的了解，不仅要研究它们的生物大分子代谢，而且还应该从细胞的相互作用，激素调节以及有丝分裂放锤体等方面进行研究，但正像大会主席加拿大的 Thorpe 在谈到形态建成的生理生化基础时所强调指出的，从目前的知识来看，我们仅仅开始触及到问题的皮毛。

研究细胞分裂，DNA 合成和代谢等基础问题，体外培养是一个很好的手段。但要使培养物能同步分裂以及能够分离出中间产物是重要的前提。这次会议有多篇控制同步分裂的报告。加拿大的 Kurz 等在大豆细胞悬浮培养中，采用每 3~4 秒钟通氮气 1/10s，在 24h 或 30h 内共通 90min，这样的处理可使同步分裂的有丝分裂指数提高 12%~15%。如果 4 天一周期，每 24h 内通氮气时间延长到 8 × 30min，则有丝分裂指数可高达 26%。此外，还采用 3%乙烯通 3h，3%CO_2通 3h，普通空气半小时的程序，也可收到明显的效果。美国的 Minocha 以菊芋块茎作材料，在培养基中加 1~5mg/L 脱落酸，可明显的刺激 DNA 合成，使同步分裂增加一倍。日本的 Komanine 等在长春花悬浮细胞培养中，用磷饥饿的方法诱导同步分裂成功。其程序是磷饥饿 4 天，喂磷 1 天。这程序重复 2 次后的几小时内细胞数目就大增，并且诱导的同步分裂至少可以保持 2 代。

会议上还展出了从悬浮培养细胞中分离细胞核，DNA，RNA 的简化而价廉的新程序。对 *Acer* 属研究证实了组蛋白是在细胞质中合成，然后转移到核中。在整个细胞周期内组蛋白都进行合成，但在 DNA 合成前达到最高峰。

细胞生长发育的调节，多数还是围绕着激素来进行。德国的 Bender 报道了培养基中的吲哚乙酸(IAA)在 3 天内由于光照大多数破坏了，同时也很快可为培养组织所降解。但是胡萝卜培养物很快在 24h 内就可以诱导合成自己的 IAA。他从而认为外源 IAA 和激动素是一样的，只是在起动时期是需要的。至于激素的作用机理方面，荷兰人 Libbenga 向大会提出了“植物中激素接受器”的评述。他认为首先要研究植物细胞中存在什么样的特殊的激素接受器，其次激素与接受器的复合物必须是一个有活性的结构，也就是说应该有一个键。如果这是一个控制基因作用的键，那就应进一步研究哪一部分基因组是受激素控制的以及以何种方式来使基因起作用。这报告给我们提出了要从分子水平上来研究激素作用的机理。

有关培养基方面也提出了一些新问题。加拿大的 Thaker 把鸡蛋白(0.1mL/8mL B_5)加入改良的 B_5 培养基中，使培养的菜豆离体胚所形成的小植株，在可溶性蛋白，RNA 和叶绿素含量上都比对照要高。日本的 Ojima 等发现培养基中氨单独作为一个氮源时，培养物只发生一点生长，但如果加入某些具高 PK 值有机酸(如柠檬酸、琥珀酸、顺丁烯二酸，丙二酸等)都可提高氨的吸收，而获得满意生长。此外，瑞典的 Fridborg 研究了培养基中活性炭的作用。说明 1%活性炭可促进胡萝卜、蚕豆和葱培养物的形态建成，甚至对已丧失形态建成能力者有刺激的作用。其原因可能是由于生长的细胞，分泌大量的酚类化合物和其他代谢产物抑制了形态建成，而活性炭则可吸收这类化合物。

有关细胞分化和形态建成的调节问题，印度 Johri 提出在苔藓培养物中，分化是受到接种细胞的密度和激素的平衡来调节的。同时还决定于顶端细胞有丝分裂放锤体方向的改变，也就是说如产生对角线的横壁就意味着分化的开始。此外，有关器官分化过程中同功酶的变化，激素对分化中同功酶的变化，赤霉素和乙烯对性别分化的作用等方面的报告也很多。

染色体数目不稳定性是组织培养中的一大难题，意大利的 Damato 对这问题有较多的研究。这次会议上他把不稳定性归纳为三个方面的来源：①染色体的核内复制，这在原始外植体中就有可能发生；②在诱导愈伤组织时，有丝分裂发生染色体断裂；③由于有丝分裂器或染色体移动受到干扰，或者某些基因组的选择有利性，造成了培养物中的增殖细胞群发生了变化。这些变化是与培养基中激素，培养物的年龄和原始外植体的类型有关。这次会议中英国的 Shillito 的报告，还提出培养基中盐的平衡对细胞遗传稳定性的影响，他认为可能与激素和维生素的成分一样重要。

植物组织培养工业应用的前景

应用植物细胞培养的方法，通过工业生产的途径来进行具特殊价值的次生物质(如甾类化合物，类萜，生物碱和酚类)的生产，这方面的研究，近年来国际上有了较大的进展。目前对某些抗癌物质，强心苷及抗植物病害的药物等都已选出了一些好的细胞株，使生产物的水平有了提高。同时在次生物质的代谢，生物转化的途径，酶的特性和它们的调节，环境因子(包括营养物质，光照等)对产物形成的影响，以及激素对它们的调节控制等方面也进行了大量的基础研究。国际上有十几个国家在进行这方面的研究，其中日本和西德的工作比较出色。当然，目前存在的问题还不少。正如西德的 Zenk 指出的，要达到工业应用的目的，下列几个方面是值得重视的。首先是应用细胞培养所产生的次生产物的产量能否等于或高于起源的植物，这里就有一个高产量细胞株的筛选问题；其次，如筛得高产量细胞株后，这些细胞株通过长期继代培养如何使它们的生物合成能力保持稳定，而不发生变异；最后，要投入生产还不得不考虑成本核算的问题。看来这些问题是造成植物组织培养目前尚不能工业应用的主要障碍。

植物组织培养本身是一个方法学的问题，它一方面对工农业生产发展起着重要的作用，同时又是植物生理学、遗传学、细胞学、形态学、病理学甚至分子生物学等基础研究的一个极好的工具。当然这些基础研究的成果又进一步推动了植物组织培养的发展。这次会议总的趋势是在继续理论研究和发展新技术的基础上，扩大探索植物组织、细胞培养在工、农、医各方面的应用。

由于植物组织、细胞培养的重要，国际上专门成立了“国际植物组织培养协会”。这协会每四年举行一次国际会议。第五届国际会议将于 1982 年在日本举行。

本文原载：植物杂志. 1979. (1): 46-47

加拿大纪行

钱迎倩

(中国科学院植物研究所)

盛大的国际学术会议

1978 年 8 月 20 日至 25 日，第四届国际植物组织、细胞培养会议在加拿大的卡加立大学召开。我国派出 8 名科学家第一次参加了这个国际学术会议。1978 年 5 月，在北京参加中澳植物组织培养会议的许多老朋友，在这里又见面了，显得格外亲切。各国的朋友们都为我国抓纲治国，科研上的大好形势而高兴。

这次会议可以说是植物组织和细胞培养方面的一次国际盛会。会议内容涉及形态建成的调节、遗传操作、花药培养、原生质体、细胞杂交等 18 个方面，共提出综合报告 48 篇，研究成果 320 篇。人们看到，随着研究工作的深入，植物组织培养在农业上越来越显示出它的重要性。正如美国著名组织培养学家、MS 培养基创建人之一姆勒谢奇所说的那样，植物组织培养在农业上的应用可以归纳为三点：一是培育植物的新品种；二是复壮特殊的无病系；三是快速的无性繁殖。这些年来上述三个方面的研究工作都有许多进展。近年还有应用组织培养方法进行除草剂的筛选等工作的。关于细胞工程的研究，目前虽然尚无重大的突破，但也有一定的进展。美国的马修斯用人造脂体(Liposome)把大肠杆菌 RNA 包裹起来，然后再作原生质体引入，从而使 RNA 受到了保护。这项新技术引起了人们的广泛注意。瑞典的埃立克逊用化学药品 Cytochalasin B 处理加上离心后，可把原生质体分为无核原生质体和细胞核外包有少量细胞质和质膜两个部分，开辟了去掉植物细胞核甚至单个染色体的新途径。通过体细胞杂交的途径，匈牙利的杜迪兹得到了伞形科的属间杂种植株。加拿大的甘博格得到了烟草与西红柿的杂种植株。在动植物细胞融合方面，英国的诺丁赫姆大学最近把胡萝卜原生质体与蟾蜍细胞融合成功。这次会议有关细胞分裂生长、分化、形态建成和它的调节，以及细胞结构、遗传稳定性等基础研究，占了整个会议内容的 1/3 以上。另外，许多国家的研究，展示了植物组织培养在工业应用上的可喜前景，应用植物细胞培养的方法，生产具有特殊价值的次生物质，如甾类化合物、类萜、生物碱和酚类等，近年来都有了较大的进展。

会议内容这样丰富，而会议只用了五天时间就圆满结束了。会议形式新颖，生动活泼，组织效率很高。你一报到，可以立即得到一本介绍会议一切细节的说明，得到全部论文的摘要和与会者名单。这次会议结合纪念著名植物组织培养学家斯特里特，特意邀请了国际上著名科学家作了共同感兴趣的报告，这就使大家对植物组织培养研究和应用的现状与前景有了概括的了解。你要了解自己研究领域的情况，可以从有关的综合报告中得到。会议为每位向大会提出报告的科学家，提供了一块两平方米左右的地方，供他们以大字报的形式，展览自己的研究成果，并规定时间由他们在大字报前解答提问，你在这里可以进一步了解有关研究的细节。如果需要你还可以在有关专业性的圆桌会议上，介绍自己的研究心得或与有关专家共同讨论问题。会议组织的碰头会、招待会、宴会以及游览等活动，都为与会者创造条件，来结识朋友，了解情况，交流经验。总之，会议组织者通过各种形式来满足与会者的要求，使会议开得既紧张又活泼，在短短的五天内收到了预期的效果。

一个高水平的实验室

会议圆满结束，热情好客的主人，邀请中国科学家去外地参观访问。位于萨斯卡图的加拿大国家研究委员会的草原地区实验室细胞培养部分，是我们参观访问的重点单位。

草原地区实验室的水平是比较高的，在国际上有一定的地位。他们的 B_5 培养基、聚乙二醇高频率融合方法、杂种细胞培育以及同功酶分析等工作，都是具有国际先进水平的。组织、细胞的冰冻储藏，是近年来保存种质新发展起来的一个领域，他们很快占领了这个领域，并且在木瓜分生组织储藏等方面作出了成果。

这个实验室的水平高，原因是多方面的。给人们印象最深的有三点：一是研究人员精悍。这个实验室的细胞培养组只有 8 名研究人员，每人配有一名技术员，人数虽然不多，加籍印度科学家卡撒博士却风趣地告诉我们，这个组是“国际性”的。原来这 8 名研究人员来自 8 个国家，是择优而来的。是的，科研攻坚，人不在于多而在于精。二是有过硬的研究技术。这个组的 8 名研究人员，在广博的基础上各都精于一个方面。研究组的负责人韦特教授精于同功酶的分析，来自西德的康斯坦皮尔正在进行次生物质代谢方面的研究。研究人员各自同自己的技术人员牢牢掌握着一个方面的研究技术，需要时，他们又互相协作，互相配合。三是有现代化的实验装备。这个不到 20 人的研究组，各类仪器，配备齐全，占了三层大楼的一半。如超净工作台就拥有 16 台，其他如液体闪烁计数器、超速离心机等，应有尽有。

这个实验室每年还接纳世界各地一定数量的科研人员来进修或读博士学位。国际上有些植物组织学者都曾在这里进修过。在我们即将离开时，甘博格教授热情地表示，他们热烈欢迎中国科学家或学生到他们那儿进修或学习。

现代化的仪器设备

在渥太华，我们用了两天时间参观了渥太华大学和加拿大农业部设在这里的研究站。同其他一些单位一样，这里的仪器设备给我们留下了深刻的印象。他们实验材料的培养，除温室外，基本上都采用人工气候箱(图 1)。渥太华大学一个大实验室里就有人工气候箱近 30 台，型号大小不同，可以自动模拟一天内不同时间的光照和气候，因而他们的试验材料一年四季都能得到很好的保证。他们玻璃器皿的洗涤以及高压灭菌等都有专门的自动化设备(图 2)。各种规格的培养皿、具盖离心管等都是塑料制品，买来时都已进行了灭菌。这些都大大节省了科学实验的人力。

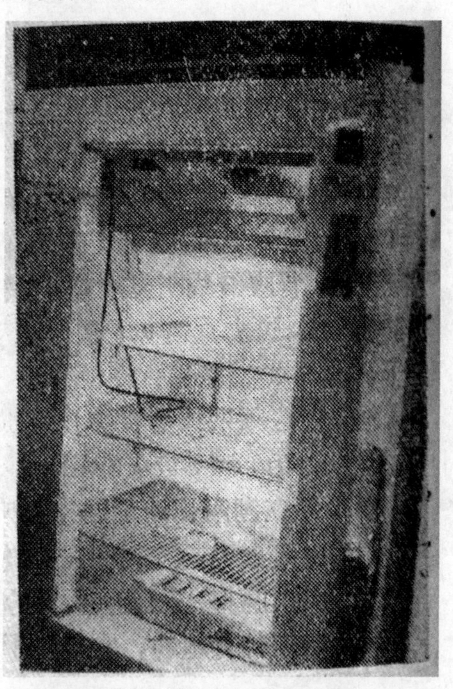

图 1　一台小型人工气候箱

图 2　卡加立大学组织培养实验室一角

右：两台自动洗涤器　左：两台自动控制高压锅

他们的其他设备也很现代化。电子显微镜室由博士水平的人来领导。扫描电镜、冰冻蚀刻、X 光分析直到暗室设备，许多单位都是配套成龙。他们放大一张照片，使用一种仪器，只要 5~10 秒钟就可以完成。还有一种差分扫描热量计，测量的范围从零下 196 ℃到零上 1000℃，灵敏度达到 1 微卡，能够监测细胞内是否结冰，并可以测定物质的纯度和溶点。

看了这些设备，使我们深深感到，科学研究要大上，实验设备的现代化是一个重要条件。加拿大的许多仪器设备都是自己生产的，在温尼伯城就有专门生产环境控制仪器的工厂(图 3)。

图 3　细胞悬浮培养卧式转床

发达的农业

由于植物组织培养与农业有着密切的关系，在参观访问过程中我们对加拿大的农业也作了一些了解。加拿大的农业相当发达，是世界上重要的粮食出口国家之一。它给我们总的印象，一是劳动生产率高；二是科学研究搞得好；这两者又是相辅相成的。

加拿大的农业科学研究，主要由农业部下属的各研究站及大学的有关院系来进行。他们的研究工作一方面与农业生产实践紧密结合，同时又注意应用基础和基础的研究。他们通过组织培养在育种方面进行了大量工作。例如大麦单倍体育种已应用于生产，油菜单倍体育种、亚麻和小麦等作物的组织培养也将在生产上见到成效。其他如体细胞杂交、突变发生及遗传操作等方面的研究，都是为进一步改造植物开辟新途径的。

在萨斯卡图地区，那里冬季气温可达零下 40℃至零下 45℃，低温与干旱是农业生产上最突出的问题。那里的萨斯卡其万大学谷物系和农业部的研究站，针对这个问题展开了一系列的研究。他们利用美国、苏联、中国和其他许多国家的小麦品种进行杂交，不断培育出适应当地环境条件的优良品种；用核磁共振测定组织内水分含量，进行品种的抗寒试验；用高压液相色谱测定含量很低的植物内源激素，研究植物内源激素与植物抗旱力的关系。在基础研究方面，锡密诺维奇教授等从膜和酶与低温的关系上进行冻害的研究，他们的工作引起了国际上的关注。

在加拿大的访问就要结束了。这些天的所见所闻一直在头脑里迴旋。与各国科学家广泛接触，加强国际间的学术交流，是我国实现科学技术现代化的重要措施，而要更好地参加国际学术交流又取决于我们的工作水平。这里的关键，就是要迅速地把自己的工作搞上去。

本文原载：生命世界. 1985. (5): 44-45

澳大利亚的试管苗工厂化生产

钱迎倩

(中国科学院植物研究所)

1985 年 5 月 7 日至 25 日，随中国科学院组织的考察组，考察了澳大利亚植物组织培养，特别是试管苗工厂化生产情况。考察组访问了堪培拉、悉尼、布里斯班及墨尔本四个城市的有关研究所、大学，并重点访问了 9 个苗圃及组织培养试管苗工厂化试验室。

澳大利亚植物组织培养研究的某些实验室，在国际上占有一定地位；在把组织培养转化为技术商品应用于工厂化生产方面，也是比较先进的，并且有着方兴未艾的势头。对于这方面的基础研究、应用基础研究以及开发性研究或生产，他们有明确的分工。基础及应用基础研究都在有关大学或研究所内进行，而且在许多情况下，这些单位只把组织培养作为研究生物学领域某些课题的一种手段。至于开发性研究及试管苗的生产，则完全在私人苗圃或专门生产试管苗的实验室内进行。

澳大利亚植物组织培养开发性研究和工厂化生产，历史不久，全澳开办最早的试管苗工厂 Micro Flora，也才有 7 年的历史，多数是近 2~3 年内兴办的。这些单位的规模都不算大，固定人员都不多。据称是大洋洲地区最大的试管苗工厂 Horticultural laboratories，包括临时工在内才有 28 人，14 个超净台，10 间共 150m^2 的培养室，培养植物约 40 种(不包括变种)。全澳设备最现代化的 Burbank 组织培养实验室，不到 10 人，6 个超净台，一大间 70 多 m^2 的培养室，用 50 种不同的培养基，培养约 60 种 250 个变种的植物，约 30 万株。还有些单位规模更小，工作人员都以家庭成员为主，一切设备，因陋就简。像 McBeans 兰花苗圃，只有 15m^2 的培养室，以培养兰花中的 *Cybidium* 为主。他们的盈利是肯定的。像刚刚开业三年的 Sturat James 苗圃，又在筹建更为现代化的实验室，就是一个证明。

从参观的几个单位来看，澳大利亚试管苗工厂化生产有以下几个特点。

一、实验室的布局合理

试管苗工厂化生产同一般组织培养实验室一样，配培养基、灭菌、接种、转移材料及培养这些环节是缺少不了的。这些私人实验室把这些环节分别安排在一个小建筑物内的各个房间里，既经济又方便。像 Valbri 苗圃就是这样(图)。为减少污染，实验室都设在远离城市的地方，建筑物的空气只从一处进入，经过过滤装置后，使整套实验室都处于过滤空气条件之下。由于室内始终有过滤空气打进来，又只有一个进出口，室内压力比室外相对要大一些，即使将门打开，空气也是只出不进，保持着室内空气的清洁。另外，门口还设有消毒池，池内放着洒有灭菌剂的地毯，凡进入实验室的人都必须在鞋外再套上一薄塑料套鞋，在消毒池内消毒后才能入内。

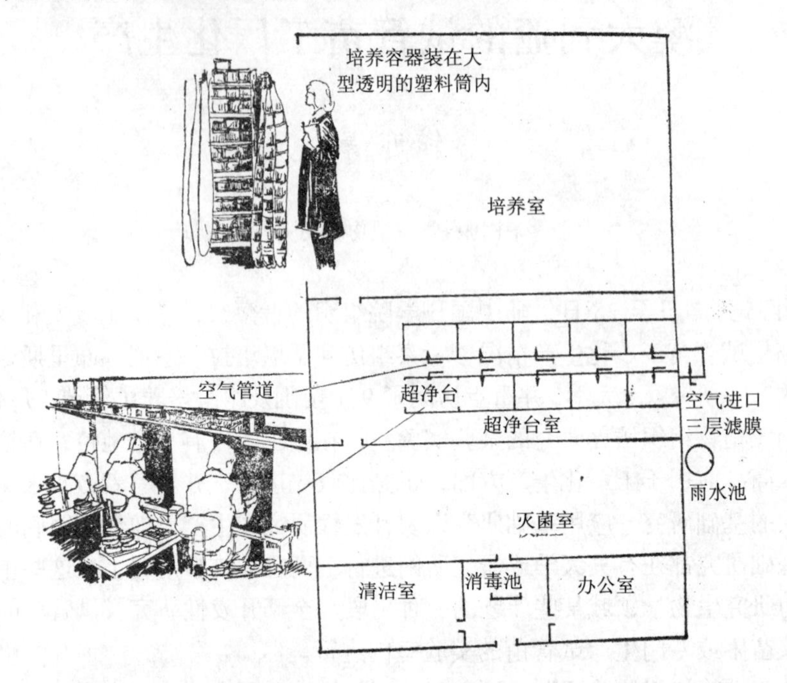

试管苗工厂实验室建筑物平面示意图

Burbank 组织培养实验室是设备条件最好的，建筑物的墙不少是用大玻璃代替的。经理告诉我们，来这里参观的人很多，特别是旅游者和中小学生，但一般都不允许进入实验室，在室外通过玻璃就可以看到实验室的全部。这个实验室的有关数据是自动记录的，主人拿出他们的实验记录本给我们看，上面贴有每次称药品的自动记录纸。这些资料都保存着，一旦出现事故，就可以从中寻找原因。他们制备培养基、洗涤器皿及高压灭菌的设备也都是第一流的。接种外植体有专门的房间和超净台，与转移室分开，以免外源细菌、孢子的污染。培养基配制后，放到 4℃的专门冷室中保存。实验室用的是经过专门设备过滤的无离子雨水，不用自来水，以避免漂白粉中的氯气。

二、想方设法降低成本

(1) 多数实验室的组成都以家庭成员为主，只聘请一位大学毕业的技术人员。Valbri 苗圃是一典型代表，不仅实验室成员是家庭成员，一切设备也都因陋就简。如高压灭菌器他们不用多数实验室使用的、价值 2 万澳币的现代化灭菌器，而用的是当地产的类似我国家用高压锅一样的大型高压锅，每个才 200 元澳币。超净台也是自己用木板钉的，过滤空气进入实验室，先进入一个大管子，然后再进入 10 个自制的具有进一步过滤装置的超净台，这样成本就大大降低了。

(2) 培养容器较普遍的是采用澳大利亚产的能消毒一次的圆形塑料食品盒，每盒可装 50 株试管苗，经济合用。

(3) 合理利用培养室的面积。由于培养容器采用的是圆形食品盒，可以 3~5 个重叠起来在培养架上同时培养；还有的把许多培养容器装在大型的透明塑料筒内，挂在培养架上或专门的架子上，这就大大提高了培养室的利用率。因此，许多实验室的培养室面积不大，而培养的苗数却不少。

(4) 培养室内白天普遍不加光照。主人告诉我们这是为了节约能源。白天气温高，有天然光，可以不加光照；晚上温度降低时才加光照。

三、小苗移栽成活率普遍较高

我们参观的实验室，试管苗移栽成活率一般都在 80%以上。很重要的一点是保持湿度。温室内的小苗都用专门的塑料罩罩住，罩内装有自动喷雾装置。喷雾装置有两种：一种是由定时计控制的，每 6min 喷雾一次；另一种是机械控制的，有一似苍蝇拍状的舌，装在喷雾器的下面，舌联结在一个内装水银的管上，管内水银能自由流动。在喷雾之后，由于舌上有水，重量加重，随使水银向前流去，使继电器跳开，喷雾停止。舌上水分不断蒸发，重量减轻，水银又向反方向流动，继电器再次接触，又开始喷雾。这种装置，结构简单，易于仿行。

移栽小苗的基质，不用一般的土壤，采用树皮、蛭石和泥炭土的混合物，用营养液施肥。移栽小苗的容器用黑色软塑料小杯，放入每穴直径约 4~5cm 的 100 穴的塑料盘，或具 100 穴的泡沫塑料盘。小苗长到一定程度，根系伸入基质，很容易地连同基质从容器中取出。装基质已机械化，每小时可装 15 000 盆。

四、重视市场信息

试管苗工厂同一般商业一样，要想盈利，不仅产品要适销对路，还要有理想的价格。因此，掌握市场信息，十分重要。现在试管苗礼品是畅销货，价格也高，一般试管苗每株 30~40 澳分，而旅游礼品可高达 3~5 澳元，所以多数试管苗工厂都有这类产品。我们在当地还看到马来西亚产的试管苗旅游礼品，可见这已不是澳大利亚的独创。

澳大利亚各城市的建筑物内，尤其是饭店、旅馆、商店需要大量的各种类型的观叶、观花、蕨类等室内植物，这些也就成了试管苗工厂的大宗的、畅销的产品。现在，多数工厂又在培养所谓“神果”Babaco(番木瓜属植物)。Babaco 原产厄瓜多尔，由新西兰引种成功，近年来传到澳大利亚，正在成为一种新兴的水果。Burbank 试验室培养的 Babaco 已移栽到温室，有 6000 多株苗，30cm 高了。主人告诉我们，这种苗子在澳大利亚零售价是 8 澳元一株，准备批发到日本，每株 5 澳元。

五、经营方式

各工厂的经营方式不尽一致，大致有下列四类：一是只生产试管苗，产品批发给其他苗圃，不经营零售。规模最大的 Horticultural 工厂就是这样；二是以生产旅游产品为主；三是以批发移栽小苗为主；四是从试管苗、移栽小苗到大苗，从零售到批发全都经营，全澳设备条件最好的 Burbank 就是这样。

在墨尔本近郊我们还参观了另外两个私人苗圃，一个是珍稀植物苗圃(Yamina Rare Plant Nursery)。苗圃经理告诉我们，他们已收集到包括中国金茶花等植物在内的世界各国珍稀植物 3000 种。苗圃工作人员只有 5 人，除经理本人外，其余是两个儿子，两个每周在这里工作 3 天的女儿。忙时找学生工来帮忙。他们一方面收集珍稀植物，一方面经营苗圃，用苗圃的盈利来开展珍稀植物的收集。另一个私人苗圃专门从事玫瑰的无土栽培，出售玫瑰的切花。苗圃有 $3000m^2$ 的温室，年产切花 70 万支，批发给花店。他们的切花都一束束地包好，每束内还附有切花保鲜剂。保鲜剂的主要成分是蔗糖、微生物抑制剂及抑制乙烯产生的植物激素。

在澳考察的时间不长，走马观花，愿我国试管苗工厂化生产事业能从中得到一些借鉴，更好的发展！

本文原载：植物杂志. 1991. 18(4): 45-47

新西兰猕猴桃见闻

——科研、生产及经营管理

钱迎倩　母锡金

(中国科学院植物研究所)

1990 年 2 月，在参加了“第二届世界猕猴桃会议”之后，我们几位中国同行由新西兰科工部(DSIR)的 Alan Seal 博士接待，对该国作了几天短暂的访问。参观了新西兰猕猴桃的科研机构、少数私人果园、冷库、加工工厂，访问了猕猴桃市场管理机构(marketing board)。下面主要从三个方面作介绍。

一、科研工作

处于 Te Puke 的科工部下属的研究果园，可大致概括目前新西兰猕猴桃科研的一般情况。该单位主要进行两个方面的工作：一是广泛收集世界各国的原始材料，建立原始材料圃；另一方面是培育新品种。中国是猕猴桃的主要原产地、全世界近 60 个种(包括变种)中，中国占 57 种。在这里的原始材料圃中及彩色照片资料上，能看到绝大多数中国猕猴桃种都已引入新西兰。同时，经多年的选择他们也得到了植株显得瘦弱的自然单倍体植株。以上这些，都为新西兰猕猴桃新品种的培育创造了必要的前提。目前，他们育种的方向主要集中在下列几个方面。

1. 早熟

新西兰的猕猴桃是1904年由中国宜昌引入的，以后在美味猕猴桃(*Actinidia deliciosa*)中选育出优良品种海沃德，垄断了全世界猕猴桃市场。近年来，新西兰猕猴桃面临其他一些国家，特别是意大利和智利的挑战。不少国家引入海沃德品种后，种植面积迅速扩大，产量急剧上升。主人告诉我们，由于季节的差异，意大利对他们还不形成最大的压力，最大的挑战来自智利。因此他们用海沃德做母本，用早熟的种做父本，已得到比海沃德早熟一个月的材料，但由于果形还不理想，暂时还不能成为商品。

2. 红肉

红肉猕猴桃的原始材料他们已得到。据介绍，红色素由于是水溶性的而不稳定，并在不同生态环境下，红色不一定成为表型。在这个研究果园，我们看到了一本日本“株式会社山阳农园”出版的果树苗木目录上登载着下列产品：无毛猕猴桃，平均果重为170克，价格为1株3500日元；赤肉，平均果重70克，1株5500日元；黄肉，平均果重100克，1株4000日元。说明红肉猕猴桃在日本已作为商品出售。

3. 雌雄同株、雌雄同花植株

猕猴桃是雌雄异株的植物，能选择到雌雄同株的，甚至雌雄同花的植株将给生产上带来极大的方便。M_{121}就是他们从美味猕猴桃中选得的一个具两性花的品系，现已结果，但果较小、耐储藏期仅2~3个月，离商品化还有一段距离。

4. 大果、耐贮

他们用雄株中华猕猴桃与雌株美味猕猴桃杂交，已得到大果、耐贮的品系，但离商品化还有距离。

5. 果柄分叉

一般海沃德一个果柄一个果实。为了增加果实数量，他们选择到育二叉，甚至三叉的品系，并都已在每个叉上挂果。由于果形还不够好，果也不够大，还不能形成商品。

6. 新水果的开发

软枣猕猴桃(*A. arguta*)是一个果实皮薄、肉细而甜的种，但果很小，仅如枣大。他们有进一步培育作为一种新兴水果的打算。

此外，围绕着育种的目的，科工部与奥克兰大学都在从事杂交后杂种胚培养、胚乳培养及基因工程的研究。有的工作是与我国科学家合作进行的。

二、生产管理

新西兰农业、渔业部下属的Morgans-MAF Tech是果园管理中心。这个中心有两个任务；一是总结猕猴桃生产及管理经验，说明各方面的管理对增加猕猴桃果数量及大小的密切关系，同时它又是一个推广站，告诉猕猴桃种植者如何才能增加猕猴桃果的数量及大小。从下表(新西兰猕猴桃生产情况表)显示的资料说明：近十年来，由于重视生产管理，新西兰猕猴桃的生产直线上升。

新西兰猕猴桃生产情况表(1983~1989)

产量 \ 年份	1983	1984	1985	1986	1987	1988	1989
树冠/公顷	3.43	3.43	3.66	3.66	3.66	3.66	3.66
藤蔓数/公顷	355	355	358	358	358	404	404
盘数/公顷	1014	3130	5255	5769	5981	6224	5570
盘数/藤蔓	2.9	8.8	14.7	16.1	14.9	15.4	13.8

注：新西兰猕猴桃产量以盘计量，每盘相当于 3.6 公斤；1988 年 6224 盘，相当于 21 吨。

猕猴桃的生产经营管理最后的目的是为了得到利润。下面的示意图告诉我们，在新西兰猕猴桃的生长受哪些环节的制约，而最后要得到利润又受那些条件制约：

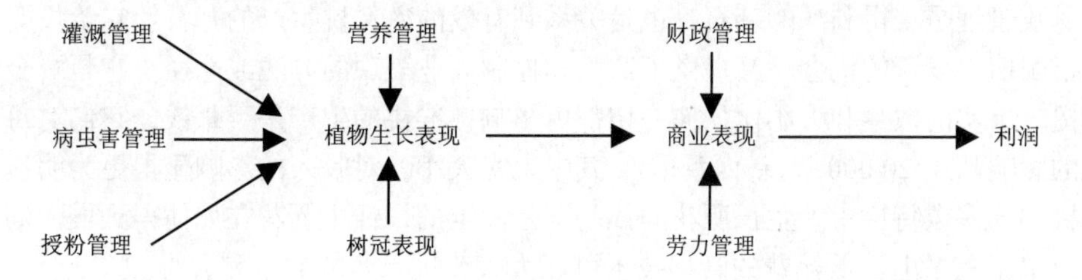

1. 灌溉管理要点

要得到最大的果实的大小和数量，对藤蔓有足够的水分供应是主要的。缺水会立即停止果实的长大，这样的损失是不能恢复的，猕猴桃市场管理机构明确表示，小果实是不要的。有效的灌溉管理必须考虑到保证不由于不合适的灌溉而使果实大小受到影响。在新西兰，12 月中旬至翌年 1 月中旬，每天果实应增重 1.2g，在这段期间内，由于缺水造成果实减小而造成每公顷每天减少新西兰币 800 元的收入。由于缺水，果实平均重量只有 91.5g，而如不受水的胁迫平均果重可达 104.5g。

2. 树冠管理要点

树冠的生长对果实的数量和大小有直接的深刻影响。树冠管理的关键是藤蔓的修剪和果实稀疏度的决定，从而导致藤蔓生长在理想的空间中。树冠管理是猕猴桃生产管理中的关键环节，并且是一个连续的过程，而掌握住时间又极为重要。修剪决定挂果的次级藤蔓和芽的生长。树冠管理的失误可使产量减半，并会影响到后三年结果量的减少。

3. 营养管理要点

有效的营养管理,对为获得最大的果量及果的大小所建立的藤蔓结构是至关重要的。营养管理的焦点是使根和叶生长茂盛，因叶、根是果实生长所需能源的源泉。关系着果实的 60%~80%的关键营养(如氮和钾)在叶中，在着果前，使叶片生长良好，肥料的用量及施用时间很重要，例如叶子出现可见的营养缺失症状时，藤蔓在这个季节至少已经丧失掉了 20%的生产能力。不合适的营养管理会影响到根的发育，并可影响到藤蔓的挂果达 3 年以上。

4. 授粉管理要点

授粉管理的目的是保证结果数量和果实大小不受不合适杂交授粉的影响。为了得到种子，雌花需要雄花粉的杂交授粉，而要得到一个大型的猕猴桃果实，需要有1000~1400粒种子。授粉的时间局限在短短的1~3个星期内，授粉的失误可减少50%以上的产量。

5. 财政管理要点

财政管理是获得利润的基石，也是关系到有效的猕猴桃生产的基石。它给投资者确认及指明值得投资的机会。又提供了监测和控制商业表现的方法或途径。它是资金保证的前提。果实的数量和大小比任何一切都更影响猕猴桃的生产是否赚钱，它们对每公顷收入的影响超过20 000元(新西兰币)。其中果实大小，对收入的影响显得更为明显。在猕猴桃的大多数特性中，生长所花的钱基本是固定的，钱主要花在如何得到最大的果子数量及单果重量上。低耗费的管理技术可以大大改进果实的数量和大小。

三、经营管理

新西兰猕猴桃事业之所以能得到很好的发展，除了紧紧抓住科研与生产两个重要环节外，在流通方面又有一个很好的运行机制。流通机制是受市场管理机构控制的。管理机构并非一政府组织，它受政府法律的制约，并要向政府注册，得到政府承认。这一机构的组成者是由种植者选举出来的，如管理得不好，有可能被选掉。市场管理机构沟通了猕猴桃的科研机构、种植者、包装及储藏公司及内销、外销各个环节之间的关系。甚至每年猕猴桃的价格也由该机构根据各方面的因素来作出决定。每个种植者根据其产品是否合格以及其他条件要该机构的承认后，才能得到由该机构颁发的一个编号。种植者收获后把合格产品送到包装及冷藏公司。这两者间无直接的经济关系。

从经济上看，种植者的所得占总销售额的比例不大。市场管理机构估计，1991年猕猴桃出售价为每盘新币9.1元，其中一半即4.55元为市场管理机构所得，在另一半中包装费占2.30元，采收费0.25元，种植者所得仅2元。种植者的责任一直要负到销售出去为止，此时才能拿到钱。在储藏期间还会发生质量问题。例如，这次会议上一个报告中提到，1990年新西兰猕猴桃产后损失达7.5%，其中果实软化占6%，储藏期间出现的病虫害占1%，其他如果皮颜色变化等占0.5%。这些损失还得由种植者来负责，说明果实的质量还有问题。市场管理机构得到的收入，除经营所需一切费用外，还支持科研。如科工部猕猴桃研究经费中的30%是由该机构资助的，其他70%由政府拨款。这种运转机制的建立，使新西兰猕猴桃事业顺利地发展。

我们也参观了号称国际上最大的猕猴桃包装及冷库公司。洗涤、包装车间的自动化程度相当高，运转由计算机控制，一分钟可装20盘。装盘、打捆成大包，先经过5℃条件下速冷，然后进冷库。冷库条件除低温外就仅充二氧化碳。该公司内有专门实验室，从事果实质量的监测及为商品目的的采后生理的研究。

四、一点体会

目前在我国，猕猴桃作为一种重要的水果已逐渐为人们所接受，并被誉为“水果之王”、“维 C 之冠”。在科研单位、农业系统及大专院校已有一支科研队伍。他们在资源调查、品种培育、杂交育种、组织培养、产后生理、贮藏等方面，都已做了大量的工作，取得了不少科研成果。近几年来，国内建立了 10 个以上的猕猴桃商品化生产基地。在猕猴桃的加工，例如猕猴桃酱、酒等试制产品上也已起步。总之，近 10 年来我国的猕猴桃事业的发展还是快的。但作为猕猴桃的原产地和种质资源量在世界上独占鳌头的中国，在猕猴桃事业的发展上，还远远落后于世界上的先进国家。我国的生产基地平均单产很低，而我们在新西兰参观过的一座私人果园，平均产量每公顷 21 吨。目前国内的产量还只能满足涉外宾馆的一部分需要量，作为一种水果还鲜为一般民众所知，市场上只是偶而见到。科研工作在个别课题或个别技术上是在国际上有地位的，但总体上看，显得零散，各自为政。规模生产管理方面的研究可能才起步或尚未起步。科研、生产及销售等各个环节也未能衔接。

上面介绍的新西兰猕猴桃事业方面的运转体制未必十全十美，由于国情不同也不可能照搬到中国来，为迅速发展我国的猕猴桃事业，认真分析研究人家的运转体制，吸取可借鉴的方面，结合国情为我所用，是最关键的问题。

本文原载：植物杂志. 1991. 18(4): 47-48

第二届国际猕猴桃会议

钱迎倩[1] 母锡金[2]

(1 中国科学院生物科学与技术局；2 中国科学院植物研究所)

第二届国际猕猴桃会议，于 1991 年 2 月 18~21 日在新西兰北帕默斯顿的梅西大学举行。来自 16 个国家的近 300 位代表参加了这届会议，其中既有科研工作者，也有猕猴桃的种植及管理工作者。代表人数最多的是东道主新西兰，有 200 余人与会。猕猴桃生产国中的后起之秀意大利，派出了由 33 人组成的代表团。法国有 11 位代表。其他国家的代表人数都在 10 位以下。我国有 8 位(其中 2 位来自台湾)代表参加。

大会开幕式后，由本届会议的主要报告人：美国珀杜大学园艺系教授杰尼克(Jules Janick)和新西兰农业、渔业部的塞尔(Pet Sale)，分别作了题为“从古老的基因来的新作物”和“1970~1990 果园管理实践的发展”的报告。

杰尼克教授在报告中指出：20 世纪前，农业的发展是朝着作物生产的中心地带远离该种的原产地，典型的例子是大豆的生产在南、北美洲迅速发展起来，而它的原产地是中国。在 20 世纪，园艺上的辉煌成就表现在诸如猕猴桃、鳄梨等水果上，它们是从单一的基因型创造出来的新的作物。育种学家的成就还包括通过种间杂交合成了如小黑麦等新的作物种。近年来，科学家的兴趣已集中在通过常规技术与添加有价值的基因的新技术相结合，以改造老的作物，从而得到新的作物。其中，得到高质量蛋白的玉米就是一个例子。杰尼克提出：21 世纪我们要找到合适的策略来增加遗传多样性以及保持农业生产量的持续发展，以适应地球上人口的不断增长。

塞尔的报告，介绍了猕猴桃作为新兴的商品水果，在 1970 年时还处于起始阶段，而在最近 20 年来，人们对这种植物生长习性的了解，以及如何能达到商品化方面取得了迅速的发展。目前，对猕猴桃成熟度的指标、叶片分析的营养标准、如何打破休眠、修剪的芽数、人工授粉以及催熟等，都得到充分研究，其成果都已可为种植者所接受并采用。新品种、改良品种的培育以及虫害综合防治等方面的研究，也已接近成熟。总之，虽然还存在一些问题有待解决，但猕猴桃的栽培已取得重大进展。

中国科学工作者向会议提交了 18 篇论文摘要。中国科学院研究员钱迎倩，代表他本人和中国农业部优质农产品开发中心俞东平，在全体大会上作了“中国猕猴桃研究的进展”报告。此外，中科院植物研究所母锡金、蔡达荣、安和祥等的“猕猴桃属种间杂交的胚胎学和胚培养”，中科院武汉植物研究所柯善强和黄仁煌的“猕猴桃种间杂交的遗传特性研究”都在分会场上作了报告。江苏邗江县红桥猕猴桃服务中心杨声谋展示了“中华猕猴桃的乔化栽培”墙报。浙江农科院园艺所谢敏的“猕猴桃的选育”因故未能作成报告。

提交会议作报告及墙报展示的论文共159篇。其中78篇分别在大会及分会场上作报告，81篇为墙报。从内容上看涉及的专题如下表：

专题	报告	墙报
猕猴桃的遗传多样性	6	3
猕猴桃育种	11	4
全世界猕猴桃的生产	7	6
猕猴桃繁殖	5	5
昆虫学	5	—
环境和猕猴桃藤蔓行为	5	3
病理学	5	6
环境和猕猴桃果的生长	5	1
授粉和开花生物学	5	10
根和水的关系	5	5
采后生理	5	3
碳和矿质营养	5	4
管理和贮藏	4	—
植物生长调节剂和藤蔓生产力	5	3
贮藏病害	5	3
猕猴桃的加工	5	2
藤蔓管理，果的生长和质量	10	12
统计方法/取样过程	—	2

以上各专题的内容都非常丰富，这里仅介绍主要猕猴桃生产国生产情况和植物生长调节剂在生产上的使用两个方面的内容。

根据会议上发表的报告、墙报及与有关国家代表交谈所得的信息，近10年来，意大利、法国、西班牙、葡萄牙以及智利、希腊等国猕猴桃生产都得到了迅速发展。其中尤以意大利和智利发展最快。而原产地中国的猕猴桃事业，虽有所发展，但在生产面积、总产量与单位面积平均产量上，都无法与先进国家相比(见下表)。

世界有关国家猕猴桃生产情况表

国家	年	种植面积(公顷)	总产量(吨)	平均产量(吨/公顷)	出口量
新西兰	1990	18000	250000	13.80	—
意大利	1990	20000	300000	15.00	—
智利	1978	9	—	—	—
	1982	—	35	—	—
	1983	470	100	0.47	600盒
	1989	10000	25700	2.57	—
	1990	—	—	—	7200万盒
法国	1985	2100	13700	6.50	—
	1990	4000	60000	15.00	15000吨
希腊	1984	618	—	—	—
	1990	3960	—	—	—
中国	1990	4000	5000	1.25	
加拿大	1990	50	—	—	

这次会议有多篇报告涉及生长调节物质 N-(2-chloro-4-pyridyl)-N-phenylurea(CPPU)在猕猴桃生产上应用的问题。CPPU 是一种合成的细胞分裂素类的激素。它可提高果实中碳的含量，并对细胞分裂及细胞增大都有作用，从而使果实增大。把这种激素配成溶液喷在幼果上，可使猕猴桃增产，到收获时果实中没有发现残留物。不同的报告中有如下不同的结果：可使果实增大 20%；在新西兰早夏季使用，使每个果实增重 20~70g；开花过后三个星期用 10ppm 溶液喷施，可使果实增大 33%；用 10ppm 溶液喷 2 次，可使每个果增重 50g；盛花期后 14 天用 20ppm 溶液喷最好。看来，在生长发育时期，何时喷，喷的次数及使用浓度，都应通过实验加以确定。

另一种提高猕猴桃产量的生长调节物质是 hydrogen cyanemide(HiCane)。这是一种打破冬芽休眠的化学物质。按新西兰农业、渔业部果树管理中心介绍，较理想的猕猴桃结果量是每平方米结 40 个果，这就要求每平方米有花 55~68 朵，相当于每个冬芽有 1.6 朵花。使用 HiCane 后，可使每个冬芽有 1.5~2.0 朵花；而不使用该物质，则平均只有 0.7 朵花。HiCane 的使用量为每升 3g。

本文原载：广西科学院学报. 1996. 12(3、4): 1-7

印度、泰国和越南生物多样性保护的管理

钱迎倩[1]　季维智[2]

(1 中国科学院植物研究所；2 中国科学院昆明动物研究所)

摘　要　管理水平的高低直接关系到生物多样性保护的效果。生物多样性保护的管理涉及很多方面，在生物多样性保护重要场所——自然保护区的评价标准，保护区内的居民问题、偷猎、偷伐问题以及调动包括领导与群众在内的保护积极性方面就 3 国的情况作一介绍。管理的另外两个重要方面，加强科研及公众教育问题也进行了讨论。

关键词　生物多样性保护的管理；印度；泰国；越南

1　生物多样性保护的管理

生物多样性保护的重要场所是自然保护区，因此首先要加强对自然保护区的管理。在这方面现从对自然保护区的评价标准、强化保护、保护区内居民偷猎偷伐及调动各方面积极性等几个方面予以讨论。

1.1　对自然保护区的评价标准

一个保护区的管理是否有成效，特别是生物多样性能否真正起到就地保护的作用，在管理上需要有一个评价的标准。印度野生动物研究所(WII)Mathur 博士提到了下列几个方面：①动物数量增长的情况；②管理水平、科研工作、设备以及规章制度制定；③培训；④与当地群众的关系；⑤有无展厅进行公众教育。

作为老虎保护区和大象保护区把动物数量增长放在第一位是正确的。自然保护区建设的目的首先是保护好物种，尤其如老虎这样的关键种，只有这些关键种在持续地增长才是管理有成效的最过硬的指标。其他的一切都是为了这个目标服务的。此外，自然保护区管理的好坏与是否有一大批训练有素的管理人员分不开的，因此重视管理人员的培训工作是自然保护区管理的一个重要方面。

1.2　强化对生物多样性的保护

这次访问的 3 个国家中，印度和泰国对生物多样性保护重视的情况给我们留下了非常深刻的印象。在印度 Sariska 老虎保护区，乘坐汽车沿途能见到如此之多的不同种类的野生动物是我们意料之外的；泰国皇家林业司副司长非常骄傲地告诉我们。“泰国目前还

保留有一大批如 Kaeng Krachan 国家公园所拥有的原始森林，这下仅是我们泰国的骄傲，也是对全世界的一个贡献”。这两个国家对自然资源的保护之所以有如此好的成果，可能归纳到以下几个方面的原因。

(1) 政府对生物多样性保护的重视　印度从英迪拉·甘地及其子拉吉夫·甘地历任总理以来，历届政府对野生生物的保护都十分重视。1984 年印度野生生物研究所新址奠基时，拉吉夫·甘地总理亲自到场并按印度传统点燃灯火，说明印度政府对野生生物保护的重视及对野生动物保护研究的重视与 1984 年我国邓小平同志为北京正负电子对撞机工程奠基处于同等重视的位置。

由于政府的重视，印度一贯被人加以“爱鸟之邦”、“鸟类的天堂”的桂冠，笔者之一在 1991 年曾参观过印度马德拉斯近郊的鳄鱼基因银行、即鳄鱼基因库，这基因库是由印度政府与美国 Smithsonian 研究院等单位联合资助、保存有世界性鳄鱼物种的一个单位。此外，印度是佛教发源地，不杀生已成为众人的信条可能也是重要原因之一。据介绍印度有 70%是素食者，这对野生动物的保护是十分有益的。此外，在印度教中有 2000 多种“神”，多以动物为其崇拜偶像，客观上也起到了保护动物的目的。而印度野生动物丧失的主要原因是经济发展，森林遭到大量砍伐而造成的栖息地丧失[1]。

(2) 有专门的经费资助　印度 Sariska 老虎保护区的职工工资金全部由地方政府负担，平时做野生动物监测的资金也因有国家的“老虎项目”(Project Tiger)而得到保证。保护区远离城市，职工除孩子上学还存在问题外，生活有保障无后顾之忧。泰国中央政府在自然保护区方面每年的拨款为 8 亿~10 亿泰国铢，相当于约 3 亿人民币。如 Kaeng Krachan 国家公园每年能得到的运转费约人民币 400 万，此外，该国家公园还有旅游者的食宿收入，基金会及非政府组织的捐款以及罚款等等方面的收入。又如 Khao Kheow 开放型动物园每年除有相当于 300 万人民币门票收入之外，还能从政府得到相当于人民币 1700 万元作为维持费。

(3) 自然保护区管理人员的培训　印度野生生物研究所是属于印度环境及森林部下属的全国唯一专门从事野生生物保护的研究所。这研究所有两个主要任务，除从事研究工作外，另一个任务是为全国自然保护区的管理和野生生物研究培训生物学家和管理干部。经费的 40%用于科研，40%用于培训，20%用于如工资及其他维持费。因此，该研究所为培训人员配备有专门的设施及食宿条件，从野生动物生物学、野生动物健康、种群和栖息地管理、自然保护区规划和管理以及促进保护意识等等方面进行系统的授课和野外实习的培训。对国家公园级的管理干部进行 9 个月授毕业文凭的野生生物管理训练，这种班同时强调理论和实践的训练。另一种班的培训对象是森林管理官员，这班是 3 个月的野生生物管理培训，结业后也发给证书，对这样的干部强调的是实践的培训。此外，由于印度是一个大国，自然保护区数量很大，研究所同时也不断地举办一些 1~4 星期的短训班或研讨班。这种班可以侧重在某一个专题或技术方面，例如野生生物的普查，栖息地评估等等。这种培训的对象是针对资深的森林管理官员、动物园管理人员、行政官员以及非政府组织人士等等。这个研究所对各类从事生物多样性保护，特别是自然保护区各级管理人员的培训，对印度野生动物的有效保护以及自然保护区的有效的管理起到积极的作用。该研究所的培训也对国际开放，包括中国、越南、尼泊尔、老挝、马来西亚、柬埔寨等的亚洲国家不少科研或管理人员都在该研究所接受过培训，这种国际性的培训，往往可得到国际组织，如世界银行，UNDP 等的赞助。

1.3 保护区内居民问题

处理好自然保护区内居民问题，往往是一个保护区能否有效保护的重要因素之一。这次访问过程中我们有意识地作了一些了解，几个国家的保护区内一般都有居民，各自有他们处理的办法，有的可以借鉴。

泰国 Kaeng Krachan 国家公园内还居住着近 1000 名当地居民。管理部门也希望他们能搬迁出去，但搬迁和安插并非容易，目前处理的办法是请居民中的一部分作为国家公园的职工，以解决他们的生活问题。

在越南参观的 Cat Ba 国家公园是一个地处热带的由石灰岩构造的小岛。这小岛基本上分为两个部分：一部分相对较平坦的地区是居民区；另一部分近 10 000 公顷是石山，这部分辟为国家公园，里面无居民居住。小岛周围是红树林区，大面积红树林改为养虾塘后，养虾业的发展使居民有很好的收入，而不再破坏国家公园的森林。当然这例子比较特殊，不一定能代表越南普遍的情况。

这 3 个国家中，总的看来印度对这问题比较重视，也已经采取一定的措施。原来保护区的居民也是靠山吃山，近二三年来，政府专门拨出一部门款子以解决烧柴的问题，有条件的地方则接上天然气或煤气。保护区内也时有发生老虎吃掉当地居民牲畜的问题，据介绍当有这类问题发生时，政府则给予一定的赔款。他们还准备成立非政府组织(NGO)，吸收当地的居民来参加这个组织，共同来决策保护区的管理和发展问题。

Primark 在他所著的“保护生物学导论”[2]的最后一章中也专门谈到自然保护区或国家公园的规划要公开，要让当地居民了解、讨论以及评估。并让当地居民相信他们在保护区的规划中能获得利益，或者说保护区的规划是与他们密切相关的。说明正确处理与当地居民的关系是十分重要的。

1.4 偷猎、偷伐的问题

即使在印度的 Sariska 老虎保护区还难免存在着偷猎、偷伐的问题。为之，保护区有 35 个人专门负责管理缓冲区的偷猎、偷伐事件，并有法律规定，一旦抓住偷猎、偷伐者，要禁闭 6 个月。但总的反映偷猎、偷伐一个比较难管理的问题。在泰国我们参观过的野生动物禁猎区及国家公园都是与缅甸接壤，据介绍虽有边防军或保护区的管理人员，但偷猎、偷伐问题也是不断有所发生。在中越边界的野生动物非法贸易严重存在，因此我们也不便于在越南对这问题作了解。总之，关于偷猎、偷伐问题是一个很复杂的社会问题，在我国这问题更是普遍而严重地存在。不是有了法律就能解决，而是与当地经济发展、公众保护意识的提高、加强教育与法律密切结合，综合起来才能解决的问题。

1.5 保护生物多样性要调动各方面的积极性

生物多样性的就地保护是主要的保护方式，就地保护首先要保护自然，当然，迁地保护也是必不可少的，不管是哪一种保护方式都要有很大的投资。在有关投资方面，访问过的3个国家在体制上也不尽一致，印度，中央政府只是作全国的规划，对设在各邦(省)的国家公园或禁猎区的维持或运转费是由地方政府拨款的，而泰国与越南则一律由中央有关部委拨款。本文已较详细地介绍印度与泰国政府对有关自然保护区拨款的情况，尽管如此，各个单位都还是反映资金紧张。本文也介绍了泰国北览鳄鱼湖动物园及 Sarafi 世界的情况，这两个单位全部都是私营，不仅不拿政府一分钱，每年都有相当丰厚的利润。当然会有人感到商业性、娱乐性的味道过浓，但从客观上至少把物种保存下来，并都能繁殖得很好，从这意义上，也应该说是值得鼓励的。此外，这些商人也捐赠一些资金用于生物多样性保护。例如，泰国北览鳄鱼湖动物园就部分支持了今年 8 月间在曼谷举行的区域性跨国界生物多样性保护会议。

在绝大多数发达国家允许土地私有，因此在个人占有的土地上作生物多样性就地保护或迁地保护已有很长的历史。私人的保护区至少是国有的国家公园或禁猎区外的一个重要的补充。目前我国也已有了一个好的开端，据报上登载建国饭店销售部经理助理常仲明用自己积蓄的32 000元资金租贷下为期 70 年的 $20hm^2$ 土地。这块土地处于在 50 年代时还常有豹、狼和狐狸等野生动物出没的北京昌平县流村乡。小小的 $20hm^2$ 土地成为我国大陆首家私人创办的自然保护区。据报道，自从封闭这片山谷以后的几个月时间，山上各种鸟类开始增多，并能经常听到山鸡的鸣叫声。当然作为生物多样性的保护，面积还过于小，但在我国的国情下，这个创举值得很大的重视。

总之，我们认为生物多样性的保护也应该充分发挥各级政府，集体以及个人三者的积极性，当然政府渠道是第一位的。目前或在相当一段时间内经济再困难各级政府也应比现在有更多的投入。个人的积极性更应得到积极的扶植，没有经费资助的可能，在政策及其他方面尽可能地创造条件，让个人的自然保护区能茁壮成长。而且要加以大力宣传。

2 加强生物多样性保护的科研工作

参观过的 3 个国家，保护区科研工作的开展情况似乎受到国家重视的程度、经费情况等因素所决定，尤其国家重视程度更显得重要。印度对野生生物保护科研工作是出色的，上文已对政府的重视作过介绍。“老虎项目”就是由印度政府、当地邦政府与世界野生生物基金会(World Wildlife Fund)在 1973 年协商建立的。老虎在一个生态系统中作为关键种或旗舰种，保护了老虎可保护住整个生态系统，“老虎项目”的核心指导思想是，在虎存在的生态环境中从大型兽类、树木、草本植物、昆虫甚至微生物等一切生命都是这个生态系统的食物链中的一个环节。一开始印度在“老虎项目”下开辟了 9 个避难所或禁猎区，到 1995 年逐步扩大到 21 个“老虎保护区”。

我们参观了在 Rajasthan 邦 Sariska 老虎保护区，保护区的科研工作做得相当出色。每天都有专门的管理人员负责做老虎的监测工作。众所周知，每个人的手掌上的纹路是不一样的，每只老虎的脚掌纹也都不一样。监测老虎的工作人员在熟悉老虎的行踪后，采用脚印技术(Pugmark technique)，获得虎的掌纹。其方法是用石膏粉与水调和后，倒在一个比虎掌大一点的框内，这框事先放在有虎掌的细沙或细土上，等石膏固化后，取出就有了虎掌的复制品。在石膏未完全固化前，在不具虎掌纹的石膏板的另一面记录上日期、地点及取样人等等必要的数据。傍晚前在老虎经常出没的地点铺上细沙或细土，第二天早上发现虎掌就用上法取得复制品，然后再用铅笔在纸上描绘出虎掌，输入计算机内，用这技术就掌握了在这保护区内老虎的数量动态并可做作行为学的研究。这方法比先进的无线电项圈跟踪技术要经济得多。就用这技术，他们确定了保护区内老虎数量近年内由 11 头递增到 25 头。每天做监测的人员只是受过一定训练的一般工作人员(甚至只有小学文化水平)，可是他们的记录却成为整个印度保护“老虎项目”最重要的原始数据的来源。

这个保护区亦定期做出野生动物统计数据报告，这报告内容包括所用的技术、具体的日期、监测所用的时间(按表上看是从第一天下午 4 时开始到第二天下午 4 时，作 24h 的监测)、温度、湿度、风速、晚上是否有月光等等。所列的表格上对保护区内主要的大型或特大型野生动物，如食肉类(如虎、豹、豺等)、偶蹄目(如野猪等)、灵长目(如长尾叶猴等)以及啮齿目等 19 种野生动物种群的具体数学，还列出有 300 种左右的鸟。有毒、无毒的蛇、蜥蜴及其他小型爬行动物都非常普遍，在报告的最后由有 Sariska 老虎保护区当地官员及野外研究负责人的签名。

我们参观的泰国 Huay Kha Khaeng 野生动物禁猎区专门设立了研究站，这研究站目前已开展的有三个科研项目，例如豹和野牛项目。他们抓了 7 个豹，在颈部套上无线电项圈作遥测它们的活动范围。基本弄清了这 7 头豹的家域(home tange)。这为保护区对大型食肉类合适的保护区域的管理决策提供了很好的基础信息。这个禁猎区的研究站经常接待泰国国内外的科研人员。有专门设施及小的图书馆为外来科研人员作合作研究。

泰国 Khao Kheow 开放型动物园也开展野生动物繁殖方面的研究，亚洲野牛的胚胎移植工作，但并未成功。北览鳄鱼湖动物园在积极地开展与鳄鱼有关的科研，此外不少野生动物的繁育工作也已解决。如该园饲养了 20 多头老虎，繁育已不成问题。

最值得提出来的是这次在印度参观 Sariska 老虎保护区时，见到一位野生动物研究所的不到 30 岁的在职女博士生在这远离研究所近千公里，只身一人在老虎保护区的工作。这位女士在 1994 年首次在这保护区发现了一种俗名为锈斑麝猫(Rusty spotted cat)拉丁名为 *Poiona rubiginosu* 的猫科动物。她以这种动物为对象，用无线电项圈法来研究它的活动范围及其他行为学。研究所为她的工作拨给她为期 3 年的 3 万美元的研究经费，并专门配备一辆吉普车、三个助手，长期在保护区做定位的工作。当地政府和保护区为了鼓励支持她的研究工作，给她配备了对讲机，有紧急事情发生立即可与当地政府取得联系。从印度和泰国的保护区来看，都很支持科研人员进入保护区。尽量在生活和工作上给予方便，并不收取任何费用。他们认为科研工作对保护区的管理是很大的支持。

WII 是印度野生生物研究的主要单位，建立于 1982 年。1984 年新址开始建设，1986

年成为环境与森林部下属的一个自主研究所。该所从建筑到设备都很现代化，在科研、行政、培训、图书馆等各方面都已计算机化。在科研方面计算机用于统计分析、绘图、数据管理、卫星图像分析等，目前国际上普遍应用的新技术所谓 3S(即遥感 RS、地理信息系统 GIS 及地理定位系统 GPS)在这里也已得到应用。WII 还利用 GIS 和野生动物数据库的资料，对印度北部大型水电站建成后的利弊作出客观评估、报告提供给不同意见的双方，最后由国会和政府决策。

研究所由野生生物、野生生物管理和野生生物扩增(Wildlife Extension)3 个部分组成。全所 30 个科学家、40 个研究生及 150 名技术人员和行政人员，每年得到政府 60 万美元的拨款，此外还从国际得到不少研究费用。

研究工作从生态、管理和社会—经济角度，在印度不同的生态和地理区域从事应用研究，在雪豹、灰色大松鼠、海水龟的生态学以及再引入自然的鳄鱼和犀牛的监测等方面已作了系统的研究。对在不同的生态系统中存在的濒危物种、严酷的生境、野生动物健康等等方面也正在开展工作，这单位是中央及邦政府在野生生物保护方面咨询的权威单位。

此外，上文提到的国际环境和森林部下属的 Zoological Survey of India 及 Botanical Survey of India 都已有近百年或上百年的历史。两所分别在不同邦设立了不少分支机构，基础研究和基础资料的积累是大量的，并有大量的出版物。政府给予较充分的拨款。他们认为还有大量分类学方面基础科研要做，并不存在“濒危学科”和后继乏人的问题。

我们在加强生物多样性保护的科研这一段介绍了不少印度和泰国的情况，从介绍的情况可得到下列几点认识：

(1) 政府应真正提高对生物多样性保护的认识。印度在经济上不是一个强国，可是对生物多样性保护在科研方面给予足够的重视，给尽可能多的经费，配备尽可能先进的设备，这点是值得借鉴的；

(2) 抓准项目，并动员各方面力量协同攻关，得到好的效果。如“老虎项目”不仅把整个生态系统或某些禁猎区保护起来，同时促进了老虎保护的科研工作；使自然保护区或禁猎区不仅成为就地保护的主要场所，也是科研的重要基地。印度的“老虎项目”应该说是政府抓生物多样性保护的有效措施。发挥了行政官员，有关研究所，科研人员以及自然保护区或禁猎区中的官员及一般工作人员等各方面的积极性，使印度的老虎数量不断地增长；

(3) 研究所通过培训与抓生物多样性保护有关的行政官员、自然保护区的管理官员和一般工作人员有了很好的沟通，促进了自然保护区的建设，提高了管理人员的水平；

(4) 泰国的经验是生物多样性保护研究已调动起国家机构和私人企业的两方面的积极性，促进了生物多样性的保护和持续利用。

能做到以上这几点，对生物多样性的保护必然真正起到促进的作用。

3 加强公众教育

访问过的 3 个国家的有关单位，对生物多样性保护的公众教育问题都比较重视，其中尤其是泰国给予我们更深的印象，政府在这方面也给予必要的投资。参观过的开放型动物园、禁猎区和国家公园，在介绍时都提到他们重要的任务之一是公众教育。每个单位都有其宣传品并有展览厅、报告厅，有很好的音像设备，中小学校经常组织学生来这里参观、学习，本文已提到过的泰国著名保护自然的科学家 Seub Nakasathein，此人热爱自然，做了大量保护自然的工作，长期定居在 Huay kha khaeng 禁猎区内，献身于保护自然，保护生物多样性的工作。他到全国各地讲演，宣传自然保护的重要性，他也反对政府建水坝。可惜的是他在 1989 年早年英逝，年仅 37 岁。原因是他认为他做了大量保护自然的工作，但不为人们所理解而自杀身亡。他的过世对泰国是一个震动，泰国有关方面设立了以他的名字命名的基金会,长期保留了他在禁猎区内的住处及遗物供大家参观。为他立了铜像及纪念馆，并用这纪念馆经常进行保护自然、保护生物多样性的宣传教育，在我们访问的当晚与其他客人在一起受了一次保护自然及生物多样性的教育。在开放型动物园及 Kaeng krachan 国家公园都配备有先进音像设备，已接近发达国家的水平。以上这些除了反映“四小虎”经济实力的一间外，更重要的是政府对这方面的重视。

在我们所见的印度和越南的一些单位，相比之下差一点，在印度结合旅游，各种印刷精制的宣传品还是很多的。目前越南经济虽不发达，但在 Cat ba 保护区也有很好的一个宣传厅，有拍得较好的录像。

对自然，对环境，对生物多样性的保护在我国的宣传教育任务是非常重的，或者说是应紧迫解决的。我们与过去相比已有了长足的进步，但我国经济不发达的地区还很多，特别是生物多样性尤为丰富的地区往往由于交通不发达而更贫穷，因此保护好生物多样性除采取其他各种措施外，加强公众教育是不能忽视的。在这里应该特别提到中国科学院昆明动物所保护生物学中心在美国麦克阿瑟基金会的资助下，在这方面已开展了不少的工作。他们主要做了三方面的工作。第一是在云南高黎贡山热带森林地区进行了为期 3 年的包括物种、森林现状以及对自然保护的社会经济制约等方面的较全面的调查和考察，同时进行公众保护意识教育，他们在傈僳村进行教育集会，与当地群众讨论他们调查与考察的结果，展示教育录像，传播森林和野生动物保护重要性的一般知识。并向群众宣传限制狩猎活动的重要性。告诉群众要以选择性的狩猎方式以取代非选择性的狩猎，并建议仅猎杀成年雄性而保护雌性和幼体，取得一定的效果。第二是与美国国际野生动物保护协会(WCS)合作，对西南地区(云南、贵州、广西)林业和环保的管理部门和保护区工作人员进行了培养。培训内容包括基本的野外工作方法，如地形图识别，仪器(指南针，测高仪等)的使用，物种识别，数量调查，保护宣传以及行政管理等，取得了良好的效果，为野生动物长期动态监测奠定了基础。第三是与云南省教育委员会及美国国际野生动物保护协会合作，在 1994 年使用由国际野生动物保护协会编写的两套教材，在云南省部分中小学进行了野生动物保护教育实验项目，他们已对昆明市及西双版纳自治州的中学生物教师和小学教师分别进行了培训。国际野生动物保护学会的教育顾问专程来担任教学工作，教材是利用该协会编写的“蟒蛇帕勃罗看动物”和“动物生命的多样性”。培训结束后，教师们使用上述教材在各自学校的一个班进行实验，取得很好的效果。这一项目对于发挥教育在推动野生动物保护工作中的作用及利用野生动物来教授基础科学知识方面都有积极的意义，学生们也学到了动物、动物生存环境和动物保护的基本知识，增进对野生动物的认识、了解和兴趣，使他们更加热爱自然，自觉的关心、爱护野生动物。总之，昆明动物研究所已为我国在公众教育方面开创了一个好的先例。

这次 3 国之行，了解不同类型发展中国家在生物多样性保护和持续利用方面的各种情况。有不少方面是可以值得我们借鉴或学习的。如能做好本文第二部分几点，对一个国家的生物多样性保护和持续利用的工作可能会有很好的促进。

参考文献

[1] Southwick C H, Sidchigi M F, Population status of non-buman primates in Asia, with emphasis on *Rhesus macaques* in India, Am J primatol, 1994,34: 51~60

[2] Primack R B, Essentials of Conservation Biology, 1993, 503~507

本文原载：广西科学院学报. 1996. 12(3、4): 8-15

印度、泰国和越南生物多样性概况

季维智[1] 钱迎倩[2]

(1 中国科学院昆明动物研究所；2 中国科学院植物研究所)

摘 要 首先涉及印度、泰国和越南3国陆生生物多样性主要栖息地——森林及自然保护区的概况，然后对3国的物种多样性以及生物多样性的就地保护，迁地保护及持续利用的情况作了介绍，并与我国的情况作些比较。

关键词 生物多样性；印度；泰国；越南

印度、泰国、越南和中国虽然都是发展中国家，但是还有很大的差别。印度的特点是地大，国土面积3 280 000km^2，人口为8亿，居世界的第二位，经济相对不发达；泰国国土仅约中国的 1/19(513 115km^2)可是近年来经济发展迅速，有亚洲四小虎之称；越南是这次我们访问国土面积最小的国家(330 363km^2)，由于连年战争，经济处于百废待兴的阶段，与我国有相似之处，是正处于改革开放的阶段。因此对这3个不同类型国家，在围绕生物多样性保护方面进行考察，寻求进一步合作的可能性，是我们这次考察的目的。本文将对这3个国家有关情况作一介绍，并与我国的情况作些比较。

1 概况

1.1 森林覆盖率情况

森林是陆地生物多样性的主要栖息地，因此介绍生物多样性就从其栖息地——森林开始。近几十年来，主要是由于人口迅速增长及工业快速发展等各方面的原因，世界性的森林面积递减速度大大增加。表1是1992年世界银行对包括中国在内四个国家森林面积的数字[1]。从表上可看到我国的森林覆盖率是四国中最低、递减率最高的国家。据Pong Leng-EE[2]报道。泰国在1940~1950年由于人口急剧增长，导致大量的天然林被砍伐以用作木材以及土地被改造成农田及其他用途。森林覆盖率由1961年的53%减少到1988年的30%，森林面积平均每年丧失5120km^2。但近年来的递降率已降低到每年减少2354km^2。印度野生生物研究所的资料说明印度的森林覆盖率在19%以下，这数字与世界银行公布的17%相近，最近50年来丧失的森林面积在400万hm^{2}以上。

表 1 印度、泰国、越南、中国 4 国森林覆盖率情况

国家	森林面积($\times10^3km^2$)	森林占土地面积的百分比	每年递减率(%)
印度	572.3	17	0.3~4.1
泰国	156.8	31	2.4~2.5
越南	101.1	31	0.6~2.0
中国	1150.6	12	3.9

注：资料来自 Braatz, s. (1992)

越南专家组[3]的材料说明越南在 1943 年时森林面积有 1400 万 hm^2，占其国土面积的 44%。而到 50 年后的 1992 年，根据越南林业部发布的最新资料其覆盖率已减少到 888.58 万 hm^2，仅占其国土的 26.9%，其中 83.92 万 hm^2 是人工林。在越美战争年代，美国释放了 720 亿立升除草剂，对越南森林毁灭很大[4]，Braatz 提到破坏面积达 200 万 hm^2[1]，森林递减的其他原因是由于人口增长，使大量森林变为农田以及过量的采伐木材造成的。至今这种过度采伐或森林火灾造成森林递减的趋势还在继续增加。每年大概还在以 10 万~20 万 hm^2 的面积减少。

1.2 自然保护区建设情况

随着世界人口不断增长、工业及经济的发展，对自然环境及生物多样性的破坏以致灭绝越来越严重。人们逐渐认识到建立自然保护区或国家公园是保护生态环境以拯救生物多样性免于灭绝并能繁衍后代的主要手段和途径。根据昆明动物研究所保护生物学中心所收集的至 1995 年初的资料，我国(包括台湾和香港)自然保护区已达 678 352km^2 占国土面积的 7%[5](见表 2)。成绩非常明显，在生态环境及生物多样性的保护方面已经发挥了很明显的作用。

表 2 印度、泰国、越南、中国 4 国自然保护区建立概况 1)

国家		国家公园	自然保护区	野生动物禁猎区及非禁猎区	其他	总面积(km^2)及占国土总面积比(%)
中国 2)	1995		951		若干	678 352(7.00)
	计划		1000			1000 000(10.41)
印度	1994	76		417	40 3)	142 020(4.33)
	计划	147		633		183 670(5.60)
泰国	1994	77		84	1177 4)	72 268(12.80)
	计划	127		100		103 374(18.30)
越南	1994	9	47		31 5)	100 000(3.00)
	计划					200 000(6.00)

1) 资料由季维智等(1995)，朱建国等(1995)及“中国 21 世纪议程”(1994)[7]综合而成；2)未包括台湾省的自然保护区 57 个，总面积近 5000km^2，香港地区的自然保护区 1 个，面积为 3.2km^2；3)湿地保护区 16 个，红树林保护区 15 个，珊瑚礁保护区 4 个，世界遗迹地 5 个；4)指泰国建立的森林保留地(forest reserves)，面积为 220 393.52km^2，未包括在总面积内；5)指越南建立的文化和环境森林保护区。

按 Rishi[8]报道，印度对自然的保护可追溯到有史时期的早期，在他们的国土上专门划出一定的地区用以保护有生命的自然资源。根据季节、性别和物种的生活史来决定禁止采伐或狩猎野生动、植物的季节和时期。此外在方法和数量上也有规定，有的动、植物物种是完全保护的，这种文化传统已成为印度民族精神的一种特征。到中世纪，大多数的统治者设置了专门作狩猎用的保护区。虽然这种狩猎保护区完整的程度不一样，但成为印度独立后发展国家公园或禁猎区这类自然保护区网络的基础。因此，印度对野生动物的就地保护不管是有意识，无意识地已有了一个很长的历史。1952 年设置了印度野生动物委员会，1972 年又颁布了野生动物保护条例。自然保护区不断地发展，至今印度已有 76 个国家公园，4l7 个禁猎区。

泰国在自然保护区方面分为 5 个范围，即国家公园和森林公园、野生动物禁猎区和非狩猎区、森林保护区(forest reserve)、植物园和树木园以及生物圈保护区。泰国在自然保护区建立，尤其对天然森林的保护着重考虑的不仅是对生物多样性的保护，还强调对水源林的保护。这个国家在生物多样性保护和自然保护区方面较重要的法令可追溯到 1941 年的森林法，以及 1947 年的渔业法，60 年代后有 1961 年国家公园法以及 1964 年受国家保护的森林法以及 1992 年的野生动物禁猎和保护法。在渔业法中已涉及儒艮和龟等珍稀物种的保护问题。1961 年国家公园法公布后，1962 年泰国建立了第一个 Khao yai 国家公园，但发展缓慢。到 1972 年的 10 年中才发展到 4 个，占土地面积 358 100hm^2。随后发展迅速，到 1994 年底发展为 77 个，并计划发展到 127 个，面积达 6 488 062hm^2，占国土面积的 12.6%。Salak phra 是泰国在 1965 年建立的第一个野生动物禁猎区，到 1993 年增加到 36 个。此外还有 48 个非禁猎区，并计划发展到 52 个禁猎区，占地 3 360 000hm^2。泰国到 1986 年森林保留地数量达 1172 个，覆盖国土面积达 22 039 352hm^2，如果把这部分面积也算上，现有自然保护区占国土面积可达到 57%。但在皇家森林司司长 Pong leng-EE[4]报道中，作为现有的自然保护区网络仅占国土面积 12.8%，并未把这部分面积及以下有关部分的面积计算在内。此外，还包括 5 个植物园和 42 个树木园以及泰国的北部和东北部还有 3 个生物圈保留地(biosphere reserve)，占地 26 100hm^2。

越南第一个国家公园 Cuc Phuong 是 1962 年建立的，占地 22 250hm^2。目前的自然保护区系统是由 9 个国家公园，47 个自然保护区和 31 个文化和环境保护森林所组成，总面积为 10 000~11 692km^2，占国土面积 3%以上。整个自然保护区是由林业部森林保护司负责，而其管理计划则是由林业部下属的森林编目和计划研究所制定。在制定管理计划过程中，国内外科学家和管理干部都认为目前的保护区面积过小，不足以保护其国家的生物多样性，而准备发展到 20 000km^2，占国土面积的 6%。

1.3 各国物种多样性概况

我国的物种多样性极为丰富是世界生物多样性特丰国家(megadiversity country)之一(表 3)。这是由于第四纪冰川期间，东亚、欧洲和北美由于地理条件的不同而受冰川的影响完全不同。东亚地区不存在北美及欧洲在冰川来临时的障碍，随着冰川的前进，生物向南退却，并且东亚地区冰川的活动又较弱，因此遭灭绝的生物少，从而保留了大批第三纪以前就存在的古老植物。动植物的特有种在这地区都很多，如中国的银杏、银杉、水杉都是中国的特有种。中国植物的特有属超过 200 个，特有种超过一万[10]。在动物方面，熊猫、滇金丝猴等特有种更是驰名世界。

表 3　我国及周边 3 国重要类群物种多样性的种数

	兽类	鸟类	爬行类	两栖类	淡水鱼	软体动物	昆虫	苔藓植物	蕨类植物	裸子植物	被子植物	地衣	藻类	真菌
中国	597	1245	385	279	850		34 000	2200	2600	200	25 000		5000	8000
印度	372	1228	428	204		5000	57 000	2843	1012	64	15 000	1940	12 480	23 000
泰国	295	920	301	105	700~800	1847	6121		560		18 000			3000
越南	224	800	180	80	471		5500				12 000			
世界	4600	9020	6300	4010				17 000		750	250 000		26 900	46 983

注：数据来自文献[6]和文献[9]。

越南的动物和鸟的种及亚种的特有比例也极高，其中有名的有越南金丝猴(*Rhinopithecus avunculus*)、黑叶猴东京亚种(*Trachypilhecus francoisi policephalus*)、爱德华氏鹇(*Lophura edwardsi*)等。越南的物种的多样性似乎还远没有被调查清楚，直到 1992 年在越、老交界处 Vu Quang 地区还发现了两个大型鹿科动物的新种，即 *Pseudooryx hatinhensis* 和 *Megamuntiacus vuquangensis*。

泰国的物种也是比较丰富的国家。也有较多的特有种。在高等植物方面特有种有 1000 种左右，占其植物总数的 8%；动物特有种在 200 种以上，其中包括 7 种哺乳类、10 种蛇、23 种蜥蝎类以及 11 种两栖类动物。表 3 说明泰国在动物区系及分类方面的研究比植物相对地清楚。按介绍，18000 种植物中只有 1/4 是已被研究并作过描述。应该说还有大量的工作要做。

根据印度野生生物研究所资料介绍，印度的物种也是世界 12 个特丰国家之一。印度不仅物种丰富、并且由于历来印度对基础研究及基础资料工作的重视，在本文涉及的 3 国中，印度对动植物物种的调查研究是最清楚的国家。在国家环境和林业部下专门设立动物学与植物学研究机构，称为印度动物调查(Zoological Survey of India)以及印度植物调查(Botanical Survey of India)，历史悠久，总部设在加尔各答，全国设有不少的站。发表大量的专著，例如包括 630 种植物的 3 卷红皮书等。并且相当一部分珍稀、濒危植物已在植物园中进行繁殖。从生态系统角度对印度老虎栖息地的植物学作了研究。在被访问的 3 个国家中是最值得重视的一个国家。

1.4　生物多样性的持续利用

生物多样性是人类赖以生存的基础，因此对生物多样性不可能绝对保护，而必须要利用。包括中国在内的亚洲这些国家，对生物多样性的利用都有悠久的文化，仅以野生动、植物作为药用而言，中国历史最长，利用得最多，野生植物就有 5000 种被用作药用。越南对生物多样性利用的工作也极为重视。在 1993 年出版了名为“越南利用的 1900 种植物”的专著，记录了越南主要用作药物、木材的植物名录、分布及利用情况，前言中说明这本专著将对农业、林业、医药、教学起到很大的作用，成为对生物多样性利用的基础。地处印度科学中心地区 Dehra dun 的印度森林研究和教育委员会所属的森林研究所的博物馆中很大部分的内容是展示印度对生物多样性的利用。

当今的世界，尤其是发展中国家较普遍存在的是对生物多样性掠夺式的、毁灭性的利用问题。因此，为了子孙万代的生存，如何合理利用与持续利用已当然地提到每个国家的面前。对野生动、植物在自然繁殖、自然更新的基础上进行合理利用是持续利用的主要方式。这里不仅涉及民众的保护意识及教育问题，更重要的应该还要针对某些野生动、植物如何能合理地持续利用开展科学研究。

印度在对野生动物持续利用的观点已有很长的历史。当然对发达国家来说，比如美国和加拿大，在某些地方狩猎是允许的，但政府明确规定只能是持有执照者在一定地点，允许对某种动物在某个季节打一定的数量，以达到持续利用的目的。

持续利用的另一个方面是对野生动物的饲养及野生植物的人工栽培，这方面中国做得较好。在野生动物方面，如对扬子鳄、梅花鹿、紫貂等的人工饲养都已有很好的经验及经济收获，在植物方面，由于地奥心血康作为药物销售的成功，薯蓣的人工栽培也已达到相当的规模。泰国北览鳄鱼湖动物园，是由一位泰国华人独资从商业及保护世界不同物种的角度，经营规模最大的鳄鱼养殖场，从刚孵化出来一个月到已有 20 多岁的鳄鱼今年的数量已达到 63000 多条，经濒危物种国际贸易公约(CITES)批准，每年能出口 1 万多条鳄鱼。鳄鱼皮的各种皮革制品国际市场价值极为昂贵。因此走商业的途径，对濒危物种的保护及持续利用应该说也是一个重要的途径。

2 生物多样性的就地保护

2.1 Sariska 老虎保护区(印度)

这保护区过去是帝王狩猎的地区，是由蜿蜒群山和山谷构成，属于荒漠的落叶阔叶林地带。树种相对地比较简单、山上的主要树种为生长在山顶部的印度乳香(*Boswellia serrate*)，在山中部的 *Angeissus pendula*；山谷中的主要树种为紫铆(*Butea monosperma*)及枣属的 *Zizyphus nummularia*、马槟榔属(*Capparis*)、*Balanitis*、扁担杆属(*Crewia*)等灌丛组成。以上树种在 6 月下旬时有一部分已落叶，但在一年四季中总是有绿叶的树种以保证羚羊、鹿等动物整年有食物。这里动物种类相当多，有大型食肉类虎、豹、豺、偶蹄目的野猪、灵长目的长尾叶猴以及啮齿目等几十种，鸟类 300 种以及各种蛇、蜥蜴等两栖、爬虫类动物在不同的季节都很普遍。

在这个保护区中我们看到了很多野生动物。Rajasthan 邦负责森林和野生动物保护的副长官非常熟悉当地野生动物的情况，知道豹出没的途径，傍晚听到猴群不寻常的叫声，就知道豹不久就会从这附近经过。清早能看到数量不少成群或单个的羚羊、野猪、鹿、翩翩起舞的蓝色的孔雀以及成群的长尾叶猴，它们不怕汽车，不怕人，自由戏耍或觅食。此外，还多次见到新鲜老虎的脚印，在这个保护区能如此容易，频繁地见到如此多的野生动物，一是说明保护区的野生动物已经有了相当的数量，另一点也说明人与自然的关系已经比较协调。老虎的数量也明显地增长，近年来由 11 头增加到 25 头，尽管这样，这个老虎保护区还只能排在全印度 21 个老虎保护区的第 6 位。

2.2 Rajaji 国家公园(印度)

这国家公园地处印度野生动物研究所所在地 Dehra Dun 附近，喜马拉雅山的南坡脚与中国接壤的边境距离才 300km。这个保护区是典型的热带雨林，植物种类要远比 Sariska 老虎保护区丰富、复杂得多，雨量也非常丰富，进入保护区要经过宽度很大的大片由大小石块，砂砾组成的河滩地。当时无水，因雨季尚未到，从河滩地上躺着不少大树看，说明洪水泛滥时大树可连根拔起。动物的种类与数量要比 Sariska 多得多，但可能由于保护区面积过大，一路上能见到的野生动物并不如在 Sariska 能见到的那么多。值得提到的是看到一大群兀鹫围着吃一只豺的残骸，虽然不知道这头豺的第一捕食者是哪一种动物，但能看到在一个生态系统中的食物链的关系。

表 4　印度等 3 国部分保护区情况一览

国家	名　称	类　型	建立时间	面积(km^2)	居民情况	经费(政府拨)	工作人员	保护站	保护情况
印度	Sariska 老虎保护区	荒漠生态系统	1978	877	核心区 300km^2 1000 人 缓冲区 4000 人	中等	官员 6 人 共 150 人	24	保护好，近年来老虎数量由 11 头增至 25 头
	Huay Kha Khaeng 野生动物禁猎区	热带雨林	1972	2780	不详	美元 35 万/年	官员 12 人 正式工 50 人 临时工 228 人	17	不受人为因素的破坏
泰国	Kaeng Krachan 国家公园	热带常绿林为主	1981	2915	缓冲区 1000 人	美元 50 万/年	雇员 30 人 临时工 150 人	若干	不受人为因素的破坏
越南	Cat Ba 国家公园	岛屿热带雨林	1985	150	100km^2 无 50km^2 渔民	少量	10 个技术人员及少数管理人员	无	渔民不进保护区

2.3 Huay Kha Khaeng 野生动物禁猎区(泰国)

泰国有好几个大的禁猎区是由分别属于几个省的禁猎区结合到一起。这个禁猎区就是与分属另外两个省的其他两个禁猎区连成一个大的禁猎区，三者加起来的面积达 8943km^2，并与缅甸接壤。为一望无际的葱葱郁郁的林海。禁猎区有一研究中心、一教育中心，有泰国著名保护自然的科学家 Seub Nakasathein 纪念馆。此地已经 UNESCO 承认为世界遗迹。称为 Patrimoine Mondial World Heritage。

这里的森林保持原始状态，可分为湿润常绿林，干旱常绿林，混交落叶林，龙脑香森林及竹林等。野生动物有大象、野牛、老虎等。其中包括哺乳类 67 种、爬虫类 77 种、两栖类 29 种、鸟类 355 种及鱼 57 种，而野生植物除对植被类型做过些工作外，普查基本未做。

2.4 Kaeng Krachan 国家公园(泰国)

是泰国最大的国家公园，泰国与缅甸接壤的边界很长，这个国家公园是与缅甸接壤。这里的森林是泰国重要的水源林，受到政府绝对的保护。国家公园内有两条河流，有瀑布、水库、山的最高峰1207m，与上述 Huay Kha Khaeng 野生动物禁猎区一样，从高处瞭望一片葱葱郁郁的林海。

这个国家公园的生物普查工作有一定的基础。85%面积为常绿雨林，10%是落叶的混交林，在落叶林区经常会发生森林大火。常绿雨林的组成很复杂，大量的藤本植物，附生蕨类和兰花，有不少木本和藤本的果树。由于 Kaeng Krachan 地处亚洲太陆和马来西亚半岛的交界处，多样性很丰富。亚洲大陆植物物种有栎属(*Quercus*)、栗属(*Castanea*)及槭树等。还有马来西亚半岛的棕榈及果树，此外，有价值的树种还有 *Afzelta*、坡垒属(*Hopea*)、羯布罗马属(*Dipterocarpus*)、紫薇属(*Lagerstroemia*)、紫檀属(*Pterocarpus*)和沉香属(*Aquilaria*)等。动物物种也是代表亚洲和马来西亚半岛的物种，有400种以上的鸟，57种哺乳类，例如，印度野牛(*Bos gaurus*)、水鹿(*Cerrus unicolor*)、爪哇牛(*Bos banteng*)、苏门羚属(*Carpricornis*)，还有在亚洲几乎绝迹的野水牛。此外，野生动物还有老虎、熊、豹、菲氏鹿、普通鹿、白手的长臂猿、两种叶猴、野狗、水獭和野猪，在这个地区还抓住过四头白象。鸟类中有红原鸡、孔雀-野鸡、颈鹳、黑鹰、啄木鸟以及多种鸣鸟。此外，真菌物种的数量也不少，如竹荪等。

对自然保护区作了实地考察，由于森林过大，沿途难以见到野生动物。但在某个路段是大象的活动范围，在不到100m的一段距离内除见到大象的足迹外，还见到多堆新鲜的大象粪便，说明这里大象的种群还是很大的。由于还缺乏专门的研究，对种群大小说法不一，在30~200头。由于是雨季，泥土较松，沿途还能见到其他兽类的足迹。

2.5 Cat Ba 国家公园(越南)

这个国家公园地处越南著名海区城市海防不远的一个岛屿上，是一个处于热带的典型卡斯特地貌的石山地区。由于保护区部分是石山，没有道路，我们深入林区作了实地考察。森林是比较原始的，有百年以上的具极大板根的大树，重要动物中兽类有豹猫(*Felis bengalensis*)、有蹄类有苏门羚(*Capriconis sumatraensis*)、水鹿(*Cervus unicolor*)、灵长类有这里特有的黑叶猴东京亚种(*Trachypithecus f. poliocephalus*)、猕猴(*Macaca mulatta*)和红面猴(*M. arctoides*)，鸟类有犀鸟(*Buceros bicormis cavatus*)等6种，其他还有啮齿类、松鼠类等。根据有关资料，这公园内有植物745种，哺乳类28种，鸟类67种，爬虫类15种，两栖类11种、鱼50种。濒危物种的动物8种、特有种1种，占优势的是灵长类及啮齿类。

在森林中作一个上午的考察，只能在边缘地区行动，除见到大量各种蝴蝶外，未见到任何大型的动物。Cat Ba 处于越南的东北部，红树林长得都很矮小，比起广西沿海一带英罗港与钦州湾的红树林还要矮小得多。由于大量地被改造成养虾池，红树林遭到严重的破坏。尽管如此，还是可见到不少成片的红树林，从远处看，物种还是比较单调的。

3 泰国的生物多样性迁地保护

3.1 北览鳄鱼湖动物园

这个鳄鱼湖不仅保存了包括中国扬子鳄在内的世界范围的物种 13 个，由于利润可观，资金大量积累，又逐步建立起一个半开放型的动物园。其中包括 15 头狮子、40 头老虎、15 头大象以及猩猩、猿猴、熊豹、河马、大蟒等大量的物种，很多大型动物大量繁殖问题已解决。

3.2 Kheo Kheow 开放型动物园

这动物园实际上是由两部分组成：一部分是半开放型的动物园，这部分规模要比北览鳄鱼湖动物园大得多，占地 800hm^2；另一部分有占地 15 000hm^2 以上的山地，在这山地上有相当数量如鹿及野猪等野生动物，这样的结构为繁育的野生动物的回归自然创造了很好的条件。所谓半开放型动物园是指根据动物的生活习性，尽可能地让它们能生活在自然条件下，而一些会危及人的安全的动物还是采用笼养或池养的办法。此处对一些飞禽及鸟类，与发达国家动物园一样，修了一个占地近 1hm^2，高约 10m 左右的大铁丝网，内设人工池塘及山坡，鸟类及飞禽可在这范围内自由飞翔，设有两道门，观众可直接入内参观。

表 5 泰国迁地保护的部分情况

名称	内容	建立时间	占地面积(hm^2)	工作人员	经费
北览鳄鱼湖动物园	收集世界鳄鱼物种 13 种及半开放动物园	1950	100	400	独资经营
Kheo Kheow 开放型动物园	该园具 200 个物种，数量达 5000 的半开放型动物园及大面积的野生放养区	1978	800~15000	90 职工 100 临时工	国营政府资助及部分收入
野生世界	商业性、娱乐性极强的全开放型动物园		80~1200		独资经营

这动物园的设施集野生动物的保护、公众教育、研究与娱乐于一身。其展览区占地 160hm^2，而繁殖区则占 608hm^2。动物在广大地区内自然摄食及繁殖，以达到回归自然的一个过渡。这地区只准科研人员进入，观众是不能进去的，这一点是这个动物园的一大特色。此外，动物园内还具占 32hm^2 的娱乐区。

3.3 野生世界(Safarl World)

这是泰国最大的野生动物园。人乘坐在汽车内参观生活在广阔自然天地中的各种野生动物，令人有与野生动物在一起的感觉。这里动物的数量很多，大型猛兽的繁殖的问题都已解决。由于动物数量经繁殖后越来越多，作为泰国的主要旅游点之一，参观的人数在不断增加，为之场地将由目前的 $80hm^2$ 再开辟新的场所 $1200hm^2$。

参观后，尽管令人感到商业性与娱乐性非常浓厚，其每年的纯收入可达 1500 万美元，但在客观上还是达到了对大量野生动物迁地保护目的。

参考文献

[1] Braatz S et al., Conserving biological diversity, A strategy for protected areas in the Asia-Pacific Region. World Bank Technical Paper Number 193, 1992. 10

[2] Pong Leng-EE, Trans-boundary biodiversity conservation, In: Weizhi Ji, Alan Rabinowitz. Proceedings for the workshop of trans-boundary biodiversity conservation in the Eastern Himalayas, Kunming Institute of Zoology, CAS, 1995. 109~114

[3] Vietnamese Expert Group. Establishing and managing protected areas in Vietnam. In: Weizhi Ji, Alan Rabinowitz. Proceedings for the wordshop of trans-boundary biodiversity conservation in the Eastern Himalayas. Kunming Institute of Zoology, CAS, 1995. 120~125

[4] Dang Huy Huynh, Conservation, sustainable development of biodiversity in the areas along the borders with neighbour countries is a contribution for enrich genetic gene of the countries in the region, In: Weizhi Ji, Alan Rabinowitz. Proceedings for the workshop of trans-boundary biodiversity conservation in the Eastern Himalayas, Kunming Institute of Zoology, CAS, 1995. 127~134

[5] 朱建国，何远辉，季维智. 我国自然保护区建设中几个问题的分析和探讨. 生物多样性，1996，4：175~182

[6] 季维智. 朱建国，喜马拉雅东部地区跨国界生物多样性保护国际研讨会简介. 动物学研究，1995，16：16~22

[7] 中国 21 世纪议程——中国 21 世纪人口、环境与发展白皮书，北京：中国环境科学出版社. 1994，137

[8] Rishi V., Trans-boundary biodiversity conservation status in India, In: Weizhi, Ji, Alan Rabinowitz, proceedings for the wordshop of trans-boundary biodiversity conservation in the Eastern Himalayas, Kunming Institute of Zoology, CAS. 1995. 50~56

[9] 陈灵芝主编. 中国的生物多样性. 北京：科学出版社, 1993

[10] 钱迎倩. 生物多样性的保护和永续利用. 科技导报，1992, 5: 36~38

本文原载：植物学通报. 1989. 6(1): 61-63

怀念我们的老师吴素萱教授

简令成　蔡起贵　钱迎倩

(中国科学院植物研究所)

今年4月16日是我们敬爱的老师吴素宣教授逝世10周年。虽永别10载，但她那和蔼可亲的容貌，对工作认真负责的精神，严谨治学的风尚，对青年人的热心培养，谆谆教导以及她那以身作则地把自己的一生精力贡献给祖国的科学事业的崇高品德，都时刻铭记在我们心中。

她把一生献给了科学事业

吴老师曾多次向我们讲述，她从小就热爱自然科学，对自然界的生命现象非常感兴趣。1925~1930 年，她在南京中央大学攻读生物学；1931~1937 年，先后在北京大学生物系和南京中央大学生物系从事教学和研究工作；1937~1941 年，赴美国密西根大学研究院深造，获博士学位。回国后，她先后任昆明西南联大和北京大学生物系教授；1948~1949 年，以特约教授的身份到英国牛津大学和爱丁堡大学讲学及从事细胞学实验研究，并考察英国生物学的科研情况。新中国成立后，1950~1954 年，她继续担任北京大学生物系教授；从1955年起，受聘为中国科学院植物研究所研究员。直至她生命的最后一息，她都在为发展祖国的科学事业勤勤恳恳、孜孜不倦地工作着。

在科研工作上，她主要是从事细胞学研究。早期的工作(三、四十年代)是关于壁虎的精子发生及鸭跖草科一些属、种的细胞学研究。她曾一再向我们谈到，在旧中国，她和其他许多老一辈科学家一样，研究工作是在十分困难的条件下进行的。新中国成立后，工作条件有了很大的改善，她对党、对社会主义祖国非常热爱，工作热情更加高涨，研究工作也以很快的速度取得重大进展。1954 年，她在对葱、蒜等鳞茎植物的鳞片细胞的观察中，发现了细胞核的穿壁运动。尔后又通过大量的研究，证明这是一种普遍的正常的生理现象。为了探讨它的生理意义，她和娄成后教授合作进行了多方面的深入研究，结果指出：细胞核的穿壁运动在细胞间有机物质的运输上起着重要作用，并与植物的生长发育有密切关系。党和国家对吴老师在科研上的创造性劳动和献身精神给予了很高的重视和评价， 1978 年授予全国科学大会奖及中国科学院重大科技成果奖；并荣获 1982年全国自然科学二等奖。

吴老师非常拥护中国共产党的领导，尊重人民的愿望。1958 年，党中央号召科学研究联系生产实际，她欣然地响应号召，亲自带领学生到广西桂林地区农业试验站蹲点，对农民育种家蒋少芳同志的水稻×高粱杂交工作进行细胞学分析。经过几年对受精作用和胚胎发育的观察，为农作物远缘杂交育种提供了重要的细胞学依据。通过这次在农村的实际考察，她深感农业生产对优良品种的迫切要求。此后，她经常向我们指出，毛主席提出的“农业八字宪法”中的“种”字十分重要，我们细胞学应该而且可以在这方面做出贡献。

她对我国植物细胞学的发展费尽心力。作为中国科学院植物研究所研究员兼细胞室主任，她深知自己肩上的责任。她认为科学研究工作的发展，不仅要有人和有设备；把握好研究方向，抓准课题更是十分重要。细胞学是生物学中一门基础学科，开展学科的基础研究无疑是必须的；同时理论联系实际的工作也应该进行。当然，吴老师说的理论联系实际，并不是我们目前说的“直接见到经济效益”，而是说细胞学可以在应用基础上发挥指导作用。经过她深思熟虑地研究后，除进行细胞核穿壁运动研究外，还选择了“性细胞发育及受精作用”，“植物抗寒性的细胞学研究”，“花药培养”，“原生质体培养及细胞杂交”等课题作为她亲自参加和在她指导下进行的研究项目。实践证明，这些项目的选择是正确的。

吴老师为祖国科学事业献身的毅力是任何外界干扰都动摇不了的。即使在“文革”的 10 年动乱期间，虽然有的工作被迫中断，但她仍然不辞辛劳地查阅文献，了解国际科技动态，寻找新课题。结果她发现，在最新文献中报道的花药培养、原生质体培养和细胞杂交可能是新的“生长点”，对细胞学的发展和联系实际将可能产生重大作用。在她的倡导和亲自参加下，使这些新兴的研究在我国迅速地发展起来，并取得了重大成果，迅速赶上了国际先进水平，荣获 1978 年全国科学大会奖和 1982 年中国科学院科技成果二等奖。使我们深为感动的是当时她已年过花甲，还亲自洗涤试管和做实验。1979 年初，她不幸身患癌症，在和疾病作巨大痛苦的斗争时，甚至在临终前几天，还指示我们如何去开展今后的研究工作。她就是这样春蚕到死丝方尽地献身于祖国的科学事业，对我国植物细胞学的发展做出了重要贡献。

严谨治学

在我们跟随吴老师的工作中，她的严谨治学精神使我们深为敬佩，受益极深。她在研究工作上要求十分严格，在进行实验中总是精心操作，仔细检查，对于观察到的结果总要反复地验证。显微镜观察是很辛苦的，但她为了获得一个可信的结果，总是不辞劳累地观察大量的切片，日复一日，直到取得充分的证据为止。她对学生们进行的工作，在听取汇报时，总是要细心地询问各个细节：采用什么试剂，何种配方，实验过程中的表现情况，结果的重复性等。为了验证细胞核穿壁运动的普遍性和真实性，她先后通过多种材料，采用多种方法:撕取表皮制片、石蜡切片、杀死固定、活体观察等多方面验证后，才予以确认。她曾将玉米花粉进行低温处理后授粉，第一年就发现有很好的低温生物学效应，但她并不因此就轻易地做出结论，发表文章。尔后，她又连续数年进行重复试验，直到当初的结果在几年的重复实验中得到充分的验证后，方感到由衷的欣慰。

在撰写研究论文上，她也是要求很严格。写文章时一改再改，不仅要求作到科学性，按照客观规律分析、处理实验结果，防止主观臆断，引文准确无误；而且要求语句通顺，字体端正，具有可读性。

她对科学事业具有高度实事求是的精神，能坚持真理，修正错误，错了就改。例如她在研究洋葱、大蒜鳞片细胞核穿壁运动时，最初看到鳞茎叶片越小，细胞核穿壁运动越多的现象。后来她的学生用萌发中的蒜瓣为材料，从外到里对各叶片进行有序的系统的观察。结果证明，不是最小叶片，而是生长最迅速的幼叶细胞核穿壁运动愈多。她对学生的此项研究结果很高兴，在尔后发表的文章中，修正了原来的报道。

热心培养青年人

吴老师不仅在研究工作中重视培养青年人，她从1931~1954年还先后在南京中央大学、昆明西南联大和北京大学从事教学工作。她培养的学生桃李满天下。1978年年底，她到北大医院检查身体时，发现她患了甲状腺癌的肿瘤科主任就是她在西南联大任教时的学生。为了提高教学质量，使学生在课堂上获得高效益，课前她以最大努力去备课，查阅大量的文献资料，以便使学生们获得最新的知识。她每讲一堂课，备课时间要比讲课时间多许多倍。记得在1965年，北京大学生物系请吴老师去作一个专题报告，规定是两节课，而她足足花了一个月时间在图书馆查阅了各种有关的新文献资料。凡听过她讲过课的人，都感到她讲的内容很实在，条理清楚，反映了科研的最新进展。能达到这样的效果，是与她精心努力备课分不开的。

她在培养学生方面的特点是：①很注意因材施教，对具有不同才华的人采取不同的培养方式，给他提出相应的适当的工作。②很重视培养学生的独立工作能力，当给一位学生确定研究方向和课题后，她总是让学生独立地去开展工作，以利于发挥学生独立思考的能力和施展自己的才华。③平时对学生倍加关心，经常热心地和细致地进行督促和检查。遇到困难和问题时，她和学生们一起研究，讨论解决的办法，提供她所看到的文献资料。她热情鼓励和支持青年人写论文，发表著作。她对学生们的习作，总是仔细地逐字逐句地阅读、审查和细心地修改。另外，对她没有亲自参加和指导的工作，决不让署她的名。这充分体现吴老师对科学事业实事求是的态度和不务虚名的崇高品德。

我们怀着感激之情回忆着这一切，并深感能在她的指导下工作和成长是很幸运的。她虽然离开了我们，但她那为祖国科学事业的献身精神，一生兢兢业业埋头苦干、严谨治学、不务虚名、谦虚谨慎、助人为乐的崇高品德，永远是我们学习的榜样，并将永久地引起我们的怀念与回忆。

本文原载：植物学报. 1999. 16(专辑): 53(55)

怀念吴素萱老师

钱迎倩

(中国科学院植物研究所)

1959年我来到植物所工作后就听说细胞室吴素萱老师治学严谨，在植物细胞学上有重大贡献，她的细胞核穿壁及核更新的研究工作受到科技界很大的重视。我很想能跟随吴老师做学问。经过吴老师的同意，终于接受了我这个学生，到植物所的第二年底就转到了细胞室工作。

我刚到细胞室工作时吴老师还是一位中年科学家，从学术上讲她的核穿壁、核更新的基础研究刚开始有很多的创始，有待更深入的发展。可是从1958年大跃进到1976年四人帮的推翻，科学工作者绝大多数时间是在参加政治运动、参加劳动、上山下乡，没有一个安定的搞研究时间，另一方面，吴老师核穿壁、核更新这类基础研究是属于脱离实际的研究。吴老师虽然始终忘不了她的核穿壁、核更新研究，但出于热爱党的热情，在行动上始终紧跟党的号召，在一定时间内中断了她的研究。

现在回想起来，到细胞室跟随吴老师后的一件件一桩桩事件都历历在目。60年代前后，吴老师响应组织的召唤，利用她深厚的细胞学基础，配合社会上掀起的远缘杂交热潮，和年轻人一起出差南方，一方面参加田间的野外工作，回所后又抓紧做室内细胞学观察。文化大革命前，她还与年青人一起到北京郊区东北旺公社去蹲点，搞育种工作。由于借宿的住处、田间工作与吃饭的地方距离都很远，吴老师不会骑自行车，经常步行或坐在年轻人自行车后面，有时因农村的崎岖小路，羊肠小道，一不小心车翻人倒，吴老师好几次从车上翻下来，但她从不计较，总还安慰大家。还记得很清楚，在号召大家“深挖洞、广积粮”时，大家都和泥做砖，这样的重体力劳动大家都劝这时已是高龄的吴老师不要参加了，但吴老师照样卷起了袖子和大家一起托土坯。她一托就是一上午，不怕苦不怕累。

文化大革命扼杀了中国的科学事业，在这段时间里中国的科学停滞了。但是包括吴老师在内的一批科学家却始终忘不了祖国的科学事业。吴老师一面参加文化大革命，一边抽时间到图书馆去查阅国际动态。中国的花药培养和单倍体育种研究的成就在国际上是享有盛誉的。这些成就与吴老师的贡献紧密联系在一起。吴老师在查阅图书馆的文献中发现60年代初印度科学家首先用曼陀罗的花药进行培养，长成了单倍体植株。吴老师根据她雄厚的科学基础，她立刻就敏感到花粉经人工培养能发育成单倍体植株，今后会在育种上作出很大的贡献。于是她就大量的查阅国际资料，并翻译成中文，供同事们翻阅，这些中文资料被装订成册，开始时在植物所当时的形态室和细胞室内广泛参阅，后来外单位的同仁们也来借阅。一时供不应求，因此有一大部分随后出版成好几本论文集。一段时间内成为花药培养和单倍体育种研究者的主要参考资料。

吴老师在花药培养及单倍体育种方面开创了局面后，她又发现国际上在60年代初又用酶法大量地从植物体细胞分离原生质体成功。并发现原生质体分离成功的 10 年后(1971年)，日本科学家和德国科学家合作首次获得了原生质体再生植株。1972年美国科学家用原生质体融合的方法得到了世界上第一株烟草的杂种。吴老师异常兴奋，虽然这时的吴老师已年近花甲，但她不停地工作，用放大镜逐字逐句地把文献翻成中文。“植物体细胞杂交参考资料”第一集终于在1974年问世。当时个人的名字是不允许在论文或释文上出现的，落款是“中国科学院植物所细胞组译”，而实际工作绝大部分是吴老师完成的。可能现在的读者感到奇怪，研究人员为什么不自己去看英文原文，非要翻译中文呢?正像本文上面提到的，1958年大跃进后，中国的科学事业时起时伏，科学工作者不是参加运动，就是上山下乡，很少在外文上有长进。因此在这个年代，中文翻译稿是很起到作用，翻译稿利用效率之高也说明起到了重要的作用。

吴老师在细胞组里不仅为大家收集、翻译资料，当时年事已高、手已发抖的吴老师还经常与大家一起做实验，甚至帮着一起洗涤培养皿及玻璃器具。植物所细胞组较早地在烟草、水稻原生质体再生上取得成果，随后在玉米、猕猴桃等原生质体再生植株或无性系变异研究上在国际上领先，所取得的成就都与吴老师的开创分不开。

记得上小学做作文时经常用一句成语“光阴如箭，日月如梭”，时间过得如此之快，我来到植物所时还是一个生龙活虎的年轻人，现在已成为一个老人。今年是吴老师诞辰九十周年，也是离开我们二十周年之际，现在回忆起来，吴老师的勤奋好学、一丝不苟、严谨治学以及她对中国科学事业的贡献都是值得我永远尊敬的、终身学习的。

本文原载：中国科学院老科学家科普演讲团感言. 2010. 钟琪主编. 北京：科学普及出版社, 93-102

从几点感想谈科普

钱迎倩

(中国科学院植物研究所)

那是1999年，我的最后两位博士生毕业，这也就意味着我的工龄到此结束了。现实的问题摆在我的面前，忙忙碌碌工作40多年的我该退休了。工作一下子停下来后，又该干些什么呢?正在这时，当年在中科院机关工作的一位同志打来电话，问我退休了是否还想干一点什么，院里有一个老科学家科普演讲团，愿不愿意参加?我从来没接触过科普工作，口才也不好，这个问题很突然，得好好想一下。工作了几十年，讲什么内容不发愁，口才不好多锻炼总会有所长进的，刚退下来精力也还比较充沛，闲着不如有件事做，就在这样的思想基础上，我答应下来了。同意参加后，当然也必然经过演讲团不成文的规矩，先去听讲过多年的、有经验的老专家的科普报告，这是学习阶段；回来后努力地准备讲稿，然后试讲；虚心地听取大家的意见，不断地修改自己的讲稿及演讲的技巧；这样终于成为了一个科普报告者，开始了我十多年的科普报告工作。十年时间就讲了300多场，与刚参加科普工作的思想基础相比，我在各方面认识上都有了提高，也有了一些体会。

要有敬业的精神

参加演讲团不久，一件事给了我很深刻的教育。那是一天下午，一个郊区县第一次邀请团里两位专家去做报告，一位是比我还大两岁的天文学家，另一位是我。约定的时间为下午1点在某个地点等，他们来车接。我们俩提前到达等候，到时间了还见不到车，到1点20分了，邀请单位的车子才到达。邀请者非常客气地邀我们上车。虽然大家都是第一次见面，可是这位天文学家非常严肃地向邀请者指出“你们为什么迟到，我们在这儿多等20分钟不重要，可我们是去给学生们讲科普的，要对学生负责。每个学生为等我们浪费20分钟，加起来一共浪费了多少时间?”对方解释说“路比较远，路上交通又有点堵塞，所以迟到了。”这位老专家又进一步提出：“这些都不是理由。你们早就应该想到交通堵塞等问题。总之，不能不负责任地让同学们白白地浪费时间等着我们”邀请者大概不久就向有关领导作了汇报。我们报告结束后，有关领导出面一定要请我们吃晚饭。我们团本来也有不成文的规定，在北京做报告，包括郊区县在内报告完是不吃饭的。但有关领导一再邀请，我们自己无车回城，在主人盛情难却的情况下，我们也就破例留下了，席间有关领导一再作了道歉。这位老专家平时待人接物都很谦虚，他是我团组团以来最早参加者之一，对科普教育一贯重视、认真、一丝不苟。这一次也就是他对科普事业一丝不苟的一种表现，对我也很有教育意义，对待科普事业就应该这样的兢兢业业。

2001年应中央电视台《周末异想天开》节目好奇实验室邀请，给同学们讲“保护生物多样”

我们团里的每个同仁，包括我在内对每场报告都是十分敬业的，这次事件后，有这样的好榜样在前面，我对自己的要求就更严格了。譬如，到各个单位做报告，场地环境差异太大了，多数单位有阶梯教室、多功能厅、多媒体设备等，条件非常好；可有些单位条件很差。我们团的同仁们到条件不好的单位后往往帮邀请单位出主意，尽可能把条件创造得好一些，让听众听的效果好一点儿。甚至即使没有条件的单位，我们还是照样满腔热情地去讲。有一次怀柔一个中学邀我去讲。学校离怀柔城还有几十里地，没有礼堂，也没有大的教室可供较多的同学听报告。因是远郊区，能请到一位专家来做报告不容易，学校领导希望能有更多的学生听到报告，不凑巧的是当天下午停电，又刮起了大风，学校领导问我怎么办?我说既然已来了，按原计划讲。因我是南方人，讲话始终保留有南方口音，怕同学们听不懂专业名词，我要求学校给一块黑板能写个字，可是学校的黑板全安装在墙上，没有活动黑板。学校领导设法搞到一把导游手中拿的小喇叭，讲课地点就在楼后的大操场。同学们集中在背风的一面，远处正刮着沙尘，我手中拿着小喇叭，就这样近乎喊地、慢慢地讲了一个多小时。同学们非常安静地听讲，讲完后还提了不少问题，说明同学们不仅听到了，也听懂了。这种条件下得到这样的效果，不仅学校领导和同学们满意，我尽管嗓子喊得很痛但心里也非常高兴。

既是学习机会又可增强健康

每次报告后我们都会留下一定的时间让同学们提问题进行互动。这段时间既是给我们创造再学习的好机会，又往往不知不觉地增强了健康。当然，互动时提的问题多数是很容易当场解答的，但的确还有的一时答不上来，答不上来时，我是抱着知之为知之，不知为不知的态度，绝对不为答不出失面子而胡乱编造。当场就告诉同学们，你提的问题很好，但我一时回答不了。回去查参考资料或请教有关专家后，记下该同学的地址或电子邮箱后回答他们。这当然就给自己创造了一个再学习的好机会。此外，由于互动时间所限，当面提问题的机会还是少，我就希望同学将问题写在字条上送上来，有时间就可按字条上的、有意义的问题作回答，除此以外这些字条还有更加重要的作用，我每次都把字条好好地收起来，到适当时候把小字条整理成小册子，然后仔细地阅读，从中能发现不少问题，既知道了哪些问题是同学们普遍感兴趣的，也知道了自己在哪些问题上没讲清楚或未讲透，对今后的讲课都极为有益。例如中学高年级的同学普遍很关心全球变暖会对生物多样性造成什么影响?我看过一些资料，但并不多，为了使自己能更深入地了解这一问题，我用心寻找了不少参考资料。实际上这些资料的收集不仅仅是为科普报告或回答同学们提问而用，后来在我的写作上也很有帮助。由秦大河主编的《中国气候与环境演变》(2005)这本巨著中的有关“生物多样性”部分是我负责执笔的。为科普报告而收集到的全球变化与生物多样性关系的大量资料，在撰写这一部分时都起到了重要作用。

科普报告与增强健康又有什么关系呢?首先是有机会与更多的青少年接触、交流很有益，他们经常会表扬你，如“老师，您的报告真好”或者“老师，您回答的问题真棒”。我想愿意听表扬可能是每个人的天性，听到孩子们对自己的表扬，心情自然是很好的。更能调动自己情绪的是互动的时候。同学们一个问题、一个问题地提，有时回答了问题后，有的同学会提出不同的看法，一去一来，情绪调动起来了，心情非常的好。看到了当代中学生求知欲非常强，了解新生事物也相当多，深深感到后生可畏，祖国下一代有好的接班人了，心情好当然就可增强健康。更让人高兴的是一次到55中去讲课，学校怕影响高三同学的高考，科普报告不让高三同学听，只让高二同学听，一切结束我正收拾计算机准备告别时，突然上来两个女同学，自我介绍说：“我们两人是高三同学，学校不让我们听但我们还是躲在后面偷偷地听了。老师，您的报告我们很受益，我俩正在做中国科协组织的‘小发明、小创造’现在农业缺水很厉害，而灌溉方式又浪费很多水，我们正在研究当农作物缺水时让作物能自动灌溉，不缺水时灌溉又能停下来，现在碰到了困难，是有关植物方面的，我们想请教您这位专家。”听完了这段叙述，我激动万分，水是农业的命根子，中国又如此缺水，一个高中生能想到这么一个大问题，又敢去碰这个大难题，我虽然不是这方面的专家，但我十分愿意尽我所知告诉她们，为她们去查阅大量文献，找这方面有关专家，尽可能地给她们帮助，后来又为她们逐字逐句地修改报告。做完这事，虽然花了精力与时间，可是觉得非常的高兴，非常值得。后来学生的妈妈还带着孩子来我家专门感谢，至今我们还保持着联系。

2001年在乌鲁木齐做报告，参加当地一位科协同志的家宴

不是每场报告都令人满意

我所经历的300多场报告中，听众是多种多样的，多数是中小学生，也有老师、干部及社区的居民等，因此可能碰到各种各样的情况。当然多数情况下听众都很集中精力地听课、提问，但也碰到过令人不满意甚至难堪的情况。多数是由于听众对你讲的不感兴趣或者环境太不好了，如在一个大剧院里上千人听报告，往往听众听不清、看不见，难免台下就乱糟糟，台上做报告，台下开小组会。遇到这种情况，我就适时结束，事后好好总结、改进。

我在这里想讲的是可能难以预测的情况。举几个例子，有一次被邀到一个社区做"以实际行动迎接绿色奥运"的报告，当报告谈到迎接绿色奥运不仅仅是政府的任务，而与每个人都有关，我们北京市每个居民都可从身边的小事做起时，突然有一位50多岁的大娘喊了起来"你们应该给领导去做报告，和我们讲没有用。"会场上顿时乱了起来。我停了下来，向边上的居民了解了一下原因，原来是由于会议组织者在会议开始时说了几句后就离开了，而这个社区环境存在不少问题，这位大娘提过多次意见而得不到解决所造成的。我及时请人把会议组织者找到，向他报告了刚才发生的情况，然后让他们离开会场个别交换意见，我再继续把报告做完。这事件说明什么问题，不是值得大家想一下吗?

第二个例子是受邀到一个技术学校做报告。按惯例我到校后就先与接待老师交换意见，可讲多少时间，又给多少时间可与同学们互动等等，不料接待老师一开始就告诉我，我们学校学生的素质很差，听您报告的学生又是学机械的，您最多讲40分钟，也不会有学生提什么问题的，一下子就让我讲课没有情绪了。教室大到能容纳200名以上学生，十人一排的课桌一排排地排着，临讲前5分钟，学生鱼贯入场，老师开讲，这次期中考试每门都及格的往前两排坐，果然前两排都未坐满，这就意味着老师的话是正确的，200

多名同学中每门课都及格的不到 20 人。但我一想我是来讲科普的，不管听众怎么样，我首先得讲好，让同学们听得有兴趣，这么一想就把刚才的坏情绪丢到了一边。结果果然出乎意料，同学们非常认真地听讲，没有交头接耳的现象，讲完了居然还有同学提问题，老师、同学和我都满意地结束了报告会。这件事告诉了我们，对待任何事物、任何人不能先有一个固定的坏印象，而是始终要抱着满腔热情去对待。

第三个例子是在河南一个离城市较远的高中讲“保护生物多样性”的科普报告。报告及互动的效果都很好，快结束时，突然有一个女同学站起来说“老师，你今天讲得这么多，也回答了不少问题，我想问你，你对保护生物多样性有什么贡献?”猛一听到这样的提问真是一愣，怎么会用这样的口气来提问题?煞是生气，本来想不回答她的提问，后来一想不能这样，这位同学很想知道你讲这个题目，那你本人又做了哪些工作呢?只是提问的方式不太合适而已。于是我还是心平气和地回答我谈不上做出什么贡献，然后如实地介绍了我在为保护生物多样性方面过去做过哪些工作，回答完后那位同学也满意地点头了。

对报告内容的一个建议

关于报告内容，一开始我只讲一个题目，即保护生物多样性。20 世纪 80 年代后期，我被调到中科院机关生物科学与技术局工作，在院机关工作能接触到各研究领域的专家，在和有些专家交谈中，他们提到“保护生物多样性”在国际上已是一个极为热门的研究课题，我国生物多样性非常丰富，破坏的现状也极为严重，而且远未引起足够的重视。也就在这时候，院里派出驻美使馆工作的、原来我局工作的同仁发回的美国科研动态中也谈到生物多样性保护正是美国在抓的前沿热点问题。这就促使我找了相当一部分资料来参阅，得到的概念是在全球、在我国生物多样性破坏的严重程度，不仅影响到社会的可持续发展，而且关系到子孙万代能否在地球上生存下去，是十分严重的环境问题之一。要进行这方面研究，我院有一批优秀的生态学专家、国内最强的分类学、系统学基础以及一批分子生物学及信息科学方面的专家，有极好的研究基础。此外，时间也容不得再等待。于是在中科院副院长的支持下，我院在国内率先组织起生物多样性保护及其持续利用的项目。1990 年首次我国生物多样性的研讨会在我院召开。从此拉开了我国生物多样性研究的帷幕，我本人不但组织了此项目，并在自己熟悉的领域中也参加了进去。十年的时间已让我深刻地认识到生物多样性在我国被破坏的严峻形势，要保护好生物多样性不能仅仅依靠政府的重视和努力，必须让广大群众都认识到问题的严重性，并能参与到保护生物多样性的行动中去。做科普报告正是向广大群众宣传的一个好机会，我很自然地就选择了保护生物多样性作为我的题目。

2001年春节前，北京三中同学来我家拜访

报告的内容要不断充实、更新，关心的问题就由生物多样性扩展到整个资源环境。近60年来，我国人口由4.5亿激增到13亿，改革开放后经济飞速增长，但基本上是按工业文明的模式在发展，以上两个方面给我国的资源、生态及环境带来了极大的压力。正像环保部副部长潘岳曾经指出的：“中央在‘十一五’规划中提出‘每年节能4%，减排2%’，但2006年主要污染物排放量不降反升；平均每两天发生一起突发性环境事故，群众环境投诉增加了3成；中央领导对环境问题的批示比上一年增加了52%。环境资源问题已经对建设和谐社会构成了严重挑战，环境问题早已超越了专业层次，成为影响经济、制约社会、涉及政治的大问题。”从中可以体会到我国目前经济飞速增长、国际政治地位极大提高、人民生活水平蒸蒸日上的大好形势下，还存在着严峻的资源环境问题。因此我在查阅大量资料基础上增加了“我国面临严峻的资源环境的挑战”这一题目，宣传中央提出的科学发展观，建设资源节约型、环境友好型社会这一指导思想。

各种颜色郁金香的花由基因控制，不同品种也就是遗传多样性

实际上，资源环境问题与其他数、理、化、天、地、生以及各种技术科学都有密切的关系。不同的学科都有可能从本学科与资源环境结合点上讲我国的资源环境问题，将可能有助于不同背景、不同兴趣的听众去关心我国的资源环境问题，对解决我国面临的资源环境问题起到好的促进作用。这个建议是否有可能实现呢?答案是明确的，完全可能，目前中科院老科学家科普演讲团中已经有从事材料科学研究以及从事生物工程研究的专家结合自己的专业，做精彩的有关我国资源环境问题的报告。

外来入侵物种水葫芦在河中疯长，其他生物无生存余地

钱迎倩演讲题目及简介

我国面临严峻的资源、环境的挑战

改革开放后我国经济飞速发展，GDP 以平均 9.5%速度增长，外汇储备至 2007 年 4 月达 1.2 万亿美元，北京市人均 GDP 已超过 7000 美元，国际地位也大大提高。但在经济大发展的同时，资源环境问题已经对建设和谐社会构成了严重挑战。环境问题早已超越了专业层次，成为影响经济、制约社会、涉及政治的大问题。本讲座将从水、土、气、生物多样性角度详细分析目前资源、环境的形势，国家正采取的措施，以及社会和个人应该做的努力。按科学发展观的指导思想，建设成资源节约型、环境友好型的社会。

一个重要的环境问题——保护生物多样性

生物多样性是人类在地球上赖以生存的基础，也是各种重要环境问题之一。近 200 年来由于工业文明的发展、人口急剧增长等种种原因，造成了很多基因的流失，森林、草原、湿地等各种生态系统的破坏，大量物种在人类尚未发现、来不及定名、更不知道其用途前在地球上已经濒危或已灭绝。这就是生物多样性三个层次(遗传多样性、物种多样性及生态系统多样性)的现状。这一切已经威胁到人类在地球上的生存和发展，从而将保护生物多样性的问题提升到“拯救生物多样性就是拯救人类自己”的高度。本讲座从介绍中国生物多样性的现状开始，分析生物多样性受到威胁或灭绝的原因以及如何拯救生物多样性。

本文原载：绿色文明——建设资源节约型环境友好型社会科普讲座. 2010. 汤寿根主编. 北京：知识产权出版社，1-14

我国面临严峻的资源环境的挑战

钱迎倩

(中国科学院植物研究所)

本讲座首先分析了我国资源与环境的形势；然后从水、土、气、生等环境因素作了进一步剖析，列举了存在的严重问题；最后指出，必须走生态文明的道路：推进循环经济、偿还生态欠债、实行绿色 GDP。

我国改革开放以后，经济社会得到了飞速的发展，不仅人民生活得到很大的改善，我国国际地位也大大提高了。

例如，英国“全国语言监督”机构主席帕亚克说：“由于中国经济增长的影响，它现在对英语的冲击比英语国家还要大。”这家机构称，自 1994 年以后新增加的英语词汇中，中式英语贡献了 5%~20%，超过了其他来源。

看来，经济实力是同“话语权”成正比的。国家之间如此，人与人之间也未尝不如此。笔者不由得想起，我国改革开放的历程自广东始，广东人先富了起来。于是广东话也吃香起来。粤话北渐，“买单”就是付账、“8”就是“发”，连举世瞩目的 2008 年 8 月 8 日 8 时开幕的“北京奥运”，也大大“发”起来了。

对于遭受列强侵略、屈辱了一百年的中国人来说，确实开始“扬眉吐气”了。请看：

我国改革开放以后，20 世纪 70 年代末以来，GDP 年平均增长 9.7%。2007 年，GDP 总值达到 24.66 万亿元，是 1978 年的 20 倍；与 2002 年的 GDP 相比，增长 65.5%，年平均增长 10.6%；GDP 总值上升世界第四位；人均 GDP 为 2500 美元(北京已超过 6000 美元、上海已超过 10000 美元)，居世界第 103 位。据 2008 年 6 月低公布的数字，我国外汇储备已达 1.8088 万亿美元，超过了世界七大工业园(美、日、英、德、法、加、意)的总和。

但是，我们必须清醒地看到，上述令人振奋的数字后面，有着严重的资源、环境代价。

一、我国资源、环境形势初析

人类文明的发展史，是从采集文明过渡到农业文明，再从农业文明发展到工业文明。世界上发达国家的工业文明已有 200 多年历史。在这些国家里，工厂林立、工农业水平空前提高，经济快速增长，人民改变了生活方式，生活水平也相应大大提高。但是，工业文明的快速发展带来了严峻的后果：资源无节制的开发和过度的消耗；人类生存环境严重恶化；生物多样性严重破坏，大量物种濒临灭绝或已经灭绝。

30多年来，我国经济的快速增长也没有离开工业文明的发展模式，经济增长仍以耗能、耗资源为主的粗放型增长方式为主，资源利用率低，GDP增长的资源消耗代价是非常高的。以2004年为例，我国消耗了世界钢材的27%、煤的31%、水泥的40%，但GDP的总量仅占世界的4%；2006年我国GDP占世界6%，但消耗了世界30%的钢材，35%的煤和50%的水泥。然而，消耗了这么多的资源，生产出来的产品质量，与发达国家相比，还相差甚远。以2004年为例，我国手表的产量占世界的76%，但从产值上看，却比产量仅占世界3%的瑞士表要低；又如芯片制造业，4年投资了上百亿美元，但芯片的产量仅能满足国内市场的17%，而且质量不高，只能用于玩具制品。越高级的芯片，越要靠进口，2004年的手机芯片全部依靠进口。

民盟中央副主席冯之浚在2005年21世纪论坛的报告中指出，中国面临的严峻的资源、环境形势，给经济发展出了六大难题：

难题一 资源总量和人均量不足。1994年前，我们普遍认为"中国是一个地大物博的国家"。但是，根据60年来的资源勘探证明，我国的资源总量并非十分丰富(表1-1)；尤其是人口的飞速增长，我国的人均资源量与世界平均水平相比是相当低的(表1-2)。

表1-1 我国一些重要矿产资源占世界资源的百分比

资源	占世界的百分比(%)
石油	1.8
天然气	0.7
铁矿石	9.0以下
铜矿	5.0以下
铝土矿	2.0以下

表1-2 我国人均资源量与世界平均水平比较

资源名称	人均资源量与世界平均水平比较
矿产资源	占世界平均水平1/2
耕地、草地资源	占世界平均水平1/3
水资源	占世界平均水平1/4
森林资源	占世界平均水平1/5
能源	占世界平均水平1/7
石油	占世界平均水平1/10

难题二 我国资源消耗增长速度惊人。仅以水泥为例，2004年消耗约8亿吨，到2006年消耗增长到13.3亿吨，占世界水泥消耗的50%。电力的消耗仅低于美国，居世界第2位。而铁、铜、铝等矿产储量，无论是相对或绝对数量，我国均无大国地位可言。

难题三 由于我国经济飞速发展的需要，短期内粗放型增长的方式难以转变，因此资源的对外依赖度还将升高。因为，产业结构仍处于重化工主导阶段，高能耗、高污染产业仍有较高需求。预计2010年，对外依赖度石油将达57%、铁矿石达57%、铜达70%、铝达 80%。

难题四 资源重复利用率远远低于发达国家。例如水资源的重复利用率比发达国家低 50%以上。

难题五 当前的环境已经难以支撑高污染、高能耗、低效率生产方式的持续扩张。

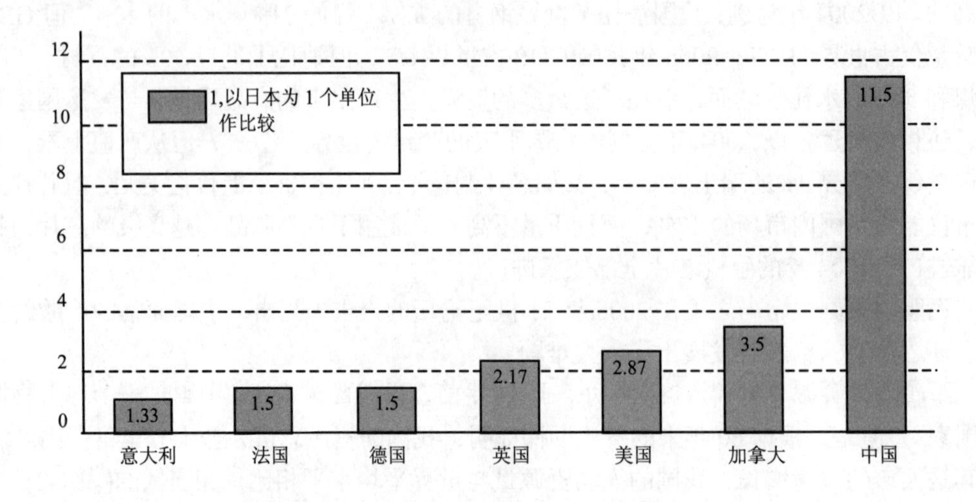

图 1-1 几个发达国家的能源利用率与我国的比较

难题六 资源利用效率整体偏低，以单位 GDP 产出能耗表征的能源利用率，我国与发达国家的差距非常之大。图 1-1 为几个发达国家的能源利用率与我国的比较。从图中可以看出，日本的能源利用率最高，若以日本的能源利用率为一个单位计，我国是 11.5，高于日本 11 倍以上。

二、从水、土、气、生环境因素作进一步分析

2007 年，国家环保部潘岳副部长曾对我国的资源环境有过精辟的分析。他指出："中央在'十一五'规划中提出'每年节能 4%，减排 2%'，但 2006 年主要污染排放量不降反升；平均每两天发生一起突发性环境事件，群众环境投诉增加了 3 成；中央领导对环境问题的批示比上一年增加了 52%。环境污染问题已经对建设和谐社会构成了严重挑战，环境问题早已超越了专业层次，成为影响经济、制约社会、涉及政治的大问题。"我们可以从中体会到我国目前环境形势的严峻。下面将结合水、土、气、生等的资源，进一步分析我国但前的环境状况。

(一) 水

水资源是一个国家的命脉。不仅工农业的发展离不开水，而且每个人的日常生活也都缺不了水。可是，我国的水资源存在两个严重的问题：一是水资源严重短缺；二是内陆湖泊及近海的水资源被污染，不同程度上存在着富营养化问题。

1. 水资源严重短缺

虽然，我国水资源总量居世界第五位，但人均水资源仅为世界人均的 1/4。全国 600 多座城市有 400 多座供水不足，其中 100 多座严重缺水。北京就是一个典型的例子：北京的水资源人均值为全国人均值的 1/8，仅占世界人均值的 1/32，人均占有量不足 300 立方米。近 50 年来，由于人类活动及气候变化的影响，内陆湖泊已减少了约 1000 个，而且还在以平均每年 20 个天然湖泊的速度消亡。有“千湖之省”之美誉的湖北省，目前湖泊只剩下了 300 个左右。目前长江流域湖泊面积共有 14000 平方千米，占全国的 1/5，而仅长江中下游的皖、湘、鄂、赣、苏几省，因历年来围湖造田而消亡的湖泊面积就达 12000 平方千米。湖泊面积减少的同时，水容量也大大减少。例如，我国最大的内陆湖——鄱阳湖，目前面积仅为 50 平方千米，而历史上面积最大时曾达到 4350 平方千米；鄱阳湖不仅面积减少，水位线也从过去的 20 米降到现在的 7.37 米；蓄水量从 1000 亿立方米，降到 1 亿立方米。又如，我国第五大淡水湖——内蒙古自治区的达赉湖，因持续干旱，注入湖内的第三条河流，有两条于 2007 年断流，湖面积比正常时减少了 500 平方千米。北京近郊的潮白河早在 10 前就已大部分干涸。

由于淡水资源短缺，全国有近 400 座城市以开采地下水作为供水水源。据国土资源部评估，我国地下水可开采资源经多年平均，每年可开采量 3527 亿立方米。两院院士张宗祜指出：许多地方没有按照地下水分布和运动规律来开采，或超开采和过量开采，使地下水无法“休养生息”，水位逐年下降。北京平均每年下降 1 米。河北平原，20 世纪 60 年代初地下水距地表只有 2 米左右，而现在沧州地区的地下水距地表深达 70 米。

过度开采地下水会造成一系列严重后果。我国农业用水要依靠地下水，地下水资源的持续减少，会使我国粮食生产无法保证可持续发展。过度开采还会引起地面沉降和塌陷，危及城市建设物。全国已有 70 座城市发生地面沉降，面积达 6.4 万平方千米，超过 2 米的有天津、太原、西安等，天津塘沽区甚至达到 3.1 米；又如，西安钟楼下陷近 400 毫米，大雁塔倾斜近千毫米，岩溶塌陷 3000 多处。此外，过度开采地下水还会导致地质灾害，如形成区域性的地下水下降漏斗。经 2007 年监测，全国已有地下水降落漏斗 212 个。更需要重视的是，沿海地区还会引起海水倒灌，造成耕地的大量丧失。如山东莱州湾等沿海地区，海水倒灌造成 60 多万亩耕地丧失生产能力，土地盐碱化，减产 20%~40%，直至绝产。

2. 水资源遭到污染

随着我国工农业和人口的快速发展，工业废水，农业用水中的农药和化肥残余，以及生活污水的排放量也不断增加，造成了淡水资源和近海海水相当严重的污染。目前，我国城市的污水处理只有 45.67%，城镇及农村的处理率就更低，因此七大江河水系中，劣五类水质占到 40.9%，70%的湖泊及近海出现不同程度的富营养化。2008 年卫生部调查表明，我国农村 44.36%的饮用水未达标，近 3.6 亿农民喝不上符合标准的水。河南的某个村庄，因水严重污染而变成癌症村(食道癌、肝癌、肺癌居多)，5 年内数十人死亡，鱼、虾绝迹。长江流域 186 个城市，接纳了 40%以上的污水，其中 80%是未经处理的。由于水体污染，20 世纪 80 年代中期在长江流域生活着的 126 种生物物种，到 2002 年时大量灭绝，仅存 52 种。例如，仅在长江下游生活着的我国特有物种白鳍豚，由于水质污染和其他因素，可能已经灭绝了。黄河流域生存过 150 种鱼类和其他水产品，已有 1/3 的物种因污染或过度捕捞等原因而永远灭绝。

水污染的另一个严重后果是频繁发生水华与赤潮。由于水体严重富营养化，在温度及其他环境条件合适时，水体内的蓝藻在短时期内会大量爆发而形成蓝绿色的水华，藻体本身及死亡后释放大量毒素，使生物大量死亡。2007 年，无锡市人民在一段时间内因太湖水华泛滥，缺乏饮用水源而无淡水供应；2008 年，安徽巢湖连续 4 个月因重度污染而蓝藻泛滥；2008 年 5~6 月间，黄河流域的最大湖泊——内蒙古乌梁素海，由于同样的原因，1/3 的湖面爆发了一种浮游的藻类植物，对水鸟、水禽造成很大威胁，渔业资源遭到严重破坏。据报道，乌梁素海还是首次发生如此严重的情况。

我国海洋的生物资源因长期过度捕捞已趋于枯竭，大量海产品主要依靠人工养殖。近海频繁发生的赤潮，对养殖的打击是十分严重的，有的海产品甚至影响到人体健康。2008 年 6 月以来，青岛及邻近海域受到一种较大型的绿藻——浒苔的袭击，直接威胁到奥运会的帆船比赛。当时军民齐动员，奋战了近一个月，打捞了 68 万吨浒苔，并布设了一条总长 22000 米的围油栏，从而保证了 8 月奥运帆船比赛的正常举行。此外，我国已有超过 100 个大中城市的地下水受到不同程度的污染。污染源也是工业废水与生活污水。用污水灌溉农田，不仅污染了农作物，而且造成地下水的直接污染。

3. 解决水资源危机的建议

解决水资源危机，除了提高认识及合理、节约利用水资源外，在技术上主要应解决开源节流问题。在开源方面：沿海地区依靠海水淡化，内陆则需提高对降水和地下水的合理储存和利用效率；在节流方面：则要依靠提高污水处理的能力，使水资源能够循环利用。应当认识到，水资源问题的解决不仅需要大量的投资，更需要相当长的时间。水资源危机是一个世界性的问题，英国、日本等一些发达国家也都经历过。英国伦敦的泰晤士河及日本最大的湖泊——琵琶湖的严重污染，都是经过了近 30 年的时间才逐步得到治理的。

(二) 土

我国的土地资源也像水资源一样，存在着资源越来越短缺及土壤严重污染的问题。

1. 土地资源短缺

我国的山地面积大大多于平原。虽然。耕地面积总量占世界第二位，但人均耕地资源仅是世界人均耕地资源的 37%，人均面积不到 1.4 亩。但是随着经济的发展，全国各地以各种名目，如“开发区”“工业园区”“经济特区”“大学城”“新修及加宽道路”“住宅区”，以及“高尔夫球场”，甚至活人墓地等等，大量占用了耕地，不少地区及县级政府为兴建豪华的办公楼，不仅建筑物本身，楼前后还有大面积的广场等，也占用了大量的耕地。已经公开曝光的右：被群众称为“白宫”的安徽省阜阳市颍泉区政府办公楼，云南红河哈尼族、彝族自治州政府大楼等。

我国目前有13亿人口，虽然实行了计划生育，但人口基数过大，绝对数量还得增加到16亿左右才可逐步减少。不断增加的人口和不断减少的耕地给粮食供应带来极大压力。

2. 土壤污染严重

排入土壤的工业和生活的废、污水造成土壤污染；一些剧毒农药和化肥也会对土壤结构和性能产生破坏性改变；工业废气导致酸雨等降落物使土壤污染加剧；掩埋处理固体废弃物，以及乱扔乱倒生物排泄物，都在不同程度上污染了土壤。据报道，按不完全的统计。全国受污染的耕地约1.5亩；由污水灌溉造成的耕地污染达3250万亩；固体废弃物堆存占地和毁田200万亩。这几项的总和约占耕地总面积的10%以上。受污染的土壤必然污染生长的农作物。每年遭受重金属污染的粮食达1200万吨，除威胁食品安全和农业可持续发展外，经济损失达200亿元以上。

土地尤其是耕地是人类生命之源。中国这样的大国，一旦大量缺乏粮食的话，不仅影响国际粮食价格，而且世界上也没有那么多的粮食可以供应中国。耕地的减少已引起中央有关部委及地方领导的重视，中央已采取了一系列措施。例如，湖南等地大量的活人墓地已拆除。温家宝总理反复强调：“一定要保住18万亩耕田这条红线。”2007年，全国已开始土壤普查，从而可以知道：土壤污染的具体地区，污染的来源、面积、分布以及污染的程度；并且可以有的放矢地逐步进行治理。

3. 水土流失和荒漠化

近几十年来，主要由于森林大面积被砍伐，大量表土随着雨水的冲刷而流失，不仅丧失了肥沃的表土，而且流失的土壤抬高了河流的河床、减少了湖泊的容积。我国水土流失的面积已达356万平方千米，占国土面积的37%。此外，全国已有近1/3的县，有程度不同的土地沙漠化现象，总数已达890个。沙化土地基本上都在北方，其中90%以上在西部地区。全国共有沙化土地173.9万平方千米，占国土面积的18.1%；荒漠化土地为263.6万平方千米，占国土面积27.46%。南方湿润的石灰岩熔岩地区会形成另一种称为“石漠化”的荒漠化现象。

我国治理沙漠工作从1949年就开始进行了，但长期以来沙漠扩展的面积远远超过治理的面积，每年还向外扩展3436平方千米。20世纪末以来，治理力度加强，治理技术也有所改进，到2000~2004年间，沙漠扩展程度已有所好转，每年净减少的面积达1285平方千米。

(三) 气

近几十年来，我国大气污染也是相当严重的。亚洲开发银行曾发表的资料指出，亚洲高速发展的大都市中，北京的空气最脏。按世界卫生组织(WHO)的安全标准，空气中威胁健康的悬浮颗粒量为 20 微克/立方米，巴黎为 22 微克/立方米，而北京达到 142 微克/立方米。世界污染最严重的 10 大城市中，中国占了 3 个。全国 600 座城市中，大气质量符合国家一级标准的不到 1%，而有 48.1%的城市，大气质量处于中度或重度污染，主要是由于空气中悬浮颗粒指标高所引起的。全国约有近 2 亿人口吸不到新鲜空气，有 1500 万人患支气管疾病和呼吸道癌症。

1. 大气污染的源头

大气污染源主要是城市及城镇工厂排放的二氧化硫(SO_2)、一氧化碳(CO)、二氧化碳(CO_2)等有害有毒气体。今年来，大中企业经过设备改造，排放有所减少，而全国的小化工、小皮革、小电镀、小造纸、小冶炼组成所谓的“五小”企业，仍旧是污水和废气的重要来源。

我国汽车工业近十年来蓬勃发展。随着经济发展，人民生活水平不断提高，据报道，北京市日增私车近千辆。汽车尾气排放的氮氧化合物，对人体健康影响很大。氮氧化物在夏天经阳光照射后产生光化学烟雾，加剧了哮喘和肺气肿患者的病情。此外，各地大兴土木，工地所造成的污染，以及如雨后春笋似的大小餐饮业所排放的污染气体也是不可忽视的。

北方的冬春时节，经常会刮沙尘暴。沙尘暴确实存在，但近年来随着沙漠治理及人工防护林的种植，沙尘暴的次数已逐渐减少。多数沙尘天气的沙尘不是从内蒙古、黄土高原或蒙古人民共和国来的，主要的来源却是本地存在的大量裸土和市民乱扔的果皮、纸屑等垃圾。北方一些城市的有关部门在清洁卫生方面存在误区。在室外扫除时，把土壤表面生长的野草全部铲除，与其他垃圾一起在当地焚烧，产生的烟雾不仅污染空气，而且裸露的土壤经人们不断踩踏后，形成大小不同的颗粒物，成为城市的主要尘源。

北方大气污染的另一个重要原因是各地农村在田头焚烧玉米、小麦等作物的秸秆。焚烧产生的烟雾除有大量 CO_2 外，甚至影响机场飞机的正常升降。

我国是一个以煤作为主要能源的国家。国产煤含硫较多，燃烧后产生的 SO_2 与大气中的水汽结合，形成酸雨，不仅污染环境，对农作物、野生动植物，以及森林、水体、土壤等都带来很大危害。福建省 23 个城市中有 21 个出现了酸雨。

2. 我国的能源及全球变暖

我国能源结构中煤炭占 66%，石油占 20%，风能、水能、核能等占 14%。1959 年后，我国没有石油的局面虽然改变，但随着经济快速发展，石油进口量却逐年增加。2007 年，我国的石油消耗 49.7%依赖进口；有关部门预计，2020 年将有 71%的石油需要进口。发达国家核能占工业能源的 16%~30%，而我国目前仅占 1.92%。从资源量来分析，能源资源今后可能成为制约我国经济持续快速增长的重要因素之一。当然，能源消耗带来的环境问题也需要高度重视。对于全球变暖，是自然现象还是人类活动造成的，国际上有不同的观点。但是，人类活动造成全球变暖加剧或变快则是肯定的。国际权威机构、政府间气候变化专门委员会(IPCC)在1990年的第一次评估报告中就明确指出："人类活动的温室气体排放使大气中CO_2、CH_4、CO等温室气体的浓度不断增加；大气CO_2含量增加1倍，未来全球平均地面温度增温的范围为1.5℃~4.5℃。"在2001年第三次评估报告中更明确的指出："新的有力证据表明，过去50年观察到的大部分增暖可以归因于人类活动。"全球变暖将会造成海平面上升，沿海城市沉浸；导致洪水和干旱，从而使农作物减产；CO_2浓度升高还会使小麦、大麦、稻米和土豆等作物的蛋白质含量平均降低15%；以及其他的环境问题。据报道，目前CO_2排放量美国第一，我国处于第二的位置，但可能在不久的将来，我国会上升到第一位。因此，控制CO_2等温室气体的排放也是我国面临的重要任务。

(四) 生物多样性

进入工业文明后，世界各地的生物多样性遭到十分严重的破坏，影响到经济社会的持续发展，甚至威胁到人类的地球上的生存。为了拯救生物多样性，在1992年联合国环境与发展大会上，由大多数国家的首脑共同签署了《生物多样性公约》。下文将从生物多样性的状况进行讨论。生物多样性一般可分为三个层次，即生态系统多样性、物种多样性和遗传多样性。

1. 生态系统多样性

1949年以来，我国的人口由4亿5千万急增至目前的13亿，加之经济发展所带来的负面影响，使我国的各种生态系统严重退化。森林生态系统，前几年仅占国土面积的14%，由于我国重视人工林的恢复，至今森林面积已达18.21%；草原生态系统中有90%存在不同程度的退化、沙漠化、盐碱化和石漠化；按照国际拉姆萨公约(即湿地公约)的规定，长期积水在6米以下的都为湿地。我国湿地生态系统中不仅大量湖泊干涸、污染，而且大批湖泊与沼泽地，由于人口增加、缺乏耕地而被围垦造田。例如，东北的北大荒就有1/3左右的沼泽地被改造。沿海的红树林生态系统与珊瑚礁生态系统也都是湿地，可是这两个生态系统的破坏也十分严重。我国的珊瑚礁分布极为有限，仅在海南岛、西沙、东沙等少数地区。据最近的报道，海南岛珊瑚礁已快被挖完。当然，我国还有其他各种生态系统，但仅从上述几种生态系统遭受的破坏，人们不能想象其后果的严重。例如，以1954年与1998年我国分别发生过的全国性洪灾比较，由于上述各种生态系统遭受破坏，1998年暴雨导致的洪水量虽然小于1954年，但给社会造成的损失和死亡人数却大于1954年。

2. 物种多样性

与国际上情况一样，我国不少生物物种已受到威胁，甚至灭绝。中国环境与发展国际合作委员会生物多样性工作组曾对我国近一万种生物进行调查评估，报告中指出，受威胁的无脊椎动物为35%、脊椎动物为36%、裸子植物为70%、被子植物为87%。2008年4月中国科学院华南植物园主任黄宏文在国内召开的国际会议上报告，近30年来，我国野生植物物种约有 6000 种受到威胁，有 104 种植物面临濒危或极危。脊椎动物中，海南岛我国特有物种长臂猿仅留下 15 头，长江中的鲥鱼以及华南虎等都已濒临灭绝。据最新调查，国宝大熊猫在野外生存的还有近 6000 头，但由于生存环境受到隔离，可能会发生近亲繁殖甚至有可能灭绝等问题。

3. 遗传多样性

遗传多样性即基因多样性，即物种下的品种、亚种等，各种性状，如抗虫、抗干旱、高产等等，都是由分别存生于各种品种中的基因来决定的，对于培育农作物和家禽、家畜都是重要的遗传资源，是关系到子孙万代粮食、肉食问题的源泉。联合国粮农组织(FAO)告诉我们，世界上 50%左右的基因资源已经丢失。我国存在的问题也是严重的。例如中国是大豆和水稻的起源地，但由于各种生态系统遭到破坏，野生的大豆和水稻资源已大量丧失。

生物多样性的丧失或破坏是生物栖息地破坏、乱砍滥伐、滥垦滥挖、乱捕乱杀、围湖造田、野生动植物走私、环境污染、外来物种入侵，以及全球变暖等等因素造成的。我国自加入国际《生物多样性公约》后，在生物多样性保护与持续利用方面以及做了大量工作，但应该说生物多样性的保护，特别是各种生态系统的恢复，任重而道远。

三、应该走生态文明的道路

以上分析，说明我国的经济发展基本上沿袭了传统的工业文明方式。在经济持续高速增长的几十年间，没有顾及到地球生态圈大循环的整体和全局，忽视了环境容量和自然资源的承载力，以致到了环境恶化和发展不可持续的境地。为了改变上述局面，中央提出落实科学发展观，建设资源节约型、环境友好型社会，并明确指出，在“十一五”期间节能 20%，减排 2%的具体目标。在党的十七大报告中又首次提出“建设生态文明”作为全面建设小康社会的一项重要目标。这就标志着我们党对发展与环境关系认识上的飞跃；在深刻反思工业化沉痛教训的基础上，认识和探索到一条可持续发展的途径。生态文明理念所强调的是按照自然生态规律办事，经济社会的发展既要考虑到人类生存的需要，又要顾及到生态、资源和环境的承载力，以实现人与自然的和谐、发展与环境的同步。

要实现生态文明的理念，下面几点是必须重视的。

(一) 循环经济

传统工业化的生产方式是“资源—产品—废弃物”，这种生产方式不仅造成大量的资源浪费，也带来了严重的环境污染。发达国家已经较普遍地推行了循环经济的方式，经济活动变成为“资源—产品—废弃物—再生资源—无废弃物”的一种循环过程。在我国南方农村已有实践经验。农村的养牛场，除生产牛奶、提供牛肉外，可将排泄物与秸秆，以及其他能利用的有机物放进沼气池里沤肥；产生的沼气，提供农户作为能源。沤肥，对现在大量使用的造成土壤板结的化肥来说，是一种极好的改良土壤的有机肥。有机肥施入玉米田后，可使作物增产。玉米和秸秆是再生资源，既可作为牛的饲料，又可将牛的粪便和秸秆返回沼气池继续沤肥。这是一个无废弃物的循环经济的好案例。循环经济的生产方式不仅农业可行，工业、环保等行业都是可行的。循环经济可从根本上节能、降耗、减排，做到“资源消耗最小化，环境损害最低化，经济效益最大化”。

循环经济在我国尚处于发展的初级阶段，要加大科学研究和技术开发的投入，要建立完善的循环经济法律法规，并要建立激励、约束和评价的指标体系。我国在2004年已建立起8个试点省，如贵阳市已出台了《贵阳市建设循环经济生态城市条例》。

(二) 偿还生态欠债

由于长期以来我国实际上走的是“先污染，后治理”的道路，造成巨额的生态赤字。国际上对生态赤字有一种衡量标准——生态足迹，即“满足人口中每个成员平均现有生活方式需要多少肥沃农田和陆地水资源”。设在瑞士的世界自然基金会《2006年地球生态报告》中称，2006年中国人均生态足迹量为1.6公顷。这表明，中国现有13亿人口，要保证每个成员现有生活方式，要么需要将土地和水域的面积扩大一倍，要么需要将生态足迹缩小到每人0.8公顷，也就是说，当年我国的生态赤字也是0.8公顷，比世界平均指数高出一倍。据专家测算，“十五”期间我国生态赤字在5万亿人民币左右。要扭转环境恶化，建设生态文明，就必须偿还生态赤字。这对我们来说，又是一个严峻的挑战。

(三) 绿色GDP

GDP是国民经济总产值，并未考虑到生产过程中所产生的一系列环境污染及生态退化等造成的经济损失。这种计算既不代表真正的国民经济收入，也不符合生态文明的理念。因此，国家有关部门于前几年提出了“绿色GDP”的概念。“绿色GDP”是从现行统计的GDP中，扣除由于环境污染，自然资源退化、教育低下、人口数量失控、管理不善等因素引起的经济损失成本，从而得出真实的国民财富总量。

(四) 加速生态文明的建设

中央提出“建设生态文明”具有划时代的意义，既保证了我国经济发展方式的转变，也保证了我国会逐步从工业文明向生态文明的过渡，并最后把中国建设成为一个生态文明的国家。对各级干部来说，除了思想观念的转变外，更重要的是改革和完善干部政绩考评标准，把以GDP为经济社会发展的主要考核标准，逐步过渡到以“绿色GDP”为主要内容的新的核算评价体系；使原来各级干部主要关心经济增长速度，变为全面关心经济、资源、社会、民生的协调持续发展。建设生态文明决不仅是政府部门的事，企业、社会、直至个人都是责无旁贷的。对个人来说，要继承勤俭节约的优秀传统，可从身边的小事做起，小到不乱扔烟头、果皮纸屑，不随便吐痰；大到有私家车的个人，参与“一个月少开一天车”的活动，都是为建设一个生态文明社会应做的贡献。

具有中国特色的社会主义，在科学发展观的正确方针指导下，必然会以较快的速度跨入生态文明的新时代。

本文原载：绿色文明——建设资源节约型环境友好型社会科普讲座. 2010 汤寿根主编. 北京：知识产权出版社，37-56

拯救生物多样性就是拯救人类自己

钱迎倩

(中国科学院植物研究所)

本讲座讲解了什么是生物多样性以及生物多样性给人类带来了哪些福祉；阐述了地球生物多样性的现状，并对我国生物多样性的现状进行了分析；提出了保护生物多样性的措施。

国际上自然保护的权威机构——世界自然保护联盟(IUCN)2008 年 10 月在西班牙巴塞罗那召开每四年一次的大会，与会的专家惊呼，地球上的动植物物种正在以前所未有的速度消失。专家们认为，这也许会是 6500 万年以来物种的第一次大规模灭绝。会议发布了一项哺乳动物的调查评估报告。报告指出，全球哺乳动物中 1/4 已濒临灭绝，一半正在消亡。这是来自 130 个国家和地区的 1700 多名研究人员参与，耗时 5 年，对全球已经定名的 5487 种哺乳动物生存现状进行调查的结果，其中处境最危险的是灵长类动物，也就是和人类关系最近的哺乳动物。哺乳动物中有 188 种处境极度危险，有大约 450 种先前被认为毫无灭绝之忧，但现阶段数量已在急剧地下降。

一、什么是生物多样性

《生物多样性公约》中对“生物多样性”的定义是指“所有来源的活生物体之间的变异性。这些来源主要包括陆地、海洋和其他水生生态系统及其所构成的生态综合体；生物多样性包括物种内、物种间的多样性和生态系统的多样性”。也就是说，地球上的陆地和海洋中存在着各种各样的生态系统，在各种不同的生态系统中生活着丰富多彩的动物、植物和微生物物种，还有物种下的品种、变种、品系等等。在生机勃勃的生态系统中，动物与动物之间，动物与植物之间以及它们与微生物之间无时无刻不在相互作用着，生态系统中生物与非生物间也在不断地相互作用者。这样就构成了一个所谓的生态综合体。生物多样性包含着这么深层次的含义，为了分析方便起见，我们往往从三个层次上来进行叙述：将物种间的多样性称为物种多样性，物种内的多样性称为基因多样性或遗传多样性，各种不同生态系统的多样性称为生态系统多样性。

二、生物多样性给人类带来无穷无尽的福祉

本文的题目是“拯救生物多样性就是拯救人类自己”，为什么提得这么高呢？我们从图 3-1 中可以看到生物多样性是基础，从物种、基因及生态系统等各方面提供各种各样的生态系统服务。通过多方面的生态系统服务，人类得到了足以维持人类生活的基本物质，维护了人类的健康、安全，以及其他直接或间接的福祉。可以这么说，生物多样性一旦在地球上遭到毁灭性的破坏，人类就不可能得到各种各样生态系统的服务，从而也就会从地球上消亡。那么生物多样性又给人类提供了哪些生态服务呢？

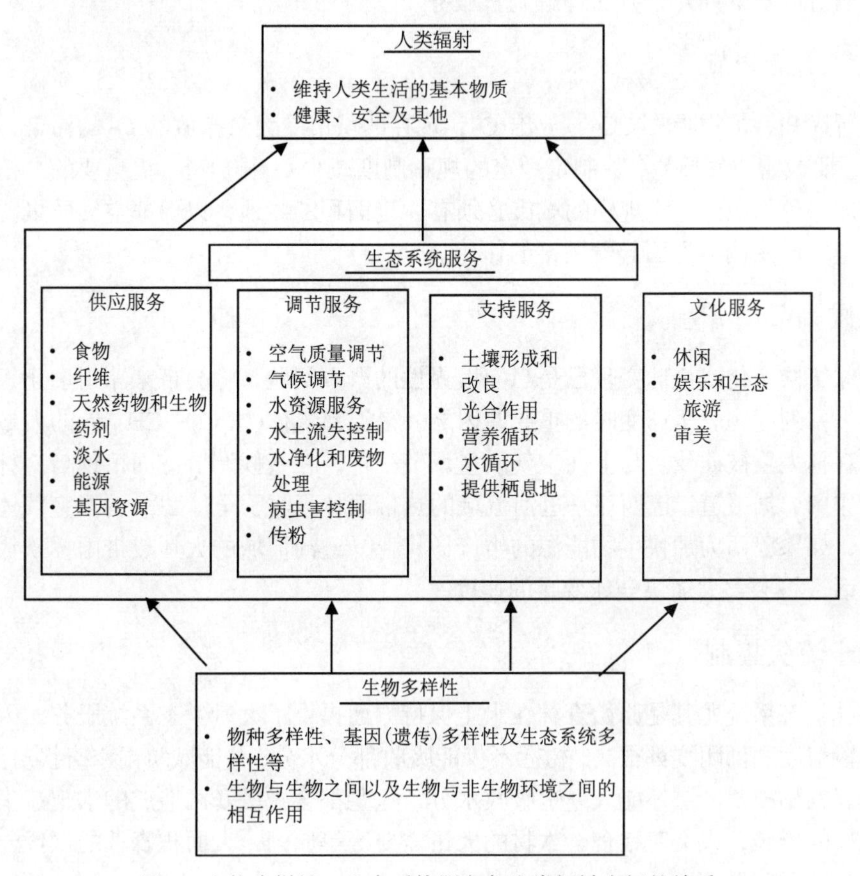

图 1 生物多样性、生态系统服务与人类福祉之间的关系

(一) 供应服务

粮食作物、家禽、家畜、鱼、水产品，以及某些野生的动植物产品是人类生存所必需的；包括木材、棉花、人造纤维、丝绸等在内的各种纤维也是人类生活离不开的；医治疾病所用的生物药物和天然药物；煤和石油等能源；淡水；农作物、家禽、家畜，以至观赏植物中的基因等等都是由生物多样性来提供的。这里将基因资料对人类的重要性

作一补充说明。基因资源也称遗传资料，包括不同物种的基因资源，也包括一个物种内不同品种、变种中的基因资源，后者就是被称为遗传多样性。以粮食作物小麦为例，小麦有各种各样的品种，不同的品种中含有不同的基因。这些抗干旱、抗虫害、高产等基因存在于不同的作物品种中。育种家要培育出高产、优质的各种新品种，这些基因资源都是不可或缺的。这也就说明了保护遗传多样性，或者说保护好农作物的各种品种的重要性。

(二) 调节服务

我们可以从下列几个方面理解调节服务。

(1) 空气质量调节

众所周知，植物吸收 CO_2，放出 O_2，现在的城市受大量排放的 O_2 的污染，空气质量很差。要改善空气质量，除制定一定的规章制度减少 O_2 排放外，更重要的是植树造林以及增加绿色面积。一定规模的城市必须有一定面积的绿地，以保证空气质量。植物及森林在空气质量调节方面起着关键的作用。

(2) 气候调节

全球气候变化或全球变暖已是当前世界性的严重问题，将会带来冰川融化、海洋面上升等一系列问题。全球变暖的重要原因之一是温室气体(如 O_2、CH_4 等)的大量排放以及原始森林大量被砍伐。与上面空气质量调节一样，在气候调节方面植物与森林也起着重要的作用。据报道，巴西亚马逊河流域的热带雨林吸收了全球 20%的温室气体。人们很担心，如果巴西为加快生物能源的生产，将亚马逊河流域的大片热带雨林砍伐后改种玉米的话，将会大大加快全球变暖的速度。

(3) 水土流失控制

森林生态系统尤其是原始森林在水土保持方面提供了大量生态系统服务。因为原始森林的覆盖度和郁闭度都很高，树冠不仅能吸收部分水分，并能减缓雨水直接打到地表，此外地表的枯枝落叶层还能大量地吸收水分，这些都会减缓暴雨造成的水土流失。由于世界人口的增长，人类对粮食、木材的大量需要等等原因，大面积森林的砍伐，已成为世界性的严重问题。

(4) 水净化和废物处理

包括沼泽地、大量浅水湖泊以及长期积水在 6 米以上的地方都属于湿地生态系统。湿地不仅能使污水内的废物沉淀下来，并经其中的各种生物的分解，使污水得以净化。应该说自然界的湿地生态系统就是一个水净化和废物处理场所，被人们称为“地球之肾”。可是由于地球人口增长对粮食的需要及其其他种种原因，大量湿地生态系统被改造，湿地大面积减少也成为世界性的问题。

(5) 病虫害控制

正常情况下，自然界的各种生态系统应该是相对稳定的，系统中发生的病虫害都能自然地得到控制。鼠害是目前我国草原生态系统退化的重要原因。草原中的老鼠繁殖快、数量大，但即使在没有人类活动干扰的情况下，草原中本身还生存着各种老鼠的天敌，如老鹰、猎隼、蛇等，因此老鼠不可能大量繁殖而发生鼠害。但目前我国草原中鼠类天敌大量减少，蛇被人类作为野味抓捕；猎隼被捕获后走私到国外可赚到巨额的利润，数量已所剩无几；老鹰也由于滥捕，数量也已很少，从而造成草原鼠害泛滥，不少草原退化严重。

(6) 授粉

许多水果和蔬菜以及自然界的不少植物都是需要授粉的。生态系统中的动物，包括蝙蝠等哺乳动物，以及鸟类、蜜蜂、蝴蝶等都是重要的传粉者，但可能由于栖息地的破坏和滥用杀虫剂等因素，全球传粉者数量正在减少，损失巨大。

(三) 支持服务

(1) 提高栖息地

各种各样的生态系统都为不同的生物提供了栖息地。当前，导致相当数量的动物濒危或灭绝的原因之一就是栖息地的丧失。如海南岛热带雨林中生存着中国特有种类——海南长臂猿，但随着海南岛原始森林大量被砍伐，海南长臂猿由于栖息地的丧失，目前仅在霸王岭一带还留下 15 只左右。

(2) 土壤形成和改良

土壤既是植物必要的支撑物，又是植物吸取生长必需的养分、水分等物质的来源。土壤在形成过程中，首先是依靠先锋植物地衣固着在岩石上，随着地衣的生长分泌出地衣酸，使岩石逐渐侵蚀，再在随后其他生物的共同作用下逐渐形成的。土壤的改良除了人工因素外，各种生物如蚯蚓等也都起着重要的作用。

(3) 光合作用

O_2是绝大部分生物包括人类的生存所不可缺少的物质。自然界的光合作用是植物利用太阳能吸收 CO_2，放出 O_2，是 O_2 制造的唯一来源。

(4) 营养循环

营养循环是维持各种生态系统正常运作的重要环节。食物链就是营养循环的典型例子。在一个湖泊生态系统中，包括浮游植物和高等植物在内的植物是生产者。它们吸收水中的氮、磷、钾等营养元素，利用光合作用进行繁殖，成为湖泊中的生产者。这些植物被一些吞食浮游生物或啃食高等植物包括鱼在内的动物作为食物，这些动物又成为食肉动物的食物，它们就是生态系统中的消费者。动植物的尸体或动物的排泄物又被湖泊中的分解者，包括低等动物、细菌和真菌分解成各种营养成分，这些营养成分又成为植物生长所必须的元素。这就是营养循环。

(5) 水资源服务

我们先举湿地生态系统的例子来说明水资源服务。如喜马拉雅山脉的高原湿地是恒河、印度河、湄山，以及长江、黄河等大河的发源地，流域人口超过10亿。因此湿地国际等国际组织与中国、印度、尼泊尔等国家政府合作采用多项措施来保护这一地区的高原湿地。此外，湿地在抵御洪水、调节径流方面也起着重要的作用。为了保障水资源的供应，各国都非常重视水资源涵养林的保护。

(6) 水循环

森林生态系统在水循环方面起着重要的作用。雨水经枯枝落叶层和根吸附，多余的一部分渗入地下，一部分作为径流缓缓地下断流向江河。地面上的植物又通过蒸腾作用把水汽送往大气，形成雨雪等，使地球上的水得到充分的循环。

(四) 文化服务

(1) 休闲

人们在工作之余，除了到电影院等娱乐场所进行休闲外，现在已有更多的人愿意到森林、草原以及湖泊等生态系统中休闲。森林被称为自然氧吧，是休闲的好去处。

(2) 娱乐和生态旅游

很多自然景观也是人们进行娱乐和生态旅游的场所，现在我们提倡的生态旅游，也就是一种只留下足迹、留下照片，不破坏生态系统中任何组成部分的旅游。

(3) 审美

各种生态系统都有各自独特的美，不少优秀的油画、照片都是以大自然不同的景观，森林、草原或湿地等各种生态系统作为主题来表达的。不仅生态系统是这样，地球上的不少动物物种、植物物种，往往以它们的整体或植物的花、叶等的美丽而被人们所欣赏。

总之，生物多样性通过各种形式的生态系统服务，给人类带来一系列直接或间接的福祉，让人类能在地球上健康、安全地生活。因此一旦生物多样性遭到破坏，必然威胁到人类的生存。

三、地球上生物多样性的现状

世界自然基金会(WWF)于2006年10月24日发表的《2006地球生命力报告》称，人类正以前所未有的速度消耗地球资源，到2050年将用掉相当于两个地球的自然资源。

在生物多样性方面，1970~2003 年，脊椎动物物种减少 1/3。检测的 695 中陆地物种、344 种淡水物种和 274 种海洋物种，分别减少了 31%、28%和 27%。1961~2003 年，生态足踪增加 3 倍多，CO_2 排放量增长 9 倍。WWF2008 年 10 月 29 日有发布报告指出，超过 3/4 的地球人口都生活在生态债务国，也就是消费超出了其生态承受能力的国度中，如果人类再从地球那里不计后果地索取，那将把地球拖进生态“信贷危机”的深渊。人类对森林、水、土壤、空气和生物多样性等自然资源不断增加的需求，已超出地球更新这些自然资料能力的 1/3。

上面讲的是一个总的趋势，就生物多样性而言，由于人类过度的开发，环境越来越恶化以及外来入侵物种等原因，地球上的生物多样性遭到严重破坏。从生态系统层次上我们举森林、湿地生态系统的例子。地球上约 45%的原始森林已经消失，占全球已知物种半数以上的热带雨林，每年被破坏的面积达到奥地利国土面积的大小，约 83853 平方千米。21 世纪初，联合国有关报告指出，一个世纪以来，世界至少一半的湿地被开发和改造，用湿地种植稻米或其他农作物，有的湿地因河流开发建坝蓄水而逐渐走向消亡。这些湿地维系着 1 万余种鱼类和 4000 多种两栖动物的生存。又如海洋中的珊瑚礁生态系统，10%已遭破坏，剩下的又有 1/3 在 10~20 年内有可能面临崩溃。又如红树林生态系统一半以上已消失，余下的也很脆弱。据科学家们评估，地球上每天，甚至每小时都有物种正在灭绝。由于人类活动的破坏，导致物种灭绝的速度至少是自然灭绝的 100 倍，甚至更多。据统计，地球上的物种至少有 1500 万种，但已定名的仅仅为 170 万种左右，多数物种虽已定名，但并不知道能给人类带来什么福祉。不少物种连名字都来不及定就在地球上灭绝了。遗传多样性为人类提供遗传资源，特别是在保障人类子孙万代的食物供应方面具有举足轻重的作用。可是联合国粮农组织(FAO)告诉我们，由于种种原因，地球上 75%的遗传资源到 20 世纪末已经消失了。

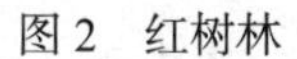

图 2 红树林

图 3 珊瑚礁

生物多样性的严峻形势引起世界各国政府的重视。1992 年 6 月在巴西里约热内卢召开的联合国环境与发展大会通过了由世界多数国家参与的《生物多样性公约》。该公约的三个主要目标是：保护生物多样性，可持续利用生物多样性，以及平等地分享因为使用遗传资源而获得的利益。《生物多样性公约》的制定对全球的生物多样性的保护及持续利用起到了非常积极的作用。2005 年 1 月 24~28 日，科学家又在巴黎召开了国际生物多样性科学和管理会议。会议发表了《生物多样性巴黎宣言》，宣言的主要内容共三点：第一，生物多样性是一种自然遗产，并不是所有人类生活的资源；第二，生物多样性正在不断地遭受人类活动不可逆转的破坏；第三，要加倍努力地发现、了解、保护和持续利用生物多样性。

四、我国生物多样性现状分析

我国生物多样性的丰富度在世界上排第八位。一个原因是我国地域宽广，有从热带到寒温带非常丰富的气候带，并且地形也非常复杂，世界上最高峰——8848 米的珠穆朗玛峰在中国，世界上第二最低点——吐鲁番地区海平面下 154 米得艾丁湖也在中国。另一个原因是我国受第四纪冰川的影响比较小，灭绝的物种相对较少，保留了大量如大熊猫、水杉、银杏、银杉等古老的孑遗生物。

正像世界生物多样性一样，我国的生物多样性也遭到了非常严重的破坏，特别在最近 50 年左右，破坏的程度尤为严重，据《中国物种红色名录》记载，在我国被评估的 10211 个物种中，无脊椎动物受威胁(极危、濒危和易危)的比例为 34.74%，接近受威胁(近危)的比例为 12.44%，脊椎动物受威胁的比例为 35.92%，近危比例为 8.47%；裸子植物受威胁和接近受威胁的比例分别为 69.94%和 21.23%；被子植物分别为 86.63%和 7.22%。其中植物的濒危物种比例远远超出了过去的统计。

图 4　生物多样性

下面我们来剖析生物多样性被破坏的状况。

(1) 森林大量被砍伐

由于人口增长，耕地急剧递增，不少森林被改造为农田。还由于经济快速发展对木材大量的需要，我国森林被大量砍伐。第五次(1994~1998 年)森林资源清查时，我国森林覆盖率仅占国土面积的 16.55%，其中幼小林竟占到森林总面积的 71.1%。人们逐渐认识到其严重性，采取了退耕还林等一系列政策，到第六次(1993~2003 年)全国森林资源清查时，全国森林面积已达 17491 万公顷，覆盖率已提高到 18.21%。但我国人均森林面积仅为 0.132 公顷，不足世界平均水平的 1/4。

森林大面积减少，使其生态系统服务功能大大地减弱。水土流失严重，野生动植物丧失了栖息地。我国人工林营造面积达到0.53亿公顷，居世界首位，但人工林呈物种单一化的现象，从生态系统服务功能的角度来衡量，人工林是远远不能和天然林相比较的。

图5 被砍伐的林地

(2) 草原严重退化

我国天然草原面积为3.93亿公顷，约占国土面积的41.7%，其中可利用草原面积为3.31亿公顷，占草原总面积的84.3%，但90%的可利用天然草原已不同程度地退化、沙化。草原退化原因除了过度放牧和被改为农田外，就是人们乱采乱挖冬虫夏草、甘草及雪莲等中草药，还有搂发菜。发菜是生长在退化草场上的一种类似头发的蓝藻，由于谐音为“发财”，因而颇受欢迎，搂耙者用编得很细的耙子搂后，草根也全搂出来，造成不仅物种大量减少，草原生态系统也严重被破坏。内蒙古草原已有2.2亿亩由于搂发菜而造成荒漠化。草原退化的另一个原因是鼠害，老鼠的天敌——蛇，已成为人们的美味佳肴，猎隼与老鹰也几乎被抓光，因而造成老鼠泛滥。

(3) 湿地大面积减少

我国湿地总面积历史上曾达到65.70万平方千米，约占国土总面积的7%，而2004年的一项调查显示，我国湿地总面积已下降为38.48万平方千米，只占国土总面积的4%；已有50%的滨海滩涂湿地不复存在；约有13%的湖泊消失，还有约40%的湿地面临严重退化的危险。

造成湿地减少的主要原因有两个。其一是不少沼泽地被开垦改造成耕地，大量湖泊被围起来，抽干水后改造成农田。其二是全球气候变化，不少湖泊自然干枯。如黄河源区的湿地严重退化，1993~2004年间减少200平方千米，水位下降、面积萎缩，并出现断流。又如有“千湖之省”之称的湖北省，湖泊数由20世纪50年代的1066个减少到目前的182个，水面面积减少60%。鄱阳湖和洞庭湖等大湖水面也大面积萎缩。据统计，现如今我国每年有 20 个天然湖泊消失。

湿地生态系统的另一个问题是水环境恶化。由于过度排污，湿地生态系统服务功能退化，甚至丧失。目前全国有 75%的湖泊水质为富营养化，被严重污染。人类又掠夺性地利用水体中的野生动物资源，物种数量和种群数量都严重减少，渔业资源衰退。水土流失导致沼泽和湖泊的湖床抬高，抵御洪水等自然灾害的能力也大大降低。

图 6　扎龙湿地

图 7　金秋的三江平原沼泽

以上是森林、草原、湿地三种具有代表性生态系统的情况。各种生态系统被破坏。会造成什么后果呢?下面我们列举两个例子说明各种生态系统破坏后造成严重的综合后果。1998 年我国长江、松花江、珠江、闽江都发生洪灾，全国农田受灾面积达 2229 万公顷，死亡 4150 人，房屋倒塌 685 万间，经济损失达 2551 亿元人民币。分析造成如此严重损失的原因，20 世纪 50 年代后我国人口急剧增长，由 1945 年时的 4 亿 5 千万剧增到目前的 13 亿左右。为解决急剧增长人口的吃饭问题，大批的森林、草原、湖泊、湿地被开垦为农田，从而造成大量的水土流失，湖泊，河流河床抬高，大量农田甚至农舍处于过去湖泊、湿地等低洼地上，这些都是造成重灾的主要原因。根据历史记录，1954 年我国也曾发生一次全国性的特大洪灾。资料证实当年的绝对水量要大大高于 1998 年的洪水量，但有于各种生态系统相对完整，功能相对完善，以长江为例，中、下游的最高水位都普遍低于 1988 年，造成的损失自然就要小得多。

再举一个由于海洋中生态系统的破坏造成严重恶果的例子。海洋中的红树林生态系统在防洪、护提、积淤等方面发挥着重要的服务功能；珊瑚礁生态系统不仅养育着大量海洋中的物种，并在防止海啸上也具有服务功能。但遗憾的是全世界的红树林由于建设港口、挖虾塘等等原因，已遭大面积破坏；而珊瑚礁由于珊瑚作为艺术品被大量开采，该生态系统中的鱼类及其他生物也遭滥捕乱杀，再加之全球变暖的影响，目前珊瑚礁生态系统已有 20%被破坏，约 50%已接近崩溃边缘。这两个生态系统的重要性，可从 2004 年 12 月 26 日印度尼西亚由于 8.7 级大地震引发海啸的反思中体现出来，印尼、泰国等国家的这两个生态系统多数被严重破坏，从而造成海啸后的巨大损失，而马尔代夫等岛国由于政府一直提倡保护这些生态系统，因而海啸造成的损失要小得多。以上两个例子可充分地说明，保护各种生态系统的重要性，以及生物多样性与人类福祉的密切关系。

(4) 栖息地丧失

由于栖息地丧失是造成野生动植物濒危甚至灭绝的重要原因。如新疆罗布泊野骆驼国家级自然保护区曾经报告说，由于采矿、探险等人类活动不断伸向野骆驼栖息地，造成野骆驼活动区急剧缩减，由原来吐鲁番南部整个库鲁塔格山区缩小到帕尔岗山区东部很小的区域，如不对这些残存区域加以保护，野骆驼可能灭绝。又如野生稻是杂交水稻的重要基因库，分布最丰富的广东和海南两省，普通野生稻1182个分布点已消失80%；云南省在1950年发现26个普通野生稻分布点，到2002年时已消失掉25个，消失率达96.1%；广西玉林发现16公顷连片生长的野生稻，由于其原生境上游被开垦成鱼塘，加之造纸厂排污，分布面积也逐年下降。这种例子数不胜数。

(5) 生境破碎

具体而言就是物种生存环境由于隔离而呈岛屿化或片断化。生境岛屿化会使某些物种长期只能近亲繁殖而造成退化。以大熊猫为例，在2008年5月12日四川汶川大地震前，野外大熊猫数量约在1600头左右，但它们的种群是分布在25个破碎的岛屿上。每个被隔离的大熊猫种群只能在某个岛屿内进行近亲交配。据专家分析，如一个岛屿上栖息有200头大熊猫，经过12个世代(约140年后)，每个熊猫将有1/8的基因完全相同，这就意味着它们相互间相当于表(堂)兄妹的关系，存在遗传多样性可能衰退的问题。

(6) 野生生物的非法买卖

野生生物的非法买卖是造成物种濒危或灭绝非常重要的原因。在捕捉、采挖、运输到买卖的各个环节，都可能造成野生生物的大量死亡。野生生物的非法买卖，在我国是非常猖獗的。以兰花为例，兰科植物有重要的生态、观赏、药用、科研和文化价值，我国有170余属1200余种，其中500多种是我国的特有种，观赏价值较高的右450种，价格当然也非常昂贵。因此，目前野生兰花遭到日益疯狂地偷挖，有的野生兰花已难觅踪迹，其中不少是中国特有种，如兜兰属、兰属、石斛属、独蒜属和虾脊兰属等。我国丰富的兰花资源正日益枯竭。野生生物非法买卖的目的就是牟取高额的利润。曾有报道说，在非洲加蓬、喀麦隆等地用8美元就可买到一头大猩猩，经长途跋涉到欧洲马戏团后，可被以15万美元的高价收购，利润惊人。但可想象，一头能到达欧洲的大猩猩，不知道是用多少头大猩猩的生命换来的。野生生物国际贸易额每年高达数百亿美元，其交易额仅次于军火及毒品，成为国际上第三高交易额的物品。因此国际上专门制定了《濒危野生动植物物种国际贸易公约》来控制国际野生生物的非法交易。为了牟取高额利润，野生生物非法贸易在我国频繁发生。2008年云南省林业厅等执法单位破案547起，收缴野生动物5072只、野生动物制品近3吨。大熊猫是国家一级保护动物，狩猎或贩卖大熊猫皮可判死刑，但这类案子仍时有发生。2003年有关部门曾在拉萨破获特大野生动物毛片走私案，收缴虎皮、豹皮在内的毛皮共1500多张。而为满足部分食客的欲望，巨蜥、穿山甲、蟒蛇等野生动物的交易也十分频繁，国内数量不能满足就是走私进口。笔者20世纪90年代在广西东兴亲眼看到，清晨从河对岸的越南芒街一小船、一小船运来的包括穿山甲、巨蜥等野生动物。藏羚羊是生存在我国青藏高原一带的珍稀物种，由于其生存在三四千米的高寒地区，皮上有一层非常柔软的绒毛，国外专门有人收购它们的皮毛，织成称为“沙图什”的女人披肩。由于非常柔软，一条很大的披肩可从一个女人的戒指中穿过，因之被称为“戒指披肩”，每条价值近两万美元。高额利润促使不法之徒大量屠杀藏羚羊，使近百万头的藏羚羊一度仅剩两万头，如不再加以制止，藏羚羊这一物种在地球上有灭绝的可能。近 10 年来，我国政府采取各种措施，对不法之徒予以沉重打击，并对藏羚羊加以保护，使之种群已恢复到 5 万头以上。

图 8　惨遭猎杀剥皮的藏羚羊

(7) 外来物种的入侵

所谓外来物种，是指在当地的生态系统中原来没有这些物种，是人类有意引进或无意带进的，也包括随着自然界的风等媒介自然进入的。首先要明确的，不是所有的外来物种都是不好的。相反，在我们的实际生活中，包括粮食、木材、花卉等存在大量的外来品种，如玉米、番茄等粮食、蔬菜都不原产于中国，都是有意引入的外来种，现已成为我们生活中不可缺少的食物。但确实有一部分外来物种造成了我国各种生态系统的破坏，并对本地物种的生存带来了很大的威胁。

举两个很能说明问题的例子。水葫芦，又称凤眼莲，是浮在水面上形状像葫芦，开紫色像兰花一样漂亮花朵的水生植物，原产于南美。在 20 世纪初期作为观赏植物被引进到我国。这种植物在各种营养水平的水体上都能生长，营养水平越高，繁殖能力越强，一棵水葫芦 90 天甚至就能繁殖几万棵。虽然植株的干物质不多，但在 20 世纪 50 年代时农民将其作为猪饲料，在植株能越冬的我国南方不推自广。在相当一段时期内，我国水体的污染相对较轻，水葫芦未泛滥成灾。随着工农业及经济的发展，包括生活废水在内的各种污水都排向水体，水体的富营养化程度越来越高，水葫芦在南方泛滥成灾，造成航道阻塞、翻船等后果。更严重的是，由于水葫芦的繁殖速度远远超过其他物种，水体全被水葫芦覆盖，造成其他水生植物由于没有阳光而死亡。大量的水葫芦耗尽水体中的溶氧，致使水生动物由于缺氧而大量减少甚至灭绝。该水体生态系统中的物种多样性也大大减少。水葫芦入侵杭州西湖，入侵昆明滇池等例子不胜枚举，至今还只能用人工打捞的方法来消灭它，在杭州一天曾打捞出 60 吨。2005 年，由于受洪水影响，30000 立方米的水葫芦等漂浮物威胁福建泉州笋江桥，冲垮了新建成的笋江桥墩。当地有关部门采取定点爆破的方法来消除漂浮物，共炸了 25 次，用掉 400 千克炸药。

图 9 水葫芦

另一个例子是引进的外来种互花米草对环境及生物多样性造成的危害。互花米草是一种禾本科植物，20 世纪 60 年代时从国外引进。这种植物对营养要求不高，繁殖能力很强，在寸草不生的滩涂上就能迅速繁殖，后被南方沿海省份广泛引种。福建省霞浦县曾报道，该地区引进互花米草几年后，滩涂上全被长得一人高的该草覆盖。涨潮时当地沿海的物种随潮水进来，退潮时这些物种都被搁浅在大片的互花米草上，或被互花米草所拦不能退回大海中。白天这些物种都被太阳晒死。几年后，原先当地 100 多个物种全部灭绝。此外，沿海有很多养虾的虾塘也都被互花米草侵占而不能再养虾，给当地渔民造成很大的经济损失。更可怕的是一旦互花米草泛滥成灾就很难被除掉，不仅带来无法收拾的“生态灾难”，也带来严重经济损失。霞浦县一度曾提出“悬赏三十万，消灭互花米草”的口号。又如苏北盐城自然保护区和长江口上的崇明岛保护区是我国为候鸟迁徙而设立的两个自然保护区。候鸟就在保护区内的湿地里过冬。可是，目前这些湿地里已长满了成片成片的互花米草，原来湿地里候鸟的食物——沙蚕、贝类等都没有了。这些迁徒的候鸟丧失了栖息地，只能待在保护区外的水塘旁。这是又一个造成“生态灾害”的例子。

图 10　泛滥成灾的水葫芦

值得注意的是，外来入侵物种的生态效应往往是滞后的，在短期内见不到。如水葫芦，是在 20 世纪初作为观赏植物引入我国的，到发现这是一种会带来严重“生态灾难”的物种已是 20 世纪的后叶，那时要除掉它已非易事了。目前外来入侵物种已有 400 多种，对我国生态系统造成很大影响，每年造成的经济损失可达 570 亿元。

图 11　互花米草

(8) 此外，对资源的过度利用、过度捕捞，以及酸雨、赤潮、水体富营养化等环境污染，也都是造成生物多样性衰退的重要原因。

五、保护生物多样性的措施

《生物多样性公约》中明确提出保护生物多样性的措施有就地保护与迁地保护等。我国履约15年来，采取了恢复退化的生态系统、为濒危物种建立通道以及应用生物技术等措施。

(1) 就地保护

所谓就地保护，也就是建立保护地，其中建立自然保护区是主要的措施。自然保护区是保护生物多样性最可靠、最有效及最经济的措施。1956年我国建立了第一个国家级自然保护区——广东鼎湖山自然保护区。几十年来，我国已初步建成了布局较为合理、类型较为齐全、功能比较健全的自然保护区体系。到2005年底，已建立各级、各类自然保护区2349个，总面积150万平方千米，约占国土面积的15%，有效地保护了我国70%以上的自然生态系统，80%的野生动物和60%的高等植物种类，以及绝大多数的自然遗迹，特别是85%以上的国家重点保护野生动植物及其栖息地得到了保护，大熊猫、朱鹮、亚洲象、扬子鳄、珙桐、苏铁等一些珍稀濒危物种的种群明显恢复和呈现发展趋势。到2006年8月，国家级自然保护区总数已达265处，面积达92万平方千米，占国土面积的9.57%。

此外，风景名胜区和森林公园也都是就地保护的好形式。

图12 西三江自然保护区

图13 白马雪山自然保护区

(2) 迁地保护

如大熊猫、大象、藏羚羊等物种由于在自然界还有一定的种群数量，可采用就地保护的措施。但不是所有的物种都可采用的，如我国的华南虎、东北虎及扬子鳄等，在野外生存的数量已经很少，人们不知道它们生活在什么地方，这类濒危物种就必须用迁地保护的方法，也就是在一定的时期内采用人工饲养、人工繁殖的方法，以增加该物种的种群数量。在我国有多个物种人工饲养与人工繁殖工作都做得很好，例如扬子鳄、东北虎，以及麋鹿等等。可是人工饲养与人工繁殖的成功还不是迁地保护的最终目标。最后的成功是要把这些物种通过人工繁殖达到一定数量后，逐步训练它们回归自然的能力，最终回归到它们所生存的原来的生态系统中去，上面提到的扬子鳄、麋鹿，还有野马等物种，我国在回归自然方面做得相当成功。以扬子鳄为例，据估计目前在野外自然生存仅 100 多头。我国首先在安徽省人工繁殖成功，并在 2006 年成功地让人工繁殖的扬子鳄回归自然，放入现已辟为自然保护区的原来的扬子鳄栖息地中。为了要知道回归自然后这些扬子鳄能否在野外生存下来并能自然繁殖，安徽师范大学的研究人员给要回归的扬子鳄安装了无线电跟踪装置。此外，野马的回归也是相当成功的。野马原产于我国新疆，后在我国灭绝，幸运的是在我国野马灭绝前，部分野马已流往国外。20 世纪后叶有关单位从国外又引回了不少数野马，并在国内繁殖成功，达到一定的种群数量后作了回归自然的尝试。第一年冬天在野外生存不成功，第二年改进后再尝试已不仅能生存而且在野外已恢复自然繁殖能力，东北虎的人工繁殖早已成功，但在相当长的时期内还不能回归自然，原因是至今没有一个自然保护区内有完整的食物链，能使东北虎找到足够的食物，而不至于伤人。

(3) 恢复已退化的生态系统

近 50 年来由于人口急剧增加，大面积的森林、草地及湿地生态系统都被改造为耕地，从而造成大量水土流失、环境污染加剧等一系列后果。20 世纪后期，我国政府实施了退耕还林、退耕还草、退耕还湖等政策，这些政策的实施实际上恢复了相当面积的各种已退化的生态系统，在改善我国环境方面起到了重要的作用。

(4) 建立通道

前面讨论过物种灭绝的一个重要原因是由于栖息地的岛屿化。为解决这个问题，政府有关部门正在准备或者已经为一些关键的物种建立了通道。例如，为了解决大熊猫不再长期在一个下范围内进行交配的问题而建立了保护大熊猫及栖息地工程。除完善和新建保护区外，还准备建 17 条保护大熊猫的走廊带，使生活在远距离的大熊猫有机会通过走廊带而相遇。为解决长期近亲繁殖问题，有关部门曾把北京动物园和四川卧龙两个繁殖大熊猫卓有成效的基地的大熊猫进行交换，将两只北京动物园的大熊猫用飞机运到四川卧龙，又把两只卧龙的大熊猫用飞机运到北京动物园，以解决遗传多样性衰退的问题。

对藏羚羊的保护，除严厉打击非法盗猎者外，在建立青藏铁路时，还专门为藏羚羊建立了通道。由于藏羚羊有一个习性，在繁殖季节它们会群集地从一个地方迁徙到另一个它们以为隐蔽而安静的地方。为帮助它们顺利迁徙，不会因为火车铁道阻碍它们的迁徙，在它们迁徙的必经之路上建立青藏铁路五道梁北特大桥，大桥下留出足够宽的通道保障藏羚羊迁徙，以使它们能顺利地繁殖后代。

图 14 “高原精灵”藏羚羊在青藏铁路五道梁北特大桥动物通道迁徙

(5) 利用生物技术来拯救濒危物种

植物通过组织培养(包括器官培养、胚胎拯救及细胞培养等)进行大量繁殖，加上快速繁殖，一年内可繁殖出几万甚至数百万的新植株。虽然不能说每种植物都已经可以用这一技术来繁殖，但总体而言，植物组织培养技术已经相当成熟了。以前只是对植物可以做到，在动物上还不成功。直到近年来克隆技术的成功，让人们看到了生物技术在拯救濒危动物物种上的曙光。1997 年英国科学家用一头羊的体细胞通过克隆技术成功克隆羊“多莉”。

图 15 克隆羊“多莉”

在野生动物上最早获得克隆成功的是美国先进细胞技术公司。印度野牛在自然界生存的数量只剩几头了，该公司的科学家用印度野牛的体细胞首次克隆成功。随后意大利的科学家成功克隆了濒危物种——东方盘羊。美国科学家从已灭绝 20 多年的爪哇野牛的冷冻组织中分离到培养细胞，用这种培养细胞克隆出已灭绝的爪哇野牛。但要说明的是，他们用的冷冻组织是从当时还存活的爪哇野牛身上取得，并经过严格的程序在深度冷冻的液氮中保存的。也就是说，在液氮中保护的组织细胞还是活的。

图 16　印度野牛“诺亚”(第一只克隆的濒危动物)

此外众所周知，骡子是马和毛驴的后代，没有生育能力，近年来美国科学家也已成功地用骡子的胎儿细胞成功克隆出骡子。当然，现今的克隆技术在技术上还存在不少问题，成功率也还不高，尽管如此，也已为拯救快灭绝的动物物种指出了一条道路。

(6) 变废为宝

上面谈到外来入侵种对生态系统和生物多样性的危害以及带来严重的经济损失。科学家已作了大量研究来解决这些问题，或者是由对环境造成危害转化为利用这些外来入侵种的生长习性来解决环境污染问题，或者是如何让它们变废为宝。北京什刹海 2008 年夏天时利用水葫芦能吸收水体大量营养来解决水体富营养化，防止水华发生，曾种植过上千平方米的水葫芦。笔者认为由于水葫芦在北京的气候条件下过不了冬，如果成本问题能解决，是可利用这一途径的。但在南方，这种方法是行不通的。水葫芦在南方水体中泛滥，目前只能用人工打捞的方法来解决，每年我国在打捞水葫芦上的费用高达 5 亿人民币。

水葫芦泛滥在东南亚不少国家非常普遍。泰国某公司在 20 世纪后期利用生长很健康的水葫芦茎，干燥后编织成粗的绳索，再把这些绳索编到椅子或躺椅的框架上做成椅子或躺椅，据报道经济效益很好。随后上海有个别厂家也做了此类产品，很受一部分白领阶层欢迎。当然这是变废为宝的一个例子，但想通过这途径来解决水葫芦危害问题是不可能的。

紫茎泽兰也是危害我国很多省份的外来入侵物种。经分析，幼嫩的紫茎泽兰的粗蛋白含量达 20%，氨基酸种类齐全，达 16 种，总量可达 12.49%，超过许多禾谷类饲料。贵州安顺关岭苗族、布依族自治区群众对紫茎泽兰进行脱毒、脱臭、脱苦处理，制成猪饲料，有效地刺激禽畜的生长发育。另一种方式是利用紫茎泽兰高大的植株，粉碎加工后制成炭棒，烧制成炭，可广泛用于生产和生活中。

六、结语

我国1993年加入《生物多样性公约》，履约15年来，政府各级有关管理部门、科研单位及教育部门做了大量的工作，已取得十分明显的效果，但应该说还仅仅是万里长征的第一步。

(1) 加强宣传教育

拯救生物多样性必须要有全国人民，尤其是生物多样性丰富地区的原住民和年青一代的觉悟和积极参与。这始终是一个十分重要而紧迫的任务。

(2) 在这十几年中也出现了不少亟待解决的新问题

由于我国各种生态系统破坏严重，特别是一些繁殖能力强的物种，自然界它们的天敌少，又是属于国家保护的物种，当自然界或保护区不能满足它们的生存需要时，就大量地破坏庄稼，甚至伤人，野猪泛滥已是遍及南北的典型例子。西双版纳的野生亚洲象也已多次走出保护区，破坏群众的农作物，也有伤人的事件发生，又如宁夏的岩羊，经过20多年的保护，已由1800只发展到15000只，已快超过贺兰山环境的最大容量。由于天敌少，发展力强，不仅践踏破坏草地，还吃灌木枝叶，造成生态平衡失调。

(3) 还有大量的科研工作亟待科研单位来解决

特别是《巴黎宣言》中提到的，发现、了解、保护和持续利用生物多样性方面应是科研的重点，同时要去发现和总结原住民的传统经验并加以推广。

拯救生物多样性，任重而道远！

附　　录

钱迎倩年谱

1932 年　12 月 28 日出生于浙江省慈溪县

1937 年　随父母迁至上海生活

1938 年　就读于上海允中女中附属小学

1944 年　小学毕业，升入上海中学

1947 年　初中毕业，升入麦伦中学

1949 年　加入中国新民主主义青年团(1957 年改为中国共产主义青年团)

1950 年　高中毕业，考入滬江大学生物系

1952 年　就读于复旦大学生物系

1954 年　大学毕业，就读于南京大学生物系研究生班

1956 年　加入中国共产党

1957 年　研究生毕业，留南京大学生物系任助教

1959 年　调至中国科学院植物研究所植物细胞研究室工作

1966 年　任植物研究所植物细胞研究室副主任，主要从事植物原生质体培养和体细胞杂交的研究

1979 年　任植物研究所植物细胞学研究室主任

1980 年　赴加拿大国家研究委员会植物生物技术研究所做访问学者,从事原生质体培养和体细胞杂交研究

1981 年　晋升为植物研究所副研究员

1982 年　从加拿大回国，任植物研究所副所长和学术委员会副主任，7 月赴日本参加第五届国际组织培养会议

1983 年　任植物研究所所长, 在任期间充分发挥老一辈科学家在学科建设方面的作用，鼓励研究人员开展国际前沿和与国民经济密切相关的研究课题；落实党和国家的知识分子政策，通过科技职称晋升、解决职工实际困难等方式调动职工积极性；为适应研究所领导体制改革的要求，探索所长负责制条件下的研究所运行机制改革；利用中科院组织的研究所评价的机会，组织研究所学科定位的研讨活动等，努力探索植物研究所发展的新途径；健全学位工作制度等,积极选送青年研究人员出国深造；大力支持在四川都江堰建立以搜集杜鹃花为主的“华西亚高山植物园”。8 月赴瑞士出席第六届国际原生质体讨论会

1985 年　任植物研究所学位评定委员会副主任

1986 年　晋升为研究员，经国务院学位委员会批准任博士生导师

1987 年　植物研究所所长任职届满，调任中国科学院生物科学和生物技术局局长。在任期间，领导和制定了生物科学和生物技术“七五”、“八五”发展规

划，部署重大科研项目；特别支持生物分类区系研究和《中国植物志》、《中国动物志》、《中国孢子植物志》的编撰，以及标本馆和植物园建设的基础性工作；在研究所发展目标制定、学科调整、国家重点实验室和中科院开放实验室建设和科研队伍建设方面做了大量深入细致的工作

1989 年　获中国科学院自然科学二等奖；博士研究生邹吉涛和张士波与硕士研究生王朵和潘杰毕业

1990 年　获中国科学院自然科学一等奖；组建了中国科学院生物多样性工作组，组织召开国内首次生物多样性研讨会

1991 年　获国家自然科学奖二等奖，获中华人民共和国国务院颁发的特殊津贴

1992 年　推动成立中国科学院生物多样性委员会，并任常务副主任，主持日常工作；在国内首先倡导转基因生物风险评估和生物安全方面的研究；积极支持建立“湖北神农架生物多样性定位研究站”；博士研究生王铁邦、于春晖和李忠森毕业

1993 年　任《生物多样性》杂志第一任主编；博士研究生郭双生毕业

1993 年　任广西壮族自治区科学院院长，在任职期间，特别支持各所的青年研究骨干的工作，组织有关研究所与中科院相关研究所开展交流、合作或共同培养研究生以加强青年科研力量；促成广西植物研究所由中国科学院和广西科学院的双重领导体制的建立

1994 年　广西壮族自治区科学院院长任期届满，回到中科院植物研究所工作

1995 年　广西壮族自治区人民政府颁发奖状，表彰他为广西科技、经济与社会发展做出的积极贡献和显著成绩；博士研究生张远记毕业

1997 年　博士研究生恽锐和魏伟毕业

1999 年　退休

2000 年　加入中国科学院老科学家科普演讲团。主讲题目为“我国面临严峻的资源环境挑战”和“一个重要的环境问题——保护生物多样性”。2000~2002 年间到全国各地演讲 148 场

2003 年　做科普报告 14 场

2004 年　做科普报告 37 场。被北京市科学技术委员会、北京市科学技术协会、北京市环境保护局等 6 部门聘为“北京绿色奥运、绿色行动”宣讲团成员，面向学生和社区居民，做“以实际行动迎接绿色奥运”的科普报告，直至 2006 年

2005 年　做科普报告 24 场；当选中国科学院老科技工作者协会植物学分会第三届理事会理事长

2006 年　做科普报告 44 场；获北京市科学技术普及工作先进个人，获北京市科普创作协会“荣誉证书”

2007 年　做科普报告 41 场；奥运大讲堂组委会授予“奥运大讲堂荣誉讲师”证书；他所在的科普演讲团获中宣部、教育部、科技部等部委颁发的全国第二届社会教育“银杏奖”

2008年 做科普报告12场，5月后因病终止科普报告。2000~2008年间，共做科普报告320场，听众达8万余人，遍及山东、江西、河南、内蒙古、河北、浙江、广西、宁夏、福建、北京、天津和深圳等地

2009年 病中协助陈灵芝将“Plants of China”专著中的一章“Contemporary Vegetation”中文稿译成英文，共91页

2010年 4月20日19时22分于北京大学第一附属医院逝世

鞠躬尽瘁　死而后已

——纪念为我国植物科学发展奉献毕生精力的钱迎倩先生

钱迎倩先生 1932 年 12 月 28 日出生于浙江省慈溪县。1949 年加入中国新民主主义青年团(1957 年改为中国共产主义青年团)，1956 年加入中国共产党。1954 年毕业于上海复旦大学生物学系，1957 年南京大学生物学系研究生毕业后，留校任助教。1959 年调中国科学院植物研究所工作，1986 年晋升研究员，同年，经国务院学位委员会批准为博士生导师。历任植物研究所植物细胞学研究室副主任、主任，植物研究所副所长、所长。1987 年 2 月任中国科学院生物科学与生物技术局局长，1993 年 2 月至 1994 年 12 月任广西壮族自治区科学院院长。先后加入中国植物学会、中国细胞生物学会、中国遗传学会、美洲华人生物科学学会和中国科学院老科技工作者协会。担任过中国植物学会秘书长、副理事长。曾任国家级自然保护区评审委员会副主任、中华人民共和国濒危物种科学委员会副主任、国际生物科学联盟中国委员会成员、主席，中国科学院生物多样性委员会常务副主任、《生物多样性》主编。2010 年 4 月 20 日因病在北京大学第一附属医院逝世。

钱迎倩先生终生从事植物科学研究和科研管理工作，为植物科学研究事业和中科院植物研究所的发展奉献了毕生精力。

他在攻读研究生期间主要从事藻类学研究，20 世纪 60 年代开始从事植物细胞学研究。他最先开展玉米花粉的人工培养，取得了很好的成绩，后因“文革”动乱，此项工作被迫中止。20 世纪 70 年代初期，抓住当时难得的恢复科研秩序的机会，根据国际研究进展，选准刚刚兴起的植物生物技术前沿领域——植物原生质体培养和体细胞杂交，进行攻关研究，并积极参加吴素萱先生主持的《植物体细胞杂交参考资料》(第一集，1974)编写工作，为当时十分缺乏国外参考资料的国内同行提供了宝贵的支持。植物原生质体的分离、培养和体细胞杂交在当时是植物生物技术、植物细胞工程领域的前沿课题，也是公认的难度极大的课题。在这一领域研究中，钱迎倩先生不仅成功地对大豆和烟草原生质体进行了分离和纯化，而且将这两种不同科植物的原生质体进行了融合，得到了异科原生质体融合后的异核体。更为难能可贵的是他对这种异核体进行了染色体、同工酶和亚显微结构研究，从多方面分析、鉴定并证实了这一科间异核体的可靠性，为鉴定通过原生质体融合获得的体细胞杂种的真实性提供了范例和方法。他协助吴素萱先生具体组织和领导了原生质体培养和体细胞杂交研究，积极开展与国外同行的学术交流，掌握国际动态，使这一研究工作始终处于国际前沿水平。在他的参与下，研究组率先在国际上成功地获得了攻关多年未能突破的玉米原生质体再生植株，成为当年该学科领域的重大新闻，受到了国内外同行的好评。在后来的水稻原生质体的游离和培养、美味猕猴桃原生质体再生植株和无性系变异以及多种植物原生质体的超低温保存上都做出了创新性的研究成果。上述研究成果获得了中国科学院自然科学一等奖、二等奖和国家自然科学三等奖等多项重要奖励。主持或参与发表论著90多篇(部)。

在担任植物细胞学研究室副主任期间，积极倡导和推动植物细胞学研究由静态的细胞形态学研究向动态的细胞生物学研究转变，建立了“细胞生化研究组”，开展DNA、RNA及蛋白的分离和纯化；引进设备，建立了“电子显微镜组”，有效地推动了细胞学研究由光学显微水平向超微水平的进步。他热情支持花药培养等植物细胞工程研究，使这方面的工作取得了国际同行首肯的成果。在十年“文革”中，科研人员长期脱离科研工作，与国外的信息交流也被中断，资料十分匮乏，对植物科学的最新研究进展缺乏了解，给当时刚刚恢复招生不久的高校植物细胞学教学和科研造成很大困难。针对这种情况，钱迎倩先生积极组织、参与编译出版了多种植物细胞学和生物技术参考书籍。如《植物细胞》(1977)、《植物组织培养法》(1980)、《染色体处理》(1982)、《植物组织培养》(1986)、《植物细胞学研究方法》(1987)等，为当时的教学和科研提供了难得的最新资料，收到很好的效果，受到广泛好评。

钱迎倩先生任中科院生物科学与生物技术局局长后，把握我院生物科学与生物技术发展全局，领导和制定了“七五”、“八五”发展规划，部署重大科研项目。他十分关注前沿学科领域动向，积极推动我院生物多样性、全球变化、细胞分子进化以及系统生物学等领域的研究。同时，在当时科研经费困难的情况下，关心和支持分类区系研究、“三志”编研、标本馆和植物园建设等基础性工作。在中科院党组领导下，他积极组织和推动科研体制改革与研究所发展，在研究所发展目标的制定、学科调整、国家重点实验室和中科院院开放实验室建设、科技队伍建设，特别是优秀学术带头人培养和引进等方面做了大量深入细致的工作，为中科院生物科学研究事业的发展做出了重要贡献。

他是国内最早倡导并推动我国生物多样性研究的科学工作者，在他的积极推动下，中国科学院率先设立生物多样性重大研究项目，争取到生物多样性研究与信息管理世行贷款项目。1990年成立中国科学院生物多样性工作组，1992年成立中国科学院生物多样性委员会，并任常务副主任，亲自主持日常工作。这一组织有效地促进了我国生物多样性领域的研究工作，为国家的生物多样性保护和合理利用提供了有力支持。他积极组织并参与中国的生物多样性现状、保护对策、理论与方法等系列研究工作，参与编写《中国生物多样性保护行动计划》、《中国生物多样性国情研究报告》等，为国家生物多样性保护的纲领性文件提供了科学依据。在国内，他率先于1992年倡导转基因作物释放的环境风险及生物安全方面的研究，并指导研究生和年轻科研人员开展转基因抗虫作物对昆虫天敌的影响，转基因作物与其野生近缘种间的基因流，建立了检测方法和研究平台。在生物多样性研究方面，开展逆境植物群体在形态、蛋白和DNA水平上的变异及其对环境变化的适应研究等。1993年因年龄原因从局长岗位退下来后，仍然在推动我国生物多样性科学研究工作，包括转基因作物释放的环境风险及生物安全等研究领域发挥了重要作用。

钱迎倩先生不仅在科学研究方面取得了杰出的成就，在科研工作的组织管理方面也做出了突出贡献。1966年2月担任植物研究所植物细胞研究室副主任，协助吴素萱先生工作，1966~1972年因“文革”运动冲击而失去工作机会，1972年恢复研究室建制后，又担任由“文革”前的植物形态学研究室和植物细胞学研究室合并后组建的植物形态与细胞学研究室副主任，1979年担任植物细胞学研究室主任，1982年担任植物研究所副所长，协助汤佩松所长工作，1983年担任所长。由此可知，在钱迎倩先生的一生中，除了参加工作后的最初8年和“文革”期间的6年外，一直兼任着科研管理方面的领导职务。1980~1982年作为访问学者在加拿大国家研究委员会植物生物技术研究所从事研究工作的经历，使他强烈地意识到当时国内植物学研究状况与国际水平的差距。1983年担任植物研究所所长后，认真贯彻执行党的科技政策，在学科建设、研究项目组织和年轻人才培养等方面做出了重要贡献。

他在担任所长期间，充分发挥老一代科学家在学科建设方面的作用，积极支持各研究室继续开展服务于国家经济发展需要的研究，同时鼓励研究人员关注和开展领域前沿课题的研究；他十分重视研究生培养，积极选送年轻科研人员出国访问或从事研究工作，一直把人才队伍建设作为提高研究水平和研究所长久、持续、健康发展的根本大事来抓。

他十分重视调动研究队伍的积极性，认真落实国家和中科院有关政策，在党委和前任所长落实知识分子政策的基础上，通过科技职称晋升、努力解决职工生活困难等方式，想方设法提高各类岗位职工的工作积极性。在他的主持下，植物研究所顺利通过中科院组织的研究所评价，为后来的发展明确了方向。

他在担任广西壮族自治区科学院院长期间，深入调查研究，通过研究机构改革、重视人才引进和培养、扩大国内外合作等方式为广西壮族自治区科学院后来的发展奠定了重要基础。

钱迎倩先生在任职期间，十分注重了解植物学在国外的发展动态，研究学科发展的规律，重视研究所发展规律的思考，努力改进管理方式，以促进研究所健康、稳定地发展。他为人正直，为政清廉，严于律已，克已奉公，勤奋努力，忠于职守，深受同志们的尊敬和爱戴。他处理管理事务既讲原则又能结合具体情况做出决策，考虑全局性问题既有发展眼光又能坚持从实际出发。对下属既要求服从事业发展的需要又能设身处地体谅他们的难处，对同事和学生真诚平和，总是以平等协商的态度待人。待人处事中表现出的聪明睿智、博学多才、诚实守信、宽厚仁和的内在素质构成了他领导能力强的重要因素。他特别注重人才的培养，把青年科技工作者当作自己的朋友和研究所发展的希望，鼓励他们挑担子，尊重他们的学术见解。他既是青年科技人员的好老师，也是他们的好朋友。

1999年退休后，钱迎倩先生以极大的热情参加了中国科学院老科学家科普演讲团和北京绿色行动宣讲团，积极从事科学普及工作。2000年9月~2008年5月期间，作为中国科学院老科学家演讲团成员，他走遍了全国10个省2个直辖市，演讲320场，听众达8万多人，他的演讲受到各地听众的广泛好评。他所在的老科学家科普演讲团获由中宣部、教育部、科技部等部委颁发的“第二届中国青少年社会教育银杏奖”。2005年他又担任了中国科学院老科技工作者协会植物学分会第三届理事会理事长，在他的主持下，协会积极开展科技咨询和科学普及服务，多次受到有关方面表扬。

钱迎倩先生的一生，是努力探索植物科学未知领域的一生，也是为推动我国植物学研究事业不懈努力的一生。他把探索真理，推动事业的发展作为平生第一追求。做研究工作，不仅视野开阔，长于提出新的思想，而且身先士卒；从事科研管理，不仅忠于职守，而且适应发展需求，努力探索新的管理方式；即使退休后，也一直发挥自己的特长，为培养青年人尽心竭力。他把自己的人生价值融入追求国家富强，人民幸福的大事业中。

（中国科学院植物研究所钱迎倩同志治丧小组，牛喜平、孙敬三、王贵海执笔起草）

把握全局，尽心竭力，推动生物科学健康发展

——纪念钱迎倩局长辞世一周年

钱迎倩局长离开我们有一年了。他的突然辞世，让我们院原生物科学与生物技术局的老同事们感到万分悲痛。尽管我们分别多年，有的走到新的工作岗位，有的已经退休，但他那挚爱事业、真诚待人、成熟稳重和令人尊敬的科技工作领导者的形象，却深深地刻印在我们的记忆里。

迎倩局长于1987年初受命任中国科学院生物科学与生物技术局(以下简称生物局)局长，直到1992年底到届满离任历时五年。当时，伴随我国不断深化改革、开放的步伐，中科院正处于科技体制改革的转型期。周光召接任院长后，提出了“把主要力量动员和组织到为国民经济和社会发展服务的主战场，同时保持一支精干力量从事基础研究和高技术创新”的办院方针。为了加强学科发展，促进基础研究与应用的紧密结合，对院机关进行了较大幅度的机构调整，成立生物局等四个业务局。以原生物学部和合同局中有关生物学和生物技术的人员为基础组建了生物局。记得当时院里只任命了迎倩局长，另外两位副局长则是由他根据推荐亲自到研究所面谈确认后调任的，分别分管微观生物学和生物技术。考虑到专业背景和年龄结构的搭配，三位局领导组成了新的领导班子。局里工作初始，在迎倩局长的领导下，大家每天忙于处理日常管理工作和院领导交办的事项，同时还研究制定生物局职能，确定处室机构设置和人员编制，调配和任命干部，工作非常紧张和忙碌。但同志们都很努力，很快进入角色，工作井然有序，很快走上正常工作轨道。

二十世纪八十年代，国际上生命科学蓬勃发展，新的学科前沿和新兴交叉学科研究不断涌现，生命科学已成为自然科学的带头学科。各国政府对重大生命现象研究和应用创新给予了极大的关注和支持。如美国制定了“人类基因组作图和测序”、“脑的十年”两个重大研究计划，日本也宣布了“人类前沿研究领域科学计划”等。分析我国和我院生物科学的学科状况，如何加快学科调整，推动前沿研究领域发展，是摆在当时迎倩局长和生物局的一项紧迫任务。为了全面掌握国际生物学发展动向和学科前沿走势，迎倩局长领导局里同志组织翻译由美国著名科学家组成的委员会编辑的科学报告《生物学中的机会》一书，组织召开了“生物科学未来十年”学术研讨会，并请邹承鲁、沈允钢、洪德元、杨雄里等十五位专家撰写文章，就生物科学学科现状及研究热点、未来十年发展趋势和展望做了比较系统和全面的阐述,同时对我院学科发展战略如优先项目的选择、条件保证以及组织管理措施等方面提出了建议。这些调研和战略研讨，为全面和准确把握我院生物科学的全局、制订“八五”规划、十年发展规划以及院重大项目、开放实验

室的组织与建议，均发挥了至关重要的作用。这些工作对局里的同志们来说，犹如上了一次专业培训课，开阔了眼界，提高了大家的业务素质。

生物局在迎倩局长的领导下，依靠各学科专家委员会指导，通过院重大科研项目和重点学科的支持，对生物学微观和宏观领域的学科进行了调整，部署了新的科学前沿和交叉学科课题，并逐步呈现出明显效果。如开展了真核细胞基因表达调控、生物大分子复杂体系结构与功能、细胞信号转导、分子遗传与发育、胚胎干细胞与克隆、神经可塑性与脑神经活动的分子机制以及细胞与分子进化、生物多样性等研究。针对国际上人类基因组研究计划，在专家的建议下，科技部启动了水稻基因组研究计划，并由我院单位和科学家牵头实施。

在加强前沿学科部署的同时，迎倩局长也十分关注我院有长期深厚积累的传统生物学学科，如分类学、区系进化、生态学的稳定与发展。一方面促进其与分子、细胞生物学的结合渗透，通过设立科研项目和建立细胞分子进化和数量生态学两个院开放实验室予以支持。同时，在科研经费十分紧张的情况下，局里研究决定拨出专门支持费，保证了“中国植物志”、“中国动物志”和“中国孢子植物志”编研工作的正常进行，支持处于极端困难的标本馆和植物园，以及菌种、典型培养物保藏等基础性工作。迎倩局长对这些工作重要性有着深刻的理解，决策是很有远见的。他说，“三志”、标本馆、植物园等基础性工作，关系到几代科学家的劳动和心血，我们负有历史的责任，不能让它们在我们手里断了香火。今天看来，这些战略资源的研究工作，不仅体现了我院生物科学的深厚基础与优势，也为国家战略需求的有关研究，对其他生物学科发展提供了坚实的支撑条件。

生物多样性的保护与可持续利用研究，是基于区系分类学、生态学和生物资源等多学科综合的新学科研究方向，迎倩局长予以高度重视，并亲自组织科学家研讨。在他的主持下，出版了《中国科学院生物多样性研讨会会议录》，引起了国内学术界、行政管理部门的重视。在充分发挥我院这些分支学科优势基础上，从物种、生态系统与遗传多样性三个层面开展研究，将其列入院“八五”重大项目“生物多样性的保护与可持续利用的生物学基础研究”，得到了有力支持，从信息系统的建立、人类活动对生态系统多样性的影响、重要野生动植物种群的遗传多样性研究、濒危动植物保护生物学和种群生存力分析、中国濒危植物迁地保护研究、重要经济动物持续利用等方面，组织队伍，展开深入系统的研究，发表了不少专著和高水平论文，受到国际同行的关注。1992 年成立了中国科学院生物多样性委员会，他任常务副主任，亲自主持工作。我院率先开展生物多样性研究，是和迎倩局长的倡导、支持和领导分不开的。这不仅体现了他对学科发展动向观察的敏锐性和洞察力，同时有效地促进了我国生物多样性领域的研究工作，为国家生物多样性保护和合理利用，为后来国家“生物多样性保护行动计划”的编写提供了科学依据。

为贯彻执行我院办院方针，生物局在迎倩局长的领导下，十分注意抓生物技术创新研究以及在农业、医药及生物资源利用等重大应用研究领域的实际应用与推广工作。由一位副局长分工主管生物技术处工作。自 20 世纪 70 年代起生物技术崛起，我院由于长期基础研究的积累，起步早、发展迅速，一直是国家“七五”、“八五”生物技术攻关项目的主持单位和主要承担者，取得40%的攻关项目经费。1987年“863计划”启动实施，生物局马上行动，组织研究所科研人员争取任务。迎倩局长派副手到上海协调有关基因工程项目的课题组和专家，避免重复和竞争，联合申请项目。协助生物物理所争取到蛋白质工程专题的依托管理单位，确保该领域的优势地位。在迎倩局长主持工作期间，生物局成立并且发挥中国科学院生物技术专家委员会呼吁与推动作用，我国基因表达调控、蛋白质工程、下游生化工程技术等领域的研发工作得到了切实的加强。生物局还注重具有战略性的管理软课题研究。如对中科院生物技术科技队伍现状的调研与分析、科技专利状况与对策研究等，统一了大家对形势的认识，为此后的优秀人才引进及专利工作的推进发挥了积极作用。我院前后有近40多个研究所、1500多位科技人员在植物基因工程和细胞工程、转基因动物、基因工程疫苗和药物、单克隆抗体和蛋白质工程等方面取得一大批科研成果，其中有些产品进入市场并取得显著效益，为国家做出了重要贡献。“黄淮海平原中低产地区综合治理开发”工作，是当时我院李振声副院长亲自抓的一项重要任务。在我局设立了“农业项目办公室”。迎倩局长积极配合，在人力、经费各方面予以支持，这项工作经常是局务会的重要议题。“黄淮海平原中低产地区综合治理开发”研究取得了显著效果，为该地区农业可持续发展作出了重大贡献。在院重大项目的遴选和组织中，迎倩局长十分关注重大应用项目的立项和实施。如农业重要品种选育的新途径和新方法、农业病虫鼠害的防治、生物资源的开发利用与新药研发、生态系统与区域整治等研究项目都得到重点支持，其成果实际应用也得以有力推动。在‘小偃6号’小麦、‘诱变30’大豆等新品种的大面积推广种植以及“地奥心血康”等药物的市场化等方面都取得显著经济和社会效益。

科技体制改革是当时我院面临的一项重要任务，也是摆在我们面前的探索性课题。按院部署，先后开始试行“所长任期目标责任制”和实行一系列科研人事制度改革，探索并逐步实行与国际接轨的开放、流动、联合的科研体制和机制。为了抓好制定研究所所长任期目标工作，全面清理研究所研究课题，突出各自优势、规划发展目标和主要研究任务，迎倩局长制定详细工作计划，把研究所分为“京、沪和中西部”三片召开交流研讨会。每个研究所都进行深入的交流和讨论。当时正值研究所所长新老交替，一批年富力强的科研骨干走上所长岗位，迎倩局长在百忙中到会指导，为研究所提出切实可行的要求和积极建议。生物局按院总体发展要求、地区布局和研究所定位，帮助各所明确发展目标，落实改革措施，在项目组织、重点实验室建设和条件保障等方面给予相应的配合与支持。

开放实验室的设立是院实施开放、流动、联合机制改革和保持一支精干力量、确保基础研究和高技术创新的重要举措。迎倩局长把这项工作作为推动学科调整、布局前沿与高技术创新研究的抓手，在局务会上反复研究，力求在地区、学科布局上合理，严格遴选。记得迎倩局长根据专家建议，支持建立昆明动物所的细胞分子进化开放实验室和植物所数量生态开放实验室，加强进化与生态学的新生长点。在后者的论证会上，他为了避嫌，派一位副局长到会主持。细胞分子进化开放实验室如今已进入国家重点实验室行列。1987年，我院利用第六批世行贷款的契机，决定建立20个国家重点实验室。生物局非常重视这项工作，面临激烈竞争，协助研究所组织申报和做好评审准备工作。在成都院评审会上，我局申报的新药、植物细胞与染色体工程、病虫鼠害、微生物资源前期开发和生化工程等五个实验室入选。这些实验室的建立与运行，为促进我院生物科学重要应用和服务于国家战略需求领域的研究发挥了重要作用。此外，在孙鸿烈副院长的关心支持下，生态站被纳入开放站序列建设。在生物局规划下，孙院长还亲自参加了生物局的内蒙古锡林浩特草原站、海北高寒草甸草原站的论证会。

我们在怀念迎倩局长推动生物科学与生物技术事业健康发展方面重要贡献的同时，也深为很多展现他那高尚德行的故事所动情。迎倩局长在研究生期间入党，当过学生干部，在研究所曾任课题组长、室主任和所长，是一位长期受党教育培养、有丰富经验和管理能力的业务领导干部。他具有强烈的事业心和责任感，工作严谨、实事求是、严以律己、真诚平和待人，是一位可亲可敬的兄长，也是一位令人尊敬的领导者。

迎倩同志是一位作风严谨、善于听取不同意见和讲究民主与集中的领导者。凡重要工作事项的决定都是在局务会上听取有关同志充分发表意见后才做出的。对不同意见，他都耐心倾听，从不随意打断或把自己的意见强加于人。平时在工作中，同事们既十分尊重迎倩局长，又能够当面发表不同意见。因为大家知道，我们的局长很民主、很尊重下级，大家在畅所欲言后，从不会因为发表不同意见受到非难，都是在促进工作的同时保持和发展了相互间的友谊，难怪局里的同志们都亲切地称呼迎倩局长为“老钱”。迎倩局长平时严于律己、宽厚待人，不利用手中的权力谋取私利，连年轻人都愿意向他述说自己的想法，争取得到他的指点和帮助。现在回忆起来，大家在与迎倩局长共事的几年里心情舒畅。共同享受着生物局这个既能愉快有效工作、又能团结和谐进步的集体的快乐。

迎倩局长是副手们的良师益友。他受命任职时，面对新科技体制机制改革的探索与实行，以及年轻科技人才匮乏和科研条件严重不足的客观状况，如何带领大家推动我院生物科学与生物技术健康发展，对他来说担子很重，也是一个严峻的挑战。他深刻认识到，要做好工作，必须调动全局同志的积极性，团结一致，相互配合与支持。两位副局长都是走上局领导岗位的新手，但迎倩同志在明确分工的基础上，放手让他们开展工作，从不随意干预和批评，让他们在实际工作中增长才干、积累经验。特别是他还放手让一名年轻的副局长具体抓综合处工作，充分调动其主观能动性，使他熟悉和掌握了生命科学和研究所的全面情况，锻炼了他的工作能力。这位副局长说，这对他今后在把握整体工作方面受益匪浅。

迎倩局长非常关心和尊重退下领导岗位的老同志。为他们安排好工作，充分发挥他们的作用。由于他们在院机关时间长、情况熟悉、经验丰富，所以遇到重大事项，迎倩局长特别注意听取他们的意见和建议。同时，他也关心并尽力帮助解决老同志在生活和工作待遇方面遇到的问题。一位一直在院机关工作的老处长回忆，老钱与有关部门协调后澄清了我的历史遗留问题，工作职务得到晋升，同时也解开了我心中的烦恼。

迎倩局长爱护、提携年轻人的佳话既多又很感人。他曾经说过，每当看到年轻人进步了就很高兴。老钱留心把有条件的年轻干部放到处长岗位委以重任，把多位工作努力的年轻人提拔到副处长岗位，让大家在30岁左右就获得了职业生涯的发展空间。当年轻人有了专业职称晋升的机会，当年轻人有了发表专著的机会，他都很爽快地表示了支持。

老钱虽然平日工作很忙，但他能实实在在地帮助年轻人提高业务水平，如他不仅口头鼓励年轻人撰写与业务工作有关的文章，还能抽出时间给予具体指点和帮助修改。在迎倩局长的影响下，局里的年轻人成长在一种健康发展的工作氛围中，讨论业务工作时常常被鼓励也敢于发表自己的见解。大家为此心情很愉悦，业务能力也有明显提高。这种环境造就的进步成为大家日后承担更重工作任务后享用不尽的精神和知识财富。

每当想起这些动人的故事和佳话，我们的内心都很感动与震撼，我们无比怀念好领导、好师长、好朋友钱迎倩局长。

(执笔：王贵海；参加：孟广震、翁延年、王晨、田彦、袁萍)

2011.2.12

青海湖边我的心在流血

阮帆

虽然年过七旬，可钱先生还格外精神，看上去也就是60岁左右的样子，他觉得，这是自己经常跟中小学生接触的结果。一说起那些孩子们，他脸上就会自然而然地出现舒心的笑容。

这不，过几天，他又将出现在“青少年科技博览会”的讲台上，话题嘛，自然是他最关心的“保护生物多样性”。

都市里的“牧羊人”。

“从小我就喜欢生物，我还养过羊呢。”喜欢古典音乐，出身高级职员之家的钱先生说出这句话，着实吓了记者一跳。

“我是浙江人，但一直住在上海，就读麦伦中学，1949年以前是很有名的教会学校，后来更名为继光。从那时起，在一个中学生物老师的影响下，我对生物产生了兴趣，我们几个同学还在学校里自己种地，养了几只羊。”这段大上海里的“牧羊”生活，让钱先生决心从事生物研究。

他家里的阳台上摆着几盆花，花的叶子黄了一半。“家里有两个植物学家也养不好花。”钱先生乐了。“我们也忙，没时间管它们，想起来就浇浇水。”

他真是很忙，1999 年后，钱迎倩先生人退休了，心却闲不下来，作为“中科院老科学家科普演讲团”的一员，他已经跑了将近20个省，西部12个省市去了10个，宁夏准备今年9月去。“退下来，事情还不比以前少。”钱先生说。

“上世纪70年代后，我一直搞的是生物技术，跟基因工程有关，以后又研究了生物多样性保护，这就与我原来的研究找到了结合点——生物安全。”用通俗的话讲，是转基因植物对环境的影响。一提起转基因，很多人会想起去年，转基因食品的安全问题闹得沸沸扬扬时，钱教授也被媒体追逐热炒：“我接受了一些采访，结果在媒体上就成了转基因技术的反对者。有些报纸甚至给了我一顶帽子:转基因技术的坚决反对派。所以我现在一般不接受这方面的采访。”他苦笑。“生物安全和转基因问题，是一个长期的、敏感的问题，短期内看不出来，科学上有不同的看法很正常，我关注它，是因为这也是‘生物多样性保护’重要的组成部分。”青海湖上演的悲剧很多人整天嘴里说着环境保护，其实对中国环境状况没有什么特别深切的感受，可对于一位经常跑野外的科学家，他是用自己的手去摸，用自己的眼睛去看那些被砍掉的森林、被一网打尽的鱼虾、被猎杀的珍贵动物、被践踏蹂躏的草原……用自己的心去倾听它们的哭泣。

青海湖，本来是著名的“人间仙境”，可钱先生在青海湖边，却目睹了一幕悲惨的场面："青海湖原来有108条淡水注入，现在少了100条！湖里生活着我们中国特有的物种'湟鱼'，它的特点是必须到淡水产卵，到了产卵季节，大批大批雌鱼肚子里全是卵，拼命挤向剩下的几条淡水河，结果全挤死在那里！密密麻麻啊，有半米厚！原来，那里的湟鱼资源有10万吨左右，现在只有7500吨！"想起那些为了生下孩子拼命挣扎的雌鱼，想到那些没来得及发育就胎死腹中的鱼卵，钱先生的心在流血。钱先生曾经几下青海湖，看着原来的草原变成了油菜田；看着人跟湖争水，湖怎么争得过人类；"青海湖的面积越来越小！按照这样的速度，如果不采取特殊措施，青海湖就有可能变成第二个罗布泊！"。

从实验室到野外。从1986年起，钱先生当了生物科学与技术局局长后，走出实验室，眼界更宽了，目光从基因、体细胞这些微观的东西，移到了生态环境这个宏观领域。当时，国际上越来越重视"生物多样性保护"问题，他和几位科学家提议加强这方面的研究。1989年，在中科院领导的支持下，中国"生物多样性保护"研究在中科院开始了，很快成立了"中科院生物多样性委员会"。

1992年，联合国召开"环境与发展大会"，与会各国都认为，全世界环境恶化和破坏正在加剧，如果不加以控制，整个人类将难以生存。大会通过了《生物多样性公约》，中国作为缔约国之一，进一步推动了"生物多样性保护"的研究发展。

"如果我以前说保护生物多样性还是出于理性认识，可之后，我的亲身经历告诉我，中国的生态环境破坏得有多严重！我跑了很多地方，野外观测站、生物定位站、西双版纳植物园……给你举一个例子，中科院在四川岷江上游有一个定位站，80年代后期，我们坐着车往上游走，江里密密麻麻的，全飘着木头！上游砍伐森林后，把树木往江里一扔，省了运费，到了90年代，江里的木头少多了，等到了1997年左右，江里没有一根木头！上游的森林已经被砍完了！还有云南的滇池，本来是非常美丽的湖泊，可90年代我去看时，污染得非常严重，水葫芦覆盖了很大面积，这就是外来物种入侵和当地污染造成的。"

钱先生原本和蔼的笑容消失了："中国生态环境问题太严重了，如果不大声疾呼，那么，我们未来的生存环境堪忧！"，顶着沙尘暴演讲。

1999 年以前，钱先生是以中科院专家和领导的身份从事"生物多样性保护"工作；1999年以后，他加入了"中科院老科学家科普演讲团"："以前，我只关注植物、细胞、生物多样性，从来没有关心过教育领域，现在，我觉得这实在是太重要了。必须要把环境意识和保护生物多样性的意义告诉下一代，让他们也树立科学的发展观。"偏远地区，往往是为了生存破坏环境比较严重的地区，这些讲座，给这里的下一代送来一个启示：是为了吃饭或者发财，砍光捞光用光呢？还是站在更高层次上，用科学的、可持续发展的方式发展经济？孩子们用自己的心做出了选择："一次我们到了怀柔，那里的学校正好停电，又刮着大风，学生们就坐在操场上听。天上刮着沙尘暴一样的大风，我手上拿着喇叭大声喊，还特地找了块黑板，把讲座主要内容用大字写在上面。就在这样的环境里，每个同学都非常有兴趣，听得非常认真。"

学生最单纯，也最热情，每次到演讲完后的"互动时间"，学生们都欢腾雀跃、争先恐后地举手，话筒在教室中传来传去；没有机会提问的同学，就传条子，每场讲座的条子都有高高的一沓。有的同学一直追到休息室，还把钱先生的地址抄下，一来二去，钱先生交了不少年轻朋友。“有一个新疆的同学对生物学特别有兴趣，他还在老师的指导下，发表了一个新种，以后，我希望他能来中科院工作。”钱先生笑得那么开心，同学们的热情，让他看到了中国的未来希望所在。

我希望领导多来听听。走的地方多了，无论是大城市，还是偏远的乡村，无论是一般意义上的好学生，还是外人眼里的“差生”，在他眼里，所有的孩子都是那么可爱，充满了求知的欲望。“让我最感动的是，我有一次去北京的一家职高，那里的老师对我说‘你要做好思想准备，我们这里是职高，下面学生可能会乱七八糟，而且不会有人提问。’可是，那天来了200多个学生，听报告时鸦雀无声，提问也相当踊跃。”这种事情他遇到过不只一次，可每次让他“做好思想准备”的人，事后都会诧异，同学们的求知欲望是如此之高。钱先生感到，要想解决问题，不是等这一代年轻人长大，而是要改变成年人，特别是领导的观念。为了保护红树林，他跟某市的领导反复解说，但人家一句话，“我们要发展经济。”一下子让他深感无奈和失落。现在，有很多地区的领导干部抢着来听讲座，最近他回了老家浙江，给当地干部讲了几场，这又让钱先生感到欣慰。“不仅仅是中学生，更重要的是给各级干部、领导来讲，他们手中握有权力，如果更重视生物多样性保护，解决起来会更有效果。”

本文原载：Journal of Integrative Plant Biology. 2010. 52 (10): 941-942

In Remembrance: Professor Qian Ying-Qian(1932—2010)

Jitao Zou[1] Wei Wei[2] Keping Ma[2]

(1 Plant Biotechnology Institute, National Research Council Canada;
2 Institute of Botany, Chinese Academy of Sciences)

Professor Qian Ying-Qian, a renowned Chinese plant biologist and a member of the editorial board of *Acta Botanica Sinica* (predecessor of JIPB) 1989–1993, passed away in Beijing on April 20, 2010 at the age of 78. Professor Qian was a former Secretary-General (1978–1988), and Vice President of the Chinese Botanical Society (1988–1999). During his long and distinguished career, Professor Qian served as director-General of the Institute of Botany, Chinese Academy of Sciences (CAS), Director-General of the Bureau of Life Sciences and Biotechnology, CAS, President of Guangxi Academy of Sciences, Chief Editor of Chinese Biodiversity (currently Biodiversity Science), Deputy Director of the Biodiversity Committee of CAS, Vice Chair of The State Review Committee on Nature Reserves, Deputy Director of the Endangered Species Scientific Commission, PRC, and Chair of the Chinese Committee of the International Union of Biological Sciences. For more than half a century, Professor Qian dedicated his life and career to the development of the plant science research community in China.

Born on December 28, 1932 in Cixi, Zhejiang Province, Professor Qian received his undergraduate degree in 1954 from the Biology Department, Fudan University. His outstanding academic performance earned him the right to pursue graduate studies, which at the time was extremely difficult to attain in China. He completed his graduate studies in 1957 from Nanjing University, and assumed an assistant professor position there immediately after receiving his graduate degree. In 1959, he joined the Institute of Botany, CAS. He had remained with CAS for the rest of his career.

Professor Qian was one of the scientists whose research established the foundation of modern plant cell biology research in China. As deputy head of the Cell Biology Laboratory in the early 1960's, Professor Qian established the electron microscopy platform at the Institute of Botany, CAS, which led to the transition of their research from light microscopy to ultrastructural studies. He was among a group of key plant cell biologists led by ProfessorWu

Su-Xuan that strongly advocated the importance of moving forward from morphological studies of the cell to the dynamic aspects of cell differentiation and development. Illustrating this foresight in scientific leadership was the fact that, despite the challenging environment unimaginable to many researchers nowadays in China, he initiated in the 1960's a "Plant Cellular Biochemistry team" in the Cell Biology Laboratory of the Institute of Botany, emphasizing methodologies employing protein, DNA and RNA analytical tools. Leading a project that made the earliest successful maize anther culture in China, he was one of the pioneers in microspore culture research, a field that inspired a generation of Chinese plant biotechnology researchers. Professor Qian was always keen in the practical application of plant research to crop improvement (Qian et al. 1981). In search of new cell technology for crop improvement, he enthusiastically embarked on protoplast culture and somatic hybridization technology. He reported the successful inter-genus protoplast fusion between tobacco and soybean, and provided chromosomal, isozymes and ultrastructural evidence to demonstrate the hybrid nature of the fusion product (Qian et al. 1982). Under his leadership, the Cell Biology Laboratory at the Institute of Botany, CAS, was in the forefront of protoplast culture technology for many years, achieving plant regeneration from protoplasts of numerous crop species including maize, rice and kiwifruit (Cai et al. 1978; Cai et al. 1987; Qian and Yu 1992). In the latter part of his career, Professor Qian dedicated his efforts to Biodiversity research in China. With his endeavor, a working group on biodiversity was set up in the CAS in 1990. In 1992, the Biodiversity Committee of the CAS was established with Professor Qian as the first deputy director. This committee had significantly motivated the biodiversity research community in China and strongly supported biodiversity conservation activities. Professor Qian had organized and directly participated in research projects on assessment of biodiversity status and strategies in China. He also studied the principles and methodologies of biodiversity conservation in practice (Qian and Ma 1994). He co-authored several key reports on biodiversity, including the action plan of biodiversity conservation and the report on current situation of biodiversity in China. These documents provided solid scientific basis for achieving regulations on biodiversity conservation and sustainable utilization at the state level. Professor Qian was also the first scientist in China realizing the significant implication of biosafety issues to biodiversity. With the fast development of biotechnology, Professor Qian called attention on biosafety research of genetically modified organisms in China in 1992, and contributed numerous publications introducing biosafety research (e.g. Qian 1994; Qian and Ma 1995, 1998). With his leadership, the Institute of Botany, CAS, established a strong biosafety research platform with dynamic research programs on biodiversity.

Professor Qian was a tireless promoter of academic exchange between China and the international community. He was among the first wave of Chinese scientists going abroad for academic exchange. Many at the National Research Council Canada-Plant Biotechnology Institute where he conducted somatic hybridization research in the early 1980's fondly remember him as an exceedingly hard working scientist and remarkably productive in research. As happened many times in his career, he placed his organizational duty ahead of everything else: he had to cut short his research visit in Canada upon a call of return to lead the Institute of Botany of CAS. As Director-General of the Institute, he opened many channels of academic exchange for researchers and students.

Professor Qian was a scientific management leader, a scholar, scientist, mentor, colleague, and friend. More than his scientific contributions, Professor Qian will be remembered for mentoring more than 20 students. Those of us who had the privilege being his students have myriad tales to tell about his kindness and generosity. Although saddled with management duties, he always made sure to allocate time for discussion and often demonstrated directly to students cell biology techniques.After he took on the position of Director-General of the Bureau of Life Sciences and Biotechnology, the weekly meeting with students proceeded normally in his office at the headquarters of CAS, and the scientific discussion was often followed by a lunch treat. He encouraged independent thinking and was always open to seeking inputs from other scientists to student research projects.

It is important to recognize that the impact of a scientist, as that of any individual, can only be fully appreciated through a prism of his or her specific time and space. Plant science research in China for the last few decades has gone through a tremendous transformation. Entrusted with many challenging management positions during the early transition phase of this period, Professor Qian made incalculable contribution to what the Chinese Plant science research is today. Professor Qian will be sadly missed by countless ones whose career has been made better by his life and career.

Reference

Cai QG, Qian YQ, Zhou YL, Wu SX (1978) A further study on the isolation and culture of rice (*Oryza sativa L.*) protoplasts. Acta Bot. Sin. 20, 97–102

Cai QG, Guo ZS, Qian YQ, Jiang RX, Zhou YL (1987) Plant regeneration from protoplasts of corn (*Zea Mays* L.). Acta Bot. Sin. 29, 453–459

Cai QG, Qian YQ, Ke SQ, He ZC, Jiang RX, Zhou YL, Ye YP, Hong SR, Huang RH (1992) Studies on the somaclonal variation of regenerated plants from protoplasts of *Actinidia deliciosa*. Acta Bot. Sin. 34, 822–828

Qian YQ, Zhou YL, CAI QG (1981) *In Vitro* plant regeneration from leaflet explants of Triticale. Chin. Sci. Bull. 26, 1121–1124

Qian YQ, Ma KP (1994) Pricinples and Methods in Biodiversity Studies. China Science and Technology Press, Beijing (In Chinese)

Qian YQ, Kao KN, Wetter LR (1982) Chromosomal and isozyme studies of *Nicotiana tabacum-Glycine max* hybrid cell lines. Theor. Appl. Genet. 62, 301–304

Qian YQ, Yu DP (1992) Advances in *Actinidia* research in China. Acta Hort. 297, 51–55

Qian YQ (1994) Biodiversity and biotechnology. Bull. Chin. Acad. Sci. 2nd issue, 134–138

Qian YQ, Ma KP (1995) Biotechnology and biosafety. J. Nat. Res. 10, 322–331

Qian YQ, Ma KP (1998) Progress in the studies on genetically modified organisms, and the impact of its release on environment. Acta Ecol. Sin. 18, 1–9.

编 后 记

一个人的一生很短暂，能够做好一件事情就很不容易了。然而，在芸芸众生中，总是有少数人会超凡脱俗，有出色的表现。通过编辑《钱迎倩论文集》，让我们再次认识到钱先生属于少数出类拔萃的人。三件事情他都作出了具有标志性的成绩：科学研究、科技管理和科学普及。在繁忙的管理工作中，他始终坚持科学研究，几十年不辍。在他早期的研究中，主要集中在细胞生物学研究，特别是关于大豆和烟草原生质体分离和纯化，以及将这两种不同科植物的原生质体进行了融合，得到异科原生质体融合后的异核体的工作具有相当的创新性。他所带领的研究组率先在国际上成功地获得了攻关多年未能突破的玉米原生质体再生植株，受到了国内外同行的好评。在后来的水稻原生质体的游离和培养、美味猕猴桃原生质体再生植株和无性系变异以及多种植物原生质体的超低温保存上都做出了具有标志性的成果。自上世纪 90 年代中期开始，钱先生在国内率先开始生物安全方面的研究，阅读了大量的国外文献，将重要的进展介绍到国内。主要从转基因生物释放对环境的影响、对人体健康的可能影响和对伦理道德的影响三个方面进行分析评述，并鼓励他的学生在植物所启动了转基因作物释放的环境效应的实验研究。在他和同事们的联合指导下，他的学生完成了辽东栎、野大豆和锦鸡儿的分子生态学研究，受到同行的好评。钱先生既是中国生物多样性研究最早的组织者，也是积极的实践者。在繁忙的管理工作中，尽量挤出时间阅读最新的研究文献，不断总结和评述生物多样性研究的最新进展，为相关的研究人员提供了重要的参考资料。特别难能可贵的是，他从多年的领导岗位上退下来之后，很快转变角色，成为一名孜孜以求的研究人员。这种平和的心态、务实敬业精神也是值得我们认真学习的。钱先生是一位具有强烈社会责任感的学者，在退休之后，以饱满的热情投入到科学普及工作中，真可谓走遍祖国的大江南北，在八年的时间里做报告 320 场。图书馆里，平日常留下他那年迈的身影。由于不断地搜集资料和丰富报告内容，同样的报告题目其内容则是动态和新鲜的。直到 2008 年 5 月在河南开会期间晕倒，才停止了外出科普活动，此时，他已七十六岁高龄。即便如此，还坚持撰写科普文章。

搜集整理钱先生论文的过程不仅是我们学习他的学术成就的过程，更是学习他酷爱自己的事业、以超人的毅力不断求索的高贵品格的过程。在钱先生逝世一周年之际，编辑出版他的论文集既是对钱先生的纪念，也是方便后人全面了解钱先生学术成就的需要。附录的几篇文章比较系统地介绍了钱先生的生平和他一生的重要活动，希望对读者体味钱先生的人格魅力提供参考。

参加文集编辑工作的有马克平、袁萍、王贵海、蔡起贵、魏伟、陈铁梅和陈灵芝同志。在论文集即将付梓之际，我们要特别感谢中国科学院原副院长李振声院士欣然题写书名，感谢中国科学院原副院长许智宏院士悉心撰写序言。还要感谢科学出版社生物分社社长王静和编辑马俊的辛勤工作，使本书得以顺利出版。

编者谨识

2011 年 4 月 20 日